Early Novels and Short Fiction

Also by Peter Cowlam

Early Novels and Short Fiction

Peter Cowlam

_____cHp_____
CentreHouse Press

British Library Cataloguing in Publication Data
A catalogue record for this book is available from the British Library

Cover image Shutterstock / romi49

ISBN 978-1-902086-31-6

CONTENTS

General Foreword

Early Novels and Short Fiction is not an accurate title, collectively. Among the earliest of my travels into fiction is *Penumbra*, a collection of short stories originally having as centrepiece the four related narratives now comprising *Entry Without Visas* – viz., 'Michael Grading', 'The House of Folly', 'Two Dissidents', and 'Homeward Angel'. *Entry Without Visas* is in itself the first of three novellas under the collective title *The Border and Back*, which became the obvious transition once I had decided to probe further into the dilemmas of Michael Grading. That exercise didn't turn out to be a novel, though *Call Bridgland Jolley* was the first extended piece of fiction I was prepared to put my name to, i.e. not consign to the bin, the one marked 'Rejects', of which as apprentice I generated many. Now comes the ripple in what has so far been an actual chronology, given that *Humber*, the centre in the trio of novellas making up *The Border and Back*, belongs with recent, much later fiction. It is the only anomaly, retrospectively, and is placed where it is as fits the overall structure.

Revisions to that initial quartet – 'Michael Grading', 'The House of Folly', 'Two Dissidents', and 'Homeward Angel' – which at the time of writing I felt nationally conscious of and referred to them collectively as the Michael of England stories, place the action much later than the date of original composition, which would have been mid to late 1970s, the Wilson-Callaghan era, and the Winter of Discontent. For example, we know from 'Homeward Angel' that Michael's return home is in the same week that Dali died (Salvador Dali, 11 May 1904 – 23 January 1989). I nowadays take the view that overall it has worked to my advantage that throughout my twenties and early thirties I was unable to find a publisher for any of my work. I suffered also from too much hope placed in a manual I always had in reach, an up-to-date writers' handbook, though eventually I came to see as lies and propaganda the assertion, somewhere in its opening pages, that publishers are always on the lookout for new talent. Novelists I read, trumpeted by the *literati* as the best of our contemporaries, all seemed to me to have the same deficiency – a rush to publication, no doubt under commercial imperatives, before having properly self-edited, or taken the time to notice that the texts they were putting out fell below the standards a cabal of tame reviewers always claimed for them. My own editing process, precisely because as a writer I am not commercially blessed, or outspoken and controversial, or prone to stand up for minority interests, has extended over decades. I am in good company. Beethoven tinkered with his symphonies, long after they had been premiered and published.

There have been other shocks too, and one of such huge magnitude no end of editing will lessen its blow. There is a cruel symmetry to it, when one tiny detail that has survived all subsequent revisions is the 'Mark of Jack' acrostic in the fourth section of the Michael Grading story. The first seven of those letters were the keys my two-year-old son Jack randomly pressed on the keyboard when, sitting on my knee, he came to help me as I worked away at the word processor, in a 1989 revision. Of importance to that Grading story is Michael's contemplation of suicide, not something I knew too much about at the time of writing. That poor victim Michael hears of 'who one early morning drove in a salty drizzle thirty miles to the coast, and high above Hastings attached a hose to the exhaust pipe', and fed it in through a window, was an actual person, one an acquaintance had told me about. Then, decades later, in 2018, when Jack had been married not quite two years, his wife Holly took her own life – a horrible tragedy in itself, and one directing me, as all-unseeing author, to the full scale of ignorance with which I had 'dealt' with the subject of suicide. It has made me think poets and writers of fiction don't really 'deal' with anything. They just ramble. And certainly in Grading's case his contemplation of that act is bookish, is merely theoretical (while in 'Triones', in seventh place in *Penumbra*, it's a taunt, to get its author attention, and in tenth place, in 'The Incredible Domenico', it's merely an element of plotting). And there's a kind of symmetry, as well, when Grading has not fully understood that his endless searching, pointed up in both *Entry Without Visas* and *Call Bridgland Jolley*, is a search for meaning (which his inventor in *his* youth sought in vain for also). That probably explains his flirtation with religion, with monastic retreat, and with the politics of East and West.

As I have said, my original plan for the four Michael of England stories was as centrepiece to a wider collection, *Penumbra* (still unpublished other than here, in book form at least). I sent it around in the early '80s, when publishers still had readers. An enthusiastic response from one of Penguin's, whose name I can't remember, though it might have been Victoria (the postcard she wrote I no longer possess), nevertheless advised I'd get nowhere without an agent. She, she said, had no power of influence over inhouse editorial decisions, which made me wonder what she was doing there and why anyone should bother employing her.

Cropping up in both outer novellas – *Entry Without Visas* and *Call Bridgland Jolley* – is the poet Humber, a post-war professional man of letters, of a kind I always found puzzling. I never quite clicked with the Beat generation, even though I have always considered writing should in some way be subversive, and hadn't got much sympathy for what appeared at the other extreme, men and women writing books who seemed better suited to banking or accountancy, poets fussing over the choice of metrical arrangement and reducing their means of communication to graceless analytics. In my mind Humber belongs with the latter, troubled as he is not just by his personal identity. He also bears the weight of his daily occupation. In a way he stands trial for it in *Call Bridgland Jolley*, that first extended work of fiction that didn't join others in the bin (there is one other that didn't go in the bin, and instead has gone missing, and will be an embarrassment if it ever turns up). The trial that takes place in *Call Bridgland Jolley* owes only the idea to Kafka, going off in another direction completely. I admit the thing goes on a bit, with its narrator endlessly re-stamping seemingly trivial details. In my defence, that's only the template by which is posed the question is his merely an exercise in rhetoric, or is his constant probing, his personal revelation of himself, key to the minute examination of a disintegrating elite. Or are the two things synonymous?

By day six of the trial his ceaseless pedantry has made him unwell. 'I am ill. I turn to a thick brown phial I picked up in the dispensary, drops for my ear, and a pipette…,' and later admits to having no grasp on events surrounding him: 'To be honest I am losing my grip….' As fiction *Call Bridgland Jolley* belongs with the uncategorised – a literary curiosity somewhere on the intersection of *Tristram Shandy* and *Ulysses*. It comes a bit late now as a millennial novel, whose opening draft was the best part of a quarter of a century before that alarm went off (when everyone was writing millennial novels). Only now, some twenty-something years past that demarcation, am I prepared to let it go, and let it be read. And I know of at least one person who will not judge it harshly, so I ask him to please forgive my tardiness.

Three of the four Michael of England stories have previously been published, 'Michael Grading' in *Valparaiso Fiction Review* (May 2013), 'The House of Folly' in *Thrice Fiction* (August 2018), and 'Two Dissidents' in *The Four Quarters Magazine* (August 2013). An early version of 'Michael Grading' won a Bridport prize (1989, contest judge Alexis Lykiard). *Call Bridgland Jolley* I have previously published as a stand-alone, as an ebook. Three other stories from *Penumbra* have been published as follows: 'The Seven-O-One' under the title 'Hollamby's Dilemma' in *Volume* magazine, issue 6, summer 2009; 'The Evangelising Power of War', under the title 'Combat', in *CultureCult Magazine*, October 2017, which still alarms me in its laying bare of the kind of psyche a modern Western education spawns, and which I am still not comfortable publishing; and 'Noose', in the *Galway Review*, May 2016.

Bim Shay I only loosely categorise as a detective novel. The several strands of the story are narrated by Adrian Fixt. Fixt works for a mysterious and little-known civil service quango called the Department, which was brought into being in a reactive age of Toryism (the book was written at the height of Thatcherism, or courtesy the US in the era of Reaganomics). The Department's sole function is to protect and uphold the virtues of capitalism. Its officers work closely with all police forces throughout the UK, and take an interest in any case where successful exponents of the free-market payola system suffer criminal harm.

Fixt is based in West London. He is called to the 'Solomon case', when Solomon, a leader in the pharmaceuticals industry, is murdered. Fixt's investigations lead him to the London home of an American adviser to the Chancellor of the Exchequer. The home does not appear to be lived in, but is used as a clearing house in the illegal trafficking of Class A drugs. Exposure of these facts is likely to cause a scandal at the highest levels of government, and so, according to a Home Office interdict, Fixt is removed from the case. When he continues to investigate in his own time, the full weight of the Department is borne down on him.

Woven throughout is a parallel plot involving the Daniel Byrne Society, an organisation dedicated to the encouragement of writing, fiction and non-fiction, on crime and criminal matters. As an occasional reviewer of crime fiction, Fixt is a member of this society. The Byrne Society's figurehead, and a committee member, is Bim Shay, a celebrated poet and leading industrialist, at a point in his career where research is under way for the writing of his biography. On the eve of an annual prize-giving, the society's three main committee members ask Fixt to investigate, discreetly, the embezzlement of a part of the prize money. At first he refuses, but the more he finds himself outlawed by the Department the more he finds himself at a loose end, and so does investigate. This leads him to some surprising discoveries about Bim Shay, while at the same time he solves the mystery of Solomon, and makes a pretty good guess as to the facts surrounding the Chancellor's American adviser. *Bim Shay* I am more inclined to view as my London novel, where I lived and worked from 1979 to 1991. It marks the end of that period, a book I was finishing off when as a family we moved to the South Hams.

Electric Letters Z, when I published it in 1998, proved to be a tortuous, agonised plaint at the state of modern publishing. I had written it out of frustration, at not being able to find a mainstream publisher. It has at its centre Alistair Wye, the narrator, a man of exaggerated refinement, or as he sees it rarefied aesthetic. He occupies the slave position in a master-slave relationship, using his 'aesthetic' in his rebellion against his master. His barrage is constant. The 'master', Marshall Zob, is a self-styled latter-day Dickens and champion of the oppressed. Zob in reality is a mediocrity, who through powerful social connections and a dubious agenting system has established himself, as a novelist, as the 'best of his generation'. He is all too willing to supply, to the mass audience he courts, a lowbrow confection of street tales in the form of novels adding up to no more than film treatments. His analysis doesn't exceed a sanified conceptualisation of street life, useful to him in the personal advancement of status and career. His dead mentor, Glaze, is a mere *buffo*, a pedantic, ill-educated headmaster-type, the *dottore* of comedic street theatre, and the butt of *zanni* jokes. All else in the book is the jangle of the English middle-class as it bolsters and prettifies itself. The plot revolves round Wye's research into Zob's archive of computer discs, emails and faxes, and his own diary entries recording his reactions to life in proximity of one of the nation's bookish heavyweights. One can't say that the long shadow of Protestantism hasn't tainted the way certain Englishmen view the world.

The book's first draft dates to 1994, and I would like to think that in it I anticipated, by well over a decade, Damien Hirst's *For the Love of God*, a sculpture produced in 2007, its structure the platinum cast of an eighteenth-century human skull, encrusted with over 8,000 diamonds. My predictive, counter-contribution to such speculative artwork is courtesy my invented character Newsome Barringer, whose *Golgotha 2000* like Hirst's piece is a human skull, but unlike it is not a *memento mori* but, in my narrator's dismissal of it, a reminder of human folly: 'The phoney Barringer finds me magnanimous, with no words at all for his stunted cave work – those rudimentary acts of discourse – and best left to the weekend's mindless supplements.'

Ironically the book was picked up by a London agent and shown to half a dozen editors, one of whom awarded it a 'near miss'. I can understand. The book was convoluted, so much so that some years later I made a better fist of it and republished under the title *Who's Afraid of the Booker Prize?* Again, irony is not lost on me when under that title the book went on to win the 2015 Quagga Prize for Literary Fiction. With what to me are its early problems fully exorcised, I have returned to the original title for the latest revision offered here. As one reviewer has said, writing for Book Viral, *Who's Afraid of the Booker Prize?* or as I prefer it *Electric Letters Z*, is 'Deliciously wicked and extraordinarily funny…satirical eloquence at its best.…'

Caliban's Machine is the only novel for which I have carried out formal research. I wanted to know what an arts college was and how it worked, and so enrolled for a course in Performance Writing at Dartington College of Arts, in 1996, an institution that no longer exists. I found it hard to connect with most of the teaching staff, who were not sympathetic to 'performance writing' as novel. At such a distance of time, I can now view that as unimportant. The novel is a memoir written from the point of view of George du Plé, a young English poet whose background is blue collar halfway to middle-class. He has got himself involved with an English family of entrenched pedigree and tradition, surname Little. There are two daughters and a son. Alice Little is the eldest, and is the daughter from her mother's first marriage, marriage dissolved. Alex is her half-sister, and is the daughter of her mother's second marriage, marriage dissolved. Roddy is their brother, and the youngest, fruit of his mother's current marriage. So, all three siblings, Alice, Alex, Roddy, have the same mother, different fathers. The two sisters' step-father, or Roddy's biological father, runs an academic press, the Tralatition Press, and because of that specialism cannot help George du Plé into publishing his poetry. However, given that George is showing too much interest in step-daughter Alex, he arranges for his removal to an avant-garde arts faculty in New York, the Donns Watson. This leaves Alex free to marry the family's preferred candidate, John Royce, who becomes du Plé's editor and annotator when du Plé writes letters home intended for Alex, which somehow fall into Royce's hands. It is these letters that form an exiled poet's memoir – a memoir of lovelorn, artistic despair. Unforeseen by anyone, a third voice is added to that of memoirist and commentator – Jack d'Ursag's. Jack d'Ursag works for the same independent press that publishes Peter Cowlam's books, CentreHouse Press, and adds his perspective on that press's behalf.

—*Peter Cowlam, South Hams, February 2020; Brislington Village, March 2022*

Penumbra

I wake and feel the fell of dark, not day.
—**Gerard Manley Hopkins**

Back to the Old Regime

The exaggerated importance I placed on my secret cipher precipitated these events, but how could I have known? After my travels abroad, and my uneasy back-door re-entry into the country (under an assumed name, with forged papers, and with the remains of my wealth, rifled from foreign accounts), I was bound to over-react.

I must accept, of course, this ruinous locality, where fearing for my life I felt that little bit safer, as most people did, in the disintegrating city. Our direction now was fixed in humiliated marble, soiled and worn. What was broken off at the shoulder had once resolved itself in a hand that pointed. But not anymore. What few critics remained, a handful of political commentators, had retreated in the dark.

I look through the dirty brown panes most mornings, and wonder. What used to thrive down there in a more colourful world has been reduced to mean imitations of purposeful human life. The square is a pocket handkerchief of muddy green, quartered by flagstones. It is fenced – at night it is padlocked, when the benches double as beds. The high terraces all round have crumbled in the salty winds. Paint peels from the windows, and brickwork everywhere stands to be repointed. The chimneys lean to front or back, geriatric.

Moments of introspection are no less bleak. If I turn my back on the roofs outside, and on the strip of lead suspended above them – the city sky – then all I see is faded wallpaper, the last vestige of prosperity. On the bare boards, my footsteps echo. The naked bulb above dangles on twisted threads. The hullabaloo from neighbours in adjoining rooms on the lower floors in the end drives me to the streets, often on windy nights, where the only welcome is a basement bar. There, I turn it all over, again and again.

I don't say I regretted I was never asked to participate fully in the Federation's aims, though it *is* a lasting disappointment that exactly why a secret organisation should approach me at all was never explained. Now in the cold winds of change, it's unlikely it ever will be. I cannot alter the circumstances of my life, yet I remain loyal to the little I know of what the members worked for – fought for even. I am prepared to stand up, at the risk of being identified, and speak out. These stark rooms, the cheerless square, the decaying city, my own nation in the grip of directionless rulers and unscrupulous landlords – what can I really lose?

Defamation was subtle, was not prohibitive. Information was hard to come by, and street declamation belonged to the half-educated, with protest chants nothing but useless rage at what was inevitable. I am still amazed at the sinister ease with which, nevertheless, the official view absorbed itself into the everyday, and how scant was resistance to its forms of indoctrination.

Less subtle was the appearance of a go-between, as I tried to concentrate, uneasily in my chair. Every so often I paused to wipe the windowpane, now almost permanently moist with condensation. I had no other reason than to keep a lookout on the streets outside. I was slow to put aside the tatty paperback I had somehow acquired, its condition dog-eared, even when that presence below was furtive and suspicious. His coat collar was upturned, and a tartan scarf was wrapped tightly round the lower half of his face. He picked his way over the frosty flags and sat briefly on a bench.

When I looked up again, an infant in a room downstairs wailed for attention, and I tossed my book aside. My wrapped-up stranger was scanning the terraces at street-level, and where it existed noted the ornate numbering. When *I* stood *he* stood. Urban decay had not yet eroded the curly black 28 on my communal door. He fixed me unemotionally for a moment or two, then turned away quickly. I waited while he strutted out across the slabs, through the barbed gate, and away under the arch.

I checked, and was out of cigarettes. On the next landing I was still struggling with my coat. In the shadows I failed to see until it spoke the bewildered presence leaning on the rail and gazing into the depths of the stairwell. He shuffled disconsolately. As I rounded him, he kicked open the door to his side. A sheath of light half illumined his features. He was squat and pale, with a two-day stubble on his face, had bleary, crusted eyes, and his hair was in spikes and quiffs.

He shuffled off the rail, only to shift his weight and support himself on the other elbow. He rubbed an exploratory palm over his sandpapery chin. I buttoned up my coat and continued to the foot of the stairs, the throaty, insistent din rising again and ringing in that dark heaven above me. I bought cigarettes and a paper, and this was the headline: 'Federation uncovered, three arrested'.

That cipher now began to worry me more than ever, even if almost useless without the key, supposing its decryption hadn't been attempted, or fallen into enemy hands. How could I protect the Federation's only two members I have known?

I remembered calling up to their room one glowing afternoon, down from the lawn where tea things were being laid out. The late sun had formed a reddish half-halo on the tips of the distant pines – my shadow with its arms akimbo long to the house, the house with its flame of cotoneaster creeping up the walls.

'Take a break,' I said.

These ghosts considered easy propositions like this always arduously, but on this occasion took to the open air, where for a short half-hour we watched that semi-nimbus go through its modulations – red, orange, pink – in the arc of the western sky.

I asked how their work was going, meaning in a specific sense, to which Hughes offered as reply something only vague and general. Already, Federation members had achieved a firm footing in important institutions and organisations: in schools and universities; in major libraries; in most areas of public entertainment; in all grades and most branches of the civil service; in a few selected boardrooms – and unions. Even in both Houses at Westminster.

I noticed too, at other times, how his eyes darted under narrowing lids, while his fingers drummed nervously on the table top, or plucked his little pointed beard. I scarcely expected his next request – i.e., that he wished to 'requisition' my house.

'To what end, why?' I asked, sensing some secret knowledge was about to be revealed.

The level-headed Denham intervened (as he knew he must). There was, he said, only one political aim, in whose service my resources would be placed. That was to soften, in so far as it was possible, the powerful forces against them.

Denham, heavy framed, ponderous, hauled himself in one awkward motion from his garden chair. He tried but failed to catch his colleague's eye, and instead carefully, thoughtfully, paced the full spiral in one of the paths – a whimsical, outdoor decoration, beginning lawn-centre, and having as destination the pond with reeds and rockery. When, in the coming twilight, Denham paused at the water's edge, he glanced back, but just too late. Hughes had already outlined his plan. He wanted to make my house a lodge, a sanctum.

'Ah,' I said, 'but what would go on here? And would it enable me to enter the Federation?'

That definition from Hughes must remain, since I was offered no other. I can describe a secret society – or nothing – whose ceremony I am able to relate only his notions of. In the enveloping dusk, he told me this: that the initiate, when called from the darkness, is stripped to the waist and stands before the inner council, alone on a marble floor of chequerboard design. Various objects are introduced, and like chess pieces arranged on the squares. Where the black queen would go is the carved ivory knob of an antique walking stick (said once to belong to the criminologist Daniel Byrne). On close inspection it looks like a gargoyle – thin, wedge-like heads and faces bunched together in a globe. Its purpose is to guard against harmful presences, both tangible *and* of an 'immaterial' world. Only then can other objects be placed, examples being a stone, a censer, a quill – also a vignette of the initiate's wife, if married.

The game, if that's the construction to put on it, is at an advanced state when there are no other pieces than these. The initiate has to say what each symbol suggests to him, then rearrange them. The council studied each new orientation and interpreted the altered relationships, and this was all the evidence they'd need. On the basis of what was left on the marble, the new recruit was either cast back into the darkness (often his own position among the emblems prompted this), or he was taken in and set an appropriate task. I took the opportunity once to quiz Denham on this, while he and I were alone. We strode through the hilly chestnut woods on a hot Sunday, to the cool, airy parish church where motets, madrigals, or sometimes masses were played. As, mechanically, he planted his light, sturdy brogues in the dust, I mentioned my earlier conversation with Hughes. Not surprisingly Denham denied there were rituals. He even dismissed everything that Hughes had said as puerile nonsense. 'Look,' he said, 'the last thing I want you to believe is that the Federation is steeped in Druid mysticism. It is entirely modern in its thought and concepts. Selection is made according to character, ability, and political leanings.'

Those days are gone. The great social cataclysm that swept everything away – my friends, my way of life, my business, my house – saw the latter confiscated. In the subsequent reallocation of wealth it was earmarked – and remains so – for one of the nation's dignitaries whose name I shall never know. (I am well aware, now, just as our impoverished masses are, who try to make sense of our lives, exactly what this 'reallocation' was.) I have reason to doubt that any such transfer will happen. I still observe the waste, with the plot and its building in lingering deterioration. The harsh winters clump by, while our sleepy bureaucrats still have their lists to process, and someone to 'allocate' my property to.

If I sought, in that political upheaval, the relative sanctuary of something like the Federation, then what is there now? The official newspaper rounded on any last bastion of common sense – or 'illegal enclave', especially if 'all-male' (which I knew wasn't true of the Federation) – and called for a purge. It was a propaganda lie, and that so-called important work, vital to national security, was no more than a witch hunt. But I am implicated, for on a cool twilit evening, when both my friends were on the train back to the city, I couldn't bear the intrigue anymore. In the dusty shadows, going over papers in his study, I marked his spiky, neurotic handwriting, then took a copy of that cipher Hughes had invented. I sealed it in an envelope, and hid it. I have a secret room for private things, and had to hope it was still there, assuming it had meaning.

Suffocating fumes filled the carriage as the engine ploughed through the countryside, the shorn hedges and wasted fields slipping by laboriously. There was a twinkling frost. Unthinkingly I bruised my hand on the cold metal of the frame as I forced the window. A howling, freezing charge of air threw me back on the seat, whose punctured upholstery disgorged its dirty clouds of cotton wool. I drew my coat closer to the warmth of my body – as it turned out, prematurely. For the third time that day my papers were checked. This had happened already on first boarding the train, when the officer barring my way stared at my photo protractedly, her hard thin lips twitching restlessly. Grudgingly I answered her questions, and was forced to agree I'd report to her station at five. Then half an hour ago a soldier in green, with a peaked flat hat and features hard to discern behind her dark glasses, went through the whole charade again – but now a shade more menacing, prodding my arm with the tip of her machine gun. An odd journey to make, she said, as if, the train lurching along a corridor of high walls and lean-tos, there were anything here to keep me.

'Just a day out,' I said.

'Huh!' She prodded me again. Her cruel features dissolved in a rapturous, toothy grin, as she chuckled, though without much gusto. Now, another just like her stood before me, the sugar-coated chequerboard of fields and hedges reflected in the black depth of her lenses. I unbuttoned the top of my coat again and pulled out those few soiled papers. These she inspected with a snort, then strutted off to the next carriage. Again I wrapped up, and pressed to the window looked out on a bright bare sun in the winter trees, and the frosted fields rushing by.

Once, out there, in a pub garden, I caught my breath, ignoring Denham for the moment. I couldn't help but watch the crimson summer sun sliding down behind a row of poplars, the last warm rays lighting the sky in a wash of streaky magenta. Dusk soon followed, and brought with it the drone of a car straining round a hill, getting nearer, stuttering through the gears. I said: 'A far cry from the city.'

He said: 'A pleasant change. I'm glad we came.'

'But don't you find it a deceptive sort of quiet? Sometimes the unease is palpable, even out here. My publican doesn't smile anymore.'

He touched his cheek then crossed his lips with one of those long, chubby forefingers. I leaned back from the table, away from the dying shade of its parasol. I lit a cigarette. He told me I should be more cautious.

'What do you mean by that?' I asked.

'Look – one of the reasons I came was Hughes. He needs time to reassess, to think.'

'I see he's on a knife edge.'

'Yes. You should try and remember that.'

He quaffed the last of his beer, and I too emptied my glass. Nothing more was said as we ambled home in the twilight. What, I now thought, if Hughes was neurotic, and that cipher was merely delusion?

The familiar oak – hanging, ornamental gas lamps – the station sign, swinging, squeaking in the breeze – all slid by as the train juddered to a halt. The ticket collector remained at his sentry post, his flask visible, his handgun not, and appeared to take in nothing (did he catch a glimpse, of me, the exiled local, an entrepreneur, stepping from an empty carriage?). I wanted to avoid any further inspection of my papers. All were forgeries, and I couldn't be sure of fooling these jumped-up, uniformed thugs forever. Therefore, where the platform sloped away, I crossed over into a potato field, and with my coat tails flying bounded over the hard, frozen clods.

The first disappointment, not really a shock, was this: the cut lawns, the clipped edges, the precise borders in symmetry under the hedges, the careful arrangement of shrubs and trees – had all run riot. The yellow path had disappeared, and the pond was rancid.

Acts of vandalism – all for the new order – included the destruction of coloured lights (nailed hardboard now spanned the window frames), a huge northerly chasm in the wall surrounding the plot (it gave military vehicles easy access), and the razing of a summerhouse, whose rubble littered its former site. I was less disheartened to see, when I forced the lobby door and looked around inside, some enterprising person had removed the furnishings, for there was no evidence of their destruction. Also, my secret room hadn't been discovered. It was still carpeted – the bureau was there un-tampered with – the chair and a low floral sofa were as I'd left them – a few reference books remained intact, and here were my decanter and brandy glass.

I scrabbled around in the disorderly drawers and plucked out at random a jar full of coppers (too bulky for the pockets of well-cut suits), a flat security key to the machine room of my old office in town (all networked computers are now centrally controlled by government), a goose feather (my house was never, I repeat never, a lodge – this was childhood memorabilia), cigarette papers, a pocket calculator, which unusually converted binary to octal and vice versa (useful when calculating hardware physical device numbers), and a brown, sealed envelope. This, feverishly, I tore open, and in a fit of relief tossed aside as I slipped out its all-important document (I had made it all-important). It was the cipher, of course, in my own hand – as unintelligible now as the day I had copied it out.

Another, long, buff envelope, awaiting on the grating back in that smashed-up metropolis, seemed innocent enough, until I picked it up and studied the inscription. My name was typed in fading uppercase – which wasn't the name my papers bore. The letter was bland and unsensational – and was printed, curiously, in the same fading uppercase, the H, L, and R in particular faint in their impression. (As I read, I worried about the cipher.) It was my instruction to see a woman called Clarke, at ten that evening – a car would call for me at nine. I gazed up into that voluminous black hell – the stairwell – and decided not to go up to my rooms. Instead I crossed two shapeless suburbs, and came at last to the hollowed stones and ancient steps of a library, where I strode across the marble directly into the reference section. Here I pulled down a single, redolent tome – a capitalised EDWA/EXTRACT in gold tooling in the leather of its spine – and deposited under ETHICS my secret, madman's ravings. Then I returned, and at nine loitered in the dark, in a doorway on the neighbouring, west flank of the square. The car, sleek and hearse-like, pulled up mysteriously at a few minutes after nine, and that same go-between with the long coat and tartan scarf stepped out. He checked his watch. He looked up at my unlighted rooms. He drummed his gloved fingers irritably on the shiny bonnet of his car. I lit a cigarette and left the match burning. As he turned he momentarily caught the eddying puffs of smoke, and behind them my shifting, ghoulish face.

'I decided to wait out here,' I said, stepping from under the storm porch, and tossing down the match. He darted in and opened the passenger door.

'Get in, Hiller....'

As soon as I'd eased into the passenger seat he put his foot down hard and motored under the arch. I quizzed, but couldn't draw him into conversation – his orders were to drive. In the city the lights were dim. In the shadows fights had broken out. Soon, the curfew. Then out, where I lost my bearings, into streets with burnt-out looted shops, a warren of warehouses, an oily wharf – it only wanted a fog to descend.

'Okay, Hiller, out! Follow the blind man....'

I stepped out in a muddy pool. The car purred away over the cobbles. A blind man tapping a cane materialised beside me.

'This way,' he said, and led me through the labyrinthine ruins to Clarke, I presumed, the bull-headed, the monster behind all this. I was bundled into a rear office by two more in city blue, where the blinds were drawn and a harsh yellow globe shone in my face. I blinked, strained, adjusted – could make out the presence, the bullish silhouette, Clarke at her work, sitting behind her desk. There was a scrape (it set my teeth on edge). A shadowy hand rummaged in a drawer, there was a pause while papers were sifted, then a photo was tossed down on the desk into the edge of that glaring yellow light. In low, relaxed, gravelly tones, the presence spoke—

'Recognise this man?' Here was Denham, in shiny monochrome.

'No,' I said. Another photo came skimming out of the dark, and the same unruffled voice—

'Him, then?'

'No. Sorry.' I didn't recognise Hughes either.

'Shame. This mean much to you?' Now, a typed folio, another reproduction. It read—

On tired grey, the fourth will remember. I shall be grieving the cynic's passing, or whatever. You review my rudimentary codes. In this climate, only the thermals and vectors.

I would be indebted to a lackey, who has no tact, is rebellious. If only you could, coin three neologisms in the sun. For a stairwell, read cerebration. On tired grey, there I relapse. A new light, severance. Jake, don't be exhumed!

We stare by gone PM. We lace the pre-prandials.

Stalin Tunnel.

Exit 39hiveclive.

It was the cipher, and I said 'No – it looks like gibberish.' The dark presence brought her fist or palm down heavily on the desk, sending assorted objects jumping and clattering back, but the voice was still calm—

'You lie.'

'Look, what do you want?'

'I want you to join the Federation.'

'Impossible!'

'Huh, I don't think so. WPC Blades was expecting to see you at five this afternoon.'

'Sorry, it slipped my mind.'

'That's not all. You've brought money into the country illegally. Your papers are forged. You're Hiller, this Hiller!' Another photo – a long-range shot – of Hiller, Denham, Hughes, drinking tea on a summer afternoon.

'Okay, so you know who I am.'

'You any idea what I could do to you? Don't make this difficult. Sign here....'

Now, out of the dark pool, an official, crested document, and a ballpoint. I read—

I, Officer Hiller, do solemnly undertake these duties, namely: To assist wherever possible in the elimination of extreme and dissident elements. To aid government in its foremost political aims: to close and police all borders; to establish the one-party State; to repatriate all non-Anglo Saxon types; to funnel endemic religions, both sacred and secular, into the one-party faith, and dissolve all others. To make all discourse the one true discourse. I, Officer Hiller, do solemnly swear....

I took up the ballpoint – the light was in my eyes – the presence calmly insisted. I hesitated...the pen was poised...and I....

Meakin

It was conceivable that the presence of Margo Quine would, in only a few days, cement his momentous decision, but before too much emphasis was placed on that event, the weary monographer dismissed it altogether. Of much more interest – in a mysterious, in a curious way – was Meakin's recent correspondence with George Kembal, whose smug, theatrical mask was known to millions nationally, and was pinned on an ebullient personality. Just what *was* his interest in a disillusioned academic? Kembal wouldn't know the professor's state of mind, particularly when, in reply to his probes, he never offered more than he had to, and rarely expressed a personal view. Now though he *was* being asked for a view. A request, definitely, threaded the bombastic loops in Kembal's newly minted note, the latest in a chain, in peril of dissolution in the steam of Meakin's bathroom.

'Huh! What *do* I think of Izzy Glicksteen?'

A flick of his hairy wrist launched that folded notepaper into short, crazy spirals through the agitated steam, but it fell woefully short of its destination – a daylight crack in the door – and plopped down among the fog of things on the cork floor: digital scales; a wicker bin, partially filled with bits of speckled tissue; blunt, disposable razors; a long-lost sliver of soap, dried out and wafer-thin at its tips.

Professor Meakin fished about between his legs and caught, swirling around, his favourite green flannel, then broke the surface of his bathwater. He wrung it out and applied its warm dampness to his face. His buttocks tautened for the moment he slid down the enamel, his hirsute torso sinking beneath the bubbles, under the bobbing luffa, under a hideous plastic frog. He stretched out an ankle heavily and searched for the hot tap with a fleshy big toe, and improvised a finger grip, though after a few spluttering warm dribbles the hot water soon ran cold. Instead, the exploratory toe hooked up the plug on its chain.

Just then the phone rang, and the surfacing whale of Professor Meakin assumed its correct *Homo sapiens* deliberation, the back foot following the front over the rim and onto those absorbent tiles. He slung on a towelling robe. We may follow the plash of his footsteps before they dry, through the door, across the hall, into the study, and glance at the broad shrugging shoulders, the receiver pressed to his ear, and take down one or two snatches of conversation: Tuesday at four – that could be difficult – Monday would be better…. What's that? He's out till then? Oh, what about later, Wednesday say…? Off to America! Lord! Back when…? Mm…. Yes, yes, of course. Tuesday at four – or could he make it five…? Splendid! Tuesday at five – I shall be out of London, you see….

He slammed down the receiver without much ceremony and thought he saw the swish of someone's disappearing coattail when he turned for the door, but knowing that to be impossible returned to the bathroom. Here with a palm to the mirror he produced in the smears and sluices something like a reflection, and pressing up to it smoothed back the sodden quiffs of his hair. Then he got down low, and flailed around in the metropolitan smog for Kembal's latest communication. All he could find was that bit of pre-war soap.

A dry and fully clothed Professor Meakin, despite his altitude above the courtyard, heard the persistent scrabbles below. Moreover, the rosy helper, doing dishes in a rear kitchen opposite his own, saw only a sedulous middle-aged man in profile at his balcony. He'd found the note, and easing up the sheet of blotting paper that smothered it took in the resultant mirror writing. Its schoolboy blobs hadn't concealed the truth: where Kembal had previously asked for samples of his work on Mahler, now he demanded his view of Izzy Glicksteen – a composer, conductor, or what? Well, perhaps the chirpy George Kembal enjoyed these practical jokes, dispatching Meakin to his *Grove's* fruitlessly. Could this have been the response to a review of a recent 'Titan' he'd sent to Kembal's office? Your lesser author hesitates at further defamation, so, when the conductor's silhouette stood on the podium, arms spread, baton maniacally raised, an unnamed orchestra launched itself Hollywood-style, its clarinet fanfares evocative of a teenage poltergeist. Meakin stuck with it, an eccentric reading, only for so long. He passed over the second movement, and in a late, redrafted paragraph wondered which of his readers had already guessed the moment he'd stormed from the auditorium. Meakin much preferred a heavyweight bout on a pub TV. One other writer summarised the whole ('Titan' that was, not the fight), as a thing charged and overwhelmed with emotional energy. But anyway. This is all beside the point.

The erubescent old char was now transfixed with a soapy little brush in one hand and a wet greasy dish in the other, and saw through all that rising steam a Professor Meakin unable to discern either her sex or her startled eyes. The scrabbling had brought him to his window, but that was an insufficient vantage. He went further, ushering in that brisk autumn air and stepping out among the dormant pots and tubs of his balcony. Scanning revealed not much more.

A dried patch of oil on the ornamental brick roughly coincided with the courtyard's southwest focus. The season had left the barbecue, no more than a built-in gridiron, with damp coals and solidified ashes. There was a triangular carousel of washing lines, folded and sheathed for the coming winter. There was, however, no explanation at all for the scrabbling.

Of course, there was one other perspective. What *he* heard, that char across the courtyard couldn't, yet her toils were unforgettably brightened when a funny academic type, whose over-large hands had tightened on the rail, bent slowly over the edge, searching. A squirrel, whose latest scramble for the wall ended in a higher assault of the pebble-dash, for the moment had failed in its aim. The hanging assortment of nuts on the balcony below Meakin's remained intact for the birds. The busy dishwasher found time in her day for a long, hearty chuckle, while Meakin, infuriated, returned to his apartment, scratching his head.

Kembal said that he wouldn't, then that he would, then at last that he couldn't meet Professor Meakin at the station, but advised that a long walk to the hotel meant a taxi would be better if his bag was heavy – 'Meet you in the bar for lunch.' The professor wasn't over-generous with the tip (since that 'Titan' review, not too much extra-curricular work had come his way), but the glass doors opened obligingly when he tramped for the foyer. The driver smirked when Meakin's gaberdine ballooned at the waist, a charge of warm, hospitable air coming up through a grating. He collected his key and an unexpected note at the desk, where the attendant's green livery no longer matched the walls, which had been repapered.

Meakin's was room 47, in the colder rear, to which he ascended in a padded lift, observing at every vertical plane another facet of himself, softened in the mirrors. Schmaltzy music accompanied: a piano, a drum, a thrumming bass.

His room overlooked the docks. He stood at the window with his note, and saw down below a laborious crane, dark and skeletal against the autumn sun, lifting its cargo hold to quay. In the distance an orange light nictitated urgently, the point where Meakin, fingering his envelope, foresaw the need for thicker fabric in the curtains. Farther out to sea, in the margin otherwise one with the leaden wash of the Channel, a few points of white or silver pierced the gathering mist. A manikin, a uniformed officer, strode across the wet asphalt and spoke. A bending stevedore released his grip on a rope, and standing, rubbing his awkward hands on his vest, revealed a red and green blur, a sword, or a heart, or a mermaid printed on his biceps. He shook his head, his arms akimbo, and smiled, the sun in his curly hair.

Meakin tore open the envelope and removed the note, and recognised immediately Kembal's over-elaborate hand, its swirling signature, and a postscript.

Professor,

So glad you made it. I always fancy an early lunch on these occasions – the bar at noon, say? Nothing too strenuous to start, perhaps a quick run through the schedule. You might even wish to toss in a few ideas. I'm open. I thought we could meet again at teatime – they do particularly good Black Forest gateau at my hotel. You know, rough out a few notes. Regards,

then, under the faultless typing, the pompous flourish, and below that, in a different shade of blue—

PS There's someone I'd like you to meet tonight, she's arriving later, unfortunately. Margo Quine, I believe you know her. Doubtless you're better placed than I to appreciate the very valuable contribution this literary lady will offer. Look forward to lunch. GK.

It wasn't what Meakin wanted to hear, but then the whole thing was becoming a fiasco anyway.

❦

In the same green livery the barman – a mere boy to Meakin – was new to the job – stuttering, nervous, clumsy. He had already soaked one frilly white coaster, and now, spilling the professor's pint again, whipped that away and tried to insert another. Failure. Attempts to mop up more pools of froth on the bar were no more assured, though Professor Meakin managed a smile, suspending his depleted jug mid-air. He scanned the full length of the mirror, through or above the inverted rank of spirits (no sign of Kembal yet), but returned his gaze to the boy's reflected occiput. The boy spoke, but Meakin wasn't paying attention. Instead he scrutinised the motif, a pink rosette, woven into the breast pocket of the boy's hotel jacket. (From Meakin's later observations red petals fringed with gold denoted management, while ushers or porters, sullen and long-faced, were granted black cockades.) The boy repeated himself, and the professor, noting a new coaster, at last saw the absurdity of his pose. He put down his drink. Then with a new influx into the bar, the boy switched on more of that groaning Muzak.

Kembal strode in – neat, trim, bouffant – and unknown to his millions, short. Meakin introduced himself and offered a drink. Kembal pre-empted that and ordered a carbonated water – very specific about the splash of ice, the slice of lemon. He paid with a flourish. He wanted to get down to business straightaway, though Meakin paused. 'Just who is this Glicksteen?' he asked.

George Kembal spread his arms and showed his palms and shirt cuffs. A craggy dimple in an upper chin formed with the elastic strain of his smile. 'You've never heard of Izzy Glicksteen!' (that voluble exclamation so ungracious in a man whose material for magazine broadcasts had ranged from Homer to Warhol). He explained. Some recent and very loud plaudits had arrived belatedly, and Glicksteen, late director of B movie, *film noir* classics, was now considered a genius of that particular genre. Sadly Hollywood, and more spectacularly America, had judged him otherwise, and the gritty realist, who brought to a starry-eyed audience the unglamorous truth of narcotics and prostitution, was made a pariah. That wasn't all. His politics and the McCarthy era spelled his professional ruin. However, no one had reckoned on his strength of purpose, and miraculously, in the cutting rooms of Europe, a sprawling masterpiece slowly emerged – an autobiography, the tragic middle life of Izzy Glicksteen.

The studious Professor Meakin, so precise and careful in his interests, waited till the beaming, diminutive George Kembal reached for his drink, to partake, no, but act as centrifuge on its ice and lemon.

'A familiar tale,' said Meakin, 'but I still don't see what you want of me.'

'Ah,' said Kembal. 'Should have explained. Need a Mahler man. I don't know why, but Glicksteen's bio-pic featured all the symphonies somewhere or other. No original music was scored.'

Meakin resisted – 'You don't know Mahler!' – though said he would help where he could. 'By the way,' he added, 'I can't make tea this afternoon, and may be late back tonight.'

This week, the nautical image, and Harry Clance, who'd consulted his almanac, and had his cards read, had searched his extensive wardrobes with more zest than usual. Beware death by drowning. No hint of his tabloid mysticism must ever reach the board, however, and on this, October's first Tuesday, the regular pinstripe sufficed as always. When he delivered his *coup*, the populist newspaper had already been tucked away in a top drawer. What replaced it in his smart executive case were some of those intolerable highbrows, all with their impossible crosswords.

His remarkable lightness of mood wasn't due merely to the glorious autumn sunshine, bewitching in its auburn showers. When the minutes of the board were gone through, and the unresolved question of Professor Meakin was raised again, Harry gently tapped the glass of his watch and smiled.

'Gentlemen,' he said, 'I can say I am ninety-five per cent sure our learned friend will be joining us.'

That twentieth, less certain part remained to be coaxed, and the professor, amazed at Harry's cream slacks, tailed him through a chintzy lift and corridors. In the vacant boardroom the pads and water jugs had been whisked away. Low lights were already on, and the blinds were drawn against the dusk of afternoon. Harry swung open the door, and in his friendly usher's pose showed off the shiny brass buttons, with anchors in relief, stitched in a double row to his jacket.

Professor Meakin stepped in, taming his curiosity: that trip to America was a vacation, clearly, and in lingering holiday mood Harry Clance just couldn't bring himself to wear a suit.

'Do, do sit down,' said Harry, pulling out the chairman's seat. He smoothed away a speck or two of dandruff and replanted the chair in front of a TV screen. This was Harry's *pièce de résistance*, the propaganda video, so adroitly slotted in by him, and switched on remotely as he departed backwards – almost bowing. When the door fastened the yawning professor had long ago formed his preconceptions, and those happy glowing cherubs, those vacuous sales associates with sporty cars and dazzling autobiographies, kept him entertained for forty minutes or so, though the accompanying music was no great improvement on the hotel's.

The doyenne of pseudo-science had persisted all these years with a model terminology, and had denied on many triumphant occasions that the theorist's vocabulary only obscured already tedious hypotheses. She was down from Olympus briefly now, and while the professor picked up a second note at the desk, she explained to Kembal that her own researches pre-empted Meakin's in one important respect. Kembal repressed a yawn and considered the rising blobs of gas in a perfect gin and tonic. For Margo, fortuitous distractions like these confirmed her presence – in practically any society – as demanding pause for thought in everyone around. Emphatic portents evolved with the sudden tautness of her oranged lips, and to Meakin – whose gloomy realisation rested in the remote possibility of passing the cocktail lounge without being seen – that smile of unassailable conviction was sharply contradicted by the merry glaze of her contact lenses. Over a dry Martini, she delivered herself with usual authority, with Mahler's predilection for boys her newest revelation.

Meakin shuddered at the prospect of renewed acquaintance, and recalled his first meeting with Margo, when one of those varsity mags sought a new editor, and put her at the head of its shortlist. Other contenders gradually fell away, and for her first official assignment she proclaimed the brightness of a new intellectual age. That fruitless retrospection, all that preoccupation with the labours and achievements of the past, could now be swept aside, making way for something more socially meaningful. Of course Meakin, with those studied views of his, those dignified articles, was among the first of the casualties (some fifteen years later, that was a matter of indifference). What palled was the problem of immediate escape, where his only solution was in feigning a migraine. So resigned, he stepped into the broad space between the door jambs, where on the evening's happy hour one of those liveried boys had bunched the concertina doors. A radiant red – a mysterious midnight blue – an emerald green – were reflected off a glitter ball above – though why a polychrome halo hovered over the plain Margo Quine he couldn't begin to guess. Fatefully she spotted him, and averted her gaze, but the slight snarl of an upper lip – a nasty orange gash – unexpectedly brought him a smile, for its exact synchronisation with a recorded round of applause – not, as it happened, for him. In the precious hush that followed, a piped cabaret pianist, no doubt wearing a sickly smile, embarked on more of that schmaltz.

Kembal, glad of this new diversion, got up and dusted down his tuxedo, wanting to shake hands. 'At last, at last – now why don't you and Margo get together over her very interesting ideas!'

Meakin turned his coat collar down. 'Not tonight, I'm afraid. Headache. Been a bad day. See you tomorrow at eight, *if* you haven't changed the plan....'

Kembal hadn't, and watched, with his hands in his trouser pockets, while Meakin trudged to his room. There, snorting, looking out over the dark Channel, at its changing points of light, he mixed a cocktail and phoned downstairs for some cherries.

Here was a new phenomenon, so hard to acknowledge, though happy good fortune made him the first, solitary witness. Kembal had followed a long, unwinding bend, ignoring his strange apprehension as only a faint, incipient thing. That was a wrong decision, for when the rising phobia insisted on life, it did so insidiously. So much was threatened – his usual equanimity couldn't be depended on – therefore potent remedies had to be tried. And wasn't this an uncomfortable truth, when he found himself shambling, when he couldn't stop watching his feet – and worse, when he suddenly tired of all the responsibilities? Wasn't that boorish professor to blame?

The banners, the diplomatic flags, then the glassy edifice of Meakin's hotel peeped out from behind a yew, while the bouncy gait that had marked George Kembal's odyssey – a long life's journey to the start of *this* broad turn – had deserted him. The sun in the morning mist smiled brightly for a moment or two, then slumbered again in its swirls of cotton wool.

It was almost eight. When Kembal reached him, Meakin had been hanging on impatiently in the foyer. He bustled out with his heavy case and grunted at the vacant taxi stand. Then he struck out past the yew for the bend, where Kembal, moving quickly for a little man, was able to flank him. He cleared his throat.

'I don't mean to press. The programme goes out at Christmas. Does this, er, commission – I mean does it interest you at all?'

Meakin shuffled, interrupting that rhythmic stride, and swung the case in a half-ellipse, round and in front of his knees to the unworked arm. A watery mist rolled in off the sea and left its moist deposits in his hair, and in damp little streaks on the flesh of his face.

'You see, Margo's unearthed some surprising facts on Glicksteen, but I need a Mahler man – or you.'

A following breeze lifted the shaggy fringe of Meakin's hair. He turned up his collar. 'Margo's always unearthing surprising facts – that's been her dubious trade from the first.'

The pale sun over the sea wouldn't ever get out today, and in the thickening mist Kembal turned up *his* collar. 'I can't comment on that, of course. I'm pleased with her work on *this* project.'

Meakin slowed up. His turn for the seafront was here, or no, just there, ahead, but had disappeared in the drizzle. Kembal tried another approach. A miner's boy who got to Oxford, his first appreciation of Meakin's work was through his early iconoclasm, and a series of essays, where the common premise rested on the eternal issue of class, in particular its English warfare. He recalled the inexorable climax, a quite brilliant and spirited burlesque of the bourgeoisie, there in its clueless charade at concert halls. Meakin stopped and sniffed the damp air, and finding the seafront, turned. He didn't doubt Kembal's sincerity, but wouldn't care to test his views, say, on the means of propaganda in the hands of his broadcast colleagues.

'There's no reason really for me to be here,' he said. 'What you want to know about Mahler I can put in the post.'

Here was the station coming up, and Kembal, for once, was embarrassed.

'Oh, that! I only chose this location because Glicksteen spent the last seven years of his life here, in a nursing home. We've talked to a few people who knew him quite well.'

An orange light far out to sea momentarily pierced the mist. Meakin thought only of his train, and began to imagine, then was there, in the sleazy lunchtime darkness of the Rose and Crown. Harry Clance, insurance consultant, had been waiting, and when he remarked on what was obvious – that the life of a sales associate was a far cry from academe – he expected an honest reply. But Meakin had already learnt it – mendacity – the first rule of commerce. The answer was, academe I care about, but this is just a job, though he explained how much he looked forward to the coming prospects, the new, exciting challenge, the broader horizon ahead....

The Evangelising Power of War

I suppose the wound I received was really of little consequence. I was, however, a young fighter – and it *was* my first wound. Almost instantly I forgot about the old men of war and the scenes of battle they'd described. I was wholly preoccupied with the terrible pain that filled my being. Nobody, I thought, can have felt this illimitable ache as I do; nobody has known the horrors of war in quite this way. I limped away. I took refuge. I would reassess the situation.

Of course, I rejected it, but the idea of desertion occurred to me – for the first time. Like everybody else, I'd been trained for war, had given too much of my forming years to that end, and would not now fit comfortably or confidently into civilian life.

I nursed my wound – I considered the various forms of revenge – and I brooded. Now, I cannot help but brood again.

I begin with the person who inflicted my wound, difficult though he is to describe. He was a man of so many perspectives, so many different guises, that from one day to the next I just couldn't be sure that, as an honest soldier, he'd ever stand toe-to-toe in combat. But of this I *was* certain. I'd never cease haunting this man, would never weaken in my deployment against him, would never allow him a moment's peace of mind – even when, this worst of enemies, a man I'd stalked and antagonised, sneered at, ridiculed, despised – even when I found him impossible to subdue. And why, why *was* that?

He didn't seem to be a man of particular physical prowess. In truth he was not strong, certainly no stronger than I. Rather, his success was due to certain flaws in his character, which would allow him to fight only within strict limitations. On first suspicion he was out of his depth he would run, hide, elude me, cheat me. It was this precise knowledge of his own fallibility that gave him his ingenuity, uncannily. Then, preferring to ignore my menaces, he showed the timid side of his nature. When we did fight, it was only after unendurable taunts and pressure. And yet – and this I can see clearly now – I was always in his mind, as he waited only for the moment when, as a genuine rival, I could see him as my equal.

Nothing escaped his watchful eye, despite my efforts to conceal much of what I did. None of my plans, conceived and calculated in every last detail, seemed enough to overwhelm him. He would clutch at his charmed medallion, his visage might suddenly change, and I have lost count of the times he stood before me – not as a fighter or foe – but as someone who wanted to be my friend, was at the very least a reluctant enemy, an unfortunate like me thrown into this senseless squabble. How could I strike out at such a man?

You see, at the very moment that question formed, I hesitated. And at the very moment I thrust it aside and looked to first principles – what had been inculcated in my remotest boyhood – my inspiration died. By then he had turned and fled, unable to make the crucial decision – either defend his own cause, or throw in his lot with ours.

Here, I have a confession. It was never my company's intention to indoctrinate anyone. It was my own idea to capture and convert this man (my family, my religion, my political affiliations – all share a history deeply rooted in evangelism).

❧

What of the early days? I can say this: there was never a more willing student, never a cadet more qualified for the grim business of war, never a trained soldier more eager to distinguish himself in his first raid or manoeuvre. But this is where my subtlety set me even farther apart from my contemporaries. Know-alls had come and gone before, and had met their various fates. *My* quality was not my fighting spirit alone, but an encyclopaedic knowledge of military history, strategy and hardware. To crown it, I had discipline and patience. I was young, I had time, and I could wait.

Or could I? When that wait turned out to be a protracted one, it was with two disturbing results. The first was my growing friendship with some of the old men of war, and my awareness of a certain coolness on their part. If they didn't say it, they had singled me out for leadership. Informed, inventive talent shouldn't be wasted. If we were going to win this war we needed individuals like me. Natural leaders. Visionaries. This was good, eventually too good for my highly competitive nature, when strange caution contradicted their intentions. Soon they showed an unwillingness to send me into the cut and thrust, into the action. Of course, when I rebelled, as anyone must, it was without authority that I gathered up my weapons, that I walked out on the plains, and, once there, that I steadfastly fixed my gaze on my target, determined not to fail.

That was how the man of the many identities became my personal symbol of all that the world must be rid of. I hunted him relentlessly, day and night, in the harsh bright sunshine or under the icy stars, in my dreams and in my thoughts.

It was never easy. At times I cursed my superior erudition, because however I designed my strategy (it was always theoretically perfect) he astounded me with something completely unconventional, and therefore unpredictable. My dignity shouldn't allow me to scuttle after my quarry in woodlands or bushes. I abhorred his long cowardly treks into unknown country – which, if I wasn't careful, would end in a sleazy night raid, and a knife in my back, my shadowy assailant slinking off without having shown his face. I was reduced to gauging all such low behaviour. Yet in meeting his cunning with my education, I never had the stealth to aim the vital blow – in fact I suffered that myself.

I fell, deeply hurt, my self-assurance suddenly deserting me. He stood in the sun, arms akimbo, puzzled.

'Why?' he said. 'Why me?'

I watched him through the slits of my eyes, but said nothing. He turned and retreated.

❧

I returned, intending to remain alone, but when those gnarled old warriors took me aside, I told them what had happened – unnecessarily, as it turned out, because they'd watched. I hadn't done badly, they said, but now it was time for words of advice. This was not a war of honour or valour, not a crusade, and in some ways not even a war to be won. It was simply a nagging question, and one we had asked more years ago than anyone could remember. No one had the answer (an important point), and it was only with that realisation that you truly knew the enemy.

'What you imply casts everything in doubt,' I said. 'Why have you never mentioned this before?'

'We're glad you have that capacity to question. It gives us hope.'

'Hope!'

'Think about what we've said....'

I retired temporarily, I was treated, and I made my way alone into the hills. Perhaps if I consider, reflect, I will overcome my doubts and difficulties (a new experience for me). But nothing, nothing – no wise words, no counselling – will ever dampen this fire, this lust that I have, this terrible desire to get down there again, when I am well, and have my revenge. To cut him down, to eliminate that other, that spineless foe, that man of the multiple identity.

Noose

Of all those once at the arc of my private cosmos, there is one who refuses to fall. He leans from remembered windows. He chatters in his nervous way with fleeting ghosts. He charms a forgotten neighbour across the hall, and with the bottle of milk he's appropriated floats to our door, his thin, bloodless lips hiding a smirk. He knows our correct relationship – classified for general use in mine, not his reflective world. I, Matthew Bello, watching from my towers, at home among the peaks and crags remote from other ways of life – I have yet to see him slide, the fire gone out, his approaching end, finality, a mad descent, a fall hardly ruffling the surface of the sea.

I am DC Matthew Bello, lost to the ills and discontents of civilisation. I trail the bereft and disaffected, men and women hopeless in their crimes, too clumsy not to betray themselves. In a reversal of old chronologies that chase is counterpoised with the vignettes I paste in a scrapbook, such as this one here, with its glimpse of Jonnie Slinger.

Briefly this is him—

Tall, thin, grey complexion, wicked blue eyes. A stoop, only slight. Abstracted almost permanently. Intelligent, clever, gifted even. A man I placed mid-forties. Odd socks (lime green and yellow are his favourite pair), jaunts to the local shops in carpet slippers. A shock of grey hair. If you're passing and have the time, look in on the breakfast room. It's a sordid mess that never sees the sun. There's a light, humming among the orange chevrons printed on its lampshade, which moves in a draught from the window, inches above the table. There are mere tokens to domesticity: yesterday's tea cups, and a cloudy half bottle of milk, already a noxious solid; a watch, a bunch of keys, an open paperback facedown in the crumbs; a packet of biscuits; a shop apple pie under a starry coat of sugar, its aluminium tray turned over and flattened. I stop short. In fact I move to reverse and clear that filth away, to put there instead, in a theatrical light, a hangman's noose, a gavel, a foreman's chair – and I shall show you why....

These multiple inborn obstacles I am packaged with look different from those seen in others, as stubborn and problematic I'm sure, yet easy to trivialise – placards pinned to people I shall never know, or not ever know as friends. I am well aware of what's bred institutionally, a salve for the conscience, a soft landing for chauvinistic bias.

That made it easy to dismiss Mrs Bishop as wholly out of touch. Quaint in her expectations, that querulous octogenarian took her social position as divine in its rights, a landlady whose demands went beyond the monthly rent and the setting out of house rules. It's the crux of my weakness, when so much human squalor has magnetised my gaze, longingly, to the clean, tidy, well ordered bourgeois house such as hers is. In time I'll admire those anodyne interiors you see in solid, middle-class homes. And look – do come and take in, for just a moment, the mottled pink marble of Mrs Bishop's hearth, or the shiny brass of the fender. Or on a dresser, mixed up with the clutter of family photos, an ornate clock, with its moving cogs and springs in regular working order under a glass dome. On sunny afternoons her airy drawing room is awash with coloured lights, through a symmetry of leaded panes. The wallpaper is a riot of pattern-book flora, while the family portraits are pompous. There are leather-bound classics, neatly aligned in period cabinets gathering dust. I ask, are these the proper attractions of, or do they render more extreme, the cold vicious winds icing our century?

But enough was enough. A long, complicated conspiracy case was reaching its climax, and I had to be at my rugged best. Mrs Bishop and her foibles weren't a great help, and nor were the legal delays. There had been several of these, all of them technical, but I could not impress on my landlady that at last a date had been fixed. Now there would be days, even a week in court, when I'd have to leave the house early, and come home late.

In our card games and imbecile chitchat, she often alluded to but without great detail the men of her family – all having had careers in finance. Last night it recurred, just as she needed a trick. She tossed a three of spades onto the baize. Her cold, wrinkled hand remained still for a moment, as she waited to gather the pack. By now my king of hearts knew he was trumped, and in his mania thrust his sword sideways through his skull. Some photo I'd never really studied now focused her attention. She glanced away – over the fireplace, over the ornamental eggs, the frogs, the silky candlesticks. Again I heard about her husband – a man fifteen years dead – in life a pillar of the Bank of England. I looked out from the fringed light of a standard lamp into the gloaming, and all I could see was this: a puffed-up portrait, a man stern, grey and Victorian. Thereafter I was in for the whole filial saga. Her first son was in mortgages, another was a journalist, his name all over the money page of a tabloid I never read. A daughter completed the set, when she and her husband worked in a High Street bank. The son-in-law I was due to meet, so now I'd be home early knowing he was coming. I spared him the embarrassment of taking me aside. *I took him.*

There had been that recent storm, and I told him, opening mildly, how the wall was drying where the gutter had been fixed. It was a repair he'd arranged.

'Redecoration next,' he said. 'For a few days you'll have to move to another room.'

'Actually I'm moving to another house.'

'Oh?'

As always in awkward moments, he fingered the back pocket of his slacks and checked on the presence of his billfold.

'Mrs Bishop doesn't relax her rules. In fact they're *more* draconian.'

He fished around in a side pocket, jangling his change. 'It's all news to me,' he said, and looked to the door. Despite all hopes, the shiny ceramic knob didn't rotate, the hinges didn't open with a squeak. Mrs Bishop was still in front of her cheval-glass, dressing.

'I don't mind the occasional card game.' I crossed the room to the bay window, where the cleaner had got the net curtains caught in a candelabrum. I unhitched them. 'But I cannot play punctually at seven every night.'

He asked if I couldn't extricate myself from a routine I must have allowed to develop.

'I have,' I said. 'In retaliation she bolts the front door before she goes to bed. It means I have to phone and get her up if I get back late, or go out. My house key's practically useless.'

He shrugged. 'She's nearly ninety. She is nervous on her own.'

'I don't think anyone now would accept these conditions.'

He shrugged again, but this time was saved, when a twist of the knob made him step away and open the door. Nonplussed – for she knew I was home, but not in here – his mother-in-law remained in the hall, where I just about made out the reddish thunder in the walnut of her face, part obscured by its layers of foundation.

'I cannot wait another moment!' she said, addressing no one.

He went out, looking at his watch. 'Yes. Better make haste.' He'd booked a table for lunch.

The front door closed. She tottered down the drive on his arm. Her daughter sprang from the waiting car and helped her in.

I still look back, to her dewy lawns, the rhododendrons, the patios and pergolas, the white gables – as all that falls behind. A hawthorn part obscures the garden stepping-stones, and when I turn – when I have to turn and look forward – mist has settled on the city and its paving slabs, where there are weeds sprouting in the cracks.

It was Monday. I picked up a paper from the stand, where a man selling flowers scratched the stubble of his chin and plucked a cigarette from behind his ear. A train clattered overhead on the iron bridge, too early to have filled. A bus pulled in, and a small boy clutching a violin case got off and ran, hopelessly, for the train. The driver checked his mirror and pulled away. The boy, having launched up the stairway, leapt from its final step, and in the flurry of his blue and white scarf tumbled onto the platform. Too late. Morning twilight filled those windows passing by, and the boy, his arms apart, could only watch a blur of nodding heads, those nameless ghosts returning to their city haunts.

I watched till the bus had reduced itself to a reddish speck, and turned for the market. Now I had the whole seedy vista, in its rows of crumbling Victorian houses, laid out motionless before me.

I came to a familiar house, with hollowed steps, and a huge front door. I ran eyes up, down, up again, and could hardly believe that up there, behind the dormer, in the dust and disorder of his attic room, I had arrested Vincent Voisard and read him his rights....

Just then his younger brother Marco slid from an alleyway, with loping strides. He had got new rollerblades. He lifted a foot and replanted it lazily, and stopped, like me, a yard from the railings. A pigeon swooped and banked and flew away. He had got an unopened carton of orange juice, which he juggled from hand to hand.

'New skates,' I said, though nothing I now uttered was welcome by the Voisard family. 'Blades,' he said. 'They're blades.'

'Oh well, they're snazzy. Suit you.'

He sneered, and bent over double, his arms dangling, and pulled up his ankle socks. Could I remember where I'd seen him last? Let's see. Ah yes: lounging – months ago – in the small hours – in his usual pose. Venue? That's inexact. A doorway. Behind it was a club – or one of many fronts in Chinatown. Vincent's kid brother Marco, in a brown leather jacket buckled at the waist, a black shirt, and dark glasses, boasted a new, expensive wardrobe. This was *before* the arrest, when all of us smiled.

I caught the twitch of a curtain where his dumpy little mother was at her bedroom window. Marco palmed his brows and ran his fingers through his hair. 'Look,' I said, 'if he's innocent, what's the worry...?' He looked up to the bedroom window, where the curtains had closed again.

The *Daily Mail*, he said, had already reached the nation's verdict. 'Who needs a jury?'

He was right, I knew, regardless of whether or not I'd assembled evidence against his brother. I changed the subject, and asked if he'd found a job. I should have known better. I had to explain that no, I wasn't puzzled about the skates (meaning rollerblades) – I did in fact believe they were paid for.

I left him. It would take months, years (I might *never* re-establish good relations), and for once was first at the office. I opened and spread out the paper, and put a ring round this—

Sharer reqd quiet nbrhood own rm gch non-smoker prefd.

Then this—

2nd prof person wanted share flat close town no pets.

And this—

Rm call any time. Short.

I waited till after eight, but the first when I called gave only a recorded message and the second had already gone. That left the unpromising third, and Jonnie Slinger, who picked up his hall receiver and put on his best telephone voice, which nevertheless hadn't eliminated, with its public-school overtones, a last trace of Staffordshire vowels. He told me to come and take a look, some time after six.

A brown sky hanging. I jumped from the bus, just as those little grey sacks – sagging and swollen – gave in. A taxi's yellow hire light went on, and its wipers – in agitated sweeps – got only faster. I tried to flag him down, but the driver, palming away a film of condensation, swung round recklessly into the oncoming traffic, and headed back to town. I turned up my collar. A dripping *Prunus* glistened on the pavement. My neck was damp. There was a patisserie. I jangled change in my pocket, a handful of coppers a shop girl had given me. An old man tottered by on a stick. His shiny mackintosh wrapped round him tightly in a sudden gust of wind. Streaks of red and amber smudged the wet paving slabs (an inverse world, in its ruffled pool the fragmented rainbow in an early English spring). My blunted optimism could not brighten even so.

There was a rising sheet of smoke when someone lit a cigarette. I glanced upward at the roofs, and set off through Slinger's breezy avenues, a maze of tiny frontages and orange slate. Eventually I stood at Slinger's outer door and spoke through his intercom. I ascended the dark stairwell, with its ancient wallpaper and a piquancy of faded cooking smells. I stepped across the threshold into his Oriental, or partly Oriental hall. All so far, as cardinal points, had brought me a few steps nearer that bizarre, eccentric imagination of his, so much more sophisticated than any I had known.

The little sign on his study door – a hortative *Do it now!* – was the kernel of his rhetoric. He alone saw the only way forward, when the whole of civilisation immersed itself in negative debate, which spawned an almost unlimited capacity for self-delusion. I liked his jokes, even though he frowned – as a man groomed for captaincy and industry. Often he thought I'd *missed* the point.

I have had my own revolution, and with pre-emptive apologies in paragraph two have overturned at least one orthodoxy – the planar world of linear narrative. Synaptic connections are put down verbatim in an alternative written geometry. There's nothing to stop me, now that I share in Slinger's departures.

His campus friends were the first not to recognise his genius – the mid-60s. There was something in the way they gripped their beer cans. In the July heat, two, three together raised their heads (headbands too). Slinger stood up and bowed – no one knew why – having calculated every coincidence of time and place, and reserved the sunny spots in his garden. They were for *his* chair. Among his evergreen tomatoes, someone pale and hirsute veiled his nakedness in the way he held his guitar, and played endlessly the same chords, the same progression.

The explanation? No one was ever given that. Certainly not me, though Slinger seemed to like me. He offered a short-term let, for which I showed gratitude.

I mentioned his little bronze Buddha in the hall, a handy place to hang a hat, and smiled at his phone, a well-trained Donald Duck holding out an earpiece on a spotlessly gloved palm.

'Is that a reminder?' I said, looking at the sign on his closed door – his *Do it now!* He tossed back that riotous grey mane and opened the study. I'd had a good look round the rest of the flat – on that day it was tidy – but here in his den was a pile of junk. An electric piano with its back off. An attractive old harmonium. Bits of computer and circuitry and other things I didn't understand. A soldering iron, sheathed, on its workbench – that instrument permanently on, with its tiny red warning light flashing monotonously.

Einstein and Maxwell hung in respective picture frames, but between them a couple of toothpaste girls spurted from a tube, their naked, nymph-like bodies fused, from the knees down, into a mermaid's fin. Then that witty contraption – his brainchild, historic work of his youth – weird depiction he was proud of as his only attempt with oils. It was signed, curiously, BLZB. Two silver shafts crossed in the perpendicular somewhere in interstellar space. Where each would touch the hypotenuse, a mirror at forty-five degrees reflected a point of light.

'It's a timepiece,' he said.

I couldn't see how, as a triangle more at home in Escher's world.

'Mm. Well. I'll take the room,' I said, 'but you'll have to explain the joke.'

He frowned. 'Another time.'

Of course. It'd take too long. I turned to go. 'I'll move in at the weekend,' I said.

He shook his head. 'No. That's not possible. I've got business here on Sunday afternoon. Make it Monday.'

Just then Donald started ringing.

'Fine. Until Monday....'

Slinger excused himself. I tripped down the stairs. I stepped out into the pouring rain.

Light, in its dimmed emissions, left its penumbral fringe, where in Slinger's midnight continuum the fourth dimension had only limited scope to regulate his life. I had problems, work, and watched him only fitfully at first, in the aftermath of his Sunday business. I was left, in the days that followed, to clear the table and wash up breakfast bowls, or a teacup – things I needed. On that sore point I asked myself, what did he do all day apart from sleep? In the evenings and into the night he was tucked away in his study – probably *doing it now* – with the radio for company. Always news or current affairs – squeaky shrills in a scrimmage with someone's grounded thoroughbass. His studied dishevelment saw him careful not to comb his hair, and particular to choose a candy-stripe for the left sock, stars for the right. On one rare morning, when I caught him wearing matching reds, I said to him, pointing down, 'You've got odd socks...' – a comment unable to penetrate the blur of his waking-up.

I know how first opinions never count for much. When I looked at the litter of technical books on the breakfast-room floor, I accepted, with reservation, that the Bohemian persona he put on, took off, a fleeting figure at his mirror every day, might really be permanent. Even if he wanted to, it wasn't possible to deter the strange-looking people who dropped in regularly in the dead hours of morning. I met them sometimes. There was a midget in leather tights and a shirt with hoops. He wore bangles on both wrists, and as earring a little brass stud. His hair he'd got up in yellow and violet quiffs (an electric shock). There was a toothy giant – another circus renegade – who arrived with his helmet still on, and with the same paperback, bearing the same fictitious name – someone called Carlos Cast – just visible and lopsided in the top pocket of his jacket. For him, the long ride here was through hellish hoops of fire (apparently).

With that pair came my first, and acutest difficulty, which I mentioned to Slinger. I insisted that professionally I might consider myself conscientious but certainly not a zealot. Implication was I wasn't about to turn him in for the sachets of cocaine his visitors delivered. Thereafter the pocket mirror and razor blade miraculously disappeared, with a 'Look! I want to be perfectly clear! If I'd known you were a copper....'

To the contrary, that comment clarified nothing. He told me that the 'real' crime was in having made, and being about to lose, a fortune. He'd built his corner of commerce with his own two hands – which he held out – but hadn't been that clever in his choice of business partner. He was talking about his theme park – games, not rides – a house with an angled floor, where balls rolled uphill. There were 3-D jigsaws, and holograms, and in the grounds a complex maze. His partner, a man named Warne, who took care of business, he suspected was defrauding on their taxes, but couldn't ward off the VAT people for much longer.

I turned to the kitchen sink, the draining board, and gazed through the nets hopelessly: everywhere, those stacks of dirty plates – those leaning towers, the slop-filled cups – the sticking pans. Everywhere, Slinger's disorder, Slinger's peccadilloes.

They shared a national tailor and went to the same optician, or so Slinger warned. One of those intractable, career-minded auditors, a grey inspector of taxes – in narrow pinstripes, in shop-front spectacles – would catch up with a hapless Warne one day, and coolly set out a list of impossible questions. Slinger had traced his partner's origins to the Third Reich, and whatever 'Warne' was an Anglicisation of, he was now referred to as Wurm, or Worm. I met him – a tall, swarthy, beaming man – but wasn't properly introduced. My hand hovered, making up its mind. Warne was jovial, even at the utterance of Slinger's new epithet for him. He offered a broad smile, and chuckled. I shook. We all went through to what was now not the breakfast room, but Slinger's makeshift courtroom.

I can explain why I agreed to this, though I now have doubts. Bear with me as I retrace steps – back a few hours, a day – and re-enter at the Crown Court, Knightsbridge. The first of ten defending barristers had stood up in the chilly forenoon and replied to the case I had previously set out. I had been watching. Counsel nearest to me kept twisting on and off the lid of his turquoise fountain pen, lounging smugly in his chair. In moments of agitation he hunched his upper frame over his notepad, and adjusted his wig. That, under its dazzling whiteness, showed Judge Brett a tidal blackness of hair, which matched his gown. He accomplished his first, most important task, well rehearsed by now, with confidence, and with a few well-chosen wisecracks drew smiles from the solemn twelve, the jury.

When he came to question me, he got what he wanted, reasonable doubt and a case for the prosecution undermined. Much did he imply as to professional integrity, as he quoted frame references from the surveillance video. To be precise, these were 211, 502, 1714–16 – which he rattled off without a glance at his notes. At those points in the video, he suggested nowhere could I seriously propose I'd identified Vincent Voisard. He turned from the jury and back to me, repeating that inanity: '*Seriously* propose, mark.' There were no words in a short reply pointing up the contrapuntal plot in the case against: the hundreds of hours of video tape I had spent months sifting, sorting, slowing, highlighting; the plain fact that I knew Vincent so well – his looks, his mannerisms, the clothes he wore, his friends. At 211, where a silver balloon bobs across the lens and takes out an ear, an eye, the glow of a cheek, the observer Bello is left with Vincent Voisard, the ringleader, that man in the dock with nine others. At 502, when he turns to a girl in the crowd (a carnival crowd, and a girl who knows his game and lunges back) – that blurry scowl is his and only his. At 1714–16, the last, that rearward shot is of him passing under a bunting. How do I know it's him? Well…the way he hitches his jacket, his cocky stride – is where I rest my case. Yet I said only this—

'I am certain that is Mr Voisard.'

The morning and its South Sea lustre. I argued even among colleagues. I asserted, more in hope than anything, and with earnest open palms, that our learned performer from the Temple, in his opening matinée, and that swagger under the proscenium, wasn't going to win. But I did not mention, even to a hangdog sergeant – a man with world-weary jowls, leaning on a forearm – how at the curtain I had sprinted down the Crown Court steps, the rain coming down, with only an evening paper in place of an umbrella. With a splash on the newly silvered pavement, I pushed my way past ten angry mothers with placards (innocent sons, police harassment, xenophobia, and more). As enemy to their cause, I retreated in the drizzle, institutionally racist, corrupt to the core, and not even worth their abuse. Their dozen counterparts within, the twelve good and true, casting round for hats and bags and buckling their coats, needed all the friendly guidance their presence asked for: something more objective than popular liberal caution tinged with the perils of the blue rosette.

Inspector Blamm wasn't sympathetic. With usual asperity, he showed me to my desk and told me to get it sorted out – the case, in all its damning detail. What bureaucratic panacea he expected me to concoct at this stage, I couldn't guess. I had still no better ideas when after 7.30 those intermittent creaks of his chair in the adjoining cubicle were brought to an end – by a sudden scrape, by the click of his light going off, by the thud of his outer door. I relaxed. Now I was free to ease pains in a softened view of opening-day disasters, and by ten had leered with fatal unconcern at a drink too many. I slid merrily off my bar stool. At twelve, loath to leave my club, Joey refused me another highball, but helped me from my seat, as somehow I slithered, a game right arm in a resisting left armhole. I tottered out to a waiting cab but came back, sure this shabby raincoat had two sleeves this morning when I put it on. Joey wiped away his irritation. He touched his crinkled brows with the braid of a cuff. He put his cocktail shaker down and whipped away a napkin, categorically refusing me another drink. I thanked him soberly only later, in the course of time – when four of those ten were convicted of conspiracy to steal, and the affable Judge Brett committed the other six to retrial – though for now he saw me safely slumped in the rear of a cab. The driver gripped his wheel, with his scowl fixed on the windscreen.

'Easy,' I said. 'St John's Wood.'

A shady green peak kept company with Jonnie's flat cap over the Buddha's knees, while two other guests, North and South at the bridge table, had come hatless. Jonnie was wearing his pale green safari shirt, with its two patchwork breast pockets and mother-of-pearl poppers. East, an emaciated, aquiline drummer, and author of lyrics, wore make-up – a touch of mascara darkened his upper lashes. He shook with laughter when Slinger gave him a 1NT to think about (that was *too* avant-garde for a poor beginner). I looked for apologetic signs – Acol, Blackwood, keep out! – and found only a pile of empty wine bottles. Slinger uncorked another, a Côtes de Provence, and applauded my timing (there went my hopes of getting to bed). When the fridge was opened again, an icy charge accompanied a hapless counter-bid, a brace of spades (a puzzling riposte, as I glanced at North's hand and saw how it was spread).

'Sit down, sit down,' said Slinger, pouring my glass.

Across the table was a new-look manikin, with still those spiky quiffs, but dyed a chocolate brown with cherry red. He rubbed at his nose, which was cold, a bit put out at the break in conversation my arrival had caused. Slinger said: 'So much for the geosynchronous satellite....' Einstein's amiable grey nimbus suddenly filled with light. Jonnie ran pianistic fingers from his brows to his crown. 'Sit down, sit down!' Now – *or couldn't I just go to bed?* – let's think this problem through. How to regulate the celestial altitude – *no, I'm just not interested!* – the orientation of an orbiting satellite – *I have work tomorrow* – with its ground track, photography the mission (that's governed, by the way, stop yawning, by a computerised queuing system). Wake up! The answer is? A moment of silence. North, whose face was flabby and round, with fiercely burning cheeks, began to foresee the undistinguished fate of his innocent spades, and wanted to change his bid – which was not the right answer. Slinger pointed out: you need, of course, an onboard system of gyroscopes; precise quantification – oh, you've heard this – of Doppler shift; coupled with, elegant in its simplicity, a triad of momentum wheels, perpendicular to one another. 'But let's hear that tape once more!' I'd made the mistake of sipping the wine.

My bridge quartet had spent the day in the recording studio, where Jonnie stood in for a missing, bad-tempered keyboards man. A hushed rattle of synthesised maracas – hardly noticed as I poured another glass – swelled up *à la page* after five identical minutes (couldn't sleep now if I tried), and with the introduction of a bass, cymbals, a neurotic snare, rose to its mid-Atlantic roar. This was the leitmotif. The doctored voice chiming in angelically belonged, incredibly, to the Technicolor pixie. We all listened hard to Slinger's masterly three chords, seamless in their transition. The drummer poured amaretto into his coffee, and stirred, and glowed at his lyrics (reprise: *You got a ugly lookin' sister*), though regretted the bass was loose (but never mind). He thought he knew exactly what to do about that 1NT. Personally I slumped, when Jonnie asked me how was the trial. He was glad to hear I thought it was under control, because tomorrow night I'd be involved in another case, namely Worm's. Was that okay?

Anything, anything – just let me go to bed!

The trial, day two. Matthew Bello arrived with propped-open eyes and a booming skull. Dionysus had taken back his mandala – a wine-dark garland – and had slept it off, but for me there was only the woodenness of puppetry. The Crown called for a complicated succession of frames, forward to the bunting (that flutter of small, triangular, blue and vermilion flags). Then back to the snatch – just there! It was all so swift, but in that gleam was the last that pretty girl would see of her gilded necklace. The bunting again; and back.... Oh, I see you're going forward – we need to go *back* to that balloon.

Bello's cack-hand on the video dials undid itself in the multiplicity of viewing screens – the one rigged up for the patient judge, the three for the eye-strained jury, the two for the barristers. An early adjournment for lunch and a point of law intervened, where in a quiet café, for all but the flap of an outside awning, I pulled myself together with sugary, milky coffee. After, a short afternoon. Then back at the office I took messages callers had left. On my way out I put papers in someone else's in-tray.

The other trial commenced at eight, when the none too sorrowful Warne sliced through the particles of spotlit dust, and with a broad beam took his place at the bench, where sat a harlequinade got up as judiciary – by which I mean those novice bridge players. That trio began to squirm, of course (wasn't this *too* much!), and might have wished for a rubber (and forget that inscrutable points system, above or below the line): was this, wasn't this a joke? I couldn't tell, but I looked to Warne's nodding, approving head. Above it, a noose – a rope swaying gently in a vortex of circulating radiator air. Off it were shadows, in a criss-cross of lights. Slinger – a brooding genius – so deceived by the world and its commerce – rapped the breakfast table with a gavel and poured water from a jug. 'These will judge,' he said, with the best of his rolling gestures. The fake, fraud, or defendant Warne, whose enormous hands danced on the table top, chuckled and trembled (so, so clever! Such a whimsical idea!). He wheeled round and with his large liquid eyes in a square goonish face sought out my own, and that was enough for me. I got up. 'Some music?' I said. '*Fidelio* – so so liberating!' Jonnie said no, no music, and I said, 'That's the phone, the call I'm expecting', though I swept past a dumb Donald Duck in the hall and groped my way to the street. An angry cabby waved a fist when I stopped him at an amber light. I crossed the road. A boy asked for change. In a window, a pink, italicised fluorescence spelt the name of our local bistro, which I hadn't noticed before. Had he ever dined there, Warne or Worm, and how was he looking now? Those chunky, burgundy brogues dangling at eye-level; the flaccid limbs, the chin on a pectoral; the swollen, purple tongue poking from a corner of the mouth; the twisted blue lips, blue face; the whole lifeless person swaying slowly in a dimming of house lights. Or, the phone off the hook (no more tricks now), would he and Slinger settle their differences quietly over a vintage Chablis?

As I expected, it began to rain.

Theodore

Growing support for combat in at least one dreary neighbourhood had done nothing to brighten its brown suburban sky, or freshen the damp air bringing to one sensitive commuter a fixed pout of resignation each time he rose from the train to the streets.

The spectacled campaigner wore *Eau de Fleurs*, and for her modish figure *couture* proclaiming identity. Chunky, masculine shoes, broad loops to the laces. An unflattering sack or duffel coat. A woolly scarf with red-green bands, angry yet ecological. And plastic badges venting her human sovereignty, in triplicate – in shorthand vegetarian, pro-abortion, nuclear-free. She was returning from the bookshop, where she had browsed through *Martha Quest* to the background accompaniment of Chopin ballades, a scratched LP. She crossed the railway bridge, noting with approval the aerosol sprayed on its brickwork: WOMEN ENRAGED. Then on a concrete pillar, WAR, the acronym for something else.

She looked up to the low-rise building where she worked. In that sturdy indifference Theodore had found unfathomable for him, she scrutinised her colleague, for the briefest moment, his figure framed in a harsh fluorescent haze, a flood of office light, a dull pearl against a dark north London sky. His own, melancholy visage had come to depict that same apparent indifference, while not the faintest smile or light in his eyes changed the resolution written in his face. Nor did he move, but hung in the weathered, flaky window frame, one hand above his head and flat on the wall's interior, the other hooked in the armhole of his waistcoat. His bubble-charts and Venn diagrams had proved to be of less interest than the dim quotidian life singled out at street level.

A small boy hurrying the other way passed Gracie on the bridge just as a local train, with its cargo of blank-looking faces, rattled away west. He couldn't care about that. Some other event or obligation pressed. The boy in light green tumbled forward into a sprint as one of the carriages wobbled laterally almost directly beneath him, sending up as parabola a shower of sparks. His peaked school cap, bright with yellow piping, rose up in the sudden onrush, but he plunged it back on his crown and held it down. A large leather satchel was strapped to his shoulder. Theodore – whose personal renaissance was a careless playground of distant memories – watched him wind his way uphill past the library. A pensioner, wearing a heavy winter coat, her ancient frame bent over an empty shopping-bag – a thing on wheels – was suddenly halted. The boy dodged smartly between her and the menace of a bulldog – it leapt up and twisted back to the pavement comically, barking on the leash where its handler had lashed it to a lamppost. Then, beyond the art shop and wine bar, he disappeared.

Theodore read the signs – too late perhaps. He thrust his hands deep in his trouser pockets and turned from the window. He studied his dirty shoes against the jumbled arrows and hemispheres woven into the carpet, suspecting things he had shrugged at, had ignored, that things not taken in his stride in his maunder through the world, were turning out to be important. But it was too late, too late.

A piece of floating black ash spiralled down inconsequentially, in a refusal to accept fully the dun homogeneity washed in an autumn sky: a rebelliousness. Theodore sat away from his desk. That floating ash, after indecisive loops and a spell when rising winds rendered it motionless, dropped in a zigzag below his horizon. His bubble chart showed the bi-directional flow of information to and from a conceptualised point of sale – an individual sink, according to *his* analysis – though the reality encompassed rows of checkout girls in a national chain of supermarkets. He sharpened his pencil for the third time and in a short energetic burst blew across its pristine point of lead. But here his resolution dissolved into the usual lassitude, and where he had planned to extend the curve of data lines, a funny little face with round glasses appeared, then a cigar, a thick moustache, raised eyebrows. That sheet of paper and with it a morning's design was screwed into a tight ball but missed the bin. If, as he thought possible, he failed to chip it up and in off the tip of his toes, the night cleaners could go on puzzling, still unable to guess that his fourteen-month assignment hadn't improved his footwork. He'd overheard his bosses discuss a tender for a top City job – wide- and local-area networks, fast information retrieval and distribution, all the latest technology – and if it came up he'd ask to be considered.

That boy with his satchel had run across the maze where Theodore had left things unresolved. He gazed at a blank sheet, a morning's fruitless work, where an immortalised image of early selfhood asserted, faded, asserted itself. His own satchel and its secrets never left him. The freckle-faced, snub-nosed girls who pulled his curly wisps of hair (when a teacher's jibes had seemed to support their condemnation of him), he never told of its mysteries, not voluntarily. He collected and traded in cards, the colourful flags of the world, granting privilege to the crosses of home ahead of transatlantic stars and stripes. An inter-war tin of lozenges, first emptied two decades before the present era, had been put aside by his chuckling, balding grandfather, and was now host to an assortment of blunted nibs. A holiday he couldn't remember – a week or a fortnight on the windy Welsh coast – was enshrined in a small bleached shell, when as shaky toddler, still unaccustomed on his feet, he looked suddenly glum as his legs gave way. So awkwardly he fell on that relic, before holding it up to the light. Other articles were: an illustrated alphabet, a legless farmer in a wheel-less tractor, feathers, polished stones, and what was it? What was it precipitating a recurrent, tormented dream (as someone, Gracie, climbed the stairs)? Ah yes, he thought he remembered.

Gracie took off her coat and glanced over his hunched shoulders at the blank sheets, and frowned. He thought of a topical witticism, though failed to utter it before she sat at her desk. She dipped incommunicado into *Martha Quest*, nibbling delicately at her cabbage and grated carrot in a piece of pitta bread. He drew another sink, another bubble, another Groucho Marx.

A gull wheeled round suddenly into his window frame and turned as he folded a top sheet under the pad. The gull ascended vertically, and by that distraction left unresolved the few strokes on a fresh leaf. His pencil moved smoothly, deliberately, from left to right. It was too tightly gripped under the tip of his index and the cushion of his thumb, and too fervently driven. It collapsed. Under a dull crunch, his neat horizontal terminated prematurely in a smudge, while a fragment of lead scuttered off colliding with his coffee mug. The diagram was little more than half-complete, though he was sure the orientation, the juxtaposition of classroom and corridor, was correct (...but just *what* was I doing, rushing from one to the other?). He glanced into the adjoining office through the open frame, where Gracie had finished her lunch.

Now then, now then, let's see – this pen will do. Jolly J. Roger must have been here, so, an X – no – a J for him. Yes. This arrow is me, walking, rather running (running?) in this direction. I can't fully remember, there weren't many others – only children – no teachers, not that I could see. Strange. What was the hurry? The hurry, the hurry? Um, don't know. Jolly J. Roger wasn't looking where he was going – huh, there's that gull again! Dull dull gull. He started to run and was talking over his shoulder, and I couldn't stop him charging into me. Those corridors were dark. The tiles slippy. Hah, I was so attached to those shoes, and they never made me wear the new ones. Anyway, the satchel wasn't done up – I couldn't stop – and crash! Right here – a star, I think, for a crash – everything tipped out just here. Sorry, he said. Though if he hadn't stopped to help me pick things up.... Tut, wonder who this is on a Tuesday morning, no, afternoon.

He picked up the phone but transferred the call when it was someone in accounts wanting to speak to Gracie. He returned the top to his pen and held the whole awkwardly before him, leaning forward, elbows on the desk. He gazed abstractedly at the unchanging brown sky. Was this the truth of it, his existential state, Theodore a long-serving employee, when now Gracie – still only a student this time last year – seemed certain to overtake him, and soon? She was the natural target for most communications from HQ – the phone, or memos – and even the client's analysts had started coming to her for estimates for non-scheduled amendments. They liked her decisiveness, her 'Three days', or 'No more than an afternoon' – preferable to Theodore's 'Well that's difficult to say', despite its weight of experience. Another thing he'd noticed: she no longer asked him for program specs but wrote them herself (she kept a copy of the original design document in her briefcase and took it home at nights). Then the worrying declaration a couple of days ago that programming was just a foot in the door. And what now, he wondered? She put the phone down and stepped into his office, but standing behind him, hovering, remained silent. It was hard for her to tell, but as a design specialist he seemed to wrestle unduly with some of the technicalities (those demented hieroglyphics on his floor plan suggested mental breakdown). He turned, suddenly animated. 'Yes,' he said. 'It was the holidays, the start of the summer holidays!'

She frowned. 'Oh. Well. That was accounts. It's month-end. Can you do your timesheet....'

He'd hung on till six and in the advancing afternoon had watched those wiry tufts of hair, the baggy eye sockets, the vague hint sometimes of a resolute mouth, his ghostly semblance gradually assuming corporeal life, or more than a reflection. In the coming twilight his window portrait had been touched and retouched at the hand of a ruthless master: the boffin's riotous coiffure asked for shears; the fleshy sacks and veiny rings under tired eyes demanded sleep; the dejected lower lip showed us a passing need for a new kind of stand-up comic. He left his desk – his head and shoulders floating up in that fluorescent ether – and put on his coat. He said goodnight and left her – Gracie – still working. There were, on the concrete steps into the courtyard, a first few drops of rain as it spattered his naked hands and face. In a sudden gust of wind a small heap of leaves and litter swirled in a corner. He looked across to the showers of electric blue sparks and the blank faces in the windows of the next train in, as it clattered to a halt at the platform. When he reached the street, the straining heavens couldn't be contained: in the light of the shop fronts, he watched the whitish pavement progressively darken. He clawed back awkwardly for his hood and broke into a trot, and at last when he sat in the train shook his dripping locks.

An older man opposite had focused his eyes on distant objects and wrestled with his own reflections – an anecdote, a ludicrous combination of circumstance, someone's unfortunate reprimand – and could not flatten its drollness. The jocose Muse at his elbow prised open his clamped jaw and coaxed a repressed or bashful smile. Suddenly, a radiance of crooked teeth. For Theodore, the leaps and bounds of his other life couldn't now be like that: every recycled event his consciousness sought to refine or re-examine was put to intense analytical lights, so that when he and Jolly J. Roger crouched on the floor, he knew for the first time just how his sense of loss was registered. His cards, his flags of the world were scattered everywhere. The tin of lozenges – which hadn't fallen open – was still that, it wasn't a tin of nibs, as far as J. Roger could tell. The white shell still slid across the floor but was destined for the feet of that bouncy group of girls, where – true to its twenty-five-year history – it was crushed and ground to powder under their feet. The illustrated alphabet was open at a smiling octopus and a lifeless pullover, while the legless farmer needed help, unable to squirm into his tractor unaided. J. Roger saw, when he bent to retrieve these and other articles, when he gathered them into the satchel, the one thing the perplexed Theodore did care about – and that was an old, ragged-looking corn doll. This he made off with, this was his prize, this in his hands gave him dominion over another human soul.

How Theodore met that loss was a complex issue, though he couldn't see why that old recurring dream had elevated one of those girls above her companions – whose eventual downfall was so much more humiliating – and who had pulled his hair no more viciously.

A hundred and something years of Inglewood Mansions (the passer-by, preoccupied, settles for approximations). That century and a bit were proclaimed in bold relief on the stucco edifice where Theodore lived. Grand steps with railings led to a varnished door, and, by contrast, led also to the tiny Yale for all those domiciled inside. It wasn't the tie trick tonight, when the reeling drunk finds that otherwise redundant garment useful for once. You slide the key down the pattern of silk to the tip of its arrowhead, which the other hand has placed at the keyhole. Tonight was reserved for other things.

Older residents remembered a portal with coloured lights – a blue galleon in a red and yellow sunset – but now those magic filters had gone. With the usual stale odour of onion soup and French cigarettes, a permanent Stygian darkness lingered in the hall. That Gaulish ground-floor spinster pervaded the gloomy stairwell for a further three flights, where her presence was subdued by number 9, the non-smoking Mr Patel with his penchant for meat and vegetable curries.

Theodore collected his mail and plodded to his own floor – the uppermost – and to his own door, where last July he'd replaced a factory 14 dating from the '50s with the classic XIV. He glanced across the landing at number 13 and listened. The girl there was Gracie's age, and on the shrill of her voice, and the bass of her jealous partner, he opened up and stepped briskly over his threshold.

'Huh, she's back,' he said. As ever his coat stand didn't reply. He switched on lights and hung up his coat on the only spare peg. He ran through his mail perfunctorily – junk, junk, more junk, a gas bill, a bank statement, a postcard from his brother in Bali (stage one, a world tour) – but tossed it all aside on rounding on the kitchen, the site of this morning's debris. The sink was black where he'd burnt and scraped his toast. That first mug of tea had left its partial rings on every conceivable surface, again. Again he'd left the milk out, and this time a mutilated block of butter too, now yellow and sweaty. That could all wait. He fetched a towel for his hair and sat down. Time to check the phone. Messages were: 'Board meeting tomorrow night, usual place – residents have voted *against* a new roof – Rich', 'Oh, hullo, son, I'll call back', 'Hmm, ahem, Debenhams, reference A for apricot slash one one four two six, dining chairs ready for collection twenty-seventh, repeat, twenty-seventh', and 'Theo – long time no see! Give me a ring on 515 3000'. He rubbed his hair hard and thought about dinner.

Then across the landing that angry bass erupted for the thousandth time, and showed no signs of dying down. The reply was immediate. Dramatic pots, plates, cups and saucers crashed – percussion added to the grate of her soprano. As operatic interlude, it went on, as miserable and hopeless as any devised on stage. Soon the performers reached their natural limit, though the props remained robust: the door when it slammed – once, when she left – remained on its hinges – as it did so a second time when he followed to the landing, with a volley of abuse into that hellish stairwell. Theodore strode to his front window and stood at the curtain. She emerged on the wet street, clutching her suitcase, her longish hair in a mess and flying, and without hesitation made for the phone booth at the corner.

'Huh,' he said, 'couldn't even have unpacked this time,' and moved away from the curtain.

Little spots of light appear on the ceiling, vibrate over the cracks in the curtains where they entered in. They lose their bright intensity, they enlarge, distend, they form a whole, a shallow pool ballooning overhead, there – somewhere – somewhere near the wardrobe. Late cars glide, drone, disappear, and as suddenly all illuminations cease. Must phone the office tomorrow, get these problems aired, when Gracie's out at lunch. What was it, what was that dream? Uh, hope his muggins across the way doesn't come calling. Can't bear another sob story. What was it – yes – what was it now? (I should get some sleep, it's late). Yes.

Then between his bouts of drifting off, he remembered. He pieced it together. The loss of that devil or corn doll – it had horns, cloven feet, a jester's grin – its removal at the hands of Jolly J. Roger had prompted lonely walks in the woods and hilly fields around the village where he lived. For an instant he was motionless, preparing to spring from his front foot, and deciding how to take in that little cluster of stepping-stones. He gazed down into the stream, where the broken pieces of himself undulated in the water. The missing fragments were another self, and where the stream had taken and deposited them, they wriggled, twisted, slotted back together. The spawned child stepped out of the water and shook himself down. Who walked in the sunshine of a parallel, infant world was a hardier, vengeful Theodore.

In the morning the radio alarm for some reason failed, though he woke all the same (and strangely the wardrobe had moved). Nor did he struggle. One of life's little processions – *Time to get up!* – for once was not enacted. Let's just turn over for five minutes. But then a decisive Theodore propped himself up immediately. He stretched, he yawned, for the moment didn't take in the new orientation. Surprisingly, he put down a first exploratory foot and found that the carpet – a bedtime blue, he distinctly recalled choosing it – had been rolled up, removed overnight, and replaced by an undistinguished lino. This was a reminder. He stumbled for the curtains, his gummed eyes unused to the suburban twilight, and when – instead of the curtains – he discovered an *en suite* basin, a narrow strip of mirror, a tubular bulb, he still couldn't guess – he still with his dreamlike tenacity clung to familiar sensations of past identity, of past habitation.

He turned on the light and looked for a sign in the mirror, and seeing only a shadow ran water for a wash, not too hot (perhaps if he bathed his eyes—). Then with the basin filling, his interrupted image caught someone looking on. She peered over his naked shoulder and acknowledged, this indeed was him. But the reflection was only partial, with the pool he was gazing in a flurry of surface agitation, with two gushing taps. His complementing parts had already reassembled, she said: a younger Theodore even now strode across dewy fields in glorious midsummer sunshine. Over there was a Norman church; there on that hillock, a clump of elms; behind those willows, a lake.

First concrete signs came later, in the interior of an ancient English house, centrepiece of a complicated maze. A chipper little Theo suspected nothing yet (in fact he was humming). He came to a stone bridge, with its onrush of water crashing through its arch. He leapt to the wall and skipped to the keystone – humming, whistling, humming – and saw on the horizon cone-capped towers. As he approached, a turret clock was visible. It had golden, gigantic hands and numerals I to XII. Beyond that a spire, its weather vane a hoer facing north. There were flags – limp – scarcely stirring on their poles. Above, a sentry gave way to fatigue, or boredom, or both, and leaned over the battlements. He blinked and raised his eyebrows, for here was a sight: a small boy ducking and weaving – a small boy running over the fields – a small boy wheeling his arms ecstatically. Whatever next!

Weeds and nettles grew in the shadow of the outer wall, which at every new latitude rose into squarish waves, where on each peak a vast stone globe was perched. Theodore came in by his usual route, from an overhanging oak where ivy growing up the wall helped him scramble down. He dropped lightly to his feet in a quadrant of the maze. He followed the wall round counter-clockwise, then turned through an artificial opening in the hedge. All so simple so far, though he knew from experience that the problem of the corn doll was a much harder challenge.

He checked his angle with the hoer. He turned, and his shadow fell before him in a line with one of the avenues, whose features were pools, birdbaths, sundials. Two pigeons had stopped to tell the time.

He paused at one of the pools, with its chutes, a fountain, a wheel, and looked down at his broken, sinistral self. There was something not quite right, yet here was only a first clue to details gone astray. A second was the squawk of a mute swan, paddling without a reflection, its neck stretching awkwardly towards him. Its powerful wings fluffed out and were about to beat. He dodged, retreated, stepped aside. It heaved itself from the water, and rose, meticulous in its flight.

He met again a company of gnomes and the flat rocks they were guardians of, or towers of remembrance. A mere touch and you remembered what you'd forgotten. So, Theo, what *had* you forgotten? With his hand to a crevice came car lights on his ceiling. With a fissure a pair of shoes. A craggy summit brought him back to winter mornings, and first tentative steps from his bed to the freezing lino…. Then that all-important corn doll.

An early riser in slippers and a string vest, who had lathered his face but mislaid his razor, leaned over his bedroom sill and saw in the fog and darkness the milkman and his float. The thing droned, its leading wheel dipped and bounced in a crater, while the clatter of empty bottles pre-empted the clunk of someone's radio alarm. A dreary newsman slurred into life. Theodore rolled over. He stretched, he yawned, he put that first foot down onto his familiar bedtime blue, and, perching on the edge of his bed, saw the wardrobe back where it belonged, the *en suite* basin like or by Mnemosyne spirited away – though these were hardly events.

Foreseeable, his latent capacity for difficult confrontations found him out. He couldn't get away, still in his bathrobe, Theodore stretching across his threshold in the act of sweeping up his pint of milk. Haynes from number 13 ensured eye contact, as he returned with his morning paper, and ensnared him by that look.

'Expect you heard the kerfuffle last night.'

Theodore stood up with his milk and tried to avoid the subject: 'Oh, that. I hear the other residents have voted against a new roof.'

'Well, that doesn't affect me, renting. I've, er, taken it too far. She'll probably get the police.'

Theodore thought, 'You're not coming in,' and recalled the terrible breakfast they'd once shared, for him an ordeal. Haynes, a callow youth, stirred honey into his coffee, and for the length of a pointless conversation – or diatribe, Theodore compelled to listen mostly – didn't retract his spoon. He stirred and stirred. His problem was Doreen. Her father gave her money, clothes, a new car. She said she never cheated. That was a lie.

Theodore was expected to sympathise, but couldn't, and in trying to leave the table, to open the curtains, to let in the sun and switch off the wall lights, had to pay attention. He got the whole of the Haynes confession. He was lonely, forlorn. Revenge alone couldn't salve his psychological wounds, though he had tried it with one-night stands. Theodore found in himself an innate prejudice hard to resist, where old-style conjugal ethics presupposed a kind of ownership, though he said only 'The sex revolution isn't without its problems.'

He took the lid off his milk and studied the grazes and lesions on Haynes's hand, as it clutched his tabloid. 'Oh, you beat her up,' he said. 'You'd better come in.'

'Ah no. No. I'm going to phone her.'

Clackety-clack. Down there a school-bound ma had tried to jump the lights under the railway arch but was shunted onto the pavement, wings clipped (husband would be furious). That burly labourer with earmuffs and a pneumatic drill (just gone!) – what was that he mouthed? Clackety. Oh, more house backs – boring!

The corner of a front page curled down over a headline, and intrigued with this: 'Lo green paper will add pornography scan'. Then agitated hands shook up and folded to pocket-size the inky leaves of a broadsheet, before smoothing out on a pinstriped knee dents in the cryptic crossword. Theodore looked up among the ads and rail maps. Insane brokers in comic strip ventured in suits and bowlers through swamps and wastelands, on behalf of their client, whose portfolio they reviewed, who lay out in the sun. A signed ethnic poem condemned in colloquial monotone the capitalist exploitation of at least one paradise island, and alongside, a foppish dragon overcame his persistent halitosis, with an antiseptic mouthwash making possible a candlelit dinner for two. Tolkienesque mythologies were reduced to this. Then again, Theodore's own dream kingdom hadn't escaped similar distortions. He never rose without a lie-in, even as a child (the lino wasn't there for long, so why had it made such an impression? And years ago his father had removed the *en suite* plumbing). Curious.

He gazed again at those city gents, swinging on jungle vines, but now not comprehending. What was superimposed on them remained obstinately unfocused: a shadow, a blur, a narrow strip of mirror, a harsh white tube of light. It was his own face, a visage almost impossible to conceive in its infant manifestation (how did I see myself twenty-five years ago?). In the pool inside the maze, he remembered a left profile. He could see the familiar nose with its ridge, the dissatisfied pout, curly hair swept off a lined forehead. He supposed that a squawking swan, detached over that glassy surface from its own, inverted image, was a clue to his other life, his dream life, a world willing to remain intact in the mire of his adult psyche. A more obvious device might have been the towers of remembrance, when so many of life's humdrum landmarks in the intervening quarter century *could* have been recalled. Somewhere however he must have appreciated the inelegance of that scenario. It was *too* easy. The gnomes, ubiquitous among a thousand housing estates beyond the fringes of his home village, were confirmation of that.

The train pulled in at the first stop, while he pieced together last night's little adventure. The man opposite snapped open his document case and exchanged the escaping odour of egg sandwiches for a part-solved crossword, then rushed, clutching his accoutrements, awkwardly for the door. Theodore watched as he gathered himself to the stream of commuters bustling on the platform: the case went under an arm, his coat went over a shoulder, he slipped his ticket from a top pocket. But this was all incidental—

The truth of these introspections was two augural doves in flight over the great house, where someone who had long been banished to the northern tower was not at peace. Theodore's radial meander brought him to the hub. There were rows of miniature conifers in tubs. Three levels of closely cut lawns were connected at intervals by shallow flights of steps. He smiled as he took in once more the extravagant urns, the chipped or broken statues – of kings or bearded philosophers. An accidental rent in the fabric of the universe, or the mysterious intersection of a world and a mind – fraught with all kinds of difficulties and incompatibilities – proposed in topsy-turvy logic, this: seasonal things were recrudescent things, but here at the maze's centre you did not set your watch sequentially. The house itself – the grand façade – its tall rectangular windows dotted with coloured lights – was a blaze of red. That hadn't changed. But the sentinels flanking the palace door had been replaced, a not so obvious fact, easily missed on a first glance at them. After all, these were the same tall hats, the same red tunics, the same gold braid. In Theodore's original dream, that dream endlessly modified since its inception, the two had appeared as older and younger – age or experience offset by youth or captiousness – and both had been smart, erect, and disciplined. In that first encounter they exercised their mindless official prerogative and denied him access, quibbling on his name.

'The O-door,' said the younger, perspiring, pointing, his neck turning purple. 'You go in by the O-door!'

'It's near the drains,' said the elder, helpfully.

That earnest jest had grown stale over the years, and the two sentinels – one might only just describe them as older and younger now – had forgotten their hard lessons in deportment. They slouched. They were bleary-eyed, unshaven. Buttons on their tunics were recklessly undone. What had they seen, what had they seen since Theodore's first visit here twenty-five years ago? When he approached, wanting to go in, they jointly lit fat cigarettes and squatted down to smoke. When Theodore put his hand on the door and pushed it open and was unchallenged by them, he stepped over those flabby torsos, flaccid limbs – two skulking war veterans – and walked into the resplendent (ah no, the derelict) hall.

There was a woven arras adorning the whole of one wall, with battle scenes. Before it had shown silver, gold, vermilion, but now was frayed by moths. Its heroic conquest hung on rusty nails, under a layer of dust. If he looked down, the marble of the floor was cracked. He rattled a closet door and pulled it open, now *expecting* an anti-climax. They'd vanished – ghosts eating toast – or were greasing their wrists in someone else's dreams. A heap of old panoplies was here instead. On three posts open visors showed fresh air in their respective helmets. He looked to the stairway, its sweep no longer majestic: that wormy banister would never support his weight, and the chips and ruts in the marble (a much abused material) made any footing perilous. He ascended nevertheless, a floating, insubstantial cloud.

No one was here. He sought his destination where a hubbub of jugglers, dancers and magicians had once repeated their routines. Behind that same door, all he could hear were low, confidential voices. He opened it. Where was that little duck with yellow feet and yellow shoes? The barber shaving a pig? Where was that jack-a-dandy on his pogo? Turns, bends, divisions. That was all junk, consigned to the loft. Props for an older anima were a long reflective table, an oligarchy in session, an agenda, pens at the ready, jugs of water, glasses. Gracie sat at the head of her cabinet, with Jolly J. Roger at her right hand: she shuffled her papers and tapped them neatly together on the polished table. 'Late again!' she said, while a wakeful commentator insisted she shouldn't be here at all (her place being that pugnacious little girl's who'd tugged at Theodore's hair). J. Roger said, 'You've lost the contract,' and Theodore thought no, the corn doll, which *you* return *after* we've scrapped it out. The other twelve – the silent members of the cabinet – assenting automata – nodded gravely, too stupid to be amused at the image of themselves in the layers of polish, where everything was a blur to him, to Theodore. City gents, the jungle, clackety-clack. Here was his stop.

Gracie on the phone, delighted, watched from that oblong fluorescence while he stumbled from the carriage, wearing his beige overcoat today. He thought as he filed past the ticket barrier, 'So bitumen for the roof again,' and when he stepped into the office and took off his coat and put down his case, Gracie was still in that animated conversation, at *his* desk, using *his* phone.

He fetched coffee, then at last she cradled the receiver.

'Great news!' she said. 'They want me to project manage the City job.'

Theodore put his coat back on and picked up his case.

'I'll be at HQ,' he said, and returned to the breezy platform while his coffee went cold.

The Visionary

Two contrasting pictures as we stoop and peer, close up – the news poles of our divided kingdom. One in tranquil, the other in benighted monochrome. In the gazette, a white shrine for the faithful. It's the peaceful reproduction of de Cort's *Ripon Minster*. A bucolic bridge, with arch in the foreground, two rustics crossing. In the middle ground, an idyllic cottage, thatched. It's reflected in untroubled waters. A broad sky, a sky for the free and rich – airy and light. Then on the letters page, the gloomy contrast. Recede slightly and note, seated moodily over some fool lawyer's smoke-filled missive, to the tune of his public feud with someone in government. He too will have noticed those typical, mean little dwellings, in post-industrial Wales. There is pebbledash. There are half forbidding nets, drawn at the top and bunched at the bottom corners, in row upon row of identical windows. There's a solitary dog or cat, or is that accidentally a photographic flaw? Clearer are the flags or slabs of concrete (hard to say which), shiny under a film of rain, gridded out in a marquetry of weeds. They disappear in a fading linearity almost to the flat mountains and leaden sky. And not a soul anywhere.

Back a little more, backward over the turf. His scrubbed pink fingers overlap the edges of this morning's paper. Continents of print reintegrate into columns, borders, hieroglyphs, then it's an overview in photos and headlines. A prolonged chortle begins and the loose folios crepitate in sympathy. But the chortle's a Gothic monster, seeking life of its own, as it finds first sovereignty, a series of guffaws. The round plastic table, with its summer scrolls and involutions, trembles – it has contact with a ballooning, vibrant waistband. Two empty champagne flutes tilt over together, chinking, then bounce on a white vine leaf. The bottle, overturned on the turf, has already been drained.

The paper comes down as we try for the latch gate, but this is the members' enclosure, and someone ushers us away. I cast a backward glance on the fleshy, pinkish face, with its bulging, toady eyes, of Paschal Brennan, film and theatre critic. I know from his reputation just what a darling he is with dull-eyed playwrights. His flunkey and chauffeur is on the steps to the bar, and to judge that toothy grin has exchanged profanities with someone in a blazer and matching bowtie. His mission is for Bollinger and two more champagne flutes. He pauses. There's a swarm of bodies, a sea of bobbing heads. He strikes out for the jazzy-looking parasol where in its deep oval shadow the redoubtable Brennan is massaging his sides.

The last race, and most had been caught in the rush for the terrace. Brennan remained seated, sipping his Bollinger, on this first of his long light evenings under the wheeling swallows and disintegrating vapour trails. He greeted it in an odour of mild intoxication. His cockney flunkey left him, at his table and parasol, one among the select few, set apart by a latch and pales – a gate, a fence, a square of turf. My curiosity had me weaving among the crowds on the narrow pavements, scrabbling for a discarded *Evening News*. I missed it by an inch, as someone scooped it up, but then tiring of the whole spectacle I joined the queue at a hamburger stand. Then I did find a copy of Brennan's paper, and leafed through – what, what on earth could be so funny? I could not say, and so followed his flunkey to Bookie Bob's, whose odds were longer than most.

'Mr Brennin wants an 'undrid on Lightnin' Streak an' fifty sovs on Miami Law Co.'

I noted the nods but can't recall that money changed hands. Then here it was, Ripon Minster from the north east – an ideal perspective – and over here, that torrential Welsh community – and what was this on the arts page?

Those distant riders came to us over the Tannoy. Brennan's so-called 'Lightning', his jockey in a cerise shirt with yellow chevrons, trailed from the start. Miami Law Co, in black and mauve checks, led. I pricked up my ears for the finish, after reading the review, whose turgid humour left the corners of my mouth firmly down, and was an outrage for the hapless George W. Clare—

This man's pontificating anachronisms are a bore. How often in his plays he wallows in homey virtues, in the belief that there *is* poetic justice, however unlikely, however steeped in petty mysticism. What's he after, what does he want, you ask? Well, I suspect it's simple. The world at last to accept his genius, and in its humble genuflection elevate him permanently over the rest. I don't anticipate that any of this will happen soon.

The Visionary, an absurd little drama, is Clare's latest attempt to enlighten us, and is an invitation into the supernatural world he is said to have researched. The protagonist – needless to say a man with a vocation – has got himself into conflict with the authorities (don't ask me which authorities). He is accused of: perpetrating malicious lies against the State; profaning the Church, which according to him is too institutionally secular; and unforgivably, corrupting the minds of the young. If you think this sounds familiar, here's the twist. His so-called Visionary is Satanic too, subject to fits of depression. He rages at his enemies, and suffers no remorse when exercising his terrible vengeful powers on the worst of them. He nullifies his antagonists, when in moments of preternatural ill-temper he reduces them to air. It is all schoolboyish to the point of idiocy, an embarrassment, a bathetic adolescent fantasy. For us, the only salvation is that Mr Clare's inner light is snuffed as promptly as whatever talent he might have had.

Wise, suited sentinels – masters of semaphore – stood straight and expressionless, arms resolutely at respective sides, when the profit and loss, the joy and anguish, were lost to the crowds, whose hoots accompanied the thud of hoofs, the flying divots, the long, fibrous necks stretching for the winner's post. Hats and caps went up in the gathering twilight, as betting slips were tossed to the ground.

The triumphant swish of mane and tail, and the snort of nostrils, belonged to that hopeful longshot whose rider's colours were cerise and yellow. I jangled my keys and strolled for the car. Brennan remained with his Bollinger, under his parasol, and greeted the news with a toast to the East. Me, I avoid all rush for the exits – the last race, the ball game's last ten minutes, the smiling prima donna under the weight of the house bouquet. These are the scenes I sacrifice – though here I imagined a someone else, a more analytical reader than I have been, who also wouldn't allow Paschal's review to pass without comment. Cue Brennan not at his reveller's table, but sitting by the phone in his weekend cottage, a cup of fresh coffee steaming in the sunshine through his window. I pictured him threading the coming week through lunch and dinner appointments, crosschecking his pocket with his desk diary. Monday p.m., hand over editorial, Gloucester Hotel, where there's an endless 'Emperor' Concerto on a continuous tape loop echoing in the foyer. Tuesday evening, Wig and Pen...but that was someone ringing now.... He lifted the receiver.

'Hello,' then the mechanical request: 'Mr Paschal Brennan, please....'

'Speaking. Who's this calling?'

'Clare. George W. Clare.'

'Oh, Clare. This is unexpected.'

'Yes, it isn't usual, I know. Listen, I've been reading your review....'

'Understand, Clare, I can't entertain personal exchanges. A job's a job, and mine is to monitor the quality and refinements of theatrical art.'

'Yes, yes, I appreciate that....'

'I answer to my public.'

'No doubt you deserve your reputation. But I also have a job too. What are called natural contrasts in comfortable society, I mark as the world's divisions, the cathedrals and the mining villages.'

'That, if I may say so, is self-evident.'

'Then you're a cynic....'

'It's hard not to be. But look here....'

'That's all!' A disconnecting click followed those two inoffensive syllables.

Brennan, astonished, replaced his receiver, and looked round the room where irreversible mutations were already under way. A glass pig metamorphosed into one of flesh and bone, and squealing leapt off the mantel shelf, then imploded and disappeared with a throaty phut, splashing headlong into what was now an oceanic carpet. That rising sea, a little choppy by the inglenook, was at first just an irritating swirl round the reviewer's ankles. Framed portraits and landscapes – familiar eyes, noses, carts and barns – dissolved into amorphous globules and slid down the walls – a sort of artless viscosity. When the grog-blossom drained from his terrified face, leaving his bulbous nose and flabby jowls a ghostly grey, those walls fell outward into a fiery waste, where the water clashed and singed. That man with his coronary, clutching at his pectorals while twitching in brimstone, could think only this – 'Impossible, impossible!' – though Clare with his penchant for the unbelievable would have given such a nemesis a *moving* peroration. His imagination was that much more exercised than mine, I reflected, driving through the gate.

Triones

I see of course what I *should* have done, to make the position clear, difficult though it is, from this new vantage, and a near impossibility, to deal in that changeable vista, the past. So hard it becomes, to acknowledge what the problem was, if any. And it's a challenge, to clarify the smallest painful detail. Everywhere I look, it's an intricate jigsaw, where the last few fragments, in whatever combination, refuse to lock in. The map is a square of shifting sand, where if the foothold is secure, it's only ever momentary. Mercifully, here in a cool room at the rear of an island house, that first anxiety has gone. I reopen the diary, a thing no more than iridescent points of light, a kaleidoscope, less than honest as a design. Its luminescent shards dissolve into first this, then that pattern, and each is followed by another, and another, and another. But can you spare the time?

For whatever reason, it seemed I should write an explanation. Spoken words always failed, or the time was inopportune. Immediately, those four old ghosts are gathered, if only for now a reflected blur. I protest at something said, because I know it implies that hardy philosophy my youth and idealism cannot sanction. But at Sunday dinner, the beef, a bloody rib, has to be carved, and with an all too symbolic wave of the knife, a discussion or conversation is murdered (could it be that my father's point of view was philosophically ill-founded, and to scratch away too persistently at its surface was to reveal, eventually, its basis?).

Elizabeth, seven years older, upheld our family cohesion – if not quite oneness – for the importance she placed on its economic unity. Her silence – the austere kind – warned that for the underdog a first victory was hard-fought, and the oppressors were two (or *I* would argue three). Anyway, now at table was neither the time nor place, my mother's 'Stop it, you two!' imposing an uneasy peace, an indignant truce.

A slight figure with pale skin, who shaved the golden down of his cheeks and chin only once in a couple of days, I gazed with a fixed scowl at the fruit bowl while the plates were passed. Etched in the distortion of the glass was a furious intermingling of apples, bananas, oranges and grapes. Again, as I think, as I recall, that swimming monstrosity, in its wash of indefinite colour, is decisive, for it's here, in this room, on a sunnier day, that I am numbed at the open French windows, the warm summer breeze playing over my face and lifting the thick ringlets of my hair. The plum that some unspeakable boredom has driven me to select and sink my teeth into has been returned, and the bowl is suspended in trembling hands above the flagstones, about to form a thousand irreconcilable splinters on the patio. Here again, the spoken word wouldn't do.

I leave the glassware hanging, poised, because my new interest is books, though not for their content. I am not an intellectual. It's their material importance – a matter of subsistence – when, as said often enough, you'd never catch me reading books at school. Their conscientious representations of the world I dismissed as an unreal sort of realism, unaware that someone very like me enjoyed a better life of sunshine, wore a smile most days, was uplifted, was not repulsed when brushing teeth before the morning mirror. The patient's occasional relief was not in the confirmation of his disease, but in the measure by which the palliative was able to soothe. If bookwork didn't constitute wonder at an astutely crafted, unsuspected otherness, it was no good to me.

Yet, it was a clumsy inconsistency when my explanation began to see the light of day. Perhaps it was. I thought all along I was unveiling something psychologically terrifying, yet all I reproduced were sample props from the annals of clichéd film and fiction. Sloppy, I admit, though the diatribe was genuine. Some men teeter on the brink of hatred for their fathers. There are some parents, well-meaning doubtless, who do make terrible mistakes. Some people have a need for therapy. Some of us cleave to the insanities of psychiatry. So it went on, until the cogs and wheels of the seasons changed the scene and ushered in a steely winter sky. A few black specks on the horizon receded. The eyes of the ghost had reddened. Nights without peace. And still no kind of explanation, nothing I charged anyone to read. Not even Harvey.

My refuge was in knowing where to find him most of the time, with *his* luck also down. Most nights of the week he played at the Tropicana, which he told me I need not envy him for. He called it, I think, a cheap nightclub for local hoydens, has-beens, bimbos and gigolos.

Christmas, not like any other – grim automata fixed round a roaring fire; the annual overdose of TV banalities; the miraculous colloquies with aunts and uncles, absent for most of the rest of the year…. Mid-to-late December, the time ten p.m., and thankfully I knew where Harvey was. His moments of respite were always at the Monkey Puzzle, where I found him propped in a peacock chair – brief calm before his night's work. There were usually remnants of a light supper on the table beside him. The evening paper he had picked up outside his West End studio had all the usual stuff – a spate, a gush of domestic drama, celebrity gossip, the compulsory catalogue of current political scandals. Yet it was precisely that predictability that brought me here, just as his passing interest in the depths of the metropolis had dissolved into a half-hearted attempt at the quick crossword.

This was his vodka period. Always a Bloody Mary, mixed and shaken by the same anachronistic barman (I'd seen him in a *noir* movie, leaning on a padded bar, with an ear and a sympathetic smile for everyone's troubles). Harvey tossed down the defoliating evening paper and in the same movement took up his glass. Grimly I crossed the lounge (deserted place), in a rush of cold air as the outer door closed, slowly, hydraulically, behind me. The gold propelling pencil would be clipped, systematically, into the inner pocket of his sports jacket. 'Dear boy!' he said, always with a flourish, and with a half-sardonic flash of teeth behind his beard, which was closely cropped. 'What can I get you?' At the stock reply (a jar of sleeping pills and a bottle of Bell's), he skirted the hat stands and potted plants, and ordered my usual (a bottle of imported lager). I lounged on an ottoman, or slouched, the furniture rearranged, in the leather swamp of an armchair. The thanks he got were this: that two across was *catastrophe* (fitting), or five down *wellbeing* (a malicious lie). But the propelling pencil stayed put. He preferred to talk.

And what he talked of had ceased to be that final defining evening, when he and his sick wife ended their holiday early, when a virulent influenza decimated half the coastal resort. As they arrived home, his drummer and their daughter weren't yet dressed: *he* was heading for the bedroom, with cocktails and a clean ashtray; she, who had seen the family car, was already remaking the wreck of her parents' bed. The luckless drummer was fired, while Natalie, coy, stubborn, unable to suffer this new parental atmosphere a moment longer, found another place to live and took a dead-end job. That hard line Harvey insists wasn't his, but he got the blame, and what for years was a rocky marriage ended.

In the gloom of that unhurried hour, in the bar of a dark hotel, its residents old, wealthy, and tucked up in bed before nine, a remoter past cradled his nostalgia. Perhaps sentimentality was his best therapy – not something I understood.

I pay Harvey this compliment: a decade has passed, yet I can still describe the triumphs, the misfortunes, the highlights of his early life. It has been gone into – endlessly – over dozens of Bloody Marys. Now where I winter there's something vodka-based and ice-cool in a glass at *my* elbow. I am thicker set, and tanned all year round: I keep under a watchful eye the hangers-on I am happy to attract (a commercial artist this time, not penniless – that's not the problem – but bent on self-destruction). I scan back through the seasons, a whorl of greens and browns and golds, yellow suns in a russet sky, the layers of trodden snow. I blink into being the seven-year-old Harvey stretching before a music stand with his first flute, or when twelve blasting out the family on Saturday nights with his saxophone, or at seventeen as leader of a twelve-piece, playing in clubs, at private parties, at fêtes and wedding receptions. Then university, an interlude that wasn't, despite reservations, a serious interruption. On the contrary, the opportunity of southern towns and cities was available suddenly.

The buzz, those heady years, could never be rivalled in his coming vodka days, when, anyway, something more sedate was planned for and slipped into (like a well-fitting glove). He married, and was comfortable with what that meant – a process of consolidation, as he termed it. I've seen the photographs, with their imperfections and glimpses into yesteryear, evidence I am guided through with inscriptions scrawled in Harvey's hand on the reverse sides. There was his exclusive tenure at the Moonshine Club, in Finchley (the contact name was Neumann, sometimes Anglicised to Newman). A dockside eighteen months at the River Boat, Hammersmith. There was a Mediterranean cruise, his only record of which was not as musician, but drinking cocktails in the lounge, in rapport with the captain. There wasn't much on returning, and for the fun of it he played for a provincial ladies' club, whose autumn masquerade of furs and tweeds had given way (there was some *coup* or other on the committee) to a midwinter show of swimsuits. For Harvey, this was his south European, dark-spectacled era – umbriferous glass, a precursor of the purplish, tinted lenses I knew in the days of his Bloody Marys and deteriorating eyesight. His band had style, turned out, he insisted, in matching velvet dinner jackets, vermilion bow ties, luminous white shirts with wing collars, and tapered trousers pressed to a razor sharpness. That got him a job on TV Saturday-night spectaculars, a contract lasting over a decade. Treated as his rehearsal, the liberated ladies of the five villages swayed to the deep purr, the discreet throb of polished jazz, and invited him back. But the purpose had been served, *his* purpose (this is what I mean about his fatalism), when the model destined to be his wife sported an electric blue bikini, and, supremely ignorant of Harvey, strode out on stage and strutted her stuff.

Could he ever get near enough, in the cold of that afternoon? Here was an answer, in the toss of her sun-bleached hair, the sweep of her arms, the flick of a wrist, a beach ball ballooning up. He hung around after the show, slipping in and out of the foyer – he made phone calls, checked the hoardings endlessly – always returning by the models' to his own dressing-room. At last he bribed an usher, a mere boy, who watched with mounting surprise each time from the leather of Harvey's wallet another note came out. He set off on his errand, and returned and tapped on Harvey's door. Harvey, opening it, suspected she had already gone. The boy said no, not quite. If he was quick he would find her at the station.

In a sudden sense of overdress he packed away his suit and slipped on a pair of slacks and a woolly (absent, a pipe with curly stem, as no tobacco ads for him: the windy musician was a non-smoker). Moments later he had swung his sporty car into the station car park, and saw her, on the platform, in the wintry gloaming, in a beige raincoat, a garment drawn at the waist by a loosely knotted belt. A fluffy yellow scarf accompanied a matching beret, under which her less golden, less silky hair was gathered in a bun. The garish, Thespian makeup had been wiped away, and in its place was a pink downy rouge, a nocturnal shade of eye shadow, and a silvery lipstick. The Tannoy hummed intrusively. Her feet stamped against the cold. The lights never seemed to change. It wasn't simply luck that Harvey was driving back to London, and could offer her a lift, but that she never knew. As the ladies of the five villages were dissolving, in taxis, buses, and trains, into the Kent and Sussex countryside, Harvey with his bride to be was speeding under a twinkle of stars to the terraces of Maida Vale.

After three days at Triones, I denied his theory of the paranormal, the only discarnate vibrations that I was able to detect being of the departed Natalie and her mother, the goddess-turned-businesswoman. If there was anything supernaturally invested in that huge cavernous household, it was Harvey's nostalgia for the voices and echoes of the past. That much I told him. I remember him going stand-offish and quiet, if only briefly, saving his trump card for a less sober occasion, as that turned out.

That said, I had shown patience and respect as he told his little tales. They were given greater and greater elaboration the longer it took to show me round the house. Frequently he found doors open come the morning when he was adamant they had been secured the night before. He asked me to explain. He spoke of ornaments and bric-à-brac, preternaturally inspired with animal volition, suddenly leaping off ledges or walls (a private entertainment for an exclusive audience, apparently – Harvey the sole witness and lone reporter of these events). Where he was keen to classify and label these weird or bizarre phenomena, as a poltergeist, or psychokinesis – anything, provided it was either inexplicable or extrasensory – without first-hand experience I could not be other than sceptical. It was not so much to humour him (suppose there *is* a collective imagination, suppose human life can survive its disembodiment), but more to get a word in edgeways that I told him so.

Meanwhile I wrestled with my 'explanation', hopeful that the quiet and seclusion of Harvey's village house would help in gathering, in ordering my thoughts. Yet that only got me down. All I ever seemed to say was this: that there was something intrinsically wrong in the grey faces and shambling limbs passing before our factory gates – 'first interest', as Lizzy termed it. But that was more a personal interest, now on the brink of passing to its third generation – or to me just another import-export firm, dreary in its labour, extensive in its warehousing. I left it. Instead I contacted a local group, an informal ramblers' troop, then in the afternoon I wrapped up and took a stroll in the surrounding hills. With a notepad and pencil, compass and callipers, I circumambulated the baronial, leafless valley until I'd confirmed what researches had shown – i.e. a resemblance to Ursa Major in the layout of buildings, as had now shifted into that pattern. Roughly I sketched its terrestrial constellation, the star-like roofs, icy bright in the pale winter sun.

Great Bear, Big Dipper, Plough – whatever – mapping a rich man's folly wasn't without its sense of mystery. There was elegance in a plan that Harvey's distant predecessor, a sheep baron, had drawn, though I asked myself why he had done it. Was he, when in odd moments not minting his fortune, got through his farming, slaughter, and butcher's monopoly – was not the man obsessed with our overarching northern sky? Or were his secret predilections aligned with classic mythology, and his second, and reputedly beautiful wife, is like a Callisto, forever celebrated in this private heaven on earth?

When my sketch was complete, and after a walk in the valley, I understood something of Triones. It and its various outhouses corresponded in position to the seven brightest stars of the Plough, which with a ruled pen stroke one imagined extending far to the north, leading not to Polaris, but to the village pub, the Pole Star.

I would have told Harvey, next time we were at his kitchen table. Instead he told me how he had informally approached two students of the paranormal. They had talked at length. Result, they were keen to take soundings, and had agreed on a visit. I laughed.

'Ought to be ashamed of yourself!' I said. But I could see he was determined.

'Pass me the butter. Don't be a killjoy.' He crunched his toast and plucked the crumbs from his beard.

He strode out to the yard, over the freezing gravel to what were once the stables, where he loaded the Volvo, and set off cheerily for his usual session in Euston. I was also busy, not with that 'explanation' (which explained nothing, but from the start was just a dismantling process), but with work. I was in the antiquarian book trade, having built stock at regular fairs at the Russell Hotel, and was about to make my biggest ever sale – to an anonymous south Californian, prepared to pay a fortune for ancient tomes on alchemy I'd picked up fortuitously. I followed Harvey out to the A2, amazed at the capacity humans have for every kind of gullibility.

I was called away semi-urgently, though my mother dissembled, giving not a reason, not even the patchiest background. She intoned through her end of the connection only a tight-lipped entreaty. 'You must come. It's your duty.' I could imagine her, uncomfortably upright in the drawing room, her rigid back not touching the telephone chair, the slender, unworked fingers of her free hand drumming nervously on the jotter, this ghost that I talked to a county and a half away. The Tuesday cleaner had probably been consigned to the laundry room and was ironing shirts – a sort of holy casting out well understood by previous domestics.

Reluctantly, I was in that same drawing room the following Friday, not in the daytime, but encamped against the cold of a late winter evening. There was a roaring fire. The reddish velvet curtains were drawn tightly to. Armchairs were pushed in an arc round the hearth. The three players in this latest charade were seated, and had been so for half an hour since dinner, their faces flushed by the heat. Ceremoniously, a tedious dynastic drama (gripping to them – this is how I guessed the whole rigmarole must be important) was switched off and the TV doors emphatically closed. My tall, suave, somewhat portly father – as usual awash in the rapids of emotional human life – one hand jangling money in his pocket, inspected the palm, now the nails of the other, but sat without a word. It was left to my mother, who offered pretty much all her maternal wisdom, a confession of fault on both sides, how we must all try again, that I would see how different things could be on my return. This much I had more or less anticipated, aware of how incomprehensible they found my rejection of the business, or 'first interest', to quote that euphemism. Yet it was pointless. These pregnant get-togethers always led to all three of them claiming victory by attrition, with the physical limitation of the outcast not out-bellowing the triumvirate. I thought of my explanation, not as a refuge, but as necessary.

Elizabeth was silent throughout, with occasional nodded approval at repeated commercial edicts, or fixing the fender with grim penetration when, for the umpteenth time, I refused to be devoured. The revelation dawned at about ten – a time obviously set aside for failure or success – when the whole thing was really a celebration. Champagne appeared in ice buckets, on the quarter-hour nuptials were announced, and promptly on cue Lizzy's groom materialised, a skinny boy with a stoop, who until then had been lurking in a remote, unheated chamber of the house. We shook. I passed into his part extended, trembling hand, a glass – and poured. This was his fortification. I said: 'You're not the first person here to be exiled to the outer kingdom.' I gestured. He, unwittingly part of the plot, only smiled, not fully aware of himself as part of the plan. It would turn out that after the wedding this limpid, chilly morsel would join the firm at the same entry point I might have had for myself – a state of affairs this clumsy rig-up was designed to make me contemplate. Still too ignorant, skinny groom sat down, miles away from puzzled Lizzy.

I resisted pleas to stay for the weekend – this is where the plan broke down – and didn't stay the night, explaining that a book fair on Sunday needed last-minute preparations tomorrow (this was their first inkling of the work I did). I left them, and returned to Triones, to Harvey's hotchpotch conception of the universe, complete with apprentices, his students of the paranormal.

In Harvey's mind, the dead were certainly dead, but in life emitted an as yet unidentified source of energy, which by a miracle of supernature reassembled the person's image, or echoed the sound of his or her voice, at any odd moment after death. This was why his late father had appeared at the foot of his bed in the night, waking him with tangible if unintelligible utterances (which notion didn't embrace the opening of locked doors). I remember quizzing him, testing him, in the early hours of a cold morning: 'Yes, yes, of course. But tell me, was this before, during, or after the divorce?' He raked over the ashes, searching for a spark, a vestige of warmth, but was evasive, unclear in his reply. 'Anyway,' he said, 'it's too cold to stay up. I'm for bed.' I knew that sign, his rebuff. But suppose for a moment he was right, or even on the right track. What about the innumerable millions of people who have come and gone? And animals, for that matter, and plants – why should they be excluded? Wouldn't our daily lives be a confusing stumble through a maze of random sounds and pictures, transmitted from the near, the middle, and the remote past? And what reasoning suggests that only our loved ones reveal themselves to us? 'It's an interesting idea,' I said, stretching, tossing an empty can into a distant waste bin, 'but I don't buy it.'

The students were of the first intake in a new department. In odd moments they read snatches mostly from Arthur Koestler, and sometimes Colin Wilson. They had professional interest in the predictions of Nostradamus, whose *Centuries* they quoted at mealtimes. In a typical working day they monitored the sub-zero temperatures of centrally heated rooms, or the involuntary swing of light fittings. They quantified invisible agencies lifting and hurling objects. The bustling little rotund one was from Smethwick, and had the unpleasant habit of regarding his interlocutor along the ridge of his nose, through narrowing eyelids. The other was as skinny as Lizzy's groom (though shorter, without the stoop) and operated as support, speaking when spoken to, lugging round equipment, preparing experiments, and fiddling with the buttons of his shirt. I arrived late (after midnight), but found them seated round the kitchen table with a deck of playing cards, a mountainous pile of empty beer tins on the drainer, the dish washer churning away in its corner. Harvey introduced me, and opened the fridge, where in the cold yellow glare all the beer had gone. He returned to the table with two bottles of cheap French wine.

They were measuring the levels of psychic activity in Harvey's makeup (this had nothing to do with ghosts in the house, but passed the time before real work got under way tomorrow), Smethwick lifting cards from the pack, Harvey guessing the suit (the normal success rate would be around thirteen in a deck of fifty-two), with the muted colleague noting down the score. This was the twenty-third pass, and everyone was growing tired, not to say drunk. But, it *did* look as if Harvey was endowed with a definite, though negative, psychical sense. His rating was consistently below thirteen. Curious.

We finished the two bottles and began a third, while a now bubbling Smethwick recalled, for my benefit, a history of last summer's hike. Imagine this. Dusk in its early descent. Two weary travellers miles from the nearest hostel. A hilly, twisting road. The lure of a room in a pub. And what *was* that pub, by a clump of pines, on the brow of a hill? 'Pole Star?' I asked. 'No. The Herdsman. In the next village.' 'Arcturus,' I said. 'That's neat.' A toothless old man sucking stout, in his regular place under the moon-flooded window – a casement, with diamond shapes – told them local tales. Silvery quadrilaterals lengthened on the bench, and overflowed into the ashtray, onto the ancient's tobacco tin, into their beer. He said that a stockbroker, or was it an accountant, or even someone high up in government, but anyway a bachelor, having built his sprawling house found nothing to do in his free hours. He led his housemaids into a mild form of fetishism, and through competition chose the lucky winner for much more specialised recreation. Alas his orgiastic nights met a premature end, our wealthy stag dying in a painful convulsion (something he ate). His winning maid and one other servant stayed on, though the latter also died, falling foul of an item of domestic machinery (something sharp through the jugular). Under her new master, an occultist who renamed the house to its present Triones, the maid's grief (or perhaps insanity) brought her to candlelit rooms late on stormy nights with a Ouija board and planchette, where she wailed diabolically, her eyes rolling. To the present day, the house was still haunted, and bore the reverberations of that miserable soul and her caterwauls.

Harvey was beaming, but I wiped the grin off his face. I said: 'First-rate entertainment, and that old man certainly sang for his supper. But there's nothing in it. Triones was built by a wealthy farmer well known in the Southeast. He was married twice, both wives dying young. He lived here for over fifty years, well into the century. Sorry to disappoint....' After that, we lurched upstairs – it was well past bedtime. It was then that Harvey had his 'proof'. Going huddled over several tomes, shivering, I noted the harmful excesses, huge overstocks, unsaleable stereotypes – everywhere. 'Antique books – what a tricky business.' I paused. Harvey was kicking up a rumpus on the landing above, where he had instantly entered the initiate's second phase of faith and devotion. One of the guestroom snecks was broken (verifiable), and so when Smethwick-born had dumped his bags there earlier, Harvey had locked the door, which would otherwise swing open, causing a draught.

'So what do you make of this?' he asked, looming large in my doorframe. He, triumphant, insisted, and Smethwick and partner confirmed, how they'd found the door unlocked, wide open, the room unbearably cold.

'Come, see for yourself!'

I did, and immediately thought of those discarded tins on the drainer.

The corners of my mouth twitch. There's an incipient smirk. I am in my lounger, gazing, in the Spanish sun, into the frost of that fantastic, spectral night. I cannot fail to be amused at its intoxicated pursuit of the truth, with its ectoplasmic manifestations (that nobody ever witnessed) emanating everywhere in the house of my lost musician friend. My sarcasm is intact. I am, always, ready for gentle exercise on those whose material lives are not enough. I reserve my human charity, as I look up, as I glance across the plastic table top, with its long, pellucid summer drinks, under a frilly, coloured parasol, for the waifs and strays of our fathomless, meaningless life.

Looks are deceptive. I have with me an elegant, long-limbed girl, whose pose is the antithesis of what had caught my eye, slumped as she was on a futon in the Monkey Puzzle (that neighbourhood the natural locality of misfits and malcontents). She tosses back her hair, sipping a Cinzano.

It is a curious autobiographical irony that where she excels, in the design of household glassware, she also experiences an indescribable loathing, having been within an inch of giving up. Grim, honourable, over-sensitive to social inequalities, nothing tempered her extremes, soothed or usefully lulled. I have amused her with my story, that agony at last subsiding, in a train of one Pagan ritual followed by another. I took the premonition, a dream that woke me with a start, to be a warning, but recalling it more fully on the eve of the wedding, saw it as one further example of that innate scepticism I shall never shake off. A thorny wasteland that I know intimately but still cannot name, we could all see in its undulations as far as the horizon. I was in the lead. The landscape was familiar. I knew the way. My sibling and the father we shared trudged behind, aghast. We halted. A church with a square tower materialised ahead, spontaneously assembled at that precise place and time from the wilds and scattered debris. Then the incredible part (it's incredible to me): at my instigation, we joined hands, we knelt and bowed our heads, and in this triangular worship offered ourselves dutifully, in the sacrifice of our souls. But our prayers were short, and ended in the horrible clang of a closing metal shutter, work of God or the devil (it is either equally well). Whatever, it acted as exclusion from a tempting other world – a kind of supernatural interdict.

Momentarily, the chain was broken. We gazed on at an excandescence, an untameable power suffusing the shutter's metallic scales. I told the other two to join hands with me again, and noted the clannish dark gowns we were now wearing, and the deadly dagger gripped where each of us was linked. I urged my people to worship more fervently, but Elizabeth fell to the ground wailing, her eyes demonic, her mouth distorted, her limbs flailing uncontrollably. I smothered her body with mine, and shook her. My father smiled. Then Elizabeth slipped her dagger behind me.

There was just no time. She ran her hand to the nape of my neck. She thrust in the blade, and wrenched. Although there was no pain I felt the warm gush of the wound she made. Frozen, I threw off the quilt even as her laughter echoed in the dark. Irrationally, and perhaps hopefully, I assumed this to be an indication that the marriage would fail, but revised that view as I sat on the hard pew with delighted relatives, while Lizzy and skinny groom took their vows. Later, at the reception, her veil pinned from her smile, minutes before the cake was sliced, I told her, half-heartedly sipping my glass, that I wished her well but couldn't imagine myself getting hitched. Her reply was a good one: 'You can't imagine *anything* family.' I looked around, at my mother in shocking pink and an extravagant, broad-brimmed hat, already in her cheeks a flush, a rosy immanence. At the earnest young men, stiffened by newish collars and singled out for the uniformity of their bow ties. At those without panache, in slacks and tweedy jackets, here because it was rude to be elsewhere. At my father with a fat cigar and an ostentatious chain slung across the bulge in his waistcoat. 'No. I can't,' I said. She wanted to know why – and if I wouldn't stay, what I would do instead. I took out a sealed envelope, my completed explanation, from where I had carefully placed it in my jacket pocket.

I said: 'You remember that time we were supposed to meet outside the warehouse, when *I* ran away…? I couldn't bear its ashen workers shambling from the siren.'

'Impressions of a child,' she said.

'Probably. But *I* can't live on *their* miserable labour.' I held up the envelope.' It's all in here….'

She understood, but pressed me on alternatives. I began to explain a little about my business, dealership in rare books, finds I had made, some staggering sums achieved. But she was called way, where skinny husband brandished a knife over a wedge of icing, a ludicrous grin stretching the freckled flesh of his cheeks. As she turned, as she swirled in her spangled wedding gown, she snatched the envelope out my hand. She walked away, and was soon engulfed by a throng of guests. The opportunity to retrieve that laboured document was denied, and there was never another – she made sure of that. Again she had triumphed, and again, in the same decisive way, she had scooped up the sentimentalised fruit bowl before it had had its chance to fall into shards on the flagstones. Once more, I was driven to the bar.

A Peacock in Paradise

An audible hum of rubber on concrete approached its source in another reality – fable and representation. A knight, symbolically clad in gold and silver, urged on his foaming horse, its white mane flying – up and across the heavens. His search for a mythical elixir had turned to this – for here was desperation, escape. Another, moonish, pursued from the rising sun, his black horse snorting – for even in modern times, that medieval reaper of souls never gave up. Half familiar objects floated up, down, across, and got in the way (scriptural revelations never achieve a lasting dominion over the fabricated world). There, a large round mirror at seventy degrees, or here, its oval reflection sliding down a wall. A giant's cloak, bent slightly from the waist, and in the shadows a hand, and in the hand a dripping blade. First faint hopes that nevertheless a good day lay ahead were shaken by an autumn gust, transforming what was a dreamed arras into real and billowing curtains. A ring of frills, tassels – an angel's fallen headpiece – resolved itself to a central lampshade. In the diminishing twilight, the throb of an engine slowly disappeared, as an early car drove out to meet the commuter traffic. She resisted – this of all mornings – and rolled on her back. Trumpeting seraphim, looping, traversing the ceiling, had gone, though still she dozed. Then she was sliding back in that dream....

Lights emerged from the mist. Then, from a dark hillside, a volcanic shower of sparks lit the landscape brooding around it. Here, like her, a peasant citizenry lingered in its first slumbers – though there the similarity ceased (life here confined itself to rustic little dwellings). Cowls or crooked chimneys issued puffs of smoke. A steady trickle of water off the roofs filled the timber butts. The procession of houses followed the sweeping curves of the road they lined, into the night hills. Closer, as the lights passed, twitching rodents scurried for cover in the clumps of twisted undergrowth. Katherine struck out for the road, and kept in her sights those glowing projectiles, rising up in red or orange fountains. She wanted to call on someone – lost, she wanted to know the way – but at the first door she came to shrank from the red crosses daubed on its panels. At the next, the thud of a cloven hoof – a Gothic knocker – echoed in the rooms inside. No one came. The god of her sleeping world hadn't nudged other spirits into life. She turned back and followed the road, to the summit, where the mists had thinned. The glow from the fire warmed and illumined her face. Then someone appeared – companion in her private hell – clipping a pen to his breast pocket, then fingering his coat cuffs nervously. His flushed face was young and fresh, though with present duties his features were drawn. 'The truth is this, I'm afraid,' he said, 'if you'll only step this way.' He took her arm and both edged forward timidly. They looked down, and in the bowels of that great, unfathomable crater, the hot, fiery magma bubbled, boiled, spilled over. 'You see the problem. You see what a task it is, getting all that activity under control.' In the heat she wondered, but then had to stand back. 'There's really no hope, then?'

'It's a difficult case.'

A sparrow had preened itself in a defoliating ash across the street, but surrendered to unexpected promptings, swooping down. Other, phantasmal wonders dissolved in the morning light, and Katherine, when she heard those vibrant wings outside her house front, had already seen a penumbral shadow dart across her bedroom wall. She shuffled off the quilt and sat on the edge of her bed, where it was clearer: that madman's cloak was her husband's winter dressing gown (perhaps Morton *could* come home today). Cold, she put it on, drawing the cord loosely to her waist, and crossed the room. Awake at last, the pink suffusion of sunshine, a morning glow through the thin fabric of her bedroom curtains, had become less harsh. She tugged them back. The world brightened, as a shower of yellow leaves swirled across the lawn – and that reminded her. The boy in the white house opposite was looking for weekend gardening work. She sat down at the dresser and saw what ghost it was – that apparition of herself – staring apprehensively from the mirror. Her hair needed another wash. And, that anaemic look – despite the supplements and all those iron tablets – somehow that had returned again. She altered the angle of the glass. A clear ellipse descended to the floor. She blamed the night's fitful sleep, when she moved up closer, and examined the faint shadows, the bluish rings under her eyes. She considered makeup, and clothes, and whether she needed petrol, but this was not a good time for coherent thoughts. She flung the mirror back to its angular plane.

She showered, dressed, applied foundation, lip gloss, mascara. She drank coffee and binned a slice of toast, burnt. She stepped outside into the autumn gusts and leaves and got in the car and drove. Out, out of town, where the country roads meandered endlessly through orchards and vineyards, and even a eucalyptus plantation. Here the mists were denser, and in all probability were not going to lift before lunch. And what were those two ragged points of yellow light ahead, bouncing, getting nearer, nearer? 'Didn't notice that last time, a eucalyptus.... Oh, here's my answer, should have guessed.' She swerved and raked a hawthorn hedge as the two yellow patches focused into a pair of headlights straddling the broken centreline. The other driver hooted belatedly, but Katherine, as she braked and zigzagged and brought her large saloon under control, couldn't assimilate that angry, shifting tone. She turned on her headlights. Then, after a few more miles, she found herself behind an empty coal truck, where a thick hairy forearm on the nearside flopped from an open window and languished in a rush of morning air. A cigarette butt slipped from two of its chubby fingers and exploded in a shower of hot ephemeral sparks in the gutter. A winking orange indicator preceded a clatter, as the truck slowed at a bend, and disappeared in the closing waves of mist down a hairpin left. It was almost eight. The next village was memorable for a timber church and a hand pump, and – what was it now? – you took a right at the crossroads after that. Nevertheless the lanes wouldn't unwind. And more: these terraced cottages on high ground above the road were impostors, and you had to wonder. Where were they – the village, the church, the crossroads? Where?

Occasionally, one, two puzzled observers came to the long colonnaded window and peered out, a frown for the younger. For the older, whose head and shoulders were plunged in the fumes of a private upper world – for him an enigmatic pose, shoulders hunched, his pipe stem cradled in the dampish warmth of an underarm. What they shared professionally they symbolised in a commonness of presentation. Their work was remedial, but here the doctor's white coat had long been exchanged for a business suit – a sober grey or plain dark blue. What they could see with their own eyes – what they'd studied and examined – belied the written history that chronicled the onset of Morton's disease. He, a mathematician and lecturer, was far from an atrophied human shell, even when officialdom had applied the term *accidie*. Only look, take a glance through one of Morton's windows, stretch up to the little arrow slit that allows a glimpse of Paradise (a glimpse from the wilderness, a glimpse away from the wrongness of the world). Here's a burly gardener sweeping leaves. Over there, a black swan flapping. Just in our sights is Adam, or without that name, a madman. It's Morton, the mandrake – busy, bustling, in a hurry, preoccupied with only he knew what. His two examiners had explored his notes in protracted, tangential conversation sessions, and in the seclusion of either man's upholstered study had kept them folded open. These days of inquiry ran on into evening, and dusk, when the lamps were turned on. Sometimes the salivary tip of a pipe stem wanders quizzically in the labyrinths of Morton's insane-looking scrawl, sometimes it's the hook on the open arm of his colleague's amber spectacles.

Morton had a theory, and in that theory Leibniz's monads had been transmuted (into nomads). Through such ideas Morton hoped to understand something fundamental about himself – while the means of *achieving* it were somewhere in the garden. For the man sweeping leaves, it was only a matter of understanding that the imbalance of Morton's mind – and not some numerical pursuit – explained why he talked to Magellan geese – that was in the lime walk – or mallards by the willow pool, or the flamingos. That simple worker only ever turned his back, unaware that co-ordinates, binomial theory, maxima and minima et al, were Morton's academic staple, though would not have been surprised that his job, held open at the sixth form where he taught, was the one place suiting his attitude to dress – rather lax.

These were the empirical facts, which of course hadn't escaped the psychiatrists. More interesting by far was his pathological need to commit the fruits of his marvellous soliloquies to paper (no one assumed that, for example, a common shoveler was capable of an intelligent reply). His notes were copious, and here at the Eden Drive Psychiatric Unit, Professor Feodore's wife – who was also his personal assistant – had noticed an increased workload in the stationery department. And what of this? Each new notebook was begun with the following, in the patient's unmistakable hand—

Mandrake, or Morton: poisonous plant with emetic and narcotic properties, with root thought to resemble human form and to shriek when plucked.

Feodore sensed the beginning of an answer, and when his paunchy colleague came to the window, pursued by a cloud of blue tobacco smoke, he offered him a hint or two. 'Look, look at him now,' he said, 'strutting, poring over those nene geese – and can't get his notes down quick enough. A mechanic of Creation.' The other put a matchbox over the bowl of his pipe, and – with increasing rapidity – sucked and puffed. 'Mm,' he said. A dragon's two hot jets issued from his nostrils.

Assuming the plausibility of recent suppositions, Feodore – if uneasily – acknowledged that the absence of evidence of Morton's religious conversion, was confirmation of that man's last act of sanity. The precise nature of his psychological metamorphosis was unimportant for the moment. The profound issue was this. God's immaterial infusion into the human vessel, if taken for blasphemy, meant that the new, revelatory aspect of Morton's life was necessarily private. While he wrestled with its terrible meaning, he protected in so far as he could that growing inner monster in his soul, keeping it from public scrutiny. Feodore, who looked to the coming millennium from the contradictory vantage of scientific scepticism and hopeful anticipation, had tried to reason, from a humanist stance, that these were prophetic days – for was not the Bible also filled with iniquity and wonder? His party peers believed and advocated that an emphasis on status was the natural adjunct of superior minds – that, in an ordered civilisation, these were inseparable – and any who opposed that view in reality believed in it, if secretly. How else to explain their inability to devise a system of everyday life that worked in any other way? The problem for Morton, in the last days of his sanity, was his despair at ever reconciling these problems. Now, as a result, it was something of the Old and not the New Testament that gripped his soul.

Since it appeared in the notebooks repeatedly – alongside a same recurring hexagram – and because the patient frequently pursued it, pen in hand, Feodore placed at the centre of Morton's animism one of the half-dozen peacocks in his collection, whose fate was seen as parallel to Morton's own. How often that one isolated figure had waited in vain for the other, who, correctly identifying the whole of Creation's indifference, consistently refused to display its coverts. It did not spread its train and rattle its quills, which remained an ornament the creature dragged behind itself in the dust and leaves, uselessly. In the *Book of Changes*, which Morton had studied while researching Leibniz, this was represented numerically as 36, a 'Hiding of the Light'. To Feodore this was the perfect sign – a precise symbol – of the prophet who wouldn't prophesy, the convert who professed no religion. Morton's own words vis-à-vis that unnatural reticence were returned to again and again in the conversation sessions—

'The pity of *this* travesty is in its infinitude, though they may seek to but never undo the righteous.'

Feodore turned from the window and waved away the smoke, and understood from his colleague's preoccupation that this wasn't the right time to voice conjectures. The danger in a diagnosis of such imagination was in arousing the suspicion that he himself had a need for more than scientific meaning to his work. He looked at his watch and remarked that Morton's wife was now over an hour late, but couldn't have guessed that moments before, headlights dimmed in a blaze of autumn sunshine, she had swung her saloon into Eden Drive, and was announcing herself to the receptionist. When there was no answer from Feodore's phone, Katherine, fretful, had to sit and wait on a huge leather chair, flicking through country magazines.

Jacobsen's rumpled suits had the shape of tobacco tins at the trouser pockets when he sat, and were lastingly permeated by the stench of the brand he smoked. He puffed abstractedly in the gloaming of that era, the late twentieth century, and even fixed his gaze on the closing millennium. He was a professional man, without culture, and without philosophy. He brought up the rearguard. He bore with him, from that point of observation – still clouded in medieval ignorance – a probing look into the history of bedlam. There were no mysterious qualities in what was after all a disease (he blamed the ancient hippocampus for that deceit). With Morton there was undoubtedly a chemical imbalance in the brain, probably exacerbated by genetic vulnerability.

They were colleagues and also friends, but Feodore's propensity – a latent interest in the faintly supernatural – he found puzzling. Jacobsen well remembered the days before drugs. He personally had supervised cold baths or showers (though never approved of straitjackets). At Eden Drive these of course were improved surroundings, if nevertheless he knew that for Katherine, whom he had gone to find, this was not a consolation. The reality was, Morton was hard to help, beyond a cure.

She, Katherine, placed him from her first and only previous visit – a dejected background figure, stolid rather than hovering – a recollection more vivid than that of the route she'd followed in getting here. He thought he might find her in reception, and slouched in the doorway. He took his hands from his pockets and approached, a short grey presence who mustered only a crumpled smile. 'Mrs Freedman,' he said, and took her hand. As she stood up and shook she noticed her car outside with the lights still on. 'No matter,' he said, and followed her out. 'That will be pleasant, a walk through the garden.'

In a pergola she commented irrelevantly on the scarcity of climbing plants, though Jacobsen, under a flimsy red vine, took it seriously and considered the point: 'Ah yes, you will find Professor Feodore has a passion for birds and wildfowl.' In the silence that followed she half expected an informal allusion – anything – to her husband's state of mind (which of course hadn't changed). The forced smile, the dimness in Jacobsen's eyes, held no news whatsoever of a cure. Three pink flamingos just coming into view seemed to confirm his jaundiced observations, in the way they stalked. She followed him into a gravel pathway, which brought them close to the conference room (where Morton already was, and Feodore expected to find them).

Feodore, who saw them from a window, ensured that the kettle was full and personally switched it on.

The peacock was suddenly plaintive: its untranslatable appeals were heard even by Feodore, who looked up again, and saw through a double thickness of glass one slim and one paunchy figure, stepping up in concert from the gravel to the patio. The peacock's throaty cries were still audible and echoing, though there was nothing to inform him more vividly than *human* transformations. The evil Dr Jacobsen had a horizontal yellow stripe on his forehead, and where his hair had once been thinning, and neat, a new wildness fluttered in the breeze. Somewhere on his stroll he'd picked up and put on his officer's coat from a former life, though his bearing wasn't so disciplined as in his early manhood. He tugged at the rope that bound Katherine's naked wrists and neck. The distortion, her anguished face under a crown of thorns – despite radiance in its paleness – reflected the doctor's cruel declarations: 'You'll never see him sane again! Your husband is mad, is absolutely mad....' He pulled at that rope a second time, and Katherine, whose long red dress had been torn in the struggle, stumbled but regained her footing on the flagstones. Jacobsen leaned on her shoulder and waved a threatening finger. The peacock protested. The officer growled. 'Don't think anyone will even try to help! Just don't!'

Now they were quite close, by the bay tree, newly positioned in its terracotta pot (there was a click, and the water had boiled). Feodore pulled out a tissue and took off his glasses and carefully wiped, breathed on, wiped the lenses. He held them up to the light, then, blinking, slotted back those amber frames. He spooned coffee into two cups but left the third empty for now. He looked up again, through clear lenses this time, and Satan's world had neatly resolved itself to God's good and mediocre. His friend the undemonstrative Jacobsen was again in his shabby suit, while the perplexed and elegant young woman under his gentle guidance brushed a yellow maple leaf from the shoulder of her coat.

Over coffee – and for Katherine tea, as it turned out – Professor Feodore explained that there had been only a minimal response to drugs, and it therefore wasn't possible for Morton to spend other than occasional days out of care. For them, too, there would always be the question of Morton's safety. For Katherine this presented the one insoluble problem – the dwindling of her finance. What could she say? She said nothing – though Jacobsen noticed, as he ushered her into the conference room, the bright tears that had welled in her eyes. They were frightened eyes. Still, she was hopeful, even when she stood at the door, looking in. Feodore relieved the nurse – in these confusing days, Morton's only real friend. Then the professor sat down at the large round table, where he as well as his colleague saw plainly what happened next. When she bent to his shoulder, with a painful smile, then with her lips brushed the coarse, bristly cheek, then her husband's temple, that same inscrutable man, with his hardened features and a malevolent scowl, waved her away.

She sat down and reached for a tissue. Jacobsen took a seat opposite, and avoided her eyes. He referred to his copy of Morton's case history, and underlined, as Feodore began, the salient points. There had been an obsession with weight, and a gruelling regimen of cruel, punishing diets. There had been this intensity of feeling, which surfaced privately, and showed itself in the most fearful moral judgement of his parents (to that culpable pair could be attributed blame for almost anything). Then came what was certain to be the end of his career, when the will to go to work was ever more sporadic.

Yet there was still no mention of a calling or religious conversion.

Feodore told Morton what his wife already knew, that was, that he couldn't go home, and that neither was it possible for Morton to remain here. What was his reaction? Immediately, he put a hand to his crown and twirled a tuft of hair in a thumb and forefinger, and looked ludicrous. 'You already know my opinion,' he said, sliding his notebook across the table, 'and anyway you'll see I have finally found the answer to *all* conceivable questions.'

Jacobsen wouldn't deny the excruciating light in the life of the faithful, or the unbearable knowledge philosophy may bring, but nor could a sensitive and practical man accept them in these simple terms. He turned a page, and noted again the mathematical interest in Leibniz, then the irritation, annoyance, the rage, at an absurd contention from one of Morton's contemporaries: that that philosopher's preoccupation with the categorical proof of God's existence prevented his one real and lasting achievement, the invention of the computer. Next one would hear that the terrifying truth of the cosmos had been assimilated into the minds of mere technocrats.

Feodore had his own thoughts on that, but the present problem wouldn't go away. 'What's to be done?' he asked.

'Put this witch back on her besom. Good God, Professor, what's going on?'

That tuft of hair in Morton's thumb and forefinger was rotating with greater urgency, while Katherine dabbed the corner of her eye with a tiny cushion of tissue paper.

The professor persisted. 'We want you to understand, to agree with whatever decision is made,' he said.

Jacobsen took out his pipe and filled it slowly, methodically, from an oblong tin. 'Look,' said Morton, his eyelids narrowing, 'you can't understand the mental slavery men like me must suffer. Look.' He opened his notebook for Feodore. Jacobsen, about to strike a match, put down his pipe suddenly, for now Katherine couldn't contain her distress and had to be taken outside. Even then, so much more remained to be gone through, Morton a man who scorned the mundane. Now at last as they sat alone, would Feodore share in his patient's enlightenment? Or ever know that life and the universe were finite in size and shape, but were everlasting, and were here, in Paradise? The underlying principle had eluded the sharpest minds, but he, Morton, had discovered it, this deception, he said, of contrasts. What existed beyond Paradise was the wilderness where most people lived – and that was infinite in size and shape. But – and this was important to grasp – that part of the All was ephemeral. The monumental strife of the human soul was a) in its striving for useless baubles in the wilderness, and b) its almost complete failure to notice the fabulous treasures of Paradise. The plight of the peacock was the perfect illustration, for here was unearthly beauty that no one cared to behold. That, Professor, had led him inescapably to the following proof—

If unholy strife in the human soul is infinite in size and shape, and the most perfect state of being is infinite in duration, it follows that strife and perfection are equal and omnipresent.

An interesting syllogism, but while Jacobsen made more tea, Katherine couldn't stop weeping.

The Seven-O-One

'*Suzy. It's me. Meet you 6.30, usual place.* That was the un-erased message on her answerphone.'

These were the words Hollamby, the beleaguered detective hack, had opened his new book with. *Beyond* these words, he'd lost all confidence.

Crank, his therapist, had pressed him to a chair and told him to renounce the bottle. At forty this was tragic, too early by far to toss it all away.

'That's too bad,' said Hollamby.

He gazed up through the sash, and through the imperfection of Crank's rectangular panes, where a pigeon flew by, then a bit of litter floated up.

'Not going anywhere near my desk,' he said. That months-old paragraph was going to have to wait.

Crank tried a different tack. 'The problem's financial,' he said. 'Or rather *not*. You're wealthy, mortgage-free. There is,' he said, 'no pressure.'

Hollamby laughed, knowing they'd been this way before. 'Somehow,' he said, 'your fees just never quite enter that equation,' and here he almost got up for his coat. Crank said don't be hasty and picked up the phone to his wife, who managed his practice and occupied the office next door. 'Libby,' he said, 'you wouldn't like to bring us both some coffee....'

Hollamby relaxed and rubbed his chin. He thought of Peter Blane, the invented, hard-boiled private eye of his nineteen bestsellers. Crank took out a pen, but placed it on his blotter, at a loss, apparently. 'It's writer's block,' he said. 'It'll pass.'

'No,' said Hollamby. 'The problem's *this* – this what-you-call-it life – I mean the flab of it.' Blane had been his crusader, a sceptic with defender's sword, a siren voice among the shallow tones of a thrusting middle-class. Twenty years ago the graduate Hollamby had penned political sonnets in a casebook, attributed to Blane. 'Unpolished, of course, but always a blast at class hypocrisy. By book twelve Blane was bored,' he said. 'In book fourteen he moved out of town.' Now, for twenty, he'd got a girl of all things – Suzy. 'Worse, there's a hint of adultery.'

Crank matched much of this to life's natural highs and lows, and stressed that the need to debunk our heroes was an important process. 'As critical,' he said, 'as the common will to elect them in the first place.'

Hollamby grunted, but didn't reply. Just then Libby clattered in with the tray, and looked scathing at her husband. Crank whipped away his pen and for now said nothing more. Hollamby watched: the bend of her knee, that way she had of leaning forward from the waist, the coffee things as she put them on the blotter. She passed a note, which Crank took up when his wife had left, and read: *Forgot to mention. Am catching the late-night shops. Meet you at home.*

Yes, he remembered. Libby was after curtains for the new extension. 'Sugar,' he said. 'Two isn't it?'

Hollamby took his cup, and stirred. Crank sipped at his, and looked out through the gloom, only partly aware of the time. It was getting late, the afternoon was wintry, a bleakness summed up in the fluorescent oblongs and weary sight in the office block across the street.

'Things move on,' he said. 'Change is a consequence of not only life, but art.' Aesthetically, he prescribed for Peter Blane a complete adaptation to his creator's over-ripeness.

'That,' said Hollamby, 'could finally break my heart.' He couldn't see the sceptic Blane in a housecoat, with a sherry at five each evening. After all, Blane's had been a persona conceived with a marked face, adolescent pocks, and always announced by what he wore – a mackintosh perpetually streaked in rain. Nights, the collar went up. And of course, Blane only ever considered his fellow human beings through the hard glaze of his eyes.

'No, it won't do,' said Hollamby. 'The truth is on the streets. Where life, where people, where everything seethes. This is all too cosy.' He got up and walked to the window, still with his coffee. Crank tried, but couldn't follow the line of his gaze.

'Relax,' said Crank.

Hollamby swilled his slops, trying to dissolve the last of the sugar, but kept his eye on the mizzle outside. The scene had been built in his mind, as he imagined for Blane his next liaison, a time and place with Suzy. He looked at the car lights, a pale yellow or shards of red reflecting off the road. He went over book twenty again, with its solitary opening paragraph. He looked down and checked his watch. Out on the street, he saw that Libby Crank was without an umbrella, and was walking east. She adjusted her thin scarf against the wind. At the corner she posted the office mail.

'Lord, is that the time?' he said.

Crank was surprised and tried to calm his client down. 'No hurry,' he said. 'No hurry at all.'

Hollamby thought there was, in the wounds of his profession. His tutor had warned against a life in books, doubting its rightness for Hollamby's temperament, a view Hollamby's father had shared.

'That was a barb,' said Hollamby, though now he saw the mistake. Blane was his trumpet, 'my agent of social agitation', a narrow character, 'but at least a man of conscience'.

Crank couldn't see much wrong with that, adding there was no need for the author to justify his work. Of course, he had long detected the rogue strain, the sense of guilt, the destructive genie tugging at Hollamby's sleeve – but played it down. 'Don't be hard on yourself,' he said.

Hard? Hollamby, turning, crashed his cup and saucer down. 'Technically I've got it wrong,' he said. Blane, scourge of the decadent rich, had shared in their luxury once too often. His hard-hitting private eye had become of all things middle-class.

'I'll pension him off,' he said.

Crank hadn't foreseen that. 'Let's stay a little longer. Try to work this through.'

Hollamby checked his watch again and said no. 'It's after six. I've got to go.' This time he did pick up his coat, and heaved it on. 'Look, I'll call you,' he said, and went.

Crank looked at his diary and put away his pen. A moment later he'd got his back to the chair and was gazing down at the street, where Hollamby stepped out. It was getting colder. Hollamby turned up his collar and lit a cigarette. A plume, then a sheet of bluish smoke wound over his shoulder. Soon he'd reached the corner, going east. Then where Crank couldn't see him, he hurried to the basement steps of the Seven-O-One Club. That had a fizzy pink cocktail umbrella etched in the glass of the door. Inside, a certain 'she' was already waiting, her coat off, her scarf folded away. Crank meanwhile turned the key in his door, and in Libby's office saw the green point of light flashing on her answerphone. He played it. It was someone wanting to cancel. He noted it. The tape overran. Playing now was history, a previous message that somehow hadn't been erased.

'Libby, it's me. Six-thirty. The usual place. Promise.' And of course Crank wouldn't know where that was, the Seven-O-One.

Hellriders

An emeritus professor holds his smeary glasses
To the fading light…

                    '…the schmaltzy poet
Didn't deserve that fabricated end, where waiting
Reporters, all from the flooded north, looked
Unexpectantly at mounting clouds of dust, and later
Traced the desert's funereal track.'

                              He scans,
But can't identify an island cone, its base of moving
Lights, and clutches at his pocket handkerchief.
His younger wife inspects concentric rings
Imprinted on a flapping parasol—

                              'It's not,
It's not our concern. Too bad for the treacly bard,
Who – helmeted and leathered – rode to a hero's
Incompetent death, who spiralled fittingly
Into those newly discovered catacombs. The vanguard
By then had wallowed in its personal angst, preferring
The rhetoric of social consternation. Where else, where else
Could his kitschy lyrics go? It's not, it's not
Our concern.'

                    She had planted a sporty foot
On a melting concrete court at noon, and restored
Its formal precisions.

                    And he: 'More terrible
Is the artificial legend, the myth that Mammon
With exclusive rights and limited memorabilia
Always creates. I see him dissemble in our civilised,

Deluded world, with something inartistic. There is a mobile
Exhibit, the poet's ersatz monogram. A rubber mud flap
Dangling from its gleaming, aluminium guard. A dimmed
Headlamp with wires and nictating indicators. A cactus.
A tailless brown lizard. Strolling deep black craters,
Imprints, the belated footfalls of curious reporters.
All in hot sand under a bright sun in electric
Blue…'

>   …though she had turned
> With the folded parasol, and was enveloped even now:
> In the apartment, in its coming penumbra, in its day-long
> Marble cool.

Mono Merriah. That was a part of it, the preparation for certain fame, though the glib biographer would pry, eventually, and the TV journalist always asks brimming questions. Mono Merriah. That was an epithet brought to a reinvented past.

A monochrome flicker is the most we should ever recall – pixels mislaid in the vastness of the new transmission medium – when the chosen illusion, marked by the usual absence of imagination, at least acknowledges the Philistine mood of his age. Some intelligence there. No one will now accept that the bard is in any way driven by sparks of inspiration (forced literary fashions resemble those of the rag trade – a Romantic poet is as absurd as a kipper tie), and so the Byronic model has to be redrawn, with its design ramifications carefully catalogued. 'MERRIAH: photo by J. Gonne, courtesy the headmistress, South Harrow Comprehensive', or 'Sea View, Merriah's holiday cottage, from the poet's early albums'. Then '*The Apple Tree*, facsimile of an original draft of the opening canto', and this, the most obvious reference, 'MERRIAH IN ALBANIAN DRESS, photo M. Sidney, courtesy the Artists' Renascent Sense Society', when M. Sidney was drunk and past caring *and* in fancy dress.

Posterity ought to be left to decide for itself what is the wheat and what is the chaff, though I offer as an aside that those seeking to define eternal noumena – of this or any other universe – haven't guessed that enormous black holes – they are everywhere – are God's cosmic garbage sacks. Because this independent voice is censored for now, posterity sustains its gentle nudge: we are binary stars, this crass contemporary and me. He shines as brightly as his juvenile ephemera. In this I have been generous (I know). In this I have engineered for half-brother Mono a permanent escape from the cosmos's all-consuming dustbin.

You've bought the lie.

❦

Here's the truth, though how at the outset could anyone conceive that his celebrated signature would one day be a rubber mud flap, an aluminium guard, a headlight, an indicator – an installation artist's articles in burning desert sands? My roving, historical eye pans back, back, a long way back, and picks out double M in sunny Elysian fields on an idle Wednesday morning – ugh! that's the lie I mentioned, the biographer's fiction! MM hasn't been invented yet. It's a breezy Sunday afternoon. The locality is sleepy, middle-class. Mumbo Messiah in those special reflective moods had the happy knack of reconstituting a Home Counties housing estate into a late twentieth-century idyll, and variously interlarded a range of ragbag images: gleaming orange house bricks – crimson tiles for the roofs, bays and façades – brilliant white barge boards – unlikely square turrets and vertical extensions. Or for the conservative and territorial, these: clipped demarcating beech hedges and conifers, neatly trimmed little lawns studded with speckled paving flags (largely without a useful destination), divisive rose beds turning semi- into three-quarter detached, so impeding the neighbourly lawnmower. His ruled pocket notebook was always teeming with observations of this kind, and there were times, certainly, when our embryonic MM couldn't snap the restraining piece of elastic off quickly enough, so urgent his commitment, those breezy folios a maze of commonplace insight. O that press! O that flattened point of his stubby pencil! For was it not out of this melting pot that the epoch-making *The Apple Tree* emerged – a thing as inevitable as any masterpiece must be, as the official biography, now long forgotten, mendaciously, foolishly asserts.

Wednesday-Sunday all those years ago (you see how I grapple with propaganda, how I aim to correct a plain life history).... Sunday saw our born-again scurry home through the windy blossoms, his shirttail flying. The Muse Erato – more properly Errata – stood at his shoulder and dictated, even as the early evening sunshine streamed in, dusty and golden, through his leaded panes. (Note how little time he made to contemplate those distended parallelograms imperfectly focused on his poet's otherwise un-illumined page.) In the morning – blue Monday, as opposed to euphoria Thursday – he did not step triumphantly into his publisher's office – publishers had shrewdly avoided him till now – but as usual strode heavily into the dark corridors of work, for how appallingly the eager fine artist suffered in his day. The pompous ledger clerk, tall, with a stoop and a droopy moustache, strolled over the cold marble, his grudging salute the mere twitch of an eyebrow. He passed in a rush of cold air.

The part-time poet in a dark suit, and with a shaving rash aggravated by a stiff white collar, stood under the chief auditor's elaborately carved doorframe, where the horizontal bore an open, canopy-like structure, in whose vacant shelter two spirits or cherubim stood by a font. Collecting himself for the terrible week ahead, he pushed open the monstrous, creaking door. He was late – artistic types left to their own devices traditionally run to a confused schedule and only half-heartedly fit with the timetables of everyday historic life. This turned out not to be a problem, because the chief auditor was at that moment swinging his way from a bunker, with a trajectory plotted through hazardous clumps of gorse, his target the first green. Having foreknowledge of this, the senior auditor had arranged a visit away from the office, with friends from his bachelor days. This left only the auditor's secretary, who only ever tutted at his timekeeping, being an amused observer of the other two. *Their* joint preference was melodrama. Vehement gestures and the mauving of cheeks accompanied the usual reprimand, delivered in blustering tandem, their familiar cycle of petty tyrannies.

Jules was wearing her skimpy black sweater and yellow beads today, and didn't look up from her filing. She tutted as he limped to his desk. The limp was an affectation and a psychological complexity, for this ensured his sense of equanimity for the moments of admonition. *What low barbarian torments a poor cripple!* was his rationale. He sniffed, at the suffusion of furniture polish that followed each weekend, but decided he'd suffer, being too early in the day, and not yet warm enough to open the sash window (it faced north).

The broad oak desks had been there for centuries so far as the reluctant MM was concerned, an arrangement suited to his colleagues, middling, introspective government officials, who in looking up from their work lit on a bank of filing cabinets, in a sombre-looking grey. Their drawers, sections and folders encompassed a not-so-secret history, a record of fees and taxes collected over the preceding decade. For a step into the remoter past, whole wodges lay moulding in a cellar. Doubtless we'll learn more of this.

The cleaners, all-night zealots, refused on principle to send out any of their number – even un-protesting juniors – into the clutter of MM's territory. His open-mouthed contemporaries had been privy to a kind of defence of this on numerous occasions. In the general disorder – the mountainous paperwork – no one had yet perceived the subtle presence of an ecological conscience, for here at least those ozone-unfriendly furniture sprays encountered token resistance. For a moment he gazed forlornly at a hodgepodge of car park and assembly room ticket stubs, their sharp perforations, then at a silvery chain of paperclips snaking its way diagonally from a top to a bottom corner of his blotter. He attempted to blow away the muddy grey eraser deposits that peppered his sea of paper, but gave up when he was too often stretching and lurching after airborne memos lifted from the chaos of his desk.

Jules was still filing the rounded nail of an index finger, with that cross-eyed intent it was always unwise to interrupt. Nevertheless, his numbing workaday boredom, and his hopeful if scant awareness of the poet's other country, the poet's dream country, were inextricably mingled again. He was compelled to say: 'Oh yes, this time I've *really* done it…' (and it was true, he had). Her glossy pink lips twitched a little then formed one of her famous dark ovals (irresistible yet ultimately frustrating for the bouncy procession of hopefuls who annually gate-crashed the chief auditor's Christmas party). She blew. It resulted in the pleasing revelation of a finely honed fingernail and a minute shower of gold dust on her desktop. She stretched forward. Full yellow cups were momentarily visible in the distended fissures of her black, knitted sweater. Her elliptical beads rattled in her pen tray. She blew again, those pink glossy lips more firmly deployed, until all traces cascaded into the worn pile of the carpet. 'Uh huh,' she said, without looking up, and in a genteel claw selected one of several bottles of nail varnish. He suspected she was wearing her tartan skirt with the huge decorative safety pin and tatty frills round the hem, which she always wore with her tight black sweater.

Solemn, misunderstood, he augmented his chain of paperclips and watched her unscrew the yellow vial. She tossed back her hair and slipped out the brush on a long, slimy stem. She spread out a spidery hand onto her own, immaculate blotter. He was beginning to sweat round the back of the neck and underarms, a sensation he attributed to the puritanical gene pool he was in. The infallible mechanism had already detected his plans, and in unfolding his weary lyric Merriah rehearsed then rejected his invitation to picnic, just the two of them together, this lunchtime (which, anyway, the sophisticated Jules would consider *passé*). The desire for fame outweighed deeply sensible considerations, however (local fame was doubtless educational, a foretaste), and not even sticky pores could deter him. Those nails acquired a hard yellow lustre under Jules's deliberate strokes. When she held up her hands for the varnish to dry – two flapping gloves on a washing line – he set down those appalling metres onto that only unsullied blotter. At Canto XIV, the ledger clerk stepped in with his burdens, a world of melancholy borne in the droop of his moustache. He tossed down a bound tome. Cantos XXIV and XXV rose up on a wave of agitated air and swirled in evasive eddies (the leaps, the contortions, the snatching bard), the bottle of varnish adding colour, upending itself in sympathy. The clerk almost smiled. Retreating he demanded the car park figures – 'before I've had my coffee!'

The irritations, the minor foils of greatness. One needed patience. One had to persist.

'Well. What did you think?' he pressed.

'Very good.' But Jules had already turned to the bottle.

'I mean in terms of style.'

'Don't really know,' she said. 'Though I'm no expert. Who's this Mono Merriah?'

'Pseudonym. Came in a flash.'

'Oh, look, that does it! My last bottle of yellow!'

Merriah gathered up his papers and returned to his wad of ticket stubs. Meanwhile, the chief auditor, with the breeze of early spring in his hair, chipped delightfully from the grassy rough to the deceptive third, where a crumpled red isosceles, just visible, fluttered madly round the tip of a wayward pole.

A man in a rumpled hat, with a simian swing in his gait, must have expected rain, but gripped the point of his umbrella and took odd swipes at pebbles on the pavement. When he looked up (for it was hopeless) it was into the coming twilight – a wash of inky blue – where an upper light went on in a small square window. Solo Mono was preparing the biographer's difficult way, and in his absurd reference book, *Scenes From My Own Life*, had come to a painful pass. But should confessions wait? And more precisely, should he have delayed, at least beyond the ghostly effects of artificial light on his page, and till after he'd studied that peculiar little man gambolling down the street, beating a jungle path with a suburban umbrella....

One asks too, how does the immured poet pretend that life's distracting obstacles are ignored or overlooked, without conceding that the stuff of art was also lost, or that decisions, when made, weren't always responsible ones? Thus the destined Merriah musing, in his *Scenes*, on his old friend Dino. How ingeniously our plunkety singer made light of imputations, carefully *sotto voce*. That historical compendium had as its lesser known intention strategies for shielding his remorse, in a litter of written dissimulations. A blond, bearded Dino rejoiced in a private blue sky and bobbed through life in the sloping shadows of an imagined, cut-throat business world. Sometimes he sat on the Town Hall steps, and in patched denims and printed shirt claimed to be the lost son of an oil magnate.

That same recollected Dino confronted him again, where Merriah's tatty denims had been discarded in favour of a dark suit and polished shoes, not to say a morning shave and haircut. Mumbled Message had to call out (in popular mysticism, the student in losing his faith gradually recedes from the master's cosmic view), and when he had turned and fixed him for a moment, Dino demanded to know what he'd done to himself. As Merriah self-consciously records—

'I've got an interview.'

'You mean for a job?' – though this was rhetorical, since Dino knew full well the meaning of society's norms.

'It's not for the job, it's the money.'

'But *I* thought,' said Dino, 'we were having a revolution....'

'Let's say my role has changed, to enemy within....'

'You can't just drop out. That's unethical.' His tone was rising. Moon Mad Crier sensed his mounting disgust.

'That's not the point.'

'The point!'

'The interview's now – in there....' He wheeled round and shading his eyes beheld the despised Town Hall, its wedding-cake edifice, its shadowy colonnade. 'You think my shoes are shiny enough?'

'Ranks of the living dead,' said Dino. 'Ranks of the living dead.'

Life had its pitfalls, even the best of us stumble. Disillusionment, its many surprising turns. 'Goodbye, goodbye.'

Translated notes from a reference book.

Professionally, it is here I deliver my *coup de grâce*, discrediting forever that unholy writer of fiction, the biographer. I assert that the new mood of liberality informing MM's masters is not demonstrable in terms of lay, bewildered reverence, profound respect for the tormented artist, the sense of awe at his ambition, whatever the biography says. It's more a case of the chronicler's narcissism as it teases out parity with his subject's. They worshipped the same god, proclaiming their offerings in the same ritual, at the same high altar. He refers, laughably, to the poet's predilections, his eccentricities, his idiosyncrasies, and claims an intimate understanding (were they not precisely his own, he reflects, pp117–18, as he crafts and labours?). For myself I would label them foibles, and anyway would take the trouble to research my material. That is plentiful – is open to all – as it's no mere accident that MM's early drafts were not destroyed, were not discreetly binned. Nor do they reveal an immensity of talent.

Any public castigation is obviated here. Private reproofs, indignant denials delivered in the mail, won't be accepted as a serious challenge. So – here are the verifiable facts, after more than two decades (for all this happened in the 1970s). Jules is married to a corporate financier and has kept her figure. You can see her punctually every morning in one of those chunky county sweaters, leaving her rambling riverside Maidenhead home with two obedient Airedales (Boesky and Mycroft). The senior auditor is now a director of housing (via an unhappy flirtation with the Department of Trade and Industry, and a long fruitless spell with a small private firm). After years of unspectacular devotion to career and domestic duties, he lives reclusively in widowerhood in a long low bungalow on a branch line into Exeter. The chief auditor has his best handicap ever and is a business management consultant in his retirement, thinking of buying a yacht. Jules has never found time to read the biography. The unmerry widower has but couldn't understand what all the fuss was about. The chief, a guiding light, was interested at the time but has largely forgotten it.

Too subtle for my predecessor's pen was the simple rudimentary fact of devious office politics, where aggravated rumours concealed a world of darker intrigues. I also have to admit that the web of hierarchical manoeuvres and inter-department deceits has proved a touch too intricate, for *my* patience at least. Still I may take the biographer to task – who fails at every turn – who never tells the truth. On one thing only I can agree – that those of us single-minded enough can sometimes frown on the worldly with damning condescension. But this was Mono Merriah, whose arch-enemy shared a car with the then director of finance, FIMTA, ACIS. If the fulminations dissolved overnight, it was through this winged messenger, whose authenticity was never in question, so exactly had he always predicted the allocation of parking spaces and the decisions of promotion boards. Nowhere did Merriah's name figure in these.

A short, squat conductor with spindly legs and a pendulous stomach pursed his dull-red lips and, whistling, filled his cheeks. You could see the rosy-looking sheen. MM emerged from his nightmare slumber – it was an accepted rule of his recurring dream that peace of mind was impossible, until, sprawling at the summit, his spiritual apparition had scaled a mountain of open books. He saw through the thick smeary glass of the window where he sat a gigantic elaborate clock hand bounce from its ultimate measure of minima and point emphatically at an ornate XII. It was ten o'clock, the turning bus was at an awkward forty-five degrees, and the shrill conductor in his shiny dark uniform was jangling his leather pouch. MM pressed grubby silver into his soiled, spatulate palm; the frog, inane, merry, assured in his trills and vibratos, adjusted his clicking dials and turned the whirring handle through three revolutions. The warm, new-born ticket he dispensed was destined immediately for the grime, for the accumulated filth in the grooves of the floor, eventually the cleaner's vacuum. Then, that anthropomorphic, whistling amphibian turned and bombardiered to the front, and our sleepy, un-shockable bard observed him fold those disproportionate legs at every joint, and uncoiling spring through the ceiling (or so his mind's eye had cast him, a regular Jeremy Fisher).

These un-remarked on late mornings (though Jules still tutted), in so far as his discernment might unravel the black art of office psychology, seemed to be conditional on the dependable supply of confectionery. The chief liked sticky, gooey chocolate with his morning tea; while the much more sober senior auditor preferred savoury, cheesy biscuits. Jules, a committed weight-watcher (she didn't ever want to wear those chunky, county sweaters for all the wrong reasons), was not a consideration, though he did offer to keep an eye on her stocks of saccharin. It was a unique principle of atonement, but on more than one occasion he puzzled on it thus, vesting in it a fraction more credibility each time. Was it part of his business as a trainee auditor to maintain a double entry and on Fridays collect the debts, so acquiring a practical appreciation of the job? The theory was set out in enormous tomes he had never cared to read.

There was a hallowed silence today when he bore these little gifts of appeasement. The chief demanded it, fixed in his charade, crouching, feet apart, measuring by sight, with masterly precision, the depth of ground the conjured dimpled ball must overcome. A caddy for once might be that senior auditor, whose disguise is a fawning smile, and whose impatient ballpoint has to be poised over a wholly confusing balance sheet – a pen that would rise no higher until the boss's club was wielded. Jules – today the purple vial – couldn't promise her undivided attention, even if the stroke had to be replayed a second time (less emphasis on the follow-through). These moments dragged. At length the chief was able to simulate the golfer's oneness or nirvana, and gazed expectantly after his bunker shot, which had penetrated a hanging calendar (it was a mere accident of available props that the pictured lake, with its solitary rower, turned out to be his target). The triumphant dénouement came with the sense of only a partially captive audience.

'Incredible. Couldn't believe it,' the chief said. 'The worst bunker on any, *any* course I've played. Ha! You know what? Holed it! Plop! Straight down! Beautiful, just beau-ti-ful!'

Our municipal singer awaited his moment, the door ajar, and broke the uneasy silence that had greeted the golfer's triumph, with *Thankyous* for his quota of confections. His hollow cheeks half concealed a smirk, though disguise wasn't his object. He suspected a maternal, hereditary halitosis, and understood without confronting it a distant, infant recollection – trips into town on the bus in his mother's rein. It was as keen as that sense the poet fights *against*, natural, bothersome, innate – the crude beginnings of lifelong, adult sentimentality. In the mornings the sensitive bard sucked chalky, eye-watering mints with good civic purpose, just as his mother had done in another country, in his remote history, twenty years or a century before.

He found refuge in his usual escape, a continuing task that regulated premium space under the yucca, which topped the filing cabinets. He retreated with a bundle of faded orange folders, whose unexceptional contents were held in place by complicated clips with springs. He closed the door awkwardly with a foot behind him, then struck out over the cold marble, and its pattern of ink stain. Below, in the underground, in its labyrinth, the corridors were dark and the floors were of blackish concrete. Running round the damp musty walls and ceilings – vertically, horizontally, severally into circular junction boxes – miles of glossed piping channelled electricity to the lighting system, a row of naked bulbs.

His destination was a huge subterranean chamber filled with historical archives. A repository – a mausoleum for the bits and bobs of unreported, unaccomplished lives. The walls were lined with sagging shelves. What they laboured to support – in the past, unimaginable years of their employment; now, today; tomorrow, and tomorrow, and tomorrow – were the serried ledgers of yesteryear, leather-bound the farther back into the crude beginnings of the century you cast a horrified gaze. Here was evidence of low office – of meaningless lives before his own – from the meticulous entries in italics in blue-black ink, to modern rounded ballpoint. Week by week, MM made his own deposits – interlacing personalised scholia that not even he would uncover again, and always the same lyric,

> Rains fill all rivers
> Till banks all burst.
> Strong men and weak alike
> Are rushed along

or forlorn little rhyme,

> There are no reasons;
> There is only the faultless
> Stride of the seasons

He pulled a wooden crate with rusty protruding nails into the harsh un-shaded hard white light, and sat crouching, a denizen of Gormenghast. He took out from the sacred, dark recesses of his jacket the itinerant draft of *The Apple Tree*, and from the pocket under his lapel the stub of a pencil, gnawed at its eraser end. He scratched his head and frowned, as poets do, and here in the cellar plied his dreadful trade – only, only as auditors do.

Up there above him in the deep inscrutable firmament, weightier bodies had already begun their great momentous schemes for his future.

❦

The ledger clerk winked at Jules on his way out, having looked closely at the golfer's calendar. He could not say where the ball had splashed down. Jules had taken a call for the absent MM, while a ponderous Fimta Acis had told his secretary to summon the urban rhymer to his office. It was known to one person at least that next month the chief would have open Welsh fields with buttercups – a less troublesome target – and in the distance a windswept hill, with circling sheep, a roving collie, and a shepherd with a crook (and no fluttering isosceles). Perhaps a new trainee also. Portly Mr Acis had eased the hydraulic backrest of his swivel chair to a cool sixty degrees, and had propelled himself on its castors to his current position. The polished expanse he'd vacated was a model for the clear-desk policy about to be launched, permitting, of course, the cumbersome telephone, the statutory blotter, also an elegant, silver-plated pen-and-ink stand (a family heirloom), and curiously a forlorn scrap of notepaper about an inch square. On this in his secretary's handwriting were the following words, a reminder to him and a cryptic warning to the muddled wordsmith: LEDGER SYSTEM.

When that creator came in, ushered from a spotless antechamber by a skinny, bespectacled spinster (who once her charge was delivered coughed awkwardly and retired, closing the door firmly behind him), MM with his inventive inner eye imagined himself summoned by Mr Minney (Academy picture of the year, 1920) into what seemed a De Hooch interior. Later reference would point up too much freedom in that association. Mr Acis wore a single- not a double-breasted waistcoat, which in keeping with his suit was of white pinstripe. His umbrella was a retractable, and hung on the semi-circular rung of his coat stand. Hats to him were anathema (only the working-classes and the aristocracy wore them). The hair was completely wrong: grey, yes, but no signs of baldness yet or even a receding line – in fact it was thick, greasy, curly at the temples. His eyebrows were bushy and still black, and belonged to the crossword addict. Imperfections were: a cratered, purple nose (the whisky drinker's proboscis); a tiny brush of cacti bristles below the lower lip (somehow the morning razor never quite scraped it away); a carbuncle in the dimple of the chin; and in the oily glow of a shaven profile (left), a hairy mole or money spider hanging on a thread. The De Hooch interior was a nearer analogy. Flooding across the southerly courtyard, with its flagstones, its wrought iron benches, its singing fountain, the afternoon sunshine filled the director's office, in its warm wheeling rays lighting up his solid grey figure, the polished timber everywhere, the gleaming checks of the tiles.

Still at sixty degrees, and with a shiny black brogue at rest on the other knee, the director bent to an inconclusive gesture, a lacklustre helix in the wag of his forefinger, exposing as he did a stripy cuff with silver link. 'Sit down, sit down,' he said. MM looked around and found a utility chair propped on the wall by the bookcase. The world inside when he bent to lift the chair was a barren one: *An Introduction to Accounts*, *An Approach to Keynes*, *Corporate Law*, etc. The world on top was happy and filial. Framed in gold, a freckled, large-toothed boy grinned out at him, and fifteen years later – a black frame and larger portrait this time – the same person in an academic cap and gown still hadn't controlled that tombstone smile.

The director examined first the palms then the nails of his hands, then the palms again, while MM considered his own – problem: where to put them? – and did his best to settle.

He decided to fold his arms and wait. The director uncrossed his legs and bent his head down, serious. You'd mistake it for attempted parody, a manic cartoon figure, surging forward – a snorting, semi-automated bull on a central stalk and five spinning castors. The multiple layers, the undulating waistcoat, whose solo thread of re-sewn buttons didn't always survive severest tests, cushioned the impact. He came to rest with his elbows on the edge of the desk, his shoulders hunched, his several chins wedged and propped in an interlock of hands, and his silver cufflinks revealed as a monogrammed pair – an elaborate G to the left with a spiralling descender, a bombastic H to the right with wavy uprights and a crossbar wound with scrolls. His ashen lids were down, there was silence, the director scrutinised his *aide-mémoire*. He took up that scrap of paper in both thumbs and forefingers. There was a moment of recognition when the shutters fully opened, when the grey lids flickered. His sombre pale blue eyes crossed and focused awkwardly – though now he *had* gathered his thoughts.

'The ledger system,' he said. 'Don't, don't! Not till I'm done….' His podgy G hand went up and debarred. MM's arms unfolded tamely, his hands fell limp on his knees. At least one urgent question was never framed. The director continued: 'Yes, I know all about it.' His hand went down and calmly smoothed away a square foot of coarseness in the middle of the blotter, where he placed the square inch of notepaper, and in turn flattened that under his heavy palm. The two plump hands came together, signalling solemnity again, and leaning over that skimpy script – he must regard it always, always – he explained *how* he knew. 'Keep an ear to the ground. Oh, I could bathe, wallow. This glorious sunshine….' The H hand tugged itself free, and again that indeterminate gesture, that indecisive helix. 'I know the distraction. You're the poet chap – which is nothing terrible, let me say. With me it's roses, with the wife origami: what you always need is an outlet….' This was the gist, the emphasis, and here he thumped the blotter authoritatively. 'You know we can't have the ledgers getting out of hand – you do understand, I can see.' He paused to palpate the indentation that his pugilist's signet ring – JJJ, grandfather – had left in the blotter.

'Fabulous, fabulous things she can do with paper – all I need's my garden. My word, yes! But you!' He examined the ring, and where powdery residues of paper had lodged in the carved Js, was moved to blow and flick at it. 'What you need's an outlet….'

'An outlet?'

'A club, a society. Academic press. You know.'

'No – rather yes.'

'Check it in the library. And look, consider this. Look. There'll be a memo – it affects everyone – look at *my* desk….' It hadn't changed: the blotter, the phone, the pen-and-ink stand, the all-important slip of paper. 'You're not the only offender. I watch and listen. Things, all things come to my attention, my ear's to the ground.' There was a cautious knock at the door, and a lady with an urn on a trolley and a floppy white hat was waiting.

'Here's your example. This is how all professionals leave their desks at 5.30. Think! Think of the cleaners!'

The radial spokes of a suddenly bashful sun were unable to penetrate an unexpected, ghostly black cloud. But the new benumbing gloom as the big man droned was not interminable. There was a second, bolder knock. The director looked up at the door and smiled.

'Come!'

At last, time for tea.

I relent as I look down. My learned friend on the windy street below is in a boxer's crouch and pushes his open umbrella against a shower of autumn rain. The tails of his raincoat flap. He was here not half a minute ago, the day's first and last visitor to my rented place, a cramped little exile. We discussed these coming pages and arrived at his verdict – 'Somewhat mordant…' – which is not discouraging when, magnanimous as I always find him to be, the solecisms and irritating points of style remain un-talked about. He lit one of his small cigars and filled my cluttered studio with smoke and its lasting aroma.

'No, there are no ashtrays,' I repeated. 'In the saucer will do – ah, too late!' A coiled spring of light-grey ash disintegrated on his sleeve.

Resolutely a classics man, the biography affronts his sensibilities perhaps more than mine. 'It's a fabrication,' he said. 'Its only truths truisms. It's also clumsy.' That was his supreme insult. Then, inspecting my drafts—

'Alas, this is no real challenge. Here are only incidents from too short a life.' He wouldn't let me protest. 'I know, I know. An incipient poet with lots to learn. You can't say what he *would* have done.'

Therefore I relent as I look down.

Jules was at the foot of the steps and astounded, for it wasn't yet nine. Mono Merriah had polished his shoes and pressed his suit. She couldn't know that as he loped in the shadows of the Town Hall colonnade, strange, sartorial confidence gave us a first sign of MM's new optimism. Shafts of sunlight imprinted angular bright bands on his jacket, just as the clock struck, though after ten, as usual, her painted lips would curl, ready to disapprove. But the trainee – his occasional limp improving all the time – missed the revolving doors and carried on instead to the library. That had the same smell of furniture polish.

The gangling assistant wanted to help, having long been slave to his index cards. He pushed a wooden tray, marked E–H, back on its wheels, then over in Reference plucked off a top shelf a neglected list of local societies, and from a low shelf a writers' yearbook.

'Anything here look useful?'

Merriah thought for a moment, then pointed out one puzzling name on a list: Old Guard Radicals.

'Indeed!' The assistant's eyebrows went up, searching for the ceiling. 'So where do *you* fit?'

'Fit?'

'Ah, so you want me to guess. Well, let me see. If I were writing now, I'd have to join the debate in the Realism versus Escapist forum. But you tell me.'

'Realism. That's definitely it. Definitely. *The Apple Tree* is a masterpiece of observation – I don't mind saying.'
'Mm. Interesting. I'd like to see….'
'Well I do and I don't have it here.'
'All up there, I suspect….' The assistant tapped his temple with a knobby forefinger.
'There it is, marvellous! Man as artist. Marvellous!'

This was a fillip, and when the assistant went back to his index, Mono Merriah sat humming with his references and notepaper. At about ten, he left the library, man as artist.

The jailer's were wicked delights. That drooping, bushy moustache concealed an evil, tight-lipped grin. His keys were hanging in a stationery cupboard but his ledgers were punched and holed at a top corner, and threaded on his hoop. When he shook them, they jangled. His one-time quarry, the late late Romantic, had said in his muddled defence that his only crime was one of circumstance. To have arrived in the desolate world circa the mid-1950s was a century too late, or early. The brake on human liberty – a kind of mental slavery, or intellectual waste – was the one essential in business-school technique. A flighty sophistication had displaced the brutish methods that in Merriah's times had survived only with juntas and Third World tyrannies. His captivity was a lifelong parole: it demanded regular reporting and daily undertakings. His bondage of course wouldn't deny him the light of day, or inflict unspeakable injuries, yet the telling signs were ignored or overlooked – his allergies, his little quirks, his emotional troughs. What was wrong, what was wrong with him, my clumsy, cadaverous, dreamy bard? Had he approached the end?

On a gloomy Monday, solar bliss. Unexpected shafts of sunlight dissolved or pushed to one side un-emphatic inky clouds, and Merriah, skulking from the post room, wanted to be out, just out there. The shallow pools in the hollows of ancient steps and paving flags were shrinking away. A diaphanous, multi-coloured bow had blurred the fountain's ragged outline. The director's grey bulk was probably lodged at the streaming De Hooch window, a lead balloon whose apex nodded at the ceiling, his chubby pink sausage fingers crisscrossed on the small of his back. His fellow traveller the jailer loomed like a mobile silhouette, passed, and receded, but it wasn't till he jangled his ledgers, stepping down on a distant, winding stair, that the unsighted Merriah began to notice his dark, lurching shape. When he was near Merriah's den, his eyes had re-accustomed themselves, but the door was ajar and light from the naked bulb showed as a thin white thread against the dark concrete. The jailer hurried himself from the foot of the stairs – all routes from there were longer than MM's, who never dawdled after illicit forays in the post room. Merriah tucked his newest stocks of A4 paper and stiff brown envelopes under his jacket, and holding them, his hands deep in his trouser pockets and his elbows pressed to his waistband, he stepped inside – and was suddenly surprised. The clerk had found his secret crannies. That latter didn't look up as he skimmed through the thirty or forty photocopies of MM's extended lyric, *The Apple Tree*. The wooden crate had been pulled out and was under the light, and on it was a pile of standard letters to magazine editors. There were also address labels, stamps from the petty-cash box, and a depleted stock of envelopes. The intruder turned abruptly and slapped the proliferated epic to the author's chest, but it fell, floating in heavy swirls and spread itself in every direction on the floor. The clerk left him but came back to the open door, now no longer speechless.

'Very, very serious,' he said. He pointed dramatically. 'Government equipment. Government property.' He shook his head. 'Very, very serious.'

Merriah gathered up his masterpiece of observation.

An Alpine fool with a red coxcomb and a white rose was not to be persuaded, or saved from himself. The sirens of worldly reason failed to drag him from his chosen precipice. Thereafter he transmogrified into a forest dweller, who, resigned to his destiny, suspended himself upside-down on a tree for as long as his impossible dream should last. Likewise the suburban poet retired – with a fabricated toothache – but remained upright, and hunched, behind his upper window, whose rectangular panes were perfectly clear to him, but a watery shiny black to the postman glancing from the street. Before the letterbox was rattled, both looked across: a raucous gull flew twice round a dull-red rooftop. It was timely augury (and that was the last refuge of anachronistic modern men). Nevertheless, a determinist theory wasn't established until the envelope was torn open untidily and read with mounting joy (a new experience). Even then, it wasn't suspected that unscrupulous profiteers, who engineered diabolical forms of human misery, had come as his personal liberators, keen to sanitise a tarnished image. They shipped their hand-held rocket launchers to remote trouble spots, but drew up battle lines in combat against the influence of ecologists and Greens, of noisy unilateralists, and, most impertinent, a sarcastic leftist press, with its scurrilous contributors. A Harvard consultant advised—

'High-profile sponsorship of the arts.'

The editors of *Old Guard Radicals*, in co-operation with the Artists' Renascent Sense Society – whose Art in Action campaign, financed by the arms manufacturer, was planned as a world event – had written a letter—

Dear Poet,

Your recent contribution has been referred to a panel of experts. It is their judgement that the very high quality of your work merits a special award in the much-publicised Art in Action campaign.

More details soon, all good wishes,

The Editors

When the hulking Fimta Acis, his thick lubberly features moulded by the gravity of new information, sat at his oceanic desk and watched the shadows form on his blotter, and as suddenly disappear – the sun and the windy clouds in combat – the transgressor chatted outside, nonchalant. He had been held in check by the spinster. He was summoned duly, and was asked to resign, but not even this dulled his spirits. Heaven acknowledged that the task was onerous, even for Fimta, a director (skills like this were only once in a while stabbed at, then awkwardly), but the reprobate didn't protest. The sun shone again and cloudy rhomboids rose instantly through absorbent layers to the surface sheet of paper. Merriah stood, dusted his suit (well, that was that over), and retreated, smiling.

That carefree mood was vindicated. Here on the mat at home was another missive—

Dear Poet,

Congratulations! Of literally thousands of quality candidates, you have been selected for a special award – the third prize, in fact.

The eco-politico-socio content of your work achieves a rare artistic intensity, and we invite you to participate in the Art in Action campaign.

The third prize has come to be known as the Hot Country Quest. So, good luck! Pack up your bags. Find the air ticket enclosed. Have a good day. All good wishes,

The Society

The eco-politico-socio(-yoyo) significance of his work hadn't occurred to him before, but now that someone had mentioned it, he could begin – well, yes – to see that point of view.

Robust Angles in checked shirts with sleeves rolled up moaned at a final photo call, which had come together hastily in a publisher's warehouse. It was a gusty night, when massed umbrellas and theatre lights had been hooked up in the building's infrastructure. The schmaltzy bard paraded in red velvet with gold braid and black buttons before three Arcadian backdrops: first, Homeric grazing sheep on rolling Elizabethan meadows; second, Byronic rills (again, Elizabethan meadows); lastly, a distant craggy mountain where the minor figure of Virgil awaited (Merriah's foreground? Elizabethan meadows). Then on to something Beethovenian, the master depicted with a square face and candid eyes, his hair made wild with a photographic retouch, but authentically scrubbed and robed, and with pen poised over an open, handwritten draft of that towering masterpiece *The D Major Apple Tree.*

It was a convenient venue. The roads at night were fast to the airport hotel, where the poet in plain grey was driven after midnight – a long sleek car with kitschy, automatic entertainment, purring through the drizzle. The Muzak, the humming fan, the weariness. From vaulted heights in a dark wet heaven mercantile gods ensured safe passage, looking out for a limousine snaking round the metropolis. The driver's splash-on deodorant.

Orange blobs overhead, their luminous efflorescence, hanging from quivering lamp poles – rhythmic lights in the prism of tinted panes – lights that quickly loomed, that slowly receded. A car with furious wipers swished by in the other direction, another poet coming home. Sumptuous leather and heavy lids. A hiker – no, a bush in a pool of headlights – had a thumb out at the roadside. Sleep, contented, uncoordinated sleep. Then hard, portentous dreams, with Dino in a business suit repeating himself: 'Ranks of the living dead, ranks of the living dead.' He shook his head, and shook his head.

Another day, and another morning, and the prize-winning poet stepped off his plane in flip-flop sandals, loud in their slaps on the soft sensitive flesh of his feet. His exotic shorts had a printed design – yellow and purple zebras under blue palms, and a fire of Biblical bushes. His angry violet tee shirt bore a sporty motif (a bat, a ball, a laurel). Karl, the liaison artist, was there to meet him, and helped with his bags to the desert buggy – 'It's a liddle bid far.' They zoomed round the island clockwise, 'Sleepy drifers heff gone over indo dhe vorder,' the huge broad tyres, the shiny snarling grille swallowing up the hot malleable road. They turned inland to a desert track and ascended, looking down on the white crenellated villas bunched in a brightness of marble patios, with glinting pools and hibiscus hedges, thriving artificially on a parched, forbidding hillside. Karl wouldn't speak above the surging, swirling din of the air conditioning. When they came down again the coming poet gazed in a new silence, a new detachment, at the hazy shapes and distortions on the horizon. A painter's brush had dabbed alternating spots of purple and pink, purple and black, black and pink, then at the base a wash of varying greens, and behold! A range of flat mountains fringed with palms.

Down, down again. The pinkish yellow sand, with its pebbles, its prodigious cacti and hardy green tufts, gave way to a blue oasis, where the palms and three tall masts of two long boats were reflected in the water. That cool perspective shifted, sifted: maroon splodges resolved themselves into live, communicating people in ruffled djellabas; the blue spangled water exceeded its momentary confinement, gently caressing a low mountain gradient. Where the mountains became rock piles in the east the blue dissolved into streaky white, and the water and sky were one. Karl drove down into the streets, squares and plazas, where there were shop fronts and orange awnings, then beyond to the ranks of holiday apartments and villas, where the roads were lined with street lamps. A man named Newman, who had survived successive pogroms, and was the founder of an arms manufacturing firm, believed, like Karl, his designer, in shared artistic experience, given his present job. Karl drew up and parked the black dusty buggy outside Newman's walled retreat, a flinty villa (one of a pair) with arched windows, abutting balconies, tennis courts, a pool. 'Snod a bad liddle place,' he said, but the waking poet, whose labyrinthine days were still a deep scar, fished unsuccessfully for an appropriate reply. Instead, he allowed himself to be led through an iron gate with scrolls and on to a patio, where a lizard had lost its camouflage and scurried past a clump of pampas grass. The courts were fenced and padlocked, though the shared pool was in regular use by neighbours (no one was bathing precisely now, but two red dragonflies, or rather a dragon- and damselfly, hovered and copulated over the shimmering water). A minty smell of eucalyptus greeted them on the desert breeze as they turned for the shade. A caged canary bobbed from perch to perch by the door, which was ajar (the maid had been in and opened up). Karl dumped the luggage in the hall, where shapes and changing contours were vaguely visible, then showed him the shower, the bedroom, the kitchen.

'Rest, dake id easy. Domorrow I'm here at seffen. Dhere's a lod of vurk.'

'What kind of work – what I mean is, what do I need?'

'Id's a problem I heff, you needn't vorry. I vont you d'understand, but really d'dest owd an innofation – you vill see. Domorrow.'

'What kind of innovation?'

'Domorrow....'

He unpacked. He found postcards on a bureau, but didn't write (they depicted topless nubile Latins with miles of idyllic beach engulfed in foam). He explored the kitchen, he tried to mix a cocktail, though with what he found couldn't fathom how (a pack of light beer, a bottle of Galliano). He went over proofs of *The Apple Tree* (how, how did that fit?), but failed again to identify its monumental flaws. He considered the political significance of an English harvest, its analysis and description, in a world where people died of malnutrition (there, there lay his drowsy humanity – Karl might wake it up!). Finally, he retired to a balcony with his notebooks and the pack of beers and, cocked back in a wicker chair, watched that blood-red ball of fire slide down, into the calm, quenching sea, where tourist clippers sailed in and out of port well into the twilight.

Tomorrow, an innovation. Tomorrow he would see.

The cigar-smoking analyst is approximately as you are now, his umbrella or bits of bat wings clinging to the rest of my only armchair – a chunky, superannuated thing, with woven rosebuds bursting open in an endless early summer, on the arms, on the cushion where he sits, under the bat's claw, even above the frills (of counterfeit gold leaf) that for thirty years have only partly dressed the castors. He isn't superstitious, but this is his disadvantage. It isn't easy, going over these closing pages, to rise, to lean forward, to prepare himself for speech. A chair for my guests is a swamp, a morass, where I ask them to examine, consider, pontificate (*he* never does, but reasons).

'I'm surprised,' he says. 'You especially *should* know better.'

'But don't you miss my meaning? That a fiction's clearer than a biography....' Just then the phone rang, but the caller wanted a mortgage broker, and had reversed two trailing digits, an unlucky 31.

'You can't mean incompetent poets deserve to die!'

'No. They deserve what they get. But what they get isn't determined by them....' I pointed to my garret porthole, in a line descending on our wonderful terrible city. 'It rests with them, with the hoi polloi.'

'They didn't shove him off the balcony. You say he was drunk on innocuous beer, and fell.'

'That isn't important – or rather, yes, it is. A mediocrity adored. Talent gone to waste. But yes, you're right. The balcony won't do. I need something symbolic of the times – of our times.'

Even so, he was puzzled, and now that I knew him I'd found an ashtray. Then the phone again, and another wrong number. (If the trailing digits were one higher numerically, would it make a difference?)

'You know, I'm beginning to like these cigars. The lingering aroma, the blue fog.'

Karl, the punctilious liaison artist, whose English had failed him on many occasions, called for the sleepy poet at seven and counted thirteen empty bottles on the drainer, though that's not to say he was suspicious or superstitious. They drove out into the arid mountains on a coiling trail of sand, though before topping their peaks, the singular Merriah glanced back through the rear of the desert hearse and reassembled, through thinning clouds of dust, the complex of holiday villas – white polished pebbles thrown down by a departing giant in the wilderness. That rear bounced comfortably on French hydraulics – as they rounded the crest and began to descend – and ahead, two greeny brown ridges crossed diagonally and formed a V, a vessel where a fleecy hand from heaven had poured a deep blue equilateral, the sea. In the whitish blue strip of sky above it, the speck of a silver plane slid round the island counter-clockwise – eerie and silent – its glowing pristine trail drawn with ruler precision from its tail, though that broke up, dissolving into wisps. Karl, no jackanapes, nevertheless parked momentarily part way down a crumbling precipice on an overhanging roadway. He pointed out that western nomads in the valley of the V were temporarily encamped – you could see the tents, striped canvas pyramids, red and white, blue and white, with flaps for porches – you could see triangular flags on poles, flapping in the sea breeze. You could see also numerous theatrical house and shop fronts arranged round a mesh of illusory streets. And you could just make out the film crew.

They drove on, and Karl explained his innovation, and how since magical Scriabin evenings it had been his dream – his special, personal, Renaissance dream – to invent, be the father of a truly total form of art.

'But a motorbike?' The poet was less inspired. He didn't understand.

'Ja, id is vy vee are here. Id is for ard, todal ard.'

They stopped again, at a lower point on the rocky precipice, and got out. Karl went over the details. Merriah – nervous, sweaty and trembling – did his best to remember. Ride in, ride in, approach the phoney town from there, from the south (the east looks the same, but that's fatal, you'll have missed it) – *If I fell now I'd grab that bulbous cactus, however prickly, and I'd pray! – When I see the film crew, I play the music and start the light show – then the other riders join me – If I fell now—*

Karl drove him to a cool, whitewashed, cubic hut with crenatures, a nibbled sugar lump in a thick rectangular shadow, and raised his hands for silence. There was an antlered beast under a dustsheet, morose, but when the sheet was whipped away by Karl (with a curious sense of his own person, with histrionics), that innovator revealed the stationary exhibit, a mobile work of art that bore its creator's signature. A medieval K had been engraved on each of the two exhaust pipes snaking from front to rear, with a curl, with a twist, with a secret flourish. Then he helped the lost bard into black, crepitating leathers and a dome-like helmet – a dark tomato with a visor, with a gold stripe at its broadest circumference, and silver stars sprayed on the crown.

'Here, led me help you on.'

A muffled gasp echoed and faded in the helmet, but Merriah, the tips of his fingers and toes electrified, stifled his objections, and vented no protest whatsoever. Karl hoisted and bundled him into the saddle, whose padded backrest with its swooping curve had been designed for a taller, much easier man.

'Dhese are some of dhe more importand kontrols: the starder (vhich alzo redracds dhe stand audomadically); dhese marked PLAY and REVIND, for dhe musik; LIGHTSHOW for dhe lights; und CLOCK...' which he activated. A light-emitting display superimposed a luminous green 1 on an evanescent 0, a 2 on an evanescent 1, a 3 on a 2, a 4, a 5, a 6.... Merriah gesticulated urgently at a separate bank of labelled, touch-sensitive switches, and finally caught Karl's attention.

'Ja, ja. Thad's a liddle komplicaded though. Don't vorry. Give me zwei minuten on dhe clock, und begin....'

He was already leaving.

'Two odher dings: dhere's a liddle probe-lem vid dhe turning circle, und avoid dhe kadacombs do dhe vest....'

'Catacombs!'

Karl zoomed to the film set in a haze of billowing sand, and found that even now the heat was too intense and his five outriders were in the makeup tent for a reapplication (they didn't detect a twitch, the nervous upper lip, when Karl put his peaked cap on, or took up his megaphone, or when he eased a little stiffly into his director's chair). Nor could Merriah detect it. He'd been too busy, and had pressed the button for music – for this was his chance for familiarisation, however brief. The result was a cacophony, as an electronic pizzicato vied with a wild piccolo or boiling kettle on a gas hob, then a voice accompanied, a moaning bass. The light show *was* a success, though that too he couldn't deactivate. Red-to-violet beams performed gymnastics on the sags and bulges in the ceiling. Then orange-to-indigo.

The cameras weren't rolling, and there should have been a script, and furthermore, flashing dimly in the bright untroubled sunshine, Merriah approached the set from the fatal east – and the rest I surmise. Perhaps Karl leapt from his chair and flapped his arms – the megaphone and waving cap going undeciphered, two high-speed semaphores above his head. Then of course the limited turning circle proved decisive, for Merriah, the flimsy props falling everywhere about him, couldn't undo his mistake. When he tried the switch marked BOOST, a mysterious cloud rose up from the wilderness and obscured his fate prophetically (here I think a velocity record might have been challenged). He pressed the switch marked BRAKE, but a rubber mud flap sprang to the right at a preconceived angle, followed by an aluminium guard, a headlamp, an indicator, which after lying in the desert sand for weeks were gathered up by makeshift trustees (as important memorabilia). CHUTE was next, but this only glorified the sad debacle: flaps on the panniers fell open on hinges and launchers slipped out on suspension rods. I theorise that the two rockets were aimless, and evidence may be inexact (a pair of massive craters might have opened the catacombs to grateful archaeologists, but are by no means illuminating to literary historians). What could he do, the apprentice, the metrical novice, when they loomed? As his hands fumbled for a switch or control, which *in extremis* might after all arrange for his grace and salvation, the redundant biographer's fidgeted, waiting, waiting for something to do, while perky Mammon turned to new hope for his ailing accounts.

The Incredible Domenico

Horton, the retired broadcaster, had an hour to spare, after a trawl through Burlington Arcade. He called on his old friend Arthur Maguire.

Maguire, columnist, had a penchant for corruption, and had spies at work, and a stream of names across his desk – government mostly.

'But Charles – it has been so long. Do let me take your coat.'

Charles Horton stood by the fireside chair, which was large, square, faded, chintzy. 'Anniversary,' he said. 'Golden wedding. Tomorrow. You know – wanted to get Abigail a special something.' He fingered the catch in the green velvet of the carrying case and opened the lid on two golden raindrops, earrings for Abigail Horton.

'Wow!' said Maguire.

Horton chuckled. 'Should bring a smile, eh?'

Maguire called it a worthy tribute and fetched two glasses, though generally he'd renounced the grain so early in the day.

'There are exceptions,' he said, 'and anyway, I've got my own milestone to celebrate.' He referred to his heap of papers.

'Oh, intriguing!' said Horton.

'A first genuine work of detection….'

'*Very* intriguing!'

Maguire assumed his Holmesian air, filling a pipe. For one brooding moment he stood at the square panes overlooking the street. Then he uttered a name, Domenico.

'Remember him?' he asked.

'You mean the high-wire man?'

'I mean *ex*-high-wire man.'

'Of course. Tragic, so tragic….'

Maguire lit his pipe and puffed away contentedly. 'Take a look at this,' he said, and suddenly produced a piece of paper. It was the suicide note—

It's all up with me. I can't live a lie.

This meant nothing to Horton, so he passed it back to his friend. Maguire plunged the stopper back in the decanter. 'Hardly typical,' he said. 'It's brief, and to the point – or so one assumes.'

Horton, who grieved that stopper, checked his watch and almost spoke.

'It's curious,' Maguire put in (a touch quizzical). 'Look at this, for example.' He pulled from his pile one of the many Domenico obituaries, ragged with the years, and urged his friend to read. Horton smoothed out the creases and read the opening paragraph—

Staff on the paper witnessed the final exit of the great Domenico, the most daring high-wire man of modern times. Some hardly believed his tragic suicide, yet the truth was plain, yesterday, under an autumn sky, in the unspoiled village of Sudbrook. Domenico had gone. He was interred, just a few hushed paces from his boyhood home of forty-odd years ago.

Horton had a deep-rooted aversion to saccharin, and stopped reading the obituary. 'I remember,' he said, 'reporting on this myself.'

Maguire put his hand on a tatty weekend review (accidentally, the *wrong* review), and urged his friend to read that too, a piece about Henri Vercune, a rising star in the French cabinet, whose European sympathies, and cynicism with the English, were well known.

'Fascinating, of course,' Horton said, though he couldn't see the connection with Domenico.

'Ah, Charles, how silly I am! Not *that* review, *this!*' Maguire picked out an earlier number from the same publication, a summary of Domenico's short if eventful life.

Domenico, or William Batt, embarked on his extraordinary career back in the 1960s, a boy of nineteen. His reaction to an inconclusive schooling? The question has been asked, yet what was it prompting the young Billy Batt to abandon everything and run off to the circus? Why not run away to sea? Or to the city? Perhaps we'll never know.

Run he could, and in putting distance between himself and home – which was solid, dreary, typically middle-class – he got himself a job with Levlins Ltd, a circus now defunct – its elephants, everything, gone. Who knows where? Ironically, his first job was as sad clown. Do not scoff. Men destined for the heights get tired of custard pies, buckets of water, outsize shoes. Batt was urbane, had charm, and didn't lack insight. He saw, with Christina Bombolino and her impetuous husband (the dashing Antonio), his first opportunity. Their act dragged on, as so would their divorce, while the anonymous Batt learned his craft as a catcher – of fallen wives, as someone remarked. Batt's place was the solid floor, with a smile, while the Bombolinos jumped through hoops.

When Antonio's troupe dissolved, as a commercial as well as family entity, Billy was still in his twenties. But it was too late for anything else, he said, and he cast around for other acts. Trapeze companies wanted him, while letters from his Kentish parents registered only protest. He ignored family pleas, and taking a new name – the Amazing Paulo – took first public steps as a high-wire artist. Nothing at first went right. He reached low ebb, and almost quit.

But good men resurrect, and the Amazing Paulo, after a new start, set about his transformation. With his small if dazzling repertoire, and a new name, Domenico,

Batt conquered the kingdom of dangerous stunts. We know the glitz, the media story, and Domenico as household name.

Thereafter Batt's was a life of ceaseless decoration. Two prime ministers brought him to Downing Street. Hollywood put him in a feature film. Bolivia adopted him. An African tribe honoured his name. He was a regular in the weekend supplements. In holiday resorts, the souvenir industry plied his image. For a decade, everything was Domenico.

His gift was daredevil entertainment. Nothing, in the bounds of possibility, seemed too much. The ever more improbable stunt – that was him. It's ironic that the great Domenico died by his own hand, life, inscrutable life, the one risk too many.

Horton scanned the summing-up, and a bibliography, and grunted, for none of it brought him to an understanding of Domenico's suicide.

Among that heap of papers, Maguire had one more accolade, from the pen of Hambro Barnstaple, a doyen among book reviewers, and not the first to try his hand at fiction drawing on the life of Domenico. Even as a reviewer, Hambro approached his subject in that spirit, with respect, deference, and highly polished critique. Maguire, again jumbling his papers, passed his friend what was intended as that review, from Dr Barnstaple's broadsheet. Horton read—

Seen here symbolically – in Mr Newby's fiery prism – a leaked memorandum and an under-secretary's emoluments: they give us precisely what? Well, repeated denials from the dispatch box, amid much braying in the House, and the assertion from one senior source that the minister's share dealings had nothing to do with inside information, despite his connections....

'Now wait a minute!' said Horton. He was beginning to wonder if, in all these 'wrong' reviews, his old friend had a motive, and was hoping to change his voting habits (which after all were the habits of a lifetime). 'What you've given me here,' said Charles, 'is a libel case, that wretched backbencher Newby!'

'Ah, I see the mistake,' said Maguire. 'That's Barnstaple sounding off on the nation state. Here, this is the piece I meant. Read *this*....'

Hambro began again—

Just now there's a glitter in the circus, and the man we all want to see is Domenico. Let me assure any sceptic: he deceives, beguiles, he casts a spell – the Incredible Domenico holds hearts in his hand. It shan't go unrecorded. I, a tired newspaper hack, whose life is the printed word, have witnessed the umbrella trick – I mean *the* umbrella trick. It's cunning, and it thrills....

The trick began with Domenico bouncing on his famous high wire – huge leaps into the big top's airy, cavernous vault – at the same time sporting an umbrella. At the peak of his highest leap he loses his balance, turning somersault, and drops the umbrella (an object specially engineered by the Rainy Days Weatherware Co). Having opened, miraculously, and turned and floated in the air, the umbrella upends itself and catches the wire with its hook. The umbrella is now a cradle for the falling Domenico, at which climax there's a crisscross of lights and a blare of trumpets.

Horton sighed, and remembered the stunt. 'Yes,' he said, 'I saw that on TV. Astounding.'

'Though I think,' added Maguire, 'the camera showed a *thrust*, not a *lost* umbrella.' He was coming to his *coup de grâce*, and had saved his final innuendo for the men of his profession. 'This is the clincher,' he said, pulling something handwritten from an inside pocket. 'I got it from a rival, who did a speculative piece on the Domenico phenomenon. Yours truly here rifled through his stuff one day when I knew he was out to lunch. What do you think of this?'

It was a letter from a man called Stockton, an early friend of the late William Batt, now head of an English department in a fee-paying school, and pompous with it. Horton read—

Dear Sir,

Your economies, especially with the truth, do great service to newspaper sales. But there is one analysis that doesn't fit that bill – where absolutely I take issue. I knew Domenico. More correctly I knew a youth called William Batt.

I can be more specific. At no time, as your article suggests, did the young Billy Batt hanker after a life of public sensation, in chasing a fortune. Nor did he analyse the dual nature of fame, bound as it is to *getting* a fortune. Those who haven't got their hands on the world's goods assume a calculating nature in those who have. Don't they know it's down to luck?

When Batt wasn't teaching me calculus (because unlike my friend, for me the school syllabus intimidated), he looked to the blue skies and told me his future life was there, as a test pilot. Yet that spelled only grief, an adventurous only child blessed with *two* conventional parents, the last word in petty conservatism (may both their souls be at peace). All along, they'd had the professions, and not the services, in mind – a safe career for William Batt. They argued, not without passion, that all men grow to the solidity of middle-class life.

Incredibly, the boy Batt chose to keep the peace, and immediately resented that decision. Then, under the parental dampener on his ambition – Batt ran away. Up and left. I groaned, from the moment he joined that first troupe. Of course, I lament his end.

That was my friend William Batt. The media Domenico – *your* Domenico – is a fabrication.

Yours, R. J. Stockton

Horton raised an eyebrow and looked at his watch. 'Quaint turn of phrase,' he said, and noted how that long spare hour had overrun itself. The decanter, he thought, had never lost its appeal, not in a long long life at the polling booth, though its content no one could rely on to loosen his elector's tongue.

'Ah, another glass!' said Maguire, who followed his gaze. Yes – ah yes – another glass.

The Invisibility Trick

Look! The magician is here – a comic, a master of guises, and a rope dancer. Follow, and how shall we tread, slung on his acrobatic wire? Oh – well here *is* a question. If art is a civilising force, what is wealth, a means of art?

Take these few back issues of *Country Life*, where a tweedy scion roams the leafy lanes, a man with a springer, a flat cap, a gun, and wearing knee-length boots. Later that same rosy presence lounges in a paddock, chatting with a square-faced equestrian. You can see, in the middle ground, a horse tossing up its tail under a cloud of steam.

Here in another shot he pauses for breath on a perron, all set (or almost all set) for those quick strides down into the waves of gravel of his drive (now I did say *almost*). A dreary columnist has called it pure dedication – departure for the office at six a.m. – though the truth of his dawns is a gambler's. After the miserly click of a roulette wheel this is his homecoming, a house girl having made his bed. His smile is a crooked smile.

In the *Tatler* that smirk is mostly boisterous, but tonight it is crumpled. Columnist, expose that duality! Forget these theories of remedial behaviour! A party starts in a handy four-page pull-out, where Sir Monocled Henry leads a flock of Hoorays in a car with an open top. Locality: somewhere in Belgravia. Time: after the nightclubs. Running our finger down, a smiling cherub picks out the roving camera, while overleaf champagne is popped and poured. Centre-left, a sequinned debutante toasts with a flute of airy foam, where two little royals have met and share a caption: *Les deux jeunes gens échangent un sourire....*

Huh! La vie est belle! For Douglas Walrus-Jones, frenzied and varied too. The centrefold charts his tireless advance to another new dawn, zooming in top left with his best friend Strang, assailing Dionysus at bottom right, and in the margins temporarily departing all conscious life. He and his acolytes are camped in a park, snoozing in dishevelled evening dress, on the steps or the benches irascible vagrants have had to vacate. That's where we'll leave him for now, sleeping it off, while the dutiful biographer considers other numbers, other magazines. For he has been: the slim idol in black shiny leathers; the Ariel poet in white flannels; a neurotic director, bane of bleary casts; and of course photographer, Thespian, entrepreneur (in fact you name it). More important than all this, he has kindled a first flinty spark as it leapt up, and in his private hall of holography has nurtured and irradiated this as his personal glow of warmth.

The sporting life had long found him out. Even in the dullest moments, in rooms heavy with drapes, and as focal point ornate, overwrought fire surrounds, Douglas couldn't bring himself to joke about the rugby fields. On that subject mute diplomacy had been perfected. No physical scars were visible, though the *emotional* bruise remained. Douglas, catching sight on cold mornings of mist patches swirling round any natural playing surface, shuddered at thoughts of his boyhood.

His tutor, a white-haired professor, remarked on other failures, and as a valediction summarised the unexceptional Jones like this, in a spidery hand: 'Brainless, clearly. There is, I suppose, an outside chance of a career in politics.' Douglas took his banishment stoically, and on it constructed his own interpretation. Those dreaming spires could continue to dream – but he – Douglas – was alive! In departing he bowed fraternally to the statue of his mentor, drowned.

What were the alternatives? An era was passing, the lumber and junk of his backroom Philistinism had been pushed out to the yard, and open curtains now let daylight in over the floral settees and deeply studded chesterfields. The once willing but fickle Everyman looked in at the hosts of bouffant fashion stags, and happily plumped for stylish hair-dos and sentimental love songs. When it began to matter that Douglas couldn't sing, and that his cohorts saw promising careers slipping away, he did what the times demanded, and in discarding his leathers and bracelets, or without regret forsaking the bright canopy of concert venues, he looked (where else?) to the theatre.

A new challenge then, and naturally no dramatist gazed with greater narcissistic penetration into modern theatrical concepts. *Sublime!* written, directed, financed by, and also starring in the central role our much misunderstood hero. This was his spectacle of nihilism, coming chronologically just too late, though as a backwash a few remained who still saw meaning in clockwork automata, mummers performing disarticulated feats, or repetition in pared-down scripting techniques. When those fashions outgrew their chrysalis, and hankered after wider worlds, what real opportunity did a prophet like Douglas have? And anyway, what did Douglas of the shires really care about chilly social injustice, or political intrigues, or the new epidemic, or the stock market, or inner-city decay, or anything?

Roses whose delicate dewy petals miraculously disappeared, then as suddenly reappeared, depending on just how you cocked your head. A momentarily riderless, momentarily mounted horse. The face of the artist oscillating between all-sensory wakefulness, profoundest sleep. For Douglas, this was a mode and a mystery suiting his ends, and offered, not a way forward, but a refuge.

New passions were extinguished with the same decision that marked their spontaneous, phoenix-like emergence – as now in the heady flirtation with paints, pungent smells and varnishes. Here Douglas never passed the imitative phase of floppy clocks, living-room locomotives, or relocated limbs, before scanning other horizons. Those were shrinking and fewer. Accommodation in parallel worlds became more, not less expensive. And he couldn't, in honesty – when his youthful claims *hadn't* been honest – rekindle his psychic or paranormal spark, where on his lonely bright island, high on a hill, fanning his modest fire, gigantic red flames leapt and danced for passing mariners to see.

He achieved profounder, ever more protracted depths of boredom, and studied with loathsome insight, sitting on his monarchal throne, twisted twigs scratching at the clear panes, or the sporadic shower of autumn leaves as the wind got up. He would look up and out, and there, sure enough, striding under the stone arch, was his gardener, shirt billowing, wheeling a rake and a spade in an enormous timber barrow.

He passed the winter as a man condemned to the doctor's or dentist's waiting room, leafing through papers, magazines and journals, mining their ores for any new innovation, or happy little vogue. When Strang paid a visit in the spring, hooting and skidding round the gravel, an idea – credit is due, an *original* idea – had formed at last.

'Incredible! Amazing! Absolutely perfect!' said Strang, and with the crunch of tyres, and a volley of tiny pebbles, zoomed away into the burgeoning country lanes.

There were little republics visible on that enormous atlas, the library, where dust had not been allowed to settle: *Strange News From Another Star, The Three Stigmata of Palmer Eldritch, Red Shift Yin and Yang, Basic for the Advanced Programmer*, etc. When he took down his *Who's Who* – of interest only when bathing in the reflected glory of selfhood – a minor gust came down darkly with him on the library ladder. A morning leafing through its pages helped him identify an audience. The afternoon saw the production of invitations.

Short-term investments included: photographic and laser equipment (diffracted laser light from any subject can be used to make a two-dimensional interference pattern in photographic film); a banquet (interference patterns, when illuminated by laser light, can produce a three-dimensional image of the original subject); and space in all the leading philosophical journals for this proclamation—

The question of will: Professor Shapkin shall prove beyond doubt that it is neither determined nor free....

After lengthy and intricate photo sessions (experts in this field joined the banquet after), a private and unpublicised function saw his friends and hangers-on, led by the speedy Strang (and in the rear the biographer), tuck into the hams, chickens, ribs of beef and legs of lamb. Witness also salads and cheeses, a mountain of freshly baked loaves, wine, champagne, and English beer – all in the sunny open air, in the Elysian fields, in his rambling country estate.

Ushers in green livery, brocaded at the pockets, cuffs and buttonholes, led the guests along a maze of little pathways, brightened by Chinese lanterns. Douglas sat in his secret room at his makeup glass, a quicksilvered oblong studded with brightly coloured bulbs round its perimeter. Part of his costume was slung on the back and an arm of a chair – a lifeless, eviscerated jacket, whose airy sleeves were tucked into the pockets. There was a pompous waistcoat, and a soft crumpled shirt, whose broad shoulders would never quite be filled again. Douglas had already put on his trousers, which were baggy and pinstripe. He sported a scuffed pair of elasticated boots, and a moth-eaten vest, to suit his new character.

He scooped up in his cold palm little gobs and dollops from a grease pot on the table, and rubbing away the deathly pallor of his neck and visage replaced it with something much older and grey. He took up his black pencil, and moving closer to that newly changed reflection, sketched in wrinkles at the jowls, at the small, pouting mouth, at the corners of the eyes – for neither joy nor longevity had planted crow's feet in that virgin snow. When he leaned back, Narcissus fled and Prospero tapped him on the shoulder. Hadn't the Siberian winters etched in lines that weren't yet there? Yes, that was so – and with his pencil again he drew tormented furrows at the bridge of the nose, and deep intellectual lines to the brows.

But the eyes were still wrong. He darkened the droopy lids with kohl (life had been very hard). With an imaginative leap, he uprooted this falsified aspect of himself, transplanting it centre-stage – the laser and light show, Prospero – and found one tiny failure of detail. He pencilled in the eyebrows generously, the rims of the eyes thinly; he applied mascara, implying long, ingenuous lashes; gloss for the snarl of his lips, and rouge to exaggerate his cheekbones.

He whisked up his iron-grey wig, with its intractable tufts and quiffs, to reveal in its place an eyeless, shiny head, and a trunkless model shocked into baldness. He pulled on the wig and adjusted it over his strands. Leaning forward again, he dabbed and patted the crown, and now almost perfect powdered the join. He buzzed for Strang, who'd polished the peak of his cap and was brushing the coat of *his* disguise (green, brocaded livery). Douglas pulled on his crumpled shirt, tucking its tails into the voluminous waist of his trousers, which he belted tightly. He spoke – 'Shapkin, Professor Shapkin' – but the words were too bright and clear. He arched his back and stooped and croaked them out.

Strang appeared – present and correct – and Shapkin shuffled to the mirror. His old youthful hands smoothed over blemishes and imperfections, then as dexterously buttoned the top of that outsize shirt (there wouldn't be a tie). Servant Strang, his quips and bonhomie left behind with his pile of everyday wear, stood by in his official capacity with the waistcoat, then the jacket, until gathered was all that the old man needed. He brushed the troubled dust of Russia from his lapels, and took up a stick to support his tottering frame. One with an ivory knob had been found.

These two – the old and the new – stepped out into the warm summer evening, under a starry rural sky, the frail professor tapping his way along the brightly lit paths – the red glowing lanterns dancing in the breeze – and leaned with his free arm on a strong young Englishman, for whom history was an ever shifting pattern in someone else's imagination.

The guests had grown impatient, seated in floral garden chairs in little cliquey groups, but were heartened, vicariously, when the show got under way and the ghostly, silvery spots were turned on. A stage with a lectern, wobbling in the beams, suddenly manifested itself where a continuation of the clipped lawns might have been assumed. Spread out on covered tables to its fore was the unearthly feast (fraudulent hams, immaterial chickens, etc.). The host had not yet chosen to make an appearance, but leaned on his pliant stick among the flowerpots and composts gathered in an outhouse. Strang was outside and clicked his fingers, and immediately another liveried attendant swooped to the door, bearing a silver platter with calling cards. Strang shuffled these, absently, before handing them to Shapkin, who was delighted to see – now looking sprightly, and with the stick under his arm – that his victims included many old colleagues from Oxford.

Among them was the white-haired Schenfeld, whose old-world sense of what a tutor ought to be had found its abrupt conclusion in that final appraisal of student Douglas (if Douglas *was* brainless, what would follow was someone else's mischief). Schenfeld struck a match and lit the meticulous bonfire in the huge bowl of his Alpine pipe, and for a moment was enveloped from the neck up in swirling plumes of smoke. He puffed away philosophically, eyeing the luminous discs of Brie (a particular favourite), an expectant gurgle from his nether world suddenly spiralling up. He would stay after all.

The other fidgets – theistic bishops, atheistic priests, atavistic journalists, philosophers (eschatological, sociological), and students largely (who were wiser than any of these) – had reached the same hungry verdict, and so no one got up and walked away. The old dodderer shook the soil from his boots and beat the heels, symbolically, with his stick, for fatigued warhorses must be spurred to action. When he took the stage and stood at the lectern with his papers, he surveyed (another effect) the backs of those learned heads: flaxen on student, dandruffy staves; the bald glowing pates of all those hallowed religious men; a cut-and-dry by a certain Duval of Fleet Street (papers may relocate, a good *coiffeur* is stuck with). A new mood of openness had extended its purest radiation even to these stuffy reactionaries, and when Shapkin spoke, rolling his r's and committing his well-chosen words to odd juxtapositions, it was of his feelings first.

'For me this is a moment poignant, most so, most so.' The cracked, eccentric, amplified voice filled the night air with strange eerie echoes, whose first issue was from a network of hidden speakers. 'I am Shapkin, Professor Shapkin.' And as he waited, watching the backs of those curious, turning heads, the befuddled audience gazed in amazement at his bright, ghastly presence. 'Much thanks in order to my friend and champion, Lord Melfort-Jones, who only this last week secured Shapkin's release from horrible Siberian camp – no doubting this you already know of.'

Schenfeld pulled on his pipe reflectively, gathered his brows, but couldn't recall the name. No one recalled the name.

Shapkin continued, his weary, tremulous voice rising and ringing absurdly round the conclave, and dissolving with each diminuendo into a rude hum from the makeshift PA system. 'It is satisfying particularly to have, I see, the broad spreads of view. I demolish, you see, not one, but two, two principles in a stroke.'

'You're going to prove, then,' Schenfeld asked, in his terrible polemicist whine, 'that will is neither free nor determined?'

'This is so exactly, so exactly. But first let me say, what about becoming, ping! invisible, how do I do it? Yes, something we all consider, perhaps – as phenom*enon*, no, but as concept we may much talk about with. I have only ask, "How would my relation to this world alter if I possess this secret?" and how much more is possible? This I ask you, please....'

The gangling professor in his baggy shirt and suit, his grey maniacal hair bluish in the artificial light, held those stunned, silent members of his congregation in a contented gaze, and marked the pause. Not a whisper, not a murmur transcended an electrified background drone.

Professor Shapkin craved forgiveness, and observed, gravely, that it had been many years since he was last a free man. He paused, and as the stiffened, po-faced clerics loosened a little and shrank back from the edges of their seats, he saw that it was necessary to explain his methods. Ideas, notions, concepts – complex and difficult to grasp – were in his experience made coherent through metaphor. Here he assumed general acquaintance with his finite universe theory, of almost half a century ago. He was of course perfectly free to discuss that glorious document now, though in a colder political climate his Soviet comrades had marched him off to a mental asylum, with the theory's lay translation into fiction having gained popularity with the youth of other countries. That little piece of moonshine postulated somewhere that the universe is contained in a crystal sphere, and that a small boy in his grandfather's study gazes abstractedly – a mere moment in eternity – into a cloudy globe, the axis of which is tilted. Occasionally – contiguous moments in eternity – he spins it dreamily, eyes wide with wonder at the rush and whirl of constellations his actions on the globe produce. (Schenfeld was beginning to see how this wizened old man had found himself in an asylum, and studied the Brie impatiently.)

'So, gentlemen, how is it, please – how does it help us, this invisibility we give ourselves to?'

There was still widespread reluctance, but a student of moral philosophy, with a penchant for obscure quotations and references (who was already looking to his next essay), entered into the spirit of things. 'I would,' he said, 'be as it were a fly on the wall during cabinet meetings in Downing Street.' This quite obviously wasn't what the aged professor wanted to hear, for he seemed to look vaguely and some way over the student's head, with its brightly burning ears, as he spoke. Then Patrick McGraw, the impecunious and little-known playwright, declared – raising a smile or grunt from his bored companions – that *he* would place himself in bank vaults, and laden with booty pursue a happy life in retirement (again that detached look from the grey simulacrum at the lectern). One of the bishops proposed that a wider acceptance of the Christian faith could be gained, through miraculous, herald-like visits to the poor and distressed on cold lonely nights, but a priest was appalled (it reduced the essence of religion to deception and trickery). Here, strong opinions might have erupted into proper debate (arms of chairs were clutched, and knuckles turned white, necks turned a terrifying shade of red, cheeks took on that dangerous, explosive look), but Schenfeld drew on his popping pipe then offered a considered view.

'Wait a minute, wait a minute,' he said. 'Aren't we losing sight of the stated objective?' 'Not I think, not....'

'Now come on, there are rules of the game. You were going to lay a proof before us....'

'Yes, so I have, so....'

'Now look here....' That, in his pompous English way, was as much as Schenfeld could say, because Professor Shapkin became at that moment, incredibly, apparently, invisible. In the dimming silver pools of light that once illumined his features there were now only rising specks, as moths and gnats and other creatures of the night usurped his throne. If that inspired gasps of amazement and dropping jaws, then the same clinical disappearance of their feast plunged everyone into gloom.

'You see, my point it is proved, it is proved!'

The dissembling image of Professor Shapkin now appeared, briefly, behind them, where the subject's true position had once been. 'None of you has the will, free or determined, but only the fancies, only these imaginings.' Again he disappeared, though now spectacularly in a puff of spangled smoke. When Schenfeld rolled his eyes to the heavens (he detested student pranks, and he was personally aggrieved at the Brie), he thought, was sure he could see the transparent arch of a dome, and beyond it, orbiting like a satellite, the cloudy compressed constellation of a child.... Look, as it comes again, there are the dark hollow sockets of the eyes, the round nose, and as it comes again, the pursed lips....

'Ah,' someone said, 'quite clearly a sophisticated hoax.'

Homecoming

Jumpy sheep and a collie on a circuit, then a bullock, then an empty pasture whizzed by. In the glossy magazine open on her lap a lay therapist singled out problems sent in by her readers. Oh, and what's this – gone all that rolling countryside. Already those sunny meadows were overrun by identical factory yards, where chunky labourers tottered on forklifts, and one even cartwheeled – cartwheeled! Above him are young female faces bunched in a tiny first-floor window. Now where did I put it, where did I put my ticket?

A head popped up under a distant luggage rack and a hand went to its crown, holding down a thatch of hair in a breeze where a door would open. Speculation: he's wearing that grey tweed suit, in this stifling heat – has it? yes, it *has* got a waistcoat! – because he's off for an interview, is a casual dresser, and this is the only suit he's got. No? Okay – he does normally wear a suit but he forgot to pick up his summer two-piece from the cleaners. Ah, here we are: damp walls – the platform, deserted so far – a chocolate dispenser – a grim-looking ticket man. Mm, better find that ticket – huff, bag's heavy! I'll get behind tweedy and he can open the door – then I can check these pockets. Leave that awful magazine!

Out on the street. Office people out for an early lunch, shoppers, no one she knew. The buses here in her hometown ran to a timetable not synchronised with train departures or arrivals. That was a point confirmed and underlined when bending under the weight of her backpack she stood at the bus shelter. She'd missed one by two minutes, and the next was in twenty. Oh well, I can take a look at the old school and wait for it there. She hiked up the hill. Fading fast from her memory were the pure Alpine air and mystical silence when she had snapped on her bindings each morning. After an exhilarating day mastering the black run a chocolate sponge and steaming coffee *après-ski* awaited. In the lead-up to that, her world trip had taken her into clear waters and coral islands, with a tour guide's commentary from a glass-bottomed boat – prelude to a closer look with scuba gear. Trudge, trudge. A trip round the globe had ended in this....

The Le Corbusier glass and concrete edifice no longer looked so brave and new (and look, the resident team of roofers were boiling those perennial vats of bitumen). That school and its blank modernity – once a prominent landmark, fixed in her consciousness – now occupied a smaller space, supplanted as it was by images of campus life. Anyway, here's my bus – by the looks of it that ghastly green uniform hasn't changed. What? They want an *exact* fare? See here, I wouldn't know what that was, and you've no idea what a fag it is getting money out of these pockets. You *can* insist – but *I've* got nothing smaller! Ah well, keep the change – that extra can help when you redesign the timetable. No, no,

I don't expect you to understand. Now, where shall I sit? At the back? No, that's too far with this load, here'll do.

The bus with its sole passenger chugged out of town and meandered illogically through a network of village lanes (the same awnings, the same grocery shops, the same war memorials were approached twice, three times, always from different bends or turn-offs). The same people, too. How could I forget *him*? That funny little man with froggy eyes – there he goes – still riding up and down on a lady's bike. Wonder if he'll see me – here I am, here. And does he still stare so? Or is that only at little girls coming home from school? Huh. Gone. Didn't look up. Missed me. Anyway, I've had enough of this. I can get off here and there's a short cut – what a weight this pack is. If I remember, it's somewhere behind the hospital. Or is it? The road's changed. Oh yes, the path. Hmph, getting heavier: suppose that stupid little man wants me to ring the bell. Ding ding. Mm, push once, it says. Hope that doesn't confuse him.

But the driver understood. She climbed down and crossed the hospital car park, her backpack jogging her shoulder blades, and now more insistently, with every stride. She turned for the rear and a clump of rhododendrons, but in passing the kitchens a mountainous chef in greasy overalls loomed in her path. He glanced inquiringly, but said nothing, standing aside, pressing his bulk to the wall. She edged round him into the shadows. She looked up and nodded, and saw the beads of perspiration on his brows, the veiny blotches on his cheeks, the green stubble to his chins. Then – it must have seemed extraordinary – she waded through the rhododendrons, hitching up her backpack. Those evergreens swished and folded like curtains behind her. She went over the fields and across a stream, then up a woodland path. Finally our world-weary traveller emerged from a grove of English oaks, and holding the sun off her eyes with first one hand, now the other, made out the rear of the house, the points and loops of its ridges, and rising through the surrounding ash trees its two enormous gables.

She came in at the gate at the end of the garden. Was it five, six years ago, when she had stepped out the other way, through the front door? Mm, she couldn't remember. And, it all looked unusually neat. The borders free of weeds for once, the lawns cut, edges trimmed. There was a sprinkling of peat where a kidney-shape had been dug for a new magnolia. And look here, a pool, with fish. She shrugged. So different.

She was behind the summerhouse, with its smell of creosote. She clumped down her backpack onto the damp grass. From here the house was visible in greater detail. Were these new window frames or was that fresh paint? Difficult to say. It's paint, I think, bright and white in the sunshine. Then she saw her father, who slid a spade in a flowerbed and pulled up heaps of clay, turning each clod, then slicing into smaller wholes these fresh new lumps of earth. He's put on weight, I see, and needs a haircut – in fact he was so much more attractive before he retired, in his business suits and his hair slicked back.

She stepped lightly over the lawn while he continued to work, anticipating his surprise. Ears have obviously deteriorated, I'm quite close, why doesn't he get a gardener for this? Hmm, stopping is he? And what's he got in that barrow? Her squat shadow fell angularly to her left, a dark movement that caught his eye. His shabby old shirt ballooned up in a sudden little gust but fell back instantly. He thrust in the spade for the last time and left it, freestanding. It's going to be emotional, I don't think I can stand it. He grunted in that special way of his and scraped the soil from his boot. And how do I tell him this is only a flying visit? He straightened up – it took an eternity – with a hand to the small of his aching back, and turned.

'Well, well,' he said, and cleaned his palm on a cuff.

'Hi there, Dad.'

'Good timing. See those petunias, and that trowel....' He pointed to the barrow. 'Pass them, will you....'

Three Novellas
THE BORDER AND BACK

Entry Without Visas

'Look homeward, Angel, now, and melt with ruth…'
—Milton, *Lycidas*

Michael Grading

His room under an icicled gable was only for now a temporary exile – this was his gloom. His evening life was a motionless life, and his eyes were wide – his mind was in a trance.

This was his remove, and here those Oriental disciplines – the discomfort of lotus and half-lotus contortions – had been tried and rejected. Endless cigarettes and hours of introspection were preferred.

His private cataclysm, swirls and eddies inches below a calm, unruffled surface, had taken in routinely and for the thousandth time the distorted ovals, triangles and shadowy little oblongs – a geometer's absent doodle – which when smoothed away curtained out the winter night. It was his ritual at this troubled hour to sit in his chair and watch for the first bright quadrant of the rising moon – in fact for anything – to illumine one low corner of his world.

Sometimes the autonomous elements offered no sympathy, he recalled, and once, on a starless, cloudy night (this exile only ever *half*-turned his back) he was obliged to stand at his narrow lookout, with folded arms. A discarded butt still smouldered among the debris of his ashtray, whose moulded inscription, *Au Bois de Boulogne*, had long disappeared under successive crusts of ash. Across the street, a connecting scene was re-rehearsed: offstage technicians cued a fuzzy yellow cone of artificial light – it issued from an imitation gas lamp – where a polar shower unleashed itself in an otherwise gentle flutter of snowflakes. The two players entered left. A man in a crumpled hat and a long coat with the collar turned up. With him an indeterminate dog – Alsatian or Labrador – sniffing territorially round the foot of that street lamp. Michael unfolded his arms and turned away, having foreseen the inevitable: the cocked hind leg – the right, the left – another confirming sniff – the right leg after all – the warm, steamy jet, the growing yellow hole, a dark gaping wound in the dissolving snow.

He guessed from the pitch of excitement in their voices that tonight's performers were a great deal younger: rosy-faced minors, with woolly scarves, and stripy bobble hats caked in snow – though Michael Grading didn't care to look.

Soon, the first guests would come (nor did he care to predict their identities), and that was much to his chagrin. He stubbed out another butt in his ashtray and lifted up the heavy encyclopaedia beside it, already open at 'Suicide'. Nothing much here, where most recent statistics were nearly thirty years old, showing firearms (which he didn't possess) in the United States (where he'd never been) as the most popular means, and jumping from high places (the summit of his college fire escape, perhaps?) ranking low on the scale.

He closed that ancient tome, and in another sudden movement tossed it down among a chaos of technical papers on his desk, then saw when he stood and adjusted his glasses those unwitting Thespians tumbling and sliding home through the snow, scarves flying. He folded his arms. In a moment he would hear two distant voices – a commanding basso first, his father's, then the reedy, staccato overlay of his mother's. Arctic conditions brought out the gregarious in some.

To his horror, the first of those guests had arrived, careful to plot the one reliable course round the family car, while at the same time avoiding swipes in the face – a fresh weight of snow laden in the cedar tree. That booming bass was a reverberation in the lantern-lit porch, and was soon punctuated by the pounding and scraping of feet on the grille – then the addition of more voices.

It was time, time to look around, time to find a plausible diversion.

Grading, a devout agnostic, didn't require the complicated paraphernalia of other religions. To him the vicar of God wore holy smiles but Druid gowns, and his choir intoned Satanic chants. In any case the sense of sin was the same. It was easy but deceitful, squatting before a grandmother's antique chest – its deep drawers for a multitude of thick woollies, huge rounded knobs for handles – where in hopeless retrospect he tried to make sense of his despair. Arriving guests looked up, and in seeing the dim rectangle of shaded light under the gable remembered their own student labours.

This was his other country, with its childhood memorabilia, its little symbols and reflections of his early life, now looking more and more like someone else's. He picked up an identity bracelet with a forgotten and now puzzling insignia, *Jtaly*, yet with it came the recollection of a freer incarnation of himself, where alone or with friends he inspected and mentally mapped each street with its houses, or the woods, the lanes, the churches and outlying meadows that together made the village where he lived. He remembered finding the bracelet in a strawberry field, while he and two others explored the rambling grounds of an ancient house, youthfully unafraid of its owner, said to be seated in the House of Lords, a man who when he appeared did so in loud checks and a flat cap.

One of his friends, short-haired throughout his boyhood, had an eye for detail. He examined Grading's find. Grading had no time for it, and in another moment sounded his war cries in a tepee frame, where runner beans were intended, Michael wielding an imaginary hatchet. In later years Grading lost touch but heard of that friend through rumours of a stepbrother, who one early morning drove in a salty drizzle thirty miles to the coast, and high above Hastings attached a hose to the exhaust pipe. The other end fed in through a window. Our driver, going nowhere, switched on. Poisonous gas, according to Michael's dated statistics, ranked closely to hanging, though perhaps not often on a windswept, grassy hillock, over the choppy grey Channel, and in driving rain. A milkman discovered him hours later, without a note.

Now, that bracelet had lost its charm (a greenish psoriasis had erupted through the silver plate): *Jtaly* had corroded to *Jtcly*, and those once sparkling links were worn to a brassy dullness. In his adult mind, such an article was stubbornly paired with hirsute Latin waiters, or with car mechanics. It slipped through his fingers and fell down collar-like round the buttoned neck of a glove puppet, whose features were Punch's. No Judy or string of sausages accompanied, so what else? A pair of stuck compasses, and still attached the yellow stub of a pencil. A plastic protractor, scratched, scored, defaced (listen. Was that one of the guests on the stairs stumbling already for the bathroom?). He swept aside those mathematician's tools and gathered up a leather purse – really a tobacco pouch, used for clandestine pipe-smoking – but before dwelling for too long on that, his mother had pushed her head round the door.

'They're all here,' she said.

He closed that bottom drawer and lit another cigarette.

The condemned man, not so much led but urged on by the executioner, paused frequently on his stairway, not for the obligatory cigarette or sentimental last wish, but for a final appreciation of another world, at all times accessible, if mostly prohibited. The steady hum of conversation and occasional hoots of laughter had been audible even in his own territory (he couldn't recall that border passes had been issued), where the interrupted past never properly offered refuge. Worse was this limbo or no-man's land, where what belonged to the outer reaches he not only heard but was menaced by. He must resume his stride, must turn his attentions away from the portraits and landscapes, graduated up or down the stairway, where the last window opened on a windy marsh at sunset – its wild geese receding in formation.

Gigantic snowy footprints in a black and orange maze had melted into watery craters, and had marked the hall carpet. How often while he sat on a low step, at the outset of a phone call, the polished receiver held dead-weight above his shoulder, with its pessimistic monotone – how often the archetypal goblins besieging his jaded imagination had swarmed in vain and in every direction over the resistant pile, that bright new path and its promise of emigration, of a cleaner air to breathe and a healthier climate. He took that eventual step, and envisaged on the other side that press of his parents' guests, behind whose party masks expectant faces watched for the tentative revolution of the doorknob, but only seeing for the moment, in the shiny brass, the kaleidoscope of their reflection.

Naturally when Michael entered, that uncomfortable impact was of a slightly different order. The pariah was in fact unnoticed and ignored, and was only gathered in by clammy, grasping hands when his appearance offered a tidy conclusion to someone's flagging conversation. The hum he had heard behind the closed door now billowed up with thick bluish clouds of cigar smoke, and the scent of aftershave and perfume, and unlike the busy little people in the hall he stood for a moment, frozen in the doorframe. He adjusted his glasses, pressing back the bridge with an accustomed forefinger, and thought about retracing his steps and collecting his cigarettes (discernibly pointless: there were always open boxes scattered around invitingly downstairs, on cocktail tables or the window ledge – a useful supplement to his student exchequer). He lurched mechanically over the threshold, a skinny, myopic, gangling youth, and on familiar ground took unfamiliar bearings.

The communicating glass doors had been thrown open, resolving the two small reception rooms into one, and where his gaze might ordinarily alight on a patchwork of bubble panes, there was now the relative sensation of depth and space, albeit populated by nodding, empty heads. The furnishings had been pushed more or less at random into the perimeters (the floral, hermaphrodite settee was wedged between its companion male and female, two high-winged armchairs, where no one as yet had thought to sit). In a corner, out of place away from the conservatory, his mother's peacock chair had a card pinned to its seat, with the following, in his father's hand: FOR OLD WARHORSES ONLY!

He struck out for the fireplace, where an open box of cigarettes and an ornamental kettle occupied an alcove, though a restraining hand gently clasped his elbow.

'You must be Michael,' someone said.

Anonymous councils had considered the pale man's life-and-death struggle and granted a reprieve, so that the next hand was not the executioner's on the small of his back, propelling him firmly, without fuss, into a closed circle, with its trials of social exchange. Priapus roused himself unexpectedly (a momentary twinge), and Michael reflected: he had never sought for salvation in group dynamics. He assumed that the elegant woman, about his mother's age, but slim and sophisticated, had observed and knew everything about him, and unlike him remained relaxed. An elbow was angled to a seam in her tightly fitting skirt. The line of her lightly freckled arm ended in a plume of smoke, an inch of grey ash, a cigarette pinked at the filter. The varnish of her nails was a dewy silver. When she sipped her Campari, the same pinkish residue left itself under the dark rim of her tumbler.

Mistimed advances (reckless Kāma or friendly jackanapes?), acknowledgments proffered in coded silences (the bigotry of Anglo-Saxons doesn't lie dormant long, and eventually solicits one reply or another), and the prompt retreat of a Sanskrit teacher (his presence represented only perfunctory service to social integration), left Michael looking quizzically after the genuine pariah (purportedly in search of a mislaid camera). The grey, paunchy, balding husband – how could she have made such a mistake? – skirted round that embarrassing hiatus. He said: 'Dad's told me all about it, Mike – I *can* call you Mike? What you get up to up there.' His flabby round face was beaming through a film of sweat, which he wiped with the melodramatic flourish of a handkerchief (its monogram 'AH'). On the last, fading cadence he gestured ludicrously with his rolling eyes and devilish brows, meaning Michael's room upstairs. Michael only half listened to his questions. What was an electronic OR gate? What was software, what was firmware? '...go on, enlighten my wife – she's fascinated...'. But that wife when her mouth went into smoky provocative ovals prompted important, tormented questions of his own.

Somehow the thrusting probes and awkward parries seemed to lose themselves naturally in the hubbub, and he withdrew honourably. They understood only too well the broad responsibility of the host, or in this case servant of the host. He grabbed almost desperately at that box by the kettle, which now contained the inverted tripod of only three cigarettes (he alone rendered it lame and useless). A cold albino hand offered a light, or the last flaming remnants of a charred match that curled towards the ceiling, a thing pushed under his nose in two pinched fingertips. When he squeezed his way to the other room, where a candlelit buffet had been laid out, the little snatches of conversation he caught revealed the significance of his father's sign on the chair. Later, he caught sight of the retired major, clutching a paper plate and serviette, bent stiffly over a bowl of rice and raisins. His thin moustache was clipped severely, leaving a narrow contour between it and the taut upper lip. Underneath the darkish, sagging flesh of his face the high lines and surprising protuberances of a rare bone structure were horribly visible. The major had been ill, and that was clear, and after spinal surgery the physiotherapist had recommended high-backed chairs, without the need for cushions.

After midnight, those child performers were safely tucked up while the hound slumbered, twitching in a cold house somewhere. Flurries of snow had ceased, but the pavements were frozen and twinkled in the moon- and lamplight. A late-night neighbour briskly walking home glanced out from the multiple wrap of a scarf and saw in the merry haven a reddish afterglow suffuse the velvet curtains. A yellow lantern light, still bright in the porch, streaked the icy fingers of the cedar tree. He shivered and shrugged, then thrust his gloved hands deeper in his pockets before hurrying on. The major on the other hand had retired creaking to his chair, and sat assiduously upright with a stiff whisky, listening – as were all the guests listening – to the night's raconteur. Michael's unease was by now well understood. He was some way back, behind those un-communicating doors, and sat with a mineral water, gazing at the depleted salads, limp lettuce leaves, chains of tomato pips, the half-eaten buttered rolls, the powdery crusts and waxy rinds in a litter on the cheese board. There was a busy clatter in the kitchen – a hot steamy place by now – and the slosh of a dishcloth patting the plates and china. His mother, now with her dull brown hair in a mess and her forehead lined with fatigue, appeared and stacked up plates and dishes precariously. ('Come on, give us a hand!') His father came out too – 'Yes, come on, give us a hand' – the sleeves of his new starchy shirt rolled up, his warm pink hands dangling at his sides, where a tide of soap suds slid from his fingers into little pools of water on the carpet. The shaving rash under his chin and on his neck had been aggravated by his collar, which his son reflected should have been consigned straight from the wrapper to the wash.

He could see in the arrangement of twining candelabra, each with its complicated network of little lambent stubs, tunnels of supernatural light, and through them remembered something he had read or seen on TV. A mother's pregnant, almost murderous agony ended with a Caesarean, where the divine expectation in all she had gone through had raised her consciousness above the delivery table, above the intense theatre lights, and for a moment left it hovering under the flaky ceiling, observing. The assistant midwife knew the sign, and called: the white-coated doctor came back immediately and led the revival. But this was the mother's farewell, who floated in a careless ecstasy and took a last look down: at the arched back of the weary, wakeful doctor thumping her lifeless body (grim, determined resuscitation); at the midwife, ready with a syringe but tearing open the packing round a needle; at the bloody, gory placenta on a steel tray; at the screaming child, hastily swaddled; and out there, through the distorting pane over the door, at her pacing husband, who had been bundled out into the harsh light of the corridor. A helix of autumn leaves whisked her away from this, an impossible world, and set her down again, in tune with a choir, at the gate of a summer village. 'Is it you?' she said, and the happy old man leaning there in dazzling cricket flannels nodded and smiled. 'Granddad? Isn't it so lovely here!' He held up a wrinkled hand, and still smiling told her this was much too soon. 'You must go back.' And she: 'But this is paradise.' And her granddad again: 'But what about the children? Who will look after the children? You must go back, go back....' Then she remembered what she had to do, just as the doctor sighed, relieved, and saw the flicker in her eyes.

A vast burning sun had rolled to the zenith of a perfect blue heaven. From where he stood on high ground, where he had twisted round awkwardly and polished his lenses, Michael could see that the major and the raconteur had tottered home for the night. He followed their intertwining prints – two drunken threads looping over the blurred horizon. Over there, where the sand billowed up in blinding sheets, a priest in a flying cassock stood at Michael's gate, one hand shielding his eyes. An impostor, or a harbinger, had arrived there first.

The priest appealed: 'Nicola – what you contemplate is treacherous, terrible even....'

The wind dropped. The holy man commanded the elements, if not the human soul: the vapours and nether spirits sank at his sandalled feet. The dust settled, Michael wiped away the steamy fog that had gathered on his lenses again. He pressed forward to the wicker gate, where on a winter night he'd come to claim his ultimate rite of passage. When the other two saw him come, Nicola turned away, and replied to the priest.

'I don't need *you* to tell me,' she said. 'Of all people, I don't need *you*.'

Michael approached, but did not interrupt. The broad black band in Nicola's sun-bleached hair was a pair of dark glasses, which with a prohibiting gesture she pushed into service. So in that pose she remained at one remove from Michael Grading, who saw in her face only the reflected sun.

The priest resumed: 'There is no resolution if this is your approach to our other world. There will be suffering.'

'There's suffering in *this* world. That is our belief.'

'It's what we inflict on ourselves....'

'Then all so far is a wrong turn,' she said. 'It isn't right.'

The priest said, 'What has been done was left to us,' and Nicola said, 'Then the outcome too, it rests with us.'

'Nicola, I command you not to go!'

She was wearing her green safari suit. She laced her desert boots and pushed her broad hat firmly on her head. The wind got up again. Bending her wiry frame into the swirling, unearthly sand, she opened and passed through the gate, still pressing her hat to her head.

'God forgives. God *will* forgive.'

Michael followed (for him forgiveness wasn't enough), but the priest restrained him, saying there were things still left for him to do.

'To do? What?'

The priest folded his hands gravely and with his cassock billowing up again (the restless spirit, the advancing storm) summoned his articles of faith. Michael, look: can you really leave when all is in disarray ('Come on, give us a hand…')? That bright sun in a perfect blue heaven began to slide away then plunge from its summit, while the priest, who was difficult to hear in the swirls and eddies and vortices of sand, assured him this wasn't the time in his brief young life for sleep ('Yes, come on, give us a hand…'), and faded with a kind of valediction. The fog came over his eyes again, and Michael's limbs and torso twitched. There were crumbs on the cloth where he buried his head in his folded arms, and it had to be shaken, though he was lost in a dream, lost in a dream, lost in a dream.

The House of Folly

These three were watching: a surprised face in a pointed arch (a determined woman who still enjoyed the plasticity of corporal life); and petrified, a pair of crowned gargoyles – two homuncular soldiers.

Major and minor, these latter two had warred for centuries, for the right to plant a national soul, and at the world's appointed hour rise to a gilded throne.

Michael had his back to them all – to Nicola, a Christian rebel, and to the bestial pair fixed in stone. He gazed down the mountain slopes, into the blue mists enveloping a now less tragic Europe (that was, less tragic by its sequestration). It was hard to believe that under the swirling cloudlets, governments persisted, their dogmas and liberal virtue a kind of bankruptcy. Harder to believe in a cabinet with ministers, and the forlorn hopes placed in a professional hinterland, in its tradition of searching, and reliance on innovation: cans on a string, or nowadays microchips.

In these quiet moments, in the tranquil suspension of Western life, Michael had turned his back on all that.

The live face, Nicola's, was no longer wedged between the inanimate two, though the towers, turrets and arches were no less real for that. Michael had paused to study his tracks in the snow – tentative footsteps winding through a continental mist – and projected their entry into that medieval dwelling ahead of him, a huge house filled with shadows. The pure mountain air had flushed some colour into his cheeks, while the cold sharp stabs of pain in his lungs were responsible for this, his sluggish pace, and all these reflections. The haven ahead promised relief.

A bell tolled and echoed moodily in the scrolls and flutes. In the body, mind, and soul of the ringer, a thousand years of analytic life had brought with it simplified hopes for a lasting inner triumph. Nowhere here had God-the-imperfect strewn that bloody symbol, the crucifix, into the world's violent tragedy and its school of benighted offspring. Here, the essential mysteries were written in the stone arch over the visitors' portal—

Abandon all impedimenta, ye who enter here.

Michael shook the snow from his feet and pushed open the door. He adjusted his eyes to the darkness, and, blinking, saw portraits, a folding chair, and over a mantel a relief in plaster, a moral depicted in three parts – but failed to understand.

Not new to these cloisters was one impatient student, who had come to consider Occidental principles – should he or shouldn't he cheat? Nicola, the most recent of Schmutzburg's guests, gazed from her dizzy summit, flanked by those primordial monarchs. Incredibly – for her own had been whirled away in the bitter night winds – another set of prints, another procession of black hollows, meandered from the vapours, like coals in pristine snow. The contest she had entered had a name – it was Frame Solutions. Her opponent had decided on his next move while her back was turned. She ignored him, musing on that solitary speck of a man (meaning Michael, a fortuitous presence, surely). If he turned, and looked up the mountain, at the sun and sky, and the clouds, it was only a matter of time before Schmutzburg, or its one last bastion, also entered his view. She didn't wait, but with a toss of her hair swung away from the ledge and faced her opponent, but did not return to their game. Even if Michael, she thought, understood the inscription over the outer door, and entered, he wouldn't last here long. For how could he remain? A cold stone floor and naked walls, a rudimentary bed, a low table, icy winds that howled in at the uncovered windows – no one was given more.

So she reasoned, while a mess of guilty thoughts in her opponent threatened to stay his hand, an impulse he suppressed once it had formed as a possibility. Words he spoke were a veil on his clumsy machinations—

'You had begun a list of books.'

Nicola studied the board and the new, illegal position of some of its pieces, and thought about how to answer. A few summarising sentences were impossible. What would a mere student of Schmutzburg understand of her own student life, with its autumn afternoons? Could it mean as much to him, those sudden gusts, the flutter and flurry and shower of leaves?

She heard the bell – they both heard the bell – and was certain of what to say, was equally positive that the broad, extended lawns in the grounds of her orthodox life, cut and rolled into alternating bands of green – that these as phenomena were another dissimulation. Yet you cannot consign everything to the world's history, from a surviving reality measured as private experience. The details were important.

One day she looked outward from a bench in the convent garden, and conjectured at the surrounding symbolism. Urns or sanctified vessels that hadn't stood the test of time, smeared as they were in lichens, moss and mould. Neither were the holy statuettes of unassailable stuff, when limbs were fractured and noses broken off. No. She, Nicola, had nothing to say, nothing at all of the books she'd read, and anyway a chilly wind was rising. (By now Michael was puzzling over that relief.) Squatting down at the board, she accused her opponent of cheating. Honourably, he conceded a fourth consecutive game.

Here in the House, a benign old mystic in a creaking chair had trained his mind to ignore the woody friction when he leaned forward to dip his pen, or back to gaze into the shadows and contemplate. He had never stopped wondering at the seasonal rites of peoples beyond the perimeters of Schmutzburg. These musings reinforced themselves whenever he beheld the careworn faces of Westerners who sometimes sojourned here, his life at a remove from theirs, invested with other meanings. They arrived with their signs and symbols and burdens of prejudice, for the wise elders of the House to examine, in the fullest flower of every human folly.

He'd dipped his pen for the last time that morning. He put it aside and glanced through his open arch. In the conical blueness, a solitary cloud had been busily disintegrating, and in that other perspective, in the oblong whiteness when he stood, a new set of prints curled up the mountainside.

The bell tolled and he left his desk. He took down a heavy book from a shelf and blew away the dust. When he opened it and turned to the page he wanted, too many hands had been here before, and he was obliged to smooth away the creases, to flatten out its script, before placing in a marker. A spiral of steps led him into the lower chambers, and here he met Nicola in one of the passages. Dusty shafts of sunshine filtered in at intervals through slits in the wall. He apologised, but handed her the book – not too late, he hoped. Well, this had been a long time coming, but anyway, Frame Solutions wasn't a game one learned overnight. The old man chuckled.

'I hear you're beating all our best students,' he said, adding, 'I shall have to see if I can't upset that winning streak,' though it was years since he'd played.

Down, down again, and at the very foot of those stairs a young English head turned with a start. The old man had begun to interpret for his benefit a plaster relief over the mantel, whose three divisions – one upper, two beneath – represented what? One in the pair depicted an unhappy village husband left holding a new-born baby, with an empty jug of ale. His suspicious wife knew his evil ways, and where you saw her creeping round from behind, she clutched at a wooden shoe and wound back her arm in preparation for a blow to the head. A cowardly neighbour, keeping his own head down but determined to miss nothing, reported what he saw. What *we* see is a luckless husband condemned by the village fathers. On the right of the pair, local worthies come together and are unanimous – the drunkard they hold aloft rides the skimmington.

Michael looked at the old man, and at the relief, and at the old man again. 'And that, the upper?' he asked.

'Ah, that is the just god in his heaven, who sees that his law is carried out.'

Here on another winter morning, the sun in its ice-cool heaven rose above Schmutzburg, a forgotten country, and forgotten its House of Folly. A hole appeared, or the tiniest chink, where a glimmer of light briefly penetrated a diffuse wash of moisture over Europe. A wrinkled old rustic in his mountain shack looked up for a moment and fancied he'd seen *something*, but heard only cars and a tourist coach.

Michael was in the gallery, where the students had gathered, all of them determined to ignore him. Neither did Nicola speak, coming in moments after and finding herself a seat. Michael nodded. She opened a book. She'd got it for its commentaries, its author an expert on the game of games. Grading was able to mark her progress page to page. Then without warning she tossed her hair back across her shoulder, in a pause from the book, taking in what changes took place in the courtroom below.

The affable old mystic sat at a bench with two others, while the man accused took his oath from a cleric standing by. That official withdrew, leaving in view a Westerner in early middle age. His dark hair had thinned to greying wisps at the temples, and had receded to the crown, and that made it all the more unclear to Nicola that a poet was about to be tried, his eyes bulging behind the lenses of his spectacles. Two deep furrows demarcating flabby jowls accentuated the flare of his nostrils. His thin lips formed an intelligent, whimsical smile. He stood waiting – a poet of the English municipality – in a shabby blue suit, a white shirt stiff at the collar, and a two-tone broadly knotted tie.

The case against was roughly this, while the three old men were loose with their metaphors. Our poet took his afflatus not from any potent commingling afloat in the atmosphere, but from something much less elemental, bound up with the naked mastery of form. This was not to deny the necessity of rules – that was understood. The objection was one of emphasis, for what was the character or ingenuity of prosodic architectonics other than plain, arithmetic workings out, and the trivialisation of lived experience?

The defence was less vague. Historical problems couldn't be ignored, and the poet confessed to a growing sense of intimidation in the presence of his technological colleagues. For example, he, the poet, was capable of this: he could conceive a regular figure, a tetrahedron, in his mind's eye, and could tilt it, rotate it, examine its lines and surfaces. But the crudest schoolboy, with his home computer, could do as much and more. Or on a grander scale, think of this inscrutable planet Earth, and make of that a vision – a blue ocean sphere suspended brightly in an enveloping darkness. Can any lyric prefigure again so stunning a photograph? Even Armageddon, that most vital conceptualisation in his repertoire, has been subsumed into mere technics and delivered up as a political possibility.

The accused was a man of conscience, whose observations had something of a Janus nature, being both involuntary and the source of ceaseless irritation. If all our medieval visions were now the acquired, bastardised property of governments and technocrats, then the only freedom left was in wallowing – an art that was bourgeois, puerile – or in the frustrations of social protest. And anyway, they seemed to want to consider his case in a theological light, with accusations answerable only in the realms of the unknowable. The four looked up. The sentence seemed a mere formality – condemnation to the world again – but Nicola had allowed that open book to slide from her knees and fall with a thud to the floor. This first session was adjourned.

Late evening. Michael sat in the gathering dusk on the edge of his bed – hands and forearms dangling, elbows on parted knees. He approximated cardinal points of the compass. North was cold and damp – the wall opposite. East was a window on a country in darkness. West, an open door on creaky hinges, allowing in the last warm rays of a world in decay. There as he guessed was the poet's dying emblem, a dull red segment as the sun underwent its final descent.

In the early morning the position was much the same, though now he heard voices and not the whirr of his thoughts. *Ab ovo*, the trial had repeated itself in all its developments, however much he disciplined his mind. He looked out of his eastern window and saw a distant country, its clouds of dust, its plumes and billows of brown smoke rising through an early frost, a dew. Nearer – below him on the courtyard – the poet had just snapped shut his tarnished cigarette case and returned it to a hip pocket in his jacket, which was crumpled where he'd slept uncomfortably. He lit up – a tarry, unfiltered cigarette – and drawing deeply looked east himself, though from his elevation couldn't see over the bright icy slopes into the valleys. Six, seven students just out of earshot had formed a circle and discussed concluding details, until at last an elected spokesman, whose warm breath Michael saw exhaled excitably into the cold air, detached himself and strode up to the smoking poet.

Later, a much older man was looking on, from the highest window in Schmutzburg's southernmost tower. What he hadn't seen – Nicola and Michael together again – was immaterial. His opinions concerning the two had already formed. Michael, immobile at the foot of the stairs, was pointing up uncertainly to the apex of the relief.

'The just god in his heaven,' he said.

Nicola, shrugging, said only, 'Just god, no. It's a landowner, that peasant's feudal overlord.' Meaning is always material – in this case a loss of revenue and the moral collapse of the workforce. We so like our parables of ownership and neglect.

Six or seven students set up a small table, while Nicola stepped outdoors with a playing board and a canvas sack for the pieces. The unbidden young Englishman followed, bewildered, while his older compatriot must accept he was guilty as accused. The poet as he loses his voice reveals his remoteness in what he says for those who have lost their faith.

Dreary grey scholars, who for generations had sneezed and drawn their secret signs in accumulating dust, consulted their archives, and were able to make one assertion: in its breadth of possibilities and relationships, that historic discipline Frame Solutions, first appearing in the fourth millennium BCE, had helped its adherents achieve superhuman powers of assimilation. If that was its extent, what of the rules? Well, exquisitely simple. The players began with twenty-four identical pieces, the opposing sets being differentiated by colour, and to each individual certain powers and scope of movement were ascribed, though not declared until its first move or capture. Thus an almost limitless range. Half a dozen students now formed a semicircle together with the silent Englishmen, while a seventh, large-framed and pale, could feel the colour rising in his cheeks. He would have to retract his confident offer to commentate on every move, or explain the rules, when almost certain to result was a first, embarrassing defeat.

Nicola considered her options but wouldn't make the decisive move. This was as much as Michael understood. The bell tolled again and the poet tossed down his cigarette butt onto the cold stone, crushing its smoky ember under a polished toe, a city shoe. A biting gust rolled in round the frozen peaks of that far eastern country, still twitching in its slumbers, under a long, feudal shadow. When the old man from the southern tower came out to the courtyard – robed, in open sandals, supporting his tottering frame on a staff – the sun in the east behind him settled on his grey hair bright as a halo. Nobody stirred.

So far this wasn't the game he'd come to see. He shuffled forward to the two seated at the board and crossed his arms, waiting. It was a hopeless position. He smiled. The student foundered. Like so many before him, he conceded – he retired, scratching his head. Then the old man put the tip of his staff to his lips (he cautioned the gasps, the hubbub, the euphoria), and next it was Michael, with a wrinkled hand pressed to the small of his back, as that pushed him to the newly vacated place. 'Play,' he was told, and unaware that the passing of only a few more days would see the commencement of his own trial, he squatted down nervously and took his place against that all-conquering female. A slight flicker of amusement crossed her features, but she restrained a smile and set out the pieces again. Michael, reluctant in his challenge, made a first tentative move. She snorted when he named his opening piece – a choice revealing a naivety unsuspected even in him. In the shadow of that tyrant god her failing religion had sought to vanquish, her compulsion to teach a lesson, and punitively, re-emerged.

The old man chuckled, but didn't remain, and when the poet took *his* place, assured that his own system could never be so vulnerable, no one foresaw his defeat, until late afternoon, when in the lengthening shadows, and a rising wind, only one spectator remained. But even he – pallid, large-limbed – shied away before the final outcome, consoled by the sure knowledge that both must turn to that distant, inscrutable country, to those shadows over the mountains, for any hope of salvation.

Two Dissidents

A cup of black coffee steamed away in the open window. The stationmaster, drowsy after an extended breakfast, had cocked his chair at a lazy angle. His head was lolling over the backrest. Tracts of sleepy propaganda, the leaves of an official newspaper – some already detached – gently vibrated with each explosive emission from his nostrils. Lunch was a long way off.

Outside, the penumbral shadow darkening the windowpanes had been granted a broader presence, and this, a fact of no consequence, was open to a chance observer, who glanced at the whole, at the accidental arrangement of sidings, huts, and offices – spread out in the semblance of a question mark. At this elevation, there were no clues – in the shade or sunshine – to more sinister signs of interrogation. Semi-darkness had arrived with the morning sun, the sun rising up behind Schmutzburg's mountain range. But a shadow would encroach – with supernatural ease – farther, farther to the east.

Michael looked the other way, to the west, on the abrupt downbeat in a distant clangour. He saw that a tiny black speck had matured since its first discreet appearance. It was now fully resolved as a blue and yellow locomotive, hot and belaboured in its jets and swirls of steam. He felt he knew personally its exhaustion – inanimate though the thing was – for even at this early hour his shirt was damp, and the ringlets of hair that were now too long down his back made his neck clammy, itchy. He sat down in the dust, in the low barren slopes. He took off his shoes and joined them in a knot at the laces, then his socks, then in the dry earth he drew a figure, a circle round a triangular group of ten. The first sign this morning of a cooling breeze twisted the thinning red heels of his royal blue socks. He gathered them up and stuffed them into his shoes. His shirt flapped when the breeze got up again, when the shifting sand smudged two of the points where circle and triangle touched, and these he redrew. Finally, a square enclosing the circle completed his symbol, though its companion formula was left unwritten, or awaited another hand.

Speculating on that eventuality couldn't keep him amused for long, and anyway further developments over in the west made their demands. The driver's mate, whose father had died tragically in a blaze, had jumped down from the engine and followed the glinting rails, his hands thrust dejectedly in the pockets of his overalls. A few moments later, when he climbed up a telegraph pole, the driver stepped down, but strolled the other way, for an exchange of views with a uniformed soldier. A carriage door hung open behind them, its window rolled down. Michael looked away, and turned to where the lean figure of S—, a dissident and self-professed enemy of the state, strode stiffly to the stationmaster's office. He rapped on the open window – loudly, a second, a third time. Had something changed? The snoozing official felt a mild rush of air as the paper slipped over his lap and onto the floor, still unread. He rocked forward on his chair – blinking, smacking his rubbery lips.

That sign in the dust was Michael Grading's first, though this, a lesser triumph, paled when set against his current situation – one he no longer attributed to social maladroitness or personal disaffection. Symptoms were not causes. In the West, the machine's strength was also its flaw, its bondage a conditioned eagerness for national competition, with the prejudice that nurtured clouded in threats located somewhere outside the tribe. Meanwhile the little hairline cracks that let in light – those faintest penetrating rays – meant something else was possible.

He stirred, and the breeze had got up again, though it wasn't *this* eroding his emblem (Michael Grading, a sand reckoner). He stood up and kicked over the traces, then slung his shoes over his shoulder and started out for the railway junction. The stationmaster, still with the taste of tepid black coffee, called for the camp doctor and walked on ahead to the train, the five o'clock express. For the dissident S—, here was his chance to revisit his secret place and carry on those despicable crimes against the state, in frail hopes, it was true, and in the remote anticipation that its evils and procedures would be dismantled by men like him.

C— had delayed the train once before, when a muted rap on his apartment door interrupted the fluctuation of his thoughts, his mind for only those few moments after midnight cut loose from his sleeping body – looping, ducking in the ether. In the absence of a response, the summoning hand tested its digits with bends against the joints, and the meticulous removal of fluff from a lapel. A limp, unoccupied leather glove dangled in the clutch of its mirror twin, while raw, flabby knuckles on the woodwork woke at least two floating neighbours upstairs. C—'s reaction could not help but be confused. If rebellious prose visited his dreams, his iron Muse exercised diplomacy in waking life, at a remove from (and in disguise of) his politics.

His bathrobe was draped conveniently over a bedside chair, but there was no time for that – this was his dreadful fate at the door. While the two thugs outside battered it down, a whitish, hairy, slightly rotund C— made apish ballet steps from the cold of his bedroom to the cold of his tiny living room. Three chairs there had been pushed up close to the chrome hearth and bar heater, and three mugs with slops and muddy rings were evidence of recent guests, but only coded references in a notebook were at all incriminating. When the door was flattened, and those impeccable officers of terror strolled in, dusting themselves down, their first illumination was the moonish radiance of two naked buttocks, quick to correct themselves to their proper detail in the person of C—. He was now standing, perplexed, and painful minutes short of a place of concealment, a safe little nook for those libels against the glorious state.

Gorilla One adjusted his dark glasses and turned on the light. Gorilla Two switched off his torch and examined a small, framed photograph of C—'s wife. The smile of academic success had been wiped off her innocent face some eighteen months before, but if her poems ever survived the camps and found their way to the desk of a New York publisher, well, we'd see.... That was of no consequence to these two, whose zookeeper had let them loose for a little Saturday-night entertainment. GT turned to GO and said aw, so touching, but doubted C— would see her again. Therefore good advice was to take every care of this last, treasured likeness. GO said pack. C—, still blinking under the bright, unshaded bulb, edged away, but the brutish Two, where he had merely teased and tested before, was first to the bedroom door. While obstructing that egress he calmly delivered a monstrous blow to the naked man's solar plexus. That had him writhing on the bristly carpet, and much as he admired the handwriting, it was Gorilla O's affirmed duty, when he bent and leafed through them, to confiscate those seditious notes. An uncooperative C— couldn't get his breath back. When his brainless friends frogmarched him out over the splintered door – gratifying labour for the repairer, an honest comrade – a few rough clothes were thrown over him any old how.

The train at the central station had already lost twelve minutes from its schedule. C—, doubled with pain, gasped through the corridors and down the breezy steps, gasped on the wet city streets, and still gasped, hoping to die, when he was manacled and hurled into a cattle truck. Those floating neighbours who had come down to earth could sigh, relieved that those midnight hands had opened someone else's door, but feared the new day nevertheless.

A paleness of sunlight striking on a grille parted into angular rays. He was among ghostly faces in a hellish twilight, where broken men wept or groaned, though C— detected *some* refinement, if, perhaps, it was time to discard more complex theories of being, philosophical abstractions he had once toyed with and taught. This was all too uncomfortably palpable. A barrister in rusty chains – his wrists round his ankles, his knees to his ears – was compressed into an adjacent square footage. This, when he'd defended one malefactor too many. C— glimpsed the sweaty rash invading his three-day stubble, but couldn't have known that his neighbour, who couldn't control the movement of that learned head, had shaved more recently than he'd sat to eat or slept in a bed. His head rolled – that instrument of illegal cerebration. It rolled intractably on the bare boards behind him, or on C—'s shoulder, or anywhere the lateral sway of the car dictated. If he muttered, that was in a monotone, though some sort of sense speared his delirium. He'd heard rumours, and was certain the train was bound for a transit camp. 'We are going to be re-educated.'

C—'s radiating pain had subsided into numbness, but the heat and stench off all those clammy bodies – their crumpled torsos, their intertwining limbs trussed in business suits – he met in a first wave of nausea, and with it the complication of noticing nowhere to be ill. A raw recruit in uniform, whose older colleagues played faro in a forward carriage, could still experience shock at all this human waste, and sympathised more or less. For that there was a cure, when a certain length of service tempered these sensibilities. He hauled back the huge sliding door from time to time and looked in on that sea of living flotsam, limp hands raised up to red eyes blinking against the sudden transfusion of sunlight. Then the moans – the perpetual moans.

C— would have to get nearer, and now regretted he'd been hurled over to the far side. That fresh-faced youth, frowning as always, was already bearing his modest weight into the door, his back rigid, his stomach taut, two rosy blobs painted on his swollen cheeks. The wheels squeaked in the runners and the flood of daylight diminished, and, when the door closed with a thud and a key rattled in the lock, darkness returned.

C— squirmed. C— wriggled. C— sustained a blow to the jaw, a boot in the groin. Doubtless he was fitter than most, yet was it worth fighting to the end, here on this meanest, most squalid patch of territory? Perhaps it was, when others mustered strength enough for a final show of dignity – C— joining them, and not to be denied his own. It was approaching five by the time he'd crawled to the door and the cadet returned. He asked the boy for the latrine, who tried to put him off by telling him that meant a difficult manoeuvre into the next truck, where anyway the latrine had been overflowing for several hours. C— had intimations of an awful life to come, and so insisted. The boy led him, clanking along the corridor, and tried to guide him from one communicating door to the next. C—, poised unsteadily between the two, with the breeze in his hair, felt suddenly free, and with the sweet air of liberty filling his lungs launched out on a last desperate leap, ending in the strangest sort of suicide. Senior officers, when the train had pulled up and they stood around in little groups, couldn't understand it. Those twisted limbs, the skull stoved in on a nasty-looking rock, and all that unrecognisable gore. D—, on the brink of making good his losses, cursed the interruption, and abandoned his bet, while the doctor, bustling in after the stationmaster, examined the scrambled cranium and pronounced C— officially dead.

The fate of a whole people had been chronicled and hidden away in a tool drawer in an engine shed. The dissident S—, who had pointed the scatty doctor in the direction of his master – that pompous official – made hasty marginal notes with the stub of his pencil. Webs in the corners and ligatures straddling the window frames glistened in the sunshine, impairing his view – his necessary view – through their massive oblong panes. He kept looking up from his work, at the rising dust, the hot barren slopes, but moistened his stump of lead with the tip of his tongue. He returned to his notes.

These were his later days of exile, and in the eleven years since his own midnight arrest – when there'd been three gorillas for him, S— a dangerous intellectual – he'd graduated from a prison asylum through a succession of labour camps, and had survived hospitalisation to be here, in a diminished state of health, for light duties at the railway junction. His eyes were dark and defiant.

His interrogators over a decade ago had enjoyed their first if Pyrrhic victory, while S— conceived and worked towards his own. Accusations against him – a research chemist and secret pamphleteer – grew out of evidence volunteered by his friend and associate Z—, who under duress described private conversations he had overheard on street corners. His two examiners were droll, for this had brightened up an otherwise uneventful day, and surely – an educated man – he could understand their train of thought, untutored as it was, and so arrive at the same conclusions as they. Or perhaps his denials were just, and it really was the case that while S— talked sports, Z— inexplicably must have thought the topic was economic management. They both smiled at that little *coup*, while one of them handed him a written confession. 'Sign,' he said. 'Just here.' S— still sat with his arms resolutely folded. He said, and kept on saying, 'But I haven't done anything', even to the point of extensive dental surgery – gratis, state munificence – signing only afterwards, in a rage of untreated pain.

The violence of those times, decreed by committee and administered by peons, couldn't control the freedom of thought that S— and others continued to cling to, and that was the flaw undermining the regime. It had broken his body in eleven years of purposeless toil, yet S— knew that connections round him were still intact. In his secret writings he recorded what he knew of poets and philosophers of conscience, those quiet political renegades – hundreds, thousands of miles apart. As he looked up into the light, into the golden gleam in the webs and their filaments, all that the proud man wanted was to tighten his links, to draw them in, yet like that patient spider suspended on a thread – in the corner of a window – could do nothing beyond this present confinement. It would need a miracle to dispatch his manuscript to the Western world, and God knew this was the critical time. For there were no calm assurances, no guarantees that some party minion wouldn't discover and confiscate his documents, and that the angel or messenger who came at last was nevertheless too late. Unless, unless, unless….

He pushed in closer to the pane and saw through his small bright window just a portent first – a few loose pebbles tumbling down the slope, and a yellow wave of sand. He put up a hand and swept a wisp of greying hair back off his brows, and watched as a minor avalanche brought in its wake a scuttling little lizard, a dry twig, the scorched leaf from a hardy mountain tree. He listened. The train still hadn't restarted. Instead he heard only the wind rise and whistle through the knot holes in the timber shed around him. He clawed at the webs and threads. Fine gossamer floated up from his fingertips, while a frantic spider, quick to investigate those first hopeful tremors, engineered a hasty escape down one of the fibres, and bounced on the floor. It darted off to a corner, its familiar universe having opened itself to looming, monstrous forces – for the first time in its brief young history. The dissident S—, whose nose was pressed to the cloudy glass, saw the naked feet of, at last, his go-between – or so he may hope.

The wind billowed up, and each foot, as it was planted slowly in the moving earth, emerged from a swirl of dust, where, whipped into a haze, and imperfectly visible to the dissident's weary eyes, the white of a flapping shirt overlapped the blue of Michael's denims, or flew up over the gold of his sun-bleached hair. Our one-time pamphleteer turned to that great endeavour marking his disrupted life, then wrapped his manuscript in an oily rag before returning it to the drawer. When Michael came down, sliding in the sand, bending, crouching, adjusting the distribution of his body weight, he saw a little man totter through an open door, bent with pain, but urgent even so. He wore a dark tunic, dark trousers, dark shoes. The creases round the corners of his mouth and eyes, and the streaks of grey in his thinning hair, were the marks of premature age on a youngish, doubled frame. S—, smiling as nearly as he could – at an unexpected guest – at a happy tourist with a holiday tan, with shoes slung casually over a shoulder – S— put up a hand again, and this time beckoned. The wind hadn't dropped, and a sudden gust got under and lifted the sand between them. Then the old man turned – intending Michael to follow – and passed back once more into his dark door, into his exile.

Inelegantly, Michael hopped, putting on his socks and shoes, then heard a distant whistle, and the clang of locomotion, as hastily he crossed the railway line. He stepped inside the shed and blinked in the darkness. Gradually the vague contours and outlines of things around him had shape and volume, and materialised – into a broken chimney stack – or over here a boiler – and at that bench by the windows the presence of S— (the dissident).

S— beckoned a second time, for here was his visiting angel. As Michael approached the bench an oily rag was unfurled and from its folds and creases a pencilled manuscript was drawn out and placed down carefully. The old man spoke to him – in French, in German – finally in broken English – but as time pressed and the train approached he made himself understood. Michael considered the practical implications of what had been said, and strangely not the dangers of the task (he was young and fit, he was strong and healthy), and they both looked up. The train was close. Soon, the platform would be swarming, and S— would have to take up his duties, with or without a decision. Michael looked at him blankly for a moment, then at the manuscript next to its oily rag. Suddenly he felt cold.

The driver's mate poked his round sooty face through the open frame and glanced to the rear, then stuck out a greasy palm in a gesture of alarm. The stationmaster, who had already edged his awkward person halfway through one of the carriage doors, ignored him. He remained with a stumpy leg raised, and with a chubby arm, his one fine instrument of balance, flailing in the breeze. He jumped, finally, on the sound of noisy jets of steam and the strain of the engine grinding to a halt. The driver too looked back with unexpected trouble in his eyes, two widening pools in the large white sockets of an otherwise blackened face. His fears were as quickly changed to peace of mind when fast footwork kept the stationmaster upright, and his dash from the moving train subsided to a trot before he and it came to rest.

The doctor stepped out next in his undertaker's coat, adjusting his half-moon spectacles. With a show of professional dignity he raised his hat before striding giraffe-like off to his waiting car. C— was slung out in a sack and sprawled on the platform at the stationmaster's feet. The living enjoyed little more ceremony, themselves shoved out on rifle points, or with solid boots planted firmly in their rears. The fresh-faced cadet still had no stomach for it, even having been through this a dozen times before. Now as then, under the watchful eye of his peers, he must show, by whatever deception, a sense of military detachment. Wherever these despairing middle-class men had suitcases, and the temerity to sit on them, upended on the platform, he kicked them away and roughly manhandled the protesting, spread-eagled owners to their feet. The stationmaster saw possibilities and anticipated a speedy turnover in expensive coats and suits. He liked the cut of that lawyer's, this merchant's, that professor's, and took to one side the reluctant youth, where after a few cool confidences he handed him a fold of crumpled notes from his wallet.

Michael stepped back from the window and put a hand to the dissident's elbow, and again regarded his manuscript, whose title page bore an inscription in a Cyrillic text he couldn't understand. 'C'est entendu,' he said, and wrapping that opus back in its rag he took it up from the bench. S— nodded, and pondered for a moment, searching out the right words. 'My thanks, good day, best luck.' Michael was already standing in the doorframe, gazing along the platform from the rear to the front of the train, and beyond to the dusty slopes. Scores of moaning men – some of them coatless – were being shepherded away – too far away – to a transit camp, somewhere over the hills, somewhere in all that sunshine. The stationmaster was back in his office, snoozing, when Michael turned, and waved, then strolled up the platform. He paused for reflection at the heap that had once been C—, and guessed, at the deep red splotches absorbed in wider and wider circles in the sacking, that a man's fate had found its conclusion here. Then from another heap – a pile of expensive coats – he slipped on an ankle-length fur and dropped the manuscript into the depths of its inside pocket. Then he looked up, at S—, a man at the profoundest milestone in his long long exile, who had a hand up again and registered a smile. Michael mouthed a simple English valediction and stepped onto the waiting train, which with convenient dispatch lurched into motion and began its pleasant journey back to the borders of Eastern Europe.

Homeward Angel

L ight, and alternating shadow, crisscross in the windy columns of lace, and with each new gesture a novel intersection either fades in the gloom, or asserts again the warm bright glow of life – made glorious, lasting. An ornamental curtain rail, with fruit at its tips, two brassy pinecones, sags mid-point. Voluminous nets, bunched into scrolls, exclude a passer-by, who sees only a dirty mesh in the window's lower half. In a far country someone's famulus conjured a multitude of faces in the clouds. A ruling magician, counting steps in his belvedere, looked out at the craggy peaks of his kingdom. It was time to wind the clocks, once he had searched pockets for that one elusive key.

A last plume of smoke spiralled up from an ashtray, but dissolved in an agitated rush of air, a breeze in the curtains. Michael reversed the direction of his coffee spoon, stirring his muddy slops, then, crushing another nub, flattened out a mounting pile of ash. Up there above the rail, strange portents offered clues and hints, if he tried to understand. In the racing clouds, in their changing faces, a much less airy drama had wanted to unfold, waiting till now, a moment of calm. This, a time to reflect, was his first morning back. An innocent little fleece suddenly ballooned in every direction into a military-looking visage. With its round cheeks still swelling, its curly moustaches twitching – detaching somehow, on the point of drifting away – it bellowed out its commands over the rising heads, into the farthest corner of its world. Newly forming troops, whose eyes and other facial indentations were still only embryonic hollows, mostly scuttled off, yet one of them emerged with dignity. Michael watched as they developed: strong young limbs, a firmness of will, intelligence. A dissenter (perhaps), the raw young warrior stood his ground, and by that action gained his triumph. Those moustaches couldn't be retained, the swollen cheeks collapsed, and in a sudden involution the galloping commander lost all semblance of authority and being.

East, a long way east, the famulus has mastered his skills – at last. The fretful magician paces up and down in a maze of corridors. Burning torches throw up on the stone walls and ceilings a ghoul, a looming shadow, everywhere he goes. Some fast clocks have already chimed, although he has the key. His young apprentice, out on the battlements, is laughing. No matter. He found and burst into the clock room, where with the bells, clangs and chimes bright in his ears, he placed that key in a slot, and wound. On the stroke of ten, a decade had passed. Nothing could now go back. Even as, counter-clockwise, our prodigal stirred his coffee again.

A testing personal history, enshrined in her faith in scientific creams, even now hadn't quashed all hopes. Here in the café the dumpy Genoese, proprietor, would have to live with an un-eradicated pencil-line – un-ladylike hair on her upper lip. They were pointless tribulations, yet even a tormented life may have its happy constancy: in all these years the business hadn't changed. The next cosmetic plan, exciting as always, harmlessly co-existed with the running of everyday commerce. Regulars had studied aspects of her being – her calm assurance with the percolator, or the shine her chequered cloth gave to her urns. But what of that? There were no regulars now, only a solitary. The clock had struck a fateful ten. She performed her chores without much haste. Perhaps, she reflected, if she turned off the heating. That was her best persuasion against that lone customer over by the window who had bought that miraculous thing, an eternal cup of coffee. Well, if that was the game, what about another cup, or breakfast, or...? Or no. What was the rush? Relax.

She palmed back a silver strand of hair that had fallen across her eyes, and put a chubby hand to her spectacles case. Then in a chance insight she saw, when she opened it and snapped it shut, how jumpy her customer was. And it was mechanical, she thought, the way he stirred his slops again. She scanned for her favourite page in a tabloid – for the uplift of its horoscope – to find only that the paper's fickle mystic had cruelly switched the optimistic trend of recent predictions. An expectant smile was as suddenly wiped from her face. When she looked up, Michael was busy with papers of his own, and her lay prediction endowed that cup with another half-hour of life. But here she was wrong again. He buttoned up his fur, and on his way out returned his manuscript to the warmth and safety of its inner pocket.

Up there in a troubled grey heaven there was no sign of peace, or a lull, and those dizzy, maniacal clouds clashed and cavorted, desperate, it seemed, for whatever their final destination was. A castle clock was oiled and well adjusted, and the wind, rising, whistling through the hollow streets and singing in his ears, whipped up the vents of his coat, or in another gust folded the rings of his hair across his eyes and over his face. The pendulum scarcely made a noise, but he held up a hand – two hands – suppliant things in an elemental rage – though couldn't keep off the winding sheets of rain, those icy eastern vapours soaking his face. The midday promised a bolder strike, when even so a midnight chime was poised to usher in a new, nocturnal life. Little comfort if it meant he wasn't alone. On the sound of a bell, not much time remained. Visible strands of angry ether whirled round a shop girl over by a lighted window, whose footing wasn't sure. The foolish resolve that had brought her out to the naked street was likely to disappear. Like his, her solo attempts to master an intractable townscape would evaporate, confounded by the same infuriating forces that had put her umbrella inside out.

Heralds, harbingers, windswept messengers – winged, mercurial bearers of the news – that tempest the novice conceived on his father's Gothic ramparts – the turbulence, those passing clouds – dissolved. The malign apprentice grew tired of his sorcery – flawed in its melodrama – and returned to his notes, to his book of spells. A decade had closed, a day had almost passed, and in the gloaming, and after six o'clock, the storm died down. A watery fog descended. Michael turned up the collar of his fur and thrust his hands far down in the depths of its pockets. In a maze of Victorian streets he stopped and looked out and at odd moments scanned the house fronts, regretting that an earlier reconnaissance had not given him the sureness of purpose he wanted. There were polychrome lanterns lighting the porches. He moved on and found the address he sought, apartment E, an attic, entered by a staircase, an unattractive iron zigzag at the rear of a period building. He clanged his way up, leaning on the rail, rising through the hanging patches of fog, and paused. Now above the distant housetops, he looked out and across his old home town, at its blobs and spots of orange light, beacons, far out on a human sea, and refracted all around him in little misty haloes. His village and his parents' house were somewhere over there, somewhere in a blur, but he turned and clattered up again – the second, the third, the final flight. What would happen, and would he be home even, Squires, the only old school friend he thought he could approach?

He pressed the luminous buzzer and turned his back on the door, thinking, hoping for something, inspiration, a suggestion. Look! Those oceanic lights! But no. That didn't help. Turning, what should he say? Squires, hello. Or not so assertive, and with a hint of uncertainty? Hello, um, Squires. And should he shake hands, and what about an explanation? Well, I was stumbling about today in the wind and rain, and saw your shop. Well done, by the way: always knew you'd make good. A fluorescent whiteness in the two bow windows brightened up an otherwise gloomy little street, once a haven of green with flower beds, a bin, and benches. Remember? Yes, of course. You can imagine how that drew me in. There was your name on the shopfront, though when I tried the door I saw the sign. Closed for refurbishment. You – I mean you should know this, Squires – I watched two workmen drinking tea and reading the paper. It got me thinking (an inner door opened and a light went on, and that did get him thinking, reflecting again). The wind had blown him round the streets and forced him to an open phone booth, where in the gale – lashing his hair, lashing the flimsy pages – he found his old friend's home address listed in the directory. A latch went back, he turned to face the door, and when it opened – only a crack at first – he already regretted his choice. A warm homey glare crept over the threshold, over Michael's shoes and up his shins. Squires, uncomprehending, stood waiting, a darkish figure in a magnolia hallway, acutely puzzled till Michael announced himself. The two deep furrows in the fleshy ridge above his nose, with his plodding recollection of the name, gradually flattened out.

A plane descended in a blur of red and silver lights, which however fleetingly caught Squires's eye in that pregnant wash of weather beyond his door. He shifted his weight uneasily. 'What can I do for you?' he asked, his tone officious.

Pastel shades and shadows flickered in the low lights of his hallway, where there was a reproduction Dali, whose obituarists had busied themselves only that week. A door, swinging in the breeze, masked, now unmasked, the radial glow of an imitation fire.

Squires's cold blue eyes fixed him intently, and couldn't disguise, in the watery brightness, in the chinks in the slits of their lids, his mistrust. Michael saw, and considered an easy exit, the fog and the dark now all-consuming for that instant, though escape didn't seem possible. Odd memories cast into useful phrases were not viable as preface should he turn his back. He studied Squires's pale, inquiring visage, which in its ten passed years had evolved from a bony oval to its present folds of flab on a squarish frame.

'I just got back today. Haven't had a chance with anywhere to stay.'

'So you naturally thought of me.' Squires pushed open the door and gathered his visitor into a warm scalene of light. On a low polished table, there was a phone.

'You'd better come in.'

Involuntarily, Michael arched his body forward from the waist – a discreet bow – and stumbled over the threshold. He took his bearings at the Dali and turned from that, and looking through a darkish doorframe faced his old friend under the slope of the roof, in his living room, kicking off his slippers. What, what should he say? Nice place. Or I've caught you at a bad time. Or nothing. He advanced, and Squires, looking for his outdoor shoes, turned up the lights at the dimmer.

'Not so easy, is it,' he said, 'after all these years.' Reunions were never quite what you imagined.

Michael unbuttoned his coat. Five or six framed pictures on the walls, photographs from Squires's own camera, caught his eye – autumnal studies mostly, sensitive, detached. Vacated park benches. Late suns in leafless trees. Muddy pools under a hoar frost. All a private departure from the commercial semi-world of wedding shots and child portraits he'd seen in his shop window earlier. Their maker kneeled in the synthetic glow of the fire, tying his shoes.

'As it happens there's a spare room.' At the last tug of the lace he stood up abruptly. 'Through here.'

Michael followed him back to the hall where Squires pointed to a door and stepped through another, and on coming back out was wearing a leather jacket, and clutching a document case. He stepped out onto the iron plinth, into the fog, into the darkness, and with a hand on the rail half turned to look back over his shoulder.

'Well,' he said, 'I shan't be long. Make yourself at home.'

Michael shut the door – 'I'll see you later' – and went to look at his new room.

The keeper of the clocks had somehow gained the upper hand, and where that mythical Orient had at last curtailed the destructive powers of youth, old men with long beards sat at open windows, and looked beyond theirs to an Occidental world. In no sense was a recurrent vibrancy the hum of strong young wings. In the quiet of a strange apartment, Michael tuned his ears and began to search for the source of a background hum. He found, as a first clue, two discarded Arts (Tatum and Garfunkel). Reflecting itself hierocratically in the smoky glass of a table top was the album sleeve for *The Rite of Spring*, and that led him to the hi-fi stack, where Squires had left his turntable still revolving. Michael switched it off at the wall.

He found a notepad and a local paper, and sitting at the table set them out methodically. A borrowed pen fell under the firm grip and mounting pressure of his writing hand. At a sudden, un-guessed at juncture – the defiant ink relenting, spurting through the nib – a gob of sticky blue developed into spiky loops on the upper margin of the listings page he was about to scan. He put a ring round this, '3rd sharer reqd own rm gas c/h quiet sbrn st', but crossed it out again at this: 'non-smoker preferred'. These were similarly highlighted: 'A vacancy has arisen…', 'Hospital porter…', 'Driver…', 'Packer… Good sal, bonus… Shift allnce' – though the generally poor wages didn't tempt him further. He put the paper aside. Instantly his gloomy conscience unveiled a latent theatricality, and Squires, transformed by a further ten, twenty, thirty years, materialised in a bright blue flash of ink. Those deep incisions in the sagging or hanging flab of his face were the marks of permanent military scheming, and the leather jacket had been exchanged for a field coat and glasses. His gloved hands came out from behind his back, and in one was a pointing stick. Michael, blinking, blew him away.

He returned to his new room and kicked over the heap of his coat, abandoned on the floor. He took out his cigarettes and lit up. A steady breeze coming in through the gaps in the sash window unsettled the first plumes of smoke, and sent them in broken waves to the open door. The window frame was stuck, wedged at strategic points with the faded leaves of ancient newspapers. Pearl Harbor slumbered, Stalin shook with Roosevelt, Hiroshima burned, but eventually he loosened it and opened the window. He put his head out and sniffed at the damp air. Down, way down at ground level, light from a patio door tumbled into the creamy swirls of fog, and illumined the reds and golds of a sumac tree. He drew hard on his cigarette – those last, satisfying inhalations – and allowed that orange ember to fall, to spiral down, and watched, in its dying afterglow, while the wet autumn night snuffed it out in its place of rest, in the crack between two flagstones. He kicked over his coat again, and this time took out the dissident's manuscript, just as a key turned in a lock, with Squires coming in and dumping down his document case, and looking surprised at the curls and crosses scrawled on an open newspaper.

Moods, those private islands. Words, marks on a page. Colours, shapes – a flicker of artificial light in an ocean of shadows, spots on a ceiling. A voice. Emotions, secret silhouettes gliding noiselessly in the half-lit alleys of towns and English cities. The spontaneity of real and imagined events, in a shady bar or a low-lit coffee lounge. Human flotsam in an imperfect world – the bewildered players living out their senseless lives in a metropolitan dream, on a continental stage. A nightmare, a treadmill. Turns, bends, divisions. The world, and everywhere you look the world's charade. Monotonous, unending. A deception, as everyone knew.

Squires clattered about with cups and a kettle in his kitchen, and Michael, who rubbed his head and turned away, then back to an empty page, began to write—

Dear M and D,

I see you've moved to the country,

but that wouldn't do. He pushed his fingers through his curls and his hair stood on end at the crown and temples. Squires ignored his madness and stood in the doorframe, appealing, a tatty tea towel slung on one shoulder.

'Tea,' he said.

Michael heard, but didn't understand. He tore off the top sheet and began again—

Dear M and D,

I see you've moved,

and this he screwed tightly into a ball.

'Tea?'

'It's nothing, nothing,' Michael replied, and turned to the dissident's manuscript, and this, with its indecipherable text, its alien alphabet, he couldn't understand either. But the voice, its words, still echoed.

'Well, it's brewing,' said Squires turning back for the kitchen.

A bright sun in a perfect blue heaven began to slide away then plunge from its summit, while S— re-emerged in Michael's recollections, lone figure in a swirl of sand, whose wise admonitions assured this wasn't the time in his brief young life for sleep.

For already he was waking, and in his half-dream dimly perceived that perhaps, perhaps one day, he would learn an undreamt-of language, and in his new resolution, in the cloud and the dust, in his life's thickening fog, would make those first tentative steps, and with quickened strides return to the hearth of his maker – a benign and terrifying father, somewhere, somewhere up there.

Humber

'As they have none of the essence, they have all the externals of men of gravity and wisdom.'
—**Hazlitt, 'Footmen',** *Sketches and Essays* **(1839)**

Preamble

The fourth Gregor Sabre was as fogged up as any public intellectual of his era, given the junk he published and the pampered grads of Exe he put on a pedestal. He owed everything – including the rise and fall of Harold Humber – to the first Sabre, his great grandfather and accidental eminence, who by a lucky fluke bought shares in a Cornish tin mine. Flukes and accidents are prevalent in the life of Harry Humber.

I blame everything on those shares, whose value went from near zilch up to the stratosphere, all on sweated labour. As an investment it made the Sabres rich, and that was the spinoff, unluckily for us – old money the block on anything new and useful. Things run rigid on ancient rules, at least where I come from. You have only to consider how, after decades of piracy and servitude, Cornwall is eviscerated, is left to its craggy shorelines and the departure of its industries, and for compensation is host to an agglomerate of biomes and a trade in pasties, Brussels-approved.

The first Gregor Sabre died in 1872 at the age of sixty-three, having put his next in line through Mordred College, Exe, whose chancellor he knew. That fraternity wasn't academic, resting entirely on an institutionalised after-dinner brandy and cigars. As you learn from its escutcheon, Mordred was founded in the fifteenth century as a Benedictine hostel, unimpeachable in its theology. You see it now as one of those least enlightened cloisters on the rolled green of Exe, its university sandstone oranged by centuries of coastal sunshine and blacked by autumn tempests. A mist winds round its spires and flagpoles and damps its golden pinnacles most months of the year, while a clear horizon and an upland radiant with daylight were never the luminous dome the Sabres inhabited. Sabre the second, whose career started mid-nineteenth century, busied himself with antique furniture, the cathedrals of England, and brass rubbing. That latter occupation was one he learned from William Morris, and turned into a hobby. He died in 1905 having had a good life, oblivious to the social recalibration taking place around him, yet outdoing the sixty-three years of his father, shuffling off his coil at seventy-one.

The third Sabre was born in 1863 and lived the longest yet, to the age of eighty-two, having survived two world wars and a spate of financial crashes. His era demanded a closer connection between the hunt, the grouse moor, and the vulgarity of enterprise. He responded, reading up on economics and starting up a firm – Sabrina Ltd. We applaud, when in the Twenties and Thirties Gregor Sabre the third had the foresight to publish the fashion magazine *How to Dress Up and Influence People*. The fourth and final Sabre (died 1986, age ninety-one) inherited what had turned into a middling middle-class Sabrina and rebranded it Sabre and Sabre (there was no living partner, quirkily). He added to *How* to *Dress Up* an array of coffee-table books on similar lines – *couture*, fabrics, furnishings, the kind of dinner service every home should have, what wallpaper, flower arranging, the typical suburban garden. He later expanded his list into popular science, populist fiction, puff-pastry poetry, drama to match, and other stuff you bought in bookshop candy stores. He was the first to publish Harold Humber, incidental poet, having in that same epoch approached one of his old cronies of Exe (Mordred College again, a family tradition) and appointed his son, Hugh Monmouth, as his first commissioning editor. Monmouth survived into the 1980s, but in the 1970s got his team of interns and researchers to prepare a Life of Harold Humber. Ergo what follows is largely made up of the piecing together of this material. My one caveat centres on a clutch of concluding events, all taking place at an Alpine retreat in Schmutzburg, beyond the scope of what is included here. For those who want to know, refer – if not immediately – to one Jeremy Gard, journalist, whose scoop appeared in the *European Tribune* back in the early Nineties. He was up at Schmutzburg apparently, at the scene of breaking news (you'll find it all gone into meticulously, but *you* can find out where. Other than that, there's nothing I can add).

But, anyway, the Life didn't get written. An aged Gregor Sabre, a grand old octogenarian, was more acutely aware than Monmouth that the company must move with the times. With resort to its pension fund he hired in his place a drunken drug-fuelled rock star (even then in decline), the fizzy-eyed Magnum Snark, whose first job was one of demolition, dismissing the Monmouth-Humber project as socially irrelevant. There's a Snark footnote, one I'm told is historically important, for having found adulation in publicly thrashing his guitar, too young ironically for the setting-in of hair loss, and prone to the lighting of on-stage bonfires, he celebrated a riotous lifestyle in the pride of his working-class roots. By the early twenty-first century he had recast his origins as middle-class, with the claim that his musicianship owed everything to Ravel's piano sonorities, which he had studied assiduously. He even got onto Radio 3 to demonstrate the point.

One other footnote concerns those interns and researchers, whose initials are all I have. You'll see what I mean.

The Signatories

First set of papers comes with the initials OFA, in blue block script, of a name I cannot guess. They're hard to unravel – sloppily typed notes where two clunky index fingers have gathered them as paragraphs. There is a soot of carbon paper, with smudges from an old portable, a machine whose vintage must be the 1970s, a model without a shriek key, or exclamation point, the one character you see inked (rather than typed) in the same blue as the signature. There are lots of them.

OFA had access to an album of black-and-white snaps, creased and curled at the edges, the lighting not so good, and the subject not obedient to the photographer's directions. He, stock still, had a finger poised for the click of his Kodak. The toddler Humber looks dejected at a striped ball rolled in his path. His shorts are baggy and his shirt is hanging out. With hands pocketed he is peering quizzically from behind a compost heap. There is a garden fork stuck in its summit. Steam rises. It's a cold day in the English Midlands. Five, six years later that same boy is dressed in a school blazer and a peaked cap, and a narrow tie, whose pattern is horizontal bars. There isn't a smile, much. There's a coy turning up at the corners of the mouth, which in later school life forms awkward shapes in reciting Tennyson at morning assembly. Our researcher sat down with Humber Senior one autumn afternoon and asked where he thought his son had acquired his unusual, prodigious talent. Did the father cast around perplexed, unable to answer? There is no record of anything Cyril Humber said of his only child.

The paternal idea of talent, the prodigious, the unusual, had more meaning as Humber and Co, the firm of accountants Cyril had started up and ran from his dining room. In his late twenties it had dawned he'd not be offered a partnership, when the practice he'd been articled to – a Courier Bell Chayne, in Nuneaton – saw better prospects in its pool of newly qualified. It cast a rational eye when looking to expand its client list, which didn't fall comfortably on individualists such as Cyril Humber. Ergo Cyril started on his own. The three stooges he planted round his dinner table – an old guy, a young guy, a ninny – with just a phone between them, soon sprouted out as six, listing as specialisms audit, corporate tax, estates management, self-assessment, trusts and executorships – and retirement strategy (useful one day). There was a host of other things the son Harold heard of all the time in the rumble of home life. There are poems about it.

Soon Cyril wished to take on three more and bring his little empire neatly up to the decade (a numbers man), but his wife put her foot down. 'Ursula said no,' not wanting any more pairs of size nines tramping over her doormat every morning. She also wanted her dining room back. 'It was never meant to be an office,' she said. It was not enough that Ursula had a life in the kitchen making jam, attended lectures at the WI, had her Tuesdays rehearsing with the choir, and in the summer did lots of things with crafts and fêtes. Cyril offered to put up an extension on the back of the house, with his gang of employees entering by the garden gate, forever thereafter confined to the Humber and Co control centre, cordoned off from the domestic running of things. Ursula still said no.

Cyril scratched around and took out a mortgage on a dilapidated property on Franks Crescent, a bustling open market a short drive away in Sackville-in-Ash, the Humbers' local town. He got the place rewired, painted up, refurbished, laid in new carpets and a phone exchange, shipped in a vanload of used office furniture, and put up a big sign – Humber and Co. He got in a receptionist, then a secretary, and reached new heights with a team totalling fourteen specialist accountants, who turned Franks Crescent into a hum of moving capital. The good thing for Junior, and for his mother, was all that shop talk banished from the house. Junior got on quietly with his books and homework, and went off passively to school each day, his satchel bulging – a pleasant stroll under suburban, war-torn skies. There was no teenage angst. No tantrums. Childe Harold was compliant and respectful of his parents' wishes. When not with his books he listened to Glenn Miller, tapping his feet in a repressed English way. On the dot of 8.20 weekdays – and sometimes Saturdays – the self-made Cyril drove the half-mile from home to office, and parked up on Franks Crescent, where he could see, from his office window, his Crossley below – a Regis, black and shiny, and a sparkle of chrome. Ursula's rejuvenated habitat meant garden parties, where with strict officiation she dealt – politely, and efficiently – with the grey men of business her husband brought to her outdoor salads and sandwiches. Her trick was in banding up with all those other wives, who showed affection for one another. Binding that sisterhood was the gentle scorn they shared at the professional world of make-believe their husbands trousered up for every day. The practised OFA cannot ignore a Harold biding his time, upstairs in his bedroom, in the soft caress of 'Moonlight Serenade', his homework done by Sunday lunch. Good boy.

Young Harold's stewardship of the school magazine oversaw editorials on a range of subjects, from handy tips for getting the best from the family allotment, to stuff he'd culled from a WI leaflet on make-do-and-mend. He shows a self-confident flourish, precise and intellectual, in writing an open letter to Air Chief Marshal Dowding. When there was no fallout from that (and probably no reply) he wrote another to Mr Churchill, a praise and a paean singling out the spire of St Michael's Cathedral, in a bombed-out Coventry – a symbol of defiance, and testament to the British bulldog spirit. His English teacher took him aside and asked him to learn by heart long sections from *Idylls of the King*, for recital at school assembly. He did as he was told, Tennyson not his obvious recourse, though the prospect of public performance inspired only diffidence, terror. Turmoil tightened his chest and knotted his stomach, and filled him with a loathing for literature, deadening any waking thoughts for letters as a career. He was treated for asthma and rashes. He learned his lines. He retreated into himself. His schoolwork suffered. Cyril nevertheless enjoyed the summer banquets, those outdoor spectaculars under supervision of his wife, heartily slapping a studious Harold on the back – for what a son they'd got.

Two important things occurred: Glenn Miller disappeared on a flight from London to Paris, and Harold didn't get his first-choice university. He idled his hours filling a notebook with inventive parodies of Victorian English verse. He attempted swing tunes with a roaming right hand, up and down the scale, using an old upright that had belonged with Ursula's family for two generations. Not much came of that. Then one bright September morning the three of them got in the Regis and made the long drive – as far from home as any campus could be – to Mordred College, Exe. There to his father's pride and approval Harold did his degree – in economics.

His room was across the quad from the snappily dressed Hugh Monmouth, whose line in bowties ran on a six-day cycle, in a change for every weekday, plus one he shared over Saturdays and the sabbath. Its pattern was an interlock of black and yellow chevrons. Harold made a note, and looked dejectedly through his wardrobe, grey and utilitarian by comparison. He relied on just two neckties – his old school thing and one in a sober chocolate brown his aunt had sent up for his thirteenth birthday. Hugh gambolled by most mornings under his window, with a smile on his face and the sun in his hair, a deep jet neatly clipped and brilliantined. His entourage was large, and numbered flighty, chatty, ambitious captains of the morrow, for whom Monmouth was the leader and a clear focus of social aspiration. When drunk, he centred the student bar, with loud garrulous talk. The place was humdrum in his absence. He invested his own pewter tankard in the local pub – the White Harp – and drank his beer like an aristocrat. He tipped well, with a vulgar flourish, in Exe's little teashops, and thought the girls there felt it a privilege to be of service. He chaired Mordred's debates with panache, and often imperiously, and for the losers reserved a polite, unpleasant leer. What verse he wrote narrowed itself on the class implications of a politics slow to change, with its raging issues only partially understood by him. If you were of his clan, he was the best man you'd find to fight your corner. Soon he was fighting Humber's.

We pick up the thread with LL, of an epicene hand whose sprawl of notes and asides and stage directions are along as many different vectors. I don't try to guess which, wherever I am – from a stopped jog to a semicoloned jaunt. All is tangled in an LL text, or L, as I was soon on first-name terms. Her specialist interest was Humber's personal interactions, having noticed student Harold's close imitation of the Monmouth style of dress, and the slicked-back look of his hair. Humber's other friend from fresher year was Louisa Muldoon, who was also studying economics. The slew of lectures she missed mid-semester she put down to the anguish of an acute family problem, her mother, father, and a younger brother a long way off in Worcester, having suddenly moved due to changing circumstances. Could she borrow Humber's notes? Why yes, she could, and was astonished at his proficiency, stuff taken down verbatim margin to margin. Come evening, under his reading lamp, there had followed augmenting material, with proper sentence structures. Laid out in precise detail, with books from the Mordred library endlessly quoted, was the sense he made of what, in almost casual throwaway, Exe was there to teach.

'You'll be lecturing *them*,' she said. 'I like the tie. Perfect with that shirt.'

That 'lecturing' consisted of tangibles someone in later decades – Paul Samuelson, and others following – set out more fully as the malady of microeconomics, firmly grasped rather than a groping after, as had been the case in provincial universities a long way off in England. Humber had burrowed into just that paperwork no one took much notice of, and had got his foretaste of at least one phenomenon of modern living, nowadays taken for granted, and something no individual can do much, if anything, about. Economists call it scarcity – not all bad, since it has its trade-offs, in consumer behaviour, in production initiatives, in supply and demand, in the whole gamut we're fed with (fed up with) daily in the news.

Louisa had a bookshop story, which she must have related to L, or Elle as I call her, as now I am almost certain of her identity. She looped arms one autumn afternoon with a coy-looking Humber, and marched him off into the parades and cobbled backways of

Exe, where she set out to test his patience, and judge his devotion, in a drawn-out expedition locating the right shade of lipstick, a process she had gone through once before in the suburb of her birth, on the Northern Line, and now must begin again in exile out in the wilds. She said as a kind of quaintness how the towns, depending on physical geography, were raked by a salty wind whipped in across the shale or sand or pebbles along the coastline, which prickled her flesh, or from an inland direction by a swirling moorland breeze, whose fungal aroma got in her clothes and hair. Humber hadn't noticed. He wondered had he got time to buy a cigarette case, one like Monmouth's, who opened it and snapped it shut with such flamboyance. For now they bought neither, as in a damp backstreet they paused at a bookseller's, whose collection of cut-price titles had been laid out on trestle tables outside on the pavement. What caught Louisa's eye was a second edition *Economics Explained: From Adam Smith to Keynes*, which neared the top of the Mordred reading list, at a price she could afford. Humber said the third edition had got new material, on wages, inflation and unemployment, which she couldn't do without, and with not a trace of smugness said he'd got it – brand new – courtesy the aunt who had sent him his birthday ties. Louisa picked up, flicked through and put down what was, disappointingly, this well-used, inferior, second-hand edition. 'Let's go inside anyway.'

They did. Louisa browsed. Humber absorbed himself in a small hardback collection of Jack Gilbey religious poems, which surprised her. She plodded round without strategy, and bought a bookmark. Humber couldn't make up his mind but went off eventually with Stephen Spender's *Vienna* taped in a brown paper bag and tucked under his arm. Back at his room he put it with his pile of books, according to Louisa a leaning tower, a precarious-looking structure on the edge of his desk. There also, spread out fulsomely, were his papers and the essay he was writing. Louisa – certain he couldn't see, but he could – pushed aside a top leaf and found underneath the doggerel he'd concocted. As a distraction from work in hand, it helped in the thinking process, which Louisa said was an interesting theory. She adjusted her hair, with that provocative, unconscious mannerism he'd begun to get used to, and would immortalise in reams to come. 'You're a very good poet,' she said, but he did not read in the simplicity of that remark what else it communicated. There was no time anyway, as now Monmouth breezed in with a *coup* for the Mordred Union, and confirmation of his next two speakers – the *for* a newspaperman, the *Sunday Chronicle* or something, and against, the *versus*, Exe's MP (a Tory). Come the day – or rather early evening, while the bars were open – the Union's tiny debating chamber was packed to overflowing. Monmouth chaired, in his usual imperious way. The motion, *this house believes* etc., was a brief distillation from a much longer statement, an article he'd read, positing the USA as *the* primary power, with natural rights in policing the world. *If* that nation's leadership could act as global overseer, was the question. The correct answer was the correct brake on a worn-out Europe and its wars. Monmouth's polite put-downs against a rural Toryism, dismissive of America as adolescent, too young in its democracy, and in its lack of wisdom liable to error, won huzzahs and chair scrapes and hoots from the floor, so you saw from the beginning who the winner was. And Louisa liked winners.

She told Monmouth he should speak to his uncle Gregor about getting Humber published, which he said he would do. 'But,' he added, 'Gregor isn't my uncle.' Sabrina Ltd had long metamorphosed into Sabre and Sabre. The fourth Gregor, scion of that clan, for the fun of it had geminated into two, with that ghostly other presence stalking his letterheads. His Majesty's stationers had co-opted his only editor, a spinster of middle years, who mainly opened the mail and made the tea. Her project to date was the production of pamphlets for distribution throughout this sceptred isle, but aimed specifically at the Home Guard, to do with blackout procedures, fuel dumps vis-à-vis the black market, and instruction on how to identify a German spy. As a publishing event it took the codename 'Hit It Home', a kind of riddle of the *Stanz*, one every villager must come to know. On the phone Uncle Gregor talked a lot of 'Hit It Home', and asked young Monmouth when would he next be in London. He didn't know, but he'd talk to Humber about putting a manuscript together, for these were exciting possibilities. When that Hugh of all hues next saw Humber he was on a park bench, under a twirl of falling leaves, a red and yellow scarf wrapped once round his neck and dangling on his lapels. This was his quiet moment of retreat as he plumbed the pages of *Vienna*, a stillness prompting the only lines of Spender Monmouth was able to quote—

The city is
A desert. Corinthian columns lie
Like chronicles of kings felled on their sides....

Humber said how true that was, as even then he'd a strong sense of ruin in all human affairs. For now it deflected talk of Sabre and Sabre, with Uncle Gregor (not his uncle) allergic to men (and men particularly) of a melancholy disposition, though Hugh was as good as his word and meant to keep his promise to Louisa.

For her there were other differences, a crack and then a chasm, between her two men. The next when partially revealed – and probably misconstrued – was when Monmouth turned pale and was nauseous, vomited copiously, ditto diarrhoea, doubled up with stomach cramps and other assaults, and was diagnosed with gastroenteritis. He took to his bed and groaned, listening for as long as stamina allowed to the crackle of programmes broadcast unapologetically by the Home Service, when a much better job he thought he could do. He wondered about an introduction, Portland Place, though the pay would have to be right. Louisa came to his rooms and read to him, though initially it didn't augur well. The tome she brought was Humber's third edition *Economics Explained*, not exactly sickbed reading, as Monmouth protested.

'I'm opening a window,' she said.

He sat up. She plumped his pillow. She remarked on the stripe of his pyjamas. She opened the book and drew out of it loose manuscripts and delivered – in her best altar oratory – latest, Spenderian versicles penned by their friend from across the quad.

'So, what do you think?'

Monmouth's judgement wasn't at its best, he said, when his mind, body and soul were clouded by illness, though – in his loyalty to her – he restated his promise to talk to Uncle Gregor and swing a publishing deal.

'You said he isn't your uncle.'

'He isn't – but it's family. Sort of.'

Next Union combat was between, on the one hand, a regius professor and Christian apologist, and on the other a Russellian sceptic – names not mentioned (Elle can be detailed, but does not tar the innocent offender, much less feather). 'I can't do it,' Monmouth said. 'Someone else will have to chair.' That someone was Humber, who lacked the Monmouth *éclat*, though by his demurs, hesitations, the involuntary rise of his eyebrows, Louisa detected not the diffidence of someone cast in someone else's shadow, rather a patrician coolness in one who knew better – was cleverer, and more thoroughly informed – than the two locked in debate.

She reported back how well it had gone.

Now come squibs and a minor rebellion, and our third expert witness, initials FO. FO was supposed to gather notes and other material in a round-up of Humber's academic progress, with its post-graduate high point beyond and after Exe. He got a first in economics, and earned his due in confetti and congrats. But then with warlike masculinity FO doesn't mention by name the college of Harold's MA. We are supposed to know it, from the allusions he offers. A clue is repeated mention of industrialist Sir Nicholas Chamoogan, as thanks rain down for his generous benefaction. That gallant knight opened up his troves on a regular basis, even, on one occasion, restoring the college library after a mains leak had caused catastrophic flooding. Humber was among the first beneficiaries, a test case for an index system long overdue its overhaul, one of those dedicated students able to sit for hours in the library's varnished pews, all of them newly hand-crafted. A lot of old books had been shipped in from Massachusetts, at enormous cost. The one other thing we learn of that sojourn is the back room in a pub in Jericho where the Exe Set, as so it styled itself, met for readings of its own and others' work. Core members of the group (FO doesn't conceal a smirk at the word 'core') were said to be Hugh, Harold and Louisa, listed in order of seniority, that trio dispersed in a triangle Marston, Summertown, Jericho. Honorary members, those picked up on the way and having no origin in Exe, boosted the numbers. Now, when we look them up – I have open under 'E' a *Companion to English Literature* – we've a roll of names of well-known journalists, TV people, poets, dramatists, prize-winning novelists, all at one time or other claiming membership of the Exe Set, 'a major force in twentieth-century life, culture and letters'.

Things turn very nasty. I can't help suspect that FO might once have been in close observation in the back streets of Jericho, but didn't make the cut in elevated company. Was the floor once opened to all-comers, and FO read a poem, or a few passages from a novel in progress, and got only distant looks and no applause, and left the pub? He goes on to say that a paper shortage delayed Sabre in its plans for Humber's debut collection, *Cracks in the Plaster of Time*, that title borrowed from a line in what was the lead poem. Here too was something else raising FO's temperature. Under the grey clouds of a shattered, post-war Europe, the victors with a threadbare economy and austerity prevailing, a select few managed easy, well-paid jobs, where opportunities generally didn't exist. He can't understand why, FO naïve enough to believe in university as preparation for life in a meritocracy. He extrapolates to less benighted days, or the period where he is called on to compile his recollections (Thatcher's boom-town 1980s), and says what a fit-up everything is, Louisa by then the matriarchal head of Burbidge and Pemburt, a Bloomsbury-based literary agency, with a long list of Booker-winning authors numbered as her clients. Hugh was always in the weekend reviews, pontificating on the English and American novel, and was on TV almost endlessly when there were book and culture programmes, and at one time had his own radio show, interviewing authors as to their intimate secrets of composition. He had a penchant for lady novelists, and had a string of affairs, news of which reached other pages in the broadsheets he wrote for. It all got out of hand, FO's notes ending mid-sentence – 'Can't help think that paper shortage should have gone on indef—' – as the commission ended abruptly, and he was no fan of Humber's poetry.

There is deep emphasis in the scoring out of FO's initials, to be replaced by OTM-E, a double barrel some may speculate on. I have discovered a Merrick-Eveleigh, a Tory politician. I have read up on the peerage and see her family had close connections with the organist at Exe's cathedral, in the era of Humber's time on the margins, as a first banishment – miles from London, miles from life – in those three precious years as an undergrad. Or there's a Matheson-Earnshaw, a tennis ace turned children's author. She signed for Burbidge and Pemburt shortly after the *coup de théâtre* that brought it into being, a splinter from a larger agency, one brutally commercial. It began with a clientele of three from a back room in Kentish Town, having learned what strictures apply in the making of jagged architectures, which the book world often is. Or might there be some other construction I haven't noticed, less attentive as I now am to the gossip columns? Whatever, Opal Tamsin Matheson-Earnshaw never looked back. She, or rather OTM-E, took on wholeheartedly the bombardiering propaganda set in train and never relaxed by a calculating Hugh. Monmouth, from the moment he was Sabre's commissioning editor, puffed out smoke signals from under the damp blanket of his little literary underworld, and never relented in its message written across the sky. That posturing made of his Exe Set one of the most important moments in modern English letters, a testing hyperbole only hardening in his dotage – when other schools had come and gone and rendered it anonymous. For even then he still talked fondly of his pet Humber as the finest poet a post-war English-speaking world had yet produced. That was a chauvinism OTM-E fully entered into, a bold skip and energetic dance where lesser angels feared to tread. For don't forget, somewhere in the rear there's a skulking FO, whose scepticism can't be ignored.

And yet that wasn't the summit of OTM-E's contribution, as, finally, my wager is that it *was* Opal. She recalled a writing epoch when everyone wanted participation in a movement, and had to admit Hugh's Set of Exe was politically the most sophisticated, having in its arsenal powerful means to position itself, with a new loud voice added to Gregor Sabre's. Its clarion was *Cracks in the Plaster of Time*, Humber's first foray into print, a thin collection of landscape poems, which – despite its long introduction, in eloquent, self-effacing prose – struggles to reach the fifty-page mark. There is not much progress, from first poem to last, when all in Humber's aesthetic is a whirr of coastal towns, wet streets, blurred suns, grey-to-tawny tides, rock pools, crevices, and thrown in at last a stick to tickle a crab. There is vague allegorical matter as to the human condition, showing in turf stacks and lone stone cottages, and the private life as a thing driven over potholed roads. Concrete pillars stride glum and majestic across the fields and over the hills. There are wild hedgerows, leaping fish in spate, a spotting of poppies dotting the ripening corn. In a collision of seasons the thatch is mossy, the well is rust, hogweed grows by the barn, plovers howl, there's a mackerel sky, and there are larches in the copse. The swallows have dropped their pellets into the saxifrage. There are festival joys when the weir is loud, and dancers dance on the lawn. (Heigh-ho.) A last sequence staggers from page forty-eight, first with a spade in pebbled earth slicing into the loam, then with a twist in dry air of a beet leaf, then, finally, with a combe brindled with primrose. It appears Humber more or less disowned his little book on its first and final printing, and dragged that diffidence with him when Hugh coaxed then actively shoved him into the arena of his art wars.

He mumbled in public debate. He baulked. That reticence all agreed was the demur of a supremely gifted intellect when Humber also had a heart. He took no pleasure in belittling those of lesser talent, or the majority put in his path. Then one afternoon Louisa got him on the phone and told him she'd arranged a spar contest as twenty-minute radio broadcast, his opponent a logical positivist fresh out of Trinity, Cambridge. One only imagines his despondency as he put on his raincoat and left his rented room, his domicile a rain-streaked, three-storey house in Camberwell, and picked up his umbrella on his way out. He got the bus and Underground to Kentish Town, intent on Louisa's calm, her reassurance, and found only the incessant bell of her phone in the shoebox of her office. Humber, pale and ashen, stood in her doorway, statuesque. She cradled the phone. She took it off the hook.

'You look ill.'

'It's this radio thing.'

She knew the other speaker, 'a boy wet behind the ears'. How was his new landlady?

'A rough sort of diamond.'

'Harry, you don't need to look so worried.'

'It's all right for you.'

'Honestly, you'll sail through.'

His sparring partner, as projected, was one David Ballard, whose argument was along the lines that it's only through logic, the language of maths, and the special sciences (define 'special', please) that meaningful statements arise and have cognitive significance.

Young Ballard wasn't purely atheist – he lived on a hop, half-in, half-out, agnostic – though he spouted a philosophy that regarded metaphysical, religious, ethical, literary, and aesthetic pronouncements as, well, nonsense. It was the job of the author of *Cracks in the Plaster of Time* to put up a spirited defence of what abstract thinking had brought that book into being, and was selling well.

'We're sure you can do it.'

NTH was sure he couldn't, but had the benefit of hindsight. I have a feeling that whoever NTH was, or is, he, she, was Louisa's friend or colleague or both. I have been looking through the author index of anthologies of that period, and arrive at the irrational conclusion that NTH was Natalie Hoorihane (1915-86), a poet no longer of our firmament, but whose subject matter was heroes, dictators, the overthrow of capitalism, above all mobilisation of the committed, though she'd nothing but scorn for the Exe Set. What did it do, she asked? It did not tog itself up in dungarees and hobnails and take to the streets in protest, and offered nothing in its editorials beyond a well-tried aesthetic, whose territory didn't extend from the drawing room. We'd all had enough of that. She tuned in to the radio for the Ballard-Humber discussion – 'if discussion you could call it'. Unlike his advocates she did not interpret Harold's haws, ums, hesitations as those of an elevated being remote in his grove, his habitat an impossible intellectual plateau. 'No,' she said. Those huge obstacles he experienced in descending, on his winged heels down to the sand-blown, war-torn, theatre kitchenette, into the studios of intelligent exchange – they weren't 'merit' (that's to say they weren't the demur of a man who did not like to humiliate others), they were 'mental'. A block. A persistent inability. I have no proof, as no recording seems to exist, and there isn't a transcript. I can say only the Ballard name did not make any later impression, while of course Humber is still revered as a swing-loving lyricist and authentic voice of his time. Louisa was slow to share the Hoorihane view, but thought that address in Camberwell was an inhibiting factor. Hugh agreed. But had a solution, in a friend of the Sabre family, whose cottage in Pinner (now demolished) was one he vacated annually when wintering in the Bahamas. The four met up on the doorstep, Kentish Town, and later, in a hotel lounge, they talked like civilised people over a pot of tea, with the net result the Pinner keys were handed to Humber.

He couldn't have known how to run a house. Bills from the milkman were tucked into the throat of the one empty he always left behind, with Humber unable to master the mechanism by which to settle up, or how to adjust when as milestone he'd attained a larder full of pint bottles. For the housewarming, he invited Louisa round for a Sunday roast, but at the last moment cancelled. All he'd got as a side serving was a brown paper bag with carrots turning black and deliquescent. She came over anyway, with an onion, and sautéed the potato. He seemed to spend a lot of his time in the tiny rectangular kitchen, with its hanging pots and pans and small utility table. There were two chairs. He was watching, he said, for what changes took place in the garden, a blank wildness under a dusting of hoarfrost, sometimes a robin on a twig. He'd a fondness for the red coffee pot

– as of all such items courtesy his absent landlord – whose enamel was chipped, but as part of his daily ritual was seldom void of the lukewarm sludge he liked to drink. Natalie was merciless in her analysis of Humber's precious hermit hours, an aloneness or removal from the world's 'real' events, a detachment spawning too many useless bourgeois poems, of no social function. She remarked that, because of his powerful friends – not least that Exe Set general, the effete Hugh Monmouth – such trivial verse Humber had a facility for had begun to appear endlessly, the stream constant, in the journals they all read and sometimes in newspapers. With the latter Louisa landed him a regular column, where he wrote about the 78s in his father's collection, as he tapped pen and feet to a jangle of unexpected syncopations. In opposition, Natalie marched to the sabre-rattle of Petrograd overtures, and dismissed his soft listening as decadent West.

She wasn't replaced. Monmouth, to his credit, put up with her jibes. He was prepared to meet her socially, and had a favourite teashop, in a quiet West End corner, where he frittered his time stirring in his sugar cubes and trying to placate her. That blue collar, belt-and-braces diatribe she said publishing was destined to become he agreed had its place, and added as caveat *his* tribe wasn't hers – 'and don't you forget that'. Humber had no lack of encouragement in the girding up for political battle, but immersion in it had to be on his fighting terms. She wanted to know what terms those were, in quoting – or misquoting – one of his new Pinner poems, as he called them. Central image was a thrush perched on the handle of a garden fork, whose prongs were plunged into a clod of frozen soil. Hugh asked wasn't it a Christmas robin? 'It doesn't matter,' she said. These were soap bubbles, a floating iridescence designed for a befuddled middle class. Their only purpose was in the preservation of the status quo. When she later met Louisa, she referred to Hugh, and the conversations they'd had, with turned, lathed, well-engineered witticisms, and none of that acerbity she had shown to him. The two girls tittered. Louisa had as like specialism well-aimed mortars. She revealed – with one of her smiles – that Humber had confessed frankly he was temperamentally unsuited to a life as public intellectual, and was ditching it for work in the bank.

'Oh. What work is that?' She didn't ask which bank.

When, at interview, Humber was asked what his dream job would be, he responded without pause, without hesitation. He envisaged himself buried in the financial pages of the quality newspapers, for three, three and half days per week, and as outcome writing up his report for the board each Friday, outlining what he saw as economic trends the bank should act on. For the rest of the time he'd concentrate on other things in Pinner. Guffaws. A cackle of laughter. Humber even went so far as to tell his friends that was the job he'd landed, a claim borne out by the facts, as it seemed, when he chose a different tie each day, and set off for the commuter train swinging his umbrella. I don't know whether anyone took the trouble to follow him on one of those three and a half weekdays, or offer to meet him for lunch, somewhere in a little pub or restaurant near his place of work – as anyway where that was, its precise location, someone known to Louisa discovered only by accident. Louisa must have quizzed, but got nowhere, as according to Natalie this was Humber at his most coy, or painfully shy, ill inclined to talk about his daily life. 'Does he have a girl?' Louisa didn't think so, and didn't like to mention he'd always had a special glint in his eye for her. That came to nothing, of course. It was well documented – it was all over the literary press and spilt into the gossip columns – when Louisa finally married one of her clients, the novelist, or writer of penny dreadfuls, Jolyon Lyons. There are photographs still in the public domain. It was a sumptuous, rice and confetti wedding, the day a bit blowy, the Ides of March, central London, and everyone was there. Even Humber.

Monmouth thought he dealt with it well, and showed no sign of regret, or anger with himself. He bought a decanter and had it inscribed with their initials as a wedding gift, and was one of the first to raise a toast when someone generously poured firewater from it. There are rumours that on returning to Pinner he wrote them a prothalamion, in a jingle of couplets. If this is so, only the happy couple has seen it.

Then his little secret came out accidentally, and was hushed up immediately. Angelina Boothroyd, one of Louisa's bridesmaids, a pretty, freckled girl, blossom-cheeked, her coiffure a mass of golden ringlets, and popular with her uncles, set off for her branch in Edgware on a blustery afternoon, with a cache of birthday cheques in her purse, a small fortune ready to pay in. Wind and rain wound round in sheets, and her beret wouldn't stay put. She folded it and pressed it into her raincoat pocket, and arrived – a wild Amazon – and took her place in the queue, in Humber's place of work, a hushed inner temple subdued in its ambience, dark with its varnished woods and a little less palatial for the ruts in its marble. She recognised her teller as that funny lean wolf of a man, quaint in his spectacles, who hardly spoke to anyone at Louisa's reception. She smiled pertly as Humber handled her cheques, though he didn't identify her – he scarcely looked up – as someone he'd previously met. It got back to Louisa in only a matter of days. She mentioned it. 'Harold, you don't remember Angelina?' A lovely girl, yes – but no, 'Should I?' He explained away his presence at the counter as a suddenly busy period, exacerbated by a high incidence of sickness within his staff, and there was no nobler thing to do than volunteer. Louisa didn't challenge. Instead she listened patiently when Humber had got himself into a spiral of enthusiasm now that he contemplated a first novel – its working title *A Girl Like Her* – and what research he thought he'd have to do. 'Oh, all well and good,' she said. 'I'll find you a publisher,' though she was less committed to that on finding *A Girl Like Her* was a girl like her.

'I will let Angelina know what a chance meeting it was, you down briefly from that ivory tower. How *is* the economy?'

He entered into great technicalities, though, in all, at least Natalie wasn't fooled.

Nor did our next expert witness allow himself to be fooled. He was astonished, perplexed. I know it for a fact, because he says so, in the bunch of papers I've been given. He signs himself ELO. Those three innocent initials appear at the foot of his last perforated page, and are there in ballpoint, circa the early 1980s, a production turned out on jumbo, green-and-white-striped computer paper, via a line printer whose dots don't always join.

I gather ELO was Humber's first editor of sorts, whom Louisa allocated to him, but not in an official capacity. The house he worked for, noted for its list in translated greats (Flaubert was one, Anatole France another), had no dealings with Humber, and would not have taken him into its fold on the strength of an editor's recommendation. ELO had freedom in other ways, as a man always in transit from one gathering to the next, and never asked to account for his time. As long as he got his mark-ups done, and on his boss's desk, he could rove the Soho bars and stroke the hand of London's intelligentsia, and smoke unfiltered cigarettes, as much as he liked.

I am not certain ELO had much to do with Humber quitting the bank. He reports a conversation where Humber fumes – in that genteel, repressed English way he had – at his bosses' inaction, and how short-sighted they showed themselves to be in ignoring his recommendations. I don't know what Louisa would have made of that. For a moment Humber looked tall in Texan boots and a broad-brimmed hat, in announcing the bank would have to do without him. 'Extraordinary,' as I quote ELO. 'My other problem,' Humber said, 'is this opening chapter.' ELO took a look. He agreed with Humber. He needed to sharpen his technique when it came to characterisation, though only an idiot wouldn't have guessed to whom the paean, *A Girl Like Her*, was addressed. I am urged not to name names, when one afternoon, long after closing time, Humber and his alter ego ELO were in a back bar in a pub at a private reading, though the poet they'd come to hear – a dipsomaniac – ended his rendition prematurely, collapsing in a heap of manuscript paper, writhing in the sawdust, his gills gone green on a chaser too many. No matter. ELO had taken a fine toothcomb to that tentative opening chapter, and showed his debut novelist, in the marks of his blue crayon, what improvements he had made. Humber scratched his head. 'Let me take it away. Consider.' He took it away, considered. He came back, having reached the conclusion that every little touch his editor had performed – he introduced a grimace here, or somewhere else the tilt of a hat – was borne of good academic training, but lacked the vitality of everyday flesh and blood. 'A good job, and thanks. But all this is learnt. Not experienced.'

They reconvened in that same back bar one evening, where a stout working type, ol' Lil, a fag in her mouth, hammered out Variety tunes on a tuneless piano, surrounded by beery cheery singers, who chorused as she sang, explosively until— *Hurry up please it's time.*

Descent. With the landlord's final bell, and a last lace of suds sliding down pint and half-pint glasses, Humber chose his moment. All for the sake of that beleaguered opening chapter, his adopted role was of theatre magnate, his spine straight, his expression overripe in teasing ol' piano Lil into conversation. He'd got her cornered, assailed – 'Gorblimey love' – and advised her to get an agent, as a gilded life on Drury Lane would surely be hers. 'And that was it,' ELO tells us. From now on Humber got to grips with his fantasist's craft in acting out parts, here on Shakespeare's stage, here in all the world. 'It was extraordinary to watch.'

A catalogue follows, of things ELO witnessed for himself. Instance Humber at a railway kiosk, where he asks for a slim panatela, first in fluent Spanish, then in broken English. He was with him at Piccadilly Circus, a chance meeting, when Humber veered off suddenly, and marched them to Oxford Street. He'd remembered the purpose of his errand was to buy a new pair of shoes, brown, pointed, unsuitable things, with a paisley pattern machined into the uppers – not his style at all. He walked round with an old shoe on, black and scarred and dimly polished, as partner to the one the shop girl showed him. As a limping Long John Silver, he got what he thought was a coarsened pirate patois. That persona changed to matador when he stood at a full-length mirror and surveyed himself toe to tip, thrusting out an arm where the cape would be. 'You've been reading Hemingway.' He started to wear bowties, and there were gestures, mannerisms, reminiscent of Hugo Monmouth. There was an occasion when ELO plus one were invited to a private showing, in a gallery in Marylebone, and at the last minute the plus one had to drop out. 'It was crazy to watch these eccentricities.' Humber made up the numbers, and examined the hangings at close quarters as if through a monocle. His imitation royalty, trained for these things, was hands clasped and kept in an interlock behind his back. It wouldn't do to fidget, a man confronted by swirling abstractions – a rampage of primary colours – or show how little he knew of what to make of them. 'Very apt comment,' was most often the utterance. He signed the guestbook Alain Patouille, in a sweep of changing shapes, with the A and the P two strutting enormities, pillars under which those other letters marched in a forward slant.

Then one day ELO had mixed blessings, with Humber one of the first to know his career had moved on, as now he'd rung the changes. His new job was at Lloyd's Register – better prospects, a solid salary. Upshot was, Humber had best find someone else – a new editor – to help him over the bumps and blocks and smooth the way for that opening chapter. 'Oh. Congratulations. But why,' asked Humber, '*mixed* blessings?' ELO had trawled his contacts, and thought the best he could do for Humber was a young theatre critic who had just set up in a flat near the Elephant and Castle. 'You'll always find him somewhere off the Shaftesbury Avenue.' Humber agreed to meet him, but had news of his own. His landlord was back from the Bahamas next Wednesday, so why not have dinner *this* Wednesday, my place, before I move out. 'Bring your friend.' Ergo the three met at Pinner. Apart from comedy and slapstick, what that has given me is another batch of papers, whose different testaments, dated weeks apart, bear the initials WEST. Or at least I thought they were initials, though I revised that view when in later phases only the W was capitalised. West it seems is a surname.

On the menu was charred offal and a baked potato apiece. When the two guests arrived Humber was in a chef's hat he'd got from somewhere, and was wielding a fish slice. 'Come in, come in.' West, who at that time knew no better, had brought a bottle of cheap wine, a non-vintage vinegar, which Humber, whose ignorance matched his guest's, opened and decanted. A long time it took to find a corkscrew. But, 'Very palatable.' Introductions were made, ELO giving us extended details as to West's meticulous decomposition of the musicals someone paid him to review – a daily – and how he liked to go backstage and get to know the cast. Humber would be interested to know that entering its third month was a show the writer had adapted from his own novel, putting up personal finance to get the thing put on. 'It's a tough business.'

It's an episode that might have gone on gently to another conclusion, the three cramped at a makeshift dining table in that tiny kitchen in Pinner, with a stack of plates, pans and cutlery awaiting the washing-up, a clutter in the sink. At ten, when Humber still hadn't drawn curtains or otherwise tucked the house in, a car pulled up. He had gone out front to the living room, looking for spirits – or anything – as a round-up on the decanter the three had emptied. His hand was on the light switch. West stumbled by in search of the facilities. ELO hooted something. Ballooning headlights swept across the hall, then died suddenly as did the engine. The car was unladed. The driver was paid. A key in the lock followed a soft patter of feet in the porch, and the front door opened. I don't propose to recount what undignified drollery West reports as the climax of that evening. I am given the spectacle of Humber in a stammer, insisting emptily that his landlord – a Douglas Pye – wasn't due back for another week, and in verification made a theatrically close inspection of the calendar hung on the kitchen door, where the fault was his own. 'You've marked the wrong date.'

Pye, a mild-mannered man, would not allow Humber to strip and change the bed – the one bed in the one-bedroom house. He was tired after his long journey, and quietly asked the other two to leave, and probably spent a sleepless night on his living-room couch. Humber, appalled at how remiss a tenant he had been, packed up his things the following day, and according to West led a nomadic existence for the next few months, eventually finding a room in a rambling house in Ealing, owned by a Polish widow, who also owned a grocery store. She had a nice back garden, walled.

He carried out his threat and left the bank. With that as his preoccupation he had no time to consider or comment on friend Hugh's next decisive move. Monmouth – who wanted more than a footnote in history – had made the political decision to relocate the Exe Set to Covent Garden (*vaguely* was the word he used). News was he'd convened its first meeting in this new, and much more appropriate setting, in the lounge bar of the Strand Palace Hotel, and of course Humber – the first poet, the era's finest – must make himself available. 'Ah very good,' said Humber. What Hugh hadn't mentioned was a new recruit, to me known only by the initials he has left, as I sift these testaments. I don't think it would take much to find out who he was, *if* I could be bothered. I know him as CLA, and that's enough. In many ways CLA was Monmouth's secret weapon. He'd edited some godforsaken journal that has long disappeared, and once had the vision to publish Randall Swingler. Or perhaps Swingler had taken pity, in granting use of his name in that middling press its proprietor never stopped bragging about. This thing I'm unravelling – it's middling in every sense.

Hugh's interest was in handing him incendiaries. These he lobbed into what for now was deemed the opposition camp. 'Opposition' was always designated 'cosy middle class', an irrepressible grouping that had got a monopolistic hand to everything, our living culture prime on its list. He didn't like to see an educated person writing streetwise stuff, when only someone like Malamud could do it. He thought there were other ways a poet should seek to popularise himself. He deplored the handful of distinguished feminist writers he knew about, but only because he liked an argument. And argumentative he was. After all, he was a general, and the Republic of English Letters was his theatre of war, while whisky and soda – that was his drink. Hugh urged him to write the Exe Set manifesto, tacitly of course.

'Another whisky?'

'Bless you.'

CLA reports, self-admiringly, that his presence at the Exe Set's centre was Humber's first serious experience of rivalry. Humber didn't take it well, baulking at every decision, and moodily silent when CLA's publishing credits were mentioned – which was often. As reviewer he'd achieved scholarly distinction, and knew his way through an amphibrachic undergrowth. He suspected others did not, and that qualified him to dismiss as 'poor' or 'pretentious' *his* rivals, mostly other reviewers. As a poet (note, Humber), he had been in the vanguard, among the first to dabble in a new, complex level of caesura, resulting in a lot of white space on the page. With those technicalities as edifice, a brick-built wall kept the masses out. Then with impunity CLA was able to raise the stakes. He took our leading poet aside on one of these Strand Palace dos, his whisky and soda cautiously in reach. His sole purpose and gift to the English-speaking world was in critiquing the latest protégé enlisted with him, with Humber expected to show good collegiate attitude. Humber did not. He greatly resented being told, so to speak standing before his headmaster, how much he had wasted his time on too many country garden poems, a dial round the seasons others had done a thousand times before. CLA had had someone copy Humber's last published piece, a quaint little lyric, its subject a young lover at her window brushing her hair and looking out to sea. It was CLA's job to make it clear: this kind of stuff was no longer needed. What an intelligent reading public should receive instruction in was a rapidly changing landscape, urban over rural, and the rush for technological industrialisation, and what that meant for the huddled mass. 'You think you can do me something like that, Harry?' Harry took refuge in a wilting Chapter One, and ran off to Louisa, complaining of ill-intentioned people getting in his way, none of whom he chose to name. What they had failed to understand was that the cycle of poems currently under construction was an exercise, the preliminary draft in the scene-setting his novel must be disciplined for.

'What people, Harold?'

'Oh just people.'

We don't get much about his new job. Monmouth, when assembling his team of researchers, by what means I don't know, managed to find one of Humber's colleagues, who signs himself SSI. According to Humber, his entry point into city finance was as strategist. His employer, a Panamanian with a taste for extravagant hats, had set up office on Cheapside, a location Humber was seldom to be found at. He claimed to have important meetings all the time, and a client list burgeoning with brokers. It took him all over the Square Mile. 'Sounds exciting,' said Louisa. Not so, said SSI. According to him

Humber's role entailed a stash of brown envelopes and the delivery of documents – contracts awaiting signature, whose locality was private addresses in Metroland, the zone he'd been allocated. He got back into town once in every two to three days, and before setting off on the next jaunt up the Met Line was seen hanging round the stage door where one of those musicals (or see above) was playing. SSI speculated on a chorus girl Humber was involved with. His only substantiation was brief sightings on a series of crisp autumn mornings, when – at a distance – Humber chatted animatedly, his interlocutor a redhead, distinct in a maroon beret, a long fawn coat, the belt tied rather than buckled, and boots severe in their lacing. She stamped her feet, either cold or angry. We are near that little café where SSI and Humber took breakfast together, though only when paths crossed, which happened when both were recalled to Cheapside, when respective brown envelopes were emptied and there were new assignments pending. 'Got to know him quite well,' says SSI, though was always puzzled at the variety of accents used in ordering his egg on toast, or asking for a second cup. 'I assumed he'd theatrical ambitions himself.'

There was one other who got to know him well, whose seal, in block, bureaucratic capitals, was STH. STH has offered a generous description of Humber's new descent with his Polish landlady, the widow Urbanowicz. The house was red-brick, rambling Edwardian, with a long frontage, fenced and adorned with trellised roses on the border with the street, the street made up of flagged pavements broad enough for two old-fashioned prams to pass, and a roadway built for trucks. The house with its roofline was an ornament of coping stones – long loops and curlicues – and had symmetry in its gabling, and at night towered with shadowy chimneystacks. The windows were leaded, and had – as special feature – a filter of coloured lights patterning the front door – an ultramarine sea, a galleon with a billow of wind in its sails, yellow sunbeams. The rear garden was a private paradise, enclosed in a high wall, whose far end – its view distant from the widow's bedroom window – was studded with fruit trees her gardener had meticulously pleached. There were flowerbeds. The lawn's insistent rectangle was broken as a spectacle by a meandering path to the tool shed. There were little statuettes, scantily clad naiads transplanted into suburbia from Arcadia, nymphs looking sad in a lament for lost lakes, rivers, springs and fountains. Nearest reminder of home was an outdoor tap and a hose coiled and hung on the back wall. STH took care to point out that all the houses in the street were of similar grandeur, but only Mrs Urbanowicz's had not been converted into flats. It was known she owned and ran a grocery business – not on the Broadway, but somewhere she commuted to – but in her personal life kept herself much to herself. Sometimes there had been hostility.

STH was an assistant librarian, and lived in the house across the street from Humber's. Late evenings Humber stood and stretched and drew his curtains, while STH – looking across – had puzzled endlessly as to what it was Humber was scratching away at, bent over his desk, a cheek and a shoulder grazed by the light of his reading lamp. He was tempted to ask, at moments the two passed on the pavement, to or from the station, or stood in the same bus queue – but couldn't ever find an intervention. His chance came on handling some publicity material, a list of nominees for the Morgan Beresford First Book Prize, with Sabre and Sabre powerfully represented in its batch of titles, among them Humber's *Cracks in the Plaster of Time*. There was a photograph, and to STH it struck a remarkable resemblance to his neighbour opposite. He mentioned it one morning, as both men left for work. 'You wouldn't by any chance be—' We don't need the whole chain of consequences. Thereafter STH was a frequent presence in Mrs Urbanowicz's back parlour, when the three played rounds of rummy or whist, and drank from a pot of weak tea, until the widow went to bed. Humber would always wait until she had ceased to move around above, then crept up and down stairs, and bolstered by his latest wodge of papers read from his ill-fated opening chapter – the thing still not right – his captive audience consisting of just the one. STH has said how enthralled he was, though in subsequent years searched in vain for *A Girl Like Her*, a book that doesn't seem to have been published – or not at least under that title. He asked why Humber never used a typewriter. Humber said because that constant clack-clack disturbed his train of thought, and anyway he'd got an agent who provided secretarial services when manuscripts were under preparation.

Others too had noticed Humber at his window, working under lamplight late into the night. STH tells us how remiss he was in failing to make connections, until it was too late. He recalled the string bag he took with him when he shopped on a Saturday morning, picking up the few provisions – mainly tins – for the shared larder space in the spooky rambling house where he rented a room, across the street from Sabre's vanguard writer. 'I'd always assumed,' he said, 'his work was in publishing, or teaching.' Humber never disabused him. Then one Saturday lunchtime STH sat in the Bear, in the public bar, with his string bag and a glass of beer. He was careful to look away but listened attentively to the conversation at the next table, as it spun on uncontrollably. A troupe leader and two myrmidons, all three in cloth caps, discussed the latest outrage. As insult added to the forced impositions of post-war austerity, were rumours of financial irregularities. Someone in that shady business – a man unnamed, who'd circumvented apparent paper shortages – was said to scribe away relentlessly, into the small hours, as a forger. Lots of fake notes had got into circulation, and someone was getting rich, while the rest of us grafted. STH saw no correspondence when a man similarly dressed – a cloth cap, a grey coat – he found prowling outside Humber's address on more than one occasion, the nights heavy with dew. The peak of the cap was drawn down tight over the eyes and the bridge of the nose, and the coat collar was turned up. Mrs Urbanowicz's gardener mentioned – and word got back to Humber – that someone rough and thuggish-looking had the habit of poking his head above the wall to watch him work – often for minutes at a stretch – as he raked the leaves or oiled his tools.

The first climax was on a foggy autumn night, when the prowler, his hands thrust in his coat pockets, pulled out a stone wrapped tightly in lined notepaper and hurled it at Humber's window. Humber jumped up mid-sentence, and saw fleeing down the street a figure in a flurry of coattails and with a hand pressing on his hat. That old cliché of popular drama didn't adapt itself. The stone hadn't shattered the window, the note not landing on the target's bedroom floor, but had bounced off. In fact it took days pondering, and Mrs Urbanowicz dismissing the thing as wanton vandalism, before Humber poked around in the front garden and made the discovery. The note was flimsy with overnight rain, but he opened it carefully and read its smudge marks quietly to himself, which he couldn't help deconstruct in terms of its orthography, a lower-school nightmare: *We now what your up too. You want get away with it. Singed ELI.* He discovered from posters pasted up on lampposts and telegraph poles what that signature denoted, an organisation he'd heard nothing of till then, that's to say the Ealing League Incorrupt. What could it mean? Humber, naturally prone to fret, ran off to his friend Hugh for advice, and got none, then off to Louisa for sympathy, and got a certain amount. 'How's the novel coming along?' Badly, as it happened. He'd started the second chapter, but having suffered crushing doubts had returned to the beginning, and was redrafting for the nth time. The girl like her wasn't turning out as he wanted her to be, and it was true what they said. Works of fiction evolved of their own accord, in defiance of their authors' intentions. 'Surely that makes it all the more interesting,' Louisa put in. Well, maybe. Frustration was the word that sprang to *his* mind.

Other things went wrong. His *Cracks in the Plaster of Time*, that debut collection of middling bourgeois poems, failed to make the Morgan Beresford First Book shortlist, as CLA had in all probability calmly predicted, a man never far from a whisky and soda. The first Humber heard of it was a note, or rather lengthy explication, from an astonished Monmouth, a facsimile of which I stumbled on in the archive, which I'll explain (it's somewhere *infra*). According to him it was an absurdity that Humber hadn't won the prize – the cash too would have been useful – let alone make the shortlist. The unassailable Monmouth was subject to the same delusion that all loudmouths in literary movements are plagued by, and had as a certainty the Exe Set, and the core of its members, as simply the best. Here we're given a new pair of initials, TE, the last imprint of someone else that history has buried in obscurity. TE was one of Hugh's tame reviews editors, who would, he said, ensure that war was waged on the Beresford committee. 'They'll be made to look inept – and publicly so.' 'Grave' was the word used, in so culpable an oversight, a slight on Humber's genius. Would they know a Shakespeare, if he came along? 'Oh. Well. Thanks very much,' said Humber, but it didn't end there. Monmouth engineered a column of his own in one of the reviews, with something specific Humber was briefed to do with it, Machiavellian as that may be, but all to the good, as all good Princes learn. Patient mentor Harold Humber, a poet in the front rank, would exercise his influence on a no-hoper chosen at random, and in his quarterly column celebrate the triteness of his poetry (some Johnny or Joe, and women keep out). As a 'major' discovery, it artificially created an enormous gulf in quality between himself and the best of the rest. Then we'd see what prizes Humber would win.

These machinations crumbled just at the moment Humber reacted with acerbity against his own middle-class, to CLA's approval (an assumption I allow myself to make). What precipitated it? Perhaps the rise and the economic reality and the prevalence of the new matinée idol, the crooner, winner hands down against Exe Set competition, and the train that followed, sons of Ganymede whose Romany good looks outdid Harry's camera-shyness, and whose repertoire of sickly lyrics no one dared critique. Humber didn't do with his reviews page what Monmouth had instructed, and instead maundered about with jazz syncopations and his Tennysonian idylls, wondering *what if* – if not that military flight, if not that crossing London to Paris, if not December 1944, if not that seminal moment in American mythology. Then on a pale, leaf-blown, gloomy afternoon the urge overtook him to put to the sword finally those multiple opening drafts, his debut novel already in its death throes. He gathered up his clutch of papers and stepped out, choking in the fume of conflicting cross emotions, and stood on Mrs Urbanowicz's back yard, strides away from her gardener, who was heaping leaves, twigs and toffee wrappers into the incinerator. The first few papers Humber added to that autumn bonfire coincided with four hooded marauders scaling the wall, a lynch mob, who trampled heavily over the flower beds and bore down on him. One of them, the ringleader, accused him of 'destroyin' heffidents', though the whole quartet was beaten off by the gardener wielding his hoe, and at one point ducking into his tool shed for his scythe. It was an episode that shook his foundations, Humber running off a second time to friend Hugh, who laughed it off – a prank. Louisa was less dismissive. 'What did they mean, destroying evidence?' Humber hadn't a clue. And anyway, he didn't now need her representation with the novel. No one records that she heaved a sigh of relief.

Abruptly STH's invitations into the Urbanowicz back parlour ceased, and there were no more private readings. The loss, he says, was cause of great regret, and sparked off troubled reflections as to what he might have done to offend his friend and colleague. Humber offered no explanation. Instead he was set on flight from the moral disintegration of his nation's capital, and after a spate of interviews was offered a Town Hall job distant in the north – north of the Wash even, a wilderness Monmouth found it impossible to conceptualise. He was furious. The Exe Set leadership and its band of loyal foot soldiers had worked indefatigably to put the correct critical elements in place for the launch of Humber's career, with the Laureateship an achievable target. London was the place to be, and Humber couldn't just abandon his station. 'Yes, but you don't know what I've been through.' Oh, well, in that case could Louisa talk sense into him? She tried, but given the unexpected rise of Jolyon Lyons, whose witty forensics apropos of upper-middle-class marriage, and latterly its family scene, had garnered enthusiastic plaudits as novelist. He was frankly a better bet for arts glitter and largesse than an emotionally crippled poet. 'I'll see what I can do,' she said, and it wasn't much. Humber settled his last month's rent and packed his few possessions into a battered suitcase, which, poignantly, STH saw him setting off with towards the station, wearing a green-grey raincoat and a felt hat. Monmouth smoothed things over with the *literati*, explaining Humber's absence as a call to important academic work. Not only was Humber a man of letters. He was an economist. This was a half-truth, when his new job was in a municipal internal audit department, where he shared an office with three others and a secretary.

There is a hiatus, a span of decades for which there is little or no information. I owe it to RA, the secretary Humber shared an office with on first moving north, for what snippets there are – a small insight into those early years of exile. She is traced to happily married life in Maidenhead, having made the move in the opposite direction shortly after Humber's arrival. This she states openly, in an apology for the little she has. 'Didn't know he was a poet,' she said, until she came across him in one of Monmouth's BBC broadcasts in the late 1970s. She'd turned on too late for *Going For a Song.*

We can see how it came about, his attention turning to urban architecture, for Humber's place of work was built in 1939, one of a series of linked municipal buildings designed by Percy Thomas and Ernest Prestwich. The vision is neo-Georgian with *Moderne* or *Art Déco* detailing. The material is brick in Flemish bond with Portland stone dressings. Humber has spoken eloquently of 'urban outdoor décor', as he termed it. He has written somewhere, with almost anatomical exactness, that the casual observer cannot help notice there's a band below the cornice, and there is one to balance it above the plinth. The roof is flat (lots of autumn repairs, with bitumen). The structure is two storeys, symmetrically splayed. I haven't been there, but the centre has three bays, and has a raised parapet adorned with a shield inscribed with a motto, *Do well, doubt not.* Flanking are giant pilasters and a round, capacious window. The window has a balcony and a stone architrave with double doors. There are two flights of stone steps, at whose base are rectangular planters, with rounded planters at the main door. All are well watered. There is a twenty-pane sash on each side of the building, with seven sashes to the right elevation and twelve to the left. The interior has a white marble staircase with a black marble plinth and coping, a semiotics of grandeur fitted to the humdrum of bureaucracy. There is gigantic scale in the pilasters, a metric continued in the repeat Greek key that ornaments the cornice, gilded. There are original circular and half-cylindrical light fittings. The council chamber, which Humber has often wandered in when empty, has a Greek fret design to the ceiling and balcony. Much of it entered the poet's notebook, while the vestibule was domed.

The offices were large and cavernous. In the one where Humber worked, his desk, dark wood, bulky, heavy, was positioned under the huge sash window. RA ran internal audit, insofar as she mastered everybody's schedule, and issued reminders two days, a day, then hours in advance. Humber's weekly highlight was a tramp round the town with the senior traffic warden, collecting cash and ticket stubs from a team dispersed in little wooden huts, those official frontiers of commerce a familiar mark of all the public car parks. RA watched him, each Monday afternoon, emptying his bags of cash on his desktop, as then began the laborious task of reconciling takings to the ticket stubs also in his collection. Recounts were possible, especially on a grey, lacklustre, sub-zero winter day, when circulation was sluggish and the central heating creaked. Windows stayed open a crack, as every office seemed to have its pipe smoker, or as RA recalls Player's Navy Cut, a ubiquitous cigarette. Humber, as the routine palled, as it dragged him below the theories of economics he had mastered, remained intent on jotting down couplets in his faint-line, single-margin notebook, though to RA this was the conscientious work of local finance. They spoke little. What conversation took place was impersonal. No one knew his birthday, so he never brought them cake. There was no intimacy. She could therefore never know him as an emaciated being of masculine professionalism who'd perfected his escape, a man ignorant of his true vulnerability, as he'd rushed headlong from the vanities fuelling Monmouth's smart artistic set and its metropolitan fires. In self-ejecting from that inferno, Humber had had to land up somewhere. His somewhere was here, where with Monday at its close he took his bags of coin to the cashier, whose door was locked, bolted, firmly secured, and the counter caged, a first bastion and belvedere adjoining the treasurer's office.

There was one job Humber said he liked, and that had similarities with the rites of double entry and the town's car parks, carried out when the assembly room ran a show or concert, and takings were dealt with. He hung around the box office longer than necessary, and one day was given half a dozen wall calendars by the plump middle-aged woman who worked there. These descriptions I lift directly from the RA apocrypha. He brought them back to the office and was asked wasn't he going to share them round. He replied no, 'They're a personal gift.' He told Monmouth confidentially, and we'll later know how, that life in the place he'd come to was slower than in London, weather-wise was never far from frozen, but the people were friendly, though everyone was generally hard up. His landlady was not like the widow Urbanowicz, and the room he'd got in her house was small, and the place poky. No garden to speak of. Just weed-strewn cobbles and an outside privy. He'd thought to brighten things up by pinning to the walls of his cell (as, monk-like, he referred to it) the pictures he'd cut from those calendars got from work. On one wall Alpine scenes, snow-capped mountains, green slopes in a sprinkling of edelweiss, and in the valleys chalet-style *pensions*. On another vintage cars. There were beaming factory girls in dungarees and chunky-knit sweaters, all with their sleeves manfully rolled up. His most devoted selection was of saints, and his favourite was St Rosalia, depicted in ethereal brightness and led to her cave by two trumpeting angels, a thought Monmouth must have shuddered at. That was how perhaps his friend saw *his* departure, or exit from a world of sin and shame, or in actuality from London.

Work he said wasn't so bad. It paid the bills and was undemanding. The two-storey Town Hall – 'I can give you its architectural history' – also had a basement, a black labyrinth opened by a heavy wooden door. Thereafter, stone steps plunged into the plutonian depths, with a more ancient parish long consigned to the netherworld there. His visits were to deposit completed ledgers, in an archive first formed far off in the previous century. We see him under a naked bulb, poring over those quill-written entries, enthralled by their paltry sums, those lost historical dates, and the exaggerated hand of a multitude of scribes as they merged into one, his predecessor. Who, who were you?

Hugh must have agonised as to Humber's rescue, from a fate he saw as narrow, dismal, defeatist – or so he explained to Louisa. Between them they couldn't find a solution. And Hugh hardly visited. Of the few entries in his diary that took him north of the Watford Gap there was an annual pilgrimage to the Aldeburgh Festival, and later the one in Edinburgh. He satisfied that paternal aspect of his conscience when after a span of three decades – or a few years short of that milestone – he pointed to the four volumes of poetry, a slender offering at under seventy pages apiece, Sabre had published, as by now added to Humber's debut were *Portals*, *Bills of Exchange*, and *Just Put a Sign Up*. Monmouth had seen them in draft, while almost his final act as editor was to commission a new poem, 'Swine', as the one on which that last collection he wished to see ended. 'I don't understand,' said Humber. Then he recalled that the opening poem, a nostalgia piece he'd written recalling his student life, he'd called 'Pearls'. Monmouth had got one of his interns, recruited from Exe of course, to write an introduction, with particular emphasis on the enormous influence the Exe Set continued to wield, in its primacy over all other movements. Perhaps this was a timely reminder of Humber as an important, central figure, with the Exe Set alone responsible for changing – 'once and for all and decisively' – the direction of modern poetry. That act of chauvinist propaganda did nothing to enhance his reputation – Humber's or his own. Its one effect on rival movements was an increase in the art of insulation, a talking inwardly that too often spilled out onto the pages of the *TLS*. It otherwise filled hectares of less prestigious print with new dimensions on post-structuralist theory, which the Exe Set was secure in knowing it could trump with its detailed mapping of *homo economicus*.

By the late 1970s even that was a clutching at straws. Monmouth must have thought it the last chance of all (in fact there was one more to follow) when he offered his protégé his final outline plan, and the resurrection of his reputation, or by extension the Exe Set's. By now Humber was lost to an inglorious cultural past, as all past cultures are, though I'm astonished – heartened even – at those gems whose survival is against all odds. But that's not the point. Monmouth was a friend of the BBC, who'd agreed to give him a camera and a half-hour slot for an intimate one-to-one, billed as special insight into one of our nation's most distinguished living poets. Strangely Humber didn't automatically dismiss the scheme, or the lubricity of Hugh's rhetoric. He phoned Louisa and talked at length, and later the predatory Jolyon wrote it all down in his memoirs. I have read both volumes, and enjoyed them – more so than the novels. A gaggle of tame reviewers never ceases to laud his works of fiction, mindful in pointing up an advanced technique in style, though stylistically they're inept. But that's not the point (again). Humber said he'd agree to appear, so long as the thing was scoped as a serious documentary. 'Goes without saying,' said Hugh. So now in a change of emphasis Humber insisted on their on-screen backdrop as something *he* would choose, and sent a list. It recalled an earlier era of manifesto drafts, and consisted of breweries (Humber drank no beer), distilleries (he did drink gin), factories (never worked in one), forges, foundries, mines, refineries, sawmills (ditto all), and sample mercantile warehousing. Hugh was appalled and tried to negotiate, and got in reply specifics: a Mitchells and Butler brewery, the Bird's custard factory, Fort Dunlop, Typhoo Tea, the Swan kettle works. 'They have all left their mark on the urban landscape.' That was quite true, as Hugh agreed, but he didn't think it was something the middle classes now wanted in their educational repertoire.

What we get is *An Open Door*. That documentary title is borrowed from one of Humber's early poems (it appeared in *Portals*, one of his best loved). It took as its opening shot the wrought-iron gateway of India House in Whitworth Street, Manchester. The building was put up in 1906 in Edwardian Baroque, as a packing and shipping warehouse. By the time Humber trundled past pushing his bicycle and dressed in a long grey coat, it was a Grade II listed building, preserved for its steel-frame infrastructure and its attractive red-brick and terracotta cladding and ornate dressings. With Humber waiting, Monmouth walks into shot. The two men shake hands, with the titling still on screen. They step inside, but in the next shot are somewhere else – a sun-splashed courtyard with a fountain and stone benches and a statuette of Galatea, and Humber's bike leaning on an ivied wall. It isn't clear just where they are, though I have found out from the research. It's the inner sanctum of a tobacco emporium, where office girls sit outside to eat their lunch. Monmouth raises his voice above the plash of water, and the conversation starts. A coy-looking Humber is prompted to recollections of his early life as a poet, when we hear the story of that Panamanian financier. There is no reference to his role in the counterfeiter theory, as I am led to believe he remains ignorant of that misunderstanding. He is nostalgic in recall of the assembly-room box office and some of the shows – *Hello, Dolly!*, *My Fair Lady*, *Oklahoma*. He still has some of the images he cut from the calendars, when he wished to liven up his rented room, and personalise its décor. His mood is Dickensian when he talks of the Town Hall basement archive, with its handwritten ledgers rooted in eras and cultures past. Like any dedicated poet, he confesses to always having about his person a faint-line single-margin notebook, where only a fraction of what goes in emerges eventually as fully worked-up poetry. He is modest as to awards he's been given, glosses over the grants (the English so touchy on public money handouts), and smiles only at the mention of rivalries (as of course the Exe Set has no serious competition). When the credits go up Humber is cycling off into an urban sunset, where on the brick horizon smoke is rising in a lazy wisp from a factory chimney. Elegiac music. The cyclist's arched back and his slow pedal into posterity.

The result as Monmouth reported to Louisa – or one of those minor details that again crept into Jolyon's two-volume memoir – was a small spike in sales in Humber's last collection, *Just Put a Sign Up*, the only one of his four still stocked by the major bookshop chains, who might just as well have been selling tinned beans.

There is one further addendum to *An Open Door*, the documentary, found in one of the few surviving letters Humber wrote to his publisher, or Hugh. He questioned what shears had been taken to the editing process, and was surprised that his revelation as to reading habits was lost from the final cut. Our poet had admitted frankly that his absorption in books had been in neither a scholarly nor a systematic way. He couldn't quote Shakespeare. That whirlwind of poems you found in Walt Whitman he remembered only vaguely as single or unitary. He liked the tone of the Lowell confessional, but had never knowingly observed what techniques were involved in making that private sacrament public. He'd never meshed his own gearing with that of Emily Dickinson, whose over-use of the en dash made her – in any case for him – unreadable. There were many other examples, the point being that Humber was acutely aware of what elements in other writers had informed his work. He found it impossible to say exactly how. He thought that was something the reading public ought to know.

I have no record of any reply, but can guess why Monmouth chopped and spliced his film in the way he did. His forward charge as General in the Exe Set had as its aim assailment of key military ground. Assimilation into the popular mind must be, in an age of pragmatism, clinical and scientific, not elusive or mysterious.

The trail goes cold for almost another decade, when all we have is the testament and other attachments of some of the people who worked with or for him at the municipality. By now Humber had risen to dizzy heights, and as Director of Finance had his own office in that Thomas and Prestwich building. By all accounts the floorspace was immense, the furnishings dark, knobby, bulky. The huge sash window opened onto a courtyard with a gently plashing fountain, and somewhere below a statuette of Galatea. His stalwart at one time was one of his accountants, who signs herself R, and is probably deceased. She could not have known about his other life as poet, in some of the descriptions she offers. Sometimes she drove to his house, a bay-fronted semi in a quiet suburban street, with its clipped frontages, not too many cars parked, and on the pavements mock-Victorian lampposts painted green. She delivered papers there in moments of panic – it was usually pressure from government – when he needed her potted overview for a meeting someone had hastily convened. She could not have ventured farther than the hall, whose ceramic wall-mounted mallards – a threesome – were arranged in formation on the crest of a sine wave, or into the kitchen, where they sat at the breakfast bar and he made them instant coffee. No mention of a living room lined with books. The closest she got to that, and quizzically, was his briefcase, if by chance he snapped it open when she happened to be in his office, and among its papers were things out of place. She remembers only three by name: *Life at Grasmere* by Dorothy and William Wordsworth, *English Folk Songs* by Ralph Vaughan Williams and A. L. Lloyd, and *The Good Soldier* by Ford Madox Ford, a name she knew from a Sunday evening TV dramatisation. I can add to that a fourth, Hazlitt's *Sketches and Essays* (1839), which Monmouth knew him to be an admirer of, and could not have passed over in his documentary (1979). How long would that have been in his briefcase?

To R he cut a lonely figure, and seemed to have no friends. His only camaraderie was with his counterpart in Housing – Duncan Summerset – the two breakfasting together on Tuesdays and Thursdays, in what passed as the town's continental café (a few wine baskets hanging up, and a string of plastic onions). R's husband, to do with import-export, and marketing, and work in the private sector, commuted daily into a hub of commerce and a city she didn't name, but had known the Summersets since university and played a round of golf with Duncan. R knew their house intimately, a sturdy, grey, forbidding, gothic-looking thing, its only brightness the plush of its curtains. Its all-round aspect was from the brow of a hill a few streets from Humber's, grander in its locality. The Rs Mr and Mrs were always last to leave that fixture on the calendar, the Summerset house party, with Duncan a contented raconteur and R's husband a wide-eyed avid listener, prone to chortle. What came out more seriously was Duncan's teenage daughter, whose bouts of anxiety their GP scratched his head at and didn't know what to prescribe, so forcing a frantic Mrs S to seek psychiatric help. That loomed up in the person of Dr Styre, whose expertise was part Freud, part Jung. Styre was a solid citizen big in Rotary, with family connections in Evanston (the one in Illinois). R mentions this only apropos of Dr Styre's double Georgian frontage, steps up, and an escutcheon a fag-smoking peon polished every day. R passed it to and from work, and in the evenings when she went to badminton, and was surprised one rainy Wednesday night, in an autumn gale, to see Humber ascending those steps, about to press the bell on Dr Styre's colossal practice door. She could not imagine what troubled the elderly Humber, a bachelor.

We know that *a priori* the student Rhea Bright reached a correct diagnosis. She was a sophomore. Her student habitat was the generic the University of the North, a seat of learning I cannot be more specific about, as all now spirals into the surreal. We find her at her most potent when, on one of his visits to her, on a fortnight's leave, is her boyfriend Michael Grading, who months before had graduated from that same fantasy institution, and had now escaped to the prosperous Southeast, where he worked in IT for a firm I cannot find in any listings. Rhea was an art student, and a big name one day in self-aware, socially challenging art installations. To that end she'd an eye on a warren of lockup garages behind a tidy row of pink and olive doors, a suburban adjunct she cascaded through every day, her gravel shortcut from her student digs to a lonely, windy bus stop on the corner. She did not know what personnel to approach at the Town Hall to register her interest, and every time she phoned was rebuffed or redirected through a labyrinth of office clerks, who eventually told her to write. She thought it must be a financial matter, so the name she picked from the municipal directory was Harold Humber's. His prim and efficient secretary placed her small volume of unanswered missives on the non-urgent pile, until one day she was on leave, and standing in for her was a girl from the typing pool, who prioritised things differently. We now know her as Y, our next witness, our fourteenth in all.

Humber couldn't have known what was on the agenda when, as an opus in itself, expertly choreographed by the artist Rhea Bright, she and her partner arrived impeccably turned out for the first of several meetings. Perplexed at first (oh yes), Humber showed morbid fascination when an unbelievably young, and savagely pretty Rhea ran through her portfolio, revealing, in living flesh, what terminus centuries of artistic endeavour had arrived at – a kind of circus. What Rhea couldn't have known exactly, but got a vague insight into, was Monmouth's latest machinations re his Exe Set, and a renewed attempt at gaining its permanent entry in *The Oxford Companion to English Literature*, with his own longevity assured. Hugh dipped into his resources, and after almost a decade of Humber's silence – no solitary poem published anywhere – urged him to assemble a *Collected*, with Monmouth his editor again, and with a lengthy introduction written by the poet himself. Hugh, as Sabre's longest serving director, was confident of a *South Bank* special aired to coincide with publication date, and the usual tame reviewers. He'd got as far as a publisher's un-proofed review copy. The cover was no more finished than someone's doodle, rudimentary titling on flimsy card curled at the corners, and no accompanying image. The author's copy sat in his office cabinet, in company of yearbooks and thick utility tomes devoted to tax computations and company law etc. Rhea, more observant than her partner, lit on it immediately, but did not allow herself to be distracted. She lunged in unchecked on her well-rehearsed proposal, the script she had brought for the man with the purse strings, and careful with her preface: 'So good of you to see me.' Humber couldn't grasp what the proposal was, and pressed for more detailed explanations, which Rhea was patient about, knowing how decisive the generation gap was, particularly in the arts. While that row of lockups had certain resemblance to an avenue of beach huts (an evocative image, as Humber complimented), that was not her interest. The next one to become vacant she would like to know about. She had already constructed the storyboard, her template for the film she intended to shoot *inside*, and it all had to be done by the end of next semester. 'I am bound, you see, by the academic timetable.'

'Why yes, of course. I will make some inquiries.'

Humber wasn't pleased with what Y had done to his diary, with its pattern of crow's feet marching corner to corner across three afternoons, in different coloured nail varnish – plums and garish purples, and dyestuff lilacs. He summoned her for one last task before sending her back to the typing pool – a little bit of shorthand. Y remembers it as something she couldn't understand, the recipient a man with a Welsh-sounding name, which entitles me to the following reconstruction—

'Miss Y, a letter please, to Mr Hugh Monmouth—'

Miss Y is seated, pencil poised. She moistens the lead. 'Ready.'

The pedant Humber towers above her, standing, and thumbs his lapels meditatively before turning, addressing not her but his own reflected being, a watery ghost of himself restless in the sash window. Below, and poignantly, the fountain is lined with the yellow leaves of autumn. Humber is at his opening juncture of strange and illuminating sessions with his therapist Dr Styre, who has diagnosed his middle-age anxiety as fear of the Other, that other being an unnamed, inapparent rival. I have made initial analysis from other sources, confirmed by a paper I have read of Dr Styre's, where he sets out his method, much of it counter-intuitive. His is a plodding, dispassionate, scientific exposition. In Humber's case the subject is asked to conjure up his rival in his sleep. The theory being that with concentrated efforts on that other, sooner or later the two persons would share the same dream, or sequence of dreams, and meet in its bizarre, fantastic landscape, where the chance was granted to settle their hierarchical difference. Styre's prescription was a notepad and pencil at Humber's bedside, and the demand that he make a record of what he remembered passing through that morphean haze – and to get it all down immediately on waking. His question for Hugh, one Y couldn't later articulate with clarity (so I do it for her), was: What were the chances of Dr Styre revealing Humber's rival in a race for the laurel Monmouth wanted his friend to have? Hugh's answer might have been along the lines that Humber didn't need to worry. There was no poet writing today – however young, fresh, whatever his genius – able to match his supremacy. That might have been of some comfort, until the name Bridgland Jolley emerged, days after Hugh's reply had been dictated, typed, dispatched. We'll come to that.

Y returned to the typing pool in blissful, native ignorance, and was replaced by her coeval FO, whose tenure – also temporary – was a success, comparatively speaking. She did her nails in private. Almost her first duty was to take a call when Humber was away—

'Put me through please to Harold Humber.'

'Mr Humber is chairing his committee. I will take a message.'

'Whom am I addressing please?'

FO gave her name. 'Secretary. Acting up.'

There was a pause, and the caller hung up.

She was present in Humber's office – more shorthand, more dictations – when art student Rhea Bright had her next appointment, again accompanied by her boyfriend Michael, whose red eyes and suppressed sneezes were the first symptoms of 'flu. Humber dismissed his secretary and asked his two visitors to be seated, Michael already clutching a Kleenex drawn from his trouser pocket. I mention so much detail as marking the moment Rhea struck her blow – her decisive blow. Since having roved over the book spines, their regiment of columns in Humber's glass-fronted cabinet, she had done her research. Humber's only title stocked by her local bookstore was his last, that wearied collection *Just Put a Sign Up*, its publication date now almost a decade in arrears, though she lied and said she'd acquired it as a teenager. It was a time in her life when she found herself keen on culture and only a half enthusiast when it came to school, and what they taught you there. She'd carried that volume of poems everywhere, she said, and quoted lines – amazed as much now as then at what the written word could do. Humber was flattered. Michael looked agog. 'Try to do something about that,' she told him later. He blew his nose, I imagine.

The flattery didn't end there. After her solitary bookshop haul she rootled through the college library, then hopelessly its archive, rekindling her spark in turning up a battered *Cracks in the Plaster of Time*, its cover design a blue-black functional disaster (as so Sabre cried out to an audience of shop-floor factory proles), and said what a huge impact it had had on first reading. Did Humber's eyebrows twitch? He softened, telling her a lockup was available, though he'd no jurisdiction, and couldn't override (or trample on, as Rhea preferred, in the cause of art) his friends and colleagues in Housing, whose territory it was. Michael said later how in such situations Rhea's look was crumpled, showing hurt, disappointment, appeal, at a single glance, for such were her talents of persuasion. Lord Byron would have melted, a parallel the demotic Humber wasn't able to draw. Humber told her not to despair, as he would make some further inquiries. 'I have great faith in you,' she said. He escorted them out, at the very moment FO hovered at the door, wanting to come back in. Just then Rhea turned. 'Can I ask one small favour?' she said.

A favour?

She couldn't help notice a copy of Humber's *Collected Poems* in his office bookcase, and if possible she'd like very much to borrow it. Humber explained it was Sabre's pre-publication, un-proofed draft, littered with his and others' pencilled mark-ups, though she was welcome to review it. 'Feel free with your own corrections.'

'Oh, Mr Humber, I wouldn't presume—'

While Humber fetched the book, Rhea summoned every sinew of politeness, finding herself confronted by a classically pretty FO, standing with her notebook at the door. That meeting was propitious, though for now its significance went unnoticed, a postponement I am willing to replicate. We turn briefly to Michael Grading, in whose presence a determined Rhea plumbs every depth of Humber's *Collected*, in search of any clue that will give a negotiating advantage. She was thorough – and lucky with her breaks. Meanwhile a doting Humber, on his next breakfast date with Duncan Summerset, his counterpart in Housing, said a very curious thing had happened, with a girl called Rhea.... Summerset pushed his plate aside and filled his pipe.

That girl called Rhea one day queued with her lunch tray in Profumo's Bakery, and found a window seat where – one of those casual acts of fate – FO was nursing an overlong milkshake, looking at her watch. 'Oh, an amazing coincidence. You're—' Why yes, it was Humber's secretary, 'Acting up.' The conversation got its motion at that point precisely, with FO's boyfriend late – 'He always does this' – and plenty of time to chat. There were rumours going round that Humber was getting therapy, troubled over something – no one knew if personal or professional. He'd been sighted ascending the steps to Dr Styre's practice, its grandiose Georgian frontage smothered in Virginia creeper, and having as demarcation elegant iron railings. There was a squat square pillar either side the gate. 'Yes, I think I know the place,' said Rhea. It was said the hall was floored with Renaissance rhombs, and the client, patient, whatever, was greeted by an alabaster Psyche. The strange thing was FO had been granted unique insight into Humber's state of mind, when – oh, a few days ago – a man called Hugh Monmouth phoned the office wanting to speak to *her*. Who was this Hugh Monmouth? A publishing person apparently. 'Miss O, you may not have known, your boss is a distinguished man of letters.' Monmouth was planning his biography, and was interviewing those who had known or knew him – over the phone was fine – and anything she had to offer was gratefully received. 'But I am just a secretary.' There was no *just* about it, Miss O. For Hugh could be so lubricious. She was coaxed, humoured. She described with what a patrician bearing Humber went about his daily work. FO was reckless enough to mention these recent occurrences to the man himself, her boss. Utterly out of character, Humber – a recluse, the epitome of private emotion – exploded, and mopped his brow, purple with rage on the word biography. So now those rumours had substance. Humber *was* under treatment, but still there was Hugh with his phone calls.

Michael, whose presence was signalled everywhere with Kleenex soaked in Olbas oil, looked on with vague intent at the forensic extravagance Rhea applied to her reading of Humber's *Collected*. One swirly morning she had read the author's introduction for the nth time (no epiphany yet), and told Michael that before his cold developed into something more debilitating he must get over to Madame Belokonsky's, that person being a national celebrity living locally, and a name he'd begun to know. 'Oh but why?' (Blank appeal.) Belokonsky had been subject of a redtop centre page only a month before, when no better story than other-worldly things had fallen across the editor's desk. She was a sensitive, delicate practitioner, in pioneering work as medium, whose special interest was deceased authors, her current triumphs numbering a warning for humanity – that meant every last one of us – from one Bertrand Russell, and an exhortation to reflect carefully on the Gospels – that was from Fyodor Dostoyevsky. Rhea wanted not only the Belokonsky name, now known to every tabloid reader, but sponsorship – actual lucre – investment in the film she now felt more than ever sure of, shot inside that lockup soon to be hers. Michael said okay, 'I'll see what I can do.' Rhea said if he pulled it off to tell Madame Belokonsky she'd get a write-up in the college rag, which for the coming quarter she'd commandeered as editor, as that too had fallen in her general assault on all political territories, and almost everything was now in place. Hugh would have liked her, fuddy-duddy though he'd seem (to her anyway). Then came her eureka moment, and a passage from Humber's introduction to his *Collected Poems,*

Prefaces, and notes in conjunction with these, the natural recreation of poets forced to wear the editor's hat...,

those first two clauses forming an acrostic, you see, and Rhea working out what it was—

PANIC with these—

meaning, in advanced middle age, fears for his loss of fame accompany the poet compiling his *Collected Poems*. Literary humiliation may not necessarily follow, though in pre-empting that possibility – why conceive this and nothing new? – he had more or less admitted that with every new day he expected a well-equipped rival able to claim his laurel (or the laurel Hugh had convinced him was rightfully his).

That night. Humber recalled his hopeless dreams of puberty, on only his first excursion. He put on a leather belt with a large square buckle, a cape, a wig. Jaunty walks in an avenue of poplars brought him – as poet – to hoarfrost on a sward, just as that turned to a flattish swirl of steam in the warmth of a spring mid-morning. A white knight on a nag dismounted under a brick arch and retreated wanly into its maw, where there was nothing, no distant point of light. Humber came across to look, and heard an equine snort, reverberant. The tail swished, a hoof clopped on the cobbles.

So no clues at all, said Styre, fiddling with his paperknife. By now he was so absorbed he absently twanged its blade. Well actually yes – there was *one* clue. A Romanesque BJ embellished on the saddle. That was something, yes, but Humber would have to try again. The next improbable set had an Elizabethan backdrop – a sylvan meadow, woolly sheep. He thought he had seen an homunculus in a knot of grey boulders, beachcombing, and was surprised, stroking his own chin, to find a beard, getting damp in the mizzle.

He walked to landward over the shingle, and saw on a green slope a forester in muslinet. Briefly someone in a long white coat stared out from a mausoleum, where the smoke cleared momentarily. Whoever it was – with a chisel and mallet – strode out of sight into a thicket. The forester's arm dropped. Humber hurried over and found an epitaph carved in marble – a sestet, a stupendous composition. The paper knife grew agitated. Its paunchy owner thought they were onto something, and could Humber possibly transcribe those precious six lines? Humber didn't know. All he could say was this: they were good – very good – even brilliant! He tried again, and again, and again, and after days of failure dreamed another dream, where in the blue shadows and sorceries a toad hopped across a dirt road. That other, that rival, that poet more accomplished than he, now in a moon-bright oilskin turned up his collar in a vortex of wind and rain. Chinks of red, orange, turquoise light escaped from the cracks and fissures in a shuttered tenement, its windows blanked against a thunderous heaven, a dark house swaying in an elemental thrash. His flat round hat stayed on in the gusts, as he pointed at a flapping door.

And that was it. In the morning Humber's bedside notebook yielded not a name, but a pair of initials, the BJ of his dream. If that was the next sensation on the literary scene, it was one he had never heard of. We now begin to learn how Dr Styre had half signed up for J. W. Dunne's experiments with time, being assured in his ideas – and in Dunne's ideas as well – that's to say ideas of the pre-cognitive in dreams. What jointly he and Humber inquired into, in a structured, scientific way, was a matter of prescience, he said. Those initials, not identifiable now, were something to look out for. Humber probably agreed, but turned to other things, and soon found himself assessing what implications there were in Rhea's latest announcement, for at last – hoops and hurdles got through – Michael, her right-hand man, had co-opted Madame Belokonsky onto the team, who was open to funding, enough for camera and editing equipment. Now more than ever Rhea needed the lockup. Over to you, Humber.

Humber's new panic was *The Spirit of '68*, Rhea's college rag (or hers for the foreseeable), when he read with escalating dread the account she gave of Michael's initiation at one of Madame Belokonsky's séance sessions, a full participant a-grope in the cold stygian darkness of her underworld. A handful of cartoon characters sat around her table, when with dubious pedigree, and with a knock three times – 'Yes, I am here, and I want to speak to Michael Grading' – a spirit was summoned. Said Belokonsky: 'Identify yourself.' Her hand to the planchette spelled out the name: 'Jolley. Bridgland Jolley.' Humber's further alarm came with his own lionisation in the same article. Few at the Town Hall, and practically no one in the wider community, were aware they had got a national treasure somewhere in their midst – the highly accomplished poet Harold Humber. I imagine he threw the thing into the bin.

Worse followed. Some fool from a local writers' circle, until then unaware of what gem lay buried in the municipal infrastructure, invited him to make a short address – a lecture. Humber ran off to Dr Styre for support. Styre advised caution, but nevertheless said yes, to a meeting head-on with his demons, and to the hand of friendship graciously offered. These were the psychological stumbling blocks it was no bad thing for Humber to overcome. He fretted as to what turn the lecture should take, and was appalled at its scale when that was revealed – an entire Tuesday morning someone spent setting out row on row of seating in the assembly room, and come that evening almost all the chairs filled. First on stage was chief of that local writers' group, one OTM, whose claims to professional status were an article on fly fishing published in an angling magazine, a short steamy romance – penname O. T. Munday – in a women's weekly, and a clever piece of casuistry in the correspondence pages of a *Daily Telegraph* of years ago. OTM made his obsequious introductions. There was a round of applause. Grading arrived at the lecture late. Others followed after. Humber paused, cleared his throat, shuffled through the pages of his notes. He recapped. Essential to literary art was the action of memory as the fictionalising application of our recall. This gave narrative forms that other dimension, the capacity to haunt, or at worst sentimentalise. Mr Eliot's dissolving floors skirted the point, but a real proof was adduced by his colleagues in science fiction, whose appallingly bad texts had imagined a future in a purloining of the past. Rhea dug an elbow into Michael's ribs. In a rush of air from a last stream of latecomers she told him this was nothing new. Worse news was, only hours before, Belokonsky had read her editorial, disappointed, and in a letter to Rhea said as much. Meanwhile Humber commended the scientific principles of modernism, but deplored postmodernist attention to useless detail, as now Belokonsky wanted to see in any new article appearing in *The Spirit of '68* something more adventurous, and more speculation. She asked, what notes had Michael made when she had listed her three cardinal points – her theory of ectoplasm, her theory of the extra-sensory, her theory of metempsychosis?

Just then a ragged intellectual got up at the front – hollow cheeks, voluminous white shirt, a shock of raven hair – and stated his opinions in staccato-driven anapaests. Humber – could this be his rival? – tried to dismiss his few interesting comments with neutral concord, the raising of a palm, but was rebuffed by a bow from the waist. Michael had got to Belokonsky's postscript, which made clear they must understand financial assistance was in her gift to withdraw. For Rhea that meant indefinite postponement of her important initiation into film surrealism. Then shockingly that intellectual hadn't sat down. As he pressed, Humber delved further into the refuge of his notes, but was unable to recover the lost thread of his lecture. He folded his papers and tucked them away in his jacket. In that one gesture Rhea read retreat, withdrawal from the lectern in a stew of academic humiliation. However. One could argue, harangue, eternally. What the renowned Harold Humber really meant was: the scandalous lot of poets is the menial chore for bread, and a light in the garret. This one had found his way in the toy reality of local government, and knew its largesse: here, he said, were the keys to some lockup garages (he held them up) – culmination of a history fully chronicled on the arts faculty notice boards a few miles away at the University of the North.

A ripple of puzzled, muted applause accompanied Humber departing into the wings, which with OTM's vigorous handclaps rose to a thunderous cascade. Our host and confrère called for quiet, and from a position centre stage took up the microphone, with the announcement that at the exit through the lobby a stall had been set up where Humber's *Just Put a Sign Up*, a handsome paperback, was available for purchase. There is no record of how many copies were sold. Rhea had the next best thing, a *Cracks in the Plaster of Time* purloined from the college archive, and thought a good thing to do was to get him to sign it, though by now the author was nowhere to be found. She left it until their next appointment, but before that she'd unfinished business with Madame Belokonsky, deciding on a plain white dress, girlish ponytails, peach ribbons, and for Michael a beige suit. Having so complied, we are shown him in Belokonsky's front porch, as the two waited to be let in. A pipe-smoking cyclist passed them by, weary from an afternoon's work on his allotment, but with a smile. Rhea smiled back. She told her friend how remiss he'd been, and asked why hadn't he pointed this out.

Pointed what out?

'This!' she said, and put her hand to the shiny brass doorknocker, whose motif was a shepherd's crosier laid crosswise on a bell.

Rhea had wanted science, he thought. Yes, but even an oaf could have identified missionary zeal.

Inside, he sat upright on a hard ottoman, ignored, and weighed a pale teacup with a heavy silver spoon, and on the palm of the other hand a slice of buttered banana bread. Belokonsky fluttered round his lady friend, straight-backed and angelic in a utility dining chair. She stirred her tea and explained (as Michael learned why science seldom succeeded). What she had seen so far, she said, was the naked seed of an extended editorial, and this had always been envisaged. What they lacked and were here for, you'd describe so: the practitioner's insight, opinion, a personal voice – Madame Belokonsky's – in tone the authority of lifelong experience. The reporter began with observable facts, but if he could just tear himself away from a delightful afternoon tea, he'd got his notebook again and was set to resume.

What that subterfuge resulted in was vindication of Belokonsky and her technique, and in the final, carefully worded compromise, justification of her mysticism, where mysterious forces used every available vessel on earth to work its ends. Cynics, who might have expected scepticism, were much put out by Rhea's plan for a later article – whose one happy outcome was the donation she'd sought. When the festive day came round, Humber brought golden shears, keys on a ring, and snipped the winner's tape draped on the lockup doors. First footage picked out a hopping software engineer in a panic and a froth of champagne. It made the local news.

It was too much stress for Humber, whose therapist told him to take a break. There must have been reference to that conversation, with its rigid professional advice, when Humber next breakfasted with his friend heading up Housing – Duncan Summerset. 'And thanks very much for the lockup.' Duncan and his wife had an annual fortnight's allocation at a timeshare, in a sun-filled Gran Canaria, one they seldom used, and it was Humber's if, as he said, he felt in need of a holiday. He did very much, he thought. Next thing was had his passport expired (last used on a daytrip to the Hook of Holland)? No. A few years to run. He booked a flight. Summerset made one further facility available, introducing him – by name and phone number – to tourism specialist Ed Nilsen (or EN for our purposes), resident on the island and a good contact if he thought it worth his while getting out and about and meeting people. You know, other like-minded holidaymakers. Said Ed: 'Take an evening suit.'

Ed had a full calendar when it came to organising barbecues, and for repeat business had got some well-connected people. Humber, who probably blushed to think of it, recalled his Ealing days and his many incognitos. If he was going to launch himself into the social swim of a tourist destination, instinct told him he needed a pseudonym. He toyed with that and settled on Peter Agurian, or P. Agurian as he'd sign himself. His little joke, as I don't doubt he chuckled to himself. I can only imagine with what jaded enthusiasm he went on to settle his wardrobe, adding as its final flourish a scarlet cummerbund. Yet Humber was thinking positively: those Nilsen dinner dates had kudos and appeal. Miles from home, there was no necessity to be himself, or what he'd become – a hermit, crabby, grouchy.

Other invitations followed. With the success of her funding, Rhea was able to branch out into an installation project going on in Liechtenstein, with her film showing in a tiny cubicle in a brick-built warehouse, somewhere. I don't know the precise location. A field, mainly of stubble, a stream running by, and a service road, with very short lampposts. Fast trains audible somewhere in the distance. An influx of students and artworld grandees were expected to attend. Grading had sworn not to miss its opening, and now Humber was offered formal invitation, as the reward for his co-operation over the lockup, without which the project would never have got started. Humber ummed a lot and said he couldn't come, as her slot in the diary coincided with his last days in the Canaries. Rhea persisted and looked at the dates more closely, insisting that as her showing ran for several days he'd do her the honour of making a call on his way home. After he'd agreed to that, all was up in the air again, Rhea getting word from the organising committee that her part in the festival had been put back a week, so now Humber could join them right from the start. 'Would be great to see you there,' said Michael.

Here their travel plan is lost on me, though it involved the three meeting up at Geneva Airport and taking the same flight to Liechtenstein. From the descriptions I have I can't help but imagine a light aircraft privately hired, catering for just our trio, though it must have been a commercial carrier and a fuselage stuffed with passengers. Anyway, the important point is this. Air miles into the flight an engine fault developed, and the plane put down on a remote airstrip that had no customs controls, and no one wearing uniform. Just a few stray buses came and went.

They waited for ninety minutes in what was makeshift baggage reclaim, where, when it appeared, Humber's battered suitcase – the one he'd kept since teenage, and his days of seaside holidays – emerged in a state of wilful evisceration, its lid half-open. Someone had purloined most of his belongings – his notebooks, his toilet bag, knick-knacks he'd bought for Mrs Summerset – leaving him only his evening dress, a change of underwear, and the scarlet cummerbund worn just a few days before, with effortless pride, and looking like a bad joke now. There was no reparation, with no one in that tiny arrivals-stroke-departure lounge in a remotely official capacity – not even for passport checks. The three stumbled out and looked for a taxi rank. The only vehicle was a horse-drawn cart, at rest at its driver's command, a blond youth in a straw hat sucking on a blade of grass. He did not understand their questions. They travelled on foot into a tiny settlement, where Humber just about made out the bus timetable. He set them on their way into the lean city of Guschfahl. There the only boarding house open for business was run by a mannish matronly-looking old irascible Frau wearing a floral housecoat, who in broken English directed them to her two remaining vacancies, a pair of rooms up in the attic under the slope of the roof. There was a window, a porthole barred by a cross, with good views into the mountains (blue foothills, a coat of icing at the peaks). 'Lovely picture postcard,' as only Grading remarked. The other two were tired.

Breakfast was a warm roll, a slice of processed cheese, and a decent cup of coffee. The Frau had warmed to their plight and produced a schedule of local transport – a funicular, a chair lift, a tourist bus, a branch line. The rest is sketchy. Rhea insists she must arrive at the venue before the showing commences, where there is equipment she needs from her manifest, to be set up and run under test conditions, preferably in the space allocated to her. She and Grading set out together as passengers on that local branch line, looking for the right connection. Reports vary. All agree they whiled away too many hours in Auerbach's Keller, where they met another English woman – a Nicola Chamoogan. The three were entertained by a magician whose name was sewn into his cape – Mario. Mario hadn't learned his craft, and amused more through his mistakes than his triumphs. Then Chamoogan pointed out a misprint in the train timetable Grading had managed to acquire, which accounted for the connection they'd waited for and missed, and explains how they had come to Auerbach's. Some tell us Rhea held Michael responsible for the delay, and stamped her feet in rage, and left. Others have the three meeting up again in a railway waiting room, where no tension exists between them – there is no sign of any tantrum – and all of them get on well. All commentaries agree that the one thing troubling Michael is his sense of having met Nicola

Chamoogan before. He is in endless search of himself trying to establish where. Finally he recalls her presence in one of his dreams, and asks her what she thinks are the chances of that – this Dunne-like precognition extended over a wider tract of time than in the original theory. Chamoogan is an acute intellectual with a Catholic background, and – if but Michael understood – won't be drawn into pagan speculation (but that's another story). There is evidence of a *third* meeting between the three, but that I cannot go into. What's certain is Rhea, under Chamoogan's scrutiny of the train timetable, went on alone to her showing, telling Michael that he and Humber must join her in a few days' time.

So finally dismissed by Rhea, Grading returned to the boarding house, where Humber's only change of clothes was his evening dress. So attired he set off with Michael in search of accommodation in striking distance of Rhea's installation, which necessitated foot-slogging, a train, a bus, a coach, and finally a hike uphill into the snowy peaks of Schmutzburg, whose monastic remoteness, the severity of its gargoyles, and a tolling ninth canonical hour, you might have thought suited the sacerdotal in Humber's priestly artifice, a lettered man whose grounding was that of *homo economicus*. Yet he said only, because he'd been thinking, and was determined to get in touch with Hugh, that he hoped they'd find a payphone somewhere. Once and for all he was going to tell Sabre to call off his biography.

'Oh look,' said Michael, 'there's a sign: *Abandon all impedimenta, ye who enter here....*'

And off he went.

And that's about it.

Afterword

I have one other biographical note, and it isn't that of Maureen Stone (*née* Sabre). Maureen (*née* Sabre) chose interior design over publishing, and as far as I know has lived most of her adult life in Amsterdam. When the last Gregor Sabre knew how Hugh was badly out of touch, unable to keep abreast of current trends, Maureen was his natural choice for the editor's chair. She declined. Sabre pleaded. Maureen didn't relent. Nevertheless he went ahead and fired family friend Hugh Monmouth, his longstanding incumbent (or rather pensioned him off), a decision one of his advisers warmed to, and saw as an opportunity. In no time Magnum Snark was asked to fill the post, and must have relished the opportunity, as under the rallying cry *Épater la bourgeoisie*, almost his first action was to cancel the Humber biography, in favour of one of David Byrne. Humber must have been relieved. Hugh was furious, and on behalf of the Exe Set fired off mortars from the pages of the *TLS*, or squibs landing on our breakfast table, which Snark never needed to deflect. But then Snark tired quickly of publishing and its people, and could not have enjoyed the lunches. He snorted up one last time in his padded Sabre office, then scuttled off back to his production base, where new pop and rock sensations were coming through on a conveyor, and were glad of his name, Snark Records. He'd shares in other labels too, I hear.

Sabre tried Maureen again, but again she refused, as now she'd two-year-old twins, a husband big in the Amsterdam art market, and a name of her own. Sabre, obliged to look around again, settled on his next best hireling in the feminist Gillian Crooks, a thirty-something academic with good telegenic ratings, and a calm incisive way of gendering her opinions. Almost the first call she took in ridding her office of every last odour left behind by Snark was from Monmouth, who was fulsome on her appointment, superficially collegiate in his gush of congratulations. Casually he reminded her of how important the Exe Set had been in keeping the Sabre name at the forefront, while beneath that façade she knew what he meant. She'd reviewed her handover notes, she said, and had no plans to revive the Humber biography, if that's what he thought. He hoped politely that might change. It didn't. Therefore Monmouth had no choice but to go public again, launching his Exocets (an epithet someone wilfully, playfully confused with a band of quaggas, a collective called the Exe Set), and did so again from the safety of the *TLS*, or if that failed any cultural stronghold willing to publish his rants. She put up with it over the years, and was admired for the dignity she showed when up against his barrage. In 1986, when the last Gregor Sabre, at the age of ninety-one, expired finally – an historical event chronicled as quietly taking place at his home in Taplow, with his team of carers weeping at his bedside – at that point she considered moving on. She gave me the inside story one day in 2013, a couple of years after Hugh too had shuffled off his coil, and almost six since Humber had passed. We were in the Sabre archive. I was interested in acquiring and in some cases republishing Sabre's translations into English of Danish scholar critic Georg Brandes (1842–1927). His urbane, incisive critiques of literary movements, drawn astutely against whatever political ferment, were the right antidote to thumbs-up social media-style, or Amazon flag waves (or droops as that may be) – a culture we're saddled with when it comes to the litmus of artefacts and their worth. Our negotiation didn't last long. The take-it-or-leave-it deal she offered was simple. I could have all her Brandes material on condition that I also relieve her of everything to do with Hugh and his Exe Set, and do what I like with it. I must have looked astonished.

'I'll leave you to look around,' she said. I was in the back room off an office in Southwark Street. There was a single naked bulb and not much natural light, its one window partly obscured by the towers of box files shipped from Sabre HQ in central London, and still accumulating. First thing I found was a facsimile of that note, or lengthy explication, from an astonished Monmouth, appalled that Humber's *Cracks in the Plaster of Time*, that debut collection of middling bourgeois poems, hadn't made the Morgan Beresford First Book shortlist. Also from Monmouth's hand was a copy of his letter commissioning a new poem, whose title he insisted on was 'Swine', as conclusion to the last collection, *Just Put a Sign Up*. I found only one letter in the other direction, from Humber to Hugh, badly typed and signed in ink that had dried up or run out before the final sweep. He questioned the choice of erasures applied to *An Open Door*, the film documentary, surprised and disappointed that his revelation as to his reading habits was lost from the final cut.

Other curiosities are lists Monmouth made of memoirs of cultural figures he intended to quote in Humber's biography, ditto articles in literary journals, scenes from films and documentaries, reviewers and their critiques, and a survey of propaganda Hugh took credit for as putting into public consciousness. There is a copy of *The Spirit of '68*, the student magazine of the University of the North, when Rhea Bright was guesting as editor. Almost the last thing of Hugh's I put my hand on was a template draft of the letters sent out asking those close to Humber for biographical information. He suggested initials as the authenticating mark on each testament, rather than a signature, and explained his plan, i.e. to circulate to all participants each of their statements, for the purpose of cross-check and verification where stories coincided. Then in a file of their own I found those very testaments, initialled as Hugh had instructed (except I think in the case of West). No recording seems to exist, but FO (Humber's second temporary secretary) recalled live Duncan Summerset in a local radio interview, after he'd retired. I also found, mixed in with Styre's published case notes, where Humber isn't named, but you infer him, some of Rhea's background notes to her film project.

Somehow not making the return post and still in the slush pile was a collection of poems from one Liza Lambeth, its title *The Waist Band*, with an epigraph: 'For HH, *Il peggior fabbro*'. A pencilled note on the manuscript title reads, 'Her poems are like pages from a homework book. Reject.' Liza, who taught at girls' grammar schools, made a name as poet in small-press publishing, never rising to the heights of Sabre and Sabre, and reviewed under the penname Elle. I have come across her homework books, or pamphlets.

Of much more interest, and tantalisingly so, was an official application to the judicial archive in Schmutzburg, signed not by Hugh, but a name I didn't recognise, stapled to a reply from Nicola Chamoogan, promising three key depositions, which I went in search of, just as Gillian brought me a cup of coffee.

'How are you getting on?'

I said I'd take her up on her offer. 'This Schmutzburg thing looks interesting.' Much more so than the Exe Set.

'Good. Feel free. Sugar?'

—Jack d'Argus, CentreHouse Press, Denmark Hill, December 2018

Call Bridgland Jolley

As individuals we are not completely unique, but are like all other men. Hence a dream with a collective meaning is valid in the first place for the dreamer, but it expresses at the same time the fact that his momentary problem is also the problem of other people. This is often of great practical importance, for there are countless people who are inwardly cut off from humanity and oppressed by the thought that nobody else has their problems. Or else they are those all-too-modest souls who, feeling themselves non-entities, have kept their claim to social recognition on too low a level. Moreover, every individual problem is somehow connected with the problem of the age, so that practically every subjective difficulty has to be viewed from the standpoint of the human situation as a whole. But this is permissible only when the dream really is a mythological one and makes use of collective symbols.

—Jung, *Psychological Reflections*

Foreword

I can't say I had much to do in that initial exchange of information between Jeremy Gard – of the *European Tribune* – and the press office here. There was, I know, a succession of persistent inquiries, whose end result was always the same – i.e., that careworn journalist passed through successive hands and finally to me. His petition varied little. The British citizen, Michael Grading, still relatively young, and a graduate through the state, had left a career in the nonsense world of industry, and had crossed our borders into Schmutzburg. Each weary nod of the weary reporter's head fell short of an accusation, though the *real* question Gard never thought to ask. Had we got Grading against his will? Our records I'm sure will show a flat denial of any such inference. No one at that time professed to know if Grading *was* here, still less as a hostage.

I suggested to Gard, a man who had roved round the troubled world several times in the last twenty years, that if Grading *was* here (and his presence was newsworthy), all he needed to know would be issued by our press office. To that dark place I redirected him. Gard ran a steady hand through the thin, greying hair swept back off his brows, and produced his business card. On the blank, reverse side he had inked in the name of the guesthouse he had chosen as base, Haushofer's, and urged me to get in touch should I glean further information. Information wasn't something I was much prepared to give him, on this or any subject, and furthermore Gard's insistent tone sounded like reformer's zeal, which never won my sympathy.

'Anyway what's so special about this Grading?' I asked.

Gard, re-zipping his jacket, didn't mince his words. The seams, he said, through our Schmutzburg traditions now only squared a worn fabric, and the final reticulation, a flimsy protection over our head, was about to tear. 'I am always,' he went on, 'at the scene of breaking news.'

We had arrived at a moment in the history of Schmutzburg when one tent wouldn't do for two camps ideologically – static traditionalists on the one hand, and a gathering mood of change on the other.

'Firstly,' I said, 'I don't accept your premise. And in any case what's it to do with a supposed visiting Englishman?'

Gard told me he knew very well that the last British official here, a plumpish mandarin with the tasteless aura of salesman, had taken soundings but had accepted failure. Grading's situation, having been reported in the UK press, had at last been reduced to a half-dozen meaningless scraps of paper, any one chasing any other five round the in-trays of Whitehall – precisely that whirl of bureaucracy the English didn't feel they paid their taxes for. Grading's close friend Rhea, together with Grading's parents, scoured the daily papers, and got, when the story was cold, on the one hand a summary of all known pointers (the broadsheets), and on the other coffee-break entertainment (the tabloids). Their ritual with nightly news broadcasts wasn't more fruitful. Planting themselves before the TV ended in nothing – from any nightly bulletin. Not, I imagine, without intellectual pain, Grading Senior composed the first of his pleas, and dispatched this post-haste to his local MP, a man it couldn't be claimed he'd helped get elected. Nevertheless this got things moving, and the next thing I personally saw was an overstuffed salesman sniffing disdainfully in our cloisters (which of course I didn't admit to Gard).

Gard well knew that envoy's velvety negotiation had got him nowhere. I remember him – a man who sentimentalised, as part of his strategy. It prompted him to photographs of Michael Grading, all cleverly, carefully chosen. One had Michael in the rolling green of campus life, in jeans and a tee shirt, thoughtful over an upended beer crate, with a chequer board and chess pieces. You could see the sun's halo in his hair, and in place of his missing king could identify the mottled texture of a pebble. Then there was an action shot – yellow beach, blue waves, subject releasing stick for brown and white springer. All of us here were united in the same blank look. As a last resort, that hapless envoy offered a quiet deal in some godforsaken corridor. He looked around, and in an absurd misreading of our plain living – the stone floors, oak chests – offered us 'new technology', on the condition of one definitive statement. Had we, hadn't we got Grading?

'That,' said Gard, 'was his final intrusion, and I'm willing to bet that was the point you ushered him out.'

This was more or less true. I watched him, with his shiny executive case clamped to his wrist, a man in deepest regrets for the 'clear signal' he'd been hoping for, but hadn't received. Weeks later there was a communiqué, then another, then with a change of government high-level interest in the fate of Michael Grading evaporated. The new minister wasn't tasked, and the case, having lagged politically to the back of the queue, dropped off altogether. It surprised me little, having seen the colour of the new administration. Its ethos was unashamedly commercial, its position centrist. Its one ululation urged all human affairs to the ravages of the marketplace.

'But really that's only a delaying tactic,' Gard, very calmly, informed me. 'You're going to have to face the fact that the old structures are breaking down. I know, for example, you've an increased reliance on tourism…. Tell me. What effect do you think *that's* going to have?'

I didn't dare contemplate – not that or *anything* his observations had implied. It was true that Europe's member states were less enchanted than at any other time with the disciplines of Schmutzburg, and saw little value in gentleman scholars preening themselves in the pomp and powders of poetics and philosophy, and the theory of social progress. Their valuable grants enabling us to enrol their brightest graduates, the lifeblood of our institutions, had diminished, and dramatically so in recent years. Couldn't we, they asked, turn our community intellect to the problems of renewable energy, or climate change, or a fix for the scourge of terrorism, or the bane of economics, boom and bust? If we couldn't answer that question, increased dependence on the tourist trade was inevitable – daily busloads driven up into our mountains and sniffing round our cloisters.

'Exactly what are you suggesting?' I said to Gard.

'That pretty soon all your students will be just like Michael Grading. Not selected by you, but here because they've escaped – thrown off the shackles of what's laughingly called democracy. Everyone wants a slice of power.'

'Well,' I said, with as much pomposity as I could muster, 'that's not a unique state of affairs. We do get self-motivated applicants, sometimes. But they're not treated any differently. All are subject to the fairest examination.'

'I know what's meant by that,' said Gard. 'That examination is done by committee, behind locked doors – in effect a trial, whose outcome is already determined. You might as well know it's the committee proceedings apropos of Grading I'll be reporting on. Even up here you can buy the *Tribune*....'

'I shall look out for it. But as I say – anything you need to know, it all comes through the press office. Good morning.'

He pressed his card into my hand. 'Just think about what I've said....'

'Good morning, Mr Gard.'

All very uncanny. Even now the committee was being assembled, consisting of Professor Hext (chair), Dr Muchello (retired), Professor Gee (international law), Professor Standey (diplomacy), a court reporter, a minutes-taker, seven other committee members, and at various intervals one or other expert witness. I did not take part in proceedings, but looked out for Gard's daily column in the *European Tribune*, a paraphrased and annotated version of which is available *infra*. Allow me first to offer further background information on Michael Grading. He arrived here with his friend Humber. Neither was dressed for the mountain environment. Humber sported a white tuxedo and scarlet cummerbund, and had a matching bowtie. This was Grading's foremost expert witness, in a 'case' Michael conducted himself. The difference in age between the two men was conspicuous. Whereas Grading was young, limpid, brown-haired, under-nourished, Humber had reached middle-life and appeared solid and contented.

One other witness – for the committee – was a third British citizen. Let me stress, she had arrived by arrangement – as a person who'd risen spectacularly, and whose position I cannot compromise. Therefore everywhere where Gard mentions her name I refer to her as Nicola.

The committee room was unremarkable, a high chamber cloaked in mountain shadow. A theatrical trick allowed a shaft of sunlight through an upper window, whose emphasis was the three main officials (Muchello, Gee, Standey). Lower windows gave onto the courtyard, and behind that, our mountain slopes. There was muted conversation. Our bell, off-pitch, tolled. When the tolling ceased, a bailiff opened proceedings, one elbow suavely to a legal tome.

Press Cuttings

I point out, because Gard doesn't, that in *our* judiciary the bailiff is not a minor figure. That's just *one* contrast to English procedure. As a new graduate of Schmutzburg, this is his first opportunity to test not just his erudition, but the range and power of his oratory – which in this example he frequently does.

So cautioned, let us resume with Gard's eccentric view of events, as printed in his *Tribune*, whose sensational introduction I am afraid I have had to replace by that foreword of my own above, pinion to the body of text I already foresee I am going to have to appropriate....

Day One

Antecedents according to the bailiff – supremely confident at the outset of Grading's trial – didn't help in a case like this, when few Europeans had made their way to the heart of our republic, or at least without invitation. He revealed the full extent of his lost hours cloistered with Schmutzburg's foremost scholars, to come up with – precisely – nothing.

'Antecedents' were the stock-in-trade for the kind of scholar he meant, who pores endlessly over the codification of our tradition. If not intended, it amused Muchello, Gee and Standey, our committee principals, here for Grading's benefit, and anxious to conclude his case. With a hint of a smile the bailiff pre-empted all three—

'Don't!' he said. 'Don't quip! Oddballs at large in the republic, if inflexible as to proceedings, I think can do as they please just so long as they keep their back-room perversions *to* their back room. If as I'm bound to admit it's been a painful half hour I do at least owe them something.'

'Oh, and what is that?'

'This useful-looking book.'

Gard questions strangely as a point of honour if levity is the right tone for something so serious, with Grading 'entitled' to a fair hearing. The bailiff had two things in mind. Central to all committee aims he intended that the defendant soon understood the tenor of debate (on our side dismissive). Muchello reinforced that, and anyway had his own view on the value of archive management—

'Those fossils are of some use,' he said, referring to the book, whose pages the bailiff would navigate with expertise, now and over coming days.

The latter gave notice of the kind of detail he was likely to refer to through it, not always true to republican law, but mindful of the barrier between himself and Michael Grading, which at all costs must be maintained. The bailiff was young, filled with the chemistry of youth and ego. He observed—

'The aficionado of Frame Solutions will be interested to know that the game of games has an entry.' He seemed to want to open the book at that page. 'More than that, its complicated matrix is one still written about. Even as we speak, there are new revelations under preparation. No matter what those fossils as you call them come across – if they find there are rules, they'll write them down. They regard it as a kind of ownership.'

I don't wish to be obstructive, and say only that Frame Solutions is Schmutzburg's national game. It is played with counters – one side black, the other white – arranged on a standard chessboard. Unlike chess, there is no fixed distribution of power to the pieces – therefore how each may act can vary from game to game. Play is according to rules that continue to evolve. A game may last from anything up to a day, though a few hours is typical.

Professor Standey didn't share the bailiff's view that our archivists, or anyone, could claim 'ownership' of our game of games. Those relicts had contributed nothing to its present state. 'That would demand imagination,' he said, 'which they do not have in abundance.'

'Well,' said the bailiff, with no reason to press the point, 'I hope we'll pursue that another time. You know we're facing a *cause célèbre*, and had better find an effective way to proceed.'

'Well, yes – that *is* unavoidable.'

'There is an icy wind blowing through our house. Our scholars will scratch away in their lamp-lit turrets into the winter. Whatever passes here, they'll classify. Therefore to business. We have at our disposal only one résumé, and very little evidence. This may be protectionist, but my career begins *here*.'

It *was* protectionist, and that, according to Standey – a grey, square-shouldered man – couldn't be deemed proper. He predicted our chroniclers wouldn't turn out to be as impassive as the bailiff thought. He took him to task for proceedings so far, which still hadn't broached the matter in hand – the illegal entry of a foreign national into our country. More seriously, there was also the question of infiltration of at least one of our institutions.

In Muchello's experience the republic's chroniclers *were* impassive, though now we hear a resounding gavel, as a sane person somewhere in the chamber (Hext, we hope) attempts to bring the meeting to order. Grown men can never resist a squabble, as happened now, with disagreement hinged on whose lucid mind it was that had left its stamp on the present state of Frame Solutions. Muchello, an old, gaunt, grey man, and a respected master, claimed that he alone had sniffed the dangers lurking behind locked doors. He feared a student populace intent on making a mere trivial pastime of the game he had given so much to.

For what it's worth, no backroom scholar had ever had a hand in the development of Frame Solutions. I know for a fact that Muchello had picked it up at a point of indifference and brought it to its present simplicity, something Professor Gee only scoffed at.

The bailiff bore these objections, protesting that all he intended was to set a framework on the committee's inquiry. 'Nevertheless you're right,' he said. 'The problem remains that here the unthinkable has happened. An Englishman has got across our borders. How shall we get to the bottom of this?'

'Indeed that *is* the question. In that case hadn't we better press on…?'

'Press on we shall,' Muchello said, 'but not without a breach I'm afraid. I'd hoped for a gentler perspective on the glassy panorama here. I thought that what we call retirement was a softening process…. As you can see, it's one I shall have to postpone – and anyway days of enforced idleness only make me restless. Things have got to the point where those of my friends still young and agile have noted my anxieties. My explanation's a bit thin, apparently. I point to a pair of hideous gargoyles flanking my windows and tell them how distracting they are when I look from my apartments.'

How [asks Gard] to explain these merry jousts? And such gravity in the situation. Well, it's true that Dr Muchello had retired from active life, and so shouldn't have involved himself in committee work. But there was a shortage of available personnel, which had seen him co-opted onto the Grading case. In this there was no impediment, though what Muchello meant by his gargoyles – a dragon and a lion – no one understood. That was also the case when he hinted that his was not an impartial relationship with the impostor Michael Grading. Professor Standey got the wrong impression altogether, and tried to cajole his comrade, believing that what he alluded to was the crumbling infrastructure characteristic of Schmutzburg's nooks and palaces.

'So many appeals,' he said, 'so in need of support!' There was a basilica roof past the point of repair, and a draughty scriptorium, not to say a bad case of damp in the library.

'And what about,' someone said, 'the limited availability of public viewing space, which cannot bode well, what with the present growth in tourism!'

'Is that so very serious?' the bailiff asked. 'After all, it's only an *enlightened* European who gets up any interest in sepulchres, dampish vaults or ancient sarcophagi. Even then he looks to his own cathedrals first.' If the born tourist had no interest, the bailiff would rather he didn't come at all.

When it came to the sensitive issue of tourism, Dr Muchello had a good grasp surprisingly, and was aware of the defects. 'A touchy subject,' he said. 'Yet I'm astonished that for so long so vital a part of general policy has been left to the discretion of booking clerks, whose teams have their own commission to answer to. They follow a single directive, cast as an inviolate set of rules. When booking forms are processed eastern Europeans are asked to part with a small fee, and are assigned in easy groups to the most cheerful guides. Anglo-Saxon detachment seems to be disdained. The English when *they* arrive are left to their own devices, having paid through the nose. I have no idea of the rationale behind this.'

The bailiff had his own theories. One particular exhibit was always on the tourist agenda, and that was a collection of memorabilia after Schmutzburg's first proclamation and the Prince Wix era, when republicanism was unthinkable, and service was to God and King. 'The chief booking clerk,' the bailiff said, 'at all times keeps a summarising paragraph to remind him of it. It's pinned to his booth.'

'Oh,' said Gee (sarcastically). 'Does that mean he has a fancy for papal recognition?'

'Actually he did once investigate canonisation procedures....'

'I wouldn't care to prophesy how the Vatican dealt with that *folie de grandeur.*'

'It was for research purposes only I believe. But,' the bailiff went on, 'we're getting off the point.'

Dr Muchello returned to a contemplation of his gargoyles, now telling us both were mute. Not even a bright cleansing shower or thunderous downpour gave them voice. That was a pity, since the view from his casement held clues as to Grading's entry into Schmutzburg's secret centre.

Silence prevailed, which Standey interrupted. 'Well,' he said. 'Assuming the elements haven't eroded our city walls – how?'

'I'll come to that,' Muchello said. 'Our first concern must be the fact of his entry. If as seems likely this was through the eastern colonnade, the inscription surmounting it was one he'd obeyed: *Abandon all impedimenta, ye who enter here.*'

'All this,' said Standey, 'I presume is in the résumé.'

The bailiff handed him the résumé, saying no, 'but you'd better read it all the same'.

'That's really why I'm here,' said Muchello, 'and not prodding the masonry.'

'What exactly do you mean?'

'At around noon I'm usually wheeled to my window, with a blanket across my knees and a mug of soup for lunch. On this particular day I had the luck to notice a new set of prints in the snow, winding to our door. One of my last official functions had been to grant visitor status to someone else from England, and naturally I thought she'd arrived but had lost her way.'

'Yes, I see.'

'It turns out she *had* arrived, some days before – though I was ignorant of this. That may be why I didn't connect those tracks with Michael Grading here. Chance put him in my way later that same day. As you can see, this makes me a witness.'

'Oh, that's highly irregular, don't you think? We'd have to ask whether you can go on.'

The bailiff thought he could go on. 'You know the pressures on our lists,' he said.

'Nevertheless....'

But the bailiff insisted. 'Those of us privy to the case have agreed. We can't afford to risk delay. If at the end a procedural change is called for we'll debate it and give it to the boffins. Now isn't the time.'

'Dear me no,' said the old man. 'Not when we see so many eager acolytes in mimicry of *that* shaven species. It's always inconceivable to me how they inhabit those dusty chambers of theirs without a seizure, or at least a fit of sneezing.'

'Well, if *I'm* to avoid a seizure,' said Gee, 'we'd better press on. Can't we get to the point!'

'If it's that simple. I came across Grading with his back to me, just as he'd passed through the portico. I nearly called out. By his clothing I assumed he was a tourist, off his course. How could I connect *him* and the tracks outside?'

'What was he doing?'

'Comprehending. What took his eye was the carved relief, in English oak, hanging with the portraits. Over the mantel. When he heard me coming he turned and pointed up.'

'Why did he do that?'

'He wanted to know what the chiselling meant. I did my best to explain, though the museum catalogue puts it more succinctly than I can.'

'It's one of the exhibits,' the bailiff said, 'which if you'll allow I shall read....' Apparently he did just that, so where Gard quotes from the catalogue I shall follow suit—

The three divisions of the motif depict a once important stricture. Note the left hand of the pair, where a disgruntled husband is left at home minding the baby, though by the empty jug on the barrel he's consoled himself in drink. His wife knows his evil ways. You see her creeping round from behind, clutching a wooden shoe. She winds back her arm in preparation for a blow to her husband's head. Now notice that cowardly neighbour, keeping his head down but determined to miss nothing – a man who goes on to report what he sees. Result, the luckless husband is condemned by the village fathers. On the right of the pair local worthies have come together and are unanimous – the drunkard they hold aloft is set to ride the skimmington.

'Yes, amusing I'm sure. Was there anything else that passed between you?'

'Next Grading asked what it was in the apex of that relief, for which we shan't need the catalogue. That I told him was the just god in his heaven, who saw that his law was carried out.'

'So now he'd had it explained, what did he do?'

'I suspect assumptions I have had to make are not satisfactory as evidence. I'm sure that while I plodded my way back through our stony labyrinths he didn't do as directed. By which I mean join the procession of tourists, from where I assumed he'd got himself detached. You so often find the party pariah, who in a search for curiosities makes his way into corners or niches, and absorbs himself in everything the guide won't show him.'

'Or knows anything about.'

'I met Grading again – a traveller, yes, but a tourist? I chanced to overhear what seemed on his part a long, one-sided conversation, the essence of which showed him as an authority on the history of two inter-war expeditions to synchronise polar and equatorial clocks.'

'Clocks?'

'Incredibly this was in the library. When I announced myself he looked embarrassed. He drew my attention to two English newspapers – one was a broadsheet, the other a tabloid. He told me he was just replying to the press.'

'It's too fantastic! Having found his way into the library – are we to believe completely unchallenged? – he's added insult by smuggling in propaganda!'

'Hard to believe, I know. And I wasn't at my best. Since our last encounter only ten or fifteen minutes before I had got a headache. I put it down to the impenetrable communications bureaucracy that has grown up around us. No one could tell me where I could find Nicola Chamoogan, or even when she'd arrived.'

'But,' said the bailiff, 'you must have reasoned Ms Chamoogan had been with us for days. I look out myself sometimes. In my apartment there are none of those demons, malign defenders of the house. All my stimuli are aeolian and come in the stench of student cuisine, in waves in draughty corridors. Driven by that to the windows I can't help but notice, day after day, the rising winds, the swirling sheets of snow. You must have known. Here was a set of tracks that couldn't be Nicola's. But what about this man from England standing in our library, I assume without a piolet?'

'What might explain that but not those newspapers was reference he made to that previous exhortation – that *Abandon all impedimenta....*'

'And?'

'He hadn't abandoned political impedimenta. He wheeled round to face me, his broadsheet open at the reviews page. He liked, he said, the ancient buildings here. With that as introduction, he showed me to what I imagine was unintended irony – at least where *he* came from. A certain school of architects had adopted as group epithet their "Aesthetes of Multilinearity", though his own description wasn't as flattering. Their labours, he told me, were under inspiration and afflatus of a hard-hat Muse, routinely carried out in the rustic gardens of rural England. The result never changed – urban depletions the usual characteristic of modern English cities.'

'I can't then see him cope with the ethos here, and the nature of *its* ironies, which *are* intended. I learned only yesterday that the director of organ music plays publicly, from an arts conurbation at the outskirts of madness – and does so three times a day. That's a dangerous thing at the height of the season. I don't dare venture near when I catch his vibrations, his thundering rococo edifice soaked in the insanity of fairground waltzes.' This, coming from the bailiff, might be construed as subversive.

'I think that manifestation is one our Michael Grading might have happily dealt with. He mentioned other reports from his paper, touching on the problems transporting bottles, bricks and household machinery to the showing space in public galleries. Or the intractability of experimentation in circular fiction, where to commence at any randomly chosen chapter meant to conclude satisfactorily at the one preceding, losing nothing of wholeness and meaning. Result: not a circle, a spiral.'

'I hope they don't get wind of that in the organ loft.'

'When we have time there are other examples. Black spots on a white canvas, an electrified frog in a bell jar....'

The bailiff was keen to hear more, but by now Professor Standey had grown bored and barely repressed a yawn. 'When, as you say,' he said, 'there's time.'

I seriously doubt Jeremy Gard's interest and curiosity as to the fate of Michael Grading, as I accuse him and his scurrilous paper, the *European Tribune*, of the most outrageous calumny, at least in its account of our doings here in Schmutzburg. I could not have known that the story so-called would run in that dishonest publication for eight consecutive days. And I didn't see his 'day one' until – to use Gard's terminology – day two. That's for the simple reason your European newspapers arrive here exactly a day late (and even then aren't for general consumption). Therefore it was not until the committee's second session that I was able to crosscheck Gard's pen against the calm objectivity of official releases from our press office.

I do not forgive the imaginative Gard his speculative 'analysis' turned out as 'conclusion' to each day's report. For example in his discussion on our attitude to the English generally he asks do we consider that he and his countrymen don't have the discipline of mind that we in Schmutzburg do? I say only that were the rest of the world to follow that hortative *Abandon impedimenta* then perhaps a more equable exchange between English diplomacy and the citizens of Schmutzburg might be possible.

Now that we come to diplomacy, Gard dismisses your UK envoy with less politeness than we did, calling him an 'optimistic fool', douched in the 'stench of affluence'. I recall long affable talks, which although they yielded him nothing did make clear our position. Yet in this Gard only mocks at a man whose stupidity is almost sublime, who glassy-eyed and smiling seraphically bade his flunkey 'open the portfolio', then embarked on a torrent of glitz, to sell us something. Gard restates it for us. Categorically *no* – our seniors have no call for a limousine.

The press office states that Grading appeared several weeks before that first official, and about his presence (Grading's) Gard thinks he detects something collusive. He alludes, melodramatically, to a 'subtext', secret assignations through the bailiff's coded exchanges, first with Muchello, then with Standey. For Standey, a swift summing-up wasn't going to be possible (Standey was a busy man, with demands on his time). Wrongly he presumed the written résumé was going to be the clincher, and would clear matters up. Of course that was not so. In fact what complicated things was the awkward juxtaposition of Dr Muchello as both inquirer and witness, a point that ought to have made his evidence void. Heretical though it is to say, Gard would have taken it as a sign of Schmutzburg's disintegration – in his view soon to be complete – when Muchello's 'observations' were not struck from the record. As you will see, something sinister was done instead.

According to Gard, it was Professor Gee who first raised this – though not as a point of law. All Gee could think about (I see this as the smoke settles, as all becomes clear) was how to fire a first shot in his own campaign. If this was something the bailiff understood, he took care not to show which side he was on. Nearer the mark I think is the bailiff only just beginning to see what Gard was here to do – to tell us that the old order – encompassing *all* our world's Muchellos – was doomed.

Yet, they were his words that drew attention to the shortage of court officials. He'd drawn up the list of locums himself, knowing the climate, the sheer antipathy, and just how much his contemporaries loathed these endless committees. We have already seen why Muchello had found himself recalled. Indirectly that was also the reason why – with Muchello as accomplice – the bailiff revelled in these opening spars, mostly at Grading's expense. Instance that carved relief, put before proceedings not as an exhibit as such, but as judgement on the kind of country Grading was from – one plagued by village sots and obsessed with public retribution. Some cosmic charter, putting God in his heaven – assuring the fitness of these arrangements – in reality secured the perpetuation of its error. It's no wonder that particular omnipresence has erased itself from Schmutzburg's constitution. I could go on at length, but remind myself that the fate of Michael Grading has to be my object. I appreciate how perplexed he must have been.

I don't wish to resuscitate the tourism debate, long dead anyway, though am forced by Gard's persistent jibes to say something. I make it clear that the tour, while important to Schmutzburg's economy, didn't give Grading – or anyone – licence to wander. Do I need to remind you that Muchello tried to usher him back to the cordons? (No, you say, I don't.) And what about Gard's deception concerning those footprints in the snow? He seems to be saying (or misreporting) something like this—

1 Tracks that Muchello saw from his cell must have been Michael's. If they were Nicola Chamoogan's, put there in previous days, the winds would have swept them away. (Put like this, the trick is transparent, because it assumes what we shouldn't assume, i.e. that Muchello was aware that Nicola Chamoogan was here. But we know, even by Gard's account, that Muchello had complained that he didn't.)

2 Ergo, Muchello must have known Grading wasn't a tourist, because tourists arrived on the bus, and didn't leave footprints. So the trick goes on.

3 It had been shown how Grading was dressed, making his journey on foot impossible. Had he attempted such, he would have perished long before reaching Schmutzburg. So, these weren't his tracks. (And on.)

4 If the tracks weren't Grading's, they must have been Nicola Chamoogan's – so after all Dr Muchello did know she was here.

Plainly 'un-logic'. Or tricks, tracks (knick-knack paddywhack), for really the point was this, which wouldn't have been lost on Dr Muchello or Professor Standey: 'I, the bailiff, for the time being throw in my lot with you, Muchello, and resist these new tensions, whatever they are. Read in my syntax the truth about Nicola Chamoogan, who was already here, and that a conspiracy of silence sought to conceal that fact from you.'

I don't give much for the old man's loss of direction, and doubt that he stumbled into the library by accident, and neither do I accept Gard's account of what he heard there – Michael Grading soliloquising. Humber, I imagine, had tucked himself away in an aisle. What Muchello overheard was one side of a conversation on publicly held assumptions re popular physics, because capital-s science, sitting in an honorary chair, dictated its terms to lay audiences everywhere, without the bother of proofs. That, to Gard, is the kind of self-justification that smacks of what we suffer from here: Gentlemen, blind faith, please! If you can't comprehend an exposition, then please accept it.... That too is the sticky end to millennia of capital-p philosophy.

I intertwine shades of my own loss with Muchello's pattern of feelings. I shared with that old man the view that Grading wasn't concerned with replicated worlds, parallel lives, reverse travels into time. He doggedly protected his ignorance as to the structure and causality characteristic of black holes (phenomena I don't acknowledge). In fact the whole garbage of modern science represented a dumping zone he'd rather not wade through. Moreover Grading, in holding to the 'old' orders of his own culture, sounded a common note in ours, and may have been attuned to some of our ancient maxims. Good, not dangerous ground, you'd have thought. Yet that seemed too suspicious when Grading changed the subject – I mean that ruse of his with the newspapers. I accept he probably didn't know that the 'literature' he bore was regarded as classifiable propaganda. Had he wished to disseminate it – and Standey was certain he did – the case, grave already, we would have regarded as excessively severe.

Further – and in this I acknowledge Grading may have been innocent – he made no attempt at refuge. Unequipped to change it, he had departed his own world, a lustreless terrace adorned with sun-basking reptiles, gasping under the ordures of bad taste. Those cheery pessimists writing for an English press made good with their correctives, and every day offered their revelations. Sometimes you'd see city architects, or as Michael put it authors of urban misery. At others you'd get bottles, bricks and household gadgetry, and idiotically long accounts as to the problems in gathering these as public exhibits, a process a great deal less difficult than getting them accepted as objects of art. Then there were 'experiments' in circular fiction, in my opinion best left with the author's jottings – and not put into print. To an extent I sympathise with the bailiff, whose hope was that the resident organ maestro didn't try something similar. I ask you to share my horror, now that that same man wields political power, lording it over the culture committees. It's not for me to apologise, but simply to state, that what Grading came to, saw, and left behind, was the infection of your mediocrity, whose incubation was encouraged in your world, not in ours. Alas, England, for me! (For what diminished scale of reason proposed art in an electrified frog?)

Day Two

What everyone wanted to know, and would never find an answer to, was how Grading, and how those newspapers, found their way into the library. What happened when that question was probed descended into spurious deconstruction of the first of those 'rogue publications', with Muchello launching into other stories Grading said he had read. That led us, uncontrollably, from art and science to two separate versions of the same piece of gossip in the society columns. The tabloid carried the following headline: 'Suicide starlet tragedy note found'. It was a Hollywood *femme fatale*, and a litter of broken families she'd left behind, and a trail of vengeful wives. Her note was the anatomy of human torment, from triangular bedroom scenes, to liquor addictions and other stimulants, to profligate spending, and to cap it jealous, homicidal lovers.

'Ah,' Standey said, 'she was too modest! And so few of the civilised pursuits of leisure. I suppose the note was found in the clutter of a dressing table, with an empty jar of pills.'

'Actually no,' said Muchello. 'The photographer had crashed around in vain for that. The best he put up was retrospectives of life back home. Distraught parents in a shabby morning room (view: Pembroke hills). The family retriever, half the dead woman's age. Some of the whey-faced dolls she'd bathed and dressed.'

Her friend and entrepreneur, a Mostyn Sanchez, refused to be interviewed. It was his kidney-shaped pool somewhere in California that the actress, half an hour dead, had been hauled out of, in the arms of a janitor.

'The good-hearted mechanical, so reassuring. I'll wager on the bulge of his biceps. If tattooed, was that a sword, a shield, or a mermaid?'

'Who can say?'

'Isn't there a violation here? I mean, is this really, *really* the proper etiquette of self-destruction?'

Her departure, though having little or no effect – because the journalist whose scoop it was had forgotten his closure myths – was dark in its judgements, with accusations implied of the bright *beau monde* she belonged to. Somehow that scribe failed to uncover popular sound advice written in her last confession, penned not for her loved ones, but for the millions who adored her. The recommendation not to follow, in a 'Don't do what I did' – it just wasn't there....

'Because,' Muchello went on, 'it wasn't suicide. Grading's other newspaper, in its crusade against sensationalism, carried its own, rather different report.'

Its editorial was usually detached and authoritative, but now there was elder-brother relish, and a touch of self-righteousness—

'Staff on the other paper had bothered to read the coroner's report.'

'Our semi-naked screen nymph had had a *piña colada* too many, and in the heat had decided on a fatal last swim.'

'Mostyn's blue pool.'

'Why yes. Though that faultless gentleman was in a heated phone discussion, in the recess of his washroom, when the janitor fished her out.'

'Ah,' said Standey, 'the note was a fabrication—'

'Not quite.'

The misfire hinged on the misconstruction of things at the time of her death, and no mention of her abnormally short attention span. If nothing was found at the scene, then an appropriate scrap of paper in her makeup things would have to do – a dictated checklist, prompts, points to bear in mind for the character role her agent had negotiated.

Standey returned to his slumbers and left it to the bailiff—

'All so routine, though you'd have thought a front-page apology would also have been a sincere good money-spinner.'

'Just the point Grading wanted me to understand. Yet I now know why my steps in the library met with these pointless expositions. I know what he was hiding.'

Suddenly here was Standey again: 'You're going to tell us he had an accomplice—'

'That would assume an accessory here in Schmutzburg.'

The bailiff tried to imagine what it was that had attracted Grading here, whose career in industry had begun so promisingly: 'The sharp air of mountain life. For some of us the short, invigorating walks. And no one here minds the philosopher's wasted centuries.'

'Perhaps Grading thinks the rarest blooms are found in stony crags.'

'That's uncannily near the point,' Muchello said. Having brought his Western material *into* the library, he proposed to take *out* of it a potted history of Schmutzburg, which he'd found on our shelves.

'Which history would that be?' the bailiff asked.

'Prince Wix. That era.'

An impatient Wix had paced his feudal chambers, having asked, under the heavy weight of oppression – all that dark air filling his castle – why it was always starless night inside. His advisers, who had never been asked to foresee the possibility of peaceful civilisation, thought one answer was to spare important enemies the conventions of war, and instead negotiate. Wix scratched his head (much as Grading must have). Having power at his fingertips, he demanded the key to the first of his subterranean rooms, which he opened. His retinue, swept in the draught of his purple, cowered behind him. To peer over his studded shoulder was to catch the regal glitter in a heap of encrusted tiaras, and the glow of an open chest overflowing with pearls. Yet these were not the totality, for what Wix picked out and held longingly in his gaze was a papal diadem.

Standey said: 'Spent hopes in a royal cornucopia, and Wix's puzzled second thoughts about governance and life, I should have thought don't really equate to a disaffected Englishman in search of a quieter life up here. Or do I miss the point?' Standey was weary already, and probably noted on his pad that Schmutzburg's oldest citizen was too prone to ramble.

'Well, it has its wider truth,' the bailiff chipped in. In another damp room, a bearded seer had almost reached his own century, and now, at an undreamt-of conclusion to wretched years of confinement, couldn't stop weeping. No one remembered how he'd got himself condemned. It must have been at the behest of Wix's father, whose severity was legendary. A great many assumptions, from that moment on, have been woven into folklore. That same soothsayer, as beneficiary of Wix's new liberalism, was anxious to impress. He sang his man of affairs as freer of serfs – not that Michael Grading falls into that category. Wage slavery is what I think they call it now.

Muchello had his views on that. 'That particular liberation ran its stunted course,' he said, 'in a cosmos suddenly twisted inside out. Somewhere in its sacred womb a new order of life waited in vain for the world to change around it. We all of us have our tenacious grip on the past – on Wix's kingdom in particular. But his experiment failed, and what remains of that airy new city he made – a belvedere – is evidence that his was a military capital – still. That structure is now a pile of stones, but an attractive ruin, I'm told.'

Standey: 'Perhaps Michael Grading doesn't feel so out of place in ancient worlds. Or in our middle world – one of shambling hostilities, and warlike theologies. But of course Wix's vision *was* fulfilled.' That gnarled prophet, led from the grime and the darkness, explained a complicated augury, watching a dove fly across a rose bed. He recalled that Wix's father – the king – had a penchant for dovecots, which were everywhere. Suddenly he knew the absurdity of divination, and became a bard.

'A bard who,' Muchello said, 'remained true to the reckless nature of his youth – though I expect wiser to the demands of patronage, declaiming only by royal approval or decree.'

'Not an ideal hero.'

'It's not as a hero we would ask a man like Grading to celebrate him. His most misquoted exhortation is *Off, the bismotered habergeoun!* It's seldom the case, despite choruses of popular wisdom, that the quill is mightier than the sword.'

'Our learned friend has spent too many years with his nose in antique texts.'

'You can't spend *too many* years,' Muchello said.

'You can if it changes nothing.'

'Change as such is an illusion.'

The bailiff said: 'You know our legacy. Wix's progeny weren't so wide-eyed at the sight of all those soldierly acquisitions. Theirs were fraternal acts. Replanting a nation's dismembered limbs, it wasn't too much to hope they would grow up whole again, citizens of equal countries.' You can see he was an idealist.

'Well, I know you wouldn't suggest that Europe's chroniclers have committed an oversight. It's open to interpretation, but some still trace a fine golden thread through all that ignorant striving. An order *has* been achieved. Here.'

The bailiff, who would have steered this whole sorry charade as an initiation designed not for Grading, but for himself, wasn't concerned with the 'here', and said it was hardly the point, given that Schmutzburg's influence had changed little of the outside world. Wix's descendants, having planted their family crest *en grande tenue* – a lion, a sword, a stave – had managed to despoil whatever virgin ground they came upon. Still kingdoms had their chair of state, and pantomime fools humble and tugging at forelocks. If there is justification for that kind of atavism, it's said to be in widening prosperity. In some countries, I hear, you can already witness the white knight on his charger, galloping for the glassy floor of the stock exchange, dutifully deprived of peripheral vision.

Am I sure that Gard genuinely knew what our three officials were up to? And are we really to accept that his subject Michael Grading could stoop to the purchase of a tabloid, and at the same time hold that object in righteous contempt (amused contempt)? I would like to know does, privately, the pragmatic Jeremy Gard read his horoscope, when an obvious trick relates all twelve? The pronouncements are all the same, with any one chosen from that dozen having potential – good copy you'd call it – when adapted to the predicted outcome here, and to the committee Gard has found himself reporting on. And is all this starlet suicide stuff only his thinly veiled invective against a rival in the circulation war? I'd have thought he'd have kept himself above the vagaries of personal fortune.

Dr Muchello, whose detachment by no means disqualified his capacity to understand these matters, I am sure related details of her death without Gard's propensity for elder-statesman, newsy sensuality, and with a dry eye. If I can only lay hands on the minutes or a transcript of the Grading case, I am sure to discover no one in the house said ah. The lies the press allowed itself in sanctifying her suicide any sane person passes over – just as the bailiff did – as a tragic waste of time. It wasn't lost on him that the fantasised norms of celebrities are reducible in the sale of column inches, and are dished up as commodified private hells. I even speculate Mostyn Sanchez thought that too, since *no, sir!* he gave no statement whatsoever, to anyone (not on your goddam life). One other fact easy to overlook is that no one asked the janitor what he thought, whose tattooed arms had scooped the girl from the pool.

I put it like this because, given the bailiff's tone – conjectural mostly – Gard elucidates our snobbery not as individual. It's something general to the ethos of Schmutzburg. What might be construed (and what Gard construes) as disgust for the world, is in fact collegiate in its objection to the way the world is constructed through newspaper stories (still a bait for sentient beings). Petty lives come to mean petty passions, subject not to events but to scripts, with lots of schmaltz. Our sour face for things machismo is at the greyness, the homogeneity of all things media-defined. It brings me to *my* pet theory. With the uncomfortable proximity of Michael Grading's world, like Muchello I can't see our little pocket of civilisation as a thing entirely divorced from Wix's past. Why else should Muchello dredge it up?

The bailiff drew certain parallels, and argued that the battery of Western journalese was not entirely distinct from Wix's chosen weaponry. The latter's wars and the protection of his tribes didn't seem more unworthy than the cold porridge of tabloid melodrama. One shouldn't overlook that Wix, not unlike Mr Sanchez, had an unblemished reputation. Mr Sanchez's dealings at boardroom, and at washroom level, were strictly legal, and to point that out demanded the integrity of Michael Grading's other newspaper, his broadsheet. Here furthermore the astute reader noted the absence of innuendo, since, in respecting the man's privacy, his words, thoughts and deeds were kept out of it, running counter to its rival, which never smothered important questions, or supposed them in the mind of its readership. (This at least is *my* reasoning.) So, what was she doing at poolside? (Nine syllables forming a paragraph!) Again Muchello directed us, quoting the coroner. A canopy of California sunshine had penetrated her barrier cream, and Priapus too had penetrated.

Was the suicide note a journalistic fake? Let me just say I am familiar with almost any device one could describe as an *aide-mémoire*. Not so common to our way of life was one like this, where the fine line sparing personal failure had been meticulously drawn. I question it simply because of its long list of the slightest things. If that impressed on our screen goddess her new role in all its ramifications, then why, for didn't script teams invest their belles with a single dimension only? I should also like to make the comment that, in its possession of the 'note' – the one supposedly found with her effects – the elder paper stooped to the level of its popular rival, gloating. That probably adds up to a thick-jowled editor, puffy with self-importance, and the kind of man I have secretly admired (I almost blush to report), though far off in the past. A dull life stuck behind the windows in any workplace generates an inordinate interest in life across the street, metaphorically speaking.

This comes close to the posture Michael Grading struck up in the library. Later it emerged that Humber, who was concealed, was nonetheless present too. Moreover he was there in the same spirit of debate, which went unseen by Muchello (*and* unheard), who for the sake of argument adopted the antithetical view. Now, if you please, I charge Professor Standey – or rather I accuse him – of deliberately twisting the facts. A first sign of that was his suggestion that a student, an accomplice, a Person X, one of our own, had abetted the nefarious Grading. How else could such a man penetrate to our inner sanctum? Alas Grading's trial will bring an epoch to an end. Change it marks will appear subtle at first. A greater but voted-for range of controls will accomplish that breakdown Gard has foreseen and thinks he understands. New laws will pass through statute virtually unopposed, each in itself innocuous, yet in totality adding up to one powerful man impossible to remove constitutionally.

For Muchello these were already intolerant times. There was no clearer indication of that when the proscribing of Michael Grading was our one preoccupation, for no other reason than the fact that he was alien. It was important to find him guilty. I do not take sides (yet), though I echo the bailiff, who hoped we would put our accusations as a polite if categorical invitation to leave, noting that in Schmutzburg Grading hadn't found his Utopia. And anyway that idea was a geographical as well as a political fallacy, the more transparent when ours was a country in crisis, having lost confidence even in its history. As you can see, Grading had little chance with us.

Blame Wix. Call the problem he set his advisers not insoluble, but only partially understood. For how do we, supposing it exists, open a window onto a breeze, onto the vineyards of civilisation? His mentors, true to the times, were men with dark capes and pointed beards, who considered that question frowning. Professor Standey couldn't condemn their want of originality (the full weight of learning isn't enough). He insisted that their acquisitiveness was natural, and to deny it was for Wix the neglect of his realm, or the want of its defence. If his enemies wouldn't see it in that light it wasn't a viable option, therefore Wix and his peoples were led to an impasse, where the grey fog of mysticism served to delay what couldn't be avoided. Aspersions had to be implied in certain acts of Wix's father, a man who'd committed all strength to the conquest of life, with the result that widespread benefits hadn't materialised. Was it in a fit of rage that his seer was immured? Could it have been expedient when Wix Junior granted him his freedom?

We are in the realm of self-fulfilling prophecy. Wix Senior could look to no predictions at all, of a vague future state, where the people were free and nations lived at one. The man who'd sung that creed – by now a nonagenarian – if his time under Wix II had come, nevertheless remained gauche, socially inept, despite decades of self-examination. Even then a ludicrous augury bound up in the cross-flight of doves confirmed him as a man of no real knowledge. Muchello used that to demonstrate *his* belief – that a liberated people meant also the birth of mediocrity, and that was an all-consuming monster.

Gard goes on recounting these events, secure in the notion that 'mediocrity' is a term applied to tabloids, and not the *Tribune*, or his newspaper.

'Why is it,' asked the bailiff, 'that escape has to be into the remoteness of mountain society?' What Wix had given up as a bad job, others who followed had still tried to achieve, though had disagreed when it came to interpreting historical data.

'Quite!'

Or not quite. A point of conflict remained between Muchello and Professor Standey, who still held that Wix's ambition was against natural law (Wix Junior, that is. Wix Senior was red-blooded and Teutonic). That, alarmingly, gives us the rationale of modern-day Schmutzburg as of insuperable difficulty, its aims unnatural. This might be a worry for the sensitive among us, if Standey hadn't professed also to have found the palliative, proposing that if what we had in the Republic of Schmutzburg was an extension of Wix's experiment, that was only in an abstract sense. To my mind, this is teleological flimflam.

Reluctantly, I am forced to appropriate much of Gard's text (I just can't stand that condescending tone) when speaking for the bailiff. He firmed his alignment with his friend Dr Muchello (the wrong horse, I think). Gard thought so too, telling us how the bailiff turned an amused gaze on the seer-turned-bard, amazed at his resourcefulness in bringing about that transformation, yet noting how characteristic it was of human affairs, placing poets shoulder-high with hypothesised entities somewhere remote in the spirit realm. Muchello couldn't fault him, though his distaste for Anglo-Saxon verse was well known.

Unhappily for Grading nothing could have gone against him more, a point fully revealed as a corrupted form of crossword clues, which I discovered in an exhibit I am about to reproduce. It was one that was never far from the bailiff. I ask myself what it is I can say about him, other than that penchant he had for deluding himself. Worse, he was incapable of ever knowing that failing, given the intoxicated pleasure he took in his debating skills. The fact is that in keeping Grading out of touch, or at bay, or confused, to the contrary his machinations gave away too much. That might turn out to be fatal for him.

It's the scandal of oratory that debate always teeters on an outbreak, grown men waxing lyrical or falling prey to fits of petty squabbling. The bailiff set out our tarnished genealogy, which he couldn't commend to the house, while I, with whatever opposition I can summon, refuse to trace it back to the double Wix era. That, as legacy, Standey expressed as the best of possible worlds (as Gard restrained a snigger). For Muchello, a man pendent with wisdom, this was a debatable point. The bailiff – wary of superlatives – couldn't see the 'best' in anything (especially in a fight for the hearth). Were I not in the glare of Schmutzburg's troubled politics, I would try to explain that in a rare moment of confidence placed in us, we took on your machines of state, clogged as they were with millennial filth, and set about their renovation. We'd like to give them back, a fully working mechanism, a slick little engine whose purpose is the broadest human flourishing. We've had, as you say, a technical hitch, and flourishing is postponed. But never mind. Those Hollywood directors are efficient with the salve, and vast populations are consoled by an all-encompassing, ubiquitous flicker across the screen.

Day Three

Day three did not commence until, armed with a notebook, I sat in on the morning session at the press office, where a withered, nasally, not particularly well turned-out official, addressed the world press (consisting of Jeremy Gard, smirking, and the tired-looking scribe from an electronic news mag). As far as I recorded, there was no official mention of the Grading case, and no intimation that a committee had been formed (or that an inquisition was under way). According to Gard the bailiff's first important contribution to the third day was a statement, to the effect that, with the recovery of Grading's broadsheet, and labelled 'Exhibit 2', the tabloid had never been found. It caused a rumble, then the minute examination of every news story carried by that exhibit, which Gard relays in full, and which I, mercifully, edit.

He likes to linger on the question of 'government', and does it in a dry tone (and means specifically British government), insofar as that had a cultural intertwining – or in other words to what extent should public coffers be used to finance private leisure? It's an important question if you believe that what populations do in their spare time is critical to the regulation of society. These miserable three columns, whose rubric was along the lines 'English toffs at work and play', tailed off in a discussion of royals hard at work with recreation – with polo ponies or on ski slopes, equine or Alpine. I touch on it as further exchange between Grading and Muchello after they had met in the library. Muchello gleaned in the Englishman an unalloyed republican, one who assumed that citizens of Schmutzburg must be too. It called for something vague in how the bailiff handled its emergence as material, looking right to left, from the purple into the grey of uniformity, and right again to the purple. I do not suspect treason.

Next came comedy, in a foreign premier, or puppet, easy to lampoon. This as Gard tells us came on an operatic first night, where the host, a sniffy English culture minister, thanked heaven for a private balcony suite and a pre-overture champagne bucket, followed by a grimace, then capacious yawns – yawns successfully stifled following the first aria. Gard can't help remark on what ignorance is shown in the terminology chosen – this after all a rival paper – for example 'unlikely countess dowager', or 'howling prima donna', or 'vast' soprano who blushed and fluttered from one emotive climax to the next.

He mused that even a guest premier couldn't, in the face of it, shake off the mental chains of trade and industry, not even in attempts to analyse the plot, where the two leads colluded in a dubious wedding plan.

The bailiff confessed his own medium had always been the written word. Tomes lined his cell. His mental gymnastics made no concessions to stagecraft. On that and other points I'm happy to commentate, especially if it means correcting that awful Gardian slant. About that I cannot allay my suspicions, Gard fully aware that the thread of debate had been drawn to keep Grading on the wrong foot, and flexed for the wrong direction. Should I ever track it down, I know I will find a fork in the transcript (which I tried to acquire later that day), and a malicious hand at work, with a litter of half-truths and emendations. Muchello spoke next, yet what he said is filtered through so many textual imbecilities I am ready to disregard it in its entirety. The light Muchello is shown in isn't credible, a man pleading with angels, the assumption being of someone greatly aged who has lost his faith in us, in what we do. Yet wasn't this just rhetoric, an appeal to the heavens given what was likely to be a long and difficult case?

'Small mercies,' he's alleged to have said, 'if it's for a thin unction that the long player puts off his night passage, or clinging with something like the rage of a toothache postpones for eternal minutes a return to the earth and its cradle. No apologies in this, a ragged metaphysics. Senescence comes to mean a helpless invocation – of whatever unlikely numina persist and are patient. Angel choirs! Let lenient appraisals still be possible!'

Standey said 'Tut!' For me it's stretching it a bit, to find in these remarks Muchello signalling his disillusionment. His lifelong atheism must by now have subsumed into itself its theological opposites, which is only to say absence of faith requires a sure foot planted in the other camp, though I haven't had time and leisure to think this through. We are meant to believe the bailiff passed over the point in a state of panic, or mild panic, or in haste. Gard shows him shuffling his papers and returning to the news, refocusing attention on Exhibit 2.

'Compelling,' he said to Muchello. 'I would like to know, are you of the opinion that the defendant forced this paperwork on you?'

'Not at all,' said Muchello.

The bailiff – whether with a sigh of relief or resignation is unclear – offered his audience a hearty rustle through the oversize leaves of Grading's confiscated broadsheet. He got on cheerily with what was the next 'inside' story – or what was said to be the next. From all that follows – or the course I *have* to follow – we are tempted to ask was xenophobia covertly its editorial position? The scoop's half page cited an Oriental ambassador, a man burdened by critique when it came to human rights. In reality his was a search for something to cure his pangs of conscience, and how to get rid of his blinding headaches. It was a puzzle to understand his manoeuvres. His opening gambit was in admitting to an addictive pleasure in the demands of particular kinds of horsemanship. It is only according to Gard that the bailiff laboured the point (as happened endlessly). But honestly, I cannot see that it adds to the weight of evidence against the defendant Grading.

You be the judge. Tell me how silly it is, as now we're dragged off with the dressage, or balletic rides round the circus ring. There is adoration for skimpy little nymphs in frilly pink tutus. And I know. We digress.

'Ah, got it,' said Standey, who'd crossed the lobby. 'It's hard to accept the genuine man of refinement when it's founded on wealth or has the stale reek of cigars and aftershave.'

'Harder,' said the bailiff, 'when the man's office employed a former gymnast as general researcher.'

'This,' said Muchello, 'is all just hokum.'

'It makes for an amusing read nevertheless.' So said Standey, who had taken possession of, and now brandished, Exhibit 2.

'You're not by any chance considering an outward trip on the tourist bus...?' the bailiff asked. Standey was more than usually animated.

'Not from his *present* office,' said Gee, who *was* still awake.

It has been suggested that a consequence of the trial of Michael Grading was a taskforce sent west to his native UK, to study the concept of 'free' elections, ignoring what awesome power is vested in media empires and corporate organisations. Standey would soon have to anticipate a new rapprochement with Western democracies and the entities propping them up, and in that sense was ahead of the bailiff in his thinking and his agenda. The latter – taking back Exhibit 2 – turned his attention to international warfare, with 'public bits of paper', as he put it, 'proclaiming the legality' of continental genocide – all dismissed by Gard as moral naivety, with ideological mores the subject the *Tribune* considered itself as expert in.

Gee asked could not Muchello's numina suggest other, less destructive handicrafts.

'That's just not at all helpful, and this is empty talk. Does he seriously try to tell us the luminaries of all these political backwaters can be taught the arts instead of war?'

'He does. But look, behold! A fresh snowfall! By the look of it a blizzard isn't far off, which means the bus can't leave. If Grading has a ticket home, he's got a long wait.'

I regret that Grading may also have made some useful mental notes, as I'm sure had Muchello, who wondered at his far-seeing gargoyles, how their primeval gaze couldn't part the northern mists, much less exorcise a Western press. What the bailiff lit on next – and I quote – was the 'bland agnosticism' as essence of Grading's English newspaper. One of its feature writers toyed with a nagging fascination for the inner life of a handful of moon-walk Americans, when one of them was running for election. A trim, short-haired, now ageing ex-serviceman had shaken his head decades after his lunar landing, and looked back on that point when the world, when his naked Earth, had made more sense as a blue ocean brightness suspended in a pool of darkness. He kicked over the silvered moondust much as he now kicks autumn leaves across the Senate lawn, his starry flag ruffled in a solar breeze. At that brief and no longer a real moment in his life, who's to say that what he encountered wasn't the terrifying silence of his maker, so at home up there in the lunar desolation? He can't utter it now, and in a vacuum no one hears a *cri de coeur*.

'We more pedestrian beings reserve sympathy for touchable things,' Dr Muchello remarked. 'We try to get elected on that basis only. A nearer lucidity. A localisation of all great questions.' As you can see, his reflections were harmlessly parochial. 'In other words can't you forget all this, and ask – because we don't know, do we – how the defendant got those newspapers into the library, riveting though their contents are?'

Not an unreasonable request, except that the bailiff seemed not only to enjoy, but to relish these shakes of his new kaleidoscope, whether that yielded a coherent pattern or not. It gave him every opportunity to dispense, ostensibly for Grading's benefit, a portfolio of tract and treatise (his views on statecraft, on warfare, on art, on government, on life life life). His Mistress Culture was a coquette, whose suitors could never be self-determining, and for Gard struck amazing parallels with that same English power base his journalese had been careful to vilify. You take an upper bough. You plant somewhere in its shade, with those who bask, the full paraphernalia an aristocracy lumbers its society with. To this the bailiff attaches aesthetic responsibility, whereas Gard from Great Britain can see only a system of deference and allocated toil.

In this the bailiff and Jeremy Gard are alike. The latter preoccupies himself with the wearisome issue of grade – a pasquinade when applied to people, a system of categorisation when applied to the things that people do. In the bailiff's mind it moulded itself as a fusion of leadership and culture, the former an involution of systematising processes, and the latter bound to its orthodoxies. To him any middle-class was a standard middle-class, whose appreciation of things outside itself was in need of supervision. Far from accidental, we are to take that example centred on a national premier (above), confused, bored or irritated at the spectacle and rig-up of operatic art. What is revealed is a self-contradiction, with art in the service of social status. Not that the bailiff apportioned to the arts a uniquely privileged position. For him their range of values usually brought too much tribal indiscipline.

I am convinced that the two elders would not have been dissatisfied with the bailiff's performance, having allowed for his inexperience. What we have, and what we are, is a people committed to the disassembly of preconceived structures, whether political or theological – even when final judgements don't concern us. The bailiff in holding to these tenets didn't seem to be alarmed when he believed, as I think Gard believed also, that Dr Muchello, under the snow-filled skies of Schmutzburg, had come to think the process of deconstruction was as applicable to us as anyone. Did that old man's appeal to the firmament indicate that as far as he was concerned the ritual brought to our chamber, with its rules of engagement, had all this time been mistaken?

Did the bailiff see these implications? Gard doesn't say, but is careful to tell us Standey took his opportunity. He showed that studious pose of his, with a thumb to his large square chin. He wore a frown. There were theories to the contrary, he said, though we'd have to accept discredited vogues in art weren't automatically impure if also the adjuncts of wealth.

In so much of this the bailiff's vulnerability was in having no contingency plan, should Schmutzburg suddenly collapse, as Jeremy Gard insisted was the case. He nevertheless showed, in a less than friendly swipe at Professor Standey, that should his path unwind itself back to the world, then that would be to the fallen house of Europe's Left – except, that is, in the case of his aesthetics, where he saw no need to apologise for natural intolerance. If ever his personal feelings got the better of him, that was now, for with underhand yet subtle comments directed at Standey, he maintained that the liberal world of debate – in a general sense – did not sit comfortably with the dogmas of our state. Personally, all I see in this is Standey having shifted ground politically. He was fitter for the world than his colleague.

The bailiff did have a point, though no amount of learning secured its validity. For was not capitalism – a system Standey must surely have come to contemplate – only a bedecked obelisk, a monument to sanctify the natural lusts? To define that system only in terms of its human element was, according to the bailiff, to confront only the usual repetition of animal barbarities, if dressed in pinstripe.

Day Four

My worst day. First I called at the records office, to be told it was now policy not to release minutes of committee meetings while the committee was still in session, then to learn – from a lank, smiling, intransigent bureaucrat – that final transcripts were now no longer obtainable in the public domain.

'But I'm a minister of state!' I fumed.

'Sorry. That's the new rule.'

'Whose new rule!'

He handed me the new directive, all vellum and crests and the trellis of Standey's signature.

I hurried out from the throbbing hub of Schmutzburg, a whirl of wet arches and flagstones, and struck down on the short winding roadway into the town below, where recent drifts of snow were banked to one side, and already soiled. A steep, pine-dotted declivity fell away steeply at the other.

I plucked out Jeremy Gard's calling card as I entered Schmutzburg proper – narrow streets hung with coloured lanterns, strung decoratively between the chalet-style houses and a line of shop fronts. I started to look for Jacquingasse, and Haushofer's guesthouse. When I entered its sunny foyer, a young woman sat at its reception desk, a pen in hand and chewing gum, careful to avoid my gaze. A crusty pensioner wreathed in a battered suit sat at one of the polished table tops. From somewhere the scent of percolating coffee interlaced itself with the piquancy of boiling sap from the log that smouldered on the open fire. To my astonishment, I discovered none of those simple peasant pursuits I had anticipated – no village musicians garbed in traditional wear, rosy cheeked and rising to a state of bliss, busily entertaining Schmutzburg's newly arrived tourists. Instead the groupings, as usual from the webs of office life, had arranged themselves in twos, threes and sometimes a quartet, glass-eyed round the buttons and coloured crystals of Haushofer's electronic amusement machines.

I tapped on the receptionist's desk. 'Jeremy Gard,' I said. 'Is he in?' She thought perhaps not, but in any case dialled his extension, then said brightly that yes, he was, when he picked up his phone: 'Who shall I say is here?'

'I think he knows.'

Gard met me down in those tourist trappings, natural dark woods, sunken sofas, a circle of tooled vines in the lounge, his mood relaxed, his bearing tired, but as usual extremely smug. His slacks, rumpled and beige, were not the right match for his fisherman's sweater, a dazzling maroon. But it wasn't in his dress that he knew how to provoke. I said,

'You'd better tell me now who's feeding you these lies....'

'Tut,' he replied. 'You surely know better than that, even on that mountaintop—'

'Don't plead confidentiality of sources. This is serious.'

'It is serious. First you deny Grading is here. Then you set him up for, well...we'll wait and see.'

'If there is any truth in what you say – which I doubt – it'll be thrashed out through the proper channels.'

'Not when you govern blind. You'll be shocked also to learn that Schmutzburg is a tourist haven of brothels, video parlours and cheap all-night drinking shops.'

'That's a scurrilous lie!'

'Look for yourself.'

Needless to say I got nothing more from Gard, bar an early edition of the *European Tribune*, where the rage over Michael Grading's propaganda materials continued unabated. Not that that alone was responsible for Dr Muchello's newly contracting universe, whose foreign and far-flung bodies were in peril of falling back to the centre. That old man and his team of foaming horses raced off on a private hub, still unable to hazard how a young Englishman had breached our security and planted his pathetic English newspapers in the shadows and sanctity of our library.

I have no alternative. I must return to this Michael Grading case, which as Gard puts it, in his usual shallow way, turns out to be a 'defining moment' here in the life of Schmutzburg. Yet nothing is more apt than Muchello, a man bewildered, who repeated several times that in all our machinations we had got no nearer an answer, to the truth.

It was as the day opened – perhaps as I sat in the varnished lounge at Haushofer's – that Standey openly contradicted his senior colleague, saying surely it was clear that the question was one of infiltration, and was bound to show itself eventually through careful examination. As Gard rightly guessed, it was something Grading had prepared for. He placed down his documents, ready to defend himself. He smoothed away the creases.

'A challenge maybe,' Standey continued, 'but now we simply have to suspect an accomplice.'

What then followed as Muchello's reply, if it reads like a *non sequitur*, I think *is* a *non sequitur* – a point I have meditated on, and in my own mind resolved, and in due course will demonstrate. In the charged melodrama of Western journalese I think you would say

I am about to propose a conspiracy theory – a topic we will come to. Muchello said that age had 'diminished' his 'compass', that the 'strain' on his 'motor' impaired his navigation (all metaphors the good doctor I knew simply wouldn't use). Every day he found himself stumbling through unexpected dark passageways, half looking out for Knossos wall paintings, or in more fanciful moments listening for the snort or the scraping hoof of a mythical Taurean. When he led Grading from the library – he hoped into safe diplomatic care – he repeatedly asked himself should he turn here, or there, or should he stride for that tiny point of light ahead? The gloom was a fuliginous gloom. Rather than our diplomat's office, he found instead the news editor of *Inner Circle*, whom Muchello quizzed for information on Nicola Chamoogan, and who against all common sense is also editor of *Bannerol*, too dry an information sheet for my tastes. The man in his dual role inhabits an old-world scriptorium buried in the mountainside, where Muchello was more likely to find a Minotaur than his diplomat. Furthermore how could he know that Grading's accomplice lurked in the shadows, and measured out that tortuous route just as he did?

Now followed one more of those irrelevant asides, with Muchello portrayed as a man unable to stick to the brief for more than two or three minutes at a time. These days, he said (or is that someone putting words in his mouth?), *Inner Circle*'s editor rounded off an unholy trinity as author himself. He preened his intellectual profile with a shadow intelligentsia that had grown up round him – though that applied its own labels. You could say a microcosmic radicalism, if that didn't stretch the imagination. His role was autonomous. It existed without emoluments, though gave us the opportunity to study his informed view on social affairs. The one impediment was a failure to compass anything farther back than mid-century (the twentieth), really when time began. I don't doubt the spirit of inquiry. That was Europe-wide, or perhaps worldwide – its central thrust a kind of witch-hunt, charged to eradicate a last vestige of poetry – a phenomenon largely viewed as civilisation's last big hangover.

With that word 'hangover' the bailiff recovered his sense of humour. 'Yes,' he said. 'At the least sign of a lyrical or softened sensibility, the poet is pilloried, and the didactic manual, thrust under his nose and opened at lesson one, bears the red-brick rubric "Social and Political Awareness". It's an activity masquerading as a kind of belles-lettres or literary art, but with the millennial apocalypse they have all obsessed about, its practitioners must come to bear some responsibility for the fatuousness of the age. Herds and cliques by their nature never glance at the rugged terrain beyond their cosy geography, while those blessed with objective sense make themselves pariahs (their plea is solitary, but hankers after diversity).'

'We can all, I think, be excused our personal deviations. I can say only I saw no sign of any such outpouring. Nor did he try to foist any of his pamphlets on me. When I handed Grading into his care, he directed me to my apartments.'

'Ah yes, he would – a chirpy *rara avis*. So universally perceptive, he knew a bent walking stick wasn't enough for an amnesic old man.'

'Alas, his ministrations were wasted. Halfway home I paused for breath, and felt that same old disorientation again. Not his fault, of course, but it meant going back to those labyrinthine yarns and chalk marks, a method by which I eventually stumbled across the library.'

'So far for so little.'

'Not entirely. I discovered that in delivering Grading I had forgotten to hand over his newspapers, for they remained in my pocket. Or rather *one* of them remained in my pocket, the broadsheet only. Here at more or less the same bench in the library, where it was now possible to see where Humber must have hidden himself, I spread out its pages, hoping I would find the tabloid tucked away inside.'

'And did you?'

'No. But what I did find was a review Grading had drawn a box around in ballpoint.'

It was an exercise in politics as surrealism. Cause for celebration was some latest Art House film, which depicted, symbolically, a West Berliner, symbolically, in a garden behind his flat (symbolically). Alert readers are assumed to understand what is really meant by a broad bed of roses, in the shadow of a wall (a high wall, again symbolically). Astoundingly we find ourselves – readers in common – at the home of the semi-Englished Adolf Hart, who has organised a private function – a garden party. The easy wealth of Western life finds its first frivolous moment (you will guess, symbolically) in a bunch of foil balloons, bobbing in a breeze. The guests, who are bronzed by distant suns, and who seem to share the same fluorescent grin, we behold melting (bear in mind that what a metaphor really is, is a linguistic figure underpinning a practical impossibility). This is in the mid-afternoon heat, an excuse for improvised fans and the loose pleats edging those summer dresses (the symbolic significance of which is lost on me).

'Ah,' said the bailiff, still young enough to enjoy familiarity with that genre. 'Imperfect ideals – best basis I know for the inevitable flaws of genius. Is this one of those stories of belated alarms and late *outré* breakfasts, churned out by the writers and cognoscenti of the Post Meridian school?'

The story goes on, with its back-garden assembly of film and theatre people, at whose centre is a magnate sent by Lucifer, a man with ashen jowls and bristly carbuncles, and – most important – a heavenly chequebook. Æthelwulf Hartmann (for so, nominally, has our anti-hero transformed himself) wants his bad angel to open that chequebook there and then, and with his plump cherub fingers, whose eternity ring has a matching gold watch, write with a pen. 'Here,' someone says, 'have mine!' Hartmann has in mind some spectacular project, requiring spectacular sums to finance it.

The script team rebels, who all along intended not theatre, but a kind of mercantile tragedy, a moral fable, the essence of which is the position of A for art subservient to C for the evils of capitalism. Result, or contrived result: the oilman and his electric blue signature can't part company quite so obediently, and when Adolphus (that name change again) pours from an icy cold bottle of Moët, a black treacly sludge replenishes the executive's flute.

To Muchello this all sounded rum. Yet Standey saw it as fitting. 'Don't they,' he said, 'in box-office circles, offer up these little previews as a sort of homily to the buying public, in order to perpetuate not a vision of the world, but the commentaries attaching to it? It's a mutually fruitful scheme, with its god-like glitterati living the transcendent life, high above the cinema queue, touching earth only to accept the next professional award. You see batteries of flashlit handshakes.'

'I shan't lose much sleep over that,' said Muchello. 'Sadly lamented is the pointless waste of a good bottle.'

But that, said the bailiff, who had examined the review in detail – *that* was the all-important symbol, symbols being the staple in this particular confection. What trickled out betrayed the same social preoccupation as a thousand other do-goody-gooders, being a neat little pyramid of stimulants (the soluble kind) heaped in a cocktail glass. A belle having no small place in Hartmann's convocation was said to be searching for a new kind of lead, strong in its therapeutic powers over a real-life Electra complex (can't help harking back to that fatality in Mostyn Sanchez's pool). In a strictly tinted setting, the nights of endless cigarettes and secular communion had left her lips, of a trillion inhalations, in a permanent rectangle. She also suffered a shadow on a lung. These unofficial anaphrodisiacs, little helpers in her cocktail glass, hadn't much helped, though they sang melodiously in the blood.

'I shall be accused of prejudice, ignorance, bigotry – but this is very, very rum, and not my kind of thing at all.'

I don't condemn Muchello, for consider this. Adolf Hartmann, a blue-eyed Aryan with a fylfot in his pocket, surpasses the champagne transformation with a reflex of his own. His curly blond crown is suddenly capped by a black yarmulke, two hairgrips holding it in place. We're shown its delicate orange embroidery. As hard to take seriously is the pen, which Adolf wields madly as a yataghan, first beheading the oil chief, because he won't write the cheque, then that resting actress, for whom there is no new work, and who has put on a yashmak. Abiding emblem at the close is a white rose reddening with sacrificial blood rising through its roots.

Standey noted drily: 'Detractors everywhere will approve of that witch-hunt aforementioned. Publicly, of course, the elimination of colour, light and movement is in only its first dawn.'

'We hope that for students of the macabre approval is a step too far,' put in Muchello. 'There's a literary source – *Terror and Non-Survivors*.'

'These cut-and-paste enthusiasts – for what is artistic creation today? – have no inclination to scale our icy slopes. They carry their mission only to climatically favourable spots.'

'That isn't strictly correct. A look at the library index told me this was a title we stocked. I haven't found it, but I don't see anything sinister in that. It must have gone recently: no dust had gathered in the rectangular darkness left in its place. But, it's a conspicuous void, bounded on one side by *Ten Visions of Freedom*, on the other by *Testaments of Reason*.'

'It hasn't been found?'

'No. Nor the paper.'

'Paper?'

'Grading's tabloid.'

'Ah yes. Clearly his accomplice will have taken care of that – no?'

'It's much more likely the stealthy Humber wedged it in a damp fissure somewhere. When he magnanimously joined his friend in diplomatic custody, his meagre effects amounted to a leaky fountain pen, a tatty notebook (quirky observations, but mostly indecipherable hieroglyphs), an initialled handkerchief – a P, strangely – a cigarette case, a lighter, a handful of pesetas. It may be to his credit that there was no sign of a newspaper, when I am sure you're beginning to see the relative importance of that question.'

Gard made it no secret that for him this side issue of the missing tabloid was a clever distraction on Dr Muchello's part (really Muchello's part?), and attributed its eccentric choice to the little the old man had travelled. It's true, and I don't deny, that our *preux chevalier*, the first man of Frame Solutions, didn't like cities. He detested their swarms. It's tedious to have to assert: that did not make him xenophobic. I don't need to emphasise the point that a man like Dr Muchello, and probably Standey too, held that no fit society started its day in the clutches of its propagandists. Morning papers were no less a flight of fantasy than a Viennese waltz. The problem assumed importance by the speed with which Grading, or Humber, or both, appreciated how critical these materials would be. They succeeded cleverly in keeping the tabloid out of our clutches. It was a cat-and-mouse game, for how dearly Muchello and Standey would like to get their hands on those trite little columns, any one of which had the potential to whip up damp tempests here in our icy groves.

When it came to further speculation, i.e. at the suggestion an accomplice had helped bring about the Grading infiltration, it – an ugly revelation – gave Professor Standey what licence he needed in gathering momentum for his own, very particular programme. He was a schemer. He breathed life into phantoms. His simulacrum, twitching in its ghostly sham of interdependence, took that notion of an accomplice and turned it into dynamite. Had I known his manifesto was in preparation – not that I could counter it – perhaps Schmutzburg wouldn't have descended to its present state. Unfortunately I came to know too late: section 14b, subsection v, paragraph 3, pledges the elimination of *all* dissident voices.

A Muchello who has lost his way I suspect is not intended in terms given here, i.e. of navigation and local geography, but again is metaphoric. The political changes about to touch us all were soon to brush him aside, at the moment you might have thought an elder counted for something – more than the grey concavity sunk in his cheeks, and the dimming of his eyes. In Gard's theatrical parlance he was a man with a bent back and a stave, white locks streaming madly in the breeze. There is something prophetic, if not fully revealed, in the confession he made. Someone I thought I knew, as I backward view him, I cannot fathom at all, prodding about in our covered ways, peering, undecided, into long shadowy passages, scratching his head at the unfamiliarity of this or that 'new' vista. Then there was his carelessness in allowing Humber to follow him, via *Inner Circle*, into the diplomatic office, where Grading was debriefed. Did Muchello shudder at the thought of yet more Englishmen, yet more of that philistia, invading our monastic chambers?

I live with the distortions paradoxes bring, that inner dimension of change where poets confidently sharpen their leads. In some ways I admire the refinement Professor Standey played his double hand with. Here in the house (house of the highest human folly) that stumpy, grey little man, with a mechanic's broad chest, successfully lied in his view of *Bannerol*'s 'narcissistic' editor, a man beneath contempt – and this not for the dullness of his 'opinions' column. To read Gard you'd think Standey despised that editor solely on his literary stance, a stiffness smugly wrapped in exactly the kind of artefact we've looked at above (re Hartmann et al). I can't suppress a snigger, and am about to stumble on a pun – only one of the hazards for spirits set free, like me, with a pen. Standey manipulated what the rest of us loathed – that gallant pamphleteering – as it fixed the still world forever, a remote sphere of activity caught helplessly in amber. It was to this sub-intelligentsia (there's my pun going off) that Standey (the turncoat) appealed, knowing its safe-house radicalism shocked only by its mediocrity. When Standey came to summon a body of opinion behind him – a wave of public support unhindered by careful reflection, which swept him into office – it was the intellectually disenfranchised whom, cleverly, he flattered.

I am a danger to clean hands, knowing how easily they get bemired. The sludge of hypocrisy makes no nice distinction for the palms it soils. In saying so I assert how our depleted, old-fashioned, undoubtedly snobby life is still to be defended. I shan't regret, should exile beckon, the gilded filigree my even hand imparts to Gard's insouciant pages, for now I have real work to do. I alone must rescue Michael Grading's name from the ignominy I have helped condemn it to, and that demands I place every one of Gard's findings into its proper perspective. I shall not blench, not even in the face of Schmutzburg's official press, whose chief is the one-time editor of *Inner Circle*, and is nowadays Standey's appointed messenger of 'taste'. Afternoons I see him outdoors in a brown coat, chewing on his millennial obsessions, with his bile and his hatred for a world that has a past. For his 'roots' he looks back no farther than forty years. With each passing decade, a decade drops off (making each one of his heroes *passé*). These are the irrational views of a man with a dangerous mission, on which I keep a watch. I see them exploited, moulded by Professor Standey, who is the first president of Schmutzburg's newly proclaimed monocracy. With a smile he turned attention onto 'the national scene', and made him, in our great and 'inevitable' history, Minister of Culture. I was tempted when I learned what office had been designed for me. It was in the 'reconstructed' judiciary, which amounts to a secret service. I turned it down.

I do not apologise for a complete *volte-face*. The best of us change our minds.

Day Five

We may now re-read Grading's predicament as a warning, with Muchello asking the wrong questions as to his presence. Dr Muchello had not understood how he had got here, and so returned to his chambers, at that time unaware of what was stirring. That was the case even when – with a shaft of anterior sunlight, and the embossed gold of a thread, a web, and a spider scuttling for the gloom – the old man pulled up and remembered the newspapers. The 'compass' that either he, or Gard, or a someone else had talked about, hadn't completely failed. He managed to find his winding way back to the library.

The library. Any talk of literary oblation should cease from this point on, but the bailiff, enjoying himself, saw in Grading's position a foil for the *Inner Circle* and its crusade (here were the seeds of the bailiff's downfall). He harked back to that fatuous attempt on the protean, with Adolf Hart in West Berlin, the bailiff going several clauses in the wrong direction, reminding us of that 'action'. His stress was on its occurrence prior to the dismantling of the wall.

There has been a rise in cultural engineering since, where money and careers join in a new conjunction, a phenomenon in itself open to all kinds of dice-throwing transformations. Presto! The banker's flame rolls itself up in a glittering plaything, once all of us have shared in a thousandth condemnation, by buying the argument and participating in its cause. What it really means is a price for our approval on one more contribution to the world's surfeit of social celebrity, by our own hands pushing its legions up the popularity lists. We witness knowing smiles under a parting of thunderclouds gathered over Adolf Hart and his cronies. Odd shapes given over on mouthed syllables are the precedent for the curl of a lip. Is it the same smile I see once its cynical owner sets its hero or anti-hero – those interchangeable entities – in that assembly of dissolute Westerners, in the silvered arc of society? Is that the Teutonic legacy seen in all our garden parties? Do I find some words unprintable?

Don't doubt Hart's inventor had been first to pay into the myth his iconoclasm affected to shatter, with an energy or commitment showing to the contrary how much he believed in everything he wanted *us* not to. That position was one my colleagues in Schmutzburg had got themselves into, and Gard had seized on remorselessly. If the world outside had been constructed by social commentary, under influence of industrial knights and media conglomerates, and bound by the mesh of trite mythology (a weave ensnaring a mobile populace everywhere), then what had Schmutzburg become? Preserve me this mountain air, a well-stocked library, the communicability of minds, because, in a generous splash of the salutary, I have come to find out. Unhappily there's more.

Much more. (And more that I deplore.) Hartmann (for so AH had convoluted himself) – or Æthelwulf Hartmann – not satisfied with the role of mediator, was determined to find largesse in one of his causes. The vast planisphere of art and mind, in a crude justification of excess, rendered his and ours practically the same co-ordinate. I mark it with a cross, where balanced on that pen stroke is one of those typical dates with Destiny, with Adolphus wonderfully assured, and adept in a change of costume. The carbuncular oil magnate sipped champagne on Adolphus's trimmed turfs, already knowing to what extent his chequebook was going to be wooed. Honestly, you couldn't expect the grandeur of an Idea to be self-financing, especially under the entrepreneurial stamp progressive in that era. Mammon had got all the money, but Adolphus – not personally short of silver – had got the age's ingenuity, and needed an angel. The scope of his mentality wasn't just enormous. It was theatrical. There would be lights, lasers, smoke effects (pardon my candour. Late as the hour is, I have Gard's column open before me). At its centre is his quasi-mysticism, terms of which Adolphus had inspirationally penned on a postcard, in the boredom of a canal tour and a desperate summer vacation. This whole contraption, this pantomime, would find its exegesis through a synthetic, robotic voice, or 'vox' as he liked to call it. As with us in Schmutzburg, Europe's choicest venues didn't appeal to him, London's royal parks being anathema, while a host of sports stadia was not appropriate image-wise. In full colour allow me to introduce his political crescendo (remember, this was before the Berlin Wall came down), for what Adolphus wanted was the remotest, dreariest toxic wasteland in the industrial heart of the DDR. Not surprisingly, the oilman said no.

I imagine even Dr Muchello might not at this stage have returned that genie, once out, to its stoppered phial. So far he'd followed the story's 'throughline', whose creator, majestically at ease in the ability to invent, invokes unstated rights in the transformation of more or less everything – a gold sparkle in base elements. Adolphus showed his rage, in that sour little trick played with a sunny bottle of Moët, miraculously decanting itself as a black treacly sludge. If only the punishment fitted the crime. Then that niggardly oilman wouldn't have the dissatisfaction of something unexpected in his crystal flute. With the wave of his pen, wand, caduceus, or God knows what, Professor Standey, having planned his campaign – in a descent to the lower echelons – attuned himself to depletions of this kind. He would never say trash. When as head of Schmutzburg's newly regenerate state he confronted our economic straitening, it was important to keep to the pulse of Western media.

Muchello lamented the tragic waste of a good bottle, whether or not oblivious to the undercurrents (it turns out Muchello wasn't oblivious). Perhaps the pull of gravity weighed the years of work behind him. Perhaps in the final analysis he resigned himself, unable to see the point of Adolphus's garden party. What can one say of that quixotic company of hangers-on? It just wasn't Muchello's sort of thing at all, as Gard has said for him. Therefore he left it to the bailiff to consign it to the bin, which the latter did, as a sort of solemn intoning, but sounding like a catalogue with tick list, more or less as follows, as tack still found in the broken house of Europe—

1 AH (Adolf, Adolphus, Æthelwulf Hartmann) is 'a blue-eyed Aryan…with a fylfot in his pocket'.
2 Turns wine into oil, then into pills.
3 Mutates himself into a weapon-wielding enemy.
4 That weapon no longer a pen but a yataghan.

5 (a double 5) Beheads the oil chief (keep yer money then), beheads his actress (who anyway would not have worked again). In wrapping her up in a yashmak we sidestep gender politics, so unmasking the protean AH as white, bourgeois, career-minded. That brings us to

6 His crowning image, those white roses incarnadine with sacrificial blood, human ooze rising through their roots.

All I can say is this: surely there's a point to that bardic rooting-out – which we've touched on above – if this is what poetic latitude has given way to.

The supposition that authentic works of poetry are still possible finds no support in reality. I am sorry if this sounds anachronistic. How often I shake my head, unable to bear those foolish remarks designed to ease our embarrassment. Still they come, those miles, those nautical miles – that cold wash of grey – that ocean of tedious playthings. This, I say, is down to the gurus running the creative industries, who blunt our attention through the calumnious arrangement of concrete nouns. All one has to do is string these together as a blueprint, and, well, with what result? Prizes and public funds.

Thankfully the editor of *Inner Circle* hadn't engineered any such possibilities, though now that he's Culture Minister I suppose it's only a matter of time. Correspondingly the dreamed Muchello, who refused to see that eventuality, wanted to remind everyone of one other maze of deceptions, that missing book in the library, his *Terror and Non-Survivors*. Its removal must have been recent, since the shadowy space it left behind was still unsoiled. Let me say I do not subscribe to a universe whose purpose is random, yet I see only coincidence in the two titles flanking its disappearance, which were: *Ten Visions of Freedom* and *Testaments of Reason*. More importantly it is here, too, that Dr Muchello had his first suspicions as to that lost English newspaper.

I have my own theories as to the shift in power, based on the events of Michael Grading's trial, all of it filtered through Jeremy Gard's insane, inflammatory prose. I find it astonishing that a small object, of no significance to the disinterested onlooker, asserts itself as a major force for change. Grading's trial hadn't in any proper sense begun, yet it was here, in those early exchanges, that Professor Standey built on his first insights into the political reversals that have now taken place.

Standey's speculation as to an accomplice, coupled with the potential for trouble in an innocuous publication – the *Inner Circle* – spread its influence well beyond the courtroom. Last month I confronted him – long after the trial, and long after Jeremy Gard had flown off to the next explosion of breaking news. I was uneasy that my own position was said, with a smile, to be safe, for here was Standey, a combative politician, signing warrants at his desk. His advisers, arms crossed, feet apart, square-chinned, stood round him in the shadows. All were looking inward – ironic given the height, the cabinet made to sit in a solid round tower, where an all-compass perspective *was* possible. I had been hard at work researching Gard's allegations, and was finding it no small task redrafting his *Tribune* eight-day wonder.

'Your accomplice,' I said, 'has been nothing but a fabrication, yet you still hold in preparation a warrant for his or her arrest.'

A grey smirk broadened his face. A sinister light brightened his eyes. He told me no clever ruse deserved the fate of a mere political squib. 'Anyway,' he said, 'I should have thought you of all people were up in arms.'

'Up in arms over what?'

'Why, that tabloid of course.'

'It's nothing we can't handle. Just a climate of prurient expectation.'

'But can we handle it? Soon even our students will enjoy good red-blooded relations with the world.' There was also the fact that some of our seniors had high-paid if low-stimulus contracts abroad, and were frequent travellers out of Schmutzburg.

Standey was not ashamed at having appropriated a kind of glad terror or voluptuous attraction endemic in consumerism. 'One has to deal in principles,' he said – though I can't recall anything quite so *un*principled.

Gard, scrupulously edited by me, recounts the sorry *coup de grâce* with Grading in the dock, and Professor Standey full of consternation. We return to the trial.

If as now seemed likely there had been an accomplice, Standey said he hoped some other document supplementary to the résumé was going to tell us who it was. It was incredible that two perfect strangers had penetrated our inner sanctum.

Dr Muchello said yes, that *was* incredible, and no, we had no information as to an accomplice. Then out came another in that series of allegories, which I am certain are not attributable to the real Dr Muchello. Accustomed though Gard is to lies, they're anything but seamless – and not natural to the flow of conversation. Here goes anyway.

'It is,' Gard-Muchello continued, 'in precisely that state of ignorance that I found myself at a loss, a creature bound for other climes, but having failed to sniff the changed air season to season.' This is typical press imagery – shamelessly banal – and couched in the cliché-ridden vocabulary of political reportage.

'I wonder,' that hybrid went on, 'do I really know there is something I don't know – an old man in a maze of stone corridors, noisy with morbid echoes and alive with the leap of hostile shadows. I no longer see magnetic lines. Helplessly, I call out names. I try to find light from a door – from anyone's door – in a cross of cold draughts through Wix's machicolations. Nothing, nothing I can do. I don't know my country.'

If these *are* Muchello's words, I have puzzled as to their meaning. Were they uttered for the bailiff's benefit, a man who got off the point too often and too easily, yet might have been teasing out a statement, a clue, anything? The bailiff could not have been at ease with talk of an accomplice, and stalled once that spectre was raised. Nor do I think he successfully faked his neutrality, a mask that slipped in sharing Muchello's views, and siding against Professor Standey. Unbelievably the bailiff said this—

'Feats of detection hadn't we much better leave to on-the-spot examination? That I'm sure will lead us to an accomplice, if there is one – who must be an outsider. What about this other Englishman, Humber? He confesses to taking holidays, but not in places like this. His last stop was Santa Lucia, Gran Canaria.'

We are told to sight him in that place, a man who flourishes his handkerchief – a helpless gesture while he pauses in rugged ascent through the mountain heat. That reveals a monogram, P.

'This you'll be glad to know stands for P. Agurian – *persona grata*, pesetas in plenty – and is the pseudonym he uses on holiday.'

What salve can I offer, except to say read on, if at least the *important* points are clear.

I detect a snicker in what Standey said next, a hearty 'Well!' He went on: 'We do at least have the opportunity to reverse the proliferation of Humbers,' or those we have seen in a fairground hall of mirrors. 'Unless, of course, there are other incarnations you'd wish us to know of. Isn't the real worry with Dr Muchello, increasingly unfamiliar with his own country?'

Gard-Muchello replied: 'It would be, if that were necessarily the result of alien infiltration. I don't accept it should prompt us, if that's what you have in mind, to a consideration of borders and border patrols. We know the concept of territory. It means a life of miserable labour and state oppression are almost axiomatic. These are the attachments of failure, therefore no – absolutely no – I can't find my way anymore. Somewhere here or there the thin band of light under a dark door, the scratch of a nib on its pad of paper, the sudden creak of a chair, cannot convince me these still signify fruitful midnight toil. I anticipate the theses of anarchy, and somewhere under wraps an evolving theory of property rights. You hear tin leaders squawk if bills of exchange suddenly seem unfair, whenever entitlements once taken for granted weigh the other way, towards the underdog.'

'This is all off the point.'

'I don't think so. The students here have learned the first principles of Western life – and cheat. Worse, it took a European to find them out.'

'All borne out,' said the bailiff, 'in the résumé – if you'd care to re-examine' (though with a weary gesture Standey did not). 'This may be a symptom of something more serious, when a puffed-up parvenu plants the shrivelled seeds of his erudition in the barren soil of ambition. Fruits form as vacant oratory, while the hand that cultivates attends to political tropisms only. Not surprisingly, with a personal future bent on bureaucratic power, he couldn't bear the unexpected dents to his pride.' (All, I imagine, carefully embroidered, to communicate everything to the committee, and nothing to Michael Grading.)

'Who? Who couldn't?'

'Our student Mephisto of Frame Solutions – a large-framed, bearded man, who rose through the cobbled floor in an explosion of yellow light, at a time when I – the past master – still flailed around in darkness. Suddenly, one of those conspirators' doors had opened. The thin luminous pencil line between his jambs ballooned out in a theatrical cone of gas light, followed by the newly defeated proponent, cussing and swearing, who strutted away in the flurry of his coat. First Michael Grading. Now this.'

The bailiff, glancing through a window, into a blaze of sunshine lighting up the glass with a dazzle of orange fire, saw the bus still parked on a wooded precipice, its interior cloaked in the tint of its windows. 'How much,' he said, 'do we have, when we have time?' More, I think, than those clueless passengers pouring in, weather permitting, week after week.

'It doesn't get us to the point,' said Standey, who was more than ever impatient.

'Too bad. Grading is entitled to more than the starless night and a few puffs of wind we've allowed him to date.' So saying, the bailiff ushered Nicola Chamoogan to the stand.

'I want to know more about this young Mephisto....'

'So you shall. The fact is he's not unbeatable. Isn't that so, Ms Chamoogan?'

'Is this entirely relevant?'

Gard didn't say. He resorted to sporting analogies in how easy it was to luxuriate in the wistful afterglow of a champion in decline, and the passing of his era, poignant in one so young. He'd researched our national game, and had concluded it was not an exclusive order. In its prototypes its relatives are easily identified, some of which are still being played. That shouldn't make it such a surprise that an outsider, in playing Frame Solutions for the first time, can pick it up and quickly be an adept. There are several figures down the centuries – one on the steps of the Acropolis, another unearthed with a Roman tile in Silchester. One has been found adorning the deck of a Viking vessel, and another a tombstone on the Isle of Man. The witness herself alluded to this.

'Our own Swan of Avon,' she said, 'celebrates it as an intellectual pastime, in a simplified, bucolic representation—

> The nine men's morris is fill'd up with mud,
> And the quaint mazes in the wanton green
> For lack of tread are indistinguishable.'

It doesn't surprise me that an overseas assailant had darkened our young exemplar's door – and that the vanquisher was none other than Nicola Chamoogan.

To Muchello that was an obfuscating tactic. 'You ignore,' he said, 'my allegation.'

'Well. Go on with your allegation.'

'The clatter of that young student's boots on the cobbles had already receded when – slow and short of breath – I stepped into his lighted chamber. There I saw a shape at the casement where a silhouette, or Nicola Chamoogan, gazed out over the courtyard. There was a ghoulish yellow light in the corner where a lamp sputtered on the table. "What was his hurry?" I asked. I had to sit down, and could see the final result of the game they'd been playing.'

'And? What *was* his hurry?'

Nicola spoke for herself, showing how hard it was to resist his conversation while their game was under way. She had no wish, either in his probing or the resulting exchange, to be drawn on her own student life, though his curiosity intensified rather than diminished, even in the latter stages, and so on to end game. Thus with her convent school he attempted to draw a parallel with the disciplines at Schmutzburg and the ethos she described. He was amused, she thought, at the juvenile melancholia still clouding those recollections – that place with its low, linear hedges, rolled turf, and its sanctified stone for so long in a shocking state of depreciation. There was a lichened St Augustine with an amputated forearm, and a blind Pope Pius X. There was a headless John Fisher. Armed with her antidotes – her modern English fiction (all too greatly empirical, to my mind), and a pocket dictionary – she came as often as she could to sit on her own.

This was a jolt for Dr Muchello, the supreme advocate of our oldest institution. 'Even over a quite complicated game,' he said, 'he prompted you to so much extraneous matter?'

The answer was yes, though his polite interrogation was only a ruse, which the no-nonsense Nicola Chamoogan was prepared to put up with only for so long. She turned her back while her opponent contemplated his strategy – illegal moves, as she saw. She remained at his casement, contenting herself with what was going on in the courtyard. That is usually not very much. Someone stacking logs. Someone scraping snow from his boots. There's a cat, which you see sometimes in the warmth of a ledge, or mewing round the legs of a kitchen boy, out to empty trash. In the courtyard here was Michael Grading, on the point of re-entering the building.

'*Re*-entering?'

Yes, *re* – but Grading wasn't alone. There was Grading and another. This was clear from the two sets of prints in a fresh fall of snow. Grading himself tottered out from under an arch and snaked his way to the threshold of every door in sight, most of which were locked. Finally one was open, and this allowed first Grading then his friend Humber a means of entry. At that news Muchello was filled with dismay.

'Old heads full of dreams,' he said, 'dizzy with speculation. I have seen the flicker of light in once familiar faces. I try to imagine anything less ghostly. Friends dotted round a hillside camp. A distant citadel. Unimportant papers turning to ash. The scions or followers of a young Prince Wix, waiting for the first shadow of dawn. Instead, instead....'

'Instead nothing,' said Standey, who couldn't bear much more of this 'hypothetical flimflam'. 'We might just as well consider, I don't know – a pair of blood-red dragonflies, zigzagging round Humber's holiday pool. All this mock gravity surrounding the life and work of a student master of Frame Solutions, caught in a professional *faux pas*, isn't as far as I can see of any moment at all. Come along! What else have you got?'

The bailiff obliged. 'Understood. Let us now take a look at Exhibit 1....'

'Which is?'

'Handwritten notes.'

Gard, with a melodramatic flourish, tells us Michael Grading moved forward, puzzled and about to speak, though was steadied by his aide Humber, and sank back in his seat.

Muchello objected. For him concern ought to be intense, if Nicola Chamoogan had accused a leading student of a misdemeanour. Who was to argue that Frame Solutions wasn't central to every other discipline? One saw in its clarity, free of the clutter of uncontrolled emotion, how some things couldn't be dealt with lightly. In the hands of a cheat our *raison d'être* was open to question. Our visitor couldn't now assume that the tainted lustre, the world's filthy commerce, was as far behind her as that haven of petrified amputees.

Standey was conciliatory: 'An unwelcome revelation, no doubt – don't think I'm pleased. It is another matter though, and what concerns us is the nature and motive of Grading's entry, and to what extent his companion humours or colludes with him. And how is it Ms Chamoogan knew they were coming when none of us seemed to?'

'I didn't know they were coming. And this is the first time I've set eyes on Humber.'

'Well in that case was Grading a friend of yours? An acquaintance?'

'No. I met him once, twice, a few times, on my journey up here.'

It seemed Grading told her about a premonition he had had, which he now saw as to do with her. They'd stopped off in the kind of place host to thigh-slapping Bavarians togged up in *Lederhosen*, where old men with tangled beards sang from a medley of *Volkslieder*. I knew the sort of thing. A ruddy-faced accordionist sat in an ingle-nook.

Be that as it may, over the timber door, which Nicola described as having a diamond peephole, a sign partly obscured by a plastic growth of ivy said this: 'Auerbach's Keller'. It was a riot of semi-Gothic script, so perhaps she ought to have known better.

'Very atmospheric.'

Inside, synthesised violins and a glockenspiel repeated short astrological themes in an endless loop. Grading had already acquired a set of programme notes, bound up with the zodiac, and had paid for it through a woman at the door. She wore a tall pointed hat and carried a besom. Her face was a chaos of stick-on warts. Nicola couldn't be persuaded to buy one (a programme). On stepping in she and Grading were the only customers. The time was not yet seven. Auerbach's entertainers tried no less hard for that. A youngish man in an explosion of stars and a sickle moon and the name Mario stitched into his cloak, in italicised sequins, loomed above Grading seated at a corner table. A candle guttered. The magician dealt three kings and an ace, and discarded some others.

'As you can see,' said Nicola, 'I was near enough to see the cards.'

They were facedown initially. The trick, at any rate with this client, was an unsuccessful one. Grading called them out correctly, whereon an astonished Mario turned them over one by one. After a short silence the magician offered Grading his wand, then turned to Nicola a few tables away, for whom he transformed tissues he'd successfully conjured up into a Paisley scarf.

'So, these theatrical goings-on naturally led you into conversation with Grading?'

Not immediately, for now they watched in the privacy of their own silences while Mario made a hasty return to his dressing room, for reassuring daubs of makeup. He re-emerged (a hollow sort of martyrdom) and returned to his tricks, though by now Mario was looking solemn. He took up that Paisley scarf, and shook it into more of the same, then those into a knotted chain, then folded that into a giant's mantilla. A shrinking and finally disappearing thing when, with a flourish and almost a smile, he passed it over a bunched fist, and revealed in an opening palm – an egg.

'Did it hatch?'

In a manner of speaking, though there were no fragments at all when he brought his two hands together, applauding himself. Instead only reams of yellow tissue paper – disposable props, which he left for his famulus, festooned over the beams, littering the tables, trembling on the stone floor. There was, Nicola recalled, an icy draught under the outer door, and – in a comic turn – faint suggestion that Mario was about to declare a new branch or category of metaphysics, a sham gesture Grading was unable to pay attention to. His eye had been caught by a moving projection on a back wall – of gloved hands that swept an arc of fire; cracked, inflated cheeks, and mouths that blew the cloudy mountaintops, where winged horses struck at the solid ice with ringing hooves. There was a funeral cape, whirled on a watchman's window, transforming Auerbach's northern night into the dizzy lights of Aurora.

The bailiff understood: 'Mario's is a thin *amour propre*. His discipline doesn't belong here, and this is all too much. What do we read in a world out there dubious in its crafts? No one seriously believes its activities have more purpose than our own – or do they?'

'You might say our own are in danger of becoming like them. Some might even want that.'

'Oh yes, and what does that achieve?' asked Standey.

'Not much. And I don't think anyone here can stand on the howling slopes, and do as Mario does, or has.'

'Chances aren't good for Mario. For none of his kind.'

Soon after the charade, Rhea, another of Grading's friends, also arrived at Auerbach's, in a flush of cheeks. She was unable to eat, she said, yet spared no energy in taking him to task. They had missed a train, and she held him responsible.

'Anything else?'

Oh, quite a bit more. The place was filling, and was soon foggy with the smoke of Alpine pipes. The last thing she wanted was Michael's laconic evasions, and flew into a rage when it was impossible to put things right. Nicola Chamoogan saw it all. The amethyst flash of rings when she smacked the table top with the flat of her hand. Spots of purple on her temples and cheekbones. The crack of her clogs on the cold stone floor when she stomped for the door, threatening to, but not walking out of his life.

Muchello smiled. 'So like the English,' he said. 'Cast on a changeable sea without a barometric gauge. The sight of land is rare, but it's so much better when a comrade's elusive island remains a blur, or is never seen at all.' If Grading wanted to beachcomb here, on a frosty shore, where the tides receded centuries ago, then that's how Muchello found him, at a point in his life where a rustic termagant is scathing of her husband, a man the whole village condemns to the skimmington. Not that that was the inference Nicola made. In less troubled moods, she had found Rhea personable, affectionate.

'You begin to see,' said Standey, 'the native proneness to wild conclusions....'

What could Grading do? He approached Nicola, opened his railway timetable, and asked if she could help. She looked, and saw that Grading wasn't to blame, since careful scrutiny might have spared them the confusion of a misprint, so un-Germanic, and so much easier for her to spot.

'Suspect Auerbach's sly covenant with the railways, his trading interests served in the sale of light beer and *Blutwurst*.' (Actually in Nicola's case *Emmenthal* and *Pumpernickel*, and at this early hour fresh orange juice.)

'Fare fit for a sybarite. Such a diabolical conspiracy going on at the chambers of commerce....'

'Well, anything was possible, given the programme notes,' which Michael – depressed over the timetable – asked Nicola to translate.

'And did you?'

She did her best. The cover photograph was an unmistakable clue, of a youth in a henna robe, arranged in the shape of an aleph, who commanded his four tokens of sorcery, the symbols of his faith, in easy reach on his workbench. A sword, a pentacle, a cup, a stave. His dignified nimbus, a sidewise figure of eight, belied his lineage. One interpretation placed his ancestry with travelling hucksters, whose sleight of hand easily gulled the peasantry.

The bailiff added his tuppence: 'My recollection puts him with Mercury's caduceus firmly in his grip – a useful tool in the charmed lives of thieves and businessmen,' and in some cases one might say that. This particular publication was knavish enough, if unpriced, a gift, part of the gloss of Mario's publicity. Its inner pages set out a complex method of astrological consultation, apparently.

'Rogue text like the train timetable.'

Except complete in its misinformation. In the index one had to read up and across for the page number, then combine that co-ordinate with another – time. The date with its full numerical representation pinpointed certain paragraph numbers, and that led to the final prediction. Grading's was this – that his ruler, Jupiter, was opposed by the unpredictable Uranus, and this wasn't a good time for travel plans – pure luck on the part of the forecaster. The coming eclipse of the full moon in Aquarius should put all that to rights, and once the sun changed signs from Leo to Virgo nothing could impede his progress, wherever he wished to go.

'A lucky divination in light of Grading's infringements here in Schmutzburg – incredibly for so long undetected.'

'Base models,' Muchello said. 'But someone should caution the twitching astronomer too. He has that monocled look – a round eye glazed by the telescope – and his theory's of distant explanations. I hear his probes have mapped the raging storms of Neptune, and revealed Triton's unexpected smooth terrain. He's scratched his signs on a copper disc, and with the recorded voice of a chosen someone has hurled them into a silent whirl of constellations. Is there a reason?'

'The spirit of scientific inquiry sets him apart.'

'Always an excuse for hocus-pocus. What was Grading's excuse?'

'That we hope we'll find out.'

According to Nicola, it was something in his blood (or so Grading had said). His grandfather had been a factory hand, who didn't live to retire from the industrial waste the accidents of birth had plunged him into. For all that, he'd put his faith in popular wisdom: that elusive cloud with its silver lining; that first failure with a draw coupon and the persistent tries again.

'What did Grading mean by this?'

He meant, or rather it is I who say that he meant, that everyone's unction was a function of his lot (unctions and functions). He had the temerity to ask Nicola – at Auerbach's, not here in the committee room – what did *she* believe in? – as if hopeless proverbs and star signs were categories of serious faith.

But Nicola's 'belief' – that was another story.

Day Six

There is this minor revelation, now that my middle-life insists on its lengthy shadow (O must it shade practically everything I turn to). I find myself less inclined to tetchy, ineffectual swipes at the all-powerful Professor Standey, and am part reconciled to the cotton-wool wrap round a life of incompatibilities, which only now do I discover *do* co-exist. This is to my chagrin. It turns my commentary upside-down, already a thing shaken, once of course I had overseen its difficult extrication from the homilies, from the homespun wisdom, so typical of the *European Tribune*. But there we are. I'd say the same of *all* organs of agitprop, if in Gard's case it is, of course, 'socially informed'.

I am forced to attribute certain floating things to our new president of Schmutzburg, or of New Schmutzburg, a man whose consciousness is frozen granite. I see him with a flexible wand of his own, having taken his cue from Mario. He's clutching a silky top hat, and is about to produce a litter of fluffy pink rabbits. Perhaps our lady in the stand was one he'd happily cut in half (so, without further ado, here is an electric saw, and a spotlight. Just step into that ring of brightness, please! Abracadabra!). Excuse the lapse. It has been, oh, such a very long day.

I remain powerless, here in the watches of my nights. I am able to do no more than pinpoint the sleight of hand, or with the restless scrape of my pen describe or depict that secret trapdoor through which Professor Standey freely came and went. I am looking for a transcript, and at long last my searching will be over. There have been deceptions, yes, but now I have the minutes of the Grading committee. If I haven't yet proved Standey was aware an accomplice wasn't involved, now I ought to be able to. Rabbits out of hats.

Not even Muchello guessed at the scope of Standey's imminent campaign. Put yourself where *I* am just for a moment. Try to think of our basis of debate, and the bright airy dome in which it's supposed to be conducted. It's not a mere nothing I can trace in its ancient antechambers, in the veins of its marble. It's a sense of grandeur, which everything here is intended to celebrate. Everywhere – in the pedestals, the capitals, the entablature – the written word is crafted, chiselled, incised. What we have raised to the highest firmament is the power of the human voice, the voice of the human mind. Therefore what we rationally fear is indoctrination by that same means.

Forgive my light-headedness. It's the nineteenth of May (not the nineteenth century). What I see in the reddish sheen of my internalised soap bubble is a kind of counterpoint, reflected. There's a damp draught under my door. I think, before making a decisive move for my diary, I expect that film to tear. Ping! All that's left is a ring of moisture on the floor. Day six, Grading's trial. Standey's insistence on a name –now a repeating leitmotif – led the committee through a thousand involuted processes. At each one, in review, I cannot deflect that same persistent question. How anyway could anyone undo his subterfuge? He succeeded, when in pressing for a name everyone thought there *was* a name.

Tomorrow is the twentieth (and in a few years the millennium). More troubles, I think. In Muchello is a first decline of his powers, when in his fifties, or even in his late sixties, I'm sure he'd have anticipated Standey's potential for current dissimulations. You can't cover up through men in white exercise of nationalist fervour. Such regrets I have, wanting – at all times wanting to report – a different course.

What I should have given then, to have been in the bailiff's seat. For he it now is, as the only credible opposition, who opens doors and cubicles, and peers into all kinds of unlikely corners. What properties I'd exchange for the muted tocks in Standey's suite of offices, a man who tells the world to stop, with a halt on time only he is able to contrive. He has some several grey entities, grouped round him in his presidential chambers, who smile if he tells them to, and who act with a common will. By the time Muchello had gone, he had done so without resistance. As for me, the light is out – and it's cold. Mark it on the wall, the nineteenth. Know from my ciphers the nights of exile roll themselves into one. These my secret pen strokes I have for the people of England – if something in the end to very little purpose. I admit, I do not know what happened to Michael Grading, or where he went. I am ill. I turn to a thick brown phial I picked up in the dispensary, drops for my ear, and a pipette…

'…pip pip sniff' (in the drivel of poets). Life goes on. These hazy lines, which all this time I have built ciphers into, are beginning to straighten out. Those fuzzy little curlicues, a multiplied full stop, a closed corridor of square brackets (I am feeling delirious) – fantastically resolve themselves into the miracle of legible print! [Let us open this corridor. Let us breathe this mountain air, which is so, so pure.] Sadly and nevertheless, it wasn't enough (as I read) when Muchello parcelled his loss as a loss of navigation. Joking aside. I believe I do an important service in removing my disguise. I am frank in the many half-truths carefully prepared for the roving Jeremy Gard. There is nothing to be gained in treading the gutters.

Let me introduce our first official opposition. Yes, it's the bailiff. I can more or less say, having little regard for dates, that the cloud that's the glass of my being began to clear only about ten years ago. Days and society pass, leaving what isn't quite graspable as foggy reflection. I can't always justify, or interpret words I may have used, or views I expressed. When I assumed in the press office a campaign of disinformation, it deflected Jeremy Gard not one iota. He knew intuitively who had engineered that deception with its emphasis on Humber. His large English hands lit on all objects – papers, a door handle, the scarlet cummerbund he wore – with the same unvaried deliberation. Someone had clipped the bailiff's wings, or kept him on solid earth, since he never got to grips with that presence otherwise viewed as Grading's right-hand man, who remained at all times taciturn. In his sad, sunken eyes he misread the sparkle of cynicism. Others saw in his square chin only a square chin. In his jowls the thick jowls of his middle age. Or in the flare of his nostrils – simply the flare of his nostrils.

I regret a difficult end to my vicarious dealings with him, and I am sorry if my reading lamp illumines as little of the past as it does of the future. Are both merely abstractions? I think so, as I share the bailiff's first doubts as to Muchello's effectiveness, who couldn't penetrate the mist that had suddenly gathered round him. Moreover if he needed the bailiff's help, what that really consisted of was a climax of puns and assumptions, not so much centred on as woven round Humber as witness. The thousand successive tails I shall try to flip (with a Spanish coin, a peseta) – that's an eventuality remote in its chances. The man's only presence to date was laconic. The bailiff – for a reason I think I can guess – had put him in the borrowed house of the hermit crab, as puzzled as anyone at the construction of Humber's exterior, which at all times was a long line of diminishing reflections. He was lean, and tall by the standards here – well over six feet. There was oneness, a healthy wholeness you saw when he was about to give evidence. For Standey it was greatly inconvenient when the multiple Humber had the stamp and personality that no fiction, not of an accomplice, not of anything, could make disappear – assuming you're willing to follow into a maze of revelations.

The professor came down hard on Muchello, given that first failure, with Humber slipping through our net, and all that taking place in the library. The more Muchello looked inward, the more he began to know what a clouded horizon was, and a handleless rudder.

I can fix his last public demonstration as an imperfect reconstruction, the surviving relic of that final committee's eight-day dream. The real world isn't concrete. It is notions and abstractions. Perhaps when I say I've no wish to get hierarchical, really I have. It's something anyway the English understand. (What sort of time do you have?) To be honest I am losing my grip, obsessed and desperate as I am to obtain that transcript, a thing I know as a monster, rearing in the dark. Construe what you will. Think, but only think, as you please. Put him on a shelf, labelled. In any case reflect that Muchello's last office was as an eminence. Since then folklore has gathered to his memory. There are many who maintain that all we ever wanted was the first man of Frame Solutions ranked against a corps of opposing students. And that is how he *ought* to be remembered. It has brought with it the careful suggestion of the game as his lasting achievement, which tells me only disorientation *was* the prevailing wind, when none but he condemned a cheat.

I have had to tell myself, at any odd moment – on the cold flags of a colonnade, in the dark air marking off a Rococo arch – and do so repeatedly, that however much I deny it President Standey is now unassailable. There's little I can do. At Grading's trial, if he began to explore his rise in power, it was not with the certainty of a single lasting blow.

He used that open forum toyingly, always on the edge of what was etiquette. All that while Muchello stuck to the rules – a point that matters little, in the days after his demise. What goes on in his absence is Schmutzburg's economic regeneration, through enterprises learned from Western entertainment, with its packaged bullion neatly tied in bows and laced with the perfumed expertise of its professionals. In sight of it all, our good president has transformed a generic sneer into the raised eyebrows of expectation, signing new intellectual trade with the West as on a higher plane. It serves the philanthropic end known laughingly as 'education'. This I shall come to.

Posthumously, Muchello has proved his point. Here in a dark room, in this wilderness of ice and masonry, my grey head nodding, I have read and re-read, and finally inked my comments between the lines, using the minutes, and now the full transcript. Like that frail man before me I have traced the disease and the spread of its infection. A contagion leaks from that single point where someone decides to change the rules. Soon we'll see a student population not restless, but clamouring. Other failures will follow, with Frame Solutions marginalised, and the recreation replacing it an evolution from the wiles of rhetoric to the peddling of merchandise, base artefacts catalogued as 'art'. Then some simple inoculation won't be enough. To Muchello it was too destructive, and the seeds of irreversible decline. To Standey it was a chance to shunt the old man off into the closed canopy of regret and recrimination.

I don't rule out some momentary debilitation when, finding himself too close to these slippages and errors, Muchello's powers of concentration lapsed. If I went in for editorial footnotes, there'd be a hook to something *infra* in the depths, outlining Nicola Chamoogan's personal metamorphoses, which the committee began to hear about. Muchello could only brood. She by contrast was a dominating force once she had taken her position on the stand. She had, she said, no qualms in the promotion of the person over the person's creed. Soon we shall see what path was cleared for her career.

Throughout all Standey chose *not* as his medium our usual tablets of text. The written somersault had to be spoken first. He made his point as reminder: it wasn't the student king of Frame Solutions standing trial. It was Grading. The shame and the dented ideal of our life and country mattered little – for now even Muchello compromised, while his colleague frankly got on with the job.

My conscience is in endless dialogue with itself – the nullifying clause. I detest German doggerel, and say so only because, were the whole rig-up my invention, I would have dropped this episode at Auerbach's – a stylistic blunder. Do I really wish to know that Grading, as Mario's captive audience, had fallen foul of a misprint, with Nicola putting him right? Or that his partner Rhea, stressed and impatient and with things of her own to do, was about to walk out? What prompted all this futility under the lights and mirages of astrology, with its complicated auguries – those tabular predictions – I do not know (dear me, no!). I can scarcely conceal my contempt, and agree with Muchello, whose glassy-eyed astronomer subscribed to the same mystic lunacy, with his probes and signals in a sweep through the depths of space. To him this was just another manifestation of blind faith, whether or not Grading knew the fatal power of human curiosity. The spooks of our ignorance are afloat in the swamps of even disciplined minds.

'Yes,' said Muchello. 'How often our blinkered pioneers stumble on a piece of precious earth, while others who follow, quick with their measures, mark it out as hallowed ground.'

'That,' the bailiff said, 'is a benighted laity prostrating itself in worship, a nation's drudgery the key to its spiritual panacea.'

For Nicola that wouldn't do – not for the visible Church, which according to her was founded for the saving of souls. The magician's deceit was his wand, and even the lapsed found his practical mysticism – well, difficult.

The bailiff said, 'Don't expect our sympathy. Baptism here is at a bureaucratised font, a refreshing bathe in secular waters. Confirmation is offered those well versed in humanity's glory in itself.'

'Then you all need the swift jerk of the shepherd's crosier.'

Grading turned these things to deliberate insults when, on the following day, he bumped into Nicola Chamoogan again, in the cold of a gloomy waiting room. Chamoogan had time to spare before her train. Grading and his friend Rhea had bought their tickets. With Rhea browsing at the magazine stand, Grading found Chamoogan alone and told her where he'd seen her before – before, that was, Auerbach's.

'You recognised him?'

No. He told her about a premonition, or a dream several years old, which had stuck in his mind. He had found himself in the desert, in a blinding sheet of sand, as it billowed up around him. A priest in a flying cassock stood by a gate, a solemn hand shielding his eyes. It was Michael Grading's gate, but Nicola had got there before him. It was to her that the priest appealed, saying that what she contemplated was treacherous, terrible even. The wind dropped: the holy man commanded the elements, if not the human soul. Grading pressed forward to the gate – his gate – wanting to claim his passage, though dressed in a safari suit, *she* was better prepared. The priest turned away, indifferent to Grading. Nicola was adamant she didn't need his commentary. Grading interrupted, asserting this wasn't a private contract. Nicola stepped through the gate, the priest still urging her to stay. There were perils along the path she intended to go, to which she said only that was the crux of their belief. There was nothing he could say or do to stop her going. When she went on, Grading tried to follow.

'That was all?'

No. Nicola met them again, despite taking a different train. At one point all of them spent a riverside evening together, breaking bread and pouring bottled water. Grading returned to his presentiment, and wondered – still in the fever of mysticism – if that wasn't really evidence of synchronicity less as coincidence and more as universal phenomenon.

'In your view was it?'

Nicola never had dreams. Anyway it was hard to reconcile a popish upbringing with the science of mysticism.

'Ah yes. Our life a life in psychic togs – or rather not.'

That, with her feet in moonlit water, was also Rhea's view. She shook her head. These things were unknowable, she said. Nicola didn't see her again, but at dawn the next day continued on her way with Grading never far behind, who was now travelling alone.

'Did he say why?'

No. Grading did not say. He had been thinking over his conversations with Nicola, and asked her if she thought that what we called God one only approached through the completion of clues in a kind of cosmic crossword. One such that Grading had made up he showed her, jotted down on a scrap of paper. Nicola remembered it, and could set down the clues from memory.

'Yes,' said the bailiff. 'Here. Exhibit 1.'

'Oh, well, please—'

You may or may not have detected reluctance on the bailiff's part as he took the floor. It was his job to read out these cryptic little ditties. My hand trembles in the orange fluff of lamplight. Now more than ever I have to take care – precondition my ears to sudden callers, or the unexpected knock at the door. This is my stealth, the certain price I pay, worth only its returns in a purse of small change. I offer you my open palm – with its few lustreless coppers. Here are my purchases. Here the illicit custom of my nights. Take or leave my hyperbole, for only now do I try to subdue, in the nocturnal watches, a last tinge of irony, a corrosion I know I shan't eliminate. I think you will have to accept that with the opening of Nicola Chamoogan's evidence (I think she lied), we are offered the tiniest illumination. Through its little points of light I plunge in with the ethos of old dead Schmutzburg. The round edge of oratory is one thing: from the wads of my cell, inept crosswording / swording is another.

It was deeply humiliating for the bailiff to have to read these ciphers, apart from speculate as to their meaning – but, as ever, he did his duty. Neither do I, in setting down (or setting right) these pages, overcome my prejudice. He wondered if what they approximated to was ancient English sonneteering, onto whose crystal *abab-cdcd-efef-gg* one transposed them one by one. The bailiff considered time out to consult a Shakespeare Complete, and the search for anything that resembled comments Grading might address to someone like Chamoogan.

Here is Exhibit 1—

Across

1 Even a secular faith, though all-conquering, is powerless. What ism is it, what ism is any belief, if not pessimism? (11)

2 Both, we would say, are open to the fickleness of fate, but fate is what they're always running from. (6, 3, 7)

3 Seeks repose, and lives inspired, but is always deceived by the dream…. (3, 7)

4 If you could see the twists in this, you'd cease to try to understand it (all this hope; all this striving on hopelessly). (8, 4)

Down

1 Ancient prophets have said it's up there in the stars, but is this only the remorseless tug of the universe? Discuss. (2, 4, 7)

2 Blessed are those content with life's finality, for they shall inherit – what? (2, 3)

3 An ism again, that proclaims in our mortality a point beyond which it's impossible to see. (7)

It is amusing to note that writers scribing for the *European Tribune* made suggestions as to a grid for Grading's metaphysics, not only shading in the black squares, but attempting some of its solutions. A notable two down Gard gave in a later edition – it ran and ran as tea-break entertainment. The suggestion *ab ovo* seems perverse, and not the right fit. A three across was *Ed's analyst* (a man called Edward, or the editor?), while another read *all England*.

Muchello had come across something similar in the retirement memoirs of one of Schmutzburg's first architects, a high-flier whose name he withheld, whose profanities had a semi-sacred look. Such persons once debagged of pinstripes find a welcome in all sorts of readerly households. It set him off at a tangent, Muchello tackling the issue of waste, and the crowning glory of waste – though I am not sure whether he meant of paper, or ink, or intellectual application. His target stayed in the climes of public service (do we read an obscure allusion to the bureaucracy here?), from which he projected a caucus of technical advisers, professional meetings-goers, and at the periphery a knee-bending cast of industrial knights, all good at crosswords. To the whole charabanc he imputed a train of social theories, handy topics useful as table talk. 'Or,' as he put it, 'a good settler in an after-dinner speech. You don't have to guess at why, when each guest, numbed at the point where coffee, cognac and cigars are consumed, has reconciled the presence of mendicants outside, dirtying the metropolitan streets, with the best that is possible in an impossible world.' At the root of Grading's puzzlers, he felt, was just such an attempted reconciliation. For the haves and have-nots, proceed. For the world's riches, read faith (for how the wealthy are chosen). Nothing but sanctified rapacity could come out of a country like England.

The bailiff said: 'The witness is drumming her fingers.' He was thoughtful, said nothing more, and let her go. Then for the first time Dr Muchello looked weary, glancing at the defendant. Standey, more than ever impatient, urged all speed with what remained of proceedings. 'After all,' he said, 'we're keeping the good Dr Muchello from his rest and retirement.'

'I don't mind telling you,' Muchello replied, 'retirement isn't a rest....'

'Oh, what is it?'

'It's a returning to a vacant house. The cold cellar has a film of water on the walls, and the lumber of early life is heaped in the corners. In the room above, a spider has woven a web in the casement, but that has long gone too. Its redundant silver threads catch the city lights as these are turned on and fill the evening sky. There are letters in a desk, and faded snaps, but when you try to force it the drawer is jammed. There is a chilly gloaming in the attic, and from the folds of its lace curtains – when you open the window, when you breathe the salty breeze – you shake the dust of decades past. You strike a match, and ghostly silhouettes rise through the floor, then sail up the walls and over you across the ceiling. There is nothing here – it is only memorabilia – the last signature of days that have disappeared – a life made meaningless by the heartless world a short walk away, a life scarcely real anymore. There's a sudden creak on the stairs, a footfall, and hope, perhaps – a familiar face, perhaps – then nothing at all.'

'Well,' said the bailiff, 'thanks for the warning....'

Curiously, when I had been entrusted with the dead man's papers, I came across a sonnet penned in Muchello's hand, whose solemn quatrains described someone returning to an empty house, lumber, a spider's abandoned web, a match light on the stairs, a footfall.... In a footnote he says this, and I quote him verbatim—

I like to guess at a player or a performer on those stairs, for just as I begin to categorise the strata of organised society, he tells me suddenly the light of a busy life is an enveloping dusk in a valley. Trees – solid oaks – are only now a tracery in an unexpected sunset. Where that shadow on the stairs really belongs, when my own eyes are dimming anyway, is among the expressionless faces inhabiting the world. What is it, what is it really that's happened?

Not that the committee came to an answer, since Standey, in the spirit of things, but careful to stamp on any vagueness, acknowledged his old colleague's new state of life – if lived in a stone turret, and fabricated on sand dunes.

Muchello said: 'A turret, yes – though what it *isn't* is a world of make-believe. Inside it you come to know your master, in my case a man of little mercy, whose vaulted night is filled with the cold brightness of distant stars, and rings with laughter.' Muchello had looked out through the fluted columns, and up at the rosy cherubim trumpeting on a gilded ceiling. 'You have to imagine,' he said, 'that when the house lights go down, anyone who stalks this private stage must look up and out, and gaze into the vastness. The thrill of it's in knowing the place for the first time, and arriving without a script.'

'Or that people who dwell in whole paragraphs,' Standey suggested, 'and not abbreviated crossword clues, will populate that kingdom. The safe cause is the hardy cause of indifference, and perhaps that's even proper. I agree, though – it's not hard to share your unease, watching those anonymous shadows swarming in the twilight, especially round a book-written faith.'

'That,' Muchello said, 'is perverse, even for you.'

'I don't see why.' He would have thought it not unreasonable to get at the defendant through the jests and riddles the defendant himself had performed.

'If indeed these *are* his jests and riddles....'

Grading must now answer a few simple questions, and began his session by introducing himself. Contrary to talk of infiltration, what the committee saw before it was an English IT specialist still in holiday mood. His was not criminal intent, he said, and he was game for whatever party tricks the committee had devised. More than once he had found it hard to suppress a smile. The chairman might like to know (so wake up, Professor Hext!) that the bizarre nature of what he had found so far in Schmutzburg tempted him into the old man's haunted house. He wanted to show us, jeering at the windowpane – if you would just pull those curtains across – a jester with reddened jowls and bells in his hat, and at his right hand a round-faced clown, with custard pies and smiles.

Now there was a lively mockery.

A good deal he'd learned, he said, from just that one evening in company with Mario. He had not expected to encounter – here with us – these *abstract* sleights of hand.

'The essence isn't deceit. What we're at pains to show is the gamble we're all engaged in.'

'Well, yes – what are we all anyway, but hopefuls bunched round the baize, and the game is the game of our occupations, chips spilling everywhere....'

'Less impersonal commerce can't be had without detaching yourself, getting out from all that polluted air of the gaming room.' Trick games for Grading didn't necessarily involve jokers *in* the pack, though I can't help thinking that the hand we held was one of wild twos and a one-eyed jack.

'I'm not against its novelty value,' the bailiff said, 'but all this belongs on the street nevertheless.'

'It belongs in the boardroom too,' Grading said. In fact he went on to say that that's where knavery was most at home. He joked about sharpers, and is where I can't help but locate veiled insinuations as to procedures in Schmutzburg, though only now do I understand. He asked had Standey got the elusive lady in his top pocket (again this has taken me time to interpret).

'Wit we all appreciate, I'm sure. Nevertheless, this crossword of yours raises serious implications, which aren't nearly so amusing.'

'Supposing,' the bailiff said, 'it *is* the defendant's property.'

Grading, who as already pointed out worked with data and information, admitted only, he said, to occasional substandard code, software pointers getting the upper hand, the odd corrupted working set, sometimes the nought in an enormity of negativeness. 'That is,' he said, 'just about my lot. Don't have much time for crosswords, I can tell you.'

This was, to quote Muchello, 'refuge in mere technics', who was more at home in his inter-stellar safehouse, and returned to its allegories. Fatigued as I become, at *all* these twisted metaphors, I know them for the larger deceit that – to our shame – this whole Grading case represented at Schmutzburg. That is not to say I am in any way influenced by the work of Jeremy Gard, whose newspaper is one of the most wretched and not much better than a tabloid. It brings me inescapably to what Muchello supposedly said next – a fabrication of lies, highly implausible as the kind of thing he *would* say, particularly in a serious inquiry. Yet I am showing you – will later reveal in full – how the committee, far from engage in public debate, stealthily and secretly decided Michael Grading's fate. For the moment you have to suspend your disbelief and accept, as incredibly I once did, what Muchello is recorded as having done next. We are shown one clear incident, ethically bound to meaning deeper than that of card play, though now the game is for the highest possible stakes, with a dealer about to remove the cellophane shrink round a newly printed pack.

Attention is drawn to the wear and tear and the diluted green of the dealer's cuffs. It was hazy. He tried to discard that now crinkled transparency, though it clung with the static his chubby fingers had generated, pork digits fluting over an overflowing ashtray. He twanged the red elastic of his braces, then loosened his floral tie another notch or two, while shifting the burnt-out stump of a cigar from one corner of his mouth to the other. Did Grading follow?

'Perfectly' – but for one important detail. It wasn't a green, but a blue shirt, with a reddish golden crown embroidered on the breast pocket.

'My apologies,' said Muchello, 'though that's not really the point. Just as in theatre, with its monologues and soliloquies, and divination as to the mysteries of life, so our dealer, mopping his brow, has come to the same pass. (I can see a crown, sewn into a corner of his handkerchief.) What's that random fall of the cards? That middling six, that mustachioed jack? That hearty king wielding a heavy blade? New games come under the rule first of a sulky-looking royal, now a clubhouse triumvirate, now a dogfight ace in a war-torn sky.... The chips are pushed into the middle: on the stroke of one, the ten of spades inherits the world. What can all this mean, this playing a hand of cards for the cosmos?'

Standey said it was nothing, and that anyone could leave the table and climb the stairs.

'That,' said Muchello, 'you'd have to do through an eddy of stale tobacco smoke.' There is a chink of light, a frosted pane, a stuck window that *will* open. There is fresh air outside, and across the fields ringers and the wag and weave of bells. There are friends outdoors but their hour after midnight precedes a transcendental dawn. Still our unshaven players continue to grope, never knowing that under the square shadow of an ancient tower a village girl in her bridal gown is coming down a summer lane on her father's arm, while an usher in range of the organist waits for a semaphore – a sure sign, and in it a simple affirmation.

Amen.

I shan't be consulting lawyers. I shall go, and without excessive baggage. Nor am I about to embark for the fantastic deceptions of Hampstead. More on that later. For yes, I have had my fill of pantisocracies, both theocratic and economic. I detest the crookedness of England – its brokers powdered up for a perpetual photocade – in its closed insularities. Unholier still, that endless family of counterfeits – I am talking about their 'good public works' – that somehow, by the perverse principles of market science, attracts the rude largesse of what is merely a book industry – where the artificially elevated saturate its market with ghost-written fabrications. As I say, more on that later. Now only let it be clear – to you, and among those learned goops at the Temple – I shall not, repeat not be coming to England.

Yes, I have got some explaining to do. First, my own part in the conspiracy against Michael Grading is (you will please sign here) very much diminished. That's surely self-evident. Is surely the call for calm. How otherwise shall you see the changing emphasis our committeemen brought to the Michael Grading trial? They were surprised at his debut. It was confident. Grading wasn't overawed. Moreover when it came to obfuscating games, which after all not only Standey but Muchello had set in train around him, he was an adept, or at the least an amused participant.

I flatter myself that at this juncture your tireless scribe found himself several strides ahead of some of his colleagues in committee, having at last worked out that the discrepancies between our press office, and what Jeremy Gard continued to report, could mean only that Gard was lying, or that Gard had an accomplice. Now who was it with a liking for that subject?

I put it down not to my perspicacity but to the clear line of reasoning that comes to those excluded or put into exile. Not unnaturally, everything the committee had so far passed, it had done so for one purpose, to bludgeon the defendant. Its stratagems failed – yet always omitted was one rudimentary question. If Grading had a games mentality, why was that thought to be the natural adjunct of his occupation, of the work he did? And why was that important? As you have seen, to us the typical Westerner is a chirpy little man with a toolkit, who seeks a haven in technicalities in uncertain moments, and probably gets damp at the underarms, whereas here we prefer debate. At the first sign of a difficult interlocutor one of us surreptitiously prolongs the debate. Our objective is always, tactically speaking, to arrive at abstract locations, all of which share something in common – places we get begrimed – and blink a lot – only to agree that where we are, in life's sooty interstices, is where no one (by definition) can hold a light to what is humanly unknowable. Sir Isaac, Albert, and all in their train (they of the watch spring, they of the supernova light show) can consider themselves dismissed. What really is the sequence of links and the particle glue of the universe is humble *Homo sapiens*, a solitary player on an unlit stair. Where that species belongs is with gamesters round a table, for whom the thread of things is the turn of a card, sometimes rites, sometimes a god, sometimes a ceremonial vow. Insanely, these are our totality.

Grading countered with a multiverse more the work of a science fiction hack, and on that basis dispensed with the chubby faces of prophecy and the manias of evangelism, which for some still infuse their life pulse into the cosmos. Muchello had read up on computers, and listened intently (you couldn't trust the old bird not to do a thing). Fable had it of a quantum processor wanting to talk to Miss Lonely Chips down south, on a plane of reality you could not pin down to its supra-coordinate. After several retries and as many checksums a faulty line is reported. The whole thing turns to prophecy, with news of ecological imbalance, and in the simplicity of paperback wisdom predicts a high-temperature apocalypse. Then with irony we are shown – after all – that the receiving processor's translation tables had transposed a fateful arrangement of bits into good wishes for a happy daylight saving, and in nanoseconds had made the decision not to respond.

'Well,' said the bailiff, masking his bemusement, 'there is I trust some sense in it.'

'Some, yes,' put in Grading, 'supposing you view our universe as a galactic matrix in a vast modularisation of relocatable machine code.' Its moment – long long millennia – is a teetering just as is ours, in the thick of a beta test site. There is, however, a problem. 'The world's first technocrat hasn't perfected the interconnectivity of flesh and spirit.' Blue-suited consultants had scratched their heads, but couldn't determine the fault, and anyway, bored by the project, suggested the decommissioning of this, followed by the costly introduction of a rival system.

'I have heard of this sort of thing,' said Muchello, who to everyone's horror was enjoying this. 'The West has spawned a professional body of consultants, but they aren't a bit inquiring. They exist merely as tools for a vending job.'

'Entertaining I'm sure,' said the bailiff. 'We are though pressing for a plea. I ask Michael Grading does he want representation?'

'He can't have representation,' Standey objected. 'Have you forgotten?'

'Forgotten?'

'Our shortages.'

'Ah yes,' said Muchello. 'But there is always one lawyer who keeps himself free.'

'You don't mean, I hope....'

'Ah,' said the bailiff, ominously, for it seemed Muchello did mean dot dot dot.

I knew the man professionally. Privately, his obsession was the photo history of vintage cars. In public he never tired of recounting his only victory outside of Schmutzburg. This, a shabby domestic affair, saw its outcome hinge on the various sightings of an infant in adult specs, who was known to have consulted a Strasbourg train timetable. (That, as so many of these themes, reprised. I wonder why.)

Muchello remembered the case. 'The child had perfect pitch, could reproduce any melody on the piano, and, the crowning precocity, could sight read.' But over transportation schedules in Strasbourg the child had no such mastery, a point well elucidated when one, then two, then five witnesses recalled that he held the timetable upside-down. The prosecution claimed this was a natural consequence of those large, cumbersome spectacles, put on in the child's inclination to be like his father – thick lenses over perfectly good young eyes. The case had by then descended into a meticulous examination of the minutiae, with its wider significance expertly overlooked.

'To this day.'

'Well that we shall see.' There had been a charge of libel brought against an assistant treasurer somewhere, who in a monograph – sensationally produced through the anti-EU press – published minutes outlining ministerial fraud. Again, the prosecution dissembled, and talked endlessly of the monograph's plain-looking cover, with its image of a tree out of leaf and a pockmarked moon dangling in its branches. On an otherwise sterile horizon, half a dozen satellite dishes, spaced at irregular intervals, and scanning an ink-blue sky, were shown under radiating arcs, of news broadcasts beamed from around the world. In the middle-ground a man, a silhouette with a Rastafarian hairdo, had his arms held out. But the diversion backfired. This was not a case of libel, but of someone telling the truth.

I will try to put a stop to this, though curiosity intervenes. For why should someone in a treasury department place so high a value on the idea of political honesty? His was a growing family, whose youngest didn't share his myopia. He was sour about a protracted recruitment freeze, which meant little upward movement and a halt to career prospects. Solution, according to the prosecution: he planted a recorder, and under cover of a train timetable expanded the shorthand notes he made from it into incriminating longhand, which he slipped in a file bulging with genuine documents. Defence, though, succeeded (our man with his vintage cars, who subsequently never ventured out of Schmutzburg).

'I can see,' said Michael Grading, 'what all this has to do with me.' He decided he too could battle in irrelevancies, and sketched for the committee one of his personal memories, from his childhood, he said. Scene: a cold windy bay somewhere on the Welsh coastline. Mnemonic: an inscription on an old faded photograph, on whose reverse side someone had printed the time, place, occasion. There was a girl with pigtails, freckles and a button nose. 'She palmed a beach ball on the guesthouse wall. You are all,' he went on, 'intent on ensnaring me in something I shall never get out of. Is that not so?'

'Certainly not,' Standey assured. 'Academics here get great satisfaction from circular argumentation,' which means to say the self-fulfilling prophecy is relied on to reconcile the irreconcilable. Like so much in the techniques we've developed, this had its fullest flowering in a Grading forerunner, a man who arrived – also unbidden – in an earlier part of the present century (the twentieth, should this reach you after that chime of bells, the millennium). He was a technician of sorts, claiming sole authorship of the first round novel. You begin at any arbitrary chapter – with a murder, say, or with the detective's summing up, or with an arrest – and continue in sequence, ending at the first chosen chapter minus one. A black art, whose impossible system insists on a prism of chronologies, with as many plausible rubrics. I hear some fool has even written a novel backwards.

'As to your analogy,' said Standey, 'it isn't the same.' (Analogy of what, I ask?)

Grading might as well have said anything. Why not talk about mazes, or labyrinths – or Russian dolls! Counter to circular fiction, or the reverse grind of authorial gears, why not ask the court to consider a wooden mummy, a thing you listened to and shook.... Within it, in a shrinking replication, one found the same plucked eyebrows or painted lashes, the same if smaller slits for the eyes, likewise the cherry blob of a mouth – a miniature hall of mirrors. Then again, what could a boy do in a diffuse, failing ocean light, when the tide was coming in and his tribe of dolls was planted in the sand, but now almost overtaken by a rising pool of brine? The fulfilment of its evolution was in its last diminutive number, or a loss in its powers of reproductive fission – and the point of its disassembly was merely its reassembly.

'I think in the circumstances,' the bailiff said, 'I'd advise against *any* representation.' To him circular novelism wasn't much different from the type of legal sleight of hand he insisted he was set against. Incidentally this rondure of a book is one I have made myself read (if laboriously), in what have become ceaseless investigations as to what really occurred at Michael Grading's trial. Any least clue I find I follow up. Like the work of my colleagues, it's a book that's fatally flawed. In Chapter Two, a jeweller, having swept up autumn leaves, sees them miraculously back on a sycamore in Chapter Twelve. He grumbles at a Russian winter setting in. The author at no point confirms the only possible interpretation – I mean the passage of years, not weeks.

Grading needed no support, however obscure, and however more than usually clouded these exchanges had become. He found in all this badinage a connection between (in his terms) 'office man', bound to his technological milieu, and 'oratory man', imprisoned by the concoctions of language. According to Grading, both belonged to systems grounded in the same ideas. Everyone loves a system.

Professor Standey was far from dismissive, and showed appreciation for Grading's defence. 'These public soliloquies on English life,' he said, 'are adapted in so many petty ways. It takes only the shortest stay to absorb our culture.'

'That,' the bailiff said, 'is because our culture is sensible.'

'It's likely these probes and counter-probes will reach a dead end. But there's plenty of time.'

'There is one inescapable question,' Muchello said. 'Do we approach these seven crossword clues in light of Grading's infiltration, or do we ignore them?' Muchello's favourite English poem was *The Rape of the Lock*.

The bailiff wanted to draw a line under all proceedings thus far. In his opinion, where we had taken a wrong turn was with those basement card players. He thought of them as inspired men urged on by worldly promptings, and asked the question: when they ran across the fields, was it because they heard the ring of bells, or was it something else? Hadn't midnight put a blanket on their chime?

'Our poker knaves need never have departed their subterranean den,' for according to the bailiff their occupancy belonged to the outer darkness. They cut and showed their cards in a cosmic rehearsal room, he hoped for the last time—

'Worlds wagered on one last trump.'

Muchello played along, and said that if now all preference was to leave those principals backstage, they would need new scripting and direction. When the spotlights come on, and the prompter reads and re-reads a first, useless cue – an opening address, and its echo – we would know what little preparation time was left, though it still wouldn't do to be hasty. The audience consists of one, who is waiting for comforting reflections on a life made whole – it requires the adhesives of the imagination – but is disappointed in making out only a glitter of brass in the orchestra pit, and the tuning of strings, all soon to be borne on a lunacy of dissonance. There is no apology, only the faint suggestion that meaning is never synonymous with harmonising truth – these two concepts having convoluted themselves into a bizarre synthesis and strangulated mutations.

Muchello, with his old man's zest not just for crosswords, but the cryptic kind, one imagined marked off as solved Grading's seven innocent clues. Frankly it's something I'm sick of. (I'm dozing at almost four a.m.) It's a throaty boom that wakes me, a low wind moaning in the towers. By dawn I expect a crystal glare in the quads and courtyards, and an icing over of the locks and bolts on the perimeter gates. (It's four, just.) Now all becomes clear. My genie has granted the scratch of a pen. That script he unrolls bears an empty stave – it is headed 'Nocturne' – and all that's missing is a vine in its inky rampancy, and on its trellis music to the beat of seven harmless crossword clues. There is nothing he can do for the slops in my cup, which will congeal and freeze.

I hear the last stroke of four fall away in the sub-zero gloom. These are my nights, you gentle people of England. All spent in the cold fringes of light from my lantern, when the one thing I yearn is the perfected hollow of a feather pillow, and the sanctity of sleep. Let me implore you. Here, in the task I assign myself, I alone unravel an old man's falsifying patter, that demon tongue somebody sought to bamboozle your Michael Grading with. There was no one here to take his part.

There's an old crone fitfully dozing, a tired campaigner with his feet in the hearth. There is a breath, a pallid whisper, when a last pale flame jets up and lights his slumbers. In the dislocations of dawn a gust goes up round the roof, where the brittle leaves of autumn rattle in the gutters. The servants have gone home. President Standey alone is left with his schemes, as he anticipates pleasant evenings ahead. But this is the wrong side of the millennium, the wrong side of midnight, the wrong side of the dinner gong.

Muchello wanted to adjourn.

Standey said no.

'We must.'

'No.'

Day Seven

An Olympian disdain for the word 'foresight' has put me in thoughtful mood, as my inkwell runs dry. Already I attribute this, and a hundred disturbances, to that passing squall in the night. I am sublimely ignorant as to the accepted wisdom on the causes of atmospheric change. I assure you, it's a quackish meteorology, which at worst only briefly discolours the dome of my interiors. I am too often taking a blunt razor to a blunt pencil.

But, that overnight dousing has pearled my sunny meads. Its brightness is in contrast to the courtroom, and everything coming out of it. It's a crepuscular place, even at the best of times. Dusting my way through its gloom with only a handful of 2Hs makes for a light script over deep indentations in my papers – a kind of reverse Braille on the underside of each completed leaf. (Not to mention writer's cramp.) Even so, I have got my second wind, having lived on, and through, and throughout these days of combat – just as Michael Grading did.

I have the benefit of hindsight. Nevertheless, I am more than surprised at the range of things Dr Muchello took into his retirement. After he died I went through his rooms, where the first thing I looked at properly was the casement (and those gargoyles outside). Its airy fore space was dominated by a large wooden chair, over whose frame a woolly travel rug was draped. His ancient spectacles, lenses highly polished, sat nearby with their arms crossed, ballooning an angular light over the sill they rested on. I found, dotted around, extensions to all that stupefying literariness – the man's sheer sense of tittle-tattle. To give an insight would mean reconstructing wodges of memoranda, ephemeral bits of paper that floated onto his escritoire. He knew in intricate detail funding policy for public services across the most powerful EU states. He had considered in depth English ambivalence vis-à-vis Europe, and what that had done to its parliament. He had read copiously on *corpus juris* and extradition. His dangerous flirtations paralleled anyone's, in a disparateness mirrored in the breadth of his appetite for games. Yet, even with my eyes open to this, I still couldn't see where Muchello had picked up so much science fiction, astonished as I was at that one instance where Grading was also familiar.

I long assumed, of course wrongly, that Muchello had invented it – that model of electronic exchange. I stifle a yawn. I see already I must sharpen the stub of my pencil – again. I persuade myself that as he got older his extemporising grew more eccentric. None had seemed more outlandish or complete in its infraction than those two digitised brains, with 'North' and 'South' performing their roles in opposite hemispheres (Miss Lonely Chips down south) – the two entrusted as they are with the world's ecological balance – if I read correctly between the lines. Irony isn't wasted when, from an incessant flow of analogue sensor information – airy, or earthy, or submarine antennae – it's the corrupting transformations found in our first paradise that are all this time being monitored. I understand the inference when, on a not very fine day, there's a communications failure. It shows itself in an erroneous prompt to resynchronise clocks. That's to say one digital hourglass, 'North', with its gemination, 'South', for these must measure our eternity to the last, to the ultimate nanosecond. That the communiqué turned out to be more important – of a thousand bright Chernobyls – was a detail lost in all that binary etiquette. You may tell me I am wrong, when Grading was not expected to have come across similar patterns of mythology. My own view has no relevance. Everyone saw the crisis, which I have no wish to deepen with a blunted 2H, where anyway such distractions only increase the throb in the flat tip to my index finger. With that my dreams of the stationery cupboard intensify. How to get there without a chit. Pause, and a chance to go back, reread.

So back it is. I uncover nothing more than Dr Muchello, a man whose autumnal locks already touched the clouds. He waved the worldling away, tolerating no other footfall in his private Parnassus. Yet Grading was foot sure over the abyss, for how often he and his workmates had approached that same fantastic decoction round the home fires of Albion. Then as always the universe was an arrangement of binary digits, a complexity beyond the reach of those blue-suited consultants who'd come to fix it. Everyone caught in its defiles was aware that somewhere things had gone wrong. Its disaster passed them by, though that they made light of. Scrap it, they said, and replace the whole system.

Muchello wriggled, getting off the hook with one of his favourites. It probably began, as I remember him, with a looseness round the shoulders, a raised elbow, the fatigued provocation of a moving hand, the whole a continuous motor, having a verbal termination. Then his usual gripe, a well-tried critique on the triumphs of commerce. (I know I shall some day acquire ink.) For myself, I have long given up on even bookish consumerism – a decision bringing calm. I am less talkative. I can promote peace, quiet, even forgiveness for the pettiness of institutions. I am able to shrug at the bailiff's failure to extract any kind of plea from Michael Grading, and see as just a diversion – just another diversion – his thoughts on a defence lawyer. That in the end reduced us to one – that *buffo* with his vintage cars. I blanch as I think of it, casting unbelieving eyes over that whole rigmarole.

Grading asked for time, and pressed for further details as to the *buffo*'s performance – accidental as that might be – in the libel case alluded to above. It wouldn't have escaped him (and for that matter Humber, whose advice he must have sought) that whatever the case – I'm not sure of it myself – decisions made at continental level *could* imply similar hubris here, in Schmutzburg. It mattered little that our car-loving senior hadn't grasped essentials: he'd won his case, even if the outcome owed much to the tactical blunders of a confident prosecution. One pictures it. A man in courtroom procession through a fog of irrelevant detail, not the best model for our own procedures, but one we're in danger of adopting. So I think of our examiners, and what they were up to. (There goes my 2H again.) *Buffo*, in a bluster of protest, showed the flower of his eloquence. The prosecution case was flawed, hinging on an upside-down timetable, and glasses good eyes couldn't read through, and thereby watched the defendant brought safely to a not guilty. To cap it came that monograph – sheer judicial lunacy! – and unanimous condemnation as to its cover design. I imagine a great deal of head scratching, when wasn't there something – some tiny peccadillo – wrapped up in that welter of minuteness?

It's not something we would easily condemn. Hard times at the office, pay pathetically low. If you wanted to talk career structures, well – forget it…. (If more complicated than that, it's gone over my head.) The thing gathers dirt to a depressing finale, where counsel for the defence drives home protestations of innocence. How was the defendant in any way guilty? All he had done (had he?) was put a few personal touches to an unimportant document, hoping that someone above him was about to retire. With the passing years, that little indiscretion would look very different – for what in social terms appears despicable initially, eventually isn't. Victory was the defence's by default, and counsel for it must surely see Grading's case as the one to get him limbered up again. Grading had none of it, seeing in that a yet further sally into the idiocies he must have thought we liked to practise here. *He* could play at that game too – and did.

He complained that an illicit hand had half tugged the wool over his eyes, then launched off on his own style of dispute, not appreciably different from ours. Our culture, amorphous and at bottom European, ensures every trope finds form in circular argumentation (as you have seen). The defendant might vent his abhorrence, but that only exaggerated our multiple effects, our geometric replications, the roundness of debate. Life is endless. Unwisely, Grading had allowed himself to be sidetracked. In walking our ceaseless circumference he had weakened his position as impostor, perhaps wanting our acceptance. But don't get me wrong. I like to see a man defend himself. Had *I* conducted proceedings there would have been no speculation on the *buffo*, as like Muchello I wouldn't have had him – an opportunist – wheezing over an over-complex caseload. I am willing to face the obvious question. Is it one of sham or shame? Or what between those two is the connection?

Muchello was perhaps secretly content to remain on the committee. That, at the close of day six, retained in its shadowy grip its catalogue of negative affirmations. Shall they, come the last trumpet, be undermined? I see through them into a dead or dying epoch, where politics encrusts itself in hard dry clay, masked in the cold clods of social formulas, in a masquerade of new solutions. You may as well unhinge the imagination, a thing still immured in a medieval wattle. Its only newness is a name (the latest, greatest counterfeits in the paper world of news), dealing as it does in human goblins, bogles and bugaboos. Did Michael Grading really believe that in ours was something superior to his, a culture, and a society, immune to the ills of social aspiration?

World of words is a world of benighted readership. I'm sorry if this goes on.

I fake, through what is still my ministerial elevation, the look of someone in the know. I have done a quiet deal with the stationery clerk. I wasn't sure, when he winked, what it was he expected me to reciprocate with. A leg up, apparently. Happily my ink quota is assured for days to come. You'll imagine my relief, getting shot of those pencils. But it doesn't solve the problem – that I still have to live under the claw of officialdom. Sometimes I swear. Then I have this foolish recollection of a cap of bells, and all, I think, is a joke. I remember cross garters. Yellow stockings. Some ghostly bard whispers through the ether, telling me the sprite Comedy has made a sojourn of my writing desk. There's no scope otherwise for deadpan, to say with a straight pen how much I am imperilled by control on the nation's paper, not to mention other supplies. Pardon – yours is a different perspective, which I always forget. You'll please forgive these lapses. If you could turn the tide of my nightly scrawls, you'd see the paper I use is the reverse side of old memos, destined for the refuse men. What caps them is a crest. What the crest depicts is a hand, a sword and a laurel. It reminds us that all, in the end, is combat – for so it was with Grading. The alarm had sounded. Its sonority shook that web of lies constructed round him. A tinkle in Muchello's voice was frangible silver, while Standey remained impatient. The change coming wasn't fast enough.

It fell to the bailiff to squeeze what he could from the case, for what evidence, really, did he and his colleagues have? Two English newspapers – or one and one other mooted. Then there were seven cryptic ditties I am embarrassed to call crossword clues. I don't feel either it achieved anything when our one independent witness was ushered to the stand. Had the court bothered to explain why the Chamoogan woman was here at all, Grading would not have had the opportunity to probe for it himself (a man, don't forget, with a dangerous sense of humour). So much was said, in the disclosure of facts about her, that I don't know why the court preferred its own description. That, again, was symptomatic of our cultivated ignorance as to social advances attributed to the world she and Grading had come from, at the foot of our mountain. When on day seven Grading insisted she submit to cross-examination, we'd already had a version of her childhood – doctored, of course – and by extension her youth. In one sense conditions of her young life offered an explanation as to the criminal acts that surrounded it, yet this was one of those determining factors Grading didn't acknowledge. He'd got that class-riven way of the English, and with it offset his own life experience against hers. That was crass, given the mysterious silhouette darkening the turf of her father's country retreat – a menace that had brought her to our door. I will try to clarify.

'Imagine this,' the bailiff said. 'Our witness, hooded, caped. The scene: a marsh, lakes, estuaries. Moon or starlight. The task – to keep her last servant faithful, and rowing. This is a northern country. Her plight will be known, but for now no one reads her tragedy. This is a last-gasp errand. What she has got with her I will enumerate. A plain casket, and a large gilt key, on a chain. There is a family brooch, which is safely locked away. A platinum maple leaf, and a butterfly carved in ivory, and rubies bunched in a blackcurrant cluster. Why is this? And why this shroud of secrecy? It's to do with revenge, and a new peasantry rising up against her, and how she has come to think of those symbols she carries, on a journey she hadn't planned for. Those trinkets aren't after all a frivolity: they're a shoring up, the necessary currency in times of confrontation.'

'Oh, come on! That's a bit melodramatic, don't you think...?'

'No. It makes sense. No one warms to the idea of a dignified, penniless underclass. It's far-fetched to say vast urban populations are reconciled to it. Only the self-deluded know they're there, but won't take any notice. The downtrodden make their stand at last. The self-perpetuating sham of the Chamoogan household they know for what it is. The world is stuff, and stuff can change its shape. As to a good marriage – that's impossible. For what is it in the conceptual union of independent entities if not the terms of contract where the ultimate clause is monetary?' The bailiff couldn't help getting heated. *You* would call him a misogynist. We have another term.

'Pretty oratory, only to tell us systems are weighted, and the well-off make capital from ideological imperfections. It's not our concern. Nor should I have to remind you what is.'

But Muchello objected. 'You won't,' he said, 'have forgotten her letters, which all of us have read. The bailiff may be wrong, but is not unrealistic. It's not hard to conjure the child Nicola, freckled, in pigtails, object of English envy.'

'There's a shadow never far away, a lurking adult, a man, whose coat collar is always turned up. Each morning he follows her with his notebook. He is endlessly fascinated, and records everything – from the features in the crowded terrace of her school, to the variants in the wearers of its uniform. Across the road are a bench, railings, a London square, where he ensconces himself. He is keen to put every last detail in his notebook, from the pink scallops of an Austrian blind to the chalk-blue tablet, its painted figure "AD 1877", visible under the eaves. There is a shiny scutcheon in the porch.'

'And an ancient hollow in the steps....'

'No one suspects. What gives him the appearance of someone of everyday ordinary life is his stroll for the bus – bound, you think, for the gloom of an office. We will dub him S (for Silent, or Stalker, or Sinister). He doesn't set off until a sleek limousine, purring through the suburbs, draws up at five to nine, with little Nicola Chamoogan sitting in its back seat, a seat of sumptuous leather. S long ago took that vehicle's registration. He knows that the chauffeur – a man in green livery and gold brocade – will open Nicola's door. That same flunkey escorts his young charge up the steps as far as the varnished hall. Here Miss Ritchie is waiting. Off they go to morning class.'

Here again was Grading's cue for comedy. 'I was,' he said, 'as notable myself, whizzing through the streets to school – in my case on a bike I shared.' Each day he and his pal took turns on the crossbar. 'The last stretch,' he went on, 'was through sunlit chestnut trees, at that stage still a young planting.' It brought him, unable to control his bell-ringing pilot, into contact with the village hag – 'Let's dub her HW' (for Harridan, Warty) – an infamous gossip, and mother, seemingly, of hundreds. She was keeper of the gates at the village school, who by a cruel twist of fate was semi-literate, and unlike S was unable to record her observations.

'Pertinent, I'm sure,' said the bailiff, who went on to say that S, years later, having been caught – his coat looking shabby – pleaded temporary disorientation, due to an intensive study he'd carried out of rats in a maze, under laboratory conditions. No one assumed this might be a metaphor. For reasons he couldn't explain, he found himself stumbling about in the grey walls of Nicola's Catholic school. It was seen with what fragility he mopped his brow, and the matter was dropped. He refused cups of tea, and was shown politely back to the world. Nevertheless, a Sister Oliver, a genteel old English lady who conducted piano lessons in a chamber no larger than a cloakroom, couldn't help see Satan at work. In her spare time she gardened the vegetable patch, and remembered clearly (and traced the sign of the cross) a months-old footprint near her runner beans. It was distinguished by diagonal treads at the toe (left and sinister), and a smoothness at the heel. Then also she recalled an older right-side print: that had Gothic castellations, and showed an arrogant disregard for her seam of radishes.

Grading responded. *His* dark pursuer, he said, back in those innocent days at school – his HW – could never rely on her wits whenever *she* was challenged. Her pram was really a bulldozer, round which her swarms of infants, spilling from the pavements onto the roads, were the cause of near traffic accidents – incidents she responded to with crude hand gestures and volleys of abuse, and got in return a procession of irate, fist-shaking drivers.

Incidentally, should one attempt to unify those three initials, it is possible to make a phonetic shoe from an S and an HW. It is not out of the question that Grading had this in mind when he said that his two tousled cyclists – himself and his friend – on lifting the tent of her skirts, noticed the harridan's masculine ankle socks. Then also, in her pauper's round-toe shoes, here was the parallel to those criminal imprints in Sister Oliver's vegetable patch. But this, in its celebration of circles, is going too far.

'All rather academic,' the bailiff said. The gym mistress took casts, and to the annoyance of the maths faculty hung them in a store cupboard full of old-fashioned calculators – you know, the hand-cranked kind. Sister Oliver raked over the kitchen garden and watched from the gates, through railings, from attic and balcony windows. Nicola, bored of piano lessons, took to books instead, and penned a few lines of her own. She sent some samples off to *Artemis*, once the flagship of the suffragette movement, though it failed her as an outlet. S didn't return, and for his indiscretion lost his surveillance job.

Grading, warmed to this as serious play, argued that his counters and interpositions were the proper comparison the moment called for. He had not been so coarse as to juxtapose a kitchen-sink reality with the glitz of Nicola Chamoogan's early life (her life now, for all he knew). To me it's a verbal excrescence, but of course I wasn't there, and have only these three written accounts to go on (Gard's, the minutes, the transcript). It was Grading's misfortune, he said, to live in an unreflective epoch, one pleased to elevate to respectable heights anything smacking of social commentary. 'And it isn't sentimentality,' he said, 'when I know how much my contemporaries admire the constancy of working people.' His HW still bore a sulphurous torch. Successive generations, boy cyclists like himself, had seen the mark on her children's brows. He recalled how the bruised cheek of one of her hapless offspring served to exacerbate vicious rumours surrounding one of the several fathers to her brood. He had returned to the hearth with his welding gear, when the wheels of the pram – shiny spokes, muddy white tyres – had been put to use for a cobbled-together go-kart. HW cuffed the responsible child. She insisted on having the pram rebuilt (for how else could she get so many kids to school?). Some years later, a younger half-brother, having no sense of the appalling march of his times, idly scratched a fylfot under the hood of that reassembled machine, where the bright yellow of a nursery chick had weathered to a few jaundiced fragments. It is even possible that a distant grandchild flies to that same local school in an imitation Messerschmitt.

Unblinking, the bailiff resumed with S. 'Whatever his redeployment – darning the holes in Balaclavas, or babysitting an arms cache – I don't know.' His successor turned up innocently a few years later, while Nicola studied a map of Oxford's city centre. She was anxious for the second post. One mediocre exam result made it pointless, and the promise she'd given her cousins, already settled in Walton Street, would have no meaning. Meanwhile a car several miles away groaned up a wooded slope and steamed to a standstill. A shepherd, sucking a stub of straw, and speaking the language of refined country gentlemen, directed the stranded driver to the nearest house, and therefore phone. The English summer threatened with a dark cloud. Nicola pushed her dark glasses up over her hairline and sat forward in her lounger. No concern. It was still a fine day: that little flurry of wire wool sailed on harmlessly, in a temperate breeze. But what was that grey shape, far away to her right, emerging from a hilly brake and lurching this way? Well, why worry? She glanced at her outdoor table, where the map had suddenly lost its attraction, but now sitting up and finding it in reach here was one last chance for that womenonly genre in fiction – here was a book at her elbow.

'A last chance,' said Standey (for a read, for relaxation), 'but a bad choice.' He guessed that all such books were careful with their disclaimers, but this one was rash with its epigraph, which wasn't womenonly in its choice. This, for example, put its author's claims extravagantly—

> I am a goddess of the ambrosial courts,
> And save by Here, Queen of Pride, surpassed
> By none whose temples whiten this the world.
> Through heaven I roll my lucid moon along....

'At around page seven,' the bailiff went on, 'the grey shape resolved itself, first to the shadow, then to the smiling person of a fellow-student – though in his case penniless, and thrown on the mercy of strangers. These were the whims of his old jalopy.'

A day servant led the luckless traveller through a maze of penumbral chambers, where anyone vaguely alert couldn't have failed to notice the architect's manipulation of naturally striking sunlight. 'Streaming in,' said the bailiff, 'through the stone casements, wiping the marble checks underfoot.' Each ambit took in the family portraits, 'all a bit prudish'. Masculine whiskers. Frock coats. Feminine smirks. 'Not to say sparkling *décolletage*.' All however hung in Victorian gloom. 'Try to imagine pyrrhous wallpaper blossoms. Carriage clocks. A lot of heavy weave.' Then on polished walnut a tray for the caller's card. That was flanked by a solid vase, which Gard insists was centred on a linen doily, though the minutes offer no such information. 'He declined to deposit anything there, but gave his name as Leo,' then at last, under the rainbow dew of a chandelier, was shown to a telephone. He stood a long time, surveying the seat, the red velvet, the mahogany niche chiselled into the curve of a stairway. The servant in tails shrank politely into an open arch and contented himself in a room full of viols and a spinet, and hung with tapestries. When – again years later – the pernicious little plan was seen to its end, this same, loyal, laconic member of the house reported that not much of a conversation had taken place, nor had it been necessary to wipe over the shiny black receiver after Leo had gone.

Puzzling too was the flat refusal to be shown along the local lanes, which were quicker, or so the bailiff underlined it – or be driven in Nicola's run-around back to his car. Hints at his purpose partially exposed themselves – 'in the veiled threats', said the bailiff, 'that he couldn't resist on parting'. He was held by a dual reflection – a bobbing, painted balloon, his own smiling face, bright in the sable depths of Nicola's lenses. He looked lingeringly at the title of an open paperback pressed to her cleavage, *Girl Valence*. For some obscure reason it made him remember last night's dream, a turbid concoction reminiscent of Jung, as someone pointed out. In it a façade and steps to a door led him not to the interior of a house, but into a garden. There was trimmed turf, a neatness in the borders, and at the bottom a rickety timber gate in a tangle of shrubbery. Someone's children played, tossed a ball, pointed up, jumped through hoops, prodded a sleepless cat with a cane. Adults – not, it seemed, his countrymen – frowned (why?). Then an infant gorilla rolled from the shrubbery, then three pubescent brothers, then a mature male crashed through the gate, rearing up on powerful legs, grunting, beating its chest (just picture those leather fists). Leo gathered up the children and ran for the door, and in his recollection succumbed to an old cliché. He fumbled, he said, when he tried to secure the latch and make his escape, but eventually succeeded, setting the children down on the road outside, the door by now being banged on loudly, vibrant. 'There had been only seconds to spare.'

A day or two later an aristocratic shepherd, serene with a malt whisky, in a gentle sway under the low beams of the Huntsman's Arms, remembered how a stupid young fop had tramped for hours across the fields in search of a phone, only to come back to his broken-down old Morris. There with a few simple tools he tightened up a radiator hose and cleaned and adjusted a spark plug. A verger, a banker, a barman roared in that free house. A groundsman absently stroked the maudlin face of his Labrador. The froth had descended in his jug of stout, as he wondered at Leo, remembered only as running through a brake.

'Later,' said the bailiff, 'someone very like Leo turned up again, wearing a white top hat and tails.' This was after Nicola announced those successful exam results. With a tremble – or so the bailiff thought – she smoothed out those all-important papers and swept away her breakfast crumbs. What father wouldn't discard the day's inglorious headlines? With some few flimsy leaves of reportage still collapsing into crumples on the floor, he ran through his pocket notebook, the tip of his index finger hovering on a list of venues and entertainers. A new dress was measured for and made – a silvery pearl with ocean spangles – while the Parnassian Function Rooms were reserved at the Hotel Pallas. The first dance was granted a junior minister from the Treasury, whose career and ballroom steps had taken on a new vigour, though older and more experienced men deplored these present days of messy resignations. An almost constant realignment in the cabinet wasn't easy to follow. A retired diplomat with baggy eyes and a watch and chain clipped a Havana and shook his head, then in the gentleman's room – a floor and walls of mirrored pink – shook his head on hearing, even in here, a piped marimba. Wafers of creamy grey ash scuttered across the tiles in an unexpected gust from the door, when one of the evening's performers hurried in for fresh dabs of makeup, remarking only on the splendour of the brass fittings and the evocative aroma of a lighted cigar. This was Leo of course.

Muchello said: 'Old men like us – like him – look on in reflected bewilderment.'

The waiter in white, his face pressed to the glass, rouged his lips. He darkened the lids of his eyes, and deepened what remained of the pallor in his cheeks. Old-world diplomacy had no place in a postmodern washroom, therefore the exponent of that art gingerly felt his way backward to the door, ignoring Leo's tributes to Nicola's *haute couture*. Having returned to the ball, his eyebrows still climbing in surprise, his greatest loss was his monocle, or so his look suggested. He declared the waiter's 'uniform' an outrage – and this before he had seen the fantastic question marks and exclamation points woven at all angles into Leo's waistcoat. The gallant from the Treasury, his grasp of economics rivalled only by his knowledge of the *paso doble*, was able to smile when – this bit of theatre the ultimate eccentricity – the waiter emerged and took up his duties. First job was to distribute cocktails on a tray, yet there was something too insistently mechanical in the way this was done – for life now imitated technology, or in his case a dreamed technology. The deliberation, the jerky motor functions, that look of the space-age automaton, a metallic, robotic smile: 'These were the curious investments of one man's voyage round the dance floor.'

More conventional lackeys had turned out in evening dress. They wheeled champagne in ice buckets to the top table, where a proud father, festooned in explosive ribbons, burst a balloon and glanced over page one of his after-dinner notes. Nicola put aside a highball and held up a champagne flute, while the waiter, supporting his tray on a single palm, cranked the free arm through several planes and, cocking his head, raised his top hat. First Nicola remembered a penetrating gaze. Second, a sardonic smile. Finally, Leo's dream. She hoped his Sinanthropus hadn't returned to haunt his nights, or broken through the door – she hoped too there'd be no car trouble after his work here now. The hat stuttered down, the smile shrank, the robot marched. Still missing a monocle, the one-time diplomat turned to his godchild confidentially, repeating his assertion: something, something was rum.

My secret life under the lamp, covert in its medieval disciplines, has put me in the market for dangerous cargoes. To date I have dealt with the assistant archivist, whose chief is busy with committee work. I bite my tongue. What jumped-up bureaucrat isn't! (Though I shouldn't get so tetchy.) The old drudge suits my purpose, half-blind, and probably deaf. At any rate I'm getting tired of my repetitions – I am finding, and might put this to him, that semaphore would serve us better. I engage him thus, not meeting that opacity of his eyes, wonderfully curious as to the lopsidedness of his shirt collar. Its buttons don't match their hooks. I lie to him—

I tell him I grow more sentimental the older I get. The bruises and bumps of freefall are soothed in a lint of nostalgia.

'Nostalgia for what?'

'What used to be my profession.'

I shouldn't laugh. Getting past that crock isn't difficult. All I have to do is be careful when concealing whatever load I have, passing through his sanctum. I come and go, to put back or filch another, and another, and another wodge of papers, the next chapter in that transcript (you know very well what I mean). Yet to my horror what else do I discover, languishing in that archive. Not only Nicola Chamoogan's letters to Schmutzburg – a touching correspondence her pen controlled though her weeping didn't – but also letters from her father, which seem to corroborate her claims. All such documents should have been exhibits in the Grading trial, but never were. Then there's a kind of symmetry, in the scraps, oddments, and other things archived that should also have been released. For example Humber's handkerchief, initialled. And remember those pesetas? I'm jangling them now.

Nicola, had she suspected malice, might guess at how all such evidence *could* come to matter. She hadn't the committee's hindsight when – in the days after the Parnassian Function Rooms, at the Hotel Pallas – she settled into her student rooms. Some old novels were packed in a family box. The spell took on a yet brighter pattern in a donnish contemporary, a man called Sear (good looks, Italianate, natural charm), who bedazzled her nights. She developed a fondness for romantic dinners, where deconstructing Roland Barthes over a fish platter wasn't the half of it. Yet soon that idyll was shattered. Stumbling into his room one afternoon, she was forced to apologise and as hastily leave, when Sear, with his shirt off and ready for his second shave, allowed his gaze to drop. She watched as it travelled furtively across the room to the boy he had got from the streets, the latter supine on Sear's divan, still clutching an electric dildo. The shock of it half drove her back to that boxed-up fiction, where a world of strident heroines writhed against her gag. She dismissed its call to arms, but in a pact with herself sought out new old voices and other acquisitions in the supermarket book trade. Preference there – if that was a conscious thing – centred on the social mire that has framed the events I am embarrassed – almost too embarrassed – to describe (see all of the above).

There was a difference between those undercover agencies she had met and the picaresque villains depicted in the escapist fiction she devoured at the rate of a book a day. She deceived herself there was something attractive in subversive establishment figures, bored by the ritual, if lacking the courage to shatter the mould of tradition. At the other extreme were only spineless lowlifes, whose argument against an elite was personal exclusion from it. One saw it in the obsequious machinations they devised for getting themselves accepted.

As the bailiff has said: 'Even here, the truth still wasn't obvious, and the imminent catastrophe was still unpredicted.'

Long walks in the pale autumn sunshine ought to have helped, but didn't. With a rising wind and the swirl of city leaves a pause at a window prompted her immediate hike away. Conveniently, a gloved hand has wiped a transparent arch in the condensation, and from *our* vantage, when *we* look in, this is what is seen. The cultured Sear with his rent boy, in a heated review over cups of cappuccino and country patisserie. Some loose change in a foreign coin has been pushed across their table. The boy drove a hard bargain, the one characteristic his gratitude at being plucked from a South American street had failed to soften. There the problems of poverty had begun to be met by an executioner's pistol. Who really needed those round-eye pleas and open palms in the heat of the morning, the window rolled down, the traffic shunting at a mournful pace through town? Rico, a brown lithe boy, had seen his brothers cynically shot, and at night shared his telephone kiosk with an effluvial pimp. Sear – a man on holiday, and in holiday mood – stumbled on him on a fateful Saturday night, intending to phone for a taxi. But is that taxi – that taxi that never came – the counterpoint these wise committeemen intended, or did Michael Grading at last outplay them at our game of games? The bailiff turned our attention to a sleek limousine, purring through a brown fog and Home Counties drizzle, pulling up and parking on a frosty forecourt. This I shall return to.

Sear, who couldn't abide laxity, put up money for a place at the local language school, and soon had his boy speaking better English. He placed him in work, in an industrial warehouse, its edifice dove-grey and corrugated, the Dickensian locale of one of many firms in the portfolio overseen by family Chamoogan – this of course not just any family. A sort of life whimpered on in the cold wintry glare of English commerce. But. Anyway. To return – for I see I've left that limousine. The chauffeur remained ensconced, his engine humming, a little less stiff in the leather wastes of his seat. He breathed on and polished the peak of his cap, the analogue clock, the luminous dials on the dash. The first of his three passengers got out, reassured at the family name bedizened over the office door. He remarked on the ghost of a dark young face when he stood at a window, half adjusting the disarrangement of his tie, his scarf falling in loose folds over the lapels of his coat. His wife was ermined, and had to be supported at an elbow (that was a job for Nicola, daughter and heiress). Ma hadn't counted on a cratered warehouse frontage. These favourites of hers, little bijou shoes, occasional party wear – having awkward stilettos and a pale blue ribbon stitched to each upper – were a bad choice. The face in the glass withdrew before she recovered her stride, and in a neon flash of reflected light a neighbouring window suddenly, noisily, closed. She could see nothing there and looked perplexed, her uncertainty turning to curiosity when, as mere transparency a well-to-do man, still young if middle-aged, smoothed the hair over a right or left temple, and tucked in his scarf. She had caught her husband's reflection, and recalled his youth.

Chamoogan was a Francophile. In the closing weeks to Christmas the season had only intensified the lugubrious nature of his warehouse manager, whose nasal sycophancy couldn't conceal his disappointment when Sir Nicholas far from admired his budgetary flair. Sir Nick surveyed dejectedly the cheap bottles of Spanish, Portuguese, and Bulgarian wine. That his minions were rallied by any relief wasn't the point. Ownership was a prerogative and shouldn't have to clarify its specialised demands. He thought on the phone he'd specified Beaujolais. 'As well,' the bailiff said, 'the engine *was* still running.' In any case this unimportant contretemps served to focus our heroine's attention. What I now relate are Nicola's own recollections—

The distribution manager, a weaselly man with a pinched nose and flambé cheeks, who chuckled uncomfortably and peered defensively over his thick jet spectacle frames, exemplified the private nature publicly exposed, being asked to perform the master of ceremony's *and* the majordomo's rites. Then the wooden-limbed workforce – instance an old village widow, suddenly muted, her pursed lips, whistles, trills up and down the scale, her tunes of popular crooners, temporarily, mercifully, silenced. Or Rico, a boy with candid brown eyes, not quite recognisable as he stood at the packer's bench, his winter jersey tucked into the waist of his corduroys, his nimble, opportunist hands turning over, stroking – not the vibrant phallus of Sear's objectified appetites – but the mammoth staple gun of his new occupation. Names were lost. At the point of embarrassed introductions the vast concertina of doors, or its ribbons of steel, were pinned to the jambs, and a reversing truck at the bay offloaded its delivery of heavy-duty tape. An influx of cold air jolted an atavistic wind machine, which, with a loud throb and an explosive ignition of oil or gas, whipped up the dust from the floor and the maze of teetering shelves, resettling it in billows and waves all over that English purgatory.

Nicola, not at home in that society, failed to give it a correct social context, and smiled at its maladroitness. She is still too pleased to dwell on the irrelevancy of a clever little chess problem, which she had left bookmarked in one of her journals in the car, awaiting on the forecourt. 'White to move and win,' where the three possibilities for the four remaining pieces seemed at best a stalemate. I have it in writing. I shall have it all in writing. The car snaked its way through the lanes, the verges lined with naked chestnut trees in the cold of that afternoon twilight. A diluted flush of marmoreal pink in the west, the homeward west, dissolved into blue, while a gloved hand up front slid from the wheel and flicked on the lights. A bishop, his a vector of black rhombs, gazed ahead into certain isolation, where an opposition knight postponed a first check. In the same sleepy mentation a half-remembered Rico displaced Black's vulnerable king, and unimpeded by the usual rules of chess traversed the white rook's open file brandishing a miniature blade and a slingshot. A *faux pas*. A sense of her parents' overdress. That's all it was. That was the irritation. That alone prevented her single-move solution, and accounted for the proliferation of doodles up and down the margins.

Sear chose much the same moment, if several miles distant, to advance certain economic theories. According to him the grey mass accepts its poor education on the assumption that its want of ingenuity renders ludicrous any other alternative, little suspecting that the limits everyone works and believes in are random and artificial. What to the young seems pernicious and unjust, to the mature – those conditioned by years of enervating labour – looks about as it should be, for how could a middle-aged lathe turner, transplanted and placed at a negotiating table, be expected to arrive at a sensible and equable arms reduction (say)? (His example.)

So, now, two problems, no solution – though plans had evolved, and a treatise. Claims, all exaggerated, were published: a revolution was well under way. In its outcome the measured tranquillity of that first among academic institutions, or more correctly the serenity of one of its students, amounted to counter-inspirational matter as Sear searched for fodder and had in mind sacrifice, and as centrepiece his altar of social progress. As for the situation soon to be 'corrected', the student he had in mind was Nicola Chamoogan.

Oblivious to Sear, she had ended the night's journey in the throes of the cryptic crossword, her car having hummed across three counties. Under the chauffeur's assured hands it swung in from the foggy lane, where she saw in a pool of swirling white light, and knew she was home, a berberis, a Gothic escutcheon, a globe on a brick pillar. She has recalled the car tyres crunching slowly on the gravel driveway, then in the thinning clouds the glow, the luminous reds, yellows and greens, as lamplight suffused the velvet drapes, and as they drew closer all those solid gables in a vertiginous depth of darkness. The weaselly distribution manager should have been summoned and ushered to the drawing room, and made to chew inelegantly on chicken wings, and with the other hand clutch at a glass – of what? – a cheap Sancerre – and made to hold his own in conversation, while wondering at his dark blue suit – his frightened eyes in a flutter at Sir Nick's loud, clubbable, affable friends. That – a malicious thought – was only a balm, and uncharacteristic, and anyway quickly passed.

Once inside, notes on a jotter listed the callers: a broker, speculating; a backbencher wanting to clarify his trade question for the House; an arms manufacturer (same line of work as Sir Nick's). Sear, and this is speculation, might also have called, professing to have got a chance wrong number – though in reality confirming precisely the opposite, that this hadn't changed since Leo had called here.

If he remained anonymous for the duration of that phone connection, it was now the proper time to declare himself with his student debating group, as he brought to its Yule convention all kinds of clever sophistry. First debts, he said, were to the morose grey masses shuffling on the frozen streets outside, when a feast going on indoors wasn't calculated to soothe their envy. A rising tide of convivial laughter crashed about their heads, while a flicker of reddish yellow light from the roasting fires had blurred the frosted windowpanes. Sear was a natural representative – was someone who'd bothered to lift the heavy brass knocker on the door, and rap. The bellboy opened up, and tried to keep him in the vestibule, but, unable to contradict the authenticity of certain academic papers he bore, couldn't hold him back from the function rooms. That interrupted a toast, and glasses were lowered. A surly coxcomb stepped into the circle of light and tried to interrogate him, and as he did so poked him in the chest. His wit was met with greater wit – all politely acerbic – for incredibly here was a man who lacked a pedigree yet outstripped them in mental agility.

Here was the point. Our class hero undertook to remain sober until after midnight when, with his new peers lost to Bacchic slumbers, Sear was free to roam the house and gather up its silverware. But to what advantage? Doubtless hanging from an upper window and showering his booty on the uneducated supplicants below would give them a champion, and might in the short term alleviate their penury. But that was not the same as seizing power, and with it initiative, and was therefore – with that new bottle of pink champagne such a temptation – futile as a gesture.

He got drunk, of course. In the delicious vapours floating up in his animal consciousness he just made out in the fumes, in his hazy imagination, two disjointed reflections coming together. The first was a blond Dionysus, stripped to the waist, his yellow curls touching his shoulders, and with a blue sword and cherry-coloured heart tattooed on his chest. Superimposed on that were details from his South American days, a centaur – or was that a gaucho? – rearing up on a palomino, tossing up his frazzled hat, a dark disc receding in a southern sky, and beneath it a man hooting, with a toothy grin and the droop of a moustache. For all I know these were the farthest ends of the pampas.

Sear's coevals in debate predicted a career in stage or celluloid drama, though the one or two sons of industry squirmed uneasily. His was a genuine threat, if a tasteless political allegory. Unnecessarily as we now know, the few wise counsellors among them advised a much less impressionable Nicola to keep her distance. What they didn't know, or guess. In the end – and this may be the end – it was her intellectual remoteness that brought to the fore bold changes in Sear's meticulous plans.

A quest for adventure could never carry him into the cut and thrust of commerce, for having gazed briefly into the muddy pools of industry Sear recoiled at that office-bound kind of power. He had always known that awaiting him was a dishevelled band somewhere, whose trail of wrecked cars and bombed-out buildings asked only the transformation of leadership, good British discipline, and funds. His opportunity came via Leo, and the ragtag of revolutionaries round him, though that brought with it one other problem. There was no provision in his scheme for a pungent distillation of theology and sexism, a ghastly cocktail sloshing around unmercifully in the psyche of his victim, and destined to be purified in the addictive ether of high Toryism. Her future among the marble busts of academe had seemed to him a certainty, where political idealism shouldn't have to dirty itself in the grim charade of everyday ordinary life. Yet of all things she embraced a practical vision, and having graduated commuted daily from a modest abode in the Barbican, to a cramped little office at Westminster. Here the phones rang incessantly – stage-struck ministers demanding a soapbox literariness, a homey warmth and falsified good will in the speeches she was called upon to write. Sear could curse that bit of secular blasphemy, but his old resourcefulness as suddenly paid off. Little Rico – after years, commendably – faced dismissal. In the end it was impossible for so bright a butterfly to settle on the dun homogeneity of an English working life – though he had always been sure to pass on all scraps of business correspondence to his first master rather than the shredder.

That semi-literate earned his patronage because of his stealth, though could never distinguish a debtor's weary explanations from a handwritten note of great political moment. To him, all correspondence was the same. Sear, point on which Jeremy Gard is much more certain then I, responded with the same inducements every time – a few crumbs in an open palm, inviting. Gard has pictured an old Italian serving cheesecake and cappuccino, and a Monday morning liaison in a marble café somewhere, Sear digging deep into his trouser pockets, able to pay his informant just so much (and no more). That was always a mark of his caution. But here, in smeary Xerox – and clownish, perhaps – was one Chuck Wiseman – a lay preacher and arms manufacturer – who enlarged on an earlier note he had passed into Chamoogan's empire. The phone, for many reasons, had been impossible. But. Here in print, this rotund little man from New Jersey made much of his ancestral commitment to Europe, and what that ancient pillar of civilisation meant in our nuclear age.

What that was was little more than the rough and smooth of commerce, with Wiseman's reputation in decline, when too many of his clients levered lids off the crates he'd delivered – the trouble spot a remote one – to find their hand-held ground-to-air devices, or other such apocalyptic weaponry, the worse for transit. Monsieur Duval, his mid-European distributor, had shown a disturbing indifference. That left it to the tireless preacher himself to organise a conference, where with flip charts and an overhead projector he hoped to convey the importance of his mission. This was at the Hotel Grünlich, where Wiseman was looking for an innovative new line in packing, and a shortlist of tenders. He knew Chamoogan had overcome the same problem, and wondered if Sir Nick was prepared to give a guest lecture....

Sear had already reconsidered his original plan, and had decided that a ransom for Nicola – who was now an instrument of government propaganda, moreover a Tory government – risked the inconvenient wrath of the British establishment, and the full force of its powers against him. Perhaps no one would risk getting quite so impassioned over her father, chairman of an arms manufacturing firm, whose commercial links to government that same establishment might be embarrassed by.

Fancifully Gard has imagined the whole scenario – with first Sear's uncertainty, then his satisfaction. We are asked to wonder at an otherwise unimportant autumn morning, when Sear buttoned his coat and tucked in his scarf, and tried for himself, as later Gard must also have done, the vacant benches dotted round the glass of an Austrian lake, where reflected in it was the Hotel Grünlich's newly painted stucco. What else would he see? There were silver birches vectored on two intersecting slopes, their yellow leaves and albata-coloured trunks mirrored in ragged lines. Or, if he got up and tramped along the path, was that a hotel clerk on his way to work, fishing in the mesh of a waste bin, too hurried to buy a morning paper – or was it only an impeccably turned out hobo?

There was a pair of swans, skimming the surface. Just as he turned to watch, and with a naturalist's eye follow their laborious efforts getting airborne, a taxi drew up. Here – joy at last – the new victim climbed out, and was ungenerous with his tip. The driver left him alone to carry his bags, a task the concierge also found it impossible to help with.

So many others, Gard writes in italics, had noted a grudging welcome at the Hotel Grünlich.

Sear stalked his quarry at the close of that first day, forgoing the *table d'hôte*, but wearing a borrowed tie when he visited the bar. He was careful to remember choice yarns picked up from public school. He held up his brandy glass, and fixing his new acquaintance repeated the name: 'Chamoogan – unusual. I'm in the other camp. John Smith.' Ridiculously commonplace, but a pleasure to hear another English voice, loud as it was, competing with keyboard violins, handclaps and yodels. They shook.

On day two they met for afternoon coffee, and just about managed a wedge each of Black Forest gateau. Wiseman's hawkish frame darkened the frosted glass in the doors to the foyer, and seemed to swell. Sear or Smith put down his fork, catching at Wiseman's conversation. He groaned. Chamoogan listened out. In demotic German, the New World evangelist attributed the loss of a *démodé* hat and cane to the sheer cussedness of the cloakroom attendant.

Smith and Chamoogan slipped out by the door to the car park and strolled round the lake. Those same or another two swans ruffled the calm surface again, Sear's cue to recite a half-dozen lines from Yeats, nearest indication yet of a political motive. Chamoogan had to get back, but lit a short cigar and pointed up to the conference-room window, where, through a plume of smoke, both briefly saw the reflected gold of sunset. Wiseman needed another hour to complete his specification. Tomorrow – the last day – he wanted to talk about procedures and timescales, and the rules for submitting tenders. Chamoogan said the day after that was going to be his last.

That was not quite right. On the following evening, after the conference, Smith, who only now mentioned he was here for his health, followed his countryman to the roulette table, where he fingered the croupier's elbow, and where both placed a bet. Chamoogan won. Smith lost and sent for a gin and tonic – a double. It arrived, with a Bloody Mary. That, Gard tells us, was for an attractive blonde, who was not just scatty but inept over the denomination of her chips. In the meantime Chamoogan had won and Smith had lost again. Smiling – for he never had this kind of luck – our businessman prepared for a final assault on black. A histrionic Sear sipped at his cocktail nervously and felt for the bulge of his wallet.

Or was it a cardiac flutter? Chamoogan helped him to the door and across the foyer to the balustrade outside, where in the cold clear night there was a hard brightness in the dusting of stars above. Smith, with his head down, took long slow breaths, and felt the pain in his lungs – that sharp, invigorating air. It wasn't Smith but Sear who straightened himself up, to behold the distant sweep of headlights and the glitter of frost under the shiny grille of a hire car. He revived – though Smith of course had died.

Sir Nicholas was granted only minor concessions after several days of captivity, when in a narrow upper room, in an Amsterdam safehouse, the door suddenly creaked and the naked bulb, having dangled idly over his filthy mattress, was filled with a blob of light, blinding after so many hours of darkness. His hands were unlashed. Here, as he blinked, was a small whisky – with ice, and with an anti-inflammatory, poor treatment for the burns and lesions cutting into his wrists and ankles. Chamoogan was reintroduced to Rico, whom he had watched pulling up in that fateful car. Had he thought hard when that slim person at the wheel slid out and opened the boot, he might have placed the face. The little South American stepped onto the terrace and unsheathed, in the warm glow of lemon from a lighted room, a gleaming dirk, which he pressed to Chamoogan's ribs. Smith had disappeared into the icy vapours, but Sear's were enviable powers of healing: no amount of resistance, protests, could stop him, and he bundled the businessman down the steps, into the open boot.

The first exploratory probe, a polite little note, a few brief sentences in idiomatic English, already awaited collection in a Paris *boîte aux lettres*. It insisted the kidnap was the work of an obscure liberation group, as yet hardly active on *this* old continent, but already on the brink of a South American coup. That ought to worry the secret powers of England, but Sear, who wasn't now so sure of himself, had cause to reflect. He leaned on a ledge as he looked out over a calm stretch of canal, with cyclists ambling by. Were his instructions a little too obscure? Both he and Rico had scoured successive editions of the *New York Times*, but a review of the personal columns hadn't uncovered the code or cipher they'd asked for, the appropriate family response. So – a rethink.

Proof of their claim – a planished silver ring, an heirloom – had now to be dispatched, with a tougher wording, and an increased demand for cash. In the days set aside for the Chamoogan household to reply – this time through the English Tory press – Rico acquired more undreamed-of skills, fighting his corner at three-handed bridge, hard though it was to follow the sophisticated conversation also taking place. He had begun to win a rubber or two when Sear, producing more whisky, anaesthetised his chief opponent. He called for Rico's dirk, who started to sever – Chamoogan gnawing the leg of a chair – the thing he wanted the heirloom reconciled with. Then they all moved on.

The cold ivory digit, dirty under its blue oval nail, was delivered in a bed of cotton wool in a schoolboy pen box. At this point the investigating detective, largely silent till now, advised caution. Amazingly, this was followed a month later by a lengthy missive from Chamoogan himself, who couldn't find the exact phrase or philosophy, could never explain or define the compelling relationship, almost the camaraderie, that had developed between him and his captors. The best he could do was relate their taste in expansive conversation.

'What now follows is what their conversation was about—' is the kind of remark the smug Jeremy Gard, no mug himself on the investigation trail, inserts towards the end of his exclusive. To what extent the committee mulled over this sad bad episode I can't really say. The minutes are terse, and the transcript I suspect has been altered. It seems clear however that Professor Standey decided to adjourn, on the revelation that – after the Hotel Grünlich – Sir Nicholas Chamoogan had planned a short stay here, in Schmutzburg. Why? Well according to Gard, and this I only now begin to believe, this came about through a conversation that had taken place privately between Sir Nick and your then Secretary of State for Defence. The latter alluded to the intellectual thaw now taking place in our 'humble', 'eccentric' republic. It meant that persons such as Standey and Professor Gee were aware that continued EU funding couldn't be taken for granted. Awards would have to be earned. As a first pawn pushed forward two squares, so to speak as an opening gambit in that game, Chamoogan was about to enter negotiations for newly developed surveillance equipment, whose overdub and sales patter Chamoogan and his tame cabinet insider agreed should be scripted by someone here.

I know. It sounds extraordinary.

Adjournment

My loquacious Aunt Maude, and this is decades back, when she stopped her chatter for five minutes, packed me off to my cell in Schmutzburg, and did so with a wave, having given me a travel bag and pier glass. The latter fell to disease, and the rash of black spots seen in cheap mirrors of antiquity. It depressed me even then. Its carven frame is appropriately Swiss, with a mesh of leaves and vines that half conceal the winged things a-flutter within. It makes easy reminiscence on an industry in cuckoo clocks, which for generations was linked to the family name. All that is only the reflected ruin of myself, a broken image, something I would catch in the act of sighing back at me, much like the boy I then was, whose consoling bar of chocolate soiled already sticky hands in a succession of railway waiting rooms. I should weep at the duplicity of being, though can't bring myself to shed a first tear, having played my double role for that Englishman Jeremy Gard. Look – I can put my hands on Humber's scarlet cummerbund, knowing its whereabouts precisely. I have got access to Chamoogan's correspondence with the selection of elders he chose to approach in Schmutzburg, a handful of documents they've vetted, edited and lied about. I'm sorry, doubly, trebly, multifariously, as I see there are few courses open to me now.

But I must go on.

With what weighty significance the bailiff whisked all exhibits away, when that adjournment commenced. Grading was left to think his position through, with Humber his adviser, and arrive at a defence. The whole day was spent on that hiatus. For me it began with talk of conspiracy down at the breakfast table. I kept on hearing the name Gee over my muesli (as you shall too). I heard it also at lunch – whose ritual was drearier than usual – thin cabbage soup, and something indescribable the chef spooned from a huge copper. At supper I fully understood the meaning of failure, which I now know translates to a series of mishaps with makeshift sticking plaster, powerless to render whole again the brittle remains of our national moral purpose. I tutted into my pottage. Further to that I find I'm in another fix, having received a note from Public Relations – a department that didn't exist a year ago – who, as no business of theirs, would like me to explain to Refuse – fancy name, meaning garbage men – why there is never anything in my bins. Of course there is no need to present myself – a few written words will do. I shall dash off a tired sentence, which for a few days might just suffice. Then on top of that I get this other note – Stationery informs etc. increased demand for ink etc.... As for my light, burning till dawn – well, I refuse, I say, to acknowledge the new slim-line budgets, not at least until the ratification process. I only hope that a non-bureaucratic flag will wave their suspicions away. Every scrap of waste paper furnishes my draft to you, to Grading's fellow-English.

Day Eight

A hobgoblin, a two-headed mutant – symmetrically over-stocked with limbs – extended its elastic arms to the defendant, and in the adjournment clawed him too uncomfortably close to a poisonous breast. Professor Gee had got to him. I look at my watch. I look at the shaft of sunlight, a reddish gold. I lean on a useless tome. It's one I have borrowed from the bailiff, and placed down with decision in a diffusion of light, where its scattered beams end as a rotating film on the floor of the committee room. In my mind's eye I am able to scrutinise every scrap of information with forensic intensity. Michael Grading, as he probably regrets – wherever he might be – cooked up his own defence, and demanded that Nicola Chamoogan be summoned for cross-examination.

Professor Gee, who specialised in international law, and as an official was no longer part of the committee, dug out the strata of black ash and for the last time tapped the bowl of his pipe on his heel. What does that signify? It meant he had done a quiet deal with Jeremy Gard, and explains, belatedly, Gard's open contempt for the press office here. Gee, I learn, has defected to England – more correctly to the English offices of the *European Tribune*, where life will soon consist of coffee slops and the endless lighting up of cigarettes, or so I suspect. The bailiff glossed over his departure, taking up much of the committee's time in deploring the loss, as all agreed that now we were minus the meticulous nature of Gee's unique talents. What he didn't say was Gee had something spicier in mind, with insights soon to be enshrined in the *Tribune*'s editorials, cheery, loud-mouthed summaries of life in a reluctant age of ecology. I imagine yards of glass, smoke-filled offices, the muddled aroma of Turkish, American, French tobacco. Bored talk I suppose addresses the many developments, concrete and abstract, at the heart of city life. To me it's a waste of effort.

According to Grading, the adjournment had seen Gee promise Humber a first-edition monograph on the game of games, or Frame Solutions, written by a man called Joseph Knecht. Yet all Humber got was an interrogation, Gee compiling his background notes on English intellectual life. In exchange was the offer of an annotated list of Dr Muchello's successes, and the pledge to teach him the rules. I guarantee that won't now happen, even should Gee return – not that he'd find either Grading or Humber still here. Nowadays he hangs on the coat tails of hacks like Jeremy Gard, in transit from Wapping to the Westminster village, a student of all things sensational, and the lingo it's obligatory to couch them in. I can envisage Gee already in his new sophistication, having forgone the first rule of Frame Solutions. You name the next piece and denomination into being when it's known for what purpose.

The bailiff paused for all dead talk of the monograph, with Grading reluctant to leave that subject.

'I think it's something you must allow me to look at,' Grading had said. 'Or even give me a copy.'

Had either of these things happened, Grading would have been happy, he said, to show Gee that the England he craved, and that Grading had left behind, was oil, sludge, canals, high winds, gales, hurricanoes, and brown billows of smoke swirling overhead and belching out of chimney stacks…. On odd clear days the blue corrugation of a paper factory reflected itself in muddy waters, or so he described his workplace – or the one he'd abandoned. I don't know where in England Grading had lived and worked.

Standey, careful to avoid reference to Gee's *adventures* abroad, spoke instead of the burnt-out ecosystem he had gone there to find out more about, a lurid image perpetuated in the Western imagination. What was infiltration of the West if not to gain familiarisation with its most recognisable fault line, leading to ultimate exacerbation of it? What else is central to the evolution of all such strategy? Rulers rule what we're induced perpetually to think about.

All beside the point, according to the bailiff, who held up his copy of the monograph so that everyone could see. What he wanted to know was how much of it was a first step towards expert tuition in Frame Solutions, and how anyone under interrogation could have benefited from reading it. In answering that, how would it help us assess the legitimacy of Grading's presence at the heart of Schmutzburg, not to mention Humber's? And so it went on, to nothing definitive, no conclusion.

Ergo, after what has been an endless process of redrafts, I am able to sum up those eight days of Grading's trial, long ago as that now seems. My record is something I at least have time to revisit, as the walls tumble, and there are new details it has cost me to unearth. There is one outcome, when Standey, soon after becoming President, showed himself at pains to justify our new, autocratic style of government. It was virtually the last conversation I had with him, when attempts were made to woo me into his cabinet, in the transition from outward-looking republic to shadow state, one in whom its fortified refuge was an increase in border control. Draconian as that might be, I couldn't fault his reasoning. These were our last days. Our ethos was less attractive to those we depended on. Were we doomed? Would a direct line into British US subservience help with the accommodations we would need?

'All that I understand,' I said. 'But are there not problems of another kind in making an example of the Englishman Grading and his friend?'

'What do you mean?'

'I've studied the paperwork.'

'Look,' Standey said, 'there's a principle at issue.'

'What principle?'

He trailed off into inconsequentialities, telling me how he had once found Professor Gee waxing sentimental over some tatty souvenirs. The worst was a yellow, typewritten menu from a Cricklewood bistro (vegan, he thought), where a first informal interview was arranged with the *Tribune*'s editor-in-chief, at a time when the Grading story was on Gard's list of potentially breaking news. It brought a tear. A thumb-printed receipt from a subway heel bar conjured the descriptive spectacle of an aproned smithy, and this too necessitated the dab of Professor Gee's shirt cuff. Now only yesterday Gee had returned to that world, taking his place on the tourist bus – a seat at the front.

I imagined clueless holidaymakers, bobbing down the pass, unable to share the professor's ideals in family entertainment. What after all was there through those tinted windows? Was it really more than a crystal brightness, with the worn clichés typical of Alpine postcards? As to my own position, I think of myself as a part of the peasantry, having no say for or against these outings. I am someone who suddenly wakes in an explosion of snores – my own. I shall take any recollection – of something blue and ethereal through the bus's skylights – and try to get a sense of Gee in his satisfaction, at how a cloudless heaven in the heights he'd left behind can compare with the brown smog of the industrial heap he was bound for. Was it really for diplomacy? Or was it a thirst for experience? Was *that* why he left?

I think not. Tittle-tattle has always been his gift, and that is the stuff to exercise his pen. A front seat on the bus was his perfect vantage. All advice is not to contradict the tour guides if in an advanced position. One microphone, two vocal ecstasies. Then I had a thought on the driver, swinging his wheel as the bus descends to sea level, a man with steady nerves and tunnel vision, and without a lasting view. Would he take at face value what he couldn't help overhear? The lyrical raptures gone into on another plain lake – yet one more described as hyaline. I could lead him, with Professor Gee, to its banks, but gazing down he wouldn't see a true reflection. Gee's lined neck, the flab of his chins, warts, carbuncles, nasal hair, black pepper on blotting paper – a clogging of pores. Or the bulge of his greedy eyes. The lake is smooth, calm, glassy. The man looking in is clean and respectable, but his nose is retroussé.

Standey, with a sleight of hand, urged on us the troublesome issue of tourism, now to be treated as of lesser importance, given what booty Gee's realignment would bring. I am talking about the kind of deal Chamoogan had in mind. 'We might even hope for an end,' he said, 'to all that amateur photography, which only makes us the butt of silly jokes for bored and boring relatives at home.' Standey actually poked fun at the 'fool holidaymaker', fresh from the slopes of Schmutzburg, regaling his family with holiday snaps. Raised eyebrows when, in a wash of polychrome, that miserable bloke called Joe issued for the first time and everlastingly – a smile. Next he's got a foot up, about to meet someone's coccyx. Then some rake he befriended sports an expensive fur and points to a worn inscription in stone, in a language no one in the party understands. Or to take another instance: Beryl or Meryl's mother's uncle is intrigued by a bell in a bell tower. There are always crowds of pensioners – round a hand pump, or a tombstone, or collectively reading a map. And there are always half a dozen who want to do brass rubbings.

'Anything else?' I asked.

'The list could go on.'

Professor Gee, and those who'd follow him out of Schmutzburg, were going to alter all that, the more so the more they were paid. No one could say how much. And would anyone lament it? Muchello, as Grading's trial drew to a close, I felt sure was one who could, yet it puzzled me that his summarising opinion didn't materialise. He chose to talk in parables, only one of which I am able to paraphrase, uncertain as I am. He told that disintegrating court that an ideal no one bothered with unwound a path through a tangle of cobwebs, and brought you to an upward climb through a squeal of mountain winds. What began as a precarious footing on a narrow stair ended in a spiral to the summit, and fine views from Schmutzburg's highest tower – a broad sweep over the inducements, or the deceptions of the world. 'What will draw our attention,' he said, 'always transcends that greater whole.'

I think of that as having little to do with Michael Grading, and am prepared to say why. If you look at his case as I have, it looks less a dismissal of him and more Standey's defence of Gee, whose actions were little short of treason. The decisions Gee had made, once they were known, Standey saw as right and proper and politic. What Gee et al had devised in a confusion of reverse propaganda, deliberately obfuscating, was aimed at that corner of the English establishment that still had Grading on its files – his case conveniently lost under mounting piles of bureaucracy.

We might have disturbed the crystal of mountain life a lot less severely, and not muddied it at all. All is murk. Even so a few things are still visible, if you're prepared to look. Dr Muchello, harmless, old and retiring, and having travelled all that way for a few sentimental possessions, I see sharply in contrast to Gee. Gee's life is an exhortation to the rest of us, to open up, enjoy. For me it adds up to no more than a sad hour at Cricklewood, looking at last Sunday's reviews over celery and chick peas. I imagine him, bound for a bus or train, and a visit to the opera. 'Relax,' he would say. 'It's once in a while.' It's depressing to think of him, late on a Friday night, consuming an egg, crêpe or croissant at a corner stand, the street vibrant, streaming with theatre traffic. One shouldn't be perplexed at the fizz and spangles of the hoardings, he'd say – and don't be indignant. Enjoy.

None of this for me, thanks. To me Gee has rubbed, breathed on, rubbed again, a piece of silver plate, and read out the inducements of a copywriter. I can't take it seriously.

'You will have to,' Standey insists. Yet if Gee's mission were authentically one of dissemination, with Grading used as pawn in his call to evangelise his counterparts in the West, why had he planned to leave before the committee had reached its verdict?

I have no wish to mislead you. I have it from a reliable, unimpeachable source that Gee the student – not the same man twenty years ago – looked to his chorister's vestments, shabby-looking hand-me-downs, and predicted a fastidious life of newness one day. Nothing would convince him that the garb usually worn in Schmutzburg, and the Spartan chambers allocated to us – so natural to the rigours of inquiry – couldn't be replaced. A man of erudition had a definite need for a mahogany desk. Then of course, in the advancing winter twilight, when the familiar shapes of a rural landscape dissolve in a gloam of ink, one instinctively keeps the world at bay. Velvet drapes, in a nice warm scarlet, were the first defence a house put up at the intrusion of cold windy nights. Sedentary men with creaking joints liked to pace before an open fire. (Not even I deny that.)

But this is hardly the point. How many, I wonder – one, two, three? – have suggested similar ideals to the restless Gee? I can guess at what he's had to put up with. An exclusive after-dinner order, un-bewitching with its few hard seats and stodge of conversation. Who wouldn't prefer some quaint little club in Belgravia? One of those idyllic spots, having banished equality questions decades ago, yet keeping on at least one in the species of 'other', whose job is to dish up late-night platters with the last of the nightcaps. Do I jest? Well, I know of one place, and am able to state vicariously (as Gard is my mouthpiece) that no one is there for the pleasure of its portraits, stout Victorian elders, stern, sturdy, bewhiskered. It's to sink in the pleasant swamps of the leather settees, with a keep-out sign in the form of a newspaper – the best from a right-wing press. You can expect, occasionally, a liveried toad, on his tray a handwritten note or a glass. There are roaring fires under every ornate mantel.

This Gee was willing to look into, or as Standey said, only the excluded put the question of exclusion in its proper context. Grading had got part way to broaching it for himself in the crossword clues he denied he had written (hate crosswords, he said), adding: 'Children of a communications revolution exchange pleasantries via uploads and downdumps' (as if that were a proper refutation). His conception of a theogonic universe was its evolution through asynchronous timers and semaphores, where all the old deities didn't trust themselves to the electronic circuitry that arrangement necessitated. Part of the technologist's training – healthy, you might say – was an indifference to the unknowable. Yet it is always in the boldness of guesswork that humanity has an opportunity to free itself of bigotry.

For me I regret it, as an attitude that had given him little or no insight into those unctuous clerics I had heard much of in English society. No more than ordinary men, appearing under media lights, who with broad smiles indulged the luxurious faith of the rich, these latter having got themselves up cleverly into the broadcast role of interviewees. It's the joy of nations when two millennia of the Christian sword end in the tickled vanities of vacant media personalities, who after hours of sentimental chitchat achieve, as the justification of worldly goods, spiritual acceptance. It ensures unhindered roaming in the afterlife, a way clear to a supernormal drawing room, where it's assumed for the music-lover and admirer of Euclidean geometry a genteel sort of Beethoven taking tea with a ninnified Bertrand Russell – grey and hieratic – who between them have set a spare place at table and kept it open all these decades. Sceptics have a right to their blasphemy, when the Lord has conceived a cosmic lucky dip.

It gets us closer to the points Gee had missed, or I suppose might conceivably come back for. Even then I doubt if a pioneering press was interested in the mysteries of authorship and the divine ripples spreading out from seven insoluble crossword clues. Were they really the 'mystical' anticipation of a future course of events? The dreamed prediction to link a young Grading and a wiser Ms Chamoogan? Or was it only chance, a smudge on a timetable, that had brought them together, strangers crossing arcs in Auerbach's ancient drinking den? In Grading's so-called premonition, the two had arrived in a desolate country, where the wind rose from all quarters, whipping the dunes and the desert sands into waves, whirls, eddies, while a priest at the stormy gate was there to confirm the depth of human doubt. His was the question of who shall inhabit God's inscrutable household. Myself I cannot warm to a politicised brand of Christianism, God's favourites gilt-edged and preening themselves, careful not to allow urban philosophers over the threshold. Atheists, once thought fit for the propaganda *coup* we like to call conversion, pottered about, digging or trimming the borders, where the perfected world was row upon row of neatly laid-out gardens. The scourge of civilisation can't get near the practical life of the faithless, whose efforts serve the faithful. The gardens are walled, to keep the enemy out. For even among the enlightened, entrenched in the bureaucracy of academe, and knowing the need for departures, the revolutionary foot forward is no more constructive than selling out to the press.

To Standey that was a hasty conclusion. To him Professor Gee was not without integrity

– though this as a subject was one he was anxious to get away from.
'What's behind us is behind us,' he said.
There was only so much information we could share.

Some night I shall wake irrationally, intent only on my dreams, and in fear of the dark shall attempt to pin my spectres down. You can't quite do that (I see I've another note from Public Relations). The truth is I have only the shadowy twitch of a curtain. There's a change in pressure when one by one the ghouls of my own concoctions leave by the door. What have I done? Mainly I have chosen to disagree.

I twirl a pen, then work my way through a vogue in gloves, getting neither pen nor gloves to fit. I have meditated, in the style of Western gurus. For good reason, I have marked the adjournment above as the moment of finality, as now I give way as events dictate. Gee with his newspaper deal and Grading for copy. Grading with Humber. Grading's deception, not a real defence. Then there was Chamoogan, at ease with herself, and prepared to submit to the political game her father was a part of. For me she flunked the cross-examination. (Quick! There's a military beat in the click of heels outside. There's a rap, but on this occasion at someone else's door, not mine. So relax.) I tell myself to be calm, and not to succumb to the exotica of Schmutzburg's new disease.

Ah, England. Can't you be amused at men like Gee? He'll applaud that quackery you vote for come the hustings, acted out under a monarchy and other anachronisms, a land that will not relinquish the flag. (Now who's moved this paperweight, here on my desk? Or is it my imagination?) Gee I sometimes see through the fog of my insights, feet up in a smoky newspaper office. I shall miss (a) his point of view, (b) his jokes, (c) those strolls in a comedy of elevated talk. I can't quite see UK sterling as compensation, while I shudder at what he's contracted to write. Imagine the headlines – 'Michael Grading's premonition'. (Now this is too much: someone's torn a page from my notebook.) And all on the basis of reputed exchange with the suspect, who with Humber spent his last hours here in a survey of our game, with rules briefly glossed. Now what would this pair want with that?

What Jeremy Gard doesn't report is Professor Gee counting on a long run in the *Tribune* in the follow-up to Grading's disappearance story. This is the point – and is also off the record – at which the bailiff took the others aside. Privately he warned his older colleague that as the trail went cold, and all that psychic idiocy lost its edge, Gee would have to look for something else, who on the contrary argued that given how anxious Grading was that his case should be heard, there must be a lot more still to come out. But by now the bailiff had tired of the whole thing, as I am beginning to. The only thing Grading represented was England as an archipelago dotted with diminishing industries. It seemed laughable that his office space, territorially fenced off from that of his colleagues, was in self-contradiction in referring to itself as open plan. He pinned his personal décor onto his partitions – photographs of loved ones, get-togethers, notes to himself – that sort of thing. He had a window view, which came with rank, rank coming with service, his service stretching back two years or so to graduation. He could look out at the canal, albeit an infected stretch of the Grand Union, as his interest had to be maintained. He could be soothed, wrestling with select-when-end constructs in the closed cotton wrap of the software those reporting to him had written, according to specs Grading had handed out.

Not, I add, that our professor was prepared to take much notice. He was full of a cocktail-style tourism, with an incurable need for London. He raided his coffers and found a ten-shilling note, and sighed at the bright recollection of how it got there. I've seen his trunk, with its pine lid. He produced from it a *Peter Pan*, a book read several times over during Gee's infancy. Later souvenirs included a Proms ticket, not from the last night, mercifully. A man called Wilson, H., still at that time only a commoner, Gee showed me had parted with an autograph. In caustic mood I blustered it mightn't have been his own. Then, behold, a bespattered menu from a Cricklewood bistro – which I am told was a winter meeting place for the capital's blue-nosed poets (I leave you to guess what I think). What, you say? The prolonged sneer, you say? Out of fashion? Ah but note the care with mine – a sneer that doesn't exceed necessity.

How, I ask, could Gee have come to break a heel? Or was it that Gee was quick to assist some floozie on his arm, who'd twisted her stiletto? I'd have been glad to see him go, if that hadn't meant his new asseverations were words of advice for the tourists coming here. Ironically they were the numskulls soon to be addressed by him in the columns of the *Tribune*. You see what hypocrisy I am having to deal with.

Had it been up to me, he'd have been forced to give up all aspects of his Schmutzburg office, on the basis of no place left for him here. The opposite happened, since at the outset Gee was pushed up, clutching his portfolio, to the highest reaches of President Standey's new administration. The president is quick to point out, now that our trade is a two-way trade, that Gee and his votaries have dual encampment here and in England – surely an advantage. Cross-continent propaganda shows the latter tenancy as under the jurisdiction of a Lord Somebody, whose gang of village boys is grouped under fervent nationalist colours. But that is a lie. England's indigenous culture is much more sinister than that, with Gee demanding its largesse, rather than a 'frank' and 'open' exchange. The president wanted his name lit up, as a condition of the commercial bargaining now under way. To that end the English concluded their side of things with an anthem, penned for the president's benefit, by one of their most celebrated, most banal of musicians ('Arm-Still Standey'). Standey condemned none of it, saying only of Gee that for someone so advanced in years, the acquisition of worldly titles was a harmless recreation. Anyway. Off my soapbox. Let's say Gee took a slow ferry to Britain, having a history of falsehoods clutched to his heart.

We never recovered the tabloid, and apart from its sister broadsheet there was one other thing Grading left us to look at – that attempt at a crossword, much as I hesitate to dignify it. Author? As yet not proven. And what about his premonition? What if Grading *had* foreseen those priestly ministrations, in a desert storm, as a chance encounter with

Nicholas Chamoogan's daughter? What if Gee's pointless dwelling on those media cognoscenti – they of the networks EU-wide – represented another foretelling on Grading's part, whose presence here with his English newspapers cautioned against involvement in a ratings war? And what of his and Nicola's respective positions vis-à-vis the Church, with its matters of the utmost gravity trivialised through celebrity gossip carried on under studio lights – hasn't something similar happened here in Schmutzburg? For what if heaven won't admit a pauper? And required is some simple translation, *Darling, I see a simply divine afterlife* rendered as *The programme planners know what the masses want to hear, so let them hear....* In recent days how I drift, and get tired. Would you be surprised to learn that Nicola Chamoogan is our new Public Relations director?

I think she's about to insist I present myself. I hope after all this time she won't have lost sight of certain English ideals in 'democracy', a public sphere where 'truth', and its fellow-conspirator 'reality', are permitted to flower. She surely knows that what she has come to preside over is rotten to the core, with men like Gee prone to rush off, eager to offer their services. I'm told that the bailiff, now heading a department called Research, is working on a new soap opera, laughably described as 'scholarly', and due to go out on prime-time TV. The script team operates out of Chiswick, and is not due back for several weeks. For me there remains this one long night, which in all its mountain clarity folds its limbs round my labour. For my serenity, for that invigorating air I breathe, I hope that Public Relations will grant me lenity, and thereby allow the completion of my task – now more than ever a secret. That is to show how Grading, a Grading you shall know – how he and Humber countered the intellectual fraud we have fallen to here, and showed us just how to read its English equivalent.

Gard with his penchant for confrontational politics couldn't bring himself to a calm or reasonable resolution. His eight-day wonder depended for success on the tension between his starlet Michael Grading and the Establishment Figure (his capitals) Nicola Chamoogan – a polarity of English class conflict, always good for sales.... To that end Gard's newspaperly dénouement resurrected Grading's so-called premonition and used it as a battering ram in the defence's cross-examination. It involved theatrical legalese, in a formation of sentences showing partisanship, and concluded with a salvo of questions for the villain (the plain Nicola Chamoogan, career girl). Gard's implication was this, that the premonition was a lie, a fabrication, but a contrivance necessary for finding out the truth, which with fist-thumping pyrotechnics Grading started to do – under, that is, the watchful hand of Gard's reporter's pen. He bullied his witness (this was the only way). Transgression, he said, was not a secular norm that somehow left the sacred untouched. Then came this regurgitated 'establishment' stuff (was this more Gard than Grading?), making *her* the political enemy (and this is what I hate about the English). This, Gard-Grading went on, looked all very well, clubby in its ethos. But then Gard – or do I mean Grading? – coaxed the committee back, returning to his dream of Nicola Chamoogan and the priest at the gate – evidence, he said, of truth he had found in the theory of synchronicity—

The wind dropped: the holy man commanded the elements, if not the human soul. Grading pressed forward to the gate – his gate – wanting to claim his passage, though dressed in a safari suit, *she* was better prepared. The priest turned away, indifferent to Grading. Nicola was adamant she didn't need his commentary. Grading interrupted, asserting this wasn't a private contract. Nicola stepped through the gate, the priest still urging her to stay. There were perils along the path she intended to go, to which she said only that was the crux of their belief. There was nothing he could say or do to stop her going. When she went on, Grading tried to follow.

Nicola, smiling under oath, offered counter-thrusts, pointing out that authors of popular mysticism made special provision for moments like these, with 'quite a repertoire', ranging from a reversal of lay and clergy roles, to the outcast's undeserved damnation. Whatever form it took, it was usually called on to demonstrate obstacles between two parties, trying, but failing, to communicate.

'Don't tell me,' she said. 'You wanted to show the priest how impossible an English life had become.'

Well, yes – albeit all Grading could utter was gobbledegook to do with his work (in itself this courts our sympathy), and rattled on about a damaged paging disc, or the intermittent reliability of his data buses and hardware drivers. To the priest the only meaning this conveyed was of worldly prevarication, with the subject taking refuge in a self-definition solely to do with his work. He'd got more weighty matters to consider, principally Nicola Chamoogan's painful departure from the one and only faith.

'That is why his word is lost on you,' she said, for in Grading all she saw was the lukewarm sense of his destiny and the pursuit of joyless pleasures. 'And is why,' she went on, 'you feel excluded, even if you aren't.' This was a deceitful heroism in the throes of which Grading wasn't alone. It was a common disillusionment. 'An unwillingness to accept that the essence of our lives isn't approached through what we do, but in how we do it.' That left Grading with the amusing question, what was it beyond packet switched data streams and network architectures, if not a deeper reality, if not some hope of finding his *pneumatikos*?

Gard-ing replied: 'It wasn't the composition of crossword clues.' This was Garding's best riposte in disavowing their authorship.

🌶

Grad-Garding resorted to jibes when in rebuttal his witness recalled her friendship and close association with one of those old-style media pioneers – a radio voice. His home politically was the wing opposite to hers. I review what paperwork I can. I say only how that manna from a paperman's heaven had no sense of the miraculous, not to me, with the witness out-manoeuvring him (as, in a professional capacity, she continues to out-manoeuvre most of her colleagues here). The argument was back where it didn't belong, in its social mire. Her radio friend – a man known for his common-sense broadcasts, back in the Fifties – openly wore his Party membership, though towards the close of the Seventies saw no option but to tear up his card and discard. Chairs creaked, and today I groan, for Grad was back on his heels.

'Can't help observe,' Nicola Chamoogan said: 'there is no action. All this indignation of yours – it's lazy armchair stuff.' The committee, suspicious from the start, dismissed Michael and his cohorts as more in the line of Wix's descendants, though she could not argue 'action' as particular to her radio friend – not in my opinion. He, with a plummy voice, easy, and known to millions, debated – and did so with extra-Gardish acumen – all known issues of his day. But the voice's possessor had not a happy constancy off air. Chamoogan was able to tell us with confidence, having known him. That's to say *known* – she and just a few others.

What kind of political beast was this? He'd a fat face and a maritime beard, and sucked the salivary stem of his pipe, a thing always with him, clamped in his yellowing teeth. In course of time he felt no longer able to broadcast. For fifteen years his chosen place had been three rooms and a kitchenette, in an all-glass view of the busy metropolis, his aura one of cold, eerie silence. One afternoon, with his friends around him – and Nicola was one – he couldn't help but sentimentalise in the dying evening light, as he poured another cup. The sun slid down behind a few naked elms clumped on a bend in the river, its last warm rays entwined in the blue-grey lattice of the railway bridge. He tossed down three symbolic coins onto the square brightness of his blotter – a pound, a penny, nostalgically a half-a-crown. Nicola followed his gaze to the calm steely water, where an Everyman, a solitary rower, bumped his little boat through a lengthening mesh of triangles cast as a shadow from the bridge.

Grade of course knew his media history, and so could guess who Nicola meant. This was the same commentator (Grade-us smirks) who had been humiliated publicly, having failed – and not just once, but several times – to explain his comprehensive change of political views. New lines have to be drawn all the time, so that declaring which was which, who are friends, enemies, and who is 'establishment', is never straightforward. Nicola and her friends rallied round. Mimics and parodists, spilling over from the music hall, and happy for any kind of work, took to the small screen and dramatised his *volte-face*, not that they understood it intellectually. This somehow involved requisitioning the basement to his tower block, where boxes were delivered filled with rag-trade off-cuts – silks, denims, wools, corduroys. These items our slapstick artistes festooned everywhere – over doors, curtain rails, chairs, tables, a sink. Leering limelight performers, lifting top hats and twirling their canes, sporting a canny resemblance to that pre-war broadcaster resident above, tried this or that cut of cloth while endlessly, endlessly imitating.

'This,' comments Gard, 'can't be seen as evidence' – its source being a tabloidism he affects to despise. Nevertheless it was the entire truth, according to Nicola Chamoogan, whose tactics were clever. She recalled that one or two autumn clouds enveloped the setting sun, while at the same time the intense white of that blotter, and the coins still resting there, dissolved into grey. By what legerdemain she didn't know, but the coins, once they'd disappeared completely, were replaced by the torn pieces of the broadcaster's Labour Party card. He it was who pointed to the rower, who by now had passed under the bridge, and was chopping as he veered for the inside bend. A crow flapped slowly from one of those elms. The rower, in taking the bend, looked tired.

'*Was* tired,' said Girdang (for it is difficult to know whom the *Tribune* is writing for), 'if *his* card was also in tatters....'

Islets on the leeward side offered the rower calm, deceptive as that might be. A flurry of yellow leaves rose up, a cascade, a vortex. Gardeners had got their bonfires – the smell of mould and fungi, and bundles of torn-up membership cards – as little puffs or lazy plumes of smoke dissolved in the tangle of branches above. Which way should he go? Well, that was impossible for him to say, like all those solitaries – stubborn, indecisive, laughably proud, and in a war-torn century complete in their loss of direction. It accentuated an already vulnerable nature, and helped to perpetuate the all-party myth: 'a man needs masters, leadership, definitive goals'. Yet so much had been learned since those golden radio days. What those basement parodists had been quick to see was a change of face. Theirs was a new way to ease the pains of work, at the end of the day and the approaching hour for bed. The world's representative rower was plunged in the florets of his armchair. Instead of a glass of stout at his elbow (the hoardings showed treacle with surmounting foam), and arcs of air to tell us his radio is on, something more potent sat on his table top. In a corner the TV ubiquitous grew hot as it glowed. Nostalgia, varsity theorists, public ululations, a nation's dampened liberalism, first signs of a leftist rot, a canker in all those English pillars, was all now the heady mix spawning that nightly flicker, waiting for the early-evening homecoming. De Grade is sure that Nicola Chamoogan's cosmopolitan friend had deserted his post not as a lost cause, but because the medium had transmuted at a rate that he had not. It was asked, what TV packaging, tricks of the makeup brush and studio lights could make a consumable of flabby jowls, and a beard that looked like barnacles? All that homey reason, its virtues of logic, couldn't compete with an angelic face, a tidy coiffure, a well-cut suit. One voted for what was inevitable.

Well – it didn't turn out quite like that. He put on his boots and left at once, and passing the janitor sitting in the basement, a plain man drinking tea from an enamel mug, struck out across the mudflats and lurched into the pale urban sunset. All left behind at the window watched him, a man hunched in a beige duffle coat, swiping with his stick or kicking what rubbish lay in his path, the shreds of old tyres, what looked like a handleless frying pan. It was going to make a good picture, so Nicola found his camera. Years later he sent her the photographs, signed and dated, with a last few words never likely to get an airing. With them he described how he'd wanted to follow the rower, tramping at the oily riverside, in a forlornness of autumn trees, through the wisps and curls of pinkish bonfire smoke. One had to imagine that boatman, resilient, weathered, at home in the elements. For his decades of isolation this much was clear, even to him: the need to look more closely, at everything, the farther away from everything media diktat took us. Neither he nor our one-time broadcaster guessed that skulking in the undergrowth, listening in and scowling at their conversation, was a wrinkled homunculus – throw of an unconscious age – who lived with the terrifying revelation of ritual life as a deluded life, and that the sole truth of civilisation was the world's materiality. This was his advice: trade well with a dirty coin, and be sure to prosper by its commerce. That, and the marketplace, and the natural order of macroeconomics, are the only meaning.

To me this is too arduous a view, from a glassy perspective – an elevation always likely to lend a poetic coloration, and never to the point of things. The sun rises over the roofs, over the wet slates of any grey suburb. A first car from the west, lights blazing in the twilight, hums with the rub of tyres on the frosty macadam. It leaves the loop of a flyover, and bounces down on silken hydraulics. A wind gets up from the east. The orange and inky streaks in the dawn sky puff themselves up and turn into lead. Suddenly it rains. The barnacled commentator yawns, stretches, casts off his pyjama stripes – showers, breakfasts, checks the mail. Friends call after ten for coffee and a smoke – for these are conversational times. Soon all there gathered are drawn to the spattered panes, and the windy rattle of rain. Down below, outside, there is real life – it somehow goes on. A hat flies from a turning head. Yesterday's news, the correspondence page, wraps itself round the fragile pole of a street lamp, but tugs itself free and spirals into the apocalyptic vault of a dead London sky. An old char on the darkening pavement crouches into the gusts, prodding an open umbrella into the sheets of rain. A new and stronger wave blows it inside out. They're nodding, those erudite observers, but turn their backs and start on the biscuits – and that is their life. Their own, and occasional walks outside spanned decades, but never in weather like this. Converts to any new faith progressively wait, and wait, and wait – for one fine day, for an autumn afternoon, for a world where the pavements have dried.

Nicola wished to put a stop to all these misconceptions. Tiny details put in the right places transformed the shambling middle-age of the man that Degrade (and I) have reimagined, to what he really was – in his youth more militant than Grading [I therefore restore that name]. He revised his views on the universality of his values – for perhaps they weren't so universal – and accepted that life in his academic tower was divorced from the street. His attempt to reverse that preference came when his coffee-morning friends numbered a poor ethnic boy who'd survived the purgatory of English PAYE, having worked in a Greenwich foundry, and having won, to everyone's surprise, an important community award. In an impromptu acceptance speech he thanked his family, but turned to the judges and despaired, for how could he go on scowling at the inequalities of English life? The thought had crossed his mind to sound a flat note (an off-pitch foundry bell) and dismiss the prize [surely the moral thing to do]? Murmurs of laughter. Gentle applause.

'And let me put a stop,' said Nicola, 'to one other deception. That priest of your premonition is after all *your* invention, not mine, and the Nicola you think you've predicted isn't the Nicola standing here.'

'Well, I think that was understood,' Grading said. He watched the bailiff take a note, and thought he might jot down instances where even insiders could be induced to speak out. It wasn't unheard of when members of an elite found themselves uneasy with – and not exactly deploring – a social system whose basis was locked or bolted doors. Muchello, dazed, by now almost completely gaga (according to the *Tribune*), chose this as the moment to ramble into fond recollections of a lost friend and former annalist, one who had been – depending on the mood – ignored or maligned, and careless with his speculations. He spelt out the first of his cautionary examples. Gard cannot reprise it without a snigger. He devotes a whole column inch to a lutenist clad in a green tunic, a feathered cap and scarlet hose, whose job is to sing under castle walls as the hour approaches twilight. You picture him lit indistinctly by the moon, a blood-red rondure suspended over a turret. At nightfall the same singer is fantastically granted a constellation. It is named after him. In its pattern of meaning it's destined to enter folklore. On a clear night we see in the bright studs of the northern sky an outline we're supposed to know as a water-seller – a man practising a handstand – and alongside him the shape of an amphora, one of whose ears is broken. All however is premature, when a torchbearer, clearing a stile on the western horizon, has already swung his back foot forward in preparation for a kick. Those cosy in their castles were in for a shower, as toe met vase. I confess (though unlike Gard don't snigger), I know not the meaning of this parable.

It was it seems Gard's pet theory that Muchello preferred *any* meditation, the more distant the better – and that was the essence of an all too evident 'failure' in post. To put it in any other way was too polite, whether or not it meant chipping away at the great man's pedestal [all mock solemnity].

I feel I can now sense Michael Grading's resignation, that look of a man putting up a spirited defence, but at the same time conscious of not being listened to.

'If that is Frame Solutions' first annalist,' the bailiff said, 'he's sadly now departed. I recall his fondness for solitude, and how he liked these mountains.'

'And knew how the climate of public opinion changed, one day fair – or so saith our committees, tapping their barometers – only for the torchbearer to kick up a storm.' How Gard describes Muchello's eventual decline is a conspiracy I refuse to enter into. It was an exercise at one moment grave, astute, monumental, at another big-booted and stumbling.

Standey asked: 'How does that help us?'

'The game's first chronicler was a man with an intimate knowledge of the peasantry, who in the short years of his youth climbed these mountains and taught himself to yodel.' He also wrote a good deal, all travel books – journeys through life – so his outings had the stamp of authenticity. His ingress was accidental, a blundering in.

'When by chance he did tumble in we all looked up,' Muchello explained. 'He tapped the cakes of snow from his boots with a stick, and there – in that one innocent gesture – everything about him was known.'

'But we can't say that about Grading, and his associate Humber – can we?'

So in fact Grading had been listened to.

I am not about to advance a new theory, though with a creature like Humber I find it tempting. Gard variously refers to him as a coxcomb, a wolf, a great big dumb ox of a man. I on the other hand muse, patiently, to myself.

Humber was slow on his feet. In the time it took him to take the stand, Nicola – having vacated it – had already sat down. She picked at her fingernails and had a long, penetrating look for the bailiff. Humber, with his cummerbund, was a rare bird in these parts – overly sartorial – for what or who could have plucked him up at a happy cocktail hour and whisked him away to our mountainside? And to what purpose? Gard unkindly quips that perhaps someone had put him on the trail of a mountain species threatened with extinction, and asked him to bring back after-dinner photographs. One reflected how little we really understood our local goings on. A few grey smudges in an Alpine waste – the last throws in a survival game – end times in the life of lost migrations, a small bundle of fluff clinging on in a shrinking natural world, epics baldly set out in a cross-discipline of scientific papers. But there I digress. Allow me to clear my throat. Lights, please!

One twitch of the head swept a strand of hair off Nicola's cheek. As I have mentioned, she reserved a long, lasting look inscrutably for the bailiff. I can't help thinking that any one of several committee members must have been the *Tribune*'s insider, its informant.

Before I reveal the astonishing facts of Grading's companion, let me just say I wouldn't be consistent with myself should I not reject the 'intuitive faculty'. (I therefore reject it as hokum.) But. My Muse has given me one of Humber's craft personae not as yet known to Michael Grading – though I suppose, with what I'm about to uncover, Grading would not doubt its place in Humber's repertoire. Humber, you see, had a psychological condition, though is that not so with all of us, in some shape or form...? Furthermore it was a poet's condition, about which professional opinion had been uniform, if not encouraging. He had the comfort of a label – I have not come across it – Minor Zelich Syndrome (or MZS). This, he told the court, was neither common nor completely unheard of. His first analyst, a callow theorist who had come by his plush practice through a series of fortuitous inheritances, probed at his client unmercifully. He was obsessed with money, and having no culture beyond the world of theatrical farce, or those glitzy transatlantic soap operas, didn't understand the basis of Humber's neurosis. That was remiss, particularly as Humber himself, bit by bit, had placed all necessary information at his disposal. What could Humber do? He'd chosen an out-of-the-way place to carry on a not very public career, yet these rail trips to London impinged on his consciousness unpleasantly, even undoing his cosy distortions of life in rural England. How many times, from the sanctuary of his railway carriage, had he watched tattooed labourers in cricket whites as they thundered up to bowl? Once he thought he saw a manic hotelier thrashing the bonnet of his car with a willow switch. Miles north of St Pancras, overalled mechanics smoked Churchillian cigars on the forecourts of the brick buildings where they worked.

'I am afraid,' Standey said, 'you will have to explain.'

Humber explained. His first day job, on leaving that dreaming city, full of dreaming spires (long before Nicola Chamoogan), took him to Cheapside, onto the commercial payroll of a Panamanian financier, a loan shark with scrupulously clean fingernails, who operated from a narrow top-floor office, but in every other respect – apart from his suits, which showed the man's taste and flair – was less fastidious. His deals were done over the phone or quietly in semi-lit bars. It would never do to allow his highly respectable clients a glimpse of the cast-offs he used as office furniture – two chairs, a desk, a filing cabinet from somewhere up the Gray's Inn Road. Wouldn't want to give the wrong impression.

It was Humber's job to rove round the city with documents to sign, a task he approached not with enthusiasm but eccentrically, changing his voice (that instrument naturally repressed and la-di-da), to hail a cab in broad Bronx say, or to buy his tea and sticky bun – haggling over the change – in a not convincing cockney. Somewhere inside him lurked a hard-bitten Yorkshireman, who came out usually at railway kiosks, to berate some sullen, unhelpful ticket clerk. That wasn't all. One idle, rainy afternoon, his nose pressed to the office window, and scratching round for work, he followed with widening eyes the bobbing black umbrellas floating through the smeary white fluorescence of the shop lights opposite. Humber dreamed on, of hot days in high summer, for which he devised the perfect counter to the hordes of short-sleeved tourists, in an endless jostle for an effective camera pose. Properties, a new costume, please. A trilby, the brim turned down over one eye, dark, Mafioso glasses, rounded off with a cruel Sicilian snarl. One hand in a jacket pocket clutched the stem of his pipe – a Peterson – able to double as a stubby little hand gun.

'Ah, I see,' said Professor Standey. 'At that time your ambitions were theatrical, but stuck in a job you didn't like you were only awaiting that first important break....'

No. His landlady, a Gdansk *deracinée*, kept a tidy house and a gloomy delicatessen in Ealing (though reports vary on that). She also couldn't make him out. Her neighbours, most of whom were indoor types, spent a great deal of time with elbows on their window sills, looking out for the bizarre Humber, a man whose gait was comic, in a loping sort of way. Even the outdoor types, whose pride was the pride of suburban ownership, who in easing back pains – after pulling weeds, after clipping lawns – couldn't resist the occasional, surreptitious, or pointedly angular glance. *They* couldn't make him out. A Saturday cinema-goer, who had concealed himself behind the louvres of a gable window, was ostensibly blowing attic dust from a school report. He followed a line of view across the street, with its interplay of shadows and afternoon sunlight. That line of view was straight into Humber's room, where Humber was seated at his desk. Rumours began to precipitate. Soon it became a pastime, to observe or spy on Humber, with his long face, up there in the evenings, at weekends, framed in a pool of glass, bent studiously over a desk, and assisted late into the night by the cone of light from a table lamp. Humber, in conversation, was cagey about his work, but had said vaguely it was to do with finance, so what else was this, in a post-war economy, but the secret life of a counterfeiter?

Next time his landlady stalked through his room, swooping down on yesterday's discarded socks, or the debris of pockets Humber had turned out, she must have borne that in mind. To the puzzlement of everyone concerned – or who had made themselves concerned – there were no fake banknotes, either hidden in drawers or stuffed under his mattress. This was a minor setback.

Humber got on with his life, and still consigned his socks to the wash. Loose coppers, somehow always rattling on the wainscot at around bedtime, he put in a lidless jam jar as always. His landlady neither pressed him to leave nor gave him official notice. She was, it is true, an old peasant at heart, her perspective broadened by the upheavals recent turmoil had inflicted on her race. So, when a few weeks later she poked about in his room again, and this time came across some handwritten pages on his desk, on a quick skim through she knew exactly what they were. In them whole paragraphs had been excised with the neurotic strokes of a fountain pen, while to the converse two torn halves of a resurrected page had been pasted together. So what of it? What makes that significant? Well, here in writing was Humber's personal cavalcade, the gambol of winter scenes, in a girl he called Jin or Jez or Jude, a hopeless first novel with its equally hopeless amour, a thing doomed and painfully one-sided. Yet here also was the theatre of Humber's mind, since it wasn't solely on those real streets that characters, voices, costumes were tried on and cast off. Note, please – the same playful intensity, the same agonised apprentice grappling with his art.

'A terrible disappointment for cinema-goers everywhere.'

Except, that is, for Humber's analyst. It gave him his early discourse on the inverted glamour of *film noir* verism, papers that in therapy circles are said to have been formative, though we shall have to take Humber's word for that. What cannot be doubted is that Humber's first analyst, in common with his first London landlady – that merry widow of Gdansk – had been shown a glimpse of Humber's extended juvenilia before it was destroyed.

'Destruction that,' added Humber, 'I now see as adding fuel for the counterfeit theory.'

After several hard winters, and the wear of city life, what had you got? A moral lynch mob hooded in a blue Christmas midnight. Its two or three leaders climbed up and over the widow's wall, and left certain clues – for example the deep impression of overshoes in the clods of frosted earth. A yellow glow in the cold of a rear window urged them over the lawn, and here, when they peeped into the back parlour, the diabolic Humber, the rose of a roaring fire in his cheeks, heaped hundreds of stupid love poems into the flames. The speculation was too much to bear, as Humber took up a poker, twisted at the tip, and quietly raked the ashes.

'That's it?' Standey asked.

Certainly not. 'There was,' Humber said, 'a last glow of sunshine in the west....' That, he said, was through a thinning wisteria, which had run its riot and had now been tamed, along the length of the garden wall – which was high and crumbling. A sour-faced gardener trundled clippings and a first fall of leaves in a barrow. Flames – or rather orange embers in a brazier – had given him his unnaturally high colour. 'I,' said Humber, 'stirred my coffee. A cab was calling. My bags were in the hall. A puff of wind rattled a scrap of paper over the paving stones.' He naturally thought of the novel still on his desk (a thing thrashing about in the sordid throes of amoebic fission, wanting to be two). The gardener, an anaemic office boy out of a job, hopped about where some fool had left a rake, then flung it in the shed. 'I fetched my papers, and I picked up the poker, and heaped all that Celtic nonsense into the brazier.' The boy went home, leaving the barrow out, and the shed unlocked. In a sense what had been destroyed *was* counterfeit, which its author refused to leave until it had turned to ashes, a few grey specks floating up in a last bid for fictive life.

'A sad end to youthful ambition.'

'No,' said Humber. 'A beginning. A metamorphosis.'

His last conscious method role had been the day before, in horn-rimmed spectacles, a bowler hat and a gaberdine. The Panamanian sat with his feet up, stubbing out a long cigarette, categorically refusing Humber's resignation – this was a bad week and everyone had obligations. But the English so attired – this one standing for too long in a pool of water – are resolute. It looked like rain again, so Humber said good morning, and not concerned at all at the things the Panamanian said about the threshold, and what would happen if Humber crossed it – well, Humber crossed it. A crier on the street bellowed out a headline: 'PM deplores black market.' In the cab to the station, smoke still swirling in his brain, you could see him sitting forward, both hands wrapped round the handle of his umbrella, a pose accompanied by a chuckle. Twenty-five years later, in the frozen wastes of northern England, Rhea, who was Grading's partner for much of his college life (and for a year or so beyond), had eyes for some old municipal lockups, which she wanted as a studio for her latest student project – a film. After a great deal of fruitless negotiation it required a petition. Harold Humber, FIMTA, ACIS, visited the campus, but with hands folded on the studded handle of his walking cane affably said no. Clearly he hadn't understood the electric combination of wit and realism in Rhea's dramatic works. Grading told her that her next step ought to be to make an appointment via Harold Humber's secretary.

Of her we have Humber's own testament: 'A dumpy spinster. Reliable.' A woman handpicked for an unvaried wardrobe. Victorian shoes, black, and brought to a sheen at God knows how many minutes to dawn. An old maid's dresses, predictable, and therefore uncontroversial, and having a seasonal permanency – printed cream and pink in an all-year bloom. Her white arms bore the mottles of forty-odd summers. Her pens – most of which were red – had always been put to sinistral labours, her robust left hand forever resisting the tides of a right-handed world. In the ordinary everyday the errors of sleepy clerks or aberrant cashiers seldom evaded her underscores, still less her amused tickings-off (they were oval-shaped).

'As to Rhea's making an appointment,' Humber said, 'Madge would certainly have asked awkward questions.' Why, for example, had the petition not been enough? Why could Rhea not accept Mr Humber's decision? 'And anyway, when not on leave, Madge always left Friday mornings free in my diary.' But now an impostor occupied his sanctum, a wide-eyed girl from the typing pool. Her spots of nail varnish – an unimaginable frost-bite blue – had left some strolling bear prints in the snows of Friday, ten to ten-thirty. 'As I understood,' Humber explained, 'there were some campus officials wishing to make union representations.'

Grading took it up: 'Rhea had considered what constraints, and had talked them over, and had satisfied her colleagues.' She persuaded them that the fact of her debut – her directing debut – wasn't uppermost in her mind. It had something to do with principle. Debate moved to the script itself, which Rhea had co-written (I hesitate to say this, but all it amounted to was a miserable assemblage of every domestic ill). However, to her credit, Rhea censored out those usual cries from the heart and spontaneous acts of violence. What she said she needed was two people only, sitting calmly in a small, rectangular, whitewashed room (or lockup garage made to look like that). To be got rid of, unsentimentally, were her co-writer's stage directions, by now the last vestige of their collaboration: Man raises bruised fist, now in frenzied grip on kitchen Sabatier, strokes, raises again. Glint of blood on steel in the moonlight. Instead, a plume of pure white cigarette smoke found its final transformation, rising in a thin vertical jet from the prism of an ashtray – a hideous knob of glass. The manias, depressions, jangling of nerves, life together on a knife-edge: all of it was seen in that white thread of tobacco smoke, dissolving into a stratum of cotton wool on the ceiling. Further, in Rhea's new scheme, she dispensed with the sudden jerk of limbs, the emotive frenzy delivered in every line, and instead arranged for subtle changes in the ambient airflow. Any notion of the dramatic depended on the whitewash, and the bright but unstated lighting ballooning ghoulishly from floor level. What makeup there was carefully paled her players' lips and cheeks and blackened their eyelashes. Bizarre camera angles put a back or forward slope into their seating arrangements, while close-ups flirted with one detail only, that huge prismatic ashtray and its trick of transformation, where the smoke – swirling and agitated – crumbled into a brown or reddish fog. They might, they said, dabble with other bits and pieces, inter-cut randomly (for how could they really know at this early stage?): a network of lumpy green veins in a bony hand, the hand itself sheathed in marmoreal cold skin; a scimitar with crescent moon, pinned to a lapel; an open book facedown on a low table, its spine creased, the author and title illegible. Importantly, a baby's rattle. Tension returns to the plot in a revised dialogue, a series of drunken political commentaries interlaced with gloomy reflections on personal failings and the problems of ambition. Needless to say, the disgruntled co-author took her original idea to an address in Wood Lane and did marvellously well, though Rhea still couldn't get her lockups.

'And?'

Said Humber: 'Those bear prints in my appointments diary I don't mind telling you I regarded as an abomination.'

This he later pointed out to a pipe-smoking counterpart – cool patrician heading up the housing department. This latter enjoyed certain hobbies after office hours, the most striking being a form of divination via the subconscious, got to grips with (apparently) only after the study of graphology. According to him Humber could now expect – the clue being those smears of nail varnish – only troubles ahead. He urged him to make special preparations for the following Thursday – which sounded mysterious – for Thursday was the obvious destination before those tracks faded under a powder of snow. And don't be surprised, he added, if 'union representations' really only means louts in studded leather, with obscene tattoos and ceremonial pins through earlobes and nostrils. (So much for men of noble sensibilities.)

When Rhea at last arrived, accompanied not by union representatives but only Michael Grading, Grading politely held open the door and pulled out a chair for his friend, whose hair was bouffant. She carried a notebook and reading glasses. Grading wore a beige suit, impeccably pressed, which he usually called upon only for weddings. He put a brightly socked ankle over its opposite knee when he sat, and systematically thumbed the plunger of a propelling pencil, which doubled as an eraser. These were nervous manifestations, followed by the twitch of a lazy heel, onto which Grading tapped his retractable lead. Humber remembered them both.

Said Grading: 'Now he knew, our business wasn't the student union.' The fact that Grading was here at all was down to a meeting of Rhea's committee, a group of theatre students who hadn't overcome initial scepticism, and didn't believe they knew sufficient protocol to penetrate the Town Hall's inner, most sacred chambers. Rhea threw up the epoch-making script – a copy, naturally – and stormed from the committee room. The angry thud of an outer door shook the water jugs, while the last of those airborne folios scuffed the plasterboard, brushed the glass of a hanging portrait, and came down prophetically over the chairman's gavel. Finished art has its look of ease. But this was the pain.

What was open to Rhea now? She scoured the local listings, and circled half a dozen potential backers. First and last on the final shortlist was Madame Belokonsky, a plumpish medium with a working interest in deceased authors, who had outlined plans to reconstruct the Synoptic Gospels in accordance with edicts only just divined from the late Dostoevsky. In exchange for a lengthy editorial in the campus rag – theme: her dramatic escape from the Stalinist pogrom – she agreed to contribute a sum. For equipment. But the lockups were still a problem.

Humber explained – it was out of his hands. The housing department had sweeping plans for the site. Rhea prodded her teeth with a hairgrip. Humber sighed.

'She saw what I didn't,' said Grading, 'saw what was in Humber's bookcase.' When Humber made notes and dropped his shoulder in a certain way, Grading was able to see only the fiscal *œuvre* – *The Importance of Being Audited* – plus, under the broad sash of a window, the pellucid red of the sun in its owner's ear.

'Let me repeat,' said Humber. 'Ours was not an obstructive municipality. Successive finance chiefs had been sympathetic to student recreation. But the site was spoken for.'

This put severe strains on Rhea's accepted style of leadership, which at that time was intellectual muscularity in preference to mindless ball kicking. Her last and obvious question framed itself a moment too late, and suffered drowning in its first abortive syllable. Humber had whipped out a large white flag and blew his nose thunderously. In the next four days Grading lost touch, first through an ear-singing malaise, then in the hot and cold sweat of a fever. He got through a drawer full of vests. The bin, overflowing with cerebral litter, had a rebellion of its own, overturning. Thence to hallucinations, where all that emptied garbage glowed in a tangerine half-light, while a grinning un-Muse picked her way through its wastes. Happily she frowned, unravelling the florets of screwed-up paper. She read aloud, imitating one of Humber's private voices from a quarter of a century before: 'Bootstraps and the public deployment of handkerchiefs are crucially important. No matter how exacting we care to make our error checks, a printer, say, or a monitor, subject to the problems of wide-area communication, is bound to catch cold. It happens. Gentlemen, I urge you to consider a cyclic influenza check. No less a commendation comes from our friends of the municipality.' Rhea, ceaseless supplier of wet flannels, told him he'd suggested running spikes for the postman and wanted that motion put to committee. Also that Humber, whose powers of healing he suddenly envied, had been sighted, mounting the steps, not of his general practitioner, but a psychiatrist. That at any rate was according to the tarnished scutcheon, with its square capitals, and its round italic in verdigris.

The housing chief, serious about his graphology, had sampled Humber's signature hundreds of times down the years, but confined his comments strictly to out-of-office hours. Over his usual breakfast of chocolate and lemon soufflé he thought he'd detected the first real signs of panic in his friend and colleague. He pushed a last bit of sponge tangentially, with a long coffee spoon, back and forth across the blue concentric rings of his breakfast plate, but at last gave it up, instead rubbing flakes of tobacco in his palms. Humber, who on this occasion shared that breakfast hour, shook up the leaves of his morning paper. Feeling conversation might be necessary, he folded the whole into quarters, putting it down when the waitress wiped the table. Interest rates were high, he said. With that the housing chief tried a different emphasis, using the word panic again, absently thumbing the shreds of his ghastly cheap tobacco into the bowl of his pipe. He lit and re-lit several times while the pair waited for the bill. He burned a fingertip when the charred extremity of a match curled up through its last sputter of bonfire smoke. Market confidence was at low ebb, Humber went on. But the chief said this: 'You should try my daughter's therapist. Here. Here's his card.'

The haze of Grading's illness lifted, the moon was out and it was sunset. Rhea decided his rehabilitation ought to be a walk through the flaming silvered reds at that moment dousing the campus, '...reflected light in the refectory windows'. She'd borrowed one of Humber's books, and picking her way through sprays, compacts and lipsticks pulled a slim paperback from her bag. Grading: 'Just look at this, I thought,' but hadn't made a mistake – for here was the name printed in ghostly lime: Harold Humber. Its draft cover design bore the funnel of a steam train, the cogs of something clockwork, a party streamer (crinkled) and an empty cocktail glass, whose stem was frosted. And, in that same ghostly lime, *Collected Poems*. Publisher, Sabre and Sabre ('very strong backlist').

You will have guessed – it belonged in that same bookish oasis nourishing good readership in Humber's dreary bookcase in his finance office, where an ear, nose or cuff was no bar to Rhea, who noticed what? I'd think, or dare to suggest, sonnets – the full-blown, edited version destined for a print run with a high production specification, on paper singled out for its colour, weight and opacity.

Said Humber: 'My new analyst later acquired his own copy of the *Collected*, but placed it on a high shelf with a few travel books and thrillers.' Tense on the couch, Humber followed the Amazonian tributaries, the cracks in the ceiling, but returned again and again to damp earth, to the *Collected*, whose modest spine one day spanned a diagonal separating *Death in the Sluices* from *Rowed to Morocco*. Far from original, said analyst was an advocate of word associations. He thought to use this method in detecting his client's old-boy old college elitism, though failed to find it (Humber insisting it didn't exist). He twitched, breathed on his lenses, wiped his glasses.

'"Each",' he said, perhaps wondering if the tyrants of socialism had found a way through Town Hall red tape.

'Peach Pear Plum,' Humber replied, recalling a publisher's catalogue of children's books – so confounding the analyst's 'equal' or 'equable'. The latter's talcum grey hair had a mad, professorial look and a greenish forelock. Catching himself in the mirror every time he turned to make a note, he swept away the showers of dandruff on the shoulders and lapels of his dinner jacket, and adjusted his bowtie. Humber hoped he wasn't keeping him, though before putting on his coat and checking its pockets for an after-dinner speech, he blundered on a touchy subject: the dichotomy that must exist for a man of letters following a dull career in town finance. Humber got away with something vague as reply. 'At least he didn't think I was showing signs of panic.'

'I think you might have preferred,' said Standey, sourly, 'Madame Belokonsky's divination.'

I think I already perceive a poet out of sorts with the greatness of things – issues, mainly – but finely tuned to the minutiae.

Back a second time, Humber noticed the analyst's copy of Humber's *Collected*, a little outpost up there among the ceiling rivers, propping up not the same but a new diagonal. As time went by that theme – if you'd call it a theme – varied, so that at times Humber's book was back to front, at others upside down. In fact over the course of numerous consultations it was seen in every possible orientation. Sometimes it wasn't even there.

Was that analyst a connoisseur?

No! He and his spare-time geneticist friend, fellows in oratory, and, respectively, secretary and treasurer to the local branch of the Long Table, between them chopped up Dr Humber's opening *terza rima* and showed a less than discerning audience how the tics and obsessions of adulthood revealed themselves, even through an intellect at its most liberated – which to Standey was banal and a *non sequitur*.

'*Very* banal!'

Rhea, whose teenage solipsism had done her no good, dissembled but couldn't repress a Wagnerian sense of artistic destiny. She ignored Humber's cunning slant rhymes when, in private, she came to survey his work.

Shaking up Michael's short-term memory – even stamping on his hat – she asked him to recount the important events preceding his four lost days. She had a pointing stick, a white board, and squeaked out her message with coloured pens. The biology lab resounded in her shrillness – bright, spotless chamber, and a conveniently empty venue. Grading remembered his 'gateway suite' – electronic egress into a thousand chattering bitstreams – and lamented that its last module still remained unwritten. But this was really too frivolous: the pointing stick missed his ear by so much, and rattled in the benches. She picked up a jar of frogs. He protested, for that really wasn't necessary. A bearded student in a moth-eaten woolly lumbered in and out, wheezing. Cautious, Grading urged her not to invoke those pickled frogs: he knew perfectly well she was after the lockups. Yet he couldn't see how Humber's *Collected*, now ironed open permanently at the preface, changed anything.

Meanwhile our analyst and gourmand – innocent son of science – stumbled about in a fog of his own. It required a large handkerchief for the film that had fogged his lenses. He wanted to demonstrate the growing (ultimately abortive) theory he and the geneticist had cooked up – one suspects over Port and one of those malodorous cheeses, though he never complained of nightmares. He marked the *Collected* at its mid-point, and an eight-line lyric. This, if the author agreed on his trade secrets bandied about or played with, he'd admit cast light on the poet's most important themes. If, as expected, *Mind* condescended to publish these findings as a joint paper, the 'lyric', cited as experimental evidence, would have to be included. Humber, admitting to the use of leitmotifs – and having dabbled in Nietzschean recurrency – at this stage of his life felt fully at home with repetitive chores. But he could not accept that his *Collected* was structured on anything as concrete as an important theme or themes. Rules, formal structures, were there to be identified, and that was as far as it went (though his friends in the psychiatric faculty didn't know a roundelay from a triolet). It was embarrassing to have to mention it, but mention it Humber did – as a clue. The word panic.

Rhea, unreformed addict of the cryptic crossword, thwacked her companions with a ruler, a book, whatever came to hand, when plain anagrams seemed unwilling to bend to her will. Acrostics were the same. She did however put down the jar of frogs, and at last, triumphantly, told Michael to read the preface, but only, she said, as far as the word hat.

This, I have it on good authority, is how in his preface Harold Humber, poet, opened his *Collected*—

Prefaces, and notes in conjunction with these, the natural recreation of poets forced to wear the editor's hat....

Rhea directed him to a preceding page, to an author's note. This amounted to a good-natured confession, with Humber regretful that the Muse had deserted him these last ten years: the *Collected* was all he could muster. That needed some choice quotation, so now she turned to the back cover, and pointed out the testimony of the Laureate-elect, who commented that despite a decade of silence, Harold Humber was still, in the opinion of many, the finest English poet now living. An unfortunate construction, since he couldn't say 'now writing'.

The geneticist worked off his Long Table dinners at the municipal squash courts, but was one day summoned to the cafeteria. He stood in a miasma of sweat, dabbing his brows with a blue bandanna. Our therapist, doctor, medic, whatever – now in a panic himself – sat with an iced soda water, the final draft of the *Mind* article, and a blue pencil. Humber sat there too, to approve his labours: excisions, emendations, even the honour of a re-assembled couplet, the sour fruit of a sleepless night. Where a first, complicated argument had dwindled to one or two casual observations, Humber was called on to chair the debate that moved to a second, a third, a definitive point of view. His Muse was tugging at someone else's coattails, eager, he was sure, to hold hands with a younger, much more youthful poet somewhere. What Humber knew and his therapist didn't was that sooner or later a rival would emerge and overtake him. If nothing else, the occasion marking that event seemed good for bogus theorising. Yet the theory Humber advanced, whose only purpose was to toy with his two psychiatric researchers, came not with prosody and poetics, but with a plunge into the arcane world of market movements. Absurd conclusions followed, while his own pen, it has to be stressed, remained safely clipped in his pocket. Febrile, industrious man, he said, had become the being he was, not through life's ceaseless ritual, and his monuments driven by aesthetics, but in his bondage to Dow Jones and that fearful index. That, Humber went on, was the last little blip on the *Homo sapiens* temperature chart.

Rhea was nearer the truth, and having approached it felt she would get her lockup after all. Bold cherry strokes on the whiteboard squeaked the discovery—

PANIC with these—

meaning, in advanced middle age, fears for his loss of fame accompany the poet compiling his *Collected Poems*. Literary humiliation may not necessarily follow, though the prefatory explication – why conceive this and nothing new? – amounted to not much more than an obfuscating ramble editorially.

It was, thought Rhea, worth finding Madame Belokonsky's card and making that visit she'd been promised, if only to test the rumour of a parrot in her Victorian parlour, able to quote everything ever uttered by Raskolnikov, together with all relevant page numbers (in a translation by Constance Garnett, Heinemann, 1914). Grading was the hired diplomat, and no, he detected no signs of bird life. Nights, invoking the dead, Belokonsky wore large hoops in her ears and a spotted bandeau. Perhaps there was someone he'd like to get in touch with again – an aunt, a grandmother? He couldn't think. Anyway, it was much better that he simply watched and took mental notes, since, he said, he planned to get something typed up for next quarter.

Humber could confess to a good but expensive joke, though the therapist's fees weren't that amusing. Noting his occasional grin, rare on Mondays, extinct on the thirty-day settlement date, the housing chief asked for fresh samples of his colleague's signature. Humber bore his losses stoically, for anyway now seemed as good a time as any for a bout of word associations – the black couch, its band of white linen where the feet were crossed – those hairline fractures in the ceiling – the bookcase with its slot for his *Collected*. The analyst's 'bead' got what he wanted at last, Humber's 'elitism', though not in a context he understood (*Das Glasperlenspiel*). Of course (um!). He got up and glanced at another of those turgid Long Table speeches, littered with the orthographical blunders of, he guessed, a bemused audio typist. Humber asked why didn't he try something else on his masticating audiences, and suggested a neurosis – his own, in fact.

Late for his next appointment, Grading tripped on Belokonsky's raised threshold and fell into the arms of the wiry spinster hired to take the phone and answer the door. She took his coat, and hung it under a portrait – of Victoria, in ample profile – where a short imitation fur and with it a man's soiled raincoat already hung. In the parlour or outer sanctum – where there was *no* parrot – months of consumer gloss, in a world of country and ladies' magazines, spilled its open leaves in flimsy waves all over the place. Grading counted four cups on the arms of chairs or on tables, all with matching plates.

The receptionist moved a lone quadrant of sponge cake to the serving hatch and examined a thin smear of lipstick on the glaze of a cup. She thought Grading might just be in time, and opened a door gingerly. Silence. He checked pockets for his notebook. Then, at an unspoken sign, she waved him in, her other palm still on the fingerplate. The door closed behind him. Its cone of light shrank to a thin line in the jamb. Michael sat down in the dusk and saw his opposite number, a man with Stalin's moustache, not, apparently, able to raise his eyes and break his concentration. Alongside him a young-looking woman in a coruscating evening dress wore a bright peach lipstick and showed, occasionally, a darkish stain to the pearls of her teeth. To his right he could just make out a plain woman in black, and facing her, at the table head, in hoops and a polka-dot bandeau, Madame Belokonsky, who held a planchette. He looked into all dark corners, but nothing was concealed. He felt the underside of the table for wires or switches. Still nothing. He recalled, approximated, the breadth of the terrace, the depth of its façade, and considered the possibility of secret rooms. And could a seam in a carpet indicate a trapdoor? He explored with his feet.

This now was Humber's position, if I have read him aright. His respective precursors a century and a half ago couldn't much care for the condition of man, and anyway, for *that*

grand theme, the work of God could still be assumed in the changing tapestry of human society – in all its divisions. Humber had his private angst to consider, and much like his humourless ancestors didn't think he'd approach it through a theory of universal exempla.

'You'd be spectacularly wrong,' he said on the couch, 'if you thought my splendid reputation was in any way a permanent fillip.'

He'd skulked for the best part of thirty years with the dark woods and rutted marble of the municipality, never deferring to interviews, biographers, public readings, not even radio broadcasts. His therapist, a man who presumed to change all this – if amusing to watch, while galumphing about – succeeded only in depressing him that much more. Why, we ask? Why do we think that was? Well, the quack asked this too, so the patient uncrossed and re-crossed his feet, making himself more comfortable.

'It's the real and tangible fear of public humiliation,' said Humber.

That made his therapist put down his list and scan the scientific wastes of his bookshelf. What, he wondered, could have brought this about? Humber was an educated man, with two careers.

'Education, pah!' was what Humber said. All learning enabled him to do was derive rogue couplets from older and anyway much more original examples.

Poets measured out a distillation of the world. One day somebody unrefined – who unlike him couldn't escape the ravages of social change – would offer up the perfect text, more beautifully chiselled, more incisive, more witty than any of his own. 'I don't want to meet him. I'm sure I shall.'

Some days after this a red-brick pedant, who knew by heart his contemporary poets, invited him to give a lecture at the local literature faculty. Under the therapist's guidance Humber foolishly agreed to it. The advice of therapists always is: Confront. Confront these obstacles. Confront them head on.

Back again to Michael Grading, where more light was cast on his role as note-taker. A remote autumn sun suffused the thin fabric of a window blind, and paled the white of the Ouija board. He studied the polite headshakes, and suddenly understood why Rhea had assigned him – specifically him – to the Belokonsky project.

'She wanted the greyness of my mind,' Grading said, a thing lukewarm in the workbench analysis of binary protocols, and having just the loathsome objectivity appropriate to that assignment. He had to avoid sensationalism, she had said (and he didn't mind that at all). He reduced the Stalin moustache to a near bootlace, and called its proprietor Jones. He relayed Jones's message, how Jones personally argued against the Third Reich. But Jones had a flaw, being the loss of all close relatives during the Blitz, which put him on an emotional, not a philosophical plane. Highly detectable was Jones's complete lack of interest in Belokonsky's moving pen, if that seemed to want to spell out 'Mother', 'Father', 'Aunt Joan' – now all forty years his junior. Jones despaired, wanting to hear from the Führer himself. When that didn't occur, the transmission had failed him personally. He wanted his moral comfort. He wanted to be sure the tyrant Adolf stalked an unendurable limbo.

Madame Belokonsky knew how to shriek diabolically, and had the theatrical knack of doing so when things went badly – so keeping to her trance and Jones in his moody silence. The cabaret woman sitting alongside him turned out not to be his partner – for this was the woman in black – and so, when a chauffeur called later and slipped on her car coat, Grading could agree – it made of her inquiries, after a succession of dead, departed poodles, something less incongruous. 'Yaye' – all the contorted medium could manage – wasn't a name the false Mrs Jones recalled, but inspired Rhea to her only editorial footnote: Yap? Yelp? The woman in black got up and grumbled – the real Mrs Jones – but sat down again. Belokonsky wailed and started to rock laterally. All present saw the film of perspiration on her lined forehead, catching the feeble glow of the blind, sluicing down into the floury foundation of her cheeks. Someone had a message – for Michael.

'I'll jot it down,' the bailiff said.

'It didn't make much sense.'

'Nevertheless....'

'The first part was this: Toad, flapped backward.'

'First part, you say....'

'Yes. The next was this: "u" replace "at".'

'Anything else?'

'Yes. Green inland bridge.'

'I see.'

'And that was followed by Adam's bruised toe.'

'Adam's bruised toe?'

'Yes, and lastly, Chiselled in italics.'

'Did the bearer of this message give a name?'

'Yes. Bridgland Jolley. But that was no one I knew.'

This is our point of balance, with the mysterious Bridgland Jolley about to enter the life of an elderly English poet. Humber stood up and straightened his tie, while the psychiatrist, baffled, and no longer keen on *any* associations, binned and replaced that smudged bit of linen. He roamed round the consulting room, and found the barometer in need of the flick of his finger. He looked out through the sash of his window and saw on a flat roof rain in black and silver pools. He turned his short broad back on the grey leaden light of the sky, and in large silhouette had the need to say something, yet only fumbled with the button of a cuff. His limp hand shook itself free, and in one chubby undulation indicated the desk and two chairs. Humber sat. His consultant continued to pace. Then he produced a postcard from Spain – a Dali clock oozing over the shifting sands of a lost Newtonian universe. He confessed that time was short. Five radiant daughters – the eldest in holiday mood – had made him a guiltless procreator, and that was why, in his mind, Freud was safely dismissed. That left him flailing around in the chthonic chambers of Jung, looking, he said, for an homunculus, though for the time being only plunged into his vast leather chair and pulled out a checked handkerchief.

Humber noticed a tic, a twitch of his right eye. He wanted to come straight to the point, he said, and mopped his brow with a flourish. Sporadic showers of dandruff sugared his lapels. Before going on, he picked up a memento paper knife and scooped out filth and quick from a thumbnail. What they needed to do, it seemed, was approach the neurosis on two fronts: its central manifestation had to be acknowledged, of course, while its dormancy must be there to trace in Humber's past. They would do it in the uncertain realm of the collective, the realm of projected archetypes, at a point where two dreams – or more to the point two dreamers – could be made to meet. Humber thought of the mounting bills, the fruitless consultations – but agreed. If he began tonight then it wouldn't be long before he and his rival sonneteer were sparring somewhere in his dreams. The postcard – that eldest daughter coming home after eighteen months – meant switching the bi-weekly sessions from Fridays to – what? Humber scanned through workaday couplets in a pocket diary. 'Thursdays, p.m.,' he said, though Mnemosyne, humming a catchy aubade, preferred dawn, and the breaking light of that waking hour.

Grading arrived at Humber's lecture late, and others trickled in after him. Humber paused more than once, clearing his throat or shuffling through the pages of his notes. He recapped. Essential to literary art was the action of memory as fictive application or light on the chosen subject. This lent to narrative forms that other dimension, the capacity to haunt, or at worst sentimentalise. Mr Eliot's dissolving floors skirted the point, but a real proof had been demonstrated by his colleagues in science fiction, whose appallingly bad texts had imagined a future in an extensive purloining of the past. Rhea dug an elbow in Michael's ribs, and in the rush and hubbub of a last stream of latecomers told him this was nothing new. Prior to this hour Belokonsky had seen their editorial draft, and had been disappointed, and in a letter to Rhea said as much. This Rhea passed to Michael, in a torn blue envelope, whose contents he tugged at – a pink headed notelet doused in the fragrance of apple blossom. A plain, round hand declared his observations nothing but reportage, and therefore uninspired. At the same moment Humber commended the scientific principles of modernism, but deplored postmodernist attention to useless detail. As to Belokonsky, she expected something speculative – a theory of ectoplasm, of the extra-mundane or -sensory, all somehow interlinked in the phenomenon of metempsychosis, even though these were impossible inferences.

Just then a ragged intellectual got up at the front – hollow cheeks, voluminous white shirt, an unruly shock of hair – and offered his reflections in staccato-driven anapaests. Humber – could this be the rival? – tried to dismiss his few interesting comments with neutral concord, the raising of a palm, but was rebuffed by a polite little bow from the waist. Coincidentally Michael had got to Belokonsky's postscript, which pointed out they must understand no financial assistance was appropriate at this early stage, so signalling an indefinite postponement of Rhea's initiation into film surrealism. Shockingly, that intellectual still hadn't sat down, and pressing on with his observations dispatched Humber further into the refuge of his notes – too late. It seemed he was now unable to recover the lost thread of his lecture. He folded his papers and tucked them away in a jacket pocket. Rhea anticipated retreat, a withdrawal from the lectern in a stew of academic humiliation. However. One could argue, harangue, eternally. What the renowned Harold Humber really meant was: the scandalous lot of poets is the menial chore for bread, and a light in the garret. This one had found his way in the toy reality of local government, and knew its largesse: here, he said, were the keys to some lockup garages (he held them up) – culmination of a history no doubt fully chronicled on the arts faculty notice boards.

That night. Humber recalled his hopeless dreams of puberty. This was for a first excursion. He put on a leather belt with a large square buckle, a cape, a wig. Jaunty walks in an avenue of poplars brought him – as poet – to hoarfrost on a sward, as that just turned to a flattish swirl of steam in the warmth of a spring mid-morning. A white knight on a nag dismounted under a brick arch and retreated wanly into its maw, where there was nothing, no distant point of light. He came across to look. There was an equine snort, which reverberated. The tail swished, a hoof clopped on the cobbles.

So no clues at all, said the medic, back with his paperknife, but by now so thoroughly absorbed that absently he twanged its blade, then fiddled with a speckled brown pebble, origin the western Pyrenees. Well actually yes – there was one clue. A Romanesque BJ embellished on the saddle. That was something, yes, but Humber would have to try again. The next improbable set had an Elizabethan backdrop – a sylvan meadow, woolly sheep. He thought he had seen an homunculus in a knot of grey boulders, beachcombing, and was surprised, stroking his own chin, to find a cropped beard. It grew damp in the mizzle.

Humber walked to landward over the shingle, and saw on a green slope a forester in muslinet, who pointed at yellow smoke in a grove of oak trees, and said there were papers there, quite safe. Briefly someone in a long white coat stared out from a mausoleum, where the smoke cleared momentarily. Whoever it was – wielding a chisel and mallet – strode out of sight into a thicket. The forester's arm dropped. Humber hurried over and found an epitaph carved in marble – a stupendous sestet. The paper knife grew agitated. Its paunchy owner thought they were onto something, and could Humber possibly transcribe the six lines? Humber didn't know. All he could say was this: they were good – very good – even brilliant! He tried again, and again, and again, and after weeks of failure dreamed another dream, where in the blue shadows and sorceries a toad hopped across a dirt road. That other, that rival, that poet more accomplished than he, now in a moon-bright oilskin turned up his collar in a vortex of wind and rain. Chinks of red, orange, turquoise light escaped from the cracks and fissures in a shuttered tenement, its windows blanked against the thunders of heaven, a dark house swaying in an elemental thrash. His flat round hat stayed on in the gusts, but he pointed at a flapping door.

Rhea judged it time for a plain white dress, girlish ponytails, peach ribbons, and for Michael the beige suit again. Having so complied, we meet him in Belokonsky's front porch, as the two waited to be let in. A pipe-smoking cyclist passed them by, weary from an afternoon's work on his allotment, but with a smile. Rhea smiled back, then told her friend how remiss he'd been, and asked why hadn't he pointed this out.

Pointed what out?

'This!' she said, and put her hand to the shiny brass doorknocker, whose motif was a shepherd's crosier laid crosswise on a bell.

Rhea had wanted science, he thought. Yes, but even an oaf could have identified missionary zeal.

Inside, he sat upright on a hard ottoman, ignored, somehow weighing his teacup with a heavy silver spoon, and on the palm of the other hand a slice of buttered banana bread. Belokonsky fluttered round his lady friend, straight-backed and angelic in a utility dining chair. She stirred her tea and explained (as here Michael learned why science would seldom succeed). The draft, she said, was the naked seed of an extended editorial, and this had always been envisaged. What they lacked and were here for, you'd describe so: the practitioner's insight, opinion, a personal voice – Madame Belokonsky's – in tone the authority of lifelong experience. The reporter began with observable facts, but if he could just tear himself away from a delightful afternoon tea, he'd got his notebook again and was set to resume.

What that subterfuge resulted in was encouragement for Belokonsky's adherents, who read in the final, carefully worded compromise, a vindication of her mysticism, where mysterious forces used every available vessel on earth to work its ends. Cynics, who might have expected scepticism, were much put out by Rhea's article – whose one happy outcome was the donation she'd sought. When the festive day came round, Humber brought golden shears, keys on a ring, and snipped the winner's tape draped on the lockup doors. First footage picked out a hopping software engineer in a panic and a froth of champagne.

Humber persisted, night after night, trying to dream his rival. Then without warning a toad sprang up into the thin jaundiced light of a passing cyclist, who'd got his head down and a hoe on his back, and somehow stayed upright in a river of brown mud. At once Humber came to the tenement's outer door, which the wind had caught and was flapping violently. The rain was full in his face. Inside, the tail of a luminous oilskin floated up and lost itself in the pitch of a stairwell. Humber started up. The wind howled in the brickwork. The door slammed shut, was flung open, creaked on its hinges. On the first floor his eyes adjusted, where a whirl of aerosol graffiti spelt out names on walls, initials, a note on current politics. On the second floor, nothing. On the third and fourth, ownerless suitcases – somewhere a pair of city shoes. At the top, more graffiti – yes – no! – a sonnet, signed on a corridor wall! Must memorise, remember, wake up! Then torrential foam flooded in at an open window. Out on a sea of moonlit sludge its author scurried into an olive grove, his black hat spiralling into the night. Humber took out his synchronous notepad and pencil, fighting for one last sleep, and in the darkness began to scribble down that little bit of genius. His writing hand clashed with his mug of bedside water, which spilt on his jotter. He clicked on the light. The fringe of his lampshade danced in shadowy loops on a few rough calculations, a financier's top sheet. His night eyes, screwed up tight in fleshy sacks, couldn't keep out the glare, so a hand had to do as his shade. He thought, remembered, began to write again, smudged out an error here, another there. Days later the analyst scratched his head, then wanted to delve into Humber's youth – for here was Mr Jolley's nonsensical sonnet, delivered untitled—

> Tenants, seen fleeing the aerosol word,
> Shoes out, bags for the boy, the last cab gone,
> Had no home thoughts for frost on Bridgland's sword.
>
> Hambert unbalanced his books, searched, had done
> With Bronx or cockney patter. He behaves,
> Fully attuned to his therapist's drone.
>
> (You replace, at symbols construed as haves
> And political have-nots, two chiselled
> Initials, spelling sludge in moonlit waves.)
>
> Then my toad, bruised by Adam's hoe, misled
> Everyone, seen flapping but not backward,
> And has got himself shamelessly libelled.
>
> Translate – in the lamp-lit, aerosol word –
> See the reflections, green in Bridgland's sword.
>
> —*Bridgland Jolley*

Standey said: 'Curious!' The after-dinner medic frowned and put a copy of Bridgland's poem in his file, then raised an arm. Now a child's yoyo fell from his open fist, now an antique pocket watch, turning in the golden light of his table lamp, a faded pearl face under polished glass, its disappearing VII, a dark keyhole superimposed on its III. Pendulous, it started to sway, to twinkle, to make Humber's eyelids heavy. His analyst dug up old ground, and having issued his fee advanced his Zelich theory (Minor Zelich Syndrome, or MZS) - though this was not an improvement on Humber's Mayfair specialist, or what he had outlined. In his paper, his subject was very much the apprentice writer, plunged in the chaos of a debut novel, who for technical reasons was in need of a wartime spiv in an ante-room - therefore author invents one and acts out the part in a railway office. Others followed: a Paris *danseur* in a bistro, disputing a bill; a loud Bronx ballplayer hailing a cab; a navvy leering; a deaf geographer. So it went on. The broad sweep of the psychiatrist's brush swept out its new definition of literary art, naming it a refuge, a safe house for any who may suffer Humber's crisis of identity. Wasn't it obvious? Anxieties over an adept young rival were no more than a manifestation of that uncertainty, yet Humber's own subconscious assembles the sonnet and sonneteer – a *buffo* sonneteer – to ease these fears. So. That was it. Cured. As we'd all see, when the analyst reviewed the case and took it to his next Long Table. Humber was invited, an anonymous guest for table one. That was the plan, but what was it that changed his mind?

'Let me be plain,' Humber said. 'I picked up Rhea's campus rag at a paper stand. In it, as double-page spread, was a seraphic Madame Belokonsky, photographed in biting wintry monochrome.'

Editorial flummery played up to her claims, but were in part borne out by an independent witness, by Michael Grading, that innocent target of Jolley's ethereal mail. *Humber's* Jolley, for how had the person of his dream leaked out into Belokonsky's parlour games? Humber immediately confronted Grading. Grading protested: he was – and still is – innocent, and now regretted taking so much time off work, all to help his girlfriend Rhea in her last college semester. The whole crazy episode now made it impossible to return to a normal working life.

'I'm going to get away,' he said. 'Rhea has this other scheme, in Liechtenstein—' though Humber followed, with Rhea unable to object, or even flattered – and via the Canaries came to an accommodation (but more on that elsewhere).

I have a need for a long cool something myself, and mountain rides, and would like to be able to report that a verdict was reached (it is certainly the case nowadays that our committees are much quicker when it comes to dispensing justice). Regrettably that wasn't so. The committee kicked its heels, bantered a lot, and made jokes.

Today I look out from Muchello's deserted quarters. I inhale sharp air at the casement, and feel myself minutely bored at the close examination of his gargoyles.

'What of this Humber?' you ask. Gard, who for all I know was invited onto the committee himself, suggested that at the end Humber put a hand in his pockets, and pulled out a silver cigarette case. He snapped it open on its hinge. A wobbly reflection of light, a sloppy oblong, set itself loose on a cheek, a brow, a temple. 'He never ever,' says Gard, 'through the course of the trial, lit up – and now we know why.' It was the cunning little compact of a man with Zelich's disease, when the mirror confirmed whatever unlikely transformation the poet had chosen next. An enlarged frontal lobe, the broad lips getting thin and beginning to snarl, the flare of those nostrils reduced to a twitching proboscis. 'What – or rather whom – could you expect of this man Humber at the close of Grading's trial? Priest? Circus master? Virtuoso? Politician, perhaps? Or what about Bridgland Jolley?' Thus the speculations of a newspaperman.

Well, to my mind, it's none of these. You should ask Professor Gee. That man had done with the conventions of Schmutzburg's old and crumbling academe. He turned to a first glimpse of the reddish gold sunset on Western educated life, with its hums, its Humbers and its hypo- or psychotherapies. In late autumn you can see an interesting light on any unremarkable factory wall. With life in the everyday, rarities like Humber have had to disguise themselves in the work clothes of ordinariness. I am to imagine – though without conviction – that a day-long conference on the rigours of local taxation is as profoundly interesting as a hatbox, as a sonnet, as an internal combustion engine, as a cry of *Evenin' piper*. These are the spotless silks our poet conjures up in the norms of his paper worlds. Yet Humber was here, in Schmutzburg, with his hands folded. Overall he melted without transformation, was someone knocking back a schnapps at Auerbach's, just another nobody among all those garrulous yokels on the tourist bus, an intruder in our house, yet overlooked in the dusky shadows, the dark winding corridors, the library. 'The just god was in his heaven,' as old Muchello had cajoled, yet that was according to one revelation only. Humber was here, all that time a dun shape on the stairs, all that time when Nicola Chamoogan engineered her new career. 'We have heard,' my counterpart Gard wraps it up, 'how deities come to look so much like prescient landowners, concerned at the moral decline of their workforce, while our Humbers remain, whatever you want them to be.'

'Well,' said the president, whom I overhear, addressing, presumably, Harold Humber. 'I see the bus is waiting, so you won't have time for a game,' meaning Frame Solutions. 'If by chance you do run into Michael Grading, here is Knecht's monograph. Tell him to read the preface, where the rules are explained.'

We play with a board, and pieces – it's rather like chess – though each denomination remains undeclared until either its first move or capture. You can imagine the complexities, and how, as the game goes on, a natural order slowly asserts itself. (The bus, allow me to reiterate, is waiting.) There is one other thing I am sure you would like to see, and I have wondered about it myself. What would happen if the bailiff. What would happen if President Standey. What, if he were still here, would happen if old Dr Muchello. What would happen if each of them held up their hands? Please. Yes. That's right. Look. Are all little fingers intact? There is just one omission, as you tell me the bailiff's too young, so that leaves – um.... Ah, a shame, the driver's getting impatient. I can see: he's drumming his palms on the wheel, checking his mirror, blowing his cheeks, while Humber, look, without commitment, is shuffling towards the outer door, and hesitates.

Scenes, acts, symbols – a change in the weather – two sets of prints in a new blanket of snow – those fixed heathen faces posted on a lookout, whose dumb lips shan't ever murmur: time to put our props away. I am all played out. And it's clear, and demonstrated, that I can't stay here now that a team of worldly geographers has appeared and is measuring our elevations. (Regardless, those fine stone projections *are* still possible.) O what is that mood of rebellion?

The driver is stabbing his throttle, checking his watch....

Humber, I see, has at last lit a cigarette, and exhales a perfect blue ring. What, you good people of England, do you think I should do? Call, perhaps, for Bridgland Jolley?

Effectively that is the end....

Down From the Mountain

A mixed pattern of light and semi-shade, for small ensemble of Western or Westernised players. (See preceding Acts One and Two – my 'Foreword' and 'Press Cuttings'.)

A Note From Your Impresario

I had of course, when I first embarked on these redrafts, only a single text at my disposal, printed over an eight-day working week in the London edition of the *European Tribune*. That I have reproduced above, in more sober, less sensational terms – the *Tribune* not a publication noted for its even-handedness. That was something I discovered anew when Gard, departing outrageously from Schmutzburg's official press releases, not only prompted my changes and emendations, but did so under suspicion.

What is clear, despite Gard's distortions – not to say plain untruths – is that Michael Grading found himself high on our mountaintop at a time when (if I may put it so) our old order had reached its point of conflict with the new. It's an accident of history that this has been represented as Michael Grading's hearing. As you have seen, that reached its climax as a straight fight between Dr Muchello and the rest – the rest being led, or misled, by Professor Standey. Only the bailiff wavered between the two camps. It was hard to choose, for after all he had the start of his career to consider. Young, and inexperienced, he'd much to analyse before settling on the best way forward – that's to say personally, for himself.

Muchello was far from that curmudgeonly aspect of advanced age and intellect, and unusually sought a middle way. He was inclined to give Grading an opportunity to prove himself, to make himself a worthy citizen of Schmutzburg, if it was shown that was why he had made his difficult journey. Standey, less tolerant, if not exactly xenophobic, was ill-disposed to the common run of people rooted in foreign soil. That makes it the more ironic that Standey was the first to applaud Professor Gee when, with Schmutzburg's intellectual trade finally seen as unsustainable, it was he who led our tenders for other kinds of work. I don't need to point out that Nicola Chamoogan proved a valuable asset in that process.

It fell into much sharper focus, despite the Gard fabrications, on day two of the hearing, when Muchello was still a credible participant (a precaution I shall have to explain). It came as no coincidence that the debate turned on the problems of a governing class at pains to create the semblance of a free and open society. If Schmutzburg is said to be instrumental in defining such a society, and how it works, already Standey showed he didn't share Muchello's analysis of that subject. He'd begun to see his older colleague as a liability. Gard didn't give much for Muchello's view either. As an average UK newspaperman, Gard represented a wearisome middle-class, poisoned by professional snobbery. He was unable to contain his glee that the Schmutzburg I had known was in its death throes. That is what led me to believe it must have been Standey – who rose above the governing quorum and became our first president – who secretly supplied Jeremy Gard with his column inches.

Allow me to remind you of how I re-crafted Gard's account of the committee's third day, opening with the following paragraph—

Day three did not commence until, armed with a notebook, I sat in on the morning session at the press office, where a withered, nasally, not particularly well turned-out official, addressed the world press (consisting of Jeremy Gard, smirking, and the tired-looking scribe from an electronic news mag). As far as I recorded, there was no official mention of the Grading case, and no intimation that a committee had been formed (or that an inquisition was under way). According to Gard the bailiff's first important contribution to the third day was a statement, to the effect that, with the recovery of Grading's broadsheet, and labelled 'Exhibit 2', the tabloid had never been found. It caused a rumble, then the minute examination of every news story carried by that exhibit, which Gard relays in full, and which I, mercifully, edit.

There are certain observations I am now able to make concerning this. The most important is this: I still couldn't verify to what extent (if any) Gard's account of proceedings coincided with the transcript. It took some subterfuge on my part to obtain that document, though when I did, and compared the two, I was astonished by what I found. For days one, two and three, what appears in the *Tribune* is at odds with what the court reporter officially recorded. Thereafter – i.e. for days four to eight inclusive – the two accounts exactly coincide. (I shall come in due course to what level of conspiracy ensured that this was so.)

I was also very much bewildered when Gard began to show Muchello as a man who saw his position in a fictitious mystical twilight. It came about with that broad sweep over a range of subjects suggested by Exhibit 2, the broadsheet Grading had brought from England. Muchello was still present on the committee (perhaps), but his utterances are reported selectively, and begin to lose context. It leads me to ask that if Muchello *was* removed from the committee – and I think he was, at the close of day three – who is it speaking for him throughout the remainder of the hearing? Gard and the transcript certainly show him as a full participant to the end of day eight.

I cannot now remember how many times I had redrafted that *Tribune* report before it became clear what had been going on. Looking back over my present manuscript, I see I must have been working on the events of day four when I first had an inkling. Then, I said this—

What then followed as Muchello's reply, if it reads like a *non sequitur*, I think *is* a *non sequitur* – a point I have meditated on, and in my own mind resolved, and in due course will demonstrate. In the charged melodrama of Western journalese I think you would say I am about to propose a conspiracy theory....

That 'due course' has come, and conspiracy is no longer a theory. Nor is it simply a question of Professor Standey telling Jeremy Gard what to write in his newspaper, or how to present our dealings with the world's Michael Gradings, at least to an ignorant Europublic. It's clear they worked in concert, producing not only that monstrosity of journalese, but a revised 'official' committee report. I am doubly convinced of this. It explains why at first it was so difficult, then later relatively easy, to get my hands on that 'transcript'. The puzzle it gives me is this. How did they script or invent the part Dr Muchello supposedly played, during those last five days?

Not long after Muchello's death I entered his cell and tidied up the last of his possessions. Most were papers, one of which was a set of notes recalling a conversation with a previous visitor to Schmutzburg. Part of that exchange was taken up as parable. It told of a lutenist under a castle wall, and magically his later transfiguration as a constellation. According to Muchello, it showed an unfair weighting in human affairs, even when raised to the heights (or in our case made law). Illegal though Michael Grading's entry was, Muchello could, in the end, come to approve it. That, I think, was why it was important to have him removed from the committee.

I decided that the proper place for that one stray leaf was the Schmutzburg archive, together with Muchello's other papers and reports. I found monographs he'd written going back decades, whose subject matter was exceptional in its range: the compass and navigation; Knossos wall paintings; the Minotaur (or mythical Taurean); our own *Inner Circle* and *Bannerol*; the death of poetry; migratory birds (what happens when they become disorientated); student activity as now more politics than philosophy; some assorted scions of the young Prince Wix (they who were dotted round a hillside camp); travel by sea and the barometer; the skimmington; astrology (Mario); its successor astronomy (the raging storms of Neptune, Triton's smooth terrain). There were samples other than these. However, I am sure you begin to appreciate that having unearthed the transcript, and having at length decided this had been tampered with, it wasn't difficult to fathom where Gard and Standey had got their source material. I don't much care to analyse Gard's motive for doing this, having generally a low regard for men like him. But what of Standey – what did *he* hope to gain?

Positioned to decode it, I can say that what he hoped was to send a diplomatic signal to the UK, whose taxpayers had fast become a reluctant contributor to Schmutzburg's copper-coloured treasury. The British have always been sceptical of grand social designs, especially the one set out as Schmutzburg's special task. Now that Standey saw that we had faltered, it was a clear indication of intent on his behalf to negotiate UK aid on a modified basis, which I don't doubt will entail internal reforms. So far as Standey is concerned, the ordinary citizens of Europe, of whom Michael Grading is the representative, may still not participate in the drawing up of any new plan, though the one concession will be to the likes of Nicola Chamoogan. She and all who follow shall have *some* say in matters.

In passing there were two other monographs I came across in Muchello's effects. In one was material reminiscent of Muchello's views on retirement, including the following lines—

> Relics. They're heaped, broken in the basement,
> Suburban lumber, beachcomber flotsam
> Left by the tides (the child grown to a man,
> And home again on a halcyon sea).
>
> Remembrance, here by an unlit casement:
> A kneehole under sheets, drawers in a jam
> On faded snaps, a girl's unsteady hand,
> Her coloured notelets headed with a P.
>
> Recalled is the clamour of voices
> Up in an empty attic. Dormer curtains
> Shed the years of dust in a salty breeze.
> The silhouettes my lighted match has thrown
> On a wall – these are student delusions
> A creak on the stairs has me re-conceive.

The other concerned an experiment in Jungian synchronicity, where two technicians attempted to communicate during their sleep, through a commonly dreamed dream.

Act Three

The snows, just a flurry yesterday – that wild wind through my keyhole – the world and its impediments to flesh – have accustomed my thinking geographically. There is a wall of shelves in my cell. The apprentice, bailiff, in his seedtime a scholarly lawyer, abandoned the loose manuscripts of however many years ago, in precisely this place (I am pointing). Why? Ah, well – by the way I'm so tired – it's because no one now reads the dry dissertations concerning an old, supplanted legal system. (So tired.) It has been, as the slogan says, a good rejuvenating *coup*. For me there's an unidentified hand taking liberties with my favourite paperweight (an ivory Buddha, which I don't think I mentioned) – though I shall finally sound an alarm. A safe house for my new account of Michael Grading, that un-aging man of these confessions, is a shelf on my wall, the right place for any passing testament, a dull coin in a tarnished mint. The end, and I admit to mild desperation, is just about in sight. It's timely, with this new bulletin from Public Relations, signed by the director – N. Chamoogan, DLitt. She's stooped again to the theme of garbage, and wants to know why my bins only ever yield up an occasional orange peel, or a few tufts of greying hair. Then there's this supply of ink that the stationer's clerk has sworn to (I knew he'd be a turncoat). And my lamp, a fatigued yellow, seen more than once glowing after midnight. She wants me to present myself.

Shall I wear my hair parted, or swept off my temples?

Act Four

'Be cynical,' the beast, my conscience, bids – though I can hardly take it seriously, as it squats at my elbow. Its blunt teeth mean I'll feed it from my hand, and in the warmth of my human fire shall stroke its glossy fur. This is a dark place. One moted beam, a thinnish gold, strikes in high and angular, an afternoon light in through a narrow arch. There are no new prohibitions, yet, to do with our archives, so what I now gather is Ms Chamoogan's file. Her depositions never got into Michael's hands. (Shall I go back, and over a boiled egg, buttered toast, read, read, read?) There is a change of air, as the door swings, but I didn't see who just came in. It's a dangerous tide. Curiously here's a note, from a Dr Blube to dearest Nic. It's addressed to her daddy's house in Bucks. It seems his lament is his semi-retirement to Princes Risborough, alluded to here, in para two, through a veil of bitter jibes. He is maladroit on what he calls 'too much TV punditry'. I detect hatred for a woman called Bickerwell. In his memoir, 'now under way', a man named Maguire 'shall taste my acerbity' (absurdity). Ah, click! and now I see – can guess who he was, or I hope still is. Blube, barnacled, parodied, that radio moralist, who tossed to an autumn wind the four corners of his Labour Party membership card – as I see he recommends all leftist 'thinkers' should now do.

Fatuous.

Fifth and Final Act

My old Aunt Maude's pier glass is my symbol of return, which I have stood before assiduously over recent weeks. I'm getting good with the scissors. It's a skill, snipping away round the temples. It aspires to an art at my double crown. I intone black magic, taking those blades to my occiput. Still, I have discharged my first grey hairs, and so on to my escape. On that day I shall assume, sweet sons of England, what is known as a flat top. A lager-sprinkled tourist clued me in, over his secular hymnal (at the demise of the football stand, and all-seating). And get this for a disguise. Item, one, a sports jacket, single vent, beige-stroke-royal-blue checks, broad lapels. Two: shades, lenses mirrored. Three: avocado jodhpurs, no crease, funny little pockets that nothing fits in. Four, five – a cream sweater, turtleneck – shoes, caramel, pointed, laced. I find we don't have buses anymore, which makes me a late booking on the coach, which I'm assured has flight facilities. That, saith the blurbist, means air-conditioning, waitress service, an observation point. There are video entertainments, for those inclined. Toilets, democratically, for all. And what about baggage? Well, my valise shan't be necessary – I have just a toothbrush and underwear, rolled up in a manuscript. I am calm, anticipating my descent. It will disperse, the ethereal air, as my mind wanders, and as I go down. (Shall my nose bleed?) A throaty Dane, a dulcet cherub crooning in her microphone – she'll sing me the sights, right, left, hyaline, as we round the corniche into Europe. And the sun, will it shine? And oh to be in England!

Chorus, Princes Risborough, where I want that pantaloon for his publisher. Exeunt all.

Curtain

Bim Shay

'In your labyrinth there are three lines too many,' he said at last.
—Borges, 'Death and the Compass'

Foreword

There must be a rational explanation for the transformations that took place, even over the writing of this account. It would not have appeared at all but for the stuttering progress plaguing my new job, in a quango I didn't know existed until I was seconded to it. I never saw the tiers above, with my reporting upwards to a sole, forlorn line manager, whose office was quiet, capacious, in a perpetual layer of afternoon shadow. When he was stuck for things for me to do he dreamed up his 'special assignment' (a joke surely). The first case I was given came with a name I knew – Solomon, an industrialist. I'd heard of him from news and press, though now he was dead – murdered – the victim of a stabbing, one that had taken place on the London Underground. One of the last persons to have seen him alive had shared his carriage. She, Frankie Reuter, was an IT specialist, born, brought up and educated in a South Africa still riven by apartheid. She was expecting her father to retire from public office and join her in England – the old country, their roots going back.

Frankie had the full treatment of my notebook, a thing I carried with me everywhere, where I jotted down the minutest details, using encryptions only I could decipher. I was still learning my new job, and was sworn to secrecy. At least that is how I explain this compulsion I had, recording *everything*. That said, what I got from Frankie didn't cast much light, though in a mingling of hope and flirtatious interest I returned to her again, and again, and again. No joy, and when the case went cold I turned my attention to Iris Cadogan, a cultured, wealthy invalid, who'd witnessed a street crime no one guessed would have political implications. When investigations got serious, obstacles were put in my way, and – as with Solomon – I made no progress – or none worth the name. Yet it didn't cease, the pressure I was under with an ill-named 'special assignment', and my boss, in his shady retreat, knowing my difficulties but always demanding progress. When I produced very little through Cadogan, attention was turned to a third case, that of a petty thief called Staverton, who for reasons I found ludicrous was suspected of base animal rites and worship of the devil. That's how frenetic they were, those days stripped naked in the excesses of market greed, with a return to the world's primeval instincts. As a kind of self-defence, I spent more time at home, in company of a second notebook, into which I decrypted much I had committed to the first, in a vain attempt to unravel these puzzling, and on the face of it disparate events. Again, not much progress. Worse, I could even believe I was suffering nervous delusions, and saw my 'special assignment' as never truly under my control. There was about it the flitting, the spectral, the work of an unseen agency. I tried to pull myself together. I tormented myself endlessly over Solomon and

Staverton, fearing I would never close the page on either file. On the verge of breakdown, I was given leave, and with nothing better to do I visited my sister, a long way west at her holiday retreat. There I learned some bitter family truths.

By then I was sure the Solomon and Staverton cases would finally elude me, but I still had Cadogan. In addition to what she'd reported there had been a second murder. I had been present at its reconstruction, and I took some comfort there. Then unexpectedly I was taken off *all* cases, indefinitely, and in the enforced idleness that brought about I took on private work for the Daniel Byrne Society, an organisation for which the industrialist and poet Bim Shay was a figurehead. Salvation.

I could not have known that in the pause the Byrne work gave me, there was an opportunity to think out and understand what links connected the three projects I had failed on – Solomon, Staverton, Cadogan. Despite bureaucratic obstructions I arrived at a solution for each. Tell me what you think, even when *I* cannot believe a word I say, with a third force at work, prying, lurking, undermining, changing my name, address, my occupation....

—*Adrian Fixt, Ladbroke Grove, September 1989*

Case Studies

You tell me that Mendelssohn (philosopher) gave up playing chess. This, too grave and serious as a game, while lacking the importance of an occupation....[1]

1

My work was for the Department,[2] whose management structure I only partly apprehended in the dusk of its bureaucracy. I was last in a line of command, a foundation of sentries and runners and upward reporting, the cement with which the Great Wall of Commerce was kept intact. There are pre-set limits to the wintry erosion the fierce winds of politics and the English system of class are able to bring about, things I was bound to the task of enforcing.

I'm grieving because I've lost my dog, a boxer called Boscy.

2

I picked out from one of Henry Reuter's tea chests a schoolroom compass, still with its pencil, an object I was fixated on.

3

Then I learned that my line manager, at home with the angular furniture and semi-twilight of his office, was in fact an academic, not a bureaucrat. I am still not clear as to his specialist subject. 'Life science' is the nearest I can get, if you want a description. I review these events – I relive them – through the contradictions of my notebook.

4

My position hardly changed. I patrolled the grey of the metropolis, which today is the changing light of summer. Drummed into me had been the importance of upholding the system we lived by, i.e. capitalism. I was bound to routine police work, though I was given only scraps, or just those minor cases where the organs of commerce had suffered attack, or were harmed in any way. Dark – or Professor Dark, as I now must refer to him – had anticipated slack times ahead, and asked me to write a training document, for the benefit of recruits new to the Department.

'Make use,' he said, 'of whatever case you happen to be on, as material.'

The case I was on was that of a man called Solomon, who was found by a station official late at night, alone in a Circle Line carriage, expertly knifed to death – and strangely expressionless.

5

I didn't know the internal structure of the Metropolitan Police, and was only ever given its personnel to work with – a situation fraught with mutual suspicion. My point of contact was Detective Sergeant Matthew Bello, a man I knew from the Drayton Arms and its pool table. We met more recently in a hotel lounge in Harrow on the Hill, under its Byronic shadow. It was the eve of Matthew's thirtieth birthday. He told me he was feeling old.

My office was a cupboard, in a dark basement in a labyrinth of cubicles, in a maze of fluorescent corridors. I talked to Bello on the phone. He told me to meet him at an address in Castlebar Road, a certain Henry Reuter's retirement pad, where Frankie, Henry's daughter, had agreed to be interviewed, she being among the last to see Solomon alive.

Rain had pearled the grass when I got there. There was no sign of Bello, so I waited. I picked up the compasses and pencil, then put them down on the ledge under an oriel window. Soon it emerged Bello had already arrived, but finding the house open, with only a removals man and a lumber of tea chests, had gone in search of Frankie.

I was never sure what respect if any Bello had for *my* work and occupation, though he knew I had got where I was by accident.[3] I viewed as pantomime certain aspects of *his* discipline, Bello prepared to stand up and play his cameo, in a shallow world of melodrama, with its climaxes and gasps around the courtroom. I cannot contain that scepticism, something I was at pains to conceal in my notebook, an object never far from prying eyes.

Compiled in my cramped, cryptic, neurotic hand, was a world of detail I could never know the significance of, at the time. I *can* say this, of the Solomon case: it was a clear blue morning, in June. The sun, its rays a warm heaven through Reuter's new house, with its many leaded panes, spilt itself in maroon and magenta rhombs – a light refracting on me.

I moved away when Matthew, who'd found her at last, entered the room. Light, through that same glassy rainbow, enfolded itself on a withered brown globe, one of many odd objects from a litter of packing cases, which without illumination remained a world of mud. The detective sergeant palmed the globe idly, and stopped its movement on the instant it squeaked on its axis. Frankie followed him in, cue to introduce me as his colleague. I told her not to mind if I took notes, while Bello asked the questions. With no sign of the devil-eyed Blamm – or Chief Inspector Blamm, the funnel of all information – Bello later explained how his boss had stayed behind at the office, fighting back his allergy with worthless placebos. How often during the summer months had Matthew watched him plunge his nose into a bunch of wet tissues.

Frankie had travelled across London under instruction to sort her father's possessions, days ahead of him. She removed a portrait from an old cardboard box – of, I assumed, the house's new owner, a man looking out contentedly from the shade of his hat. The brim was broad. Elsewhere I noted schoolbooks, lettered in the turquoise ink of Frankie's young hand. Once or twice we were interrupted by the removals man, who was plump and perspiring. Outside on the rose bed, beneath the oriel window, the deep shade of his van cast itself from where he'd parked across the porch. She adjusted herself, walking to the window, in her lightness of tread caressing the open boards with her espadrilles. By now I had picked up and weighed with satisfaction those compasses.

6

Outside, kerbside, sitting in Matthew's car, I glanced over papers and photographs he agreed to show me from the file – the Solomon file. I had made a point of memorising Frankie's home address and place of work, and at the first opportunity put all of it in my notebook. I'm not so clear as to the conversation I had with the removals man, before he had shown me into the house, a note on which I expect to find with the marginalia, and the summarising streaks, belonging with those other entries. In itself it amounted to nothing. He'd a lasting impression of a high wind overnight, which a few miles away where I rented had gusted through my open windows. To him it was malign intervention, as he looked at a fallen gutter, and used the word 'apocalyptic'. His name was Cramp.

It's puzzling.

7

Later that evening. I returned to Castlebar Road, to find Frankie, and Cramp, and the removals van, still there. In the room full of tea chests I asked exactly those questions the detective sergeant had put to her earlier. There was a breeze (intoxicating). The thorn of a rose scratched at a windowpane, in a corona of yellow petals. Frankie's thin reflection resolved itself as a distant summer bloom in the late sunshine. I turned, having once more picked out those compasses, which I didn't reveal until our conversation reached its close. She put a hand to the blonde quiffs of her crown, and the spiky crop at the back of her head. Old Henry, she said, was now expected one day late.

'Him?' I said, with a nod to the photo. She lifted it up and rubbed at a smear in the glass. Him. Old Henry's smile looked brighter, benign. She put him on the ledge, a face tanned and lined in a gilded frame.

'You're probably the last person to see Solomon alive,' I said. 'Apart, of course, from the murderer. What was the time, approximately?'

Her hand was restless. Her short strong fingers combed through her hair. A late train, she said, and couldn't be more specific.

But where did she get on?

'Victoria.'

'What time was that?'

A shadow darkened her lips, her chin, the small chasm of her mouth when she spoke.

'After ten.'

I looked up and saw Cramp, or rather his arms and his torso, in the red checks of his shirt. He stopped – in a wave of clear glass – a hand fumbling, turning a loose cuff, rolling up a sleeve. There was something she wanted to say to him, though when about to his drill boots crunched on the gravel. She let him go. I watched her come down on her heels and took out those compasses, setting their legs apart. The joint was stiff.

'Good size, good weight,' I said. 'Handy.'

I re-opened my little book and began, adrift and hopelessly distracted by a legion of minor peripheral things – a distant siren, the concise rustle of leaves in the breeze, the hanging limbs of a yew. An aqueous smear, crimson through those oriel filters, slid off my margin and over my hand, and re-illumined my page. I wrestled with her account. She'd worked late, and with her briefcase and an overnight bag got on her train, at Victoria. She came here via her only interchange for Ealing, and to Castlebar Road. One other person occupied her carriage, a spindly, youngish, middle-aged man. His bright hazel eyes flickered open, where he'd slumbered over a newspaper column – its pink financial pages. There was no sign at all that he feared an assassin – a man hatted, Matthew Bello thinks. For one thing the victim rolled up his paper and chuckled. Later, when I looked through the carriage – now at Paddington and out of service – I chuckled too – at the overhead ads – at the bright beautiful lives of dawn coffee drinkers – at the mantras of an insurance firm, gold-plate policy trussed up dismally in Goethean doggerel.[4]

Frankie, leaving the train, saw nothing unusual. Solomon – for such at least has been the identification – when he rattled into Paddington had by then lost that sparkle in his eyes, now fixed blindly on the arm of his seat. A cold broad blade nestled warmly in his breast. A station official, emptying the train, stumbled on the corpse.

'I would like you,' I said, 'to cast your mind back to the photograph the detective sergeant showed you earlier.'

It was a blurred still, or extract from surveillance footage, which Bello had floated down into Henry's gilt-edged gaze. It wasn't clear – in fact was a wave of black specks in a tide of intermittent greys. I explained. This was a rear view, caught on a station camera. It probably represented Solomon's killer. The elliptical blob – though to my mind this seemed unlikely – experts thought to be a fedora. What looked like a doctor's coat was an open gaberdine. A belt was visible, trailing. Later frames pictured the dislocating flats, squares and ovals of someone in a hurry, hurdling the ticket barrier and sprinting for the street above, all the time outgrowing that coat. An arm, badly unfocused, jerked, and the hat – it at one point changed to a trilby – skimmed, then banked, then slid down the station foyer's ancient-looking wall tiles, where it missed a wire bin. The discarded coat – which Chief Inspector Blamm described as new and costly – had been picked up by PC Rudge on the stairway. The hat had not been found. A man hailing a cab was bundled aside, as someone nabbed his hire from under his nose. An artist's impression reconstructs the back of that departing head, which of course is practically useless.

Henry's little smile looked smug. The retired barrister, who had spent his working life in Pretoria, had seen much worse – limbs broken or blacked, skulls crunched under successive blows of the sjambok. His little girl was adamant. No she had not seen that man, coated, fedoraed, or otherwise.

The breeze in the yew lightened, darkened, finally streaked the downy peach of her cheekbones. When emphatically she turned, I thought she'd remembered the thing she'd needed to say to Cramp, that overworked but friendly removals man, who clonked up the stairs. In fact a shower of yellow petals had caught her gaze.

'I hope,' she said, 'I won't have to identify the body.'

'No. That won't be necessary.' I passed her, and she passed back, the compasses. 'Ah, no – they're yours,' I said. 'From out of that chest. Thanks for your time. I'll keep in touch.'

8

I can't deny that as things stand I am acting out of mistrust, as revealed in the sweep of my pen, which with each closed loop is always hiding something. It rarely communicates thoughts, as that would render the theft or loss of my notebook terrible to contemplate. My handwriting – once an elegant, schoolboy italic – looks like spiders from an inkpot. I go for the added confusion of abbreviations. Some I invent. Others – the orthodox q.v., cf., cp., etc. – are in no danger of interpretation, so entangled is the mesh I hang them in. I add a mathematician's vectors – arrows that I number – to point back and forth from page to page.

9

By mid-July the chief inspector showed his alarm at the lack of progress on the Solomon case. He and Professor Dark must have had a phone conversation, as now I was sent to the chief inspector's office, in haste. I found him with Bello, openly hostile, and preferring, he said, to think about his holiday. Instead he was here, with his few exhibits, and not his man.

'What good,' he asked, 'is a gaberdine and trilby?' Yes, a trilby. It had finally come to light.

That of course was rhetorical, for wasn't there also the knife? My mind wandered. Blamm droned on impossibly. All I could capture was an image of myself, striking out on the gravel of Henry Reuter's drive, not quite focused on the dead man Solomon – as it turns out *the* Solomon, a name huge in pharmaceuticals.

'And what,' asked Blamm, 'has this Castlebar Road got to do with anything?' A large house with two over-sized pineapples on its gateposts, on its lawn a chalky *amoretto*, a thing petrified on a raised slab in a rock pool. It had a hand that couldn't pluck, three of its digits having broken off. Bacterial green attacked its fundament....

Bello gave him what answers were necessary, revelations Blamm had already turned his back on. He liked to look out – for naturally his turret had windows. He questioned Bello's methods. Angrily he waved in his face a weekend newspaper, open at the column he'd been reading, the parting public pronouncements of a retiring academic, his last post a provincial university. He'd given his career to the analysis of poverty and crime and the relationship between them. That whole fabric – crime as a social phenomenon – was openly disputed by the then home secretary, whose two-sided flesh-and-blood bookkeeping reduced the evil humans do to individual acts. It was a controversy setting the implacable Bello and Blamm in opposing camps, which now in the latter's office dramatised itself in a history of break-ins and car thefts. The chief inspector, so like that quack in the cabinet, gave this newspaper dissertation little of his time. He tossed it down on his desk, an action raising one other question. Had too much laborious reading dulled his criminal mind?

I was staring. A dry streak in the damp creases of his shirt showed as an island, a brief stretch of land, a soap-powder blue, marooned between the chief inspector's shoulder blades. He swung round and faced first me, then Bello, and held on his palm a tiny yellow tablet, which the detective sergeant said was futile. The chief inspector shook it respectfully, then closed his great bear's fist around it, and tossed back his head. Bello applauded. The chief inspector popped his bitter pill. Not yet eleven, I thought. The mail unread. Already the chief inspector's bin overflowed with the soaked inflorescences of a dozen discarded tissues.

'Try that Reuter girl again,' he said. He couldn't see, flat and limp – and reflected in a dome of glass – the first faint twitch of a smirk, as Bello beheld the office urn, and tugged at a paper cone.

'I don't think she'll add to her story.'

'Which is what?'

Well, Blamm, this is how it was. At six, left Puddle Dock for Victoria. At ten, stepped onto fateful train. Got off Notting Hill Gate, Solomon still alive, having rolled up his paper, chuckling.

The detective sergeant opened the tap on the chief inspector's urn. A clear cupola rose to its glassy ceiling, and lost its shape.

'Here,' he said. 'Have some water.'

Blamm said he was open to any new premise, and studied that disposable cup. 'Even if it means you invert it,' he said, referring to his paper cone, 'and wear it, marked with a D.'

Bello had no answer, and nor, as he looked at me, had I. All I could know was this: that near my feet a procession of screwed-up paper tissues had ended their parabolas in the shade of the chief inspector's bin.

'Nothing to add,' I said.

Blamm, as riposte, ran an eye on the sharp creases in his trousers, having sat at his desk and put up his feet. A large heel left its dent in his blotter. I wanted to get away, and didn't sit down, though Blamm, in the movement of his hand, somehow kept me in his spell. To Bello he pointed out a large manila envelope among his papers, which Bello found, rummaging. I cast around, resting momentarily on a desk portrait of the chief inspector's bored-looking wife. Uncomfortably I met the big man's diabolism in the pink glaze of his eyes, till at last he smiled, professionally, reluctantly.

'There's stuff there,' he said to Bello, 'I want you to read. Things to check out. Nothing to do with the Solomon case.'

I edged from the big man's office, ahead of Bello. The back of the chief inspector's chair sprang suddenly, as his phone began to ring. Bello shut the door and strolled in the gloom of the corridor. Light – a pale barley – crept to my heels, then overtook my stride, thinly spread on the nap of the floor tiles. Then here was Blamm again, poking his head round the door.

'Remember,' he said. 'No fancy theories.'

Then there was thunder, a Gargantuan sneeze, which shook the walls of his cavern.

That, as his valediction, I took down with me onto the street, where I was sure of his eyes drilling my back. Not hard to imagine also a hand to his tissue box, a shake of his head, that weariness, as again he deployed himself on the rough terrain his differences with Bello placed between them. I shrugged. Under my feet was rough ground of another kind, through an age of hard heels, hobnails, stilettos, having left its ruts and veins in the pavements.

I crossed to the other side, then called out to Bello: 'Meet you for lunch, the Hoop and Grapes. My round.' Then I slunk away, out of his and the chief inspector's view.

10

Hurley, whose kid brother Bello, with my help, had put away twelve months ago, stepped from a shopfront, clutching a carton of pineapple juice. We exchanged glances. He thought better than to speak, and moodily walked away. I turned and went in the other direction, into the cool ruins and thick midday shadows, where the street, a long line of late Victorian terraces, was a crumbling edifice, collectively speaking. I rummaged in pockets and pulled out Frankie's number. I stumbled on a bright new phone booth, a tent of tinted glass outside a corner shop. I plundered pockets for coins, hauling out a corrosion of coppers. Farther on an excavation – its house bombed-out and boarded up – laid claim to last week's news. A page of print wrapped round a lead pipe, sprouting through a clod of earth, blared its headline: 'Kosher pig saves the rabbi's bacon.' It was hot.

One street farther on the terraces were bleached, a chalky white. A small boy on the flagstones chased, and never unravelled, the barber stripe of the ball he bounced. A curtain twitched. Under an ebony hand a column of lace shed its motes of dust. I glanced up to an open attic where in a wave of mechanical Motown a falsetto pleaded its case. A car – its headlights on – rounded a corner. A sycamore dappled the macadam. Bindweed curled up a fence. The driver, who wore a fluorescent smile, raised his hat. It was Joey, barman at the Club Sportif. I waved.

He grated his reply in the misalignment of his gears. Then, distantly, the screech of warm tyres, then a moving siren, and flooding back the frenetic life of the city – three, four blocks away. I stopped in the fragments of shade dancing under the sycamore. I caught the last of Joey, a receding paleness of taillights, and turned where a wire fence had snapped into ladders, and was overrun with bindweed.

On I tramped, into a street with beech trees, and a square with a bench and railings. I found another corpse, stretched out under an Indian bean tree. What a nuisance that would be, as now I'd have to rummage in the musty drawers of officialdom, and pull out a mask, its wearer detached and solemn, and begin to make notes. Then happily that wasn't necessary, with the corpse miraculously twitching back to life. A sudden jerk of limbs turned the bottle it had drunk from back into the upright, chiming on the flagstones. A last dribble of liquid spelt, in amber ink, in Gothic script, a hearty name in cider. The bottle did a pirouette.

I knew by the cut of his sack that this was a sophisticate of down-and-outdom, off his accustomed shop front and sleeping it off in *my* chequered vale. Should I ask him for silver (that phone call to make)? Or join his vagrancy? Or write a note and plant it in the neck of his bottle? 'Now we are two. Washed up. Marooned on a shared traffic island.' Then I found my phone card.

11

You begin to see how important my notebook is, to me at least. Its flow, contiguous on the page, is not in line with the linear pattern I have so far followed. I am going to have to break that sequence, at some point, with Iris Cadogan, another call I made, conspicuous for the time she made me wait when I went to her house. All I could do was ramble in written words. But that's to jump ahead, which I do not wish to do. Eventually I found a phone, and dialled. And waited.

Certain other incidents I record, with the call I am making slow to be connected. A fat city pigeon plunged from a whitewashed recess and dipped under the ribs of the railway bridge. A man in a grey suit and brown flesh having merged in a throb of silver made the reverse journey from a newspaper stand. Waves of heat rose from the pavement. He was bent at the knees, and supported on a stick, the ferrule of which he prodded at the pavement. Bar to his progress were two younger men, their bloom the deserts of finance, who jointly fisted the air at the latest index prices, with the FTSE 100 up.

The pigeon crossed their path and landed. All three, puffed-up and lolloping, vied for the yellow bay of a taxi stand. I waited – for someone on the other end. Should I hang up? I was about to, then with a train and its overhead clatter my call was answered. 'Frank—,' I said, but got no further than that, the first truncated syllable, which floated off and hummed in the mist. A few yards away that pigeon was nodding from all elevations at a nub of dried cement. I rattled the handset and put it back to my ear, where there was now recorded music – an electrified twang of strings, and as background a pan of boiling eggs. Again I shook the earpiece. Not so sweetly two castrati whined in the solitude the lovelorn always feel they have to sing about. As such I waited.

Above me on the platform a bald man in a black suit made a jump for the train, and didn't succeed. His forward foot, then only his document case, got wedged in the doors, which he wriggled free. All this he followed with a trek across the footbridge, having tried for the wrong train anyway. It cued my telephonist in Puddle Dock, who put a peg to her nose and showed the powers of her index finger, flicking off and finally emasculating those heartsick singers. I said 'Frankie Reuter,' and was put through immediately – though Frankie was flustered.

'I'm on my way out.'

I explained. 'It's Solomon. I expect you can guess. Just one or two more questions. I'd like to meet....'

Not possible, she said. She was heading out for the Tara Hotel, where she'd got a lunchtime seminar.

'I'll call for you there.'

Later, at the Hoop and Grapes, with Bello. I didn't tell him I'd tried her again, and awaited my opportunity. Once he'd gone to the bar I leafed through Chief Inspector Blamm's manila envelope, whose paperwork was to do with a man called Staverton. Blamm had made notes, schematics, and a timeline. Bello said nothing when we parted on the street, where I returned to the station. On the platform, in the squat shadow of its canopy, I unknotted my tie. A sad clown in a beige suit on the opposite platform took out and waved the burgundy checks of his handkerchief. He looked west, where there was still no train, then dabbed at the long pinkish scar on an otherwise smooth-looking chin. That was enough to persuade me our summers had got too hot, and I slipped into the waiting room – a place cool, stinking and littered. In a foam of script, its walls trumpeted a man called Agg and what he'd done to a girl named Rose.

Professor Dark, the Department, and all in authority above me, cannot overstress how important it is to observe and record, to pry into almost everything. It's a habit I've acquired, having learned to sift what seems to be important. According to the chief inspector PC Rudge had 'definite' views on the 'recidivist' Staverton – a man Bello knew from his days on the beat. I had seen the red box Blamm had drawn, with a broad arc and arrowhead pointing to an address – Staverton's. I remembered it, and given Staverton was 'probably a Satanist' I'd pay him a visit. Now.

12

I can't be sure when Professor Dark first had serious doubts as to my suitability. If there is one decisive moment, I'd trace it to a magazine a bemused colleague skimmed across his desk, one of several articles seized in a dawn raid. I had watched that operation, whose scene was a cul-de-sac off the Harrow Road. The target – a man called Josh – scrambled to his bathroom and flushed away a cache of cocaine, just as a trained gorilla broke through his door. Our victim lunged for the fire escape, and fled, wearing just the bathrobe he managed to fling on. That garment I later examined – black towelling and a pattern of gold stars – after we'd picked him up, in the cemetery, Kensal Green, where he put up no resistance. He was cornered, in the faded grandeur of so many gilded mausolea, and held up his wrists as the cuffs were snapped in place.

I was shown round his room, an interior hung with damp green wallpaper, and a gallery of colour pinups, only one of whom I recognised (Hendrix, the era *Electric Ladyland*).[5] There was printed matter, among it the magazine referred to above, the spring quarter issue of *Outer Fringe*,[6] whose editorials were under the rubric 'News From Lesbos'.[7] It was here its editor named a certain Adrian Fixt as a man you couldn't trust, and showed, provocatively, my obsession with narcotics as not entirely professional. Furthermore she regarded me as too closely connected with the forces of fascism. All this I tolerate for her quality of information.[8]

On that same day I was treated to the vacant leaves of Dark's five-year planner, and wondered what was ordained.

'You can't go round advertising yourself like this. It's not only you, the whole department is jeopardised.'

'It's not that serious,' I said. 'The *Fringe* is small circulation. Lucy can say what she wants.'

'I don't like it. I don't like her connections. And another thing. Your relationship with Bello is getting too fraternal.'

I denied it, though admitted to myself it might be true. Dark had only to invoke those profile notes he had looked at on the eve of my appointment, and there was his justification. Fixt, a loner, prone to close in on himself after the premature death of his parents. One living relative, a sister, her remoteness exaggerated by the money she had made. A man probably craving friendship.

'Don't get too close.'

'Don't worry.'

'And why haven't you made a fortune, like your sister?'

'One day I'll tell you.'

13

Rudge's theory of Staverton rested on a number of local disappearances, some reported directly to him. By 'disappearances' I mean not of people but domestic pets – mainly canines. That had been the fate of my faithful Boscy.

Bear with me, as I put my notebook down. I need to think. I can hear Blamm, see him holding court stirring sugar in his coffee. He tells his colleague Bello how remiss he's been. It's not this alone that makes unbearable the limbo he's condemned him to, so hot, and clammy. For my part my windows are open. I am fanning myself, and have my back to the desk, which is dark, inanimate. I have looked at it without its pens and reading lamp. I had the foolish idea of draping over it the embroidered marigolds of my one and only tablecloth, with a chair reserved for Frankie. I even went to the trouble of getting in more bottles, for cocktails – of course futile. For at no time has Reuter put down her glittering powder bag – not anywhere here.

It's too bad, there's a phone downstairs – ringing, and ringing, and ringing. What I need is a breeze, not a headache....

I pace out these square yards in the voids of my attic. I am tired, and want to shut my eyes. I stumble. I try to spirit myself back to the professor's paper world, which has become increasingly impenetrable. I'm not even sure if the notelets I write ever reach his desk. Now this incessant bell, in an empty flat below. I open the skylight as far as it will go, and strain for a better view. A wingtip catches the sun in a brief arc of gold, the next plane in for the airport.

Ah, at last. That phone has stopped, just as someone across the street has come to her window, hair wet and wrapped in a towel. A black cab below stutters through a gap in the traffic, yet still is trapped in a yellow box. Just as that phone starts to ring again the girl across the street starts on the meticulous application of mascara. I thirst for the bar. I sit – my head and that phone in counterpoint, an onslaught I don't think I can tolerate. Let's just try the notebook.

14

Overtired, you'd say, or stress. And yet my figments won't be blinked away. Insane scrolls in a margin have life in a wrinkled face. My hand shows signs of resistance, the image twisting itself in a malicious grin. It suggests new information, words that aren't there, secrecy in my glyphs. It pronounces one impossibility – that it's Dark, miles away in his lair, with his office phone, the receiver to his ear, crossing back and forth on that Stygian lake, the shadow cast on his floor, an agitated figure as he tries to get through on the wrong number downstairs.

I reach for the knot in my tie, but see it limp and discarded, dangling over the back of a dining chair. I can't stand the heat, and the grime. I'd douche down but for the lack of pressure in the water main into the building. There's a sun-mottled ancient downstairs, who lives alone on the ground floor, who spends his evenings hosing a brown slab of earth in the communal garden, and that doesn't help.

But enough. Be gone, mirages.

15

It boiled down to petty supermarket thefts as the definition of Staverton's recidivism. Items Rudge has enumerated include tinned pineapple, sliced ham in a vacuum seal, a small carton of continental cheese, a plastic washing-up brush, and an apple (Braeburn). These things had found their way into the lining of his coat because, said Staverton, the free market placed him outside its economic covenants. He'd enough education to make that claim, and insisted he was unfit temperamentally for the rigours of industry. That psychology Blamm had puzzled at, Staverton having had the kind of job you'd call a career. But not anymore.

Though that was not why Rudge had shown new interest. In the years since Bello left the beat, Staverton's record had either improved or his skills were better honed. Now he could boast only a distant acquaintance with those 'pillars of rotten English life' – by which he meant the magistrates. These, so far as Staverton knew, were dull, conventional men who raised their palms minutes before lunch, asking that reason prevail – but outside in the corridors, 'and do not trouble us again'.

I knew Staverton's neighbourhood, and ignored Blamm's endless navigations written in those papers placed in Bello's care. The best route began on a dishevelled street north, where I caught the smell of laundry flapping in the yards. I knew of a book collector somewhere, a long-nosed, rosy Czech, in whose terraced house I had offered what I could for the *Collected Letters* of Daniel Byrne,[9] whose insight into the criminal psyche was one of Dark's set texts.

I don't necessarily share his opinion. The letters ran to three large volumes, a triad the bookseller wasn't prepared to break up, and a sum demanded I couldn't ever muster. Nostalgically I found myself outside his house again, with its tremble of nets in the window, the red door, the Georgian front, a fanlight. I was tempted, but didn't go in, so would have to make do with the abridged paperback I'd got instead.

A hard beamless sunshine poured from the heavens. I looked up and saw only in the crumbling edifices a line of cornices in bad repair. A long broken scroll capped the terrace. Across the street, a Chinese boy scooped up a coin from the pavement – eyes low – and in the brassy glitter of his smile thumbed it into the patch of his pocket. He tucked in his shirt. Someone I couldn't see rolled up a ground-floor window. I moved to the street corner and headed west for Staverton's – not a house, but a room. A woman, of approximately Frankie's age, whose stone face fixed itself immutably in a scowl, held out a palm. For a moment I scrutinised the straps, buckles and pouch, and the soft clawing hands of the infant pressed to her bosom. I dug in my pockets, knowing words wouldn't do. A dry cough saved her my sympathy. I just handed her my coins.

I crossed her busy street and got round to the back of Staverton's, through throngs and a hubbub of traffic, into a closed world of heat and noise.

16

Now that I'd trodden Rudge's cumbersome terrain, I followed in his steps to the cobbled square soaking up the shadow of the tenement Staverton lived in. Its ground floor was a Chinese restaurant and takeaway. A chef in a grimy tunic stepped out and tossed away the gore of something's entrails, but missed the bin he was aiming at. He parried with his knife. A skewer of bruised innards clung in elastic gobbets to the blade, which he flicked away.

A man in soft shoes and with short flapping sleeves and a colourful shirt flowered past my shoulder, waving a boater, which he plunged back on his head. The chef returned a nod. The hand with the knife flopped down. That passing acquaintance had a bloomer tucked under his arm, and a red rose and Labour Party badge pinned to his lapel. There was an emerald sheen in his unshaved profile.

The chef shrank back in the depths of his doorway. I noted in Staverton's window the plant that had first attracted Rudge's attention.

I still shake my head. I still have the chill of that tenement in my scalp and hair. I pushed my weight against an outer door where the paint was peeling and the sun had bleached its timber. I knew from Blamm's manila envelope what Rudge had reported, in the dead prose his uniform demanded: '…was proceeding south from Portobello…', not that he guessed he was on to something. He called in on that old recidivist, a favourite word by now, and touched on the terrors in all dog-lovers' hearts. 'You know anything about these disappearances – pets? Seen, heard anything suspicious?' His gaze fell on what was on Staverton's window ledge, a parlour palm (or *Chamaedorea elegans*), and wrongly identified hemp (*Cannabis sativa*).

Staverton professed ignorance, at all missing canines, especially where theft was implied

– nor had he noticed odd goings-on in the neighbourhood. The constable, avoiding the slope of the ceiling, careful not to allow flakes of plaster onto his sharp lapels, made a mental note of other things he found there. Mostly he records the portents of Staverton's preoccupation with Satan. A pair of spiked handcuffs hung from a ceiling hook, its origin the medieval confessional, a pendant you consciously avoid on crossing the room. He must have passed some innocent remark on the clatter from the kitchen below. 'Busy restaurant.' He scanned walls for the prints, likewise shelves for the books and magazines, and saw as I was about to too the likeness of Matthew Hopkins, and the woodcut of a determined-looking succubus. He browsed through a *Malleus Maleficarum*,[10] which he found open at S for Strappado (he mentions this impeccably spelt). The conclusion is one the chief inspector doesn't arrive at himself, i.e. that here under the eaves of a crumbling house PC Rudge had found our man, whose rites and religion called for animal sacrifice.

I came in at the rear of the tenement and climbed the back stairs, a cold flight of steps up a square well. Soon I was breathless, and leaden at the calves. I paused to read the graffiti, spawned under a prolific hand – its owner schooled in the New York subway – with a list of groups of people connected with the locality back in 1968. Then a man named Armist, twice in '82, then in '83, then after a pause in 1985, wrote volumes on the probes of Suzy Sucro's expert lips and fingertips. He'd omitted to give her number. Rose and Agg had got here too.

A grille or window someone had left open had let a sparrow into the stairwell. Dazed at the scud of my tread, it bounced on the brick, skimmed the handrail, and only just avoided collision. I held out a forefinger, gallant and idiotic. In its madness, in its whirr of beating wings, the bemused creature returned to the chalky smears of its perch – an ornate, candleless lamp bracket, all twists and scrolls, an adornment wildly out of character.

I crossed the top landing to the foot of the last half-dozen steps leading to Staverton's garret. Steam, dissolving into falls and rivulets, sluiced down a frosted pane of glass in the bathroom door. A glug of water swirled in a waste pipe.

I climbed steps and planted my feet on the cold of a lino floor, alone in Staverton's room. First of Rudge's clues I found was of Hopkins (died 1646), in what kind of iconolatry I couldn't guess. I studied the portrait. Nowhere in his large eyes is traced the least sign of brutality, and I liked the hat. Among other images was Hogarth's *Credulity, Superstition, and Fanaticism*, which Staverton had snipped from a Sunday supplement.

I circled the hanging cuffs. I found, taped to a mirror, a page torn raggedly from a book the size of an encyclopaedia. Its grainy depiction was a witch or peasant woman, in a heretic's mitre. There were keys on Staverton's dresser – a Chubb and a Yale. With a red crayon he'd circled and later removed a letter to *The Guardian*, with one of its correspondents in trouble on a theological matter, pressed to explain a report a Joseph Garle from NW4 had taken exception to. The rant opened 'Repeatedly your column overlooks…' and went on, 'It was, with the close of the fifteenth century, and the Inquisition busy with the witch delusion throughout Europe, that the authority given the inquisitors, *in* Germany, *by* Pope Innocent VIII, was extended.' The lesson ends, 'I hope this corrects some very misleading points.'

Such a ragbag of bogus scholarship we suffer through the newsstands. At 13.05 a radio reporter crusaded across the cobbles. That did not check with Staverton's wall clock, seven minutes slow. Then with my weight the floorboards sagged, as I stepped to the hub of his room. I picked up from a table, and rotated in my hands, a forehead tourniquet – a model. A door creaked on its hinges. I glanced angularly, expecting to see over my shoulder Staverton's trembling bulk on his threshold, but saw only the threadbare chasm of a wardrobe, whose door continued to open. A flash of silver slithered over the ceiling. In the door's interior, in the dark pool of its mirror, my own vexed profile glanced back at me over the hunch of my shoulder. I shuffled up immediately and adjusted my tie (the broad end, always a testament of haste, inches too long). I moved closer, to another of his cut-outs, this one gummed into place. I had seen it somewhere before, in a supplement, a welter of column inches as it catalogued the arts of erotica – '...from Father Mathias de Giraldo, *Histoire curieuse et pittoresque des sorciers, augmentée par M. Fornari* (Paris, 1854)'. The subject was a naked succubus, on her haunches. A large man supine, in the drain of his ecstasy, with his beard turned up, his eyes closed, bore her on his torso. I opened the wardrobe's other door. That too was grotesquely decorated, with a full-length hanging of a peasant woman – this one eighteenth century – who was plucking out the teeth of her goonish-looking mate, hours dead, swinging by a noose.

I sat down to the remains of Staverton's breakfast, a few sodden squares of something wheaty, and on a chopping board the last crumbs in a chunk of cheese. A homemade banana chutney had been opened but abandoned. Its lid was facedown on the table top. A pale green mould had begun to weave its fibrous structure inside the jar, which had not been tampered with. In the foil of a pie tray, a white cigarette butt was squashed at a right angle. A book of matches (Hotel de Verdun) had an *aide-mémoire* penned on the flap: someone's initials – 'AL' – and the reminder, 'phone PM'. I listened out for Staverton (still no sound), and picked up a pocket address book – owner anonymous, though for its maze of entries various hands in as many inks had left their marks. I smirked at the potted palm (I correct myself: I smirked at Rudge), because here was a hand mirror, and on it a razor blade. Again I flicked through the address book. When Staverton wasn't slicing powders, he was chopping out the rear pages – all entries under V. Why?

Just then a frenetic radio voice, eager with the day's politics, was swamped in the vibrant electric of a bass guitar, with that underpinned by a drum. A scrubbed hand, in the heat of the kitchen, turned the volume down. Did a deafened waiter – a rage in his slanted eyes – screech for battered cod or Peking duck, and make himself heard? It was the lull I stood up in, and was where I took my place at Staverton's window, ready to turn, and protest that his door had been open (and whose confidence I intended to gain, through swipes at PC Rudge).

17

Not much came to light. My silhouette, to Staverton without his glasses, was a blur at the window. He pulled himself up abruptly, and halted. His mouth, an angry elliptical O, collapsed in a pout.

'Police,' he said, the tone weary.

'Well, sort of.'

Steam followed him in from the bathroom. In the moisture he polished his glasses and pushed them into place – two heavy oblongs perched on his nose. His robe was a muddy coffee colour. Its age I guessed in the fluff of its pocket, frayed and hardly a strand remaining. He fumbled with a tissue box and pulled one out, and wiped his lenses again, this time in great deliberation.

'My colleague,' I said, 'is young and over-zealous. He thought he could book you on the grounds of a potted palm.'

'You *are* Police.' He kept his roving eyes from the vanity glass. I coaxed him, fixing mine on the razor blade resting on and reflected in it—

'PC Rudge is conscientious.'

Staverton's reply was a short, laryngeal rasp, his ritual preparation for speech, if, on this occasion, words failed. There was dumb silence only. I waited, and got for my answer only a plunging-on of those glasses once again, and an owl blinking.

There was a fume of singed pork over the courtyard. Staverton, in need of something to sneer at, repeated the name Rudge, in a jingle of cockney rhyme. The pitch of his voice was high. I waited, thrumming on his windowsill, sticky to the touch.

'Place needs a clean,' I said. I looked at him in the mirror, framed and pear-shaped. In the passing of years, sun, air and wind had changed his hair from the straw of his stubble to the mouse of his crown, just a few dark wisps remaining. I didn't like his hairdo, too long over the nape while cropped above the ears.

'Dogs are nothing to do with me...'

'...*and* cats.' I asked him should I take notes?

'Notes?'

'Cats, dogs. They're not what Rudge frets about. But *I* do, having lost my hound. I'd have to admit, there *is* an explanation needed.' I looked at the tourniquet.

He, only an arm-length from his Hopkins, made a flourish of his index finger, sliding the bridge of his glasses tightly onto the ridge of his nose.

I played out his melodrama, benignly as I could, exactly as the yobbish Rudge would do, though mine was a different purpose. I closed round with a casual grip on the stub of my pencil. 'Don't let it bother you,' I said. 'I *am* taking notes.'

He sized his voluminous denims, torn at the knees and scored where he turned them up, but decided not to dress. With a vengeful heave he tossed them onto his quilt. I caught his glance, a flinty glaze under the fleshy lids of his eyes, and followed his guilty digits in the debris of his breakfast table. He attempted to deceive me, taking, turning over, discarding each chance article. He compressed a perspiring gob of Stilton under a thumb, and aimed it at a bin. It scudded high and wide, and ended with his coffee mugs. He picked up that duplicated razor, teasing its edge, blunt, and destined, he said, for the rejuvenating air of a pyramid he'd made. Careful not to make any such his last action, he whipped up the Chubb and the Yale – two keys swinging on a ring round a small, fat finger – and slung them into the folds of an ornamental lily pad, home to a collection of paper clips. From its packet he eased then wriggled out a cigarette – French, pure, white. He was confident. He snapped his Zippo open, shut. He surveyed the room.

'The evils of any creed,' he said, 'are just as much its truth. Not something your flatfoot understands.'

'Don't blame me. That idiot was sent by someone else – another department.' Curious at his philosophising, I took out and blew into the steel-grey florets of my handkerchief. I itched for the novel depth and texture of my other notebook (the private one. I'm referring to it now), though that would have to wait. Incisive questions – soliloquies – speculation – all were best left for the midnight lamp.

He followed the jerk of my forearm, and smiled – a thin twitch in the pout of his lips. He said with a sneer it wasn't the witch-finder who'd pushed him over the edge. There was another Hopkins, a point I didn't let him enlarge on. I left it there, certain, I said, we'd talk again.

The door shut behind me. I looked up and saw the doomed sparrow, perched in its smears of chalk. Staverton, social freak and malcontent, clattered round his room, putting out of view his incriminating objects. That though was belatedly, for as always I'd registered everything.

I'd got down to the next landing when that ill-nourished sparrow winged its terrified way over my head, in search of somewhere safe. A middle-aged browbeaten woman stepped out from Flat 15 – two rooms and a bath – as I hooted in the stairwell (a merry Papageno), trying to shoo the thing outdoors. She did not flinch or unbend – in fact stooped to knot her garbage sack. Dark specks ribbed the finger of ash curling from the filter clamped between her lips. Her housecoat was blue, translucent, knee-length. The scarf, nylon, was knotted at the crown. She stood upright. Ash fell on her sack. The butt dangled on her lower lip – though she remained speechless.

'The sparrow,' I said. Then, outside, I blinked hard, thinking about those Byrne volumes.

18

I'm what you'd call computer literate, though there's something I don't understand about the word processor, accessed via the Department server. Professor Dark asked me, in that cheery way he has, how my document was coming along – the one for training. I was about to print its opening sections, or anyway the first draft. I'd give him a copy once I had proofread. I'm glad I said that, as certain things aren't as I wrote them. My opening ought to have section and paragraph headings, like this—

1 The Department
1.1 Management Structure
1.2 Commerce and Industry

For some reason it doesn't. I shall investigate.

19

In the meantime, here is a feat of extrication, for let us decamp to Scarsdale Place, and the Tara Hotel, where Frankie was due to deliver her seminar.

I got there too early (or too early for the late lunch I had planned). What to do in those precious idle moments before the appointed hour? I tried my jacket hanging from either shoulder, the casual look, and left the hotel. This would not be relevant documentation, except to say I can always tell, in the varying grades of pessimism, the extent of what is wrong with anyone, in my case by the shop fronts and their reflections away from Scarsdale Place. Back, arched; collar, crooked; tie, ditto; shoes scuffed; hair, a mess.

I straightened the tie, in the blind gaze of a quintet of tailor's dummies. A dresser, her mouth full of pins, appeared behind a cardboard tree. My presence didn't distract. I watched as she levered an inanimate forearm up from its elbow, and gave to her leading man a cocktail pose, in the raising of a glass not there. *Prosit*. She moved sideways across the display and bent down, so that now I caught my deeper reflection – gloomier still – in the seat of her jodhpurs. Baggy eyes, a resolute mouth – sufficient shock to make me smile, to want to look pleased, anything. She tugged at a shirt cuff hidden in the sleeve of its wearer's jacket, an adjustment ending in the tarnished gleam of a cufflink. It did not seem to perk him up. The hardness in the hollows of his cheeks remained. The square discourse on his lips was a heckler's. To his left a senior, two to three yards back from the windowpane, had raised a knee, showing how even the primitive moccasin could be worn around the office. Uppers were leather, embellished. That same boyish coiffure was plastered on his scalp. The rest of the band made do as sleepwalkers, vacant extras waiting for a change of gear.

I returned to the Tara, up its nondescript alley, still too early. There was billing on a sandwich board, and for delegates a black arrow in the direction followed for sign-in. The concierge, a man with an exact parting but a lopsided bowtie, acknowledged with a nod and the flourish of two pink chins. He handed me a programme, which I have kept. It's here in a drawer with my totality of theatre mementoes – a Fo, a La Clos, a Pirandello. The bar had sides and a corner missing – a sliced octagon, pulled out unevenly at its angles. It was imitation marble, cocoa or chocolate coloured, and cool to the touch. According to the barman, there was nothing stronger than coffee. He poured me one with cream and showed me the *table d'hôte*, a dual sitting starting at noon, with an Atlantic salmon appetiser in a *chaud-froid* sauce. Highly recommended.

'Thanks, but I'm too late.'

I studied the programme. Page one pictured a trio of speakers, a pair from a New York business school and a wild savant from academe. The redshirt poured me another coffee, and couldn't resist his repertoire of jokes. Instantly I recognised his toad's eyes, the fat jowls, the thinning stubs of his hair, and knew him from a short-run TV sitcom, subject the lives of London's security men.

'Good luck with the next audition.'

20

I turned to page three of the programme, which introduced the firm hiring F. Reuter as its consultant. The text was drear, agonised over in a stifling office somewhere in Puddle Dock, the reflected Thames a glitter of rivulets, a minor cascade on its author's interior walls. In vendors' prose, here is what we had come to the Tara for, and was how the world was shaped. First the chairman's threefold vision of prosperity (investment, growth, stability: thesis, antithesis, synthesis). His commitment was 1) to research and development, 2) to products into the future, 3) to the customer.

I turned to the seminar agenda, whose opening paragraphs explained how an XYZ Plc had sustained its market lead. The morning's first session discussed the market XYZ was in – the new digital infrastructure and the breadth of its communications. Frankie's pitch was technical and sales. Next came an interlude, then the savant – a short, talcum-haired man—

An approach to IPC: language or pseudo-code? S. Magus

All that had passed, and now at three o'clock the schedule had got as far as this—

Signalling asynchronous events: enhancement tools for semaphores and timers. F. Reuter

The barman said what a refreshing change – not like all those stuffed shirts whose only evolving feature was a salary. He had taken her bags, when she'd got to the Tara with minutes to spare. She looked over the seminar room. Her blouse, white and diaphanous, was half-buttoned. She told him what a morning she'd had, at Puddle Dock, launching salvos, all because her overhead slides – she'd laboured on them half the night – the technician assigned was adamant couldn't be produced – not at short notice. Frankie said, 'You need to try harder.' Further headshakes. She went to the basement herself, where the acetates were made. There a man rolling tobacco had as assistant someone poking pen holes in a polystyrene cup. She stood over him, and made him do the work.

I heard her at a distance, surprised at the easy tone, with none of that reedy unresponsiveness I had encountered so far. She had style, panache, authority. She told me later when I congratulated her that much of this was due to the work of her script team – though did not say, and left it for me to discover, that *she* was the team. She had three distinct keys: mood one, levity; two, decision; three was application. Her asides were of real-world analogies, as she explained, and I vaguely understood, her asynchronous timers. A low boom of laughter swelled the seminar room, as she must have told a joke – a joke I didn't catch. I listened harder, as endemic to London life is rudimentary air-conditioning, and the door was ajar. A house flunkey fussing with a screwdriver was assailing the plug on an electric fan, and drew blood. An explosion – a guffaw – raised the few loose papers inside – his cue to down tools and disappear.

I put my head round the door and looked in. One of those transparencies coloured the air, swirling on her chin, on a raised hand, a cheekbone. Her thick green marker pointed at the screen, and a flyspeck on it. Result: more guffaws, though of course I'd missed the pun. The performance went to the first of her miracles, and the mystifying artefacts of digital technology. I, of the Department, the only man here who'd seen her stolidity – the pauses, the monosyllabic replies – must now reconsider the remoteness of her nature, nimble in its mastery over a crowded room of listeners.

She crossed her heart with the green marker – not for verity's sake – and cartwheeled the other arm frontally, and held it in a pose pointing at the ceiling spots. For the sake of argument – an argument about to be unravelled – we had now to think of her as a kind of marionette, at work in the storerooms in a supermarket. Eyelids drooped, cheeks wooden. The mouth, if not stupid, is expressionless. This was our flesh-and-blood representation of the semaphore system XYZ was selling, her dumb show a parody of the work the storeman does, his job to re-stack shelves as soon as they reach a certain stage of emptiness. His position – one arm crossed, one pointing up – is transitional, and coincides with a half-dozen cans of pimentos. Frankie called this diminished stock an asynchronous event. He, the semaphore, signalled it. Someone, in all probability idle in the stock room, is tasked periodically with getting up and walking to the door, on the lookout for these signals.

Frankie went on, her marionettes standing in as subroutine primitives, or technically her semaphores 'wait' and 'notify', essential in internal software timing. When two or more processes are active simultaneously, it's because there's a limited resource, usually. 'Just like here with the air conditioning.' Laughter, applause.

What notes I managed to make, when tired and under lamplight, are ended here, in a natural prohibition of frantic crossings-out – though a further brush with Frankie's mystical art has since entered the record. It happened later that summer, when I needed her expertise, and called at her flat in Holland Park. When she knew what I was after she pointed to a set of manuals, directions I followed in a trail of floored undergarments all the way to her nightstand. There an insane text, by a Donn G. Krinkel of Framingham, Massachusetts, only stirred up deeper mystification, and was where I had to give it up. But anyway, we'll come to that.

21

I chaperoned Ms Reuter to an afternoon lunch, through a maze of irradiating streets. I pointed out – our conversation thin – a man in blue shorts, his tan an inferno of flesh. She smiled, already used to our English eccentricity. The man wore city brogues and swung his document case back and forth rhythmically, an umbrella hooked in its straps.

Why had I come, she asked – an abrupt question I took wrongly to mean the seminar room, where I had hovered on the threshold.

'It gave me the satisfaction of watching a room empty. There is humbling desolation in the aftermath of human activity.' In detection, just as in modern poetics,[11] one pinpoints self-evident things. I could not help but notice the polite reserve of those who'd attended her seminar. There were other things I'd spotted. For example moving trapezoids, a mobility of angled patches, a dance on every workbench, the result of drawing the strip blinds, the sun's beams in the windows, a stencil effect and the medium of water.

'Water?'

'Yes. The water jugs.'

'You serious?'

I put a hand to my brows (I am English. It is hot). 'A good lecture means your listeners don't get thirsty.' The jugs remained full. Not two minutes ago her computer buffs trooped out over the raised floor, a tramp of feet that made it shake. Then the benches shook. All that iced water found new lines. That wasn't all. One of her students – wiry haired, late thirties – had found her semaphores hard to grasp. Her timers impossible. 'I happen to know he left his complimentary pen, with a pad of headed paper. I mean to say nothing, yet explain my method.'

I knew these streets. There was a café, Dino's, one block further west, a few more strides into the burning sun.

'Ah no,' she said. 'Why did you want to see *me?*'

Ah, that was simple. 'I have gathered so little on the Solomon case that the details are important, and you are a source. Let's take an instance. What was in Solomon's eyes, when you saw him alive? He seemed worried, perhaps? Did he doze? Fidget?' She repeated what she had said at our first interview. She'd caught his smile, but hadn't thought to look again.

'Okay,' I said. I pointed out a rococo D – Dino's distinctive insigne etched in an upper window. 'You'll have some lunch?'

A sturdy Florentine moved in a wave of stale air from the reaches of his kitchen, and composed himself. I closed the door. He forced a smile. A few spots of spittle bejewelled the barbs of his beard. His two giant paws, dark with follicles, skimmed the undulations of his vest. He bowed, minimally. Wiped tables (we seemed to need a choice). Late as the hour was, he conjured a menu, from a depthless arch to the rear. He dredged and repeated a mantra: 'But see, so!'

Frankie sat down, not now hungry, and ordered a lime juice – plenty of ice. For myself – as I also sat – a Pilsner. A reflection aqua-light in the tan of her neck slipped away on the pleats of her blouse. I mentioned how quaint it was, a wall trellis hung with empty Chianti bottles and a string of imitation onions. No answer. The waiter stepped in, having mined a precious six and a half syllables, asking was she ready to order. 'Oh,' she said, and folded the menu. 'The *crudités.*'

She stretched away her pains, the accumulated pins, cramps and aches of office life. Her blouse when she stretched shoulders went briefly from opaque to see-through. The cups, loops and frills of her bra were bright maroon. I looked at her brooch, in form the leaf of an oak, in miniature, its design an autumn film of frost. But no conversation there. 'Exquisite,' I said.

The giant's thick shadow loomed. I ordered. A sauce, I said – the one with pasta hats. He scribbled a note. I thumbed my pockets, waiting, turning over everything I'd wanted to say. How, please, to begin? With a word, a phrase, a smile? Frankie sighed. She had to be back at Puddle Dock by five, she said. Her shoulders hunched. An elbow tested the table. 'I shan't take long,' I assured.

I looked from the table again and saw that sluggish Latin, more morose than when we had entered. His vest, a soiled, cinerary grey, retained a vestige of its original fluorescence. His broad back, enveloped in darkness, threw onto the brick arch into his kitchen a new dimension. My face was flushed with the heat of his oven. Distractedly I felt in my jacket. I pulled out an envelope whose frank was the Byrne Society logo, and inside an invitation. We will I'm sure return to this, though let us first look at the drawing I had done on the outside – a rough diagram, my mock-up of the platform, the carriage, Solomon's seat, and diagonally opposite his, Frankie's. I explained—

'A certain chief inspector sometimes lets me see his working papers. My own thinking contradicts his. I believe the assailant may not have been wearing his coat and hat – not to begin. He could have pulled them on after the murder, in the next carriage.'

Frankie did not raise her eyes from the table top. It wasn't that she *meant* to be evasive.

'It means,' I went on, 'I must ask you to think again. Do you remember a man with a package, or a light gaberdine under his arm, or over? And the hat.'

The giant recovered his swagger, coming from under the arch and out of his cavern. An ashy brightness lit his vest. He uttered his mantra – 'But see, so' – and planted down a vinaigrette, then with more care Frankie's glass of juice.

'It's okay to talk,' I said. I thought even now she didn't want to, but then her bowl of *crudités* appeared, followed by my pasta. She smiled.

'I'd like to help, of course,' she said. A first hopeful flame, a suffusion, a warm rose under the flimsy satin of her foundation, ebbed from the thin flesh of her cheeks. Again, the runnels, sluices, the remote little ripples in the life of her feelings, were stilled, were calmed.

She reiterated: 'It was late. I was tired. I didn't take much notice. Sorry.'

I plunged my fork in the folds of a toyland panama, then pushed it and a topper through the garlic mire of my lunch.

'Well,' I said, chewing – to no loss of appetite. 'Should anything occur....' My one final question, for Gino or Dino, was: really how to drink my beer without a glass? I looked up from the table, still unable to plumb the midnight of his arch. I only imagined him, in the darkness, roasting the vastness of his bulk on the heat of his gridirons. He no doubt listened to the patter of our chow, emerging again, with banana fritters, ices, mixed fruit, and more we didn't want.

Frankie fingered my envelope, its outlines of murder meaning no more than the chance journey home I wanted her to recall. She studied the crest, damaged where I'd torn the envelope.

'Byrne,' she said. 'That name's in the news.'

'Yes. Byrne, Daniel. Dead now, but made a name in crime. Reporting.' He disappeared from city life when someone paid a large advance, then published his chronicle on the most notorious crimes he'd reported on – murders mostly. Some financial swindles. He took it seriously and wrote letters to law lords, prison governors, chief constables, the probation service, academics, the villains themselves, reformed or otherwise. 'It's those and the replies he got that the department I work for classifies as a primary text, and is out now as a TV series.'

'Exciting.'

'The society thinks that too.'

'You are sceptical.'

'I try not to be. I'm a model of politeness. The committee boasts the world's leading expert on Daniel Byrne. There are questions I wanted to ask him.'

'And?'

'He replied with his hourly rate.'

'You had to pay him?'

'Not exactly. I don't control the training budget. I got myself an invitation to hear him speak at a garden party, given by the Byrne Society. There's an awards ceremony, overseen by someone else you've probably heard of – Bim Shay. The society's figurehead.'

'You're a member?'

'Not anymore. Its committees like clear blue skies, and things to celebrate. They know delusions are born in English winters' – so don't, Frankie, allow that season into your house. Stay indoors come November. The streets are a crawl of cold shoppers coming in from the pavements, into the warm up-draughts and anaesthetic of shop-soiled air. Predators are waiting, with worthless heaps of things to buy – a glitter on so much trash glossed as regenerated life.[12] My feet thaw, but not the nausea. I think of that one dustcover too many beaming at a book-buyer's world, retiring civil servants, journalists, politicians, TV people, all with their memoirs.

But not to be coy about this. The letter enclosed had the automated signature of Paschal Brennan, the society's public relations guru. I can say from meetings I have had and other sightings, and photographs always in the press, that his is a satisfied smile. The jowls are thick, the proboscis rosy, the locks raven. There is world-weary mourning in his fast, intelligent eyes. Brennan it was who raised cash for the Byrne Society prizes, given out as awards to those contributing most to our insight into modern crime, and into the criminal mind. I flicked open the envelope. 'The invitation is for two.'

'Where?'

'A private estate, Sussex.'

'Sounds lovely.'

'Weather permitting. Why? You'd like to come?'

How could she refuse? *Mirabile dictu* – after weighing certain possibilities, she didn't. Surprised and elated I walked her back to the hotel, where over a cup of coffee I watched her put it in her diary.

'We'll call it a date,' she said.

'Look forward to it. Till then don't be surprised if Detective Sergeant Bello gets in touch, and asks you pretty much what I have....'

22

It's perplexing. Having reversed those aberrations in the corrupt draft I printed from the Department server, I find they've re-emerged, and what is more are headed by an epigraph, to do with the philosopher Moses Mendelssohn,[13] and the game of chess. This could prove a serious problem, now that Dark is asking about the training document. But never mind. Must press on.

23

That clash of personalities in the case Blamm versus Bello was no more than two distinct ways of looking at the world. Nothing to date had brought this to a climax, except now there was no movement on the Solomon case. It increased the tension between them. It also meant that at meetings I went to, where Solomon was on the agenda, the two found it easier to talk about Staverton. I at no point admitted I'd interviewed him myself. I tacitly encouraged Bello, who rejected the ritual theory, which the chief inspector thought he oughtn't to dismiss – or not hastily.

I returned to Blamm's office often, late in the evening, in the expectation of not finding him there. Dark had begun to apply more pressure, and shared with Blamm concern at the lack of progress. 'The problem,' I said, 'is a dearth of information. Blamm is secretive. To a lesser extent so is Bello.'

'I don't care how you get your information....'

I rifled through Blamm's papers, and photocopied everything I could. If I got back before he'd gone home to his wife, Bello was usually with him. Blamm hovered at his window, at pains to emphasise whose aegis we operated under. Whenever he did so Bello looked frail, but told me nevertheless he'd just the right particle of faith necessary for long-term survival.

I tried to lighten these triangular loads with diversions into the Byrne Society, a shapeless, shambling group of enthusiasts I wasted more time on than was strictly necessary. I had told Blamm what it did, and stood for. He shrugged, and said nothing. He didn't need to. Bello smirked, though he as well as I couldn't know, without glancing forward onto its path of salvation, how Byrne would represent a reliable escape, given the purgatory the chief inspector felt instinctively was good for my soul.

Blamm slumped in his seat. I looked through the window behind him. A plump gull, a mile out from its earthy mounds of refuse, adjusted its wing tips, turning its feathers into the thermals off the chief inspector's tower. It circled, buoyed up on the waves of heat, but finding nothing to attract it banked from the square of the roof above. Blamm's lengthening silhouette detached itself from the slope of its backrest. He got up, a man quiescent in the relative cool of evening. He strode to the window. Glued to the open slats of the blind, he raised an arm. A hand went to his brow. His weariness was Bello.

Bello had nothing to say, unable to address the hunch of the chief inspector's shoulders. He checked through his mail. Blamm moved to a corner of his window frame, and with a huge thumb and forefinger prised open a wider gap in the blinds. He, and now I, caught the first flaming streaks of gold, the deep flashes that, as I decided to go home, had darkened to red the day's last fires, a sullen glow in the vacuum of closed windows regimented in the shops and offices. I could hear water – from a hose in the yard – then a girl's laughter passing by. I hardly expected Blamm, never far from a tissue box – never conceived, dreamt, imagined what he would now attempt, just for Bello's benefit and mine. A lyrical depth. A gentle frame for the hooks and blades of his philosophy.

He said, slowly, 'This is our metropolis.'

They troubled him, the colours of a July sunset. I hung my jacket on a chair, apprehensive. I waited. On the half-hour I heard a distant bell, a chime or curfew as complement of his mood – declamatory. The Blamm I knew had transformed, and acting as his own forerunner, in his squat little tower, was not the same man looking out, into the shadows and crags of his kingdom. He was a man aloof in the squares and twilit corridors of his crumbling urban domain.

'I send out my envoys,' he said.

What he sought out, over the villa parade, in the depths, cavities and recesses, what he saw through his blind, was this—

'A fractious element.'

I took a step back, convinced I should not have put my jacket down.

'I close in,' Blamm said, 'on any least suspicion.' In his tone was a touch of melodrama. 'Why? Because I hold to the status quo.'

'That's what we're paid to do,' I said. I picked up my jacket and searched its concealed pockets, wanting the certainty of incriminating papers folded up and safely put away.

Said Bello: 'I'll get onto the Reuter girl again.'

Blamm flicked his wrist and the blind snapped shut. He was emphatic. 'Do. And ask the right questions.'

I buried my photocopies in the depth of my wallet pocket. I looked askance and cast for a first spontaneous spark, a thought, light words in the over-shrouding immensity of what was gathering in the detective sergeant's night. For all that, I couldn't find the right escape.

The big man stood waiting in his damp shirt, a hand pertly on a hip, and saw – in those papers I had Xeroxed – what the deceit of my toil hadn't concealed, in the bulge of my breast pocket. I presented only the disarrangement of my hair, and steely determination in the clamp of my jaw.

'Some water,' I said, and watched for the explosion of rising air as I drained a cupful from the chief inspector's urn. 'And by the way, Blamm, here – you look terrible. Have a tissue…. Ah, no – that box is empty….'

With a flat palm Blamm crisply smacked the desk. 'I'm watching,' he said. 'Closely.'

I begged anyone – a night cleaner, anyone – to enter, and take the insanity out of this. Then that big man sat down and swung a leg free.

'Okay,' I said, and hoped it implied I had entered his rulings, now that he wanted to make it his job to 'classify', to identify a 'type', to reference the world not through the middle path of defeated English liberalism, but according to popular nostrums.

'You know how I hate to theorise,' Bello quipped. His head jerked back. Something twitched at the corners of his mouth – not a smile, quite. 'It's my humble opinion,' he went on, and stopped. Blamm had found a pencilled note. He looked at his wall clock, then at his watch, then at me, then at his problematic detective sergeant. That spouse of his, framed on his desk, managed a vicarious frown in the tropical half-light, too well acquainted with her husband's late arrivals home, the lost hours, the fever of his timekeeping. She had learned, too – as something I guess, in the thunder of her husband's homecomings – that Matthew Bello's opinions never were humble.

That note he had written to himself, a reminder to get home early. He'd read it a dozen times, and of course hadn't gone home – yet. I smiled, unable to share in the irony of that observation. He went on, with felicitous unconcern, as to *why* he must get home – some business with a man from Kenton, a roofer. It seemed in the vast cosmic scheme of things a practical joker had put Seamus O'Cleary here on planet Earth to unhinge the un-blissful domestic life of Bob and Betty Blamm.[14] Seamus inspected the ridge tile that had got itself dangerously loose in the storm, as Blamm had asked him to do, but then slipped awkwardly. O'Cleary wasn't hurt, only shaken, and was sent home, and immediately Blamm's wife picked up the phone.

The chief inspector, in the wave of sympathy Bello and I sent out for the poor woman at home, instructed his detective sergeant to take a second look at Staverton – that far from innocent prey to the disenchantments of suburbia. Mark the occasion. On the descent of that ridge tile, then the crash and tinkle, a glasshouse monthly had found its way to the floor, having fallen from the hands of Mrs Blamm, so now at last the chief inspector, hooking an arm in his jacket, was on his way out. Then only a head, a long arm, a briefcase were visible round the door.

'Just get more on Staverton,' he said, departing.

I watched at the window for his car. I waited for Bello to go. Then I rummaged through the chief inspector's papers.

<h1 style="text-align:center">24</h1>

Was I being allowed outdated information? I suspected so when according to what gems I had plundered, I had Staverton's occupation as hospital porter. I out-sat my welcome in Outpatients, where after an hour hidden behind my daily paper that subterfuge proved unnecessary. The last page I read rattled with celebrity gossip from the pen of its resident wit, his *nom de guerre* Rodolphe. Monsieur Rodolphe carried a baggage of English aphorism, as I found from his trip to the theatre, where no debutant could truly tread the boards till able to peel and eat a tangerine in the style of the leading man he had just borne witness to – and so on.

The paper fell to my knees in rumples. I gazed down at the photograph of a US diplomat collapsing into the cross-eyed inspection of a Havana cigar, as that in turn suffered its first Cubist disassembly. It tried, it didn't keep its shape. I looked up. A physiotherapist, a Ruth Eastley-Something – for so read the fleeting double barrel of her name badge – had walked from Orthopaedics and waved a swollen tennis ace out through the exit. Had he mastered that stick? Lean! Lean to the left!

With still no sign of Staverton, I would have to ask PC Rudge where *did* he work?

When, later, we met, Rudge had the flat of his hands pressed to the crop of his crown. I began my questions. He chortled over spillage from a discarded cup of coffee. Staverton, he said, was a hotel skivvy – the Green Parakeet – not far from a bookshop owned and run by someone I knew, whose name was Lawcom. Lawcom was an Orientalist. His shop was a haven – so yes, I knew the Parakeet. I would find Staverton running errands – on Wednesdays it was Moon's Market, Chinatown. Business-wise, the Parakeet was owned and run by an Anglo-Sino couple, whose duotone, chanted mostly at the chef, insisted on good relations East with West. It was a conference hotel, which one day a week treated its delegates to authentic Chinese cuisine.

So to Wednesday, and Chinatown. Almost immediately I bumped into people I knew, not least the bank branch manager whose car I had once seen impounded. He had hired and clung tightly to a Japanese working girl, who showed him the way to an upper-floor boudoir, in a maze of brazen-looking shop fronts.

Moon's was a glass and poppy red façade, on the east side of a brightly oranged precinct. I had tried to get discreetly out of the way, when abruptly that banker above, hot in his short-sleeved shirt, doubled back and brushed against my shoulder, in a sudden change of heart. In the window was a hanging fowl, and no sign of Staverton. The banker, who refused to step aside (he knew it, but couldn't place my face), was on the point of an expletive. A first semi-eff lived a brief life, lost its shape, and dissolved. He strode off to the next corner quadrant, once more magnetised at the prospect of rentable human parts, eyeing each sunny intersection, and this time went in pursuit of the pale flesh, the red hair, the unbuttonable seams of a girl of sixteen, no older. When he accosted, she shook her head.

A man with a stiff back and a wisp of chestnut hair in a whirl round an abscess on his crown dropped a can of lychees. It rolled listlessly over the threshold of Moon's, where he bent to the full revelation of his outgrowth. He got up. He brushed the dandruff from the lapels of his blazer, which was shabby and blue. He looked left, turning right. It brought him, apologetic, into contact with my shoulder. That's okay – and anyway I needed postage stamps, and shambled into a tiny confectioner's. I had grown weary under the psychological weight of last quarter's bills, the full set – phone, gas, electric.

For reasons as follow, I never got those stamps. A street vendor, in sandalled unsocked feet, blocked my path, hawking his newspaper – at that moment for me exclusively. He sported a neatly trimmed beard, pared to the roots. The time was noon. His subject, resurgent fascism. On his stall he'd set out a collection of coloured stickers. I tried to move on, having not yet abandoned those stamps, and managed only to position myself in the full onslaught of his volleys (he addressed *me* – 'Yes you sir!'). In the clangour, with its barbed headline scratching at my ears, I'd suddenly got a headache. Should I get some analgesics?

I watched the ghoul of my reflection, fluctuating, cramped, thinly etched in outline, an innocent glassed in a tapestry of window ads. All this time my tie had been hanging inside out. The lining, ardent in the shiny black of its arrowhead, fringed the enlarged D of a soap powder. Just while I caught the giveaway price, a swinging hand, a plumpish pectoral, then a nebulous ring of elastic, then the ponytail it gathered from Staverton's hair – these also reflected themselves. He was here for his bean sprouts.

I formed a half-eff of my own at the foam and wrath and cacophony of that purveyor on his soapbox. I asked how it was I had allowed myself into a shady underworld of work, so unlike my friend Lawcom, whose life had taken a more pacific turn (that was even the case in our student life, Lawcom about to graduate in Semitic studies).[15] His purview has since spread west from the Levant, and east to Beijing, and he is never far from one of his Waley translations. It has placed his life in a valley of green moss and abundant bamboo, a calm retreat I hankered after helplessly.

To my left, in K'un Mo's Garden, my eyes roved up the pilasters and across the lintel, their ideograms newly touched in silver – cranes in flight, bright icy pools, blossoms, people in a squall. And look, there's Staverton, crossing the road to Moon's....

I forgot the stamps. I forgot the analgesic. Two pale streaks of occidental sunshine formed as smears in the thick pebble of his lenses. They were little mincing steps that carried him along. There was added, as a part of that movement, the girlish toss of his ponytail. I followed him into Moon's, at a distance. Inside I weighed two tins. I earnestly considered, a bean or a fish soup?

As he made to leave he saw he'd overlooked an item on his list, and turned abruptly. I waited, then followed him out, surprised at the happy bounce softening his gait. He turned south, dodging a deep black ordure fronting a fruit stand, a freshly manufactured left-hand swirl. I hung back, and was immediately approached. Did I want a girl? Er well no. In that moment Staverton disappeared through a plain white door.

It was firmly shut when I reached it. A few frilly knick-knacks framed themselves in the adjoining shop front, where flakes of green paint peeled from the timbers. In the window a life-size dolly, with a sultry, broad-lipped smile – a vulvar pink – belied her mummification in the endless removal of one last garment. Had I got money (the perennial jangle of coins)? The despair of my wallet – these days a model of stoicism – said no. Could I write a cheque? A muscular doorman, with arms folded, and wearing a tuxedo – he too seemed to say no. There was a half-blocked sign on the closed door – FREELOVE's – and below that the legend: FOR ALL YOUR ATTACHMENTS. I went in, expecting the hum of low lights, Perspex fitments, starry hangings, a lot of plastic. The door closed quickly, and here in a concrete yard I found only a dark man squatting, his hands to the raised head of a spaniel. I sidestepped, but the man, who stood and palmed the strain in his back, inadvertently got in my way, having tied those canine ears in a handkerchief (a sling for the jaw, a knot to the crown). It had a mournful look of dentistry. I said hello. The man smiled, nodding at, and through, a whitewashed arch. 'That way,' he said. The spaniel stood, bobbing its tail, wanting to walk, or to talk, or to tell me something new. I thought of Blamm, for should that dog disappear, or go missing, in his mind that would surely be linked with Staverton.

I walked through the arch. A cavern with a counter was managed by a blonde. She – in a malaise – wore one of Freelove's tightly fitting shirts. Lethargically she showed me a list of credit cards Freelove's accepted.

Downstairs, a damp tide had swept through the crumbling plaster. I sneezed. Large-handed suddenly, my newly huge knuckles pulsed through my pockets, reaching for a tissue – old, compressed, and suddenly remembered. A salty brightness, as counter to the violet throb of a strobe, squared the walls, which to the contrary were knobby when touched. They withered away in the revolving shafts of light, which intensified. In a front seat a youngish man had already unbuckled his belt. There was a stench of human sweat. On stage in her leather camisole a leggy brunette, with her two props – a whip and a high stool – tossed back her head – in a lash and thunder of her thighs. A pool of red velvet lit the spot she occupied. The boy with his belt off – a not so random volunteer – shuffled from his seat, where he'd left his jacket. He couldn't wipe away a sheepish grin. Nor could those milky orbs, his buttocks, conceal themselves, his trousers now ankled, as the lights turned again – making this, only a chance copulation, just slightly too methodical.

I reported much of this to Matthew Bello.

25

Matthew Bello asked me to report it to Blamm.

26

Blamm by contrast enjoyed more wholesome pursuits, getting out whenever he could to the shale of the south coast – not necessarily on weekends. He sailed. One of his barrister friends, with a yacht, was someone he skippered for. This, on his return to work, gave to his long stride through London's clammy heat the outdoor man's athletic look. The sign was his leathery sheen, enhanced – the chief inspector's all-year tan – which had a depth and an alien glow, and which, he complained, didn't always signify robust good health – not when those allergies had got the upper hand.

27

With a hint of vengeance, Professor Dark urged caution. If Blamm refused to give us quality information, why should *we* furnish *him*? 'Anyway,' he said, 'it's not up to us to do their work for them. By the way how's that training document?'

I wished he hadn't asked. To be frank, those earlier invasions had begun to develop a much fuller life, which I couldn't now put down to a fault with the word processor. Nor was this the work of a hacker, since I'd disconnected from the network and now used a stand-alone PC. Was there a creeping virus?

'I'm afraid the news isn't good,' I said. 'Due to technical problems I've had to switch to different hardware, which has put me behind.'

'Well just don't neglect it. I'd like to see something soon. I'm giving Blamm a ring. Try and get him to co-operate.'

28

You'd interpret the extent of Blamm's misfortunes in one of two ways. First, as a procession of medics – men and the occasional woman – quietly calmed by the years of priestly self-assurance, who shared a poor sad smile when the chief inspector (you'd think a rational man, yet finding his case hopeless) was ready to consider any unlikely remedy. He was looking at New Age crystals. Numbness in his hearing plunged our quippish jokes low on the horizon, with Bello – especially Bello – muffled in his laughter. In the floor space between us, in the illusory light-and-dark of his corridors, Blamm invoked the grey lines and horseshoe of his south-coast bays, choice locations where he'd never been known to sneeze. His mind wasn't completely on the job, understandably.

His other form of palliation was the sweep or dab of tissues into those tired-looking eye sockets, where the fog blurring his vision wasn't easily dispelled.

He'd wearied palpably of Bello chasing round in circles, who today rose helically round his object, the detective sergeant trying to approximate the rise in viscosity – that factor critical to his boss's mood – by the volume of mucus in his binful of paper hankies. Bello's witticisms fell flat, his jokes about Staverton, his jokes about canines, with Blamm's persistent malady having spread to places no one suspected. He only now mentioned his hatred of dogs, and for that matter cats, whose fur made him wheeze. He went on to tell us how his wife, with a bundle of women's weeklies, had ordered him to read their resident GPs, whose wise words were a help to countless thousands apparently.

29

A succession of progress meetings with my own boss, Dark—

How did Blamm seem now?

Well, having offered him – and having offered Matthew Bello too – fruit of my recent toil – propped under those Chinese logos, or tailing their suspect through the markets of Soho…. We'd got no farther than prurient quips on a straight-legged Staverton, emerging through that white outer door, blinking. Like me he'd passed that madly hungry dog, whose checked face wiped its bowl clean. That constituted one other flaw in the Rudge theory, for I knew there had been, in Staverton's string bag, the doggy lure of a tin of coconut rolls, bait that Staverton didn't employ. If Blamm's department wanted to proceed intuitively, these were my findings.

And the training document?

Well. Um.

30

What's happened to the training document is this. Some rogue hand, preferring the imprecision of fiction, has twisted practically every detail of the case. It seems I've been given a name, which is just about the only thing I've managed to excise, in what is becoming an alarming rate of redrafts. Also you know how writers of fiction can't avoid certain devices: it seems this one views overt romantic touches as important, and insists I am falling for Frankie Reuter, which I utterly refute. No single exchange with Blamm goes by (to him he assigns another ridiculous name)[16] without casting him as court jester.

You begin to see, this is not something I can possibly release to Dark (Dark!).

31

Again, Dark has telephoned Blamm, and again Blamm (the tight-lipped Blamm) twitches in the first vague apprehension of a smile (oh hand him that jester's garb, that quartered red and yellow). What in fact I provoked was rage in the chief inspector's brows, a toxic puce that has coloured his complexion. I held up a palm, smiling.

'Now don't get me wrong!' I said, trying to back off.

'Why yes, don't take it like that,' said Bello, supportive.

But the chief inspector was hotter round the neck. He stood up. He towered to the ceiling on his long flannelled legs. Not so cleverly, I allowed him the last word, and somehow separated its sense from its thunder – that this was no good, no good at all.... It wasn't on.

'I absolutely insist,' he said to Bello, 'you bring that man in! I'll question him myself.'

That, as ultimatums go, was not the one I'd predicted for Detective Sergeant Bello...

32

...and now I too have an ultimatum, with the persuasive thud of Dark's tightly closed fist in its hard descent on the desktop. 'Adrian,' he said, 'you've held out long enough. Now you might be a perfectionist...'

'I am, yes.'

'...and can't bear to publish a document until you think it's finished.'

'Exactly so.'

'But....'

Big but.

'I want to see a draft training document first thing tomorrow morning...on my desk....'

What am I to do? The more I work on this, the more I lose control....

33

Somehow I feigned the condemned man's gaiety, a last grasp on life as cartoon entertainment, and descended from the kerb. I'm sober now, and remember the terrifying ease of my tread, how without effort or apparent weight I spiralled down to the Club Sportif – a low-lit basement with tinted table tops. The time was six – according to the bar clock. Joey, who wore a saffron necktie, held the polished stem of a brandy glass in the scrubbed tips of a thumb and forefinger. He'd seen me – of this I am sure – but raised that receptacle up to the lights in the ceiling. A frown, then mobility to the tight grey curls at his temples, were cue for a rim he would have to wipe again. Out came his starched napkin.

Here, for the natural pause of his ritual, I hopped up on a padded stool, and lounged.

There were murmurs behind me from a corner table and two big men hunched and shirt-sleeved. The first was damp at the underarms. Joey, fussing with his cocktail shaker, still wasn't ready, so back I glanced. The two shared a bottle of spring water. In their tumblers was a remnant of crushed ice, yellow in the glow of lemon rind. Systematically, the second scratched the small of his back with the awkward probe of his ballpoint, then pulled at the lampshade over their table. A soft pastel light diffused itself over their papers. I imagined, in the hushed privacy of their conversation, a brewing city scandal, a mortgage or insurance scam. Both went quiet. Efficiently, those papers were whisked into the void of an executive case.

At last, with his white grin and cuffs, my barman finally lit on the parched earth here on my island (glad you could come). 'What'll it be, Mistah Fixt?'[17] I remembered his car lights full on in the sunshine, his driver's eccentricities, though had nothing to say about that. The vodka, scotch, Martini rosso, all those big bottles inverted to his rear, fell under my roving eye. I shut my mouth in a tight thin line. Then foolishly I allowed him one more distraction. In an impossible contortion, his big candid eyes, rolling in his round unclouded face, watched the light in mine, yet caught the sweep of someone's sleeve in the kitchen, behind and over his shoulder. When I still said nothing he called for a tray of tortilla chips, keeping up that grin. Somehow I got off the point, caught, and momentarily confused, in the glare from the cooler. This I was certain had been moved from its last arrangement under the TV set. That in turn brought me to a po-faced, made-up newscaster, in funerary black, but jaunty nevertheless on the latest slide in the pound (*against* a basket of currencies). I decided on a fancy lager, with its snazzy label and Mississippi steamboat, its bottle square at the shoulders, the neck long, the stopper white. With the tortilla salt sticks also arrived. I insisted Joey pour. He put down a frilly coaster, meticulously.

As I now know, this was the year an Italian diva was touring with her swansong. I was to witness one last well-wisher, who try as she might couldn't get to Earls Court in appropriate style – all while I sipped my lager. Her flat was in Rothschild Mansions, where her dressing table overlooked a lawn with swings and plane trees. That was the problem, she said. She got up on a bar stool, just as my two fraudsters left (one had gone off for a haircut). How could she know, putting on her tints – a rouge, a blossom, a midnight eye shadow – with no one at her shoulder to warn of a team of truckers, one good and one bad man, who lifted her sporty run-around onto a trailer? 'After all, I *am* a permit holder!' Joey, a forearm to the bar, stuck with his grin, and told her how seldom it cut any ice, as now she appealed only to him. She'd double-parked because, what else could she do?

Good Joey got her a dry Martini and planted the phone at her elbows, then dialled for a cab. A tide of froth slid down my empty glass. He guessed my mood (ah yes, another if you please!). I thumbed away the heavy stopper of bottle number two – a sober, translatable object, still within my reckoning. I saw in the opera-goer the first signs of age, in the loose flesh of her upper arms, and how her grip on the handset had no effect on that. I could think of nothing, no friendly quip, and was struck only that her deepish monotones curled upwards at the ends. I fixed my eyes on the diamond glitter, the moving coruscation of her evening dress, and at last had something to say. I quaffed – in a sense inspired – but was put off suddenly. One of those city mobsters returned through the louvred door, a man cropped at the temples, and damp at the crown. He asked for the phone, then hung back, on seeing it in use. She turned her head away, sifting her one blonde streak in the cut of her bob. I twitched at her perfume. I sat up straight with my glass. She recited couplets, mock heroics, with her catalogue of pleas to the cab company.

Still waiting for the phone, that city gangster unburdened his pockets of change in a corner with the fruit machine. Me? I needed another drink. Then the phone came free, and remained so, for with a line of lime-coloured sevens a volcano of silver oozed from the fruit machine. Now I *would* have another. I waited. Joey put the phone under the bar, and flicked with his napkin where it had sat, and fussed with a hundred other things.... I poured, thinking it might be my last. Then that rattle again, a cascade of coins, and huzzahs, and the jackpot almost. In the euphoria scraps of conversation diminished to a hum. I lost myself, in a low throb, and was warmed at the ears. Amber, a velvety red, an egg-yolk yellow – these were the dabs I eyed in Joey's palette – bottles all doubled in the narrow band of the mirror behind the bar.

I found a table, one all my own under the brassy blades of a ceiling fan, and was ready for a peppered steak. Joey crushed ice – my ice – but someone – the cabby – buzzed at the outer door. The two spent a few moments vying in sibilants over the intercom. Result: one fine lady left her Martini for the Earls Court opera. The city partner (partner B) returned, his mop of hair intact but holding a golf ball, and got no sense from partner A (the other). A had got too close to the jackpot. B called for the phone, which delayed my cocktail again (vodka, orange juice, a splash of Galliano, just a hint of ice). B tapped out a long number, and at last settled back. Surely, I thought, time to loosen my tie, as I caught its reflection, and plunged my gaze into the darkness of my table top. Watch...watching...the wide sweep of the blades above. Wumph. A breeze as it flattened the bounce in my hair.

The cocktail came, but by now I was dreaming. Five, six, a dozen more people took tables or propped up the bar, though I was less preoccupied with them. I had found, in the wall hangings, the ease of an earlier world – a tailed, hatted gentleman, aloft on a penny-farthing, not much concerned at the falling rain. I snatched at my drink – I added another, and another – more vodka, orange, Galliano – and somewhere let the menu slip to the floor, where a procession of smart city shoes scuffed it, or kicked it in a corner. I lost count and overlooked the time, or didn't care, only guessing my condition. Folds of blue cigar smoke swirled, hung, got wrapped round a hundred bobbing heads, then with the cold shrieks of someone's laughter I detected the mingling odours of two tactless aftershaves. I slumped back in my cane chair, long edged from my table by two robust men and a loud woman, big, as I'd heard, in the boxing game. Insanely, my eyes went round and my head tried to follow the blurred circles of the ceiling fan.

My shirt fell open, and after the heat – minutes, hours, I don't know – and before he strode the vacated floor, I watched the barman Joey, who was holding the phone. A and

B had closed a property deal – 'That's rat, Add-ri-ann, prop-ah-ty' – but then getting a connection and holding up a muddy palm he stemmed my abuse. He talked, and immediately swam out of focus. The saffron necktie, fringed. The white of his cuffs. The velvety texture of his waistcoat buttons.

The next cab to call was mine.

34

So you can see how well I have learned my mantra. I am Fixt. I am Adrian Fixt.[18]

35

The interview room, one day later. A low shaft of sunshine came in at the meshed window, and struck brightly on the dampness of the wall opposite. Blamm, in the role of tormentor, placed down a packet of cigarettes, deliberately on the table. They were English, low tar, were not the Gallic brand I had seen in the suspect's garret. At times the chief inspector had such a tough streak. He explained, and did so carefully, that smokes, for now, were prohibited. This Bello confirmed, stepping from the shadows.

Staverton sat tight-lipped. His face and a denim shoulder caught the light. He was sweating, but clear-headed. I, I'm afraid, was not (I mean I wasn't clear-headed), and now regretted all those cocktails. Regrettable too, I had sat at my window till well after three, re-crossing my feet on the sill. Those feet being sockless, the total sensation was pleasantly cold. I had poured endlessly a sickly liqueur from a silver bottle, as I clung to the last shreds of impossible ideals. Those – whatever they were – involved the occasional sweep of car lights in and around the box junction, or rare silhouettes in the blind across the street, all of which were important to scrutinise, or so it seemed. The rest of my neighbourhood – that was a blur. I admit I am losing my grip.

Blamm aimed his fist at the table top, so that the packet, a full one, jumped in the air. Outside in the yard, someone dropped a spanner on the asphalt, and this – for the duration of its tinkle – lit up a blue electric spark in the fog of my eyes. Blamm turned his back, to the suspect and to me. I took out my notebook and leafed through several pages, though shrank finally from its convolutions. Blamm spun round dramatically, all fire and malicious teeth (it was, you see, how angry a man could be). 'Come on,' he said, 'just what do you think you're up to!' This was Bello's cue, in an effort to be nice and good, to catch the suspect with his eyebrows raised, mouth puckered. When, croaking, he found his voice, it was subterranean (a first symptom of 'flu). What he intended, a sympathetic *What the chief inspector really means—*, instead sounded bored and disrespectful.

Today Staverton had looped his ponytail in an ochre-coloured band. He had a plastic carrier, into which he had slipped a comb and a paperback – reading matter I later inquired after. I retreated to Blamm's peripheral vision and folded my arms, aware, vaguely, that in turning to the light the slow, deliberate, animate man had merged with the inanimate white of his shirt. I supposed this marked a new line in washing powder, one perhaps less abrasive on his rash. He did not sneeze (though certainly thundered).

Bello's response (to the thunder) was well-rehearsed and a salve – a soothing word or two – which in theory should have had our suspect confide in him or me. Yet that wasn't a workable proposition. Staverton, too over-indignant, and a great deal of steam to his lenses, sounded off pertly. Here were some of his observations. 'Come off it, Blamm! I know my rights! Anyway what's the charge?' He looked tired, but not intimidated, and calmly wiped his glasses. I glanced at the tattered book in his bag and asked what he was reading. 'It's Gothic,' he said – and that was it. Gothic, horror, sci-fi. Oh – and a bestseller.

I turned to the wall and wondered where all Bello's brightness had gone, his colours, his defiant quips for the endless purgatory of routine police work. If he kept his thoughts private that was because, ostensibly, he gave the chief inspector's victims hope. At least, that was as Blamm calculated, a sure method of turning one small error into an escalation – if not now then later – supremely confident of an end point in the conviction he was after. I ran my gaze up and along the sooty brickwork, and again down, where at the seam with the concrete floor movement had taken place and water had seeped in. Blamm said something in an undertone – which I didn't catch. I felt one ear lobe warmer than the other, and a cheek that had reddened. Bello moved more fully into the light. In the greyness of my hair a nimbus began to glow, or so it seemed. Then it was clear what Bello had to do, and for whom.

'You can go,' he said, turning once more, where he beheld a limpid Staverton.

'But don't worry,' said Blamm. 'You'll be back.'

36

Dark, as I had probably expected, summoned me back to the office. There had been no sign of my document on his desk that morning. I alluded vaguely to my difficulties, but delayed the inevitable in saying I believed the Department had suffered a breach – an infiltrator. He immediately got on the phone to our technical people.

'Keep chipping away at Blamm,' he said, his hand over the mouthpiece.

'That's not easy,' I told him. 'He affects to be helpful by allowing me to witness unimportant interviews, but gives me nothing at all on the Solomon case.'

37

I can't say I find it amusing that the chief inspector, a man wise to the flaws of our passions, could construct on the basis of a hangover – that pale throb I had at the temples – a loss of self-esteem. This was a term he used more than once, during a turgid, headmasterly pep talk, directed more at Bello than at me, though he did mean me.

It had the character of formal interlude, and an unexpected conciliatory tone. The talk took place in his office, where one of his minions, probably barked at over the internal phone, had positioned a whiteboard. It came with a squirter, a roll of heavy tissue, and marker pens – tools that the chief inspector had no inhibition in the use of. In fact, when he'd managed to get both Bello and me obediently seated, I detected in the chief inspector – well, what shall we say – *relish*. Steadily the accumulation of ink strokes emphasised his salient points.

On first walking in I had no inkling of what was to follow. I found him seated, while Bello, as always, paced. Or rather Blamm was slumped. There was something – I can't say what – in the tired glaze of his eyes. Was this one of those odd cool days, when he was clear of his sneeze, had broken free of his pink stigmata?

In these new warm wads of relaxation he adjusted the rest of his chair, and folded out its arms. His great shoveller's palms cradled the back of his head. He assumed, which did not come unnaturally to him, the absolutes of monarchy, with a range of modern facilities, feet up on a tidy desk.

He said he thought our whole approach had become too bookish, though he meant journalistic: in the next breath he talked about the West and its press. For myself there's a grain of truth in this, though the pestilence *I* suffer, this whole fiction at another's hand, is something I neither shape nor approve of. To Bello he ascribed tracts of social theory derived from the paper he read (probably *The Guardian*) – an insult the detective sergeant bore stoically.

Blamm added quickly how much he sympathised with Matthew Bello in the management reports we were expected to read, huge tomes suffered in tablets of A4, an excrescence in semi-literacy which, as a thorough pro, Blamm claimed to absorb. 'The reality is,' he said, 'ours is a world of sloppy memoranda.'[19]

'I can't imagine,' Bello said, 'this is why you asked us here. But since you've raised the subject....'

'I am, Matthew, listening.'

'Acknowledgement of intelligent life in newspaper offices isn't necessarily perverse.'

'Did I say it was?'

I can't be sure of conveying what followed in anything like my appreciation of it. My personal notebook says one thing, these ceaseless draft documents another. If I could have my say for one moment, I would plead the case of Detective Sergeant Bello. What I find he ceaselessly questions is the things we accept as lying outside our interest. That sets dangerous limits.

Blamm did not like that at all, but then having to answer the phone he didn't elaborate. Bello tried something else, though not as I show, or attempt to show, as now we enter a narrative sphere I am powerless to wrest from my rival—

'I predict histories of hindsight as a consequence of doing things in the way we do them.' As you can see, my shadow likes his rhetoric.[20]

With an accidental sweep of the hand, the chief inspector's unsuspecting spouse tilted forward, and on a cushion of air fell gently onto her glass front. This he ignored. He got up, a tall man almost touching the ceiling. He put his hands behind his back. He paced to the window. He inspected the Venetian blind.

'You should know better,' he said, 'than that.' He tugged at the cord, and left us to guess, in the onomatopoeic rush of fins, what cynical frown was thumbed into the fixed stone of his face. When he turned, his glare was icy. No doubt he thought Bello was being sententious.

Then, behind those umbral bars, in a slant on the floor, a wall, the cage of Blamm's desk, his gravitas shut itself away. He grinned. He would have spoken, but just then Ms Flint came in, a temp he had brought off the High Street. 'Your report,' she said, adjusting the aloof angle of her glasses, frames a shade of vermilion matching her blouse and shoes. Blamm, as everyone fully understood, preferred old Miss Chadwick, at this time attending a bridge convention. He bent himself forward, stiffly from the waist. His captive wife, who was still facedown, felt the breeze on the back of her neck, while a new report from Rudge – orthographically a nightmare, despite the efficient Ms Flint – she tossed down on the big man's jotter. Ms Flint closed the door behind her.

The chief inspector snatched at his black marker pen and levered off the cap. He turned attention to a case one in his team (and not Bello) had cleared up in the previous week. Pointedly, this was his first *exemplum*. What took shape under the seamless gestures of his hand – a ragged myrmidon – was his implied criticism that Detective Sergeant Matthew Bello did not conduct his business in the same methodical way as his unnamed colleague. 'What I'm saying,' Blamm said, 'is that upwards of a dozen witnesses had reported a ruffian in armed retreat from a security van. You remember?' Those investigating, operating on a hunch, felt sure one of the twelve must know the thief's identity. Blamm drew an oblong with wheels representing the van. '*I* have a hunch, too, Matthew. I think your Staverton is hiding something.'

I see it as a fluke on his part that this turns out to be right.

By now the whole rigmarole had assumed rainbow proportions, the chief inspector dabbing in new details in violet and cerise. Then he grew bored, attacking it with water and wiping it away. With a flourish he binned the tissue. He turned to Bello. His tone, still benign, dropped a semitone – a slide marked 'confidential'. 'Now,' he said. 'I would like to show how *I* think *you* think.'

He drew – this time in bottle green – a saintly circle, not quite closed at the top, an imperfection representing tufts of hair. He dotted in four points within that circle, its eyes, a nose, a whistling mouth. This was Bello's face of man – 'man' meaning *Homo sapiens*, millennial-style. A squeak and a downward vertical stroke ran the neck, chest and waist into one. Four jointed lines attached the limbs.

'You, Matthew, think of man like this.'

I tried to follow, and watched him add – now with a dangerous red – atmospheric lines with arrowheads. These he explained were external pressures, and placed Bello firmly in the environment lobby. According to that, the world, the inexorable world, determined what an individual life would be. His *coup de grâce* consisted of a second, and larger-looking skeleton, livelier in its dance. *Its* arrows were centrifugal – for here was humanity seen as it was – as a conscious agent, and here with the pair he'd chosen was the verifying glow of science. I don't say I entirely disagree, yet one might just as well abandon rats to a shoebox, in which some levers *do* and others *don't*, on a chance depression, serve tasty little tidbits.

The big man sighed and came down from his plateau, and rested on his hypotenuse. Quietly he crossed his ankles over that latest of Rudge's reports. Then came that thoughtful way he had of fisting the left, the right, and the right palm again. I knew, and looked away, how he'd now interlink those ten great digits. Could anticipate the stretch, the straightened arms, finally the cradle for his head, as that supported his gaze, somewhere into the shadows on the ceiling. I looked at his two puppets, playthings in an evolutionary ball game. I asked myself, were they beginning to smirk, as Bello smirked, and to look like him?

Finally Blamm broke the silence, with clichéd allusions to the Darwinian plane he had drawn, and its two types of people on it. Bello started forward, but thought better of it – and didn't take the bait.[21] Blamm went on to say, or repeat, that his men were out there – that his men were his ears and his eyes – were men who knew the deviant life of the street. On what other information could he base his decisions, given that Bello had placed himself outside that arrangement, had conceived the world through the social pressures that made it?

Bello strode to the window, planting his feet oceans apart, doubtless amazed that the plain PC Rudge had somehow penetrated the city's soiled concrete, its glassy front, and had perceived the life pulse of the cosmos, in its seething criminality.

Reserve a fast train, two spare seats, the next waiting liner – there's still a welcome on Fixt's island. A beach, palms, a tower (ivory), heaven's vast timepiece over our heads, and look, down there, at the spangled sea.... Here are the steps. Careful how you climb! And see how smooth!

The earth has a broad horizon.

38

Now. Where did I put my notebook? Ah yes, the kitchen – which is full of steam. And, under the attic window, here is my final draft document – or is it my rival's?[22]

Currently I have a tendency to re-boil the kettle, having thought of tea without ever making it. I have done this on five, six separate occasions. There are definite signs of dilemma, as the clock shows a minute past noon. What has led to these pauses is dumb comprehension at the crude melodrama my co-author cooks up on behalf of Detective Sergeant Bello, but more strikingly the humble PC Rudge. He wants me to accept there is mutual hatred between them. He insinuates that a prejudiced Matthew Bello has studied the PC's CV, with nothing but sneers for his list of leisure pursuits, which are sports, TV and DIY. I am shown evidence of this in a kind of nightmare Hitchcock fairground I have supposedly visited, but have no recollection of (I advise you not to skip this note).[23]

Bello, in graphic detail, told me how he'd got first-hand evidence of Rudge's community rapport and took it to be typical, and asked what *I* thought. He (Bello) was unseen at a newsstand, but only yards away when it happened. Rudge, with a knowing smile, had passed him by, where Bello had queued for his morning coffee and slice of toast. Bello put down the PC's irritability to the exceptional heat, intense even at that time (it was before 9.30). Rudge carried on. He placed himself under the fringed awning of a ladies' salon. On the same pavement, about to have her hair done, was someone Bello knew, a young wife and mother – and recently the target of obscene phone calls. In tow was her bored child, who tugged at her hem. He couldn't get the breeze, because there wasn't one, into his pinwheel, whose vanes were an alternation of cherry, Wedgwood blue, and a milky mustard yellow. His mother said something like, when the wind stirs is a matter of time. For the time one asks a policeman. PC Rudge, whose mood was zealous, stern, was fixed at the jaw, that jaw an uncommunicating oblong. Humourless, he strode into the daylight. He pointed up – into a sky of steely blue, where visible only, either pencil-thin or fluffy, were the white ethereal trails of holiday jets. That was not what he meant. So now he pointed up but not so far, to a weather vane, which, in the form of a cyclist, head down and pedalling madly for the Baltic, was the uppermost adornment on a building and its spire. Below it, in a brick façade, was a pearly clock face, its Roman engravings an ornate I to XII. The boy performed tortuous calculations, which availed him nothing. The clock, as Rudge knew, hadn't worked since Christmas. Its short finger, quaint with curlicues, was stuck fast at XI, in a kind of self-perpetuation of humanity's last uncertain hour. The boy wheeled his arm, which was enough – more than enough – to put a breeze in his tricolour – though time and the wind stood still.

39

I would not have chosen the above example (assuming I *have* a choice), except that Blamm, winding up another of his pep talks – this time without the whiteboard – suggested I might spend a couple of days on well-earned leave. I viewed it with intense suspicion when Professor Dark, at more or less the same time, made the same recommendation. In the meantime my hacker problem had been bounced from Technical to Security. Perhaps I should get back when the dust had settled.

'Oh – I don't think so,' I said.

40

Nevertheless, Professor Dark insisted. 'You'll feel much better.'

41

About this time of year my sister Cecilia escaped the city heat and decamped, still with her workload, to her Kernow estate, a revamped castle in whose extensive grounds were the ruins of a Benedictine priory. It went back to the twelfth century.

'By the way,' said Dark, wishing me *bon voyage*, 'yesterday I spoke with Blamm. One of his men now questions this Reuter person's train times.'

They had found a further witness to Solomon's last journey, which placed him on the train *before* Frankie's.

'Here,' said Dark. 'He's documented it.'

42

I tried to phone Frankie, first from the hum of my office (without success – Miss Reuter was out), then from a street corner (when she'd 'flown' to a meeting), then – third time lucky – from a café. It was lunchtime, when without appetite I left the stale bread and warmish pips of my cheese and tomato sandwich. The purr of her voice told me distantly she was in transit virtually all day – between Victoria, Chiswell Street, Puddle Dock. She could spare five minutes at her flat in Holland Park that evening.

Did I kill time till then? That impostor at my keypad writes that I did, in a lovelorn state. I in fact phoned Cecil (or Cecilia) to say I'd been delayed. Then I studied that latest document from Blamm. Then I took a red crayon to my, or to our, latest draft. None of this of course is varied enough for the fictions of our time, so it's suggested I frittered away an hour or so in Peter Lawcom's shop. Lawcom, as I have previously tried to make clear (I now know unsuccessfully), is a Sinologist. He lectures and writes articles. However, ghostly intervention casts him as an unworried bookshop owner. I am surprised to note my co-author agrees on him as my sole surviving friend from the gloom of our campus years – but goes on to say how predictable it is whenever I call on him. It's a bad day. He greets a long face. He can guess at my fatigue as that affects my pulse, which quickens at the tinkle of his bell. The mat says ONE SMALL STEP. His shop is musty – though as an example of Lawcom's market sense there's a cut-price Mauriac in his bargain box outside. On this occasion we had long cups of coffee and reached perfect agreement on the place of the English civil service, as somewhere in the basement. It meant that when, at about eight, I had reached Reuter's flat, I had dispelled much of the pessimism Dark had earlier made me suffer.

I found Frankie preparing dinner for two – lethally she answered the door wielding a Sabatier, which, when I followed her into the kitchen, was her chosen implement for slicing ripe pears. As something I studied, I can say her hand was at times unmerciful. In the window was a mother-in-law's tongue, and beside that a litre of Claret, part decanted. Two silky rouge candles in an outlandish candelabrum reproduced themselves feebly in the dull polish of a dining table, which I saw across the hall in another room. Beside that, through one other open door, I sifted my glances over a duvet, a double – which alas was not for me to share. I smiled and took out my notebook.

'Your daddy's move go off okay?' I asked.

She sliced chicory on a chopping board. 'A few problems,' she said. An ivory Buddha had gone astray. Had this been set roaming, I joked, when the house, packing itself into tea chests, paraded its counter-philosophy, its ornaments of materialism? A twitch in her thin lower lip challenged the fixed composure of her jaw, though she refused to smile. She took up a garlic press. I considered the shape, a distorted figure-eight, in the microscopic links of the gold bracelet she wore on her wrist, then watched, in the full span of her smallish hands, as they closed on the handles of the press. Three small cloves of garlic collapsed under the whitening pressure of her fists and oozed from the press's pores. A spell, a charm, a piquancy suffused the air. I unclipped my pen.

'Make yourself useful,' she said. It was my job to recover the page she'd lost, a recipe for pear and pecan salad. The book, *Vegetarian Suppers*.

'Ah yes. Page sixty,' I said. 'Oh, clever. The dressing's yours.' It was for her clear skin, her clean blood, this penchant for garlic.

I said I hated being a bore. Our tireless investigators had produced another witness in the Solomon case, 'a man', I said, 'in your line of business' – that's to say the marketing director of a small software firm, whose office was in Reading. 'He states very precisely that at 9.50 he saw Solomon – alive and well of course – in the train he had also caught. He was in a hurry for his Paddington connection.'

There was a problem with timing, when this was the train *before* Frankie's. For one hopeless moment she assumed she was now a suspect. It required assurance. There was no doubt, I said, as to the train Solomon was finally on. It was taken out of service, when the corpse was discovered. We had statements from station officials. One might only speculate. Had Solomon, for example, arranged to meet someone *on* the train, and realising he'd got on the wrong one, got off and waited for the next? Was Frankie certain she had seen no one, at whatever stop, looking in before stepping on – checking for someone there? I had my pen poised over my notebook. Frankie thought, but said no, there was nothing. She was sorry. She segmented an orange.

'That's okay,' I said, and closed and put away my notebook. She cracked an egg in a bowl, then placed a pan of water on the hob. 'I'll keep in touch.' That said, I made no effort to go. She put a hand to her head and ran trembling fingers through the spiky nap of her hair. The tail of her blouse rode up. She eyed the dusty shafts of light across the hall in her bedroom. It was time for her shower, and to get herself dressed for dinner.

I stumbled out, blinking in the crimson light. The last of the sun left a maroon flicker in the leaves where the street was lined with flowering fruit trees. The path from her pillared doorway was paved in a polygonal interlock, where I paused ludicrously, in a belated reflection on how I looked. Jacket not too rumpled. Tie, loose, yes, but straight. Hair oh a little dry – in need of a wash, and a cut. Then of course my shoes, laces broken, knotted together.

I moved on. A cat, a tortoiseshell, arched its ribs and stretched its four limbs, then retracted its claws. I stopped, pursing my lips, rubbing a finger and thumb. The cat shrank down, sleepy again, into the warm contours on the bonnet of an old blue Morris.[24] Higher, in the depths of a bedroom window, a girl with long straight hair brushed at it furiously, making a face. Someone was coming my way – I assumed Frankie's date – youngish, late twenties, in a bottle-green suit, and a yellow tie. His shoes were a ghastly tan. Unmistakably that was a *vin de pays* in one hand, wrapped in pink tissue. The pavement between us diminished. He looked away, or rather downward beneath my feet, where the slabs in a lunacy of straightness made any diversion awkward and unnatural. His glance fell from its target (the target was nonchalance), in a feat of introspection at its worst. Therefore I call on my countrymen to end these conceits, and send our planners back to school. 'Friends, we have got it all wrong!' So I mused on our civic sensibilities, insisting on the tearing up of crested documents, that tonnage delivered up ritually onto the desks of our city fathers, men in whose monstrous vocabulary are the words 'approval' and 'ratify'. It's all an affront to my best ideals in geometry,[25] what with their plumbs, perpendiculars, and all those wrong right angles.

I cast around hopelessly, from the luxuriant tortoiseshell, to the dark panes where the girl had worked up static in her hair, and finally to him, the focus of all those parallel lines, bent to a single point. He was sallow, Italianate, and wore his short hair longer to the collar and ears than did Frankie. His stride was long and athletic. He stepped aside.

I shall write it down, one cool evening, with a breeze in my curtains, and the moon – a suffused red or clementine – rising up over the dark crowded plateau of my rooftops. I shall call up the thin vapours of the night, and shall have my pen ready – here in the cone of my desk lamp, over the pages I abuse with a hundred crossings out. Perhaps in some far-off age, boffins gathered in a backroom shall unearth my untidy scrawl, and remote from the cold metallic surfaces of the world's new brightness – a place of winking satellites – shall piece together these little broken bits of written lumber. Who, they'd demand, would wear such a tie, a faded yellow? And this patch of fabric, a frayed bottle green: our friends from the rag trade attest to a two-piece, a man's suit, circa the 1980s.... A ring, found with a shirt stud, seems large even for a man's hand (we consider this an ostentation). Then take this leather belt, looped in a man's trousers: elegant, yes. But the watch, and its strap – are these not the property of a deep-sea diver, which have somehow got mixed up? I, Adrian Fixt, am never likely to know. I noted in passing, a few yards from that old blue Morris, the pale green pyjama-stripe of a computer printout, tucked under his arm. I reiterate, I deplore these straight lines, as I envisaged Frankie's romantic evening over a hex dump, and chuckled.

Oh, and by the way, that computerese was something I subsequently learnt from a man called Dunne.[26]

43

Yesterday, in a pause from these reconstructions, I returned to that phantasy above, its object Frankie Reuter, and rounded off with an hour at the supermarket. I had acquired a *Vegetarian Suppers*, and now needed fillo pastry. You might question my rationale, yet I counted on Frankie's sympathy. I had the threat of removal from the Solomon case, the plan being to spend more time on the training document. In light of that hiatus, would she now relax our over-formal link, and sit, if only once, at my dinner table? Yes, it was makeshift – and rickety – one I had picked up in the Grays Inn Road, which made me think suddenly how doomed a plan it was. Still, I could not help project cool Frankie Reuter, *en brosse*, with a smile, in a soft glow of candlelight, cradling a first aperitif.

I got to know a man at the corner delicatessen. His shop uniform was a dirty apron with vertical blue stripes. His hands were large and ungainly, were awkward with the bacon slice. In stature he was short, and squat, with a padding of flesh that oozed from zips, buttons and seams. The cherry of his grin was permanent. The dimples, the fixed distensions about his eyes, chin and jowls, went with his sixth-form humour. When not at his counter he sat in the recess of his backroom, drinking tea on an upturned crate, or demolishing ham and pickle sandwiches. I sometimes overheard him in scurrilous phone conversations. I was once in a queue behind two sisters, who shared in his humour. One was giggly and thin. The other showed fortitude, not at peace with her waistline. I knew them, from house calls I had made over recent months. I even recalled, in its pendular regularity, the capacious tick of their drawing room, with its collection of clocks. They had the ground-floor flat in a grand, deteriorating corner house, and ran a colonial regime re lawns and the privet hedge. Whole teams, a hired succession of boys, had learned how to mow and cut.

I told myself to stay outside, and having examined the deep serrations in the wheel of his showpiece, a Saxby pie, I was better advised to go back home. Instead I blundered in, intent on Feta cheese for the *hors-d'oeuvre* I had in mind. The two sisters dislodged the soft silver fluffing of my cloud. The first had her mind un-made-up on tinned *champignons* – which she took up, put back, took up from a low shelf. She remembered my face, wrongly, as one that belonged to the force, and right there out loud deplored the shocking state of police inertia, in view of all those missing cats and dogs in our neighbourhood. How many more were going to disappear? Foolishly I protested. 'First someone needs to report a crime, but that hasn't happened.' That burst of outspokenness plunged my act of purchase into a scowl of embarrassment, as now I learned that only yesterday a sympathetic PC Rudge had found more fuel for his theories – his Satanic practices, here in our midst. Did I know the pensioner whose long rear garden abutted their own? Well, he'd had a pane cut from his glass extension. In the blue night a gloved hand had eased in and lifted the door latch. A trace of pig's liver and, with it, two spots of blood in the soiled nap of a carpet tile – did I want more evidence than that? It had entered Rudge's notes as Rex, an un-regal, sloppy Alsatian, plainly duped into a stroll outdoors.

'Okay,' I said, and turned to that jolly porker at his counter. 'I need seven ounces of Feta cheese. Got any?'

44

I have abandoned any thought of that dinner invitation, and am looking carefully at my notes. What begins to take my interest is that two-day pleasure trip to the grassy castle heights of Fixt Senior– she who exercises endless fascinations over my boss, Professor Dark. To some extent, there is reciprocal appeal: Fixt Senior, in the odd hours she sets aside for leisure, is intrigued by the world of espionage he operates in, and is addicted to spy fiction.

I took my file and other things to study on the train to Penzance. There was, inexorably, a mix-up with seats, a frail spinster having reserved the same one I had – both non-smoking. Then with unforeseen staffing problems the bar was closed. On the other hand, three taxis vied for my cash at Penzance, though the one I plumped for was reluctant when I named my destination, Castle Fixt, summer retreat of that successful Eighties girl, who had moved from hose to investment, and saw no contradiction with her faxes and screens and her medieval chambers.

I was, she had said on the phone, 'welcome to spend a few days', yet for that whole afternoon I failed to pin her down. A servant dusting the porcelain led me across the hall, that place with its stags' heads, suits of armour, timber balustrades, and with galleries overhead. I thought I detected a presence at my heels as I browsed the tooled leather tomes in the great cavern of her library. I heard footsteps fading over a cobbled square, though looking out and leaning over the casement I saw no one. At five in the afternoon, her manservant – elderly and local-sounding, in a black suit and carpet slippers – said he'd received instructions to boil me an egg and serve a pot of tea. Could I make my way to the dining room? 'She will receive you shortly' – was the reply I got to the repeated question, 'When is Miss Fixt available?' The dining room – when eventually I found it – was a conference suite, having a long solid table running its length, from the stone fireplace to a tapestry hung on the opposite wall, a dusty red and gold. The tea was stewed. My egg had overcooked itself, left for too long in its unopened shell.

Things didn't improve the following morning, when for long periods the only evidence of other beings was the caw of a crow. I pulled up and swung round, snatching at the air, only to grasp the disappearing bunch of her shadow, as it slid round a door. Several times I found an open book, facedown and indented at the spine, just *where* I cannot be specific about (on a window seat, then in a niche with an alabaster bust, then on a kitchen dresser, where it shared a shelf with a fine display of Wedgwood). I picked it up, always to confirm her reading was lowbrow fiction.

I discovered certain anthropocentric obsessions, relating to the genealogy of our family. She had identified a Caledonian branch, warring and wielding claymores. By an accident of fate, her papers got confused with my own, among them illicit photocopies where I had pencilled notes on cases I was working on. They found their way into that paperback, and acted as bookmark. When the book next turned up, it was minus my papers.

A change of air, brought in on the afternoon tide, blew through the rocks, reeds and grasses. It crossed a sandbar and rolled inland over the tufts and fringes – the older Fixt's feu and pasture – finally it squealed in the fortifications round the estate. Instead of returning that book, I withheld it, hoping to draw her from hiding. I found myself objecting to the printed flap of its dustcover, where a weight of excess was extraordinary things written about the author. I killed an hour, and read. The prose style (bland), was apparently 'deceptively transparent'. The plot 'clever', 'unexpected' in its twists. Insight into the criminal mind – that was 'profound'. The book overall was 'millennial', with its central character a parallel to the 'real' Sir Geoffrey Kite (a name I did not know). He had a natural flaw, but in his heart was the 'quest for greenness'.

The flag room was no more rewarding, with its hoisted crowns, its crosses and thistles, though as I went on with my search I found her chair at the hearth, threadbare, its comfort the deep hollow of its cushions. The fire was remnants of ribbed charcoal in a bed of white ash. Her heraldry, a sword, a sash, and a vertical stave, was beaten in the planished copper of the canopy above. Passion had been tamed as an obeisant docile lion, prone and asleep. Through what point of reference I am at a loss to say, yet I was reminded of Blamm – the monarchic chief inspector – eyeing his ethnic suburb, where the streets were unsafe and morally disintegrating. There were bordellos. There was an evil trade in evil powders. People had lurid beliefs.

I glanced from beam to beam (where, where was the other Fixt?), and studied the surface gloss of one of the hangings, a portrait – head and shoulders only. The subject, a hermaphrodite, my hostess had dredged up and labelled as a Great Great Someone. It was an unsuccessful inventor, always fiddling with prototypes, a first precursor of all she regarded as 'in error' in the Fixt line....

The breeze recharged itself, a crumple in the grey-green surface of the sea. It combed through the ferns, was a sly invader over the castle wall. As I looked out it became the sweeping change in the rub of the nap, in the short blades of the lawn. Something moaned in a keyhole, then a susurration in the chimney's velvet brought a fall of soot. I turned, and unexpectedly came across my papers once again, which I slipped safely in a pocket. I stumbled, trying doors, heavy and creaking. 'You have to be somewhere,' I said, and put a foot forward, now at the bottom of a spiral staircase. High over my head a door closed in a tower, followed by a thud, then a smothered echo in the gloom. I climbed up and round monotonously, pausing at every window slit. To the south I saw the flap and billow and the red checks of a tablecloth, pegged on a line. West, a dark rent over a luminous thread of skyline was in reality a kestrel, suspended in a buffeting wave of air. On my second and third turns north I looked out over a larger and larger patchwork in the squared fields and feudal birthright Fixt the Elder had worked to recover. I called out again, and strained for the reply. The door, eerie on its hinges, let out a dusky shaft on the curve of the stairs, a crack through which was tossed a coloured marble. It was one I recognised. Its inner bud was a collision of cherry and russet. Its surface was scored. It bounced and tinkled on the stone, and rolled where I trapped it, under the fading sheen of my shoe.

I scraped my heel and picked it up, and remembered its little history, and reflected how cunning that other Fixt had become, and put it in my pocket. I looked up and followed the slow distensions, a hinted profile, a woman's jittery silhouette in the stairwell's yellow dust. Shadows on the wall had transformed the stub of her nose into one that was long and thin, and the flat crown of her head to a point.

I took another step forward, willing to agree a truce. She, the once bright child, rosy for an hour, all verve and *élan*, and happy for the first gold strands of life's little tapestry, had since not regretted the passing of her innocence, and had hardened in her adult life. Yet that same innocence was something I could flatter her with, as I played up our infant closeness. I would (would I?) try to explain, not the lunacy of my metropolis, but how a decade there can change our human perception.

I got out that marble, as I was probably meant to do, and closed my palm on the cherry and russet voids it had prompted me to.

'You're going to tell me you have a theory,' she said. The penumbral yellow glaze shortened on the wall. I slowed, I moved up more carefully. A last hollow step brought me to the highest point above her acreage, whose labourers had decamped to the towns and cities decades ago. I pushed open her door and walked in, and for a moment took in the wide panorama – light in a gilded wall mirror, an overhanging sky – green shades, dapples – the gold of a distant spire – how the rays of the sun concisely emphasised the smallest smear in the windows. She had set herself at ease in a movable chair, where banked before her, on a system of interlocking shelves, were her fax and telex machines, a clutch of modems, and at least half a dozen computer screens.

'A theory…' I repeated.

'If nothing's changed,' she said. 'Wouldn't that be, Adrian, along lines of the way we live, and the economy that shaped us?'

(Don't call me Adrian.)

I shuffled uneasily, hard soles on a cold stone floor. I unavoidably blinked at the sun's brightness.

'Well,' I said bluntly, 'money has always been our family's problem.'

'Not simply money, Adrian – it's what it can buy. In your case an aesthetic.' It seemed I was in for a lecture, with that intruder, bearing his baggage of fiction, wanting to reinvent me in his alien image.[27]

That marble was a poor sort of ploy, she explained. It was supposed to conjure, because she knew for me it would, a lost country, the idylls of childhood, those few precious years before the Great Fall, by which I mean our lost family fortune. Children of good families brought their playthings into Leagues Fixt, for such is the vanity of men made rich by trade. There was a fissure between an outhouse wall and a loose flagstone, in the corner of an enclosed patio. I recall it as latticed, in summer a riot of wisteria and honeysuckle. Boys lost their marbles if careless enough to allow them through that fissure, an event I feigned puzzlement at. When they had gone home I collected the lost marbles, knowing precisely where they had lodged. That was with the wine bins down in the cellar.

'There was a pergola,' I said. 'And a passion flower.'

'And a bond between us.'

'Oh yes. Your inflated sense of elder-sister responsibility, I a brother half your age.'

'Perhaps *yours* was inflated.'

'Memories are precious.'

And recall was the problem – this was the point she insisted on. A transference had got under way, so her notion ran, when an unremarkable girlish vision of herself found itself impossibly elevated through the counterfeits of *my* adulthood. She was not at all uncomfortable, and allowed her phone, when it rang, to keep on ringing.

'You surely knew that nothing would remain.'

'And you, being that much younger, didn't know.'

'How could I? Nothing around me changed. A flat country of fields,' I said, 'and poplars. There was a rhyme you used to recite for poor Reynard, pursued by the hounds, to the cries of *Tantivy*.'

'Adrian. This is sentimentality.'

Perhaps, but I remembered also, under that pergola, a valedictory couplet, and how we sat together while she said it sing-song-style. Then all the money had gone, and the removers were bringing their vans along the drive. Since then she'd reflected[28] on the fact that our father had ventured into modern life without first shaking off the dust of an older world he'd come from. In later years he turned grey and shaved unevenly, and adopted soft collars. She humoured him – this before she'd matched the vastness of his fortune – buying him a schooner of sherry, and ensuring they were photographed. It was a week before he died. The deceased man's fault, she said, was in harnessing horse to plough, when commerce had long fired up the engines of sweated labour (and that was the full extent of her metaphors).

She, the other Fixt, answered her phone, and immediately hung up. She told me that in the years I'd numbed myself to or ignored her better luck, she'd fled her ideal and made a City career. 'Only picture it' – a woman in a man's world, kept waiting impenitently in marble or mahogany foyers. Our family bankers were shrewd, and for as long as possible secured themselves behind closed doors, dusting off the last of our documents. A quirk they chortled at, in holding up a soiled parchment, was our ancient Fixt watermark. Miraculously, they put a hand to one last let-out, and pulled out with it a last sprinkle of cash. Across the street, where that rugged female thawed her hands at a brazier – the other Fixt's figment of herself – she warmed to that final opportunity for making good. I said I didn't much care for this, and asked her about my photocopies.

'You've been prying,' I said.

'No.'

'Your bookmark is no longer at the page you're reading. You've reached page ninety-three.'

A mild flurry of damp air flapped round my earlobes. She had stood up. 'Let's,' she said, 'be sensible.'

'Those photocopies came from my office.'

'Adrian. I thought they were simply scraps. Doodles. It's tragic if they *are* important.'

'You've read them?'

'I have.'

'But they're private.'

'And not my sort of business. This man Rudge you don't seem to like, and the chief inspector – and Dark, your boss – what you say of all three typifies your attitude. They don't share your views, therefore they're stupid.'

'They're prejudiced.'

'Everyone is prejudiced.'

'You cannot build objective work on a personal preconception.'

She paced backwards awkwardly, while in all this quiet pugnacity I smiled again. My roving gaze had lingered on an inlaid casket, with elegant twists and silver scrolls. Absently I opened it, and found inside, in a padding of blue velvet, two polished duelling pistols (convenient symbol). Heavens, how would she ponder my reversals, this habit I had of running time backwards? Back, breezy charge! Back from these machicolations, back from the dun fringes! Back, I say, over the coarse grass, the jags, the sandbar! Back, back a hundred times, back through the reeds, back (over the dark tide)! Go back to your medieval homes!

45

'Ah!' she said. 'I've been looking for that....' She snapped shut the lid of the duelling pistols and took the casket from me. Then, her voice distant – 'I shall put that away.' She retreated through a studded door into an adjoining room, and left me with her computer screens, a palette of red, white and blue repainting the day's share prices – very patriotic.

I listened out, but heard only the casket as she put it on a table. 'Nothing to say. All right. But look, perhaps there is something you can help me with....' In the silence I reflected on how in my twilit garret at home I needed not a flambeau (as round here) but a pen torch, for the nights I spent with those illicit photocopies. It seemed the neighbourhood's entirety of city dust, in the rise and fall of a summer storm, in a swirl outside, had at last settled, coming in across my balcony. I went over the record – Rudge's absurd probes, the marginalised Staverton, the unobtainable Frankie, Blamm, man of men.

'You still there?' I said. Silence again. Perhaps she measured the duellists' twenty paces. Then I heard the creak of a hinge, and asked myself had she picked out her pistol, fingered its mechanisms, assessed its weight, one against the other, on her open palms?

'Listen,' she said, but nothing in her voice resolved our differences. She even closed the door. Therefore here was my *Doppelgänger*, not the spectre of my keypad, but the era's new Victoriana, a woman dark at the brows, her look ferocious. Did she bluster? Did she gaze at the door panels? Would she make this a matter of honour, and pride? Doubtless I would find her, should I follow her in, in striped trousers, an eye firmly shut, the other taking aim. My last ever sight would be, behind her through the window, a kestrel, a piece of black cloth in a moving plane, and the barrel of her pistol.

'Really, Adrian, you need to wake up,' I heard, muffled through the door. '"Fairness" at best's an indecent scramble for affluence, then in middle-life the warm glow of charity as that's dispensed on the failures.'

'You've reneged,' I said. 'You aren't my sibling, and can't be.' I put my weight into the door, and rattled the knob, finding it stuck. Some other sound issued, the swish of a coat or cape. Now I shouldered the panels. 'It's gone on long enough,' I said, despising her lands and all that puffed-up heraldry. I describe it thus, as I embark on clichés: the plainclothes man, head down in a shoulder charge; the cocked chair wedging the door. If the medium was film or TV, I'd have cooked up this hopeless moralising on an oily shoreline, where a fifty-minute dramatist, lined and bearded, kicks the shingle in an endless interview, able to articulate a titanic addiction to caffeine. What else is there except asides? I am blameless, an abstraction. I am merely the author of standard office reporting. I flinched, eyes tightly shut, and for the moment of impact entered in rearward. That, of course, revived old pains, a scapular twinge, though I thought at last I'd got her pinned in a corner. However and but. The triumphal fist only punches vacant air. There followed a split second only – a temporal bit of circuitry in an over-hot connection – when the patched-together years, the failures, were past, future, and immense. I looked around. Here was a cheval glass, which someone had re-silvered. My reflection gazed back at me astonished, framed in the scrolls and twists and vines from the lost Eden of childhood. A gold wafer moving on a low beam crowned my thoughts. Where was that other Fixt? How had she got out? I cast around the room, by her standards uncharacteristically Spartan: the glass, a broken chair, a window seat, in a corner a single screen with its shares. Then here as I expected a low table, and no sign of the casket, *or* the pistols.

I gave up the search, having looked for other doors. I picked up a tide chart. Scholia, page seven, enciphered someone's hasty retreat by sea. I moved to her windows, where a continental smudge, the vague shape of Africa, had compressed itself in the vertical. Then I saw how I'd beaten her back to her breakfast quarters. There was a plate in the window seat, in the clear-up missed by her *bonne*, its blue china smeared in a congealed dribble of egg yolk, with a dash of peppered toast crumbs. I picked up the eggcup, knowing it immediately (hers, from the days of our infancy). It had been hand-painted with a procession of play-box trumpeters. One had a torn sleeve and severed forearm. Pink cheeks had faded to orange. The terrier bounding at a raised heel had transmogrified – was a poodle. I looked out, instantly puzzled, in anticipation of a nineteenth-century horseman in a gallop across the fields, but saw no one. My hand was unsteady. I moved uncertainly to the glass and supervised new knots in my tie. I glanced down, to a small walnut table, where there was an overturned goblet, and half a bottle of Burgundy – cool but still *chambré*. The sun had moved. The flake on the beam had moved. Gold in the silvered glass – that had moved, and hurt my eyes. I adjusted its reflective angle and shrugged at the trapdoor this simple action revealed. Shrugged at what it concealed, her escape.

46

I offer a theory of time, establishing one only as the unifying 'law'. 'Action', 'events', traditionally the record of a passage or sequence, are terms I banish, especially when applied to written accounts. 'Time' is curvilinear, beginning randomly wherever I start to internalise or reflect, and runs in every direction. That is how I treat my notebook.

I dismiss, but shall not forget that other Fixt,[29] in whose castle I roamed, rattling her cupboard doors. I sprang from her dark hallways, lurked round her corners, put myself always at the ready, yet each time I failed to pounce. She did not reappear – and left only clues. I cite, as deliberate in their choice, the red heel in a mazarine sock, a cast-off from schooldays, and a loose shirttail, all that remained of the garment whole. There's an airman's hat – one of mine, whose colour and style she never liked. I have catalogued, with a long flaming torch lighting the racks of her cellar, what memorabilia is salvaged from our youth. Soiled tennis whites, where years, or centuries before, she had hurled them into a corner, with a ball and racquet (a bad loser). There was a galleon, with fractured mizzenmast, as yes, I had crunched it underfoot – the result, more midnight oil, more glue patiently applied. I found a crutch for her broken ankle, as once I had dropped a banana skin. She had decided to replay that incident *ad nauseam*, for I found the crutch everywhere I looked – on a chesterfield, propping a table, twice by my money pig (yes. I understand. *Mea culpa*). So now, gentlemen, the Department's Adrian Fixt, irrepressible taker of notes, has acquired these coloured hoops, brought forward from his boyhood. These lilac ones have ribands. I have learnt to curl them in the air. I can spin them in reverse, as I wheel them on the ground. Others I hitch at my side. I require, demand, I automatically decree: that boyhood figure is going to jump, high, higher, what-ho! jump through every one!

47

I returned home from my 'holiday' one day early, on a Sunday – prominent only as the anniversary of my transfer to the Department, sweetened by a pay rise. It was almost a relief on the Monday, stepping out into the cold morning air and tramping into Staverton's neighbourhood, where I mused on what can be termed seven ambiguous kinds of trivia. My censor has since been busy, and will allow me only certain details. For example, Staverton's small round window, open on its hinges. There's also its surrounding gable, with faded yellow stains, behind which, under the pitch of the roof, I could if I wished locate his communal bathroom. Forbidden, however, are these – a long way down on the pavement – and unlikely to survive a further draft. One, a confectioner's swirl, a glistening brown. Two, a flaky white ordure – even though so many canines had disappeared on Staverton's streets.

I crossed the boundary between his and my neighbourhood, and saw, behind park railings, through shrubs and English oaks, the peak and the candy stripe of a helter-skelter, here for several days, which I only now took notice of. Then the loose flaps of an amusement tent, sandy circles, hoops hoisted up a pole. The shrubs thinned and I understood more clearly what had numbed the back of my head. It was the distant hum of a generator.

So must a man maroon himself mentally.

48

Of course, theoretically, under threat of losing the Solomon case, I am in danger of light duties, and am stuck with this infernal training document. I'm suspicious, as in Dark's sweeping generalisations, on the brink of lightening my load, the other case he named was Staverton's. He hadn't so far mentioned another, that of Iris Cadogan, which he knew I'd a passing interest in, and showed no sign it might also enter his prohibitions, as now I began to think of hers as the most important – to me at least.

I met Bello privately a few days later, wanting whatever smallest thing he could tell me about her, which, as the outcast I was rapidly becoming, I didn't find easy. He told me Blamm had bemoaned his summer shirts piling up in the laundry basket, with domestic ills infecting the plumbing. He'd spun round the office with his sleeves rolled up, and toed his colleague's chair legs, clumsily. They discussed Rudge, a subject Bello was tired of. Rudge it seemed had answered an emergency call, and had gone hotfoot to the scene of an attempted rape, in Paradise Alley, a few streets short of Staverton's address, all this occurring before he'd shown interest in that freak of nature, where he later discovered that potted palm and its owner's instruments of torture. From dustbins in Paradise Alley,

Rudge retrieved what was said to have been used as a disguise, a mask, one that had also been described by the crime's only witness. Blamm produced it from his top drawer and showed it to Bello. Bello also saw a copy of the witness's statement, and an open paperback on Blamm's desk, its subject the role of animal sacrifice in occult rites.

'What kind of mask?' I said.

'A toytown gorilla.'

I have since seen it, a piece of cheap plastic, whose elastic strap had broken free of one of two retaining staples. A piece of its mauve chin was missing. The lips, which were yellow, showed a symmetry of cracks, and the gums, a cherry red, were split. There was a dent in the nose directly above the nostrils.

'A toytown gorilla,' I said. 'I wonder....'

The statement, which I haven't read, I have only his word on. A tenant, newly arrived from West Africa, not adapted to the fumes of inner-city life, had suffered an asthma attack after she had gone to bed. She flicked on her bedside lamp, and rummaged through the drawer where she kept her inhaler, but couldn't find it. Meanwhile the scene in Paradise Alley, which her room overlooked, was a patchwork of city lights and reflecting pools of oil. Below her was a car mechanic's workshop. She got up and moved to the window. An assailant, hidden with the refuse sacks, lay in wait. His victim, unsteady on stiletto heels, made her way awkwardly across the cobbles. Our witness, whose inhaler was on the window ledge, ingested its cold tang of vapours, and looked out, where a half-tame gorilla was in the act of unbuckling his belt.

It just had to burst out – lights, a sudsy iridescence, the throb, the pulse in his loins – the whole visceral fantasia. Somewhere a dustbin lid flew off, which slipped the gorilla's cover prematurely by mistake, and fell with a thud. Close-ups, please. Net stockings, neatly worn. A shiny black. Voluptuary. A lady's silky shoes, in accelerated crossovers. Would she get away? The sham gorilla emerged from a heap of litter and kicked at an apple core. A cat yowled. A light went off. Only one person watched, from the Côte d'Ivoire. If there were others, no one came. In a first headlong rush, a bifurcated crisp packet fluttered from a dark lapel. The victim was ruggedly his match, and had already wound the straps of a leather bag round the flat of her hand. The primate, steaming, thrust down his head and painted face, the real face the face of Staverton (according to the newest of Blamm's hunches). One imagined his disgusting little paw whipping up the skirt, fumbling for a band of fabric. Yet, our mock gorilla received a buckle in his ear, its force and momentum the clout of a shoulder bag, which surely would have raised a bruise.

'I want you,' Blamm instructed his detective sergeant, 'to get him in again.'

The mask having slipped, the gorilla found a knee firmly in his groin. In the blue light, our witness saw no more than that. But someone called the police.

49

Precise timings I don't have, but that was followed by an attempted burglary at a private address near the Club Sportif, which PC Rudge investigated, a matter of days after his call to Paradise Alley. This, on the face of it a routine break-in, developed into a murder inquiry. Rudge discovered the corpse. A young woman had become that corpse at roughly the same time Staverton had felt that blow to his ear. The break-in was reported by Iris Cadogan, an invalid, who I later learned was terminally ill. She lived life in a wheelchair. She witnessed the crime from her window. Dark, who at that time hadn't devised his final test for me, briefed me to collect her statement, while Blamm and the chief superintendent began their examination of the house opposite – the murder scene. This – as it now turns out, a conspiracy of events – puts me on the brink, in so far as I follow that inferior philosophising at the start of Section 4.6, which my censor has revised, calling it Chapter 46, and has otherwise messed with my chronology. It leaves me committed to a case higher powers would have me abandon, but as you will see I don't give up easily. It's a paradox too, as this was a crime Blamm had deigned to tell me about as soon as he was on to it, though left it for several days before mentioning the lesser matter of attempted rape. So I mused with my notebook, on a day I sat waiting for Iris Cadogan. Investigative work is like that, a process of constant refinement.

She kept a rambling house, where her nurse, red-necked and dour, showed me up several flights of stairs, into a kind of waiting room, where I sat for an hour turning everything over, as usual inconclusively – Solomon, and apropos of Solomon Reuter, then Staverton, and apropos of him the remorseless PC Rudge. For my sanity I allowed myself a diversion, off into Byrne territory.

I sank to a *chaise longue*, and fingered its gold brocade impatiently. I crossed legs, and for a moment scrutinised the dull gloss of my shoes. I tugged at an inside pocket, and re-crossing legs held the envelope I hadn't yet filed at home up to the light of the window. Not *the* window, from which Cadogan had seen the crime – I was on the floor above. As for that envelope, only now did I note an error in the postcode. The address label, like the enclosure, was computer-printed. It was my letter from the Byrne Society, my invitation to the awards ceremony and garden party, an occasion I now had good reason to look forward to.

I returned to it, struck by its choice of fawning word and phrase, now that the great man Bim Shay sat in on Society meetings. The light of publicity, to which most of its admin wasn't yet accustomed, had brought about a mixture of coyness and self-inflation. Retained were certain indulgences, one being an ornithological crest, pre-printed at the pointed seal of the envelope. It was a highland eagle, Aquila's head in profile, its feathery shoulder fluffed where wings were about to beat. Nor was this in any way arbitrary, since a trio of specialists had approved it as genuinely Byrne in character. This same figure, in three rather than two dimensions, had first been found as a carved ivory pommel topping the handle of the walking cane Daniel Byrne most often used (much scarified when it eventually came to light).

At his death an anonymous bidder – or 'Benefactor X' – saved the Byrne estate, the rural parts of which a developer wished to turn into housing. 'X' privately examined the author's effects. Curiously – for numerology had been a Byrne obsession – this revealed ninety-one replications of the eagle motif, mostly capping the eraser end of pencils. One other, or the ninety-third, was discovered by a lay reader living in the Home Counties (Sissinghurst). It was the brass knocker on Byrne's old cottage door – an adornment before his days of wealth. A handful of scholars emerged and had their say. They went on to uncover a further three replications, which were later thought to be the originals, and prompted speculation as to the unconscious mind of visionary first, criminologist second, and now numerologist Daniel Byrne. One theory repeated itself, with the idea of 'threeness', mapped to the *ménage à trois* of Daniel's childhood household. No other exegesis seemed possible, therefore in a kind of intellectualised tabloidism, the extent of Byrne's penile fixation was publicly aired. Did not these ninety-one pencils, when erect, tip themselves in ninety-one swollen extremities? And consider, how handy to the grip, that cane! This – the phallus 'shared' by Daniel's parents, who 'shared' a male lover – now placed the man's *œuvre* in a startling new perspective.

Worse followed. A collector, who raised sums in a lifelong commitment to the author's original drafts, found yet two more in the succession of eagle motifs. These turned up intermittently in the margins of discarded typescripts, where Byrne had left doodles, and which he did not go on to develop as case histories or theories – a discipline he wearied of in later years, and I suspect found loathsome. Then another four were stumbled on, when plans for the Byrne museum began with a survey of the author's last address, in Hampstead Hill View. A consultant architect, whose watchword was 'preservation', had strong opinions on the bathroom, and did not want to see a complicated run of copper pipes (to replace the existing lead) traversing floors or running up walls. Incidental to this, it was found that Byrne's last quartet of eagles presided over ablutions, being doubly engraved on the hot and cold faucets original to the bathroom. This of course was the home he departed (for what afterlife I cannot guess), and so made intrinsic the material value of that highly ornate plumbing. We're allowed a smile, for having raged at the refined inanity surmounting Haverstock Hill, in particular the bookish set – finally, moneyed, Daniel Byrne joined them. In passing, we have now a total of 102 representations of the eagle motif. The sum of those digits is three.[30]

50

I uncrossed my legs. By now twenty minutes had passed, and Cadogan, unable to do anything before her medication, and her makeup, had still not been wheeled to the lift and brought upstairs. I stood up under the rosy dew of a chandelier, and thereby recalled old Henry's happy lights at Ealing, those filters I had seen empurpling his daughter's pectoral. On the sound of a something, I walked to and opened the door, though released its ceramic knob slowly. Somewhere down in the polished depths of the house, a phone tinkled cavernously, and was answered.

There are things I remember, but see from my notes were not written down, or were erased. For example (moving across, looking out of that window again), the arrival of a dispatch rider, who angled his bike on its stalk, then casually strode to the police cordon, which of course the efficient Rudge had established. He carried a large padded envelope.

Systematically, Rudge held up his palm – allowing neither person nor package to cross the line. Rudge, I reason, even insisted that the courier remove his helmet, whose visor was tinted. The constable studied the envelope address, then pointed to the porch next door. So on and so forth. In that porch next door, a spindly man with steely spectacle frames appeared and received a by now un-helmeted caller, and being very tall stooped for his package. The courier was short.

I still clutched that Byrne Society envelope, about to pocket it, though paused for a brief survey of the sketch I had drawn on the back, of Solomon's last ride home.

51

Now, I would like to propose – for you, Professor Dark, and for the chief inspector – that Adrian Fixt's repeated failures, which I don't find easy to write about, are really the essentials of success. Sometimes you have to gather a plethora of detail in order to possess the one important gem. You see I shall solve your crimes. I shall solve them because I have gone into untrodden territory.

52

The witness Cadogan – of precisely what crime I shall come to – still hadn't got her chair to the lift. Again I am here at that upper-storey window, with its strawberry-coloured drapes. There is, in the broad sweep of the street below, a litter of vehicles, among them the chief inspector's saloon. I rake up, down, laterally, over a line of solid houses, over the kinks, twists and bustle in the ornamental railings. I am half in a dream of a young A. Fixt, who grew up in a street like hers. I know how, Mrs Cadogan, in that moment of homecoming, the dusk of a July evening blurs the architectural lines, or how up there – wide eyes open to the night – the bright amber of a rising moon flames the roofs.

53

I turn back into the room, to take in the formal suite I have been ushered to. On a half-hour chime, I rest my gaze on two impossible cherubim, floating, trumpeting, holding up an iron over-mantel – caryatides, twinned in a deified system of vines, shrouds and vapours. One, great, heavenly timepiece, with its glass, gilt and spinning wheels, bears down its weight off-centre, while above it, on the chimneybreast, a vision in oils is glorified in harps, robes and levitating saints. Another, a portrait of Wellington, signifies the Cadogan ancestry in world affairs. Here is a bookcase. Here Trollope's *Pallisers* – a Folio edition. It contests a middle shelf with Gibbon. Waugh's *Decline and Fall* rubs shoulders with an unimportant Tolstoy, which I am now squatting down to. There's a flaw, a hairline crack running from lead to lead in one of the panes, which is heart-shaped. That little blemish stencils itself on a Somerset Maugham, over the spine of a *Collected*. I try the door. Locked. I look for the key. Fail. Hard now to keep amused, I light on the diamond knob of another door – one in a pair – and open it (into a walk-in cupboard). I refuse to confront what is in there – shoes, hats, furs – or whatever....

54

I hear the lift cage rattle. But this is for the cleaner, and not Iris Cadogan, as is heard from the mop and pail – not on mine, but on the landing below. I return to the wild strawberry framing the window and fold my arms. Across the street, in the light dapple of maple trees, I can see the fine mousy strands, the thin middle years of Blamm's double crown. His large head he has thrust out, the neck tense, in the open sash of a window. He can't expect to find a footprint there. Again I return to my pocketbook, and again, with those pale blue rules in a waste of paper snow, I stray from duty. Shall I write the date? The name, 'Mrs Cadogan'? Or make my comments on the chief inspector's isometrics (a man whose vertical gaze is now fixed on an external cornice)? The pages of past weeks slip through my hands, and here in a dog-eared corner I still trace the perfect scent of Frankie's perfume – *ma griffe*, as I think I said. Is there too a frothy smear of spilt cappuccino? (Ah. Now. There's Blamm with a forensic brush, which he had better return to its owner. I am up here with a smile.) How shall I ever get out of this maze?

I'm rambling.

55

I have a flair for crossword puzzles,[31] those teasers beloved of hacks and amateur sleuths, yet here at Cadogan's I have nothing beyond a scramble of clues. This excess of time and test of my patience is down to her appearance, which cannot go on in the absence of cosmetics. I sympathise, knowing the demands of each new day. In my case any such preparation is undermined by the reduced role I have of chronicler, when far from raising a phoenix my professional fortunes have gone the other way. I spend a lot of time at home, a pen raised. My notebook is constantly open. It and my draft document are a labyrinth of criss-cross crossings out. Professor Dark, pending 'certain internal investigations', and a definitive statement from Security, who state that nothing is wrong, has reinforced the threat of indefinite leave. He demands handover of the training document, but all I have to show is a contents page (would *you* give it up, in that state?). Still, I try to imagine an audience of one, a sole reader somewhere[32] – let's say plunged in a homey lamplight, or in the sordid fumes of a railway waiting room, doubling as overnight *pissoir*. I have need of someone prepared to believe in an infiltrator at the heart of the Department.

Again I come back to that room at Cadogan's, where all I could do was look out. The chief inspector's disparate cranium mushroomed behind a pane of frosted glass. I could tell, in the forthright ripple of his arm – a long arm – that the minutiae (perhaps he'd picked up a tube of toothpaste) 'just couldn't you know be overlooked'. Ah, the victim's sense of order: she squeezed the tube so, from the bottom up. Rudge, at this time reiterating something non-committal for the press, had admitted the doctor. The constable stood under the carved Pans of the porch, shaking his head (to unanswerable questions). Someone arrived with sniffer dogs. There were postings on every exit.

I folded back a frayed cuff over my wrist, which because of a rash was watch-less. That comes to mind because, when last I watched TV, the screen was overrun by a man freakishly skilled as fork-bender. According to him, sunspots, 'in a chance *cosmologia*', will retard the luminescent green digits of my timepiece. Cadogan, whose preference was for orange lipstick, had set my continuum to her own kind of slow.

Another look at Rudge. I winced at his flat feet, his square chin. Having been spoken to, a slackness round his mouth, only transient, returned to its former rigidity. Passing clouds had no power of transformation – the slant under the peak of his helmet thickened. (Fidget. Boredom.) What other observations? Well, the chief superintendent hadn't yet arrived: the only smart car was Blamm's. Here, at Cadogan's window, I measured its oblongs against my thumb. It has given me the following ratio: 1, the saloon; 2, the bonnet; 0.75, the boot – room there for the chief inspector's case and wellingtons. The colour is metallic blue, which shaded into bright anaemia in the shadow of an acacia tree. Then there was something more in Cadogan's books. They had been shelved not authorially, but relative to size, therefore Austen and George Orwell – again both products of the Folio Society – were juxtaposed. From here my mind wanders to sandwich plates, in a corner cabinet. One in particular caught my eye, not for its design, a Randallesque forge,[33] but because one of the corners had a bite-size chunk taken out. What does that conjure?

Heaven forbid.

56

So on till finally a made-up Mrs Cadogan was wheeled into the room. She found me just as I had picked up a framed photograph and wasn't about to put it down – a verdant wash, subject darkness in a lane in the green of a moonlit sky, ruts from a coach's wheels, a bend, a few leafless elms. A high moon left its pearls in the mossy pools, and at the lane's end, pale and ghostly, a chalky gable floated supernaturally – all so out of place among these airy upper rooms.

I caught myself rehearsing the official line, but bit my lip. The nurse's face was livid walnut. Cadogan's was thin, mask-like, emaciated. It looked up at mine with an open, unspeaking mouth. The nurse backed off, in a flourish, hoping I wouldn't be long. She returned almost at once, fussing with a microphone in her mistress's lap. 'You may not hear,' she said, and showed me how to turn it on, where to hitch it up. It made Cadogan irritable, angry, and was a sign for the nurse to leave. She had, she said, to re-check brakes (one, last, uneventful push on the chair, which she had already immobilised). Here for the nth time I felt for my notebook, while a distant flame in Iris Cadogan's eyes wasn't yet extinguished. A dull ember – the afterglow of a mind hardened to life experience. I got out my notebook, and, carefully, structured my first question. 'Supposing this is the room downstairs, you,' I said, 'were sitting where?' I paced to the window.

Crisp white sunlight crossed the lines of her face. A long life in the sun had left its silvered bronze in the tautness of her flesh, a few mottles on the backs of her hands. I thought of my mother. (Why? Because I put them at roughly the same age.) What preoccupied *her* was the loss of her youthful figure, not the Fixt family fortune, to her alien built as it was on trade. Moulded with my teenage years is a post-war photo from the bloom of her youth – a starlet, newly married – a faded sepia stuck to the rounded door of the fridge. Older, plump, a mother of two, her own hand had appended the caption: 'Remember, this was once you....'

Now I imagined props for a younger Iris wearing a printed frock. In the nimbleness of one hand scissors, in the other daffodils. A tall green vase, sunshine, a burst of light in through the kitchen blind. Outside in the gardens, plum trees, a hammock. The young Cadogan had fire in her eyes, preface to her steely coldness now, and a mouth formidably stern. I glanced up again at her moonlit lane and saw, under the dark solid trunk of an oak, two cloaked figures, a misty lunar haze in their hair – and how they hurried home. I tested the tip of my ballpoint, a sign, then urged myself to business.

57

She wore a peach smock and had both hands in her lap, inactive. The morning sun streamed in. Her makeup hadn't taken well, and was smudged. I looked away. I returned my gaze to the house across the street, where I saw Rudge, police cordons, dogs – a doctor – still no sign of the superintendent. Those boffins from Forensics had put away their samples into plastic bags.

'Two little black boys?' I queried.

'I believe that's what I said.' Her soft voice had a hard tone, as she explained once more that the nurse had opened the mail, and left her sitting, reading.

'I just want to get this straight,' I said.

'You *have* it straight. If you'd be so good—'

'How did they arrive?'

'I said. In a van.'

'Colour? Size? Registration?'

Registration! How did I suppose she'd remember that? In her mind it was more marked out for its orthography, she said. 'The logo was "Glaciers". "City Glaciers".'

'Anything else?'

She was not in need of a glacier, or a glazier. She'd ignored it. 'Until I had read my mail.'

'Go on.'

'They removed a window pane. One had been shattered....'

'Then?'

'Then they left, in a hurry.'

'That was odd, don't you think? Who lives in the house?'

'Lives' was hardly the word. It belonged to an American, who wasn't ever there.

'Wife? Children?'

'No.'

'Mrs Cadogan, about what time did these supposed glaziers leave?'

'Eightish.'

'You called the police – when?'
'*I* didn't call anyone. Hilda did. I don't know, ask her, an hour later.'
'A long delay.'
'I thought those boys had gone for their breakfast.'
'Mrs Cadogan, I think that's going to be all for now. Shall I send the nurse, Hilda up?'

58

I pulled up with my first step onto the scrubbed checks of Mrs Cadogan's front path on the distant phut of air brakes. PC Rudge across the street – a cube of refrigerated flesh – swatted flies buzzing round his helmet. A passing cyclist found this the perfect opportunity to mend his tyre. He stopped and unclipped the front wheel, and produced a spanner from under the saddle. He began, in a mist of perspiration, a not convincing repair. I crossed the street, passing close enough to make out the motif on his shorts – a laurel, a globe, a winged hat. He bent to the sprockets of his rear wheel, too theatrically grave, a keen eye to the goings-on in the house cordoned off. His spanner hand went limp. A plain sparrow bobbed over the roofs. Thus omened, I mustered a nod, bypassing Rudge, stepping into the house he was sentinel of.

Inside was a great deal of memorabilia, in a haphazard arrangement under multiple layers of dust. Among the miniatures was a Chinese pagoda in jade, and on the same shelf a scale reproduction of a Cadillac. There was an obese Buddha in bronze. Others proliferated, in light woods, with one in ivory. Niches, ostentatiously Romanesque, were the display place of porcelain clogs and a maroon beret – all as I say under house dust, which hadn't been disturbed. On a correspondence table I poked my pen at the mud flaps of a Model T Ford, assembled and painted from a toy construction kit. From another production line a Warhol hung from a picture rail. It was paired with a framed photograph of bathers in the Ganges. The wallpaper was sweet peas on a dark green trellis.

The phone was in the shape, form and stance of Mickey Mouse, acting as room servant, the earpiece held out on a gloved palm. I don't know where you talked. He was wired to a message machine, which was illumined (a red, and a green point of light), though the tape had been removed. Here, uniquely, the dust *had* been disturbed, which seemed to be a clue. I went on to find Blamm at the top of the stairs. I rose to the upper steps, where I tried him with that little lead.

'Yes, I know about that. Not now, please!'

The big man was bent from the waist in a hairpin, at the sneakered foot of the body, a blonde with gore in her hair. He puzzled over a ring of blood in the woolly pile of the carpet, and muttered. The girl was prostrate over a bedroom threshold.

I said 'May I?' and came into the room. His reply was an uncertain gesture, one of those handy whirlpools with a long, extended digit. He remained distant, in one of his moods, still piecing together the girl's last movements (obvious though her terrible outcome was). I crossed to the room she had tried to leave. In it was a modern pine chest, five drawers – two paired at the top, three full-lengthers underneath. Among its ornaments was a basket, with assorted objects, some I recall. A toffee hammer. A pictured airman, his gaze directed up at a war-torn sky – or may have been a blueness in the heaven over Wiesbaden. There was a tiny globe really a pencil sharpener, with its two halves thrown together in an alliance of North America and the bulk of southern Africa.

I turned these things over with the flat blade of my pocket knife, and kept that big man huffing in my sights. I unearthed keys on corroded rings, for their power to conjure padlocks vanished in the night of someone's former life. Clocks didn't tick, having stopped. The woodchip walls were a museum. I looked at the sporty pennants from upstate jamborees, which went back years. There was a large photograph, signed indecipherably, of a smooth-chinned football player, a man with a clumsy profile, exuberantly cleansed by the razor he'd agreed to promote. So on, and a much-thumbed Whitman, exemplar of pan-American incontinence (or that's *my* opinion). Its paper spine was creased. Not unlinked, a batch of tatty programmes featured the New York Jets. The whole nation summed itself in its flag, part unfurled on its pole. It had in its undulant silk a definite stripe, red, white, a splash of blue, and the point of a star.

The chief inspector, metaphorically with tweezers and a magnifying glass, laboriously straightened up, placing both palms to the small of his back. His large youthful head darkened in a gloomy depth of ceiling. As I spoke, the weight on those asinine shoulders lightened a little.

'The pathologist,' I said, 'has been his usual helpful self, I assume.'

Blamm emitted a sigh, at which I abandoned those trinkets. I feared the Arctic freeze of his mind. I moved, in the stale air of his exhalation, to the body, the corpse, the brutalised victim. He asked how I'd got on at Cadogan's, to which I replied evasively.

He thought. 'Okay,' he said. 'A truce.'

I told him what I'd found. His response, arrest those two little black boys.

'That's ludicrous!' I said. 'You don't think *they*—'

'I suspect everyone,' is all he said.

I bent over the corpse's beaten head, and couldn't help reflect on the cold war between our two departments, now at its keenest. I didn't talk. I looked at the girl. The girl had a short skirt, plum coloured, cheap-looking. It matched her canvas shoes, and had ridden up over her thighs. Her woolly top was a matrix of knitted holes – snakes or reversed esses – and was an egg-yolk yellow. It was half-length, summery, and showed her perfect navel. She had no bra, no straps to her shoulders. The thin chain of a necklace had got caught up in the tangle of her hair, which was long, newly washed, ash blonde. Her bag was some way from her feet, and this, of dark leather, was an overkill of zips and thongs.

The chief inspector softened. 'All right,' he said, 'here's what you don't know about Solomon. We're certain someone was blackmailing him. It's in the notes.'

59

Blamm said he'd go no further until he'd conferred with the chief superintendent. Bello was more at odds with the latter than he was with Blamm, consumed as he was by left-wing politics, a distraction he should have been more careful not to reveal. But he was young. To him Sparling carried a sharpened sword in the rear of an antiquated Toryism, and viewed the world according to two certainties: its statistics on serious crime, and the moral disintegration of modern city life. 'I hate to tell him,' Bello had said, 'of other things also at the world's end.' Said Sparling: 'We face, gentlemen, an ethical flab generally.'

The man had visions. He perceived, in the fabric of national life, uncleanliness brought upon us by the unrighteous. The siren of Finchley had shaken her priestly robes. By day she followed a moving cloud, a cumulus. Nights she communed with a ball of fire. Her half-sibling, of Number 11, held up his free-market rod before the tribes. *She* went up in the mount. There the Lord Mammon spake unto her, saying, 'And I will give thee tables of credit, and a law, and commandments I have written.' And the glory of Mammon abode upon the mount, and the cloud covered it six days, and the seventh day he called the siren out of the midst of the cloud. And the sight of the glory of Mammon was like devouring fire on the top of the mount. Then she went into the midst of the cloud, and gat her up into the mount, and *was* in the mount. Then were the Heathites wroth, and was Sparling, and wanted to smite her.

But then Sparling always said *this*: 'There will be one bright day.'

<h2 style="text-align:center">60</h2>

Murmurs, then a chatter of basso voices rose up through the closed window, yet when I glanced no one had breached the cordon or had followed the chief superintendent. He was a short man, with loose, bluish flesh around the eyes. The largeness of combat had filled his shoulders and upper torso. Nicks on his dimpled chin, and a rash to the larynx – not new, but an exacerbation – were the signature of Sparling's morning razor, never sharp, or almost always blunt. There was a smell of lavender. Blamm responded first, in the turn of his head and a semi-elliptical loop around the ceiling lampshade, which hung above us crookedly. He was careful with his huge laced shoes, and stepped over the girl's bag, the feet, those unlucky legs. Sparling moved to the doorframe and checked his watch – a digital, with a squarish face, and a brown strap, tatty, worn.

'What have you got?' he asked.

Blamm looked to the landing, and to the baseball bat, lodged in part in the banister. 'Just a vague idea,' he said. I knew that tone. I knew we were in for some theatre.

'Thought you'd be on holiday by now.'

He probably wished he was, the outsize Blamm better scaled to the ropes, beams and sails of his boat or yacht or whatever. Here sheltered from a powering wind and its salty spray, he went to some pains to show us his other, professional persona, not a life bowed and skulking, rather Blamm a fatigued athlete shut up in the darkness, doomed to the internal babble of aloneness. He'd hinted more than once at an unhappy marriage, and that was the truth of his yearning for escape, for the sea, for the open air, for the haven of lost horizons. Land had not suited him since, or his ordinance there, where the solving of crimes invoked reason, logic, the strange fire of causality, intrusion into the criminal mind. We were hearing awkward phrases ('In so far as we can gather'), things dreamed up over a test tube, and cast in bold type for the exercise of classification ('That's as it appears to be'). Sparling came into the room, a good man for grim charades. I could see him uneasy, askance, crooked in his looks, but amiable, and for the moment open to any hypothesis.

Blamm threw off his lab coat (so to speak). He called for more props, trying on the villain's mask, an article he pulled from a pool of shadows up in the ceiling. He took out a ballpoint and angled it up. This, in his great hand, was mightier than the sword, and for the purposes of simulation approximated to something much larger. I am talking about that baseball bat, which he told us was clean (no prints). If Sparling cared to step in, Blamm would reproduce the blow. Herein is the disadvantage in the chief inspector's height, who saw the world's pates from an upper elevation – in the crowded train – in the sandwich queue – from the seat where he sat in the dentist's waiting room. Dry scalps had come under his scrutiny, as too the receding tides, the waves of masculine hair thinning with each professional decision, which roused his sympathy – especially so in a younger man like Sparling. Sparling stepped in, balding, stony (for him the Thespian life was anathema), but put up a show in the victim's role. The chief inspector stood behind the door.

Blamm talked us through his imitation of the crime, despite my doubts, and the smirk I shared with Sparling. The chief superintendent had a silky spotted handkerchief, and here, tracing the girl's steps, dabbed its patina to his shaving rash. Blamm excused the breadth of his angles, bearing down on Sparling's crown – or, as the head turned, onto the temple. The climax came on the extensible point of the pen.

'The orientation tells us something,' I said, in its fit with Sparling's physique. It was porcine, and didn't match the victim's, but – I guessed their height was roughly equal. 'The chief inspector wants to slice off your ear.' A shorter man – six to eight inches, say – would have had the right angle for the killer blow (a man like me). Here Blamm acknowledged what might be a useful contribution, but as usual our commerce had its caveat.

'Where she is, isn't where she fell,' he said. In fact she'd broken her arm – the left one, which was partly tucked away – and the pain of falling on that a second time, half on her knees and crawling for the door, had probably finished her off.

I winced. Sparling said 'Good!'

That was some small glee. And perhaps all of us were pleased at that interlude, calm if brief. We strolled down. The men with brushes could keep that room forever, for the whole long length of eternity. Blamm, whose sense was temporal, lured me into the confines of his car, and drove us out. I should have known the kind of exchange we'd have, a sweep on his diagnostic curve, yet I allowed the tint of his windscreen to put my mind at rest, a filter on the morning sun, which had given me a headache. He wanted, he said, those boys masquerading as glaziers – he wanted them rounded up, and if necessary charged.

'I suppose,' I said, 'one sat on the other's shoulders, wielding the bat.'

Blamm turned on the radio. The weatherman predicted rain, a storm. The chief inspector, proud of his thoroughness, said only this: 'At no point other than the window are there signs of forced entry.' Keys hadn't entered his speculation.

On we drove. With those large hands to the grips of his wheel, the chief inspector swung his car into a one-way system.

61

Someone had appropriated the chief inspector's parking bay, ignoring its sign. In a show of impertinence, some other car had filled its parallelogram. This, provocative territorially, had been done to make a point – highly necessary when the chief inspector didn't understand the work its owner undertook, all as a matter of conscience. He chaired a group of neighbourhood vigilantes, which Bello had kept an eye on. It had passed too under Blamm's shadowy veto, to which our chairman responded. The disenchantments of the middle-class were tolerated 'at the nation's peril' (he was a small man, and had probably never graced a playing surface). Blamm only sneered at the impostor in his parking spot. 'Hah! A Citroën...' for this, to a certain kind of Englishman, is a highly insulting remark. He positioned his own long car just so, to block that committeeman's exactly where it stood. 'That,' he said, 'should do it.'

I had remained with my jacket off. Blamm's, on a hanger at the back of his car, had beards of new cotton at the cuffs, and was baggy at the elbows. There were no, absolutely no signs of a storm. I rose, stepped out. I turned to face a glare of windows, the full reflection under an intense summer sun. The chief inspector's silhouette loomed in a jangle of keys over the car lock. 'No sign of rain,' I said. I led the way. Blamm shook the silver in his trousers, loose change for an early lunch. I opened the vestibule door. A mid-morning drunk, or a madman, or a park vagrant – I wouldn't see, couldn't know, didn't care – had kicked at a panel in the door and left his impression. 'Ah, that's too bad, look here!' The chief inspector rolled his eyes. By now the sun had warmed my back, a cascade in the billow of my shirt, and yet, as I stepped inside, my blood had cooled.

'You absolutely sure about those boys?' he asked.

Well, I wasn't, though I turned and held the door. He was looking gloomy. Wheeling for the handle, I disregarded the blur of shapes indoors (momentously). Staverton sat there patiently, having been brought in once more by Bello. I said to Bamm: 'All the clues are there – the missing tape, the girl (when we know her identity), what's in her bag – when *that's* known – whose house....'

Blamm came in: 'Plus whatever you're *not* telling.'

In fact there was nothing, and I smiled, unable to correct him. Then I turned to Staverton. Remarkably, his hair was now double tone, with shades of grey, an effect of the height of the window and the warm rays of sunshine slanting on his shoulder. I advanced. 'Well, thanks,' I said, though my hopes for reform in one other zealot I knew – a WPC Shutt – were dashed when she crossed the floor, to tell Blamm the vigilante was here to see him. Her brown eyes looked electric under the veil of her brows. The twitch of her lips – that one fragment of communication – failed in its smile. She nodded, I believe at me, before marching back to her office, years too young, I felt, and too suspiciously clean. By contrast Staverton looked beyond his age. Nausea, or a bout of dyspepsia, had exaggerated his usual pallor. Those flabby cheeks were looking hollow. The quiffs of his new coiffure were a loud wild strawberry when he stepped from the light.

'I won't talk to *him*,' he said, with a sullen look for Blamm, whose jacket was over a shoulder.

'You won't have to,' I said. 'Here's Detective Sergeant Bello.' Bello was stirring tea, a mug.

The chief inspector, rolling down a shirt sleeve, looked weary and Masonic. I knew his technique at interview. To be blunt, Blamm was a bully. Yet here after all Staverton was reprieved, as that jumped-up committeeman suddenly appeared, on the explosive sound of the door's hydraulic hinge.

'Hoy, Inspector Blamm!' he said. He brandished a trowel, which he'd recently bought, still in its moulded wrapper.

Blamm put him right: '*Chief* Inspector.'

Nobody smiled. I studied the gloss, the viscosity, the thinnish amber in the open boards beneath my feet, and put a finger in my ear. Blamm's voice reached me on a random tide, and in its jumble – *piano*, *fortissimo*, rest – the confused message spelt out five precious minutes he'd allow the vigilante. Bello asked, in the new *détente* that had begun to flower between his department and mine, if I wanted to sit in on the latest interview with Staverton. What I could say?

I looked at Staverton. Twinned grooves in the fat of his hand had grown pink under pressure of the string bag he was clutching. It was stuffed with a magazine called *Fear*, which he'd bought in the Charing Cross Road. I shrugged, expecting political matter.

'Well, we'd better get on,' Bello said.

Staverton showed no inclination to move, not till Blamm and his vigilante, not till the last turn-up and shoe, and a fading bass note, had disappeared up the stairwell. Then he lurched forward, knowing his way to the interview room.

Blamm sent down one of his seniors, a man with a stoop, who long ago had tired of criminal psychology. His eyes had been magnified, a muddy brown, and were afloat in the squares of his lenses. I read there the texts of a dozen unsolved cases. Now on a hard chair he might content himself with mere mechanisms, unfolding his arms, about to push buttons, asked to work the tape recorder.

Staverton needed smokes. In the deepening rut of his pauperdom – a card he was always likely to play – he'd been reduced to green Rizlas and loose tobacco.

'You've rolled that one a bit thin,' Bello said.

Times were hard.

Bello hedged. Since, he said, a serious crime had occurred not a hundred yards from Staverton's room – 'A few nights ago' – he was going to account for his movements. 'And another thing.... We'd like to know if you keep an ape's mask with all that medieval paraphernalia....'

Staverton's fingers shook, failing with the first grey wafers of ash, as he missed the round aluminium tray. He didn't know how to speak, or what to say, and stuttered, clownish, but not incoherent (he expressed himself in the plaintive rise of his eyebrows).

'Plenty of time,' Bello said, and crossed his arms. That, I thought, gave me the chance to understand the suspect's brand-new hairdo. I could not fathom a reason for the close crop to his temples, the rakish quiffs forward from the crown, the accentuated ponytail (in a beige ring today). Then, astonishingly, he confessed – *he* was our man. *He* was that masked gorilla.

Bello uncrossed arms. 'And the mask?' he said.

That, explained Staverton, he had won at the fair (three ducks down under the barrel of his gun). His remaining account differed only in severity from that of the witness – that witness from the Côte d'Ivoire, by coincidence a woman he knew.

62

That appeared to wrap it up neatly for the chief inspector.

'It's no bad thing,' Dark told me in confidence. 'Now he's had you as sacrificial lamb, perhaps he'll give you this blackmail stuff. Why not get over there. Sound him out.'

'You're probably right.'

'How's the dreaded document, by the way? It's a riveting contents page – though I *would* like to see more.'

'To be honest I thought you'd lost interest.'

'Ah, no, Adrian....'

'Well then let me see.'

'What *is* the position?'

'Um.'

'Well not to worry. Just don't tease. If you haven't had time to work on it, just say.'

'Okay. I haven't had time.'

'Fair enough. Now why don't you try and tie up this Solomon thing. Then perhaps you *will* have time.'

'I'll do my best.'

'And don't let them tie you in knots on the Cadogan case.'

'The Cadogan case. Right.'

63

That – Section 6.2, or Chapter 62 – is a clever move by that ghost in my word-processing machine. I'm completely thrown. It's a chronology that has its own logic. So the question is when – when exactly did Bello also accept Staverton's confession? His contradictions did not help the Department answer that question. And here's a thing – the freak Staverton, in owning up to the attempted snatch of a handbag, had described the struggle lucidly, but was not able to show signs of bruising to his ear. Odd, since his victim fought back with that same bag, an accessory said to be heavily strapped and buckled. To the chief inspector this was all unnecessary detail. There were a thousand explanations. Furthermore, it was Blamm's instruction that Bello should press for a full confession of attempted rape. Theft was no good.

64

Blamm, after two thoughtful days, adopted new tactics, and was friendly. For once he sat upright in the fusty shades of his office. Two symmetrical smears exuded from his upper lip (it looked like gum for a stick-on moustache). I saw he'd been pacing with the phone, which had come to rest on a grey filing cabinet, not his desk. 'Told you so,' he could, *should* have said, but only expressed satisfaction at progress we had made with Staverton.

'Yes,' I said. 'Surprisingly easy to wring that first confession.'

'Of course,' he went on, 'this ruse with the handbag isn't going to wash.'

The bad sign, I felt, was the chief inspector wanting me to sit down. Thus he gained the high ground, as he himself got up.

'Stuffy, isn't it?' (A belated observation.) He put his big paw through the Venetian slats and opened a window. That let in noise and air, and raised the dust, and with it a twitch of his eyebrow. His portrait frame, with its angular stand and backplane, was in range of my chair. I read, bunched in a corner in Blamm's untidy hand: 'Marjorie, Lyme Regis, 1986'.[34] I was about to speak but the chief inspector sneezed portentously. Submissive and automatic I passed him the tissue box. He took it in a hurry, but was hasty with something else, a silver chain with a cross, a trinket he'd been fingering all this time. He plunged it into a trouser pocket.

'*Gesundheit!*'

The chief inspector smiled. There were a few things on his desk, from the murder scene opposite Cadogan's. 'What now?' I asked.

He trumpeted into a tissue, which turned his nose a springtide pink. I watched him with the telephone, at how without disturbing the bell he lifted it clear of the plastic tray it somehow came to be nestling in, home to an array of cacti. I sensed he shouldn't have done this. The dark frown and the drawing in of his eyebrows showed me his regrets. He put the phone down, miles out in his sea of working papers, and tried to lead me away with a crumpled smile. That didn't work. In the assortment of articles on the chief inspector's desk – nothing I'd consider unusual – I held my gaze and tried to fathom what was going on. He twittered about his committeeman, 'a buffoon', and with forced laughter told me he'd cut their conversation short when something else had come up. I felt we were now in a labyrinth. I approached with caution. I chuckled, hearing how our hapless Citroën man had enraged himself in the parking bays, waiting for the busy Blamm to move his car.

'He'll know not to park there again,' I said, and looked at the handbag, the one that had been the murdered girl's. Some of its contents were out on his desk – keys, an organiser, a concierge's business card (the Hotel de Verdun), a blue crush pack of cigarettes. Blamm, casually, picked out and leafed through a wodge of stapled notes. These, in his varying hand, touched on his chosen extremes – red, turquoise, a nice royal blue. About a week ago life had been leisurely, but then we'd come to today, and – well – those floating bars that had missed their t's were the sign of his neurosis. In fact his handwriting generally had a frenetic look.

'Ah,' he said, 'here.' This was his trump card. I watched the twitch of his mouth, and the way he read, and knew instantly his 'here' was too clumsy. Of all things, Blamm wasn't a man to improvise. By 'chance' his notes slipped down onto a polythene sachet, a consignment of cocaine. The big man craned over on his hands, and in part read to me—

'Sparling's been sat on by the Home Office. *Your* department, *my* department – we're all of us off the Cadogan case.' That left me with the prospect of no case at all and a return to the dreaded document.

I sat back, and I suppose should have been relieved, my errors eclipsed for the moment in the grandeur of higher counsels. However, I replied spontaneously—

'You didn't need an *aide-mémoire* to tell me that.'

65

So, we are now at the point in my tortuous little history where I was put exclusively on light duties (and of course when that didn't work out I was urged to return to sister Cecil down in Kernow).

'It's absolutely right,' said Dark. 'We're off the case. Now perhaps we'll get that document.'

'Not quite,' I said. 'I do not buy this Staverton confession.'

'Sorry to say, Adrian, we're off that case as well. Fact is there are moves afoot to take us off *all* cases. So, the document. There are no excuses now.'

'This is so unexpected.'

'Don't dwell on it.' There was something just too ominous in this sudden U-turn.

The phone rang. Professor Dark answered. When I had left his office, he covered the receiver and mouthed something at me, which I thought I understood, through the panel of glass in his door. I stepped back in. I re-crossed his floor. He had, I saw, a hand to a newly opened file (new orders, I assumed), but then he put the phone down, and the file in a drawer.

'You wanted something else?' I asked, to which he replied, could I just get him a chicken-with-mayo bap....

66

A cream filament, the first stray cloud in a light blue sky, unfolded its single limb and spread itself out. I had begun to feel the breeze at the back of my neck, and the sweat in my hair. For some time I had tried to avoid that road, street or avenue destined to lead me home, therefore each turn I made was less than mechanical. Result, a thousand yards added to my route.

A firmer breeze stirred in the street awnings. At an outdoor display of fruit and potatoes, I bought a peach. The stallholder palmed his chin and quizzed at the weather.

'Stormy,' he said (not quite the tone of a question). A swathe of grey dust puffed up from the gutter. 'Stormy,' I agreed.

On I went, to the Club Sportif, at whose much-wiped bar I drank one beer only. I paused at a late-night mini-market, certain I needed nothing, though nevertheless bought a carton of soya margarine – adding to those already in my fridge. Too late for an evening paper, I arrived home, finally, too late also for the news. I switched on my standard lamp. 'Nothing quite right,' I said. For my answer there was only the lacy silhouette of my lampshade, its tassels on my wall. I turned to a box of books acquired from Lawcom's shop. Again, I mulled over circumstances, which had not quite culminated in the professor's chicken bap, which I'd refused to go and get. I had insisted, edging from his office, on everything he knew on Solomon, before I signed off. If, as he said, there was anything new.

'Well, if there is,' I'd replied, 'it's better from you than Blamm.'

To my astonishment he told me tomorrow.

I picked out an ancient atlas of China, but did not get past the key to its references. I lingered over an account of odd things to find in the Rue Neuve-Sainte-Geneviève, but abandoned that for my window. I looked outside. The world was airborne. So much litter swirling round.

'Stormy,' I said. 'A dun light.'

I fetched a knife for my peach, but didn't go on to slice. It had got muggier – '…dun to saturnine…' – and I opened a window. 'Ah,' I said, 'the first few spots.' Outside, far below me on the street, a group of theatregoers ducked for cover. The hoardings were a fantasia of Broadway song and dance, and a Fifties revival. I looked out at the only man with a cummerbund, who clutching a tabloid pitched it above the gloss of his head. I loosened my shirt, pulling its flaps from the grip of my waistband. A square of corrugated cardboard spiralled up from a shop front. A light flickered. Somewhere an alarm clanged. Across the street, in an insurance broker's office, a fluorescent light had failed, plunging the glass door into a pool of darkness. Night, and its vapours, diffused the mottled reds of each passing car, whose taillights left their streaks in the wet roadway. It was suddenly raining hard.

A rent, a silver thread in the greyish blue, compressed itself, then yawned open into a radiant chasm, a golden bow over the roofscape. Something had troubled the minor deities, who were hurling boulders. There was a distant rumble. The storm opened with a boom. I checked my clocks. An electric zigzag – a streak of blue lightning – singed our concrete planet. A prolonged crack loosened the flakes of my ceiling. The first fresh douche of rain released its scent.

A faint trick of the light constructed a thin reflection in the inky translucence of my window, a face reminiscent of that other Fixt. It had that lean concavity under the cheekbones. Light, a presence ghostly in its eyes, flickered in its brows. Not greatly unsynchronised, thunder over my roof lent my apparition one further illusion – a voice. A second flash stirred the shadows angularly across a cheek, the nose, an eye. The mouth moved, as in a match light, shaping to tell me exactly where it was that I'd gone wrong. I imagined her mornings, Cecil in the dawn of new wealth, a woman strolling in her paddocks, trussed in country tweeds.

The light in her eyes faded. I had not forgotten – nor shall I – the easy action of her hand when slowly she unscrewed the diamond-studded top of her fountain pen, an heirloom whose pattern was tortoiseshell. 'The decline of our house has been irreversible.' Now she blinked lazily. 'In a decade I shall have re-introduced the wine bins.' The face in my glass receded, though another blue streak revived it. Its lines converged, it wobbled in my window frame.

I put *my* predictions to *her*, and described what her new great house would be. 'A few stone steps in open air. Eviscerated doorframes. Detached oak panels. A suspended window….' A hard rain lashed at my panes, where already the imprecision of her brows rippled and dissolved. The wind whistled in the ornate twists of my ridge tiles. The rain, now permanently filming my window, wiped away the blue lines of my ghost, my other Fixt. The deities boomed, beating their hammers on flint, prelude to the launch of their chariots over my housetop. Then, with the passing of their thunder, a straggler drew down a black arras, those brooding clouds, as I closed my curtains. The sill was wet. A damp shadow had left its impression in the carpet. I looked up into the triangles of my roof space, then at my wall clock, listening to the continuous abrasion, the pouring rain on the imbricated slate. Later, on the radio, there were Byzantine chants. A West End playwright talked of political ambition, and a seat in the Lords. I made my bed. I drank whisky. I came across and tucked away my Byrne Society tickets. Should I phone Frankie, to confirm our travel plans (now only a week and a half to the garden party)? Or should I wash this glass?

Doors, everywhere, had closed.

67

I had still got the smell of damp pavements in my nostrils, and the warmth of the sun on my back, when I arrived next morning for my meeting with Professor Dark. He had begun to smile, briefly before lunch, having sent someone out (not me) for a smoked beef sandwich. His appetite was back. I sat down. I took out my pen, without the intention to write, contenting myself with its mechanism. Extending, retracting.

'So,' I said. 'What's the final state of things, before I close the files?'

He shuffled his wodge of papers, and told me that according to Blamm Staverton still stuck to his version of events, having confessed to the attempted theft of a handbag, but not attempted rape. He'd begun to complain of police harassment, at the hands of PC Rudge, abetted by Detective Sergeant Bello. Blamm wanted the rape charge, so turned a blind eye.

'But why the Home Office? What's their interest?' To me it didn't add up, Staverton a petty thief after all.

'Beats me,' said Dark, who steered me into the safer waters of the Solomon case, passing me papers, and easing himself, legs crossed, into the lazy angle of his chair.

Blamm had got corroborative statements from Solomon's friends and relatives, and had built up a profile of the murdered man. His youth was where you'd start, when Solomon had shown a crank's obsession with shoes. That trait had climaxed years before in a ground-floor flat – the first property he bought – only yards from his mother's house, a large, modern, fortified palace on the outskirts of Stanmore. We knew of three overnight guests, female and olive-skinned, who had gazed up, on separate occasions, through the young Solomon's plain white shower curtains, and out through the barred window – in the matriarchal shadow of the adjacent house. Its high wall, with a triangular coping I later verified, was crowned with the jags of broken wine bottles, in effect a *cheval-de-frise*. An alarm bell in a painted box, in those days a stoplight red, was fixed to the gable. There was a security sign, and on it, in silhouette, an Alsatian, head and shoulders only. There were blunt words of warning, though to read you would have to stand at the wrought iron gates.

Solomon's depravity – if that's what it was – was reflected in his footwear. It was a nervous spasm, which repeated itself for that succession of overnight friends, his accessories of bachelor life, not that *I'd* have called them that. They numbered more than Blamm had been able to interview, but all had been an influence on what was already characteristic – his habit of acquisition. It had not yet reached the spectacular breadth of his later adulthood, and still showed itself only in the stiffness of his tread. Three such persons had remained in the neighbourhood – a span of twenty years – and had each, in Chaucerian story-telling style, come forward. Curiously, all remarked on the orientation of the shower cubicle, under the gaze of his mother's gable, which made them think of Alfred Hitchcock. For myself, this is no more or less than the dark hue of our common imagination, and I was not surprised therefore that Professor Dark chuckled. Here though parallels with fiction end, since Solomon's bathroom heralded nothing more sinister than its poor provision of towels – the host's persistent gaffe. There the sore-footed Solomon was always found wanting by his lady friends. One, large, fluffy, peach-coloured wrap, was all he ever put out – swaddling enough, he must have thought.

One in that procession was a brunette, a Mrs Pinkus, *née* Rosenbaum, whose expert powers of description Dark told me I'd enjoy. All those many years before, her hand had reached for the cupboard in Mr Solomon's shower room, groping for the turban that – as you and I know – was not there. A left-foot flipper fell down and slapped the lino. The right, a stickler for equipoise, followed, as so did an avalanche. A fell boot struck her shoulder. Yachting shoes, tied at the laces, toe-danced down the mirror. Sandals, and a sturdy brogue, then something elasticated, then an odd gym pump, then the partner brogue, all tumbled out. Finally an errant slipper. 'Of course, it couldn't go on.'

The redhead, now a Mrs Schmidt – who at that time lived and worked in Hendon – was better adapted to on-off affairs. Hers easily spanned in excess of twelve months. She threw down the gauntlet finally, having squeezed him in on bridge nights, just – Thursdays, she remembered. The quick fire of that once-a-week coitus ended in mild exasperation at his floating shoe shop, which she threatened to incinerate. On Fridays, her arrival late for work was down to his flippers. Her boss's jibes – a frantic, smiling man – had become indelible, launched as he scrutinised his wristwatch. 'Friday again!' he would say. Well, after so long, that did it. 'If this is to go on,' she said, 'you'd better buy a bigger place.'

By now Solomon had cast off his student rags, but had exchanged them only for the rumpled suits that went with his first job as chemist. This had its perplexities, since Solomon refused to consider the forfeit of his weekly jousts. 'Incidentally it was around this time that his hair began to thin.' This was critical information. That's because, despite decades of exaggerated claims in magazines and newspapers, what we of the moral high ground might suspect might be true, *was* true – all those miraculous tonics are useless. A toupee Solomon tried he discarded as gauche. He counted the cost of his thousand and one hair restorers, then got to work on his own concoction, which he marketed. This was phase one of Solomon's sudden wealth.

A blonde enters the scene, a Miss Pym – not exactly kosher, it has to be said – and someone these days going by a variation on that name – Ms Pym-Wilcox. The hyphenated afterglow, adopted in a belated doff to her ma (God rest her soul), 'resuscitated mater's lost sovereignty' and at the same time lent support to her social activities – with straitened interest groups, sparked into life on the fringes of politics and activism. She was responsible for a quite dramatic *coup*, inveigling a well-known lady novelist into addressing her members, in the beating of her pliant breast, and a cheery snarl. Such good fun. Her Solomon era, she said, owed its cause to her fascination for life in a kibbutz, an organisational concept she had since put before a quorum of single mothers. For that particular project, she had had an eye on the West Country, or Wales, or the Highlands, though it remained an ambition only, falling short of necessary funds. Dark, who had not had the pleasure of her company, stretched out his legs and allowed himself a smile. 'Crazy!' he said, and shook his head. Blamm had noted her use of tobacco – an endless parade of mentholated cigarettes, which, once lit, she discarded almost whole. 'And perhaps you'd know the meaning of this,' Dark said. Blamm had described the logo on her headed letter paper, which was a short-haired nymph dressed in a jobber's stripy shirt with tie, brandishing a roll of cash.

Miss Pym, so called in that first life, witnessed the proliferation of Solomon's shoe cupboard. Added to that, with his popular counter to baldness, she watched also its expansion geographically. Stanmore lost a chemist, suddenly, and unexpectedly, and Miss Pym had to re-think her Thursdays. That now meant a trip from Hendon to Finchley, where Solomon had stationed himself in an airy semi – 'Complete,' the agent had said, 'with original dados, balusters and fire surrounds.' Soon the recesses filled up, and Solomon, a man of many pointed shoes, began to prioritise his soles and uppers according to an all-weather life in the boardroom. His favourite brogues predominated, usually black, though an alternative range in tan or in ox blood began to extend that choice. He rebelled once with a brushed suede. Thankfully all those heavy boots had disappeared, though Miss Pym, opening a kitchen cupboard on Thursday number one, half expected a deluge of footwear. 'Not a bit of it,' she said. 'Brooms only, and a vacuum cleaner.' The amazing fact of his hair loss was this: that in turning the male world's pattern baldness into cash, his heavy walking gear had been removed. His boots were filling the voids in a dampish stone cottage he'd acquired on the edge of the Pennines.

Ms Wilcox had told an unflappable Chief Inspector Blamm she had only one caution, clear in her own mind as to the inevitability of time and its passing. Accumulating decades were a question of magnitude. 'One always assumes,' she said, 'the blunting of recall.' Ergo (she phrased it) a month of Thursdays later – or perhaps a leap year – the non-smoker Solomon spoke of a special commission and a lucrative contract with the tobacco lobby. Incidental to this, an artisan he hired delivered up a fine piece of handiwork. It was a cigarette box, a Swiss chalet in miniature, with movable shutters and pebbles glued to the pitch of the roof. There was a musical action, and anyone tempted by an English cigarette was treated to a burst of *Ach, mein lieb!* – Solomon's one real regret.

'Well, there is a point?' I asked. I seemed to echo that query of the former Miss Pym.

'Arrogance!' said Dark, an opinion I hadn't asked for, and as usual didn't share. Solomon's ostentation was never more evident – and this was Blamm's view too – than in the fully dimensioned holiday chalet – I don't mean that bagatelle, that little imitation – our hair restorer acquired. His passion for real estate was suddenly an Alpine whim. You would think this a provocation specifically aimed at Blamm, when the twanging cigarette box was an exact replica, 'even to the carven name!' But this was without originality, and perhaps he meant 'graven'. The chalet's name was 'Edelweiss'.

There were more disappointments for the chief inspector, none more poignant than in further revelations from the sophisticated Ms Wilcox. Her script is marked *vivace*. 'He filled the place with skis,' she told him. The professor opened the span of his arms. Cocked on his chair, he appealed to an airborne sprite that only he could see. 'I ask you!' Predictably, the chief inspector had fried in the heat of disapproval, wiping his brows (according to Dark). Blamm had, Dark said, a picture in his mind, and must have seen himself as the only man so endowed visually. Me? Well, I knew my smile was wearing thin.

Then Dark attributed to Blamm the crassest remark I think I have ever heard him utter: 'Of course in the Solomon household, successive Yules went uncelebrated.' Solomon and the blonde Miss Pym had their bags packed and ready in the hall in Finchley, and watched for the snow reports.

Miss Pym remained in tow, to the start of Solomon's era as mogul. As an individual she had no qualms, since his playgrounds were (her terminology) 'but a small archipelago', formed 'as a matter of cause and effect' around his business empire, or dominion might have been a better word, she thought. After all, this possession of land was only the footsure symbol of a small man finding his step. I am told that for Blamm 'step' didn't quite do it (sometimes he was wholehearted in his metaphor). It was, rather, a rapacious march, a 'sweet doing nothing'. There was envy in his tone, which had aroused the professor's suspicions. It made him wonder how the chief inspector analysed his data.

After a further read I completed the catalogue, and was able to state out loud what Dark already knew, i.e. that Solomon had soon got bored with his marble apartment in Gran

Canaria. Its problem – its drawers full of flip-flops – he resolved with a further property deal on the Costa del Sol. He took on a Moorish villa and hacienda, which he kept for the low season, generally avoiding the warlike English abroad. For the spontaneous drive out of town, a round house in Leicestershire did nicely, and was the right habitat for his leather riding boots. I had only puzzlement for his Languedoc vineyard (more correctly, his part interest through an independent *viticulteur*). 'What could one wear treading grapes?' Dark didn't see the joke, because his lunch, a pastrami sandwich, had arrived, an event that prefaced the disintegration of one of his molars. The fact that he departed the Stygian shades of his office, cradling his jaw, had nothing to do with my judgements. So we *didn't* get on to Cadogan, the real cause of Home Office interest.

68

Ms Wilcox had wrestled with the monumental problem of her hairdo (happily, no sign of baldness). This I know, since I had now been left with the untidy disease of both the chief inspector's and Professor Dark's handwritten notes. Let me explain.

Nowadays, details of her private life were open to examination, due to her public engagements – things no one would have guessed when Solomon first routinely bedded her, in Stanmore. A throbbing Professor Dark, coming back for plain yoghurt lunches, contained himself, in a fixed static smile, his cheek and jawline swollen after his hour in the dentist's chair. Ms Wilcox claimed special foresight, derived from a careful study of 'the prevailing political ego'. As Blamm had learned, across his desk, at interview, she'd anticipated the savagery of mid-Eighties hair artistry, getting herself cropped a good decade earlier, under comrade André's flashing scissors. 'Ah,' I said, because the detached Frankie Reuter came to mind, whose styling was the same. She was left with her natural coloration, blonde, which no longer suited her image, jet, auburn, or *châtain* a better fit for her public militancy. She persevered and in front of a flashlight eventually found the desired effect – a dye of the right androgynous finish. This was what kept her in the van – which, as conclusions go, possesses a certain logic.

Solomon had long moved into pharmaceuticals, and as such did not do his deals *coram populo*. In his shoes and sharp suits, in his general tenor, even Ms Wilcox finally saw the man in his chosen context. Hers was what spare ground there was – I mean in available news media – and that is how she left him. 'A hard man,' she said, 'negotiating.' But, she went on, too gentle by half in his personal life. The vile gods of commerce are never placated. They can 'never abide', Dark observed, 'the cul-de-sac of affluence' (the rule of wealth is it swells or contracts). Economically bubbles began to burst, and gleefully various schools of commentary – right, left, centre – rubbed their hands. Their predicted demise of England's first female prime minister was not as confident. Ironically, that iron mummer represented Solomon's constituency, and that meant more, not less discomfort, each time he sat, stood or chatted under the flimsy arch of the Conservative Club. For his rivals and colleagues, their adopted stance in the same Tory tent meant no such obstacle. For one Mr Whoplode, still bemused in the rose tint of Conservatism, a decline in

Solomon's fortunes paralleled increase in his. Output from Whoplode's factory, whose product line had overlaps with Solomon's, went up. Correspondingly Solomon's shrank. This was 'riveting' to watch. The florid Mr Whoplode kept a finger on this of all pulses, dispatching his best, most persistent reps to all the important drug lunches (large ears listening out), while *he* remained staunch, a Thatcherite, brave, imbecilic, unafraid in the coming storms of recession.

My next meeting with Dark took place on the following day, by which time he had come to salute his wife as I had never known before. In the ebb and flow she'd responded to the surgical ache in Dark's upper jaw. He needed his emollients, shuffling his Whoplode papers, and come midday was able to chew on that man whole. 'Aw, just look what she's done!' he said, and showed me his inaugural lunch pack. Cream cheese sandwiches, no crusts. 'Thoughtful,' I acknowledged. Perversely I remained shut to the potential he attached to the statement Whoplode had made. After all, *he* had come to Blamm. I learned he was ruddy, and saw by his signature (a round sweep with a fine nib) that his glory was superficial. 'An employer's bombast,' nodded Dark, but *I* said more a possessor's. I had no choice, but followed the tentative wheel of the professor's mastication, hoping for conversation. For a moment I beheld his bottomless silence, not seeing other than offence in the muddy pool of his eyes – sombre, thoughtful, alarmed.

Instant impression of Whoplode was of a man at home in the hotel lounge. He stirred endless cups of morning coffee, beating the fire of his gossip, assured of a profitable end, no matter what pose. He'd mastered the pharmaceutical convention, the one-day seminar, and revelled in its recreation. Nor did this depend on any particular attitude. That could involve legs crossed at the knees on a regal settee, or saw him standing under the brass trim of a wall light, about to swoop for a biscuit. As time went on, his rival delegates scuttled back to their respective UK hideouts, flushed with the evolving 'sad news' on Solomon. Whoplode was first to talk (i.e. openly) of that person's financial reverses, a catastrophe beginning with rumours, in the end 'tending to a bush fire' – as Dark put it eloquently. Solomon was losing business, was holding off his creditors only through the sale of personal property. The chalet went first, with its skis thrown in. 'How do I know this?' Whoplode protests. The overblown tiers in Solomon's management structure threatened collapse, thanks to a wholesale defection to Slough, 'to my own good firm....' Technical staff were coming over too, and as everyone knew, they were the last to know anything. It was suggested that confidential papers had found their way west also, the blueprint for Solomon's salvation – a miracle drug for weight watchers – for that too was now set to be marketed by Whoplode.

Dark said that having got excited the chief inspector danced a jig with his finger ends, saying: 'Whoplode's got this irritating habit.' The chief inspector forgot himself, imitating Whoplode, removing a notional pair of glasses and breathing on each lens in turn. Dark said: 'Now I'd know him anywhere.' Blamm got upset at that, and brought down a hand hard on his desktop. 'Is that really the point!' he said. Dark agreed it wasn't but told him he'd spilt his paper clips. Then they argued (which I might as well render as one of those kitchen-sink scripts)—

BLAMM That doesn't help at all.

DARK You want to tell me this is Solomon's murderer?

BLAMM No, but something's wrong.

DARK Well? What?

BLAMM Whoplode rubs his hands while Solomon sells off his houses.

DARK It's business.

BLAMM Later he's shocked at his murder and wants to tell us about it.

DARK Because.

BLAMM Because what?

'Because,' Dark said, 'he wouldn't want you to think he'd bloodied his hands for the sake of a weight-watchers' pill.'

'No,' said Blamm. 'I've thought of that. It's too simple.'

'That,' Dark replied, 'is my line.'

69

I tried to call Frankie, and at last caught her – 'with a million things to do' – before breakfast. The mail – and with it the local news – cascaded onto my mat, its WELCOME a bristle of inhospitality. A lathe started up in the flat below, when I said to her, not quite honestly, 'It's a very bad line.' The handset needed a clean, and the thing generally, an unhygienic white, had had its day. It had similarities with the conventions of home – that's to say home after the fall, which felt like a century ago, where the configuration was a 1960s hall, with stairs running off, and a telephone table.

Then I was pre-empted, about to strike my heels on a floorboard. That rumble suddenly ceased, and absurdly I, not Frankie, was shouting. 'Do beg pardon!' I said. A pause followed. I envisaged her, fingering an ear lobe, when again that rumble started up. I just about caught what she said. 'Ah yes, understand,' I replied. She had friends down in Sussex, where she'd arranged to spend a long weekend, to coincide with the garden party – the Byrne Society. 'Meet you there,' she said. (Infernal noise!) 'Meet me outside,' I corrected. 'I've got your ticket.'

70

'Outside' was Sir Geoffrey Beaufoy's gatehouse. Sir Geoffrey – as with the succession of Beaufoys before him – was an old Etonian. Unlike them, he'd opted for backbench life. From its hard pew his objection to European integration was exercised with great curmudgeonly relish. He was a patriot, especially on matters of currency. His other passion – a point I could but won't debate – was as public diarist from the tea rooms and bars of Westminster.

The Beaufoy signature was a line in foppish garb. In public he charmed. His friends, we knew from the tabloids, were circuit judges, Formula One drivers, TV chat show hosts, and whatever obscure MP he could mould for leadership. It was after Wolverhampton, with its prophet Powell, that life in a political grey suit appealed to him, though he wasn't at all like his learned model. Philosophical scrutiny was too finicky for him, and what erudition Beaufoy had, had long ago localised to his solar plexus.

Today, Sir Geoffrey had got his chairman's hat, and welcomed all guests, all-comers, mellifluously. I caught sight of him as I hung around in the gatehouse. I paced the parquet floor, sporadically looking at the clock – and clutching Frankie's ticket. I glanced out through the stone mullions, which had yellowed over time. Sir Geoffrey wore cream slacks and sported an old school tie. He bounded, an arm outstretched, in almost perpetual salute, in and out of the topiary. There was one fleeting instance when I saw him emerge from behind a giant fowl, which had a beak, an eye, a coxcomb. He greeted a plump young woman, whose smile was overshadowed by the extravagance of her headgear.

The waiting got worse. A Mrs Madox-Smythe, who presided over the official register, and handed out programmes, didn't want me loitering. 'Time's getting on,' she said. Her cheekbones protruded, and as remedy were too overtly over-farded. A lifetime extruding aristocratic vowels gave her lower jaw its acerbic disjunction. 'You're Fixt,' she said, 'or Thorpes?' She looked up from her list. 'Fixt,' I said. 'Mr. Two tickets. Waiting for a friend.' Ah, yes, that she already knew and had made a note of. 'The young lady's already gone in. Ms.' I surrendered the two tickets and in return was handed a programme. Thorpes, a DLitt, bowled in behind me, a boyish man in a tawny suit, clutching a large brown envelope. His limbs and little soul were awash with professional joy. Perhaps his cargo, which I assumed was an A4 typescript, bore with it great commercial value, and it was this that hummed in his being. Naturally I dismissed him. Briefly Mrs Smythe lost his name on the list. He told her to look up her entry, to which he added, as an aside intended for my ears only, an obscene innuendo, which I'm sure she heard, her colour high, her smile teetering on collapse. Thorpes breezed out to the chalk path, where I followed. His trousers were rumpled from the train, and a muddy hue in sunlight. I noted how bizarrely he comported himself – madly over the clipped lawns. His arms, legs, and his bobbing red head were a miracle of uncoordinated motion. I allowed him to get ahead, in his manic strides for the house. I looked out hopefully, into each secluded folly, for the waiting Ms Reuter. Right here, perhaps – where for no good reason an octet of flagstones had been part-enclosed in a perimeter of quick-growing conifers. Yet no, what they confined – a bench with memorial plaque – was unoccupied. Or here then? Sorry – no again. Soon there was a swing, in the arms of an oak, moving but empty. 'She must be somewhere....'

In fact she'd been singled out by the society's public relations man, the West End reviewer Dr Paschal Brennan, whose path I have crossed before. She smiled, and must have found it amusing. By some ruse or other he'd lured her from the green sward and away from the plastic blues and reds of the bunting, and the breeze in its little flags. Should I attempt a vocal shrug, surreptitiously as I emerged from an arbour? Whether or not, I had reason to wince at Brennan the private man. His life was bent to his addiction, treating on equal terms the grape, the grain, the hop. His look was Romantic, and trussed.

He offered himself gift-wrapped wearing a bowtie. All that lightness around his temples was a vapour of champagne, which is not in need of explanation (his flunkey drove him everywhere, having first placed bottles in the cool box). In the remote shades of Beaufoy's little princedom, that same lackey had positioned a moulded garden table, which in its weathered state was looking less than white. We were near some potting sheds. Brennan had placed centre-stage his own champagne bucket, and in addition had asked for a second flute to be brought (for Frankie), and one more bottle of Moët. The scene was incongruous, a paunchy middle-aged man bearing his weight on a lightly rusted drainpipe, wooing a shorthaired girl. She smiled and sipped, on the safe side of a water butt. 'Typical,' I thought.

A plant pot and a window box lightened Dr Brennan's seedy grey profile, where a gardener had left them on a sill, above the height of Frankie's shoulder. She looked good – shoes white, leggings electric blue, blouse the burnish of nasturtiums. The sheen of her hair fronted a blue and purple wave from the box's trailing lobelias. When she moved, to put down her glass, a crimson-leafed begonia appeared from behind her head.

For Brennan – in the high gloss of this first of his champagne breaks – my appearance dampened his mood. He must have recalled how for the space of a week, if several years ago, our paths crossed repeatedly. First in the Grays Inn Road, where I was surprised to find him looking elderly and ashen at the temples. I had made no account of the dictates of TV imagery, and had only ever known him for his wispy tufts of hair assiduously blacked. He plodded gloomily from the façade of the *Sunday Times* building, at that time shared with an engineering firm. He had been on a TV show, from which I also recognised his Bacchic jowls: some jolly music quiz – guess the composer, the opus, or watch a stringless piano pedalled and struck – all kinds of brainless parlour games. Perhaps that was the day he'd lost his review work – if no great tragedy, a loss nevertheless. The general opinion seemed to be that the solid Brennan had found himself at odds with the latest tyrannies, the smart talk, the scandalous profiles, awash in the arts supplements, when what was wanted was a punchier kind of wit.

A day or so later I chanced on him again, much the worse for wear. We were on the threshold of the Wig and Pen. Brennan was on his way out, the time two-ish. He thought my long gaze was going to precede requests for an autograph, but of course, having not much interest in the demotic of his pen, I didn't oblige. Towards the end of that same week, from the studios of commercial radio, an arts and current affairs presenter dragged him to the discussion chair, with a programme edition banal in its titling. It was something like *Pandora's Legacy to European Letters*. I forget the exact construction. Moments before, he wriggled his way ahead of me in an upper room of the Cheddar Cheese, where he quaffed a quart of Marston's – even before my one and only pint had been placed on the bar. Then, for over a year, there were no more coincidences. Then, at a meeting of the Daniel Byrne Society, when I had offered myself in view of a vacant committee post (application rejected, albeit an interesting CV), his little bloodshot eyes widened in confused recognition. 'Dr Brennan,' I said, and shook his hand. 'Fixt. Adrian Fixt.'

Let me see if I can remember that meeting. Sir Geoffrey wore pretty white pumps and a striped business shirt, having adopted a behind-the-scenes democracy, proposing then seconding himself in the continued role of chairman. Unwisely he kept to the same committee consisting of four, an even number, which of course denied him the casting vote. He was arrogant enough that aristocratic flamboyance would always carry the day. Sir Geoffrey pointed to Dr Brennan's invaluable connections, mostly media, and so urged him to stay in post (all this took place in Beaufoy's London office). Brennan, smug, heard from the rest of us how no one else could as effectively fill his role – the PR role. All this I knew was true, for Brennan was a man able to persuade supermarket chains to part with useful sums in sponsorship. He did have intellect, though nowadays that was something he liked to conceal, preferring to cobble together acerbic book and theatre reviews for glamour magazines (sometimes) and the tabloids (mostly).

His critical work was admired once, for which he researched minutely and wrote with a youthful flourish. Despite the blunders of at least one archivist, and the problems of a lacuna, his biography of playwright George W. Clare remains, I am told, a classic. He was also one of Byrne's favourable reviewers, having described his populist theories as 'a project', and as 'syncretised disparate source material of unusual invention'. And yes – he was also voted back. So too was the third man, Bim Shay, another literary type.[35] There was no practical value in *his* appointment. His post was secretarial, and he was there as a 'figurehead only', as Beaufoy put it.

I bumped into Brennan again, on a grey day in the St Paul's precinct, where, waddling over the flags, he greeted me asthmatically. 'My dear chap,' he said, arms open, a bit unsteady. I cast about for something automatic, and alluded promptly to what was by now his successful re-inclusion on the committee. 'That,' he said, 'is all bunk,' and got on to something more pressing. His diurnal oblation to Dionysus had fallen overdue, so now he insisted on a remedial glass of Bass at the Blackfriars. 'It'll have to be quick,' I said. At that he scoffed, though I protested I'd got an appointment. He asked only what a good Oxenford boy like me was doing in the crime business. 'Actually,' I said, 'I'm redbrick.' That cheered him up. 'I'm glad,' he said. 'Not much good goes through those English portals.' That cheered *me* up, and now miraculously the man had colour: a ruddy tweed suit with a mauve fleck, a yellow waistcoat, an immobile puce around the cheeks and the dimple in his chin.

He failed to settle himself when we got to the bar, where he grumbled at the dried egg rolls under a glassy electric glare. His solution was a plate of ham and a crusty chunk of bread, a few doors away in the medieval gloom of the Ludgate Cellars – a minute's walk. That was his cue for one, perhaps two bottles (I can't now remember), of an oaked Australian white. 'On this I shall pass,' I said, and ordered still water – 'with a slice of fresh lemon.' It didn't trouble him to drink alone, even when those gigantic quaffs were smaller than his thirst. He became jovial, expansive, then wide-eyed with disbelief – not when I told him I'd never read or heard of Clare – but when I said that in Lawcom's shop, on a very high shelf, ancient and redolent, a slim paper volume called *Stargazing* bore a certain

Paschal Brennan as its author. He put his napkin to his mouth and wiped away a blade of cress.

Euphonious angels had hymned the intoxication of his youth, and now that the fat man had got out – that bigger Brennan lurking in an undernourished frame – the rhapsodic smile of his inebriation served notice of at least one regret. His young heart's song had made him coy, and was the residuum of a feverish, former Celtic life, which he couldn't now brazen out in conversation. 'I don't want this to be generally known,' he said. I watched him. There were furrows in his flabby brow – this was how he schemed – and immediately his bearing changed, was pendulous. Somewhere near the bar a coin dropped on the cold stone floor, and here, at our rough wooden table, the Dublin hack was grey, despondent, thoughtful. He planted a firm handprint in the condensation sheathing his bottle, and poured. 'I suppose I *could* get that one back,' he said – meaning Peter Lawcom's sole copy of *Stargazing* – though logistically the elimination of all traces of what he now saw as his little indiscretion, was beyond his resources. 'Well,' I said, 'that would be a falsification anyway. You are – or rather you were what you were.' That only qualified his mood of confession, for now, with the breeze of early manhood back in his hair, he bemoaned his subsequent life of 'hackery', those suitcases full of newly bound books, destined for the glare of his reviewer's lamp. 'They're hardly ever worth a read,' he said. Desperation had long set in, though in its first hiatus he attempted to conjure back, into fictive life, a dozen, twenty, a hundred novels that had engraved themselves as the meaning of his early years. That – the re-read – shattered his illusions. The deep significance of almost all those texts was a soap bubble. 'I am just so weary of books,' he said, and poured himself another glass – something he *could* still do.

71

As such Brennan breathed his fumy verity. With the grape his only consort, the deluded scribe sat out his nights in the cone of his lamplight. He rocked to the rhythmic clack of his typewriter, in a tiptoe of sport, jest or waggery – and 'alive to the smell of garlic and steak in other people's passageways'. Cartoonists depicted him as Paschal wolf (a theatrical sobriquet, picked up I know not where), a seedy-looking reprobate prowling at his keyboard. Careers, he knew, could be broken, for Brennan's hand could be unmerciful. Too often his appointed goal was the castigation of whoever happened to be the current *farceur*, some young hopeful laying out his wares on the West End stage. Then, briefly, a kind of rehabilitation seemed plausible, when Byrne's penal theories, now that a right-wing intelligentsia had decided to re-evaluate them, prompted a debate that Brennan participated in.

In the re-parcelling that now took place – our liberal democracy gone soft on the causes of crime – things unspeakable entered the character of Daniel Byrne. His studious image took on menace. For the benefit of an expanded middle-class, with its book-club audience, nothing could now be sacrosanct. Twenty-five years after his death, a handful of marketers – operating strictly paperback – offered the usual platitudes as to the nature of his genius, at last seen as ahead of its time. As spinoff the realist Byrne garnered a new generation of readers, a crudeness that filtered into almost everyone's longhand.

Decades after that, our clever raconteurs of late-night television, in the spar of studio critique, are unable to discuss the icon Byrne without a pitying smile – something Professor Dark seems wholly unaware of. Their argument is this: to find sympathy with Byrne it's necessary to look back on a society whose 'natural' order has been subsequently challenged, at the same time performing the sleight of hand that ignores this latter fact, with its leaders, patricians, still propping up a causal world in a shared sense of what its authority is. There are still those who cling to the notion of good citizenship as a hierarchical thing.

72

I emerged from the rhododendrons, and felt sure – so soon as I showed surprise – that Brennan knew all along that I, Fixt, had been lurking there. He was flippant. 'My dear Herr Ficht!' he said, in that permanent miasma of alcohol. Frankie allowed herself a smile, a twitch that unsettled the constructed contours of her lip gloss. 'Fixt,' I corrected. 'Mr. Glad you weren't kept hanging around,' I put in, at which Frankie thought for a moment. 'It's all so wonderful!' she said. Brennan laughed. 'Bit off yer beat, old man.' I found my riposte a split second too late. Just then the tall apparition of Beaufoy's chief gardener rose through the turf, a crotchety man with a weather-beaten face. He clutched at a hose, and a sprinkler valve, and was tetchy, with as yet only a drop of water. Brennan I knew would not resist some quip, the exact nature of which I tried to predict – a waspish man and his blockages. He was unsteady on his feet (so early in the afternoon, I thought), and with an effort of concentration edged a timid little step into a depth of shadow, into the shade of the brick building behind him. His shifty little eyes, bulging at the best of times, were streaked with blood. 'My dear fellow,' he said, exhorting the gardener. 'Do, but do keep an eye on these' – meaning his table, his bottle, his two champagne flutes. 'And do organise two nice garden chairs!' I looked into Frankie's face, with its hint of glitter round her eyes, and divined, in her radiant smile, the pleasure she took in Brennan's buffoonery.

The gardener's irrigation problems were not ours, happily, and the three of us turned away. I took up the rear. The lush Brennan put his tremulous paw to the small of Frankie's delicate back, and escorted her onto the sward. They crossed to a line of topiary, where in the shade of an exaggerated cock Paschal at last shared a pun: infecund Adam with limp hose; contrariwise, this giant fertility – but how Brennan phrased it I can't precisely remember. I followed them up to the first of the buntings, which harmlessly lisped in the breeze. I stepped off the path and paced hard into my own shadow, away over the clipped lawn. In a yellow tent, which served beer, a loud group of newspaper people had gathered themselves. They had at their centre a small man with a ruddy complexion, and, unspectacularly, a grey suit. His big, grandiloquent gestures, set off in a blaze of Delphic anecdotes, had reduced his acolytes to helpless mirth – cloned, curiously, in the same carmine necktie. Egged on by their prodigious guffaws, and beaming smiles, he predicted heroic failure for the cranks of the Daniel Byrne Society. It was possible he was right. New dawns, eras, epochs were all a bit back-yardish. The whole thing turned to farce when, with the outdoor scent of pork on a rotisserie, a jongleur, a man from Frome, entered the tent – his get-up a quaint stripy hose – and ordered a soft drink. 'O my! What these rustics get up to!' The player left with his tin of fizz, unaware that the squeaky titters behind were aimed at him. I checked my programme, which had him listed as part of a trio, here to perform their pantomime – St George in pursuit of a dragon. 'Revisionist slapstick', as someone said.

Another beer, please! Why thank you again! I sat outside at a table, which sloped dramatically, its parasol printed with the word 'inzano', the C having faded. A sallow roué with a viridescent moustache attempted to sell me honey-roast nuts from a pannier. I flicked him away with my programme. I studied the timetable. Family shows were under way – a mummer with life-size fantoccini, over by the south gate, and the St George group. In the lime walk, not far from Sir Geoffrey's water garden, a medievalist recited a versified riddle. Someone was going to swallow fire – none of which I cheered to. Then, thankfully, at one o'clock, the long beige buffet tent opened to an accumulation of queues, which I joined, with the eventual reward a dollop of potato cubes in Mornay. A jocund chef in an open shirt and a tall hat carved from a spit, thence tossed two slices from a flitch onto my paper plate. His accomplice was a formidable woman, who bawled her victuals capaciously, and squished something indelicate into my sauce – a chicken wing packaged in a paper napkin. I waived a half-glass of tepid *vin de pays*, not having the circus know-how to juggle that, a plastic fork, and to weigh my lunch in a steady palm. Soon enough I saw Frankie again, though by now the crowds had gathered – hordes in weekend casuals bowling over the grass – which blocked my view. I munched over their heads, setting my gaze on the distant gables of Beaufoy's country seat. Someone had threaded morocco-coloured streamers in a cypress tree. A Grimaldi in draughtboard checks rose up on stilts and stalked round a bronze statuette.

In a parting of summer frocks and seaside blazers, I caught sight of her again, still with the vile Brennan. That sad man had a grubby hand between her shoulder blades. She, so thrilled, had hers in Sir Geoffrey's, who shook it with vim. It bore simultaneous fruit, because something Paschal said had tickled him. He couldn't help that toss of the head and a belly laugh. Then Frankie laughed. Then I caught the glitter of gold braid and ostrich plumes in the person of Miriam Beaufoy, and she laughed. Funnily, I didn't. Instead I found a wire bin for my chicken bones. I walked off (farouche, yes), madly waving my programme (having disturbed three wasps, who were now in pursuit). A game old buzzard with a wrinkled neck plodded to a halt and braced his forward momentum on the shiny aluminium of his Zimmer frame. A stroke had partially eclipsed the colonial ferocity in his martial-looking face, the thin latex of which, now only semi-mobile, balanced a half-smile under one bright, one dead eye. Enough was enough. My intention at all times now was not to see the joke, even were I capable. In ringing endorsement, a cackle of laughter went up from that gaggle of newspapermen, somewhere behind me.

Folly that it was, for I had no hope of transmuting them to stone, I glanced back across my shoulder. I bore perhaps the only true witness to their grouping, that's to say closed to the outer environs, and tight in a circle. I waved away four wasps now, and completed the quintet with swipes for the crock on his Zimmer frame. I headed for an avenue of maples, one of many dappled walks irradiating from the heartbeat of Beaufoy's house and acres. What was I missing, if anything?

A troglodyte with a fractious infant – both wearing dungarees – had raised her voice and gesticulated wildly. The child, reluctant, waded from the centre to the edge of a pool, which had as its ornament two preening swans chiselled in stone. The surrounding disc of water, a reddish, rusty brown, was without motion, that stasis undermined by little spots of sunshine fragmented through the trees, and in a quiver on the pool's still surface. I sat on a stone ledge, waiting for the grunts to die down, at a distance round a bend. It was cool and I rolled down my sleeves. Again I looked at the programme. After lunch – it said – we had an inaugural lecture to look forward to, 'a purely light-hearted affair', to be delivered by Mr Simon Kennedy, our man from the City. 'Light-hearted' probably meant a string of usual anecdotes concerning the life of Daniel Byrne.

For Byrne the story began in a garret and ended with lionisation for his popular works of criminology – some I have mentioned. Sudden celebrity, and lots of invitations. I am unsure of what stage someone taught him how to speak effectively in public, when there were moves into radio, and later TV. In one fell swoop his coffers were filled, and that attracted leprechauns. We can guess at what that was code for, an occupational hazard set out whimsically when Byrne was persuaded to write his memoirs. He showed us his full eccentricity, bringing to his pages the first of his little people, an allegorical being spirited into life in the glow of what treasures he'd amassed. He had with him one practical purpose, that poor, pale, blinking little man. That herald from another world tugged at the confused undergrowth of the master's beard, Brahmsian in extent, and told him 'Hack it off!' Was this a joke? We don't know, but in any case, presto! Imaginary beings were now the bottomless material of his once-weekly radio show. That, if filled with social intent, nevertheless transformed the rites of his everyday life, which bordered on the mystical. The letters he wrote to his London property agents, his 'honoured gentlemen', were prefaced by a visit to the barber. A city tailor cut him a suit. Then he needed a valise, anticipating travel. Having sold his terraced two-up two-down in a cheerless north London suburb, he holed up in a hotel on the Strand. From here his 'honoured gentlemen' chaperoned him into the solid estates of Highgate and Hampstead. He liked the look of the heath. He remembered a cousin in Kentish Town, and that was near yet not too. So it was settled. Those happy intellectuals in his new social calling went out of their way to humour him, though couldn't conceal smiles when the new-found Celt in him butted in on their conversation. They drew him out on his projects, nodding gravely (woods, streams, runes, a vaulted sky, a soft-edged parable for the deceits of civilised life), but privately did not fear a challenge to their privilege, whose outlet was media and academe.

You can see what has attracted Beaufoy to Shay, an outsider similarly.

73

I listened to Kennedy's incessant drone, an excrescence much better suited to the boardroom pulpit. What shaky aesthetic had called him to the lectern – today of all days – I didn't try to guess. Most seemed to share that scepticism, preferring the bar, their lunch, their talk. It was a performance lacking key variation, and was easy to ignore. A group behind me had important bits of gossip – I heard it rumoured someone had been asked to research and write Shay's unofficial biography. I caught the name, Grace Fowler.

Kennedy's *pièce de résistance* – the handing out of prizes – he acknowledged as Sir Geoffrey's bonny brainchild. I remembered the debate, from one of those early society meetings. 'You would have to demonstrate,' was one objection, 'that the terms of competition were genuinely open.' Sir Geoffrey, a raging backbencher, a man who supported the establishment from a privileged position outside it, palpated a palm over the swart stubble of that grey square chin of his, and considered that point (unusually). 'Ah!' he said, and all of us knew that tone. He tugged at the shiny knot of his tie, and adjusted it. The thing still didn't sit centrally, and now over-compensated its former rightish bias. A thin light swept up the wall, as someone, probably me, passed him the water jug. 'It *will* be genuinely open. Entries won't have necessarily been published.' That set us muttering. A blazered yachtsman under a brown fug of pipe smoke thought this might be counter-productive. 'That could put off publishers,' he said, 'who might not want to risk their authors. You know, outdone by a novice.' The committee thought hard, but, in the end, opted for an open charter. The cosy world of publishing had lost its notion of democracy if it viewed this as a disincentive. And, well – 'Let the competition be devalued if the big players do abstain,' someone said with defiance. At that point Dr Brennan suffered an indisposition, albeit brief. The man was mute under a gale of un-exhaled laughter. This was because he knew our human vulnerability, and the scale of the prize money. He recovered to raise his glass, and shared his merriment, one eye glaring moistly. That seemed to settle it, and at the vote the ayes had it.

74

I came out, and walked, and put those preening swans a long way behind me. I personally had life, and a will to stretch my legs, and pointless reflections like these. Astonishing that an architect must once have designed that everlasting pool, so that it, and the mute swans, and their pedestal, the polish of English outdoor life, were among its models of petrifaction. A green maple leaf spiralled down behind me, crosswise over my shoulder, with a turning sun in its veins. I fought off certain suggestions, without success. I recalled, inescapably, an autumn afternoon, and the same sort of leaf, its colour a burnt cinnamon, the thing beaten by a horizontal shower onto my windowpane. I was at home, at my desk, with a *Crime Quarterly Review* open at an article on the quirky psychology of *noms de plume*. I mused on the real identity of the author, and weighed my conclusion with a burden of inevitability, and in an inspired moment, void of constraint or logic, supposed him to be the fickle simulacrum invading *all* our texts. This one gave us a nice little murder with a Chinese box motif, bent to one further figure of penmanship, a man who has his back to us, and is hunched at a desk. We're shown his perfect hands. They're pale, naturally, and the digits are long, with spotless nails. The leaves of half a dozen typescripts, pristine in all ways, remain unmoved in the breeze, pinned to the desk under a glass paperweight, which is etched with an Arian ram. It's a starless, restless night, and here, atmospherically, is the total of things from the props department. Patio doors, ajar. Curtains, open – in a bit of a stir. Outside, a shapeless rustle of black foliage, and the moon's yellow crest, as it fails to scythe a passing cloud. Shall there be rain, lightning? It doesn't matter. What's important is those typescripts, for behold, they describe a man at a desk, immaculate hands etc., the glass ram, troubled night, moon, foliage, a mauve cloud, and so on, and of course typescripts, which describe a man at a desk, a moon, a scythe, a ram (let me apologise now). Zoom out to the apogee, the biggest box. Our subject puts his pen down. Thunder, lightning. He turns (are we going to see his face?). Someone steals up with a knife, from behind, and stabs, but of course our victim puts his pen down. Thunder, lightning. Someone steals…etc.

I regarded that whole contraption as pointless, as I tend to think of anything in racy prose. Its title, *Concentric*, ought to be *Ec-centric*. Its best invention in metaphor was that hall of mirrors shown above. Anything – a wing beat, or a bouncing ball – has an implied replica, usually embedded triumphantly in a distant latitude of the narrative or text. I wouldn't bother you with this, except that its author had reached the Byrne competition shortlist, with an essay on the troubled identity of Peter Sutcliffe.[36] That (the shortlist, and later the awards ceremony) had run to problems of its own, timewise. The blade of one of Beaufoy's sundials extended a penumbral scalene well past two o'clock. The ceremonial lectern, a throne and platform rigged up outdoors with a microphone, remained eerily unattended, a long twenty minutes after the prize-giving should have commenced. The guests were restive, checking, re-checking, watches. The four silent trumpets, grey loudspeakers, were a hum. One was on a flagpole. Another was entwined with a passionflower looping round a pergola. The third, put up to vibrate the canvas, was aimed across the bar in the beer tent. Anyone in or around the lime walk would hear the fourth, it was hoped, hung in the arms of a bronze Pan. Eventually Sir Geoffrey emerged, having exchanged his cream slacks and old school tie for a Forties-style pinstripe and a matching, monotone bow. He didn't seem pleased. Nor did Kennedy, who shadowed him to the lectern. Brennan, his usual russet, managed a smile, but remained by an open French door. The blessed Bim Shay[37] hovered more remotely, quitting oak panels for a window. Beaufoy spoke, or rather mimed, and was prompted by Simon Kennedy to switch on his microphone. That accomplished an anxious caesura, with monophonic buzz to accompany. Then when Sir Geoffrey cleared his throat – a metallic ahem! – the catch in his larynx made way for something sombre.

His orator's ease, the thick trickle of his voice, that plummy basso so fitted for public use – all this had deserted Sir Geoffrey, at least for now. Audibly he resembled a cheese grater, mincing his phonemes, acutely embarrassed. There'd been 'a bureaucratic foul up', and sadly the winners' cheques weren't where they ought to be, 'that is to say not here!' – and what could anyone do, really? Somebody sniggered. Not I promise Fixt. I had got myself in a position to the rear, and watched over the backs of heads as he squirmed. This was, after all, comic. Nonetheless all good things must be cut short – that is a maxim. A cherub tugged at my elbow, whose purpose was to end my fun – or so I thought of it, a conspiracy. He wore a stiff shirtfront and a waiter's black tails, and passed me a note. *Please make my way to the great hall – immediately.* Beaufoy was on the point of announcing third prize, unbelievably for the Sutcliffe study, authored by a man called Sam Cornelius. Thorpes, who'd been sitting at a lunch table, suddenly got up, and having realigned his crotch sat down again athletically. Then came Cornelius, whose limp wrist feebly brushed my cuff (yes, he'd been that close). He skirted round the crowd. One of his friends, a loud Falstaff, roared his applause, his abysmal throat a luxurious tinct of claret. In a few hoots only his black beard was silvered and bespittled. Then that pestilent fool made *me* his object – only because I had dared to stare back. A house of misspent plaudits followed, singling out me for one of the laurels, but of course that only mistook my stroll for the great hall, and not for third prize. In the end their handclaps rounded on someone else, a more genuine fake, so that at last Cornelius rose at the lectern, his brows knotted and limpid. All saw the circular flash of gold, the reflected sun in his round lenses, though I didn't stay to hear his deepest gratitude.

Brennan ushered me through a studded door, still affecting not to use my name, his 'My dear fellow!' a discourtesy marking his full absorption into our social system, with its classes and classifications. I paced across the floor, as seemed to be indicated. He examined his shoes, nervously. I gazed up into the roof, at a recent renovation, sure that while I paused he'd at last cast off that shabby cloth of English etiquette. My eyes dropped from the stained timbers onto his rotundity, that lost little man, a plain, bombardiering, idiotic littérateur. His veiny lids fluttered. He was sheepish. I asked myself why, how. Such befuddlement wasn't due just to the charge of his glass – after all, he hadn't got his crutch here now. He was hangdog, tentative, grandly over-spanned, a diminished man under an ancient architecture, those replicating hammer beams holding up the roof. They'd all of them, all – Beaufoy, Kennedy, Brennan – all earnestly beseech that it wouldn't fall in.

'What's it you want?' I said, and heard Sir Geoffrey's blaring laudations echo in the air outside. Fantastically the second prize had gone to a youth. For a moment, when he looked up, a transom in the silhouetted arch of a window striped his face. Then he came towards me, crisscross over that web of Gothic shadows. 'Fact is, old boy,' he said, 'we're in a fix.'

Bejabers, was that all!

75

Brennan traced nervous circles with the stub of a little finger – not, apparently, to mesmerise. He'd positioned himself at an arras under a pointed arch, whose stitching glorified house-of-Beaufoy chivalry, its detail an embroidered knight swishing a sword and bearing up a cup. The appropriate caption was missing (I thought): *Determined defence, ancient site, Threadneedle Street.* A barbarian with a halberd, too apish even for today's counties, was pitted against him. The duel took place under a stylised vine.

I said to Brennan: 'One intrepid age to another,' the 'another' being much less certain, our own. He turned but didn't really look, in full compliance with that tradition he'd come to uphold. Its demand is preservation, in this case of the good family Beaufoy's bequeathing of vulgarity.

The jousting was obscured when Brennan, plodding, occluded all but a velvety tuft of grass – though as that sank another detail rose, diagonally over his shoulder. I made it out immediately, one of those unlikely juxtapositions of English heraldry. The Beaufoy house proclaimed itself in two crossed spears crowned by a coat of arms, a design splashed in the subdued colours filtered through the mosaic of a window light. A painted feather emblazoned the curved shield (silver and ostrich), whose quill (gobony gold and azure) was the triumph of ink over field sports. For me, it presupposed one further analogy. I am thinking of Sir Geoffrey's improbable profession, whose emblem is a head in the sand.

Brennan, unsure of his step, began. I watched him open his arms (with mild horror, I anticipated a bear hug). To my relief, this only prefaced an unfinished sentence: 'All I ask....'

God only knows what's happened to Frankie, I thought.

There were no portraits, surprisingly. All had been shipped to another wing, which was never named – east, west, whatever. I did, later in the day – at teatime – glean an explanation. I had followed Sir Geoffrey into the drawing room, where Miriam fanned herself in the shade of a potted palm. But that is all to come.

By now the overall winner had sprung to the lectern. I hoped it wasn't Thorpes. Both Brennan and I had half an ear to his sibilant grind – as someone later remarked, the default medium of an over-*risqué* speech. 'Let's not be long about it,' I said. Brennan, with another seedy gesture, showed me the way. I followed, uncomprehending, the flaccid pointer of his index finger, to see only the scarred lintel of a fireplace, a slate hearth, a demijohn with ornamental grasses. 'Ah no!' he said. 'Here!' The 'here' was a silk screen, un-concertinaed, and behind it a vast double door, through which we passed. The plebeian rabble outside, wide-eyed at the nonsense still being perpetrated, expected tea in the hall, where Brennan had no wish to be overrun. 'Discretion,' he said – and anyway, before that, we'd have to give way to an army of white-capped ladies, and the wheeling in of trolleys and urns. We squeezed up a turret, on a winding stair. We doubled back, across, over, finally up again, an assault that sent us through a succession of doors, galleries and furnished rooms. The point of that final, dizzying spiral was a studio. It overlooked lead moulding on a huge flat roof, and was filled with the incessant tick of meters – mournful on an un-plastered wall. Brennan, wheezy, asked me to sit down. I did so, in a window seat. 'The others will be here,' he said.

'I live to see it,' I replied. I half turned away. Then, at the sound of footsteps on the stairs, Brennan looked suddenly, quaintly Mephistophelean. I hoped it was Beaufoy coming up, to give this whole rigmarole its quietus. Brennan paused mid-sweep, in the theatrical wheel of an arm. Something – some private thought – had blanked his eyes. Someone or other's ghost swarmed over the floor and up the walls. Slowly, a pale jaundice showed itself in the loose flesh of Dr Brennan's overfed face. I could not sympathise. He grinned – not for the last time embarrassed. I turned attention to the folded acres of lead, a blue grey, and running from it an aluminium duct, ablaze under the angular rays of the sun. From there I traced the exact flight or lethargic flap of a crow, an old black glove in a steely sky. Then finally his clever deceits brought back my eyes, and I watched – his entire frame askew in the vertical. The much whitened, un-protesting stubs of his fingers bore his terrific weight with fortitude, as they pressed into the plastic yellow glare of a table top. Here we were still, in the contrived set of a silent movie, just short of a pirouette. Majestically, with the claw of his free hand, and from the concealed fold of an inner pocket, he produced a cigar. Ludicrously he offered it. 'No,' I said. 'I don't. I hope you're going to get to the point.' He may have, of course, to the accompanying tock of those meters, but that was a song drowned by the prodigious clonk of Beaufoy's tread.

So to Sir Geoffrey, who now assumed the lead. His entire head rose above the stairs, then above the banister. Then up too came his slim shoulders, shrugging themselves. An itch, was it? Once here, he did not share the doctor's reticence, able only now to put behind him the 'prattle' of speechmaking. He shook hands vigorously, dragging me up. In a rush, and since we had graduated to the talkies, the dramatic Sir Geoffrey introduced me to his script (he allowed me certain improvisations).

HE [*a bright ponceau*] Mr Fixt. Very pleased.

I [*stoutly amused*] A lovely place. Nice day.

HE [*casting for a hook*] Really too kind. Um. [*Interlude, no music, no confection*]

I That was Thorpes was it at the winner's post?

HE Thorpes good gracious no. Fellow called Higgins. Fact is we're in a spot with the winners' cheques.

'Yes,' I said. On cue, a grey Simon Kennedy mushroomed out of the woodwork, here to help his little Punchinello. He assumed authority to the best of his vocal range, filling our human silences with careful words (as again, those pendulous ticks threatened to conquer our soundscape). He explained the problem so. The committee, at its final meeting late last week, having decided on its trio of winners, could not decide on the placings – the one, two and three. Each man went away into the lamplit night, having pledged in democratic ink – all somewhere scrupulously for the record – to bring in his preferred placings today – i.e., on prize-giving day. 'A consensus wasn't possible,' he said. 'Therefore, a hasty ballot.'

'Yes,' I said. 'I see the dilemma.' Kennedy, with a fond thumb to a shirt cuff, appealed to my maturity. We were all professional men (that, in *our* day, was a bastion). 'Go on,' I said, and asked myself did I need my notebook? His cufflink was engraved, not as I'd assumed with a vine on a trellis, but with a C, which was looped with coils round the angles of a K. He went on. He described the moment he and his three committee colleagues looked out on the dawn-white pavements. The anaemic glow of Sir Geoffrey's London desk lamp had proved to be useless. It was here that someone suggested the ballot – in principle fine – yet all had an itch to write the cheques there and then. 'Presumably, that would save time today?' I said. 'Well frankly yes' (Sir Geoffrey, back to his script). The two signatories were before me – Kennedy and Beaufoy – and couldn't help looking, feeling stupid. 'Okay,' I said. 'Let's get this straight. You signed and dated the cheques, leaving the payees blank.' Brennan, compressing his cigar at its open end, had breathed in the scent of honeysuckle, and recovered himself. 'Absolutely. Mr Shay committed all three cheques to respective envelopes – that was certain.' It was Shay's inimitable ballpoint, the sweep of a poet's hand, labelling each exterior – a FIRST, a 2nd, a THIRD. 'So then what?' Well, that much done, Brennan inspected the water closet. Sir Geoffrey rummaged in a drawer for his House of Commons diary. Kennedy, his mind still clear, stepped into the hall and rang for a cab. Sir Geoffrey went to the door and bellowed out a phone number. 'And?' Really that was it. The envelopes went into Beaufoy's wall safe (nothing untoward). Sir Geoffrey slipped them into an attaché case this morning. 'What we now find is one of the envelopes – empty.' 'Oh,' I said, 'empty....'

All of them sighed. Then, by some mysterious compulsion, Brennan sought out and found the silver tube for his Havana. He fumbled it, sliding it away somewhere, which allowed me to study his Englishness, a poodle he'd trained and adopted. It kept in step with the others, properly co-ordinated when the three of them closed round me in a semi-circle. It shared a common perplexity, the cold fear of professional taint, given the least scent of scandal. Here there was Beaufoy, who envisaged a bad press, those acres of newsprint hot from the doings of or around Westminster. Kennedy reserved a prayer for himself, a man of finance. How he knew those mad, bad dogs, and the salivating handlers, in a relentless scourge of every square inch throughout his Square Mile, nostrils keened to the least whiff of dishonesty. Then of course Brennan owed his sheen to the brightest media lights, as a man permanently made up. He was opposed to the release of information, with its possible accretion of myth and speculation. 'That I think is unlikely,' I said. They echoed the word 'unlikely', yet prudence led them to make their benediction. I, Fixt, would (wouldn't I) be glad of a little extra work. Paid. Discretion the watchword.

'Gentlemen. You want a private detective.'

Beaufoy: 'Yesinessence.'

Fixt: 'I'm afraid that's quite out of the question. Emphatically no.' I had not given up on my career, and I still had the problem of two unsolved murders, whether or not Dark had taken me off those cases. 'And I am not,' I added, 'trained in police work, as I think you assume. You, Sir Geoffrey, I'm sure know all about the agency I work for....'

76

Far be it from me to disguise my smiles, having got to the accidental truth cloaked in Sir Geoffrey's veneer. Those innocent fires – abated little embers, really – were just a dull red on just an unimportant horizon, no matter how he might predict an unstoppable conflagration. 'It's a figment,' I said. Nevertheless, he'd sensed the possibility of flames, even as a man who'd bragged that the febrile swish of party whips had scarcely licked or tickled the hairs of his back. It was hardly a comfort, when all that backbench barracking was likely to dissolve in bluster, just when the party looked vulnerable to change. 'Not so,' I said, and followed his troubled step, though by now he had come to view me as an obstinate schoolboy.

77

I was unable to match his un-rhythmic strides as he led our group away. I paused often, to look at his trinkets, in the tiered succession of galleries I followed him through – more sunlit space than the typical house-dweller dreamt of. 'Charming,' I said, at a wreathed infant, carved in the same dark wood as the curved balusters. 'It's got velocity,' and indeed it hung there, suspended in air, in the open apex over-spanning a doorframe. 'No time for that,' he said, and pointed down another flight. Even so I stopped at a niche, where an ancestral bust dignified the curl of the family upper lip. 'Ah, that,' he said. 'Miriam always ribs me.' The sculptor, he said, was a social climber and sycophant, who'd taken this particular scion of the Beaufoy line – in fact Sir Geoffrey's grandfather – and performed surgery on the nose (a repealed wart to the right nostril). Still donned in his beautician's cape, that same artist had applied his neat cosmetics to the eyebrows, with a trim and transformation, where now a single bed of thorns fell apart into two elegant pencil lines. 'Well,' I said, 'I can believe it.' I felt no disrespect given the peppery craters embedded in the flesh of his proboscis. His eyebrows came from the maternal side.

In the drawing room, the ample Miriam cradled her cup of tea. Sir Geoffrey made only fleeting introduction, perhaps regretting I had come this close to the core of the Byrne Society. Miriam – her backdrop a burgundy coloured curtain – was discussing her favourite inanities with one of those cynical newspaper people. His was a poised cup and nodding head. At least she had the shade of a palm, if not really his ear, and explained why the family portraits had been taken from the hall, where I was shortly to take my tea – not here among the elite. 'It's because of Sir Geoffrey's hobby,' she said (his soul's submission to music). Weekends, Renaissance song sharpened the acoustic depth, which the presence of hangings tended to diminish. Ms Kirkby was here often. His passion for the human voice extended to Byzantine chants. Then there was 'his spiritual at-homeness in the Baroque', which had brought young Mr King and his consort – 'ah, so memorably' – on two, possibly three occasions, she recalled.

Beaufoy tried to whisk me away. The sweep of his pinstriped arm, the direction of his open hand, insisted on a succession of closing doors between me and Mr Bim Shay, poet, who'd now caught my eye. The great man had knotted those wise brows, having been

pinned in a torrent of nothings in a godforsaken corner. 'Time,' I said, and took in the
bobbing heads, the stifled yawns, when to me only Shay cut a decent figure – doubly
crowned by a presentation plaque and beside it the head of a stag. It was the surefooted
Thorpes who'd approached him as quarry, unleashing vapours on the one authentic man
of letters in our midst. Beaufoy glanced, and misunderstood. 'A quarter past,' he said. I
shrugged, not keen to take tea in the great hall. Nevertheless there Sir Geoffrey pushed me
into the hubbub, before parting, his eyebrows raised. His frown dissolved, and he relaxed.
He eventually picked out Kennedy – Brennan a moment later – and sent them back to
their duty, socialising. A rosy char thrust a saucer of tea under my chin, with its cup afloat.
'No thanks,' I said, and cast about for Frankie. She'd got herself with one of Brennan's
coevals, aglow with uncontrollable smiles. That set me striding for an early train.

78

Semi-supine in my chair, legs a-dangle over one arm, head gratefully tucked under the
opposing wing, I had closed my eyes with the radio on, and had dozed. I was troubled by
a sense of grief, applied to I knew not what. I woke up, neither to silence, nor to a voice or
music. I rose to stamp, but not to stamp-out the hum of that lathe downstairs.

My curtains waited to be drawn. The moon's bright quadrant paled an ornamental frog,
put to work as paperweight – feet, legs, a bloated belly anchoring my private chronicle of
Staverton's first arrest. My problem, I felt, was the case we'd all been taken off – or was it
merely intrigue that had heightened my curiosity?

The streets buzzed, which meant plenty of cabs. I took one – not to Cadogan's, but to
the house opposite – and later stood under the orange flicker of a street lamp, from where
I made my way to the murder scene. That's to say yes, I broke in.

79

By morning I'd a lightness of tread. There was a scent of dew and garden roses.

Towards eight I went by bus. At a quarter past I had claimed my usual café stool, where
I picked at the buttered flakes of a croissant, served in a plain serviette. It was approaching
nine when a first cloud squeaked across the empyrean, and with it a rumour circulating
from my boss's office. Absurd to say, some fool had suggested that despite a serious blow
to the head with a baseball bat, the girl hadn't died (Dame Nature's clever trick was a state
of hypothermia, duping all but the doctor). The result (highly questionable), and destined
for a file marked scandal, was the tenacious victim under round-the-clock surveillance,
fighting for her life in intensive care. Or so ran the fairy tale. To me it didn't make sense.
And surveillance – wasn't that the fatal flaw?

None of this deterred me. I even brought a shine to my sword, which I hoped to cross
with Dark's. I advanced through the labyrinth, to the door of his lair, without the
assistance of thread or chalk marks. Once at his threshold, what did I find? The door was
ajar. On first looking in, I saw Dark slumped in a crosshatch of shadows, legs crossed, a
secretive phone to his ear. He chuckled cautiously, to, or with, whoever was on the line.

After a pause he said: 'Of course, yes.' There he put down the phone and swung round, surprisingly animated, stirred by the swish of air as I closed the door. I would begin, I thought, with a bright 'good morning', but managed only a 'goo—'.

He brought the flat of his palm down hard on his desktop. This was catastrophic for his inkwell, which fell from its stand and pirouetted into the waste bin. Professor Dark asked – at which point I recall the blaze of his eyes – what did I think I was doing...?

'Doing?'

He stood up and strolled to his notice board, thumbs tucked under his armpits. 'Don't think I don't know,' he said. 'You were careless. You were seen. I am talking about last night.'

I replied to his broad back, to the formation of creases in his polyester shirt. What he abhorred was lawlessness, especially among his staff. That he would not tolerate.

'Ah, but I've found,' I said, 'something significant.'

He turned, shaking his head. 'I see from the chart you've got outstanding leave. Take it!'

'But—'

80

A little light headedness, in the days that followed. It made my dilemma exquisitely domestic, breakfast being a toss-up between the tang of lime marmalade and the fruity gel of a blackcurrant conserve. Should I have toast, left whole or triangular? Brown, white, wholemeal? The bedrock of how much butter?

Indecision, though it cannot define ends, isn't fate deferred. It is resolution postponed. This was a lesson I learned.

All kinds of trivia are open, suddenly, to scrutiny. That flutter of mail on the WELCOME mat, if not exactly hailed, is an opening on a specific kind of comparison – of size, weight, texture, typeface. A bill is a masterpiece of dry formality. Circulars are an attempt at sunshine. The chirpy insurer exhorts us to life, supposing he's a grasp on that. Eventually none of this is distracting enough, and frankly I remained in a huff that Dark had refused to listen. Should I phone, write, somehow let him know my thoughts?

No. But what they are, Dark, are this—

For was it not suspicious that a large family house, under the eye of the witness Cadogan, had only the semblance of one that was lived in? I found nothing out of place. No rumples in the easy chairs. No ashtrays to empty. The beds, though neatly made, unslept in. I could find no books, papers, magazines, left half unread. In the kitchen the bin was clean. The cold jaundiced glare from the fridge, when I opened it, revealed just a solitary can of pimentos. Good staffing, you'd say – yet there were layers of dust, everywhere. 'That may or may not be so...' you would say. Didn't I understand? We were *all* off the case.

Ah, but why?

Day two, Fixt's exile. I took half a dozen newspapers and settled on their distribution throughout my living space. Two tabloids for the throne room, where the strains of credibility met a counterpart materially, with plosives. In my bedroom a rightish highbrow, whose twitterings I balanced, in the hollow of my easy chair, with distortions from the other wing. That had only the lure of the crossword to keep me awake. It left two others – one, laughably, claimed to be 'independent'. I bothered with that only at the breakfast table. Its front-page headline was an unadorned 'Chancellor won't resign', with the perverse conclusion that perhaps you thought he would. News content was a froth of indignation, as a catalogue of his, and his government's blunders—

1 Legacy of credit boom still leaves personal debt at all-time high.
2 Property prices fail to recover.
3 Credit economy now untenable with decline of housing market.
4 Prime Minister restates government targets for inflation.
5 Small businesses continue to fail, houses still repossessed.
6 So on rather dully.

All this took precedence over what at one time may have been good spectacular gossip, if the City's shady doings ever can be. That, as an inescapable institution, had been relegated to the gloom of an inner page, under the banner HOME AFFAIRS. Elsewhere, in the profile of someone new to the shadow cabinet, we find an outline plan for the unemployed – all of whom he assumed to be athletic. His brainchild was a cross-county federation for the furtherance of amateur sports. An obituarist on a following page summed up the life of Professor Walter, OM, whose pronouncements on education hadn't gone completely unnoticed. Then in the finance section I found another slant on the chancellor, pictured in a flashlit handshake with Mr Alastair Vercelli. Mr Vercelli, an Italo-American-Scot, had resigned as the government's economics adviser and was on his way back to Washington, followed by his daughter Alison, who'd been studying at Goldsmiths, but would finish her degree back home.

Day four or five. The blue-shirted mailman bore up on my desolate altar something other than a final demand. It gave me pause for nostalgia. Oh for those perforated dispatches, mostly red, rolled out dispassionately from a network of corporate print rooms. The headed, typewritten page I un-quartered I systematically palmed flat, so far as toast crumbs allowed. Its culmination was the insane sweep of someone's signature, underlining itself without the smallest hint of hyperbole. That was to say my leave had been extended indefinitely. Therefore Adrian Fixt, a small man in the grinding quern of officialdom, should either sink to oblivion, or in the best traditions of Hollywood acquit himself through every court and committee for the reparation of his honour. Thankfully a cloud of English pessimism at that point descended. We all at some time find ourselves helpless under the steadfast wheels of bureaucracy. For me that meant one more bout of indecision, a fog in which I did not call Dark (I imagined anxious moments, his effort of composure each time that phone clanged impetuously on his desk). Instead I tried to track down Sir Geoffrey Beaufoy, an act involving a long succession of unattended phone extensions. I redialled repeatedly, and eventually got through. I told him I would take his case, and found only that he couldn't really talk, or had cooled over recent days. His 'Yesofcourse' dissolved to a 'Beintouch', which I took as a polite brush-off.

Perhaps it was time to tackle the complete works of Shakespeare, or Proust, or anything...the *Encyclopaedia Britannica*....[38]

I thought about how to assemble my four main, and at this stage only suspects – those giants of the Byrne Society. It turned out that Brennan was behind locked doors, somewhere off the Edgware Road. This had been the case for several days, having been pressed – with not too strong an arm – to the solemn joy of a wake. A gnarled Irish poet, a man of flights and flatulence – harmlessly cocooned in lyric rusticity – had taken the trouble to die. As a poor sort of epitaph, this was a matter of days after finding himself a pillar of contemporary culture, with awards and medals for his work. Brennan drank himself under the table, aided by the added intoxicant of Celtic *vers libre*, which as literary hack he was called on to recite – strictly in honour of the dead man. In the days that followed – because I did wait patiently on this – Paschal groaned on his back, gouty and a new shade of green. His appointments were cancelled, or in fact slipped from his diary like spectres. What remained to his gaze, if intermittent, were the cracks and the yellowed mouldings, the floating rose of a ceiling somewhere in Kensal Rise. This much he told me himself, when eventually I'd got the quartet together.

By contrast Kennedy shook his head severely, or so I divined when I phoned. He announced that for him any day *would* have been fine, but for a tricky takeover with a security firm. This was one he had to oversee himself, though at reasonable notice he'd spare an hour one evening. Beaufoy, on his side, or rather from his backbench, had scented blood. Now that the hunt was on, he saw his government turning in a major U, and wished only to heap fuel on the fires of revolt. Shay I couldn't get hold of.

Had they jointly backed down? It seemed that way. I let the thing drop – not without a twinge of regret. Thus my first week of leisure was destined to complete itself in a mountain of half-read papers, when in skirting the foothills for news I was surprised to hear from Sir Geoffrey. His late-night call came just as I had made a virtue of trashing the crossword – or was about to – this being no great effort of will, as something I'd abandon. I had already cleared the way for stage-one Shakespeare – a paperback *The Tempest*, with scholarly annotations. Amusingly, Sir Geoffrey saw my magnified eye in a Holmesian glass, and wondered how I'd been 'progressing' with the case. I resisted the impulse to laugh, telling him, in the gaps between his yesindeeds, that what I needed was his and his colleagues' co-operation, without which nothing could be done. His response was lukewarm. The four couldn't possibly assemble themselves till at the earliest next week, he said.

'That, Sir Geoffrey, makes it very difficult.'

He replied with an um, and went suddenly quiet, thinking. Finally we compromised, with the venue for preliminaries. This was his London address. More precisely the study at his London address. Here, under the gaze of Beaufoy's snooty servitor, I was able to inspect what evidence there was – 'Though I can't begin to guess what that might be,' he said.

'Well, there's one thing,' I pressed. 'If you've still got them, I'd like to take a look at the original envelopes.' He was sure they were somewhere, since the prize-winners' cheques were eventually mailed, registered post, with profuse notes of apology. Even then I wouldn't let him hang up, and came right to the point. What about the *missing* cheque?

'A sum must by now have been drawn in favour of someone,' I said.

I gathered from a second silence that yesinfact this was the case, though the someone stayed unnamed. 'We'll talk about that,' he said.

81

Allow me to state, hypocritically, that I have never liked the mummery and fancy dress of police reconstructions, preferring to balance the likely event – in this case the removal of a blank cheque – with its probable cause (someone in need of money). What follows must for that reason read as a confession, or *volte-face*.

Beaufoy's man below stairs, who only gradually won my respect, watched as I approximated the dimensions of Sir Geoffrey's study. He – Mr Snoots – stood at its centre, his nose turned up. I paced the perimeter walls, counting – and converted the figure to feet. I didn't let him go immediately, asking him, telling him, to be at the ready. I completed the sketch at Beaufoy's roll-top, determined not to hurry. The furniture took most time. I wanted it positioned accurately – a *chaise longue*, two filing cabinets, on the wall at a right angle to these a glass-fronted bookcase, its content a lot of legal tomes. It was just about beneath Mr Snoots to sigh, though I could tell he needed to. I smiled. Even with my back turned, I couldn't rid myself of his zoological image, an anthropomorphic penguin hovering at my shoulder.

'Ah, elegant!' I said, having at last stood up, with my hand poised, and my eye focused, over a piece from Sir Geoffrey's chess set – a knight of course. 'Indeed, Mr Fixt. Crystal and jasper. An heirloom.' I didn't think I needed to note that. 'Where,' I asked, 'is the wall safe?' Snoots showed me to a Tuscany landscape, whose brush strokes were recent, and lifted it aside. I asked him who had got access, but that, he said, was a question for Sir Geoffrey. I pressed. For example did he? 'Decidedly not, sir.'

The question was put to Sir Geoffrey, late one evening, when that hapless quartet had scratched around and drawn a blank. By then I'd adopted blunt trades parlance, or union obstinacy – the only way of getting my prime suspects under the same roof. Again, that brought me to Beaufoy's study, whose scale diagram I referred to at odd moments, often when a crossword anagram hadn't become obvious. Brennan was in an after-dinner glow of cognac, and quoted Tennyson—

> Let us swear an oath, and keep it with an equal mind,
> In the hollow Lotos-land to live and lie reclined
> On the hills like Gods together, careless of mankind.

Shay shifted his weight to the other foot, because, I imagine, Brennan's rendition made him uneasy (its pigment, its distillation, more than the attractive notion it expressed).

Kennedy, impeccably dressed for business, repeatedly checked his watch, though remained neutral. Beaufoy sat at his roll-top, with just a twitch of political triumph, used as he was to the wave of an angry order paper. He showed scepticism, in light of his three envelopes, streaked as they were in the chlorotic gleam of his desk lamp. He offered them up with an implied 'Youseeitspointless', though an initial glance made this far from so. 'Thanks,' I said. 'Now we're going to stage a little charade, for which I would like you to take your places.' The reply, four blank faces.

'It's just routine,' I said.

I arranged them according to that night of indecision, and asked for a re-enactment. Shay turned pale, but remained inscrutable. Had he finally regretted artistic links with so questionable an organisation, despite the perquisites? Beaufoy, his look incisive, I sensed doubted my effectiveness, and might have been pleased to exchange opinions with Chief Inspector Blamm, were I to realise that option. Kennedy alone was game, un-cuffing his Rolex for the last time that night, and with that impulse showing me a sporting unconcern at the hour.

'As I recall it,' he prefaced, 'you and I were here – just here – where we signed the cheques.' He got together with Beaufoy at the desk, where he arranged three notelets, as simulation, on which I made them both scratch signatures.

'And what of Mr Shay?' I asked. He had been sitting, he said, but told me this reluctantly. He eased himself into the *chaise longue*.

Dr Brennan remembered the pulse of a high-performance engine, which had prompted him to twitch the red velvet of Beaufoy's long, sumptuous drapes, then to gaze down into the halo of a streetlamp. A loud, convivial giggle, then a car door slamming, trained his attention on the end house at the curve of the terrace, though he missed the glow of car lights. He was sure, he said, he had seen a golden Porsche in the neighbourhood – days, a week before – but had missed it zooming off in the night.

'So, what next?' I said, by which I did not have in mind the ins and outs of finance, though I coaxed out Kennedy. He, having understood the deeper mysteries written in our living balance sheets – he alone had overall mastery. I took advantage. He set events before me. Now I have a numbered list as attachment to the diagram. With embellishments that's as follows—

1 B[eaufoy] and K[ennedy], the host seated, the other bent from the waist at the roll-top, scarcely wait for the ink to dry, and in the shade of the desk lamp share a contented grin. The cheques have been signed, post-dated.

2 S[hay], the one real poet of our times, because the others have stirred him to do so, lumbers up from the *chaise longue* and opens one of those filing cabinets. Here with the wodges of memoranda, behind a fin marked STATIONERY, is a handful of envelopes.

3 Good time Br[ennan], who has sampled the cask in a not distant keller, is a few rooms away with the plumbing.

4 K is unsure of public transport – this, after all, is London – its being so late. Before stepping into the hall to call for a cab, he passes S the cheques, who, standing at the filing cabinet, has already marked the envelopes. For this he has used his own ballpoint, that stupendous instrument of his Muse.

5 B sees S place the last of the cheques in its respective envelope, and steps outside (to advise on a cab firm he is able to recommend).

6 Severally, B, K, Br return to the study, where B sweeps aside his Tuscany landscape and commits those cheques to his wall safe.

Form might move us to a 7, being how on the morning of the ceremony Sir Geoffrey transferred those cheques to his attaché case, whose ancient leather is embossed with his monogram, initials that had also been his father's. It ought to have made him my leading suspect – though of course he, as I had seen with my own eyes, had turned puce at the loss, and had laid out his own private cash for me to investigate. I asked him about the wall safe, and who else had got access.

'Only myself,' he said, impatient. So to the key, and where was it kept? 'Here in my drawer.' Finally the missing cheque, and who was the eventual payee?

Not guilty (chorus). (Was this too close an inquiry?) The remote Bim Shay showed me his poet's troubled brows, and exchanged a side glance with Brennan. That reprobate flushed, first through a shade of morning breakfast peach, then to last night's lobster. He squirmed, I think. Beaufoy got huffy, prey to some straitened emotion detected only in the vehemence of his shoulders (shrugging). What he wanted to say *was* couldn't I do better than that, but this wasn't his backbench, and so he kept shtoom. Kennedy alone evaded my dumbing anaesthesia, preparing himself with the strum of his fingers up the sensitive cut of his suit.

'Immanuel Ashby,' he said, naming the name. Ah, good. Now we'd got a lead. 'Well, not quite,' he warned, and shared with me everything he'd got from his old grey boys in the network. Mr Immanuel Ashby had ceased all movement through his current account five years ago, despite pleas from the bank that the administrative overhead made it uneconomic to keep it open. Nor had Mr Ashby kept the bank up to date with at least one change of address (though of course Kennedy shouldn't really be telling me this). I must have looked puzzled.

'Dear boy, what Simon's saying is this,' said Brennan. 'We've visited the poky flat in Camden where this how you call Ashby used to live.' Its tenant was a man with biker's leathers and a pin through his nose.

'Who presumably has never heard of Ashby,' I said.

82

A masque then, and puppets not willing to be obedient, their limbs under control of a hand I couldn't see, and someone concealed in the void, scheming for a closure whose nature I couldn't predict. That meticulous choreography amounted only to puzzling faces: Solomon's, blanched and lacking life; Staverton's, its flabby cheeks and pert little mouth; now Ashby's, ghostly and yet to be constructed. And now it turns out, through a back channel kept open by Matthew Bello, that the dead girl opposite Cadogan's (dead indeed, and not in suspended animation) had been so for days before Rudge found himself called to that address.

I withdrew, into the news headlines first, thence to the *ante meridiem*, and the oppression of my attic. The afternoon approached, and dragged, its hobnails clumping by. A brandy soothed in the minutes after midnight, all crosswords abandoned. Then, and only then, if I opened my windows wide, might a cooler air deliver solutions with it? I probed that absurd notion, leaning out on my ledge over the deserted pavement. A stray car, a few late cabs crossed and re-crossed the yellow zones and broken white lines. No. Of course not. One had to be seen doing, not thinking. That was the first rule of Western meditation. Therefore had you considered, Fixt, a visit to Camden? Why yes, and that would yield nothing, except possibly some well-priced bric-à-brac. And what about the four? Shouldn't I interrogate them individually?

Kennedy and Beaufoy I relegated to the lower half of my list. Dr Paschal Brennan I never liked talking to, much. That left Shay, who had shown only the remoteness of a man among fools, and about whom there exists a swollen file and a flutter of press cuttings, in the keeping of one Grace Fowler, someone I wanted to meet. I could see easily how Shay reserved judgement on his more successful colleagues, and had a reluctance with social issues – affairs best left, he says, to professionals in other fields (he has in mind journalists). He is impolite about newspapers. Is scathing of broadsheet critique. This set the seal on Shay's isolation, and placed limits on his public opportunities.

The *TLS* flexed itself to one cautious summary, unable to fit Shay, if there *is* a poetic mainstream, into the current of demotic verse. Nor did the Poetry Book Society rubberstamp him RECOMMENDED. There was one unintended result, when ex-Professor Chekhovsky[39] – of Cambridge, Massachusetts – a man always on the lookout for literary outsiders, sounded off once he'd safely retired, egged on by a young magazine editor, interested in his views on 'the best writers writing today', the result being a long list that didn't include a single Nobel laureate. It is certain Shay was not expecting this, and didn't really know who Chekhovsky was. Chekhovsky had concentrated on one of the few new books Shay had published in recent years, his *Lyrics*, pages he had filled with light and sound.

The night, added Chekhovsky, is long, and the audience is fickle. There is only so much wonder in a fizz of golden stars. Dawn approaches. His poet, Shay, or the one he has singled out, trudges through the dewy grass. He's stubbed his lighted fuse on the stone wall of an English castle (so long as there's life, it smoulders). We can identify him, wading through the vacated seats of last night's revels, now striking out for the highways of twentieth-century life. Regrets? Well, yes, but not at abstractions like these – it's only the fact that they set him apart.

The Chekhovsky plaudit emerged in an era when wide-angle shots of emasculated colliers filled our little screens, men beaten back to their pitheads by armies of police in riot gear. A Roy L. Hapgood, having a distant connection with Chekhovsky, was able to trace and publish, as foil for these social upheavals, an exchange of notes, where the Chekhovskian half had also got into his possession. One of his former students, who only now discovered a Hanseatic ancestry, outlined her objections, having interpreted in Chekhovsky's literary hit list improper aesthetic snobbery. Chekhovsky remembered her, and was polite in his recollection. He even referred to her cited authors not, as you'd expect, with a strong opinion, but with delicacy. In passing he again mentioned the thoughtful lyricism of a neglected English poet, a Mr Bim Shay.

I placed back the stopper in my brandy bottle and considered the voids in my diary, a sequence of days – white, lined, and bottomless – frosting the months to Christmas. The same exclusivity affecting the Byrne Society – its appointment of Shay as figurehead – clouded my better judgement. Of those I had jotted down, his was the number I sorted from my notes. In the morning he wasn't at home, and his phone rang and rang (this, in a cloistral hallway). It was the same after lunch. By seven p.m. I'd prepared an apologetic opening, but had no opportunity to utter it. Even at ten, his receiver was obdurate, cradled. On to the next day, and still nothing, so by the third I'd bounced on the back seat of a bus to Highgate, where I tapped on the door of his flat. An old char in a sky-blue babushka crossed her arms and gazed up the stairwell from the floor below. A toy dog yapped from the doorway behind her. Across the hall at number 5, Bim Shay's neighbour – a youngish man in an olive bathrobe, and with combed wet hair – came out and stood on his mat. He'd got a half-pint of water in a milk bottle, which he was about to pour into a potted bonsai. 'He's out. I mean out of town,' he said, having watched me stretch to the fanlight. 'When's he back?' I asked. 'Always hard to say....' I penned a note and put it through his door. On the Friday I'd still not heard, and so went to the library for a trawl through the press guides. I phoned his publisher, a man with a high, artificial voice, who didn't want to talk. Mr Shay, he said, was closing a twenty-year labour, a *magnum opus*, and didn't want to be disturbed. 'That's exciting,' I said, 'though I do need to track him down.' A long pause dealt artfully with the urgency in my voice. 'I'm sorry, that's quite impossible.' A note to Shay (c/o his publisher's office), which he was happy to pass on, was as much as he could do.

83

I turned all night, mangling the quilt and flattening the foam of my pillow, until at four I abandoned sleep altogether. I put on my dressing gown. I still wasn't dressed when, at the Georgian sash – that tiny transparency abutting the eternal bewilderment of life – I watched for the first rosy flush of dawn over the coils, loops and tiny spires forming the ridges topping the buildings opposite. Irrational suspicion didn't, I felt, become me – except that now I wanted to know what it was that Shay was up to. A first swill of tea, with its leaves, did not give up its secrets. The glaze of my emptied cup reflected back on me blankly. Nor would my Muse of new domestic life wave a wand when I surveyed the debris of my breakfast plate, its crumbs of toast and gobbets of raspberry jam. There was a rush of traffic. As it faded, I searched for Grace Fowler's address (I'd remembered her as Shay's biographer), and found it – a late, and not alphabetical entry to the Byrne Society's members' list.

She lived and worked in a riverside apartment, a warehouse conversion, still with its brown brick and corrugated roof. She was averse to the fixed subdivision of space, a point I appreciated on glancing in over the hat on her head. *Lebensraum* – of which there was much – she had squared off with a criss-cross of screens, to partition bed, basin, bath, workspace. She allowed me in grudgingly. 'I don't think this should take too long,' I said, though already she felt intruded on. She unhooked and swept up a man's city shirt (from where it hung on a nail). She put it on over the electric zigzags of her swimsuit, a one-piece. 'It's a very unusual place,' I said, and walked to the open rolling doors, where she returned to a canvas chair and a newly turned sheet on her notepad. 'Spacious.' A pulley outside over the lintel, no longer commercially active, served for a hanging basket, thus far filled with rich peaty soil, but sprouting only a dazzling pair of gardening gloves. I looked out over the spangled Thames, its succession of silver crests slapping the green slime, those years of decay in the timber of her wharf. She put on her sun specs and pressed them down at the bridge. She shook a box of matches. 'Bim Shay,' she said, 'info on,' though her final syllable lisped to the unlighted cigarette now bobbing between her lips. 'Shay, yes. But then as I say, this shouldn't take long.'

The broad brim of her sunhat lolloped half over one of her lenses. In the gloss of both those pools I beheld the miniaturisation of me, shirt-sleeved, arms uncomfortably folded. I explained my position with the Byrne committee, not at all discouraged at the front she put on, in that neutrality of headgear, glasses, the hard little mouth (in an intimated snarl). 'I'm acting for Sir Geoffrey,' I said, and underpinned that revelation with expansive gestures. Two fine jets of white tobacco smoke snorted from her nostrils. With the dismissive wave of her hand a light flake of ash rose up and disintegrated. 'Bit late to vet his own people,' she said. I corrected her. 'I'm doing the vetting.'

She had decided, she said, to renegotiate her advance, and so had suspended all work on the Shay biography, publishers being what they were. 'That's to say low on the evolutionary scale.' There I had no opinion, having an eye not to her pay but her play. Shrewdly, she'd got in help from three starry-eyed students, who for no or low wages had agreed to carry out research on the Shay project – 'with the added promise of an author's acknowledgement'. Clever, I thought, but persisted. 'I don't wish to pre-empt their findings. I wouldn't mind seeing their files.' Across the water, a tall docklands surveyor, a man with tangerine chevrons welded to his boots, pushed a wheel on a handle along the wharf. Ms Fowler flicked her cigarette out through the doors into the wide blue, and got up abruptly. She led me to a bundle of working papers, ranked in heaps. To the touch they were brittle, positioned as they were under the dejected grin of a ventilation grille. 'You'll have to take notes,' she said. She hadn't read them yet, and didn't want them disordered. She went back to her keyboard and screen.

I began, over-optimistic, pen poised, and already deaf to the plastic clang of her keystrokes. The unmistakable fires I imagined at the heart of Shay's life, that hilltop beacon alerting us – the passing ships – to his glory, had not been lit, or had escaped the full view of Fowler's three investigators. I put my pen down. I read, and found contradictions. I scanned from one to another, and was pulled under, not up. Then in a wordless rethink I looked across at Grace Fowler, who'd relaxed, with her shirt off again, stretching her legs in the sunshine. Warm for her, I thought, and considered myself, here in an underworld, my hands palpating the crystal wetness along a cavern wall, in search of a spark. Take the simple point of Shay's graduation, and what each of his three researchers had to say. They signed themselves MS, GM, and JMcD. MS had him as a BSc (physics, no college named). GM mentioned a BA in English, but was undecided as to whether that was Nottingham, 'or possibly Manchester'. JMcD, almost certainly wrong, described Shay the student poet as an angry young man, and one who had left school at sixteen. McD quoted one of Shay's magazine editors, when according to him for five or six years the young Shay had a working life as a factory hand.

It was not until that trifold history intertwined itself in a single thread at the subject's mid-twenties that the ground felt sure. Shay's father bought a partnership in Wester Dein, a start-up firm whose business was electronic sensors, or the assembly of. Shay was ushered in through the backdoor, and from a workbench and drawing board began his career in the electronics industry. Not a poet's best perspective, I couldn't help think.

Ms Fowler made herself a glass of lemon tea, putting on her partner's shirt again (white, with red pencil stripes). Other signs of him were a suit in a press, grey and sober, a suede shoe in reddish chestnut, and a holiday tie, or it may have been a bandanna. I asked if she'd discussed these notes, and received an abrupt 'No time' for reply. Then the post arrived, and that distracted her, a returned draft, unhappily. She winced too obviously and left it unopened. What I needed, and lacked, was a strategy, and as such I pulled out the research notes according to GM, whose age I could but sex I couldn't determine. Prominently, he/she bathed in the afterglow of Shay's industrial career. Wester Dein proved only a stepping stone, and after half a dozen job changes – that, incredibly, in a five-year span – the quiet and undemonstrative Shay had arrived at the boardroom. This was with a mid-size firm, with offices in Nottingham and Manchester. The chairman, otherwise glued to his shareholder reports, looked up and out on the rain-swept gloom, apparently ill at ease. The era predated the free-for-all of market conservatism, yet on the other hand his pessimism had little to do with health-and-safety regulation, and all the red tape. Shay caught his eye, in part because he rejected the sycophantic style of his management colleagues. 'One might wring hands,' Shay is quoted as saying, 'at the trend to de-industrialise, and not know what to do. That would be wrong.' The chairman showed his cordiality, and invited Shay to a working breakfast. He poured the coffee himself and offered his congratulations. 'Nicely put,' he said. 'But why is it wrong?' Shay's answer, which to an extent is vindicated, showed him as no analyst of industry *per se*, but more of its mood. It need only be generally thought, and not necessarily true, that our industries can't any longer compete – and, well, they *will* no longer compete. That brings a new broom, and new brooms sweep in new technologies. A full-blooded embrace was the best thing (decades before PCs arrived on everyone's desk). That won him a seat, a brief, and a portfolio. Here over their cornflakes the chairman sketched out a path for Shay with an emphasis on special projects.

Grace, pianistic, lifted her hands from the keyboard. The sun doubled itself in the flash of her glasses. She tossed her head, and rocked her seat, and laughed. I assumed at nothing in particular, then imagined that ingrate hapless enough to return her draft. Was that someone she was even now re-scripting, an innocent in for much worse through the next depression of keys? I said goodbye to those epicene testaments signed GM, and turned to MS, whose calligraphy was tall, accelerated, and laterally compressed. It was a feminine sweep of the hand, and belonged – graphologically speaking – to someone attracted to causes. About Bim Shay's there wasn't much to say, except that quiet thoughts behind those lofty brows had triggered his pure disdain for the English establishment. Rather than fight it, he had found a way of holding it at bay, distantly. His mother Rebecca hadn't the same inwardness, and before becoming a parent – and before her problems with that – she laboured nightly over a manifesto, in reality a catalogue of personal disgust at a world of anachronisms. How one dressed. Dietary constraints. Observances. She told a friend she'd never go anywhere near a kibbutz. That same friend was magnetised to Rebecca's brother Ben, who at the time was high up the synagogue's hierarchy.

So much for her ailments of mind. And anyway, those who presumed to know her – most culpably her relatives – were aware only that she lived under a flat roof, and had a palm and a cross-lineation of paving bricks, to the rear of the house, in its courtyard. What they failed to note, and what the Fowler commission uncovered, in the grim years of Rebecca's adolescence, was political subversiveness unable to connect itself to the politics of nationhood. Affairs of state were no more to her than ritual, convention. She had rebelled at the person she was assumed to be, and gave notice of that at each of life's little milestones. Any who crossed her mat with a view to her long-term commitment to the faith was immediately asked to re-enter. Amulets on doorjambs were ridiculous. Friends rash enough to wish her a happy Bat Mitzvah had that sentiment returned with opprobrium. 'It was,' notes MS, 'a frustrating time.' Rebecca wasn't communicating, though she softened towards an uncle, who, having restated the parental view, acknowledged her independence and did not condemn her obstinacy. It took her into the balmy courts outside the faith, whose wicked allurements she found attractive. She said wryly she preferred indecision to certainty. Those she went around with were indifferent to *all* religion. Then, finally, she completed her excommunication, which took the form of a duplicated note (it announced her elopement with and subsequent marriage to – Mr Philip Ashby).

84

To those initials I fitted a name, MS becoming Many Sidedness and finally March-on Supposing. She was prolific, if slipshod. She bowled on unstoppably in an avalanche of notes. Yet hers was important knowledge – of Bim Shay the pseudonym – without for several sides of A4 confirming what I expected, offering no hint at the poet's forename (that forename was Immanuel). It goes like this. Mrs Philip Ashby's early married life was the magnet for her researches, with its history of failed domestic appliances. I was swept into

Smethwick, impatient, casting round in a damp kitchen. As a kind of rebuke, I can tell you categorically, Ms S, that an ancient wringer with a handle obdurately stuck was not amusing (your handwriting tittered). Nor was a lentil soup that plastered the ceiling – to do with the perished seal of a hand-me-down pressure cooker. One other tale, still of abandoned dinners, gave us the charred maw of a gas oven, which after years of loyal service resigned its post with a spectacular explosion. Ho. Then meantime the deplorable Philip enjoyed certain mechanical perversions, always having a car or bike in bits around the yard, which brought in on his boots, his hands, in his golden hair, oil, or grease, or autumnal flakes of rust. Had Many Sidedness a cartoonist's hand, this is what she'd draw – a grin on Philip Ashby's blackened face, his hand and his naked forearm holding up a gasket.

Ashby showed respect for the commercial acumen his wife had brought, and was not impervious to her musings – little asides, really, at a one-bar heater. He threw in the towel at the municipality, where he worked. Eyebrows rose collectively, for few on the ground staff were as diligent and seemed so happy. He moved into the garage business, and ran his own shop, and hired labour. Later, as a student of change, he knew the right moment with rivals in decline, and learned what a death throe looked like. He spread his interests. It's why I malign MS, who marched on – not with Immanuel's, but with Philip's biography – on the assumption I shared her relish. The point was this, if over-elaborate: by the time of Immanuel's birth, the one-bar heater had gone and the house was prosperous. From this must follow, or so ran her theory of economics, Immanuel's childhood bliss – a boy with everything he wants. What she had overlooked was the strain of recrimination running through that family, a point she had only skirted round. For Ashby Junior's childhood, and a less racy prose, we turn to JMcD, whose sense of his unhappiness with spanners, wrenches, all the garage tools, had more validity. I might as well offer Ms MS my parting shot now, dismissing as sentimentality her explanation as to how our subject got his name. Immanuel Yaeger, the sympathetic uncle Rebecca Yaeger sometimes drank coffee with, enjoyed the honour of passing on his forename. But you haven't pointed to this – that from Im Ashby, or even I'm Ashby, is formed an anagram someone should have noticed.

85

An outer fringe of lamplight was the probable and unearthly illumination accompanying JMcD's meditations, supposedly poetic. I guessed at a male imagination attempting to comprehend another, in the subject's own words. The biographer's probe, a pale torch, cast its single, speculative sweep over the jags and flints of Shay's adopted country – an exile, or distant cell, from where it was possible to see, in thin luminous outline, a streak of natural light over the clefts of his horizon. Wrongly, in my view, it was here McD looked for an inspirational source of what, in later life, were Shay's exotic works of poetry. He approached a bewitching twilight, yet stumbled frequently on a stump or a plain grey stone. Things crept in the undergrowth. A favourite serpent, uncoiling the lunar gloss of its scales, sliddered from a bough. On one other excursion McD breezed his ankles on the shore of a lake, and saw, over the rings of black water, and in the gloam of its lanterns, a passing craft, its movement painfully slow with the ghostly flutter of its one red sail. He mapped out the hillsides, a burnt brown, and saw them lit under fiery gobs of magma sporadically tossed in the air.

There is a point where daylight warms the air of Shay's desert. McD, who has entered his landscape, is majestic with the sun on his back, and gazes down from the mirage of a ridge. He picked out three figures in an encampment, two of whom, at a bend in a sandbar, are scooping up water. A line of distant palms mirrors itself in a blue oasis. McD thought he understood. It was Shay, he said, in the foreground. Standing apart from him, the man wrapped in the deep maroon of his djellaba was a father figure (he says this, even when the name Philip Ashby is known to him). Nor does he name Rebecca, remote in the background, a crouched figure at the campfire.

McD, as he tells us, tried to get down, somehow to place himself among these inventions. This, he thought, was the clue to Shay's art. Yet the pictures so formed were dissolving, an illusion. By this I recognised the early pages of *Lyrics*, a text McD used in his translation of life into art (not the reverse, curiously). At page twelve (McD's page twelve), the system collapses. Night falls, to enshroud the Ashbys' desert, and leaves nothing resolved. It doesn't deter McD. He turns to another, this time an extended poem. This he says 'papers' a technocratic Caliban in a voluptuary moonlight. That hunched-up brute is a man hobbling from the edge of a lawn. Cascading water silvers the stone petals of a fountain. Its soft tinkle, carried on the night air, intertwines itself in the thrum of electrified strings. Somewhere on a wall there is a harlequin in rhombs. Someone, we hear, plucks at an old violin – a pizzicato. A juggler, quartered in red and yellow, has plonked down carelessly 'four to five' torches, which are smoking. Gone, too, is a highborn lady, who has left an amethyst on the ornately wrought tracery of a garden table.

> Light from the chandelier through an open door
> Sprinkles coloured dewdrops
> Over the ballroom floor.

Caliban, with a sack of human bones slung over his shoulder, scurries across that chequerboard. There is a discarded lute on a footstool. Revels have been abandoned. Uneaten grapes in a bowl. Pools of claret. An overturned goblet. (Oh what is that hum?) The beast Caliban pauses at a stone stairway, then follows its spiral down, into his cavern, where the air is cool and the stonework damp. Little tongues of flame lap at the stubble of his horny flesh, at his inhuman hand, when he opens the furnace door. That sack has the powdered bones that he heaps in as fuel. The fuel is to drive the pipes and wires and wastes whose furnace is their heart, and which circulate the house. And welcome. Welcome to *Caliban's Machine*.

To me, it seems faintly ludicrous even to suggest, as does JMcD, that unveiling the life of the poet is only a matter of decoding his symbols. Nevertheless McD had put a finger to Shay's unease with his working life, when the specialisms his CV listed reached an abrupt end with his last assignment before he retired. Technology, in *Caliban's Machine*, cannot support itself without human sacrifice – that furnace with its human fuel. In 'Eclipse', a short poem towards the close of *Lyrics*, a tired officer stretches out a booted leg and pours himself more brandy. One of his three fellow-officers, who sucks at a cigar, bids an opening bridge hand (1NT). Another has moistened the lead of his pencil, and notes the score at rubbers all. His is the partner not seated, who, having shown anxiety all night, now, as dawn approaches, parts the slats in the window blind. (Oh what is that thud?) He puts a hanky to his neck, to dab away the dampness round his collar. Outside, barred by the blinds' louvred light, the thin arms of a prisoner raise a hammer wearily. His backdrop is a moonless sky. The hammer swings. What is pounded in the sludge, remorselessly, at an unlit roadside, might be material rocks, but as Shay has them are just a representation. They are worlds gone wrong, the worlds Shay has inhabited.

86

McD, having flirted with the idea of his subject as marked from the beginning, veered off noisily from that. He at one stage showed him transfixed at his summer window, a boy in an idle dream, his pen poised. More soberly, his index to the real life of Immanuel Ashby he found in the family dossier, abruptly meandering off into the gloom of mechanical labour. All that grime on Philip's hands.

The boy, naturally – this was Philip's first mistake – would follow his father's curiosity into the oily den of his workshop, that jolly corner where the hobbyist spends so much precious time. Bim Shay loathed it utterly, its bits of engine, its carburettors, its imperial spanners etc. I accept without obligation this particular circle of hell might have been the unworked material of *Caliban's Machine*, though that cannot explain the imaginative process, with demotic experience turned into art. Take as comparison our poets in a lesser mould, those the establishment upholds as paradigms, whose objectified world is trite in its representations (a dipstick, a fumy spark plug, an adjustable spanner, a sump nut).

I stress, much of this is my interspersion, with JMcD venturing only guarded opinion of Shay's contemporaries. Moreover I bow to the sheen of his researcher's escutcheon (no social blots, no smudges), since according to him – and here's the nub – what we are always being shown is an acute sense of public humiliation. This, as a condition, is neatly wrapped up in an acrostic. The line beginnings of 'Eclipse', of its final sixteen-line stanza, spell out this: MALVOLIO'S GARTERS. I am amazed. I know not how the historian uncovers his subject's life, or ensnares its ephemera. Yet here I must pay attention. McD, always cogent, remarks on it so: 'It finds its origin in a home construction project.' He goes on to place before us the young Immanuel holding a lump hammer in one hand – in the other a bolster. This – what shall we say – senseless role of navvy, has been arranged by his father. New slabs on a patio are about to be laid. There is a small difference in horizontal levels he insists on chiselling into a slope. This was a project in itself – hard labour. Yet Philip and his bar companions are grouped in a semi-circle on an afternoon filled with sun, and find tremendously amusing the boy Ashby's thin arms and ineffective swipes. 'A piece of juvenilia predates the mature poem,' McD further informs. This has to do with a convict in a quarry.

By now McD had come to play out his secretarial brief without my criticism, and could afford to digress on any chosen axis. He had schooled himself on common-sense psychology. Point in case is a scatty Russell lookalike, a man retired to Tring, and bleached by the sun of eighty summers. McD tracked him down and got him to recall his editorial days, in particular the small-press profile he had once penned on Shay's behalf. Shay had already published a triple sestina, one (and one only) quite awful villanelle (as they mostly are), plus a handful of sonnets – all through his quarterly magazine, whose covers were plain. 'A small point and very important' he deemed it: 'Shay, at that evolutionary rung, hadn't invented his *nom de guerre*.' A kind of self-hatred, suddenly, or hatred of the Ashby clan, threatened asphyxiation, for now he had seen that bestial name in print, and he wanted to bury it. A declaration was needed, and was worded for the profile. That informed what was likely to be an indifferent readership that Immanuel Ashby had been his pseudonym. Now the author wished to resume his baptism. Bim Shay. I repeat, Bim Shay.

87

That letter, c/o Shay's publisher, would not now do – a conclusion I arrived at plunging a knife blade into the orange on my plate. To my complete satisfaction the peel came away in a contiguous spiral, with the sun going down, in a prolonged Homeric blush, its deep maroon and streaks of gold, and rays that reddened the façades across the street. Here I was, home again.

In the cold dawn I was still dozing. I had added a brandy glass to my plate, the plate crossed by the knife, all of it a mess of pith and orange peel and one uneaten segment. I imagined all kinds of possibilities, and could see them, an unravelling weave, in the anagrams and acrostics of Shay's esoteric little books. I soaked for an hour in a hot tub, drinking tea. At nine I phoned Lawcom's shop (no reply). At ten I got through and talked to him, or rather issued my commands. 'What I need,' I said, 'is the three published volumes of Bim Shay's poems.' He looked, and found that he possessed the third, was able to borrow the first, and by the following lunchtime knew how to acquire the second.

So began my lazy assembly of spelt-out clues – up, down, across – the mad reconstruction of Shay's thousand-odd stanzas. Lines two to six of his villanelle offered me HUMBL, though I'm stretching a point, arriving at it through a tortuous mathematical series. An ornate rondeau, consisting of clocks, tides and a table of motion, yielded LOIT. It came from word beginnings, and was a pattern broken abruptly by the fifth letter, a B. I'd had more luck with a man (or mask) called Spartak, a compiler of word games, who for years had held half a page in the local rag, tucked away with the flotsam of planning applications. 'Give it up,' I said to myself. Then naturally I thought of Frankie. 'Surely,' I said, once more evaded on the phone by her, 'there are machines, and software, able to scan a text....' Familiar silence. Then one dusky evening I stood on her Holland Park doorstep. She ushered me in. She showed me to her manuals, in a trail of floored undergarments up to her bedside stand. Here, an insane text (Donn G. Krinkel, Framingham, Massachusetts) stirred up even deeper mystification. It's where I needed help. 'Okay,' she said. 'I'll give you a name, and a number.' They belonged to a specialist in the field, from the something-or-other research institute. Eventually I met him outside a spaghetti house in Southampton Row, a pale, nervous man with a tonsure, who put his cold fishy hand in mine, and shook.

We did business over a laminate table top, where we sat in the half light, in a noisy corner he had chosen by the kitchens. Dunne (for such, reader, browser, reviewer, whomsoever I've ensnared – such was his name). Dunne, I meant to say – or 'Do call me Don,' he said – took refuge in the breadth of his chequebook. It was, he said, *his* treat, an invitation he rattled off as a kind of background Muzak, a tickling of the chimes of petty wealth. Irritation induced me to eat. He ordered pizza, and I a bowl of ravioli with a side serving of garlic bread. He fingered the chilli dispenser, using that as an explanation of his work. One moment it had the role of free text, onto which one hooked key words, in which guise he slid it to the table's open edge. Next, it was a key word itself, and skated back to centre table – with a cruet, an ashtray, and with Don Dunne's Pentel dancing in its train. 'It's all about associations,' he said. 'Understood,' I put in, and produced Shay's three volumes. 'I'm trying to trace the author, whose work's all trickery. It's just possible he's embedded a place name, a resort, a favourite retreat – or any clue – somewhere here.' Don Dunne raised a self-effacing eyebrow and said that was interesting. 'He's a man fond of anagrams, acrostics, acronyms.' Or indeed any such device.

These days I spent my mornings propped on my pillow in thrall to an encyclopaedia article on encryption techniques. Dunne's final liaison, arranged within hours of that man's last-minute flight to Tenerife, had me lurching to my sill in the whiteness of dawn, that sturdy volume left unopened at my bedside. I tramped along Finsbury Pavement before the morning rush, where we were due to meet. Another cold handshake. A dew prevailed, which cooled the air. Dunne's olive suit was fresh from the cleaners. Again, business brought us to the meal table, and to breakfast (Dunne was in holiday mood. He took us to a continental bar). I fixed on his *pain au chocolat*, which he had dangled for an alarming duration over his coffee cup, sodden. He was blasé over his 'key-to-disc girls', who'd 'clattered in' every word and semi-colon at a morning's sitting. 'Mind,' he went on, 'selecting the right algorithms wasn't straightforward.' Nevertheless the end result was a wodge of printed output, which he put down on the table, and scanned through with his ballpoint, which trembled in his grip.

I couldn't fault his curiosity. Nor could I ignore that sedulous instrument, that sucked pen of his, tracing its hairline ink over the jumbo stripe of each printed page. 'I don't know,' said Dunne, 'what this man's political affiliations might be.' He alluded to the incidence of acronyms, the most commonly embedded being hope – shall we guess – for world order. UN cropped up a lot, though more often traceable to words like 'unnecessary'. 'Possibly,' Dunne mused, 'this Shay's a committed European.' The pair EC was prevalent, as were EMU and ECU. 'He's a poet,' I said. 'He looks at the human soul.' Dunne leafed to some latter pages, where Psyche's presence might have been referred to (there was a PSIKEE). JUNG was there once, and also incidentally GUNJ. Freud, with a FRUDE, may also have made an appearance. 'Yes,' I said. 'Clearly some of these are coincidental.' Statistically Don Dunne disagreed, pointing out that FRUDE had been identified three times. 'You could even argue for religion,' he said, giving me a JEHO and a VAH not once, but twice.

That brought us to names, and of rivers we had an EXE and two WYES. CODU you might construe as County Durham. There was something similar with IRE. The breakthrough – and this urged me to my feet without a thought for the bill – came in a four-part poem, 'The Architect's Son'. It had been composed in blank verse, and had an epigraph—

> The offender's sorrow brings but small relief
> To him who wears the strong offence's cross.

The whole was overarched by an opening and closing acrostic – line one, line ninety-nine respectively. 'The thing's gobbledegook to me,' said Dunne. It opened with the word 'Fitzpaine', and described a man obsessed with architecture: spires, golden domes, a winter palace. The last piece of scaffolding came down in the steel of an August sky. The contractors went home. The designer's intolerance showed. Worse – his robed wife insisted on overseeing all aspects of the interiors. She banished him from the drawing board. 'I think I know what it means,' I said, and explained. 'The architect needed a show of solidarity.' His son shared none of his enthusiasms, and when asked, cajoled, then bullied into work – which now centred on the winter gardens – his response was sullen. 'He objects to the linearity of his father's thinking,' I said, whose contrast is the fine beaten silver of Bim Shay's verse. 'That's the whole point.'

Dunne, who began to warm to the game, detected a repugnance for the perpendicular intersection of flagstones. That was good, I said. An oak was lopped for an oriental folly. A pagoda, centrally viewed from a tower, had not been given its best position. Arbours were too predictable. The vast lawn, squared and hedged, was a patchwork of symmetries. The pump station was not ideally situated. Plumbers – in teams – rigged up a crisis of concealed pipework. It ended in a hundred rhythmic parabolas, where the cool crystal of tap water was an infinite resource. It was ingenious how on the sound of a voice, or a tread, or the echo of Pan (in a distant wood), it was all made to jet from the mouths of writhing dolphins – each with a nymph straddling its spine. 'The end comes for the architect's son,' I said, apart from what had gone before, 'on the installation of an altar.' 'Well, not quite,' said Dunne. 'The end's a closing acrostic – "bridge".' Therefore our subject over-spanned itself with a place name (Fitzpaine Bridge). This, by a fluke, did mean something to Mr Donald Dunne, BSc. He had spent, he said, his last bank holiday seeking out a flamboyant TV chef, who'd acquired the Maltsters in a picturesque Wiltshire village, Middle Widney. 'Fitzpaine Bridge,' said Dunne, 'is a touristy place not far from there.'

What I needed now was an ordnance survey map, but on my way out found DD's sticky business card pressed to my palm.

88

I wrote in my notebook (the unofficial one) 'a triumph in air over water', when two at least of the world's elements had been conquered. To the architect's son, that was by virtue of wealth. To Shay, whose not disinterested hand had shaped the scene, this was not to confuse the serrated blades of technology with the fine lines of architecture. I congratulated him. With his father dead, his rejection of paternal expectation he had put to the public gaze, yet no one was likely to read it as such.

I took with me on a fast train out of London a survey map and books by Shay. With the city's backyards outrun by the serenity of trees and fields, I dozed or made notes. Finally, I clutched my grip, swaying in the carriage aisle. The engine maundered into a small town a mile or so from Middle Widney. I stepped out under its Norman bailey.

89

There were no rooms anywhere, even at the Harvest Inn, on the other side of town. A man with wiry hair playing pool overheard the landlord telling me no, and said – nervously chalking his cue – he'd got a spare room at home, and suggested a sum, undercutting B&B. I was tired. I listened. He streaked his shirt with chalk, wiping his hands, and left his opponent sizing his shot. He came back beaming – it gave him a rakish look – then led me across the street. 'Here?' I said, and watched him fumble with his keys on the narrow, neatly flagged pavement. The house he had brought me to was like a shop, fronted with large panes and a mass of green timber. Below the windowsill, as of a butcher's or a fishmonger's, the black and white tiles were drilled with holes, where a chemical had been injected. 'Here,' he said, and ushered me into the gloom of his house. I hitched my bag to the opposite hand and felt the warmth in the last of a reddish sun, which sank below the rooflines behind me across the street. Its beams filtered through a wave of dust. 'Here,' I thought, and beheld – what? Perhaps only the unchallenged twilight of a distant life. Or was this really my unbearable office I'd begun to shudder at, getting closer to Shay? I could hope and even deceive myself it was an allergy of dust, or the air of mid-renovation, the fated revision of ancient shop space, not fully metamorphosed domestically, a project abandoned for want of cash. 'Excuse...' he said, motioning wires (exposed), and a confused mesh of pipes. The floor, solid with a bituminous skim, was uncarpeted. In the next room, life! There his wife sat up, where the gore of televised surgery was camped on their set in monochrome.

The room they gave me was large, with a desk, though the final notes I made were superfluous. I knew – I even foretold our exchange – exactly the words I had for Professor Dark. How though to broach this knowledge I had of Shay? It wasn't straightforward. I stretched on the bed and pushed off my shoes, and dozed. Then I rubbed my eyes in a veil of dusk and saw – in the far corners – how the clear dimensions of my new locality, the shapes, the lines, the relationships, had turned themselves into a tumble of blurs and smudges. A dream, or snatches, refused to return whole, as I tried to remember: was that something said between a man and boy (or it might have been a girl)? Animal hoots – from the inn across the street – rose up to my window, and were the alarm that had pierced my sleep. I turned on my light at the bedside and saw what my host had left me there to read: Agatha Christie, *The Labours of Hercules*, then someone called Raphael, interpreting dreams. I looked up BOY. That, if at play in my dream, was a 'good sign'. GIRL, conversely, signified I would 'shortly be engaged'. Downstairs I asked for a local map, and asked them to mark, in an orbit circling Fitzpaine Bridge, a series of crosses – these being the likeliest lunchtime venues. X, Y and Z, with their brews and seating, looked improbable. 'But this White Harp,' I said, 'at Widney Hall....' Both were blank. 'That,' I went on, 'is the arts centre – yes?' Why yes. 'Good,' I said. 'Perhaps tomorrow, or Sunday....'

90

So to Sunday, just after noon. Nothing – no faint breeze – touched the grass or lifted the flag on its pole, or twisted the vane over the Widney clock tower. I walked the flagged way and skirted the Great Hall. I, Fixt, entered the crowded bar, the White Harp. A thin-faced man mentioned the Brodsky Quartet. Another, plumper, had the Tagore name on his lips. Guffaws, a struck match, a surge of blue cigar smoke (its tails and its swirls, hanging at shoulder height). There was a jewelled woman, not prepared to step aside. For a moment we were tête-à-tête. I studied, intimately, the lined bronze of her neck, the discoloration of her teeth. The man with her, bobbing at my shoulder, was a portly beau in khaki shorts, with spindly legs. He clutched a Campari under his chin, divining meaning in its melting cube of ice. Everything here was 'so nace', she declared, and expected me to agree (I didn't). There was a Glyndebourne connection, she felt sure. I squeezed between her and her consort, and wriggled away, into touching distance of Shay, who hadn't yet seen me, on his way to the garden. He had bought his half measure of English ale, and a wodge of Sunday papers – and clamped in his teeth a packet of roasted nuts. Should I, shouldn't I follow? Of course yes, though allow him a minute.

I came out, with a glass of beer, and with papers of my own. I watched him, loitering on the lawn, where the waiting paid off. A fat man, ludicrous in a navy beret, vacated a table. Shay sat, and in the slanting shade of the parasol I tossed down one, two, the three slim volumes of his poems. 'Clever,' I said, and added a fourth piece of work, that remorseless list, that output from Dunne's computer.

'Please have a seat,' said Shay. I moved my chair, so that now as I sat I had my back to all that human traffic in and out the door. He ran a hand through the dark wisps in the talcum grey of his hair, and swept it all back. 'A fine warm day,' he said. A few suds of froth mingled with the beads of sweat on his upper lip, as he sipped his beer. He asked – 'How did you know?' – calm at that confession. '*Know* is wrong,' I said. 'I found out. In fact I wanted it to be Beaufoy.' I ran through the theft once more, all the way back to that late night in Sir Geoffrey's study. Brennan stepped out to admire the washroom. Kennedy went to call a cab. Beaufoy followed. Shay had got the envelopes, and pocketed one, now that, miraculously, he found himself alone. 'That meant finding a replacement and writing on it quickly.' But Shay penned 2nd, not SECOND, which didn't correspond with the FIRST and THIRD of the other two. 'The cheque,' I said, 'was drawn in favour of Immanuel Ashby. Im for short. Or I'm. I'm – that's to say *you're* Ashby.' Fastidiously, he selected one roasted nut from the torn packet on the table, and crunched it in his molars. 'I expect,' he said, 'you would like to know why.' On the contrary. I knew why. 'Grace Fowler was about to begin your biography. Her minions had been busy, getting all the facts.' Shay's doubtful academic background was going to be public knowledge. What I didn't understand was the anonymous advance to that same biographer – from Ashby via the Byrne Society – an advance inducing her to research the life of someone more prestigious. 'But that would only postpone her revelations.'

'A postponement is exactly it,' said Shay, and explained that his lifelong labour would not finally come to fruition under the weight of public humiliation. Life had caught up. All had come to pass. By now he wasn't quite able to despise Sir Geoffrey's hypocrisy, sharing at least one of its obsessions – that notion of public opinion. 'That,' I said, 'is too typically English, for you.' He feared Grace Fowler. He feared her biography.

'All right,' I said. 'How long do you need?'

God knew, the world of English letters was comatose without him.

91

This was in no sense the force of irony, nor could I question what Shay had settled on long ago – his *Snares in a Sacred Gateway* – as the working title for his *magnum opus*. 'The curse,' he said, 'is the elevation of art over religion, idolatry over worship.' He had completed that nostrum in a redevelopment of an earlier draft, where his 'Machiavel' acted as guide through the barbed circles of an everyday upper world – Shay, of course, now well qualified in its deceits. I left him on a thread, with the tortures of just not knowing (shall I, shan't I expose him?). 'After all,' I said, 'persecution sits at your engine.' I packed my overnight bag and settled with my stand-in landlord, hoping he would find a plumber and electrician before taking in another paying guest. He laughed that off, walleting the money. The journey home didn't at all drag. It consisted of a succession of experimental notes pencilled out for Beaufoy, which refined to just two. *Dear Sir Geoffrey, You'll be pleased to know....* Or *Dear etc., Regrettably I can't progress this case....* I needed, I knew, a return to work, but I chose a bad time – a Monday morning – in a last heroic attempt. I sat by my phone, having in mind Professor Dark seated at his desk, and dialled. Engaged (so wait, try again). And at last....

'Ah, Fixt, good to hear...' he said, and so in like terms I parleyed, up to a certain point. The man's floating presence gravitated itself when with one stroke I knocked the calm wind out of his sails. 'You're going to tell Blamm to rethink the Staverton confession,' I said. After Cadogan's, I couldn't help noting the murdered girl's effects waiting for classification on the chief inspector's desk. A packet of Gauloise. The concierge's business card from the Hotel de Verdun. Sachets of cocaine. 'That case,' said Dark, 'is closed.' I replied: 'Staverton confessed. But that was to a crime he didn't commit.' On that visit to his garret, I had taken my opportunity during those final moments he spent in his bathroom. What had I seen on his table? A packet of Gauloise. A book of matches (Hotel de Verdun). 'Someone had penned a note – the initials AL, and a reminder to phone.' The professor groaned – at me – but pulled himself together. 'What are you saying?'

Staverton's history as petty thief was well documented. I theorised he'd lifted the living girl's bag in a shop, on the street, or in a café. 'Other contents were an address book, from which he'd removed the V page – and a set of keys, a Chubb and a Yale. And of course cocaine.' Nowadays I see in the press that the chancellor's economics adviser had resigned unexpectedly, with no explanation other than the usual – he wished to spend more time with his family. His daughter Alison he was taking back to Washington with him. That man, as the professor knew, was the American-Italo-Scot, Mr Alastair Vercelli. 'And his daughter. Was she Al among friends?' Unlike me, Staverton correctly decoded that AL, for after all he had got the help of that address book, where he found Vercelli's entry, Alison Vercelli's, who used the property her father rented not as her home but a clearing house. 'I'll wager Staverton phoned, and only ever got a recorded reply.' Finally he left a message, to say that he'd got the cocaine and was willing to trade.

'That's good work, of course, Adrian – very well done. But a big step, you know, Vercelli's daughter and cocaine....'

Was it though? Was it such a step? 'And is this your tacit acceptance that the house across the street from Cadogan's *was* rented by Vercelli?' He returned to his usual icy calm, which turned to tetchiness as soon as I pointed out that to open Vercelli's door you needed a Chubb and a Yale. Staverton turned up, late at night, and finding the place in darkness, but the curtains open, decided to let himself in and have a look round. Once upstairs, with all that Americana, he heard someone else come in – the girl, with a spare set of keys, and another delivery, or was she there for a pick-up? So now what? Well, she doesn't turn on a light, but climbs the stairs. Perhaps Staverton's in the very room where drops / pick-ups are made. But here he's in his usual cowardly lather, and clutches the baseball bat – not, however, so in a panic that after that crack to her skull he forgets the tape. This he plucks from the answerphone before he leaves. I allowed a pause, certain Dark couldn't bear to hear much more. We had, he said, to consider Staverton's medieval perversions, the mask – for all we knew the Satanic sacrifice of all those missing pets – plus, too, his confession.

I said, 'You don't believe that. It was his alibi. The two crimes took place at the same time, miles apart.' Those boys posing as glaziers had pulled their little stunt days after the girl had met her end.

'I don't think that *quite* wraps it up,' said Dark. Well, no, not quite. Solomon's pharmaceuticals owed its success to laboratory research. 'Do you think,' I asked Dark, 'or perhaps you know, that this involved animals – for example domestic pets (only heaven knew why)? Was this something his blackmailer knew? Had Solomon reached his wits' end, about to expose his blackmailer?'[40]

Had the professor, now in a dark night somewhere, put his phone down? I said hello, two, three, a fourth time, sensing he'd regressed to a state of statuary. Then I heard him clear his throat. 'That case,' I said, 'is still open – or ought to be.' I couldn't hope to guess his mind, and parted on the sounding of a car horn. Then, at my window, the world reintegrated itself, and rushed back to my sill. A long way down, on the buzzing street, a trick, a slant shadow. A squashed penumbral oblong glanced off an awning, and thinly cloaked a shop front. Then here was someone – fresh from his 7.30 shave – who opened up a tabloid, centre page. Or now – it seemed newly born to my ears, almost – a cacophony of traffic noise as it swelled to my ledge. A train, rattling at its points. A line of cars, hooting through a change of key. Its lip gloss and aftershave applied, the metropolis woke finally, and I had woken.[41] Cool, reserved, futureless, I looked out through the houses, over the roofs, into the hum and ether of the day's new doings. The real failure, not in the end mine, was a collective, was down to this great and terrible city, for that had its rules, its foppish life, its jaded literature. No. Our dilemma was Shay, Bim Shay. Bim Shay.

Enough.

Notes

[1] Mendelssohn, Moses (1729–86). Jewish Enlightenment philosopher, and a Leibnizian. He managed a silk firm, while defending his loyalty to Judaism under pressure from Christian controversialists. His son was a banker, who brought up *his* son, Felix, as a Lutheran (J. L. F. Mendelssohn Bartholdy, composer of the *Reformation Symphony*).

[2] The Department. One of those secret civil service quangos spawned in a reactive age of Toryism, whose sole function is to protect and uphold the virtues of capitalism. Its officers work closely with all police forces throughout the UK, and take an interest in any case where successful exponents of the free-market payola system suffer criminal harm.

[3] I worked, conscientiously, if at times a little lugubriously, for the PSA – or Property Services Agency – before its business was privatised. From here I was drafted to the Department.

[4] Ironic that the poet, statesman, theatre director, critic and scientist – genius unlimited – grounded the Human Soul Romantic in the banality of rhyming jingles (If I could view the world from on high / Cultural flatulence I'd descry).

[5] The list of celebrated rock musicians, whose lives ended prematurely at the age of twenty-seven, continues, eerily, to grow – Hendrix, 1942–70.

[6] *Outer Fringe*, one of those ragbagmags that come and go, owned and edited by Lucy Diamond, a visiting lecturer on the arts college circuit. Her *BlowJonnieBlow* (latex penis or umbrella, limp or fully erect) was a prize-winning exhibit at the ICA (1987).

[7] I had once been treated to an evening of topless Sapphic moonbathing on the flat roof of Lucy's apartment, when a power struggle at one of our prestige universities ended in the outspoken suicide of its chancellor. He'd also had longstanding marital problems, which research suggested had a lot to do with Lucy.

[8] Nor can I fault the spectacle of her writing. Here's one of her texts I was taken with – whether written in a haze of hashish smoke I cannot say—

Minions in a free press, let loose with a vision, have washed a tide of stucco from the blades of their trowels, now that their work has ended on a coastal tower. Theirs was a decade long promised as a refuge for the world's put-upon, in its failures of completion – the last little twist of gold leaf. Walk here on the shingle and know for the first time how it appeared as architecture (it's a thing built in suffrage at the world's roaring tide). An old mariner and watcher of portents, who numbered the educated inhabiting his lair, succumbed to that tidal obsession, as is shown in the lines of his charts. The curious, their hair damp in the breeze, waited, immune to the cold night and its bright northern stars, and remained at a steep elevation until it was dawn. All put down their trowels, and looked in from the scaffold. The storm had gone on for centuries, but now that ancient had found anchorage, his Arcady. He paced – distracted – in the dome of his observatory. He gazed up into the airy curves of a pendentive. He looked at himself in a pier-glass. He tuned a vintage radio, and heard the subhuman hum of news people gathered round a table. He hung a map in a spandrel and placed a setsquare at thirty degrees on a cloudy constellation. He'd sent for a boy, who came in panting, for the steps spiralled for nearly half a mile from the well of the basement. He gasped at the peach marble, the red felspar, the green serpentine. The boy looked to the elder's chair and divined the start of one last voyage. 'Time?' he puffed. 'Is it time?' The grizzled seafarer picked up a pure crystal and tossed it from hand to hand, then put the boy to a handle, whose radial was half his own height, and made him turn. Slats, louvres, creaked open on lubricated rollers, the dome cranked out its telescopic eye over a grey-green sea. 'Music,' he said, 'an ocean interlude,' as already the headlines were written ('...amazing to think, in just ten years...!'). But look, see, here, a red sail, as the boy is urged to the heights. Turn! Turn! Eventually, the mariner put down his crystal, and all outside saw the points of his callipers, the dark firmament, a cigar shape, a saucer, a blinding white light. And there were headlines, and there was reportage, and talk round a table.

[9] Byrne, Daniel, *Collected Letters*, three vols (New York and London, 1966).
[10] *Malleus Maleficarum*, the *Hammer of Witches* or *Hexenhammer* (first printed 1486). Said to be the most sinister work on demonology ever written, codifying prevalent black-magic folklore and Church dogma concerning heresy, and perhaps partly responsible for all that inquisitorial hysteria. One might conjecture that Staverton was easily seduced by any delusion that seeks to dignify itself theologically (Exodus, xxii, 18: 'Thou shalt not suffer a witch to live.'). Other texts I found in Staverton's possession were of the English occultist Aleister Crowley (1875–1947), *The Book of the Law*, and a torn page from an anthology, Sidney Keyes's 'Gilles de Retz': '...for never / Since Christ has any man made pain so glorious / As I, nor dared to seek salvation / Through love with such long diligence as I through pain'.

Crowley rejected his family's faith, the Plymouth Brethren, and followed more esoteric interests, in 1898 joining the Hermetic Order of the Golden Dawn, and training in ceremonial magic. He married in 1904 and on honeymoon in Cairo claimed to have been in contact with the supernatural, with an entity named as Aiwass dictating to or giving him *The Book of the Law*, a sacred text urging its readers to 'Do what thou wilt,' or submit to the 'True Will' through the practice of 'magick'.

Crowley wrote prolifically – poetry, novels, the occult. In 1920 he established a religious commune in Sicily, the Abbey of Thelema, where he lived with his followers. A libertine, his lifestyle led to denunciations in the British press, Crowley notorious for his use of recreational drugs and his sexual orientation (Crowley was bi). He was called wicked and regarded as a Satanist, epithets easily understood through Rudge's peasant conception of upper-class degeneracy, aided and abetted, or perhaps encouraged, by Chief Inspector Blamm.

Gilles de Retz (1404–40) was a Breton baron and marshal of France, and a man of wealth and distinction, whose career ended in a trial for Satanism. He was accused of abduction and child murder. He fought in the wars of succession (1420) and, in 1427, for the Duchess of Anjou against the English. He served in several battles with Joan of Arc, notably in the relief of Orléans in 1429. He was at her side when Paris was attacked, returning to his lands in Brittany only after her capture. There his court was more lavish than the king's, and much of his wealth was consumed in maintaining his châteaux – their décor, their army of servants, their heralds and priests. He was a generous patron, with much of that maintenance devoted to music, literature and pageant. His family, with the king's help, alarmed at so much frivolous expenditure, prevented him from selling or mortgaging what remained of his lands. At that point he turned to alchemy and developed an interest in Satanism, hoping to acquire knowledge, power and riches through invocation of the devil. He was accused of abducting, torturing and murdering more than 140 children, and was arrested. He was brought to trial in Nantes, first before an ecclesiastical tribunal, then a civil court. He refused to plead until, threatened with excommunication, he acknowledged the court's authority and denied all charges. The ecclesiastical court condemned him for heresy, while the civil court found him guilty of murder and sentenced him to death. The calm and resignation with which he greeted his execution (by hanging) were lauded as proper Christian penitence, though critics have pointed up irregularities in court proceedings, remarking on the financial implications of his ruin, and on the fact that confession was obtained under the threat of torture. The de Retz name was later connected with the story of Bluebeard, the murderous husband in Charles Perrault's story *La Barbe bleue*, with its locked, forbidden room, wifely curiosity, then her timely rescue.

[11] I am perplexed at that comment, which I cannot recall making – almost as if another person leads a Department life in lieu of me. I don't know why I should have to invoke anything as alien to me as poetry, a subject I haven't studied since sixth form, and only then under duress. I can't see it other than one of those slipshod disciplines I was glad to abandon once I had finished with school and university. I can't of course escape those primitive dirges printed in certain daily broadsheets (all that friend-of-a-friend-of-the-editor stuff), or those quaint asides in the cul-de-sac of 'Poems on the Underground'. I'm not the best judge, as you see, and I take it on trust there is currently a 'Renaissance' in modern poetry. Or so say my one or two bookish friends. That still doesn't explain how this comment, and the note I'm obliged to make about it, have crept in at all.

[12] Opinions it is wise for a man in my position not to express, yet the civil service is full of weary people eager to tear down the structures their lives and careers are sworn to uphold. I am told even Professor Dark is tempted to chronicle an 'interesting' life and career, and is waiting only for the bell to toll on his retirement. I don't expect too many revelations.

[13] It was Moses Mendelssohn, one of the most famous philosophers of his time, and an important influence on Kant, who applied to the latter the epithet *Der Alleszermalmer*, the all-pulveriser. Kant had shown how certain claims to knowledge were beyond the realms of sense.

[14] A not so innocent aside, in the gradual unravelling of the riddle-as-logos I seem to have strayed into. We shall return I'm sure to 'Bob and Betty'.

[15] I shared a student house with Lawcom and two others, he a year ahead and researching his dissertation. Among some many esoteric books piled on his desk and scattered round our living space I recall only some: *Avot, Tanya, Zohar, Sanhedrin*, a commentary on Exodus, various texts on Maimonides, Sala W. Baron's *A Social and Religious History of the Jews*, a new interpretation of the Seven Noachide Laws, and an appreciation called *Life of the Alter Rebbe*, whose author's name I can't remember. On Fridays he would not allow his party-going friends to enter his room, and sat quietly with his books and his radio on. In those days Callaghan had lost the election, with unrest on the streets and the IMF underscoring the nation's humiliation. Lawcom vowed not to leave the Party, but lectured us on how everything must change.

[16] The name Blamm in fact. Each time I restore the chief inspector's correct name, I subsequently find it superseded. The same goes for Bello, the same for Dark…and Staverton is a place name, made use of in more than one county in England.

[17] Fixt. Adrian Fixt. I am therefore Adrian Fixt – which you know to be false. In reality my name is Adrian Fixt.

[18] I shall I swear slug it out, even if that means here in the relative shade of our document, determined not to allow that nefarious hand to thread its pretty emblems through my text. (Oh now look what's happened to the previous note!)

[19] It can't have escaped anyone that whoever my gate-crasher is, his motive isn't social justice. I shan't bother to review this hybrid thus far concocted by the two of us, but merely reflect at random on those various prints he has left in my flowerbeds. He is, I begin to see, some pale reflection of myself, who can't stick to the job at hand, but must aim his barbs at the fully paid-up members of the institutions I'm involved in. Admittedly I can see how his escalation of untruths is focused on my civil-service ethos, and places it against a scheme of other things he'd *prefer* me to talk about. There's Lawcom and his welcome world of books. The use of anagrams. The Byrne Society. Byrne's *Collected Letters*, on which I continue to place so little value. Rodolphe, whose cultured newspaper prose I have no opinion on at all. Other odd things are a chalky *amoretto*, Blamm's Gargantuan sneeze, all those props belonging to Henry Reuter – a globe, rhombs, compasses, coloured lights. Nor should I omit Lucy 'the Sky' Diamond, nor that paperback trash I am supposed to take an interest in through Staverton. But anyway, please stop me now, before I get carried away.

[20] I shall also have to acknowledge my ghost's political temperament.

[21] But *I* do take the bait, in a rage of exclamation points!!! In the human animal kingdom, isn't it the survival of the slickest…?

[22] 'Document' wouldn't be the right word – not in any case in civil-service terms. Dark's, and indeed my own expectations could not have been farther from the intellectual phantasy that shadow of myself deposits in my nest. Only think, those colourless, sombre tomes lining the shelves of a thousand cheerless offices....

[23] It seems I do at least have some powers of negotiation. Here are some highly inaccurate observations on the person of PC Rudge, which I have repeatedly excised from the main body of the text, and which, finally, my cohabitee relegates to the notes section—

1 Dirty Old Town

I (not Fixt, but that other, who shows his prejudice against the police) pursued but lost him, somewhere in a backroom full of cobwebs, here in my dream of his hometown. My train had stopped between stations, and I dozed. The embroidered chairs were under wraps. The light, which was off, was an unshaded bulb. My footsteps clattered on the naked floorboards. I cast round hopelessly for a plan of the house (I don't know, Doctor Wide-Awake, why I'd expected to find such a thing). A distant light, or the orange glow of a city, attracted me to a window, where I stood for a moment before turning back.

A shelf sagged, but not with the weight of books. Rudge as a boy had tinkered with electronics, and as testament to that here were the remains of a television set, the chassis of a valve radio, wire (festoons of), circuit boards, and a ham's headphones. There was a writing desk, whose drawers were unlocked, and these I emptied into the cold shadow of the chimneybreast. Articles were: a child's comics, with picaresque infants; a truncheon (Uncle Eddie's, home after his travels); a toy soldier, a long-limbed boy in combat dress. A photograph torn from the pages of a tabloid newspaper showed a one-time defence secretary with wild blond hair, wearing a flak jacket, and ensconced in a tank, in a prowl territorially on an English hillside. There were two family snaps, chewed at the corners and badly faded. One was of Rudge's kid brother, attempting flight with an off-road bike. The other caught the same boy dressed as a sea scout, sitting on a tree stump, sharpening a stick with a Swiss army knife (Uncle E's again, I assumed).

I made a grab for the light switch, which was loose, and connected to nothing – all it was was an old brass fitting. It rattled, hollow, as I flicked it up and down. I came to the window for air, and saw two points of silver, two stars in a stormy cosmos, sliding over the wet roofs of Rudge's grey city. A sunset, a dull ember, instantly flared up in a burst of cinnabar. In its explosive dusk a huge, ungainly bird, whose wings were a steel mesh and an imbrication of leather, wheeled heavily in the purple base of a cloud (this a private sundown.)

I took off and searched his empty streets for cars, pedestrians, a stray cat even, and saw only the taillights of a van, parked and unattended in an alley of walls and back doors. Its engine throbbed, disturbing no one. I shambled down and caught the night smell of frying cod, but where were the seaside restaurants? Not, it seemed, among the overhanging façades of the constable's winding back ways, where the quaint cobbles, mewses and mechanics' yards peppered his northern hill town. I tried, shook the door of a jeweller's, but it was locked, and here, if I looked closely, was a broken star of David, faintly embossed in a cross panel, and painted over in treacle. Away through a round arch I pushed my face to the sable breadth of a windowpane. A man whose shop name was Mehmet traded in fine silks and damask. Then I heard a drone, a fishmonger's Morris straining up and around the bends. When I stood back, its two dancing beams came together slowly, a blurred disc of white reflected light. Ghoulishly it swelled up, and the van, hard at work, swept through the arch. I ran into the street, shouting. The van swerved, dodged, then ducked into a steep by-road, and leaning to its offside halted in a ditch. In a blush, the driver stepped out smartly and smoothed down a wisp of hair. I called out, but he wiped his hands on his apron. I called again, but he scurried away.

A rear light was out. A door flapped on its hinges. The van's cargo littered the street: pressed lamb, pistachios, carob ice cream, jars of hot mango chutney, Boursin, plantains, yams – a bird's nest. I walked, much farther, more steeply down, and meandered across the shingle. The evening was penumbral – starless. The dark waves and the receding tide had left their dissolving spume in small, desolate pools. I tickled a crab with a stick, I hurled a flat pebble. I thought I'd a hint of what the cosmos was when I found, but couldn't decipher, a bottled message. It said, 'Ecce homo. As ever the times are petty, and good advice never changes much. Go. Throw this away. Cast it to the winds, to the outer darkness. Nothing matters. The universe is closed, opaque, elastic.' I placed it down with a ribbon of seaweed. I tried to invent a morning sun, diffuse in a coastal mist, its first cold radiance albata bright in the band of wet silicon, that sandy outer edge of the bay. It wasn't possible, now. The mounds, the waves of rounded pebbles, crunched and shifted under the fall of my boots. I slid on my heels. Then when I stopped I saw, looking out to sea, a point of white light. I could conceive nothing, no chance vessel risking a dangerous shore, and knew, in the crisscross of timber, the posts and lintels, gradually the rows, the columns, the bolts, the tourist's long pier, and at its far end a solitary lantern only.

2 Seaside Entertainments

I climbed up. A man named Butler, a cheerful hair stylist, had opened holiday premises, and under the candy stripe of his pole had positioned, in shiny cut-out, a smiling Sweeney Todd, who stroked his razor on a leather strop. I checked the knot of my tie and stumbled, trying to guess to which yuletide it belonged. A trinket came into my hands, a silly necklace, a chain and pendant. I found it snaking over a gap in the floorboards, and picked it up. It was meant for PC Rudge, whose admirer couldn't have found it easy declaring her affection. You imagined her giggles, and such cute dimples. The pendant formed a disc, which Rudge had to blow to get it spinning. Its inscription, partial on either side, thereby resolved itself from the enigmatic I I C /L to I LOVE, etc. Don't destroy the evidence.

I had a few coins. One of these I dropped in a slot, and turned the handle for the peep show. A dark-eyed nymph with a tropical tan unfastened a rear clasp and tossed her head, now an unfocused blur in my viewfinder. Boredom, or indignity, had hardened her mouth. A rehearsed wave, an approximate sweep of her hands and arms, freed then exposed the two palpated nipples, pink and erect. She slipped off one other garment, a token isosceles, its loops and frills of lace dissolving over her thighs, knees, ankles. The light flickered (a hand enveloped a pubis). I thought I saw the gleam of a blade, a Swiss army knife held up high in a half-lit casement behind her – then a blue flash, then a white brightness, then – as the twilight out on the pier ended the show – a blank.

Some dream.

3 Walpurgis Night

A door – the wrong one for me – had a wild pink rose in its fingerplate, and a hand, gigantic and pointing. The mat said WIPE FEET PLEASE. I stepped inside. I unclipped my pen. To the north was a long low window squared to the night's transparency, as it hung on the pier, abutting the bay. I pulled up a gauze. I tried, but couldn't make out – for what was it, high on those sandstone cliffs – a dome, a telescope? An old man, perhaps full of youthful dreams, searched for signs in an untranslatable sky. Below, a wave with a crest of grey foam slopped against a post. (I believed my train to have stopped in a tunnel.)

A ball bounced in behind me through the door (that's to say a rugby ball, for Rudge was a man among men). It flopped down, thrashing for continued life. I watched it coil up on a point of its oval, then slew in a pirouette. It turned round finally, falling on the solid claw of a table leg. I sniffed the air (a mingle of cigar smoke and furniture wax). I found the last green ember of a Havana, a butt only, smouldering. I picked it out from its charred niche in the rail of a snooker table, which I like to think prevented a conflagration. One other sign of the absentee was a bottle of beer – a stout – as it warmed itself to room temperature.

Fluff, Holmes, on the baize, indicated amateurs, and this I wrote down. Three reds remained. The board showed two low scores. Was this time to go? A TV, somehow suspended in the cigar fumes, clicked on and roared with laughter. (I'll watch. Only for a moment.) An unctuous compère with a solarium tan and a bootlace moustache, and loud checks, and a line in humiliating asides, beamed at a gangling clerk. *He* had a stiff new shirt and a company tie, and couldn't keep to the right spot, and had to be constantly tugged at the elbow (this was uproarious). 'Here – it's a red cross – it's painted on the studio floor!' Life for the tall was cool, dizzy. Perhaps, that compère said, the cross was too far down. The clerk, vacant and open-mouthed, tried – it just wouldn't come – tried to name – oh these questions were a tease – the last prime minister but one. Dong! I'm afraid that's out of time....

A crowd of bobbing shadows, long to the door, scrimmaged for the open air, but I managed to shake them off. I struck out. There was a clangour of bells, alarms. I left my trail as a waste of white powder, when from above I was showered in theatrical snow. The black pointing hand was at odds over destinations, as now it inclined its index down to a watery grave. Light, in a fire of celestial orange, seeped in at last through a rent in Rudge's cosmos. A moon, a drunken sickle low over the flimsy streaks of silver, brought life, then death, to Rudge's mermaids, bobbing on his sea. I sniffed the air again, in blank recognition of the piquant smell of vinegar. Ignore the alarms, I had thought, that muted rattle of electric bells. There was a silhouette, and guffaws from behind a tobacconist's booth. A forearm swiped the air, and a heel clipped the timber. Then briefly, the swish of a quilted coat. Then – a thin blue flame arched and looped into the night ether. For a moment the footfalls ceased. Rudge had a companion, a man who messed with gunpowder. I watched for his firecracker scudding down onto the cold planks. Its fizz of maroon sparks squirmed between my feet. I dodged to the balustrade and called out non-specifically – 'That's cheap, Rudge, that's really cheap!' A swash, a murmur, then a moan came up from the grey tide below. A flame, blood-red, then an aluminium white, then the two in combination, fountained up, then an explosive purple, finally a floral dance. In its kaleidoscope another sign was lit – it said BELOW.

I tumbled in below, missing the bottom step. An obscene shape, an expletive, touched but didn't leave my lips. I pawed at a cobweb in my face. I stamped on a spider and sneezed. That shook the dust from an arras. A coin dropped and whirred gyroscopically, somewhere above me in the coal dust, in the stairwell. The door creaked high over my head. I looked out through its chasm, seeing only that lunar arc, a pale cheese, a slim crescent in the inky oblong of the doorframe. '*Really* cheap,' I repeated. The coin with its whirling glissando flattened down into an uneasy quiet. I expected bats, squeaks and sonic chatter, a chained spook from a closet, recorded bassos in diabolic laughter. Somehow that brought down a second arras, a fairground mantle that I could, then couldn't get off, then shrugged to the floor. That in some way left me at a hall of mirrors, about to learn a first decree: these phalanxes, these ever more diminutive reflections of me, these were the distances of being, and the perfection of being was less than a tiny dot. I understood his observations. I stepped away from the wheel of my replication. I managed a comment. Told him I wouldn't recoil from his gestures. That I'd plod on through their venue. That I understood their desperation – not to say the wet streets, the shingle, the dark bow of the shoreline, the un-sailed-on sea, the starless night. Even the televised babble and vacant personalities, for that's to be put up with. Yet I did take exception to two things: that ghoul, with his hand, his foot, his coattail skimming round a corner; and the trick silvers in PC Rudge's playpen, where I now stood in his seaside hall of mirrors.

A wave, ripple or convexity in the looking glass, if I raised a magnified hand or counted tombstones in a lopsided grin, allotted the same emphasis in Rudge's caricature of me as I foresaw in mine of him. Then again in the sidereal pallor of another, and taller glass, the flabby city-dweller, trimmed to a thinness at the waist, parted, returned to, parted company at last with his pantaloons. That garment boasted an unbelievable range – windy, capacious one moment, the next a pool of linen on the reflected floor. The floating torso took on a cartoonish flexibility. Huge lungs inflated an unreal machismo after a thousand press-ups, and from the seams, the nervous strain in the shoulders of my jacket, I could infer solidity in my newly toned-up deltoids. The head, alas, too heavy with brains, shrank under a carrot tuft of hair.

So *should* I see myself, according to Rudge. I aimed a heel at his crystal. A momentous blow, you'd think. Yet the shards of a man's mind were holographic, and here in Rudge's sideshow that travesty of fluctuating images was retained in each. 'Ah,' I said, and I picked up the arras, though had lost him. I shook out the dust. I invoked – heaven knows – a vengeful god, who in cloaking the heavens had snuffed all distant points of light. I extinguished or barred from my mind Rudge's mosaic, and walked for an outer door. The first I rattled stayed closed, leaving its plastic knob in my hand. The second opened on the tide, whose grey waves roared round the struts of the pier. The third was a cupboard full of junk (a tenon saw, hammers, a mallet for my toes, one spokeshave, one bag of nails). The fourth promised new contact with life, for now my train had jolted to my stop. Here I stepped out onto the platform. I looked up at the screens, where London's underground life had its likeness in lighted black and white. I glanced down at the swirl of litter. I turned my back to the gusts of wind. A long walk, I thought, but here luckily were the emergency stairs. A spurt of blue sparks, as the train lurched, recalled that floating firework, and I remembered my escape. There was a low beam through the keyhole of door number four. A band of golden dust crossed and re-crossed the knuckle of my hand. It pierced Rudge's midnight: this was a trickle, then a flood of sunshine when I threw the door back. A crescendo, icy waves crumbling into foam through the crags and hollows of a cliff face, were now restated according to the rhythms of my London suburb. I brushed out the creases and stood, blinking under the keystone of an arch, a door swinging behind me. Somewhere on a distant block a giant of a man from County Kilburn, bronzed and swarthy, pounded an oblong of tarmac with a pneumatic pummel, and wore mufflers. A cab, a blinding sheen in its windscreen, turned and bobbled up the kerb on a single tyre, and in its rear view caught a dispatch bike buzzing like a hornet. A lazy forearm unrolled itself from a wound-down window. The fist gathered itself for an uppercut, and at its zenith, as it punched the hot air, snapped out its chubby middle finger and poked it at the sky. A bus from Cricklewood clanked into gear and lumbered into the broken thread of traffic. In a lower window a man with wiry hair and a perpetual grin watched me stride from the closed door of the Underground, sole user of its emergency exit. Joey, my private barman, about now would be wiping cocktail tumblers. The last of his daughters was here, on the street, a lithe jet girl in a stained pearl dress, hobbling and clopping in her mother's silky high heels.

I looked up at the clock tower and as usual it was stuck at a few minutes past eleven (time, ever static, recorded the vain cyclist no nearer his Baltic goal). Across the street, Rudge, beheaded in the shadow of an awning, marched into the heat and pointed out something high over the shop fronts. A young wife and mother, newly mauved in her ringlets of hair, put hands to hips and tried to fathom his meaning. She glanced up at the glitter of holiday jets. A boy tugged at her hem and scuffed at the pavement. A squared hanky dangled from his pocket. Rudge – a man new to his beat – wasn't going to help, for she wanted to know the time. Perhaps she sought out the amused twinkle in the eyes of passers-by. *I* don't know, I was too far away. A truck sneezed (of all things it wanted to turn, reverse, unload). I thought I might be seen, or might have to turn to the shop fronts, where I had planted myself in the glaze of a lighting emporium, and had at my back its shades and wall lamps. The boy ducked and dived, filling the vanes of his pinwheel with a makeshift breeze, which deflected the constable's gaze. I wondered – which way would Rudge turn now? – and thought I saw what Blamm had refused to, an athlete, blue and uniformed, a man programmed for one task only, the city's crusade against evil, when evil was sought out everywhere, even among the innocent.

There was a hot mirage of wet macadam. In the liquefied bends, there was a logjam of traffic.

---

[24] My counterpart is a draughtsman, but instead of elevations on a drawing board, he uses signs. This Morris is one of his many symmetries. See his novella, *Endnote Twenty-Three*, 'Dirty Old Town'.

[25] Apologies. This is you-know-who at work – and what did I tell you! A draughtsman!

[26] Don Dunne, a systems analyst we shall meet, a man with a maths degree.

[27] I begin to understand his little game, this wraith among the electronic pulses of my word-processor. He's doomed always to be a figment, having set himself at odds with the cynical demands of public life, with its value on fame, its submission to political manifestos, and the pronouncements wrapped in its social programme. He has risen above all that, and must see himself therefore as a new kind of aristocrat.

[28] There is nothing much reflective in her now, a financial magus of the Thatcherite years.

[29] Now I'm suspicious, seeking for clues, connections, any crossword deceit in this elaborate little rig-up. I remember those partial letters in PC Rudge's pendant, and ask if

in this instance an F is an unformed E, and Fixt is an anagram of exit, a portal I cannot find. What do you think?

[30] Three is a prime number. Three was his number of parents in their prime. Ninety-one is not a prime number, though on first appearance you think it might be. The sum of its digits is one (9 + 1 = 10, 1 + 0 = 1). One is wholeness. One universe. One god. I don't pretend to know by this what Byrne's numerology meant.

[31] As if we didn't know!

[32] So the duplicity of binary fission, where nepotism is the central statute written in indelible ink and upheld by the legislature in the Republic of Letters. The reader reads the writer if the writer reads the reader. Dry country. I am now tempted to let this cuckoo in my nest fly free.

[33] I knew, fellow-scribe, that finally you *would* counterbalance Hopkins Matthew with Hopkins Gerard Manley—

...Ah well, God rest him all road ever he offended!
This seeing the sick endears them to us, us too it endears.

[34] But didn't I read somewhere that Bob Blamm's wife was Betty? Could this be the turning point in my contest with that other?

[35] It's typical of Beaufoy that he should have chosen, as figurehead, a poet outside the academic tent, as literary artist not acknowledged by the academy. Nor did Shay belong in the populist camp, remaining a virtual recluse when it came to the treadmill of workshops, festivals, and the handing out of prizes. He had enemies, and the worst of them implied he'd only got published in the first place when, as a prominent industrialist, he personally knew our captains of industry, including Lucinda Munney, a principal at Leader Books. Leader was his publisher. Shay's fortunes have changed since. I understand he lost a lot of money in an ill-fated venture somewhere, and having retired has little chance of recovering it. Oh, and by the way, the cuckoo has flown the nest. He soars! He sings! *See note 32, above.*

[36] Sutcliffe, otherwise known as the Yorkshire Ripper. Yet don't these few paragraphs also serve to show an important aspect of the layered technique that guardian of my bitstream brings, with his cloud-capped architecture – all dizzy heights constructed on a wedge of Civil Service stationery.

It's worth recalling how the press had first claims on a killer dubbed the 'Yorkshire Ripper', a leader writer's inspired, popular sobriquet, long before arrest and conviction, Sutcliffe going down, eventually, for the murder of thirteen women, and the attempted murder of seven others. He was awarded twenty life sentences, to be increased to whole life at a later date. His attacks began in residential areas, but moved to red-light districts, Sutcliffe drawn by the precarious situation prostitutes have in our society. It's possible he had regularly used them himself. When interviewed he claimed that the voice of God had sent him on his killing spree, with murders carried out over five years (which included women who *weren't* prostitutes). West Yorkshire Police were criticised for the time it took to pin down Sutcliffe as their man, despite interviewing him nine times over the course of their investigation. The high-profile, sensational nature of the case resulted in a plethora of information – among much else – including a recorded message and letters from the Ripper himself, revealed in the end as a hoax, work of the infamous Wearside Jack. At his trial in 1981, Sutcliffe pleaded not guilty on grounds of diminished responsibility, having been diagnosed as a paranoid schizophrenic, though a majority verdict saw him convicted of murder. I think Blamm always half-expected to find tribute to the Ripper among Staverton's effects. He must have been disappointed not to. He had good reason to see Staverton condemned as a woman-hating monster.

[37] From the seedy world of commerce, into the seedy world of public life, here was a hearthside poet warming his feet with the minor deities...

[38] ...and so I have to concede, my counterpart has claimed all my paper territories.

[39] Chekhovsky, Dmitri (1909–87), now safe in contemporary arms, though his origin and literary evolution are traced, according to Grace Fowler, to Russian and European Symbolism. He was born in Moscow, but under the Cold War's first chilly breeze sought asylum in the USA. Running through all his work – the fiction, poetry and drama he chose to critique – is his antithesis to the deterministic order of the nineteenth century, which had cast its long shadow. There is film footage of him and Derrida in conversation (French with English subtitles).

[40] It is now obvious that Blamm had worked out long before I had that the near simultaneity of the two crimes – the murdered drugs girl and the 'attempted rape' – raised questions as to the likelihood of both being committed by Staverton, someone only ever known to the police for petty theft. Given the pathologist's report, which Blamm was privy to and I was not, all knowable timings would have shown the girl's death as days before those bogus glaziers, arriving in their van for their abortive break-in. Blamm also knew before I did of the Vercelli connection with the address where the break-in occurred, in part witnessed from across the street by Iris Cadogan. I don't need to stress that the Home Office would not have wanted the chancellor's close advisor or his daughter mired in scandal, i.e. student Alison Vercelli living a high life off her London clearing house – a political imperative the chief inspector was forced to acknowledge (or so I would reason). It was for my confusion alone, and therefore that of the Department, that he led the trail up every wrong alley, wanting our fake glaziers arrested, and even putting about the rumour that the dead girl wasn't dead after all. That said, he wanted a conviction, and tried hard to put Staverton away for attempted rape – even when the victim of that allegation hadn't come forward. All he'd got was a witness. So you see, this is what I've had to deal with, though have to admit the chief inspector isn't so stupid after all. I'll give you that, Blamm, though of course like so much fiction leeching on the human propensity for dishonesty and crime, his is an instance deserving only the footnotes of literature, which dutifully I have consigned it to.

[41] So as the burden of my day job dissolves into London's light air, a fully emergent Adrian

Fixt breathes palpable life into the ghost in his word-processing machine. At last I am alive. I am a writer.

Electric Letters Z

Amusing, perhaps, to transpose that human geometry found in a *roman-à-clef* to the solid planes of reality, yet this is not, reiterate not, a *roman-à-clef*. Characters resembling etc. living persons etc. are an amazing coincidence....

Foreword

Whether Zob really intended the commemoration of John Andrew Glaze's death, and a celebration of his life, is open to question. A great deal went against it as a project, whose perils should have been eased through Zob's profession – though that in itself is complicated. By whatever chance or accident, those of us at work on the 'inside' – so to speak in the boardroom of English letters – have come to know Marshall Zob as wholly constructed, borne up on the vanes and social wing beats first tested by his father – by Zob Senior – two men inclined to act depending on the scale of reward.

Worse still for me has been Zob Junior's personal weather map, his London clouds – I mean his sullen brown drizzles – and at certain other times his tumble of intoxicated sunbeams, all bound up with his flight up the fastseller charts. This has made his house – or rather my former place of work – unpredictable atmospherically.

Astonishing, no – but it *is* ironic that Glaze should come under my pen, an instrument I'd hoped to keep free of any such taint. By contrast this is so unlike the golden quill the mercenary Zob is obliged to wield – this by his family's rules of fortune – practically every working day of his life, in a padded cell. In just that ramble through another man's life (and death) is an often unbearable strain on my nib, host to all kinds of opposing forces. This is the point, the sore point, that I note even now.

Do I feel embarrassment, discomfort, shame, when what I have spawned, under the privacy of my editorial lamp, is the full revelation, and of not just any diary? It's *my* diary (excerpts below), a document I kept for scrupulously professional reasons. I cannot be blamed if it tends as its seed the fullest vulgar exposé. Plus there has also been the problem: how to contend with the sheer ineptitude of John Andrew Glaze's death....

My name I shall hardly need to stress is Alistair Wye. A ragged-trousered visionary, up on a purple moor, has told me that numerologically this is a sign of passion – he means my name numerically transposed. Apart from that I have been, and I admit laboriously, Zob's amanuensis. Marshall Zob, should you not already know, is the perfection of the dead Andrew Glaze, PhD, whose brightest student he was. This was back in the early 1970s, in the cloisters of Modern College, Exe University, where the writer and academic, and Blagueur Prize-winner (twice), the witty Zob Senior, had passed before him – many years ago.

So. Gloves are off. I shall refute mythologies. Shall prick that iridescent bubble, a falsified lament over Glaze's death. Shall go on saying that this has been no loss, a passing that hardly caused me to put down my coffee cup, or extinguish my cigarette.

I drove Zob, in Zob's silver Mercedes, to the stone parish outside Exe, while over preceding nights I had smiled patiently at his oration, which somehow he'd rehearsed with a straight face. The priest, a man in a newly ironed cassock, beamed throughout. He remarked of Glaze what bookish soil that gifted peasant had tilled, as a form of compliment – in truth a slight on the class origins of a respected academic. Zob, whose pallor through recent small hours was aghast, had reached that point of luring a procession of women into his lair. One, a red-haired girl of twenty, less than half the littérateur's age, sought his assistance for a thin collection of poems, with an eye to his publisher. It meant that she, like me, had the pleasure of his funeral oration, though unlike me tested the tog of his duvet. Her night-long amplitude dispatched Zob throughout the next morning to the first, then to the second, then to the third bathroom, I later deduced in search of that cream, potion or palliative for his poor sore phallus. His redhead had tongued, petted, squeezed, caressed – once too often.

I slipped away before Zob's last farewell, and with the engine running warmed up the Mercedes. By now I was well versed in that mendacious act over Glaze's mortal remains, soon to be incinerated. Zob commended his fumes to the cosmos, assured of the 'greatness' of his achievement, for had he not laid down his lucid path, through 'a continent of English culture', for less certain feet to tread…? Perhaps depressingly that was so, though I cannot be fagged to talk about it now. Here should end the life, work and attainments of John Andrew Glaze, whose second journey out in a void I'd rather contemplate across the street, in the Forces Inn, where I could weep into some lovely local beer.

Therefore in some sense our latest Zob masterpiece – a novel he has tactfully called *Gimme the Cash* – is overshadowed by the demise of his distinguished tutor of Exe, a man wholly without insight. May the Lord protect his soul.

(By the way, Merle, what did you think of that capon?)

—AW, Highgate

Diary

'Diary' is not a term I should choose, as this implies adherence to one clock alone, that remorseless timepiece of our daily lives. Time is the soil of my adventure, and is measured retrospectively – once, ineptly, as a chance remark by Andrew Glaze, and now on a separate occasion by me, with editorial amendments. If as a kind of second I am acting with professionalism, I do so as Zob's assistant – a post I shall shortly have to resign – and not as Glaze's apologist.

Politically Zob has had me partitioned in a small, interdependent state of his household up in its roof space. It amounts to two large rooms, with extensive views of the neighbourhood, and a hazy glimpse of the heath, green at its edges. I am equipped technically, having a networked IBM-compatible, that constellation linked to another, the phone with exchange and fax system. The central heating, which Zob thoughtfully modernised before moving from Wandsworth, extends its pipes considerably into my attic. One of my rooms I set aside – this is for me personally – with a divan should I work late and not wish to go home – home being another garret, this one in *West* Hampstead.

Zob's father had Anglicised himself decades ago, shedding his eastern European Zoblinski, or Zobilinsk, or something like that, in favour of that sole syllable much simpler for his post-war English hosts. He too was once of Exe, as student and professor (and colleague of Glaze), and sportingly approved my wallpaper, a plain cream with gilded crowns – as I feel is only befitting. Zob's mother, twice a divorcée, and famous for more than twenty novelettes for the lady's romance market, didn't like his Wandsworth furniture. She told him to sell it off in exchange for fine mahogany and walnut, country pine for the landings and bedrooms (of which there are seven), and sumptuous chintz for the living rooms.

It has to be said, it wasn't without assistance that Glaze, the immortal Glaze, had shuffled off his coil. That was back in the greys of November. The saleable Zob, at this stage a *near* millionaire, stamped his feet on the cold parish pavements, shuddered, and wrapped himself more snugly in his coat. In the glove box in the Mercedes, I found, and avoided, his emollient.

In December that same Zob trimmed his wisteria ruthlessly, the thing having overreached its green reticulation, and pulled it from its gable. Now it was late January. From that same eastern perspective my view was of emerald crocus stems and the lawns sugared with dew. *Gimme the Cash* was due to appear, and was an automatic choice for Best Novel to be Published This Decade, or of those on its committee. I shan't have to add Zob even now dreamed up something 'special' for the millennium.

Innocence is everything. Zob's with that plaything the microchip is spectacular, and gives us some curious mishaps. Take for example that item of email, addressed to me upstairs, to prepare him and his agent a pot of ground coffee. They had their feet up and were sucking cigars in the drawing room. But this was a communication the benighted Zob - novelist, columnist, critic - delivered to the wrong queue, dispatching it to his publisher's office as a fax. I gathered as much one morning in a whirlwind, from an energetic intern robust enough to work there. It was therefore to my immense surprise when I did receive instructions, on January 27th, a Thursday, when the moon was auspiciously full. It came as a genuine email, smooth as winged Mercury over cupric ether, so sure had been Zob's touch over his keypad—

MZ to AW: 27/1
Al. Cheers for the mug of chocolate. And ta for telling Annie I was out. Some thoughts re Glaze, that is I think two months a decent interval. The hacks have sharpened their nibs, so why not me too? Anyway I've got material on Glaze. Please make time to talk about this, before lunch say. By the way the second, as well as first bathroom, is now out of bounds to you. And please could you smoke outside. Marsy

Why thank you, Marsy….

January 28 As a matter of fact that meeting was postponed, because Annie - a redhead, with a redhead's temper - hid behind a forsythia, and must have seen Zob step out to his Mercedes. He'd gone to retrieve his briefcase, and possibly his lotion, though I'm sure there were several jars in bathroom one. Zob was in the doldrums all day - I know, because he kept playing that Albinoni Adagio - and sent me home early for the weekend.

Albinoni's too Gothic for my taste.

February 1 Yesterday I didn't see him, hear sound of him, or manage to intercept phone calls. He remained in his study throughout. I smoked my afternoon cigarette over the ledge, exhaling white cloudlets into the dry, cold air. In a patio corner, where Zob's gardener Adam had carelessly left a rake, a jasmine showed its tiny yellow flowers, its dark green stems.

February 2, a Wednesday At approximately 9.30 a Mach One courier delivered a padded envelope, moments before I arrived for work. Zob put it with the other mail and told me to deal with it, delicately and as a matter of urgency. I took all correspondence up and had my morning cigarette.

Later. The tireless Annie Cryles, poet, I now know as the co-ordinator of that Mach One courier, a 'lively bloke', she said, with a cockney patois, and an acquaintance of hers. Her covering note set out Zob's appreciation for the material she'd enclosed. It was a thin collection of verse, its title *Keep Off the Grass*, packaged with half a dozen photographs – portraits, in monochrome. I select just two. The first, a close-up, shows an outraged snarl. The other is an action shot, of a young cosmopolitan wearing leggings, arms wide to a swoop of pigeons. The scene, Trafalgar Square. Her scheme disguised itself as divine intervention, with Zob supposed to declare his 'discovery' to his publisher, and launch himself ecstatically into a foreword, as detailed by her. This, in his populist, popularising style. One other trumpet was that institutional weekend column of his, for a broadsheet whose name I'm unable to utter. In its postures of debate I cannot detect that independence it claims to have. In it Zob's social percipience ranged over all human commerce, and lent us his wisdom on everything, from petty crime to the papacy.

Shall Annie see herself heralded? For her sake I mention Zob's debut novel, grey prose for a grey Western world, whose clever title – let me remind you, *Aristotle's Atom* – he claims to have plucked from a dream of blue wood smoke. This as you'd expect, Zob being the son of Zob, was well received, and is retrospectively hailed for its astuteness, and is hardly a fiction at all, with its emphasis on all kinds of political cover-ups. Since then the whole panorama of Western rapacity – an ape who pales under the spotlight – is persistently the subject of the younger Zob's newspaper work. Annie Cryles stepped forward centre stage, to take her cue.

Alas intuitive as to the making of careers, she hadn't accounted for all those satin-faced beauties – her many competitors – whose rise was doubtful when dependent on Zob's initiative. What he did for her he must for them, being, as she now knows why – nothing.

A second collection – *No Ball Games* – is currently being assembled – and there's one for her projected continental audience, *Cédez le Passage*.

February 3 (a.m.) I paused before going up and slipped into the press room, or I should say basement, which is full of tea chests, these being stuffed with unread publications. That was the far end. Better lit and more often frequented was the near end, where Zob kept his wine bins. I eventually found the article Annie had referred to in her note, and was able to verify what critical approbation her poems had attracted. All this I discovered in an article whose author constructed a complete social thesis on the solitary seven lines of her title poem.

To her it must have seemed a natural extrapolation, when on the strength of these and other plaudits she envisaged her future as performer, critic, competition adjudicator, sometime workshop and summer school guru. But I'd got my instructions, and knew what to say of those flimsy leaves she'd lumbered a courier with. 'Marshall,' I wrote, 'is grateful for the opportunity of seeing your work, and greatly looks forward to a second collection.'

That afternoon. Another cigarette over the ledge, and the thought that technically I was unsuited to the work Zob was asking me to do.

And by the way, Adam had moved his rake.

February 8 In two days we will see a new moon. Mrs Clapp, the Thursday cleaner, seems to have got her days muddled, and was in the laundry room hectically ironing shirts.

February 10 That new moon, and an explanation re Clapp. Today it's her brother's funeral, after a prolonged wrestle with an incurable disease, which afflicted his throat.

I have noted our metropolitan sky as a distant zinc, extending its cloudy arcs over the neighbouring roofscape. Chimney stacks, those at any rate I can see, if only in a blur of burnt orange, dissolve then reintegrate through a sodden streak of mist. Adam, a man who has rendered me two syllables only since arriving after New Year's Day ('Thankee' - for the mug of tea I proffered), has put down certain markers, though I can't yet see *him*. There is for example a heavy bloom of footprints over the dewy lawns. There is a barrow with a tool bag.

I see already the crocuses want to reveal their sumptuous blue. Daffodil buds - one day these will be a riot - just begin to show yellow. There's a thin pink blossom on the cherry trees.

February 11 The traditional path of strife, where two roles are cast - i.e. villain equals indifferent establishment, which holds back all natural genius - has no appeal for Annie. She was here just now slamming doors, which shook the whole house. She had gone by the time I got down, leaving Zob ashen in the doorway of his study, still smarting at her valediction. Bad taste makes that highly printable in a novel of his, yet finds no place under a stylish hand. Farewell, Ms Cryles.

Ash Wednesday That new moon ushered in new realms of adventure, for only now do I discover how Zob, among his twilit mountain spectres, has tried out his electronic bulletin board, whose Stateside calendar defaults have temporarily thrown me. I have though sorted that out. Here's something he posted almost a week ago, and two weeks *after* that first Glaze memo—

Subject Professor Glaze   **From** Marsy
Date 2–10, 16:10:51   **Reply to** Box #1, Ext #1, Zob
Text: Al – Well done for not upsetting Mrs Clapp. More than *I* managed.... Cornelius phoned me all last night on the Glaze project, so I think I'll resurrect it. When can you spare some time on this? Any idea why these screens sometimes lock up? Marsy

There was another, which through an automatic generation of software pointers (so saith the user guide) encamped itself on my screen, though I had tried manfully to escape (intending to pick up the phone. Intending to tell Zob this wasn't the best medium for spontaneous exchanges). This was as follows—

Subject Professor Glaze **From** Marsy
Date 2–10, 16:19:32 **Reply to** Box #1, Ext #1, Zob
Text: Forget that about the screens. I had my NUM LCK down, its little red light.

February 17 A bronze sky today, without that sheen, and with patches of turmeric. A week ago Adam, or so Mrs Clapp reports, expected a boy on work experience. He, 'bless 'im', only now turns up. Adam wanted to dismantle a timber chalet that had been assembled directly over a concrete oblong, which with the years has meant a bad case of rising damp. The boy, or pouting youth, arrived in denims – shirt, jeans, half-length jacket. No boots, but canvas shoes, in a nice matching blue.

Mrs Clapp took a hand-held vacuum to the drapes. Zob was out, so I left him a note on his desk.

February 18 Zob, Wye, finally meet to discuss Glaze. Good-time Marsy, over a glass of Merlot, has been talking in the hamburger bar to Cornelius, who wears thickly framed glasses. When you add in the nose, which has the look of rubber, it only *seems* like comic garb. Cornelius (Zob's agent), having considered the Glaze angle, has now got bored with it – and so it follows has Zob. Zob Senior drew attention to the year of our Lord the next. This – *annus mirabilis* – would see the sixtieth anniversary of Glaze's birth, in a Cornish fishing village. Zob Senior sired his only offspring in the Valleys, in a mining town, and told us how much both he and Glaze loathed Dylan Thomas. Zob Junior, a man immensely more successful in money matters, now tells the independent Wye that next year is therefore a good one for a commemorative book on Glaze, a man 'who has done so much' to promote understanding of present-day letters. I'm to forget all this for the moment though. A TV anchorman, who had the good fortune to encounter Zob's last novel, *Hype*, was taken with its central character, or more correctly his absorption in televised sport, in particular soccer. The character is Tallon. Tallon seemed so 'knowledgeable' that naturally his creator must also be – and would Zob care to participate in a TV debate, entitled 'What's Wrong With Our National Game?' Zob said to me, 'Well. What *is* wrong with it?' Should I reply so, that it's something *he* should know, with its muddy palms firmly to the levers of the marketplace? For myself this is too gloomy a picture. I am hymned by those angels in my native Manchester, who have combined Gallic poetry with Celtic persistence, and in a season of triumph, and of double triumph (as I am now able to insert, joyously, gloriously), are the velvet contrast to the prosaic Annie Cryles plus troupe.

I told Zob I would give this some thought, and pen a script to rehearse.

February 21 The problem as I see it, with Zob and the TV debate, is this. Zob had a precariously wealthy father, and this had a bearing on Junior's school life. In the particular fee-paying institutions I have managed to document, soccer is and always was anathema. I ought to advise Zob to contribute only on that other, that barbarians' game – i.e. rugby. Though I think Zob was always one for smokes behind the bike sheds.

February 24 Mrs Clapp, arriving shortly after ten, has placed a tray of snowdrops on the kitchen table. I say this because Zob sent her out for steaks, an avocado, prawns and button mushrooms, which she also placed on the kitchen table. That by the way is a dark antique pine, which bears the incisions of cooks galore, going back to Victoria. There are, pretentiously, hanging from ceiling hooks, redundant utensils, also from Victoria's reign – booming copper receptacles, much tarnished today, and iron ladles. Zob interceded as I made a mug of chocolate shortly before midday, and asked me to bring a cup for him, strangely on the middle landing. He sent Mrs Clapp out again, this time for a single carnation, at which she huffed, wanting, as she put it, 'to hoove'.

On the middle landing. Zob had opened a door into a room I had not been in before, whose sash overlooked the corrugated carport between *his* house and the lower numbered neighbour's, who is a liver surgeon. Zob cradled his mug of chocolate. The sky was a patchwork of ochre and lead. The room, said Zob, represented Wandsworth. By this was meant its contents, which had padded out the *Lebensraum* at his last address, a poky flat. Statistically it's not worth the trouble. There were papers, so many papers. A Neanderthal hi-fi, able to play tape and vinyl. A bookcase, not square but a parallelogram. Prints. Posters (one of M. Jagger). Frames, and separately pictures. There was much tasteless bric-à-brac. There was a roach clip. There was a personal computer, also from the Neanderthal period, with several five-and-a-quarter-inch discs, still neatly racked in a tinted library box. I remarked on the wallpaper, whose regular pattern was an aquamarine seaweed threaded through a violet trellis. I picked up a long-play Rolling Stones (*Around and Around*). I put that down and picked up a Telemann, an earlier starlet from a later period in Zob's aesthetics.

Before I went home Zob insisted I make a garlic mayonnaise for the prawns and avocado. He wouldn't tell me who that 'someone special' was who was coming to dinner. While I did this he poured me a gin.

If you want my opinion, garlic's not a suitable dressing.

February 25 Adam and that laconic boy have at last got around to the chalet, or its reassembly. Much of its lumber, loungers, garden tables, a wheel from Zob's very first bike – a BSA Bantam – has been stacked for the last week or more in the laundry room. I hardly need mention Mrs Clapp's chagrin, perhaps shared by Mrs St John, the Tuesday cleaner, who having 'reconsidered' her position is to return on St David's Day. As I suspected, those flanking borders, a quincunx of circular mounds and a northeast heart-shape, are a ripple of daffodils, yellow smears in the condensation of our northern Europe crystal. The chalet's going up on risers this time, which Adam assures his master have been treated. I have refused to work in a room draped with seaweed.

Let me be precise. That old personal computer is not one the clever Marshall Zob ever mastered. This has something to do with Glaze, who had a big-bosomed secretary, a spinster who typed, typed, typed. 'Don't trust 'em,' he said (computers. Bosoms he adored, especially big, and was faddish about. Zob observed this, observing Glaze, observing Zob's then-partner playing squash). Glaze, almost two years before his tragic demise, and after decades of philosophical consideration, took a sabbatical. It was a wholly personal matter, though he dressed it professionally, a sleight for the casual observer, who might have expected the fruit of his metaphysics served back to the world as lecture tour. This did happen, but not in Britain – small and provincial and always slow to accept revolution – but among our friends across the pond. Because yes, the tour took place, though has not as far as I can tell changed Western thinking at all. Glaze kept in touch with his friend and former disciple continually via airmail. Zob, whose first novel had not yet attracted Hollywood, and in fact was almost pulped, still scratched for a living in Wandsworth, doing hackwork. He replied to 'all' the professor's correspondence somehow, using a proprietary word processor running on a PC. This was one of those antiquities not yet touched by the tentacles of Microsoft. I have looked but cannot now find the printer, which I expect to be a Microline.

Zob's professional vanity, if it persuades *him* doesn't persuade me, and the commemoration – *The Zob-Glaze Letters*, in his eyes a milestone – I see as fodder for the trade's funeral parlours, those many remainder outlets up and down the motorways.

'But there's plenty of time for this,' said Zob. 'So keep it to the background.'

'The background,' I echoed.

'Yes. Get on to it *when* there's nothing else.'

'When there's nothing else.'

St David's Day To be honest the task's not that easy. Having brought that old PC up to my room I find that the fixed disc is unreadable. Nor are the professor's writings easily found. His letters, in no particular order, are scattered among heaps of other material. And get this. Cornelius was here to shake my hand, wearing a black shirt, a yellow tie, and with a daffodil pinned to his lapel. Mrs St John threw out that carnation, which had expired badly, and which was still in the green flute Zob had planted on the dinner table.

March 3 Mrs Clapp I heard warbling, singing and whistling, while with gusto she was cleaning bathroom three. Cornelius, who has taken certain soundings and is again warmly enthusiastic on the Zob-Glaze project, sluiced his personal Niagara over the falls of bathroom two. I therefore deposited certain evidence in bathroom one, which I later flushed away, having had plenty of time to take in the new Jacuzzi, with its brassy pristine fittings.

March 4 I have found a start-up firm under a railway arch, near my home address in West Hampstead, who will restore my 'lost' data and write it to a reconditioned disc. You can get excellent kebabs in West Hampstead. The bill of course goes to Zob, to include the *per diem*.

March 9 Now this is what I call droll. Zob, for whom the world of practical science is a blur, had created a new directory (DIR1, DIR2, DIR3…DIRn) for each electronic letter – those not always dispassionate epistles – that he laboured over in replying to the hapless Glaze. I have no doubt he referred to the section 'Sample Setups' in what at the time was the current user guide (a document somewhere, somewhere in that seaweed room). I have coded a zippy macro, to gather them together to a single, saner harness. That, as I patrol the environment, reduces to sixteen letters, written over a period of twelve months, occupying forty-five kilobytes of disc space. Zob, with both Oxbridge and Exe degrees, is a man only commercially literate. That old pile of junk he sweated over myopically in Wandsworth takes up too much of my desk space.

March 10 As usual I made my chocolate, in a mug that bears the legend 'Genius at Work', which is Zob's little joke. I overheard Mrs Clapp in a protracted exchange with Adam over chrysanthemums. Adam invariably wears navy blue overalls, with a tiny pink tulip stitched into the corner of one of its pockets. Now that he's creosoted the chalet, Zob says he doesn't like the new colour. Too dark.

I am beginning to tear my hair out over the professor's unknown number of letters, only three of which I have so far found. Much of what's in that Wandsworth room I think would prove highly combustible, not least a purple review of *Aristotle's Atom*. This, a cutting from a risible Saturday supplement, had been penned by a Cambridge confederate, who has himself gone on to win the Booker, and has not ceased since to pontificate. This is chronic among public diseases.

March 11 I am in possession now of five of Glaze's letters, all in black ink, on carmine notelets, and strongly doused in the scent of apple. The next stage is this. To recover them all, then key them to disc, interleaving them chronologically with Zob's. Zob will write a foreword. One of his cronies – perhaps that anthropologist Simon Macamister, himself a graduate of Exe – will write one of those tedious introductions.

March 14 Six letters now, and by chance a Xerox of Glaze's lecture notes. I have found them amusing. According to him – or I should say according to notions attributed to him, and known in one or two campuses as the professor's 'quotidium' – according to Glaze time is a spatial continuum. Moreover it is linear, extending infinitely in two directions. This makes us eternal travellers on a regal strip of carpet, a thing unfurling endlessly under a cold sprinkling of stars. (Cold showers I recommend.) The mistake – or as Glaze had it the 'grand fallacy' – has been to pin our lives down cyclically (sunrise, and after a period of twenty-four hours, sunrise, and after a period of twenty-four hours, and so on *ad nauseam*). This is the *false* measure of time, recurrence being – not a circle – but exactly that, the repeated occurrence of, of, of, not things, rather 'doings'. 'Doings' he attributes discretely to men, and in some lecture halls women also. Thus Shakespeare finds his repetition in someone like Larkin (in itself an inexcusable flaw in the whole theory). One reason that Shakespeare can't shake hands with Philip Baboon is this. Although essentially the same they are nevertheless products of a different time. Time is therefore only a separation in Glaze's system, and is measured in terms of distance. So. Why can't I step back a second or two? Answer: each 'second' is an enormity.

I can see we are going to have to return to this, Professor.

March 15 I paused on my way in to work today at Annie's forsythia, which is a bloom of fiery yellow. The first presage of Zob's new woman, apart from that garlic mayonnaise, came via Mrs St John, who handed me the mail, wanting to polish the hall dresser. I sorted it, dealing to the top its smallest envelope, which was white, self-seal, with a window, and not of recycled paper (tut). Its franking, as I later saw I'd misconstrued, showed the fragmented scales of a cobra, charmed in part, and had as caption 'British Open Tanka Society' (or BOTS). From a glance at my society listings BOTS was an organisation started up in 1989, and run by Fiona Trethowan, DLitt, from an address in Woodstock.

March 16 Cornelius, a big man whose sporty jacket was patterned with corn and lilac checks, today had an ash-grey silk to the top pocket, and brought us his business plan on floppy disc (which he calls 'flaccid'). It was his strategy for *Gimme the Cash*, which as party worker it is my job to place – among his other business plans – in its own square mesh in our network: C:\PLANS\GIMME.DOC. Thereafter Zob will expect it on his desk, laser printed. Cornelius's secretary, a wondergirl for whom I once stirred a Martini, is orthographically astute, though it's not always the case these documents pass through her hands. I shall therefore run GIMME.DOC through the spellcheck.

How's this for an afterword! An *ible* for indispensable, a capital C for cockney, and among the many possible suggestions for the name Philip, 'phallus'....

St Patrick's Day A spin-off of the Japanese Festival, which was not that long ago, gives us the minor academic masterpiece *Western Culture and Oriental Short Forms*, a survey by Fiona Trethowan. In her preface she explains that the book grew spontaneously from the many readings she had organised during that festival year, usually in the open air on campus sites. Some, under threat of our English summer (i.e. rain), were 'conducted' in the bar, 'inevitably' (concealed laughter). Zob was browsing through a signed copy, which I later picked up and skimmed through myself. This more or less confirmed my opinion of Bashō et al as literary cul-de-sac, that short if perennial thoroughfare wherein Zob also excelled.

Inadvertently, and while I made a salami roll, Mrs Clapp unplugged the laser printer, about 'to hoove'. This has 'unprogrammed' my preferred font, which supports the use of italics.

March 18 Cornelius's business plan is just like the others, consisting of these points—

1 Posters on metropolitan street corners and in every bookseller's window, to proclaim: GIMME THE CASH: THE NUMBER ONE BESTSELLER.

2 Blurbists to be quoted on the paperback edition, with turns like this on the book and its author: 'A remarkable *tour de force....*' 'Indisputably the best of his generation....' 'This very important book....' 'The two extremes of Marshall Zob: you love him, you loathe him, you can't ignore him....'

3 Myrtle Bloge, by now famous for the sheen of her round spectacles, should agree (Cornelius thought) to chat on camera during one of those incessant late-night media shows, with Zob himself as studio guest.

4 The usual two-page splash in at least three of the weekend broadsheets.

5 All the obvious interviews, where of course Philip Mastabyle should prove indispensable, a critic who loved a cockney yarn.

I'm supposed to make *my* suggestions before delivering up the printed copy, but all I can think of is—

6 Am working on a book myself, I mean a good one....

March 21 Zob's drapes are a peach velvet. Today when I arrived they were still drawn – that's to say they were tightly sealed on all three sides of his bay. It means retreat, and calls to mind those odd moments I have witnessed his crises of conscience, and how debilitating. Zob well knows his 'difficult' reputation. On that subject he said to me *reconcile, please!* as a sort of exam question. This was under the moulded vines of a Victorian ceiling, where the light was poor, and the tables rough. Growing warm under my restless hand was a plain Greene King, and under his of course a London Pride (then another, and another). The question unravelled itself with each successive quaff: 'Harmonise the formal Marshall Zob, who was charm's paradigm at dinner parties, and the sluttish world of his fiction.' Often he's remarked on the parallels with Dickens, a feat not thought possible in the frozen soil of modern public life. My answer is therefore always this: 'Irreconcilable' (and for me another failed exam). Those drapes, whose graded peach has filtered too many rising suns, were a veil on the gloom and a match for his mental atmosphere – thin inky clouds a pall on the sky's luminosity. Nothing stirred or twitched. In the kitchen I found his brandy glass glued centre table. The study, whose fug of spent cigars I sliced through angularly as I opened the blinds, awaited the remedial hand of Mrs St John, who was not due in till tomorrow. I made no attempt to rearrange the suite, whose leather is always cold, and whose tone is a perplexing acacia. I checked his desk diary and discovered today's entry sporting a matchstick man but no appointment (though M. Bloge was penned in for the twenty-second, as was Cornelius). Later I would confirm that electronically. For now I removed the remaining residue of cognac, a nut-brown pool at the foot of the bottle. I spent the day quietly, mostly rummaging in the Wandsworth room. I was, I thought, able to report a breakthrough...

March 22 …though that had to wait. The barrel-chested Cornelius, faintly incongruous in a blue business suit, incarcerated the protesting Mrs St John in Zob's den of solo Sunday revels. Moreover he helped with the dreadful machines of her trade (spray cans, a carpet talc, the elephantine vacuum cleaner), by bringing them all in. As a rule, she said, she mopped the kitchen floor first thing. 'Rules, Mrs St John…' he countered, and you yourself may articulate the rest – there to be broken etc. – for so England's most gifted social chronicler had demonstrated. Frankly that blossom of creativity was still hungover, having flirted with that hair-of-the-dog maxim, dining last night on a bottle of claret. That was in the hamburger bar, where I have established a network of spies.

Cornelius rechecked his watch when Zob, still in the natal wrap of his bathrobe (its texture a fluffy *café crème*), slumped down exhausted. Approximately, this was on the middle step, back staircase. Was there, he wanted to know, coffee on the hob? Cornelius respectfully advised a shower and a shave, and assured him that while he got dressed a freshly percolated cup would be brought to his room. In the meantime agent Cornelius again consulted his watch, hoping, 'Goddammit', that the small-faced Myrtle Bloge – 'so incisive an intellect' – would arrive even later than she now was. She did. By about half an hour. That gave Cornelius endless opportunities with the violet silk to his top pocket, which he repeatedly flattened on the kitchen table. I watched him fold it, and endlessly refold, into the three prongs of the trident that now adorns his breast. In the meeting that followed, designed to settle questions before they were asked – to be aired live on television – the pertinent Ms Bloge fired salvos from her notepad. Zob, by now sober if sluggish, defended his art. Cornelius, as apart from prompting his client, took the minutes…

March 23 …which not surprisingly have landed on my desk, for me to transfer to disc, and laser print, a rigmarole bulleted as—

1 MB's apologies for the delay, road works on the Euston Road.
2 A question-and-answer session on Steven Kiff, a petty criminal centrally lit in that belated success *Aristotle's Atom*, a character resurrected for *Gimme the Cash*. A guarded exchange, ranging from Zob's self-styled precursor, Dickens, to his enemies in the feminist camp. With care and caution Crouch remained nameless, as did all other belles in that biz. Finally—
3 Any other business.
CS It's important to mention the Best Novel to be Published This Decade award, for which *Gimme the Cash* will certainly be short-listed.
MB I'll put that in the summary.

I happen to know that Zob returned to bed, the moment the door had been closed on the trenchant Ms Bloge. I heard her little Skoda phut from the drive.

March 24 Her reply to my fax came stapled to a handwritten addendum to the minutes, a caveat to her final comment above. She was, she said, prepared to furnish propaganda *time permitting.*

Palm Sunday I am powerless in this involuntary sense of gallantry at the plight of my landlady, Mrs Isabelle Lavante, an attractive widow in her mid to late forties. Her athletic son Michael – academically brilliant – this morning kicked out a back-door panel and headed for Dollis Hill with his football. It was the old argument. She, of course, trumpeted the virtues of higher education. He, a café existentialist, rejects all forms of learning designed for the needs of commerce and industry – institutions that to him deserve only our contempt. I'm bound to say he does have a point. Nevertheless, that does not console our middle-class mater, who wants only the best for her darling. Temporarily, I found some hardboard for the panel, as the weather was damp. I looked up, where intertwining ink-blue ribbons tumbled in our sky, as disconsolate almost as she. Her claw hammer I left on the drainer, with the box of remaining panel pins, and invited her out for breakfast. She said no, then well maybe, then okay yes, and offered unilaterally that it was quicker in her Citroën, ageing as it was. 'Certainly less irksome,' I said, 'than the Ford,' a decrepit servant mottled with rust, and lumpy where once there was firm upholstery. I chose one of those pretentious little places in Hampstead, where everyone vied for the supplements. Those who went without consoled themselves in an endless supply of coffee (at least, had there been a waitress). For me I ordered scrambled egg, pepped up with cheddar and textured with slices of mushroom. The distracted Mrs Lavante had lemon tea and a croissant. These details I remember well, as they were repeated on one (and only one) further occasion, when I knew I ran the risk of meeting my employer, who couldn't himself boil an egg. I was deflated, suddenly, on catching sight of him, over in a window seat. His hair was impeccable, washed, brushed and blow-dried. His laptop was open on his knee, though I'd count it a minor miracle should anything get recorded there. He had with him, I saw, Fiona Trethowan, whose face was honest, naïve, dimpled. Too late to change it, Mrs Lavante sallied on ahead to the only spare table, a pocket handkerchief of timber, whose seating was a bench – a singleton – recessed into a stone wall, and a milking stool. Marsy called out as I ducked the low beams. The litany followed. Marshall Zob, Isabelle Lavante. Alistair Wye, Fiona Trethowan. Isabelle dissolved, tossing back her jet hair, and to my astonishment looked girlish. Later she confided privately over the flakes of her breakfast that while 'not exactly' an admirer, she had read both his books. I squirmed uncomfortably on my milking stool.

March 28 I was, incidentally, sleepy. I met, incidentally, Fiona. This was, incidentally, on the back stairs. That was her *first* mistake. She had on those same leggings and pleated blouse I recalled from breakfast on Sunday. Moreover (second mistake) she had no overnight bag. She fluttered past and out of the front door sheepishly. No matter. Let me

announce my breakthrough…. Can you confirm, I asked Zob, that I have found the first
– i.e. number one – in that series of Glaze letters? Why yes. Yes. He could.

28a Scriveners Mews
University Place
Exe
13 December 1991

My dear Marsy,

I don't mind saying I've got some messy personal business to attend to, which
forces me into this US thing. It's so long it seems since my only other visit there,
in happier times. Luckily I'm able to fund it with a lecture tour, though have no
idea what I'll lecture about. I have often pondered on the literary lineation of time,
purely as a metaphor, because metaphor I think has truth-bearing possibilities. So
perhaps I'll test that out on a student populace. We'll see.

To be honest am leaving behind some pretty awful domestic probs – of another
nature, yes, though not unrelated. Giles, that fool son of mine and *flâneur*, has
switched to the wine trade, off on some regular jaunt in Provence, just when he'd
got on his feet in the luxury car biz. Why oh why wasn't he gifted like you! How I
could have guided him – and so patiently – through the hallowed halls of Exe.
Jessica's no better. Wants to marry a mechanic. Rich as that good sir might be, I'll
have none of it. I told her mother as much, who said to me blimey Andrew don't
you ever let go!

All right for her, Marsy, but let me tell you never, never trust a woman! You'll
know by now, after the break-up – or I should say precipitating it – that bitch on
heat fell right into the arms of New York's fattest banker. I have the luck not to be
so corpulent eh, don't I just! Ah well. A life is a life is a life. Not sure yet of my exact
itinerary, though first stop's not surprisingly home from home. Will write you
from New England.

Loved the book. Get that weather-tanned yachtsman, what's-his-name Snell, to
swing a film deal.

The best for you, your Andrew….

It's to the exactness of my craft that I point out humbly that in December 1991 the
thirteenth fell on a Friday. I do not intend by this anything sinister or ominous.

March 29 Apparently all day yesterday Marshall fiddled about, first with an up-line
dump, then with a down-line load, but could not retrieve those notes he'd made on his
laptop. I put him right, and found preliminary sketches to *Bust!* – his millennial piece.
Futuristic (not his strong suit), pornographic (Zob well practised there).

In the afternoon, giddy under the load of cheese sandwiches – pale, and orange, and double Gloucester – I broached what I saw as the problem of Glaze. Firstly, only by luck had I found other letters in a shoebox, to which Zob said, Micawber-like, the rest would turn up. More importantly, necessary editing raised the possibility of an over-trim, leaving little of the original correspondence. 'That's a bridge we'll cross,' he said.

March 30 Zob was in and out of bathroom one pretty much all day, and I don't think did much work. Cornelius dropped in for a 'last' run over those minutes, at whose addendum he took issue. He did so vituperatively, with little spots of foam to the corners of his mouth. Try as I sometimes or intermittently might (to kick a foul habit), those sublunary anti-tobacco lobbyists still couldn't claim the amanuensis Wye as an adopted son. Why, Wye? Well, my addiction was exotic, that fatal blend of an American cigarette. It's so-so that I prolong a contented puff into the marine tints or wash of our English seasons. I note: it was three days ago – Palm Sunday – that British Summer Time began.

> On my ledge, leaning,
> I saw Adam, preening.
> Tufts of grass from a corner plot
> Are all that his stationary barrow
> Has got.

Then Adam straightened up, as I remembered not to propel my butt to the patio. He scratched his head at the first blood-and-pearl blossoms of a magnolia, which to his mind was not advantageously placed. Sir, I envy you your simple occupational complexities, though not your meteorological terms of employment! Ash on an old man's sleeve, and so forth....

At four I got sent home. Adam, a hoe strapped to his back, had already cycled forth – as I told Zob – through a mizzle and over a brown horizon. Our master wanted womb-like conditions, and a medicinal Scotch, being the correct preparation for his appearance on TV, though the experience was not new to him certainly. I parked my Ford and saw that the London Pole Co had hung a sign on widow Lavante's gable. At eight she asked me to macaroni and Pesto, with herself at the table head and son Michael at the foot. He had at least temporarily capitulated, and so spent remaining hours in his room, with his books. Isabelle poured wine, a repugnant Lambrusco, of which I managed a half glass only. At about 9.30 I caught her in a huff at the local news, having adjusted her two-bay settee. She had already hollowed a round cushion (in the glow and tasselled shade of her standard lamp). Then at ten she observed loudly from her listings that 'leading writer Marshall Zob' was this week Myrtle Bloge's studio guest. She decided to stay up, and yawned a lot, with a certain fatigue round her eyes, and a heaviness to the lids. 'May I,' I asked, 'borrow a tape, record?' Yes-of-course-by-all-means.

March 31 How I have studied...

April Fool's Day …and studied that recording. Item one, a film montage, featured the work of a sculptor operating out of Plaistow. His artefacts were a social thing, manifested in heaps of household recyclables – beer bottles, supermarket tins, Patak's chutney jars – which he arranged and colour sprayed in a warehouse somewhere off the Old Kent Road. Item two was a poet-dramatist whose texts were in fact 'stigmata'. Item three – an equally sunny soul, but unlike the others fabulously wealthy – was an ageing rock star, who by some artifice had persuaded an otherwise reputable string quartet 'to do some material' (I think that meant a forthcoming album). The engaging Myrtle had that harmless smile pinned to her visage throughout. She reserved for Zob's entry, the last item, a deep, bosomy breath, which at last revealed the full circular extent of the legend on her sweatshirt. This, as a studio light caught first one then the other round lens, read as follows: 'WELL, WOULD YOU ACCEPT A SECONDHAND SOLECISM?' It meant perhaps that the deity Zob was merely a grammatical blunder, there to be erased. To be fair she stuck scrupulously to the plan I had outlined in the minutes. She uttered the 'Marsy' diminutive. She even mentioned Zob's new book in the context of Best Novel to be Published This Decade, as 'surely a strong candidate'. Zob could have no complaints, even as I pointed out it was no fault of hers when – in the enforced ease of his studio chair – Zob had worn what seemed a shifty look. Nor did I think his choice of black suit and white shirt open at the neck made the right contrast. 'You can't,' I said, 'be top card and appear half respectable.' He should also consider, I thought, a haircut, being just too long to the collar. And those fat thumbs of his – best to keep them out of sight, not twiddle.

It is pointedly so that Zob never once took my advice. Nor did his gardener, who wanted to hack down that magnolia, and to my astonishment later did so.

April 5 Isabelle, only just back from a grey Easter in Worcester, was this morning on the phone to the London Pole Co, wanting to know why there had been – as she put it – 'no action'. Zob was equally querulous, in his case at the fellow-critic Philip Mastabyle, who had not shown up. When, later, he did, it was with a photographer – a man with a beard and perpetual smile. The Glaze book – or I should say its primitive beginning – now had the authenticity of a second voice, but of course a third, those editorial lies so well rehearsed in Hampstead, had not been invoked. Mine, for now, was muted. Here was Zob's first reply—

Flat 5
147 Trefoil Street
SW18
18 December 1991

Dear Andrew,

It's bound to shake up those too many nannies in our industry, which God knows needs a prod just now. Be sure to send me a transcript of at least one lecture – this idea of yours so fascinates me. By the way thanks for those kind words. It's just a pity that weather-tanned yachtsman (yes, Snell is his name) can't find someone like you. There has been not one sympathetic review. And get this! The rampant Geraldine Crouch, that fat-faced 'masculinist' (as she calls herself), described my sober Steven Kiff as 'highly implausible' – though of course she herself has been nowhere near a pool room. I am at the moment ploughing through her *Geishas in Godalming*, which as geishas go is godawful! I shall return the compliment, one reviewer to another. And don't by the way be too hard on Giles. I thought immediately, on that only occasion I met him, he had got your sense of humour – ever so slightly acerbic. That should carry him through. Not much I can say about the rest.

Keep in touch. Marsy....

As so I conclude it is the frailest error, and a substantial world of vanities, that Zob supposes a footnote should demand our attention.

It is mildly unpleasant to think of it as publishable.

April 6 Meanwhile a scaffold has been erected on the brown brick façade of widow Lavante's, right up to the ledge of my garret. The purpose, as has now been intoned by a bicephalous foreman (to his client he presents a lamb's head), is to remove those elegant, nevertheless disintegrating sashes, and replace them with uPVC imitations. For the one member of his team (who is particularly oafish) he reserves his rhinoceros head, ducking it down in a preparedness to charge. I cannot describe the profound warmth I tend to feel when Isabelle wears what for me is *her* colour – a luxurious, almost hyacinthine blue.

April 9 I have been summoned to Isabelle's two-seater, now that the boy Michael has finally gone to bed, at way past eleven. Accidentally her ivory hand has brushed my knee, but has retracted itself respectably. Then I find she wants nothing more than to smooth Mastabyle's two-page Zob spread jointly in her lap and mine. It's killing me, therefore I make my excuses. I spend too long in the bathroom, and hear her try the locked door, then the patter of shoeless feet. She has again I see bought toothpaste with red and green stripes. Someone, Michael, has used my blue mouthwash....

April 10 Wind, clouds, rain, intermittent sun. A lot of greenness, moisture, not to say the wet lawn outside. I find these new windows deeply disturbing.

April 11 Auspiciously, a new moon. I ask Zob for his thoughts on CD ROM, which as a new toy may make my afternoons less tedious. He glowed significantly, and made *me* a mug of coffee, even before I had opened the mail. How Mastabyle had marked the launch of Zob's new book – with a career profile, of the author at forty-plus – appealed to his sense of sycophancy. That bearded photographer had, also, entered the conspiracy. He gave us a reclining Zob in sturdy brogues, backed by the marble of his fireplace, and flanked by two Victorian caryatides.

April 12 That panel the boy Michael tested with his heel still hasn't been replaced. But the news is worse than that. A wizened mechanic, here last evening while Isabelle fried onions, overhauled my makeshift patch, with – a cat-flap. I am assured that a cream and marmalade kitten, a 'cutie' with darting eyes, is to take up residence. It's going to make me sneeze.

Zob when I got to work was up, and had scoured the morning papers over his toast and coffee. There was only one book review, by Geraldine Crouch – not, however, of *Gimme the Cash*. Her opening gambit, ringed in red marker, and awaiting on my desk, read: 'Forget Marshall Zob. Now at last we do have something to shout about….' In ballpoint Zob had put it so: 'Al – thought this might amuse you.' I am able to report, with not much detachment, that the new voice is sure of itself, possessing 'a youthful resonance' (an echo, and a re-echo, in a sealed glass dome we still call English Lit), and belongs to Justin Simms, a twenty-four-year-old. His debut novel was, *ahem*, 'stunning'. Simms has proved a thorn in Zob's flesh, being got up in war paint in Crouch's rival camp – which means, regrettably, more of him too soon.

April 13 Next in that important sequence of correspondence was a postcard from Glaze. Its picture is an ink-line reproduction of Andrew's church at Exe. It's known for its Perpendicular Gothic, and distinctive squared-off top to the tower. I went there once, where a guide for a party of six drew attention to the font and its motif, in 'harmonisation', he said, with the surrounding arches, windows, etc.

> December 27
>
> Refused – categorically refused – to spend Xmas with Jessica, whom the mechanic has managed to impregnate. The girl must know how I loathe Cambridge. Am going to talk to my only contact in film about your wonderful book. A prosperous New Year. Andrew

To which Zob did not reply.

April 17 Slept late, as did widow Lavante, who appeared phantom-like at the foot of my bed, and whose negligée – brief and diaphanous – should prove no real obstacle to our morning of love. She had found me so hot. 'That,' she said, 'was Mr Zob on the phone,' who had invited us to breakfast. The Citroën was having its hydraulics refurbished, so, after queuing for the bathroom, and finally a hurried shave, I fired up the crock (the Ford). Isabelle appeared on the doorstep – in slacks, a jacket, a lemon bowtie – just as my cassette tape wound to its first crescendo, a Mahlerian clash of cymbals, which in deference to her I turned down. Our venue was as before, where Zob had reserved a bench and two chairs in the window. Fiona, who was there again and had her briefcase, and whose small lively face had a girlish intelligence, showed Isabelle a warm welcome. I asked myself what was going on. Zob only smiled, smugly. Already he had started coffee, a saucered droplet of which he inadvertently spotted on the white acres of his woolly – a crewneck – to which Fiona immediately took a tissue. Waitress service had been restored (there had been problems over pay, it turned out). A pretty teenager with mousy hair and a frilly pinafore moistened her pencil while the petition was gone through. Bran flakes for Fiona. For Isabelle a croissant. Me – oh scrambled egg. That's the one with cheese and mushroom. Zob, who chose this moment to check pockets for his credit card, ordered a Scotch woodcock. Then in the lacuna someone mentioned Mastabyle, whose article Isabelle said she'd enjoyed. (To *my* taste, that pungency of anchovy is too overpowering, even for a pizza, though that's another mealtime.)

I ummed, yet the widow, a not exact admirer, used the word 'delighted' when Zob invited us back for sherry, 'or even stay for lunch'. There was a first hint of sunshine, though the wind was cold. Its little gusts brought a pinkish under-tint to the satin of Marshall's cheeks. Fiona had put her hair up in a bun, because last night she'd been busy, when it missed its wash. It showed us in full the pale rose of her face. Isabelle, in that tumble of vernality – those pregnant clouds before, above, behind – looked less than her middle forties. I go further and say that her tread was light. Although. And of course. Nothing. Nothing upsets me more than the ride she took to Zob's – not in my Ford, but to the throb of jazz in the relative luxury of the Mercedes. My point being that while you have in Mahler the tenacity of consolation, to arrive, to re-park, to agree that all was well, even as Fiona stooped over a plastic tray of primroses, doubtless to do with Adam – to do all that when polite laughter mutes itself on the cadence of a saxophone – this is all barbaric.

At noon we had sherry. That was in Zob's study, raked by intermittent sunshine slanting through the blinds, and of course it was muggins here who poured. Nor was that just for our cosy quartet (or trio-plus), because now a procession of Western miniaturists, members of BOTS, the British Open Tanka Society, descended on our doors, in from the cold from every major compass point. It meant, smiling, I exhausted the medium dry. For the old crones it didn't matter much as I switched to sweet, asking myself what in heaven *were* they (something I soliloquise), the room filling with hubbub. Most were greyish, advanced in years, in a babble of conversation I still can't close from my mind—

One, a language teacher – a greasy man who gibbered. Two, a spindly, overworked-looking female, described (first by herself, then by Trethowan) as a special-needs therapist. Three – if not their leader then certainly a figurehead – an emeritus professor (once of Exe), who was dumpy and at all times wore an enraptured smile. Four was a collective four, being a half-dozen retired dilettanti, who had difficulty apportioning equal time to the pursuit of Zob on the one hand, and on the other the professor, who remembered Zob Senior. There was in addition, and somewhat out of sorts, a curly-haired youth here in a vaunt of credentials, having won top prize and money beyond his dreams in a national poetry comp.

So I repeat (and repent of my sins, which are too many for one man to bear), and all to what purpose? Fiona, indefatigable, had moons ago set in train a postal renga, a verse structure I am not sufficiently interested in to describe. Each recipient pens what approximates to a couplet, and, re-stretching that tensile elastic, mails the whole job on to a next on the list. We were, ceremonially, a couplet short, with the convocation in Zob's study here for the *coup de grâce*. That fell to the elected hand of their guru (the professor), who honed his curved sword in an air of Arcadian worship. All trooped out into Adam's bit of England, or Zob's walled garden. A brown wind whipped over the roof. In central London there was rain, a dampness streaking the concrete. The professor, compacting the wet grass under the tramp of his feet, admired the chalet, from behind which a suburban Pan kept an open eye. The professor took out his notebook, then raised and put away his pen – his xiphoid pen. The language teacher gasped. I turned away. Fiona, with a studious grin, had seen it all before. The professor wrote, not that remaining couplet, but a haiku – as 'a loosener', he said. It went like this: 'I saw a daisy / As I walked across the grass: / Summer afternoon.'

Huh?

Okay, 'afternoon' would just about do. 'Spring', when I took issue, the professor claimed not to 'scan', and defied syllabic stricture. As to that solitary daisy, when a hundred others, plus buttercups, constellated Adam's turf – well, he had a mind very much for the particular (though I could question his choice of words). Worse followed when the professor added majestically his last masterstroke. The group renga, or resultant 'piece', was in patches scatological, and trivial throughout – and was handed on to me. 'Be a dove and produce that on your laser,' said Zob.

So that was the game! I went puce. Fuming, I visited bathroom one, for a splash. There I found, in burnt Paisley, an alien toilet bag, overflowing with feminine contraceptives. Someone's bath cap, an olive green, nonchalantly topped a three-quarter towelling robe, hanging up. And what was that, swamped in the shower tray? Ah that, Horatio, was an anti-friction gel, a half-used tube. How – as I interrogated the mirror – to extricate? Solution: key renga to disc, direct output to laser in the study. I did so and made my apologies, leaving Isabelle and friends to their ham baguettes in the kitchen. A few days later I intercepted a note from Fiona, which thanked Zob for a 'lovely' weekend. Amazingly his next conquest was Geraldine Crouch.

April 18 Monday morningish. Someone in that foul assembly knew the art of laser printing. Not Zob, for sure – maybe that yellow-haired youth – who anyway has left a copy of the final renga on my desk. Can't help reflect on a wiser, Chinese parentage, having brightened our wastes with a better model altogether. Do I see, in the fragments of its inversion, a Confucian temple, its hues reflected in a lake? A boatman? Or again a stillness of twilit cloud capping a purple ridge? And what is that decrescent moon, that sickle of luminescence silhouetting not one, but two distant pines? Instead it begins: 'A Pelagian / ruse…'.

I penned a few notes, 'winds', 'leaves', 'mountains', and crossed them out, then turned to courtly chambers, the destinies of wanderers, city towers, a boatman rowing on an autumn lake. Then I folded the cover back in place and quietly put my notebook in a bottom drawer. Time to journey on.

April 20 Malkin, that marmalade feline, has marked out the elevations in his new demesne. I can't argue with a sheltered spot outside, under the bay window, where his alert, inquisitive round eyes follow every passer-by, from under the bowed stem and green-white bells of a Solomon's seal. Less easy to accept is his appropriation of Isabelle's two-seater settee. If I sit there – rarer nowadays – there is soon the swish of Malkin's tail, right under my nose. The two rear paws test the resilience in my groin. My eyes stream. I sneeze. If Isabelle hears – in the kitchen opening a tin – she laughs. Malkin I shoo off, who returns in a scowl of neglect, finding that tin is tomato or beans.

Tonight the widow was tired, having helped Michael with his French, an essay on life in Grenoble. Unnoticed, I put Malkin out with a note for the milkman, and returned to the living room just as Myrtle Bloge launched on her full half-hour. Tonight's was given up exclusively to the 'phenomenon' Justin Simms. As a simple fact of TV scheduling, it was one a remiss Zob had failed to point out – at least to me. But I knew he'd be watching. This remarkable man (Simms) wore (note, Zob) a Cardin shirt and an Italian suit. He was – and didn't blush to hear it – of gentle birth. Throughout his boyhood he tinkered with a red Bugatti, which even before he was licensed he drove direct to Vire (he drove circuitously back, upsetting the gendarmerie). His first efforts in creative writing were naturally brilliant, winning him a prize. So I could go on, and as a point of order so Myrtle did – and on and on and on. In researching his debut novel Simms wanted to know what was all the fuss about in post-industrial Britain? He lacerated his yachting pumps, which had cost hundreds. He fished out his striped rugby socks, his school wars fondly remembered. Some dungarees he had sprayed the Bugatti in served as principal garment, enhanced authentically by a few days minus shaving tackle. The hair, bleached by a long weekend in Key Largo – where he was best man at an old chum's wedding – would grow out over time. So got up Simms set a course into the disintegrating streets of his and your metropolis. North of Oxford Street he sang – outside the Cambridge, with its early-evening throngs, where coins were pressed in his palm. He moved on to the Blue Posts, with a fabricated life story for its drinkers, or, he corrected, its drinkers outside under parasols – who urged him away with cash. For his nights he acquired a polythene wrap, into which he mummified himself, mostly in a doorway off the Strand. From that he graduated to a cardboard coffin in the precincts of Charing Cross. So on for a long three months, where his street life gave him – a verism actually lived through – the germ of his 'powerful' first novel. For Myrtle the palm was already his, alluding to the thing close to Zob's heart. I mean that Best Novel to be Published This Decade.

April 21 As might have been predicted, a bright-eyed Cornelius, in exaggerated gestures – first one then the other hand – was here in good time. Before ten. He and his winning client went into conclave shortly after the hall clock struck. Yet Cornelius couldn't think. Repeatedly he demanded fresh cappuccino, so that the reluctant Mrs Clapp had to keep switching her Hoover off and on. My three puffs of smoke, as they wound into grey sheets and departed from my ledge, did not, at about lunchtime, coincide with any solemn declaration. All I saw in that line was Adam's weathered face, as it gazed up. Not at me, but at the pale green fringes at the extremities of Zob's wisteria.

April 22 There was an attempt, which failed, to keep their conclusions from me. I had a call from Snell's secretary, who was trying to send a fax, but got only a sequence of unintelligible error codes. I checked our software at our end and found the server had got itself in a loop, which I corrected, halting then restarting. When, techno-naïf that he is, Zob told me to output the Snell fax direct to his laser, he couldn't know I had read through it on my screen. It was Cornelius's five-to-six-point plan as to the problem of a dangerous rival.

1 A declaration of 'war' is inadvisable, as that could leave you vulnerable.
2 Conciliation is a best first step, with a public laudation, such as 'Welcome, colleague'.
3 Open camaraderie between you and the new boy. By that we mean friendly, professional rivalry. This is the surest way to undermine the Crouch link.
4 Remember, Crouch is a raging suffragette, and as yet no one has sounded out Simms on that score. Ideally he'll be unsympathetic.
5 Finally Simms was born with money, and is bound to get bored with work. If so you might lead the rest of us in regretting his premature retirement.
PS **6** Have a party. Invite Simms, and Crouch. And me!

St George's Day Malkin, whose four paws prodded my duvet at precisely 9.45, alerted me to the basic facts of breakfast, mewing. What he meant to say was the widow wasn't there to provide it, so could I get down and open a tin?
Why anything you say, Malkin….

April 24 Ditto.

April 26 So to that hand-washed environment, and the spotless ambience I saunter in most days, with a great deal of help from Mrs St John. She, slave to a dirt economy, and today luckless, has been unable to dust the lampshades, because someone has failed to recharge the hand-held vacuum. *I* blame Mrs Clapp. Zob spoke nostalgically of the Wandsworth room, where a whatsit, a feathered cane, he was sure he'd put there once. I led her with my gaoler's key.

And so what, Christopher Robin, did you find? Well now. In a valise some curious items of lingerie, to do with the great man's research for his *first* book. Would Mrs St John disguise, I thought, her peasant disgust, as I held to the light a first and a second pair of panties, swart, frilly, crotchless. Nor, I said, did I see utility in this, a cupless bra. I tipped out knee-length boots and remarked on the sheen of their leather. When I found a stylised cat-o'-nine, just right, I thought, for the lampshades, Mrs St John shuddered. An article, 'Masturbatory Deceits and the Over Forties', by Professor Hand of Edinburgh, I spared her. Why do I relate this sordid interlude? Because...

...with the wodge of transatlantic mail found in that same valise I am able to reconstruct the following sequence—

300–506 29th Street
Astoria
NY 11102
22 January 1992

My dear Marsy,

A slight detour, as first lecture, about which I'm strangely nervous, isn't for a few days. Samantha – rather that bull-necked sugar daddy she's somehow ensnared – has rented above address, whose furnishings I loathe. She says 'for the kids'! Oh how she lapses into Americanisms. This is on the off chance they would like a break. For Christ's sake what about me!

I MUST have it out with her re this mechanic – I mean, can you imagine, a grease-monkey grandson! She couldn't seem to care less. By the way that contact I mentioned is filming in Toronto – for another six weeks – which I *can* coincide with. Promise to have a word.

The best for you, your Andrew....

Flat 5
147 Trefoil Street
SW18
2 February 1992

Dear Andrew,

Please don't fly to Toronto on my account, though that is such a clean city. Certainly not like this one, infested. Speaking of which, the fatuous Crouch, despite my efforts, has got her suburban geishas onto the shortlist [Best Novel to be Published This Decade]. It's rumoured she once lit a cigar for Maxwell Hayste, who as you know took over the chair. Her advocates are also her friends, with CVs all listing time on the committee. You know. All those TV journalists she hangs out with.

By the way your banker friend made a splash in the news here, having bought and sold a tyre company. Lots of redundancies. This he defended in an interview on the Plymouth Hoe, for which, ancestrally, he feels an affinity.

The best, Marsy

1655 Sherbourne Street
Apt 1313
Toronto, Ontario
13 February 1992

Dear Marsy,

Really it's not out of my way. In any case Shayle and I go way back. Shayle's my film man, and for other reasons is a joy to talk to. Samantha, as I suppose I should have guessed, has proved intransigent. Some stupid ideal in New World denial, conjured up to add a youthful figure to her empty-headed middle-age, has made her short-tempered – infinitesimally so. She allowed me five minutes in her apartment. This is in Fifth Avenue, from where, when she isn't jogging through it, she trains her binoculars on Central Park. I tried to raise that not inconsiderable problem of Jessica, to which she said 'Goddammit Andrew you're so – English!' This is how she lives. She dialled for her escort, who turned me out onto the street. And I mean *of course* I'm English!

Shayle's had his own problems (low budget equals ragbag cast), but I'm delighted to say has read and enjoyed your book. We talked about it over a fish supper, which the restaurants are very keen on here. I attach his card. Get that Pantalone Snell to call up his office.

Don't ever talk to me about the bull-neck.

Yours ever, Andrew

Flat 5
147 Trefoil Street
SW18
19 February 1992

Dear Andrew,

Snell has been hospitalised, with quite literally a balls ache (a virus, which they say got up through the vas). Thanks for the card.

My toes have been warmed by a many-headed dragon, meaning Crouch and friends, whose shared halitosis is, well, *ugh*. I am accused and found guilty of anti-feminist activities. Sentence: my *Atom* will not share space with her shortlisted geishas. Apparently there are other punishments under consideration, on which the sisters will have their say.

Doesn't she know the cold war's over?

Marsy

Glaze wrapped up this particular conversation via picture postcard – a pale view of rounded hills, and the caption 'Little Rhody'. I quote in full: 'Providence, 26/2. As I said, you can't trust these women. Andrew.' As a postscript he sent another (this one was sunset, Narragansett Bay): 'First lecture delayed – but watch this space! Report coming soon....'

April 28 Mrs Clapp, whose waxy complexion I watched slowly metamorphose to a shade of aggravated nectarine, tossed down Mrs St John's note on the kitchen table, having laboured to read it. This of course was to do with the miniature vacuum, and the importance of recharging – which was a slight, I might say, on both ladies' professionalism, which to that point had been exemplary. In reality Mrs St John didn't wish to repeat the Wandsworth experience.

May 1 I am uncharacteristically moved by a Hollywood B movie, which Isabelle recorded weeks ago, reserving for tonight a request for my company. I smile to think it has been just the two of us alone, with the flicker of her TV screen, in the seductive lamplight of her living room. And with such a gooey soundtrack.

May 2 Bank holiday. More trouble with Malkin, Isabelle having left her bed early, and not returned till noon. For a change I tried one of my science journals, as a break from those idiotic proofs Zob insists I take home. He thinks I will learn something. Michael, rehearsing low hard penalties against a back wall, instead has got me anticipating his thump-thump, thump-thump. I go out and keep goal, which prompts an ironic smile (one of the glories of English football). He will learn otherwise, but doesn't think I can play.

May 4 I have concocted a melodrama – *The Guilt That is Hampstead's* – or at least Act One, as I recall the days of my childhood, when Aunt Alexia bombarded us with opera—

Scene: Balcony above. Below, patio. Enter at balcony bored office worker Wye, who lights cigarette. Stares out wistfully. Enter, below, Adam, chief of ground staff, taciturn. Stares up at thick green wisteria fringes.

WYE [*flicks ash*] There are plans, I hear, for that magnolia.
ADAM [*leans on rake*] That's as may be.

WYE [*heated*] I tell you I don't like it, this – conspiracy!

ADAM [*unmoved*] Folks should mind their own.

WYE [*stubs cigarette*] I'm not going to allow this, Adam!

ADAM [*surly*] Don't see as 'ow.

WYE [*passionate*] I'm going to save that magnolia....

ADAM [*saunters to rear*] 'S not as the marster sez.

WYE [*as vow*] Well let me tell you one day you'll have a *new* master. This can't go on.

Exit Adam, shrugging.

WYE All of them, fools! [*Exit.*]

The earthy R. Quiggly-Walsh is cast as Adam. Wye plays himself.

May 6 Zob has been depressed, and suffers more than is usual for him from writer's block, not a condition medic Wye acknowledges. He spends more and more time in the hamburger bar, drinking coffee and Marsala. But. Even the deepest human flaw can be assuaged – and Wye is the man with cheering news. It comes with correspondence from a continental admirer – a Miss Overmars from Amsterdam. Amazingly her envelope bore no finer detail than this, in a capitalised hand: 'Marshall Zob, London, England'. Her note, with photo attachment – she's a sunny blonde, and freckled – was appropriately dated April 30th, which according to the diary was Queen's Day, Netherlands. Miss Overmars is determined to make her pilgrimage, with rucksack and sandals. I expect Cornelius will advise against a reply.

May 8 Malkin, as I spy through my one open eye, is ermined in the sleeve of my dressing gown – draped on my chair. As usual it's Sunday, and the widow is absent. Time to get up, get down, and rattle tins. There is a note for Michael, who has taken up tennis, pinned to the kitchen notice board: 'Bacon in fridge, eggs in basket, bread cut. You need to plug in toaster.'

I'm going to nail up that cat-flap.

May 9 Morning. A brown drizzle has dampened my hair, badly in need of a trim. I calculate how much time to allow in paying my barber, George, a visit. George is a corner-shop Greek, safe with his scissors. I hold him responsible for the sheer mental energy I expend on our English weather, in all its disappointments. I tell him, every time I visit, how, in a process of opposites, I've lived my life in a pellucid dream of the south, with a yellow sun and vineyards, and somewhere the dapple of eucalyptus leaves. The reality's abrupt, for here in the northern hemisphere most of the time it's cold, and *I'm* cold.

That doesn't deter Zob's merry English postman, a man I met in border country – the driveway. His boots had been polished, and I couldn't help notice the super-sharp crease to each trouser leg, in tone a shiny charcoal. His shirt was sky blue, and I mean by that a British sky, and sported little maroon insets – and the sleeves were rolled *up!* I exchanged pleasantries and took the mail. Much of it was uninteresting, marked PRIVATE (Wye, keep out!), though a package from the Miracle Book Club has been a distraction. A Mr Tom Corbiere, Miracle's marketing director, pinpoints Zob as 'perhaps the most socially astute among our leading intellectuals'. Please, a moment – allow me to compose myself. He takes a bold step, enclosing 'sample material'. This, a *nouvelle* (a modest 80,000 words), is by a 'bright new talent', whose concoction of art is reflected in his photo, printed on the dust jacket. It takes the latter of two available options – smug, or genius frowning. It was a dull book, for I read it, yes. It *was* professionally turned out, one of those artful tales of life in the basement, whose final chapter saw an impoverished cleaning contractor cuckolding a dealer in rare ceramics, a man who was – and this was the book's subtlety – despicably rich. Mr Corbiere sees 'top writer' Zob as his organisation's figurehead, and offers to print his autographed portrait regularly in the Sunday supplements. This of course meant potent advertising for both parties, the full thin face of Marshall Zob topping the embossed spines of Mr Corbiere's most recent publications, and all to a jingle: 'The miracle of Miracle!' One could easily underestimate what price Zob might otherwise pay for the name – Zob, the mighty Zob – permanently before his public. It raises that long contentious issue of Zob's entry in *Who's Who*. Cornelius wants to see the address listed as care of the Snell agency. There are all sorts of nuts out there, some prone to write letters.

May 10 I cannot say what murders the earthy Adam has begun to contemplate. Nor in a crosshatch of rain can I see what lights his face. Is it manic? Benign? He's examined the first fruits of a fig tree, which small as they are *are* visible through a fringe of leaves, which are still very sparse.

May 11 It's the same with a clematis, whose wonder cascades up and over the near wall of a red-brown, hand-built enclosure, soon to be swollen with compost, with steam rising off, and a fork stuck in.

May 12, Ascension Day We leaden mortals I'm afraid are rooted in earth, still with our petty tropisms. Cornelius, who phoned at ten, said he'd be here at noon, then, arriving at one, wanted to go straight into a 'luncheon situation'. I reserved a table at the hamburger bar, the place deserted when we strolled in urgently. A short, hirsute waiter, whom I knew as Andreas, had set aside a shaded recess, under a winding stair and a solo ceiling spot. Cornelius flatly rejected that, choosing instead a table at the front. I switched off to his drone and followed the contours etched in a frosted hexagon of window glass, its glaze a Twenties belle (or the head and slender shoulders of), with a coy little smile for her cocktail, its cherry impaled helplessly on a stick. Cornelius removed the following to an adjacent table: 1) a glass ashtray, which Zob retrieved, 2) a white carnation in an aluminium vase, 3) a chilli sprinkler (he was newly allergic to capsicum). The big man Snell was voracious for information (quite apart from his peppered steak, which came with *pommes allumettes* and a coleslaw salad). Affable Marsy was a lot less ravenous, chewing his Mexican cheeseburger only intermittently. The miracle was Miracle, about which he hadn't been sure, though under the aegis of Cornelius's grin he was now certain, we thought. 'Why of course go for it! Eh, Al?' Why-of-course-yes. I myself ate ravioli, and extended a long arm for the chilli, to which I am partial (it's the spice of my professional life). Cornelius was resolutely against Miss Overmars, a name Zob intended to put on his guest list. It prompted a good many paternal observations, which I am able to condense as follows: 'Why Marsy she could be a nut, out to knife-shoot-blow-up a celeb. Five-minute fame.' That had to be thought of, Zob conceded, though he couldn't recall ever upsetting fundamentalist Hollanders.

So to dessert, and Snell had a strawberry sundae, Zob the lemon sorbet, while Wye said 'I'll pass.' Cornelius left his hologrammed plastic on the saucer, getting in return, and declining the ballpoint, the chit with peppermints. He would, he said, unscrewing his fountain pen, negotiate with Tom Corbiere. As, a strain to his hand, he signed, he left me with instructions. 'Liaise,' he said, 'with Merle,' with whom I envisaged drinks at happy hour. 'What we need's a proper guest list. Get her to show you the mailing package, or software whatever-you-call.'

I'd be delighted.

May 13 (Friday the 13th) Merle this morning had a tooth extraction, and is too numb to talk mailing lists. It's no matter, I said. 'Monday. I will call in on my way to work.' That leaves me in company of Glaze, whose next batch of four I have sequenced, though I have no enthusiasm. Instead, over a pot of Assam tea, I have an Act Two, *The Guilt That is Hampstead's.*

Scene: 'Top writer' Zob's study. Mahogany, walnut. Somewhere a PC plus laser. Hangings: a white background, reddish orange sun; cranes; a lake. Books: *Dictionary of International Biography, The Zen Book of Bedtime, Aristotle's Atom.* 'Miracle' price list open at page two. Enter Wye, bearing flattish glass bowl filled with magnolia petals.

WYE [*puts down bowl*] I'll fix *him*. [*Wye goes to computer, types. Enter Zob.*]
ZOB Ah, Al, hi…. What's the buzz?
WYE [*hammers keypad*] That – gardener…does this! [*Indicates magnolia bowl.*]
ZOB Does what?
WYE [*prints page to laser*] The magnolia! Adam has chopped the magnolia!
ZOB For a moment you'd got me worried….
WYE [*takes printed page from laser*] Oh come on, wake up, Marsy! Where's it going
　　to end! The fig tree? Clematis?
ZOB Al…!

WYE The last thing anyone wants is trouble. But when I tell you there's a laburnum.

ZOB Of course that would be tragic. This is so unlike you.

WYE Call him in. I want you to call him in.

ZOB Al, now listen....

WYE Now, Marsy.

ZOB [*shakes head*] Okay. You insist. [*Goes to door, calls Adam.*]
Enter Adam.

ZOB Mr Wye laments the magnolia.

ADAM Can't say as some folks 'as noticed.

ZOB And is concerned for the clematis (which one's that, by the way?).

ADAM As grows up the—

WYE [*flourishes paper*] That's quite enough!

ZOB Oh come on, Al.

WYE This is not gardener's question time! Here is your resignation! Sign! [*Presses paper to Adam.*]
Adam, astonished. Zob, astonished. Wye, perfectly serious.

Zob is played by any fortyish male accustomed to sitcom. R. Quiggly-Walsh as before. Wye, again, Wye. Inadvertently a note on my Assam tin has this to say: 'Tea animates the intellectual powers', it 'maintains or raises lively ideas', 'excites...sharpeneth the thoughts', tea lends 'vigour...to invention', it 'awakens the senses', 'clears the mind'. This, an extract from *Discourse on Tea*, by Dr Thomas Short, published in 1750. 'Nother cup, please!

May 15 Widow Lavante. It's Sunday. You know how I groan. I woke to the sound of what, I suppose, was your Citroën. I'd follow – yet...where are my keys? Malkin-*gesund*, that's Malkin-*gesund* (that's a poor chap, hah-*heit* in a sneeze).
    One sorry result of Isabelle's Earl Grey, which I have had a small china mug of.

May 16 Snell's leafy neighbourhood, in whose graceful deceptions your jongleur sings his suburbia, is enchanting on a day like this. Yes, there's a drizzle, and as usual I have had to wrap up. Yet in no sense is it irksome, switching off my Szymanowski, and parking up my Ford. Listen. That's the chirrup of a blackbird, whose now vacant gatepost has a fresh smear of chalk. There are no ground staff, no sinister someone whose saw has plunged him into the destructive manias of open-air life. There's a laburnum, whose sap shall be spared, its limbs already a glitter of gold, and so on as I strode to the door....
    Merle, pearl, received me. Cornelius, puzzled, re-crossed the hall and took off his glasses, wiping them. He remembered why I'd come. 'Al,' he said, in a tone that meant we *will* see Marsy through, given his turmoil. A client called him on the phone, a television chef, while I, in the drug of Merle's scent – that touch to her delicate ears – found myself led (or a dab to those opulent wrists), or *mis*led into the seductions of that opium.

We decamped to the dry dust of her office, where I adored her filing cabinets, a chipped grey – Snell's cast-offs, she said. I adored too the floor-to-ceiling shelves, whose dipping contours bore the weight of innumerable dead histories, pretty much the Snell agency's entire ring-bound clientele. Her small iron fireplace was once, I could hope, more elegant than now, though I worship that too in its overlay of curd-coloured paint. The view to the garden outside was through her French doors, with scroll handles and a security lock. Here was her lawn, which at 9.10 was laved in dew, and here her pear tree. There shall we sit on its circular seat, and is there honey still for tea?

She wore – what did she wear? A knee-length skirt that this morning she'd glanced with an iron (her colour is black. Black). A hooped blouse, piratic. She smiled and laughed and raised eyebrows, those very same plucked in a hand glass a mile from home on her commuter train. Snell she said was such a fidget to work for, and indiscreet with gigantic tactile paws. I said to her, 'How is that tooth?' (so young, and such wisdom). At coffee time she shared her doughnut, which sugared her fingers and oozed strawberry onto her chin. By twelve, when Cornelius went out, I'd browsed through her mailing lists. How many editors? (I forget.) Publishers? (Too many.) All right. Name me three reviewers. (X, Y, Z.) Writers. (Oh, they're such a bore.) In that case other agents it's important to meet. (I don't deal in subspecies.) I wrote a little program, its tune goes SELECT_IF_THEN_ELSE (which Merle said was clever). That has refined her multiple lists to one, which I have copied to 'flaccid' disc, and this afternoon will load onto Zob's network. Merle, when she'd finished on the phone, went to work on the invitation card, which she plans to have printed and framed in cloudy albata. She got so far – 'You are cordially' – which she scrapped.

'Have you,' I asked, 'an idea when the party will be?'

She had. 'Cornelius fixed that days ago.'

No one tells me anything. 'May I, as time gets on, buy you a sandwich for lunch?'

Sorry, no. She was too busy running Snell's agency.

May 17 Now, my first and lasting premise vis-à-vis the professional life of Marshall Zob, with the kind of recollection requiring a handful of props. First, a pub sign, to simulate the Golding Hop (why we were there I no longer know). Authentication is two pints of beer, placed on an iron table. We are in a garden, on the edge of an escarpment, terraced. If I can then just summon the first orange flame of a Kentish sunset.... There! That will do! Now to proceed....

It was a break in one of those long drives back from the bells and spires of Exe. That would have made it a detour, off the A2, and would *not* have been my suggestion. Zob defended his 'English' novel, which meant only I'd annoyed him with car talk. As ever he upheld his predecessor Dickens, and added to that famous name his famous name.

'It's precisely my point,' I said, implying that the English, turning to books (to write them), do not rise above social chitchat. He told me I smoked too much, yet demanded an explanation. 'Exe is a long drive without a fag,' I went on. 'Anyway. You know what I mean. Different kinds of chitchat belong to different kinds of context. But context is mostly *out* of context, when writers don't *understand* their context. By that I mean the context the market requires of them. See. It's simple. That's the writer out of context. It's a drag.' His dashboard had, and still has, a no smoking sign. He said I'd a penchant for convoluted argument. And what did I mean by 'context'? Context I told him was his English novel as political manifesto, and was therefore out of context and did not belong to the dreams of fiction.

'What then does it belong to?' he asked.

'Journalism.'

May 18 It's a premise I demonstrate, in the printed guest list I placed on Zob's desk for ratification. 'I see this as falling into three strata,' he said. 'Take away. Rework.' He thought I should know what distinctions he had got in mind, but now had to explain them patiently. The result was my addition of filters, as an extended coda, and a chord crashing out with that merry jingle I'd made, that SELECT_IF_THEN_ELSE. Grade I persons, who were to receive invitations two days before Grade II, rejoiced in the following roll (with harmless elaborations penned by me)—

> Mastabyle, a sickly smile,
> And Crouch, who hates a masculine slouch.
> Simms, Simms (an effigy, pins).
> Snell. Well!
> Bloge, Myrtle (attractive skirtle).
> Professor Emeritus, once of Exe
> (A man whose renga looks a mess),
> Then, my stars, Miss Overmars!
> The last – man's – dead!

Grade II consisted mostly of authors and agents he considered subordinate to Simms and Snell, who were to receive their invitations one day before Grade III. To the latter he penned the name Lavante, and to which I appended Merle's and mine.

May 20 Snell it now turns out has been circling the young, exciting, minimalist composer Royston Flude (let me apologise now for all these hammed-up names, upper-middle-class and only lacking titles). It's lost him rounds of cards at the Ritz, and has gone on late and many gins into the night, and has cost a fleet of cabs. Snell is gentleman enough to see his charge up the flared steps to his door, under a Georgian fanlight somewhere close to Randolph Avenue. Why I am instructed to add his to the Grade I names I hope will become clear. For the moment it leaves me groping for a rhyme (crude, Bude, rude, nude. Pseud). The same can be said of Shayle, that master of the low-budget clapperboard, and the fizzy Tom Corbiere – two other top-drawer afterthoughts.

May 22 I owe the relief of Malkin in a purr round mamma's bedroom to Michael's precocious backhand, he having progressed to competition tennis and now due at 9.30 in Weybridge. That's an anti-clockwise whizz round the M25 – 'one of those nice blue roads', as Isabelle has put it. She fed the cat before they left.

May 25 I do still refuse your modern coat, that quilted gaberdine, purveyed by the ubiquitous Despair Bros of Oxford Street. Yet, and yet. For one vertiginous moment I have stood on volcanic heights. The sky here, a crepuscular turquoise, is lit by decaying stars. There are intermittent jets of flame, a mauve or lilac edged with blue. The ground shifts and is basalt, fringed in its fissures. There are flattish towers of stone in a cinerary grey. Why should I follow Glaze here especially, having no investment in that man's death? And anyway my accusation is impersonal (please, Sam, don't go to litigation: there is no scope here for your New York attorney). I charge Glaze with the worst deception, seeking not to define those irretrievable grains of time, but to reverse the trends of posterity. This is of course to do with ideas of value, and is a spell of fine weather. Our English suns shine haphazardly. They assert themselves counter to the winds of their provenance. What Glaze inspires, with his sempiternal macadam, is the construction of a monolith (inscription: 'Here was a man'), visible from all points on that extensible vector, the future. It's a notion he has passed to his protégé, for whom I have spent all day backing up to tape his disc system, after which – tomorrow – I must drive to the bank, whose vaults he has begun to use for his offline storage. When I yawn at this, incredibly bored, Zob argues that the computer salesman spelt out the problems of disaster recovery.

(Marsy. The only disaster's this. That someone should consider printing, publishing, promulgating what today I have had a hand in preserving so religiously.)

May 26 The tapes, the labels, the red flashes, triangular windows – the space to write. I wrote. Then added corresponding entries in the log. Drove, in an atonal swirl – the Violin Concerto, Berg – to Zob's bank, which for historical reasons is in Brent Cross Gardens. Not a journey I recommend. Further, the fool clerk beheld me blankly, never having heard of Mr Zob, and ignorant of the bank's data-storage facilities. I called for the manager, who took him aside, and in an undertone told him *wake up*. The poor boy took out a pocket handkerchief, to wipe, from under the blue tufts of his fringe, the silver sheen that had filmed his brows. It wasn't, I remarked, particularly warm that day. Handed over this, in return for last month's tapes. Manager was unctuous, vulpine. 'Mr Wye, I think I can clear up this slight misunderstanding. Adrian here wouldn't have been expecting you. Our arrangement's you'll recall for the last Tuesday in every month.'

Suddenly remembered: consented to pick up Malkin, who is at the vet's a second time (he is wormy and prone to vomit). It makes me late back, which seems to have irritated Zob. He's in a lather over Royston Flude, who, according to Snell – who has again bought lunch in the hamburger bar – is actively seeking a librettist. Coming shortly is the Free

City Festival, for which Flude has a commission from the Coliseum. I sat down with Zob for over two hours, excessively worn at what importance he attached to this. It amounted to a showcase, 'for new work', he said. Flude was contracted to compose a short operetta, which, as an artistic descendant of Offenbach, he envisaged in satirical terms, a slant on our times. Could I, Al, give this some thought – perhaps draft a synopsis? Mercilessly Zob meant now. Worked late and, finally switching off his desk lamp, saw moonlight barred through his blinds – its stencils on my moving hand. Zob poured me a glass of beer before I went home. Refused to show him my synopsis, 'until I have slept on it'.

May 27 Have slept on it (to Zob I would not have had to offer the following preamble). It recalls elements of the uneasy conversation that ended our second interview, and signalled, I thought, failure to get the job as Zob's assistant. Exchange took place in a grimy café off the Portobello Road, after a first bout of research in a sparsely patronised snooker hall. I stirred my coffee. He reviewed, prosaically, his first impressions of that game. Looming large was a peppered yellow snooker ball in an isosceles of light, scudding over the baize, uncontrollably fast. Zob inadvertently had made his cue ball spin, in a forward direction. I watched as, dotted in a battery of overhead spots, it ploughed the nap against the lie. 'It's not a game I've played,' I said. He apologised, meaning that his life had not always been so leisurely (for now he lived in the expectation of royalties, advances, the sale of rights). Nevertheless, hackwork had bent him to a thousand impostures, and at one point the adoption of a *nom de guerre* – his Marcia Esbaroz, a spectre my synopsis would shortly revive, indirectly. The fraud 'Marcia' was Zob's frustrated attempt on the world of women's magazines, that web of emotional deceit. It cost him pains, with an editor (and one only) taking pity. She had noted the name. She had rejected a sixth trite story. Her view, I may guess, can be paraphrased: No lack of potential, etc., haven't quite understood the genre, etc. Suggest following reading, also these useful courses…. Happily there was no need, when just at that moment his friend Andrew Glaze stepped in, having had a quiet word through his connections with a paperback firm. So, now, if Mr Royston Flude has tuned in and is listening, that is how we have come to the following scenario—

Genevieve Purefoy, sole issue of Sir Walter Purefoy, wealthy industrialist and sometime government adviser. Mother, deceased. Enjoys sweeping views of South Downs from family home near Hailsham. Sir Walter has long been generous contributor to Tory coffers, and has mapped out career for Genevieve as party worker. But. Genevieve falls madly for daddy's driver and protector, Lobridge, who is blond, tanned, virile (and nocturnally a student of chemistry). Won't on that secret ground move to Ealing, where Sir Walter has handed her the keys to a handsome-looking town house, somewhere in Montpelier Road. Sir Walter blunders in on their night of love. They are in the stable, where the buck, in a ripple of moonlit buttocks, is up on his toes. Miss Purefoy, whose knees are spread, is perched on a sill. Later, in daylight, and fully attired, Lobridge refuses to be bought off. Sir Walter's hand is forced. Decides that he will risk a scandal. Fires his man. Only now does Lobridge reveal a political identity, which is nondescript, but vaguely Liberal. He campaigns for electoral reform, but at a rally has his foot crushed under the wheels of a pantechnicon. The foot is amputated. Lobridge, convalescing, completes his degree (I don't need to stress with distinction). He acquires work and limps into the office each day. This is with a petroleum firm, from which platform he invents, patents and markets a miraculous new plastic. Now a millionaire, Lobridge hobbles back to the South Downs, where high on a green hill, and with the wind in her hair, Genevieve has all this time been waiting. Lobridge goes down on the knee of his bad leg, weeping. *She* proposes to *him*. Tears escalate, to a deluge of joy. There's a no-fuss wedding, which Sir Walter misses. He is heartbroken, literally, having not survived surgery. A last word goes to Sir Walter's obituarist, who is certain an elevation to the Lords was likely. The house is shut up and sold, while the dream couple move south to Antibes, where Lobridge is determined to overcome his handicap.

(A note on the cast. Lobridge is a tenor. Genevieve, soprano. The problem of Sir Walter gave me an interrupted night. In the end, opted for baritone.)

May 30 A quiet weekend, bar that marmalade Malkin, the arch of whose back and lazy tail I saw silhouetted through the thin mulberry blind in Isabelle's laundry room, late on Saturday evening. Michael and the widow zoomed in and out with the Citroën, whose lugubrious grille is spattered with flyspecks. It seems that the boy is a tricky left-hander. What's current – and timed for the bank holiday – is an under-seventeens tournament, located somewhere 'between Reading and Slough', where he's progressed to the quarters. It has involved a return to wash, dry and iron his tennis whites, which Isabelle insists must at all times be impeccable. She did not thank me – in fact was disparaging generally of what she called my 'awareness' – when I, and not she, had failed to encounter recent confirmation of Malkin's green malady. I didn't offer to scrub the affected carpet tile (that was in the laundry room, whose odour I had often wondered at).

May 31 Zob, in a distant grin, has had time to think about the synopsis, sharpening his focus to matters that don't concern him (notably staging). He is adamant on one prop in particular, being a *trompe-l'œil* – and seen to be a *trompe-l'œil* – depicting three birds on a wall, very English in their grading – small, to medium, to large. For an adopted Hampsteadite, this is the proper emblem of Lobridge and his working-class origin. Zob, at home with the status quo, does not seriously believe in reformers drawn from any other stratum.

June 1 He committed one further indiscretion. This was some sample dialogue, predictably the stable scene, over which he and Cornelius chortled. In a meeting scheduled for tomorrow, Snell will put this, the synopsis and a proposal to Flude.
RIP.

June 2 Mrs Clapp has developed a dangerous rapport with that insane gardener Adam, who has cut three peony stems in exchange for a mug of soup. I watched her arrange their white tissue of flowers in a vase, which was round, gently while she hummed. I am afraid I shattered that equanimity with news that Zob, Snell and Flude had been in conference all morning, and would appreciate tea. Or rather that Flude had brought his own – a peppermint and limeflower bag – which I dangled from its thread. The others would take whatever was in the caddy. She huffed. I stepped outside and lit up, with just a glance at Adam, who eyed a bank of irises tragically. The surgeon's hawthorn capped his backing wall with a wild breeze of crimson in its flowers.

Took my time driving home, enchanted at the chestnut trees. There is a superabundance this year of red candles, that burn brightly in their boughs.

June 3 I see it was as long ago as May 13th – a fortuitous Friday – that I numbered the professor's series of four, in its following imperfection—

c/o 'Biltmores'
Empire Street
Providence
RI 02903
5 March 1992

Dear Marsy,

I least expected first-night nerves, which is as well I opted for yesterday's dry run – mercifully a non-specialist audience. I was overwhelmed beforehand, adjusting my necktie, with that sudden absurdity, that tissue of human doubt, that I know has accompanied great ideas.

I am indebted to a man called Spinks, from the *Providence Phoenix*, who had assembled three collaborating workshops together with a writers' group – though the hall was gloomy. I got over my attack, emphasising purely the literary aspect of my theory. Surprisingly, few latched onto my examples, not having heard of most models I mentioned, and a tenth, Janus-faced Muse I've invented. One dear boy muddled that flighty tart Mnemosyne with my own strictly desolated cherub.

Did anything happen? I threw the whole thing open to questions, permitting myself a smile (you know: the fidgets, consumptives, chair scrapes). A tatty, malnourished, New Age-looking creature, whose day job was in the electronics biz, thought he knew what I meant. His, he said, was a perennial toss-up between, and I quote, 'synchronous and asynchronous switching'. I told him not to talk gobbledegook, which raised a laugh.

There is a postscript. A short piece appeared in the *Providence Journal*, then a few days later, in almost the same column, an open invitation – for me – to a lecture on McTaggart. I suppose I shall have to go. News to brighten my path is that Jessica insists she won't marry the mechanic, or so Samantha says by phone (our one civilised means of communication). That leaves only one problem. How to dispose of the offspring, when it comes.

Has that clown Cornelius got in touch with Shayle's office?

Hope all's well, your Andrew

Flat 5
147 Trefoil Street
SW18
14 March 1992

Dear Andrew,

McTaggart's a killjoy – unlike Snell, who needs only the least success to drag off his clients to the wine bar. He was fine, once on a course of painkillers, and tries to laugh off the indignity, whose high point was a green-coated specialist, a man who compressed his scrotum under an ultrasound scanner, while Snell himself pinned back his pinkie in a thumb and index finger. Nor could he quite see the funny side of the invoice, which listed his genitalia as, I suspect appropriately, 'small parts'. The sort of thing Burgess does so well, whom Crouch, in an interview, has claimed to out-drink in Monaco. She gets around. And yes. Cornelius has passed papers to Shayle's office. There will be a meeting.

The best, Marsy

1422 Sayer Street
Providence
RI 02903
24 March 1992

Dear Marsy,

Absolutely right about McTaggart. It tells me that I don't intend to get embroiled in a cosmic wrangle with philosophers or physicists (but think I can probably just about handle computer people). Last night's lecturer reserved, when glancing away from the lectern, his self-assured looks for me, which is comic. How do I accept a premise – McTaggart's I assume – whose vocabulary of time can't be abandoned in the denial of its reality? This only affirms my belief that 'time' is a function of the way we think, and that therefore we *are* its progression. Have you by any chance bumped into Giles? I write and I write. No reply. By the way I'm moving on tomorrow, so mail me at following address etc.

Yours, Andrew

Flat 5
147 Trefoil Street
SW18
1 April 1992

Dear Andrew,

As a matter of fact I did bump into Giles, though before your letter came, and in none of the usual places. Snell's arranged for one of Shayle's assistants – Gloria Punch – a bubbly little redhead, who seems to be here every other day. Should the project go ahead, and should I decide to write the script, she has gone over – thoroughly, tediously – Shayle's entire specification, which is incredibly detailed. Somehow she'd got a trade invitation to a wine tasting at the Strand Palace Hotel, where Giles chinked my glass several times, 'to the ebullient Mr Blass'. A nice '87 Shiraz. Gloria had to be taxied home.

What the high-profile Crouch incessantly sees as war attracts its recruits to both sides. Blandford – you know his magazine well – has signed me up for a regular column, with no particular job description, and gives me only this aside: 'Pull no punches.' Speaking of which, Gloria's been rearranging my flat. Can't find anything.

Honestly.

The best, Marsy

4143 Bay State Road
Boston MA 02215
9 April 1992

My dear Marsy,

Forgive an old man his wonder. *Don't* get embroiled in other than a work relationship with Gloria, sumptuous though the girl undoubtedly is. The next step is conjugal. Then it's homemaking – furnishings, curtains, a dishwasher. Babies follow, and are not of our species. These let me tell you smell, are noisy, and require food (even at night). They grow. They learn infallibly to upturn porridge plates on heads. This is irritating, if it's you who has to clear the mess. Then there's the whole business of education, which is costly, and is no guarantee of adult life as learned, as accomplished as your own.

How many times during Jessica's teething did I long for a sabbatical like this....

Be warned. Andrew

Flat 5
147 Trefoil Street
SW18
17 April 1992

Dear Andrew,

Have decided to go ahead with the script, as Gloria doesn't convince me it's that difficult a job. Snell's doing his bit, throwing his not inconsiderable weight about – not with Shayle, with the publisher. He suggests that rather than allow my *Atom* to be remaindered, an important book like this should have had its sales performance predetermined. Of course, authorial hype is at the moment reserved for those already at the top – they have their fame or infamy.

Best. Marsy

Glaze's blessing came on another of those postcards, this time sunrise over Cape Cod, 23/4. 'If,' he said, 'you can't beat 'em....'

June 5 It's usual for Isabelle, when not in transit over Michael's tennis, to arrive home Sundays at about noon. I have come to set my watch by it. Figuratively. (It's years since I've worn one.)

June 6 Snell, in tasteless checks, made all the more hopeless by his two-tone shoes, and with golfer's slacks, has earned his reprieve. I refer to polite if outmoded gestures I watched him enact at the passenger door of his car, which when opened gave us a tall, bright-eyed, refulgent Merle. Merle had the document case, which she handed to Zob in his study, then as a matter of priority went up to bathroom one. I'm sure she powdered that freckled little nose. No Clapp, no St John, ergo 'Al will make the coffee.' The fourth mug, mine, did not join theirs. Nor at one o'clock did I share their table at the hamburger bar.

June 7 Zob's diary had one entry, 'British Library', where he seeks obscure references to a physician called Golde, to be found, he's been told, in a Renaissance tract on alchemy. Someone has asked him to write a small piece on the divergences of science. For me he has left the following email—

MZ to AW: 6/6
Al. Snell's got a lovely little girl, but a bit scatty. All of us knew I'd overlooked Corbiere, but, great though her smile is, she has managed NOT to get him a printed invite. It occurred to me after they'd gone. He's a Grade II, so, if she can get one made in the next couple of days the Grade I's can be mailed, as planned, this morning. Please phone her. Marsy

The expanded date/time stamp pinpointing the memo's inception (it appeared on the queue as MEM001), was, according to the system log, 94-06-06.20:24:44.MON.

June 9 Another (94-06-08.18:56:32.WED, MEM002) read—

MZ to AW: 8/6
Al. Thanks for giving Merle a shake – that problem's sorted. Snell's giving it some thought, and I'd like you to too. Have agreed to read, South Bank, as part of promotion, new book. Consider the usual format a bit bland. Any suggestions on how to pep it up? By the way I see you're 'invited' to the party. Would like to talk to you about dress. Marsy

I discussed it with Isabelle over a supper of noodles with courgettes, but got nowhere.

June 10 Often, approximately fifteen years ago, mid-summerish, usually in a liquefying ray of sunshine – usually early evening – the solution to practical problems was no more involved than the right degree of detachment, attained through the lotus position, a posture I abandoned, as I did also its associated pattern of respiration, hard to accept as mystical afflatus, though it *is* a mode of consciousness. For me the floor didn't rush away. I can't candidly report an elevated perspective on what was then my room – rectangular, with further oblongs shaded in, to show a bed, a desk, some drawers. The manual, which I have kept and refer to, describes the next stage so: 'a headlong rush into the astral dome'. I was supposed to see the bluish charcoal in the slates of the roof. The whole terrace of houses. The winding street. An aerial projection of the Hertfordshire village I at that time lived in. Then the cold brightness in a canopy of stars. 'It shall be granted,' the book says – though not, alas, for me. So and therefore.

Does eventually the Westerner return to the gurus of his own hemisphere? It is often the case, though in mine Freud was rejected, on the ground of that seedy aspect, and anyway I wasn't after something so potentially tyrannic as his 'id'. Jung appeals to literary minds, with his structure of psychic meaning and a tapestry of coincident mythologies. I deal, don't forget, in the fiction of Zob's life, that flimsy, virtual tent frame he floats and suspends his existence in. But of what relevance is that to the flux of activities that – as a frail mortal – I am lumbered with today? This whole thing with the South Bank reading, which I am supposed to co-ordinate – frankly it's getting me down. On the tail of that, the Gothic extravagance Morpheus has conjured I cannot now attribute to the wedge of Brie I scoffed – with a water biscuit, just before bedtime. Nevertheless, it is after that Jungian habit of fifteen years ago that I am starting to draft these most vivid of my dreams. Shall I let you see?

(Note. Fifteen years ago I was a stripling, of twenty, having triumphed in dogged resistance to the formal notion of education. In those breezy days the detachment I prized couldn't be accomplished through the Jungian discipline of dream evaluation. *My* dreams had much to do with high-performance cars – the sensation of speed – and one of those second-rate poets, whose term for this was his *Erhebung* without motion – i.e. a levitation I hadn't achieved through yoga. On one occasion I veered my shiny red Lotus into a swamp. The next moment I hovered over a revolving planet, whose sprigs of green intermittently flecked an unending acreage of black-to-purple vegetation. O we who eternally travel.)

What follows is a draft. What precedes is a pre-emptive apologia. The grey sleet this miserable oneiromancy delivers itself through is due to two things: the inordinate influence the gup of Hollywood has had on our time, and the monochrome receiver this son of science, as a boy, absorbed it through.

Having said that, I recalled nothing of last night's dream till late afternoon, early evening. The scene was Zob's cellar, a location geographically broader, with a higher ceiling, than I'd encountered awake. A barred, thickly glassed arch, to the rear, admitted the last, almost horizontal rays of a June sun. There was – where I assume tiny chips of ice random in the bloodstream – a hollowness of echoes at any slight noise. I recall a heel on the stone flags. A human voice. Above all, the rattle of chains. Let us go in. The walls, in a dampish black stone, are lit by flambeaux, whose tongues of orange flame are edged with blue. There's a rope, hanging, for strappado. There's a table with thumbscrews. That vermilion glow, in the perforations of an iron brazier – ensures, does it, a white heat in the embedded tip of a poker, whose brass handle I can still see. Enter, to the rear and left, Adam, in a friar's gown and open sandals – a hunchback, bearer of a surgeon's tool roll, who shambles into a circle of jaundiced light. The patient Zob is etherised on the table (and is strapped). Cornelius, whose terms are strictly ten per cent, has scrubbed up and is currently representing the surgeon Alistair Wye. [So far I resist a second draft.] I have, as I am now forced into this subhuman view of myself, a green cap, white mask, a medic's freshly laundered gown. There are Teutonic overtones, a lost Englishness to the way I speak. 'Tsob, ja, iss here?'

Zob, yes, was here – dark-eyed, supine on the table. Small, circular contact pads dotted on his torso, chest, on his upper arms, and to the cheeks and forehead, are connected to copper wires. These latter snake over the cold stone floor, and up to the terminals of Dr Wye's 'un-patented' thought machine (I wear a perfectly straight face). It's a Victorian monster, with a dial that calibrates voltage output. 'Svitch on, switch on....' My famulus Snell, a man tremulous in the newness of his task, passes a large gloved hand over a stalk marked ON and OFF. He looks at Zob's chart. A valve, which is pear-shaped, lights with a blue electric zigzag. The beast Adam on a secret sign shuffles to the light of the operating table, tugging at his chin, which is carbuncular. I turn the dial, just ever so. There's a twitch to Zob's ankles, Zob's wrists. The beast cowers (a freakish mechanical, whose reactions are slow), and with Snell's intervention avoids, narrowly, the depression of my rings, chunky and oversized, as my hand rains down. That same hand calms itself as the tools are unfurled. They are mostly razors and a few spiked chains. 'I vont more umph!' Snell, ashen and perspiring, turns the dial. This satisfyingly puts Zob's entire being in a spasm. 'Ja! Thed iss it! OOMPH!' From a vial of orangey brown sludge I fill my hypodermic. In the machine's flicker I test the action of its syringe (this is a touch sardonic). Snell protests, but this I won't have. In what's now the thrash of Zob's poor sedated body I steady the forearm and choose a plump green vein. I jab, pump, the patient shrieks, though of course can't sever the bonds of his strapping. 'More off thed umph!' So Snell turns, unsure yet obedient. The beast groans. I in this mania pull a paper from my Doktor's gown, while the machine begins to spark. 'Ah, zo,' I say, 'to dis Sudbenk. Ver I vont you NOT to read off dat new Buch.' Zob's eyes open, saucer-like, streaked with blood at the whites. His hair is on end. I want his confession – his writer's confession. Snell says the machine is too hot, which observation is borne out by the helix of sooty smoke from its backplane. Zob vibrates. The beast crumples to the floor. Snell at last accuses me of insanity, at which I cackle, reading from my paper. 'Tsob's Buch, nein,' I say, over the noise, the heat. 'Here! Here!' – the 'here' being the Herr Doktor's lecture, of which my Jungian pencil recorded only six key words. The machine arced. Zob's cellar filled with electric flames. The floored brown habit that was once the beast Adam shrank away as a liquid down a drain. Snell would turn no more. My phantasmagoria, once Zob's cellar, rolled itself up, and in a tight ball of biblical smoke receded into the dark and over the horizon, in what was otherwise a peaceful night. In the morning, having failed to slice Zob's frontal lobes, these words only were on my bedside pad: 'subterranean', 'refracted', 'peaks', 'mapping', 'confession', 'razors'.

Zob, in the late afternoon, early evening, asked me if I'd had any thoughts. I said I'd give it my best over the weekend.

June 12 It's Isabelle's birthday, which means her secret Sunday morning breakfast liaison is today cancelled. Michael had no luck at all boiling an egg, a failure he told me of just as I had propped my pillow and was about to read a treatise on recursion, and the uses of in 3GL block-structured computer languages. He looked pathetic in my doorway, still in the candy stripe of his pyjamas. I helped him, starting with the saucepan, whose light brown, lightly speckled egg had cracked along the long circumference of its oval. With the resulting seepage, a mingling of white and yellow slime had pervaded the water, which I told him had boiled too vigorously. 'Throw away, rinse,' I said. I produced toast, lightly buttered. A nice little egg in a nice china cup. From the garden, a half-dozen moon daisies, which looked well in a slim green vase. To these I added Michael's card, and the morning paper, and placed all on a tray. The boy, of course, got all the glory, backing into his mamma's half-lit boudoir. The mistress hitched herself up onto the brassy vines of her bedstead. This I know, because I brought up the rear with a small pot of tea. Malkin turned full circle – twice – before re-sinking into the hollow of the unused pillow (and a shame, I thought, that it *was* unused).

June 13 I now know why Zob was so interested in the physician Golde, since I have had to dust down that pointless article of his. It is couched in professional journalese, for one of those semi-mystic science journals. Its topics, typically, are UFO sightings and remarkable acts of clairvoyance. I am told that once it carried a two-pager on Watsonian pyramids – the kind one sharpens razors in. Ironically, Zob's little piece is an assault on our present age of cynicism, which, according to him, has its origin in the current remoteness of science, or its 'practical unintelligibility' to ordinary educated men and women. Golde is Zob's sample of mid-world man, a being capable of grasping all essentials in the total of human knowledge – a feat impossible today. But then Zob performs a stunning *volte-face*, in the space of two sub-clauses, positing for Golde a universe that had still not lost its primal magic (even though, for the physician, all things knowable – were known!). Golde – whose sublime, symbolic approach to the cosmos meant a change to his name from Orr – believed in the transformation of base metals, devoting much of his talent to that branch of alchemy (cf. Jung, a post-Newtonian). I pointed out the inconsistency.

'What inconsistency?'

Marsy! That to Golde, confident in his awareness, there was no scope for conjuring tricks – or should have been no scope. While for us – or for most of us, with no grasp at all of the sub-atomic – our present age of science looks like hocus-pocus.

'Pedant!'

June 14 More about that journal. Zob has a back issue, whose glossy cover is a blue illustration of the sapphire Earth, a low sickle washed in darkness. This is 'home' as photographed over the moon's silver horizon. There is a caption: 'Is this a figment of God's mind?' As it prevails in one campus, physics and theology are parallel lines, bent to a single point in a distant shade of eternity. Besides, Zob has thought about my objections of yesterday, and says, to the contrary, they 'prove' his point. Golde, for whom no schooling remained, located our common mystery beyond the bourn of epistemology. That puts the kicking boot on Zob's flat foot, which gives him renewed courage on the South Bank question. What had I thought of? I can hardly relate my dream, and the flummery I began and restarted several times, only to cross out all such efforts in the margins of my jotter. Remember those key words?

> These medics, pale and subterranean,
> Unbending in the shafts of refracted
> Daylight

I tried again—

> Ah, noting the moist brow, what confession
> Is likely? Our patient's of Alpine peaks,
> Ethereal

and again,

> You know the patient's history. His peaks
> Of fame. The base of learning refracted
> In a glowing populism. The mapping
> Out of friendly reviewers

and one last time,

> Seen here in the filth, in the refracted
> Motes, cankers, tumours, nothing the razor's
> Poised to restore

and finally gave up, because as you can see I'm no poet. I suggested to Zob two, possibly three speakers, and a selection of pages thick with dialogue. 'With a duo, or trio,' I said, 'and do it in the round.'

That brought a smile.

June 15 I am suspicious. The rough texture of everyday life has, for one of those rare brief moments, worn its surface of sandpaper into a smoother, single plane. My sweet widow has somehow learned whose genius it was behind her birthday breakfast, and for once, in her overcrowded kitchen, showed no menace at all in that serrated flourish of the bread knife. In fact a lyrical intensity glazed the sunny reflection in its blade, whose pale transparencies oscillated in the grainy pine of the cooker hood. I am sure I blushed when she planted a little coy kiss on my cheek. At this point I didn't suspect conspiracy when she told me I should treat myself sartorially. I wore the same old denims, the same yellow jumper, the same same same....

Later, to the shrug of Zob's black-shirted shoulders – this was in the middle of my office – I encountered something new (for him) – a first dramatic sign of indecision. Was this, was this not, a soliloquy, and our own Marshall Hamlet? Well, not quite. Adam outside, topping his ladder, passed the time of day with his master. He had his trowel to a new window box. This would give me: trailing lobelias...petunias...a geranium...a sprinkle of alyssum. Adam, who saw me over Zob's buttoned epaulette, said 'How-dee-doo-dee.' He turned the peat, once only with his trowel, before descending. I'm sure I could smell honeysuckle.

Zob smiled pleasantly. I couldn't pretend not to notice his critical eye for my décor, while his two plain eyebrows converged in a wavy line. 'It's dreary,' he said (here was the rub, Horatio). His preferred decorator was a man from Purves Road, in Kensal Green, as now Marsy had begun to torment himself as to the room's refurbishment – soft peach or apple white? 'Anything,' he said, 'but gilded crowns.' I happened to like them, but the subject changed, politically to books. You remember, Marsy, how you scanned my shelves? He knew I liked to quibble. Therefore the thesis, to my mind Exeish, was solely to do with the disciplines of reading. Yet why *this* moment particularly? To him it was self-evident that those who professed themselves 'bookish' went cover-to-cover mechanically, and dutifully, while the real 'thrill' of it occurred no more than a dozen times per life. I said his success had jaded him, and added, while I had no real objection to soft peach, I needed to see a colour chart. 'So you shall,' he promised, and took me to the one he'd spread out, downstairs in his study on the escritoire. The other thing was hair, meaning the fuzz that was mine, and clear precautions against the Greek barber George, whose creations were only of workaday inspiration. 'Remind me,' he said. 'We'll drive to my club – what about tomorrow afternoon? We've got a decent *coiffeuse*.' It didn't end there, as the real point was the role planned for me on the night of his party. There were, he said, doubts about my wardrobe. As an aside I said to him this need not be constructed in the language of international diplomacy. Quite. So then couldn't I spend the day in Bond Street? While the decorator was here....

So that was it!

'Exactly. Do bring me the receipts. And remember. Smart casual.'

I tried to have the last word. 'There's a shade here called perfect peach,' I said.

'Al, that is just – perfect....'

Episode Two. Have realised – as a sudden revelation – what a rigmarole tube travel has become. It makes of them distant, impossible memories, those leisurely journeys in from the garrets where I've lived, all of them west London. It goes back to the work I had in theatrical properties, in Mortimer Street, a brief personal history I shall some day write an anecdotal book about. Today it's a catalogue of eccentricities. I shooed a pigeon on the platform, looking for and not finding any least morsel. There was boredom at the newspaper headlines. There was nothing to buy, with the shutter closed on the confectionary stand. Then at last the little silver train, glum-faced and trundling to a halt, perversely opened its doors just where I wasn't. That small fact was large in its impact on the seat I got, which placed me opposite the world's only morning drunk, a man with a loud shape to his mouth, a chasm carefully avoided in the wall of tabloids erected over the seats around us. One youngish girl, who seemed to have too bright a spark in her eye, had been reduced to the nth hundredth page of a blockbuster – an activity I realise it's impossible to imagine. The drunk combed out the dry curls in his mattress of hair, a weary-looking shade of brown. He told me what kind of society this was (he thought I didn't know). He went on, one hundred per cent counter to the rhythm of the train, to spill lager on the green dye of his shirt, asking me, now fully bathed in madness, what kind of bloke I took him for. 'A musician,' I said, seeing his guitar. 'Play.' That was a service he told me I'd have to pay for, and held out a hand. 'You should,' I said, 'get those eyes seen to' – they were rounder, redder – which stumped him. I got up – 'Alas the factor is time' – and got out at Belsize Park, re-joining the train a carriage behind, where there were no vacant seats.

I took the commission conscientiously, as Zob had suggested rejecting the standard man's shop. It meant mild revulsion and a twinge I couldn't repel at sight of those dummies, with white, expressionless faces, all such a resemblance of humanity, limbs bent to the pose of the cocktail lounge. I found eventually a talkative Jamaican in a corner for the plainer man, who nevertheless wished to sell me a white tuxedo, a bowtie with zebra-style chevrons, and as the clincher a lime green fedora. These he saw neatly contrasting with a pair of snakeskin shoes, and trousers an olive green. 'I don't,' I said, 'wish to take the wind out of your sails…' I tried to attract his senior colleague, '…*but*—' His boss was like myself, a cool, monochromatic Caucasian (such thoughts spark solutions to crossword clues). Under wiser auspices we arrived – happy trio – at a plausible outcome. That's to say beige slacks, which I'm assured are *à la mode*, with just the hint of a flare, and narrow turn-ups. Brushed suede shoes, a ruddy brown. And because I foresee a night oppressively warm, a short-sleeved, floral shirt, whose autumn tints are gold, russet, chestnut. Certain other incidents found their way to my scratchpad. For example the round, rosy burgher who asked for directions to Marble Arch, yet who smiled and shook his head (apparently in disbelief) when I pointed out a traffic sign. Then in Oxford Street, under the pale sentinel of Centre Point, a girl in baseball boots, who kicked at the poppy-coloured panels of a photograph booth, to the mingled strains of Orff (*Carmina Burana*, from shop front X), and an '80s crooner ('I'll be watching' etc., in an adjacent shop front Y).

I passed my old office in Mortimer Street, now in the hands of a telematics firm. There were no personnel, merely a populace of modems and multiplexers, whose open chassis of racks, shelving, mesh, ensnared itself in its loops and coils and cabling. Hard to think, eh, Wye, of a time past, in its glassed golden front, posing on the telephone for passers-by…. Such-and-such remembered: One horse's head, for a panto, Stratford East – will see what I can do. Rapiers, *Hamlet* in the Park. Difficult. We've had a run on rapiers. Will ask around. And how's this! A Broadwood piano, for a première, Hammersmith Lyric, a three-acter the resourceful playwright has penned under the simple heading *Ludwig Van*. Surprisingly I've just the thing…. I stumbled away into the metallic azure and chalky white street, not really humming to myself. In a basement off Castle Street I bought a finger roll with frankfurter, whose amber garnish with surfeit of stringed onions was just that little bit cautious – in fact insipid, bar the mustard I added (which was hot and English). So on and outside Foyles, where the smug Zob beamed from his posters. Here I caught sight of the blond crown and striped shirt of a man I thought I knew, though when he turned, to the puzzle of an expectant look etched on my face, it was a stranger, bearing no resemblance. This had happened oh so many times before.

Got back about two, having found, then lost, then re-found the receipt, which Zob raised a theatrical eyebrow to. 'It's cheap,' I said, and lied about the snakeskin shoes: 'They were just what I wanted, if not quite right for what you have in mind.' How else to make him aware, as he raised a finger for hush, that in forgoing them I had effectively halved his bill. Shush! His radio you will see is marked ON. In an interview, in the broadcast foam of a woman's magazine, Geraldine Crouch stuttered to a yes, she did expect men to open and hold the door…. I went out, and shut Zob's securely.

June 16 Our man from Kensal Green has got this far precisely: my books are in boxes, the shelves are dismantled. My DTE – which he hasn't dared disconnect – is shipped to the middle of the room, under a sheet. Mrs Clapp says 'It's shockin', luv' – because Zob can't say when he'll be back. 'I am also,' I add, 'profoundly unsure about that peach.'

June 17 *Between two and three a.m.* It emerges only now that at approximately 5.30 yesterday afternoon Michael, overstretching himself – attempting a left-hand smash over his innocent right shoulder – fell awkwardly behind the service line. It was not a grass court, whose surface, he protests, is unpredictable. It had the painful consequence of a grazed elbow, which I've no doubt puckered his lip, and a turned ankle, *its* consequence a twinge he was able to walk off at the time, but is excruciating now. My dear, lovely, sleepy, un-winnable Isabelle, though she did touch my arm only yesterday, is not at her best in a crisis, a failing exacerbated since the loss of her husband – a loss by drowning. I have never pressed her to complete that tragedy.

The light from her landing below, filtered through the deep plum of its shade, stencilled its mystical blue in all three dimensions of my room, which I always leave open. That, to the tune of a high twangy voice that woke me, was supplanted by a refrigerated yellow when the bathroom globe was turned on. In the hullabaloo – as I calmly put on my robe – I should expect, should I, what? Um. I went down. What I found was Michael, in that same candy stripe, semi-supine on the pedestal, with the afflicted ankle perched over the bath's plastic gunwale. The pain of it contorted what was the usual moroseness in his usual teenage face. Here too was my nubile widow Lavante, whose contours left nothing to doubt through the thrills and frills of her negligée. She tested in alternate palms the weight of a rolled bandage against a jar of paracetamol. I swear as I advised something stronger I had not consciously noted the brownish pink in what I now know to be stupendous areolae. It's the same with that dark, inverted equilateral – that same priapic interest. (But wait. We are not at that moment yet.)

She followed me – 'Shall I call,' she fussed, 'a doctor?' – to my room. There was, you students of Glaze, an imagined future, where a Y-fronted Wye made his bedding seductive for two. Woe, Wye, is flesh. (I shall be and was and *am* oppressed by the present.) I opened a drawer, not on a bottled aphrodisiac, but painkillers. Next she followed me to the kitchen. You ask me why go there? (She asked it too.) Well, omitting for the moment that long-nosed tap on the outside brick, here was the only prospect of water from the main. It was already known how solemnly I urged against drinking the bathroom water, which came through an old lead pipe from a tank in the loft. This, as I bore in mind Michael's debilitating pain, was a dictation I didn't repeat – though I did point out the rampancy of the plant she called her string of hearts, slung in a pot attached to the lintel over the window. Botanically I can't hazard a nearer exactness, though in any case that description will do. Look it up. Its leaves are cordate in shape and thumbnail in size, are a pale green with dark mottles, and grow in chains, voluminously. You replanted its occasional corms. Of course this is all voluptuous in its irrelevancy, because back up in the bathroom we found Michael hopping mad, bad and sad. Nevertheless by three o'clock my paternal morphine had him tucked up and soundly to his dreams. Isabelle followed shortly, into her boudoir, where for seconds only I hung around in the doorway. This, in my mind, was no more than an inconclusive little query – whether or not to leave her my pills. I remember she winked, switching off her bedside light. That is what I said – winked, switching off her bedside light. Shall I repeat? Winked…whaddya know…I shall was, I be – I therefore am.

Coffee, mid-morning. It's a situation to which I am forced, a man indifferently propping up the kitchen freezer, which hums and tinkles its incessant electric medley, a succession of polar ditties I'm in danger of learning. Grey Kenny from Kensal Green, in applying his peach overcoats, warbles to a synthetic brand of misery – one that our radio goops, O they of the Corporation, rashly term entertainment. Between plaints there's a frenetic over voice, its owner's chin held high to the challenge of a broadcast smile. This somewhat forces my retreat behind the closed door of the Wandsworth room, where with renewed reluctance I extend my forensics over that Glaze debacle. Zob does not yet suspect (and I shan't disillusion him) that all these private letters – these notelets in the life of a son of Exe – are of no public interest, and certainly of little value.

At and about noon. There was one high shelf I hadn't tried, because it required a stepladder, which the warbler loaned me (while devouring a bacon roll – still, incredibly, warbling). Here a cardboard box, with its flimsy corrugations, yielded an assortment of pen trays and inks dated to a desktop Zob has long abandoned. These I put aside, and later took to my room. Then, again, that decaying scent of apple, so soon as I put my hand on a sachet. Its charm I put down to the legacy of Gloria Punch, the bubbly redhead. A car passed by on the roadway below, and from the reflective angle of its windscreen danced its squibs across the ceiling, just as I lifted the box. You will have guessed. Herein another wodge of the professor's tormented outpourings.

As usual I couldn't be bothered, and made sure only to put them aside, with the pens and inks. They had got themselves shuffled into a handful of old photos, which caught and held my attention, a power of attraction the late Andrew Glaze continued to lack. I deplored his society of mutual handshakes, the fraternal clasps, the closed circle he and the Zobs belonged to. Individual reputation is built on the precept of internal consent, but our tabernacles are not meant to be the tents of exclusion. I cite a specific example from his ephemeral, and already dated *Companion to Writers Writing Now.* It's a document where many hands in its making have co-operated in the professor's editorship of it. You won't be surprised that in his preface Andrew Glaze is quick to acknowledge Marshall Zob as among those 'who offered critical suggestions and were tireless in their support'. Zob's entry itself, a good two inches deeper than Mr Burgess's, is out-distanced by Glaze's own, whose only contribution to English letters is as flatulent commentator. The poet Shay (that's Bim Shay) gets no mention. Nor does Ad Dawilde. Nor does his biographer, Frank Argyll. What should one expect from Exe University Press? Not to worry. My cool summary shall some fine day see light, ten per cent of which I shall shine on a man very like Snell.

In the meantime I have got these photos. The oldest is inscribed so, 'Jasmine, '69', which I see from her pose is nothing to do with that particular coital variation. Jasmine's a little bit plump, is stretched out alone on a stripy beach towel, and is wearing frumpy, old-fashioned underwear. She represents Zob's first goodnight. Another is dated 1974, and is one of three that feature the Glaze children. Giles, about seven, is wearing turquoise shorts with a tee shirt, whose print is a domed Shakespeare (inappropriately, as it now turns out). At a perspective of twenty years you can identify the germ of failure, as I look as the professor would, in hereditary terms. But the Giles I see here, his hands behind his back, wears the contented grimace I imagine still persists. As for Jessica, Glaze had no ambitions, other than planned introductions, whose rosy culmination was naturally nuptial. One hardly envisaged it, other than meaning the mixed seed of two 'good' families – or as the professor might say, 'sturdy', by which he meant English middle class.

Now, please, permit me to point out the gloved piper lolling on the departed's tombstone, whose word in my ear is of Jessica. The girl is liquid fire. There is mud on her denim dress. Her little red boots are on the wrong feet. That impish grin for the lens is the prefix for what was to come, when in semi-adulthood she traded pens for swords. Nowhere where Glaze instructed her was wisdom genuinely taught. He is – I think I can hear her say – that clueless un-family man, who years later can't bear her sardonic frown – a plasticity reserved for Exe's voluted interior. I shall contradict that insubstantial ghost (Andrew's) to say she's a clever girl. Didn't she decline, on grounds of health, to browse his shelves and pluck out any one of those sedated tomes, those great slabs of parasitic English life…? He taught her to recite names. She uttered them all with a lisp. She has insisted since, in the shrugs and tobacco stains of her adulthood, that a working girl hardly need reiterate, in deprecation of her daddy's 'importance', to what extent she has despised 'the book' – its spawned professorships, its dead industry, its stifling symbiosis. She will I am sure drink Zob's champagne, and perhaps even raise a glass to that one contributor more (or Zob himself) to an already overflowing trashcan.

Marsy, this is strange, but there is also a family portrait minus the professor himself – so do we assume that Glaze was the photographer? Here in the professor's wife is the overweight of resignation. In our proletarian grandmothers this is also called 'character'. But Samantha has never worked. 'Character' – *en famille* – is mid-life loathing, even if an impish Giles has a winning smile. Jessica, whose fingers pull at the corners of her mouth, is a round-eyed monster. And so on.

Our trio of snaps, completed in 1982, centres tall Professor Glaze in full regalia. This time it's Samantha's hand at the camera, who just for the moment has frozen the breeze in her husband's gown. The sandstone, after twelve years a faded yellow, is anaemic in the gargoyles, is just a little less so in Exe's castellations. Giles, in mid-flight as song-and-dance man, is a swaggering teenager. Jessica's mobility has turned to a pout. This all takes place in a quad outside the library, with speeches and a ceremony due to begin. No tourists. This is the way it will end, with *no* domestic bliss.

Hum....

Afternoon (afternoon of a writer). The last of us from Albion's golden shore to see those gilded crowns, ever more rare under the remorseless hand of the Celt Kenny, with his glistening tracts of peach, was a man called Zob, who leaned across my sanded sill to see...what? The blue denims, the yellow jumper, the frizz of their possessor's hair, who under a wisp of cigarette smoke gazed into a niche in one of the garden walls, host to the mauve bells of Adam's campanula. Zob said he had a spare moment, and so, he saw, did I, and 'what about that haircut?' (which sounded rhetorical). Unavoidably this was an opportunity to be driven in a car by *him*, where I noted anxiety in that way, that knack he had, of shifting gear from fifth direct to second. He ummed a lot, about but failing to speak. He switched radio stations, settling, moronically, for news. He was I believe courteous for a Bentley. For a three-wheeler, nosing into the traffic stream, he reserved weary hand gestures – terms of abuse properly understood – and pulled the face to match. Finally parking up he hinted at what was on his mind. Zob was surprised not to have heard from Flude, 'given the project's timescale', which was limited. (That was it, the operetta?

Apparently.) The sign on his health club door was a circle, meaning wholeness, pierced at its centre by an arrow, meaning death (actually fleetness, he corrected). The receptionist was a ruminant. She chewed gum. She stood in the shade of an oversized yucca. For Marsy she smiled. To me she handed the guest book and pen, disconsolate. Was it the hair or the garb or what? Well, it's been a long day. I signed. I followed Zob to the hospitality lounge, where he brightened. That was because, in time, just, to avoid the club aficionado, and a squash champ – who approached perspiring and bandanaed – he got himself smothered by Madeleine, or 'Maddie' West, whose youngish flesh was a shade of solarium bronze. You will know this girl, famous for her sequinned leotard, whose fullness she pressed to Zob's elbow. She I held responsible for the exhaustion, and perhaps the despair of millions, via her breakfast-show aerobics, with the promise of a video to follow.

'You must,' she urged, 'try the new flotation pool. It's the outer space experience. Do you have trunks?'

It has been, as I say, a long day.

'The *coiffeuse*, may I ask?' They headed off for a dip.

'Oh, she's that way' (indeterminate hand signal).

Evening. One grave question, which the restyled Wye can't answer: 'Où est Malkin?' Malkin, who hasn't come home, even for the rippling entrails – even the chopped head – of Isabelle's fish supper.

Malkin. Here puss puss.

Night, and not surprisingly the sweet potions of sleep, which my Morpheus has soothed with, as I now primp the quilt and pull it to my ear. Did I say it was *oh* such a long day?

June 18 Isabelle, who now maintains she has always taken a second liking to me after a haircut – but a pity about the jumper – has me reflecting on that wink, that flutter of her eyelid, that meaningful seduction, as I watched it close blissfully for that short eternity. She has, she said, after a lapse of years, joined an art group, whose leader gave her, insistent despite her refusals, a walnut whip. She placed it in the gilt reflected light from the carriage clock, off-centre over the fire, douching its chocolate pyramid in a yellowed veil of cellophane. 'Please tell Michael.' Michael is being coached by a man whose name is Moncur, and this will go on, and on, for successive Saturday mornings. 'He's an ex-pro,' she said, one who had once covered ground over the outer courts in the early rounds of Wimbledon. He is said to have had quarterfinal potential, though never overcame the glaring predictability of his cross-court forehand. Majestically his lob, though tirelessly accurate, lacked sufficient pace. Moncur, alternately sullen, jolly, sullen, was fifty-ish and now pear-shaped. That was the gravitas from which he was able to flash winners, after the briefest sidestep, past the best of all his students – who was called Michael (whose ankle is strapped).

Still no sign of Malkin.

June 19 No. I am not your father. Trust you to turn up when mamma's gone. And take that tail from under my nose. I'm going t', t', t'…snATISHOO!

June 20 Isabelle has torn a page from an infuriating supplement – Saturday's, I think – and has left it on the kitchen table just as I'm about to spread my morning toast. It is no fault of my own, fighting back the nausea, that the complacent Zob now invades my breakfasts. Here's that surly grin, over that inventive caption, 'The miracle of Miracle'. The good widow Lavante it seems to me is duped by its cynical ploy (and some miracle that is), and has ringed the Jane Austen 'complete' as the free inducement to join, even though it exists, in unread paperback, on various shelves round the house. Concerning Miss Austen, Zob supposedly has this to say: '…today's readers still find in her letters certainly a wit, and that occasional coarseness that has so surprised some admirers.' Coarseness he knows about (knows how it sells).

June 21 Mrs St John has refused to phone the wine warehouse, in West Ealing, where Zob, through Giles, has explained he knows the management. Instead she has filled her miniature watering can and taken its enormously long spout to a basket of white fuchsias. It's something Adam has thoughtfully provided in an angle of shade from the patio wall, just outside her ironing room. There is also a bench, a trellis for a climbing rose, and a terracotta tub with a cane and a *red* fuchsia, in whose orbit I see there are mauve and pink petunias.

June 22 The party's on Saturday, in three days' time. Tomorrow there's a full moon. Zob, who's in a twitch, suspects that Giles's friends in the trade have let him down. He begins to contemplate, and to retrieve the situation has started to consider a selection of supermarket wines. Oh what madness.

June 23 Oh what joy. (Thanks to me, of course, who knows how to word a fax.) Mr Pagliari, who had been attending to Mr Zob's order personally, apologised profusely. The fact is he has had a couple of days in Burgundy, with M. Ramonet, because he likes to stock his cellar from source, having tasted in barrel. The van followed shortly, though I did not supervise its unlading. Some cases I saw. There was a Louis Roederer Cristal champagne, a bottle of which I persuaded Zob to put aside. There was a 1989 Château Latour. Then some of Ramonet's white Burgundy, a selection after Mr Pagliari's heart, which thumps ecstatically. There was, too, some mid-range Rioja, and a 1982 Meursault-Perrières, at least one bottle of which Giles later discovered had oxidised. As a token, which assured his client of only his best intentions, Mr Pagliari gift-tagged a 1978 Bâtard-Montrachet, which Zob placed in his private rack – to be followed by another, when on the Monday Giles also felt obliged to address that imperfection. Mrs Clapp glanced over the invoice, and no doubt setting that alongside her wages viewed the whole spectacle as a shocking waste of money.

June 24 The caterer, a Mrs Obernau-Ombercrombie, is a reliable Finchleyite, used by Snell for literary buffets. She comes recommended, having gorged the Conservative Club at three of the last four Tory election victories. Snell, who invents epithets, tells me she's an acquaintance of – and I quote – 'the harridan of Number 10 (RIP)'. She prefers to be called Olga (though I call her Agent Triple-O), and is here to finalise the menu. Agent Triple-O isn't Zob's type, being lined, a bit brassy-looking, and too old – too old for intimate use of that triptych of mirrors framed on Zob's dressing table. He seems to me gloomy, and offers as explanation Kiff's moustache. Kiff he has resurrected for novel number four, and the monumental problem is this: was that moustache full grown way back at Chapter 5, or was that merely the point at which he stopped shaving? This leaves Zob with the depressing task of rereading his work, and leaves me with OW, I mean OOO of Finchley. She's quite a girl (daddy was Luftwaffe), and has a categorical style. She marched to the kitchen, opening her heart, mouth and nostrils to its facilities. On the patio she told me yes-very-good-SO. Then in the drawing room, whose oak partition opens to the TV/music lounge, she suggested a rearrangement of the furniture, if, as she understood, the buffet would be served ah-so-here. (I wasn't sure Zob would approve this.)

So, over to Obernau-Ombercrombie, who was (you'll excuse me) 'yes down the middle' certain to get here by ten tomorrow morning, having shopped. Her codas were symphonic – and lasted for as long as I held open doors for her to sail through. She said there'd be dips, as an artiste who so objected to the easy option – things like tortilla, too dry to perk up our taste buds. She conceived she said on an exquisite scale, and even now envisaged chopped Parma ham in a creamed whisk of avocado. Nor had she ever failed in her creation of chickpea, that speciality appearing in endless variation in best-selling, vegetarian cookbooks. Quintessence was garlic and lemon and a hint of root ginger. I was surprised when she re-inspected the patio and sat on the bench. She produced a cigarillo, which with practised inattention she inserted into a smoke-coloured holder. Then she pressed, did Agent Triple-O, an elbow brazenly into my ribs, on accepting a light. Ah so! If the weather held, she said, she would bring her assistant Peter, who could set up her gridirons – anywhere here – for the one or two morsels she'd thought to barbecue. What inspiration. Shish kebab in her famous marinade of oyster sauce – and banana, or peach, in a sprinkle of muscovado sugar. 'That all sounds fine,' I said, though later, when Zob told me to meet her here at ten, I was not inclined to state that view. It also meant showering, later, in bathroom three, and changing in my newly painted room into my party garb.

June 25 [plus appropriated small hours of following morning] No doubt in some distant circumstance, with the grey-haired Zob's hilarious memoirs – a sad waste of paper I wouldn't at this stage bet against – I shall share the joke, me with a crooked stick (when I am not, that is, in the mobile rage of my Bath chair). He rang me at nine. Rather he rang me in a panic at nine. With that my poor damp Isabelle, enfolded in the soft pink wraps of her ablutions, re-plugged her bedroom phone into the point on *my* landing. That's her nice blue one, whose receiver bears the sweet imprinted scent of *eau de fleurs*, from her wrists, from her little white ear lobes. I rolled out of bed. I held that exotic instrument against my dreaming ear, and begged him what, what was that he said? Miss Overmars?

Why yes. That leggy lass had arrived from Amsterdam, not especially now but several days ago, whence – sandalled and rucksacked, and with an impeccable smile – she had hitchhiked to Oxford, to Cambridge, and staggeringly to High Wycombe (in that triangular order). Now, after an early start, she'd camped herself on Zob's doorstep, having left it late, but not she hoped fatally so, in replying to his invitation (because all I'd recall were RSVP). That in itself did not unnerve him (I am looking down through the part-open bathroom door at the nakedness of Isabelle's ankle, and now as she plants herself backward, at a sumptuous thigh). It revealed that, the juncture an awkward one, my deluded employer had all this time assumed important professional status in every one of his 100,000 readership. Only now do I recall a frosty morning, complete with vibrant exhaust, and the silver Mercedes, whose jet of carbon monoxide corrugated that crisp November air. I had sprayed a cloud of chemical vapours onto the windshield, while Zob, the huddled passenger, waited for the heater, still at the point of exhaling the breaths of Siberia. When we drove – I can't now recall where, some bleary meeting somewhere – he must have imagined that most of his readers did as we now did, but every single working day – smart executives equipped for the week with the insights his books had given them. Miss Overmars, who proclaimed herself his 'number one fan', with such charmless grace seemed likely to shatter his myth (not to say mirth).

The girl was gankly frangling. (Now let's try that again!) The girl was frankly gangling. She wore shycling sorts, in black and lime-green stripes, a tight fit, rather longish to the knee. The inky circular imprint on her tee shirt named as its logo Georgia Tech, where she confessed she'd never been. She was oh so tall. Teeth, tombstones (with gap for feeler gauge between foremost two incisors). The flesh of her face was a lactic white, and at the hems of her shirtsleeves, in graded hoops, was a rare to medium roast. When I got there – moments before Agent Triple-O – Miss Overmars was all leg, somehow concertinaed in one of Zob's cane patio chairs, or tappit-who-cares. I put her at twenty-five, six, no more than seven. Zob fumbled over the kitchen drainer, with what courtesan still abed I don't know. He was scything through the foil seal in an opened jar of decaffeinated coffee, while Miss Overmars had left un-drunk the orthodox sludge her host, startled, surprised, had already made. On the table, humble gift, was a packet of Dutch crispy toasts. It was paired with another in Miss Overmars' rucksack, which before tossing it onto the back seat and folding herself up in my Ford, she took out and gave me, with a 'Zenk you'.

I am not a man for Wagnerian explosives (sometimes unfortunately). My tape had wound itself not that far forward into its opening *lento*, by which I mean Górecki's Third Symphony, Opus 36 (1976). Okay I know. Our classic broadcasters can press little more to over-do (Miss Overmars) this piece. For you see, in that reverberating cocoon, I was not able to stifle whatever conversation our lank soprano might embark on (ergo better to gabble myself). Here was my subject (and here my aside: for I did, Scylla, I did, Charybdis, have the presence of mind to wind down my window and issue a cheery wave. This of course to Obernau-Ombercrombie, whose puzzled approach crested itself in the flash of metallic blue, the colour of Triple-O's Espace). 'You like music?' I asked, to which I got a 'Yar, Dire Strades.' 'Never mind. Am straitened myself,' I said, and got on with the lecture. Let us put this utterance in context. (I am talking about this symphony – yes at the moment it *is* quiet.) Dawn, imagine. September 1st, 1939, imagine. A sly old battle cruiser, in open emulation of 'exercise', coolly departs its anchorage outside Gdansk – till then a free city – and caddishly opens fire. Caddish? To us English that means un-gentlemanly conduct – very very serious. We have these English sayings. For example: 'Sobriety is the vice of life'. But to go on. It meant that Europe was at war. Now I shall skip some, since I wasn't actually present. A half-century later I want you to imagine this time that event's fiftieth anniversary. A faceless mass, the media man's dream, notionally linked itself up through its multiple television screens – for a relay from the Opera House in Warsaw. The schedule, inevitably, included Beethoven. Also Mahler, also Schoenberg, also Penderecki. There was, too, the commentary of a survivor from Auschwitz. That is what I said, Auschwitz. And why, Miss Overmars, Auschwitz (or as is said in Poland, Oświęcim)? Because. Oh now you've made me miss the lights! It's because what you are listening to is in fact a prayer, we might say a prayer for the whole of humanity, who knows no end of oppression.

I pulled up on Isabelle's drive next to the low-lying Citroën. I chaperoned Miss Overmars in, even to the point of bearing her vigorous rucksack, and debarred Michael on his way out. My un-merry widow, clued up to the day's changing arrangements (according to the guru Zob), left her milk and her cat tins and came to the hall with a newly laundered dish cloth. I told her I had lent Miss Overmars the privilege of all my acquired knowledge apropos of Górecki's Third, over the whole car ride, *in extenso* – to which Isabelle said 'Poor girl!' Then I addressed the entire amphitheatre, saying if Miss Overmars liked tennis at all Michael would be more than happy to give her a knock-up. 'Isabelle will lend you a racquet.' Yes yes this by the way is Isabelle. Now I must officiate, you'll excuse me, in Master Zob's castle. At which locale, when I re-arrived, a tarty blonde wiggled under the portcullis and stepped into a waiting taxi.

Obligingly the tyrant Olga, in the van of her tyro Peter, who was yet to arrive, had left visual markers as to her rampage through Zob's ground floor. Zob, one guessed, occupied a higher elevation, perhaps naked under a cone of diamonds from the nozzle of his shower. Here on a wire hanger, slung at a perfect horizontal from an end peg on the hall dresser, was Olga's short jacket, to which I later found the matching skirt. Each article proclaimed itself in a residuum of *eau-de-Cologne*, and, more strikingly, a tangerine blaze of velvet. Her colours were autumn. In the kitchen, on that famous table, over whose scored surface the trivia of Zob's estate had so often been discussed, Olga had parked her supermarket parcels. One had Greek olive oil, in another was a bunch of celery, its green coxcomb overflowing its cellophane sheath. A breeze, intermittently gold – as it passed through sun, then cloud – lifted the nap of the carpet, here where I now stand in the drawing room. A Limoges perfume boule, in blue porcelain adorned in wild roses – one of a pair the strident Annie Cryles had a liking for – had been moved from a low table to a niche. Some similar transference had visited Zob's bone china trinket box, a gift I recall from Fiona, whose gilt *fleurs-de-lis* I eventually located in the prismatic glass of an ashtray. These were the first superficial precautions our in-residence caterer, whose beringed hand was around those oak panels to the TV lounge, had fittingly explored. The panels slid open. She wanted to know, she said, how best to deal with her client's semi-precious egg collection. She of course meant those exquisite samples – some in jasper, others in spangled quartz, one in alabaster – that as details one might rightfully expect, though never come across, lighting the grey monolith of a text by Marshall Zob. It was the same with his chiming exercise spheres, whose principle was acupressure, as you rolled them in your hands and so massaged the palms. These, she pointed out, in *cloisonné*, had departed a long way from their brocade presentation box. 'Perhaps remove these delicate things to the study,' I said.

Her assistant Peter, a dejected man in a white shirt and grey flannels, somehow wedged a small refrigerator on an extended hip while braying at the front door. I allowed him over the threshold and led him to the kitchen, where he humped the thing down. His station wagon – a mauve with punctuating rust – had its hatch door yawning, out of whose maw he produced folding buffet tables. Then the gridirons. Then those one or two priceless utensils his mistress could never be without (for example a giant slotted spoon. For example a 1970s pressure cooker). I thought I might hazard a catalogue of further edibles – this from both cars – though when I looked inquiringly at sardines in a bed of ice chips, our auburn-ash-to-blonde, to a flourish of culinary trumpets, shooed me from the kitchen. Symbolically I washed my hands, informing Zob, through the interdict of his closed bedroom door, that 'all' was under control, and that I could no longer prevail on mother and son Lavante for the diversion of a gauche Miss Overmars. 'Come back at five,' he said.

'Come back at five.'

Home again. Is that a crooner I hear, from Isabelle's radio, through Isabelle's open window? An autumnal russet splintered the jet of her hair, through the many angles she wielded her garden shears, whose oily blades glittered briefly. What had to be done, she did, and oh how she scowled, expecting me – yes *me* – to roll up sleeves and help! I protest! I am just not the homeowner type – the man whose decisions, and precisions, and excisions, are the popular mires good minds are contaminated by. There were tufts of grass fringing the rope twist edging the path. 'Your birthday...no, that's gone,' I said. 'Christmas! I'll buy you an electric strimmer.' I stepped inside and switched off that crooner, to which she said illogically she wanted the news: 'Switch back on!' 'And Miss Overmars?' I asked. Well, apparently, that perinatal gazelle had seriously understood my promptings, and had propelled the innocent Michael – each bore a racquet – to the local courts, which to his mind were hopelessly substandard, being potholed. For Miss Overmars, well, hers was not naturally a tennis nation.... One thought, and none too profoundly, of Betty Stove. Perhaps of Tom Okker. In fairness these were exceptions. My approach through the park was no more eventful than a first spontaneous pause at a rock pile and anemone. So far my distant matchstick figures only bounced on elastic in and off the net. Next I saw clearly the demarcation in the stripes of Miss Overmars' shorts – the black to lime green – and at this point plucked and tossed back a ball from a rose bed, whose yellow fur, I now recall, re-palming it reflectively, had scarcely been ruffled. Michael served a gentlemanly underarm. Miss Overmars caught her return on the rise, in a zigzag of limbs, scooping her racquet under the ball, without – as Michael stood there, arms akimbo – that flick of the wrist transmitting topspin. The ball found its own angle over the perimeter fence, and joined, as I tramped to discover, a half-dozen others in the flanking boscage. Carved on a bench I learned that the prime minister – or someone who shared his name – was a *souteneur*. We have educated graffiti artists here in north-west London.

Lunch (at Isabelle's). It consisted of cheddar, ploughman's pickle, and crunchy Dutch crispy toasts. Miss Overmars told us her daddy was a dentist, and that she too wanted to work with people – though with more than their gums and teeth. What she felt strongly about, and Zob please note, was adult illiteracy. And youngsters with learning problems.

Four-forty p.m. Have left Miss Overmars – unfurling, unfurling, unfurling an endless unfurling gown from her rucksack, for which Isabelle prepared and cooled an iron.

Five, or thereabouts. Zob, with more or less permanent prehensile fingers and thumb round the eraser end of a pencil, is feeling tense. He paces a lot. Agent Triple-O has run the dishwasher several times. She explains she has made her dips and plugged in the baby fridge. I imagine she has therefore racked them, in all three dimensions, at a cool degree

Celsius. She has, I see, prepared four salvers of trout, each in a simulated sea of cucumber. There have been carrots, and there has been, Captain Cook (see below), celery – and these have suffered the same fate. That is to say we have amber and chlorotic three-inch oblongs arranged in tumblers. (We have crunchy Dutch crispy toasts.)

The assistant Peter was having his coffee break in the TV lounge, where the buffet tables were erected, dressed and adorned with china, cutlery, and also with serviettes, whose paper is a bright ponceau. He has the TV tuned to Teletext and takes issue – mawkishly, retrospectively – with its weather forecast. This I have no particular opinion on, but am concerned at how close his elbow is to an Alexandra vase – gift courtesy Zob's plump ma. It is reproduction creamware, moulded with leaf and bead borders. Its six sides are hand-pierced in open symmetrical petal work, and the lid is crowned with an oak-leaf finial. 'May I draw your attention to this,' is what I say, and precede that sullen man, whose empty cup shakes in its saucer, to a low marble table by the door, out of which I hope he will progressively go. 'An amusing pastime....' Blank looks, so let me just take his coffee cup. '*Prima facie* it may seem simple, and is in point of fact cleverly strategic. It is called, and I'll explain that, the Captain's Mistress. I urge on you the spectre of our own Captain Cook – those long lonely nights in his cabin – after whom, for so I perpetuate our English legend, the name is gamed I mean game is named [see above]. What you have to do is line up four of these hardwood rounds – there, I'll start – ahead of your opponent. As you can see, in its finely styled cabinet, with its burlwood inlay and brass fittings, the whole is not without ornamental value, as is the case with so many objects here. Well. I see you're pondering your move, wisely I might say. I shall of course allow you to pink in the ace I mean think in peace [away, typographic sprite!]....'

The phone rang. When I lifted the hall receiver, Cornelius was already babbling. Briefly, I followed his avuncular outpouring, in full expectation of the usual staccato response from client Zob. Snell said he'd get here early – 'at around eight' – and would help receive guests. When Zob next saw *me* he was looking for a pencil. Olga expressed it so – 'Dat's nerfs, zo relax!' – when I pointed out the one he clutched, though by this time he'd forgotten the important name or aside, got from that colloquy with Snell, as the one he should have written down.

Eightish. Cornelius, good as his word, is here. In a slight *crise de nerfs* myself I am in the bachelor's den, striding self-consciously into those beige slacks. No adjustment I can make to Zob's minimalist cheval-glass quite dispels the late rush of sartorial doubt, almost overwhelming when I button up that floral shirt. It seems author and agent have secretly conspired, each in his hired tuxedo. And get this! Snell's cummerbund is in a drowsy shade of poppy, while his fluorescent white shirt has textured stripes. Zob's is a palace mauve. The bowties are complementing, my master's having a sort of *chevaux de frise* design, in a staid navy blue with white. Snell's is a riot of 1960s psychedelia, the decade he was sent down from Oxford.

At 9.02 Cornelius placed his outsize paw on the knurled knob of the Yale, and with a plasticised grin prepared himself for the first guest(s). That (or these) happened to be

Miss Overmars, who found herself ushered over the threshold by a dissenting Isabelle, whose intuition told her the party was some way off its start. She wanted, she told me later in bed, to drive around the block several times more. Zob had run away, ostensibly not having heard the doorbell, for a final dab, he said, of kohl to his nervous eyelids. At 9.30 Cornelius, prowling in the kitchen, had demolished a remaining half-packet of peanuts. Olga, noting a can of Pilsner – this her slobby assistant had perched at his elbow – told a tired-looking Peter to get up and check the barbecue. This had been lit at 7.00, then relit having sputtered out, had reached its correct cinerary pallor at about 8.30, and probably now needed more charcoal.

It's 9.31, 2, 3, and there's the doorbell, in evocation of quaint Respighi airs. Cornelius opens up, to find in the reverberant porch that flesh-and-blood rotunda Mickey Blandford. As ever here was a man distracted by the day-to-day of politics, that twilit arena his editorials had long and impossibly strayed into. I never tire of telling Zob that the man's dubious leftism is already *passé*. For some reason he hadn't properly read his party invitation, having brought a bottle – of middling champagne, beribboned. He passed it to Snell. He grinned through inelegant brown whiskers – one day I shall have to take him aside and lecture him about that. Zob was of course overjoyed, because this let him slither off the Overmars' microscope plate, who as social fanatic warbled to a much reprised chorus from a stock set of plaints focused on juvenile crime.... Zob squared to his friend (beams, guffaws, handshakes) and was particular to round his vowels.

Isabelle had sneaked a crab *vol-au-vent* and was ticked off by Triple-O, for these had not yet been 'pud owt'. Blandford, who had just come from his club in Shepherd Market, apologised for Sir Maxwell Hayste, who even at this hour was transacting pressing commercial business, with his stockbroker.

I have this empty-to-full queue theory, and am tempted to take it up with a software engineer. It operates empirically on the simple principle that once you have decided to step into an empty shop or vacant railway carriage, it fills up immediately. A procession of Zob's guests, on the tail of the apricot-jowled Blandford, tripped in over the threshold. Here was 'Maddie' West with effeminate, and only slightly madder escort – 'But darling!' – each with dewy spangles in the same solarium shade of hair. Her poncho was 'parfickly nase', which in its black and white checks, or rather rhombs, matched her partner's waistcoat. 'Actually wescot,' he corrected....

Shayle I found had an endless capacity to depress, having a jaundiced tan with accompanying spleen. The in-Gloria Punch found the right words elusive: 'Where's that flunkey for coats? Oops! Here! O well, ta, ha!' Merle uplifted me – said I was looking 'sharp'. Zob undid me, his finger and thumb to my elbow. Confidentially, *sotto voce*: 'Al, be a whizzo. That lovely boy Andreas promised to come and serve drinks, but alas....' No sign of Andreas. 'Why not start with Gloria there. Al, you won't let me down....'

Marsy. One day I will.

Gloria's vogue in the aperitif line was at this time a sickly orange liqueur, whose shade, in the wrong tinted glass I served it in, was only a touch darker than the sunned exterior of the Glaze boy, Giles, whose carroty hair and complexion had metamorphosed under his Provence *soleil*. He and his partner – a dark-haired girl with frightened green eyes – had a Pimm's No 1, and roared to an after-dinner *faux pas* – this the raconteur Blandford had recorded, and now looking every inch a salty dog, related. He clutched a cold beer, though I had offered him rum.

Jessica – sister to Giles, in love with the 'mechanic' – entered stage left, Act One, Scene Two. As to points of restitution, the despised prospective son-in-law, as it relates to that high-flying literary man, now deceased, was a charming Mauritian whose name was Vic. He I discovered was an engineer and not a mechanic, and ran his own electronics firm from the Cambridge Science Park, in the assembly of asynchronous signalling devices. He thought there might be something in my queue theory. Their lovely twenty-two-month-old Amanda was at home being baby-sat.

Time presses. Zob has told Olga to tell her slob to tell me to open wine, so here in a blur of integrated polychrome is my whirligig – what remains of the guest list. The cynosure Justin Simms, who arrived with the 'masculinist' Crouch, and got chatty with the minimal Royston Flude…. The pugnacious Mastabyle, fist semi-permanently clenched. He in the tireless probes of his newspaper work had persuaded the bruiser Crouch to the pillory, on 'poor Tom's' turn to be manacled there (meaning Eliot). Today Crouch's poor toms were overripe Jerseys, for whose plop and dribble of pips she had a pristine new target, the Anglican Church, meaning death. Another Tom – Corbiere – kept a more-or-less constant, uxorious arm to his wife's attractive waist, where her rose-coloured dress was gathered by a broad green belt. Haphazardly Myrtle Bloge walked in, with a much older and balding man in a business suit. Simon Macamister sported a joke tiepin, which depicted the head of Lenin. He had long wanted to write a travel book based on the real-life sojourns of a cricket captain (this is a tedious game, therefore I fail to remember all but its most famous English names). What did Myrtle think? (Nor is her answer something I'd remember.) There was one other, the liver surgeon, oh and another, that hobbit of BOTS (Professor Emeritus, once of Exe), plus motley authors and agents now only a whirr of half-remembered, and anyway misleading conversation.

Cleverly I put that 1989 Château Latour among the boxed debris, or aftermath of Olga's day in the kitchen, and placed another (open) bottle discreetly in the shade of Zob's cooking sherry. It replenished my glass. For Giles, in tandem with his green-eyed beauty, I naturally reserved the Meursault-Perrières (which had oxidised) – with the result that he got on the phone immediately. For the Philistine horde I uncorked that mid-range Rioja and took it round on a tray. At this stage Crouch, who quaffed and knew no better, had got Simms and Macamister in a huddle under a bluish pall of gunsmoke (those disgusting English cigarettes of hers). 'No,' she corrected, at which Macamister bit his lip. 'The fact of a popularised following, is that growth, especially worldwide growth, is achieved only through the lure of one or other career path. This has been a disaster for Christianity. Its original thrust was secularised….' Bloge, in the adjacent circle – Bloge, Mastabyle, Blandford, Flude – drifted over on the sound of that salvo, which was Simms's cue to step aside and swap his place. I noted he couldn't help but finger his glittering Rolex.

Zob, pulling at his shirtsleeve, where only now I noticed his iridescent cuff link, began to entertain Bloge's sirocco-blown escort, who had heard – indirect from his mindful Myrtle – that Crouch had only yesterday been appointed to the committee, Best Novel to be Published This Decade.

Snell I don't think knew this, who had only himself to blame, having got himself cornered. At each new incorrect detail I heard him blithely impart that 'that was not quite so', or so he'd been informed. Merle, bright droplet of jewels, centre to my pagan altarpiece, put her boss and giant panda right. He was telling the widow, one wisp of hair over her face, and wearing for a moment a smile that had set, that having swung a recent TV deal a ninety-minute adaptation of Zob's second novel *Hype* would soon reach the nation's crepuscular living-rooms (barring mine, the discerning Wye's). An impatient Miss Overmars overheard him say this, and now told us she had read, and of course reread, and of course re-reread, and of course of course etc. double-re-re, that masterly opus two. To her mind here was one of few genuine works of literature cohesive enough to tackle the underlying problem of democracy in a capitalist state. And how ingeniously so, when in a careful choice of words his stance was firmly opposed to the structures propping a constitutional monarch. To that Merle, proceeding gently, said: 'How so?' The answer, if rambling, I précis so: Function of hereditary monarch is to encourage in the individual citizen (or actually 'subject') reverence for the state. The state is a complex organ both operated by, and in service to, its 'democratic' elites. Ergo, hereditary monarch is the highest symbol of social oppression. But let us not sermonise. Particularly as the night is young, and the Rioja's so, so, so…middling….

Prosit, Miss Overmars.

'Woss iss dis middling?'

'*Prosit!*'

Isabelle followed the laden tray. The laden tray was in my hands. Together we found out Corbiere, symbiotically attached to his wife, his wife's pretty dress a shade of rose I liked. He was telling Maddie West, which meant also her animated twin, how the miraculous jingle – 'the miracle of Miracle' – occurred to him in a four-second burst of genius.

'Incredible!'

The sullen Shayle took one of three last glasses on my salver. Symbolically Zob turned up then apologetically turned down the central chandelier, via the dimmer switch. An escaping cramped ellipse of light from a table lamp, in a burnt hue of burnt sugar, illuminated an eye, a sallow cheek, an ear lobe, as Shayle began to speak. He'd had a problem with extras – this on a shoot in Exeter. I don't propose to make doubly clear that his job is largely low-grade entertainment, and that his lode is a TV production house I have the foresight not to name. 'It's what you get,' I said, 'for falling short of Equity rates' – because, brothers and sisters in servitude, picture the scene—

Director circles that particular section of supremely pointless script where hero, an

Italianate youth, whom ignorant author has named Sancerre, enters private casino. Silence. Action. There are six extras seated at each of three round tables, above which gaffer has suspended lights from makeshift gantry. Dealers deal cards onto green baize. This is draw poker, the rules of which are not entirely grasped by all eighteen. Other props are: a Churchillian cigar, numerous cigarettes, cold tea in whisky glasses, water for gin, where only the lemon is genuine, and low-alcohol lager. None is to be drunk, as no top-ups between takes. There is an imitation haze, and several thousand pounds in sterling, all in bank notes (and there, gentlemen, is the rub). There is one camera only, and this means an interesting interplay of angles is, well, frankly troublesome, and in the end a little nicety Shayle – already over budget – decides to abandon. Sancerre strides to table where great rival Anjou (I'm sorry, that should read Andrew)—Cut! Move table, this one here. Makeup, silence. Action. Sancerre strides in and takes his seat, and because the scriptwriter has no grounding whatsoever in mathematical probability theory fleeces his opponent, first with a full house, then a straight flush, finally four of a kind. This – as I yawn – does not conclude the story. The casino is folded up and put away. The players break up for coffee. Those bank notes are counted. They are recounted. Then they are endlessly recounted. Here we arrive at the brink of an accusation, though directed at which of those eighteen? Or perhaps the star Sancerre himself is underpaid…. Here I turn to the liver surgeon, whose surprised left eye socket seems momentarily monocled. 'Do please have this last glass,' I say.

I retreat to the kitchen, into the welcoming glow of my private Château Latour, and am unfortunately observed by Gloria Punch. The professor is here too, moistening a pencil, with an open notebook, and with something to say on 'the pleasance of sodalities' (!).

How shall I wrap up this dismal scene? My departing Muse, in a lightness of tread, and with that cool air of exile she fans to my brow, has preached detachment. Gloria finished my bottle. Giles – who stumbled on my semi-hidden stocks – as haphazardly usurped the role of major-domo, at least insofar as Orphic revels needed to be supervised. Ms Crouch and Miss Bloge processed through the buffet lounge, where the former delivered her new tractate, *Women and the Priesthood*. Here I cannot take issue – without, that is, looking stupidly solemn – when that whole charade was essentially fun and games for the male of the species, a 'poor chap' who sought to dignify his workhorse status with the magic rain of mysticism (there I go: solemn). Flude, Snell and the impeccable Simms picked at a raspberry-coloured pâté, and were otherwise in conclave. Merle – star of my studded heaven – had got Isabelle and Blandford into the laundry room, and needed only the unsuspecting me for a hand of solo. Merle, my precious Merle! How could I disagree with your *abondance* (or agree with your *misère*)? It's no matter. By two a.m. I had had enough, therefore dissolve, I say, inebriate diplopia! The smiling Wye could find no right bid…

…for a twenty of diamonds…a duopoly of spade queens…a quartet of black twos…

…and was it you, was it you who put me to bed, shoes by the door, beige pantaloons overhanging my chair, shirt on a hanger?

Merle!

June 26 Am I or am I not that floating cloud, a dazzling white in a wash of pure azure, scorched at the fluff of its fringes…or am I in a doorless dream, about four feet, about a yard above this mattress?

Bump (of course the dream)! Here is that perfect peach, where there were once my gilded crowns. Through there's my DTE. Amazingly shoes by the door – and what! beige pantaloons overhanging my chair – that Tropicana shirt on a hanger…. Aw now Merle, my pearl! For these things yes, a double, a treble, a multiple affirmative (why yes, why yes, why yes yes yes)…. Then for one sodden moment, as the man who never suffers hangovers, I and my many morning identities trooped to bathroom one, and briefly caught the spectre of Geraldine Crouch, attired only in an oversized pair of Zob's boxer shorts, returning – not to a ring with awaiting heavyweight – but to the *auteur's* lair, whose bedroom door she quietly closed behind her, dampening a cascade of thunder from the cistern.

Moreover other regions of the cosmos have suffered disturbance. I find when I get home Isabelle is still in bed, and not at her regular Sunday morning jaunt. She insists I sit by her. She says 'heaven' when she has me massage her shoulders (one sharp scapula slips the hook of its negligée, then the other), then she collapses, prone. 'Only think,' she purrs, 'those shining Hampstead lights!' That's what she *called* a party.

I go to my room, where I find Miss Overmars – a sack of limbs – who all night long has pummelled my duvet. Categorically no, I shall not massage, Miss Overmars, *your* shoulders.

June 28 Mrs St John, in Lutheran disgust at the sight of all these empties, all these catholic indulgences, hopes sincerely I will clear the kitchen and her laundry room, and get me to a bottle bank. Obernau-Ombercrombie, a surprise visitor, checks in in a banana trouser suit, having reasoned that her lost slotted spoon must be here somewhere. I thought she must be right, recalling the maladroit Blandford, whose obese chuckle was fully exercised when someone suggested a game of charades. He purloined that handy utensil, and with it swatted the smoke-filled, slightly acrid air. This did not mean 'Bane', as would have been logical, but 'Lord', *Lord of the Flies*. A rosy Gloria Punch, who at that hour secreted musk to her underarms, triumphantly guessed it, and followed on – in my view this was apposite – with *Diary of a Nobody*. I found it – the spoon – down the back of a leather settee, though the double-dealing Triple-O could not reciprocate with a trip to her nearest recycling centre.

I shall look out for her invoice, ensuring its longevity in the heaps of my grading system, that is to say submerged in the least urgent correspondence pile.

June 29 I have puzzled on one curious fact concerning Miss Overmars, for it seems to me that her left profile tends to a scimitar, while the right is more to the gibbous. She has spent these last nights on a zed bed, in the spare but really Isabelle's utility room. There is a table with typewriter, and an easel someone has folded back and pressed to the wall. There are the games, jigsaws and a dumper truck that have outlived Michael's childhood. More poignant is a desk and secret effects, these being under lock and key, bound up with the late Michael Lavante. Here is his portrait, a large smiling face in the vigour of its manhood, a fullness avoidably cut short in the port of Zeebrugge. That understood, I have resisted offhand remarks related to anything maritime, however unlikely it is our talk will go there. And I am careful not to fall for our island fascination for disasters at sea.

Happily Miss Overmars is re-shod in those sandals, and courtesy Isabelle has a newly laundered shirt and shorts. She is on her way and has promised to write. Having so much enjoyed talking to the professor, on Saturday night – he of that 'pleasance of sodalities' – she is setting off on a pilgrimage to Exe. I have agreed, among the sonorities of a fugue, to drop her on the West Way, where with her map and her rucksack I can see, in the departing mirror, she has stuck out a thumb. *Bon voyage!*

June 30 Mrs Clapp – who finds everything almost back to normal – has been run ragged by Cornelius. His incessant demands for cappuccino she tells me detract from an extended assault with the oven spray.

Later I was called to the meeting, where I found Zob slumped in his study, and Snell poised with clipboard and fountain pen. I drank Earl Grey. Snell could not resist the raw laughter of commerce, observing that now that the harpy had been bedded – by Zob – a place for *Gimme the Cash* on the shortlist – Best Novel to be Published This Decade – 'of course' was assured – for had not the winged, taloned, 'man-hating' Crouch been appointed to the committee? Zob, darkish, shifty – a mien reminiscent of its screen manifestation – said only this, that for a misogamist the pugilist Crouch had an expert hand in erogenous electrification. Excuse the coarseness in Snell's guffaw. That, he said, in a multitude of exclamation points, was exactly the colour of present business. I finished my Earl Grey.

The 'colour' was purple, 'present business' was Zob, apropos of Cornelius's drawn-up plan for the South Bank reading. 'By the way thanks Al for that excellent suggestion.' Snell had marked his selected passage from *Gimme the Cash*, along following lines, as I subdue vipers, as I battle digestive turmoil generally—

Scene, rambling Edwardian house off quiet lane in Cookham. Kiff, a street entrepreneur and supplier of all cargoes, has trawled a King's Cross *trottoir*, and has brought to client Ambrose (a bored lawyer) a teenage brunette. He has brought also a sachet of yellow powder. Also a camcorder. Events unfold in the drawing room: thick pile carpet, heavily woven drapes, the latter drawn, though it is daylight outside. Certain theatrical arrangements have been introduced, notably a foil-lined umbrella, fully open, and a desk lamp, which has been turned on, and is craning its neck. Ambrose emerges from a Chinese screen, from where he's exchanged his daytime clothes for two lone items. One is a pair of surgical gloves. The other, shield to his throbbing rhapsody, Zob sheepishly terms 'priapic overcoat'. Kiff co-ordinates his client's home movie show, whose male lead jokes that this is what makes of him that hungry *Homo erectus*. Organ probes pimply-cheeked rectum of lily teenager, who is obliged to stand and not turn round. One of those gloved hands caresses a thigh, her groin, massages her clitoris. It's a scenario I don't mind stating I don't find easy. I fear the public, *and* my public blushes. I bottle up my squirms – that internal writhing of liberal toleration. As to overall ambience, shall there be motes, dust, fug, a heavy atmosphere? Cigarette smoke? A blue filter on the lens? The cast is read, the die is cast. I object. Cornelius bellows 'Intransigent!' That is because there's a gloss on my chivalry, and with it I will not see his assistant step down off her pedestal. But I am patient, as the walrus Snell fabricates our trio and narrator so—

Cornelius in the part of Kiff. Low-life patois. Think of Ealing studios. The supposedly comic. Al is Ambrose, and that's because I'm so stuffed-up, exactly like a filthy lawyer. Zob does the introduction and sundry interpolations. The teenage brunette is played by my thirty-ish, dark-haired, light-skinned Merle. It's a human tragedy, on a scale I can't overstate, that the climax is ours—

NARRATIVE Lubricants, insertion.

SHE Cor blimey mate wotchya think I am!

I This, my pet, is your *annus mirabilis*, and is established. You'd like as it were to renegotiate terms. Yes?

A pause in the whole disgusting episode was Snell's insistence that Merle had been sounded out on this, responding with customary equanimity.

July 1 So to my second cigarette of the day, where a loose co-ordination of hand, eye, thoughts floating in cotton wool has brought me to my ledge. Ah my, this enveloping perfect peach! Adam I couldn't help notice seized on a kebab skewer, petulant. No one can possibly know (Blandford) how that had got embedded in a tract of newly turned soil, home of those first enamels in a clump of hydrangeas, pale blooms just beginning to show. It reminds me that somewhere beyond is a shattered wine goblet, which the bibulous Gloria Punch drummed with a dessertspoon, a contact resounding, she claimed, to the rhythm of the *Marseillaise*.

July 3 Isabelle again missed her Sunday morning rendezvous. I know that because, having slept fitfully – shall I call Merle or not? – I swept back my curtains, the time approaching dawn, in a first flush of orange. She and Michael were loading the Citroën: the boy's five racquets, one set plus one change of whites, tennis shoes, sandwiches, a yellow Thermos. He had made progress in a round-robin tournament, on his preferred all-weather surface, and now faced an older, much taller boy, in the first semi-final. 'How I beat him,' he said to me later, 'was with topspin to feet. Made him bend.' That strategy had occurred to him, thinking back on Miss Overmars.

The conclusion was this. He went on to win his first final, and came home with a lightly tarnished cup, whose wooden pedestal sat on a square of blue baize. He showed me his medallion.

Michael: bravo!

July 4 To work, and a fine day indeedy, as I smoke out more of that Stateside correspondence. This next collection I found in a cyclist's backpack, scrunched in the bottom drawer of a chest, so stiff I jerked it open one resisting knob at a time. Zob admitted he had never really curbed his appetite since the banquet of his youth, though naturally his metabolism hadn't kept to the same pace, and exercise now was more than ever a need, yet couldn't be remoter. In passing I found an air filtration device (for mouth and nose, with strap), and one of those elliptical helmets in a luminous red, which he must have looked attractive in, pedalling the gutters of southwest London. But enough. Let us amuse ourselves with that studious corner the futile Professor Glaze gradually, imperceptibly, painted himself into.

4143 Bay State Road
Boston MA 02215
27 April 1992

Dear Marsy,

Safe ground, I assumed (the wonderful, wonderful Updike), and a fitting audience, as I thought: academics, book people, students. Ah but no. Having declared a moratorium on that unimportant 'time' element, which might just as well NOT be a component of my theory – I might say my GIGANTIC theory (because I know you understand)…well! Words almost fail. Some fool student of theology asked me if I had invented my solid continuum after St Augustine, i.e. from a co-ordinate somewhere outside it. 'Only in the sense,' I said, 'that literature has a beginning, which may or may not correspond with the book of Genesis, and is probably approaching its end, given that other continuum the TV.' Waffles of dignified laughter. Then at that precise moment the tubular bulb in my lectern began to blink, then fizz, then went out. 'The way,' I said, 'of all contrivances, which it's as well we all take note of.' I was handed a pocket torch, but of course by now was irreconcilably parted from my script. Inevitably *Four Quartets* crept in, as it were through a fire exit, or someone at the back. 'I might as well tell you now,' I told him, or her, I don't know which, 'I regard that as a complete waste of, yes, time.'

A day or two later I found myself in the university bookshop, and picked up a student magazine, mostly poetry, mostly trash, some of it promising. You know the sort of thing. The cover had an ink line drawing whose background is suggestive of an arch. On a closer look the heady vortices of hair belonging to the five persons seated round a dining table were in fact birds' nests. Hands looked like mittens. The carafe they all poured from was bottomless. Well, I didn't expect to find this on an inside page: *so then time unwinds / its macadam, right and left / lanes, past and future*, which broke the first rule of haiku, bearing a title: 'Lines for a pioneer, Professor Glaze of Exe'. Touching. I shall keep as a memento.

Keep writing. Yours ever, Andrew

[I might address these further lines to the transfigured professor, whose visage I suspect is a radiance of fool's gold, whose cloud is a cloudlet, and who shall pluck the electrified threads of a lyre in everlasting solitude. Is this memento not more of that trickery from the McTaggart tome of pressed flowers? Given the vantage, far from our temporal intersections, permit me to ask, on this so-called unwinding macadam: what is the traveller's perception? Of the past as it approaches the future? Or vice versa, the future incessantly tumbling into the past? Also I hazard the view that in correlating 'right' with 'past', the author was probably English, that's to say a left-lane driver. AW]

Flat 5

147 Trefoil Street

SW18

5 May 1992

Dear Andrew,

There are bound to be misapprehensions. God knows I've suffered my own – at the hands, guess, of Gloria Punch. I'm sick of her tyranny, the sound of her clarion: ah but have I considered the 'cross-write'?

I don't suppose I have to tell you. It means fitting up the script for more than one audience, my job to place it hand-in-glove with a uniquely English social system (she thinks I haven't noticed, there are strata and there are substrata – lower, lower-lower, middle, lower-middle, and so her lecture goes on). What drives me barking to my breakfast is that habit she has, taking as example random chunks of dialogue, and shortening them more than they already are. Still, I think of the money.

By the way I've advertised for an assistant. Am about to process applications.

Don't let them grind you down.

Marsy

[My own, highly decorative application was not among that first batch – nor, incidentally, the second. I can't begin to conjecture as to his strategy at that time. It was one that attracted a retired batman from the flat vistas of Leicestershire, a typist from Pinner, 'keen on Agatha Christie', numerous school-leavers, still unimpressed by the unsettling discovery of life and the world as NOT a media network. There was also a professional minutes-taker, and there were a great many people who described their work experience as in 'human resources'. My first task on accepting the post was to file this correspondence. AW]

c/o Roland Spatz
Long Island University
Greenvale NY 11548
21 May 1992

Dear Marsy,

Now it's getting silly. What do I find, on opening my first bundle of mail! That I'm a man pursued. In this instance by the *Boston Review*, which carries a lethal broadside. I am condemned for, and I quote, my 'cheap deconstructions', where for every text I disassemble I have substituted my own 'pet literatures'. That process functions as the sole synchronic code where writers and academics like me find their preordained role in life. This, I learn, is mighty useful in propping up and dignifying my 'absurd' notions of time, as a sort of clearing house, from which those authors I envy are banished, while their lesser agonists are encouraged to the best wine in my cellar. It's news to me.

Thank heaven for your letter, kindly forwarded by Professor Happs. (In my opinion there's plenty of time to choose an assistant.) Needless to say I have made what's in all probability my final visit to Fifth Ave, where Sam and her voyeuristic binocs have unthinkingly lit on a mugging (three Hispanics closed in on one white American) in Central Park. There was a gum-chewing cop when I got to her apartment ('Just go over that, huh, lady....'). When, amazingly, I squeezed in five mins – this was with my ex-wife, that sole partner in the moulding of my mattress – she said to me 'For Chrissakes, Andrew.... Nothing *needs* to be done about Jessica.'

I shall tell that cop I have been in the museum of natural history, where I met his contemporaries in a display labelled 'Ancestry'.

Let me know how you get on re assistant.

Yours, Andrew

[Author's note: the walrus Cornelius related with some aplomb the news that Jessica was again 'with child' (his biblical way of putting it). He was less animated in the serious declaration that she was unwilling to participate in a commemoration of her father's life and work. He couldn't understand it.]

Flat 5

147 Trefoil Street

SW18

30 May 1992

Dear Andrew,

Tell them philosophy's like those certain fruitless variants of courtship – a dead end. Some academics feel too safe in a cul-de-sac. Perhaps that'll be my next book, though I don't fancy the research.

I just can't imagine how so many unsuitable people have come across my advert. Hundreds of useless applications. It's exhausting, but I have a shortlist. Top currently is a clean, wholesome girl from Bath. She's back from a teaching job in Cadiz. Before that her 'pastures' – her words – were the 'untroubled' spires of Exe, where her specialism was Virginia Woolf (before you ask, I don't hold that against her). We had a long chat in a pizza house. I'm tempted.

Most recent interview was in the pool hall. Since *Aristotle* I go there a lot – it helps me think, and relax. I couldn't make it – or rather him – out. A native of Manchester, yet talked like colonial Tunbridge Wellian. His name's Alistair, though he didn't hint at a Scottish connection. He seemed – which is perhaps the operative word – seemed (stress) well informed generally. He assumes I'm of the Left, because he's seen my byline in *The Observer*, and told me he'd read and liked my lampoon on the decent, genteel exterior of former Tory prime ministers. I didn't say hear hear.

For all this his degree's in computer science, though the man was evasive about his university – a sleight of hand I thought these boffins weren't capable of, having no intelligence outside that realm of the microchip. He could be very useful, as I wouldn't mind all that hardware paraphernalia – though God knows I can make nor head nor tail of the box of tricks I have got. He works, he says, for a theatrical properties company in Mortimer Street, for whom he designed, wrote and installed a stock-and-order system. He reads a great many science books, and for that reason thinks he can talk down to me. I showed him a thing or two on the pool table.

I'll see what I can do through the *Massachusetts Review*, through one of my contacts, though this goes back years. Try and scotch this time thing, which is getting out of hand, and not you at all, I'd have thought.

The best, Marsy

[I *shall* have my say. First a note about that 'colonial' Mancunian, whose early travels south revealed his as an alien tongue, where his 'bath' to rhyme with 'hath' was just one of several vocalisations completely unintelligible to his school-fellows. Solution: watch the mouth move, and imitate those 1960s BBC news broadcasters. Now can yuh hear me, mate!

I stumbled on Mr Zob's advertisement in a barely current issue of *The Author*. It was left on my desk by Playwright X, a boy of twenty who, having been handed the palm in a drama competition, now thought of himself as a theatre mogul. His play, *E for Euripides*, was due for its 'world première' at the Riverside Studios. He wanted, he said, an Attic ambiance, which to him meant square columns on pedestals, with capitals clouded out under the gantry lights. He insisted – he thumped my desktop – on statues with scoured faces, and once ostensive, now truncated limbs. Did I have a monument of Semele? If so how could we rig up a low flame above it? Let me say now that X's *Bacchae*, if given authenticity according to period, was brought to life by moderns, with dialogue in the vernacular. Dion, X's Dionysus, was a West Indian with shaven head, and the purveyor of amphetamines. His Meanies, or Maenads, rapped a lot and danced. A magazine astrologer, the amazing Theresa, took the role of the blind seer Tiresias.

'Why,' I asked, 'truncated limbs?'

'Huh?'

'Wouldn't they be pristine, all that long time ago?'

Look! Had I *read* the script! Er, no. All I can find on my database is a Cupid, but that's at the Nottingham Playhouse.

I jotted down Zob's box number. I penned, I sent off my joke application. Did I expect to hear from so busy a man of letters? No, and so gave him no second thought – until I did hear.

The conversation we had in his pool hall was over a best of three games, which did, it is true, end on the final black. This, naïvely, he potted. The light from the canopy above parcelled its tiny quanta in a varied dilution of yellow. Here perfectly was Zob's imperfect illumination, in whose glaze I remarked on the soiled nap of the table. 'Successive smokers,' I said, and chalked my cue. Together we bent to those grey-green archipelagos, those swipes of ground ash. 'I am interested in music,' I said, in reply to his question what existed other than the written word. When he talked about literary prostitution this was, he said, merely a term in a very long series. According to him, we who worked prostituted ourselves in one way or another. In a glumly glibly status quo few authors had the courage to challenge anything. Did this, I asked, not leave your fellow pool players intellectually *in vacuo*? And to talk of society's imbalance, wasn't that merely society's impregnability? That was more or less it, he said, never having claimed that the elevated tribes and scribes to whom he belonged really did have a social conscience.

He potted a first yellow, calmly: wasn't he after all on the comic side of fiction, and therefore exempt? Then, he imagined, he snookered me.

'Let me show you,' I said, 'how to bend a ball….' Awkward, of course, to cue, just as our human quarks or men of conscience can't with certainty cast their vote. To the *massé* nevertheless. My stolid white dragged its heels round an interposing yellow. It struck a side cushion and my object ball simultaneously. Result: not the pot he'd expected. I allowed him, O ye dumb angels, bearing the professor's footstool, just one more visit to the table. I took that first game, it has to be said without much effort. The second I gave him, only because he bought lunch, which consisted of egg, cress, warm mayonnaise, sandwiched with expert inattention into two squares of foam.

Now, as for those levitating letters tailing my surname, I cannot legitimate the embossed sheen of a doctorate, the gold plate of an MSc, nor even the albata filigree of a lowly MA. As a short-trousered first-former, and I agree a touch Romantic, I took Browning – with his 'Vanity, saith the preacher, vanity!' – and that ricochet off the book of Ecclesiastes – '...all is vanity' – somewhat to heart. What after all is 'education' but the remorseless hum of commerce? At seventeen I wrote a one-page constitution, governing the life, aim and ideals of Wye's pantisocracy. The project was doomed, naturally, depending for sovereignty on a deserted, disintegrating cottage just outside a tiny settlement called Capel, where I was known and loved. That wider kingdom sent in its head-shaking yeomanry, blued in look and uniform, with arguments against. Their central thrust was the minor matter of ownership. Our adopted country or cottage belonged to a Medway vicar, while the 'discovery' of marijuana also helped break up our experiment. This was one smoke-filled, winter afternoon, when the sky was a blossom pink (as I looked out, and up, through a weald of elms).

I told Zob my qualification was as a computer scientist, though I have only a BSc, so in terms of the actuality that wasn't entirely untrue. I watched him on that final black, which he'd failed to spot was equidistant from two corner pockets, making predictable the white as it holed itself too. Lucky we didn't bet, eh, Marsy? Amazingly our second interview took place in a grimy café not far from his snooker club, and for a third he sent me to see Cornelius.

We shall ride, Professor, this heavenly ether again, I am sure. Signing off for now. AW]

c/o Crispin J. Tucker
University of Pittsburgh
English Dept
Pittsburgh PA 15260
9 June 1992

Dear Marsy,

At last a clear blue sky! No barracking. No flame-bearing guide to those catacombs or damp under-culture we're pleased to call 'time'. And NO awkward questions. In fact a civilised reception altogether. Why? Simply I've changed tack, and last week dusted down and delivered a decades-old paper on the prolix Thomas Wolfe. And what about this? In a long spell of applause I found myself presented with a bouquet of lilies, from such a lovely bridesmaid – all courtesy and violet bows....

I hear from Sam that Giles has got himself a supermarket deal, with the Château Le Clairiot. And what should I make of this? Is about to buy property – in St John's Wood. It's shocking! Years of harassed parenting have done *something* for the boy....

By the way anything you now send will eventually reach me – albeit through a cascade of forwarding addresses. Now follows a storm warning. I'm not sure about this Alistair, and I personally never trust a scientist. In many ways those scholar clowns have put our thinking back, what with their absolutes and objectivity, and a slavish adherence to 'facts'. They never seem to accept that facts are only temporary, yet the merest glance at the history of scientific disciplines should tell them just how tenuous their mastery is. Your Bath candidate sounds a good deal more wholesome. Keep me informed.

How easy are the habits of the tourist and sightseeing. The Frick office building has white granite exterior walls with stained glass in the main hall (by a man called John La Farge). It represents Fortune at her wheel, I hope a good omen.

Seriously. Give your Alistair a miss.

Yours, Andrew

[Adieu, dull sprite! AW (with sword)]

> Flat 5
> 147 Trefoil Street
> SW18
> 17 June 1992

Dear Andrew,

Good luck to Giles! I'm also up for a house move, now that a first trickle of real money peps up those dreary quarterly bulletins. You know, boundaries of overdraft pushed into unknown territory. 'Dear Mr Zob, I do not recall' etc. This has been my own bank manager imitating any other.

The Alistair question is more amusing than you realise. This is a man who is highly opinionated, yet whose arguments lack formal precision – in fact are typically redbrick, a point he's rather coy about. For him the purpose of 'literature' is light entertainment, but of a kind directed to the brain's higher centres. He offered me his discourse over a gladiatorial game of pool, which, after mainly flukes and one or two quite good trick shots, I hadn't the heart to let him lose. His ethos is industrial, being quick with – and not much else – technology and its playthings. This has its uses, and is so much fun when observed close to. If I *am* to see him again, I shall ask Cornelius to give him the once over.

My man at the *Massachusetts Review* says he'll publish whatever I concoct on your behalf, if only to take the emphasis off this time thing, which *pro tem* is the best I can do. No pun intended. I hope this will go some way to put present efforts in a better light.

In the meanwhile, I have this unctuous estate agent – Hoop and Spaghetti and Co – phoning me with house details every twenty minutes. He doesn't cease to remind me that he's also a chartered surveyor.

All the best, Marsy

[Let us pass over these injurious asides. The laxity in Wye's pool-hall dialectic won't embrace E for Ethics, not today. So, on to that interview with Snell, whose solid slice of England was fronted by a square of lawn, at its centre a well of soil, the surround a stone jigsaw held static in a mesh of sun-bleached cement. Outdoor décor was a symmetry of herbal niches, where Merle had grown thyme and oregano, and a smattering of sage. Tubs – asymmetrically arranged – would one day sprout bunches of begonia. A stone hollow on a stone pedestal cupped a collection of pinecones, not as far as I could tell from any near location. In defiance of secateurs a cotoneaster climbed the porch, with just a hint that the Snell escutcheon (a copper blaze in oblong) might soon be overrun, a thin finger of green scratching away at a comma, a stop, a parenthesis. There was, intermittently, the scent of honeysuckle. The mat outside said WIPE FEET. The one inside, WELCOME. Merle, who moments before had admitted *her* guest, tapped on her boss's door. She introduced me – not to him – but to Delilah Scuff, whose *No Nonsense Farmhouse Recipes* was a runaway bestseller. Scuff had a withered look. It framed a misanthropic mouth, as opposed to the smile the world's wistful cooks examined on her dust jackets. Merle and her client went off into conference, into the back room, a room with French doors – doors that would open to the pear tree outside, with its satellitic bench. Cornelius – a man avoiding landmines – stepped into the hall, a passage over-stocked with polished wood, oppressively dark. A grin he'd pinned on suddenly as suddenly dissolved. His giant hand ushered me to his office.

What, my late professor, is left to relate? Well, there was agent Cornelius in an endless infraction with his phone exchange, as he tried hard to persuade the busy Merle to bring us each a cup of coffee. I shouldn't smirk at this, Cornelius stooping finally to walk to the kitchen himself, at the point when his handset buzzed, and the extension lights were aglow. 'Oh thanks. No sugar – absolutely right.' There were other absurdities, none more stereotyped than the way he reclined in his chair, his fingertips together, and none more shallow as he announced, in a grave hour of English social history, men of Zob's vision were ignored at too high a cost. Thankfully that squall was quick to pass. We joined 'the girls' in Delilah's latest celebration, and shared their delight at a series of TV kitchen shows, a deal done all on her own by Merle. I had the supreme honour, Merle having poured out drinks for all but herself, of stirring her Martini, and setting within it a cocktail fruit. For hark, Professor, and consider fresh evidence below. I have stolen in at a quiet hour, into Zob's study, and have plucked a leaf from his business correspondence file. It means you may never, never trust a technologist. AW]

Snell Literary Agency
12 New Caxton Grove
London NW8 5HL
19 June 1992

Dear Marsy,

Saw your boy today, quite a personable young man. Hung on my every word when high importance of your work was explained. Am sure you'll have no trouble kneading him to fit your purpose.

As you say, seems pretty clued up technologically. Sorted out my phone – that incredibly complicated new exchange I've got. Some of the things it can do! It so happens we celebrated one of Merle's recent successes with a little lunchtime splash. Alistair proved most accommodating in passing round the drinks. I think he'll be okay.

I will as I promised phone Maxwell Hayste.

Best wishes, Cornelius

[Zob had taken a pink highlight pen to that closing pledge of Snell's. A stroke filled with deliberation swept across that important committee name. AW]

July 5 A coincidence, doubly so, whose significance only the passing of time will unveil. I was feeling, at ten thirty, 'eleven o'clockish'. That impulse welled to a descent of the front stair, when I'd got in mind Zob's cache of coconut cookies – which I knew Mrs St John wouldn't demur at, if I did the dispensing. O that crooked smile of hers. At this same moment, what perversions, discursions, and kinks in the kitchen curtains. The plain Geraldine Crouch honked at the horn of her soft top, out on the drive, or demilitarised zone. This got Zob up from his chair – his blinds drawn, the desk light on – and if not exactly into his flak jacket certainly on the defensive (their war of the cognoscenti sexes). She was toesy. She was rosy. She was ever so ever so posy. Of course Zob 'hadn't' forgotten their appointment, and if hush-hush I did get all the goss from a third party. Anyway...

...Zob cast around for keys, assuming they would go in *his* car. (They did, but *she* drove.) Here Geraldine darkened to a shade of outdoor rubiginous and entertained *me*, the only onlooker, with true-life stories of suburbia. (She was frumpy, she was scrumpy, she was ever so ever so lumpy.) I don't know where she lived, though I gathered not in a house. I imagined Gothic corbels, ivory turrets, broad pearly apartments among Highgate's moonlit mansions. She told me the buck-toothed girl in the garden flat – snub-nose, freckles, ceaselessly up to her elbows in mud – had recently shown her a squirm of leggy tadpoles, each the size of a thumbnail, in a bucket of orange water – though now I misquote, for it must have been the bucket that was orange…. Anyway, this was floating with mosses, and this being the nub of Crouch's *entente* with Nature, she was agape at the tiny frogs sloshing around inside. 'What a bright kid can teach you,' she said. I crunched my cookie disrespectfully. Fortunately Zob emerged from his door frame having chanced on his keys, and off they zoomed (she was driving. She was thriving. She was ever so ever so blithe-ing).

I phoned Merle. We had lunch. Our first few words in an amazing subplot were spoken. But that's not really the point.

I got home in a flush – because, Merle, you accepted my dinner invitation! – and was there a full half-hour in advance of Isabelle. She, 'dead' on her feet, slumped in her two-seater, and dumped her shiny black shoulder bag down on the floor. Her feet, lethargically shod, extended over one arm. Her drowsy hot head indented the other. 'Make your landlady tea.' Tea I made her. 'These! Pull!' I tweaked off her buckled shoes. I whipped off her ankle socks. I stroked an exploratory hand up her – SHAME, oh Zob's infection! out, vile fiction! Actually I filled the plastic kitchen bowl with warm froth, and remained on duty with a cup of tea, the first of two lay witnesses in Isabelle's beatification, or the soaking of corns, just as Michael thrummed in, with his tennis racquet standing in as rock guitar.

She had been (oh Michael don't) to a private viewing. To prove that was no hoax she produced a printed card, which I read. *You are cordially invited* etc. *to an exhibition of 'art objects'* etc. *by the 'visual block builder and* [assorted epithets]' *Newsome Barringer*, who was from Phoenix, AZ. This had taken place at premises in Soho. 'Funnily your boss was there,' she said, 'with that, you know, that what's-her-name. Always on TV.'

'Crouch.'

'Uh?'

Relax, my pink-ankled dunkle. 'Geraldine Crouch.'

'Yes. Her.'

'What was it like?'

'What was what like?'

'The exhibition. What was it like?'

'Oh, that.' Apparently lousy. The centrepiece was an enlarged human skull, got up with zonal streets, pendulous lights, midnight cars – all emblematic of the Western City.

'That sounds a gas,' I said.

July 6 Drove up, not particularly early, through the street to Zob's, the neighbourhood still in a yawn. Next door that liver surgeon, whose life to me was bleary and insubstantial, had got in a flap over his wife's dipstick. Buy her these toys, what does she do!

I parked alongside Geraldine's soft top, where in its plump upholstery I noted volume two of her memoirs, whose catchy subtitle is: *I go up to Oxford*. That car, and that car's autobiography section, wasn't there when I stepped out for a walk at noon, though I hadn't heard her go (hadn't heard her at all).

July 7 A note from Zob on the kitchen table. 'Dear Mrs Clapp – Don't, repeat don't do my bedroom today' – which had that good peon in a puzzle all morning. Bedroom-wise he was generally 'most p'ticular'. I wondered what order of gymnastic apparatus Geraldine, now living out her volume three, had left there. (She was spacious, not curvaceous, she was ever so ever so voracious.)

July 8 I reappraise my Englishness. That, with its aptitude for comedy, looks naturally feeble on stilts out on a pier end, but that is deceptive. It does not need to transform itself, or be any more successful when put in the open air. For what is its sideshow, and who is it asking that question? I shall try to be brief, fumbling for an answer. Here, if you look, is a trio of painted clowns. Here is a raised structure, glued together on the paved outskirts of insanity, a location starred in a crisscross of light. Enter, platform left, 1) a trumpeter in big red shoes, who puts an occasional leap in his gait. His trousers, baggy, are in black and white checks, a bouncy panta-balloon too large at the waist, and so held up with braces. Fanfare, please, as that announces 2), solemn and whey-faced, the bearer of a single snow-petalled rose. Should I scent its fragrance, I would find it squirting water in my face. Ha-ha! Finally 3) a pierrot – just look at those pompons! And what's that, a platter? With a card, and inscription?

Merle O Merle. Regardez. Pierrot's platter here. That is, that was, for you.

July 9 I am just the kind of dupe, lashed to that turning wheel called capital, who possesses a business address book, if by now it is twelve years old, or no more than thirteen, or fourteen at the very outside. This goes back to my time in King's Langley, or to be perfectly frank a backwater there, known as the KL Western Meditation Centre. Hold on to your chair leg. There *is* a point to this story, though I know I digress.

I was, personally, an inmate – not you understand in any ordinary arrangement. What those sandalled, shiny-pated elders – the serenely robed of the institution – what they wanted, because business was good, was a computerised booking system. They could not afford, they said, investment in expensive time-sharing. Nor could they consider buying in equipment. This meant selecting, liaising and finally co-operating with a suitable bureau, and for this they wanted my services. At interview I must have come across as neither smirking nor poker-faced, the two kinds of sceptic they knew. Nor were they surprised when I negotiated almost wholly by barter. I would take, on a rolling weekly basis, cash for expenses – and treat the whole thing as a break from routine. A retreat to the wooded knolls, the dewy brakes, to those one or two diminished tracts of rural England, at that time had its attractions. Of course 'so-called' civilisation – as for brief weeks I came to refer to it – was not that far away, with the railway nearby to Euston and Milton Keynes, and God-knew-what in the world beyond. There was a golf course. There was a particularly rancid stretch of the canal. There was, as seemed the case in England everywhere, insipid commercial property. There was also my address book. I do, I know, digress.

Induction came with a fresh wave of 'students', from as far afield as Smethwick. Introductions were under our shaven guru, a youngish man whose interpretation of capitalism was from strictly the lotus position. I shall paraphrase. Capitalism, which one may scarcely regard as a 'philosophy', was a system doomed never to penetrate the surface gloss of our cosmos. It involved immense pains on the part of its practitioners, in what was merely the co-ordination of resources, which were mainly people, the goal being material. That translated meant the uneven distribution of power, and importantly wealth. Individuals were the component force in no profounder reality than that. I acknowledge that for all my attempts, which gained no more than a semi-whole, or a wrestler's half-lotus, the fragmenting parts in my 'personal', 'more meaningful' reality could never transcend the vaulted roof, never mind take in atmospheric views of the railroad. Nevertheless I pressed on with the bureau, and found one off Oxford Street. The system – the capitalistic system – that I finally delivered involved form-filling, dispatch to the punch centre, daily program runs, plus weekly and *ad hoc* reporting (*ad hoc* being in response to a phone call). I learned in exchange and I quote that 'Life is a mystery.' Nor did I surrender my worldly address book, which *is* the point I promise.

The publishers (of that address book) had inserted an index of restaurants, with cinemas, cinema clubs, and music venues also thrown in. Yesterday – before I knew I'd summoned those clowns (it will, it will be explained) – at what time I don't know, one of my ball-nibbed disposable pens quivered in detection of desert water (so to speak), and finally magnetised to an exotic list of entries under M: Ma Cuisine, Mes Amis, Mon Plaisir. Ludicrously these were the names I offered up to Merle, on a comic platter – because after twelve, thirteen, fourteen years, did they exist? There now. I think that about wraps it up. Inscrutably, that's to say without irony, the bright Merle or pearl of my life rallied with a counter suggestion. At the same time she insisted that I did not wear those beige slacks, which after several hours of duty were host to an ocean of crests and creases. (Endless apologies. It cannot be the air.) She lived with wonderful desires, and was refulgent, and under a glistering nimbus improvised lyrics, and on one occasion sang me an Oriental house front. [Get thee, tired critic, to a bunnery. I repeat, bunnery. Don't tell me this is all impossible. That is only *your* fatigue. Get thee to a bummery, you reviewing tabloid hack. The wily Wye is in love.]

Her Chinese shanty had maroon pilasters snaked in painted dragons, and a great many rickety chairs inside. Try the yam cakes, she said (divine). I had to pause, that address book firmly pushed aside, when she ordered Hung Shao chicken – delicious. And why was it, Merle, our short smiling waiter lit us a candle? And served us coconut egg rolls compliments? And gratis too a final pot of perfumed tea?

In that contention for the bill our fingers briefly intertwined. My map shows me how for that one charged moment we were in the aerial ken of Eros, though should he beat those wings I begged him to fly no farther than the south canopies of Carnaby Street, through which we later strolled. A gaucho in a broad-brimmed hat strode in off the street and showed me a cargo of roses, wrapped singly in a film of frosted cellophane. Music, please, a violin, something Brahmsian, gypsy! 'I will,' I said, 'have that snow-petalled one.' Then a few streets away came a place she knew, a nightspot she called Extasis. Here we sat on padded bar stools under a tropical awning, and in secret hatched our clever professional plot. That, as I'm sure you'll understand, I cannot divulge to you now. Anyway mine was a coconut cocktail. Then I unzipped my cardigan. Then, Pulcinella, we danced the night away.

July 10 Dawn. Something in the club coffee has had me bowling mummer-like and Bacchic out on the grey pavements just off Monmouth Street, but the fact it was laced with rum and Tia Maria is not the only explanation. I recall the black cab that resolved itself to a shiny cabbage green, in response to my dumb show, plodding to the kerb. Advertised on its passenger door was stranger transport even than this, and a number to dial to hire a mobile sandwich. The sour cabbage-soup cabby wasn't pleased to take us to the suburbs, where over his dashboard, and the back of his head nodding, he complained when I opened my door into the line of traffic (what traffic?). That, when I looked, was a solitary jogger pounding the gully thirty, thirty-five yards in his mirror. Well, there goes his tip! I paid when he'd set us down, but even so did not escort my new business partner, my Merle, to the pattern of her door, with its mosaic of leaded sunset. That's because there was, at a slant from her bathroom window, and at an angle to her neighbour's washing pole, a dewy triangle of uncut grass that had...

...one pair of rubberised swings, a tyre on a chain in a frame, a silver slide, three concrete cylinders, one for base, two for vertex, and in the shape of antlers a seesaw...

...where in the glory of her adulthood I swung, rocked, walked her through the park. All is, she instructed, play. My tensile grin, when later I shuffled to my own door, must have passed that information on to Isabelle, who by now had resumed that Sunday liaison, and whose damned Malkin mewed at me in the hallway. I am exhausted (hope she puts that rose in water)....

July 11 Geraldine's soft top again, and this time her morning face, when she showed it round the kitchen door. 'Marsy would like coffee taken up,' she said. I therefore made another, in that mug whose painted design is the unstoppable ascent of six red with one plum-coloured balloon, all threads dangling. Geraldine left with her briefcase, having left certain large wear in Zob's attractive Ali Baba laundry basket.

Zob, bored and argumentative, later replayed Part Five in his radio masterclass, which the design team shamelessly titled *Art of Modern Fiction*, the whole series having been broadcast after that surprising, belated success of *Aristotle*. Today's lesson – again, and again, and again – was 'Characterisation'. Here was Zob's five-hinged framework onto which you stretched the fabric of a dreamed-up, fictive persona. 1) Think of a name (amazing how that simple act is decisive psychologically). 2) Appearance. Is your invention dark, light haired, a redhead? 3) Dress. Someone always in a business suit is not of course someone always in sloppy strides and a sweatshirt. 4) Gestures/mannerisms.

Once established, these are pretty reliable, announcing your hero's return to the action. Instance my own Steven Kiff, that swagger from the jeaned hips when he walks the west London streets. 5) Dialogue. Cannot be underestimated. Compare: 'My dear chap'/'Oi! You!'

Here is my own quintuplicate, a five-fold, quintessential opposition, where I disagree with our 'master', condemning these as only the superficial vestments of personality, but which somehow seem to be the obligatory notation in popular forms of story-telling. 'She swept back that wild gypsy hair. He, with his strong arm, held her back from the cliff edge,' belongs untransplantably to the filmic deceits of narrative, which you, Zob, have adopted for the same purpose – what your friendly reviewers call 'literary intent'. But this is mechanistic, and belongs to that vacant hour of early evening soap (of which Zob is the middle-brow equivalent). How then, he asked, would I deal for example with a heroine? Well, Marsy, I should not confer anything so trite as a 'gesture', which is after all a motor function replicated *ad nauseam*. She might I think be a ghostly presence, whose streaming dark locks are notional, as I swing her on a child's swing (say), and whose smile is of pearls and rubies, as I try to catch at her wrist, where I the 'author' give chase through a triplet of hoops (fumbling for my notebook). Her voice might also be a reed, a sympathetic oboe, one that I insist is seldom given to the rough and tumble the trade terms dialogue. She is a levitated presence, whose sole vestige (unfashionable now) is her creator's metaphysical goal, and does not belong in that realm of simulating cut-outs, so patiently folded away, as the hack, writer or romancer approaches the closing paragraph of his book.

'A profounder fiction,' I said, in my best headmasterly monotone, 'once opened up lets out one genie at least, and is impossible to re-stopper.'

'Are you telling me, Al, I don't write thoughtful fiction?'

It didn't float. It didn't dress its silks – didn't abstract that place called readerdom or subjugate the hard folds of reality.

'This is fanciful.'

'Precisely. That is, by certain definitions, fiction.'

'I think I can see, Al, why I'm the writer, why you are not.'

'I think I can too.'

July 12 Mrs St John, not typically succinct as to Zob's shammed world of aesthetics, has suggested through Adam an assortment of garden flares. This is for the terrace party – or dinner for four – that I now learn Zob has got planned for later this week. Adam, who in general can't be trusted with missions in diplomacy, I am astonished to learn has made of this a first representation to the 'marster'. More to the point, as reward he shows off, and I say this emblematically, the yellow, beribboned medallion someone has pinned to his chest. At the time he was dressed in overalls. That is why, on the kitchen table, there is now a potted coleus, on whose variegated leaves – a ruddy brown fringed with green – Mrs St John exudes syllables so ineptly. This is the first such coleus she's come to possess. It likes the light, he advised. Zob remarked on it only when she, and it, had gone.

Geraldine – grumpy, stumpy, ever so plumpy – dropped in for an hour-long 'minute', the time taken to retrieve a document that, as it turned out, had slipped behind Zob's *bonne nuit* TV. Zob, whose created characters were 'substantial', did what he could to transcend this embarrassing episode.

Cornelius, driving back from repairs to an erratic screen-washer – if it rained, it worked, if dry, it wouldn't – gave us the news and authenticating obituary that had somehow escaped us. That is to say our emeritus professor, once of Exe, had dutifully expired – on the final and unspluttered phoneme of a haiku—

> how in the quiver
> of a dragonfly's wing, words,
> ah, here where I—

May I suggest the appropriating 'ping'? Though 'sing', with its violating rhyme, is probably what that daring rule-breaker had in mind. Snell of course was quick to appoint a broadsheet obituarist, for whom we may invent a soliloquy,

> how in the quiver
> of a dragonfly's fang, words,
> ah, here where I—

'clang', 'bang', 'harangue'.... Or suppose we erase 'fang' and choose something like 'dragonfly's eye', which leads us plausibly to 'here where I lie'...'lie' of course meaning that style of things common to Master Zob's circus, to deal in untruths.... But don't let me keep you.... Who gave us testament was none other than Mastabyle, naturally in one of those reactionary papers, which happened to be Snell's daily.

This was a quaint piece of sophistry, whose artifice had been well rehearsed – for compare any review of any piece by Zob. The sole ingredient in any such tissue of propaganda is the dead man as one of the world's elect, a commodity gift-tagged as 'champion of the people' – 'people' conforming to all properties of a colourless vapour. One merely imagines it enveloping our globe. This, you'll note, is polished, high-class journalism, where you will ask what was it Philip had to say of our departing professor. Or how shall I get out of this maze? The professor had many distinguished cronies when up at Oxford in the Forties – a difficult time. This explains why so much frankly commonplace 'material' (a cubic yard of undergraduate verse) wound its way from that self-esteemed pen – which was prone to discharge, furthermore in unpredictable turquoise – to so many prestigious journals. We were quoted something in full, the tedious account of 'Under Cover Glover', a man in a death throe with rifle and binoculars, on a remote or dangerous border. Remember, these were the days of the professor's 'dynamism', when he had not yet metamorphosed to a hobbit, and whose style prompts my *docteur* to pronounce a bad case of Bloomsbury.

Alas, those 'connections' formed no automatic circuit – electric and eclectical – into the soundwaves of celebrity. This I shall remind you is Mastabyle's terminology, which I decline to take issue with here. He tells us that irresponsibly younger and lesser poets, bright working-class boys from the shires, who in golden times pursued professional cricket (as a possible career), now found themselves lauded in print, to the partial eclipse of our middle-earther, and just when the mantle of public acceptance seemed a formality. What could he do? Um, well, two things, according to Mastabyle. He could and did become an Orientalist. Also he might apply himself to much of that inferior verse touted in school anthologies. You know, those dreary evocations, the dun granite of a man's mind possessing, oxymoronically, mesmeric powers to repel. In the terrors of our own times this is developed in the rise of Zob – which regrettably doesn't belong to the annals of science fiction. That I shan't stress is not Mastabyle's opinion, as unlike him I cringe. Unlike, too, I pass over our professor's parallel career, as practically worthless, in the sheltered porch of academe. I force, urge, condition my resumption, where he, Mastabyle, closed with that touching reference to the professor's life as miniaturist, 'perhaps the finest these isles have known'. It's a claim I greet with sceptical hilarity.

Our deceased hobbit was found in his hobbit hole, poised, or rather slumped over a bamboo table top, by his friend and colleague Fiona Trethowan (finally alarmed that his phone had not been answered in two days). 'Nobly' Professor Bilbo, man of 'great academic integrity', was found, 'even at the last', in the spell of his Muse (a freckled girl I envisage with a lollipop). Here, friends, simple genius – a very last summery exhalation—

> how in the quiver
> of a dragonfly's wing, words,
> ah, here where I—

'zing', was Mastabyle's speculation, conferring a timely harp.

'Here,' said Snell, 'keep it,' and got up to go. 'I see Al's really interested. Hope you've got your dinner party organised. Merle's really looking forward to it.'

Zob said he had, and avoided my quizzical gaze.

July 13 A first and last rehearsal. I am glad it's not Friday (superstitiously speaking). Zob drew up his leather sofa, which someone, Geraldine, had saddled with a woolly poncho, so that the backrest – in every other sense an atrabilious shade of pea – was centred by that garment, its pattern of rose and cobalt folded in a V. The short-skirted Merle sat at one end in style and imitation of a teenage brunette. Zob was at the other in the majestic pose, co-ordinator. Typographically, or topographically, or in a more objective analysis geographically, I, with my open copy of *Gimme the Cash*, stood behind her, clutching – and this time pornographically – an imagined tube of lubricant. I found it all so visceral. For an Ambrose I needn't change my voice – which, correction, certainly isn't colonial, and isn't Tunbridge Wells. Cornelius, a less likely Kiff, outside of money talk had not a lot to say, which inhibited the perfection of his dialect. Then of course the whole thing couldn't proceed without debate, to which the following alludes—

AMBROSE This, my pet, is your *annus mirabilis*, and is established. You'd like as it were to renegotiate terms. Yes?

WYE Obviously I understand *annus mirabilis* as a pun (as probably the kind I, Wye, would make). But what 'is established' – that isn't clear.

ZOB You'll suspect me, Al, of modelling Ambrose on you.

Slight murmurs of laughter.

WYE Nevertheless....

ZOB [*to Merle*] Be a sweetie. Run through that last line again.

BRUNETTE Cor blimey mate wotchya think I am!

ZOB [*to Wye*] Now you.

AMBROSE This, my pet, is your *annus mirabilis*, and is established. You'd like as it were to renegotiate terms. Yes?

CORNELIUS Al, it's so clear. Anyone can see.

Wye still not convinced.

ZOB No?

MERLE [*side of head to poncho*] Ah! Got it! What's established is what she is – an angel of the night....

ZOB Though as she learns, Al, that coition is in fact going to be anal...

MERLE ...she'll want to up terms.

KIFF Aw for fuck's sake!

ZOB Not yet, Cornelius.

CORNELIUS Sorry.

ZOB [*to Wye*] You happy with that?

WYE Ecstatic.

July 14 Mrs Clapp, in the transient role I have had to invent, I cast as one of those boundless underlings summoned to the Holmesian detective agency, with domestic brief. I know, Watson, that the dinner party took place here, last night. Good Lord, Holmes! What leads you to that? Instance these garden flares, charred at the flame end. I calculate these sputtered out in the grey hour of dawn. Then these longish corks, having escaped their usual fate (the bin), and all this litter on the terrace. I have an inkling as to the guest list. Crouch, as was fairly usual now, we crossed on the threshold just as I got to work. Merle (because the walrus let that sacred name slip). But duty, Mrs Clapp. Duty. The dining room crumbles in an effluvial air, where time in its new medievalism has left a bismotered heap of crockery. There is I observe low tide in the gravy tureen. Why yes. Someone did gather the cutlery. Unfortunately shoved it, handles down, in that fine Florentine piece otherwise used as a wine cooler, such is the style of Italian terracotta. Now what's that you've got on that indignant-looking tray – that's right – there among those glasses? A Rolex, you say. Now who do I know would leave behind his Rolex? Thinks....

July 15 Thinks, Sherlock Wye....

July 16 Thinks.... And what an itch this is, now as that testing hour is here. (Thinks.) It has found me, having taxied not only Zob but the walrus too, to a vibrant South Bank foyer, where in the shallows of pre-performance the unruffled, unruffable Merle is cross-legged in a low-backed chair. She sips coffee with Justin Simms, who I note is attentive to every word and gesture. To him Zob restores the Rolex (no more thinks). Polite smiles. Reintroductions. Cornelius does not suspect a conspiracy, and flatters himself that the teenage brunette, or Merle, short of skirt and half in part, will attract Zob's rival, a man ready market packaged. That's not in the sense I fear, but into the protected twilight, under a darkening wing, into the poison of Snell's commercial underworld. I measure his Cheshire grin. Some rictus that is.

Forgive me, my people, for this was all my, Wye's, idea. As I ignored the fidgety heels and gazed out over the nodding heads, I feared for our performance, beginning in a hollow and quickly gathering too much pace. Zob, as is his usual inclination publicly, sought authority in a change of voice, with an appropriated bass, as if plucked from the fluff of passing clouds, given his gestures hand and arm (and if you understand my metaphor). I, as he, doff to that vain meteorology, whose injunction was to seek escape in self-apology, which is so often, Cornelius assures, the 'burthen' of genius. It didn't matter to me, though I was bitterly affronted, wanting above all to reach our co-ordinated *finis*, when a heckler, on the stroke of my *annus*, stood up and interjected: 'Filth!'

'...*annus*,' I continued.

'More damn filth!'

To that a concerted *shoosh!*

It did not take long to eject him, because he went quietly. He looked *so* young to be so zealous, for did that boy shave I wondered? Zob, having at last learned the dignified stance of greatness, left it to the martyr Cornelius to resettle our throbbing audience, which to me was a Cubist's dissection of eyes, noses, tufts of hair, where in renewed calm he restarted our recital. Afterwards, at the book signing, I pulled out of boxes and opened for Zob's abeyant pen in excess of one hundred copies. Oh my! One hundred stooges, gambolling off through the reflected ripple of that wise brown river, the Thames.

There is a footnote, divorced as you see by a blank horizon, an uncertain space on the page, demarcating my Saturday the sixteenth. That white chasm above denotes hindsight, because strictly this is an appendix and belongs to a later time. (I have, for a floating fourteen days, lived in the padded glow that comes with a publisher's advance, a sum thoughtfully negotiated on my behalf by the constant Merle, who is now engaged, and rightly proud of her new topaz. This is worn on her maiden finger.) I am in a stone cottage, with my standard lamp on, under a southerly spur of Dartmoor. I am reviewing, revising these pages.

That 'heckler' I have learned from Merle was an implant, carefully and secretly arranged by Snell. He phoned the said agency. It was several days after the press furore, the consequence of that staged indignation, though in this instance indignation was genuine. That fresh-faced youngster didn't much appreciate the elasticated cheque Cornelius had written for his trouble. Merle had to phone him back, having investigated, because of course Snell was out at some book launch or bistro. For some reason his emolument was paid from a suspension account, which was highly irregular, and that was why the cheque had been stopped. 'I will ensure,' she said, 'Herr Snell gets you another cheque off asap.'

I would like to add, that topaz is set in a starburst of diamonds. Meanwhile those raggy tabloids, whose shared olfaction is often infallible, had the spice of prurience in its collective nosethirles. A 'story' had 'reluctantly' appeared, several square feet from the photogenic dugs of student, model and playgirl Cindy, whose profile was set off by silky high heels and a string. The story was our South Bank foray. In that handy currency popular with newsmen, it had ended in 'near riot'. A gaggle of cameramen planted their tripods at the extremes of Zob's drive. Reporters with hand phones rang, knocked at the door, solicited comment. In the end I struck a deal, which, having declared it 'a bargain', these moral folk of Wapping stuck to. I read out a statement – in fact a disclaimer – with the taciturn Zob cemented to the doorstep behind me, his arms folded. I am tickled to report that 'spokesman Wye' was quoted in subsequent issues, from one or two choice sentences voiced in that driveway manifesto, if much embroidered. The spinoff as they say was a photo opportunity. My own handsome features have brightened a muddy corner of certainly one gossip column, as complement to that used-car-seller's look, so intrinsically the characteristic in Zob's public image.

Cornelius advised that sales increased significantly at this time.

July 18 Zob's is a whole life honed to communication—

> From his home
> A Mr Drone
> Has dialled us on his telephone—

a life nonetheless prodigal—

> It's lax, very lax,
> Zob's ignored another fax—

is as well a life plugged at its ears—

Our medium's fibre optic,
Yet might as well be Coptic—

for all the attention he paid. I got rid of Drone – a salesman – without those usual lies of etiquette, i.e. very impolitely, because no I could not (understand?) bear to talk 'replacement windows', which he insisted thermo-efficient households must nowadays acquire. The fax I was more than happy to intercept, being electronically doused in Merle's hypnotic fragrance. Cannily she imparted that the rough beast, not only as it slouched but bore itself to Bethlehem – all under solar flares – was what we might nowadays call the investigative journalist. She had just talked to one on her office phone, and was able to warn of his fraternity, a caravan about to decamp to Zob's oasis, or the neutral pavement outside. Click.

Zob, as usual, could not stir himself to the puerile chime of his doorbell. Eventually I answered it. Ah – a commercial traveller, I assumed. He on the porch mat – thinnish, twenty-five-ish, wiry hairish – didn't exactly deny this. His grip was broken at the zipper. It bulged, yes, but not to the strain of unsold gadgetry – nor kitchen nor garage. What he wanted to sell me, so unalloyed his faith in the largesse and culture of Hampstead, was a collection of thirty poems. This he had gone to the effort of printing privately. I must warn, I said, that my litmus is generally acid, though all the same I opened its yellow covers. 'Honest work,' I went on, 'which puts it at a disadvantage straightaway.' Its mood was its central fault, belonging as it did to the *belle époque*. I gave him a few pound coins, being some way short of the price he asked. 'Mr Zob,' he said, 'I appreciate your frankness.' There, I pointed out, was his second mistake. To all intents Zob wasn't at home. 'Anyway he'll comment only on the work of immediate rivals.' If he didn't mind, I'd been detained for long enough, though of course I returned to the drudgery of Glaze's correspondence with that accustomed lack of zeal.

Remember how I soaked poor Isabelle's tired feet? Well...

c/o Crispin J. Tucker
English Dept
University of Pittsburgh
Pittsburgh PA 15260
28 June 1992

Dear Marsy,

Dr Tucker has a wonderful daughter, which one lusty cynic, who personally knew her medic, puts down to her 'pneumatic implants' – so vividly phrased. She isn't the only girl got at here, under pressure of smallness – for in every sense this is a vast and overwhelming country. How many more I can only guess have felt the need for similar amplification. Truly this is a market for your books, Marsy.

She is the star student in a recently rehashed writing course, and is about to do her dissertation. I saw her taking notes at one of my lectures, which I promised to enlarge on provided she discuss a vacancy I have. Silicone or no, Exe demands the highest calibre, and I always need researchers.

Dr Tucker has professional and personal connections with the visual block builder Newsome Barringer, a deeply tanned native of Arizona, and an awesomely confident man. His *Golgotha 2000* – a 'masterpiece' of postmodernism – was at a private showing on the plush fifth floor of a life assurance firm (all glass, aluminium, plastic), who as investors and promoters are by far his major sponsor. The said piece, *Golgotha*, is a 'staggering' achievement, which sadly knows no counterpart in contemporary writing – with the possible exception of certain descriptive interlocks found in your *Aristotle*. *Golgotha 2000*, an enlarged human cranium, models that patchwork we know as the modern city. You can see streets, the lights, the cars. The whole is bathed in a glow of fluorescent green.

Barringer, over a fleeting handshake, assured me that all exhibits would at some point come to, ahem, 'Lunnon, Ing-lan'. So, if you have the chance, be sure not to miss it. Because, Marsy, that would be a pity.

Mercifully this 'time' question seems to have subsided. Thanks again for your support. I have had to field several off-the-record queries, the most persistent from Penny Tucker, naturally. Happily I seem to have persuaded her I was never promoting a theory at all, but rather have had one thrust upon me. Sunny days, I hope.

Signing off, Andrew

I can correct one misapprehension – and only one. The phoney Barringer finds me magnanimous, with no words at all for his stunted cave work – those rudimentary acts of discourse – and best left to the weekend's mindless supplements. That's where the *Golgotha* sample caught my eye, over a much more alluring breakfast egg. I am, as I say, magnanimous.

Again to the satin of time, with its shimmer on all of our dead yesterdays. I checked out certain items from the universal properties dept, in particular a nice pair of clocks, each consistent with theoretical relativity. What cosmic pyrotechnics shall I envisage or reflect on, when Glaze's dated missives form a symmetry with mine? *His* June approaches *my* July, and that makes it possible our changing day and month may correspond at some point, though our year never will. You will please permit my third timepiece, a projection into that floating fourteen days, where I live in the warm glow that comes with a publisher's advance. Here in a stone cottage the winged light of my standard lamp washes the quartered hues – there is ochre, yellow, blue, green – on a stud wall backing, its dabs of paint more subdued in its yellow than in natural light, or daytime. The table is round, dark red at its surface. Somewhere is a stylised bowler Merle has got from a joke outfitter's – one she found locally. The location, a southerly spur of Dartmoor. I pore over, review, revise this page, paragraph, *this* very sentence. Time, or the question of time, shall not allow Professor Glaze off its general hook.

Did Marsy really care? You be the judge.

Flat 5
147 Trefoil Street
SW18
8 July 1992

Dear Andrew,

I knew you'd sort it. Really it's down to that way you have of not standing for nonsense. Bravo.

I'm going to upset you. These conflicts of interest put the decision against the golden girl – Miss Clean from Bath. I've gone for the technician, Alistair. I am tempted to have a go at something sci-fi. You know, one of those turgid, futuristic things. He'd make good material. I hope he lasts that long. Though I've a feeling the real world of books will be a jolt. A blip in his microchips.

My man from Spaghetti and Hoop keeps driving me up Haverstock Hill, and points to all those rock star mansions. O what illustrious company. Seen one or two things I like. Any chance you might get back for the housewarming?

Onward. Upward. Marsy

Clocks one, two: all movement suspended. Clock three, a quartz, tockle me a heraldee across my firmament. To re-announce, verbatim, what?

> Time's abundance,
> A maze of intersecting lines.
> Zob, his doorbell's profundance:
> Can any bright note out-ring
> His chimes?

…is not the right sequence. I'm tired, and my mind has strayed (to that wiry poet, with his yellow book, his grip, his two pound coins). More coffee, I think. Perhaps this—

> Time's implacable layer,
> Layer on layer on layer—
> Is there no restitution,
> No de-laying of each new layer?

Yes. That is better. Now, 'time', for the duration of what amounts to an editorial interlude, is as accords with quartzy clock three. That is after the death of Glaze, and after the death of Zob, metaphorically. It was he, my unwitting master, who suggested the stone cottage, with its little square panes set off icy in its cold solid casements. There is so uncluttered a view of the plough, whose studs of varying brilliance, in the clear canopy of night.... Forsooth! I detect that yellow poet, back with his wiry book.... A third cup of coffee.... Must try to stay awake....

Now. Let's run that again. It was Geraldine's idea, and *her* exclamation: 'Wouldn't it be lovely! Property! I mean round here!' To me it betrayed premeditation. We later discovered, over an outdoor table, where my notebook records the White Hart at Dartington, that a firm called Stags had given her printed details of several such dwellings, all similarly isolated. She drank, I recall, a glass of iced Bacardi. Zob, having bought but showing no thirst for his continental lager, shuffled those stag-emblazoned photographs (a predictable logo) under the deep cigar-shaped shadow of our parasol. Again Crouch fingered, mulled it over, longed, she said, while the sun caressed her sandalled foot, for a look at *this* one (here where I pen my corrections), on the southern slopes of the moor. A handwritten addendum, or rather vortex in ballpoint, confirmed that while the vendor sought a buyer, short lets might be considered. I drove them over – not in the silver Mercedes, but while they canoodled, a riot of limbs in my rear view, in Geraldine's soft top, with white hood, grey flashing. We found the garden overgrown and filled with potential – as, execrably, I paraphrase the blurb. Sole heating was a multi-fuel burner, a black monstrosity monopolising the irregularly shaped sitting room, a rectangle with one corner sliced by a diagonal, on whose far side downstairs facilities had been added. Zob could smell damp, Geraldine only honeysuckle. He said – or did he ruminate? – that as brilliant London writer now wasn't the time for country retreats. Though it has to be said it *was* very quiet, 'perfect' for revision work.

The den off the sitting room was adequate as a study. You entered via an open arch, which the three of us did, singly. Of course, *I* brought up the rear, subdued and not at all talkative, and lost to a private swirl of personal thoughts. On the day of our viewing, its sole furnishings were a stuffed, old-fashioned armchair, whose two front feet were fitted with castors, and a four-legged, iron-framed table, where someone – a previous occupant – had left a water jug. Its glass was filmed in a residue of orange juice, and there were two accompanying tumblers, one of them brushed with mould. The colour scheme lacked symmetry, reminiscent of Zob's first creative era, with its free love, summer festivals, and the problems of intimate relationships. In those days these had been aired under a blustery sky, when Zob took part in a lot of public gatherings. The walls (see above) were blocks in yellow, ochre, blue, green. The wood floor was a brown-orange burnish, with marks and stains dating to the last period of redecoration.

Geraldine remarked how easy it would be to do the place up, and went on and on, about the money for one thing – no problem there. Then the beaches, which were all so near, yet to Zob so highly repugnant. He, a pale metropolitan, fried in the sun. Then there were the walks brrrng! I said the walks brrrng!

Time tells me clocks pressing one and two will supersede. Away, quartz three!

c/o Maura Grimm
Department of English
Bowling Green State University
Bowling Green OH 43403
17 July 1992

Dear Marsy,

Regrets re Miss Clean, not that I remember her – though I do recall, on numerous occasions, the question have I been to Cadiz. I haven't.

Make sure this Alistair doesn't overstep his brief. It's fine if you want all that techno stuff, complete with its man with screwdriver. Electronic inroads – if that's what you have an eye to – are merely an adjunct of the way our network already works, and as to communications generally, that you should leave to the publicity people. They are (I understand) more than usually clued up.

I worry about computers. I worry they will offer scope to any old blagueur, those who rely on calculated luck, and are never in the sense that we understand professional. Anything new to unsettle the status quo is always appealing to outsiders, quick to accuse *us* of lacking in principle.

I'm not sure that a foray into the swamps of sci-fi is advisable for you. I can't help but think its mystery is really a kind of *mysticism*, its prophecies a cloak on what at its heart is medievalism. Real insight is in the here and now, and yours is the crystal analysis of England as is now experienced – all done it seems so effortlessly. I think you'd waste your time trying to understand madmen like Hawking, whose chapter 'The Arrow of Time' – in view of my present plight – I did attempt to read, someone having rudely thrust it under my nose. Alas that whole question has resurfaced. A bonny-faced youth from some godforsaken faculty asked if I saw parallels between that conception and what's alleged to be my own. I would have liked to tell him the future is dead, as are all who pass over its horizon. All life will end, he said, in a black hole. It's tedious.

By the way Penelope Tucker pressed her implants to my elbow, and asked me to do a piece for her quarterly review. Said I'd have to think about it, but with no real hesitation eventually mailed her a double-A4. It's called 'Marshall Zob, First Man of English Letters'. Hope this helps to raise your profile here. The market's so enormous, if you can tap in.

The best for a red-hot housewarming. Shall be there in all but the flesh.

Andrew

No comment – despite the insistent alarum, which on the flimsiest strand of midnight my quartz clock three interjected with. It was later, while I watched its thin fingers jointly overshadow a long Roman I, that I abandoned my manuscript, tossing it into the hollows of my rented sofa, thence clattered up the wooden stair to bed. This morning it is grey. My copper-green ashtrays, full from the night before, I see have new and incredible niches. All my north windows, whose complex is multiple, show me their varying angles relative to that single vista, the moor, whose hue is a distant *verd-antique*, and whose peak is still tonsured by the hanging mists of dawn. Those tufted blades of grass in the fringes of my garden arc to the pendent glue in the ensnared, yet inexorably earthbound droplets of dew. Of what prophecy is this, my wilderness? And shall I beat an egg for breakfast, or simply break bread? And there is one other important point to debate. Shall I renew my depleted pack of cigarettes right now (and that means a drive), or sharpen the red crayon of my trade? Where did I leave that manuscript? Where?

An hour's work. Then the drive. Then I get back, having bought a yellow coat with scarf to match, as well as cigarettes – in a charity shop. The coat has buttons at the cuffs, a pair. I keep it on indoors, where in all weathers it is cold and damp. I sit glumly with my smokes. Writing is a solitary occupation.

> Flat 5
> 147 Trefoil Street
> SW18
> 28 July 1992

Dear Andrew,

Tucker. I know that name. Did Crispin J. once have something to do with Blandford? Or was that Tusker? Maybe not.

Don't worry about Alistair. I am hiring him only for the job of technician, and he doesn't in any case start till I move. On that I shall have to delay. That's because I've landed the first couple in London whose conveyancer I expect will sign himself Pedant from Edmonton. He is determined *not* to exchange. Question: Can I provide evidence of damp proofing? Answer: No. This is a first-floor flat. Question: Well, if not rising, penetrating. Counter question: Have you read your clients' surveyor's report? Answer (intransigent): Evidence of all precautions taken against a propensity to penetrating damp must be supplied. Answer to answer: My own surveyor, on *my* purchase of property, did not draw attention to that problem.

I'm sure we'll explore similar pleasantries re timber infestation.

Can't agree, Andrew, with your assessment apropos of sci-fi genre. If (big if) I went that way, I couldn't be bothered with Hawking, Penrose et al. I think I would – in fact I've started to do this already – absorb the 'culture'. You know, take my cue from others in that field. Books. Movies. A glance at the 'zines.

Method. That's the real science.

All the best. Marsy

By my three clocks I denounce, categorically, that commercialised decade recalled in assassinations and a moon landing, a time of easy terrestrial trade in the moulded goods of psychedelia. It makes it hard to admit an unexpected visitor, who comes as an invasion of my page, and whose name is Max. He wears his hair long. Stitched to the unholy knees of his denims are patches of Paisley. He has parked his station wagon under the greened filigree of a roadside hawthorn, a utility run-around whose livery is a nondescript brown, but augmented with gold pentacles in enfolding clouds of tangerine. A ram, its coarse pelage a muddy cream, has poked its black muzzle through the dilapidated pales of my fence – a picket fence – and is munching weeds. Max – a man without a business card – I note with fatigued alarm is encrusted at one nostril with paste or a gem. Which, I shall not inquire. He has a portfolio. He wants to sell me 'artwork'. I am obliged to look, and therefore hum and hum.

'Well?'

'Well what?'

'Like it?'

Guffaw (beg pardon). Isn't – isn't that dusky Pegasus, afloat in the radial spokes of sunset – just a bit *passé!*

'Oh well something classical.'

Ah now what's this? The pelagic, tragic Triton. Now really! I shall have to explain a long and recent history with my landlady's cat.

'Landlady's cat!'

Yes. It's made me phobic. Even at the sight of what shall we call these, fish scales…? It reminds me of Malkin at meal time. Anyway, those translucent waves, that phantasised element your mythologised merman seems to command: it was done with briny lips to a twisted seashell, not as you have it here a cream horn. Sorry.

I closed the door. I heard phuts of exhaust, then the souped-up tune of his engine. My reading lamp, with its pyramid of thinning light, eerily diminished the rose amendments and emendations encrypting this present leaf. Time, as I hold to the square panes a glass of falling sands, had fused the sovereign anatomies of three distinctive clocks. I tossed my crushed cigarette pack, whose inflorescence was red and white, over a chair, and watched it rise and spin over a rug, then fall on the line of a parabola into the shade of my bin. For a moment I transposed its flight to a sky of perfect peach, so that I recalled now that I do not mention this, once when I had written this journal, or that I overlook certain cold articles junked in the Wandsworth room (excuse – an unavoidable collision of tenses). Here there was row on row of science fantasy tales from the house of Gollancz, and here too, in Zob's old video library, were those technicolored, outlandishly creatured yarns, all of galactic warfare.

Must get back to my manuscript.

c/o Finnegan Rich
Cleveland State University
RT1216
Cleveland OH 44115
9 August 1992

Dear Marsy,

Rabbit is, Finnegan isn't, rich. My host's a man obsessed with his failures, notably Broadway in the mid-1970s. If not for his critics, he says – 'foul sons of art' – New York's big box office would long ago have showered him with gold. He doesn't hide his disaffection with his job. He tells me he's discomfited – and wouldn't anyone be? – by the threadbare socks he wears, though there's absolutely no need for this. It takes all sorts.

I got Sam on the phone today, increasingly girlish. The bull-neck, whose virility's the platinum tint of his credit cards, wows her nightly, in a range of bowties, through an endless chain of hotels and restaurants, some of which he owns. The man is all dinner dates. We, Marsy, may smile. Last week she met the mayor. Also a billionaire attorney. And seems to think it significant human experience!

Grave interjection (because there's worse). She's got herself light-headed and grandmotherly, because Jessica's boy is due in less than a week from now – or so I'm told. The bull-neck's going to put her on Concorde, and will arrange for a limousine from Heathrow to Cambridge, where I've told her to investigate care options. Not such a blue sky.

Take care. Andrew

Hasty PS. I committed the hideous error of allowing poor Finnegan Rich a preview of my lecture notes, who perused, then passed them on to an assistant. I really don't deserve this. That person views my repeated disavowal of 'literary time' as unduly modest, and has given it the full dignity of philosophical discourse. I find myself with St Thomas, opposing Duns Scotus (a quite terrible fate), late to the gatehouse with my own 'fascinating' slant on the 'principle of individuation'. What does this mean, Marsy? As far as I understand it, it's this. Take two individuals that belong to the same species, and ask: are they different in essence, or are they essentially the same? St Thomas – and so, it seems, do I – takes the latter view, in respect of material substances. Duns Scotus (c1270–1308!) does not. St Thomas can justify it so: that matter consists of undifferentiated parts, to be distinguished only by a difference of position in space. Of course fool that I am, a chance remark I made once and unthinkingly is seen as the metaphoric unravelling of time, and furthermore something I describe spatially.

PPS. What a relief! No one brought up this mumbo-jumbo in the lecture, which went well and precisely to my pocket watch.

Andrew (born 1935!)...

...round all of which the moor-ish Alistair Wye has inscribed a crayon mark, in stoplight red. That's specifically for Merle, when on those dampish green evenings she will join me here, and under the prowling tock of my quartz clock will read my manuscript. (I note that, in its titanic force of anti-climax, a temporal clash of heads has been avoided, which is perhaps why our shared universe still squeaks along undisturbed. I refer, of course, to my eighteenth of July – overtaken without incident by Glaze's August. Also see above his hasty PS.)

Flat 5

147 Trefoil Street

SW18

20 August 1992

Dear Andrew,

I get the picture – being repetitive. How we've all discussed this, endlessly into the mornings. Don't you remember you told me on the one hand there are challenges it's useful to take up, while on the other there are mostly academic oddballs. I'd avoid them, which I seem to recall was your advice for me.

You can see my address hasn't changed. It's exactly as predicted. That is, having never treated the timbers – because there's been no need – Pedant of Edmonton wants guarantees against dry rot, wet rot and insect infestation. I'm about to withdraw and re-launch under another agent. I think that's my quickest option.

Blandford wanted me to do a quirky piece on that Nostradamus you can sometimes see at the intersection of Oxford and Regent Street. You'll have heard him, will have seen his sandwich board. Sins of the flesh. End of the world is nigh. All that spittle on his beard gave me reservations – would give anyone reservations – when Blandford proposed an interview. Ergo I talked to passers-by, shop and insurance people, for *their* impressions. Yes, I thought, an 'impressions' piece. Blandford will like.

Now who should happen along but Giles, who was on his way from Hamleys, with a mobile, a cuddly chick and a string of brightly coloured plastic balls for the cot. I assume you've heard the news, so I shouldn't have to explain. Giles was even joyful, and thinks *you* should be. *I* think you should be.

Easy. Marsy

I have smoked almost the whole new pack, and am reminded, as I flick at a warm crust of fallen ash, that Glaze set certain cold limits to all probable eventualities, after so much life as airsmudge. [Merle, you will have to believe me, as I explain that volcanic deposit above. It's untimely, yes, in a Glazean sense of the word. I promise you, it's the unwitting censor of only one costly syllable – that syllable is 'mail'. It's by no means the worst infelicity I am sure to brush up on, come evening – over a glass perhaps of local beer. Anyway in framing this the following comes to mind: so much life as hot air. But enough of that.] Glaze's response was quick, laconic, and sour, and was penned in large schoolboy letters on a postcard, whose scene was an ink line drawing of the Old State Capitol at Springfield—

Evanston IL, August 28th. Marsy. There are things you don't understand. You're a bachelor. The family's 'joy' isn't even at a boy. If I've got this right they're going to call it Amanda. This is precisely the tribal infiltration that dilutes first local then national culture. It doesn't have my blessing. You I thought knew better. What's worse is this week I have felt I do want to come home, but not for that reason. The weather here's subject to extremes as well.
Yours. Andrew

So too here in the wet verdant future on the fringes of Dartmoor, a privileged perspective I shall shortly cast back into its proper chronology, an all-day deluge, a constant film on my windowpanes, is also a pattern of lakes in that rustic wilderness outside, my garden. Shall I, booted, caped, sou'westered, splosh to the pub on that Ariel stroke of nine, or stay home with a *vin de Bourgogne*? Whatever. I must get back.

July 19 Zob, cocooned in his study, with a tall glass of coffee courtesy Mrs St John, intercepted the day's first call before I could reach my extension. I returned to the windowsill, whose pattern of accidental burns this morning's cigarette had added to. By now the campanula had gone over.

I looked at today's mail, bum phodder all (pardon that eccentric spelling. I happen to like it). I struggled on with it gamely, to the point of an nth loan offer, with a competitive APR – and noted Zob's extension light as the thing went out, then immediately relit (its little amber oblong). Zob had dialled out, I learned, to Cornelius, who was not at his office, and who called back at about midday, by which time Zob had gone out. Ergo—

'Merle's given me an angle,' Snell said, defiling her name, 'on this new scheme of Philip's....' I grunted knowledgeably, the result being that a whole lit roadway unwound itself, with following milestones—

1 Raptorial Mastabyle had wheedled his way into commercial radio.
2 His brand-new show, slanted with bias, which he claimed was intentionally unoriginal, announced itself under a much thought about and finally insipid title.
3 After much deliberation, that was *Talking Music*.
4 Marsy, proposed first guest, would talk conversationally about his 'interesting'

life, with eight chosen discs interspersed, from which extracts would be played, and discussed.

5 The show would go out to coincide with the nation's Sunday lunch. That's something Jimmy Clitheroe had done.

'Marvellous opportunity, don't you think?'
Yes, Cornelius.

July 20 Adam has broken his hoe.

July 21 A proposed meeting, with a ten o'clock start, was not convened yesterday, because there would have been no one but me (I, of course, must take minutes) to keep Snell copiously topped with coffee. 'Fresh. And I mean fresh.' Poor Mrs Clapp.
Adam has broken his toe.

July 22 Thank heaven it's Friday.

Subject Talking Music	**From** Alistair
Date 7-22, 11:41:36	**Reply to** Box #2, Ext #2, Wye

Text: Marsy, this insofar as my minutes record was the course of yesterday's discussion—

1 Snell very alive to this as further publicity opportunity. Urged that you know what public you want to reach. His preference, as usual, is as broad a church as possible – all ages, all walks of life. *Point was agreed.*

2 Important you present very human side. Talk about family life as you grew up. Reflect on: parental influence (wholesome), schooling (irksome), school friends (harmlessly pranksome), holidays (never exotic). Crucial to claim ignorance of father as establishment academic. The masses, which means mostly life's losers, are always so touchy on nepotism. *Point was agreed.*

3 Student life. Play down elitist nature of Exe's ancient institution. Point up camaraderie with working-class contemporaries. Abiding image is: receptive young man taking first tentative steps across threshold of twentieth-century literature, as opposed to Oxford classics. *Point was agreed.*

4 Professional life. Can make much here of initial commercial failure, i.e. *Aristotle's Atom*. Implication being society's usual tendency to value its gifts belatedly. *Point was agreed.*

5 Current activities. Short break after immense labours over *Gimme the Cash*, a chance to reiterate that this is currently on sale, and, you believe, shortlisted for Best Novel to be Published This Decade. *Point was agreed.*

6 Plans for immediate future. Keenness to participate in commemorative process re Andrew Glaze – 'friend, mentor, brilliant academic' – who died so tragically

only last year. A tremendous, appalling loss, not only personally, but to English letters generally. *Point was agreed.*

7 The long term. Your most ambitious undertaking, a millennial novel, whose panoramic survey is a broad sweep across the whole Christian era. A tapestry of social history embossed with futuristic speculation. *Point was agreed.*

8 In summary. A kind of conclusion, to put those eight chosen discs in chronological perspective – i.e., what each piece of music has meant at its corresponding stage of life. We have to be careful here, given that all eight selections must in totality have that same broad appeal your comments are tailored to. [This being in Snell's view so critical, it forms separate bullet points, at 9 (below)].

9 Discs.

i. From Sixties/childhood Snell recommends cherubic Beatles as opposed to *your* preference, rebellious Rolling Stones. We want to keep it clean (so perhaps something to sentimentalise the dead John Lennon: *There are places I remember…*).

ii. The emotional pyrotechnics of youth. Snell advises avoid at all costs the grotesquerie of a Mahler say. Keep it simple, effective. Suggested candidates were: 1812 Overture, Beethoven's Fifth, Brahms' Piano Concerto No 1. Slight hints here at the avant-garde could be along the lines of, for example, *The Rite of Spring* – but nothing that is now controversial. We don't want a Boulez creeping in.

iii. Solace. Everyone needs it when things don't go well. So, early professional life could be accompanied by: that Albinoni Adagio, or the Pachelbel Canon, even a 'Brandenburg'. Or what about some jazz?

iv. An all-time favourite. We all have one. That piece we never tire of listening to. There are some obvious choices. The Elgar Cello Concerto, perhaps with du Pré (who in herself elicits sighs). Or that Rodrigo guitar piece, which is still v popular. Or some good old Haydn rum-te-tum.

v. Opera has a surprisingly large following, even among those without much money. This is an easy one. Domingo or Pavarotti, with a Verdi or Puccini highlight. Something that really grabs. Italia '90 springs to mind.

vi. Contemporary awareness. One could acknowledge those minimalists, just to show interest in progress in other disciplines. But *don't* choose any rhythmic drumming, handclaps, or syncopated vocals!

vii. Personal horizons. By this is meant a composer you say you know little of now but would like to explore. That doesn't mean someone obscure. It's something you've never quite got round to. You could try Wagner.

viii. No intellectual it seems can overlook Mozart (bit like Shakespeare). Understand *The Magic Flute* is highly thought of.

Points, Marsy, agreed.

July 23 Isabelle, who has bought a jade bikini, refuses to put it on. We talked about this in the bathroom, where we met accidentally, and where I mentioned Adam's toe. She pressed my hand to her midriff, though the seduction ended there – with litany and variations on her accumulated pounds.

Isabelle! You look, you feel, just fine....

July 25 Oh what a yawn, being Monday.

> **Subject** Talking Music (minutes)   **From** Marsy
> **Date** 7-25, 10:11:41   **Reply to** Box #1, Ext #1, Zob
> Text: Al – That's fine, that looks about right. Any chance you know *why* this *Magic Flute* is so regarded?
> PS How do I direct a copy of this via fax to Cornelius?

Well.... It's why you always need a man with a brown lab coat and a screwdriver. So...bringing my massive intellect to bear...I shall, Marsy, take these queries in reverse order—

Item. On that simple technical question, really all you need to do is export the bulletin to the outgoing fax queue, led by the prompts up to and including a request for the target fax number. 'Export' can be done in one of two ways, either by source filename (which in this case happens to be c:\B_BOARD\SEND\T$0059), or by date stamp, which is of course DS7-25_10:11:41. EXPORT appears on your foreground list of options.

Item. This too is a technical question, but at the borders of metaphysics. Perhaps I can put it so—

SYNOPSIS, The Magic (Hampstead) Flute

Cast Queen of the Night
Pamina (her daughter) – played by Wye
Veiled ladies, boys – of the Queen's retinue
Papageno, a rustic – played by Snell
Sarastro
Monostatos, a lustful Moor – played by Zob
Papagena, a wrinkled hag – played by Crouch
Tamino, a handsome youth – played by Merle
Attendants, priests, mechanicals etc.

Scene Rocky terrain, dotted with twisted trees. Distant hills. A temple. The sky, azure graded to scarlet. Enter Tamino (Merle). Enter serpent, scales a lurid green, eyes a reddish yellow, fangs. Tamino (Merle) overcome by reptile. Three veiled ladies, each armed with Olympic javelin, appear and together rescue Tamino, who is now unconscious. With reluctance they abandon him, bound to report the event to their mistress, who is of course Queen of the Night. Enter Papageno (Snell), royal bird catcher, who stumbles on a waking Tamino. Cannot help but claim, in usual good-natured mendacity, that he (Snell) has fought off the serpent. Merle, Tamino, is grateful, though returning ladies berate Papageno on learning of his or Snell's dishonesty. Queen of the Night has dispatched three ladies with portrait of her daughter – Pamina, played by Wye – with which Tamino becomes enchanted. As you can see, this was a bad mistake by Zob, and allows me to put on my four-cornered lecture hat.

Aria: This portrait so enchanting etc.

Scene Resplendent chamber. Sumptuous drapes, gilded chairs, refulgent candelabra. Queen, Tamino. Queen insists that if Tamino (Merle) rescues her daughter – Pamina, quietly played by Wye – she (the Queen) will offer Merle Alistair's hand. Pamina is held captive by Sarastro.

Recitative and aria: O tremble not, dear son etc.

Scene Rocky terrain (again). Sky a steely blue. To keep him from danger, Tamino receives from ladies first a magic flute, then additionally a copy of *Strong Opinions* (this is a book of wisdom by the incredible Sirin). Papageno is given a miraculous chime of bells. Queen summons her boys to guide them to Sarastro's palace.

Scene Egyptian chamber. Sculpted sphinx. A casket inlaid with hieroglyphs. Faience cup in form of lotus flower. A wall painting, depicting slaves with a tribute of ebony, ivory, pelts, a leopard, a monkey. Attached to a wall is a throw stick. Above this is a mounted scarab. Monostatos, who as Moor is played by Zob, has foiled Pamina's attempted escape, therefore Wye must suffer his captor's bookish halitosis until he is rescued. Monostatos is intent on making her, Pamina, servile, but runs off distracted when Papageno (a strange and bucolic-looking Snell) tumbles into the action. Papageno has arrived ahead of Tamino, and of that comely youth he informs Pamina.

He, he, he – he loves me then?

Scene A leafy grove, with blossoms. To rear, temple colonnaded to two others flanking. On a lintel is engraved TEMPLE OF WISDOM, while those flanking are TEMPLE OF REASON, TEMPLE OF NATURE. Tamino has reached the temple, which is ruled by Sarastro. Pamina (the bewildered Wye), escaping with Papageno (the cheery Snell), is again checked by the evil Monostatos (envious Zob). Zob is prevented from inflicting permanent harm only by that magic chime of bells.

Enter Sarastro, with entourage, also with triumphal car, which is drawn by six lions. The two lovers (i.e. Al and Merle) meet for the first time. [Starburst, in enriched purple.] Sarastro deems that Zob be punished, and that Tamino and Papageno be brought to the temple for trial. He escorts Pamina to his sanctum. I'm sorry if this goes on.

Chorus
Ah, divine wisdom – long live Sarastro!
His rewards and his punishments
Are one manifesto.

Scene A palm grove. Silvered bark, gilded leaves. Eighteen thrones are arranged on a sylvan floor. Each throne accompanies a decorative pyramid and inlaid cornucopia, the largest of which are set at the centre. Sarastro explains to gathering of priests how he abducted from the tyrannical Queen of the Night her daughter Pamina (who is played by Wye, and who will win out in the end). He states that Pamina (Wye) is destined by the gods for Tamino (Merle). This will take place in an Olympian heaven. Pamina he is about to admit to the 'Consecrated Band'. Tamino (dearest Merle) must now prove himself in a preordained trial of (and to Zob these are alien concepts): steadfastness, constancy, courage. To the Queen too these matters are alien, who now tries to persuade her daughter to murder Sarastro (as if I would!). Zob, that lustful Monostatos, in creeping up slyly on Pamina gets wind of the Queen's ideas, and hopes to inspire an enraged Sarastro to revenge (but Sarastro isn't enraged, and instead banishes Monostatos). Now, as this is getting all a bit too saturnine, we need a comic aside. Let us again to Papageno (that periphery man called Snell), a gourmand, who in his earthiness cannot himself be consecrated. We witness his ribald exchange with the hag Papagena (enter, stage left, our own Geraldine Crouch). Presto! Crouch suddenly seems attractive, and will satisfy his bedsprings.
Ja, mein Engel!

Scene Small garden. Perhaps a well. Perhaps a little pond. Trees certainly. Three boys prevent a disconsolate Pamina from committing suicide (not that I would ever consider this option), and lead her to Tamino. Allow me just to scratch my head as I tilt my four-cornered hat.

Tutti
Two intertwining, destined souls
Can't be bound by commercial roles,
While PR men in their media den
Advocate only accountancy goals.

Scene Two mountains, one with the loud, subterranean, gem-encrusted torrent of a waterfall, the other erupting fire. Cavities in the mountain walls make these visible. To the sounds of a magic flute, and clutching a book of wisdom, Tamino and Pamina traverse these caverns (i.e. fire and water), and survive their ordeal. This is a moment of genuine celebration, because of course art as well as life is affirmed. The works of Monostatos (or the novels of Zob) may be banished to the flames. The night will consume its Queen.

Chorus
Triumph and victory! The destined pair
Overcome each snare
And achieve their consecration,
Their very-cel-e-bra-tion!

Scene Garden again. Papageno/Papagena in symbiotic embrace. They plan for several children. Then final onslaught from Queen of the Night, who in alliance with Zob, I mean the Moor, is thwarted.

Scene Radiant sun. Sarastro brings lovers together, O happy dénouement. Tamino and Pamina attired in priestly garb. So fortitude has triumphed, even in our Zobbish era of media cynicism, with 'Beauty', 'Wisdom', finally and everlastingly crowned. There are few who believe this still to be possible.

Chorus
Heil sei euch Geweihten! etc.

Here. You. Hang up my hat. It might just be better to show Zob an open page of Kobbé.

July 26 Here is one of those miracles of muffled suburbia, its signature a zing of warm blood, or now as it mounts to a torrent the physiological roar of selfdom in both my ears. The milkman did not clatter his duellist's bottles at dawn. You, my seconds, must believe I woke other-worldish, in a woolly cocoon, in the womb of my duvet. My drawn curtain simulated twilight. Then came the mild thud of my radio alarm as this, itself in a dream, ushered in the tender beams of a 'Moonlight', or an opening piano movement played by Alfred Brendel.

The house was deserted. No Isabelle, Michael, Malkin. Nor did I find Zob, nor Mrs St John, who was on the trail of vacuum bags, on arriving, quietly, at work. Zob's business diary, open to today's page, placed him with Philip, who had arranged for a rehearsal without engineers. Adam, somewhere hopping for his breakfast, remained absent too (away, curl of his lip). I smoked my cigarette out on the patio – slabs a chalky white, with lacquered, alternating charcoal blue, a design that Zob had fondly called 'Renaissance'. A demotic cabbage white opened, closed, reopened its wings, considered, then abandoned the mauve tips of a buddleia. A first pale flicker danced on the dewy crystal, that over-spanning arc, whose brown vault is London's northwest sky. A nice day coming.

July 27 Isabelle has car trouble (suspension), and has left her Citroën at Dollis Hill – in the hands, she says, of a meticulously oafish mechanic. That 'nice married man' across the road (it's irksome I have never noticed him) helped her shuttle to and fro. Zob was equally perplexed, checking his inside pocket, thinking he'd seized on, then knowing he'd mislaid his small red pocketbook – in fact a diary. 'You haven't seen it, eh, Al?'

Um. No.

July 28 I find, because Merle faxed me her minutes, that this morning's meeting – not here, but at New Caxton Grove – had been convened for the discussion of one further enterprise at the hands of Philip Mastabyle. This was very much to do with contact he had made with Jacqueline Keys, a new name insofar as my memoir goes, but someone I instantly remember I have met. Let me call your attention to that happy occasion.

She was and remains a tea-drinker, and is, as Philip suggests, 'quite big' administratively in the Free City Festival – in fact she's the co-ordinating director. However. That's jumping ahead. I must go back to Zob, at about this time last year, who had got himself in a lather over something (don't know what, don't care). His repeated failure to hire a dispatch rider – being early on a Saturday – meant muggins here eventually drove, foot flat on the gas, to the brakes of Great Magner, with a package. At that time I had only recently acquired that battered Ford. Miss Jacqueline Keys, a remote sheen in her hairstyle – a bob – I had been briefed to identify.

'Look out for a tartan Thermos.'

I parked with confidence under an eddy of maple leaves, in the shadow of a tower – both the shadow and tower Gothic Revival. I opened my door to the sound of crows. Atmospherically I crunched across the gravel….

I had arrived for the last edifying moments of her summer school, her class of '93. Her many students, majestically hungry and rumbling, had been bewitched by Scandinavian culture, and under present auspices termed themselves 'Hamsunite' – even during a tea break. They weren't particularly young, though lounged in the typical pose of youth, in twos, or threes, or singly, where there were benches screened in arbours, or plainly on the lawns. Zob's package was addressed to the Great Magner School of English.

'Is that too,' I asked pointing, 'a part of it?' I had my distant gaze on a circular folly, matted in moss from the ground to the cone of its roof.

'All you can see,' she said. Such Attic tranquillity our Hamsunites reposed in. A sigh….

Miss Keys had the seat of her jodhpurs firmly to a woodcutter's log, whose remnant of bark was mottled with fungus. Scars of damp sunshine crisscrossed in auburn in the light chestnut of her bob, but dissolved abruptly – a cloud, a wash of blue-black distemper, cancelling that English moment of sun. Her flask was horizontal in the short grass and decapitated daisies, though its plastic cup of muddy-looking tea sent up a column of steam, which my few steps nearer agitated.

'Miss Keys,' I said, and motioned the package, which was important and padded. That passing cloud, now in the rotating shape of a wildebeest, parted at its head and torso, allowing one liquid fragment of sunshine.

'Now please call me Jacqui.' She removed from her knees (and brushed down her jodhpurs) a Scotch egg in a paper serviette.

'Urgent dispatch. From Mr Marshall Zob.'

She quizzed, in the pucker of her lips, which continued, meekly, to smile. Then having thought a bit certain questions in *her* mind must have been resolved. That I could see in the bright arch of her pencilled eyebrows.

'Ah yes,' she said, 'I know....' She stood up and put her cup of tea on the log. She took and ignored the parcel, because – what a nice place, I said. She told me about the inception of her summer school. Why do I encumber you with this?

Well. I drove away, just as a crow flapped around that ornamental tower. I pulled up for sheep in lanes. Was rounded by a collie. I emerged, in a dream of country spires, with a fan of red mud to my offside wing. I forgot, with my wet tyres to the motorway, all about Miss Keys – until, that was, today. Careers of course move on. Her borrowed venues for books, with now no sign of Hamsun, was through her links to the world of trade exhibitions, and a role these days as festival organiser. For that she'd been wooed. Mastabyle had bought her, intellectually, an after-dinner drink. Something he said over a calvados had secured him a slot at the Free City Festival, the real *coup* being for the opening day. The programme was yet to be finalised, with the event now imminent. Naturally he had thought of friend and top writer Marsy, who when sounded out agreed to a lunchtime session, whose format the two would meet to discuss. Of course Cornelius had to thrash out details. (No word by the way from Flude, which might explain this fax from an enchanted Tamino.)

Here was the set-up. It is assumed (it is assumed by Cornelius) that any paying audience, and here I quote Merle's fax, 'will be composed largely of would-be writers....' Joint abettors are Philip and Snell. Glazed bust with laurel is that of Marshall Zob. The belief – and I am afraid this is inveterate – is that no one within that shaky circle, blue on road maps, and in all ways London's orbital – and certainly no one outside it – is capable of approaching the impossibly high standard set by a text by Marshall Zob. (Allow me to snigger into my flight bag.) Let me say in passing that for Cornelius it was never worth his while to open the mail, except of course to clip to its contents that standard, and by now well rehearsed *Dear X, Regrettably our client list is currently full*, X being a Tolstoy or a Bloggs. These are the parameters I want you to understand, since, as I now float free of my worldly obligations, with such sweet joy in a publisher's advance, I am able to paraphrase that deliciously practical ethic our world-led trio beat out with Hephaestus's irons—

MZ Okay. We'll be seated, on a raised platform, with microphones. You will ask questions.

PM Absolutely.

CS Moreover, Marsy – questions on how to get published.

PM Got it in one, Cornelius. Propaganda line is this. You try and try and try. Eventually you write a good book. This is the only way.

CS Good books always find a publisher. Caution: don't analyse 'good' and 'bad'. And DON'T discuss the net book agreement.

PM/MZ Okay.

But enough. A filter on this tragic scene. (I, Wye, have been huffing all day, and must buy myself an expectorant.) Contain your contumely, you fellow-scribes in vain. Pay out, I say, good money for verse (not festivals). Look at what I find, still unwashed by a bookseller's tide—

> Let those who are in favour with their stars
> Of public honour and proud titles boast,
> Whilst I, whom fortune of such triumph bars,
> Unlook'd for joy in that I honour most.
> —*Sonnet XXV*

Away, sons of Art!

July 29 I should have known, I suppose, from what occurred before breakfast. My planar dreamscape, transparent dome of idiotic conversation, collapsed in a half-remembered echo, with mine as the high ground and a verbal exchange I only semi-recall. It was under a ferocious assault of decibels, or really quite quiet voices active on the street. It is Friday. I twitched my curtains. I can now say with certainty that the nice married man across the street is from the italicised *Number Nine*, whose anachronistic door, in imitated Georgian, is flanked by hollyhocks. Their flower's a deep luxurious red. To him it seems clear that having got her suspension right, Isabelle's starter motor has given up the ghost. Tacky French (he did not say, himself having a cherry Peugeot). I hope it's not the start of something, in that receding grind of his gears, because, nervously, he's giving her a lift.

Later that day. Zob, I find, is in levitating shoes. I discover this routinely. 'My liege, here is the morning mail, or what of it I designate as personal.' I am completely unable, with that flutter of charismatic wings, to tie him to the floor. His feet are an inch or two above the bin, as he floats. He passes a green hand under the green shade of his reading lamp. We are, I am not too delighted to hear, 'getting away for a few days'. The unbeautiful Crouch, loud on the phone just now, has got us an invitation. This is *en masse* to the ancestral home of 'esteemed family Simms'. I try and cobble together a large, plausible lie protesting my commitment to the Glaze project, and for once this is not technically beyond him, though like Snell he is troubled by the terminology. 'Take the laptop,' he says. 'Put what you need on flaccid disc.'

At midday I packed my canvas bag. I wrote Isabelle a cheque (yes. She was home. Here was my July rent). A man on the drive rattled spanners, having lifted her bonnet. He, superfluously, I have remembered, his hair sandy, with a green gob of grease above his right temple. Fell boots! Not too filthy overalls. Even at six in the evening I couldn't quite erase him, by which mellow hour the Mercedes' dusky rear view gave me a dozing Zob in the plush of his upholstery, at which point chauffeur Wye turned the radio off. The car turned. The haze-capped Quantocks shrank over my right shoulder. Soon that golden disc, the western sun, in its descent to the squared fields ahead, to the bluish ridge beyond, would blush crimson, would halve itself, would abandon to darkened roof space its last loose threads of scarlet.

I am looking for somewhere whose address is – now what is this hasty scrawl? – 'near Ashburton'.

Darkness. In it is the emerald luminosity of the dashboard, with its flicker of orange needles. The swish of passing headlights – an effervescence over the ceiling, across that thundercloud soon to be Zob's brow, and out through a rear quarterpane – has woken him, unfortunately.

'You know, Al,' he said, or rather these words rumbled from his core, his mind still swaddled in the motion of sleep. 'That diary did turn up.' It was all too terrible.

'Yes,' I said. 'It was in this morning's mail.'

He told me – because he was infuriated – that having left Philip, who had ordered an early lunch (all this was on a Tuesday), he told me that he, the deep-breathing Zob, went across Covent Garden, intent on an antiquarian bookshop off the Charing Cross Road.

'Why?'

'Al, don't interrupt, but to get an illustrated Le Fanu, a present for Merle.'

'Oh. It's her birthday…?'

'Yes. But as I was saying.' He checked pockets for cash, but this was an expensive Le Fanu, so he pulled out and put on the counter, in precisely this order, his claret-coloured pocket diary, his chequebook, a ballpoint, lastly his concertina of bank and credit cards. Of all things a Nabokov caught his eye, an *Ada*, first edition, though on handling it he passed it up. 'Condition didn't match its price,' he said. Mere slip of a girl at the cash desk, standing in for her monocled grandaddy (who frequently needed to rest his hip), received Zob's signature with a capacious, not to say stupendous yawn, and even held his cheque to the light. No fame for him here. He marched out, to the Dickensian tinkle of a bell, leaving his pocketbook on the counter. It returned in the post this morning, which restored his faith in shop people. Not such fun were the quirky witticisms penned inside it, in a violent red in an alien hand.

'I want you to write, Al, first thing tomorrow. Demand an apology.'

'Ah,' I said. 'Now here's the Newton Abbot turn. I'd say we're getting near….'

I remember Isabelle's mechanic. I recall a sudden pool of light, a slow truck groaning round a bend. A green gob of grease above the right temple. Tired, very tired....

July 30 There are, my fellow-subjects, things I cannot believe. I say this as I recollect the high-browed Justin Simms, who last night perched on his balustraded steps, smoking a cigar. We shared the same moon – I, who glanced up through a tinted windscreen – and he, whose shadows off his sycamores were lost to a rising bank of cloud. I had got us, Zob and myself (that babble from the back), recurrently lost. In honesty what did I care for his diary?

Crouch, impossibly animated, had parked – oh hours ago – on the yardage of gravel half-circling the house. The house mid-Georgian (circa 1758). The conducted tour was this morning, naturally, though I remain stung by the night before – when, having had a longish life of useless toil, any last thoughts I had on the politicisation, the non-literariness of the putsch I had jointly planned, seemed not out of the question. Simms, whose father was just now buying companies abroad, and whose mother sunned herself in Tuscany, directed me to the attic, i.e. the servants' quarters, but told me which suite of rooms to drop off Zob's baggage in. Guffaws from Zob. Here, ye put-upon, is one of those vagaries of workplace bureaucracy. In its train are reproaches aimed at the masters of industry, of whom Simms is a legatee. It raises questions as to that structure called the labour force.

At a few minutes after ten, Saturday a.m., with the four of us crunching the driveway gravel, I rejected, feeling touchy, the symmetries in Simms's seven-bay façade – its stone quoins, the plain ledges, each offset above by a winged lintel, the three centralised bays, all doubly pedimented (porch and roof). Then those balustraded steps ascending to the door, to each side of which is a Palladian pillar. I do not allow the randomness of hierarchies, as exemplified in that social quartet, ever to smudge the dappled complexion, the robust good health of my mind. I told him I didn't care for his stucco, whose caramel was not the right shade. Nor have I been driven to the arms of a trade union. Simms had a look, a sneer, but had no answer. Had I made my point? Perhaps so, as my blood rebels.

I declined coffee on the terrace, for that would have meant their insufferable chat, three important nobodies very pleased to be so. After all I'd got work, of a spectacularly laboured kind, wherefore in the shade of my garret I prepared that penultimate chapter in the epistolary life of John Andrew Glaze. Notes all flat. A celestial twang. A lead angel, tone deaf, a dead reverberance in Zob's heavy laptop. All that coaxing with abysmal harp. Understandably I needed my breaks, for what sane man can bear these doses of academic blather?

I saw for myself that Simms, like Zob, had an outdoor man to keep his world prosaic. I leaned from my attic window, and just about made out a murmur of conversation as it layered itself in the warm scent of coffee beans. There was, at a distance, a hotchpotch of palm trees, pine trees. The cut lawns and dusty paths were littered with cones. There was – and I shall write down, record – a tamarisk tree, helplessly out of place, as it lent shade to our trio, in a clatter of spoons and coffee cups. Distant gunnera dotted an ornamental lakeside. Beyond that a square of sunshine caught on the cedar shingles slating a boathouse roof ('nicely weathered' – as I would hear Zob say). An extended roar from Simms, whom I imagined hirsute, stripped to the waist, combined itself with other effects from Crouch, who imitated steam through a whistle. That did not indicate he'd squeezed her in a bear hug (not yet), rather that Zob had told a joke.

I went down. A nylon coated flunkey, oldish, brown-haired, a villager, a widow creased at the sacks of flesh that enthroned each eye – had come from the terrace. She bore her master's tray with a world of moulded ceilings awhirl in the dome of the cafetière. That and three china cups were bound for the scullery. I went to the dining room, where the rectangular windows were duplicated in the lacquered table top. I reached out a hand for the russet and green of an apple, which until that moment topped an assortment, a yellow, peach and orange flame of fruits in a finely stencilled bowl. Simms came in too, just as my newly capacious jaw closed on that innocent English apple. He had changed – miraculous click of fingers – into cricket whites, and had since angled a croquet mallet jauntily on one shoulder.

'Marsy's looked high and low,' he said. 'You're *here*….'

Why of course. Far away as possible….

He directed me past the boathouse to the croquet lawn. There I found Zob whooping, Crouch giggly. Her all-live sculpture I might later invoke in some pretentious critique somewhere – a perfidy that common sense won't allow me to unleash – though the couplet

> Zob, pathetic,
> So unathletic…

was one I later penned, though never found time to develop or recapitulate. But. I should put this to rest, with our two children of destiny instantaneously locked in shoulder-to-shoulder combat over the linear path of Geraldine's croquet ball – unerring through its hoop. After that Marsy, elbow to vertical mallet, ankles crossed, exhorted me to all-day sobriety, since he wanted me to drive the three of them – 'just before nine' – to the venue of Simms's birthday celebration. He was twenty-five (a boy with a sycophantic publisher), and was gathering his tribes for an all-night bash. That was on a pleasure boat, up, down, then at its mooring somewhere on the River Dart.

'And I hope, Al, you've got that letter for me to sign.'

Geraldine had already detected blankness: 'Oh Alistair really!'

Zob, in that incipient flab of his forty pointless years, swelled up from the waist. He had noticed his counterpart, loping past the boathouse. For him this was no fun, and so had gone to exchange his mallet for a lemonade bottle.

'Al, I'm frankly surprised.' What had I been doing?

'I'm trying to close off the Glaze project – at least my part.'

'That buffoon!' said Crouch. She'd had her ear to reliable gossip, an odour so far seeping no farther than a fluorescent web of corridors, and of course the odd cocktail lounge. Officially his death had been 'comic'. For commercial reasons there would probably be – in ten to twenty years' time – a reappraisal. Zob smacked his heel with his mallet head uncomfortably.

'Okay,' I said. 'I'll do the letter. You'll need to give me the name, address.'

Simms interrupted. 'Anyone for lemonade?' Then I left them, deeply conversational on the condition of those shingles.

July 31 It has been an interrupted night, and is now five a.m. Sleep, impossible sprite, has goaded but failed to seal my lids. They droop and do not close. Therefore in the gloam of a strange and creaking house I have sat in the glow of the laptop, waiting for Simms, or Crouch, or Zob, or someone's drunken call. It came at minutes after three. Add to that, I have been thinking. Most persistently about last night, when in all but cap and livery – for such is Simms's way – I opened the car doors to three fizzy partygoers ensconced in Zob's saloon, whom I'd delivered quayside. Only imagine what social equality the three merry hacks put their pens and bankers' cards to.

Merle, with pearls, and a high neck – a gorgeously fitting evening dress, in coruscating henna – had already boarded (and this is *not* my joke) the *Penelope*. That simple craft, awash gently in a first ladle of punch, compulsory for each new arrival, had the kingfisher flutter of bunting attached to its mast. Friends – for Simms unbelievably had these – had inflated twenty-five party balloons, not with human gas but with helium. They bobbed on the rails, on whose painted ironwork Merle rested her naked forearms. Odysseus, by whom I mean of course the chauffeur, at last smiled. Merle waved vociferously. Simms, who at that moment sidestepped a capstan, waved back importantly. Heads turned to the fitful explosion of music and laughter, which melted into balm. Cornelius, in a white summer suit with carnation for buttonhole, stepped meaningfully from below decks, where a portal swung to. He had brought them punch, but shouted ahoy (to Zob, who was now at the gangplank). You can see how this plays on my mind – yesterday, today, and tomorrow it's August.

I returned to the house, with instructions to wait by the phone for 'whatever eventuality'. I have dozed here at the laptop. Have reflected endlessly, groggy sentry as I am, on the imitated throb of gaslight, a splutter of yellow condensation in the *Penelope's* portholes, as that vessel bounced on the tide. Ah me those windows! Convivial and trivial – rondures dabbed in on a foam-crested wash, all under, Merle, a canopy of stars.

I dashed off that letter – Dear Mr Mansard, I must protest etc. – though Zob later dismissed it as old-world gallantry and made me rewrite. I stumbled about on Simms's oaken landings, and sniffed at his chambers. I tried hard to avoid, when I shambled into his studio, a large room in a gold south aspect, the diluted prose of his current parturition – doubtless the next fastseller. I found its casual folios loose on a secrétaire table, and discovered later that this was material Snell was keen to see. We may anticipate Zob, or what he intones: 'Judas'.

In another room bolection mouldings framed the fireplace, with the central asset a mahogany tester bed. At the window a history of south-westerlies paralleled the transoms with lines of black pencil, where well into the morning two woven drapes, which I shook for dust, continued to be drawn. It turned out that the walrus Snell would snore here till just before lunch, while for brief visits only the rampant Crouch – who scarcely drew a veil in the composition of memoirs – settled her feet first to the foot, then the pillows, then again to the foot of his bed. Yes. I did say a tester – its frieze and cornice a graphic evocation, or wooden firmament of thunderclaps.

My own room, Justin, had a night commode, which I took to be a birthday joke. Your rapacious elders had cluttered their boudoir – into which I glanced, and out of which I marched – with a mahogany linen press. Also in mahogany was an attractive sofa with a serpentine design. Over the fire was a giltwood pier-glass, and under the centre window a Queen Anne chair. Outside a longcase clock had stopped at a quarter to two. The landing generally, cloaked in historic shadows, rendered tasteless the celebration of a name – Simms, the name Simms – with its posed-for lineage, a projection into history any sanguine person ought to find depressing. One shuddered not only at the roll of antecedents, their august beginnings the self-made house whose name had sprung from the clammy mists and the halcyon years and heroic age of J's paternal grandfather – a man spotlessly bald. That glossed portrait offered background clues as to the primal source of all those Simms doubloons (beaten silver in a Moorish arch; the fringe of an olive branch; a distant hacienda). Evidently Spanish trade, and not a picture I liked. Another showed a woman with chihuahua.

I am exceedingly bored. All I have for these sleepless hours is the Glob/Zaze correspondence, which is still in a jumble, and is sizeable as refuse.

At three-ish – or on that landing still at a quarter to two – I received my 'final' directive, via the slurred imbroglio of Simms's telephone voice. I got in the car and turned on the radio – a mistake. Its sultry waves brought all-night news from the world of adult therapy, whose vocal incisions deepened, before they could cauterise, lifelong psychic wounds – or some such technique. My car lights ballooned over the hedgerows. My engine purred on the riverside streets, with its velvet echo: the stone elevations, all those timbered gables, crowded shop fronts, some with painted gargoyles. On the pleasure craft the *Penelope*, over the starboard side, Crouch threw up, and was cured (felt 'marv'lous!' she said). Cornelius, on the white bonnet of his Jaguar, bellowed that he never got drunk, and would drive (critically with Merle, who was flushed). 'Just lead on, eh, Al....' Simms dozed in the back. Snell's neon headlights cascaded over my rear bumper and re-silvered the mirrors. Marsy had the window down, his blurred eyes lolling over the squared red fields. Crouch, whose hand touched my knee, my thigh, then casually stroked my loins, got distracted when I swerved and retuned the radio. Nevertheless. Not half an hour ago a night-capped Cornelius (brandy) checked into his guest room – 'Wow! A four-poster!' Simms disappeared to bed half-undressed, with a last suspiration for his party blower. Marsy said 'Night' but made mountaineer's work of the stairs. I myself saw Merle to her room, while I am more or less certain Geraldine retouched her rouge, for the woman was insatiable. Ten minutes ago I happened to look out from the open door of my attic (because I can't sleep. Because I want to shake off this purgatory called Glaze). What did I see but this, Geraldine as she lumped from her *en suite*, and again minutes later as she shambled loudly from the deluge of a toilet flush, whose cataract I have learned to sing—

> She was bra-less,
> She's not harmless,
> She was ever so, ever so
> Parlous.

Zob it seemed couldn't be roused, so she abandoned his and tried Cornelius's room, remaining there for some time – and so to those thunderclaps. Should I, with candelabra, tap on Merle's door? Well...
...perhaps not tonight.

Footnote. I am inclined, in the first orange streaks of dawn, to entrap the erase key, though this I resist. Try, please, to understand that I have spent an exhausting night with the fatuous observations of the late Professor Glaze, not to mention the goings-on of aged teenagers. Is it enough that my horoscope has assured of at least one bright day? Mr Patric Walker, I shall hold you to this.

August 1 I poached myself an egg for breakfast, and left enough devastation in Simms's country kitchen that I hope will weary his hangover. The bright Atlanta of his quarry tile floor I have spotted with toast crumbs. On his sunny worktops I have left a Lakeland system of tea stains. Latterly I have found and connected the laptop to his laser printer, which action results in something quasi-baroque as typeface – substance as follows...

> c/o William Spiegelman
> 2001 Benson Avenue
> Northwestern University
> Evanston IL 60201
> 31 August 1992

Dear Marsy,

I am sure the power of foresight is seated in the prostate, since the bonhomie with which I was received, driven about, and made to feel at home, was responded to by a long bout of jitters in approximately that region. Spiegelman is scatty and really quite charming. On the first night we had dinner, accompanied by aeolian harp, courtesy his aged gramophone, whose sound, although spiky, was not intrusive. He told me about his daughters. One is a dental technician. The elder's an Egyptologist. All this over a nut roast with green salad, which he'd prepared himself, and to *my* taste over-peppered. Spiegelman's a pale vegetarian.

He told me he'd lost his wife, a vegan, ten years ago in a boating accident. He'd kept certain of her artefacts exactly as she'd left them – for example her shoe rack, with all its shoes, bar those that went down with the boat.

Apart from those two lovely daughters, of whom photos were proffered, we discussed my lecture – not I regret in any great detail. We easily drifted into asides on the latest Kennedy biogs, which is an industry he's morbidly keen on.

So to my prostate, whose soundings I shall learn in future to take note of. What I have found – and this was accidentally, several days later – was an entry in the notices, which listed my contribution, a rumour now hard to quash, as Professor Glaze's 'Theory of Literary Time'. Of course, these misapprehensions have to be corrected, which on this occasion, in the half-light of the lecture theatre, it was impossible to do. My disclaimer, which I assumed was clear, was met with chair scrapes. Someone stood up – her appearance recalled one of the Spiegelman girls. She articulated a single word – 'Nevertheless…' – with what a world of subterfuge lurking in those innocent four syllables.… Soon she'd got me having to justify myself.

Let me remind you of where it is said I stand. It's with St Thomas, on whose opposite bank Duns Scotus posits difference – i.e. of essence – between individual things. My own metaphors are strictly to do with the action of writers writing books, for which articles my commentators substitute 'matter'. To St Thomas this 'matter' is or suggests undifferentiated parts. Distinction is merely a difference of spatial position, a co-ordinate tantamount to time (they say) in the Glaze system. Here unfortunately it doesn't end, because Scotus and Aquinas stand to be dismissed before we have a proper view in 'modern' terms. Enter Leibniz, who rejected the distinction of essential from accidental properties. So, now, for 'essence', read 'all the propositions that are true of the thing in question'. It is not possible, for Leibniz, for two things in this sense to be exactly alike. This, I'm told, is a principle he has termed the 'identity of indiscernibles'. It didn't go down well with physicists, who declared that two particles of matter may differ solely in terms of temporal and spatial position. That view has since been rendered problematic by relativity, which disposes of space and time as relations.

The problem is further modernised when the conception of 'substance' is challenged, or making of a 'thing' a package of qualities, its having no longer a core of 'thinghood'. This is to circularise the whole argument (which in my view is what the entire canon of philosophy does), since, in not acknowledging 'substance', we arrive at a position more reminiscent of Scotus than Aquinas. This highlights 'faults' in the 'Glaze theory', and leaves us once more with the 'problem' of space and time. I am sustained, Marsy, in the calming resolution that there is no reason why I shouldn't cut this tour short. Please let me hear of the real world, for example more about your house move.

Take care, Andrew.

Flat 5
147 Trefoil Street
SW18
11 September 1992

Dear Andrew,

Glad to see you've risen above these pointless researches. Must say the minutiae of everyday metaphysical life hold no clues as to how to pay the bills. I'm put out because Blandford rejected – yes, rejected! – my Nostradamus piece. This while my book's a top-ten bestseller…. Should have thought the name alone was worth something. In the end he commissioned a gloomy poet from West Yorkshire, whose approach was predictably anti-Thatcher.

Mixed fortunes on the house front. There is a crotchety octogenarian in the adjacent flat, which belongs to the house adjoining. The outflow from her and my gutters is carried by a downpipe on her side, which over time has overgrown with moss. As a consequence a prolonged downpour caused seepage under the eaves into her dining room. Because she can remember paying £10 several years ago to have her gutters cleaned, she assumes all is down to a lack of maintenance on *my* side, and holds me responsible.

Comically the story doesn't end there. Next day a man resembling a sumo wrestler arrived with a ladder, not exactly to remove the moss, but to transfer it into my gutter. He did not flinch from this action even though I watched from an open window.

Better news with the new agent. He's found a buyer who wants to move quickly, and whose conveyancer is sane, rational, businesslike. I'm satisfied the whole thing will now go through quite quickly. But I'm tired.

All the best. Marsy

c/o Dr George Stanford
963 EPB
University of Iowa
Iowa City IA 52242
19 September 1992

Dear Marsy,

Things don't pick up. My contact here, Kathryn Fitzgerald, having carefully denied improper relations with one of her students, could not finally refute evidence of a parking lot surveillance camera. This has reputedly shown, in ankle-to-thigh close-up, how, after a late-night party, she 'arranged' herself on the hood of someone's convertible. This while her innocent protégé, whose penile tip was also the subject of close-ups, pulsated in anticipation. How true this is I don't know, though she has certainly gone, and has left no forwarding address.

Dr Stanford is her successor. Although a mild-mannered man, he is just that kind to get my back up, whatever he says or does. He knows nothing about my visit, has received no handover notes, and anyway would rather accommodate me as guest at an extramural workshop group. He would like me to talk about the sestina (as a man profoundly in the grip of extinct poetic forms). I am afraid I snapped at him – and have been doing so ever since – though in the end did agree to the workshop.

Phoned Jessica, really to see what arrangements Sam had managed to make. She has made none. Worse. I have been given a christening date, and am expected to come. Worse still. The godfather's some kind of activist (and has links with the European Union, which I told Jessica doesn't make it easier). To cap it all, I have committed an abysmal *faux pas* with the workshop group, calling one student's work a hangover of 1960s psychedelia. It turns out she is synaesthetic, and her 'sights of sounds' and 'tasted shapes' are an attempt to encapsulate her 'natural' sensory experience.

I keep getting a rash round my ankles, and in scratching abrade the skin. Need a holiday perhaps.

Andrew

Flat 5
147 Trefoil Street
SW18
30 September 1992

Dear Andrew,

I've followed up these time/space propositions in a book by Venice Schiff, whose gift is the gift of elucidation. It tells me you are right – perfectly right – to remain airborne above that murky water. It's so obvious that the corridors of fiction open doors to far richer vistas than the circumlocutions of philosophy.

I'm sorry to say Blandford's gone overboard on this professional Yorkshireman – a versifier who is big, I'm told, on the performance circuit. That's amazing in itself, because to me he is virtually inarticulate. I say this not without having gathered empirical data. I was at the Blew Nose Café – I was working with my assistant – where he recently topped the bill. His rendition was a first-person dirge called 'Elaine'. Elaine was a childhood girlfriend, a year above him at the secondary mod. Wordsmith from the frozen wastes first had the hots for Elaine during a school holiday in Dunoon – or so the dirge ran. What was he getting at?

Well, the relationship – which had always been coy – spilled over into school life well after the holiday, though never developed beyond walking home from the bus together. These walks – and this is the point – were never accompanied by conversation, except to say 'See you tomorrow' at the point where they went their separate ways. His summarising stanzas were a focus for the whole, and seemed to ask to what extent do TV and video condition the minds and behaviour of the young? Disgruntled from West Yorkshire thinks he has an answer, having shown that as recently as the early 1970s innocence was possible.

I had been asked to produce a not too detailed critique, while as you know I am not the best person when it comes to talking poetry. This lowlife from way up north does seem to be a phenomenon, therefore I got this Alistair to do it for me, as a test piece.

See a doctor about that rash.

The best. Marsy

Zob, we shall see, whose life is a sequence of pragmatical illusions, shall come to consider that an act of plagiarism has been perpetrated against him. That is my point of issue number one (and on it more later). Point of issue number two concerns the epistle above, addressed to the late Professor Glaze, which amazingly Zob intends to publish. Alas I no longer have the immediacy – of not one, but two foggy London nights. But never mind. Step this way please, into this vaporised ring of light, a lemony halo, where my wounded capacity to reflect reconstructs that fateful September of 1992. (O what is that noise?)

It is not that difficult, on the streets of north London, to identify the slop-shirted poet, for this is its habitat. It is a species well known for its violet proboscis. Its fraternity is such that whole groups get together on alternating Tuesdays. Zob, through an understandable blunder on the part of Blandford's administration people, chose the wrong Tuesday, therefore we unwound our thread – among those brown brick terraces – to the café door on workshop rather than performance night. We sat down unsuspecting, and were asked by a sour-faced cocoa-drinker if one of us would like to read first. Zob shook his head, and I also passed, though composed something suitably trite, under the table, on my knee. Meanwhile someone read a spectacular piece about a pogrom. (I am not being facetious. As framework or substructure, that grim subject was the underlying point, given the writer's experience, which was discussed. The poem's moist jewel was its cluster of personal things, in prismatic detail – a button or a photograph – so making more monstrous the evil ranged against it.) The team's leading coffee drinker, a paunchy middle-aged man clad entirely in denim, dismissed this kind of thing as okay when it came off. Only one jaw dropped. Then we moved on – to a thing in nursery couplets, whose jangle related a string of commonplace encounters, Christmas shopping, a glass arcade. Blue denim critique pronounced it 'definitely' competition material. That made its author flutter her eyelids.

That fog was no less pendulous when, on the following Tuesday – and this time alone – I strode through a brown mizzle under the street lamps, or later, in an onrush of blue smoke, wiped my shoes on the stunted bristles of the café doormat. I now regard it as a tragic mistake that I took my seat to the rear of the audience. That action's memorable result was prolonged embarrassment, when – with hacking cough – I walked out during a long insistent encore.

Here briefly is or was that evening. As preamble two straw-hatted yokels, or 'word painters' (I anticipated polychrome), launched into diatribe, subject – or I should say premise – that unmitigated social evil the supermarket. Other artistes bemoaned the lot of the minke whale. Another offered the fist-clench in an onanist's angular variations, using an adjustable cheval-glass (imagined). From a performer unnamed came the 'phraseological' truth of war (how much wiser I now am, politically). Finally we got that theory of innocence (and everyone said aw!) from our yellow-hosed adventurer late from Dunoon, which it is irksome to see as paste-up in Zob's letter to Glaze (September 30th, 1992). He does not even take the trouble not to sound like me. The piece, originally for Blandford's quarterly, was turned down by that editor. The truth of the nation's poetry scene was not sufficiently mythic, and that was of little interest to the purveyors of our culture. O what is that noise?

That noise is…is Merle, who was in the kitchen, the twisted bombsite of which I wanted Simms or Crouch to encounter first. Ah me. The others have proposed snacks, I am told, so here she is, afloat on that mosaic in the hallway, as she turns and turns a plastic handle on a device she's found for wringing out lettuce leaves.

'You hungry, Al – like some lunch?'

'Why yes. Just let me gather these papers.'

'We're all in the garden.'

Snell was sockless on a stripy lounger. Crouch touched his knee in passing the cutlery—

> Light that you see,
> In his eye that you see,
> Is mingled with overnight
> Ecstasy.

> Ecsta you see
> In the night that you see
> Is jingled with midnight
> Chimes you don't see.

Begone, impish Muse…. Let me just sit here on these moss-encrusted flagstones, on the patio, and examine my papers. Ah now what's this! A history lesson, plus cant from Kant et al.…

c/o J. Anthony Spatz Jr
Andrews Hall
University of Nebraska
Lincoln NE 68588
14 October 1992

Dear Marsy,

My host has salted a wound. His intervention ought to have warned me. My arrival – I shall go further and say optimistic arrival – was crowned by a lecture he took me to. It told me all about the place. Here, Marsy, is revealed truth (see enclosures)—

In 1838 a commissioner sent by the US government, whose brief was to settle Indian disputes, reported on the salt basins of Lancaster County. These amounted to smooth floors of hard clay, covered with a layer of crystallised salt, which definitely glistened. In 1856 these were brought to public notice by government surveyors – which attracted the first permanent settlers into the region. A number of smallish salt operations thrived in the early 1860s, though were seen off by the railroads – they of course facilitating competition from eastern manufacturers, whose production methods were that much cheaper. In 1886 the state sank a test well, which although deep was disappointing in its result. No serious efforts were subsequently made in the use of deposits for salt production, with one of the larger basins converted into a salt lake, and developed as a pleasure resort. I am trying very hard to remain rational. A hamlet called Lancaster, serving as the county seat, survived these experiments.

Now, Marsy, it's important to know that the state of Nebraska's first legislature empowered, in 1867, a commission – its remit site selection. That was for the new capital city. The new capital city was to be named Lincoln. On July 29th 1867 the commission chose Lancaster, no more than ten or so stone and timber houses situated on the prairie. In all a hundred miles from the nearest railroad, though progress was swift. The city was incorporated and declared the county seat in 1869. In July 1870 the first railroad – the Burlington and Missouri River – reached Lincoln. It was followed by several others.

Why do I tell you (refer now to those enclosures)? It's because Spatz is pseudo-Betjemanesque re the buildings here. The State Capitol (he tells me with relish), completed in 1932, has been one of America's 'best architectural achievements'. For him it's a concrete link direct to all of that preceding history. From its massive two-storey base emerges a central tower, to a height of 400 feet. It is surmounted by the figure of a sower. I am now talking guidebooks. The architect was B. G. Goodhue. The sculptor was Lee Lawrie. The interior mural décor was by Augustus Vincent Tack and Hildreth Miere. The inscriptions and symbols were chosen by Hartley B. Alexander. A statue of Abraham Lincoln, by Daniel Chester French, is at the western approach to the Capitol grounds.

But here's the thing really. The genial Spatz thinks I can view the insane philosophers of Europe in the same pioneering light, and has even assumed my life and career owe them a debt. It is becoming, Marsy, intolerable. I sat for an hour, for the commencement of my lecture (this a few evenings ago), while one of his trained monkeys primed my audience with irrelevant gibberish, which I have since had to revisit, and still say is gibberish. As preparation for what I was supposed to add, I had the spectacle of multiple exhumations, Kant first, or the Kant external world – which also belongs to us – causing only the *matter* of sensation. If there are sentient beings who mentally arrange this matter in space and time, that is how – *quid est veritas* – I am dragged in, as according to Kant, and now this minor Spatz school, 'things' – like railroads and towers – i.e. the causes of sensations – are inherently unknowable, are not in space or time, and being subjective are merely a part of the way we perceive. I did try to look at my watch, or the time (I am not joking), as Spatz, nodding in my direction, showed himself hugely interested in how the Glaze system fits with Kant's, with human experience only ever a mapping onto our perceptual pattern of geometry and time. If spatially, temporally, we 'experience' grains of salt but do not 'know' them, for example, what correspondences do *I* attribute, in *my* conception? Is geometry 'true' only to the point of our experience of things, but not of those things in themselves, or am I going to offer something counter? If space and time aren't concepts but forms of intuition, you might as well say a book isn't a book, but so far as we're concerned it's a book – or would I say that?

Hegel is even more confused. For him the process of time is to the more from the less perfect, in both an ethical and logical sense. He needn't really bother with what is 'ethical' and what is 'logical', because his theory treats these as exactly alike. Their perfection is the same, i.e. a closed whole, a complex of interdependent parts all working to a single end. That end, which is the fulfilment of history, concerns the progress of 'spirit' – I think he means human spirit – whose object is to be free. Spiritual freedom comes about, Marsy (surprisingly), through the mundane system of monarchy. People spend whole lives in the study of these propositions.

I have some sympathy with Schopenhauer, who abolishes time and space, and subjugates everything to 'will'. Will, he says, is the source of human suffering, made endless because it has no goal. It has no goal because we pursue what can't be achieved – happiness. I'm with him there. What we mean in referring to any happiness that *has* been attained is no more than satiety. Conversely an unsatisfied wish results in pain. It's with this reasoning that Schopenhauer turns to the doctrine of Nirvana, which prescribes that the less we exercise will, the less we shall suffer. To see through the veil of maya (or illusion) is to see all things, really, as one. All things being one, he cannot differentiate himself from another, or for that matter from any given object. Armed with that knowledge volition is quelled, with our will repelled from life in a denial of our nature. Time and space being the 'universal forms' of will, these are also denied. What then the cosmos is, is nothingness.

Spatz cheerfully intervened at precisely this point, on the understanding that I would now deliver my own extension to these ideas, with 'further illumination' on all this gobbledegook. I did consider a way in with the veil of illusion, interest etc. in Eastern thought etc. that has fed into modern literature. Etc. I recalled my earlier studies of Pondicherry and the British Raj, and might have rattled on about this. Instead I retired with a migraine.

I'm not putting up with much more of this. Plus that rash has spread to my underarms.

Andrew

Glaze's enclosures, which I vaguely remember – having come across them in the Wandsworth room – were a dozen or so photographs of the State Capitol – not that I ever paid them much attention.

12 Hampstead Hill Drive
NW3
9 November 1992

Dear Andrew,

Made it at last! And in the end with hardly a hitch selling off the flat.

Must say the garden's a mess, by which I mean it's not to my taste – so shall have to get a man in to sort it all out. Alistair likes his two-room garret, whose sloping ceilings are a permanent reminder of his position. From there he'll co-ordinate much of the administration. For the rest of the place I shall need domestic help. The neighbour, who's a liver surgeon, has lent me his directory, his 'list of mops', as he terms it.

So, Andrew – how has all this come about! Yours is no small part in it, and nor is Snell's (you may be surprised to hear). He has only to get the scent of money in his nostrils and suddenly he's motivated! Film rights, TV tie-ins, you name it!

Andrew, I feel fantastic! You must see a doctor about that rash.

Marsy

Demurely at first, I contemplated a spring onion, though before I had poured salt onto the raised circumference of my plate I rejected that idea. I left my lunch as a reluctantly chewed circle of baguette, with a cream cheese I had failed to taste.

'Why Al you're not hungry after all.'

Merle, on the thick uppers of her flip-flops, flip-flopped into a cane trellis festooned with the flaming girandoles of a passionflower. She had tennis shorts in washday white, and a transparent blouse, checked in a shade of lemon peel and apple-green – a cheesecloth whose exquisite tail she had bunched and softly knotted at that perfect navel of hers. The long-lashed Simms, who was now on the connecting red brick, a pathway locked together in zigzags, filled the opposing arch. This one had honeysuckle, and one other withered bloom. I overheard their conversation. Merle, in the kitchen, had come across lemon grass and tamarind pods, with which, she said, 'I can cook up something exotic, this evening if there's time....' Simms, with his smooth brow in a garland of fading honeysuckle, and his whole upper body swimming under those mad wild scents, said,

'That would be charming, delightful.'

Crouch took the point of a pair of manicure scissors to the quick of her toenails, showing us the dark fringes of forest pubis under the cocked leg of her khaki shorts, which had turn-ups. Snell, flourishing a blue hanky, said he was hot and would take another shower. She followed him not ('Insatiable,' she muttered). Simms I noticed now had his hand to the small of Merle's back, flesh on flesh, and steered with good-natured precision over the green sward, I felt sure toward the boathouse. Crouch asked would *I* like a shower (not tonight, Geraldine). 'Or a bath?' Thanks all the same. I shall I think take a stroll around all that mare's tail, to the far side of the lake – which I did. Casually.

Geraldine finally cut her nails, shovelling what clippings confronted her lunch plate (O her brittle rhino claw) into a Chinese bell pot – whose design was dragons, willows, pools. She used it also as a spittoon, getting up to go somewhere – as it happened a potting shed. Here, under the larded luminosity of her cold feminine buttocks – the flab of her stellar revolutions – a startled garden boy limped from his climax. It's that kind of thing, according to certain purple passages singled out by the Sunday reviewers, that her most recent memoir revels in.

I examined a dovecot (peripherally), then a dark chalet on its backdrop of unhurried blue sky. Simms, his legs wide to the stern of a newly painted boat, the *Venus*, may not have suspected my scrutiny. I am often that man with hands deeply pocketed, who likes to be alone. He helped Merle aboard and seated her aft, then wobbled to the bow, where in the reedy lakeside – to Crouch's same slow rhythm – he at last dipped oars. It was so romantic. I imagine it stirred the rainbow trout. Or that Merle, with a lazy hand in the gathering foam, lolled as she watched for the golden slither of carp.

I was eventually satisfied that they talked only, and began to walk back, but was not so sanguine when centre lake they seemed to confer.

It was approaching the cocktail hour when Zob presented his gift-wrapped Le Fanu, and wished her a happy birthday. Merle was a capable thirty-three.

August 2 Snell, who'd got through the night without the intervention of his succubus, made his dawn resolve, and at ablutions decided to push on back to the office. 'Wonderful, Justin, to see you,' I remember was his valediction, with a gigantic hand proffered.

'Tremendous bash!' Merle, who handled the maps, pointed out – pointed out by a back route – how it wouldn't be substantially out of their way if they called in on one of their clients now living in Lyme Regis – an old '*trouvère*', or so he described himself. Cornelius must have agreed, because, in his novelettish way, that grandee plied them, in the weave of his drawing room, with tea from a silver service and endless refusable rock buns. Recently he'd acquired a parrot (needing the companionship), which aside from stocks in piracy had since learned to imitate the revolving whine of an auto alarm. Merle pursed lips and tried to teach it pretty things. Really-must-be-going Snell couldn't see how to utter it (the verb 'to go'), until a wall clock tinkled. It was as well it did. Our two got back to New Caxton Grove a little before five. In the back office Merle's answer machine winked its little green light insistently. Poor tired Merle! I don't need to imagine, how in that next hour or so, she returned calls, having no time to change, so remaining for one added hour in the dampness of her tee shirt, its print the Sistine Chapel, its excerpt Adam's ceiling electrification. The vague scent of pear to her perfumed wrists was past its ripeness. Then to top it Cornelius came in with urgent, days-old mail to reply to, while *he* ran a foam bath.

My own daylong cast me in the role of chauffeur again, this time dropping off those three colossi at a place Simms, as far back as boy with fishing rod, knew of tucked away in a coastal corniche. It opened to a path, which under its canopy – a padded oak and pine quilt, peppered with silver birch – cut a conical section into the bay, secluded, and to all intents private. Zob, unsteadily sandalled (those dry, lumpy clods), carried the cool box, with its cold beers, its pasta and potato salads, its spare rib in a spicy marinade. Simms took the towels, which were bagged, and the barbecue. Geraldine the tongs and charcoals. Driver Wye had the laptop and was told to kill time till rain or sundown. I drove to the next touristy town, where I parked the Mercedes, and got out and wandered.

Not much to report. There was a bric-à-brac shoppe, with large etched windows, whose display was miniature brass boots, a collection of toby jugs, and a lamp with a pewter base and frosty globe. There was, in the doorway, a basket full of plastic footballs. Nothing much else. In a low-beamed tearoom, all stone walls and horse brasses, I amused myself with a glass of frothy coffee and a plate of Danish pastry. Not that I was hungry: bored. Soon the next table gave up its starched cloth and napkins to an outdoor type, a man in sturdy new boots, flecked grey ankle socks, cotton trousers, and a lumberjack shirt. His charges were female. I say this because I met this party again, not long after in the tourist information office, where I scrutinised stratified 3D models depicting the local coastline, with its steep slopes and 'hog's back' cliffs, now a rare nesting site for the peregrine falcon (he said). He also told the story of Exmoor's paths, with its colour-coded walks. One of his companions touched his elbow sourly. Nevertheless he rattled on. I came away with a dream of wild brown trout in the cellophane glitter of the rivers he named. I might soon have to visit the barrows of Hangley Cleave. Shall tramp one day among the purple moor grass, or the reddish bell heather, listening out for a curlew, or a snipe, or a plain mountain blackbird. Could find myself in pursuit of a fritillary, or an emperor moth. 'One other thing,' he said, though he found himself dragged to the car park.... 'Uplands', I heard, 'bog asphodel', 'heath spotted orchid', something about wild cranberry. We crossed paths again, this time as he reversed his orange camper truck. He acknowledged the nose of my car with a wave. Has he hired a boat, I wonder, and is now out at sea, casting his line for heavier fish...? No matter. For all I knew, for all I intended to tell Zob – whose car at dusk I left with hazard lights on – and for all Zob had learned of the great outdoors— But what could I say anyway? With its naked sun slanting over those narcissistic rock pools, everything he now knew was summed up in a nasty pink imprint streaking the tops of his shoulders. I carried the cool box. Geraldine squirted him with a lot of white lotion – and rubbed. Simms had a contented, and not altogether a friendly smile.

August 3 This was the day we left Justin in peace, at the discretion of his Muse, who as scion of street-corner antiquity never made the least suggestion as to the use of waste bins. Perhaps she was timid. Geraldine on the other hand wasn't, and in no matter what public place (I recall a mini-market, a town square with fountain, a very crowded post office) lifted Zob's shirt and palmed in yet more of that salve.

Yes (as I refer to notes). It was despite everything the day we stopped for drinks. At the White Hart, Crouch had already scoured the local agents, who had compiled a portfolio of 'character' properties. So so wearying. Nor, as driver, could I, as driver, do justice to the Blackawton brewery, whose beer was on tap.

'Blackawton,' said Geraldine. It was where they did the worm charming.

We are – as I must just adjust this parasol, in a table that's wobbly all over – we're in many ways privileged to know that.

I have the benefit of Crouch's most recent memoir. Her vulgarity is southern in its lighting, and has a lot to do – in that political stance she adopts – with coaxing out the machismo she knows to exist in her men friends (to demonstrate *what* obscure point I do not know). She dragged us to the edge of Dartmoor to look at what is now a small stone cottage rented by me, in whose cool shadows I complete my memoir, a place then as now peaceably set in a wilderness. Zob looked at the roof slates, some of which hung by a last, fragile-looking corner. Inspected with a wilful eye the angular inclination of much of the pre-war guttering (a subject he'd involuntarily researched, back in Wandsworth). He prodded with the toothy blade of his house key – rather sullen, I thought – an infested lintel, and followed up with a wormy-looking post. He sniffed at the damp air inside and announced remotely that this was not a place he could get on with (anyway he had long thought of France and a gîte). Geraldine laughed it off – 'Marsy, you're not looking at this in the right way' – and wanted him right now to get down to the agent's office and write out a deposit. 'I mean the place has *so* much potential.' Zob's only comment was huh. I scraped back the kitchen door, where we'd managed to gain entry, and quietly pocketed the agent's blurb.

August 4 Was the day we left Simms altogether, Geraldine with pyrotechnics, Zob and I awkwardly. Breakfast was cereals and orange segments, whose tonic of bitter-sweetness was one I still recall light-headedly. A second pot of coffee arrived stage left – that's to say a double oak door under a precarious set of antlers. Geraldine roared at the housemaid – her laughter a show of astonishment at the woman's servility, or quaintness. There was a definite hint of a curtsey. Simms pressed the enfolded corner of his napkin to the enfolding corner of his mouth. Zob looked on with terrified eyes. I myself cast about the room, for would a paunchy Belgian detective with waxed moustaches enter stage right – I mean by the patio doors – to dissect the monstrousness of our crimes? Not regrettably this time. Geraldine left slops in her saucer and mentioned that her bag was packed. So soon as Simms got one of his flunkeys to stow it in her boot she was off – '…it has been such a pleasant break.' It left Zob with difficult diplomacy, his relation to Simms never quite exceeding its present concordat, respectful only. 'Perhaps in the circumstances…' he said, meaning I don't know what. 'Huh, eh, Al?'

'Why yes of course,' I said. 'Geraldine's so right. We can't keep Justin from his work.' I have recorded in my notes that when, with our humming tyres to the motorway, we overtook her just this side of Bristol, Zob was browsing through the Glaze letters and failed to notice. It has to be said that Geraldine was drumming her dashboard, to the frenetic rhythms of her radio. This, I believe, is a measure of her inanity – brilliant though she undoubtedly is.

August 5 A curious reply, from not Mr but Dr Mansard, whose gum-chewing grandchild you'll recall returned Zob's diary. Mansard quotes his granddaughter's transgression as 'spontaneous', a note in the lined rectangle for Tuesday the twenty-sixth of July. Silly me, she writes, left my diary behind. Mansard, though apologetic, puts this down to youthful high spirits, and points out that she *had* troubled herself to return the thing. It is a fact that the bin was never far away, under the bookshop counter. Zob, whom I have never seen with white knuckles, and who is generally mild mannered, upsets a lot of negligible objects, bringing both fists down on his desk – for example an ivory paper knife, which has surprise in its leap. There are obscenities, he states, under the early dates of autumn (is this prescience, I ask?). 'You can't call that high spirits!' I am to draft another letter to Mansard, making all this clear, and asking (rhetorically) should Zob seek legal advice – an area of professional life he does in fact venture into – in my view incautiously – though in quite another connection.

August 7 Malkin strayed in, during Isabelle's Sunday rendezvous, with an ear half-chewed and the remaining velvet caked in blood. The Citroën's on the drive, so the mistress is out in a borrowed car – not, as I view from the window, that cherry Peugeot.

What am I going to do about Malkin?

August 8 Zob, as tetchy as I've seen him, now cracks the whip on the Glaze project. 'Why, Al, is it taking so long!' (Lucky I've worked on this!)

I tell him I'm there or there about, and will do my best to close it off. Therefore…

…day one, endgame—

c/o Ludo Marcinkiewicz
University of Denver
Denver CO 80208
20 November 1992

Dear Marsy,

Glad the move went well. Mine, into host after host's, is weighing dreadfully. Not the least distress was the quack I saw about that rash, who prescribed a powder for athlete's foot (of all the things it could have been). He suggested I might be diabetic. Me, diabetic – after all these years. Still. In a few days the powder did work.

It's almost certain now I'll wind this tour up, with Denver the last straw. Some hoaxer thought it might be a wheeze to jet in from Europe the world's leading Nostradamus scholar. I can't seem to shake off this time-watch thing. Added to that all my lectures are now preceded by any other speaker, to whom I am usually expected to reply. Hence our Dr Xavier Rée, whose ideas were along following lines—

First (disputed) premise is that Nostradamus 'knew' of events occurring since his death. That was in 1556. This does not imply a predetermined universe, because with it is implied the notion of parallel realities, and the essence of time not as a flow but branched. Behold the time tree. We see boughs, branches, twigs, though there is no mention of foliage, or even the fruits and flowers of time. Our world and our cosy reality, which most assume to have no parallel, is (it is posited) merely one twig among many, its past being unique only from the point of its first sprouting. Other twigs represent times, worlds, cosmological culs-de-sac similar though not identical to our own. Not quite the funniest part is this: that it all comes about through sentient beings exercising their prerogative of choice. Choosing to do one thing rather than another results in a new twiglet, so that you, or a replicate you, when you didn't get up with the alarm, spawned another you, complete with universe, who did. Where, Marsy, does all this end, when you can't begin to consider all the multiplicities? With not only human choice but animal? Or with the consciousness of plants, responsive or not responsive to whatever tropism? With intelligent machines perhaps?

Can anyone take this seriously? Rée evidently does, and even thinks of it as science, asking us to rethink our reality as one permanently sliding into a plurality of worlds, only one of which we can ever experience. Mostly life never evolves across these other worlds, though in some it is scarce, and in just a few is abundant.

How does this relate to Nostradamus? Rée says we're to regard him as an adept in tree climbing, a man who's tested the branches and glimpsed the many boughs. Why most of his predictions are plainly wrong is that his purview has been across so many parallel worlds, where things don't happen quite as they do here. I should have chosen a career teaching infants.

Hope to see you soon. Andrew

Zob, who glanced over my shoulder – up there in my heaven of perfect peach – picked out that penultimate paragraph as I just ran over it again. I had been testing out some fonts I had never used before, and felt quite taken with a castellated italic. Zob, who had scanned that paragraph too, said to me 'Don't saw the branch you're sitting on. Try to predict why I can't get hold of Cornelius. He doesn't return my calls....' Well, Marsy, unlike you I had the benefit of special agent Merle, and knew – through what I'd describe as time's unruly undergrowth – precisely what Snell was up to. He was wooing Simms. What prescience the forces of parallelism attributed to me (in the sense of prophecies synchronised to the human tide of all that is self-fulfilling) suggested it was time to resurrect my three-act soap. Do you remember *The Guilt That is Hampstead's*? Somewhen is a little bird perched on a branch, to tell me I should finally pen its finally disintegrating scene. Finally. Perhaps I will some day.

12 Hampstead Hill Drive
NW3
4 December 1992

Dear Andrew,

Just about getting straight (so now life begins!). All that junk from my Wandsworth days – all those age-old accoutrements – I have consigned and locked up in a single room. Edith was here with catalogues [Edith Zob, née Parkes, the writer's mother, by then a divorcée], so I have been on a spree in the department stores. Michael has dropped in too [Michael Zob, OBE], and gave his seal of approval.

I shouldn't if I were you, Andrew, persist with this tour, which I see is taking its toll. At bottom you're dealing with a gun culture, so it's no surprise to me you're up against people who want to make a fight of it.

And what about this! Yesterday Blandford tried to fob me off with a dog (actually a bitch, actually a pup), which he thought I'd be just right with, strolling on the heath. Sounds too much like hard work. But a nice-looking animal. I allowed him to exercise the thing on the front acreage of concrete, which I *must* dig up and properly landscape. It was a definite put-off: the bright ordures Blandford took a makeshift glove to, and the long hunt he had for my dustbins (as I laughed).

So, Andrew, when shall we see you? There's going to be lots to catch up on.

Take care. Marsy

This was Zob's last letter to Glaze, bar some final scrawl daubed on a picture postcard.

August 9 Endgame day two—

> c/o Antony Lester
> Box 9131
> Berkeley CA 94709
> 23 December 1992

Dear Marsy,

Feeling much better, having spent a few days in San Francisco. My hostess, an authority on the SF streets and boulevards, yesterday walked me round, and drove me into Lombard Street, and down. I've got some snaps, which I'll show you. I'll also show you a *Five Dollar Review* I found by chance, whose poetry is full of tanned leathers, tabloids, soap suds, printers' inks, serums, the smell of gasoline – the kind of thing your daddy sat up half the night to write himself, though of course England's overripe for that.

I will see you some time in the New Year, which is when I'm heading back.

Happy Christmas. Andrew

Curious how Glaze, in his moments of deepest uncertainty, resorts to that professorial fallback, the catalogue, though this one not nearly so elaborate as his missive from Nebraska, dated October 14th.

Marsy's reply is via picture postcard from Rome, whose quartered laminate I review through the gloom of English rain (it's that sort of day) – the Colosseum of course, with pedestrians, cars and coaches – and a night shot, all of it made a luminescent green with artificial light. There are other things besides (and besides the young Michelangelo's chisel).

What's indented on the reverse side, in deeply felt ballpoint, is not so high-flown. As a matter of fact Zob is frankly vague as to the importance of Rome come the frosts of London's January. I, Wye, have some recollection. To do I think with an American beauty, robust and a strawberry blonde, who said *aw!* in so many ways (her winks, her wrinkled nose), once having somehow allowed herself to be cornered by him. I imagine that took place in the platinum foyer of one of Zob's smart new London friends, where he lingered on a cocktail, she an heiress to a perfumery. When Zob learned she had business in Rome he of course hitched up his trousers and chased after, though there is no clue to this in what was actually written on his postcard, dated January 11th—

> Greetings from Rome, where I am spending a few days. Small world, isn't it! Shared a taxi from the airport with Sir Maxwell Hayste, who initially didn't know

who I was, and yesterday, at a *bureau de change*, on the Via Palestro, which is near my hotel, caught sight distantly of Geraldine Crouch – who doesn't seem quite the lioness one recalls from TV, when tearing strips off complacent men. Glad this tour of yours is at last near an end. See you soon. Marsy

As we can see, Zob's pursuit of American collateral pre-dated Geraldine's election to the committee (Best Novel to be Published This Decade). I go further and offer my personal view that Zob had not previously met her. I say also, and with absolute certainty, that we had not yet entered that vigorous media vortex, one of whose sickly green symptoms was Crouch herself, as a regular visitor to Hampstead Hill Drive, in her cabriolet. From here on it becomes a circus, in sight of which the best of it is from my loge. Zob adopted his *faux bonhomme*, in which at least one person saw salesy possibilities – I mean Mastabyle, who could not, as parasite, raise his own profile without fatuous men like Zob. That happy *rapporteur* had links to the committee that weren't only professional. And don't forget his was a good line in after-dinner patter, exhaustively round the dining rooms of Hampstead. Philip ensured a *succès fou* for whatever the marketable Zob might turn his hand to (*Gimme the Cash*, as it happened). It's so asinine I know – yet typically Philip. (Now then. It seems some obscure communication from the worshipful company of turners has got itself mixed up with these last letters from Glaze. More research, I assume, which Zob has since dropped. But this is beside the point.) Where was I? Ah yes, these letters from the hapless Glaze. There are – as I informed my employer – only two others we might bother to consider, which strictly speaking didn't belong with that previous correspondence. I have named these the Rosewood letters, as the kind of dramatic epithet the world of Anglistics likes to adorn itself with (this is also very asinine). These two received no written reply from Zob, all of whose gossamer had borne itself up in an airier calling (or evacuant).

The evangel according to St Andrew (that late competitor with harp, St Andrew Glaze) has given us the last months of his life in his favourite south-eastern corner of England, that garden paradise he has somehow made his own, the place as well as the person still large in our memories. Rosewood: that was the name of the nursing home, its setting tall pines and clipped Elysian lawns. There from an upper window a sedated Glaze cast eyes on the surrounding hops and freshly painted oast houses. More remote are fields of corn and chestnut woods, a pastoral into which I have driven Zob often, up, down and a meander round those Kentish hills and lanes. That being a course of events touching on three distinct seasons, I am able to pass, with a single page of my album, from the feathered trees with photosynthesising shafts of light, over a woodland floor of bluebells, to the ghostly fields and brushstrokes of snow on all those five-bar gates.

Zob, a mere entity one is entitled to think of as squashed to the shape of a sigh, or perhaps a sluggish ampersand, recalled a more voluminous exchange of letters than in fact was the case. I don't think he faced this position with quite the commercial acumen he had so far demonstrated as purveyor of fictive trash. His first thought was to exclude the Rosewood letters, as not suitable to the commemoration of Glaze's life and work. Later he performed an about-turn (acknowledging the need for padding), and wanted to see them included, as an appendix he now referred to as the Rosewood testament. For the time being I was instructed not to produce a manuscript.

August 10 Unable this morning to park my car, whose offside wing (I note with no immediate prospect of remedy) has broken out in a nasty rubiginous rash. The obstruction amounts to two beefy shot-putters, in shorts and perspiring vests – one with pneumatic drill, and wearing headphones, who bores at the concrete once Zob's drive, the other with a pick, lifting flagstones. Zob, who will surely find a distant lunch appointment (and travel to it now), is also in headphones, and is hunched in his study, it only *appears* with neuralgia.

I had just about dealt with the mail, being a half-dozen letters I marked 'attention', the rest a paper mountain my foot compressed in the bin. I was asked to move my car, to make way for the rubbish skip. Once down there I saw that pneumatic drill replaced by a ballpoint, for what was now enamel mugs and a tea break. Remarkably its sausage-fisted owner made short work of his *Times* crossword – which I mentioned to Zob, eliciting a well, didn't I know, there are all sorts of people out there? Why thanks, Marsy, for that insight.

Could not help but notice, shunting my Ford through an adjacent parallax, and stepping onto the paved vista abutting the liver surgeon's, how an uncertain shrimp of a girl – in her mid-twenties, about – tested, with the point of her Victorian shoe, the disrupted purlieu of Master Zob's castle. Her jeans were a faded blue – studded, not zipped.

I locked up my car. The tea drinkers caterwauled. One of them catcalled. Would see, would they, a *danse du ventre* (as somehow figured in that crossword)? The diamond mesh of her knitted summer top, ending in elastic versts above the navel, part revealed in apricot cross hatch a firmness of young fruit. A hand many times to a strand of loose hair, she skirted the rubble to our door. Zob, who at this time discerned the flagitious in all human motives, now had reason to soften. Her presence here I later learned was 'completely' unexpected. After five minutes or so they went out together.

August 11 I am apprised of 'certain' explanations. That's because Zob, whose husbandry is again open to the charge of incompetence, launched first one, then a second official communiqué, over the kitchen table. Politely he had called Mrs Clapp Mrs St John, having framed, against her protestations, the following question: 'Well? What's *wrong* with these brushes?' (I am incredibly bored by now.) Mrs Clapp did not control her indignation, and scurried off, clutching her brushes. In no logical connection I could see, Zob told me he was having the front landscaped, though his workmen had abandoned their rubble and so far hadn't come back. He said also that a girl I might have seen yesterday was Dr Mansard's granddaughter – Arabella – whose plea of innocence he had 'totally' accepted. Tonight she would leave her toothbrush behind.

August 12 Last night she left her toothbrush behind (in bathroom one). I noticed because its bi-directional handle, so styled in an ebullience of market waffle, was a bright shade of saffron. Its bristles were fiercely mauve. One other clue was the toothpaste tube. It had two pristine indentations to the breadth of its shoulders – cool signal of contempt for the neat little folds Zob had engineered over several weeks to the other end, to the wedge of its foot.

August 14 Somehow one of Isabelle's house-and-garden magazines – a tonnage in my hand – had found its way to my bedside table. It's not all bad, for a Sunday morning read. Its voluptuous double-fold depicts perfect people in a perfect conservatory, the full course of their lives completely untouched by a permanent English mist. The floor is burnished marble. Everywhere are potted palms, wicker chairs and glassy table tops. An average housewife wears radiant *charmeuse*, while a happy husband has a knitted cardigan. There are, and this was obligatory, prone children messing about with construction kits. And smiles.

Unusually for a Sunday Isabelle got home in time to make us lunch, of macaroni cheese. Michael, his appetite only whetted, rattled his dessertspoon just as Isabelle retuned her all-booming radio. A first decisive cue was a sudden soprano, who told us 'Now, *Talking Music!*', point at which Michael went off and ravaged the freezer, re-entering with a swirl of Neapolitan ice cream, under a glistening chocolate sauce. Very pleasant intro was a background dream of Delian poppy fields, followed by the baritone unmistakably Philip. Perhaps I should not have to reiterate the accustomed lie – '...my guest today the writer Marshall Zob, whom many regard as England's finest...', Wye having by now adopted the saneness of detachment.

I listened....

Some short audible mummery placed Zob as an innocent in public affairs, a man who could not impose the rules of society, or do anything but submit to its markets. He therefore penned comedy (a grim sort of comedy) for the delight of his audience everywhere. Zob was a universal.

Philip: 'Was it always so, Marsy, or did you have to work at this?'

Work of course, stupid.

'Your first record, then....'

Well, as someone who grew up in the 1960s, something touching from the dead John Lennon. (There were places he, the dead man, remembered.) Lovely – but it surprised widow Lavante. Moving on then, and here Mastabyle summoned his plummier tones, for what about family life?

Answer: very caring – with the emphasis as you'd expect on communication. Zob though was left alone a lot, and that naturally explained the unusual, even extraordinary development of his imagination.

Another record. Zob recalls a very first trip to the Festival Hall, for a performance of Stravinsky's *Rite of Spring* – exhilarating!

Student life.

That of course was hardworking at Exe.

'You got a first.'

Philip. Zob wasn't about to boast. Here you're supposed to point up camaraderie with working-class contemporaries. Abiding image is: receptive young man taking first tentative steps across threshold of twentieth-century literature (as opposed to Oxford classics).

Never mind that. Let's have some more music.

Well, things didn't exactly go swimmingly after Exe (it took a long time just getting hack work). Even now, in irksome moments, 'I still have recourse to that wonderful Pachelbel Canon' – which is news to me.

'Success did eventually come....' We are referring here to *Aristotle's Atom*, a quite staggering first novel, which was remaindered, and might have been left to its unmarked grave but for the tireless Glaze, who nudged it without the tiniest blush into the lucrative world of low-grade movie-making.

'These things are sometimes slow to take off – but let's have some more music.'

Zob professed an old favourite in Elgar – the Cello Concerto – which I'm certain does not have a place in his CD library. Cynically du Pré as soloist (we imagine much head-shaking, and we hear the word 'tragic').

'So, Marsy, what's going on in your life *now*?' A chance to promote *Gimme the Cash* – on sale in all good bookshops and incidentally shortlisted for Best Novel to be Published This Decade. Accompaniment, Italia '90.

'Now. What of the future, Marsy? What does that hold?' Plans, stupid, for the Andrew Glaze memorial, with a lot of nonsense here interspersed: 'friend, mentor, brilliant academic'. Music that followed was: 'I'll Stake My Cremona to a Jew's Trump'.

'So to the long term.' Don't, Philip, encourage it – that whirl of saccharine, that ambitious air, that placenta Zob has termed 'millennial' (meaning we're in for a novel, dodo size).

Conductor taps lectern, wields baton, launches elastically from podium. A leather-clad demiurge clashes cymbals in the cloaked halls of Valhalla, and we're away, winged with the Valkyries.

Can't, I'm afraid, stay for *The Magic Flute*: 'I don't think, Isabelle, I can finish this Chardonnay. I shall I think just put it in the fridge.'

Be gone, salesman Zob.

August 15 Adam, more nimble on his feet, left – in a nightmare of infantile handwriting – a recipe for Mrs St John. It was in turquoise ink, with spots and spider's threads, scrawled on a sheet of crumpled notepaper, which I see he has pinned under the weight of the steam iron, prominently in the laundry room. I had wandered in there while the kettle boiled. The recipe was for pumpkin chutney, which nicely I later connected with just such a plant, whose fruit – the size of my fist – and whose loud orange trumpets shaded themselves at the rear of the chalet. Zob complained that he was still not getting through to Snell.

August 16 Mrs St John held that recipe amply to her bosom, sighing deeply. Zob said, 'For God's sake, what's happened to Cornelius!'

August 17 Zob said the same thing again. I said it so happened Merle was having problems with her new file-transfer software, $$TransPlant™. On the pretext of helping out with that, 'Shall I get over to New Caxton Grove, see what's going on?'

'That's the first sensible thing, Al, you've said. What does she want with file-transfer software?'

'She'd like to work from home more.'

'Oh.'

August 18 Merle was tied up for most of yesterday with one of her TV gardeners, with ideas for another book. Here was a man whose varicoloured flowerbeds, and a haze of patio mosaics, had livened up the rectangular plots of new housing developments everywhere – a trade he had made his own. This being so she agreed to meet first thing this morning, which means not later than ten.

Cornelius I ascertained was 'in'. His contented purr, punctuated less and less often by a second, and boyish voice, emanated through his closed door. Eventually he and Justin Simms exploded in good days and handshakes into the thickly carpeted hall, where Snell passed his prospective client to the 'very good care' of his 'right-hand man' (meaning Merle). She got up from her chair, which turned a half-revolution on its stalk, wearing an impish smile. Snell closed his door and picked up the phone.

Merle's 'very good care' was of course too good, for now, while I checked her protocol tables, she and Simms talked unguardedly of the rival agency she was about to launch and run from home. She was sure, she said, of Delilah Scuff. Simms confirmed she could also count him in. Yesterday she had worked on her TV gardener, who as loyal, earthy type was unlikely to desert Cornelius. 'Even our technician has certain ideas for a book – isn't that so, Al?' Naturally I equivocated, passing to that other field of communications. The PC, which she intended for home use, and had parked temporarily on the floor, under the desk, had been connected to the phone network, but not to the closed world of Snell's office system – which sounded to her 'grimspeak'. 'Never mind,' I said. 'We can run tests between here and Zob's.'

I told Zob, having picked my way across the rubble of his drive, that Cornelius must have been out on business.

'This file transfer,' he said. 'Is it something *we* should be using?'

August 19 Zob – and I confess I've rarely seen him puce – is today furious. The steel-tipped toe he aimed at the hall skirting board, till then an attractive pine, and perfectly mitred, and with so many intricate knots – that size nine has, I'm afraid, left several indentations. He danced on his hat, a flat chequered one he bought for but never wore on country walks. This new mood is owing to the worst trinity, which I take in reverse order (I have vegetated before too many TV game shows lately): 3) there has been no sign of his garden landscapers since that opening destruction; 2) Simms's much vaunted book has been put on the shortlist, Best Novel to be Published This Decade; 1) Zob's own – of which I have spoken many times – called *Gimme the Cash* – has been removed (from the shortlist, that is).

I was told to get Snell immediately on the phone, and succeeded only in his recorded voice. 'Then for God's sake send a fax!' which I did, though not to the precise wording Zob set out, this his moment of rending spars or shipwreck. The reply, which arrived at close of business, was from Merle, and said only: 'Cornelius out. Will call you Monday morning. Pleasant weekend.'

August 20 A profoundly mottled Volkswagen, a bright yellow where it hasn't disintegrated, has been parked on Isabelle's drive most of the morning, and lives on stoically without its front bumper. Lent to her, she explained. Someone from her art class.

August 21 Similarly a Saab, of about the same vintage – its colour a charnel-house ash – but absent of course for her secret Sunday liaison. She was not home in time for *Talking Music* – Mastabyle's guest this week a pustular Tory (once of its cabinet). Atrabilious swirl of dance music, mainly.

August 22 The political Cornelius Snell, in an extraordinary meeting – which I had the misfortune to chair – reveals only now what he has long suspected, i.e., there have been moves to have *Gimme* rescinded – a development he sees as 'retrograde'. The reason he gives for his own last days apparently incommunicado – a removal Zob was rash enough to cast overt suspicions on – is that behind the scenes he has moved 'heaven and earth' to get that important piece of work reinstated. 'You know,' he said, 'I detect Geraldine Crouch behind all this. Never trusted that woman….' Snell's large hand on the table edge, perilously near my own (of a more modest, and artistically chiselled design), thrums nervously throughout, and seems likely to slap my wrist should I casually mention that not only is Simms in town but was witnessed in his office. Zob wanted to know what to do about Simms, whose precious throne of literaturedom he seems to have usurped. This all took place in Zob's kitchen, where I also had the job of making coffee.

Cornelius: 'Well you know Marsy in the press only this weekend I see that the gal widely tipped as the first female poet laureate has challenged Moorland Frames' – Exe Professor of Poetry – 'to a public poetry bout' – a challenge whose bait the latter wouldn't rise to. 'Here's your precedent. I mean, why not do the same to Simms!'

'Now what is all this debris?' is what Snell said, in departing, as I waved him from the threshold.

August 23 Not the easiest day to get through. Hourly it seems Zob is undergoing change

– is the enraged parody of that drama I have cast him in, as my adapted Monostatos. He breathed fire, sulphur and garlic, in a reprimand for Mrs St John, who scuttled home at noon dabbing an embroidered handkerchief to the runlets of tears stinging her cheeks.

I kept more or less to my peach domain (décor having lost, as I turn my head, none of its silk). I am blessed with the charmed whispers of delicious anticipation, and cannot usher in this evening (this of all evenings) at the same accelerated rate as the thump of my heart, which I find is inditing. Eventually my hour came, and I drove – not home – but to the cambered crescent abutting the green railings, the park and its paths, which Merle's little place overlooked. I left my car. I did not climb her stairs, or tap at her door immediately, but took a first evening stroll (this one alone) along the shaded walks, over the greens, in an arc round the cricket pavilion. I plucked pink anemones in a rocky garden round an ornamental pool, and laced that little bouquet with ferns. These, when I handed them over, wrinkled the freckles of her nose, and were scissored over her drainer, where she arranged them in a vase.

Her suppers were simple. Then over pots of tea we talked business. Simms's revamped *All That Glory*, about to peak on a wave of new publicity, was a youthful tale of erotic self-realisation, and would head her list, in a glow of prestige. The stalwart Scuff, whose down-to-earth cuisine you'd depend on for hundreds more titles, was core income. *My* contribution, diarial insight into the life of a deposed prince, should some day find its market niche – and as a matter of fact she knew just the publisher.

'I'll arrange an advance.'

Merle – this was all too fast!

At sunset I needed guidance, therefore in an orange glow through a silhouette of hawthorn trees – on that second, and accompanied stroll through the park – she categorised each media snare it was wise for debut authors to avoid, as we walked. (As we walked.) I cannot describe this twilit sorcery, with its first dim stars over the roofs of her suburb. Cannot describe its narcotic pulse in my veins. 'I shall need time,' I said, for even under the dead weight of commerce there were still those who sweated over redrafts. 'Also I shall have to change all names. We wouldn't want a succession of lawsuits.' Was there, she asked, somewhere I could get away to – to finish off?

'There's a place on the fringes of Dartmoor.'

August 24 Zob, whose acuteness is the test of Snell's loyalty – something Zob would like to see nudged to the margins of adulation – fired a salvo in that direction over the fax network. His next great masterpiece takes as its subject literary rivalry (it said), with a working title *Gatekeepers*. For this he demands a colossal advance.

August 25 Snell said a million was 'steep'. Zob said he'd throw in his Glaze memoir (material he seriously overestimates).

August 26 Free City Festival, day one. It's my fact-finding mission, here where I sit with the ghosts of a famous, not so ancient venue, the Royal Albert Hall, where I can't help muttering....

Strange is this convergence. There are opposites, contraflows, a collision of echoes, a resounding theatre space, Handelian joy on one hand, hearty hymns launched up to that brightly enamelled cupola as it over-spans the whole incredible creation. On the other, a randomness of people off the streets, having flapped sodden umbrellas in the foyer, sits through a handful of poets down on the stage. Subject matter has ranged from infantile to adult masturbation (these things have to be confronted, we are told). Someone I noted plumped part way through for the sheets of rain darkening the pavements outside. Unlike him I did not have an umbrella – for which reason I learned minutely how I must 'rethink' my genitalia. O for the want of shelter....

August 27 Day two. Had the pleasure of Isabelle's company, who held my arm as we walked across Waterloo Bridge. There, in one of Zob's cosy back rooms in the South Bank complex, his interviewer – the prickly Philip Mastabyle – seemed ill at ease, persistently adjusting his lapel, which interfered with his microphone.

The structure underpinning this well patronised event was approximately so—

PM A welcome, with slimy residues, or a frog that croaked in his throat, which he never fully evacuated into that Kleenex. Such an encouraging audience.

MZ Okay [*in answer to appeals*]. Will sign books later.

PM Am proud to present, etc.... (AHEM!) who will talk today about the whole business of publishing a book – a business more open than ever before.

MZ Yes I will field questions...

PM ...time permitting (cough!), excuse! For most people it's a question of try, try, try splutter!

MZ Why absolutely Philip I couldn't have put that better.

PM Eventually you write a good book. This is the only way.

MZ The *only* way!

A raised hand, a question from the floor: Does that mean good books always find a publisher?

PM Caution: who's to analyse 'good' and 'bad'?

Another question (stifled).

PM No. I don't think we want to get into the net book agreement. Spit.

MZ No absolutely not there isn't the scope not with the ground we've got to cover.

PM Absolutely...

...and so on to the book signing, at which Isabelle got her *Gimme* bombastically monogrammed, where I swear I detected a twinkle in her eye.

In contrast Bloge and Simms had a wonderfully nostalgic time, in open discussion of Justin's woodland unbuttonings – usually with barmaids – material that constituted the kernel of his forthcoming book, *All That Glory*. Good audience response, belly laughs.

Isabelle told me, going home – an arm through the vent of my jacket, her hand flat in my rump pocket – that the Citroën would one day return. At the moment it was garaged somewhere in Kilburn.

August 28 Day three. Some quite tedious lectures at the ICA – biographers waxing unashamed on yet more truckloads on Shaw (yet again), on Wilde (yet again)…. Turn out the light…is there an author in the house!

August 29 Day four. Flude's operetta, a matinée performance, which took place in the rough and tumble over in the Coliseum. Not only did I see Snell queuing for a programme, in a quite unusual lounge suit, whose shade was a shiny anthracite, but *he* saw me, though chose that same instant to retreat to the cloakroom. I bought a programme too. On a first, superficial glance at its cover (with artwork by Julietta Simms – someone's coz) I thought little of it. Welkin was a pastel blue. Under that was a green hill. On that green hill was an expansive Georgian house, its stucco a sickly caramel. In the grounds around that house was a buskined tenor (actually a half-buskined tenor, having had a terrific accident involving one foot). It began to seem familiar.

I took my seat, and felt that tingle of excitement when a bassoon, a piano, a mellifluous horn began to warm up. I turned to and read the synopsis – a few straggly paragraphs penned in the best pugilistic prose of whatever movement the writer belonged to, which I translate roughly as follows—

Genevieve Purefoy, sole issue of Sir Walter Purefoy, wealthy industrialist and sometime government adviser. Mother, deceased. Enjoys sweeping views of South Downs from family home near Hailsham. Sir Walter has long been generous contributor to Tory coffers, and has mapped out career for Genevieve as party worker. But. Genevieve falls madly for Daddy's driver and protector, Lobridge, who is blond, tanned, virile (and nocturnally a student of chemistry). Won't on that secret ground move to Ealing, where Sir Walter has given her the keys to a house (in Montpelier Road). Sir Walter blunders in on their night of love. This is in the stable, where the buck, in a ripple of moonlit buttocks, is up on his toes. Miss Purefoy, whose knees are spread, is perched on a sill. Later, in daylight, and fully attired, Lobridge refuses to be bought off. Sir Walter's hand is forced. Decides that he will risk a scandal. Fires his man. Only now does Lobridge reveal a political identity, which is nondescript, but vaguely Liberal. He campaigns for electoral reform, but at a rally has his foot crushed under the wheels of a pantechnicon. The foot is amputated. Lobridge, convalescing, completes his degree (we don't need to stress with distinction). He acquires work and limps into the office each day. This is with a petroleum firm, from which platform he invents, patents and markets a miraculous new plastic. Now a millionaire, Lobridge hobbles back to the South Downs, where, high on a green hill, and with the wind in her hair, Genevieve has all this time been waiting. Lobridge goes down on the knee of his bad leg, weeping. *She* proposes to *him*. Tears escalate, to a deluge of joy.

There's a no-fuss wedding, which Sir Walter, who is aptly heartbroken, misses, not having survived surgery. A last word goes to Sir Walter's obituarist, who is certain an elevation to the Lords was likely. The house is shut up and sold, while the dream couple move south to Antibes, where Lobridge is determined to overcome his handicap.

Lobridge is a tenor. Genevieve, a soprano. The problem of Sir Walter, Flude, the composer, had overcome. Sir Walter is a baritone. Justin Simms – that rising star in the world of popular fiction – had written the libretto.

I note in passing some peculiarities in staging, rendered difficult, problematic, when Flude was a *bare* minimalist. For example Genevieve's split loyalties were almost always illustrated at the zenith of her register – parturient shrieks, and the wave of what looked like an order paper. The accompaniment incredibly was a hundred kazoos, blown by the children of the Moonshine Choir, or so it says here. Or take that steamy love scene. This had Genevieve couched on a hay bale, in a pool of red light, unrolling from her thigh, round her knee, over an arched foot, with toes pointing to the gantries, a silky black stocking. Flude's writing here is for raucous trumpet, muted. The choreographer – by coincidence another Flude – places Lobridge in a pool of purple light, at some distance stage left. For this we had piano thunder. Sir Walter enters to the querulous meander of an oboe.

The reviews were gushing, one rounding off with this: 'Precisely what *does* make a city free.'

August 30 No sign of Mrs St John.

August 31 Zob, who only last night found time for a whole week of reviews, is furious, and says he's been plagiarised. He can't get Snell on the phone, only his pleased recording. What about Merle? 'It appears,' I say, 'this is one of her days working from home. I don't know where she lives.' Towards sundown, in reply to his of the forenoon, he hands me a fax, a smooth reflective script that Zob has earlier crumpled in his palm, but has since smoothed out at its creases. It's from Cornelius, who advises that plagiarism's sometimes tricky. Circumspect Snell suggests a polite note to Simms. That advice Zob does go along with, but only to a certain point, wanting to tramp through anything he says to Simms with the foot-stomping threat of lawyers.

September 1 No sign either of Mrs Clapp.

September 2 Stayed off work for the whole day with a headache. A succession of old jalopies, camouflaged according to provenance – baked potato skins from sun-beaten southern plains – rolled on and off Isabelle's drive all day. Some she drove, in others she was passenger.

September 5 Am asked to scrutinise Simms's reply, and for the record key it to disc. Here goes—

Justin Simms

c/o Erlem Management

97d Cromwell Heights

London N6

2 September 1994

Dear Marsy,

So nice to hear from you. Confess to bemusement, am certainly the innocent in all this. Flude gave me synopsis – *his* property, I assumed – from which I worked libretto. Hope this clears things up.

Festival an unqualified success, I hear.

All best. Justin

The only point I can raise, but didn't, is that Erlem is an anagram of Merle. But. And as far as I know. She hasn't yet resigned from Snell's.

(Okay. I'll own up on the address too. It's undeniably hers.)

September 6 Don't really know what Marsy now intends. A letter he wrote to Flude, as an aubade after a long sleepless night, he thought better of. Come those first spiralling motes of dusk, he binned it.

September 7 Adam, who has not so far mutinied, I saw this morning bent double – concerned, as he reported to 'marster', at the continents of moss engulfing the rear lawns. Only this afternoon, after a light lunch, I took my second smoke, having slung myself low in a cane chair outside on the patio. A still air. All my blue rings softly melting. This was while, with the crash of kitchen utensils, Zob – and I did say Zob – Zob made us coffee. 'What, Al,' he asked, 'do you make of it all?' I saucered my spoon reflectively. 'Well, Marsy....'

September 8 A joint manifesto delivered by Mesdames St John and Clapp, in a black-bordered envelope gummed, I can only guess, with snake venom, the two want Wye personally to pass on to the ill-fated Zob. It has to be said, he's got his share of trouble.

September 9 An encouraging sign. That's to say a builder – a third face – arrived and strode grim-necked among that rocky Armageddon where I once parked my car. Zob says how fed up he is of leaving his Mercedes on the road. They exchanged unpleasant pleasantries, with this new contractor predicting that the golden seams at the heart of Zob's bank vaults – not even they would ever be enough to put things right. He would, he said, prepare a 'quote'.

Too late, there are two letters of dismissal awaiting signature on Zob's desk. I have not seen St John and Clapp since yesterday. In passing he asked if I knew what a Hoover was for. Obviously I said no.

September 11 Strangely Isabelle asked me the very same question, shortly after she had parked up (a dilapidated 2CV, whose folding window plates looked to me like washing hanging out). At this I smiled, and later checked her broom cupboard. Bourgeois preference here, I saw, was an Electrolux.

September 12 The Zob household – and this the great man himself intuits – takes a different brand of weekend propaganda from that of widow Lavante (a point I *shall* explain). I found him in presidential mood, Arkansas heels planted firmly on his desk. He was on the phone, in an unfamiliar pose, talking to Snell, who in a change of direction was keen to respond, and at length. Why was that? Because, of course, his sense of outrage matched that of his faithful client – his star client – the capricious Simms having signed with that er who whatchamacallit, Erlem (a firm no one appeared to know much about).

I trudged to my peach empyrean. There Zob had kindly left open one of his weekend supplements. Its scoop (or so I regurgitate), and I am just too refined to quote it in full, it said was its 'vibrant' excerpts from Geraldine Crouch's forthcoming memoir, produced with provocative *beau monde* photos, a succession of flashlit poses. Crouch shakes hands with Mrs Thatcher. Reads proclamation to Lord Longford. Is gowned at Bristol for her honorary DLitt. Is shown with an ageing novelist – or is that a toad shaking his chins? It's hard to see in this light.

Crouch invents names, for example Arthur Pole, while Larkin (who is now deceased) can safely stay as that. Her memoir turns tables she says on all her accusers, whose cartoon-like misconceptions treat her sexual mores always in connection with college girls. That she rebuts with another name, one Martlesham Sob, whom she insists is not a good lay. The same can be said of Clerihew Snail, whose seed is explosive, with the flavour of vanilla. Some men she finds are priggish and unyielding, even in the rub of her matchbox cockroach, a sickly puerile pun her punctuation sniggers at. A certain Elasticare Wile is a case in point, whom she describes as 'boorish'.

I can't say I'm shocked. Certainly not to the point of Martlesham and Clerihew, who I see from the exchange lights are still gassing on the phone.

September 13 A clean yellow sunlight at certain times each morning pours in through the miry windowpanes. In odd movements it is apt to transmute that clinging fur, where cornices meet in corners, or where the line of a staircase intersects an upper floor, into ripples of quicksilver. All goes unchallenged by the duster.

The hall carpet begins to suffer, not now having that two-headed whirlwind, St John and Clapp, in and out with the Hoover. Despite all this, Zob is cheered.

September 14 Apparently there has been a letter from Glaze's executors in Exe – a tired trio of academics – who after much deliberation are able to release papers intended specifically for Zob. Zob, clearly, has the breeze of publicity ruffling his shirt cuffs, and says he is now interested in the Rosewood letters (which I have foolishly mislaid).

September 15 That drive to Exe now contemplated. Certain memories revived. Foremost, of course, on a leaden day in February last year, was the news of Professor Glaze – a man convalescent, not peripatetic. It did not come from him directly, but from Giles, who phoned to tell Zob, who in turn told me (as, I recall, my two blue hands were wrapped round the warm glaze of my coffee mug). I said something like 'Oh', the whole scene amounting to one of historical unimportance, which nonetheless repeated itself with the much later news of his death.

We did not fly to him immediately (I mean during that fated February). Zob was at this time toasted in every West End restaurant, and kept a punishing round of social engagements – not to say Aphrodites warming his bedtime quilt. It must have been early March, with the sunny wag of daffodils, that we passed through Rosewood's massive pillars and first snaked up the loose gravel drive. Zob and I stood momentarily at the great studded door of the sanatorium.

Glaze liked his many affectations, not more so than now. The plight of his exhaustion – that electricity of mental enervation – had plunged him irreversibly into a Bath chair, complete with equipage, the woolly red check of a rug for his cold blue knees. 'Good to see you, Marsy,' he croaked. 'You must be Alistair Wye.' And of course, I was, with the job of wheeling that defunct ante-postmodern to the vast glass canopies that had – as a photograph reminds – views of the surrounding pines and Kentish rhododendrons. Glaze had the pale auburn stubble of a man who now only occasionally shaved, and wore the soft tieless collars of a man whose wardrobe was limp.

His room if sparse had a table, at which, in his moments of renewed inspiration, he pursued his transatlantic Muse, or in a squeak of schoolboyish handwriting still attempted 'once and for all' to set the record straight. He imagined a late flashlight, beyond it a night of furious scribing – his prize the prize of salvage, those first rising bubbles off his very own *Titanic*. He could still believe unverifiably in a man's recorded life, thought and experience as simply an inexorable passage of time. Yet there was, he knew, no convenient detour, no theatrical sleight of hand – however conscientiously he harvested his past.

Our next trip, in the days before I kept a diary, I am nevertheless sure came at the end of March. Then our concern was the recurrence of Glaze's rash, which left on his cheeks a large angry blotch in the shape of a butterfly. A visiting GP prescribed ointments, which with persistent use held those fires in check, though stress (and not the post-traumatic kind), a reasonable diagnosis, was one the invalid argued with. He insisted his health generally was in decline. He repeated it often, and found Jessica – having arrived from Cambridge earlier that day – indifferent and tutting. She had got her gurgling Amanda awkwardly sitting up in her car carry, into whose elastic mouth I watched her spoon a pulp of sweetened apple. Needless to say this for Glaze was overly visceral, and so – and not solely for his sanity – I wheeled him through the sun and polish of Rosewood's long hollow corridors, to the glassy cavern of the reading room. It wasn't without incident. He insisted I took with us, though I never saw him walk, an aluminium stick, which had a fearsome ferrule. He brandished it poetically – his rage the rage of genius – at almost all passing staff, none of whom seemed perturbed at his insults. Jessica burped the baby (I am told). She mentioned to Zob that Andrew's bad temper was down to the bull-neck, who was footing the Rosewood bill. 'I can see,' said Zob (later, to me, in the car), 'how that must hurt.'

Other trips, should I try to remember them chronologically, show in the red trace on Andrew's chart no recognised pattern of decline. Sometimes he was up. At other times down. There is a moment of recall that illustrates it well. Glaze watched us to the gate after a last pot of tea. I checked the time, and as we set off agreed with Zob it was early enough to try a variation on our route. His car I plunged into a dappled forest, Zob in his cosy corner tossed around on the back seat, our tyres gripping each new twist in the road with a squeal. Bluebells, a radial sunshine, the flash of silver birch – and Zob watching none of it. Instead in the dampish brakes of his own, internalised bucolics, his one shady thought turned its all-bright flower to the rays of the woodland roof with a single admission only – that certain critics had yet to be won over. To me it was clear why, though I made a show of checking our roadmap. His pursuit of mass popularity, and that addictive desire he had for respectability, were not *both* his to satisfy – though naturally those persons he had called to duty round him accepted that they were, or themselves fell silent.

Glaze was at his gravest when attempts to shave – I noted the tremble of his hand – made of his face a colourful patchwork, with V-shaped nicks and interconnecting clumps of stubble. Our journeys there were then at high speed, memories of which are no more than a whirl of village greens, with a haze of newly flowering orchards. Glaze on one occasion was very acerbic, even with Zob. Jessica had preceded us by a few days, and had left him things to reflect on. A tooth mug on his table had been part filled with water for an arrangement of campions, with just a swish of spurge. There was an empty tin of something for Amanda in his bin. Zob was talking about film, radio, TV tie-ups – media media media. Glaze, with an issue of *The Five Dollar Review* nestling in the hollowed rug of his lap, kept telling us 'Now – now I'll read you that poem' – something he had long promised to do. He in fact broke down in a tremulous fit of sobbing, not having reached the second stanza. He waved his stick and us away, but that was just one in a catalogue of scenes for which there has been no explanation. Others were—

A broken bed head. Post he returned to the mail unopened. Two bedding sheets tied together (Glaze's room was ground floor). A letter to the bull-neck pleading for Jessica's (yes Jessica's) release. A refusal to eat breakfast, unless under the watchful gaze of one of two women who cleaned his room, who was too busy to do so. Zob, I have to say, never noticed much wrong, or as policy failed to react.

He was better in June. Deteriorated slightly in July. In August the GP pronounced him in the rudest health, when a relieved Zob bought his old mentor a psychedelic tie (apparently a joke. Zob inscribed the gift tag so: Andrew, remembering the Sixties!). Then, in September, Giles had to sit for long hours in the dome of Rosewood's reading room, of all things ploughing through Ginsberg. Only this, it seemed, could smooth his daddy's crumpled brow, and shut his eyes peaceably. Then one Wednesday Giles got suddenly called away on business, and did not thereafter see his father alive. Samantha I don't think ever visited, but kept in touch by phone. She even phoned Zob, notably one mid-October morning, in a panic over something Andrew had said. Was Andrew at this point raving? Did she believe in Zob as the only being on earth capable of pulling him through? I am, I hardly need say, the disinterested Wye, and just don't know, though of course was asked to drive, through a child's wonderland – clustered dew drops on a thousand ghostly webs, a bright distant sun, we in our dusky Mercedes cruising east, as a single morning ray transfused those swirls of English mist. Unexpectedly we found Glaze rosy and jovial, and discovered that the bull-neck had arranged his membership of a nearby country club. We repaired there buoyantly, where Zob plied him with sherry. That obeisance performed, we returned him to Rosewood, gushing and flushed. A crisis, Zob assumed, averted, though it was there, for the last time, that we left him.

Jessica, the rebel Jessica, was the last member of his own circle to converse with him, to touch his warm flesh, though like us knew nothing of the monsters invading the dark pool of Andrew Glaze's final November night. He managed to noose himself, in a psychedelic tie, and was found – jowls a deep royal purple – his socked feet dangling lifelessly in a circle, somewhere over that overturned Bath chair.

September 16 Number 28a, Scriveners Mews – Glaze's modern three-room flat fronted by a stone façade. Although it belonged, as part of its worldly estate, to Exe University, in deference to its otherworldly resident its rooms had been left uninhabited since his passing. The three academics who showed us to the professor's roll-top were comfortably dull, comfortably archetypal. The first had a shiny dome. The next was thinning, the day's detachment clinging to his shoulders. The last was quietly wrinkled. What they gave us, or rather gave Zob, was a bright yellow folder containing a handful of loose papers. There was also a bundle of business correspondence, tied with string. It included Zob's postcard from Rome.

Glad to leave that sepulchre.

September 20 A fourth builder, whose truck was compressed under the cargo of sacks of sand and a cement mixer, arrived to survey the ruin of Zob's frontage. Noting ever new measures taken from his rule he traversed the graded circles of that particular purgatory, and breathed in sharply. He left a card (not his, but a colleague's), then drove off forever westward into the mildness of the morning.

September 21 Zob, having left that yellow folder on my desk, now asks me to add to it one more paper – his programme for the thanksgiving service, which he has kept in a drawer since November 1993. Its cover layout is worth reproducing—

> THANKSGIVING SERVICE
>
> FOR
>
> JOHN ANDREW GLAZE
>
> PROFESSOR OF ANTE-POSTMODERNISM
>
> EXE UNIVERSITY
>
> on
>
> Tuesday 23 November at 1.00 p.m.
>
> in
>
> Sir Galahad Hall, Exe University

Zob is keen that I 'study' what are now referred to as the 'yellow' papers, should they cast light on that extinct theory of literary time. In Zob's mind it has a bearing on the Rosewood letters, and will determine whether I am to resurrect them. Let us, however, take a closer look at this programme – a service I did not attend, and which Zob has not much spoken of till now....

Page one is headed by the service commencement, or the playing of music for cello bows, by S. Collerant, a rhythmic percussive piece for an ensemble of bows (with no accompanying cellos). A welcome and introduction by the Rev Jonathan Dyke, followed by presentation of emblems and diplomas. It consisted of Glaze's many degrees, most of course honorary, preceded by Giles with Daddy's ancient camera, Samantha with Inveraray toasting fork (acquired on their honeymoon), and a J. Hunter with brass rubbings (whose significance is lost on me). Then a reading from *Rabbit Redux*, by M. Pritchett.

Page two, from top to bottom, was: 'News of the World III', a poem by George Barker, recited by M. Zob; an organ transcription, *Fanfare for the Common Man*, played by Mrs F. Deboyes; then tributes (various names); followed by readings from a selection of Glaze's own works; ending in prayers, silence, a hymn, 'Jerusalem', then the final blessing.

God grant him peace.

September 23 The harpy Crouch, which is Zob's touching epithet, not mine, whose branch of humanity exempts itself from all tones of reconciliation, positions herself in the booms of theological bravado – or so I read it – in her invitation to Zob, apropos of forthcoming festivities: public/private celebrations of her fiftieth. Zob is even vain enough to accept.

September 27 Have now had a chance to study the 'yellow' papers. They range from notes, references, embryonic essays in Glaze's immature hand, to press cuttings and torn pages from a number of American journals. Between them they shed no light at all on the absurd theorising of an English academic, who it is clear spent much of his sabbatical attempting to demolish – without success – opposing points and arguments posed in both print and the lecture hall. I am sure he cannot have seen justification for that intellectual slip of the wrist, and in my view sought ways of establishing one of two things – either that his 'literary time' was in fact metaphorical, and not to be taken literally, or some further complexity that rendered the whole sorry hodgepodge deeply impenetrable, and in the short term – i.e. the duration of Andrew's American jamboree – unanswerable. Glaze was not above this latter option. Let me direct you to one of his Stateside critics, some of whose published comments Glaze himself draws attention to, via highlight pen. I quote the last sentence from an editorial found in the journal *Hesperides*, summing up his rise in the early 1970s: 'You shouldn't doubt that no one ever really knew what Glaze and his confederates were getting at, though they collected many prizes....'

It is amusing too that far from bin those many objections previously touched on, Glaze actually toyed with some. I see that time tree notion at least made him think, for he has worked in intricate detail – on the back of an envelope – some highly deleterious future for his beloved Samantha – all based on the decision to blow his nose.

September 28 Much as I enjoy the exercise and the poison of my pen, in its tussle with the lights of our time, I am not wholly without sympathy. As I've come to see it now, the disaster for Glaze was the lack of any ground plan, and what he imagined his shoddy, cobbled-together thoughts aloud were going to be – a lucrative waffle at young adults who'd not had sufficient time on planet Earth to think about anything very much. Yet people won't be palmed off, either in the virgin territory of youth or in the remoter accretions of age.

September 29 Glaze, Glaze, Glaze.... Everything Zob says is Glaze....

October 3 I have, Marsy, as requested, considered the commemoration project. Some trick of literary time means you 'remember' a great deal more correspondence than is actual. So – let me furnish statistics. It's an exchange that began on December 13th, 1991, and ended with the second Rosewood letter (both of which I am now instructed to drop), on April 21st, 1993. Approximately 13,000 words were penned or keyed. There are in total forty-one letters and cards (a thirty-five/six split). Nineteen of the letters were written by Glaze, and only sixteen by Zob. To Glaze's five postcards there is one, Marsy, by you (remember that trip to Rome?).

'Thirteen thousand words, eh, Al? That's going to take some padding! Got any ideas?' Well, Marsy – just a couple....

October 4 National Poetry Day, and the spectacle of Annie Cryles, the redhead, who has somehow scooped a string of awards-with-bursaries, reciting her catatonic dirge on early evening TV. I am in favour of promoting all high-ranking Arts Council persons to the first manned exploration of Mars.

O that studded crystal, our modest little solar system....

October 7 Zob Senior, acting for Zob Junior, has been talking to one of his learned friends of the Temple. This morning we received a high-quality vellum, with medieval illuminations, whose unpunctuated blocks of type culminate in an indecipherable signature (a balloon dissected by a pen stroke). This confined gas of a man has agreed to take up the young Zob's allegations of plagiarism, now directed at Royston Flude.

Beg pardon, Your Honour, but....

'What was that, Al?'

'Why nothing. Except to say Merle wants me to test that file-transfer software, tomorrow...Saturday....'

October 8 Merle, I find, is in a state of euphoria. That is because her paperwork has progressed with unexpected celerity. The point is that on Wednesday she anticipates clearing her desk at New Caxton Grove, and on Thursday officially opening Erlem's for business. I cannot prevent her floating to the various ceilings. Nor will an innocent smile depart for any clockable duration – not that I, the amused Alistair Wye, ever wear a watch. That slightly pinked satin, that happy, that gorgeously animated face! I am asked subsequently shall I propel her on those park swings near her house, where the breeze gets in her hair, and the points of her toes score two ecstatic arcs in the light bright air of our heaven.

She insists on buying me a seafood lunch, somewhere on the brink of Ealing, and drinks too much vintage champagne. It's the kind of celebration that goes on, and on, and I therefore postpone our file-transfer tests until tomorrow.

October 9 I arrived at Snell's, Snell in his white bathrobe with a clutch of Sunday papers, on whose doorstep I intoned much mysterious gibberish concerning $$TransPlant™ – which Snell assumed referred to something called – or *he* called – 'electro-surgery'.

'Why of course come in, dear boy!' he said, and ushered me to, and left me with, the dotted lights and humming fans of his computers. I constructed a block of ASCII text for a first test transmission, but that was not a success. Zob's receiving equipment did not, for some reason, respond.

I drove over. I had, I was certain, installed the software. I parked up behind a Renault, whose coachwork was a muddy-looking beige, peppered with brown to burgundy rust. I picked my way over the rubble, reflecting that yes, I *had* set Zob's FT server running. What – as I slipped in my door key...yes what (for this was all so irritating!)...what, I couldn't guess, was wrong?

I blundered into the study, where Isabelle, in only a lemon bowtie, plus matching ankle socks, was prostrate on the desk, but supported at the dugs in the squeeze of Marsy's palms. Zob – the hirsute Zob – throbbed, and I suppose shrivelled in her loins, and in his exertions had toed and unplugged the modem. I said something like 'Oh', as did Isabelle, though hers was really a gate in a whole fence of exclamations. Zob, not unreasonably, said only 'Get out, Al!'

October 10 Not surprisingly Isabelle, who has 'gone away' for a week, expects me to find other lodgings before she returns. Zob, for whom these things are merely a recreational hazard, did not expect me to fill my briefcase with computer discs, and resign.

October 12 Merle also resigns...

October 13 ...and so Erlem is born. That firm's senior partner is shrewd enough to set aside sufficient start-up capital for three-months' rent re that delightful damp retreat on the fringes of Dartmoor. Here my first task is to write a synopsis, which she expects to discuss over morning coffee with one of her publishers. It's a man called Dr James, who runs a highbrow, independent press. Dr James is primed.

I chose the den adjoining the sitting room, with that stuffed, old-fashioned armchair – a good place for relaxing with paper drafts and a red pen. The four-legged, iron-framed table, with a red cover, I used for fag breaks. For work I shipped in a light deal desk where I had the laptop – the laptop I'd purloined from Zob, as a kind of poetic justice. The abrupt lack of symmetry in the colour scheme turned out not to be a distraction, the walls a chequerboard of yellow, ochre, blue, green (see my entry for July 18th above). Said Merle: 'We will need a cover portrait.' She sent in her photographer, who set me at my table and asked for a disdainful look (one has only to consider everything I've been through). The book front will show the author at work, or rather meditating, with a lit cigarette. He has his yellow coat and scarf to match, and has chosen as headgear a joke bowler hat acquired on his travels.

November 27 Have begun the second redraft. The main problem is to invent fictitious names. I have to keep a balance between the real and the bizarre. Incidentally Merle, who was here this weekend and only a few hours ago caught the London train back, has told me Snell is more enthusiastic over Zob than ever – and is pressing for that million. She was sure that what had changed his thinking was a recent campaign – TV, street hoardings, every bookshop window – proclaiming Simms, her own Justin Simms, 'the number one bestseller'. I am told bookmakers make *All That Glory* clear favourite for that peculiarly English accolade, Best Novel to be Published This Decade. However I, the unassailable Alistair Wye, know better than that.

Such a bleak glorious stroll we had, this afternoon over the moor.

Christmas Day A capon I brought up from Riverford Farm is in Merle's oven. We are at her kitchen table, whose centrepiece is the manuscript she completed her first full read of only last night.

'Fine, Al,' she says (uplifting tone), 'though I don't much recognise this Merle.' Today her yellow hair is in a tight coil at her nape. 'Also, it needs a foreword.'

'To say what?'

'Something anticipatory.'

'How about *The Guilt That is Hampstead's*, third act, in which the first gardener Adam is granted new life – fairer, more meaningful employment....'

My job to peel potatoes. Though I cannot first resist a mild gin and tonic.

Merle says, 'Now seriously, Al....'

Well now, let me think. In my memoir of social decay, which has been after all the catalyst of artistic regeneration, I shall start I suppose with a fatality. The corpse is symbolic. Some time hence its transmogrified mulch is the moving ground that the grandeur of a renascent literature flourishes in. It shan't be compacted – not by those clumsy hobnails our many Marshall Zobs tramp in our world of printed pages in.

Why yes, Merle. I should do that this afternoon. Probably after lunch. What we're talking here is best novel to be published this, and the next, and the next decade.

Allow me to raise my glass (that gin, that long cool something), and drink your health (that is to you, genteel reader). As for me I *shall* remain your faithful Alistair Wye – and this you will see...

...and yes, I *shall* return I promise. Shall certainly smile for the camera.

Click!

Caliban's Machine

…they who are so fond of handling the leaves, will long for the fruit at last.
—**Sheridan,** *The Rivals*

Publisher's Note

Caliban's Machine is a series of fragments or missives, penned towards the end of 1998 by the English poet George du Plé, using a laptop he'd acquired, with a prefatory note (as follows) and annotations by his editor, John Royce.

Du Plé is looking back in several different ways. Large in his thoughts are the late 1970s, and his connections with a publishing family living in rural Kent (Tralatition Press). Grafted on is his experience of the early 1980s, a period that saw him document student experiments at the Donns Watson Research Institute for the Performing Arts, in Lower Manhattan. There is, as a direct development of that, his subsequent editorial role in *Village Id*, a New York journal, or nowadays 'zine', followed vaguely by the mid- to late-1990s, when he roved the world in pursuit of no profession in particular.

Du Plé, at the time of writing these fragments (1998), had returned to the rural setting of the 1970s, aware that the family, which still owned the property (called Middlecross Towers), had now gone back to London. Du Plé's return was ostensibly to recover the various books and papers that throughout his travels he'd sent back for safe-keeping.

These fragments or letters, composed during his time alone at Middlecross, are all addressed to Alex (*née* Little), a member of the departed family, and the member he was closest to.

Officially, these letters were never delivered, an omission compounded by du Plé's disappearance before their completion. It was in this state that John Royce discovered them, and made a copy, and later added his commentary. There are certain clues to be found in du Plé's text indicating that this is what he intended. By 1998, the time of composition, the internet had made it relatively easy to locate people, in their work and habitat. Du Plé had remembered the name d'Ursag, Tralatition's last commissioning editor, and approached him with a view to publishing his memoir. D'Ursag told him that Tralatition had long been subsumed into Leader Books, but only for the sake of maintaining its backlist. However, as he knew of other small independent presses, and also knew John Royce, a deal might be possible incorporating both authors under the same title. Royce took up his pen again, and enlarged on his commentary. Here it's important to say he is not a neutral observer, having kept up his own connections with the Donns Watson, particularly with Robert Quay, founder of the course in poetics that du Plé found himself overseeing. By then du Plé had also added to his text, so the two were faced with having to re-evaluate each other.

Royce, when presented with George's newly revised papers, was probably expecting a written retrospect, in dry academic terms, and a calmer examination of his experience of the Donns Watson. So to speak with the wrong reading glasses, he mused on what to him was the flaw in George's summary, and put this down to du Plé's family characteristics (see his prefatory note below). Du Plé's father was a draughtsman, whose library consisted of battered engineering books, and in whose household, a 'part-timbered dwelling', the young George played with marbles and messed with Meccano, never learning how to analyse *social* machinations.

Royce, of course, would know all about du Plé's various predecessors, and most probably sympathised with the elder Crane, 'a man', according to Waldo Frank, 'of turbulent and twisted power…outraged by the jest of fortune that had given him a poet for a son'. That son of course was Hart Crane, author of *White Buildings* and *The Bridge*, whose biblical resonance du Plé – half a century later and on the Atlantic's dormant side, bookishly speaking – briefly emulated in his student days as poet. On that note we think John Royce has the *right* glasses on, and in a sense is reading *for* us, in the pages that follow. Yet those pages might not have happened at all. In 1998, there were things in George's text Royce insisted he excise, and there were interpretations Royce had made that du Plé vehemently disagreed with. The two squabbled, to the point of mixed consent as to what the book was to consist of precisely. Then, finally, later that year, the project was shelved. It is now 2017, and the thing has been revived, long after each author's purpose would have been served (du Plé wanted his first love back, Royce wanted a divorce).

One thing still puzzles us here at the press, in the unique position we are placed in, never having met either du Plé or John Royce. We were approached in February of this year, not by either of the two authors, but by d'Ursag, through whom all negotiations were mediated. Therefore we ask, is John Royce the figment of the author's self-policing process, let loose with invented crossbeams over that other figment du Plé, whose poetic gift is ceaselessly prone to social and academic irritability – or is there an objective purpose in what is first a textual syntagm (a publisher's note, an editor's note, edition notes, epistles), but in the end is a textual logjam (all that and two sets of comments, rooted in distinctly different times)?

Perhaps you should decide.

—*Christian Patmore James, CentreHouse Press, Nelson, New Zealand, 2017*

Editor's Note

Theoretically these fragments, whose premature end is an ellipsis, meshed together tardily in George du Plé's hand, add up to a 'confession', his friend Alex (*née* Little) only superficially the addressee – or Alex perhaps the decoy. Let me add too, in that same spirit of confession, that these few helpless spasms – du Plé after all a minor English poet – have been crossed with *my* pen purely by accident. Though there is no mercy, while I sit here sharpening my nib, the role I hope is a transient one.

No one should be fooled by the infelicities the galled du Plé offers his Beatrice, as an explanation for his departure, a sudden departure back in 1979. Did that leave the house and family, where much of his time had been spent, as bewildered as *he* became? Du Plé can blame everything on Marcia Copparo – 'Copparo, who plunged into these isles chaotically in the summer of 1979', to use his own turn of phrase. How he followed her Latin lures, not quite into the hub of the New York gallery system – her own hand the prohibiting one – is somehow an excuse. First we get his brooding, then later his indifference. I think the latter state is the one that must apply when du Plé abandons himself to the Donns Watson, an artistic haven in west Greenwich Village, noted not solely by me for its pioneering work.

I cannot imagine that throughout these sixty-five agonies (or I should say LXV), du Plé has in mind an audience of one. That 'one', in the intervening years, has had and now puts behind her a career in the theatre (not that du Plé knows much about that), and I suspect is well acquainted with the tricks and artifice of *his* trade. Take for example his fragment numbered XXVI, where the Donns Watson firmament converges on the back doorstep of George's charnel house, a gathering we're shown a glimpse of before it's consigned to a poetry of flames. Robert Quay, whose brainchild the Donns Watson is, I see is singled out for lasting detention (our beleaguered Anglo Rose somewhere uses the word 'condemn', which as too prevalent in a poet's vocabulary is thereby meaningless). All bears the hallmark of intellectual indolence.

Not that I defend Quay simply as a colleague, separated less by an institutional idiolect than an eight-hour flight – a flight incidentally bi-directional as well as transatlantic. In the collision of cultures whose end in du Plé's mind can only be disaster, we ask is that the New World as a tarnished outgrowth of the Old, or the Old addicted to the tarnish of the New? It is du Plé himself who skews his reality, and not the environment he's at odds with, a process of self-delusion I see him habitually stoop to. There are numerous examples. It's a fact that Alex Little never played Brahms intermezzos (fragment XVII). Never at any stage were there wine bins in Middlecross's cellar (fragment III). When there exists a slim ancestral connection with the Dodgson family, it's almost certain that the *Fiery Sickle* (fragment IX) is a fabrication intended to link the anonymous Alice Little (in part Alex's sibling) to her near namesake Alice Liddell. I am sure also that Michael Trent (friend of the Little family, see fragment VIII) is an impostor in emulation of Alan Mitchell, whose *A Field Guide to the Trees of Britain and Northern Europe* was published by Collins in 1974, and whose Pinetum at Bedgebury is only one setting in du Plé's distorted rig-up (note 1, fragment VIII). I'll add that the 'bandeau' of fragment XII is one of du Plé's many samples of exotica, like those Gallic cigarettes he smoked (fragment, or figment XXIV – du Plé a non-smoker). Alex wore an Alice band and not its French equivalent. The whole dubious edifice is of a cultural provenance pre-dating and therefore blurring that of the Donns Watson, an exercise in self-authentication du Plé is never entirely free of.

And why, I ask, does he adopt that distant tone in his dealings – his dealings at one remove – with Marcel D'Orbieu, whose *Geometry of Everyday Life*, in particular its essay of page 66, is given its own plateau in du Plé's circles of brimstone? D'Orbieu only seems to me to make the suggestion that the planar dimensions we live in, our Cartesian intersections, our angular disjunctions – are the reality all human grammars operate from. Yet here again is George, pre-empting his first pen to paper, to commit his hapless Marcel first to the US then to the UK postal system, urging his Alex – his Alex of two decades before – to retrieve it from the mail, and read ('Please do this now', fragment VIII). One knows before long that the only 'grammar' du Plé is open to is a kind of fictive revitalisation, though it's never certain if his future is the cliff face ahead, forever crumbling into our present, or if that present is an Eleatic arrow, permanently failing to meet its target.

As for du Plé's personal past, or origin, his father was a draughtsman, and worked as an engineer. If we fish in that gene pool long enough we'll probably explain du Plé's fierce objection to D'Orbieu's *Geometry* – a technical arena he regards as out of bounds to those entrenched in a world of letters. His mother was a music teacher. The family threesome lived at the margins of the hop industry, in a grey-roofed village equipped with a pub ('Gaul's Head') and a corner shop, whose pre-war 'Hovis' sign remains. The family home was a part-timbered dwelling in an oldish Kentish cottage style, flanked on one side by an apple orchard, and on the other by a tributary of the Medway (riparian walks and an iron bridge, in battleship grey). One sees geographically where his lyrics were birthed.

It was Alice who first knew him, having met him at a public reading, or public lecture, with one of its speakers a William Morris enthusiast, who had put together as a connected narrative an excerpted *News From Nowhere*. Her then current book group congregated at a private address in Capel, a venue where du Plé later gave *his* first reading (doubtless one of his Crane derivations). Alice subsequently introduced him to her sister Alex, at a chance meeting in a large walled garden in Frant, where a troupe of medievalists had come to re-enact a joust.

At this stage that's as much as I should say, except to add that all Alex remembers of this, apart from those thundering hoofs, is having heard some folklore surrounding du

Plé Senior, who'd had a brush with the law. Days before, he'd forced off the road the local Tory MP, whose car – a vintage Alvis – careered into the plate glass of the town's only stationers (one of several businesses owned by that member and his family). No fatalities, no cuts or bruises. However, in replying to the magistrate, in answer to the question 'Why?' the engineer said only this: 'Because he deserved it.'

That, as an introduction, just about wraps it up, except to point out that a preliminary note like this is really an afterword, a pre-emptive summing up. I would like to point out too that du Plé is a figuration of the word 'duple' [f L *duplus* meaning *duo*], suggesting masks, doubles and even duplicity.

Can you believe the duplicitous George du Plé?

—*John Royce, Hampstead and Middlecross, 1998*

This Edition

In 1998 I told du Plé that there was very little chance of finding a publisher willing to take on the autobiographical ramblings of an obscure and little-known English poet. George moreover hadn't been too bothered about getting his poems known, either through the West's multitude of literary journals or through a programme of public readings. Nor had he financial independence and could call, like Proust, on a young, progressive, Grasset-type to help him into professional publication. The cost then of doing it yourself was still relatively high, and pads, tablets, kindles and other e-devices were yet to be invented. All that was doubly inconsequential when his dispute with his editor dampened the enthusiasm each had had for the project, which has since lain dormant for almost twenty years. But personal circumstances change, as do our family and public relationships – as also has publishing technology.

I met him in London in the winter of 2015, after we had emailed extensively, George from his frame house near the ocean road, on Waiheke Island, a shoreline exile that explained the ravages of sun and wind and his weather-beaten look. We arranged a 2.30 rendezvous in the Café in the Crypt, St Martin-in-the-Fields, where I found du Plé already at a table, not yet having taken off his scarf and coat. Even indoors, England in November was an inhospitable exterior better buttoned up against. I picked him out by the book he said he would show prominently, a paperback edition of *The Way by Swann's*, which he left face-up alongside his cup and saucer. (I knew that addition to the Proust industry – a translation by Lydia Davis, under the general editorship of Christopher Prendegast, published in 2002. The series came out with great fanfare.) George still had that image in his mind of our meeting in 1998, when I claimed to be a youthful fifty-something. Now it was hard for him to adjust to the rotund, completely bald figure extending a cheery hello. I had not aged as well as he. Du Plé approached his sixtieth birthday wild-haired, greying, slim of build, and still with a spark in his eye. He was a poet after all.

He told me he had worked for the last fifteen years as a language teacher in Tokyo, where he had crossed paths with James Kirkup, though had read his *Gaijin on the Ginza* (with its Tokyo setting) only after his death (Kirkup, 1918–2009), by which time du Plé had retreated to Auckland. For his brief visit here in England he had used Airbnb. The place he'd found was near a station on the Hastings line into London, and close enough to Middlecross for a stroll into Church Lane, where he could photograph its gables. He remembered a classic geometry etched against a clump of pines, and in spite of surrounding property development would continue to think of it in that way – the James Little little princedom, as he called it. The whole plot had had an infusion of cash (the dirt of new money, he said), which he regretted. Gone the brick paving as frontage, where Marg had parked her Morris Traveller, a permanent presence under the drawing-room window. It had been replaced by speckled macadam, with the surrounding shrubbery uprooted, and was a much larger-looking expanse. There up to four vehicles were parked at any one time (a Range Rover, a Volvo estate, a sporty little Mazda, a VW plastered with stickers). I asked him frankly if he would like to meet Alex, which I thought I could arrange. There were hardly two days together when he didn't think of her. But she'd had a career. There were two grown-up daughters. The young woman he had known had married, twice. A reunion he'd find awkward.

He showed similar agitation about the book. Now that there were three distinct timeframes he wondered if the thing wouldn't work as a whole. All he'd wanted was to encapsulate that poetically charged moment in the late '70s, early '80s, when two diffident people – himself, George, and James Little's stepdaughter – had formed their union, with Middlecross as its backdrop. What he insisted had been a 'first' exile in New York he feared had made his reflections over complex. He wondered if, in 1998, he'd quite captured the threefold vision that had sustained him throughout that loss – of Alex, of Middlecross, of Tralatition Press – and to what extent Royce's annotations had dented the personal mythology vested in that trinity. Now in 2015 the past had changed again, and some further commentary on it, or the bit we were dealing with, seemed necessary. He asked if I would write it, something beyond a few words of introduction, and launched out passionately on the need for a second tier of footnotes. The mechanism for that I said would prove a challenge. Nevertheless I promised I'd give it some thought. He'd read reviews of mine online, and trusted me.

We talked much about the medium, with du Plé adamant that if the thing came out as an ebook – to which he had no objection – it should come out first in print. I suggested that the press I had found would prefer electronic publication, the advantage being that with three voices and an intermesh of notes and counter-notes, the ease of forward and backward referencing was a feature easily facilitated. Du Plé understood. 'But I am old school,' he said, 'with an unbreakable connection to the book as object,' what with the cover, the weight and feel, the turn of the pages, ultimately rank and presence on a bookshelf, which for the years of our lives is intimately presided over.

He was in England for just another five days, during which time I met him only twice more – very briefly – so that once he'd drunk his tea and filtered out onto Trafalgar Square, and had subsequently returned home to Waiheke Island, it was back to our email negotiations. The result is this, a primary and an underlying text, du Plé's and Royce's, connected by an elaborated system of notation. The Royce text, or the Commentary as listed on the contents page, is governed by a supplementing system of endnotes, and access to it is tagged as of this example, [R:I.n1.pn], which means see the Royce text, Section I, note 1, page n. As you follow these navigation points you will sometimes see reference to a further text, because I have done as George requested and added, in the terms he has spoken of, the third time signature, my Envoi. The return flight from any leap forward is via backward references that follow the same principle as outlined above, where [dP:I.pn] means the du Plé or primary text, Section I, page n, while [See dU:VII.pn] means refer to the d'Ursag Envoi, Section VII, page n. I promise, you *will* get the hang of it. But let me warn you now: for this book you will need three bookmarks, or for the electronic version just follow the hyperlinks forward and back, and ignore the page numbers.

—*Jack d'Ursag, Denmark Hill, London, 2016*

Middlecross Towers, Highwicke, RO5 1ND

I Regrets

The storm-tinge of confession, now that I am back. You were right, sitting here with me – when? – almost two decades ago. I admit this. Nevertheless there are mementoes, among the books I begin to unearth. [R:I.n1.p637]

II Cradling

You were also right about this house, whose approach is a maze of undergrowth. Somehow my keys no longer seem to fit the door, or aren't the keys I thought they were, or remember. Eventually I found hand tools in what used to be the workshop, and prised open a service hatch to the cellar, which came away at the hinges (here, Alex, much of the timber has rotted). I try, but cannot imagine in words the hollow clang as the jemmy struck the cellar floor, or the vibration of feathered air, when a flock of pigeons left the trees and circled the chapel.

Yet certainly I see, in the first deceptions of sleep, that bearded Roman whose eclogues were (you said) initialled under the winged augury of a dove, in flight over an atrium, towards the peppered green of an olive grove. [R:II.n1.p637]

III Speak, Mnemosyne

Nor could I quite remember that labyrinth in the depths of Middlecross, in whose sepulchral twilight I tripped on a bicycle wheel, and in so doing disturbed the dust on an old heap of hat boxes. I clattered into wine bins. I tempted, furiously, a switch for the bulb over the table-tennis table, then groped my way to the wooden stairway steeply angled in cobwebs, and plotted my way up into that huge, haunted, starkly tiled kitchen (mugs of coffee drunk here endlessly, once).

There is, today, a reddish tinct of reflected maple leaves, coming in through the stone casement, over the pine table, over the quarry-tile floor, which without its mop is a dull maroon.

Did I hear the deliberate crunch of car tyres out on the gravel?

IV Point, compass point

And did I get my bearings? Well. No. Not immediately. Amazingly I'd forgotten about the enamel mosaic cemented as a kind of mandala and centrepiece into the floor of the hall, and had forgotten too how small a rectangular space that was. Disturbed by this (disturbed by this amnesia) I stood here. The barometer said fair. There were, Alex, half a dozen walking canes stacked neatly in a corner by the door. No post on the mat.

The dresser still has its clothes brush. The brush is supine. Its black bristles haven't lost their gloss – they point to the moulded laurels in the ceiling.

V Dead letters

As you suggested, all my belongings are here and hereabouts – some in the walk-in cupboard, some piled on the workbench in Alice's lumber room, where she first used to paint furniture, for her market stall. There are papers, which mostly I'd forgotten, but among them I have found my letters home (or letters here). This I regret. Why do you not possess them, Alex? There are other things I'm looking for, though what I have so far gathered I have taken to the small round studio. You never liked it there. Cold and easterly – forbidding, you said. You remember, when all but you, and I, and Alice....

VI What kind of vista

The view is not the same. No life on the lawns, which are clover and weeds. Hedges gone wild – are the ragged delimiters in what was a squared geometry, the tiers and terraces plunging down – in a summer haze, in an autumn mist – to the boating lake. Fractured statues. A first hint of winter in the movement of every branch.

The phones don't work. Theirs and other ornamental tables are layered in dust. The fob light on my key ring pales. I shall find matches, and roam in the cellar again, where I shall turn on water, electricity, gas.

VII Dead letters read

Have started to go through my papers, their bundles tied with yellow twine, which I see have been thrown together in no particular order. Some few lines dated – dated when? – remind me how I *imagined* my return—

> Orange streaks
> across a southern road....
> [R:VII.n1.p638]

I did not anticipate then that the house would be deserted, its life extinguished, and all of you fled.

Just now I was certain someone glided in through the doorway, but there was only a breeze in the wash of blue curtains.

That vane, that man with his hoe capping my eastern tower, squeaks in the wind.

VIII American

Two more of my books from that lumber room: an *Alice* (I bought this and had your sister in mind), and Trent's *Trees of Britain.* [R:VIII.n1.p640] This I took with me – I don't know why – but must have returned in the post.

Talking *of* America, please refer to that D'Orbieu I've sent you (I mailed it to you yesterday). [R:VIII.n2.p640] Please do this now. Because…

…I still have etched in my walking consciousness the paths as they circumscribed that Long Islander, who fatally was Alice's friend, and whose name you won't have forgotten – Marcia Copparo. Copparo, who plunged into these isles chaotically in the summer of 1979. By then she had tramped across mainland Europe lovelorn after a Frenchman, a plan she had to give up, finally. With what adhesive I don't know, pasting the fragments of her broken heart – but her smiles, that incessant chatter. She spent a sullen few days weather-wise in London, having arranged it with Alice, we learned only belatedly, in one of those weeks when you and I and Alice were at Stoneridge. [R:VIII.n3.p641]

I remember the four of us together, and a pointless stroll through the cemetery in Kensal Green, and how under the gaze of her Italian eyes she wrote herself into my address book.

IX Flame bright

I have found candles, stockpiled in an era of strikes and blackouts – politics not in those years able to ruffle my moonlit waters. They were in the utility room next to the cellar door. Your mother always thought ahead. It means I've been able to get back to that murky wonderland we shared, and reconnect the services. I noticed – and it's something I never noticed before – a huge, pot-bellied, solid-fuel stove, a coppery gleam in my candlelight. There is a mesh of pipes and wires proliferating up the walls and under the ceiling, and entering the house from under the floorboards. I came across that bass guitar you used to play (it's now stringless).

I tested the taps – a gasp of air followed by a splutter, then explosively a torrent. I stepped outside and walked through the grass, under a first twitch of falling yellow leaves, down to the lakeside, where your *Fiery Sickle* – last moored to its present grave – is a skeleton of peeling timber. (Life. What is it but a dream?) [R:IX.n1.p641]

> Row,
> Over stars,
> Endless lakes,
> Into nights, days.
> Let invincible dreams
> Dream, endless love,
> Love….

Go, and catch a falling star. Amazingly, many of the light bulbs do still work.

X The Donns Watson

A vapour of sunlight, a smear in the citrus filters banked in a soufflé of lemon clouds, at this early hour make lace in a silhouette of hilly crests and distant pines. [R:X.n1.p641] I intend to walk round the whole perimeter before I close this note, but am stuck with interiors – this house of abandoned rooms [R:X.n2.p641]. Yours is cryptic, with its empty wardrobe. There is one old suitcase still on the bed, redundant but for its lid, in a gape of expectation. Drawers are lined with newsprint (a headline: 'Pound devalued'). Only three of the four wall hangings remain – a fragment of song, a miniature reproduction of someone (a face I have never met), a photograph of the Pont du Gard. [R:X.n3.p641] There is a large rectangle of not so faded wallpaper – this is above your dressing table – where Roddy's portrait used to be, a swirl of engine oil on rusty water. It's the one Marcia shipped back home, selling it not through Kunstler, but in East 4th Street. I wrote to her. I phoned at the end of July. Then in late September I arrived at her office – at that time in East 70th. She ought to have been prepared, but seemed surprised. She gave me the key to her apartment, on the corner of 30th and 29th (take, she said, the second elevator), where I skimmed through her magazines and met her housemate. She was an entrepreneur, she said, selling bagels from a handcart around Fifth Avenue.

I meant only, Alex, to remain for three weeks. Then I was introduced to Robert Quay, who after a long portside evening told me he'd been asked to show me what went on at the Donns Watson, where I was given a guide, Myrna Molloy. [R:X.n4.p642] Myrna, an associate professor, who to stay one step ahead of her students was cramming on D'Orbieu. Did I want to help? I was handed a wodge of unpublished papers, and a highlight pen – an event that set the tone for the whole of my sojourn. [R:X.n5.p642]

XI Planar

So you see, Alex, my New York – that city I absorb as a set of spatial elements – persists as a private cartography, whose internalised compass points are a ragbag of grid references (those intersecting avenues and streets), points of gravitation, for example steps skirting Fifth Avenue and the 82nd Street entrance (Metropolitan Museum of Art), or another, a few deeply engraved codes, important to the traveller (bus 300, bus 107), or incidents (a lucky escape, in broad daylight, in Central Park), finally a blurred retention, things as things but divorced from their locality—

- Point Mercer Street, with its Museum of Holography, a walk from the Donns Watson – *due piedi*, as Marcia would say.
- Point Central Park. I cannot now reconstruct the whole beat of a city from this rectangular strip of green. I recall, first, sitting on a park bench, which I shared with an adult male, who was trying to get to grips with his paperback edition of *Brer Rabbit*. [R:XI.n1.p642] Second recollection, time approximately noon: attempting to leave the park, but surrounded at my exit by half a dozen mixed race, who demanded cash, but who relaxed their menace so soon as I spoke. One had lived in Ladbroke Grove, and said he knew Viceroy Road. [R:XI.n2.p642]
- Subway train RR. Into whose moving carriages I gather my reflections on the river, on Manhattan, on Queens, on my daily hike, on Fifth Avenue, on that bar I drank at returning to Marcia's....

- There are blurs. A Chinese restaurant, somewhere, somewhere in Chinatown. The Spring Street Bar (telephone 431 7637): was this a meeting place, whose interior I lose?
- A fleapit, and its movies: *Phoenix Tree*, whose written account I still have, whose cinematic images I don't; and *Sycorax*.
- Empire State Building: I saw it, I wrote that I saw it, I forgot and am still forgetting that I saw it.
- The roof of Marcia's apartment block. From here from Marcia's reclining chairs the whole cityscape fell away – for Marcia as she sunbathed, for me as I roved through her *Brothers Grimm*.
- 59th / Lex, NE corner – was important once, is a dead shorthand now.
- Port Authority, gate 243: hugs, my brief goodbyes for Marcia.

Do I have regrets? I have none. [R:XI.n3.p642]

XII Terse

It's alarming how quickly my room needs a tidy up – and how easily I'm distracted. Something, or someone, below me on the gravel – or is it a trick of the light? – catches my eye – and is gone. There is a teacup – design poppies, a faded pink – detached from its saucer, which at certain times of day is a pool of ceramic light. There are books, all of them floored. And papers. The jemmy, which I hung on a radiator – will that heating system work, I wonder? – I returned to Roddy's workshop. I could not help remember how I had looked with nervous detachment at the wreck of his MG, and was surprised when it didn't go for scrap, and was kept, a memorial, after his accident. Had it ruined his life? That stutter, that slowness, that hesitance in everything he did. Not the blond, bright-eyed fourteen-year-old of his photographs.

'Yes' – is all you said, one syllable more than I heard you utter in the presence of your father. [R:XII.n1.p642]

I have come across that bandeau you sometimes wore, playing table tennis (perfunctory strokes, I recall).

XIII Post-portside

How did Molloy describe her boss, the busy Robert Quay? She couldn't find the right word, and coined a portmanteau – 'dynantic' – her best term for a pedant and his dynamism, which in Quay's case I came to agree was as good as any. He invested an abundance of nervous energy in routine motor tasks, with a wildness of upper limbs, gestured underlines and drilled full-stops, expansions at their severest on the occasions he taught, which were rare. He was demonstrative and not didactic, and was famous for the markings entered on his whiteboard, a collision, at lecture end, of words, phrases, arrows and underscores, arcs bending back and forth, indecipherable once the lesson was over. He did not share in the aleatory fads his visiting practitioners brought for hire on sunny afternoons, a fraternity Molloy told me she also had no time for. Historical strides, she said, were not the sole property of chance combinations of the found and the stumbled on. As for the performative, its confinement wasn't just to a 'lost' mode of consciousness, recoverable only in unexpected associations of the tribe and its built environment. These things when brought to our attention weren't necessarily a challenge to our 'preconceptions'.

I had no opinion, and that surprised her. Nor did I express any personal view on Robert Quay. But it was odd, she said, that once she had joined the teaching staff the poetry Quay was known for – all of which existed in five slim paperbacks – was removed without explanation from the Donns Watson library, and disappeared completely from its index system. We were having our first real conversation in a crowded coffee lounge, in what she assumed was a protective hubbub around us. I have reason to think we were overheard, as all she now knew of Robert Quay the poet was dead flotsam left on a whiteboard after one of his classes – a jingle I later saw recorded in one of the washroom cubicles—

> On the walls and floor,
> On cellophane,
> In a circle (enclosed)
> Or forming a cross –
> Tammuz, [R:XIII.n1.p643] Gilgamesh, [R:XIII.n2.p643]
> Pepi's papyrus. [R:XIII.n3.p643]

In its doling out as Quay's teaching material it was written in lime-green marker as a bullet list (which I don't punctuate above), but in the washroom appeared with a cartoon caricature of the poet himself (a fat nose, large ears, a bald pate, all these features exaggerated).

The Donns Watson interior matched the dejection of Lower Manhattan. Quay's office was a flood of fluorescent gloom, no matter what time of day. The windows were high and lost to a crowd of taller buildings round us. He shared his cell with a visiting sound artist, who shuttled between here and his schedule in Chicago. I told him how Spartan I found it, after Middlecross – with scarcely room for its desk and a bar heater. We spoke a lot, though I never gauged his origin exactly, intellectually speaking. Only a fraction of what he read was piled on his shelves. Some books were the property of that sonic adventurer, after his soundings off away in his second city.

Quay was tall and powerfully framed – a distant ancestry in mid-west farming stock – and wore what remained of his hair, which was brown and straight, ragged round his ears and to his collar. His wardrobe was overstocked with billowing shirts and jeans, most of them needle cord. He wore his collars open, no tie. There were lakes of perspiration to the underarms. His style of teaching was avuncular – he liked to joke. He didn't mind quips directed at him. [R:XIII.n4.p643] I found him alone one afternoon, perched on the edge of his desk, that surface a cascade of books, papers and footnotes. I had brought with me and was clutching it nervously a portfolio titled *English Poems*, a subject he evaded with jerks of the head and a faint miasma of musk. [R:XIII.n5.p644] He asked me how I'd got on with Molloy.

Her sessions were dull, I had to admit.

XIV Langer

Molloy did not exempt from criticism even those specialists she had booked for afternoon sessions. Langer she grilled in the student bar, a few feckless days before entering her signature on the job offer approved and printed off and sent to him. He was a lone figure on the theatrical fringe, a short stocky man with a pronounced public lisp, and not open to interruption once he'd got a head of steam. This is what an open-mouthed Molloy, unable to get a word in, found to his discredit. He explained the ins and outs of a recent piece, astonished she hadn't come across it, a civic project designed to siphon words and abbreviations from hoardings and noticeboards. The resultant cargo was thrown in a heap, out of which he devised arithmetic procedures – or dice throws – for the extraction of a new textual order. The technique was varied endlessly, and a fortnight later was passed on to one of Molloy's students, Beckie, who had ambitions of bringing the creative arts into the workplace. Her daddy ran a gas station south of Vancouver, north of Seattle. In her revamp of a postcard home she 'factored in' a fire roster from the Donns Watson coffee lounge, and in a group session intuited from it large doses of meaningless verse, like this—

> Gigo the gigo mesh mesh.
> Joel Joel fetch me your.
> Support support the mood chord.
> Up across down fire base.
> Carried exist carried exist carried.
> [R:XIV.n1.p644]

Langer asked – that if, as materialists, we are prepared to rearrange objects in a room (though I can't quite judge that parallel), or props in a performance space, why should we not be prepared to juxtapose words in the same concrete way? Could we not stand at one remove from the words we use, and regard language as having a 'life' of its own?

'Huh!' I hear Molloy say. [R:XIV.n2.pn]

XV Appreciation piece

Langer, before his return to the fringe, set a brief: 'Make a piece of writing through / in / as / out of / for performance. The piece can relate to or be produced as part of a live event, and / or show traces of a prior performative action / process that was part of its production, and / or be built / made exploring performance visually or materially.' [R:XV.n1.p644]

XVI Paper sculptor

Molloy, accustomed to argue from the fine scenic views of her specialism, the Empty Space (that theatrical void that has to be filled), for a range of political reasons I don't pretend to understand now found that standpoint less straightforward. [R:XVI.n1.p644] She had been thrown into an off-campus project she saw no point in, and immediately phoned her agent. She lectured conscientiously, and stooped to all kinds of impostures. I found her, on a gloomy Monday, engineering a three-dimensional letter from a sheet of A4, without the aid of scissors, glue or tape. It was the handcraft called authorship, she quipped. She followed that with a film show, and for its twenty-minute whirr sat smoking in her office. The film featured: a word written in leaves floating on a pool; an arrangement of pebbles on a step, to spell the exhortation STAY; words burnt into wood; a Sumerian text incised in clay with a stylus. [R:XVI.n2.p645]

When I phoned you you were out, so I spoke to your mother. Try, Alex, to think of her, forming those very precise vowels in a gusty hallway, the wind and rain lashing round the house, howling, she said, in a vortex above the solid brick and shiny slate of Middlecross. She hoped you'd be all right in your car (because branches were plummeting down and blocking the roads). I almost told her I was on my way home.

I attended only one more session supervised by Molloy, which she had called 'Writ'. [R:XVI.n3.p645]

XVII Lacuna masquerade

A short break. [R:XVII.n1.p645] I am standing, Alex, in the music room, having closed the cellar door, which I cannot remember leaving open. Here is the music stand – those twists and extravagant loops in its wrought metal – where Roddy, before his high-speed collision, used to play (you said) his violin. Here is the piano too, a Bentley, where you practised that Brahms intermezzo, over and over. A swirl of yellow leaves sweeps across the patio outside, which is squared with weeds and barnacled with moss. One of Alice's nightscapes, a balletic Arlequino pirouetting round a moonlit obelisk – five stars in a blue romantic sky – still hangs over the fireplace. That fireplace, mahogany and dust. [R:XVII.n2.p645]

XVIII Colorless

Molloy went on sick leave, and that was the moment I tried to cut my visit short. She phoned me from her deathbed, in a whip of jaundice-coloured clouds (am happy to say she did resurrect herself). She attributed her sudden ill-health to student rebellion.

'Oh, I hadn't noticed any rebellion,' I said.

What I also hadn't guessed was its connection to me. I, a rose-complexioned George du Plé, an Englishman with a taste for Gallic tobacco, was the only mediator her students would accept.

XIX Question, Alex

I met their leader Brad, alone, one quiet afternoon in the refectory, where I watched him stir his coffee. He told me the institutional problem he and his comrades had begun to experience was the plethora of unwritten edicts, at times full-blown as tyranny over the individual. In his case that compromised his artistic method. He thought the whole idea of the Donns Watson was a freedom of expression, or escape from the magnitudes of power usually found in cabals or committees. His DWRIPA.LIT.2219, the course he'd enrolled for, had been an awful disappointment, underpinned by a body of learned goofs intrusive in their bias. DWRIPA.LIT.2219 was a strange string of digits he had first encountered in the prospectus. It had floated mystically in his consciousness, borne on those free bellows he assumed were his lifelong licence to practise. But there were things he'd found – all bad – hidden in the Donns Watson rulebook. As I write this, Alex, one blue talcum of wood smoke disperses lazily over the pines and chestnut trees beyond the lake. Brad dreamed up a hundred impossible questions, hostage thus to the free air of creative meditation, in an attempt – in a vain attempt – to banish those scars inflicted by Quay and his troupe. As reminiscence, it presses down insistently. There is no escape, not below in the cellar, not in the glassy reflection of the clocks still here, nor as I sit with my elbows propped on the kitchen table. What has gone wrong?

I will tell you.

XX A tower of Babel [R:XX.n1.p645]

It's the tide of regret, Alex, having breezed through your house, and scattered the dust the years have settled. The spectre Mnemosyne I see from the corner of my eye, always somewhere, somewhere unattainable. It does no good to adjust the luminous point of my compass. Wherever I go, it aligns itself to the magnetised letters of a dead magnetic north. What is my homecoming, when I live in a vista of weeds, and search for its hidden pole in the codes of a depersonalised history? My work is the work of paper, into whose architecture I incise alphabetic signs, and in the pauses between attempt to reconstruct my past.

Yet I cannot reconstruct my past. [R:XX.n2.p646]

XXI Theme and variation

Brad, when we next liaised, this time in the Museum of Holography, on Mercer Street, confided that, perplexingly, his instincts told him it might be in his best interests to allow limited contamination of his portfolio, using matter not interdicted by the Donns Watson.

'You mean find common ground?' I asked.

'Sure.'

I reported back to Molloy, and repeated what he said.

'What ground is that, George?'

'He didn't say.'

'Oh well, it's progress I suppose....'

I find calm in that wood smoke, and watch as it melts, under a pellucid sky, over the patchwork of pines dotting the chestnut wood, which still exists as an arc round your house, despite a new road layout. I dreamed up a hundred possible evaluations, and ways of diminishing all recollection of the Donns Watson – Quay, and Brad, and Molloy, the lot (that whole tapestry).

I will if I can. [R:XXI.n1.p646]

XXII Mutiny

I found myself in yet another basement, drinking coffee with Brad and his core of the disaffected, not knowing how to extricate myself. It was his gang of five, dressed uniformly in leathers and bikers' boots, studs, buckles, tattoos. There was traffic noise overhead. Brad (from Ithaca) was an armchair deity. That status he had won through the complexities of his vocabulary (he turned a decent essay). I noticed how careful he was, planting the fuse of rebellion, on the point of retreat from the packed explosives his flame-bearers were still stepping forward to, intent on setting it alight.

They drafted an ultimatum, in respect of shortened lecture time, late notification of marks, tutorials and absent tutors, an over-zealous application of business methodologies, and the exorbitant cost of canteen meals, which only just undercut the hamburger bars. It was Brad's second in command who held the poison pen, the natural designation when he was also the student rep. His name was Budd. Budd, with partial success, had tried and teased the same thesaurus Brad had always used. This is beside the point only insofar as it's beside the point, for of course that lent further motivation in the flourish of his pen, an instrument pregnant with bile.

The Donns Watson reply was a refusal to budge on any point.

XXIII Is this house haunted

A dawn mist rolling in off the Manche left its foggy crystal in the wilderness outdoors, in the weeds and fallen leaves. A damp raven sat hunched in its old-man's overcoat, then flew from where it had perched. I stood, Alex, at the window, in the round room, fixated on this catalogue of non-events.

A clangour of hot-water pipes echoed in the depths of the house, under my feet, a metallic thunder turning into a tinkle of troika bells. It followed the circuit of central-heating, and chimed in every room. The raven flew back down. Autumnal heat, in its spokes of sunshine, cut its golden swathe through the hovering mist. I bent to the radiator, and listened (earth, air, fire, water, music). It was cold.

In the cellar when I turned it on the light burned with a yellow glow. That pot-bellied boiler I mentioned had its doors and its gaping maw wide open, in a swirl of sooty dust, where it had just been raked and cleaned (though no sign of anyone else). The service hatch, which I had closed, was again open. I followed the intruder out, and emerged in a radiance of evaporating mist. There was a distant volley of gunfire.

I find this a complete mystery.

XXIV Workers of the world, unite!

How, Alex, to describe student subversiveness, after the 1960s? Our gang of five, by the start of its last semester, had diminished to a triad – Brad, his sidekick Budd, and me (as moderator). To anticipate a long, hot, cloying New York summer, a now nonchalant Brad shed the studs and snake leathers of his calling, and replaced them with soft shoes, pressed slacks and open-neck shirts, bright and scented from the Laundromat. Budd, resistant to practical examples, came round slowly. He drew the line at razor blades, and left intact the blond down glued to his chin. I smoked crush-pack cigarettes and relaxed in a floral tunic.

When I next saw him, Bradd was perched on the edge of a desk, one foot planted to the floor, the other swinging. He was tired, he said, of Art as the poor relation, and Science the all-conquering. It was an issue the hard hammers of Donns Watson oratory never looked like cracking. Could an adequate challenge ever come from here? You only had to look around. The facilities were rank. The lighting inadequate. The furniture castoffs. And look at those shoeboxes called studios and lecture theaters! Budd had written it all down, in preparation for a broadside someone must deliver, and asked could I make representations?

I said I could, to a point. Today my routine took in the delivery of flowers and fizzy pick-me-ups, which I took with me to Myrna Molloy's bedside. She told me that mentally she felt exhausted. For Brad that wasn't enough. He always aimed high, he said, and did I, or did I not, have Robert Quay's ear? Wasn't I part of his School of Deconstruction? I said up to a point.

'Point? What point?'

I had seen Quay's 'The Myth of a Man Called Shakespeare', a piece of his he'd written for *The Chicago Review*, complete with lifts from one of his protégé's poems—

> send for an English scaffold co
> build the man and his theater
> with sellotape epistemes and timber [R:XXIV.n1.p646]

'Up to that point,' I said.

It had no relevance for Budd. 'What's it supposed to mean?'

'You should start a student rag.'

Brad put himself forward as editor, and wrote a commentary piece called 'Caliban', though no publication was launched. His essay (or its Xerox) languishes in my files. [R:XXIV.n2.p646]

There's a troubled grandeur in all such failure.

XXV Budd

He was a different Budd when Budd was solo. Brad, whose companionship he couldn't rely on, was the priest underwriting Budd's conversion, while I – an exaggerated Englishman – was a curious blossom blown over the wastes of college concrete. Afternoons I found him scribing the rounded aluminium of a coffee spoon in the granules of spilt sugar in his favourite basement bar, with the remains of his lunch, always a seeded roll. A question for George du Plé, formed after weeks of negotiation, was why me, here – and why *was* an Englishman here? Ah yes, I said, England, with its rills, meadows and mists, and a shrouding of fairy dust on the du Plé family castle – a hilltop construction with candied turrets and ivory crenellations. There I dreamed silver dreams over the chalk gorges and river valleys, where plush green meadows rolled to the sea.

'It's the spirit of adventure. Plus of course Fate usually intervenes when it comes to a failure in relationships.'

Budd couldn't hide the desperation of his choices, which depended on mystical essentials under the cold pepper of science – God looming sceptical in the institution's sooty chambers. It was a reflex, a natural retaliation, a swipe of the hand, a swish of air round all these sons of Frankenstein, spawned on a bleak mountain – black clouds, dark pines – and re-electrified in the labs and on the operating tables of the Donns Watson, with its Molloys, its Langers, its Robert Quays. He shook his head. On that path, Budd said, he was halfway a disciple – no more. That in itself was an act of social hypocrisy, for once he'd got his degree the last thing he would do was follow Robert Quay out to the dreary suburbs, that haven of the gardened agon, the agon reduced to a kind of backyard book talk. I told him Molloy would soon be coming back. He pricked up his ears, not at that, but at the toothy bark of traffic noise lolloping in from the street overhead. A taxi. Then the intervention in a mingled fury and the multiplications of a car horn, as a thin-browed sedan nosed ahead, straining at a stop light.

'Time to go,' I said.

He thought I meant for good, though I had in mind only that afternoon. I spent an hour in the Donnell Library, having walked up the Avenue of Americas. I phoned, or rather dialled, then replanted the blunt receiver when Copparo's bell clanged in the clean air and consumerised art in her office, in East 70th. Bought papers, confection, gum, chewed a hundred unanswerable questions, went home – went home and ran a tub of warm suds.

XXVI Brad

Brad had toiled with the intricacies of a new Philishave, which his kid brother, Harvard-bound, had packaged up in Ithaca, and dispatched, three days late, through the US Mail. It was Brad's birthday, twenty-first or twenty-fourth – I'm not too clear. What followed was a friendly nudge at his new clean looks, and the colour match of his sneakers and jogging pants. They were smoke grey, with dewy flashings – not that I ever caught him pounding the sidewalks.

He held one court card, but did not play it royally. He flushed with embarrassment, having called a truce with Robert Quay. That brief episode was sunlit through an orange smog of tobacco smoke. He'd got his entourage, propping up the canteen furniture (decrepit polished amber), and with an official communiqué revealed – what? Well – that the manifesto was dormant for now. The strategy-minded Brad would judge the right time for its release, for his phoenix out of the ashes.

Budd rebelled, but he too was silenced – a bright star extinguished in the coffee-slop firmament of the Quay school of contemporary art – an academic suburb whose interdicts were against forms of communication 'wide' in scope. 'Wide' was an audience exceeding one hundred. All else was commercial and belonged with the evils of capital. Nevertheless the rose tints of art sometimes coincide with the rose tints of politics, and there were murmurings. Others stood at the brink, able if not yet ready to debate with Robert Quay, or finally condemn – publicly – his school of hangers-on. Quay went on with his handshakes, and with secrecy drew up his covenants.

Brad had a song in his heart for the virtue of unseen mechanisms. I fell similarly to that inverse elitism I found rebarbative in Quay, and entered into Brad's small, closed, sententious cliques, of a format suggested in the mauve crêpe and court of Robert Quay, his private rooms where all of us sometimes gathered. Brad sparred, with demotic verse, and meanings you could argue. Budd rambled pseudo-philosophically, assured that we took as a sign of mental labour his catalogue of specialist terms, long in their evolution, and wrapped tightly in clauses, sub-clauses, sub-sub etc. I couldn't tell if – in his blank response to ours as its preface – his end had been achieved. Brad, in a kind of détente, kept up careful eye contact with Quay, the enemy, in what seemed an unspoken relationship, about which I could go on and on, unimportant though it was, though there is just this one other small point I would like to make [*excised*] […].

XXVII Marcia

I called Copparo again, this time from the glassy canopy of a public kiosk. She sparred with someone on her other line, in the pauses telling me she'd meet me for lunch, at the Brittany du Soir, Marcia still nostalgic for everything French. She was precise about the time – 13.20. I got there – the interior an after-blush of pink and peach – to find she had left a message at the desk, so sorry she'd had to cancel. My gaze intensified. I studied the *table d'hôte*, but abandoned that for the defunct hollows of my diary. I called her again, but now she said no, absolutely no – no prospect of getting out again this week. Not for lunch. She agreed to meet me six-ish, 'for a Cinzano', in one of her plush velvet lounges off Fifth Avenue, where with coy devilment she swung her legs from her bar stool. I remained patient, Copparo munching thoughtfully through a tumbler of salt sticks. I asked her what had gone wrong.

'George, I've a helluva lot on.'

'I gather.'

One of her colleagues, an older, square-shouldered woman, wrapped up to the tips of her ears in a false fur, passed by then doubled back outside, a hand to her forehead. She crouched and looked in, through the criss-cross of light in a glitter of tiny bulbs recessed round the window. Smiles, mutual waves. Introductions (George, Hope, Hope, George). George is an English poet. That so really. Hope here runs *Art Day News*. Pleased to meet.

She wore gold streaks in the ash of her hair. She like Copparo drank vermouth, and stirred into it the cherry she had skewered on a plastic trident. I drank too. Or rather I watched, for the rising fizz, in the frosty glass of beer the barman placed at my elbow, centred on a coaster. His smile was thinly moustached.

'You're tired, Marcia. Should get more sleep.'

'Why thank you, George. Aren't you so – English!'

'Blunt. That's English abroad.'

She and Hope pattered over the week's gossip. One Newsom Barringer, from Phoenix, AZ, whose airy cellophane 'inflatables', anchored by elastic attachments to all sizes of desert boulder – sun, sand, the barren wastes, each rock in the thick black pool of its shadow – had conquered the centrefold of a rival mag printed in Philadelphia, using photographs the artist had supplied. Barringer was just out of college. The whole thing dissolved into an impromptu business exchange, and I left them (my few feeble goodbyes), Hope in the muted clash of her over-sized earrings (silver-plated cocoa beans), Marcia with her light Italian freckles and tired-looking eyes. The next time I spoke to her, Marcia was trashing trash, as she moved from door to door in the basement of her apartment block, a place mazed with cubicles – a soap, a linen, a garbage room. An Escher-like escalation of angular concrete steps, sloping up (north, east, south, west, wayward to the lodestar) merged on a common, and for me an impossible destination. I descended, Orpheus in the laundry room, and wheeled from the entrance, from the utility door on 30th and 29th. It wasn't just any Sunday. I'd left some disconsolate badinage abandoned on my notepad, [R:XXVII.n1.p646] under a mercurial sky the colour of mud. [R:XXVII.n2.p647] She had sent me one of her gallery postcards (her gallery was Kunstler's, East 70th). Jocosely this was a *David*, in three-quarter view, with mint-stripe boxer shorts, mirror-coated sunglasses, and a digital watch for the left wrist. In the billboard of her handwriting she let on that Alice was due at her apartment this weekend – a chance to meet up.

'Oh hi George,' she said. 'Go on up. Gotta do the garbage.'

'Garbage, Marcia....'

'Excuse me!'

'That's nothing,' I said.

Upstairs I found not Alice but Copparo's mother, in pressed slacks and a short blouse, its intricate design an infolding of miniaturised checks. Her lenses were tinted and were set in an amber frame, and were perched on the tip of her nose.

'You must be George. Olga Copparo.' An olive hand, stained with verdigris, discarded an LP sleeve and reached for mine, a paler, ghostly hue. That LP was *Switched-on Bach* – jazzed up, synthesised partitas – too neurotic for her tastes, she explained (the disc revolved, but the needle had been raised). We shook. 'You're a poet,' she said. 'English. That's something.' I was so glad to know this.

Marcia percolated coffee, and produced fruit cake, whose glacial exterior she sliced with a bread knife. Her seating was shabby and low to the floor. It was an effort to disengage once you'd sat down. I picked at my fruit cake, but drained my coffee to the sludge. Olga – her conversation a succession of family bulletins – never stopped, so that pageboy du Plé might some day act as fully apprised go-between of these and other confidences—

Harry Copparo, Marcia's opera-loving pa, was holed up in South Dakota, doing a long bruising deal in kitchenware (that was his business apparently). Chrissie (Copparo's sister, a slim twenty-three) thought she might now quit her job at the RKO, having said last week that definitely she wouldn't. Uncle Cy had been discharged from the Bellevue, and could walk with the aid of a stick. Two boys from Brooklyn had been found, and arrested, in a parking lot at the Giant Stadium, having smashed up Larry's Chevrolet (it had been stolen. It had been missing for over a week). Dale had started his legal proceedings against the crosstown buses....

I retreated into a cascade of daily papers and Marcia's glossy magazines found on a table top. That included *Art Day News*, and that whole postmodern, pre-literate rigmarole with Barringer, currently one of the world's most frequently commissioned artists. I looked at how slowly the clock moved, and began my long, awkward, backdoor process of extrication, until finally I said I had things to do at home, [R:XXVII.n3.p647] and left, vowing I'd catch up with Alice later in the week. In fact I met her on the street, climbing from a cab.

XXVIII Paper cargo

Another caesura, and an irregular, hollow thud, which I traced to the damp recess of the pantry, its shelves lined with that shiny blue tissue Roddy once spent a morning snipping into rectangles. Its window's uppermost pane has a green diagonal crack, in a gentle curve, corner to corner. Outside I discovered the cause. It's the fig tree, now a giant, the hard knuckles of its limbs prone to catch even the slightest breeze, then clump away at the glass. In its shade, someone had propped a vintage lady's bike, which had fallen over, spilling the contents of its basket (mail, whose frank read *Your personal invitation from Amex*; a box of Swan Vestas; and a month-old *TES*). The front wheel hadn't ceased rotating on its spindle. There was a glitter in its spokes.

XXIX Alice [R:XXIX.n1.p648]

She wasn't surprised to see me on the sidewalk, holding the cab door open, Alice half in, half out.

'You coming, George, or going?'

Going, I said, and looked at her. She was fuller in the face, but it wasn't that that took my breath. Her once alluring smile showed signs of freezing over. Her eyes were rounder, with a shard of deceit lighting each iris.

'Marcia home?'

'With her mother – Olga. How is Alex?'

'Alex has given up waiting. Did you know she's at Manchester?'

'That came as a shock. She is every inch Goldsmiths. Your mother said....'

She paid for the cab. 'Why don't you come on up...?'

'No. I'm wrestling with zip codes.'

'Zip codes, George?'

'Never mind.'

She walked to Copparo's street door, in a billow of masculine shirt tails.

'It's the second elevator.'

'Thanks. I *have* been before.'

'Oh. Okay.'

Her cab roared away.

XXX Gunsmoke at OK Corral

Sensibly Quay remained on his ivory ski slopes during a first, and in my case effectively the last work-in-progress – an event Molloy chaired, still pale from her sickbed, and which I minuted. It meant showings, or lead-up – or a trail of gunpowder – to that bad odour, or singe of brown sugar, which Quay in his post-practice called 'offerings'.

Budd had been egged on feebly, and as feebly glopped at his bait, having got it into his head that the constructed reality he for one called humancraft (Blake, Wake, Bleak, Finnegan) owed its metastructure to three transmission media. These were the Word (or Logos), the particle waveform light (Light), and the limitless conflation of finite genes (compare the words 'genetic', 'genesis'). For this he sought willing participants in public acts of coitus, under the glow of stage lights and the banner *Logos as Factum*. What he hoped rescued his 'piece' from the mires of pornography was his on-top male, dressed in a periwig, his point being that in matters penile and factory, fully birthed status into the Law of the Word as Law, is the Word, since she with her dumb knees spread has a strip of surgical tape plastered to her mouth (all of which is a contextual frame unlikely to be clear to the casual spectator). Various performers had given it the nod, but had all backed out – notably a Lou Licksenberg (I knew him but we never spoke), who having said *Sure!* now said *Not so sure!* He wasn't clear about his girl, whose first doubts hinged on the moon cratered surface a lost adolescent war with acne creams had left her as profile. In principle they were still willing, but after long, careful preparation did not feel Budd had given sufficient thought to the 'liminalities'. By this was meant the first twinges of Lou's erection (or that was only one example). Should the piece start where his untrousered monster was a *fait accompli*? Instance two: those not so final sighs, that ocean of flaccidity, when the two unglued themselves – but unglued themselves to what? A fag-sucking recumbency? A shuffling offstage? Or what? [R:XXX.n1.p648]

All such meditations – perhaps I mean mediations – had to be thrashed out openly in a closed circle, on a bare floor, under naked lights, in one of those gloomy college studios (cola cans and candy wrappers in a plane of geo-stationary orbit around the empty bins). Brad the Slack'd, whose smile was aloof, and whose careful comments must now be weighed with correspondingly unsubtle medicine balls, had at this time dismissed the mystical Budd and found a new sidekick. This was a lank-haired realist from Ohio (from Cleveland, Ohio).

Brad said: 'The problem is choreography' – for choreography belonged not with the theory of an implied Word, but the theatrical glitter of the premeditated Deed. The 'deed' for Brad, and for Brad's new sidekick, whose name was Mirtch, was 'essentially' a social sleight of hand. You read that 'essentially' everywhere.

Only one other student brought text, an upstate New Yorker – little A5 cut-downs, into whose fresh air he had typed his on-the-road lyrics. These were sensitive and gentle, and on the whole favourably received, though even here Mirtch wasn't short of firepower (his smoking Smith and Wesson). According to him, lines like 'I can handle rain, but not critique' took us into that whole 'tricksy' area of legitimation, 'text' the ultimate architect of its own undoing. Tablets delivered in the wilderness presuppose an aimless polity, whose sterility of purpose is mystically identified by that one man among hordes onto whom unseen presences have hitched the purple of aristocracy. Yet we cannot believe now in a naturally priestly order of scribes. This made the Word both a class and a legitimation issue.

'I don't think,' said Mirtch, 'text as such is any longer possible. There has to be another way. You have to *find* another way.'

Molloy chaired a second work-in-progress, a few days after 8 December, in a smaller studio, whose interior showed residues of a Duchamp retrospective (not his pissoir, but a variant – a series of suspended flight bags). [R:XXX.n2.p648] True to Mirtch's new leadership – in report of which I poured her endless cups of coffee – with Molloy endlessly rolling up a cigarette – her students by now had abandoned the 'impossibility' of text as such, and had come empty-handed – even those who could write. However, what happened on 9 December, throughout all windswept corners of the Donns Watson, with Mark David Chapman having murdered John Lennon, was an outpouring of greetings-card grief – a lot of amateur verse, where you detected the 'old' ethos of warm human feeling – a huge spontaneous charge in the aftermath of that emotional man and his music. Some people even threw themselves from rooftops.

'How's this square,' Molloy asked, 'with our shining new world of gone or deferred text?'

XXXI Cheap day return

Alex. Yesterday the gold dip of my nib performed frantic pirouettes round a quaternary of Mirtches, and in a final caption, balloon-like, crossed its feet. This is now a permanent deformity. With its insect trail of blue ink perforating a self-burlesquing name, it resigned its post. At that point I decided to come and see you. This was still early enough that a surface dew covered the platform, and left its charcoal pools in the slate of the station roof, its slope in all other respects dark grey, the lingering signs of a weary world circa the 1970s. In the waiting room – which was cold, and deserted, and whose interior I looked at through rainbow ripples in the glass of its door – a potted history of adolescent rendezvous had been painted over in magnolia ('Rose and Agg'. How I remembered that inscription, 'Rose and Agg'. Can we wonder, Alex, wherefore art thou, Rose, now...?). [R:XXXI.n1.p648]

A shower of sodden maple leaves, in a swirl over the escarpment, un-flapped itself and settled on the glistening curve of the track. The hum and clatter of the Tannoy announced all trains running late. Mine when it huffed to the platform, shrugging its shoulders, bore only the late remnants of its commuter population, the carriage I mounted cradling one occupant only, wiry haired, pen poised over last night's crossword, the margins littered with clues in initial workings-out. The whole tabloid, dog-eared, he had spread out over his document case, which was flat on his knees. Mechanically, he palmed away the creases. These articles he gathered up hastily at Tonbridge, where through the window I tracked the olive flecks in the steely wool of his suit as he hurried along the platform. At Sevenoaks I dozed. Approaching Waterloo, I dreamed. At Charing Cross – an innocent abroad – I lurched among those eager bestsellers in the glass and plastic tents of the book and burger stalls. I bought, Alex, my ticket for the Northern Line, and yet, yet, descending into that helix of wind and dust, on the first steps down to the ghostly grime of a metropolitan underworld, I slowly about turned, then plodded my way up to St Martin's Lane, where an Italian café I had known had changed into the velvet lining, into the plush interior of a restaurant. Here I ate lunch. Then I returned to Middlecross.

XXXII Logos as factum…

…and those final days at the Donns Watson. The next tragic event was a *public* showing. Mirch took control of the programme, and oversaw production of an attractive, glossy catalogue, fully representative of that class of '81, bar one – that pariah of text, rain and critique, whose on-the-road lyrics I have quoted from above. Somehow Mirch also organised batteries of volunteers, who arrived with ladders and pots of paint, from whom the Donns Watson received its matt or pastel facelift, in preparation for the New York art world spinning through its studios. *His* piece of work transcended all of this. It was positioned in the library (irony intended), on an upper floor, where the windows overlooked an artificial-looking line of fruit trees. I recall standing in a queue for a glimpse of whatever this 'piece' might be, for all the leaden ache in my legs, and the moistening of my eye – a thorough glaze by now. After an hour or so I gave it up.

By contrast Brad had moved into the heritage business, having reconstructed, in a blacked-out Studio 41 – with only a pale saucer of light from the gantry – one of those makeshift nuclear shelters featured in government information films, of the '50s and '60s. A note on the studio door traced the word 'shelter' through a propagandised etymology, in terms of age rather than meaning (a derivation from the provincial English *sheld*, or nowadays *shield*, according to Webster's, or at least my 1880 edition). The central exhibit was encircled with luggage labels, which I knew to have been left over from the job lot he'd bought for a previous project (to do with travel writing), on which we as spectators – despite this nuclear shroud of darkness – were expected to respond. I said something flippant about Medici gazillions, and the miracles thereby chiselled from slabs of marble, and asked what could the Donns Watson bring to our culture, supposing more than the $50 budget per student per showing per annum.

As to Budd, he by now had suffered the final falling out, not only conceptually, this phallogocentrism thing not something he wanted to think about. Only days before, damp in the basement shower, in an echo of giggles and the hollow drip of a tap, Licksenberg was found cheating on his girl. That meant she wasn't answering her phone. Budd finally overcame that drawback and opted not for human sculpture, but a model. Lou rehearsed one last plea for his outraged ex, or soon-to-be-ex ('Aw honey, don't you see Budd's piece it's made for us now....'). In the end not. Therefore Budd's answer was a double helix, which he remade from its original wire and plastic, a model he borrowed from a biology lab, College Physicians (630 West 168th – quite a way away). This he hung from the lighting rig in Studio 21 – the largest of all the Donns Watson studios – and passed through it a violet beam, which somehow formed, in the shadow it cast, the word 'factum'.

I still possess a copy of the catalogue. It's incredible to think it's now almost eighteen, and has come of age.

XXXIII Anonymous

At breakfast time, this morning, a spatter of rain thrummed on the windows. I looked out, as the wild grass flattened from its partings, and the gravel darkened. On the kitchen table I came across an empty spectacles case, in a soft blue leather, into whose dark hollows I searched for a clue to its owner. I found none. The rain eased, or rather rolled itself up into little hanging cloudlets. I continued my search outside. A grey twist of rope, ending in a damp fray of fibres, was all that remained of the *Fiery Sickle*, whose tinder had been gathered and removed ('Row, / Over stars'). I paused at that little arbour which used to be surrounded by bamboo, was hung with wind chimes once, whose scarred bench I remember walking miles to, obliged to return your short-sleeved pullover. At that time our physiques were similar.

No one sat here reading today. I wonder if you recall, Alex, that penny-in-the-slot weighing machine, which Roddy undid with a screwdriver? Today I found its rusty clock face. And there's an outbuilding full of discarded RAF coats. (Alice's? Theatrical costumes? Stuff from the war?)

When I returned to the house, that spectacles case had gone.

XXXIV Handshakes

I turn it all over, I go way back. I guess at how an irritated Robert Quay viewed my evasion of his year group, as it prepared for a first public showing.

'You *must* come,' he said.

'Not sure I can make it.'

Quay looked disgruntled. 'Not seen the works in progress? Not curious?'

Well yes – I'd seen Budd's witty piece called *Intrastate*. Mirtch had come up with a pun called *Bibliofile*. Brad had called his *Transire* – a word not normally part of his American vocabulary.

'I'll check the diary,' I said.

XXXV Prismatic

A rainbow, and under its arc not a crock of doubloons, but that arbour, formerly all bamboo and a tinkle of wind chimes. Propped up against our bench (initialled still, 'AL

GdP 1978') I found that same lady's bike, with its silver wheels and a black saddle, in whose wicker basket strapped to the handlebars was a local newspaper. It had been folded into a square at the bed-and-breakfast ads.

Twelve to fifteen pounds per night.

XXXVI Tucker

I was surprised when both Alice and Copparo came to the showings. They were joined briefly by Hope, the last day. Hope wore a floppy hat and a conic coiffure gathered to a bun. The world we inhabited was turned kaleidoscopically inside out if you spoke to her, with reversals and unexpected emphases in the marine blue of her sunglasses. Her lips, which were oranged, had a loud shape when she talked. She talked a lot.

Repeatedly I crossed Hope and Copparo's path. They decamped often to the studio tables set haphazardly outdoors, where the umbrellas had the same concentric stripes. In the cool of defunct Gallery C (its curriculum dead) hardworking staff hired from the Rosebay Café – a place Molloy frequented, on Sheridan Square – spent all day cutting sandwiches, the fillings salmon and ham and a shredding of lettuce leaf. Hope remembered me (George, English, poet). Copparo said I'd left it late (by now it was four in the afternoon). Alice huffed and said that was typical.

I said not at all: 'I've been here an hour.'

Hope wanted to introduce me to Crispin J. Tucker. 'Didn't I see him roaming, Marce?'

'Yes. That was in the library.' He'd been bending his monocle to Mirtch's *Bibliofile*. 'Cute piece.'

'Who's Tucker?'

'George! He's the editor, *Village Id*. You didn't know?'

'No. I didn't. Sorry.'

That planned introduction didn't take place till sundown, when I had picked my way through the rising waves, the heat a corrugated heat, stumbling into darkened studios, shambling in and out of blacked-out labyrinths, space formerly the grey-lit infrastructure of lecture and performance theatres. To my astonishment, in Ginsberg B – it was a shoebox with spotlights – Alice extended handshakes, then a warm hello, then her calling card, to an artist responsible for a phone exhibit, an ancient piece of office junk the programme listed so: '…bridge between language…language's formulating objects'. At certain random points the phone rang. She repeated much the same performance in a remote, cobwebbed corner on campus, where a slim-hipped, sleepy-eyed entrepreneur had rigged up a sickle moon, an image not quite pointed at by a silvered fingertip. I don't know what broken theory this was meant to demonstrate, and I forget what it was called – *Pro-verb* or something like. Some things I leave unexplained.

Early evening, Hope having disappeared – and still no chit-chat with Tucker…. We few remaining flat-foot mortals enjoyed the first of three celebrity appearances, i.e. of Newsom Barringer, all the way from Arizona, whose airy, cellophane 'inflatables', anchored by elastic attachments to all sizes of desert boulder – sun, sand, the barren wastes, each rock in the thick black pool of its shadow – had conquered the centrefold of one of Hope's rival mags (as I previously mentioned). O now and here was Hope too, on the same raised platform, to interview said prodigy.

'Let me try, Newsom, somehow to get at what this is' (loud shape, oranged lips).

In a series of replies, to her series of probes, Barringer catalogued his art as shifting points of light, which he as planner, who like all of us lived with a sense of cosmic darkness – life of course a transient life.… Or as I meant to say, he attempted to cast familiar things into unfamiliar shapes, or an unfamiliar otherness in the way he arranged them. To this his audience responded not with sounds, but silence. Not to be discouraged, he summed up his rationale as an attempt to show that measurement is not a matter of abstract calibrations, but is a navigation process through the encounter with, and the defining of – objects. Hope opened the floor to questions. Alice elbowed my ribs.

'Cynics' forum,' she said. 'Here is your chance, George. Speak.'

Resolutely I stayed silent.

Those two other celebrities were Rosetta Taype, a performance poet / writer, and Henry K. Myres, her publisher / critic / sponsor, whom Quay had put on the panel, supplemented by four others, whose recollection I am finding vague. As preface to their views, Mirtch had prepared a keynote statement. [R:XXXVI.n1.p648]

Molloy, chairing, got Myres to answer first, whose less than friendly smile saved itself under the hugeness of his black, ragged, Nietzschean moustache. Taype, by contrast, delivered a crunching metal salvo, with its main point of reference a selection of short staccato pieces under the collective title *Cognates*, designed, she said, as a corrective for long-held middling muddled views. That muddle she also was guilty of, but only because it was spawn of the social world that conceived it. It was 'accessible', and had an opaque, thickly laminated cover. All answers we ever want, find herein. Again Alice, again that elbow in my ribs.

'Now here's a real old harridan,' she said. 'Surely, George, she tempts you in….'

'Taype's last crap,' I said. I fanned myself, finding that programme useful at last. My jaw was firmly clamped, but with a smile.

Then I was introduced to Tucker, who over the course of the day – and several glasses of lemon tea – had established a good working rapport with one of the Rosebay staff, whose only task was to butter baguettes, an assignment that didn't stop him waiting lavishly on Tucker's table. Hope and I drank plain black coffee. Tucker was plump, spoke breezily, and wore his hair pageboy. I gazed into the silken paradise of his shirt, with its passion tints (greens, blues and sunsets), with its palms, sandy beaches, its tropic of exotic birds perched or in flight. Habitually he slid that monocle from his top pocket, to breathe theatrically on its lens, or bent it to his programme, where he strenuously sought my name. Then abruptly Tucker had another appointment, at a private address in Jackson Heights, though he did not depart before handing me his card. As an afterthought – having already stepped from the shade of our table umbrella – he asked me for a contribution. Yes. That was right. For *Village Id*. Of which a unique English number was in preparation.

This, Alex, was not a publication I had studied, therefore I sat open-mouthed, agent Hope acting on my behalf—

'Sure. George'd be delighted.'

Then that most English of honorary Englishmen set off for Jackson Heights.

XXXVII The café of conspiracy

Copparo gave me five minutes of her time when, ten days later, we were *en route* to the Café de France, where – due to the fragile *détente* between her and her boss (a rampant capitalist whose bargains were hard) – she was planning to do a deal. It was to do with one of Hope's leads, and Hope had agreed to meet up.

'Talking of Hope and leads,' she said, 'she wants to know did you follow up on Tucker?'

'No.'

'Well don't let the grass grow.'

XXXVIII Pyrotechnic

Alex! That bicycle again! This time with a flimsy polythene bag protecting its saddle, abandoned in range of the lake and its willows, where the trees in the arms of the wind shake out the residue of last night's rain. From here I look out across the water, to the brick-built boathouse, where on late summer nights Alice had her fireworks. An explosion of silver spangles, gold froth and starbursts. The boathouse, the cone of its roof coated in lead.

XXXIX Ratiocinative

So then what about Tucker, and *Village Id*? False, tempting trails of enthusiasm led me to exhume my zip code poems, yet in only now confronting their paucity I couldn't consent to send them, anywhere. I scoured my notebooks. Barring indifferent commentaries on those showings above (XXXVI), I couldn't find anything. So on, or back, to ancient writ, to things I'd abandoned, in the hope of reworking a phrase or passage. Result, some lethal concoction I persuaded myself was new – or rather New – and packaged the whole thing off to Tucker before doubt had set in. This, Alex, is the life of the poet. [R:XXXIX.n1.p648]

Tucker acknowledged receipt – I say this because his promptness surprised me – in a minute hand (this also took me by surprise), scratched or so it appeared with the point of a pin, on a plain white postcard. Some weeks later he returned it, thoroughly tea-stained, and with a scent of lemon, trussed up in a padded envelope, with an accompanying paperback. By now I was into night lamps, and tedium, with work I had taken proofreading, for a firm in Chappaqua (zip code 10514), whose guide books you saw on every corner stand.

After several more weeks I heard from Tucker again, this time in a panic on the phone. Having written to just about every English university (some didn't respond, some said no, most passed the buck), Tucker had at last arranged a four-month sabbatical at Benbrook Height College for the Performing Arts, in sight of the Tamar, Ing-er-land.

'Know much about them?' he asked.

'Not a thing.'

XL Lake eerie

There is no sign of that bike, but, as I stand at the lakeside – a blow of afternoon air at play on the light of its surface – I see the door to the boathouse is open. There's no sign of a boat. It has meant a long walk in wet grass for whoever…oh now I swear that's a hunched grey profile I can see at the window…. Gone!

XLI Dead weight

Just cannot rid my mind of Tucker…

XLII Medieval

…whose inaugural reading in the Great Hall, at Benbrook, as I gathered from the first of his high-speed postcards home, went well – an epic whose subject was Lenin and, curiously, mushrooms. [R:XLII.n1.p650] Though that is to jump ahead. [R:XLII.n2.p650] What happened next is as follows.

XLIII Paper chase

When he had booked his flight he met me at Washington Square, where in a drizzle of exhaust fumes, under a lone trapezium of blue remembered sky, he launched on one of his publisher rituals. He'd garbed up in one of his usual Hawaiian shirts, a little damp. He was with a man he named as L. Ray McNally, and to that static figure Tucker handed a large, bulging, battered brown envelope.

'Assistant editor,' he said – for now in him were entrusted plans for *Village Id*, the English edition. 'This here is George. George being English, you can count on his expertise – ain't that right, George…?'

'Oh absolutely.'

'Sorry, George, about that "Logos".'

'You don't want it?'

L. Ray clutched that envelope, and from the woolly foothills of his height above me (he was six foot two or three) beheld me in his unerring, unerringly shifty gaze. That look I encountered again when he called on me late one afternoon. I had reason to note the time. My wristwatch (an old, boyhood analogue, which I left by my bedside phone), refused to restart on being rewound. At precisely 16.16 I had reset its hands according to the luminous green digital – faultless and dependable – recessed into my cooker front. That moved on but my wristwatch stuck to its time shift (or is it a time shift I live in?). [R:XLIII.n1.p650] Before 4.30, L. Ray said that the brown envelope – more battered by now – had been stuffed in the mail, and soon I would find it on my doormat. His pretty wife, he said, had emptied a drawer full of kitchen utensils onto the floor, and had walked out – gone back to her ma in San Diego.

'San Diego?'

'Where *I'm* headed.' Only thing on his mind was to get her back.

XLIV Kindling

Some maniac has taken a saw to our arbour bench (bamboo, wind chimes, readings from Keats – things of beauty, joys forever), and reduced it to a neatly stacked pile of timber. Weather's turning cold. Then that bike turned up again, in a softened glitter of autumn sunshine, which I can still see from across the lake – it and the red brick of the boathouse palely lit.... The boathouse where, Alex, your bike – yes, *your* bike – has been leaning innocently all morning, its front wheel turned inward.

XLV English village id

Momentously Tucker called me up – a disembodied plunge into the warped continuum, or the spacetime of our transatlantic phone connection – and somehow, in the assorted staggers and delays, conveyed the whole week from his diary. Then he listened intently as I gave him news of McNally's resignation. No matter, he said. The order in which he'd arranged those loose English papers (editorial bulldog clip, its years of use, its years of invasive rust) was more or less in order of importance. All I had to do was hang them together, with whatever else he'd put in the mail, then get off down to the printers, whose address I would find in any recent back edition. Why thank you, Crispin J.

'It's just great here,' he said (in Ing-er-land), and regaled me with all that Benbrook offered, or had done so on his sojourn thus far.

XLVI Mercurial

My oblation is to you – Alex, to you – with the probability that at last Marcia Copparo no longer represented that dark-eyed Sicilian beauty, whose discarded hair ties or minutely embroidered handkerchiefs I picked up and clutched to my cheek. She remained absent in the hundred places we agreed to meet. Alice is blessed, a hard-mouthed young woman who nevertheless took tack and string to the fractures of my heart, as a staunch on the vagaries of Fate – Fate, whose patterns of romantic force had contrived only bends and repulsions. She phoned just a day or two after Tucker. Her hair was turbaned, she explained, and her flesh goosy from the shower – therefore I couldn't make claims on her time. A lot more I guess at. The truth was that somehow my little plaints, whispered loudly in Alice's ear, or self-evident in the way I screwed the pages of a magazine, or tossed away the supplement or pull-out – it had all reached Copparo in a roar of lover's despondency, a throb that couldn't help but go on gorging itself. Alice well knew, from their tear-stained intimacies – that bud of blushing roses round their talk – how Marcia was also alone on lovelorn shores, and hadn't lost hope for her Frenchman – a blade whose last *au revoir* was waved from a railway carriage snaking out of Paddington.

'That apart,' Alice said, 'Alex has a right to know where *she* stands....'

'I'd like to know myself.'

Latest news from Queens was another retraction, Marcia pleading a two-day headache and jumpy thermometer ride. It left me in no doubt that tomorrow at the latest, the work-weary Copparo would sink into the satin of her bedroom, with a jar of aspirin, and lemon spooned with honey steaming at her bedside. I cancelled our evening (the hitch was that Alice couldn't take her place), a perfect two hours in company of the Arnolfini Quartet – a sacrifice I chose, having seen them months before, in a chilly parish church, one foggy autumn under the lamps of St Mary Cray – all a misty orange blur.

I shook my phone. Alice, spectre, a floating voice, drifted round the mouthpiece, as she stooped to tuck her towel. She complained, in a loud purr, then in a rush, that the breeze of her air conditioning blew its Antarctica into every corner of her apartment, and had begun to ice her limbs.

'But thinking of you, George,' she said. This she made clear wasn't personal affection. In essence this was double jointed as communiqué, as she and a Kleenex-dependent Copparo, after an afternoon drawing up their lists, had pencilled me an invitation to Kunstler's next exhibition.

'Honoured,' I said. 'What exhibition's that?'

Alice said she'd drop that in the mail.

XLVII Yesterday's news

I am certain I saw again that grey profile, the one from the boathouse. Just a few hours ago. I had walked round that clump of rhododendrons between the allotment – a bed of weeds and wild flowers – and the edge of the estate, still marked off with chestnut pales, having so far survived the axe. A stray leaf from yesterday's *Times*, where in its tablets of print there is a long article on the history of Sarajevo, had gusted up and lodged in those evergreens. Indistinct it might be, it was human in shape. I caught one further glimpse in the tool shed, but with the angle of other outbuildings – the laundry room, workshop, chapel – it wasn't possible to keep it in my sights. I approached, folding and pocketing that article. On a stretch of lawn, still pearled by this morning's dew, a line of prints of medium shoe size meandered to the rose bed, and over its mounds of clay. I jumped. Then I was past the swing, its little wooden seat – a small cut of wood – swaying on its two ropes knotted in the oak tree. The door to the tool shed was open. I went in, and stood on its sagging floorboards, looking. Not much there. A short flex hanging from a nail. An old-fashioned hand-push mower (which I do not recall in use), its blades a spiral of rust. A broom head and broom handle, the two having parted company. On the bench a slab of Carborundum, its spangled charcoal under the smear of spittle its possessor had worked with an edge. There was a wooden stepladder, splashed with paint. I looked out and across, where a pale shaft of sunshine besmeared the lichened panes in the roof of the glasshouse. No sign of anyone.

XLVIII Kunstler

Copparo's invitation arrived in a swirl of gold letters on a pre-printed card, an italic framed in a red-ink border. An engraving in the top left corner was a sprig of lavender.

Subject was Agnes Mombert, now in her seventies, once well known, according to Alice, as an American Impressionist (Agnes, one of those artists late to the gallery). An enterprising friend of the Kunstler had rediscovered her, not for the pointillism she had perfected when young, but for a body of Surrealist work Mombert had turned out in the '40s, from her studio north of Patoka Lake (a place called Shoals). My firm instructions, for how well Copparo knew my wardrobe – happy if hangdog – were to find something semi-formal for the occasion, and not to forget the invitation, without which I wouldn't get past the desk – an insistence I found overly bureaucratic. I was hard up, with not much coming in. Work for the publishing firm in Chappaqua was finicky and not well paid. Yet – I somehow transformed what Copparo saw as peasant simplicity with a motley of pressed, pristine add-ons, which in the angles of my mirror – profile left, right, chin to shoulder – I knew were outlandish. A narrow-lapelled, white tuxedo, whose texture was crêpe to the touch. A striped shirt with a wing collar. A bowtie whose yellow silk found my several thumbs, and which I exchanged for a clip-on. Pants, by which I mean trousers – which didn't, Alex, fit my persona (perplexed and penguin-like) – these were too tapered, or sat too broadly on my shoes, which were pointed at the toe.

These, atrocious sophistications, weren't the prompt access to East 70th Marcia had seemed to promise, given the interdicts the desk and receptionist insisted on. The latter was ash to blonde to strawberry, a rainbow shadowed at her crown, and wore a bowtie much like mine (hers though matched to a waistcoat, whose faint pinstripes were the same flame red I caught, in a certain light, in Marcia's hair). She couldn't extricate herself from the glue of her phone, whose caller seemed to ask – question she repeated, and repeated, and repeated – not *Where* but *What is the gallery?* I passed my invitation into the smile of her gaze then attempted to walk to the elevator, an action she checked theatrically with frantic gestures. Then again those explanations, patiently for her caller, the subways, the bus routes, and again the *not where*, the *what*. In it loomed a long tractate on the infestation of capital in art, a Marxist outburst she wasn't prepared to listen to. She attempted one final description, at the same time waving me off into the plush of a leather settee, a huge, studded, blood-coloured beast under a Hassam reproduction (poppies, a bay, a two-masted pleasure craft). So back to her caller, and repetitively *what* is the gallery?

Why, exhibits of course…. Some people!

She put her phone down and cradled it on her desk. I watched a girlish toss of her hair. Again I passed her my paperwork, whose name she checked against a list.

'Mr Dew Play, go ride on up.'

XLIX High life

'Up' was to Larry's penthouse, a sunlit firmament woven with perfume and a billow of blue cigar smoke. A sad- but bright-eyed Agnes, in a plain grey frock, and a hat whose brim was pinned at the front, had both hands occupied. In her glass was something thinly green, with a sparkle, and a cube of pineapple impaled on a cocktail skewer. She'd got herself besieged by a posse of men in business suits, a situation Alice, bound to the forced *politesse* in a group of younger men, kept a cautious eye on. She rolled, then unrolled, the exhibition catalogue, which she referred to superficially, then used as a fan to breeze her brows, which until she caught my eye had darkened. Marcia was talking to the steward, a boy in mid-stride – hair slicked, jacket meticulously white. I awaited the clatter of his tray as it tilted through several teasing angles, yet remained intact over the clutch of heads, its load of empty glasses a cargo he delivered somewhere cloaked from view. Alice looped her arm in mine, and at last escaped her school of connoisseurs and newspapermen. She pressed her elbow into my ribs, and was slow to retract it. She nudged me again. I stepped back – a manoeuvre planting us both in the shade of Agnes's conversation, so attentive were all those newfound friends and admirers.

'Looking sharp, George,' Alice said, whose drop-waisted dress and art deco hairdo I complimented.

The steward paused in slipping past, his tray static, and horizontal, and crowded with newly replenished glassware. Marcia edged closer, but stopped to talk with Larry. Larry, Alice said, was a good but exacting boss. For today's escapades Marcia wore a leopard-skin blouse, in contrast to Hope, who stepped from the elevator just a minute behind me, in something plain and white. It had lots of pleats, and she looked, well – fulsome.

That abundance lent its shape, sack-sized and gregarious, to that special knack she had in fitting names to faces, their owners returning puzzled handshakes or apprehensive smiles (all too English, I thought). She wound herself, through the wreckage of interrupted conversation, leaving in her dust trail those same setting smiles, knitted eyebrows, lastly a flurry of catalogues ruffling the air, by now stale with tobacco and perfume. She over-did her hugs for Alice, whose mind wasn't on the conversation we'd been having. It was to do with you, Alex, and how 'impulsive' I had been. I was too ready, she thought, in accepting this as my exile, with the wind at my tail, and how I'd departed the weatherworn shores of England. 'Alice,' I said, 'there are things you do not know,' but she did not ask for more. Instead your sister turned hips and shoulders in the direction of Agnes and her entourage – a genteel old American sipping at her drink – where a grey-faced entrepreneur, in square-framed glosses and a fluorescent white shirt, was busily describing views to be had from the heights of Charlie Cowles (another house like Kunstler's). [R:XLIX.n1.p650] CC had a gallery in Soho. Somehow some crank had bypassed the switchboard and got through to him – to *him!* – personally, and asked repeatedly: *What, what is the gallery?* Mindless.

Hope said 'Why George!', and I said, 'Good to see you….' She'd heard all about *English Village Id*, and asked how that work was going.

'Sort of stopped,' I said. [R:XLIX.n2.p651]

Eventually Alice got her wish, when Larry and the leopard-heart Copparo trailed off in different directions, circulating news of the exhibition, which had opened. About half the company tramped downstairs to the viewing, cue for Hope, who chose just that opportunity, intercepting New York's newly brand-made celebrity. She introduced Alice, who fingered the embroidered adornments to her bag. She introduced me, as editor of *Village Id*, 'a cute little lit mag'.

'That's not technically accurate,' I said. [R:XLIX.n3.p652]

'Why George, don't be so self-effacing – it's so English.'

I left them, and made my way downstairs to the exhibition, where a self-portrait had attracted attention, a work dating from the early 1950s. That crowd I bypassed, and found myself in her '40s corner, with plenty of elbow room, and time to browse at the samples that between them Larry and Copparo had chosen from Agnes's Impressionist era (an excursion now considered naïve – though of course Agnes was then in her thirties and hardly known). Naïve or not – which meant really 'anachronistic' – these were her lightly coloured byways, delicate sprigs, trees in a sumptuous haze of afternoon sun, remote hilltop homesteads, lakes reflecting moss or amber, leafy pools, her skies an electric blue by day or burnt, burnished and auburn at sunset – and people, leading far-off lives, in a cupric-coloured shadow. Her *Bridge* (terse titles all) was twilit, while its actual construction showed itself in only a dove-grey metallic rib, a road bridge spanning a waterway, whose grading went oily to turquoise, and at the middle of her canvas a ghostly silver, which from portside was dotted and streaked with pale orange lights. *Nightscape* was a fractured moon, in the broken wrap of tinted yellow clouds, suspended over the charcoal chimney stacks of a plain-looking factory. Her *Parade* (of 1945) was an East Coast city street, in a cross-sleet of sun-licked tickertape, whereas *Orchard* (1948) was a swag of white blossoms in a wreath round a clapboard frame house.

When Alice appeared, it was side-by-side with Agnes – she and Hope having somehow wrested her, temporarily at least, from that corps of aficionados. I had got to the self-portrait – just those sad eyes, a straight nose, a limpid brow, and only a suggestion of framing hair, all part submerged in the nether tones of green. Shortly after that, Alice had pressed her card into Agnes Mombert's hand, and not half an hour later your sister and I had looped arms again, and with Hope at our rear sauntered through that capacious foyer and out towards the doorway, then on to the dappled street outside. [R:XLIX.n4.p657] Here a man with a toothy grin, and wearing a tall black hat, handed out varicoloured leaflets, which in a crossfire of printer's fonts and point sizes said

wHat Is tHE gaLieRy

– and underneath this a date and venue. I screwed that paper up, but didn't discard it. I put it in my pocket.

L A snake in the grass

I don't think I can be here much longer. It's not the cold and damp, the biting air, or the wash of condensation filming the windowpanes each morning. It's the changes going on around me. The metallic clang of tools, or the ring when a wrench or spanner is dropped in the cellar onto the concrete floor. There are echoes at any time of day. They reach me even at the summit of my tower. I'm tired of having to investigate.

I had made up my mind, arms folded – a dejected pose. I had looked out from my window beyond the boundaries of Middlecross, into the patched light and yellowing leaves of the orchard. Now a new sound – the high-pitched whine with woody incisions, thrumming in cyclic waves, its source an electric saw. I put hands in pockets, about to go down, and came across that scrap of paper I had earlier put there, now screwed up. I mean the Sarajevo piece, on whose reverse side was the correspondence page, whose longest, loudest, most minutely detailed missive was a defence of the sale of Tralatition Press, to a soulless conglomerate. [R:L.n1.p657]

I stepped outside, and traced – snaking through the clumps of grass – that cable I had earlier seen hanging up, from where it was plugged in down in the cellar – I traced it to its other end. Flakes of white paint, and golden flecks of sawdust in a trail that petered out, were the only evidence of anyone's handiwork, which led me back towards the tool shed. An aluminium house ladder, its lustre dimmed in the moist atmosphere, was propped against an oak bough, from which your swing had now been cut – two knots binding only the remaining tufts of rope.

I remembered instantly how once I had stumbled on you here, in a white frock and open-toed sandals, hair pinned up and you still damp from the shower, rocking gently in the rays of morning sunshine, reading a libretto, *The Mikado*. On other days I heard you singing in the music room, your mother at the piano running on ahead. Soon after a whole troupe from school filled the same space, rehearsing cues and choruses. Everyone appeared mid-afternoon – robust smiles and ringlets – when Alice brought out jugs of iced lemonade and served it on the lawn. I'd been omitted from the party that drove in convoy to the final performance. There was last-minute confusion over ticket numbers. But for me it is this, as memorial: a week in spring – forsythias blooming, cherry blossom soon to appear, a magnolia, with a scarlet blush. In the woods, bluebells....

The Mikado had its last night midweek (not a Friday, unusually). You went with your father in his car, which had to leave ahead of the group, he having arranged to meet one of his new authors, or a prospective, who was driving down from London. The meeting took place in the lengthening shade slanting over the quads and courtyards of the Dame d'Hautpoul, a mark of the pine trees in that Arcadia. [R:L.n2.p657] According to Alice, he sat through the performance, but had to get away promptly on the last curtain, and did so swinging his briefcase.

The whole thing was a huge success.

LI Stoker

You cannot forget the autumns here. They are subdued in the dawn fires of sunshine, a pale yellow flame briefly through the Kentish mists. They're a satin weave suspended over the river valley, or trickling through the chimney stacks of Middlecross. Today dew in the tufts of grass turned to foam with the swish of my ankles when – with that scrap of paper pocketed again – I tramped from the tool shed, around the rhododendrons and back towards the house. I paused because that flex, with an undulation of its head – its dead electric head – slimed its way back to the cellar, where a pair of unseen hands rewound it. For a moment I bunched my fist round the handle to the service hatch, about to throw it open, and in that underworld confront whoever it was enacting these systematic deconstructions going on around me. [R:LI.n1.p657] Instead a squeal of hinges, then the thud of a door to its jambs, followed by the hurried escape of a hunched up, coated little being, who with grunts and stumpy strides skimmed the lawns and diminished to a blur as he ran round the lake.

I followed tentatively.

LII To the boathouse...

That little man wasn't in the boathouse. Your bike was. Its treadless, faded tyres were blackened by the rain we had had that morning. Also here was that suitcase I had last seen open-mouthed on the mattress in your room. Its lid was up, on the workbench, under a vertical rack now emptied of oars and boat hooks. Someone had begun to pack things into it, but had got as far as three articles only. There was, first, that colour print of the Pont du Gard, in a myrtle-wood frame. Second, that portrait of someone you knew – a boy with rosy cheeks and a retroussé nose. I'd never thought to ask you who he was. Lastly an A4 padded envelope, stamped but not addressed – not yet. Inside was a sizeable hardback, its cover black, and its spine tooled with Tralatition gilt. The monogram is a swirl of curlicues, as I find it all the harder to accept that the press has been sold. [R:LII.n1.p657]

Just then I caught a shard of light through the square panes of the boathouse window, and looking out over the lake saw a lime-green car nose to a halt under the fig tree. Sunshine, intermittent in the mist, caught the violet tint of its windscreen. A muffled thud as the driver door closed did not coincide with a clear definition – there was a ragged outline only – of the person who'd emerged, a man instantly cloaked in the shadow off the pantry wall. He was, anyway, consumed in a re-gathering of mist that suddenly fell in shrouds. I left the envelope but took the book, and dropped it into my room before looking in on yours, where, as I expected, the last remaining hanging had gone. [R:LII.n2.p659] Here though a large-framed pair of glasses, arms crossed and masculine, rested on your dresser – an excrescence I removed and re-sited in the music room.

LIII Billet-doux [R:LIII.n1.p659]

A dribble of rusty water from the inlet valve to my radiator has left a copper-coloured sickle in the grain of the floor – first sign that the system will soon be switched on. The mist outside has thickened – this when I thought it might disperse – and hangs in broken waves, clouding the upper extremes in the stonework, decorative loops atop the walls and their coping. From here in the round room I just about make out the headless statuette of Pan. Sliced tangentially, there's an exaggerated acorn crowning a brick pillar. I can just make out the headstone to Porthos's grave – 'Here lies one who barked.'

I shall make time for that book I've borrowed, which adds to the long list of Dante translations already in print – it's yet another *Inferno*. This one's the work of a man called Royce (a name I vaguely recall, though I can't remember why), which although a reprint isn't at all recent. There's a handwritten dedication penned in faded green ink to the half-title page, which reads: *Dearest Myra, all love, John.* [R:LIII.n2.p659] Inside it I found a sheet of cheap headed notepaper, a shiny white, and smooth to the touch, its origin more than coincidental. The crest is a red hart, done Cubist style, and the place is Benbrook Height – that college of performing arts where aeons ago Crispin Tucker did his sabbatical. In John's same green hand the note began *Myra, thought I would*, in a gambol of half-crossed t's and open loops, which in a self-involution ceased contritely in the blankness they abutted. [R:LIII.n3.p659] The page this note happened to bookmark coincided with a few verses part way into Canto II (lines 59–70, if you would like me to be precise)—

> O courteous shade of Mantua! whose fame
> Is as durable as spacetime,
> My friend – though he does not share my status –
> Is in the deserts of his middle life –
> A man so burdened he's about to quit the fight.
> He veers from his former path,
> To a point where I cannot turn him back
> (If what he says is true). I ask you,
> With speed, dispatch, and all the eloquence
> I know you to command, to help, assist –
> Allay my fears. Who asks you this
> Is Beatrice....

I'm not sure about that *spacetime*, nevertheless God speed Myra, Beatrice.... [R:LIII.n4.p659] There are interruptions, I hear...

...and an indescribable clatter, which I assume is from those goings-on in the cellar – a metal pale, tools, a burst bag of nails, rattling centrifugally, contrapuntally, in an empty oil drum. This time I did investigate. What I found, on an upturned tea chest, was a tabloid open at yesterday's gossip. There is a slow reader, somewhere in Middlecross. Part of that tattle was a succession of captioned photos, location a cinema foyer, whose dome above was the glitzy skies of Leicester Square. The culminating snap was of a thrown shoe and a smudge to a silk shirt, whose owner's profile wasn't one I recognised. Added was a sprinkle of crumbs, and nestling in the centrefold a part demolished cheese and gherkin sandwich.

Some old junk was being gone through. On the bottom step to the kitchen I found this, Alex – the plinth to your record deck, its vintage the '70s, its arm in two parts and dangling by its sinews – and plugless.

I have rescued it, and brought it to the round room.

LIV Black mantra

Alice and Agnes honed their good professional links, right up to the time of Mombert's death, which I heard about after I left New York. Alice had one filthy habit, always jangling my loose change, and did it again on the sidewalk, your sis with me in a saunter from Agnes's exhibition (others here from Kunstler's followed). The probe of her fingers worked their tips to a friction, then lit on that paper I had screwed up and left there dormant. She pulled it out and undid the creases. One day after that, friend Hope phoned and asked had I any thoughts.

'Any thoughts on what, Hope?'

'On what is the gallery.'

'Well,' I said, 'it's typically Greenwich Village.'

'Aw now George....' Nevertheless, she offered an assignment, with a copy deadline midday Thursday, she and *Art Day News* unlike Tucker running to a calendar.

'By the way,' Hope asked, 'how is Tucker?'

'In thrall to Benbrook, I should think.'

'Uh?'

'I don't know, Hope.' Hopeless. [R:LIV.n1.p659]

Sceptical as I was, I have reason to be glad I accepted her commission. It didn't lead to an end of the James Little du Pléian curfew – schemed Atlantic style, and broader in scale than even I'd imagined. Nor did it lighten what Machiavellian weight bore down on my shoulders, Alex. [R:LIV.n2.p667] Yet, I had come to read his conspiracies. I put up with my vapid city life, with its dose of English pragmatism, its emphasis on over-caution. Anyway, I was too put off by the disciplines of journalism, in my view a kind of affliction – a malady yellow at its edges, whose media-borne pathology taints the newsprint in almost every arts capital. I wore that half-serious smirk – the one your mother understood, and in certain disjunctions connived at – when having drunk to the dregs my afternoon coffee, I slipped into my seat pocket a miniature notebook, faintly lined. [R:LIV.n3.p668] If not exactly raring to go, I perched the stub of a pencil behind my ear. By foot, subway, and foot again, I descended into the threads, slants and shadows of sunset, and emerged finally in the black pools and reddish gold reflections intermittent in that concrete weald (an encircling city of windows). The address – which Alice had underscored on the flyer she'd de-floreted – turned out to be a cancer of warehouse space in a cranny off Canal Street. It had been vacated by a corrugated box firm – Usdyke Inc – whose blue, pellucid logo still adorned the glass plate, in a door intense with neon, or it had that appearance in the last broken shafts of sunshine.

I went inside. The guest book, large and grey-leafed, was open on its pulpit – two amber, burnished wooden steps up, and a music stand. A proliferation of today's date and dittos marked its two facing pages, which had been signed numerously, in different shades of ink and a range of styles (most notable: medic-like illegibility, and its offset, copperplate calligraphy). I scratched in my own mark, a few cursory strokes – its gobbets and blacked rusticity carefully concealing my name. I took stock of entries ahead of mine, not from today's alone, as with puzzled curiosity I leafed back to the opening page. As a first salvo a cramped if tidy hand connected itself to a previous two, in a languid stretch diametrically across the Pacific. A trite jingle emphasised their scale of geographic separation, set down in verse in the comments column. Why should this have been noteworthy? What was my interest in someone who, however remotely, had paired from an arbitrary list of addresses its two farthest points, these being Phoenix and Dunedin? And why were my suspicions not dispelled? I think because of those many *other* signatures, mostly listing Ithaca as home. The only person I knew from there was Brad....

Alice has told me repeatedly that no PoMo catalogue – with its bits of bootlace, factory springs, a butterfly clip, always lots of cutlery – can ever inflate itself without invoking safe-looking chapter heads. After Usdyke Inc, what else could evolve but the tired designation 'Found Performance Space'? From glances through Brad's ragbag of names, light led me away – as I pocketed my pencil – to a shimmer of ill-lit drapes, rigged up over one of those science-fiction voids where double doors ought to be, or were folded back. I parted them. Their sooty linings inside, and my hand briefly, were touched by silver – as contrast to the dejected twilight everywhere else. All was, Alex, highly reminiscent of Brad, Mirtch, or both. Aesthetically this was their signature, their showing room a shying room, because blacked – just like my name, outside and beyond my control in the foyer. But now I discovered I wasn't alone. Through this inferno swam or galumphed the detached limbs, torsos, the bright buckle on a belt or shoulder bag, those monochrome shapes that only integrated into wholes when the eye adjusts to the light.

I knew with what mockeries the coiffed Brad had turned out his intricate tractates, in the sullen hours or grey mornings that seemed to hang on the Donns Watson statuary – all that lichened finger-pointing in an ancient modern underworld. His perfected themes had varied not at all from the ones handed down, in tablets of diktat, the heaped cumulus, or the rarefied prophetisms of the poet Robert Quay. Quay, who in recent times had been bureaucratised by a set of rules – or portents really – written into the Donns Watson handbook (I mean specifically course number DWRIPA.LIT.2219). Limits, liminalities, contexts, constructs – these were the magic mantras chanted by rote, in a collision of cultures – which all of us sucked our fagends in – there to perform the metatext – the thing that surrounded, subsumed, or in the end engulfed our fatalistic little turns, this dance with our robotic Muse some still regarded as Individualism. Brad, having sacrificed his, was wing-clad nevertheless, and could hover at any requisite altitude with his pocketbook or microphone. Some audible clashes culled from a civic construction site I heard had been recorded to tape, and now thrummed monotonously in the simulated depths, somewhere in the performance space above. Overlaid onto this were the startled, or puzzled, or hard-hearing phone respondents, unable to comprehend that cultural survey in its single point of focus – Brad's, or Mirtch's *What is the gallery?* There were faint titters, sniggers, and in them a knowing condescension – this post-Usdyke audience, wraiths of an early evening midnight, having come down off Canal Street briefed or well informed. Still most answers singled out another, an irrelevant question: *Where – where is the gallery?*

Actually Hope could see the column inches it was possible to distil from the barbs of my editorial re these student escapades. She had had – when I showed her my draft – a sad, and as she put it plum-coloured morning. She slammed phones. She overturned the paper cascade of her in-trays (I watched her do this several times). Then she couldn't find her diary (though that didn't matter now).

'It's nearly three,' she said, and meant it must be time for lunch. She produced crackers, decisively. Then with more care a chive-mottled cheese, which was foil wrapped, and whose packaging showed two slim slimmers slimming. Oh and why not, a *pinot noir*, from the vineyards of Santa Barbara – 'Could you open George please—'.

That distant mourning I saw in her disappointed gaze lightened at a first heady hint of the bouquet, always her genie to spirit away the workday whims. I poured (one small glass for George too), and at close quarters was sure that the pallor of Hope's complexion wasn't cosmetic. Peach infused her cheekbones just as that first sip of nectar softened her palate. She coated her biscuit in cheese. When she nibbled, an orange-cornered crumb lodged in the fibres of her sweater, a steel-grey knit. Then a chopped chive gummed itself to the bud of her upper lip. There were miracles too – the three to four hairline furrows in her forehead dissolving in that sunshine of indulgence. She read my draft (I knew she would re-draft), and cut to the chase immediately. Not the name Usdyke, the pulpit, drapes, those ever-revolving sound-overs, or that afternoon cradle of night. What after all intrigued her was the exhibit Brad and Mirtch had chosen to place in an outer rim of darkness, on the surface of a glass display case, under a phalanx of light, or tiny pinpoints.

What *was* this exhibit (and what was the gallery)? I am, Alex, very tired. The cold and the damp in waves off the walls and the floors at Middlecross begin to be invasive. I shan't last here much longer. Therefore I wearily admit that the tape loop swirling in that black ether somewhere metaphorically over our heads made attempts on the question *what*. I shall not state the obvious. Our social norms and the scales of predictability were what this whole dusky setup sought to undermine. Here galleried, given its context, glassed, in the end faddish under a cosmic shower of light, was a cassette tape – very like the one we listened to – except *actually* rather than only *linguistically* deconstructed. [R:LIV.n4.p668] Its five bright retaining screws sat thread-up in a quincunx. Next to that – a shape and a pattern of stars – was one half and the black velvet of the outer case. Then the first of two membranes. That, in a procession long and linear, was followed by three plastic wisps (grouchy mouth, Groucho eyebrows) – loose, floating apparatus to do with tension in the tape (I am told). Capstans were two, and the spool itself, then finally those other halves (membrane and outer case). And all pedantically neat.

'That's unmistakably Brad,' I said, and told her what I knew about him.

'Quite a guy,' she said.

She gave me a paragraph – George du Plé, freelance for *Art Day News* – somewhere in the lower reaches – but with editor's reservations. Where I had begun 'Roland, Michel, and now the lost triumvir', Hope had overruled: 'Two bright boys from the Donns Watson....'

The centre spread couldn't be other than a sun-baked profile and the floral dress of a diffuse Agnes Mombert. [R:LIV.n5.p668]

LV Family snaps

A freak howl of wind rattling the sashes in the round room presages a hard Kentish winter, with no sign yet that the mechanic, commuting cloak-and-dagger between the cellar, the tool shed, and the boathouse, has succeeded with the central-heating switch. [R:LV.n1.p668] The cold needle pricking at my fingertips – breathing on them does no good – delays any parallel breakthrough with that record player of yours. To be honest I didn't expect to be here for as many days as this – I can no longer tolerate the changing English seasons. I have found a plug, which I've attached. Even then, the turntable – whose rubber grooves I have run my house key through, to remove the quick – is stuck.

The whole pointless exercise made me think back to one of those accumulated spells in Middlecross's populous times, when the silence was hard to penetrate. Mere days – not the march of past decades now coloured in regret. The thing's almost antique (the record player), and was lugged round with your mother's mountain luggage back in the 1950s. In an attempt to give up smoking, she packed up her cross-country skis, having paid a deposit and a few months' rent on a small, modestly furnished flat, in the sharp air of Schwamendingen. She was single, with a first honeymoon not far off. Some of this you know. A lot you don't.

The firm Marg joined was Anglo-American, and needed interpreters and translators. It turned out not to be good for her health, the office she worked in swarming with close-cropped, newly qualified engineers, dollar rich and loaded with unfiltered cigs. You recall how Alice sketched in other details, in later years coaxing out names for faces – carefully haphazard in a box of grey photos. I remember, over the dents and polished scars of the kitchen table, or pouring afternoon tea on the lawns of Middlecross, how girlish she could be, unearthing, then in an adult way re-emphasising those rumours surrounding her suitors (but not her husbands – Alice *knew* about these). [R:LV.n2.p669]

Marg smiled when one in her list of admirers brought Alpine gifts, varnished knick-knacks – then a bottle of schnapps. One small glass capped his evenings in her flat. Then the stroll home, the man weightless under the starred guide or twinkle of frosty porch lights. Soon came the vinyl – for so our circle of Paradise at certain moments approximates to divine ordinance – and anyway the schnapps didn't last. There was a lot of Mozart (an 'Eine Kleine', a 'Jupiter', a dazzling array of piano concertos). Then came a *Matthew Passion*, followed by Adrian Boult, doing the 'Enigma'. Some few other conductors tucked under Eddie's arm were Klemperer, Barbirolli – Beecham. Beecham had written sleeve notes, setting out his thesis on attractive versus ugly women, and the distractions of both in the workplace. That same passion livened up his baton, where the sore-headed Russian bear, Mussorgsky, boomed and hissed in a mountain storm (Ravel orchestration). Twenty years ago, these items were extant in the Little collection, if superseded electronically now.

Ed had to get back to Philadelphia, having decided to switch his interests from post-war Europe – all heavy plant and rebuilding – to the US leisure industry. Marg followed, and did her dutiful rounds in all branches of the family. Trousered aunts showed her the stores. A trio of high-school nieces whiled away a week of afternoons just to entertain her, in the ceramic reflection brightening their indoor pools. Week two she spent alone, but shopping – up and down Fifth Avenue – her base a Central Park hotel, and the bustle of New York, which Ed had carefully arranged. The wedding – a social and theatrical opportunity – called for broad-brimmed hats and a catalogue of long-haul flights – and was synchronised to coincide with the English buds of May. Colours were pink, white, violet. It took place in the old Saxon church in Elmshurst, a dormitory village on a commuter route between Hastings and central London, whose leafy solitude was shattered one Saturday afternoon by a fleet of limousines, though seamlessly returned to its dreams and tradition shortly after that.

Years later – in fact four years later – one other sacrament fulfilled itself, also at Elmshurst, where the hospital hill climbs were flanked or fringed with silver birch and rhododendron, the vast sprawling layout ringed by a chestnut wood, where oaks and solitary pines grew also. A bespectacled stork with well-wisher telegrams dropped Alice from the clouds and into the safe hands of one of its maternity suites. [R:LV.n3.p669] There is much Marg told me. And there is much I have for you, Alex – here, now and at Middlecross, where the hydrangeas are rich in enamel, and the buddleias have gone over. I look down where Alice used to hand out cake at her hatter's tea parties, now where continents of moss invade the lawns.

A new century beckoned circa 1960, at a time when all that headgear had to be dusted down or replaced, for a new bride, with a new itinerary now drawn up. Marg had entered her phase of British politics, and categorically wouldn't move to Philadelphia. The house she rented both of us know by its glaze and rose façade, which in the albums look like streaks of rain. She and Alice overlooked a snaking stretch of the Medway (accented by two short straights), whose steely grey ribbon washed a mud or grassy bank, depending on the season. The same record player sat with its mouth open on an upended trunk in the dining room – small, square, and lit by a single bulb – though now with Rachmaninov and Beethoven bagatelles added to its workload.

When Alice was two, the house acquired a dog and an au pair. Marg got a part-time job as party worker. She canvassed for the Liberals, whose ragbag at that time a star-eyed mother of one saw sanctified, as if in golden dusk. Or was that the twilit sheen dusted from an old lapel? The dog was a Lab and border collie pact, whose shiny black coat was dipped in a murky white at the forepaws, with a dazzle of Alpine snow at the chin and between the pectorals. He'd survived suburban nightmares, a first and last unsuitable home, his dog life there numbered by the furnishings he'd gnawed through. His next stop was a concrete yard and a community of wire enclosures, compounds marked out under the collective name Angel Pet Rescue, an epithet locally derived. I remember a hotel in Tonbridge, whose long narrow bar was black beams and horse brasses, with an escutcheon sharing that Angel engraving. It – the rescue centre – had charitable status. Its logo was a flop-eared woe-bitten corgi, on good terms with a black and white cat, demure in its feline gaze through a furry *bandito* mask.

Swashbuckling Porthos – so-called – came with his vaccination card, and a name that (to me) is portentous only in retrospect. I sit here fretting over Mrs Little's record player, scratching notes on the reverse side of an envelope, and see for the first time Porthos is almost an anagram of Thorpe. That latter name attracting so much scandal. [R:LV.n4.p669] Porthos, as a pup of fourteen months, was ransomed to the scale of doggy years that soon put him in advance of Alice – Alice, who only in June had blown out two pink candles on a home-baked birthday cake (see photos). [R:LV.n5.p670] He was happy, wacky, full of motive power in his long, slender, lurcher limbs (Porthos, a mutt of cloudy lineage). It took time to discover how the mush of his diet had caused his copious diarrhoea. Yet here in those riches of his bowels dude Porthos – now the sophisticated town dweller – found his poise, choosing as his scratching place the blue slate in Marg's ornamental fireplace, where he squatted after midnight, when Marg had gone to bed. It ensured a very nice start to her days (dog days). Booting out the hound at night, if under a blank sky or a studded dome pearled with Mondschein, wasn't an answer, as Marg found out. [R:LV.n6.p670] Happy Chappy, a toothy grin to his muzzle, and a pink tongue glossed in saliva, hummed funny tunes to Alice's rabbit, a mere ball of grey fluff, its ears quick and alert to that terrorising hound prowling round the hutch. [R:LV.n7.p670] Quaintly Marg had named that rabbit Russell. Russell, cold, naked fear in the roundness of its eye, bounced at high velocity off all its four walls of chicken wire – even at the faintest sniff of dog breath on the wind.

More good work had seen Ed, who never failed his firstborn, [R:LV.n8.p670] set up arrangements for Marg's au pair, dispatching across the Atlantic the blondest of his nieces – a pneumatic Rose-Anne, whose high-school years had been in Vermont. [R:LV.n9.p670] Rose-Anne found the dawg kinda ca-yute, and didn't object at all to late-night walks along the Medway, which under the diffusion of northern stars, or a sackcloth pallor of clouds, varied in its ripple and tincture, passing from the brittle gleam of gunmetal to the dull brush of battleship grey. The vet did her bit too, injecting antibiotics, and proposing a diet of short-grain rice whisked with scrambled egg. Marg for her part set the alarm for six, and in the dews, hails and frosts of all those Kentish mornings, exercised pup Porthos along the same riparian ways (the same as Rose-Anne's). All this seemed to be the remedy, the dog squatting either in a dawn wind or under the cloak of night, and left at his various staging posts a good-dog glisten of caramel-coloured swirls, all artfully suspended in the clumps of riverside grass.

There was a problem Marg *never* overcame (the solution lay in the process of years, and the dog's descent into age), and this was the habit Porthos had – when it was time to attach the lead – to roll on his back and zigzag on his spine. Paws you saw folded limply in the air, two muddy white mittens dangling on a washing line. In this pose too, young Porthos jawed his chain and gnawed at the leather loop. The reverse process – *removing the lead* – wasn't nearly so indecisive, its end result, among howls of human protest, delivered in a bound for the kitchen, where a Rose-Anne not properly awake saw Alice's morning rusk added to the dog's breakfast, snaffled. So much for Porthos.

If not also of the Liberal tent, but a man caught up in one of Marg's rallies – this is where your daddy made his footfall onto that crowded stage. [R:LV.n10.p670] One fine, if chilly afternoon, Marg got his attention, and handed him a leaflet. Since noon no end of makeshift banners had swayed above her head. A look at her watch showed that the trek home – a slow draughty train in a clatter from Charing Cross – was imminent. You could see the few long shadows falling slantwise over Whitehall, in a criss-cross through the vortices of autumn leaves. It was almost four, and a Sunday. Progress is so far good, yet here I'm stuck for a name, Alex, having got this second and third hand, and over the past fifteen to twenty years having made no particular effort to remember it. [R:LV.n11.p670] Someone hand-delivered a petition to Number 10. The Prime Minister, who at that time was Harold Macmillan, was not at home – at least not at *this* home. This in itself could not be enough to deter the Marg *I* came to know, over a decade later, when now she found herself alone, and of not much use to the cause. The location was one of those city squares, with seats, a perimeter railing, a mulch of rotting leaves, and where, under the desolate arms of a beech tree, Marg sat on a bench, consoled by the dregs of tea that remained in her Thermos.

Fortune cues in a certain Cecil Gale, still in a dazzle of euphoria at the CBE he'd recently collected, and added to the professional letters of his name. Did he come always to the same iron gate, the macadam path and assortment of seats inside, to glance – whatever the season – over the columns of his *Sunday Times*? Ah no – no! They talked about Suez, her leaflet, the grouse moors, that cloth cap called Wilson. He jotted down her phone number, though Marg didn't think (or didn't appear to think) to ask for his. He called her, on the following Wednesday, when Marg was out walking the dog. He got Rose-Anne – whose telephone emphasis was a *why sure* reiterated *ad infinitum*, rounded off with decision in an *okey dokey*. To put this into context, she was attempting – with limited success – to spoon-feed a wailing, recalcitrant Alice (Alice, who always *knows* what she wants). He tried again a few days later, this time when Marg was in a rush to have her hair done. With not quite the same haste she agreed to a night out at the theatre. Cecil's tastes were bland, so this would have been a West End farce.

Those subsequent weekends out of town must have been in the comfort and woolly succour of Marg's living room. A hot teapot, homemade banana bread, a north aspect. In the latter a reflected whiteness of frost. The Georgian sashes were over-borne by a garden full of fruit trees. Inside, the twin bars and fanlit artificial fuel of the living-room heater had not yet been superseded by an adequate central-heating system. Moreover Cecil didn't like the dog, as a very general thing. House pets made him sneeze, and loose-haired house pets mostly succeeded in setting off his asthma. This one slobbered on his ankle socks. Shockingly, it also sniffed at the bifurcation of his trouser legs. And too often to laugh off, it pressed the moist black button of its nose into the innocent palm of his hand.

I am vaguely aware of the thing, or things, that Cecil did – I mean his work – before that private implosion. [R:LV.n12.p670] There were strategies in what Marg has termed, generically, 'economics'. Its twinned portfolio, personal and professional, was property and investment. There was a hotel of his off Praed Street, which overlooked a lawned, leafy square, crumbling when he took it on, yet able to fly ambassadorial flags once he'd touched it with his wand. Firms sometimes sent him off into the lush vineyards of monetary Europe, the brief an advisory one. It was, latterly, Rose-Anne herself who supervised the dawn of his flights – she did this many times – ensuring Cecil's gloves, scarves and his suitcase found their way safely to the airport. It happened whenever some urgent dispatch took him into the bitter winds of Scandinavia. His trips into Kuwait restored his tan, when attire there was shorts, sandals, barrier creams, a sun hat and glasses.

He curtailed his country weekends in winter. Too often it crippled the rail system, through its network of frozen points – just as he'd clattered loose change into the cashier's trough, in exchange for a ticket. These were fruitless half-hours stamping his feet and hugging his sides, on the cold concrete of Charing Cross, devoid then of its brightness now. (It's a bamboozling linearity, with slabs of scrubbed marble, baguette tents, and freshly painted burger bars.) When he did get down, Rose-Anne baked bread and kept Alice warm, while Cecil, if the two were out walking, suffered all Marg's ministrations while hurling sticks for Porthos. This wasn't without sarcasm, when infallibly Cecil's marksmanship took in the icy murk of the Medway, and the dog was ever willing.

Next thing, Cecil found Marg's musical Saturday nights too difficult – the merry tunes of Mozart, or the painful incisions in the arithmetic counterpoint of Bach. He brought his own offerings, with a clutch of LPs in the burnt orange of late-November sunshine. In that van came Oscar Peterson. Fats Waller. Then his collection of Dizzy Gillespies. (All of it eventually found its way to Vermont, as did Dave Brubeck.) When it was too cold even for these, Rose-Anne tucked Alice up, and with the babe a-slumber – sweetly, under the spiral of her mobile – the three adults retreated into the glow of the kitchen stove, and dipped bread into a pot of fondue.

There was the probability of marriage, and wider transformations. A cold pattern of stars promised to plunge not only lovers, but the whole nation in an ethereal, sub-zero crystal of poetics. It's not a versification I remember clearly, whose imagery and jagged lineation belong to the oral tradition, though it certainly did enshroud municipal offices, in its prison bars of ice. There were parts of the country barred by drifts of snow. Not quite in the thick of it, Cecil removed the entire ménage to his own, much roomier place, just a short stroll from Kensington Gardens, where Porthos was relegated to the basement. He had a rug, a basket, and a rubbery bone to chew, yet kept his dogged eye on the grille above and the shafts of light from somewhere at street level. Come the dawn, that mad, canine chevalier barked ferociously, first at the distant hum of the little electric milk cart, then at the chink of empty bottles, then as the milkman galumphed to the doorstep. The postman came next, and found himself not nearly so tested, receiving a low, throaty growl. On the pips for the eight o'clock news, Rose-Anne, cued to rattle his tin for breakfast, would listen out for his snorts, whines and whimpers. He could ascend his wooden stair only when Cecil had left for the office, when the throb of his enthusiasms, in the wag of his tail, beat a hollow good day into the booming panel of the refrigerator door.

You, Alex, entered the house in an air thick with scent and the ripening fruits of August, a few months after the wedding – a birth whose anniversary I still celebrate, in a flute foaming with champagne (when I'm drowsy with regret). Citizenship there, cut short in the sudden lead weights of Cecil's credit rating, extended over several years. There were blooms, among all that personal flower in a garden of childhood recollections, adding up to much more than the repetitions of a bedroom wallpaper (that's one example), or the suffusion of outside light in the flounces of your curtains. These were the things you told me.

For two, three years Rose-Anne learnt French and Italian through books, discs, and at night school – and was quaintly impressed at the grandeur of Cecil's skirting boards, knee-high almost, and the deep pile everywhere underfoot. His trademark was a royal wash to the walls – reds, purples, maroons.

Marg continued to pay the rent on her rose-tinted country retreat, having mopped the flood and got in a plumber to mend the pipes. Then in her new London garb she set off – by bus, bike, or taxi – a spring in her stride, or a leap in her centrist crusade. Cecil, whose touching sobriety owed its reliability to the depths of his Tory stronghold, and as a man whose spouse was the purveyor of gauche or fantastic notions, was pressed in and gawked at on every side. 'Every side' was the nooks and crannies of pre-war Conservatism (Marg declared), in a dusting of empire, four worldly corners hung with cobwebs. What were these (she asked, rhetorically) but an accidental structure?

Weekends on the Medway, Marg cobbled together her lecture notes, Porthos by now filling out at the ribs, and inclined to snooze under the kitchen table. This was how your mother worked. The soft sell of Liberalism, or the fruits of those rare hours, came wreathed in a tender complexion bright with golden down, which she delivered on weekday evenings, often in chilly public halls (her auditors solemn-faced and restless, and numbering no more than half a dozen), or in women's clubs (against a background rattle of tea cups, where the tweed was ubiquitous). [R:LV.n13.p671] There were better returns at Speaker's Corner, where Marg's calm oratory – over the course of at least one missed lunch – was witnessed by your stepfather, monarch of Tralatition Press, who plucked at his ear lobe, and must have begun, carefully, to think. [R:LV.n14.p671]

That snap of broken bonds, and the glassy disintegration of first this, then a bank trove of holding accounts, when it came was effortless. Worse for Cecil, the thing tinkled in his hearth in a bewildering absence of marital recrimination. Marg merely sat in her chair – a bow-back Windsor, destined for the auction rooms – brushing out the pony tails in the girly jet of Alice's hair. For once all Cecil really wanted was to loosen his collar and drop the knot of his tie a notch or two, the correct application in a man whose apparel is an outward sign of despair. I am not as dispassionate as might appear from this written re-assembly. You have to remember, it's a lifetime I've sustained of scattered jigsaw pieces. On those half-dozen or so occasions when, Alex, you and I called to see him – at what he called that 'poky' little flat off the Fulham Palace Road ('poky' it wasn't) – it was then I learned to like him, and liked him through you.

Marg wouldn't allow him to tear his hair or even privately to weep. She supervised the dispersal of personnel and much of their worldly goods. The maids, cleaners and kitchen staff were given intricate variations on the same simple testimonial, all exemplary, and signed in a shaky hand under the solitary glare of Cecil's lamp – a banker's lamp. For Rose-Anne this didn't become necessary. As dog handler, nanny, and now a linguist, she set off one damp English morning, for a café life in Paris, followed by the suns of Provence – after that a long slow hike along the Tyrrhenian coast to Palermo.

To Cecil came men in brown coats, into whose top pockets were tucked thickly leaded pencils. They arrived in very long pantechnicons, which Porthos barked at incessantly – this the wild world of investment, his a last echo carried on the wind, and for everyone the discomforts of a grey London dawn. Marg ushered them in (fags rolled behind their ears), and very slowly out. This latter manoeuvre took till the first flush of sunset, and flirted with further catastrophe. First the un-dignifying weight in a trio of longcase clocks – doors wouldn't stay closed, pendulums be stilled. After morning tea the flash, and almost a rhyming crash of Cecil's giltwood pier-glass (circa 1765, and an heirloom). Then came a logjam in the servants' stairwell, because someone – a buffoon or what! – tried to wedge a mahogany linen press down its narrow curve. One last little detail, till now eclipsed by the master's Bang and Olufsen, was Marg's ancient Alpine record player, retrieved from under the beams of Rose-Anne's newly vacated attic room, and for sentimental reasons commandeered by your mother.

'Ah no, not that,' she said. In the years that followed, it passed by default to you, Alex.

Cecil now had to confront the hollows of his dukedom, stripped of its assets, his plaints a ghostly reverberation through the cold depths of all that naked marble, or the vacuum of his oak-lined chambers. Good old-fashioned Tory that he was, here was the moment to cloak his armorial bearings, and for the honour and appeasement of Gales past, and new Gales present, fall on his sword. Doubtless this was a gesture Marg dismissed, and whatever other metaphors, as foolish and ridiculous.

Ergo, second marriage dissolved.

LVI Back track

I don't think, Alex, I can hold out much longer. A dawn vapour in off the river valley wrapped its cold confection round the slate cap of my tower. Windows – on other days a hard whiteness after first light – this morning were filmed with dusk. A fox barked wretchedly somewhere beyond the perimeter of Middlecross, that movable line skirting and eventually fading from the red brick of our walls, the pales of our fence, the holes in our hedges. I gathered in more tightly the scarlet quilt of my sleeping bag, but couldn't sleep, and kicked it off finally.

I begin to understand just what a distraction your record player has been, as I now take credit for a warm hum when I plug it in, having removed its shell and blown across its carcass – a storm of fluff that stuttered across the floorboards. Still elusive is a first click of the pickup arm, or rotation of the turntable. The situation has bothered me to the point that I hadn't noticed the removal of that *Inferno*. It was here on the desk – yet this morning I cannot find it anywhere. Also, navigationally speaking, I left my laptop pointing at a document file, but now find someone's been messing with the control panel. Who's been here?

LVII Hundred motels

I was heading for the lakeside again, but stopped before leaving the house, in the dining room, where the French doors open with a squeak, over a step to a patio, that place squared with weeds. My one overwhelming impression is of a man – of me – who lives in a stasis of relics, of final things. Here is yet one more recollection, centred on this room, when nothing was more conclusive, or could have turned my life so completely upside-down, than the magnanimity of James's fountain pen, in its little detour across his chequebook, as he sat here calmly, releasing a sum, unrolling his signature on the dotted line. [R:LVII.n1.p671] When *was* this, Alex? And did you know what had happened?

It was exam time. You were tetchy, and not very talkative. James couldn't get through the weekends without being called away, or hosting get-togethers here at Middlecross. One such spilled over into the gardens and glasshouse, a den of mossy panes and painted timbers. Jack d'Ursag (and you know the name), a frequent visitor at that time, then in his early thirties, and known for his technical know-how, had taken James aside. The gloom was palpable, a human mirroring of the blustery skies above, typical of spring or early summer. A last round of cocktails, neutralised gins and a sea of unfiltered tap water, was without the usual London troupe, though of course Jack's was a face I recognised. He had come to talk business, when offloading the press's back list was now an inevitability. D'Ursag, having anticipated openings the great digital revolution promised, was a keen bidder, and must have made a good impression. James gave him plenty of his time, as now we see the full outcome of their talks.

Your Wenover high mistress was also there, in a long pleated skirt, its colour somewhere between dark lemon and sharpish English mustard. She smiled very positively. This she managed to do even when a North Sea wind tinkled in the trees, and wound round our heads in a spiral of smoke – thick, grey, pendant with paraffin fumes. Chipolatas were lost to a leap of barbecue flames, the sausages were charred. The burgers Marg rescued, trimming to something edible and restoring on the kitchen griddle.

I was standing then approximately where I stood this morning, on the mossy, or rather the clean sunny bleach of the patio. I could see your high mistress nibbling at a salad, and heard her choose the right moment precisely – James refilling her glass with orange juice – to butt in on his conversation, with a middle-aged woman I hadn't seen before, their talk a trajectory into the decline in standards of state education. She must have been one of your teachers, as she assured, unbowed by the drive for technology, and an ever reductive bureaucracy defining the Western workplace, that Wenover would keep up its banner. Its laboratories of learning had been, and would always be, applied rigorously to the etiquettes of independent thinking. I was not able to follow her argument further, as Marg was in need of help. James refilled his own glass – again, orange juice – and led the two ladies and the circle that had gathered round them down to the lakeside. You'll be relieved to know, Alex, Cecil *had* made the right choice – for you, for Wenover, for its labs and its teaching staff.

A squall peppered the lake, but passed swiftly enough that James remained without a sweater, and with his shirt sleeves rolled up. He hadn't yet given up on the barbecue, its ashen glow intermittently swept in a sheet of water slipping from the trees. Those old folks from the rectory were here – a Mr and Mrs Gurney – he sandy haired, his face the florid history of nights garrisoned with his decanter. The moustache was thinly clipped. His wife was pale, despite the dusting of peach in an arc from temple to cheek bone. To them both, the Little genealogy was vague, and perhaps unfortunate, the one unvitiated heir to the union not being me (as, with a case of mistaken identity, I had to explain). They kept on calling me Roderick – poor Roddy, who since that spin in a grove of oak trees has never been in party mood. (I'd wager at this moment your brother was filing a shaft of metal in his tool shed.)

'You had ambitions once to be a race driver.'

'Ah, hadn't he!'

'Not me, no. Roddy.'

'Ah of course Roderick. So which one is he?'

Mrs Gurney elbowed her husband's ribs.

Alice had got down from London that afternoon, with a bag filled with bagels. These she put in a bread basket and handed round.

In those days Ed was phoning her all the time, unable to get across too often. A blue crest and a highly tooled letterhead, on a memo from one of his English clients, had happened to coincide with the busiest point of his working week. He told his Italian wife, who told Olga, her New York sister-in-law, whose daughter Marcia shared her uncle's whims…and perhaps it was other factors too that nudged him into London real estate. Alice had done her degree and was filling time. She joked – at least with me – that a student life north of the Elephant and Castle, in combination with her father's new decree, had qualified her uniquely to run checks on certain city streets. Ed's pin in Ed's wall map in Ed's office, somewhere in Philadelphia, cast a bright nimbus over all postcodes irradiating from Baker Street – a good place, he thought, to get off a tube train. After all, here our nation's dummies were all holed up at Madame Tussaud's, and what better place to check compass and chronometer than the Planetarium? But seriously, what with his daughter's career about to begin, the thing Ed deemed most important was good communications into town.

How had Alice got on with her commission? Well, if *I* didn't know, and the basket was still almost full on getting round to me, she didn't stop to tell me (she did pause to say *something*). I was still up on the patio, and still gazing out over the grey foamy crests a persistent wind had whisked up on the surface of the lake. She said to me then, Alex – in that confidential tone she'd learnt from James – that if I, George, didn't know by now, I probably never would.

'Didn't know what?' I asked.

She nodded over her shoulder, with a 'Here' – which I misunderstood.

'No. I don't want a bagel – thanks.'

She couldn't avoid those other two, and told the Gurneys – before she told me – of the house in Viceroy Road. I remained unmoved, looking distantly from shore to shore, and only now understood her 'here' as James's weekend folly. It was one he'd made himself, which over the dinner table had been referred to – in that quaint Jamesian way – as a 'reading bower'. The thing was no more than a half-dozen planed, painted crossbeams, closed on three sides by a lattice, their mesh an interlock of diamond shapes. The plan was – Marg herself having glanced across his drawing board – to transform the walls and open roof with natural scents and climbing plants. Your mother suggested a wave of honeysuckle, a clematis, a passion flower. Ahead of this, a bench had been positioned.

I could not have said how long you'd been sitting there. In fact I hadn't seen you much at all since the night before, after coming home late, in the cold and damp. You're taciturn mostly – now exaggeratedly so. Marg was bitten by fatigue, having cooked for five, and in a quake of indigestion had driven halfway to Rye. This was for a car you didn't like – bonnet too long, you said – and didn't subsequently buy. You were glum, bookless in that bower, in a white dress – which I'd never seen you in before, but recognised. It had been bought by Cecil one muggy morning, in a spotlit boutique – an interior filled with stars and filters – somewhere at the Bond Street end of Oxford Street, where he promised a course in driving lessons (your birthday a few months off, but anticipated). I could see your hair blown madly in the gusts of wind scything through those wooden rhombs. I could see someone with you, a foot up on the bench, an elbow drilled in that one raised knee, a youngish man whose red sweater and olive green trousers I made a mental note of. Impressive too was the fact that he'd judged the venue correctly, a book lying open in his hands. [R:LVII.n2.p671]

The gusts, squalls, winding sheets of smoke, and now the hurricanoes, tumbled together in a coastal downpour, sweeping in from Wight, Dover, Thames – or somewhere. [R:LVII.n3.p672] James mastered his helm, and brought everyone running for the glasshouse. Your high mistress trotted round the lake, her salad disposed of, while the paper plate she'd served it to hadn't found the bin. [R:LVII.n4.p672] This as best she could she umbrellaed, over the darkening gilt of her hairdo. The Gurneys smiled, then ambled in with Alice through the French doors to the dining room. Your sister left her bagels on the dresser and rummaged behind cupboard doors, looking for James's last bottle of Islay (the one he always hid). I followed them in, but didn't close the doors or make my way undercover to the glasshouse. Very gallantly, your reader disembowered himself, and taking your tiny frozen hand led you on a detour under the trees – a sweeping diversion that even so got you to the glasshouse ahead of me.

Rain thrummed on the roof, its dome streaked in a palette mix of rust and slimy green. All the panes were misted. James, having checked the morning press, had weighed the probabilities of two fronts competing for supremacy over the weather chart, and had shown foresight, lugging up a barrel from the cellar. Someone, a man in a natty floral shirt – now sodden at its tropics – had stayed outside to poke the coals, but breezed in with a stupid grin. A Wenover pair, whose elder daughter had left only last year (and now studied cello at Dartington) clapped him on the back. Their other daughter *was* here, a pale-eyed pixie, sucking fizzy orange through a straw – yet even she didn't complete the entourage. Somewhere outdoors, and by now getting very wet you'd think, was one of their annual students, a dark-eyed Catalonian girl called Federica. It had been her first time in England – in Herstmonceux – where she had enjoyed nine northern days of sunshine. Said Marg: 'George – will you take a look…my umbrella's there.' George opened the door. Your all-weather *cicerone* helped himself to beer and rattled on about Arthur Sullivan. *You* didn't, but James did agree, that Wenover had some special relationship with that musician (antique though it was). That in hindsight probably gives him away – your Jim or Joe or John, he none other than had watched a lengthening shade slant over Wenover's quads and courtyards. There the tablets and carvings in stone commemorate – among all the things they could – the patronage of one Dame d'Hautpoul, whose name is everything to me. In its last fading echo, J signed himself up as Tralatition's latest author, then strode into the sunset swinging his briefcase jauntily on his hip and whistling a tune, 'I've Got a Little List'. [R:LVII.n5.p672]

Federica, when I returned to the glasshouse, had sunk the serrations of her canteen knife into a wedge of goat's cheese, and was about to embed its rock-fall of crumbs into a limp-looking stick of celery, which she carefully balanced in a paper serviette. I shook out Marg's umbrella and hung it on the door. James and his protégé Zhay (I mean J), whose present confinement ended in a joust of quaeres, quips and barroom quaffs, replenished their beer jugs while chortling privately at jokes about the Frankfurt book fair (a closed conversation lost on me). This, Alex, was an opportunity you seized – or is how I continue to construe it. If no one else took note, I certainly watched. Having scarcely touched a glass of crushed pineapple, you abandoned that, *and* an empty plate, and slipped quietly out of sight. J looked lost at times, but refrained from asking where you'd gone. Then our cavorting weather fronts performed loops and a final somersault, a reverse wind with radial sunshine suddenly sweeping all that rain away, and ringing through the trees in little golden droplets.

Other guests followed in the fire master's spray, a man new-born, skipping across the glaze of the lawn. He puffed his cheeks and blew with Promethean gusto into the damp coals, yet raised as his only spectre a rain of liquid charcoal, neither flame nor phoenix stirring from the ashes. James was the last out, and glanced back briefly over that sunlit crystal, now that *all* his guests had vacated it – its cold condensation already displaced by greenhouse humidity. He tried to walk on, yet in the second or two before he raised his wrist and checked the time, I couldn't help but notice him – transfixed. The air shuddered. A moist fringe of sunshine darkened. Here your small hand, which had remained on the latch of your bedroom window – and having pushed it open – now withdrew itself into the shadows, where, fretful not at the age of Marg's old stylus, but at the vinyl booming through it, James glanced at his watch. It was too early for that transatlantic call he needed to and did eventually make, but for now only mused on. All of us knew his loathing for Mozart, which was 'awkward' if James was quizzed by friends. It's a problem I think that cannot delude itself as 'taste', when there exist inflexible tools of measurement good breeding fills its suit pockets with. Applied to the wrong mechanism – in this case the laconicisms of Frank Zappa and his Mothers, revolving on Marg's turntable, in a cacophony you had chosen, Alex, to shatter his English Sunday – in this case taste didn't enter into it. There were frowns of accusation directed across the lawns at me.

The night led you into bookish revisions under the faults and flickers of the bedside lamp, and tempests from across the sea. The sky was red electric. Its storm and thunderclaps darkened your stepfather's tread. Inexorably that man went – a stranger really – into the hallway and over the threshold of his study – a closed tent whose last solemn office had hosted Marg in party conclave, there with her Liberal friends on the back (the very broken back) of electoral defeat. On that occasion her puff or two of smoke had endorsed a new local candidate. James only lifted the phone, and dialled. [R:LVII.n6.p672]

LVIII K'an [R:LVIII.n1.p675]

I am leaving, soon. There is a first bitter wind unforgiving in its barbs – icy. What were small gusts yesterday tomorrow will freeze the dew, even before that forms. It's a feral, weed-strewn place, with a lost garden and an orchard abandoned to its fate. By mid-afternoon, my hand can barely move.

The loss of Royce's *Inferno*, having got me thinking again about the boathouse, took me on a detour. It led to an overgrown trail of paving stones – a route already slanted in shade, and crossed with cobwebs. [R:LVIII.n2.p675] Why had I come this way, with its cold muddy pools? It's because I begin to unravel the final involution (or I *hope* final). Here I almost *see* Alice, once more with her bread basket, active in a world of Gurneys, all wanting to be led, cherished, above all warmed at James's hearth, with its glow for his trusted few. Could it be possible, just, that *they* aren't, and that blustery, sunlit, long vanished day of theirs *is*, prophetically, alive? I have spent too long in the company of ghosts.

There were less inclement times for James's folly, when, duly, a first few strands of honeysuckle started to thread its open structure. There is one occasion I moodily recall, which couldn't have lagged far behind that windswept barbecue. There was an interplay of sunshine and shadows, these thrown down by racing clouds, while you, Alex, sat on the bench. If symbolically or not, the book you'd got with you was one of Alice's paperbacks – a cast-off Brecht – his *Caucasian Chalk Circle*. [R:LVIII.n3.p675]. James, at the best of times morose – the Little disease – was more than ever detached. He had somehow to deal with a new stampede of oxen, bursting the palace bounds of academe, graduate authors, young men and women pushed into centre stage in a flourish of trumpets, and already signed to London's leading agents, a cartel whose operation was a revised scale of advances, and sums that Tralatition couldn't hope to meet. [R:LVIII.n4.p675] A coffer full of lost pennies for his thoughts, James maundered off to his office, now at ten each morning, with lead in his step and a heavy tread to the station. Mostly he was home by four.

You with Alice's Brecht, me with a hoe somewhere, Alice making sarsaparilla, and Marg tuned in to one of those studio newsrooms, with its radio debate.... She looked up and saw James – more darkish at the brows – arrive. It was early even for one of his early weekday afternoons. And it was plain to see, that he had folded and put away the day's agenda, making time to sit beside you on that bench, with specific and special reference to a *New Book of the Road* (or something). It had among its endpapers, as a two-page foldout, a pale green Great Britain veined with a mesh of A roads, and arterially streaked in blue – the then completed lengths of motorway. I remember at that time the London orbital was a mere crumpled smile connecting Sevenoaks and Dorking.

Just as, independently, Cecil had done a fortnight before, James anticipated your half-a-dozen campus interviews, and had marked an itinerary accordingly (long drive, I think, to Leeds and down to Canterbury). [R:LVIII.n5.p675] The result, which was multiple, was this. Marg looked out anxiously from a low embrasure. Alice (who confided it only later), lost her daddy's recipe behind the fridge. I, if indeed it *was* a hoe, blunted that tool on a lump of buried brimstone. [R:LVIII.n6.p675] You, Alex, only pressed that open paperback – I mean the Brecht, and not the map – more tightly to a shrewish little nose. James – *And what to do now!* – only scratched his head, and with his road book clutched to his lapel strode for the simpler climes of his potting sheds. More fruitful soil in there.

Alice found time to talk about it, one late afternoon in Queens, while Copparo whisked eggs in her little kitchenette. All day the sky had frowned, in a mood black at its jowls. A hard rain beat its palms all round them on the windows. Your sis had succeeded in remaining dry, having found indoor work for a man with an I Ching factory, though she was out of breath, and filled with curiosity over a sample she'd been given. The phone rang just as Copparo dipped hands into an open packet of flour, and Alice, forced to turn from her package, intercepted yet another pointless call from me. Ah no, George, please understand – Marcia's pale, and has very cold hands, and pastry's not her best cuisine! Well, never mind, for here were miraculous forecasts – odd strands of meteorology linked to our phone connection somehow.

'You know, Alice, I have seen one.'

'One what, George?'

I meant one of those Taoist-Confucian life kits. They're boxish – a sort of cardboard booklet – with nooks and a ring bind – and three oracular coins, which tarnish. There's an index of illustrated hexagrams, rendered as a kind of Sino pop art, on laminated pages.

'*Why* won't she speak to me?' I said.

'Wow!' said Alice.

'What do you mean, *wow!*?'

A fork of black and violet lightning wrought its transformations in a wave of surfaces, where Marcia's furnishings and odd little ornaments found themselves shifted – if ever so briefly – into an adjacent or overlapping plane. I heard the crash.

'Yes, I got that. You think she can phone me back....'

'Her yin, George, definitely mitigates *against*.'

'Alice! What are you talking about!'

She told me about that factory commission. 'You look at these things, George? I mean you do philosophise....'

I had to describe my only excursion into mystic divination, with Alice now keen to change the subject, and no doubt Copparo gesturing frantically. In our young adult gloom, the pair of us mutually bored, you, Alex, having served the winning ball at table tennis, now wandered aimlessly up and down the four grumpy strings of a bass guitar. You tossed that instrument aside. You also resisted my arm as it cradled your waist. You took my hand instead – in these days a rarity – and in the flush of its novelty led me all the way up to the kitchen, where Marg – that cavern filled with a sense of someone's absence – had signed your departure in an aroma of oregano. Its dried leaves we found sprinkled on a casserole.

One of your new Kentainer friends, a bald-headed, buskined Thespian, who lived in the blue pines and loggias of Woodhill Park, an enclave southwest of Middlecross, had spent fruitless hours wrestling with Heidegger. For him there had been too many failed exercises, philosophically. He was tired of the twittering graphologies that evolved with the world's socially changed vocabularies. [R:LVIII.n7.p676] By whatever mischance – and here slabs of text could be offered in speculation – he had pressed on into the tall green avenues as a first step into the open air, or so you said figuratively. Once outside, he stumbled on A. E. Waite and an interpretation (meadow-scented, hence your metaphor) of the Tarot. I imagine, and don't have the gall to inquire, how easily you warmed to his enthusiasm, so delicious – so *non*-academic. Was it one nervy evening, sitting in the green room, hailstones thrashing at the roof lights, while everywhere thunderbolts strewed their gobbets of fire, both onstage and off? He called himself Reach, an old family name, he explained, and whether as a post-exam reward or a pre-birthday greeting (I don't know to what extent Reach had gleaned these personal data), these Tarot cards you now set before me were from him. They came wrapped (or should I say enshrined?) in a sash of maroon satin, which he had carefully wound several times round their cardboard presentation box.

I don't think I had witnessed more impatience in the thrum of your fingers, or the cross and constant re-cross of your hands, more usually contenting themselves with the grooves and grain of the table top. Miraculously too, a hard brightness – almost diamantine – thawed the inhibitions in your gaze – a lover's gaze – where I saw, in a flicker that has died since, the burnishes of summer. You removed the sash then handed me the booklet, whose cover illustration – of the world – bore no resemblance to the automatised marketplace we merchants of the West grow up in. Where the elect live is nakedness, and freedom of the dance.

You somehow expected me to lead your trembling soul through the pomp of Waite's hyperbole – prose soaked to its fundament in vulgar perfumes. That preface I recall as wafers dipped in gipsy musk, Eucharist he and his followers administered in a thousand humble offices not of the house of God. To what purpose? The process was 'chemical marriage', supposedly to raise our shallow being through a series of transmutations, in a mental habitat adorned with Renaissance ornamentation. Its purple design sent us on our journey into higher mystic schools (whatever these were intended to be), incidental to which was a symbolism, necessarily crude linguistically, whose veils of concealment hinted at timeless truths. You could invoke Yeats, or J. M. Barrie, or the Order of the Golden Dawn, or any number of expert witnesses got up in priestly vestures.

To my detriment, Alex, I have had no success at all in reading your tree of life, though Alice told me how – on that day on the phone in Queens – she had developed a knack of knowing which half of her half-sister belonged to her. It's possibly something you also learned, reciprocally, and with a mass of newly mastered lines took back with you to the green room, where for you it was easier to act like someone else. If pressed, I would cast my lot with Alice's, and not with any Tarot hermeneutics. She found the floss and douche of that divinatory fairy dust a shade too green, or miasmic (or in effect bilious). [R:LVIII.n8.p676] According to hers, which after all is as good as practically any cartomancy, there is no viability in the concept of human flesh rooted in worldly soil, whose eventual fruit is a purified soul borne to heaven's gates on a brush of metaphysical foliage. I would say in passing it puts her beyond those holistic flavours spicing much of our current eco theory, where the world is a unitary system, and everything in it is intra-dependent (my life is contingent on an oceanic whirlpool, just as that whirlpool is contingent on me). Alice viewed any sequence or arrangement of cards as arbitrary, and therefore unrepresentative of spiritual journeys, bound up as they are – and for a certain term – with the world's estates, offices and institutions. Rejected too is the culmination of this in an ungraspable offer of enlightenment.

Either consciously or not, your half-sis had put individualism at the hub of your universe – therefore we shall have to call your psyche – to facilitate this present exercise – the measure of absolutely everything. That I think requires less quackery than some might say, and brings with it interpretations not altogether lacking science. Alice told me that what she always saw in the fall of your cards (or her own cards for that matter) was reflective and self-generated, that inner bit of you (or her) projecting whichever of its own elements were called for, to correspond with whatever depictions were there. The cards in the end were the products of other human minds. At that time the one most often recurring for you showed paupers in the snow, one of whom was a cripple with a bell round his neck, in a scene where the world's unfortunates clumped along outside a lighted window. After that came a messenger on horseback, bearing a laurel triumphantly. Next was a merchant or squire – a man who carefully weighed his alms before dispensing to the poor. Your knight on a charger (a white charger) I don't think could have been your poet, marooned across two continents. For you it's likely he's metamorphosed to a combative stranger surveying his landscape, whose dreams have put you in a garden of vines, in a life lived out under a fantastic yellow sky. [R:LVIII.n9.p677]

I remember trying to grapple with the predictive meaning attached to the nine of swords, and what that signified for you. [R:LVIII.n10.p677]

LIX Long ride

For you class ends in a haze of summer, with a last removal from the revolving shafts and shadows creeping over the quads, the crannies and the orange brick of Wenover. Is there a plaque to the Dame d'Hautpoul, still cloaked in dusk? You told me, one day when we caught the London train, how you could *hear* – in the removes of lost but recollected things – a family of rooks, wheeling in all that placid air above the hockey field. We were on our way to a cul-de-sac off the Fulham Palace Road, or Cecil's place, a 'poky' little flat, in reality extensive ground-floor rooms in a huge, solid-looking house. Its brickwork was a tinge of seductive darkness. Inside, the walls were hung with elaborately textured papers, whose clambering buds and tiny flowers spiralled to the intricacies of the ceilings – borders a rope twist of finely moulded plasterwork.

I can't remember if this was a Saturday, or whether all days to Cecil were the same. He wore, over blue slacks and a turtleneck, a silk dressing gown, with a hem that fell below the knee. Its large breast pocket boasted the maroon stitching of his monogram. From somewhere – a room he didn't ask us into – you could hear the jaded quips of a Noël Coward sound-alike. It was a recording – if made by Cecil I don't know. It faithfully reproduced the original vinyl, complete with scores, craters and potholes. That whole battery it scourged us with, hissing in a stream of cassette tape.

Marg had told him about me, in an afternoon phone call. Even before you lit the gas under the kettle, he handed me a folded newspaper. Its part finished crossword was flanked, in the margins, by pencilled attempts at a solution to one of the clues down, all of which looked wrong. The puzzle was authored by a journalist called Cross Stitch, with a penchant for anagrams and other figures, with this last one remaining, which Cecil had wrestled with without success. [R:LIX.n1.p678] The clue, which I wrote down and couldn't get out of my mind for the next few days, read like a lyric— [R:LIX.n2.p678]

> Distancing our yens, or unhooking remote, entangled, anchorless dreams. More
> endless journeys over harbourless nights

Cross Stitch was looking for a five-word solution, of two, three, four, two and four letters respectively. From solutions across we already had an r, an m and a j.

'Stumps me,' I said.

You looked at it yourself, Alex, sure that the two shortest words we ought to be able to guess. Could that lead to the rest? Cecil asked if the *yens* and the *harbourless nights* were not a tangled allusion to Pearl Harbor, which led to *The Mikado*, and your part in it.

'Alex is too modest,' I said.

'She has great talent.'

'Yes. Our local press was in raptures.' The reviewer was besotted by the costumes, the makeup, the lighting. Still you said nothing, Alex.

'What did *you* think, George?'

'I couldn't get there. No transport. The Tarot had me un-starred.'

Cecil, whose fortunes had come undone at the combination of swords and crowning cups, frowned at that, and later repeated that look, when in sheer boredom Alice constructed a tree of life. It was a hot afternoon. There was lemon tea and Harvo cake, the three of us having come by bus and tube from Viceroy Road, all the way to his place. Cecil said that with only six weeks to your birthday, he wanted an idea of what to get. He offered heirlooms – a necklace, brooches, costume jewels. There was a carriage clock, its face mottled with age. He said he'd have it restored. If you wanted something of less intrinsic value, then what about perfumes, talcs, cubes for the bath? (Look, Cecil, we all took showers, down in the mists of Middlecross.)

What about car accessories? We had to tell him Marg hadn't bought you a car, yet. Cecil finally went to his bureau, with its boxed compartments puritanically tidy, a regiment of documents and paperclips. Its hidden depth was a cornucopia, where with practised certainty he put his hand to his chequebook. This when he brought it into the light of day I could not help but note for its leather wallet, and the gold plate of Cecil's initials stencilled in its bottom right-hand corner. Carefully, he unscrewed the lid of his fountain pen, and signed away a sum that made you gasp but were too refined to utter.

'I have been thinking about that clue,' I said.

'Clue?'

You were, as ever, subdued, sad in your petiteness, as we set off for home. I asked myself was it our life's monotony, or the more intimate failure to name our togetherness into being. We left our seats, with the soot of London slipping behind, then the hoardings of Sevenoaks passing out of view.... I stood for minutes together with you, a tentative hand to your elbow, two lost souls in the opposing motions of a last train home – you, me, in the connecting passage halfway between first and second class, the window down. The night breeze caught your hair, and showed its under-sheen. Empty shapes and a string of softened silhouettes jigged with the rattle of the tracks. A vast orange moon dangled on a thread, which any moment now would tear – for these were our endless journeys – these, Alex, our harbourless nights.

LX Jet trails

Then your mother felt the flicker of *her* compass, its needle a fading luminosity when your granddaddy – five years a widower – quit the last estate of all, in a sunny Kentish dawn. In the pristine white of his bed sheets one of his helpers discovered him – resigned, she said, and glassy-eyed. [R:LX.n1.p678] Those lands long in his family, on a border with two other counties, had gone to seed. For the last twelve months he'd worn a beard, his hand too unsteady for the razor. He was used to a cutthroat, and couldn't be persuaded to use an electric shaver. They never cut cleanly, he said.

There remained this question of orchards, whose blossoms he and his wives had spent a lifetime watching over, from the upper windows. The hired labour he depended on to clear and trim – now that work had picked up in the towns – was scarce and too expensive (or so it seemed to him). In these days, a sky full of fruit fell to the ground and rotted.

I am not clear what the legal problems were. The will was a mess till James got help from his friends in Lincoln's Inn, who phoned him often. [R:LX.n2.p678] Not long after the last receiver click, and eventual sale, James bought a place near Parliament Hill, whose suburban brick and sun-bleached timbers you refused to look at (ever). I could see the point. You and Alice went your separate ways. For James this was a practical decision, with his journey home to office and back made simpler. Belatedly I ask, from the ruins of Middlecross, that first and last place of ours, now that it's a husk, haunted by echoes, or lit sometimes with the spark of your eyes, or suspicious looks: if James is there, is Marg too? [R:LX.n3.p678]

Ed's final commitment to English real estate was of that era too. As a matter of chance he was followed into Heathrow by Marcia, just one of his several nieces. I remember I was there myself with Alice in Viceroy Road, stubbornly running my eye over the long, gradual bend in the terrace, with its low walls and linear paving. Bar colour schemes and a difference in the front doors, all these other houses were the same.

'This the place you want, honey?' I heard Ed say. His billfold bulged in a back pocket, in a burst and strain of sterling.

Alice cajoled, and chaperoned him on her arm. Why yes, it was. And just perfect.

Copparo touched down on the last night of his hectic weekend ('Cute little house,' she said), and kept to her rendezvous. That, the dramatic fringe, was at a theatre club, with the magnetic lure of a handsome Provençal – a man who'd toyed with her passions all summer long, in her native New York. Rose-Anne was also in transit, having holidayed in Crete. There from its pillars and pastures, half a dozen carefully written postcards had been circulated among family and friends, and were currently in Ed's possession.

'Rose-Anne,' he said, 'she's sure something else!'

That one-time au pair had been to the caves of Mt Ida, finding scenes unmatched anywhere in Crete for grandeur. She should know, having seen the world, having seen its spectacular limestone grottoes. The guide leading her at last showed caution, where the rock plunged sharply for 200 feet or more. Both were transfixed. She used her flashlight, and saw suspended above an icy pool ghostly-looking stalactites. Halls with fretted roofs opened onto halls with fretted roofs – a labyrinth.

'Wow!' said Alice, for so began her brief flirtation with classical themes. When the shops next opened, she bought herself a local guide and three new rolls for her camera. When Ed flew home, Alice and I returned to Middlecross. You, Alex, were in Wales with Marg, levering mussels from a rocky Pembroke shore.

LXI Deal half done [R:LXI.n1.p679]

James took his opportunity decisively and well. After his calls to Lincoln's Inn, and a last staggered interchange into the hub of New York – five hours adrift across the Atlantic – he called me into the study. Marg was away. She had taken her party work with her and had left with her luggage. With Marg not there the room was fringed in semi-darkness, its walls looking less than something solid, and absent altogether at the borders of floor or ceiling. Isolated spots of rain plashed at the window, where James had drawn the square velvet drape without precision. He sat at the desk, his face aglow in the nutty gleam reflected in its polish, his pale hands uncomfortably interlinked under a thin stream of light from the reading lamp. Just by him was one of those last old-fashioned big black phones, with a dial. It sat there plump and expectant, just waiting at his elbow.

'I have been making inquiries on your behalf,' he said. The fact was a talented English poet wasn't best served by a life in the shires.

'That's a great pity,' I said. 'For one dizzy moment I had hopes for that old patronage system – a revival.'

'That's very amusing, George. But believe me – you need to get out there.' He wanted *me* out of *here*.

I watched him unlace his hands while he spoke of that programme of student experimentation now taking place at the Donns Watson. This he said was a research institute, geared to the performing arts exclusively.

'Where?' I asked.

'Lower Manhattan.'

Robert Quay, whose brainchild it was, James knew sufficiently well to make an introduction – which hadn't quite clinched it. I needed to go there. A desk drawer rumbled open. In the gloom of that half-light, James took out, and carefully opened the Tralatition chequebook.

'It doesn't sound quite *me*,' I said.

'Think of it, George, as a research project. Why not phone tomorrow for a flight.... I am offering to fund you.'

'Hart Crane, James, is all I know about America. *And* its Second Amendment. Dangerous place.'

'Hart Crane isn't necessarily a disadvantage. How much? A thousand? Two? Five?'

'I'll have to think about it,' I said, and left him, his pen poised and whole upper body bent over a blank cheque.

LXII Stoneridge

Ed bought his daughter's little house with cash, which he wired direct to her account. Therefore it wasn't very long before Alice completed on the deal, and began to choose her furniture. Marg banged together pots and pans for her new kitchenette. We two helped her settle in. (There is something I discover only now about the boathouse, Alex. That new road behind it: just how long has *that* been there?) [R:LXII.n1.p679]

Plus, John, I find I have very mixed feelings about that brick-built house in Viceroy Road. Its hall was dark, was awkwardly narrow, and always a squeeze – Alice insisted on hanging up her bike on the wall where just inside were the electricity meters. The kitchenette was not a good space for chopping at the chopping board (not after Middlecross, whose every room was a continent). From here the sink and single drainer overlooked an outdoor tap, whose last swollen drip hung in sunny suspension – never quite crashing down on the small isosceles of concrete below. Too tiny for me (I personally never ventured there), and black and cankered at its edge, this was a half square yard or so, ground for a sole garden chair, or the carousel where Alice hung her smalls and jeans and sodden tee shirts (never the two together).

The bathroom one trooped all the way downstairs for. The suite was a shade of darkened avocado, and the bath was a corner fit. Its inner moulding was a kidney shape, with a dimpled recess for its two brassy taps. Attached to these was a shower, whose scaly shaft and snake head, though they pulsed with a vehement hiss, never mustered more than a trickle. The basin was endlessly lined, its tidemark swelling or receding with the ebb and flow of our life (we were, briefly, a trio).

The dining room was windowless, and in its absence of natural light Alice used it for quieter recreation, under the intense glow of two yellow ceiling spots. How often I have wiped her hand mirror, plonked down with her sachets and razor blades, and a rolled-up ten-pound note. The living room, where daylight might have crept in, Alice barred with a blind whose slats were permanently closed. Floor space was a litter of canvases and frames. The shelves sagged under the weight of her albums, and the march of new paperbacks always coming in, and never back out. The workbench, where she also kept a soldering iron, showed the strains and stains of her busy working life. Her jars for the darkroom splashed chemicals everywhere and haphazardly.

Carpets throughout were flame red, a loudness she replaced with understated mauve. The staircase creaked. Above there were two rooms on the only upper floor, and one of these was bedless ('Just have to share with us, George'). Her boudoir was rugs, silks, and erotica. In here, John, she filmed endlessly.

One thing I didn't like was the house name, in blocks of silver paint on an oval plate, whose screws in the pointing above the front door had weathered to two tiny spots of rust. Stoneridge.

LXIII Monumental

Marcia – whose hair in those early years she wore in ringlets – stolidly brushed from view that sad-eyed smile, pinned to her being throughout her days in London. She was, according to Alice, confessedly lovelorn, though in the end had given up on her conquest from Provence.

Her flight home, if imminent, wasn't *yet*, so Alice found a camp bed and sleeping bag, and put her in that other room. You, Alex, spent a lot of time on the phone, while your sister and I consoled her coz with walks through the avenues of All Souls. I glanced through Alice's guidebook.

'Ah,' I said. 'Here's the dissenters' chapel.'

That, being both Greek Revival and grade II listed, found itself under the lens of Alice's camera, on this and numerous other visits. A good place, she said, for her classic tableaux – planned for one of those canvases back on her living-room floor. [R:LXIII.n1.p679] She struck out alone and gauged the light as it dabbed itself in little breezy streaks across the flanks or colonnades, which were curved. A flock of pigeons fountained up, and circled around us above those peeling capitals. I strolled with Marcia into the lime and poplar walks, in a pomp of leafy decay, and dotted with obelisks and urns.

'It says in this local guide,' I said, 'that the cemetery was first laid out in 1831.'

There were tombs for two of George III's children. In another rested the first husband to Disraeli's wife. For yet others novelists Thackeray and Trollope. Trollope had a granite marker, which I failed to find.

'There is, curiously, a Frederick Albert Winsor,' I said, 'a man famed for civic gas lighting. And someone called Cobbett, a cricketer.'

'You're an Englishman, and don't know your cricket, George.'

'It's despicable, I know. Look. Here's one by John Gibson, done for his sister Mary.'

'Who,' said Copparo, 'are they?'

'Beats me.'

She snatched the guide from my hand, and pored over it. Copparo smiled – just as Alice took our picture. Snap! (When that had been developed, I put *it*, and Marcia's address and home phone number, deep in the warm recesses of my wallet.)

LXIV Deal done

Long goodbyes there were, when Copparo jetted off into a clear blue sky. Some few days after that I remained afloat, when only lead shoes could bring me down to earth, back with James in the study again.

'We'll make it 5,000 then,' I said. 'And I shan't see Alex again. Meaning *ever*.'

Very slowly, your stepfather unclipped the lid of his fountain pen.

LXV Finally, Alex...

Those little white winds icing the Kentish dawns have made me pack my sleeping bag away. Now comes that slow, final decision as I detach myself – once and for all, Alex – from the gusts and ghouls of Middlecross. I wanted to possess that Dante – a last enduring testament to Tralatition Press. For that alone I have set off for a final look round the boathouse – a place more deserted than ever. On what impulse I cannot freely say, when with frozen hands I parted the lifeless brackens in the shadows behind it. Here I found not that old track, where Roddy zoomed around on his off-road bikes. It was a highway, metalled and macadamed.

A swathe of elms has been cleared, and in a cutting off the road is a steeply gabled, old rambling house, living out these last days of the century as a bed-and-breakfast place. On the drive was that lime green Passat. Stacked neatly in its boot were those bits and pieces from your room. Parked alongside was a dapper little Fiat. I walked to the end of the drive, then up a stony terrace into the reflective glaze of the breakfast room. Two people were seated – a man in a red sweater and olive-green trousers, and with him his Myra (you remember those billets-doux, at LIII above). A triangular slice of toast sat in the rack. A pot of marmalade was orange gold in the dappled morning light. My Dante was there too, John, inches from your hand, which across that starchy tablecloth was intertwined with Myra's. [R:LXV.n1.p679] Van Elph looked up, and for the brief moment before I left I could see her puzzle at my gaze.

I returned to Middlecross, and the remains of the reading bower – a crossbeam, tangled with roots, and rotten at its extremities. Here I had left a saw, and – to finish the job John's homunculus had set in train – I sliced up that last of our mementoes. I transferred its pieces to the cellar, and stacked them neatly where all that other firewood was piled. There, too, was a bar of meticulously filed metal. [R:LXV.n2.p679]

Soon our life will be flames....

Commentary (John Royce, 1998)

I[1] Foremost of which is a thickly laminated, nevertheless severely battered paperback by Marcel D'Orbieu. As du Plé's makeshift editor, many of those books and papers he mentions are temporarily owned by me. Du Plé it appears didn't sympathise with M. D'Orbieu, leastways as essayist (the title of the book sent to Alex was *The Geometry of Everyday Life* – see note 2 to Section VIII, below). [dP:I.p581]

II[1] Not a reference I understand, though Alex has talked of her sister Alice's theatrical soirées at Middlecross, frequent when still a girl, less so in adolescence, and resurrected nostalgically in teenage, when George first appeared. By then a Mediterranean warmth had given way, in Alice's consciousness, to chilly Nordic breezes, a meteorology George was at that time suited to. Alice's devised piece, *Frieze*, whose scenario George is referring to is prefaced by this—

> The ice like a leaf
> is thin;
>
> and though we can hear
> through a twist of winter'd trees
>
> that polar music
> crystal over crystal ground,
>
> for us
> we know
> it is
>
> the coda ice-cold code.
>
> On the leaf-thin ice,
> with theo-rhetorical device,
> how for an ever shall we slide?

The supporting material du Plé is calling on regarding his electronic letters ranges from scrappy to quite meticulous, and isn't hard for me to find in the papers, notebooks and diaries he's so 'carelessly' left around. This I unearthed from his 'red book'. [dP:II.p581]

VII[1]Supposing it exists as more than fragments, here is the final sequence. Du Plé's anticipated re-entry into his first cultural milieu is scattered throughout several notebooks. Its four completed verses are like this—

>   **1** Orange streaks
>   across this old south road
>
>   have flamed
>
>   these English ghosts
>   of sunset:
>
>   here is the house
>   of my cradling,
>
>   blacked at the windows,
>   rose at its western roof,
>
>   capped
>   with a golden vane
>
>   (that's a man
>   with a hoe,
>
>   whose brightness of diamonds
>   breezes in the ironwork
>   of his painted hair).
>
>   **2** Opening
>   the gate.
>
>   An oval in its scrolling
>   alters the shape
>   in its shadow,
>
>   is long
>   on the rectangular slabs
>   of the path.

The door's fiery
bleach;

a squeak,
a hinge.

A thud to the gatepost....

3 'What hat,'
I had always asked,
'shall I wear?'

I can't now reconcile
that fuller face
somehow made
exotic in the silver.

A gilded creeper
frames the mirror's arch
where I have paused
in the hall,

whose golden leaves
entwine themselves

to a crown of knots
at the apex.

4 Embroidered panes
in the stairway's niche

are the filtered lemon
of sunrise,

low to an oblong sea
(which is ultramarine),

anachronistically a galleon.

Above those lights
a cooler stair

winds against the clock
to the timbers of my attic.

Here I shall find
my fell boots and bedroll,
importantly a quilted coat.

A compass, callipers
and set squares
occupy a broken chair.

Zero, my fool of a friend,
says he has packed
leads and erasers.

I shall need that tent
and groundsheet…

I shall need tobacco.

I shall find my Zero
on a rutted track.

All of which we shall have to view metaphorically, since du Plé preferred to contemplate the great outdoors from the comfort of his window, or from behind the wheel of a car. Let me add also that my oculist is right (because somehow that lineation doesn't look quite as it should): for although I can fight this eye strain, in the end I need my newly prescribed glasses. Now where did I put them…? Ah, that's better (left them in the music room – not that I remember doing so). [See dU:VII.p681] [dP:VII.p582]

VIII[1] Du Plé, in an act of brinkmanship, having so often tested the weights of confession in his writing hand, in a bucolic setting mostly – that meant usually the Pinetum, a plantation near to Middlecross – left many cancelled lyrics, one of which begins—

That Kentish sunset when I touched your hand….
[dP:VIII.p582]

[2] The book he refers to is here, with my research notes, and is called *The Geometry of Everyday Life*, translated by Randal Neve (Cleveland: Cleveland State Press, 1985). What I am sure du Plé remembers, or reinterprets, is the essay 'Reading and Routing the City',

which appears on page 66. In it, D'Orbieu claims that the act of walking in a city in some way corresponds to a written grammar, whose vocabulary is the sequence of paths or steps taken – or 'trajectories' – which vary from walker to walker. In theory, our steps are a kind of enunciation – in what is otherwise an unspoken language, whose diversity is nevertheless unlimited, and is not reducible to a graphic trail. [dP:VIII.p583]

[3]'Stoneridge' is a house name, going back to village London, the place itself a small redbrick terrace off the Harrow Road. Until recently it was kept in Alice's family as a *pied-à-terre*. Alex used it frequently when visiting her father (Alex and Alice, half-sisters). Du Plé – whose diary is often explicit, or too explicit – with Alex *and* Alice – spent the summer here (of 1979). With that address as base, our trio mounted an exhibition in Cricklewood, which Marcia tried to transplant into New York. Despite her connections with the Kunstler Gallery, that plan failed. [dP:VIII.p583]

IX[1]There are references I know I overlook. This one is to Lewis Carroll, in whose 'A Boat, Beneath a Sunny Sky' is an embedded acrostic, which decodes to ALICE LIDDELL, and which supposedly recalls a boating expedition of 4 July 1862, during which the Reverend Dodgson first related the story of Alice. Acrostics I know interest du Plé a great deal. [dP:IX.p583]

X[1]It is supposedly Trent, Michael (see my Editor's Notes), or his *A Field Guide to the Trees of Britain* (London: Collins, 1972), who provided the indispensable handbook of du Plé's early constructions throughout the 1970s, in which his ghostly lyrical landscapes were routinely planted with Scots pines, regimented poplars, and unearthly, leafless elms, under the changing lights of sunset. It becomes clear why this could not be carried forward into his New York era of metropolitan poetics, which explains its return by post. [See dU:X.p683] [dP:X.p583]

[2]So to D'Orbieu again, for whom there is a rhetoric of walking – a phrase, once turned, like a path now formed. Navigation is taken as language, as subject to artistic style as it is to practical use. Style is a linguistic structure employing symbols and images, and bears an individual stamp. Use is a social fact, is a tool of communication. Style and use are both inherent (in the way we speak, in the way we walk), with style a symbolic process and use the manipulation of a code. [dP:X.p584]

[3]Alex did not inherit religion from her grandmother, who knew her Bible as well as her *Lives of the Poets*, but was given a parchment, inscribed in sans serif text, and framed. It was a quotation from the Song of Solomon (3: 1–4), lines beginning

By night on my bed I sought him
[dP:X.p584]

[4]I don't think du Plé appreciated the extraordinary lengths a lot of people went to to make this introduction possible. [dP:X.p584]

[5]This is an understatement (or litotes), particularly in light of references du Plé has already made, but more particularly with a view to what is about to follow. Allow me to anticipate—

D'Orbieu points out that, in one sense at least, synecdoche, as a figure of speech, extends any given spatial element in order that it might imply a totality. He cites an automobile or a domestic appliance in a shop window, items representing a whole street or neighbourhood. By contrast asyndeton, in its function of elision, creates disjunctions, with the retention or selection of parts amounting to no more than relics. Synecdoche constructs fragments into wholes; asyndeton, by its disconnecting process, reduces a whole to fragments. Synecdoche brings an intensity to detail and miniaturises the broader application. Asyndeton excises, in an affront to our sense of continuity, and in so doing undermines its plausibility. A space treated in this way – more importantly a space du Plé or you or I might walk through – is thereby transformed into separate archipelagos.

Whether intentional or not, du Plé effects both figures simultaneously (synecdoche, asyndeton), in his writing thus far. For those familiar with the past life of Middlecross Towers – for example Alex, for example Alice – du Plé's voice in this opening preamble is the voice of omission (asyndeton). For myself, largely unfamiliar with the doings of Middlecross at that time, a life and a world are constructed on the fragments he has chosen (synecdoche). Here I think is precisely where du Plé would disagree with D'Orbieu, proposing instead that experience, all experience – be that walking in the city or looking in a shop window – is evaluated, and often later recalled, only through the medium of language, with its grammar and syntax and imagery. In other words, it isn't correct to say that an order inheres in the action itself, an order obeying similar rules to that of the linguistic order – rather it becomes subsumed into it. [dP:X.p584]

XI[1]'Symmetry' is something neither du Plé nor D'Orbieu has much to say about. J. C. Harris (1848–1908) was famous for his *Uncle Remus*, and a folklore supposedly related to a small boy, though not on a bench in Central Park, but interspersed with comments on a range of other subjects. [dP:XI.p584]

[2]Stoneridge (see note 3, Section VIII, above) is situated in Viceroy Road. It was sold – and sold so recently it remains in the auctioneer's catalogue. [dP:XI.p584]

[3]How often du Plé trails off his sentences like this…. [dP:XI.p585]

XII[1]Du Plé means step-father. The tension pervading Alex's household at that time is unravelled in the circumstances of its family life. Alex had been given Alice as an elder sister (by her mother's first marriage, marriage dissolved). Her own father had been ruined (second marriage dissolved). Roddy was the fruit of this third and current union. [dP:XII.p585]

XIII[1]Tammuz, the Sumerian, Babylonian and Assyrian god, who annually died then rose with decaying / reviving vegetation. A dirge for Tammuz's departure recalls the Babylonian hymns that compare him to transient plant life—

A tamarisk in a garden without water etc.
[dP:XIII.p586]

[2]Gilgamesh – re the *Epic of Gilgamesh*, known mainly through the royal collection of tablets made by the king of Assyria, Assurbani-pal (668–626 BC), for his palace at Nineveh. The epic is rather an odyssey, similar to George du Plé's – or anyone who writes things down – where the journey is undertaken in search of a foil for the ultimate decay, that being death. My surmise for du Plé is that where he doesn't want to die is in Alex's heart.

Gilgamesh made his dangerous journey searching for Utnapishtim, the survivor of the Babylonian flood. It was Utnapishtim who would show him how to cheat his mortality. This required a plant whose powerful properties revived the vigour and grace of youth, though unfortunately for Gilgamesh once he'd obtained it it was seized by a serpent, and he returned unhappily to Uruk. [dP:XIII.p586]

[3]The known origins of writing are roughly as follows. Fourth millennium BC: some 2,000 pictographic signs, cast in Sumerian clay tablets, followed by cuneiform writing (earliest known). Third millennium: Sumerian poetry laments the death of Tammuz, the shepherd god; first epic tales of Gilgamesh (recorded 1200 BC); cuneiform writing reduces number of pictographs still in use to about 550; Pepi's papyrus, 'Instructions to a Son', which as literature is one of the earliest preserved documents.

The view of some theorists is that the transition from hieroglyphs to linguistic signs was also the transition from orality to ideology. Ideology is something du Plé doesn't believe he subscribes to himself, but so deplores in others. [dP:XIII.p586]

[4]I cannot recognise anything of the Robert Quay I know, whose visits to Europe over the last twenty years have been frequent enough. All I can guess is that du Plé here gives back, with careful elaborations, one of those figures of speech important to Quay's research at that time. Antiphrasis is, of course, to express by the use of opposites – is a figure of speech by which words are used in a sense that's opposite to their meaning. Quay is short, slight, dapper, and enjoys a thick, steel-grey, professorial mane, which he sweeps back off his forehead. Quay is not noted for his sense of humour. [dP:XIII.p586]

[5]These do not appear to have survived, at least under that collective title. [dP:XIII.p587]

XIV[1]An outcome borne out among the mountainous notes du Plé disciplined himself to make at that time, whose accompanying scholia in a more recent ink betray his later analysis. See next note. [dP:XIV.p587]

[2]Not difficult to draw distinctions and similarities between du Plé as therapist (Molloy and her frustrations) and du Plé as aide-de-camp. Where his NY trip first found its voice through Molloy's controlled subversiveness, those same forces of opposition, in a red ink boldly contrasting with the faded turquoise of his diary, are brought to bear in the battledress of counter-argument, intended as ammunition for Molloy. On the question of chance and randomness in nature, which art may choose to imitate, he quotes the physicist Richard Feynman (1918–88), who in a lecture called *Atoms in Motion* describes a drop of water magnified a billion times, whose appearance is of twisting bodies with wiggling cilia – a mass of teeming particles that attract each other and are, it would seem, glued together (though if squeezed too closely, repel). This is the subatomic world where electrons perform quantum leaps, vanishing from one spot and appearing in another, without having traversed the space between (unholy dice-throwing Einstein so objected to). Language on the other hand belongs to the macro system of information exchange, and is not reducible to quark-like terms – which is not to deny chance elements in the *evolution* of language. Du Plé also ventures into the world of genetics, and points out that the chance combination of genes, which gives rise to variation within any given species, isn't mere evolutionary recreation, but a kind of life assurance. Where one genetic configuration can't adapt to universal change, another can. [dP:XIV.p587]

XV[1]Molloy was left to assess the pieces that resulted from this, and conferred with du Plé. Du Plé notes elsewhere that for *her* offering Beckie presented a menu, from O. Henry's restaurant, 345 Sixth Avenue, which she'd marked at the top margin—

Diner » waitress » chef » restaurateur » supplier: script

Molloy was furious, and awarded a fail. Beckie complained to Quay, and after delicate negotiations the fail was commuted to a pass. [dP:XV.p587]

XVI[1]The curriculum here it seems required Molloy to send her students off-campus and distil creative possibilities from a world of workaday life. Du Plé considered this as an exercise for himself, having been struck at how dwarfed were the churches dotted round Manhattan (for that matter the synagogues and Buddhist temples too). All were in many ways subservient to that enveloping steel and concrete – those great shrines to Commerce, its brave new skyscrapers. How far he went with this he doesn't make clear. [dP:XVI.p588]

²Elsewhere in his notebooks du Plé does try to put himself in Molloy's difficult position. Langer has looked at her course notes, and has drawn her attention – not without ironic self-awareness – to an entry she has made on the subject of graffiti. But this is not just any graffiti, or graffito. This is one attributed to Greek soldiers in Nubia in the seventh century BC, the whole point being it reveals their good elementary education.

That same century saw Egyptian hieroglyphs adapted to demotic script, Sappho of Lesbos, completion of the Indian *Vedas*, Arion (Greek composer and poet), his strophe and antistrophe, also the library at Nineveh, with its poetry, educational texts, and its manual of grammatical translation (Sumerian to Semitic). Du Plé concludes, without sounding at all convinced about this, that the dual theology offered at the Donns Watson (the role chance may take in the creative act, and the physical limitation imposed by whatever happen to be the tool and medium of production), encourages us to think not in terms of personal genius, but of available technology. As marginalia I found this—

> Your pariah,
> Outside these city walls,
> Has scratched his name on a temple stone
> And wields his heavy sword.
> [dP:XVI.p588]

³Not his idea of 'writ', though he can't bring himself to talk about this with a very much older Alex, whose interests he probably suspects have changed since their earlier times together. I have exercised care in my reconstructions, having sifted methodically through his papers. I'm sure that Molloy's position was ambiguous, her unstated view being that according to the Donns Watson, 'writ' was more generally relegated to the status of footnote, historically speaking. For Molloy, unable to muster more than token resistance to the debates she'd stepped into unsuspectingly, there still remained possibilities for certain texts as relevant for study, with no necessity to embark on long and tiring pilgrimages. [dP:XVI.p588]

XVII¹Meaning, it is only parenthetically that the author is present (du Plé likes parentheses, if on this occasion they're merely implied). [dP:XVII.p588]

²A series of dreamy night scenes (oil on canvas), all firmly rooted in the *commedia dell'arte*, which coincided with Alice's Glum Period. She exhibited locally, and sold all but three – according to my information – of which this may be one, or on the other hand may be an unsuspected fourth. It becomes clear what an influence these have been. [dP:XVII.p588]

XX¹Here is an epigraph the poet du Plé was fond of, and recycled many times—

> And the whole earth was of one language,
> and of one speech.
> —Genesis, 11: 1 [dP:XX.p589]

[2]An alternative, and abandoned Section XX, is the beginning of a *terza rima*, and stutters to its second en dash like this, with impatient punctuation—

> It's the tide of regret, Alex, having
> Breezed through your house in its cradling of dust
> (Spectral Mnemosyne always waving).

> The point of my compass – absolute must –
> [dP:XX.p589]

XXI[1]Brad does eventually articulate a position, without ceasing to rebel. He doesn't deny that the craft of writing can't remain static, an amber perspective forever hardened on the past. What he reacts to is the ninety-nine Donns Watson variations played against his own. [dP:XXI.p590]

XXIV[1]Quay a Foucauldian, and Shakespeare's literary longevity an exercise in institutional construction. [dP:XXIV.p591]

[2]Brad's lengthy diatribe, in whose tone I uncover anti-American activities, is convoluted. He finds that 'everything is political', and that to scrutinise a literary artefact is to scrutinise a political structure. His first expert witness, you'd think aided and abetted by du Plé, is by proxy – the Englishman Francis Bacon, first Baron Verulam and Viscount of St Albans, who lived from 1561 to 1626. The mid-nineteenth-century proposition that it was Bacon, and not Shakespeare, who authored Shakespeare's plays, is a theory based partly on internal evidence (of the plays themselves) – author's knowledge, vocabulary etc. – and partly on external circumstances – Shakespeare's sketchy biography, and the assumption that the son of a Warwickshire husbandman would not have been up to it intellectually. The word 'husbandman' is an archaism, and arrives as a Middle English compound meaning 'farmer' – therefore objection to Shakespeare as dramatist is on genetic grounds, which of course is propaganda. Moreover it's the kind of propaganda propping an elite, which doesn't maintain itself through a voting system necessarily. It succeeds through resisting infiltration from any lower stratum, be that a Victorian proletariat or a post-Beat NY arts student. [dP:XXIV.p591]

XXVII[1]A pencil draft, on what was a jotter, bears 'Disconsolate Badinage' as a working title, and reads as follows—

Your chipper rhetorician will deny
My taxonomic claim (the 'facts' you found
You cleverly misconstrued, to imply
I err: must you prepare rhetorical ground?).

The Donns Watson's a wilderness of limpid
Superstitions. Its students all worship
Plasticated pyres, which in turn out-bids
The goat Mammon, fleet with commercial ships.

You can't absorb the witty ripostes
His miraculous ineptitude
Is able to conjure: subtlety is lost
On a marketplace crowd – art is that crude.

Enough to deny, and not disprove?
Your so-called 'facts' it seems are actually true.

Du Plé's taxonomy pins the label 'rhetoric' to almost any form of art. In a magnetised field of opposites, the 'facts' of *contemporary* art are really its fictions. Its wilderness (with statutory prophet, ignored, and a whole gamut of deaf ears) is a wasteland of commercialised trash, just waiting to be canonised. It's usual of course for gems to await the ritual dropping of scales. The twist or involution rests with the cloven-footed vendor, that purveyor of art in its shop-soiled state – devil who knows his deeds, and lies for human profit. Denial, for the non-participant, is not enough. If Robert Quay's school misrules itself, this is an issue for mathematical proof, all wrapped up with a QED (if, that is, du Plé can persist in this vein). The word 'plasticised' is struck out, restored, then doubly dealt its death blow. [dP:XXVII.p594]

[2] The colourist du Plé, who always signs his canvas. [dP:XXVII.p594]

[3] Home. I find nowhere any reference to du Plé's street address or neighbourhood, so it's not for me to guess whether like Copparo he lived at Queens, or not. There is a triptych of poems, whose twinned themes are the domestic irrelevancy of locus and habitation, and the sense of at-homeness as more a personal attitude. Copparo's talent was her ease in practically any closed environment, whereas his own was haunted—

Zip Code Nowhere

Wake up's
a clatter on the sidewalk,

with a dream
only half-dissolved.
[dP:XXVII.p595]

XXIX[1]'What mattered it to her just then that the rushes had begun to fade, and to lose all their scent and beauty....' *Through the Looking Glass*, Chapter V. [dP:XXIX.p595]

XXX[1]'Fuck-sagging', parenthesised, is scored out, is scored out, is in triplicate scored out. [dP:XXX.p596]

[2]Marcel Duchamp (1887–1968). [dP:XXX.p597]

XXXI[1]According to Alex, back in the platformed soles of the 1970s, every nearby bus shelter or station waiting room had been tipped with the silvered moon writing proclaiming the two, who are otherwise anonymous, as star-crossed and eternally in love. [dP:XXXI.p597]

XXXVI[1]Du Plé might overlook personnel, but he noted that address as follows—

1 Our question is that of diversity, regardless of medium. With what foreseeable consequence do we address our practice to the shifting boundaries of literary art?
2 How do we resolve evident tensions between, on the one hand, our tendency to shift those boundaries, on the other the limits of critical categorisation?
3 Boundaries, categories: don't these lead us to discuss all art in a reductive way? If so, how is renewal ever possible?
4 Do we ask too much that the social world change with the same flexibility as that of our practice?' [dP:XXXVI.p601]

XXXIX[1]It's a rehash going back to the red notebook, but with a new title, 'Logos as Factotum'—

Not exactly in the past. Forgotten
Yet foreseen. But without question
Here.

You knew my thoughts,
And for a moment wouldn't let me
Speak. A calming gesture of the hand,
A friendly smile, and what surprised me most,
The familial address:

'You half suspect
That what is here is a fact, it exists. No object
You see is at an obvious remove from the world
You know. In each, the quality of light
Imparts a range of attributes: this atmosphere
Is not unknown. You recall a thousand summer
Or a thousand starless nights – or only one.
Or have seen in dreams the weird and the bizarre,
Conformed to an order they themselves create.
Therefore, with a question half conceived,
You approach....'

I said: 'The word
Is last. Action obviates my speech. This level
Of communication – new to me in waking life –
It suits. I waive the usual pleasantries, and anyway
The question has escaped.'

She: 'What is it matters?'
'The world.'
'Why?'
'Simply that I'm here.'

'Only a vague connection now exists. That world
Is somewhere over there. Here is now. The now
Is as unimportant as the past.'

'Since in a dream
I have foreseen it all, I disagree, and in this sleep
Have had a point of view. In the world or the past,
I have climbed the tower and fallen to the streets
A hundred times. Or drowning seen a serpent sliding
On the surface of a twilit lake. I half suspected then
That what I'd glimpsed was real. But always in its blur.
In the fall and then submerged remained this vague connection
With the world. A correspondence carried on a month
Ago, or a year. Or how with easy unconcern I had routinely
Shuffled through the dirty streets of North West 10. That history,
Fragmented as it is, I carry with me now.'

She again:

'A dead

Woman's red world became an omniverse. Freed by the fires
From incarcerating ice, the dark infant uncoiled from the flesh
And bone of its mother's ruined body.

'All these

Things have passed, yet none exerts an influence upon your life,
Your world, your universe. All that have lived, have lived
With the silhouettes of evening. All that have lived, have lived
Again. All that have lived again, have lived again with the word
As last, where action obviates our speech. All that is action
Without speech is communication new to us in waking
Life, is as broad and silent as our universe—

'Your little

Life an undiscovered country, with only one, with only one invented
Chore....'

Hard to say what Tucker made of this. Anyway he returned it. [See dU:XXXIX.p685]
[dP:XXXIX.p602]

XLII [1]Tucker is well represented in the Benbrook College library, where his *Bookmark E*,
one of three collections of that era, has as its centrepiece the Lenin poem. This, in the
bronze-to-pinkish tint of butter mushrooms, is a huge, breathless, unpunctuated sweep
over sun-fringed birches, the law, prison, Siberia, sledge rides and book piles, marriage,
the British Museum, fishing with Gorky, Cracow, Switzerland, cards to the Bolsheviks,
forged passports, haylofts, haystacks, the Whites, the palaces, an assortment of generals,
retreat from Poland, a bullet lodged in his shoulder, a first stroke, the world and Stalin,
mushrooms again – pink to snow-white – all in the shade of those ghostly birches. Just
the kind of list du Plé always found inept. [dP:XLII.p603]

[2]Herein du Plé admits to a memoir (and I thought these were letters). Tut. [dP:XLII.p603]

XLIII[1]Yes, George, it is.... [dP:XLIII.p603]

XLIX[1]'Wipe your glosses with what you know' is Martin Gardner's usage, borrowed from
James Joyce, and applied as epigraph to his *Annotated Alice*. The edition George
possessed was much thumbed, and after its travels was now in a state of disintegration, a
paperback with a yellow cover and Tenniel's illustrations, published in 1970. [See
dU:XLIX.p689] [dP:XLIX.p607]

[2]George here glosses over (glasses over) an arty falling out with Tucker, and does not allude to his seat of editorial power, throne from which the new *Id* edicts, according to du Plé, proscribed everything (yes, *everything*) its proprietor had intended for the English number. This included a series of poems and essays by Adrian Purch, whose CV at that time ran something like this—

> Member, Irish Academy of Letters; Professor of Poetry, Exe University, 1980–; Professor of Rhetoric and Oratory, New Wye University, 1975–79; b. September 1937; educated Pembroke College, Cambridge University (BA first class, 1958); H. H. Munro Award, 1961; Marchioness Award, 1962; UK Book Award, Viscount Award, 1963; the Queen's Medal for Poetry, 1973; H. H. Munro Award, 1975; Commonwealth Book Award, 1977; European Book Award, 1979; publications range from 1959 to present.

From a carbon I found, of a typewritten letter to Tucker explaining his decisions, du Plé 'assesses' Purch through a rambling critique of the poems (some of which are translations), and a dry counter-dissertation regarding one essay in particular. One of Purch's translations is a revision based on a bilingual edition, published in 1907. Its basis is a manuscript from Languedoc, written in the late seventeenth century, whose author put the original at somewhere between 1270 and 1350. Critical to it is an event of 1209, when the pope (Innocent III) ordered the Cistercians to preach the crusade against the Albigenses (heretics in the south of France in the twelfth and thirteenth centuries). The result: an implacable war, which threw the nobility of France's north against that of the south, destroying what was then a polished Provençal civilisation. The war ended, politically, with the Treaty of Paris (1229), which curtailed the independence of the princes of the south, but did not extinguish the Albigensian heresy, in spite of the wholesale massacre of heretics.

In Purch's view, the original might have been composed soon after 1229, the product of a mind counterbalanced by the dominant Christian ethos and temperamentally something much older, which for the Church remained a recalcitrant presence. Purch saw it as unrelieved tension between the free imagination and doctrinal, political interdict. Du Plé, though he understood the attraction of ancient texts, failed to see why this one had been chosen as the source of one of Purch's own. Did it mean that the modern imagination had lost its artistic integrity, in accepting the constraints of domestic obligation, and could not find itself again except in the remoteness of an extinct civilisation?

As du Plé puts it: 'At one extreme is the academic poet, whose staple erudition is in the recycling of the conventions of tradition. Between this and any other extreme there is nothing – only a "free play of imagination", in a smug reflection on the tack and trash of everyday contemporary life.'

If du Plé found the poems 'grey', or 'insipid', the essays were worse, were 'an indulgence' (I merely quote him. Don't ask me if I agree). Purch once described himself as a favourite of one of his grandparents, who noted that the new village hall came into being in the same year as Adrian's birth (1937). This, says du Plé, is a generality assumed to be particular, but is written in such a way as to privilege the poet's as unique experience. I do not think that anywhere Purch makes his own a special case, if to the contrary du Plé appears to think he does. I'd just add that if Middlecross is legitimate material, then Purch is also justified.

Nevertheless, says du Plé, he doesn't value as Purch does Purch's sense of community. His great tussle is not with the conundrum Art in Life, or a Life in Art (du Plé's capitals), but with poetry as a sentimentalisation, given Purch's peaty lyricism or parochialness. That village sensibility seems to du Plé confirmed for Purch when still a young man, with just a handful of poems printed in various newspapers – but noticed, and commended by an elder of his trade. Du Plé even states, with disapproval, that ever since then an entrenched Adrian Purch has set himself against the aestheticism of, for example, Roland Barthes (Purch has frequent sideswipes at that fraternity), in common with many since the 1960s. The reaction against that cigar-sucking guru has been a reaction against his sales pitch, his line of luxury lit items, trinkets to match the kitchen whites – while the world of kitchen whites is also where we live.

Purch's hymn to a more congenial predecessor – a poet and essayist conservative like himself – reads like a homage to a senior, with the supplanter still in need of that final leg up (Nobel Prize, du Plé thinks). In Purch on Black Consciousness, and on Eastern Bloc poets, is implicitly the West as finished, as final, as a culture played out. He wants us to believe that without the marks and stigmata of colonialism, or a heroic resistance against the State, greatness can't be achieved, but of that he can't convince du Plé. All that's now left to the Little Englander (or Little Briton) is the over-wide margins of journalese, documenting nothing outside itself. Du Plé by contrast sees it as self-fulfilling, the natural outcome of academe and the grant-aid system – a stupendously grey monolith whose practitioners palpate the margins while persistently looking inward. The common centre – du Plé means Purch's centre – is a locus of mediocrity, which won't allow anything other than itself – therefore its view prevails.

The proof of Purch's argument – or in fact only opinion – is poems he cites written under duress. A poet acquires authentic rights only through an act of heroism (Lowell in jail, Plath on the brink of suicide, Eastern Bloc writers defying their political tyrannies, the post-colonial after the yoke of colonialism – doubtless other samples abound). Here in England there has been a kind of heroism, but long incommoded. [dP:XLIX.p607]

---

[3]This I think not a reference to its 'cuteness', but to *Village Id*'s editor – an office du Plé couldn't now be said to hold. We have already seen his attitude to Purch (above) – a weary scepticism – which without over-taxing the issue I can tell you is evident in practically all his treatment of Tucker's material. On that English number's Jesuit contribution, du Plé says this—

'The poetry of hard-won faith, thrashing for continued life on stony ground. In all a summary of what is so difficult about Christianity – necessarily painful, necessarily so unrewarding in its initial steps. I can't imagine many think like this now.'
Of its up-and-coming *young* poet, this—
'He shows promise. Some of the poems have verve and wit, and are a pleasure. On the whole his metaphors are too insistent.'
On Benbrooks's Professor of Creative Writing – a Philip Nodston, PhD – whose theory of the novel was after D'Orbieu, its structures akin to a mental geometry – angular planes, dark sections, tangents off other people's curved horizons, happy parabolas, other-world parallelisms – here du Plé resorts to satire. Tucker had evidently sent an outline of the theory, and intended it as a late inclusion. The reply was the following, a du Pléian philippic or war song—

Nodston was Arting

Nodston's overt dilemma:
Straight technical overabundance
Never will astutely serve
A readerly togetherness,
In novelised geometries.

What excited his volcanoes was the reviews section, whose sole author took in, among other things, a new translation of Dante's *Inferno* (Tralatition Press), Purch's latest collection, *Organ Stops* (EUP), a new appraisal of Herbert (OUP), and Purch's Exe Union address, since it was Purch, and not Borges, who won Exe's vacant poetry chair. Du Plé is calmly incensed at the reviewer's explanation of that choice, where Borges's 'slender' eloquence is subordinated to Purch's more 'muscular'. Du Plé, for whom the Argentine is a celestial being, prefers that the ultimate subordination belongs with Purch, in Dante's Hell, where sinners get their reward. According to Borges, Dante authored the apex of all literature, and cast himself in it, taking as his guide through Hell and Purgatory the Roman poet Virgil – a pagan, but only by two or three generations (Virgil, 70–19 BC). Virgil's *Aeneid* is the legendary account of the Trojan prince Aeneas, who after the fall of Troy laid the foundations of Roman power, whereas his fourth eclogue, in its celebration of the birth of a child to a Roman official, was thought in the Middle Ages to be Messianic, a prediction of the coming of Christ. Borges, in an essay on the *Commedia*, which du Plé is able to quote, describes himself as a hedonistic reader, who never reads a book merely because it is ancient, but because of the aesthetic emotions it arouses. 'Aesthetics' and 'emotions' for Borges belong to a very particular area of literary specialisms, and are not simply matters of imagery and musicality, of joy / sorrow, pain / pleasure, etc. Nowhere in Borges's *œuvre* is it evident that the literary aesthetic is reductive to its corporal state, the body as the site of the senses and therefore prime in everything that is sensorily received or given (which is so unlike Purch). His sensibility doesn't have much commerce in the quotidian exchanges of everyday human life. What he responds to, and is bewildered by, is *objectified* emotion, which frames the notion of beginning as an infinite regress, and completion as a geometrical progression, to whose nth term can always be added another, plus an ellipsis. In this sense he *can* be a lover of Dante, but unlike Dante not a committed Christian, in whose beginning is God, creator of heaven and earth (Genesis, 1: 1), and whose end is the Resurrection ('...Jesus shewed himself to his disciples, after that he was risen from the dead' – John, 21: 14) – or at least whose *temporal* end is the Resurrection, without which mortal redemption is not possible (and neither is heaven's populace).

Borges points to the *Commedia*'s 'aesthetic' emotion in the relationship between Dante and Virgil, which he describes as 'filial' (Dante the son of Virgil). Virgil, because he's a pagan, cannot accompany his charge beyond Purgatory, in fact is a sad figure forever condemned to that *nobile castello*, which is 'filled with the absence of God'. Dante by contrast will see God. Dante will know, and understand the universe. Further than this, Borges isolates Canto XXVI of the 'Inferno' as the *Commedia*'s high point, perhaps because, for several reasons, it is representative of metaphysical being devoid of Christian hope. It, Canto XXVI, is the episode of Ulysses – 'who is in yon fire' – in a reprise of Homer's Odysseus, who has been, in the pagan world, a traditional emblem of the soul's journey, without a guide (without God as guide), to its celestial destination. The Greek word *nostos* describes that journey as circular, starting from and returning home, with life's adventure in between. According to Homer, Odysseus completes his journey, returning not only to the bosom of his family but to the throne of his kingdom. According to Dante, Ulysses is punished for daring to seek out the mountain of Purgatory, at whose summit is the forbidden knowledge of the universe, a complete and ultimate meaning that it is not granted to mere mortals to know. This leads Borges to speculate that Dante in some way sees himself as Ulysses, a poet who has dared to impinge on the mysterious laws of God. It leads du Plé to speculate that Purch can never be this, and that somehow Borges is *also* Dante's Ulysses, a triform who lives on that shifting dune whose origin is indeterminate and whose end is one of perpetual transmogrification.

On the Herbert study from OUP, du Plé feels justified in citing Borges again – specifically *The Book of Sand*, in whose closing paragraph an attempt is made to conceal an infernal book among the ranks of the conventional. One can't help reading in this a coded message for Tucker (the code itself not difficult to decipher), where du Plé casts the fictive Borges into the same blur as his biographical senior, posing as narrator of *The Book of Sand*. In a dream of himself, in a dreamed apartment in a dream of Buenos Aires, 'volumes', or books that the wraith called Borges has so often handled, include encyclopaedias, maps, sacred tomes, the world's fantasies concerning itself. Someone very like him, whose domicile is Belgrano Street, in Buenos Aires, receives a caller who initially introduces himself as someone selling Bibles. Bibles aren't the requirement, so the salesman, a Presbyterian from the Orkneys, instead produces an octavo volume, bound in cloth, on whose spine are the words 'Holy Writ', and 'Bombay'. On opening the book, the pages appear in double columns, ordered in versicles, as is so in a Bible. The bookseller advises a close look at the page, since it will never be found, or seen, again. He states that he acquired it in exchange for a handful of rupees and *the* Christian book, from an owner who did not know how to read. It is impossible to find its first and last page, and is called *The Book of Sand* because it has no beginning or end – its very pages are terms in an infinite series. As to the bookseller's conscience, it is clear: he feels sure of not having cheated the native in exchanging the Word of God for this, a diabolic trinket. Hume is mentioned, as well as George Herbert ('Thy rope of sands', which forms an epigraph to the whole destructive rig-up), and the book is sold to the citizen of Belgrano Street.

Du Plé offers us further background information, telling us that George Herbert – 1593–1633 – balanced a secular career with a life of theological contemplation – was ordained deacon circa 1624 – and was, in 1626, installed as a canon of Lincoln cathedral and prebendary of Leighton Bromswold, near Little Gidding (which only tells us of du Plé's own access to literary encyclopaedias). Herbert, he claims, is in all guises in conscientious pursuit of a 'transcendental signifier', God's summarising logos, the last syllable of recorded time, as the divine extension of the Book of Genesis (*In the beginning, God said…*), a suspiration that renders as revealed and knowable everything that has been uttered and written in between – life and the world as a sacred inscription—

> Thy rope of sands,
> Which petty thoughts have made, and made to thee
> Good cable, to enforce and draw,
> And be thy law,
> While thou didst wink and would not see.

Above all, Herbert wants us to *see* God's revealed truth – which the Presbyterian bookseller believes is written in a book, in *the* Book, to the extent that his evangelism extends to the Hindu caste system in Bombay, where he has found what to him is the opposite of incontestable writ, with its textual flickers, its presences, its absences. Note that Presbyterianism occupies an intermediate position between episcopacy (the Church of England is Episcopal) and congregationalism, whose form of worship has been marked by extreme simplicity – this explains its appeal to Cromwell and his Puritan followers (du Plé says). One imagines that to the average Presbyterian, God's truth is a simple truth. By contrast one can't ever imagine this being the case for Hume (1711–76), himself a son of Presbyterianism, whose 'persistence in irreligion shook the conviction of Boswell, and provoked some particularly unpleasant comments from Dr Johnson'—

> Hume owned he had never read the New Testament with attention. Here then was
> a man who had been at no pains to enquire into the truth of religion, and had
> continually turned his mind the other way. It was not to be expected that the

prospect of death would alter his way of thinking, unless God should send an
angel to set him right.
—Boswell, *The Life of Samuel Johnson*

According to Hume,

> …evidence…for the truth of the Christian religion is less than the evidence for the
> truth of our senses; because, even in the first authors of our religion [whose texts
> are founded on the testimony of the apostles], it was no greater; and it is evident
> it must diminish in passing from them to their disciples; nor can any one rest such
> confidence in their testimony, as in the immediate object of their senses….
> —Hume, *Enquiries Concerning Human Understanding*

It can be by no means accidental that Borges as author (as author of *The Book of Sand*) has
passed into the simplified hands of an evangelical Presbyterian an 'immediate object', the
sense of which undermines plain faith in a Christian eschatology. Any one page of an
infinite book, for the moment we contemplate it, is the central term of an infinite series,
yet is merely engulfed by that infiniteness during those other moments when we don't.
Du Plé goes further and says that this counter-Book posited by Borges is in fact an
interpretation of *the* Book, to whom he has called Herbert, Hume and a Presbyterian
Bible-vendor as first witness. *The Book of Sand* is the Book of the basis of Western
Christianity, decentred.

Tucker did eventually complete his English edition of *Village Id*, using that bundle of
material du Plé so curtly cast off, and Benbrook's own press. There is a copy in Benbrook's
library. Furthermore the long laborious process of transferring journals, papers and
dissertations from that library's archive to Benbrook's website is well under way. *English
Village Id*, and the issue that followed, I have been able to examine at:

http://www.benbrook.ac.uk/~journals80-89

There is more on this at Section LIV, below, and at d'Ursag XLIX, but du Plé rounds off
with this, regretful of Exe's newly warmed poetry chair—

> Destiny of Borges,
> To have erred in the labyrinth
> Of scholarship

– which Tucker didn't publish either.

When du Plé was first pointed out to me he had taken himself off to his and Alex's
bench with a paperback edition of Dante's *La Vita Nuova*, which I later found
bookmarked on a mantelpiece – translated and with an introduction by Barbara

Reynolds. *La Vita Nuova*, a treatise for poets, written *by* a poet, on the subject of – poetry. Yet Dante like George ostensibly recalls a dead or departed woman. [dP:XLIX.p608]

[4]Throughout the 1980s, Alice showed great entrepreneurial flair, and made a success of bringing US artists to the UK. [dP:XLIX.p608]

L[1]That 'soulless conglomerate' was Leader Books plc. At that time Lucinda Munney was in overall control of the smaller imprints it had acquired. [dP:L.p609]

[2]I don't know where du Plé would have got this appellation, for in fact Alex's school was called Wenover. Its shield bore the motto *Hinc lucem et pocula sacra*. It must be a private joke. [dP:L.p609]

LI[1]George grew up in a post-structuralist era, and as we have seen likes to intertwine letters with life. In passing it is just worth saying that according to the Swiss linguist Ferdinand de Saussure (1857–1913), language pinpoints itself where auditory images – those mentated pictures formed in response to the sounds of words – are inextricably bound to concepts. A succession of concepts sometimes isn't for du Plé spawned only by its antecedent succession of words, since a single concept alone (for example Alex's swing) can give rise to chains of other, *unrelated* concepts (*The Mikado*, a lost English summer, the purchase of theatre tickets, Dame d'Hautpoul, a car drive no one else recalls from twenty years before). It seems that for him the destruction of one is necessarily a break-up of all the others. I wouldn't go that far, though I don't disagree that an attempt to deconstruct a text is an attempt also to deconstruct the world from which it came. [dP:LI.p610]

LII[1]Tralatition Press was founded in 1894 by Thomas Little, who was born in 1852 in Walthamstow and died in 1919 in Plaxtol. His father had spent much of his early life in the colonial East. His family house was embellished by an Orientalism that didn't suit Thomas temperamentally. Thomas didn't rebel, but as an adult was curate in a string of parishes, an existence he couldn't reconcile with the currents of debate that then prevailed. He was not at home in a Victorian English society that Matthew Arnold (1822–88) had carved up according to manners and taste. Flitches from that table were shared unevenly by the 'Barbarians' (or aristocracy), the 'Philistines' (an entrepreneurial middle class), and the 'Populace' (the rest, the uncultivated – poised but not yet equipped for social action). For Arnold this was an age of disintegrating creeds, where if religion had failed then poetry must adopt and revive its role. Yet poetry since the Romantic movement, for example in the troubled shape of Doktor Faust – a Master of Philosophy, of Law, of Medicine, and sceptically of Theology – had anticipated just that impasse. Faust was obsessed with the 'things of Nature's secret seal', which Thomas resisted, but which Darwin demystified reluctantly. According to the latter, the twenty-one land-bird species endemic to the Galapagos Archipelago were *not* the work of an all-encompassing deity. They were the products of natural selection. From here it wasn't difficult to arrive at the disheartening corollary that the average English country gentleman couldn't assume divine provenance either, but shared the same ancestry with Arnold's 'uncultivated rest'.

Under Thomas, Tralatition published sparingly. Its books, without exception, promoted Christian orthodoxy, through mild-mannered theologians with benign if dilute pen and ink. Then the press was dormant, and had all but died by the turn of the century, and didn't revive until the 1920s, when Edward Little (1888–1963) decided to take it on. Edward had lectured in politics, and in his first venture as Tralatition's new proprietor diagnosed the problem that men like his father hadn't faced up to. This was in a book he wrote himself under a *nom de plume* – *Century Street*, Jack Gilbain (London, 1922) – which was published in the same year as Joyce's Paris *Ulysses*, Eliot's *The Waste Land*, the death of Proust, Hesse's *Siddharta*, Wittgenstein's *Tractatus*, Spengler's revised *The Decline of the West*...etc. The book was not a classic.

The press's fortunes dipped again when, in the post-war years, Edward (whose obsession was politics) brought the hard edge of his conservatism into contact with the fading outlines of English liberal tradition, publishing a slim if far from modest book, authored by a man called Adam Wright, in support of a eugenics programme and a revised international banking system. The reviews were calm, the debates indignant, the sales good, the world lurched on. Soon the books and commentaries were focused on other things to dispute.

Unlike his two predecessors (his father and his grandfather), James Little (Alex's stepfather) entered the industry as a professional, not as a dilettante. He learned the business through a career in London and New York. When Edward died in the 1950s, the Tralatition James inherited – and decided to reinvigorate – listed art, belles-lettres, biography and memoir as first among its interests, had strong ties with education, history, philosophy and science, and was still open to theology and religion. Though it boasted an impressive backlist, by now it traded in an academic marketplace, and this gave James limited scope to keep it as his day job. By the early 1960s, his new list had extended into popular culture, and in the '70s had an emphasis on personal awareness (I was shown and commented on an illustrated handbook on Gestalt therapy). In the '80s it followed the post-graduate work of archaeological teams combing the world for standing stones and ancient astronomical sites. In the 1990s, with the gloss and waxed paper, and the brand-new tinsels a post-postmodernism gift-wrapped round earlier evolutions, Tralatition entered the resurgent wave of semi-academic publishing. James as much as any other beach-dweller raked his twentieth-century coastline, and to the driftwood already there added to the growth in books of literary theory, gave voice to the previously unvoiced – populations living under a colonial legacy – and couldn't ignore a new wave of feminist writers. He also found access to popular art movements (with the kind of book that explained the vogue in art installations), and towards the close of the century published authors dissenting from these views. Interestingly, and as an unconscious echo of

Tralatition's earlier *Century Street*, one author James signed up wrote a series of essays under the collective title *Cents and Centsibility* (where art, as Matthew Arnold suggests, has assumed the role of religion). That author's name was Power McTeal, better known as a children's writer, but a graduate of an MA somewhere whose ethos she finally couldn't share. She had been harshly dealt with by politically correct, North American tribal edicts, when she had published a children's picture book about the son of an Indian chief, subject matter that as a white, middle-class Englishwoman she did not 'own'. She took it personally, and ended her career as a writer for the very young.

I have to admit that the particular institution to which McTeal directed her invective is not well known and is not considered important, though in it I think James identified – sensing that the tide had begun to turn – an impassioned outcry against the role of higher education in contemporary arts practice generally.

That said, I am grateful to James that he still made room in his list for modern translations in what remains of the canon, ranging from Virgil to Verlaine. But, all is now in flux again, and with James past retirement, and having seen his offspring bar his son Roddy out on their own, his friends and colleagues – wise and well-meaning counsellors – are unanimous that Tralatition's days as an independent are over. [See dU:LII.p692] [dP:LII.p610]

[2]We are back to the Song of Solomon again (see note 3 to Section X, above)—

> …I found him…
> I held him, and would not let him go….
> [dP:LII.p610]

LIII[1]See notes 2, 3 and 4 below. [dP:LIII.p610]

[2]This is the Myra van Elph about to take up her new lecturing post at Benbrook. Our connection is initially through Exe (postgraduates, early 1970s), and there have been occupational crossings of our paths ever since. I cannot put into words how much of an insult all this is, since the book du Plé deems it appropriate to thieve belongs to her. I offered to sign it when, in a fulsome thank-you note for my part in Myra's appointment, she happened to mention this as a book she'd been reading. Whatever du Plé is trying to insinuate, is in poor taste. [dP:LIII.p611]

[3]Again this is scurrilous innuendo. [dP:LIII.p611]

[4]*And* again…. [dP:LIII.p611]

LIV[1]I know, because an automated archive makes it simple to know, that Tucker had carried over into Benbrook's house mag (*Campania*) one aspect of his guest lectureship, and had – in the sepia of hindsight – discussed this more delicately in the alumni broadsheet – an annual, which is nowadays a tabloid (and hugely more colourful. See http://www.benbrook.ac.uk/~journals80-89). One of his students – male, maladroit, and a sycophant – wanted to stage *The Two Gentlemen of Verona*, but in a feminist version, outdoors, under an English moon, and in a variance of theatrical light, citron to indigo – this presupposing that any lunar base cloud able to make that shift couldn't be relied on. One other student (female, formidable) argued that *The Two Gentlemen* was already a feminist text, since both heroines, constant and morally erect – in fact unwavering through *all* entanglements – could never allow us to see them as objects. By contrast Proteus lived up to his name, transforming himself from treacle-tongued lover, to betrayer to rapist to skulking contrition over the short course of all five acts. Not surprisingly this was not a reason to change anything, since nothing much changed anyway, with Tucker acting as editor and overseer of what was eventually a revised script, an abstract of which anyone worldwide can access from the archive—

Two Men With Diplomas

I.1 VAL PAL prepares for his new job in the West End of London, in the marketing department of the Italian shoe giant Kudos. He ribs the philandering PROTES over an infatuation with JULES, which keeps his friend in the country.

> **VAL PAL** Dunno what you want to stick around here for, Protes. You know sooner or later you lose that edge, *outside* London....
>
> **PROTES** You *would* say that, with a plum job to go to. Anyway, I'm after other exploits. And women you can get anywhere.

I.2 JULES asks LUCY, the home help, what she thinks of JULES's many casual boyfriends. LUCY prefers PROTES, but JULES says she can't stand him. LUCY gives her a note from PROTES, delivered by SPEED, but JULES affects to be aghast at this, and tears it to pieces. She sends LUCY away, regrets her action, and reads some reconstructed bits of the note.

> **JULES** Of all the guys hanging out, which would *you* go for? Lamourge with his polo shirt? Mercatio, and that lovely red Lotus of his? Or what about Protes, who was lead in a rock band?
>
> **LUCY** Oh, definitely Protes! Such a baby face!
>
> **JULES** Him!
>
> **LUCY** You did ask. [*On her way out*] Oh, nearly forgot – got a note. Here.
>
> **JULES** [*begins to read, then tears letter*] Do leave it out, Lucy! What do you take me for...!
>
> **LUCY** Now what did I say! What did I say! [*Exit*]
>
> **JULES** Can't help thinking I slightly over-did that. Can't stick all *these* back together....

I.3 ASTON, who is reading his morning paper, is fed up with his son PROTES forever sponging off him, and plans to pack him off to a law firm in Serjeants' Inn, where he has heard of an opening. PROTES on the other hand has received a note from JULES, which he pretends to his father is really from VAL PAL.

PROTES [*glancing up from note*] Now *that's* a surprising turn of phrase. Wonder what the chances are of....

ASTON [*from behind newspaper*] Of what?

PROTES You know it's nothing really. This is just a note from Pal.

ASTON [*folds and puts down newspaper*] And how's Pal getting on? Can I see...?

PROTES It's mundane stuff. If you really want to read about commuter jams....

ASTON Not something you'd know about, eh, Protes. And do stop moping.

PROTES I'm not moping.

ASTON You are. If *that's* how you repay me. To think, the money I've spent, and for what? A useless education.

PROTES Please don't start that again.

ASTON You're right – you know we *should* change the subject. An old pal of mine in Serjeants' Inn tells me he's got a job for you.

PROTES A job!

ASTON He'd like to see you tomorrow.

PROTES Bit sudden isn't it!

ASTON Frankly no. I've had this cooking for quite some days.

PROTES But of all things Serjeants' Inn!

ASTON Nine-thirty prompt.

PROTES What's Mumsy say about this?

ASTON I do wish you wouldn't call her that. If you want to know, a good opportunity, is what *she* said.

PROTES But—

ASTON No buts. And *you* know as well as I do – if I don't make that phone call *now*, the stock market's bound to crash. It's an inverse law. Take the Fiat. Launce will drive. [*Exit*]

PROTES Gawd!

II.1 VAL PAL has evidently fallen for SILV, who in her student vacations is working in the marketing department of Kudos, where her father is MD. Hearing that VAL PAL is a graduate of English Lit, she asks him, on her behalf, to pen a love sonnet for someone she has recently taken to (in reality VAL PAL himself), and which she intends to dispatch through Kudos's internal mail.

VAL PAL I've given it a go, and that's the best I can do I'm afraid.

SILV [*takes sonnet from him, reads*] Not bad. In fact a lot better than I could do.

VAL PAL I wouldn't be so sure of that. It's tricky, not knowing who it's for.

SILV Look, if you're not happy about this—

VAL PAL It's not that. It's just—

SILV No, look, here – you take this back. I shouldn't have asked.

VAL PAL [*takes back sonnet*] Don't get me wrong.

SILV No. Honestly.

VAL PAL Silv!

SILV Look I'm *really really* sorry. Gotta go anyway. Meeting! [*Exit.*]

VAL PAL What meeting!

II.2 PROTES and JULES exchange rings before his departure.

PROTES I'll be back whenever I can – weekends and everything.

JULES [*gives him her ring*] Put this, and keep this, under your pillow.

PROTES [*hastily pulls off his own ring*] You do too!

Long embrace.

II.3 LAUNCE, one of several retainers kept on round ASTON's ancestral home, is instructed to go up to London with PROTES.

VOICE OFF Launce. Get the Fiat.

LAUNCE [*ironic, irritated*] Launce! Get the Fiat!

VOICE OFF [*louder*] Launce!

LAUNCE Coming!

II.4 PROTES in London, in a Fleet Street bistro. He has met up with his friend VAL PAL, who has brought SILV with him. SILV's father, Kudos's MD, wants her to form a marriageable liaison with SIGNORE THURIO, here on a business visit from head office in Milan. However, VAL PAL and SILV plan to marry quietly in a register office, VAL PAL having had the ruse with the sonnet patiently spelt out to him.

VAL PAL So how's Serjeants' Inn?

PROTES I suppose bearable. Might be quite good, if Julia worked in town.

SILV Invite her up.

PROTES She couldn't take my bachelor pad.

VAL PAL You think *you've* got problems. You'll never believe this, Protes, but Silv and I are madly in love – aren't we, darling…?

SILV Madly.

VAL PAL Problem is, the wedding's secret.

SILV Fulham RO.

PROTES What on earth for?

SILV Dad's the MD. Dead set on a geezer from Kudos Milan. Wouldn't be my choice at all.

PROTES Parents!

VAL PAL Oh so what! Let's have another bottle!

II.5 LAUNCE tells SPEED PROTES and JULES will marry.

LAUNCE Protes and Jules will marry.

SPEED Never you mind that. You just keep hosing the Fiat.

II.6 PROTES intends to leave JULES and betray VAL PAL, by telling the MD of SILV's plans for a secret wedding. PROTES is intent only on bedding SILV himself. He is at home, in his bachelor pad, channel hopping, but not really watching TV.

PROTES Oh now what's this! Some dreary soap opera, the same old worn-out plot. *Ménage à trois*. Still, these things do happen. I mean, what a triangle *I* am getting into! And why does it have to be Val Pal! For Christ's sake, does he know just what he's got with Silv! Thinks. Should I give her daddy a call…?

II.7 JULES decides to follow PROTES to London, disguised as a dude.

JULES [*eying herself in cheval glass*] Is this right? Of *course* it's right! He never phones, writes – nothing. So about these strides, then? You know, Jules, deep down, they need taking up. Okay. The jacket. Yeah, well – a touch deserted at the shoulders. But the shades, definitely good. And the hair, *very* authentic. [*Deepening voice*] Here's a bit of a strain, but….

III.1 On a memo from PROTES, MD now foils VAL PAL's plan, and fires him. For VAL PAL this change in fortune occurs in the Kudos front office, where he is exchanging sweet somethings with SILV.

SILV I don't want to rush you, but – if we *are* to make Fulham in half an hour, we'd better leave *now*.

VAL PAL That the time already!

SILV Kudos has got to you.

VAL PAL It's the ClimberBoot campaign. Heaps to do.

SILV Well delegate. I'll see you in the car park. [*Exit.*]

Enter MD, *with memo.*

MD Val Pal, the very man! And looking well! That's good to see.

VAL PAL Morning, Mr K.

MD Good good good.

VAL PAL Isn't it your board meeting?

MD *I'll* worry about that. Your prob's the new line in climbing boots. How *is* the campaign?

VAL PAL There's a lot of paperwork.

MD Don't let it get you down.

VAL PAL That's not what I meant.

MD Absolutely no need to apologise. I *can* see the problem. For example – the way you've tackled this rope ladder business – how the boot fits the rungs.

VAL PAL That *has* been tricky, I admit.

MD I shouldn't sweat on it, Val Pal. There's an hour before lunch. I'm sure together we'll thrash it out.

VAL PAL I – er – don't *have* an hour.

MD [*momentary stunned silence*] Mr Val Pal, perhaps you aren't aware. Competition is fierce. Timetables here are market-led.

VAL PAL I'm sorry, Mr K. At the minute, my diary's full.

MD Full, perhaps – but *afloat* – and a floating diary always spells success. Success, Pal, is commitment.

VAL PAL I *am*, sir, committed.

MD Good. I'm glad that's settled. Fresh coffee awaits us in my office. There's a great deal we now need to get through.

VAL PAL I'm afraid I can't.

MD Mr Val Pal, you force me to reconsider your continuing position here.

VAL PAL Then I'm utterly powerless.

MD I ask you to resolve this, here and now.

VAL PAL [*voice down a semitone*] You want me to clear my desk?

MD Not at all. That task has already been performed. [*Exit.*]

VAL PAL Do what!

MD OFF And don't expect to find Silv in the car park....

III.2 Fleet Street bistro. PROTES, maligning VAL PAL, and talking up THURIO, in a somewhat specious effort to bring SILV and THURIO together.

PROTES A bad lot, Val Pal. To me though you two are made for each other.

THURIO Sí!

SILV Leave it out, Protes!

IV.1 Somewhere on the outskirts of Epping Forest. VAL PAL is now manager of an ill-reputed tyre remould shop. He is in conversation with that business's proprietor.

PROPRIETOR So how *do* we turn the business round?

VAL PAL It's to do with image.

PROPRIETOR Image?

VAL PAL And a change of culture – right through the organisation.

PROPRIETOR Sounds difficult.

VAL PAL Anything wholesale is – and takes time.

PROPRIETOR What can we do in the short term?

VAL PAL Well, for one thing – these cheap remoulds.... You'll have to *describe* them as that, and charge accordingly.

PROPRIETOR But that'll affect margins.

VAL PAL On the one hand, yes. On the other there's repeat business.

PROPRIETOR Repeat business?

VAL PAL It's a concept you ought to get familiar with.

PROPRIETOR You serious?

VAL PAL Absolutely.

PROPRIETOR [*meditative*] Let me think this over.

IV.2 JULES, as the dude SEB, sees PROTES fawning over SILV in the Fleet Street bistro, as all share a bottle with THURIO.

SILV What a day I've had!

PROTES Me too. All I do is sift through long spiteful lists for tedious divorce suits.

SILV Should have thought that at least had entertainment value (lucky you!). [*Sighs*] Suddenly the fun's gone right out of Kudos.

PROTES You, and Thurio, could liven things up eh?

SILV I don't think *anyone* could.

PROTES Seriously. You two – you ought to get together.

THURIO, *in a slight blush, mumbles something that, although long, is coy and incoherent. He rounds off this show of affection by replenishing* SILV*'s glass.*

PROTES Well if that's the best he can do. I've got these two tickets for Covent Garden, Silv – *La Sonnambula* – why don't you come?

SILV Not my poison, Protes. And anyway what about that girl you left behind – Jules? What about her?

PROTES That affair's dead.

SEB [*furiously gum-chewing*] I'll get them to turn the music up. [*Stands, heads for bar*]

THURIO Sí!

A pounding of piped music, hard to make conversation over, and the chart-topping refrain—

> Who's this chick
> The lonely guy flew for,
> Who is she
> We're all in a queue for?

SILV [*shouting above the din*] What was that you said?

THURIO Sí!

IV.3 LAMOURGE, friend to SILV, agrees to help her on her way to Epping Forest, to meet up with VAL PAL. We find them in the front office at Kudos.

LAMOURGE At last, Silv, I *have* tracked him down – to a tinpot tyre firm over in Epping Forest.

SILV You're joking!

LAMOURGE [*brandishing notepaper*] No – no joke. Look!

SILV [*takes paper, reads*] What's he playing at!

LAMOURGE It's early onset short CV. A sacking from Kudos isn't exactly a platform to bigger and better things.

SILV Sounds like martyrdom to me. Look, Lamourge, I'm going to the rescue. If anyone asks where I am, you'll have to think of something.

IV.4 The Fleet Street bistro, lunchtime. SILV has rejected a gift of a dog from PROTES, delivered by LAUNCE. PROTES now asks the dude SEB (or really JULES) to deliver a note and JULES's ring to SILV. In exchange, SILV gives SEB a passport photo of herself.

PROTES Launce told you *what*?

SEB That Silv kicked the dog out when it pissed on the floor.

PROTES That was a chihuahua. It *cost* a fortune.

SEB Well I can't help that, Protes.

PROTES Look – I've got to get back to the office. When she comes, give her this note [*fumbling in pockets*] – and also this ring.

SEB Ring!

PROTES Why ever not?

SEB Just seems a bit premature, that's all.

PROTES Your trouble is, you don't understand. And Seb, do you *have* to wear those shades indoors!

SEB It's the light. It's—

PROTES I don't want to know. I'm off…. [*Exit.*]

Surreptitiously, SEB *slips into the ladies' room. Enter* SILV. *Re-enter* SEB.

SILV Where are the others?

SEB Protes had to rush back to work. He asked me to give you these. [*Hands over note, ring.*]

SILV [*hands back ring*] Not his to give, from what I've heard. He dumb or what? What's he up to?

SEB I think the idea is you reciprocate – a token of esteem.

SILV [*tears note, hands back pieces*] Tell him where to stick these. And give him this [*takes passport photo from purse*].

SEB [*studies photo*] I have to say, Silv, this isn't exactly you.

V.1 LAMOURGE sees SILV onto tube train, Woodford-bound.

LAMOURGE Don't forget – at Liverpool Street change for the Central Line.

SILV Got it. [*Gets in train, train pulls out.*]

V.2 MD, THURIO, PROTES, the dude SEB, about to take Kudos's limousine (SEB *driving*) over to Epping Forest.

MD Hope you know how to drive this thing.

SEB Not a problem.

PROTES Anyone know how to get there?

MD Who's got the *A to Z*?

THURIO Sí!

Car roars off onto highway.

V.3 SILV in the Epping Forest tyre remould shop, treated brusquely by one of its workers.

WORKER Who wants 'im then?

SILV Silv. I'm his friend.

WORKER Well 'e ain't 'ere, see.

SILV You any idea when he'll be back?

WORKER That'd be tellin', wunnit.

V.4 Near Epping Forest. The limousine, nails in all its tyres (a whole bag having been carelessly left in the road), is towed to the remould shop, with PROTES and SEB onboard the tow truck. They step down and rescue SILV from the verbal barrage she is now having to withstand. PROTES sees this as his best chance of imposing himself on SILV, but she repels his advances. Frustrated, he tries to force himself on her, but at just this moment VAL PAL pulls up in a transit van. PROTES, shamefaced, now simpering and unctuous. MD, THURIO, arrive by taxi. THURIO can see where he stands, and tells everyone he must get back to his aging mother in Milan, and some important business he has with a football club, which leaves the way open for SILV and VAL PAL. JULES sheds her disguise, and having delivered a strongly worded feminist tract, amazingly will still marry PROTES. MD offers to buy shares in the remould business, enabling it to invest in new equipment, staff retraining and better quality stock.

ALL Adieu!

Curtain

This, the highly compressed version, is the one appearing in the alumni journal mentioned above, under the sweep of Tucker's editorial pen ('dude', 'highway', etc.) – dipping ink that has paled, come the last scene. Article concludes with a brief discussion, also by Tucker, honed exclusively to the student debate preceding its composition. A first option – rejected, self-evidently – saw Val Pal and Protes as the two heroines, with Silv and Jules as male partners in tow.

There is no record of *Two Men With Diplomas* ever having been performed, though Benbrook being Benbrook, it is likely that in some form it was. But this is nearly twenty years ago. [See dU:LIV.p695] [dP:LIV.p612]

²This, out of context with what precedes it, I admit I find puzzling. [dP:LIV.p612]

[3]'Over-caution' is a euphemism. The notebook he mentions has a blue paper cover, and in its opening pages was used to record the cost of post and packing, of items including contributions to a press in Berkeley, California, and a publisher of sheet music in Dean Street, London W1. Could the latter have been song settings? The few 'notes' he musters, and must have later worked up into his article for *Art Day News*, are monosyllabic, and to me remain cryptic. The word 'mard' appears more than once, in an association I only guess at. [dP:LIV.p612]

[4]I have heard it said – mostly in Alice's set – that ever since his youthful shipwreck in the USA, George has contrived to meet nothing but obstacles. He never looks *through* the swathes of repackaging (or as he'd term it circles of deceit), or the re-hash that *is* twentieth-century art – or much of it at least. All this remains merely a question, for is everything really only as defined in its relation to everything else? This is straightforward, I think, and hardly warrants so much soul-searching. Had his thing been science, he *would* have found something problematic. Does a sub-atomic particle *really* subsist in *all* of its possible states *simultaneously*? Isn't this the kind of question George would have been happier wrestling with? [dP:LIV.p614]

[5]What George doesn't mention is that the photograph is courtesy the Alice Little Archive Ltd, which it's not quite accurate to say is now located in Roehampton. The whole thing was digitised some years ago. [dP:LIV.p615]

LV[1]I can't help thinking George is now attempting to close some of the circles he has re-opened. His draughty round-room window came with a scholium, which I'm sure he wants you to have, Alex (see note 1, Section VII above)—

> Pallid mists
> across this old south road
>
> have damped
>
> again
> my English ghosts
> of winter:
>
> here is the house
> of my cradling,
>
> filmed at the windows,
> frost on its western roof,

and capped
with a cold metallic vane

(that's a man
with a hoe,

whose whiteness of diamonds
freezes in the ironwork
of his painted hair).
[dP:LV.p615]

[2]I don't think anyone took these quips as seriously as George seems to. Alice tells me her prime interest was forming a reliable address list, anticipating her European year backpacking. It was never her intention to file every résumé, for each of her father's predecessors (Edward Book). [dP:LV.p615]

[3]So on, in a spiral of fiction…. [dP:LV.p616]

[4]Jo Grimond was born in 1913, in St Andrews, Fife, and died in 1993. He led the Liberals in their resurgence after the war, having been educated at Eton and Oxford, and called to the bar in 1937. He served as an officer in the British Army from 1939 to 1947, after which he was made Secretary of the Scottish National Trust, with interests in the preservation of historic buildings. Grimond was elected to the Commons in 1950, and was soon Liberal whip. In 1956 the Liberals made him their leader. It was Grimond's determination to revitalise the party that so fired your mother's imagination.

He was opposed in 1957 to the Suez invasion by England, France, and Israel, and pitted his party against the idea of Britain as an independent nuclear force. The Liberals were the first party to favour EEC entry – that was in 1955 – and Grimond was especially vigorous in promoting that policy. He proposed increased expenditure on welfare and education, and he called for partnership in industry between management and workers. His approach and force of personality brought him success in 1958, with a by-election victory, and increased support for the Liberals in general. In 1959 they more than doubled their 1955 tally, though won only six seats. In 1964 they had nine constituencies. In 1965 they won a by-election. In 1966, although the party won twelve seats, Grimond was dissatisfied with the rate of progress, relinquishing leadership in January 1967. He came back again for two months in 1976, as caretaker. That was until David Steel replaced the charismatic Jeremy Thorpe, under whom the party had won twenty per cent of the popular vote – this in the 1974 election.

Thorpe as we know was destroyed politically by personal scandal, when money was alleged to have been paid to silence his former lover – moreover a homosexual lover.

Under Steel (1976–88), the Liberals retained their position as a significant national force, and didn't lose your mother. With the manoeuvrings of Dr Owen et al, and other liaisons, they did. A book never far from your mother's hand was Grimond's *The Liberal Future* (1959). His autobiography, *Memoirs*, was published in 1979, and that also she devoured. [dP:LV.p617]

[5]New York, and those early 1980s, where I surmise the Alice Little Archive (see note 5, Section LIV above) existed in embryo, as a paper portfolio, which I just see George trawling through endlessly, his so many hapless hours…. [dP:LV.p617]

[6]George in the remoteness of his references. A youngish Brendel, hands poised for an assault on popular Beethoven, at this stage entered that record collection. Incredibly, that's *what* this is all about! [dP:LV.p617]

[7]That archive again. A search through on the keyword 'pets' throws up photos of: a Dartmoor pony, a gerbil, a white rat, guinea pigs, a monitor lizard, stick insects, a roadside goat, cats, dogs, parrots, a budgerigar. Not all of these belonged to the Littles. [dP:LV.p617]

[8]Did George ever meet Alice's three other half-sisters? I don't know. [dP:LV.p617]

[9]Curious that our poet mentions nowhere in his text that she who had so seduced his eye – that is to say, Marcia Copparo – was one of Ed's nieces too. Or, for that matter, that Stoneridge, in Viceroy Road, was bought by him, and given to his daughter. [dP:LV.p617]

[10]Cecil, if du Plé can't see him as a man to declare his politics, wouldn't argue with Marg, for whom the essence of social progress was the free exercise of individual aptitude and energy. What had so attracted her to the Liberals, and especially their revival under Grimond, was the formula by which the thrust of individualism could somehow benefit all. Liberals at this time were keen to adopt radical, even innovative approaches to reform, and that often brought them ideologically close to the Labour Party (which Cecil would not have objected to either, since the driving social analysis was not, unlike Labour's, bedded in class loyalty). [dP:LV.p618]

[11]Can we regard this as a slight, Alex? George as well I drank tea with you in Cecil's flat, in the years after your father's economic 'restructure', with its reduced gentility. All these things – rallies, petitions, and who organised what – he talked about endlessly. [dP:LV.p618]

[12]George, otherwise so astute, in what amounts to a long linked list of memorabilia, I can't believe will have overlooked the facts of your father's interests – destroyed, as we *all* know (though never talk about), by investment scams in the 1970s, mostly in oil. [dP:LV.p619]

[13]This on George's part is, I'm afraid, too mechanical. And this was hardly a 'crusade'. I think I speak for Marg when, with pseudo-socialism on the horizon, conviction to one can look to another like proselytising. Moreover Marg's 'lectures', as he calls them, were less about policy, and more to do with the history and ideals of her party, with the Reform Act of 1832 always her starting point. [dP:LV.p620]

[14]For the record James, in a series of subsequent meetings, helped your mother gather these 'lecture' notes into a coherent manuscript, with a view to publication. Marg, who had not expected to turn political, personal passion into a book, refused to pad it out with pap – therefore as things stood in the late 1960s there was not enough to justify hard covers. Apart from that Marg was aware of the Liberal Party as driven by an *attitude*, rather than inflexible ideology. Her trust in life in itself was also her party's trust – with its creed of rationality, its value on progress, the importance it placed on individualism, *and* on human rights – not to say the emancipation of underprivileged groups.

Is there a Liberal legacy, and a book that Marg *might* write? She teetered under David Steel, party leader from 1976 to 1988. In return for support of Callaghan's Labour minority, Steel negotiated certain concessions, including Liberal consultation on legislation prior to presentation in Parliament. This was the 'Lib-Lab' pact, which foundered in 1978, at a time when Marg was disillusioned. The Liberals went on to do badly in the 1979 election. However, their strategic importance remained, even with the arrival of the SDP, in 1981, when Marg *should* have written her book. An 'Alliance' was forged, the two parties coming together for the 1983 election, winning twenty-five per cent of the popular vote.

Marg – a party worker and not now so faithful – bowed out altogether in 1988, in the wake of party tensions. Senior figures had doubts over the Alliance, while the SDP was viewed as elitist. Of the two parties, the Liberals fared better. They, rather than the SDP, retained the right to field candidates in most of the winnable seats, with historic ties in national strongholds still intact. As well as their resources, theirs was the organisational infrastructure on which the new party – now known as the Liberal Democrats – was built.

Before Tralatition was sold, Marg was urged to write her memoirs, though the point she made against was a valid one. Was this merely a family gesture, for who would read the ramblings of someone whose public career was not in the public consciousness? [dP:LV.p620]

LVII [1]Are you sure this wasn't at Marg's instigation, George? [dP:LVII.p622]

[2]Not for the first time, George's memory plays its tricks. That's not to say I doubt the breadth of its feat in all this attention to detail – or does he somehow feel he can live with his past only in its reconstitution? The book in fact was open in *Alex's* hands. That was because, again, she was learning her *Mikado* part. It had had its last night at Wenover weeks before, but was due a second run by the Kentainers, for which Alex had auditioned. [dP:LVII.p624]

[3]A list of sea areas named in weather forecasts, grouped from under the Arctic Circle to the north-west tip of the Iberian Peninsula, is—

•Viking	•Biscay
•North Utsire	•Trafalgar
•South Utsire	•Finisterre
•Forties	•Sole
•Cromarty	•Lundy
•Forth	•Fastnet
•Tyne	•Irish Sea
•Dogger	•Shannon
•Fisher	•Rockall
•German Bight	•Malin
•Humber	•Hebrides
•Thames	•Bailey
•Dover	•Fair Isle
•Wight	•Faeroes
•Portland	•Southeast Iceland
•Plymouth	

[dP:LVII.p624]

[4]Her name was Miss Harlie-Scott. [dP:LVII.p624]

[5]See du Plé's Section L, and my note to it (admittedly confused). [dP:LVII.p625]

[6]That candidate's name was Matthew Pier. Although young, and keen, and up-and-coming, he had very little chance. He began to find – like so many others canvassing on opposition doorsteps – no safe tack through the rising sea of Thatcherism, and so returned to his career in insurance. That aside, there is need of a sort out here. I will do my best.

Notably, James was lukewarm on Mozart, whose C Minor Mass was the only thing he liked. Frank Zappa he could tolerate, whose *Orchestral Favorites* he listened to with patience. And again, it isn't true to say that the whole episode was really a question of Marg's musical long-play investments, cheapened by popular cults, the sacrifice being her old and sentimentalised record player. I think to the contrary George believes it was – for why else so conscientiously map it out (Klemperer, Barbirolli, Beecham etc.)? George forgets – or isn't aware – that James's own adolescence was largely unaffected by teenage rebellion. Moreover James knew the advantage of upholding family tradition, which for him meant Tralatition, an ambition Alex couldn't, for many reasons, inherit.

As for aesthetics, I don't call it hypocrisy on George's part, exactly. If, as his own paragraphs decree, there is a quality cut of cloth appropriate to the James Littles, with a pocket instrumentation awkwardly left-handed in sudden untried moments, then to what intellectual motley does George *really* attribute his own? I am not inclined to ask solely through the mental interiors his pen lights us to, here in his present text (or George's present tense). This is something anyway he re-jigs and augments each and so far *every* day. It comes back to Alex's last year at Wenover, Alice having introduced the pair to a local *son et lumière*, with its softened medievalism. Autumn sunshine, spit roasts, spirited menfolk dressed for the joust. She met him again the following week, this time by arrangement – once for a game of tennis, which ended in three lost balls, and once for a pot of tea. Both took place in the grounds of Calverley Park.

His subsequent visits to Middlecross were reciprocated by only one, on Alex's side, to his own small place, a thatched cottage on a corner plot, in a sleepy village a bus ride from the nearest town, whose frontage was whitewash and hollyhocks, with a back garden sprouting potatoes, cabbage, beans. His father – who for one week was infamous, at the hands of the local press – led a team of drawing-office juniors at an engineering firm (which ten years ago went into liquidation). I chanced to witness its corrugated premises, when I had very bad business with a book bindery. It had a double frontage, on the first turn of a long road snaking its way through a regiment of ornamental fruit trees, at the heart of one of those old-style industrial estates. His mother taught piano, and lived with a litter of ashtrays, and use of a mouthwash. Alex recounts a glass on the piano, one in the bathroom, and one on the kitchen sill – all of them green and fluoridic. There weren't many books, which surprised. There was an atlas. A French primer. A manual for the home mechanic with family car (a Ford Capri). And recipes by Clement Freud. Du Plé, as of this era besotted by Hart Crane, had a personal library consisting only of *The Bridge* – and this a tatty paperback picked up second hand in the shop where George bought and resold all his books.

As a poet, du Plé looks to have got his juvenile exotica direct *from* Crane. I have only to pluck certain lines from his early notebooks, for example

A black cat tensile at the campanula root,

to make the point, for one has only to compare, in this instance,

The tarantula rattling at the lily's foot.

His brief sojourns at Middlecross turned from long weekends into weeks at a stretch, with occasional visits home to pick up his mail or fill out a job application. At one stage he mustered part-time work in the wholesale department of a music publisher (here, again, another of those industrial estates – as martyrdom this was bleaker than most). When, after just a few weeks, he failed to get himself transferred to the West End, where the firm had its fashionable shop front, he resigned. This his mother must have found embarrassing. It was through a connection she'd had with the trade management there that she had made possible his initial interview.

Marg found him rash, and stubborn, but personable. She spent hours, when Alex was at school, with coffee on the hob, prepared to sit, at the kitchen table, talking to him. She read and discussed his poetry, and through the probes and critiques arising out of that, divined for herself the personal implications lurking in his pencil strokes (a system tensile at its root). His creed *then*, as I think it still is now, was psychological, not pragmatic. This of course was of no utility whatsoever, and less so given the flimsy foundation a young, and disillusioned George du Plé had built it on. He could not, and has not rid himself of the mania or suspicion that education – specifically university – years he went through grudgingly without distinction – merely supported a wider conspiracy. Why, Marg might ask?

According to George, it was a new order of individualism that, having shed the cocoon of its medieval European mind, raised its thirty-fold telescope to the Venetian night, and thanks to Galileo discovered a scientific universe. In its four succeeding centuries science had accelerated the rate of technological change, and in the service of industry had lost its human scope. Now, it was *Homo economicus* in a recruitment drive, in control of the university clearing system – learning not for learning but for profit. Our sense of 'individualism' had been lost to the dead wastes of celebrity. Add to that, politics never worked, for one had only to look at what was purportedly a new revolution – its adherents Stage Right sharpening their utensils – and you'd predict easily an atrophy in lies, frauds and corruptions. (Such prescience in one so young.)

Was George filling time? Well, yes – but not, he would say, in the same sense as the bursary poet, whose frail mementoes shored themselves up on a tide of public funds. He couldn't help but belong with the centuries-old adventurer, whose tent you saw at higher points each afternoon, ascent being of a misty mountain, on and on to a crystal peak, whose all-round panorama was broad plains, a lilac flora, all of it gently combed by Mediterranean zephyrs. I can't help think of Plato and his cave, its flickers on the wall, when all the time a du Pléian Olympus was there outside.

Marg watched from the scullery window, or the French doors to the dining room, or driving in, or reversing out in her car – watched as her kitchen poet crowned his martyrdom in the demi-role he chose for himself. Individualism, now that the lava has cooled, and its glow is millennial, we inherit as a household factotum. George cut the lawns, or turned the borders, or put a posy on Porthos's grave. From somewhere down in the boathouse he emerged with a large drum of yacht varnish. His rival – his Jim or Joe or John – would sometimes glance out from the depths of James's study, at a George who spent days (apparently) with an upturned row boat. Here in his memoir this he renames the *Fiery Sickle* – which flame-bright or not, soon caught a certain angle of the sun, in the drying grades of its lacquer, its hues a reddish, nutty brown.

Marg cut him sandwiches for lunch, but could never reconcile the remoteness of his audience with the exercise of his talent. This all went on up in that round room, its squeaky weather vane atop,

that's a man with a hoe,
whose brightness of diamonds
breezes in the ironwork
of his painted hair –

and to be devious and indirect, opened up the bookcase on all of James's Tralatition publications. Could George read in a well turned preface or introduction the written oratory one nowadays had to perfect, in order to spark our grey, and entrenched, and badly neglected television mind? He devoured the entire list, and did so without comment, though in an after-burn of smirks and cynicism. Marg guessed at what the young George got from James and his family press. The pretensions of something vaguely centrist. Marg wasn't offended at all when told her liberalism was dead.

Her mealtime vision of Middlecross's future excluded personal ministrations over the ashes of George's youth. James, far from offer the solution – this one of many domestic problems – responded positively when Marg placed him as George's protector, whether he wanted that role or not. When, eventually, he made that telephone call, it wasn't because each quarter brought in larger service bills, or would herald Alex's departure. Marg trusted her adoptive son to do the right thing. Having diagnosed his English despair – quiet and unobtrusive in a remote corner somewhere – she prescribed travel, the open practice of his art – all a better option than rural husbandry. The fact of Robert Quay was immaterial, and anyway James had at his fingertips a much longer list to go through.

I would say George was horribly ungrateful if I didn't think he was ignorant of much of this. [See dU:LVII.p697] [dP:LVII.p626]

LVIII[1] In the *Oracle of Change*, the abyss. [dP:LVIII.p626]

[2] I will remind you – it wasn't du Plé's to lose…. [dP:LVIII.p626]

[3] 'Symbolic' I think in only *George's* mind. [dP:LVIII.p626]

[4] And George wondered earlier why Tralatition was sold! (See his Section LII – 'I still, Alex, find this hard to believe – that the press has been sold'. See also my note 1 to that.) [dP:LVIII.p627]

[5] As George well knows, the final choice was Manchester. What he may not know is that was followed by RADA. [dP:LVIII.p627]

[6] That rock or hard place always prone to flame up wherever du Plé decides to plant his feet. [dP:LVIII.p627]

[7]Martin Heidegger (1889–1976), whose spectre has more to do with George than with, Alex, that 'buskined Thespian' of yours. George after all – as I read on – found more solace for the changes wrought by existence, in a pack of medieval playing cards.

Without Heidegger perhaps Wittgenstein wouldn't have been possible, so depriving du Plé of an all-time hero (this at any rate according to Alice). If our poet in his early twenties could construct lines like this,

> The dead woman's red world
> Became an omniverse...

he would point to their inherent instability in terms of logic, correspondence with reality etc., as no less an example of language as social activity (no less, say, than Melissa shaking her doubtful curls).

If language can't be relied on to describe our world or our experience of it, that doesn't make it legitimate to invent an arbitrary vocabulary. It renders meaningless du Plé's couplet above, and grants no significance to his dead female world. His obsession is a new kind of syntax, and the pursuit of alternatives to everything – for him that's the challenge. For the rest of us, reading becomes less a matter of appreciation, and more to do with decipherment.

In institutions like the Donns Watson, which du Plé had little time for, the debate is as much to do with meaning, and takes two general approaches – one semantic, the other pragmatic. Semantic theory places metaphorical meaning in the language system itself. So, if metaphor has cognitive potential, it's the system that gives rise to it (see du Plé's Section XIV, with its pillory of Langer). Pragmatic theory links metaphorical meaning with specific utterances, where cognitive potential is much more to do with formulating responses, which language users are always required to do. In a more radical theory there is *no* metaphorical meaning, either semantic or pragmatic. The meaning of a metaphor is therefore the literal interpretation of the words that construct it, which leaves us with Melissa's curls, and not Melissa, as doubtful – the purpose of this sort of utterance being to jolt us into new ways of thinking. But poets, in an evolutionary sense, are different. To them, the first thing a syntagm suggests is an image, while synaptically speaking the rest of us extract a meaning. Sometimes du Plé thinks he can build an edifice on one, while ignoring the other.

> O destiny of George's,
> To have erred in the labyrinth
> Of scholarship.
> [dP:LVIII.p628]

[8]Arthur Edward Waite published *The Key to the Tarot* in 1910. The edition referred to was produced by Rider, an imprint of Hutchinson, in 1972. Alex still possesses those Tarot

cards, which remain on a high shelf in a blue presentation box – though not tucked up in Reach's satin. Where that has gone – a scarf, bandanna, whatever – *I* cannot say. The cards themselves were designed, under Waite's supervision, by Pamela Colman Smith, taking as model a range of packs lodged in the British Museum. Smith also did stage designs for Yeats's plays.

On that same high shelf is another of Alex's books – *The Oracle of Change*, by Alfred Douglas. This was first published by Gollancz in 1971, though hers is a Penguin edition, reprinted in 1974. [dP:LVIII.p629]

[9]You force me, George, to reach that high shelf (see note 8 above). In Waite's pack these cards would be, respectively, the five of pentacles, the six of wands, the six of pentacles, the knight of swords, the three of wands, and the nine of pentacles. No cups, I see, and a preponderance on battle – on the getting and giving of wealth. [dP:LVIII.p630]

[10]With Waite-Smith the nine of swords depicts a youngish woman sitting up suddenly on her couch, head in hands. Her quilt is squared, and embroidered with roses and mystical symbols. These are arranged in a regular pattern on a background of blue and yellow checks. Having said that, I find it hard to believe that after a period of almost twenty years, George can remember – not so much the one Tarot reading he was called upon to make (at least for Alex) – but six or seven of the cards that featured in it. I don't think I'm wrong to suspect deceit, or even a coded message. (As is so often the case with George, we're obliged to unravel the detail before we step back from the canvas. There are things that he says he doesn't know, that he does; conversely there are things that he doesn't know, but acts as if he does.)

This quilt I think is probably important (given what follows in George's paragraphs), though I cannot read much purpose in its astrological figures. Nor will I immerse myself in the frankly ludicrous literature turned out from our presses, almost daily, on that subject. However, those roses *are* a different matter.

The rose, because beautiful and fragrant, is a prevalent symbol. In the Occident, its status is similar to that of the lotus in Asia. It was sacred to Aphrodite, and the *red* rose (which we see on our quilt) supposedly came from the blood of Adonis. Its symbolic meanings can be: love, affection, fertility (of relevance to George's first life at Middlecross), also reverence towards the dead (by which one *could* categorise that era). Roses were woven into garlands for Dionysus and his revellers, when embarking on drinking bouts. Like the violet, the rose was thought to possess properties able to cool the brain – a treatment I would strongly recommend for all poets everywhere. Importantly perhaps, roses were supposed to help in remaining tight-lipped over sensitive information when intoxicated. The rose *and* the cross formed a symbol of secrecy in early Christianity – and secrecy in George's semi-public sense I think is an underlying factor for him.

The rose offers numerous meanings in Christian symbolism: the spilt blood and the wounds of Christ (would these have currency in du Plé's solipsistic worldview?), also the chalice or Holy Grail that received that blood. Because of the Resurrection, the rose is also a symbol of rebirth, as of course George stokes the cold ash of a long dead fire, in futile hopes of rekindling its flames.

In the Middle Ages, the rose was a symbol of virginity (I cannot speak for either Alice or Alex, in this their last year at Middlecross), so also consequently of Mary. The red rose is a symbol of divine love generally, which to me, George, is taking things a bit far. However – to return to our Tarot cards – the rose windows of medieval churches were related to the circle or wheel, and probably to the sun (itself a symbol of Christ). Two of the Greater Arcana are, of course, the Wheel of Fortune (Trumps Major X), and the Sun (Trumps Major XIX). In alchemy, the rose, usually seven-petalled, was an important symbol where complex relationships were concerned (and George has certainly made his relations complex). Plus I can't help thinking he similarly attempts to turn base metals into gold.

As for his nine of swords, some form of combat is depicted as a tooling into the couch's timber panels. The swords themselves – all nine of them – are racked one above another horizontally over that figure of lamentation. As for the card's divinatory meanings, these are death, failure, miscarriage, delay, deception, disappointment, despair, or if the card appears in its inverse, imprisonment, suspicion, doubt, fear, shame.

There are several orders here of hocus-pocus, much of it George's. [dP:LVIII.p630]

LIX[1]Cecil at that time took *The Times*, the *Telegraph* and *The Economist*, none of whose crossword compilers I recall went by that Cross Stitch sobriquet. [dP:LIX.p630]

[2]Even then, George not only wrote everything down, but stashed it. It was Shakespeare who said,

Rest easy, and do your own undoing….
[dP:LIX.p630]

LX[1]This is du Plé's imperfect recollection of how the estate was disposed of. That 'helper' – as in fact you told me, Alex – you who are mindful of half-lines everywhere – was a daughter by your grandpap's *first* marriage. [dP:LX.p631]

[2]All from disjointed table talk, I think. George – familiar with the tools you harvest orchards with – is ignorant of how Marg's father planned to subdivide his. When he died, negotiations with a property developer had reached an advanced stage, with no contract having been signed. The 'sale' George goes on to talk about was of two entities – land for housing, and the rest of the estate. [dP:LX.p632]

[3]One of those not quite ingenuous questions, prompting *me* to ask just where he was

planning to go, in his Section XXXI, via the Northern Line, or whom he expected to meet. There is also one other small detail. The letter our twenty-year revenant wrote 'home' to Middlecross, six to eight weeks ago, I personally redirected to that other 'place' near Parliament Hill. It clearly wasn't Marg who replied to him. [dP:LX.p632]

LXI[1]I wonder what kind of transaction George really thinks this was. [dP:LXI.p633]

LXII [1]Roughly eleven years. It's part of the Middlecross bypass, so I'm surprised he didn't notice it coming in, or hasn't heard its traffic. [dP:LXII.p633]

LXIII[1]That possibly clears up one puzzle, or at least is a clue. See George's Section II, and with it my note 1. [dP:LXIII.p635]

LXV[1]And we were bookmarked, George, to this passage here—

> …not reverence
> For my father, and not the force of love
> With which I should have crowned Penelope with joy,
> Could curb the eagerness I had
> To know the world, and its ways of life,
> Man's evil and his virtue. On I plunged,
> Into the seas of life…
> —'Inferno', XXVI

That aside, what Myra and I were here to discuss, in the rare opportunities we had, was her new EU lectureship. There was one proviso, that a module on the Treaty of Rome was a cornerstone of the curriculum. [dP:LXV.p636]

[2]It is no exaggeration to say, Alex, that I never met your George at Middlecross. I don't know if his abandoned locus there is one he will ever return to. As I said to you a few evenings ago, it was only by default that I was asked to make these trips to Middlecross, to tidy up and gather the mail, most of it junk. I ought to have used that pot-bellied boiler in the basement, which as focus of George's memoir you revealed the significance of, only days ago. In his youth Hart Crane was *the* American poet. George it seemed lit on an English counterpart, the lesser known Bim Shay, whose final collection had as title *Caliban's Machine*. I have found a copy. Its epilogue describes a technologically minded Caliban. It is moonlight. That hunched-up dwarf is a man hobbling from the edge of a lawn. Cascading water silvers the stone petals of a fountain. Its soft tinkle, carried on the night air, intertwines itself in the thrum of electrified strings. Somewhere on a wall is a harlequin dressed in rhombs. Someone plucks at a violin – a pizzicato. A juggler, quartered in red and yellow, has plonked down carelessly 'four to five' torches, all of

which are smoking. Gone, too, is the lady who left behind an amethyst, in the ornately wrought tracery of a garden table. Light from the chandeliers through an open door sprinkles coloured drops of dew into the ballroom. Caliban, a sack of human bones slung over his shoulder, scurries across its floor. There is a discarded lute on a footstool. Revels have been abandoned. There are uneaten grapes in a bowl. Pools of claret. An overturned goblet. (Oh what is that hum?)

The beast Caliban pauses at a stone stairway, then follows its spiral down, into his cavern, where the air is cool and the stonework damp. Little tongues of flame lap at the stubble of his horny flesh, at his inhuman hand, when he opens the furnace door. That sack has the powdered bones he heaps in as fuel. The fuel is to drive the pipes and wires and wastes whose furnace is their heart, and which circulate the house. This is your welcome, your *Caliban's Machine,* and here is my farewell.... [See dU:LXV.p699]

Fare you well, George du Plé, poet. Can you really suggest, Alex, that the one double bed in Viceroy Road I have threefold misconstrued, through Alice's silks and rugs and erotica [See 'The Five Families'.p701]? [dP:LXV.p636]

Envoi (Jack d'Ursag, 2016)

VII Dead letters read

[1]And on Royce's part we're in for fragments of another sort. I have got to know him, first in Saussure's, then in Derrida's foothills, adding research papers to the vast accumulations still accreting, and sorted into heaps. The argument never varies, though the detail does. A metaphoric frame erected on a metaphoric base is the totality of language, demonstrating what – that this is all it is? Metaphor. It was something I mentioned to George in our first internet exchange, Denmark Hill to Waiheke Island, over a Skype connection, as that became less and less useful as a debating medium. Email turned out to be our tool of choice for conversation – or writing.

I was surprised at how unwilling and resolute he was with any sparring opportunities I offered. I had good reason for wanting to draw him, if not into critique then at least comment on his tormentor, the scholar John Royce. I wondered how often Royce went to his optician, a man for whom the changing fashions would always call for a change of frames. And that was just the preliminary, when I wondered how often, in looking at the world, he needed a different lens. Du Plé took that aside literally, in an act of sublime non-committal I found to be his policy throughout, mostly. His only comment was that he had faced up in his mid-fifties to the fact that even he – the clear-eyed poet George du Plé – needed the use of reading glasses. He added a caveat, telling me his reading was not so voluminous as it once was. It was more careful though, with John Alexander Gunn the last author he had read, and John of Patmos on his list.

And no, the nearest he'd come to a calling was in the secular ambitions nurtured as a poet. Poets are prophets in the wilderness, and sometimes they are persecuted. Most often they gather as geese, and honk at the world that will not pay them due respect, and call this honking a literary form of art. He had long given up going into places where, as individuals, they gathered in groups, or a gaggle, to declaim, often in over-furnished, ill-lit rooms above a bar, or the aisles of a bookshop when the shop has closed, or a small theatre, or the foyer of an arts institution when the main event was going on inside. The ethos is gauged by the first speaker, the co-ordinator (or now called the facilitator), whose act of self-congratulation is at the small number assembled – in sight of practically no audience. That is sure indication either of exclusive fraternity or a lack of engagement by an indifferent, ill-informed public – ignorance whichever way you'd describe it. Du Plé professed not to know the truth, but whatever it was, this was elitism performed by a non-elite, one that had lost its way on the page, but continued to publish nevertheless.

I asked him what, now, after a chasm of decades, would be a likely fifth added to the four home-comer poems reproduced by my older colleague Royce. Royce, whose annotations I am footnoting (and yes, I *am* aware – in the same spirit of plunder or excavation). He told me that since moving to Auckland he had keyed Middlecross's postcode – RO5 1ND – into Google's search engine, and through the Earth pane planted on his screen had skimmed the roofs, the lawns, the terraces, the lake, the boathouse, the backing bits of smallholding. It was an outing he'd had to abandon – 'I'll never do it again' – on a trundle up Church Lane and immersion into its 360-degree street views, where new roads off – or roads off built in his absence – had given rise to depressing outgrowths, flimsy orange-brick houses with uniform, mass-produced roofing slates, parked cars everywhere, wheelie bins, an excrescence where once there had been fields, oaks, a grassy knoll. All had been swept away, a burst bubble in the mystique of his first world, in the uniformity and greying-out of its prime iridescence. That, in its remoteness, now seemed only a foreshadowing on the poetry he would write, a lost ticket he'd always try to recover for the voyage he'd embark on, where the vessel – chartered because of its equipment, built on the newest precisions – is one he'd commissioned to ply the latitudes of his human imagination. I took that as a no, there was no fifth poem, and accepted that reply. Then a few days later he emailed these following lines as an attachment, with the proviso that the lineation he was so adept at then – in that displaced first settlement – wasn't now possible, with its air and space and freedom. That was all now under constraint of a man contemplating his mortality, which eventually the young must face—

Five Point Eight

This and all other numbered paragraphs
I misplace, with the accumulating instruments
Scattered on the decks. All is debris
In the analysis of standard text,
Even with an aide-mémoire.

A word is just the index
Of another. A dial of numerals etched in sentence
Case is official as notation, a shorthand
Into lookups, a meaning written
Into superscripted read-offs
Up, down, across.

Yet I see only saturation on the page, a filter
Occlusive in its opacity,
And a scope I can hardly look through.
I don't make out the friends I had,
And the places familiar to us, and ask,

And want to know, what were the conversations
We'd had, and the music they were set to?

The answer is processed
As tabulation, where no written monument
Is raised to the dead, and the graves are dug anonymous,
North to south.

I wondered about the title, until George told me that 5 and 8 were adjacent figures in that *jeu d'esprit* also known as a Fibonacci series – 0, 1, $^1/_2$, $^2/_4$, $^3/_8$, $^5/_{16}$, $^8/_{32}$, $^{13}/_{64}$, $^{21}/_{128}$, etc. (Leonardo Fibonacci, born circa 1170, died after 1240.) If the *n*th term is $un \div vn$ its connection with its predecessor is

$$un \div vn = un_{-1} + un_{-2} \div 2vn_{-2}$$

I can't say I automatically gleaned as much in looking into du Plé's long-term conclusion to those four youthful poems. [dP:VII.p582]

X The Donns Watson

[1]I wondered how it felt for du Plé to reflect on ties and events in his current remoteness from them, and not just geographically. After all, that brief span of years we're focused on is one small locus in the atlas of time that has since expanded, with deserts and sierras between him and the book we are now constructing. He said it was doubtful such an artefact could have come about without John Royce – without that agon entered on between them. That is also *my* assertion. But George had said it himself, in awed reflection on the advances digital techniques had made available, for *our* communications. And that was not just desktop exotica. There were phone apps we'd also begun to use, with new ones added all the time, and finally a system of convergence I directed him to, able to funnel designated text into one, meta-tagged heap. What that gives is ease of access in a hyperlinked grid of multiple cross-reference, so you have to be disciplined as to what those references are. Here are some examples—

I told him that since his sojourn in the 1980s, at the Donns Watson, a general purge had transformed it from cold exercise space for the drilling of a new avant-garde, to a clearing house for young performers. He asked what kind of performers. The type, I said, wanting a first break in Hollywood or a career in TV, sitcoms etc., or voice training for markets in musicals, Broadway and London's West End, or for *a cappella* theatrics. Robert Quay had been a first casualty, and was last known to have taught in Oakland, California, where he printed one-word poems onto coloured paper and hung them in frames. Not much future in that. Having professional connections, however tenuous, I knew many who had been left in the wreckage of Marxist thinking, in its social permeation of our arts. One in particular – a Ricardo Solomon – had written a brief history of the Donns Watson, from inception to its final days under Robert Quay. The book had appeared as a single volume, large, perhaps over-large, in a glossy yellow cover, and carried an end section devoted to author interviews with former staff and student alumni. This I now learned was not news to du Plé, who had been approached by the author, Solomon, when both were briefly in London in the 1990s. Solomon recorded their interview, aimed at extracting George's thoughts and reflections on the time he had spent in close proximity to the Quay experiment. But Solomon was imperious in his application, and refused to make available a transcript of their discussion. It was therefore impossible for George to review thoughts and opinions Solomon had attributed to him before they were put in the book. He tracked down the publisher, who in a rare moment of sobriety agreed to show him the transcript, but then retracted that offer when Solomon heard of it and imposed his usual veto. Du Plé referred the matter to the Society of Poets, Scholars and Literary Critics, an institution at that time Cambridge-based (i.e. Cambridge in Massachusetts). He had been in its membership for over fifteen years. One of its officers – guardedly faceless – wrote a letter on his behalf, a masterpiece of bureaucratic disinterest, whose closing paragraph implied the veiled threat of legal action. Du Plé's participation in the book was immediately withdrawn. I now knew I must tread carefully.

The fine line was in representing George, on the one hand, without forgetting his personal life and privacy, and on the other the publisher, the only one I'd found with an interest in his book. I had the impression that publication wasn't dependent on the du Plé-Royce rivalry (as Dr James, the press's owner, had chosen to term it), though emphasis on it, balancing true human drama against academic careerism, would help the project along. At this stage nothing more was required than a prefatory note, where I (my *nom de guerre* is Jack d'Ursag) am the go-between. It's worth stating I am not a professional agent (for there are no fees involved). What is wanted is someone, somewhere, to find the commercial angle, or that overarching small talk to satisfy bookseller circles. Our best option yet was choice academic gossip his five-star reviewers on Amazon, and in other places too, could use as a launching-off point. It was part of my remit to include in the chaos of intellectual sparring George's painful position vis-à-vis Robert Quay, about whom much has been written elsewhere (he is a poet, a teacher, a theorist). Characteristically, du Plé wouldn't be drawn, and made the point that an extended introduction along these lines was in danger of portraying him – of portraying George – as intolerant and reactionary. These were the two words he reserved for Solomon, whose research into the Donns Watson was highly selective, and whose left-wing credentials du Plé regarded only as a psychological lint, applied unwittingly to soften his incorrigible social climbing. Unlike Solomon's, du Plé's disagreement with the institution was personal, not philosophical (or for *philosophy* we should say *politics*). He had found himself dumped on that co-ordinate by accident, and soon discovered in its pioneering spirit an ethic unlikely to benefit his talents, or be of any use, except – as he learned only later – as a stimulus to opposition. I could not get him to utter a word against Robert Quay, whom he liked personally, and disagreed with professionally. When the Donns Watson was forced to abandon its op art, pop art, sound art, its counter-culture, its spasms, its chasms, its isms, its meagre little binarisms, and reinvigorate its flagging funds as a shrine to consumerism, its terms of dismissal were a catalogue of mishaps, of value to the avant-garde, but regarded as pretentious.

There was one other criticism – quite stinging. It was bound to the question what had been the institution's terms of debate, if more than a dead conversation lost to the realms of pseudoscience. Du Plé said he might once have agreed it was pseudoscience, but had since revised his views – not once, but twice. And it's a separate issue as to whether the Donns Watson has broken new ground, artistically. In an attempt to do so, novel grammars have to be found, where there is to-and-fro, or borrowings between disciplines, and the redeployment of useful terminologies. (He recalled over-use of words like *valency, synergy, quanta,* as applied to frenetic happenings or static installations.) Du Plé offers as a first defence Robert Quay as not only an artist and course director, but administrator too. The institution has its bureaucracy, and the bureaucracy has a form-filling, memoranda-style linguistics, a patois unstoppable in its permeation of the briefs it handed its students and the assessments it asked of its teaching staff. It was there George thought the charge of pseudoscience *could* be levelled, as an accusation I have not known in others. He changed that appraisal according to what, in decades past, the Quay *he* knew had tried for – a new way to develop or enhance creative thinking. That, with its freshly minted theories, necessarily emerged with insufficient tools, so the push to invent probes in a scientific sense must look artificial. Nowadays science itself had begun to interest itself in the essence of innovation, at the neuronal level, so any latter-day Quay-like investigator has a ready-made vocabulary centred on the brain and its processing. When scanned, bits of that biological machine light up in the act of complex tasks: musical improvisation, word associations, checkmate in three, cartoon sketches, sporting actions actual and imagined, etc. Its two halves are wired differently, so a left side will approach a task or problem in not the same way as the right, where the dendrites follow a variant pattern. Which you make best use of makes you either a left- or right-brain person. Interestingly, the capacity for original thinking is greatly facilitated by deliberate variations to the way we carry out routine chores and motor functions. With that translated to the production of artistic texts and other artefacts comes a sort of vindication of Robert Quay's Brave New School of Poetics, where his students were encouraged to form words into phrases and sentences on non-grammatical templates. Or to put it another way, to use language according to lesser structured neurological pathways. So his project had a scientific basis after all. [dP:X.p583]

XXXIX Ratiocinative

[1]Tucker's was not a name I recognised, but it's not hard to imagine the remote corner of academe – in a research pool or creative-writing class – where if I'd bother to look I'd find him. That I am not going to do. Du Plé tells me he came to regard him as an honorary Englishman, at least in his editorials. Like all English editors, of presses, journals, zines, his responses juggled the constructive against the disparaging every time he turned down

George's work. It reached the point that George gave up – first on Tucker, then on his countrymen. He looked elsewhere in those rare moments when he tried to publish his poems, an act he came to view as the despoilment of his notebooks. Those notebooks he ranked according to the colour of their covers, and that was all he wanted to tell me about them. I don't know if this is a clinical condition, with a formal name and a background in research papers, and the centrepiece of conferences. Is there such a thing as reverse narcissism?

I asked him to tell me more about these notebooks, but he darkened, and was cryptic. He said only that over the years he'd gone through the spectrum several times. Currently all entries were made in something pocket size, with a hard cover, of a blue-grey marble design and a red cloth spine. I pressed, as frankly I couldn't see why there had been such a problem getting his poems to press, but there had. It had got to the stage where he found it too much of an effort even to try. Publishing, he says, is more a social than a creative activity, and as his is an inclination to solitude the book trade has never been open to him, with its fairs and its magazine write-ups and all those artful cocktail parties. (George, I'll invite you to one.) Yet he had got faith in himself, he said, and that would be the case for as long as his was a post-cult creed, where fortified by the spirit of his calling there was no urge to see his name in print. If that *was* a creed, I told him, it was one void of any recognisable name. He insisted, his ambitions were profane. To find out who he was in the public realm was an itch that sometimes had to be scratched, which sounded unduly harsh. If he'd produced texts others would want to read then all this internal agonising was unnecessary. From there I prodded further, and was allowed, finally, a glimpse into that same red notebook Royce had somehow been privy to, with its 'Logos as Factotum', a pillar I am now able to use as a staging post to others of its kind. Here's an example – George's 'Interpretations'. It's a dialogue, with the poet as first speaker, though I couldn't guess at who the second was—

'What was seen, and known, and understood,
Bears no exactness to the flabby mind
The larger concepts are reflected in.'

'That's to the good.
Delusions can't persist – or are a kind of framework
Where the fabric of the concrete world
Will come, in time, to cling.'

'That cathartic
Glimpse in the dark – grave, fantastic, and immense –
Urged on this self-destructive thing: the fathomless desire
To see some private revelation in exaggerated
Waves....'

'The terrible labours of the great.
The luminosity of moons.'

'Our world
A palely moonlit alphabet...'

He'd imagined having to answer to the supernatural being he couldn't believe in, in written vignettes, in dreams, nightmares and essays, in an endless ceaseless fidget refusing to be stilled. He was uncomfortable with the West's prevailing discourse, one that categorised worship of a deity as mere superstition, and dismissed as quackery its material presence on earth – its cathedrals, churches, its written encyclicals, its hierarchy of clerics, its lay personnel. Objections were seldom on the basis of a detailed study of the practice and its theology, but had sprung from the same mechanisms of intuition they purported to expose. That the world was explained in newsprint or in economic theory, or that science would reach that final frontier, was no more believable than anything else. Phrases like 'cathartic glimpse in the dark' belonged, in the collective mind of the editor, to a post-Victorian elevation where the norm is social privilege, comfortable living, and self-asserting soul-searching. Poets like du Plé, long after that age and its melodramas, may not have noticed the aftermath of two world wars, the wrench and enormity of social change all over the civilised globe, the restitution paid for colonial rape and rapacity (all that theft and slaughter), a shared burden that has now become bureaucratised and weighed with guilt. These things and more a new canonicity is forced to acknowledge as it strives to overthrow the old. But as George points out, the problem of the moulding of a bright new canon is, as before, in the limitations of its makers, whose range is banal and clichéd at one end, and unassailably lettered at the other. They and no one in between can agree on what this canon is, but only that the old was an artificial construction and has therefore met its end. This is especially troublesome for the future of aesthetics and poetics, when in extreme latitudes the practitioner has drawn up a spiritual programme, with no sure way of explaining what spiritual experience is. The resort is to homespun pieties and a vague vocabulary attuned to the wonders of the cosmos. This won't do for the academy poet, who dignifies the project of composition in a rarefication of verse matrices and metrical templates. Is the foot trochaic? After which foot in any line do we identify a medial caesura? The lines are patterned as couplets, tercets, quatrains, or what? And rhymes, when present: they are end-line, internal, interlineal? They are masculine or feminine? To answer with certainty supposes that each of us sees and hears stress motifs in exactly the same way, and therein is incontestable justification for the engineered reductionism of written and spoken verse. However, George du Plé knows that a poet is not an engineer.

There is a halfway house, between private belief in a *something* (i.e. meaning in the universe) and public careerism, complete with a grammatology intended to impress. Its occupants are the authors of political manifestos, and are sometimes seen on the street with placards and banners. Because their social crusade is important, so is their poetry, however unthoughtful it is, and however much it lacks in learning and accomplishment. The one other canon we don't have to consider, because it does not need to compete with the others, is that bound up with money, status, celebrity and television fame, which the rest secretly aspire to (those having spawned martyrs to the sub-canons and their causes). Du Plé does not follow the conventions or employ the idiolect of any of these groupings, and so isn't understood. It can't be understood either that anyone – poet or otherwise – cannot be categorised, as there is no taxonomy for philosophical uncertainty in an unreflective age. This is du Pléian agnosticism, and with it comes another of those poems he failed to find an outlet for—

> Moderns deny the holy sovereignty
> Allotted the living state, but to make
> Our cosmic aloneness a certainty
> Requires profoundest steps, which some can't take.
>
> A life-long, unholy exorcism
> By the least devout may eliminate
> Worship and the religious catechism,
> But for the rest will only abnegate.
>
> If visions, saints, if demons are subdued,
> The light of the world hasn't yet gone out.
> The doubters don't feel that anything's proved
> Whenever these questions are paramount:
>
> A life-long, unholy exorcism –
> Or worship? The religious catechism?

He didn't disagree when I suggested that the essence of his life in poetry was doubt – all kinds of doubt, doubt in the world, self-doubt – though was evasive in his reply, which he framed as a series of questions. Self-doubt, uncertainty as to selfhood, in truth didn't that spring from the family unit (however organised), from relationships, from the workplace, from the workplace hierarchy, from the law, from the constitution, from the way we live, from the way others have told us we should live, from how we contemplate our death? He had theories as to why this latter was a subject he'd written about when young. Ideas then about his mortality must have rested on the short time, necessarily for one still in his youth, he had had a corporeal existence, a first limited span present on the plane of being, a life still relatively newly squeezed from the enormity of our cosmos, through and out of its birth canal. He showed me another dialogue—

'It looks as though this shrine means nothing
To him now. A monument constructed more to celebrate
A misconception than a principle.'

'Ah yes, the scene
Of one who dreamed. Who at the end has paced
These seedy streets, and in that moment has been stripped
Of everything he values. Still alone? Look carefully,
And tell me what is there....'

'The irony of unconnected lives
That randomly inhabit the remote, independent islands
Of the universe. Of the thousands their inventiveness
Conceives, one overseer is raised to unimagined heights
To regulate their days.

But that is encumbered,
A few uneasy steps beyond the corner
Of his life. He flings his abuse up here, his unlit
Heaven. Death, the undiscovered country. Life,
The unrewarded, arbitrary chore. The desolation
Of the spheres.'

'A cry as long and silent as his solitude lays bare.'

As an aside those 'few uneasy steps' were something he still foresaw with the same clarity as almost forty years ago. The difference now was its ritual as an almost daily event, whereas back then it was only occasional. Or as du Plé himself put it, 'It was a passing thought that now becomes a fixture.'

I wished him many more productive years to come. [dP:XXXIX.p602]

XLIX High life

[1]I told du Plé I had sought out Tucker's *English Village Id* in the Benbrook archive, where a comprehensive image bank had been added. That entry point Royce mentions – the journals '80 to '89 – has become one of four, the three most recent spanning the decades 1990–99, 2000–09, and 2010 to the present (and counting). A scanned, digitised photograph of Tucker himself shows him flamboyantly dressed, in a maroon jacket, a broad-brimmed hat, and a large, old-fashioned, dotted bowtie. It's an outdoor shot, in autumn sunshine, the sky cerulean and puffed with little clouds, and a row of Spanish chestnuts in the background. There are other shots cataloguing Benbrook's central

campus, its main building – a great hall and clock tower – in a red-looking sandstone in a slant of late sun, that sun October-ish, and about to set. Benbrook's vast estate – 132 acres – has settings in other seasons too. There is the tiltyard, flanked on one side by a paved terrace, and on the other by a yew hedge. The site of medieval jousts, blood sports and other tournaments, the yard is now enclosed in grassy terraces and reclaimed as an open-air theatre, which for his duration Tucker appears to have made his own. There are modern roads, apparently, but campus approach is on foot under a Gothic arch, which abuts a cobbled drive circling a central lawn. Here I discovered other photographs, mostly of student gatherings, in all weathers – scarfed, coated and booted in winter, in shorts and rubber sandals come the summer. I asked du Plé if he'd ever set foot in the place, and if not would he like to? No to both. He couldn't see himself returning to England for any length of time, as he doubted anyone there would remember him. It was painful too to reflect that its editors and publishing people would not have heard of him.

It led me to ask how he had come to settle in New Zealand. He wasn't sure that 'settle' was the word, but told me that while working in Tokyo it was one of several holiday destinations (Hong Kong, Singapore, and Australia's east coast were others). He'd backpacked all over the North and South Islands. He'd lost count of the number of times he'd come, but always gravitated to Auckland, where he'd got friends in Devonport, Ellerslie and Glen Eden, and spent much of his time in the public library. In the late '90s, having read of it in a pamphlet, he tagged along with a group of readers on the Karangahape Road, whose venue was the Dead Poets Bookshop, run by a former student of Professor Brian Boyd (a Nabokov scholar and biographer, University of Auckland). So, for a short time, on Tuesday evenings, he tried out some of his shorter poems on an audience of half a dozen, or ten at most. Applause and percolated coffee. He regretted the bookshop had ceased to exist, and I agreed, that was a shame. I said though New Zealand overall was a happy coincidence, as the publisher I was more or less guaranteeing him was run by the Dr James we'd talked about, whose base was across the Cook Strait in Nelson.

Ah yes, Nelson he knew well. He had once met there the Bishop of Christ Church Cathedral, whose niece, a physiotherapist, was visiting at the same time. She had trained in Shropshire, and of course they'd had to talk about *A Shropshire Lad*, which according to du Plé was not a lament on death but a loathing of life. But what, George asked, had brought Dr James to Nelson? I explained he was descended from immigrant Germans, arriving in the nineteenth century. That was in the wake of Edward Gibbon Wakefield's grand but doomed attempt to colonise the country, a scheme set out in the New Zealand Company he'd founded, where he encouraged his fellow-English to sail with him, in ostentatious realisation of that vision. History did not unfold so favourably, so now there are many like Dr James. He traced his ancestry to farming and vineyards, and had shares in a brewery, and an interest in a motor museum and a small fashion house. Literature he encouraged for love not money, and was therefore not a Johnsonian. James – a pseudonym – was one he had chosen (real name Gebhardt) for his publishing. He admired Rilke, but he did not like living literary people, who according to him were vain, spiteful, solipsistic, with an inflated sense of the group. Group mentality he regarded as a self-conscious, self-exaggeration, whose primary aim was the assertion of social and professional standing. He held to the line that posterity, and not the fraternity, decided these things.

In face of that monomania, and as far as its members knew, he remained a recluse. He named his press, but not himself, on his company website, and the only images he carried were of covers of books he'd published. His star author was an elderly playwright, also known for his biographies of figures from the English stage. He devoted a page each to his authors on the website, but said nothing about himself. The portrait or icon he used on his Facebook and Twitter accounts was a cartoon-style line drawing of a gentlemanly, Jazz Age reprobate, a connoisseur of cocktail lounges, stylishly posed with a long cigarette, against a cover photograph of Venice. He posted on both these social networks intermittently, usually when sales of his books had diminished, but sometimes when one of his authors had something to celebrate – a review, a prize, an invitation to a festival. He did not publish poetry, but in du Plé's case was interested in the inclusion of poems for the current memoir, only because of what that memoir is – the anatomy of a poet. He did not invite submissions, and had a tersely worded, polite refusal for unsolicited approaches. In his real life he was much the opposite of what little of his public image he presented – a non-smoker, teetotal, ruddy, robust, and with a fondness for the great outdoors. He skied at Mt Robert and Rainbow Valley, and tramped the forested mountains backing the glacial lakes to the southwest of Nelson (one hundred kilometres plus), an earthly paradise bordered by beech and flax. In terms of masks, deceptions and concealed identities, I told George the two of them had much in common. He said he'd write the Herr Doktor Gebhardt a poem.†

'Perhaps I will get you two to meet,' I said.

†Equations of Turning Circles

Like you, I could not settle
To the planar certainties
Of written epochs or their identities,
Spheres of action distorted into the vectors
Of place, direction, magnitude.

I cannot see round every argued
Point in two-dimensional space,
And live with the quackery
Learned as a trick in the curve these mirrors
Make. They're engineered to reflect straight lines
Back onto my planisphere.

I travel north,
But on the meridian not convergent
On a pole, where the back roads pale
At noon, and the traffic is ghosts
Who walk in circular words.

You hear truncated sentences
Curling halfway up.

Dr James told me he liked the poem, and would quote it on his Facebook page. [dP:XLIX.p607]

LII To the boathouse…

[1]It was well understood why the last generation of Littles to have overseen the work of Tralatition ended that work where it did, and why the project couldn't have passed to Alice and Alex (neither of whom was truly of that lineage). Roddy, whose fate du Plé was not aware of, would not have been capable. Alice, never bookish, preferred the brash materialism underpinning her friendships in Astoria, and would not have had patience for the drawing-room reflections and the ponderous ramblings of educated Englishmen (or sometimes an honorary woman). As for Alex, du Plé was always struck by what, to him, was the unendurable tension existent between her and her stepfather whenever the two were in the same room. She was victim to the moods and depressions of teenagers, not helped by her later immersion in popular psychology, with its underworld of obscurantist explication. To what extent she was marked by the experience of family breakup, I don't know. James Little she didn't like. Du Plé probed at it cautiously when the two were alone, knowing only superficially how it had polluted *all* her relationships. She was solemn and quiet with George, but agreed to long walks and country treks – muddy lanes, ploughed or fallow fields, strolls into the lawned, picture-perfect, picket-fence hamlets they knew. She didn't say much about things personal to her on most of these occasions, when of course all George wanted to discuss was her proximity to Tralatition. There were meetings chaired by James at the long oval table in Middlecross's dining room, when people like Royce arrived, rumpled from the train, with briefcase and papers, young intellectuals filled with verve and enthusiasm, eager to project their academic sensibilities into the future of commercial publishing. New horizons open to the Little press were all those Eastern disciplines in their rapid consumerisation by the West, with its cults and High Street bookshops. The promise was not so much a 'new way' as a new hierarchy in commodities, attractive alternatives to the Judeo-Christian legacy, to go with the kitchen whites. Royce was adamant that the kind of book popularising science could do the same for culture. He was insistent about this, and would have been James's obvious choice for series editor. The nearest they got was something coffee-table quarto-size, with sumptuous colour plates and strange mystical maths applied to the pyramids, with adjuncts in primitive hand tools.

All this was at its height when George called in at Middlecross, on a dead Sunday, after days of torrential rain, and found Alex in her room. She was sucking her pen, her chin propped gloomily over an A4 photocopy. Her class had been given homework by the philosophy teacher, Mr McAde—

> Scientific rules about the real world are correctly stated, verbally or mathematically, only when we know the context and circumstances to which they apply, and to apply them with confidence we probably need to know the context and circumstances to which they *do not* apply. But what does 'to know' really mean?

She put on a long woollen scarf and wound it several times round her neck. With that question in mind, and the two short of an answer, they stepped out through Middlecross's main gate – left open in recent storms – and walked casually arm-in-arm along Church Lane, where I passed them, just as they turned into a public bridleway, its single track in a flanking of hawthorn, bright from its sprinkle of overnight rain. I had business with James, but had returned to the station, and the London platform, long before they were back from their ramble. On it no end of hill climbs, tramps through a darkening undergrowth in the pine woods all round Middlecross, the woods loud with foaming blue rivulets, vigorous streams…. Absolutely no, no end of bracing Kentish walks helped Alex with her homework. And nothing George suggested hit the mark, when her problem, she said, was of *being* not *knowing*, a metaphysical void illumined not one filament by a 'bug-eyed Sartre' and other existentialists. Du Plé remembered the line, and scribbled something later. Now though, under sheets of descending mist, they made their way back to Church Lane, coming in at its other end, and got home cold and wet. James's wellingtons were cross-ankle in the porch. There was a light on in the kitchen. Outside the rotavator was temporarily abandoned where James was ploughing solid, stony ground. He stood by the range in socked feet, a grey-knit sweater, soiled, baggy, corduroy trousers, and stirred a cup of coffee, greeting his stepdaughter and her pale-looking beau with silence, and no change of facial expression. Alex returned to her homework, and George walked back into Church Lane, where he waited for a bus (long time coming). He told me, yes, he did remember that Sunday of his youth (the rain, the philosophy, the rotavator, James warming himself at the kitchen range), but had no recollection of me as, briefly, we passed at the opening with its fingerpost onto that narrow bridleway. Me, the d'Ursag of yore, one of James's bright young grads with briefcase and working papers – and perhaps just as well.

And why? Well—

From Thomas, to Edward, to James – Tommy, Teddy, Jim – the problem with Tralatition was how to keep it going, but with its current custodian the challenge, suddenly, was how to save it. I was at meetings – at that oval dining table, on firelit, autumn afternoons – when the point of discussion (agonised musing is a better description) was whether the press should publish its first living poet. A bemused, initially sceptical James had heard of the Liverpool trio, and asked should *he* seek out a similar regional phenomenon, with a line in stand-up, hairdo *à la mode*, a telegenic smile. I probed the circuit and came up with a couple of names, but it got no further than that, except to say that when news of the proposal, doomed necessarily, leaked out and George got wind of it, and knew there was a list of candidates, he was incensed. But it wasn't Alex who told him. *She* had gauged his sensitivities as on a knife edge like her own. It was Alice, quite carelessly one afternoon, when the three were ambling round Dunorlan Lake, in the wind and rain, the café they had left just a painted blur, its colours a streak of blue and green running in the furrows of the water. George crumbed the crust they had brought and scattered it angrily for the swans. Alex slipped an arm round his waist and consoled with the briefest hug. Alice noticed nothing, and wondered what it would be like, hiring a boat in this weather. I got it all described with the greatest precision in a conversation I had with him, after I had promised to send him pictures of Ruskin Park, which is just a few metres from where I live, and a part of London he didn't know. He said the real anguish was not the descent of Tralatition Press into the realms of third-rate scholarship (I don't doubt it was John Royce he had in mind), and the demotic writings of media-savvy authors (that accent on prize-winning formulas), for that was only a symptom. What he regretted was the passing of a culture, one already disappearing at the moment he felt comfortable with it, and seen off implacably by its chrome-plated replacement. But he didn't dwell on that, and instead complimented me on the pictures I had sent. He thought Ruskin Park looked a pleasant one to walk through, and I was lucky to have it on my doorstep.

'Talking of walks,' I said, 'you mentioned you'd scribbled something on that dead Sunday all those years ago. You happen still to have it?'

He said he would look through his files, and a few days later emailed me this, which I was the first to see (he'd been careful *never* to show it to Alex)—

> Our flight,
> a kind of benign
> calenture,
>
> sent us
> in one feverish trek
>
> over the damp
> landscape
>
> or our joint, agonised
> soul,
>
> only to find
> in the rush back

home

the bug-eyed
Snark

aloof

and calmly drinking
coffee.

Not one for the Facebook page. [dP:LII.p610]

LIV Black mantra

[1]Du Plé couldn't recall ever seeing a copy of *Campania*, but would make time, he said, for a trawl through Benbrook's archive (benbrook.ac.uk/~journals80-89). After he left the US, Hope was the only one of his associates who kept in touch, systematically updating her address book with every move he made, which was eventually to Tokyo, where the one graphic novel he wrote was turned into a narrative poem, after he had found an artist but not a publisher. Its repeated refrain has echoes into the present era, and is a reminder of the permanence of economic mismanagement—

> Cancel all the debt.
> Tell all our economists
> Their sums are incorrect.
> Round up all the arms
> Dealers
> And tell them pack a case,
>
> And put them on a one-way trip
> Exploring outer space.

I told him to send me the whole thing, but it was one of those projects, he said, that lost its impetus, and after an initial burst of energy degenerated into doggerel much worse than that only salvaged bit above. At that time, and in a strange way, he was missing New York, from where he phoned Middlecross often, always finding Alex not at home, or in bed. Despite pleas for her to do so, and assurances that Marg had written down his number correctly, she never returned his calls.

'You were lonely,' I said.

'Except for Hope.' She sent him copies of *Art Day News* wherever he was, one fall issue carrying fractured, limbless poems Tucker had written when in Benbrook, propositions that began like this,

> another stress
> is the can
> subtle factor

or

> only argument
> I know
> are
> away ulceration—

the sort of thing Robert Quay would have viewed as 'important'. In a spring issue Tucker was interviewed, and used that premeditated mouthpiece to tell his fellow-New Yorkers what an amusing race the English are. How friendly and hospitable, and open to new ideas, he had found their country, if lacking in economic clout. He'd got good US schooling in the vital disciplines of self-promotion and entrepreneurialism, and was arrogant enough to think the next generation of RSC actors, directors, producers would fall over themselves for sight of his *Two Men With Diplomas*. He wooed their fresh intake, the youth of England past the mewling, puking stage, on the basis that the New-World Tucker would lead his Old-World cousins into fresh insights into the Bard they might have thought they knew. The offer was declined with gratitude and politesse. His next conquest took him into film, buttressed by a longlist of festivals he was sure he could enter, in the UK, Europe-wide, into other blinkered cultures. Seems he got involved with a small video firm in Whitechapel, who would not consider his proposal until his *Two Men* – no more than theatrical comic strip – had been turned into a film script. By then Tucker had tired of English pragmatism, and offered only to transform those stage directions at the start of key scenes into a chorus, and hoped they'd see the joke when he called the chorus Gower. No sale. Tucker returned to what George calls the Quay school of obstetrics, otherwise known as poetics, a placental avant-gardism in the parturition of pieces like this—

> Another is the
> or the mental, the physical, the
> tensile can I know
> absorb only
> fire, lacerations, the cent
> uries. Begin.
> Away.
> I know. It all
> afloat

on the estuaries
lost islands only
argument I know.

It was published not in *Art Day News*, but in one of those zines that flicker in and out of life – and not his own, not *Village Id*.

The problem for du Plé he insists was never personal, but professional. His CV preceded him in the flight from New York, and at job interviews he was careful to explain, while the team of interrogators looked puzzled and furrowed their brows, that no, he hadn't been a student at the Donns Watson. He'd had certain private funding for observation of, and inquiry into, its methods and working practices, with developments and offshoots in performative art seen as a good basis for the study of modern neuroses, which he'd considered as a possible basis for his PhD thesis. It's poignant to have to report that good brains such as du Plé's are wasted. As poet and potential ethnographer he never went near a masters, let alone a doctorate, citing the climate in academe as clique-ridden, mercantile, unbelievably bureaucratic, and run by intolerant elders.

Censorial editors defended
In public debate their 'emendations',
But in private defer to my student
Scholia, and secretly theorise.

Choice tutors connived, of course (commended
My texts), made haste with the explanations:
Graduates learned what was always prudent,
If not to overlook, then sanitise.

Let me predict: the tactical footnotes,
Mountainous litter, foil for my learned
Paper, swamp what I have in the margins
Of combative life. The Westerner gloats,
Lettered in the learning of his wealth, earned,
Note, where a profession of lies begins.

As his CV lengthened, he quietly dropped any reference in it to the Donns Watson. [dP:LIV.p612]

LVII Hundred motels

[1]To the question *What are you working on at the moment, George?* I got the reply a short piece with the working title 'What You Learn in Exile': its theme was reversals – the perverse ones we're prone to make. Centrally lit in a world starting to disintegrate is the

figurehead of Marg, not James – Marg the protector. If he had told her the party was dead – or *her* party – all that soul-searching at her kitchen table didn't occlude the liberal sensibilities the faithful still upheld. That to George was an internalisation better dissected in individuals than in the gore of organised politics. James ran things according to the latter, but inescapably into an impasse – James Little vis-à-vis the poet George du Plé. Each regarded the other as the barbarian of the steppe, if that was only a half-useful metaphor. George cautioned, from his cell halfway round the world, that *everything* is halves. The Republic of Letters had turned into capitalist diktat, run on private investment, with James one of its accountants, poring over balance sheets. That was what had seen ambitious 'hacks' and other littérateurs setting out so enthusiastically for Middlecross, and on Sunday afternoons passing through its gates. James, always ready to receive them, discarded his gardening gear and put on cotton slacks. His shirt was open at the collar and his pullover a V-neck. His pomaded, short-haired, closely shaven visitors were the machinery of Tralatition's stripped-down lubricated future, their proposals running the gamut from Anodyne to Gestalt, from Hieroglyph to Noumena, from Orient to Unisex. At the tail end Vishnu lumbered into X-rate. The papers they'd brought with them were gone into in great detail in James's study and at that oval table. He checked his charts, graphs, projections, forecasts, the profit and loss. Where the sums added up (see LIV above) the project moved forward into modelling. A bewildered George protested, to Marg but not to James. George was so expert in aiming at the wrong target, especially now as he did not feature in James's plans, James not so much the barbarian who'd stormed the citadel, more the new possessor of something rotten in it, with the Treasury running a deficit. Privately he remarked to his wife that he did not intend reading even the smallest sample of George's work, as that could be an embarrassment for both – for the reader and for the poet. It was a conversation Alice overheard, just as her new boyfriend arrived clutching a Humble Pie LP, a live recording from the Fillmore where, with a headband, he could claim to have been in the audience. He and George had the briefest rapport, which in James's mind linked the rural du Plé with a suburban Stevie Marriott, though without the Essex accent. Alice was never discreet, and her boyfriends didn't last, though her current candidate was here long enough to know what Marg had said to James. *Au contraire des autres, George is a very good poet.*

I was able to tell du Plé that James had died in 2007, long after he had given up on Tralatition. He and Marg had gone back to Cambridge, where in the ashes of a failed marriage apiece they had booked up for a lecture on education – 'what do we mean by it, what do we want from it?' – given by a young John Royce, whom the pair had later talked to over a glass of wine. His end came after a short illness, during which, on a daily basis, Marg wheeled him to the French windows of the small village house they had bought. He said little, apparently, looking out at a diminished birdlife, at the squirrels gambolling on the ridge of the party fence, a division of amber panels. His reintegration into the cosmos was via the crematorium, after a perfunctory service in their parish church, where Marg had run an art history class, which she kept up after his death. She had only Roddy for companion at her husband's passage into the night, with Alice bogged down with business she'd got in Cape Town, and Alex directing a première somewhere in upstate New York – a play by an ex-SUNY student, said to be an inquiry into genre and gender. In their absence I paid my respects, with my hat off most of the time. George wasn't at all surprised at Alice, but was astonished that Alex had gone on the stage, and had carried that career into coaxing other people wanting to do the same.

'That is what you get,' I said, 'from a repressed English upbringing.'

Marg, now in an even smaller house in Cambridge, followed James almost five years later, in 2012, and this time the half-sisters – both very tearful – attended the funeral, where I was asked to read from her favourite poet—

> Sunset and evening star,
> And one clear call for me!
> And may there be no moaning of the bar,
> When I put out to sea.

George said he was sorry to have missed that – sorry to have lost touch with the whole family almost twenty years ago. [dP:LVII.p626]

LXV Finally, Alex…

[1]So into the furnace is heaped that human fuel, as the flames leap. By that action is powered back to life a Middlecross lost to the hauntings of a poet's imagination. I told him I might make New Zealand my next holiday destination, having read an atrocious *Guardian* account of his adopted country, a catalogue of sybaritic pamperdom, chic restaurants, wineries and olive groves, tacky, overpriced folk art, where remote hospitality offered massage, yoga, the whole range of 'chill-outs'. Du Plé said he could show me simpler pleasures, and as for cuisine a recipe he'd devised had at its core polenta, peach mostarda, kale. I looked forward to it, I said, and made the point that before delivering the final manuscript to Dr James in Nelson, perhaps I should put it to Alex, who may not approve of dredging up her family history.

He wavered. 'Would Dr James,' he asked, consider publishing just the poetry, and leaving out the commentaries?'

'Let me talk to Alex first.'

'Please give her my regards.' I was to be sure, he said, to look him up on Waiheke Island, a place he'd discovered before the arrival of bling millionaires, with its bays, coves, inlets and beaches, its galleries and craft shops, its rustic outdoor eateries, the rocky, terraced gardens under a patchwork of sun-dyed awnings, a retreat for those tired of the West, or wearied by its monumental histories. On one of the headlands were the remains of a Maori pa. The whole island could be explored in short time on a pushbike, available for hire. From his phone he sent me video images as he moved from room to room around his well-lit house, one of a pair on adjacent plots two thirds to the summit of a steep incline, where there were breath-taking all-round views of the Hauraki Gulf and the Tamaki Strait, calm waves under the flame of a setting sun.

'You have found your Paradiso.'

'Yes. But not my Beatrice.'

Tutti: Fare you well, Alex Little. [R:LXV.n2.p680]

The Five Families

1

Eric and Kathleen du Plé (George's parents). Eric was a mechanical engineer, whose family history is traced to the Fens. He was born in 1916 and died in 2002. His wife Kathleen was six years younger – born 1922, in Solihull, the year of Eliot's *Waste Land* and Joyce's Paris *Ulysses*. Mrs du Plé (*née* Wrazz) learned to play the piano through her mother, whose gift was a natural ear and an extrovert personality. She never learned to read. Kathleen did, and in later life was qualified to teach. She and Eric met in a Birmingham engineering office, where in his late twenties du Plé Senior was working as a draughtsman, while Kathleen Wrazz was doing secretarial work. This was in the last year of the war, World War Two. They married. Their first house was in Perry Barr. Eric had practical things in common with Kathleen's father, who was a toolmaker, though the latter's love of the pub and the song-filled revellers grouped around the pianist wasn't among them. The elder du Plé had the kind of work that took him into Europe's post-war reconstruction, and finally to an engineering firm in Greenwich, which he commuted to by car from the part-timbered family home in oldish Kentish cottage style. He enjoyed the scenery – the hills, the pines, the chestnut trees, the hop fields, the apple orchards, the Medway walks – but he couldn't understand how much of this could have given rise to his only offspring as poet. His own passions were maths, physics, chemistry and metallurgy. His hero was Isambard Kingdom Brunel. The only music he responded to was Beethoven's Fifth Symphony. The Ninth he said was a shambles.

2

Marg was born Margot Hall, in the Home Counties. The first of her three husbands was the Philadelphian Edward Book, or Ed. Ed was a Republican, a patriot, an admirer of Abraham Lincoln (above any other US president), was a committed capitalist, and took a keen interest in his country's history. Whatever town or city he travelled to, he did not leave it until he had seen the local memorial centre and paid respects to the fallen. His knowledge of the Civil War, and with it the politics of slave emancipation, was regarded by other family members as near encyclopaedic. There was one story or Book family myth that recalls an excursion to Tennessee, where Ed strode solemnly round Andrew Jackson's Hermitage, and almost shed a tear. He had a brother, two sisters and several nieces, among them Rose-Ann, who au paired for Marg (and kept up a correspondence with Alex's mother until her death). His third wife Ell was a Copparo, whose older brother fathered Marcia Copparo, making her another of Ed's nieces. As we have seen, Marcia was the main reason – and not the Donns Watson – for du Plé's flight to New York. Ed and Marg's only issue was Alice (Alice Book, but known to du Plé as Alice Little). Ed married twice more after he and Marg divorced, and as a result Alice had three half-sisters, whom du Plé never names. Of course, Alice's two other half-siblings are Alex and Roddy.

3

Marg's second husband was Cecil Gale, CBE, a tall man with the hint of a stoop, whose first fortune was only part self-made. His grandfather, and then his father, had been in the footwear business, but after Eton and Oxford Cecil sank much of that family money into property and stock-market speculation. He saw more of Alice's growing up than Alex's, the first his step-daughter, the second his own flesh and blood. Marg insists, it wasn't his personal financial crash that put a strain on the marriage. Within easy reach of their family home, west London, were concert halls, opera houses, and the theatre. There performances of Verdi, Puccini, Ibsen, Chekhov, Pinter came and went, but all Cecil could dress for, and order a taxi, was stuff churned out for fatigued businessmen in thrall to their trophy wives: *There's A Girl In My Soup*, or *No Sex Please, We're British* – that sort of thing. He was over-fastidious as to décor, furnishings, and how spotlessly clean all of it must be, and could therefore never get on with Porthos, Marg's dog, whose later passing at Middlecross left her heartbroken. It appears Cecil and du Plé got on well with each other, George always welcome when he and Alex called on him, in his reduced state, at his flat near the Fulham Palace Road. According to George, their host was always warm and open. From the age of thirteen, Alex was paid a monthly allowance direct by her father, an amount du Plé had seen reckoned up, and knew to be adjusted with inflation, and rose annually on Alex's birthday.

4

The first Mrs Little James met in the early '50s in New York, when his career strategy had taken him past the major London houses, and there were opportunities to broaden his contacts into Manhattan. He may even have met a young Robert Quay at that time, who as a door-screen poet – door-screen poetics, the genre he invented – already had his imitators. (He had his detractors too, Quay having been accused of the plagiarism of ideas, when after a spell in Berlin he brought back something he had seen, a cabaret *Balkontür Poetik*, a *Brüderlichkeit* he had seen in performance but has not been heard of since.) It was while away that unexpectedly James inherited his father's Tralatition Press, a hotchpotch of art, belles-lettres, biography and memoir, with interests in education, history, philosophy and science, and less so theology and religion. I don't know much about Miranda Goodrich. She was some years younger, was gregarious and a party animal, and worked as an agent to international opera stars. I was once present in James's study, in Middlecross, when he was trying to make space in an overcrowded filing cabinet. He was surprised and silenced momentarily in putting his hand on a souvenir programme for a Metropolitan Opera gala, in the November of 1954. Clipped to it were reviews by Howard Taubman of the *New York Times*, Irving Kolodin in the *Saturday Review*, and Arthur Bronson in *Variety*. The occasion is remembered for the largest paying audience in the opera's history, as with closed-circuit television excerpts from Leoncavallo, Puccini, Rossini and Verdi were telecast from Broadway and 39th (the 'Old Met'), and received as far afield as Philadelphia, Chicago, Indianapolis, St Louis, Denver, Los Angeles and San Francisco. I could see, it meant a lot to James, and was probably where he met Miranda, or was a performance they attended after they were married. Miranda it was who encouraged James to take on Tralatition and fully embrace popular culture as that overtook the 1960s, with that natural outgrowth in the next decade manifested as an obsession with personal awareness, vogues in therapy, a fascination for Eastern religions, and ancient forms of divination. I was not close enough to him in that era to learn how the marriage ended.

5

Margot Hall, Margot Book, Margot Gale, and now Margot Little, a soft landing finally in the James and Marg ménage. There were no children by James's first marriage to Miranda Goodrich, so the family set-up, when established at Middlecross, consisted of James, Marg, Alice and Alex. Roddy was the only full issue of this final marriage, arriving when Tralatition was a loss-maker (financially) and James was past the peak of his earning power, and probably floundered in an industry whose change was too rapid for him to keep up with. For Marg, arrival on the scene of George du Plé – first through Alice, then through Alex – was the coming of a surrogate son, an attachment James could never share. Further, Marg could offer no guidance as to Roddy's obsession with everything mechanical. To compound it, James could not indefinitely bankroll his only son's ambitions for a playboy career in motor sports. I know nothing of the accident and Roddy's MG. It must have happened on private ground, because, at the time, Roddy was not old enough to hold a driver's licence. It was a tragedy, resulting in brain damage, and I do not know the subsequent fate of Roderick James. I do know Marg's memoirs weren't ever written. That was not because of what George had told her – that Western liberalism was an ideal and not an actuality. She would have known its politics by its moribundity, but would still have spoken up for the forces of proper action, for a world in our custodianship rather than its brokers'.

Select Bibliography

It is by no means perverse, compiling the bibliography of a writer who has published nothing – or nothing in book form. It tells us something of the era. That said, there is no lack of material du Plé had it in mind to collect and format, supposing he had that opportunity. That project might have come to fruition. Here is the list *I* would compile. From first to last, from *English Poems* to *Waiheke Poems*, I am struck by what begins as no more than diffuse, transformative energy – a dreamy confection of teenage poeticising – as that arrives gradually at its hardened contact with the world. That's a curve I've arranged (without dates) according to that chronology.

English Poems, mentioned in dP:XIII. According to John Royce, they haven't survived (R:XIII.n5), but the author has other information. Du Plé has a name for the kind of verse he was writing under this general heading – or rather two names. Sometimes it was *obverse*, sometimes it was *blanket verse*. The only rules for writing are these: that any one piece is brief, consists of one or two sentences, that the lines are short, and that as well as punctuation there are lots of blank lines, a lot of white space.

Nodes, Lodes, Zip Codes, alluded to in XXIX, XXXIX. These are representative of George's Donns Watson era, and chronicle his departure from English rurality and uneasy arrival in an urban landscape—

> So,
> when I got my wings,
>
> all the resolve
>
> (a thousand oaths
> amassed
>
> in jumping from
> that other life),
>
> all the predictions
> dissolved:
>
> toes hang, get scuffed,

first something sinks,

old familiarities—

next, a shadow,
dark vanes over a city,

spires,
a village thatch,

squared fields,
the sea...

Tralatition Reviewed, a collection (projected only) of George's reviews of books published by Tralatition, those books being critical studies of Baudelaire, Verlaine, Rimbaud, Valéry, Rilke, and translations, with commentaries, of Dante, Machiavelli, and Montaigne. I have seen the notes and some of the essays.

Gaijin Off the Ginza, biographical reflections, character sketches, drawn from du Plé's time spent teaching in Tokyo.

Somewhat More Than Ellerslie. Ellerslie is 'Auckland's lucky town'. There is a racecourse, which hosts, among others, the New Zealand Derby and the Auckland Cup. Throughout his early visits to the North Island du Plé got to know its racing fraternity – punters, bookies and others – and remembered, imperfectly, lines from Damon Runyon – *Only a rank sucker takes two peeks at Dave the Dude's doll* ('Romance in the Roaring Forties' in *More Than Somewhat*, Damon Runyon). It seems he quite liked the idea of constructing Runyonesque stories from the time he spent in Auckland's lucky town, where he stayed with friends off the Ellerslie-Panmure Highway.

Waiheke Poems, a project still in the making, and one we have already glimpsed. I don't know how many hundreds of pages it consists of to date, but here is one further insight into it, with a poem title – 'The Idiocracy of the Aesthetic' – recalling Terry Eagleton. It represents another brief chapter in George's volumes of horror at the invasion into literary art of petty social and political material—

I crossed the jagged line and landed
Two to three days late, sole envoy
Of an argument our first proponents
Couldn't quite articulate. Those against
Had lined the streets with flags, in knowing
The Opposition looked or sounded
Absurd. Those of us for, in the prospect
Of defeat, still tussled with the problem

How to alchemise politics into words.

The horizon is one long pall, singed
With electric alerts, turning
Into thread. Most of it won't be deciphered,
A filamented atmosphere burnt a battle shade
Of red. There's nothing here, no two premisses
I can connect, only the rumble of presses,
Fuelling the same, unmoderated idiolect.

What You Learn in Exile

L ast rites were read at what was
A foolish escapade, while decades on
The dead are still alive and crawl
Across my page. The press of bonded
Friendship valued for the talents
It comprised, now looks like something
Inward-looking no one can escape
Or cauterise. The watered grove
Is silhouetted trees, at dusk, where
Orange rings of smoke damp down
The spoken words connecting
All of us. A sacred institution
Like a natural law is not a sacred
Institution anymore, and no one knows
The banalities the mass will still
Applaud. Yet I am not enraged. I shift
My gaze to where the dead are still alive,
Still vibrant on the page.